Edward Duffield Neill

History of Freeborn County

Edward Duffield Neill

History of Freeborn County

ISBN/EAN: 9783741123733

Manufactured in Europe, USA, Canada, Australia, Japa

Cover: Foto ©Andreas Hilbeck / pixelio.de

Manufactured and distributed by brebook publishing software
(www.brebook.com)

Edward Duffield Neill

History of Freeborn County

Edward Duffield Neill

History of Freeborn County

HISTORY

OF

FREEBORN COUNTY;

INCLUDING

EXPLORERS AND PIONEERS OF MINNESOTA,

AND

OUTLINE HISTORY OF THE STATE OF MINNESOTA.

BY REV. EDWARD D. NEILL;

ALSO

SIOUX MASSACRE OF 1862,

AND

STATE EDUCATION,

BY CHARLES S. BRYANT.

MINNEAPOLIS:
MINNESOTA HISTORICAL COMPANY,
1882.

CONTENTS.

PREFACE.

In the compilation of the HISTORY OF FREEBORN COUNTY it has been the aim of the PUBLISHERS to present a local history, comprising, in a single volume of convenient form, a varied fund of information, not only of interest to the present, but from which the coming searcher for historic data may draw without the tedium incurred in its preparation. There is always more or less difficulty, even in a historical work, in selecting those things which will interest the greatest number of readers. Individual tastes differ so widely, that what may be of absorbing interest to one, has no attractions for another. Some are interested in that which concerns themselves, and do not care to read even the most thrilling adventures where they were not participants. Such persons are apt to conclude that what they are not interested in is of no value, and its preservation in history a useless expense. In the settlement of a new County or a new Township, there is no one person entitled to all the credit for what has been accomplished. Each individual is a part of the great whole, and this work is prepared for the purpose of giving a general *resume* of what has thus far been done to plant the civilization of the present century in FREEBORN COUNTY.

That our work is wholly errorless, or that nothing of interest has been omitted, is more than we dare hope, and more than is reasonable to expect. In closing our labors we have the gratifying consciousness of having used our utmost endeavors in securing reliable data, and feel no hesitancy in submitting the result to an intelligent public. The impartial critic, to whom only we look for comment, will, in passing judgment upon its merits, be governed by a knowledge of the manifold duties attending the prosecution of the undertaking.

We have been especially fortunate in enlisting the interest of Rev. Edward D. Neill and Charles S. Bryant, whose able productions are herewith presented. We also desire to express our sincere thanks to the County, Town, and Village officials for their uniform kindness to us in our tedious labors; and in general terms we express our indebtedness to the Press, the Pioneers, and the Citizens, who have extended universal encouragement and endorsement.

That our efforts may prove satisfactory, and this volume receive a welcome commensurate with the care bestowed in its preparation, is the earnest desire of the publishers,

MINNESOTA HISTORICAL COMPANY.

EXPLORERS

AND

PIONEERS OF MINNESOTA.

CHAPTER I.

FOOTPRINTS OF CIVILIZATION TOWARD THE EXTREMITY OF LAKE SUPERIOR.

Minnesota's Central Position.—D'Avagour's Prediction.—Nicolet's Visit to Green Bay.—First White Men in Minnesota.—Notices of Groselliers and Radisson.—Hurons Flee to Minnesota.—Visited by Frenchmen.—Father Menard Disappears.—Groselliers Visits Hudson's Bay.—Father Allouez Describes the Sioux Mission at La Pointe.—Father Marquette.—Sioux at Sault St. Marie.—Jesuit Missions Fail.—Groselliers Visits England.—Captain Gillam, of Boston, at Hudson's Bay.—Letter of Mother Superior of Ursulines., at Quebec.—Death of Groselliers.

The Dakotahs, called by the Ojibways, Nadowaysioux, or Sioux (Soos), as abbreviated by the French, used to claim superiority over other people, because, their sacred men asserted that the mouth of the Minnesota River was immediately over the centre of the earth, and below the centre of the heavens.

While this teaching is very different from that of the modern astronomer, it is certainly true, that the region west of Lake Superior, extending through the valley of the Minnesota, to the Missouri River, is one of the most healthful and fertile regions beneath the skies, and may prove to be the centre of the republic of the United States of America. Baron D'Avagour, a brave officer, who was killed in fighting the Turks, while he was Governor of Canada, in a dispatch to the French Government, dated August 14th, 1663, after referring to Lake Huron, wrote, that beyond "is met another, called Lake Superior, the waters of which, it is believed, flow into New Spain, and *this, according to general opinion, ought to be the centre of the country.*"

As early as 1635, one of Champlain's interpreters, Jean Nicolet (Nicolay), who came to Canada in 1618, reached the western shores of Lake Michigan. In the summer of 1634 he ascended the St. Lawrence, with a party of Hurons, and probably during the next winter was trading at Green Bay, in Wisconsin. On the ninth of December, 1635, he had returned to Canada, and on the 7th of October, 1637, was married at Quebec, and the next month, went to Three Rivers, where he lived until 1642, when he died. Of him it is said, in a letter written in 1640, that he had penetrated farthest into those distant countries, and that if he had proceeded "three days more on a great river which flows from that lake [Green Bay] he would have found the sea."

The first white men in Minnesota, of whom we have any record, were, according to Garneau, two persons of Huguenot affinities, Medard Chouart, known as Sieur Groselliers, and Pierre d'Esprit, called Sieur Radisson.

Groselliers (pronounced Gro-zay-yay) was born near Ferte-sous-Jouarre, eleven miles east of Meaux, in France, and when about sixteen years of age, in the year 1641, came to Canada. The fur trade was the great avenue to prosperity, and in 1646, he was among the Huron Indians, who then dwelt upon the eastern shore of Lake Huron, bartering for peltries. On the second of September, 1647, at Quebec, he was married to Helen, the widow of Claude Etienne, who was the daughter of a pilot, Abraham Martin, whose baptismal name is still attached to the suburbs of that city, the "Plains of Abraham," made famous by the death there, of General Wolfe, of the English army, in 1759, and of General Montgomery, of the Continental army, in December, 1775, at the commencement of the "War for Independence." His son, Medard, was born in 1657, and the next year his mother died. The second wife of Groselliers was Marguerite Hayet (Hayay) Radisson, the sister of his associate, in the exploration of the region west of Lake Superior.

Radisson was born at St. Malo, and, while a boy, went to Paris, and from thence to Canada, and in 1656, at Three Rivers, married Elizabeth, the daughter of Madeleine Hainault, and, after her death, the daughter of Sir David Kirk or Kerkt, a zealous Huguenot, became his wife.

The Iroquois of New York, about the year 1650, drove the Hurons from their villages, and forced them to take refuge with their friends the Tinontates, called by the French, Petuns, because they cultivated tobacco. In time the Hurons and their allies, the Ottawas (Ottaw-waws), were again driven by the Iroquois, and after successive wanderings, were found on the west side of Lake Michigan. In time they reached the Mississippi, and ascending above the Wisconsin, they found the Iowa River, on the west side, which they followed, and dwelt for a time with the Ayoes (Ioways) who were very friendly; but being accustomed to a country of lakes and forests, they were not satisfied with the vast prairies. Returning to the Mississippi, they ascended this river, in search of a better land, and were met by some of the Sioux or Dakotahs, and conducted to their villages, where they were well received. The Sioux, delighted with the axes, knives and awls of European manufacture, which had been presented to them, allowed the refugees to settle upon an island in the Mississippi, below the mouth of the St. Croix River, called Bald Island from the absence of trees, about nine miles from the site of the present city of Hastings. Possessed of firearms, the Hurons and Ottawas asserted their superiority, and determined to conquer the country for themselves, and having incurred the hostility of the Sioux, were obliged to flee from the isle in the Mississippi. Descending below Lake Pepin, they reached the Black River, and ascending it, found an unoccupied country around its sources and that of the Chippeway. In this region the Hurons established themselves, while their allies, the Ottawas, moved eastward, till they found the shores of Lake Superior, and settled at Chagouamikon (Sha-gah-wah-mik-ong) near what is now Bayfield. In the year 1659, Groselliers and Radisson arrived at Chagouamikon, and determined to visit the Hurons and Petuns, with whom the former had traded when they resided east of Lake Huron. After a six days' journey, in a southwesterly direction, they reached their retreat toward the sources of the Black, Chippewa, and Wisconsin Rivers. From this point they journeyed north, and passed the winter of 1659-60 among the "Nadouechiouec," or Sioux villages in the Mille Lacs (Mil Lak) region. From the Hurons they learned of a beautiful river, wide, large, deep, and comparable with the Saint Lawrence, the great Mississippi, which flows through the city of Minneapolis, and whose sources are in northern Minnesota.

Northeast of Mille Lacs, toward the extremity of Lake Superior, they met the "Poualak," or Assiniboines of the prairie, a separated band of the Sioux, who, as wood was scarce and small, made fire with coal (charbon de terre) and dwelt in tents of skins; although some of the more industrious built cabins of clay (terre grasse), like the swallows build their nests.

The spring and summer of 1660, Groselliers and Radisson passed in trading around Lake Superior. On the 19th of August they returned to Montreal, with three hundred Indians and sixty canoes loaded with "a wealth of skins."

"Furs of bison and of beaver,
Furs of sable and of ermine."

The citizens were deeply stirred by the travelers' tales of the vastness and richness of the region they had visited, and their many romantic adventures. In a few days, they began their return to the far West, accompanied by six Frenchmen and two priests, one of whom was the Jesuit, Rene Menard. His hair whitened by age, and his mind ripened by long experience, he seemed the man for the mission. Two hours after midnight, of the day before departure, the venerable missionary penned at "Three Rivers," the following letter to a friend:

"REVEREND FATHER:

"The peace of Christ be with you: I write to you probably the last, which I hope will be the seal of our friendship until eternity. Love whom the Lord Jesus did not disdain to love, though the greatest of sinners; for he loves whom he loads with his cross. Let your friendship, my good Father, be useful to me by the desirable fruits of your daily sacrifice.

"In three or four months you may remember me at the memento for the dead, on account of my old age, my weak constitution and the hardships I lay under amongst these tribes. Nevertheless, I am in peace, for I have not been led to this mission by any temporal motive, but I think it was by the voice of God. I was to resist the grace of God by not coming. Eternal remorse would have tormented me, had I not come when I had the opportunity.

"We have been a little surprized, not being able to provide ourselves with vestments and other things, but he who feeds the little birds, and clothes the lilies of the fields, will take care of his servants; and though it should happen we should die of want, we would esteem ourselves happy. I am burdened with business. What I can do is to recommend our journey to your daily sacrifice, and to embrace you with the same sentiments of heart as I hope to do in eternity.

"My Reverend Father,

Your most humble and affectionate servant in Jesus Christ.

R. MENARD.

"From the Three Rivers, this 26th August, 2 o'clock after midnight, 1660."

On the 15th of October, the party with which he journeyed reached a bay on Lake Superior, where he found some of the Ottawas, who had fled from the Iroquois of New York. For more than eight months, surrounded by a few French voyageurs, he lived, to use his words, "in a kind of small hermitage, a cabin built of fir branches piled one on another, not so much to shield us from the rigor of the season as to correct my imagination, and persuade me I was sheltered."

During the summer of 1661, he resolved to visit the Hurons, who had fled eastward from the Sioux of Minnesota, and encamped amid the marshes of Northern Wisconsin. Some Frenchmen, who had been among the Hurons, in vain attempted to dissuade him from the journey. To their entreaties he replied, "I must go, if it cost me my life. I can not suffer souls to perish on the ground of saving the bodily life of a miserable old man like myself. What! Are we to serve God only when there is nothing to suffer, and no risk of life?"

Upon De l'Isle's map of Louisiana, published nearly two centuries ago, there appears the Lake of the Ottawas, and the Lake of the Old or Deserted Settlement, west of Green Bay, and south of Lake Superior. The Lake of the Old Plantation is supposed to have been the spot occupied by the Hurons at the time when Menard attempted to visit them. One way of access to this secluded spot was from Lake Superior to the headwaters of the Ontanagon River, and then by a portagė, to the lake. It could also be reached from the headwaters of the Wisconsin, Black and Chippewa Rivers, and some have said that Menard descended the Wisconsin and ascended the Black River.

Perrot, who lived at the same time, writes: "Father Menard, who was sent as missionary among the Outaouas [Utaw-waws] accompanied by certain Frenchmen who were going to trade with that people, was left by all who were with him, except one, who rendered to him until death, all of the services and help that he could have hoped. The Father followed the Outaouas [Utaw-waws] to the Lake of the Illinoets [Illino-ay, now Michigan] and in their flight to the Louisianne, [Mississippi] to above the Black River. There this missionary had but one Frenchman for a companion. This Frenchman carefully followed the route, and made a portage at the same place as the Outaouas. He found himself in a rapid, one day, that was carrying him away in his canoe. The Father, to assist, debarked from his own, but did not find a good path to come to him. He entered one that had been made by beasts, and desiring to return, became confused in a labyrinth of trees, and was lost. The Frenchman, after having ascended the rapids with great labor, awaited the good Father, and, as he did not come, resolved to search for him. With all his might, for several days, he called his name in the woods, hoping to find him, but it was useless. He met, however, a Sakis [Sauk] who was carrying the camp-kettle of the missionary, and who gave him some intelligence. He assured him that he had found his foot-prints at some distance, but that he had not seen the Father. He told him, also, that he had found the tracks of several, who were going towards the Scioux. He declared that he supposed that the Scioux might have killed or captured him. Indeed, several years afterwards, there were found among this tribe, his breviary and cassock, which they exposed at their festivals, making offerings to them of food."

In a journal of the Jesuits, Menard, about the seventh or eighth of August, 1661, is said to have been lost.

Groselliers (Gro-zay-yay), while Menard was endeavoring to reach the retreat of the Hurons, which he had made known to the authorities of Canada, was pushing through the country of the Assineboines, on the northwest shore of Lake Superior, and at length, probably by Lake Alempigon, or Nepigon, reached Hudson's Bay, and early in May, 1662, returned to Montreal, and surprised its citizens with his tale of new discoveries toward the Sea of the North.

The Hurons did not remain long toward the sources of the Black River, after Menard's disappearance, and deserting their plantations, joined their allies, the Ottawas, at La Pointe, now Bayfield, on Lake Superior. While here, they determined to send a war party of one hundred against the Sioux of Mille Lacs (Mil Lak) region. At length they met their foes, who drove them into one of the thousand marshes of the water-shed between Lake Superior and the Mississippi, where they hid themselves among the tall grasses. The Sioux, suspecting that they might attempt to escape in the night, cut up beaver skins into strips, and hung thereon little bells, which they had obtained from the French traders. The Hurons, emerging from their watery hiding place, stumbled over the unseen cords, ringing the bells, and the Sioux instantly attacked, killing all but one.

About the year 1665, four Frenchmen visited the Sioux of Minnesota, from the west end of Lake Superior, accompanied by an Ottawa chief, and in the summer of the same year, a flotilla of canoes laden with peltries, came down to Montreal. Upon their return, on the eighth of August, the Jesuit Father, Allouez, accompanied the traders, and, by the first of October, reached Chegoimegon Bay, on or near the site of the modern town of Bayfield, on Lake Superior, where he found the refugee Hurons and Ottawas. While on an excursion to Lake Alempigon, now Nepigon, this missionary saw, near the mouth of Saint Louis River, in Minnesota, some of the Sioux. He writes: "There is a tribe to the west of this, toward the great river called Messipi. They are forty or fifty leagues from here, in a country of prairies, abounding in all kinds of game. They have fields, in which they do not sow Indian corn, but only tobacco. Providence has provided them with a species of marsh rice, which, toward the end of summer, they go to collect in certain small lakes, that are covered with it. They presented me with some when I was at the extremity of Lake Tracy [Superior], where I saw them. They do not use the gun, but only the bow and arrow with great dexterity. Their cabins are not covered with bark, but with deerskins well dried, and stitched together so that the cold does not enter. These people are above all other savage and warlike. In our presence they seem abashed, and were motionless as statues. They speak a language entirely unknown to us, and the savages about here do not understand them."

The mission at La Pointe was not encouraging, and Allouez, "weary of their obstinate unbelief," departed, but Marquette succeeded him for a brief period.

The "*Relations*" of the Jesuits for 1670-71, allude to the Sioux or Dakotahs, and their attack upon the refugees at La Pointe:

"There are certain people called Nadoussi, dreaded by their neighbors, and although they only use the bow and arrow, they use it with so much skill and dexterity, that in a moment they fill the air. After the Parthian method, they turn their heads in flight, and discharge their arrows so rapidly that they are to be feared no less in their retreat than in their attack.

"They dwell on the shores and around the great river Messipi, of which we shall speak. They number no less than fifteen populous towns, and yet they know not how to cultivate the earth by seeding it, contenting themselves with a sort of marsh rye, which we call wild oats.

"For sixty leagues from the extremity of the upper lakes, towards sunset, and, as it were, in the centre of the western nations, they have all united their force by a general league, which has been made against them, as against a common enemy.

"They speak a peculiar language, entirely distinct from that of the Algonquins and Hurons, whom they generally surpass in generosity, since they often content themselves with the glory of having obtained the victory, and release the prisoners they have taken in battle.

"Our Outouacs of the Point of the Holy Ghost [La Pointe, now Bayfield] had to the present time kept up a kind of peace with them, but affairs having become embroiled during last winter, and some murders having been committed on both sides, our savages had reason to apprehend that the storm would soon burst upon them, and judged that it was safer for them to leave the place, which in fact they did in the spring."

Marquette, on the 13th of September, 1669, writes: "The Nadouessi are the Iroquois of this country. * * * they lie northwest of the Mission of the Holy Ghost [La Pointe, the modern Bayfield] and we have not yet visited them, having confined ourselves to the conversion of the Ottawas."

Soon after this, hostilities began between the Sioux and the Hurons and Ottawas of La Pointe, and the former compelled their foes to seek another resting place, toward the eastern extremity of Lake Superior, and at length they pitched their tents at Mackinaw.

In 1674, some Sioux warriors came down to Sault Saint Marie, to make a treaty of peace with adjacent tribes. A friend of the Abbe de Gallinee wrote that a council was had at the fort to which "the Nadouessioux sent twelve deputies, and the others forty. During the conference, one of the latter, knife in hand, drew near the breast of one of the Nadouessioux, who showed surprise at the movement; when the Indian with the knife reproached him for cowardice. The Nadouessioux said he was not afraid, when the other planted the knife in his heart, and killed him. All the savages then engaged in conflict, and the Nadouessioux bravely defended themselves, but, overwhelmed by numbers, nine of them were killed. The two who survived rushed into the chapel, and closed the door. Here they found munitions of war, and fired guns at their enemies, who became anxious to burn down the chapel, but the Jesuits would not permit it, because they had their skins stored between its roof and ceiling. In this extremity, a Jesuit, Louis Le Boeme, advised that a cannon should be pointed at the door, which was discharged, and the two brave Sioux were killed."

Governor Frontenac of Canada, was indignant at the occurrence, and in a letter to Colbert, one of the Ministers of Louis the Fourteenth, speaks in condemnation of this discharge of a cannon by a Brother attached to the Jesuit Mission.

From this period, the missions of the Church of Rome, near Lake Superior, began to wane. Shea, a devout historian of that church, writes: "In 1680, Father Enjalran was apparently alone at Green Bay, and Pierson at Mackinaw; the latter mission still comprising the two villages, Huron and Kiskakon. Of the other missions, neither Le Clerq nor Hennepin, the Recollect, writers of the West at this time, makes any mention, or in any way alludes to their existence, and La Hontan mentions the Jesuit missions only to ridicule them."

The Pigeon River, a part of the northern boundary of Minnesota, was called on the French maps Grosellier's River, after the first explorer of Minnesota, whose career, with his associate Radisson, became quite prominent in connection with the Hudson Bay region.

A disagreement occurring between Groselliers and his partners in Quebec, he proceeded to Paris, and from thence to London, where he was introduced to the nephew of Charles I., who led the cavalry charge against Fairfax and Cromwell at Naseby, afterwards commander of the English fleet. The Prince listened with pleasure to the narrative of travel, and endorsed the plans for prosecuting the fur trade and seeking a northwest passage to Asia. The scientific men of England were also full of the enterprise, in the hope that it would increase a knowledge of nature. The Secretary of the Royal Society wrote to Robert Boyle, the distinguished philosopher, a too sanguine letter. His words were: "Surely I need not tell you from hence what is said here, with great joy, of the discovery of a northwest passage; and by two Englishmen and one Frenchman represented to his Majesty at Oxford, and answered by the grant of a vessel to sail into Hudson's Bay and channel into the South Sea."

The ship Nonsuch was fitted out, in charge of Captain Zachary Gillam, a son of one of the early settlers of Boston; and in this vessel Groselliers and Radisson left the Thames, in June, 1668, and in September reached a tributary of Hudson's Bay. The next year, by way of Boston, they returned to England, and in 1670, a trading company was chartered, still known among venerable English corporations as "The Hudson's Bay Company."

The Reverend Mother of the Incarnation, Superior of the Ursulines of Quebec, in a letter of the 27th of August, 1670, writes thus:

"It was about this time that a Frenchman of our Touraine, named des Groselliers, married in this country, and as he had not been successful in making a fortune, was seized with a fancy to go to New England to better his condition. He excited a hope among the English that he had found a passage to the Sea of the North. With this expectation, he was sent as an envoy to England, where there was given to him, a vessel, with crew and every thing necessary for the voyage. With these advantages, he put to sea, and in place of the usual route, which others had taken in vain, he sailed in another direction, and searched so wide, that he found the grand Bay of the North. He found large population, and filled his ship or ships with peltries of great value. * * * He has taken possession of this great region for the King of England, and for his personal benefit A publication for the benefit of this French adventurer, has been made in England. He was a youth when he arrived here, and his wife and children are yet here."

Talon, Intendent of Justice in Canada, in a dispatch to Colbert, Minister of the Colonial Department of France, wrote on the 10th of November, 1670, that he has received intelligence that two English vessels are approaching Hudson's Bay, and adds: "After reflecting on all the nations that might have penetrated as far north as that, I can alight on only the English, who, under the guidance of a man named Des Grozellers, formerly an inhabitant of Canada, might possibly have attempted that navigation."

After years of service on the shores of Hudson's Bay, either with English or French trading companies, the old explorer died in Canada, and it has been said that his son went to England, where he was living in 1696, in receipt of a pension.

CHAPTER II.

EARLY MENTION OF LAKE SUPERIOR COPPER.

Sagard, A. D. 1636, on Copper Mines.—Boucher, A. D. 1640, Describes Lake Superior Copper.—Jesuit Relations, A. D. 1666–67.—Copper on Isle Royale. Half-Breed Voyageur Goes to France with Talon.—Joliet and Perrot Search for Copper.—St. Lusson Plants the French Arms at Sault St. Marie.—Copper at Ontanagon and Head of Lake Superior.

Before white men had explored the shores of Lake Superior, Indians had brought to the trading posts of the St. Lawrence River, specimens of copper from that region. Sagard, in his History of Canada, published in 1636, at Paris, writes: "There are mines of copper which might be made profitable, if there were inhabitants and workmen who would labor faithfully. That would be done if colonies were established. About eighty or one hundred leagues from the Hurons, there is a mine of copper, from which Truchemont Brusle showed me an ingot, on his return from a voyage which he made to the neighboring nation."

Pierre Boucher, grandfather of Sieur de la Verendrye, the explorer of the lakes of the northern boundary of Minnesota, in a volume published A. D. 1640, also at Paris, writes: "In Lake Superior there is a great island, fifty or one hundred leagues in circumference, in which there is a very beautiful mine of copper. There are other places in those quarters, where there are similar mines; so I learned from four or five Frenchmen, who lately returned. They were gone three years, without finding an opportunity to return; they told me that they had seen an ingot of copper all refined which was on the coast, and weighed more than eight hundred pounds, according to their estimate. They said that the savages, on passing it, made a fire on it, after which they cut off pieces with their axes."

In the Jesuit Relations of 1666–67, there is this description of Isle Royale: "Advancing to a place called the Grand Anse, we meet with an island, three leagues from land, which is celebrated for the metal which is found there, and for the thunder which takes place there; for they say it always thunders there.

"But farther towards the west on the same north shore, is the island most famous for copper, Minong (Isle Royale). This island is twenty-five leagues in length; it is seven from the mainland, and sixty from the head of the lake. Nearly all around the island, on the water's edge, pieces of copper are found mixed with pebbles, but especially on the side which is opposite the south, and principally in a certain bay, which is near the northeast exposure to the great lake. * * *

"Advancing to the head of the lake (Fon du Lac) and returning one day's journey by the south coast, there is seen on the edge of the water, a rock of copper weighing seven or eight hundred pounds, and is so hard that steel can hardly cut it, but when it is heated it cuts as easily as lead. Near Point Chagouamigong [Sha-gah-wah-mikong, near Bayfield] where a mission was established rocks of copper and plates of the same metal were found. * * * Returning still toward the mouth of the lake, following the coast on the south as twenty leagues from the place last mentioned, we enter the river called Nantaouagan [Ontonagon] on which is a hill where stones and copper fall into the water or upon the earth. They are readily found.

"Three years since we received a piece which was brought from this place, which weighed a hundred pounds, and we sent it to Quebec to Mr. Talon. It is not certain exactly where this was broken from. We think it was from the forks of the river; others, that it was from near the lake, and dug up."

Talon, Intendent of Justice in Canada, visited France, taking a half-breed voyageur with him, and while in Paris, wrote on the 26th of February, 1669, to Colbert, the Minister of the Marine Department, "that this voyageur had penetrated among the western nations farther than any other Frenchman, and had seen the copper mine on Lake Huron. [Superior?] The man offers to go to that mine, and explore, either by sea, or by lake and river, the communication supposed to exist between Canada and the South Sea, or to the regions of Hudson's Bay."

As soon as Talon returned to Canada he commissioned Jolliet and Pere [Perrot] to search for the mines of copper on the upper Lakes. Jolliet received an outfit of four hundred livres, and four canoes, and Perrot one thousand livres. Minisister Colbert wrote from Paris to Talon, in February, 1671, approving of the search for copper, in these words: "The resolution you have taken to send Sieur de La Salle toward the south, and Sieur de St. Lusson to the north, to discover the South Sea passage, is very good, but the principal thing you ought to apply yourself in discoveries of this nature, is to look for the copper mine.

"Were this mine discovered, and its utility evident, it would be an assured means to attract several Frenchmen from old, to New France."

On the 14th of June, 1671, Saint Lusson at Sault St. Marie, planted the arms of France, in the presence of Nicholas Perrot, who acted as interpreter on the occasion; the Sieur Jolliet; Pierre Moreau or Sieur de la Taupine; a soldier of the garrison of Quebec, and several other Frenchmen.

Talon, in announcing Saint Lusson's explorations to Colbert, on the 2d of November, 1671, wrote from Quebec: "The copper which I send from Lake Superior and the river Nantaouagan [Ontonagon] proves that there is a mine on the border of some stream, which produces this material as pure as one could wish. More than twenty Frenchmen have seen one lump at the lake, which they estimate weighs more than eight hundred pounds. The Jesuit Fathers among the Outaouas [Ou-taw-waws] use an anvil of this material, which weighs about one hundred pounds. There will be no rest until the source from whence these detached lumps come is discovered.

"The river Nantaouagan [Ontonagon] appears between two high hills, the plain above which feeds the lakes, and receives a great deal of snow, which, in melting, forms torrents which wash the borders of this river, composed of solid gravel, which is rolled down by it.

"The gravel at the bottom of this, hardens itself, and assumes different shapes, such as those pebbles which I send to Mr. Bellinzany. My opinion is that these pebbles, rounded and carried off by the rapid waters, then have a tendency to become copper, by the influence of the sun's rays which they absorb, and to form other nuggets of metal similar to those which I send to Sieur de Bellinzany, found by the Sieur de Saint Lusson, about four hundred leagues, at some distance from the mouth of the river.

"He hoped by the frequent journeys of the savages, and French who are beginning to travel by these routes, to discern the source of production."

Governor Denonville, of Canada, sixteen years after the above circumstances, wrote: "The copper, a sample of which I sent M. Arnou, is found at the head of Lake Superior. The body of the mine has not yet been discovered. I have seen one of our voyageurs who assures me that, some fifteen months ago he saw a lump of two hundred weight, as yellow as gold, in a river which falls into Lake Superior. When heated, it could be cut with an axe; but the superstitious Indians, regarding this boulder as a good spirit, would never permit him to take any of it away. His opinion is that the frost undermined this piece, and that the mine is in that river. He has promised to search for it on his way back."

In the year 1730, there was some correspondence with the authorities in France relative to the discovery of copper at La Pointe, but, practically, little was done by the French, in developing the mineral wealth of Lake Superior.

CHAPTER III.

DU LUTH PLANTS THE FRENCH ARMS IN MINNESOTA

Du Luth's Relatives.—Randin Visits Extremity of Lake Superior.—Du Luth Plants King's Arms.—Post at Kaministigoya.—Pierre MoreaF, alias La Taupine.—La Salle's Visit.—A Pilot Deserts to the Sioux Country.—uaffart, Du Luth's Interpreter.—Descent of the River St. Croix.—Meets Father Hennepin.—Criticised by La Salle.—Trades with New England.—Visits France.—In Command at Mackinaw.—Frenchmen Murdered at Keweenaw.—Du Luth Arrests and Shoots Murderers.—Builds Fort above Detroit.—With Indian Allies in the Seneca War.—Du Luth's Brother.—Cadillac Defends the Brandy Trade.—Du Luth Disapproves of Selling Brandy to the Indians.—In Command at Fort Frontenac.—Death.

In the year 1678, several prominent merchants of Quebec and Montreal, with the support of Governor Frontenac of Canada, formed a company to open trade with the Sioux of Minnesota, and a nephew of Patron, one of these merchants, a brother-in-law of Sieur de Lusigny, an officer of the Governor's Guards, named Daniel Greysolon Du Luth [Doo-loo], a native of St. Germain en Laye, a few miles from Paris, although Lahontan speaks of him as from Lyons, was made the leader of the expedition. At the battle of Seneffe against the Prince of Orange, he was a gendarme, and one of the King's guards.

Du Luth was also a cousin of Henry Tonty, who had been in the revolution at Naples, to throw off the Spanish dependence. Du Luth's name is variously spelled in the documents of his day. Hennepin writes, "Du Luth;" others, "Dulhut," "Du Lhu," "Du Lut," "De Luth," "Du Lud."

The temptation to procure valuable furs from the Lake Superior region, contrary to the letter of the Canadian law, was very great; and more than one Governor winked at the contraband trade. Randin, who visited the extremity of Lake Superior, distributed presents to the Sioux and Ottawas in the name of Governor Frontenac, to secure the trade, and after his death, Du Luth was sent to complete what he had begun. With a party of twenty, seventeen Frenchmen and three Indians, he left Quebec on the first of September, 1678, and on the fifth of April, 1679, Du Luth writes to Governor Frontenac, that he is in the woods, about nine miles from Sault St. Marie, at the entrance of Lake Superior, and adds that: he "will not stir from the Nadoussioux, until further orders, and, peace being concluded, he will set up the King's Arms; lest the English and other Europeans settled towards California, take possession of the country."

On the second of July, 1679, he caused his Majesty's Arms to be planted in the great village of the Nadoussioux, called Kathio, where no Frenchman had ever been, and at Songaskicons and Houetbatons, one hundred and twenty leagues distant from the former, where he also set up the King's Arms. In a letter to Seignalay, published for the first time by Harrisse, he writes that it was in the village of Izatys [Issati]. Upon Franquelin's map, the Mississippi branches into the Tintonha [Teeton Sioux] country, and not far from here, he alleges, was seen a tree upon which was this legend: "Arms of the King cut on this tree in the year 1679."

He established a post at Kamanistigoya, which was distant fifteen leagues from the Grand Portage at the western extremity of Lake Superior; and here, on the fifteenth of September, he held a council with the Assenipoulaks [Assineboines] and other tribes, and urged them to be at peace with the Sioux. During this summer, he dispatched Pierre Moreau, a celebrated voyageur, nicknamed La Taupine, with letters to Governor Frontenac, and valuable furs to the merchants. His arrival at Quebec, created some excitement. It was charged that the Governor corresponded with Du Luth, and that he passed the beaver, sent by him, in the name of merchants in his interest. The Intendant of Justice, Du Chesneau, wrote to the Minister of the Colonial Department of France, that "the man named La Taupine, a famous coureur des bois, who set out in the month of September of last year, 1678, to go to the Outawacs, with goods, and who has always been interested with the Governor, having returned this year, and I, being advised that he had traded in two days, one hundred and fifty beaver robes in one village of this tribe, amounting to nearly nine hundred beavers, which is a matter of public notoriety; and that he left with Du Lut two men whom he had with him, considered myself bound to have him arrested, and to interrogate him; but having presented me with a license from the Governor, permitting him and his comrades, named Lamonde and Dupuy, to repair to the Outawac, to execute his secret orders, I had him set at liberty: and immediately on his going out, Sieur Prevost, Town Mayor of Quebec, came at the head of some soldiers to force the prison, in case he was still there, pursuant to his orders from the Governor, in these terms: "Sieur Prevost, Mayor of Quebec, is ordered, in case the Intendant arrest Pierre Moreau *alias* La Taupine, whom we have sent to Quebec as bearer of our dispatches, upon pretext of his having been in the bush, to set him forthwith at liberty, and to employ every means for this purpose, at his peril. Done at Montreal, the 5th September, 1679."

La Taupine, in due time returned to Lake Superior with another consignment of merchandise. The interpreter of Du Luth, and trader with the Sioux, was Faffart, who had been a soldier under La Salle at Fort Frontenac, and had deserted.

La Salle was commissioned in 1678, by the King of France, to explore the West, and trade in cibola, or buffalo skins, and on condition that he did not traffic with the Ottauwaws, who carried their beaver to Montreal.

On the 27th of August, 1679, he arrived at Mackinaw, in the "Griffin," the first sailing vessel on the great Lakes of the West, and from thence went to Green Bay, where, in the face of his commission, he traded for beaver. Loading his vessel with peltries, he sent it back to Niagara, while he, in canoes, proceeded with his expedition to the Illinois River. The ship was never heard of, and for a time supposed to be lost, but La Salle afterward learned from a Pawnee boy fourteen or fifteen years of age, who was brought prisoner to his fort on the Illinois by some Indians, that the pilot of the "Griffin" had been among the tribes of the Upper Missouri. He had ascended the Mississippi with four others in two birch canoes with goods and some hand grenades, taken from the ship, with the intention of joining Du Luth, who had for months been trading with the Sioux; and if their efforts were unsuccessful, they expected to push on to the English, at Hudson's Bay. While ascending the Mississippi they were attacked by Indians, and the pilot and one other only survived, and they were sold to the Indians on the Missouri.

In the month of June, 1680, Du Luth, accompanied by Faffart, an interpreter, with four Frenchmen, also a Chippeway and a Sioux, with two canoes, entered a river, the mouth of which is eight leagues from the head of Lake Superior on the South side, named Nemitsakouat. Reaching its head waters, by a short portage, of half a league, he reached a lake which was the source of the Saint Croix River, and by this, he and his companions were the first Europeans to journey in a canoe from Lake Superior to the Mississippi.

La Salle writes, that Du Luth, finding that the Sioux were on a hunt in the Mississippi valley, below the Saint Croix, and that Accault, Augelle and Hennepin, who had come up from the Illinois a few weeks before, were with them, descended until he found them. In the same letter he disregards the truth in order to disparage his rival, and writes:

"Thirty-eight or forty leagues above the Chippeway they found the river by which the Sieur Du Luth did descend to the Mississippi. He had been three years, contrary to orders, with a company of twenty "coureurs du bois" on Lake Superior; he had borne himself bravely, proclaiming everywhere that at the head of his brave fellows he did not fear the Grand Prevost, and that he would compel an amnesty.

"While he was at Lake Superior, the Nadouesioux, enticed by the presents that the late Sieur Randin had made on the part of Count Frontenac, and the Sauteurs [Ojibways], who are the savages who carry the peltries to Montreal, and who dwell on Lake Superior, wishing to obey the repeated orders of the Count, made a peace to unite the Sauteurs and French, and to trade with the Nadouesioux, situated about sixty leagues to the west of Lake Superior. Du Luth, to disguise his desertion, seized the opportunity to make some reputation for himself, sending two messengers to the Count to negotiate a truce, during which period their comrades negotiated still better for beaver.

Several conferences were held with the Nadouessioux, and as he needed an interpreter, he led off one of mine, named Faffart, formerly a soldier at Fort Frontenac. During this period there were frequent visits between the Sauteurs [Ojibways] and Nadouesioux, and supposing that it might increase the number of beaver skins, he sent Faffart by land, with the Nadouesioux and Sauteurs [Ojibways]. The young man on his return, having given an account of the quantity of beaver in that region, he wished to proceed thither himself, and, guided by a Sauteur and a Nadouesioux, and four Frenchmen, he ascended the river Nemitsakouat, where, by a short portage, he descended that stream, whereon he passed through forty leagues of rapids [Upper St. Croix River], and finding that the Nadouesioux were below with my men and the Father, who had come down again from the village of the Nadouesioux, he discovered them. They went up again to the village, and from thence they all together came down. They returned by the river Ouisconsing, and came back to Montreal, where Du Luth insults the commissaries, and the deputy of the 'procureur general,' named d'Anteuil. Count Frontenac had him arrested and imprisoned in the castle of Quebec, with the intention of returning him to France for the amnesty accorded to the coureurs des bois, did not release him."

At this very period, another party charges Frontenac as being Du Luth's particular friend.

Du Luth, during the fall of 1681, was engaged in the beaver trade at Montreal and Quebec. Du Chesneau, the Intendant of Justice for Canada, on the 13th of November, 1681, wrote to the Marquis de Siegnelay, in Paris: "Not content with the profits to be derived from the countries under the King's dominion, the desire of making money everywhere, has led the Governor [Frontenac], Boisseau, Du Lut and Patron, his uncle, to send canoes loaded with peltries, to the English. It is said sixty thousand livres' worth has been sent thither;" and he further stated that there was a very general report that within five or six days, Frontenac and his associates had divided the money received from the beavers sent to New England.

At a conference in Quebec of some of the distinguished men in that city, relative to difficulties with the Iroquois, held on the 10th of October, 1682, Du Luth was present. From thence he went to France, and, early in 1683, consulted with the Minister of Marine at Versailles relative to the interests of trade in the Hudson's Bay and Lake Superior region. Upon his return to Canada, he departed for Mackinaw. Governor De la Barre, on the 9th of November, 1683, wrote to the French Government that the Indians west and north of Lake Superior, "when they heard by expresses sent them by Du Lhut, of his arrival at Missilimakinak, that he was coming, sent him word to come quickly and they would unite with him to prevent others going thither. *If I stop that pass* as I hope, and as it is necessary to do, as the English of the Bay [Hudson's] excite against us the savages, whom Sieur Du Lhut alone can quiet."

While stationed at Mackinaw he was a participant in a tragic occurrence. During the summer of 1683 Jacques le Maire and Colin Berthot, while on their way to trade at Keweenaw, on Lake Superior, were surprised by three Indians, robbed, and murdered. Du Luth was prompt to arrest and punish the assassins. In a letter from Mackinaw, dated April 12, 1684, to the Governor of Canada, he writes: "Be pleased to know, Sir, that on the 24th of October last, I was told that Folle Avoine, accomplice in the murder and robbery of the two Frenchmen, had arrived at Sault Ste. Marie with fifteen families of the Sauteurs [Ojibways] who had fled from Chagoamigon [La Pointe] on account of an attack which they, together with the people of the land, made last Spring upon the Nadouecioux [Dakotahs.]

"He believed himself safe at the Sault, on account of the number of allies and relatives he had there. Rev. Father Albanel informed me that the French at the Saut, being only twelve in number, had not arrested him, believing themselves too weak to contend with such numbers, especially as the Sauteurs had declared that they would not allow the French to redden the land of their fathers with the blood of their brothers.

"On receiving this information, I immediately resolved to take with me six Frenchmen, and embark at the dawn of the next day for Sault Ste. Marie, and if possible obtain possession of the murderer. I made known my design to the Rev. Father Engalran, and, at my request, as he had some business to arrange with Rev. Father Albanel, he placed himself in my canoe.

"Having arrived within a league of the village

of the Saut, the Rev. Father, the Chevalier de Fourcille, Cardonnierre, and I disembarked. I caused the canoe, in which were Baribaud, Le Mere, La Fortune, and Macons, to proceed, while we went across the wood to the house of the Rev. Father, fearing that the savages, seeing me, might suspect the object of my visit, and cause Folle Avoine to escape. Finally, to cut the matter short, I arrested him, and caused him to be guarded day and night by six Frenchmen.

"I then called a council, at which I requested all the savages of the place to be present, where I repeated what I had often said to the Hurons and Ottawas since the departure of M. Pere [Perrot], giving them the message you ordered me. Sir, that in case there should be among them any spirits so evil disposed as to follow the example of those who have murdered the French on Lake Superior and Lake Michigan, they must separate the guilty from the innocent, as I did not wish the whole nation to suffer, unless they protected the guilty. * * * The savages held several councils, to which I was invited, but their only object seemed to be to exculpate the prisoner, in order that I might release him.

"All united in accusing Achiganaga and his children, assuring themselves with the belief that M. Pere, [Perrot] with his detachment would not be able to arrest them, and wishing to persuade me that they apprehended that all the Frenchmen might be killed.

"I answered them, * * * 'As to the anticipated death of M. Pere [Perrot], as well as of the other Frenchmen, that would not embarrass me, since I believed neither the allies nor the nation of Achiganaga would wish to have a war with us to sustain an action so dark as that of which we were speaking. Having only to attack a few murderers, or, at most, those of their own family, I was certain that the French would have them dead or alive.'

"This was the answer they had from me during the three days that the councils lasted; after which I embarked, at ten o'clock in the morning, sustained by only twelve Frenchmen, to show a few unruly persons who boasted of taking the prisoner away from me, that the French did not fear them.

"Daily I received accounts of the number of savages that Achiganaga drew from his nation to Kiaonan [Keweenaw] under pretext of going to war in the spring against the Nadouecioux, to avenge the death of one of his relatives, son of Ouenaus, but really to protect himself against us, in case we should become convinced that his children had killed the Frenchmen. This precaution placed me between hope and fear respecting the expedition which M. Pere [Perrot] had undertaken.

"On the 24th of November, [1683], he came across the wood at ten o'clock at night, to tell me that he had arrested Achiganaga and four of his children. He said they were not all guilty of the murder, but had thought proper, in this affair, to follow the custom of the savages, which is to seize all the relatives. Folle Avoine, whom I had arrested, he considered the most guilty, being without doubt the originator of the mischief.

"I immediately gave orders that Folle Avoine should be more closely confined, and not allowed to speak to any one; for I had also learned that he had a brother, sister, and uncle in the village of the Kiskakons.

"M. Pere informed me that he had released the youngest son of Achiganaga, aged about thirteen or fourteen years, that he might make known to their nation and the Sauteurs [Ojibways], who are at Nocke and in the neighborhood, the reason why the French had arrested his father and brothers. M. Pere bade him assure the savages that if any one wished to complain of what he had done, he would wait for them with a firm step; for he considered himself in a condition to set them at defiance, having found at Kiaonau [Keweenaw] eighteen Frenchmen who had wintered there.

"On the 25th, at daybreak, M. Pere embarked at the Sault, with four good men whom I gave him, to go and meet the prisoners. He left them four leagues from there, under a guard of twelve Frenchmen; and at two o'clock in the afternoon, they arrived. I had prepared a room in my house for the prisoners, in which they were placed under a strong guard, and were not allowed to converse with any one.

"On the 26th, I commenced proceedings; and this, sir, is the course I pursued. I gave notice to all the chiefs and others, to appear at the council which I had appointed, and gave to Folle Avoine the privilege of selecting two of his rela tives to support his interests; and to the other prisoners I made the same offer.

"The council being assembled, I sent for Folle Avoine to be interrogated, and caused his answers to be written, and afterwards they were read to him, and inquiry made whether they were not, word for word, what he had said. He was then removed under a safe guard. I used the same form with the two eldest sons of Achiganaga, and, as Folle Avoine had indirectly charged the father with being accessory to the murder, I sent for him and also for Folle Avoine, and bringing them into the council, confronted the four.

"Folle Avoine and the two sons of Achiganaga accused each other of committing the murder. without denying that they were participators in the crime. Achiganaga alone strongly maintained that he knew nothing of the design of Folle Avoine, nor of his children, and called on them to say if he had advised them to kill the Frenchmen. They answered, 'No.'

"This confrontation, which the savages did not expect, surprised them; and, seeing the prisoners had convicted themselves of the murder, the Chiefs said: 'It is enough; you accuse yourselves; the French are masters of your bodies.'

"The next day I held another council, in which I said there could be no doubt that the Frenchmen had been murdered, that the murderers were known, and that they knew what was the practice among themselves upon such occasions. To all this they said nothing, which obliged us on the following day to hold another council in the cabin of Brochet, where, after having spoken, and seeing that they would make no decision, and that all my councils ended only in reducing tobacco to ashes, I told them that, since they did not wish to decide, I should take the responsibility, and that the next day I would let them know the determination of the French and myself.

"It is proper, Sir, you should know that I observed all these forms only to see if they would feel it their duty to render to us the same justice that they do to each other, having had divers examples in which when the tribes of those who had committed the murder did not wish to go to war with the tribe aggrieved, the nearest relations of the murderers killed them themselves; that is to say, man for man.

"On the 29th of November. I gathered together the French that were here, and. after the interrogations and answers of the accused had been read to them, the guilt of the three appeared so evident, from their own confessions, that the vote was unanimous that all should die. But as the French who remained at Kiaonan to pass the winter had written to Father Engalran and to myself, to beg us to treat the affair with all possible leniency, the savages declaring that if they made the prisoners die they would avenge themselves, I told the gentlemen who were with me in council that, this being a case without a precedent, I believed it was expedient for the safety of the French who would pass the winter in the Lake Superior country to put to death only two, as that of the third might bring about grievous consequences, while the putting to death, man for man, could give the savages no complaint, since this is their custom. M. de la Tour, chief of the Fathers, who had served much, sustained my opinions by strong reasoning, and all decided that two should be shot, namely, Folle Avoine and the older of the two brothers, while the younger should be released, and hold his life, Sir, as a gift from you.

"I then returned to the cabin of Brochet with Messrs. Boisguillot, Pere, De Repentigny, De Manthet, De la Ferte, and Macons, where were all the chiefs of the Outawas du Sable, Outawas Sinagos, Kiskakons. Santeurs, D'Achiliny, a part of the Hurons; and Oumamens, the chief of the Amikoys. I informed them of our decision * * * that, the Frenchmen having been killed by the different nations, one of each must die, and that the same death they had caused the French to suffer they must also suffer. * * * This decision to put the murderers to death was a hard stroke to them all, for none had believed that I would dare to undertake it. * * * I then left the council and asked the Rev. Fathers if they wished to baptize the prisoners, which they did.

"An hour after, I put myself at the head of forty-two Frenchmen, and, in sight of more than four hundred savages, and within two hundred paces of their fort, I caused the two murderers to be shot. The impossibility of keeping them until spring made me hasten their death. * * * When M. Pere made the arrest, those who had committed the murder confessed it; and when he asked them what they had done with our goods they answered that they were almost all concealed. He proceeded to the place of concealment, and was very much surprised, as were also the French with him, to find them, in fifteen or twenty different places. By the carelessness of the savages, the tobacco and powder were entirely destroyed, having been placed in the pinery, under the roots of trees, and being soaked in the water caused by ten or twelve days' continuous rain, which inundated all the lower country. The season for snow and ice having come, they had all the trouble in the world to get out the bales of cloth.

"They then went to see the bodies, but could not remove them, these miserable wretches having thrown them into a marsh, and thrust them down into holes which they had made. Not satisfied with this, they had also piled branches of trees upon the bodies, to prevent them from floating when the water should rise in the spring, hoping by this precaution the French would find no trace of those who were killed, but would think them drowned; as they reported that they had found in the lake on the other side of the Portage, a boat with the sides all broken in, which they believed to be a French boat.

"Those goods which the French were able to secure, they took to Kiaonau [Keweenaw], where were a number of Frenchmen who had gone there to pass the winter, who knew nothing of the death of Colin Berthot and Jacques le Maire, until M. Pere arrived.

"The ten who formed M. Pere's detachment having conferred together concerning the means they should take to prevent a total loss, decided to sell the goods to the highest bidder. The sale was made for 1100 livres, which was to be paid in beavers, to M. de la Chesnaye, to whom I send the names of the purchsers.

"The savages who were present when Achiganaga and his children were arrested wished to pass the calumet to M. Pere, and give him captives to satisfy him for the murder committed on the two Frenchmen; but he knew their intention, and would not accept their offer. He told them neither a hundred captives nor a hundred packs of beaver would give back the blood of his brothers; that the murderers must be given up to me, and I would see what I would do.

"I caused M. Pere to repeat these things in the council, that in future the savages need not think by presents to save those who commit similar deeds. Besides, sir, M. Pere showed plainly by his conduct, that he is not strongly inclined to favor the savages, as was reported. Indeed, I do not know any one whom they fear more, yet who flatters them less or knows them better.

"The criminals being in two different places, M. Pere being obliged to keep four of them, sent Messrs. de Repentigny, Manthet, and six other Frenchmen, to arrest the two who were eight leagues in the woods. Among others, M. de Repentigny and M. de Manthet showed that they feared nothing when their honor called them.

"M. de la Chevrotiere has also served well in person, and by his advice, having pointed out where the prisoners were. Achiganaga, who had adopted him as a son, had told him where he should hunt during the winter. * * * * * It still remained for me to give to Achiganaga and his three children the means to return to his family. Their home from which they were taken was nearly twenty-six leagues from here. Knowing their necessity, I told them you would not be satisfied in giving them life; you wished to preserve it, by giving them all that was necessary to prevent them from dying with hunger and cold by the way, and that your gift was made by my hands. I gave them blankets, tobacco, meat, hatchets, knives, twine to make nets for beavers, and two bags of corn, to supply them till they could kill game.

"They departed two days after, the most contented creatures in the world, but God was not; for when only two days' journey from here, the old Achiganaga fell sick of the quinsy, and died, and his children returned. When the news of his death arrived, the greater part of the savages of this place [Mackinaw] attributed it to the French, saying we had caused him to die. I let them talk, and laughed at them. It is only about two months since the children of Achiganaga returne l to Kiaonan."

Some of those opposed to Du Luth and Frontenac, prejudiced the King of France relative to the transaction we have described, and in a letter to the Governor of Canada, the King writes: "It appears to me that one of the principal causes of the war arises from one Du Luth having caused two to be killed who had assassinated two Frenchmen on Lake Superior; and you sufficiently see how much this man's voyage, which can not produce any advantage to the colony, and which was permitted only in the interest of some private persons, has contributed to distract the peace of the colony."

Du Luth and his young brother appear to have traded at the western extremity of Lake Superior, and on the north shore, to Lake Nipegon.

In June, 1684, Governor De la Barre sent Guillet and Hebert from Montreal to request Du Luth and Durantaye to bring down voyageurs and Indians to assist in an expedition against the Iroquois of New York. Early in September, they reported on the St. Lawrence, with one hundred and fifty coureurs des bois and three hundred and fifty Indians; but as a treaty had just been made with the Senecas, they returned.

De la Barre's successor, Governor Denonville, in a dispatch to the French Government, dated November 12th, 1685, alludes to Du Luth being in the far West, in these words: "I likewise sent to M. De la Durantaye, who is at Lake Superior under orders from M. De la Barre, and to Sieur Du Luth, who is also at a great distance in another direction, and all so far beyond reach that neither the one nor the other can hear news from me this year; so that, not being able to see them at soonest, before next July, I considered it best not to think of undertaking any thing during the whole of next year, especially as a great number of our best men are among the Outaouacs, and can not return before the ensuing summer. * * * In regard to Sieur Du Luth, I sent him orders to repair here, so that I may learn the number of savages on whom I may depend. He is accredited among them, and rendered great services to M. De la Barre by a large number of savages he brought to Niagara, who would have attacked the Senecas, was it not for an express order from M. De la Barre to the contrary."

In 1686, while at Mackinaw, he was ordered to establish a post on the Detroit, near Lake Erie. A portion of the order reads as follows: "After having given all the orders that you may judge necessary for the safety of this post, and having well secured the obedience of the Indians, you will return to Michilimackinac, there to await Rev. Father Engelran, by whom I will communicate what I wish of you, there."

The design of this post was to block the passage of the English to the upper lakes. Before it was established, in the fall of 1686, Thomas Roseboom, a daring trader from Albany, on the Hudson, had found his way to the vicinity of Mackinaw, and by the proffer of brandy, weakened the allegiance of the tribes to the French.

A canoe coming to Mackinaw with dispatches for the French and their allies, to march to the Seneca country, in New York, perceived this New York trader and associates, and, giving the alarm, they were met by three hundred coureurs du bois and captured.

In the spring of 1687 Du Luth, Durantaye, and Tonty all left the vicinity of Detroit for Niagara, and as they were coasting along Lake Erie they met another English trader, a Scotchman by birth, and by name Major Patrick McGregor, a person of some influence, going with a number of traders to Mackinaw. Having taken him prisoner, he was sent with Roseboom to Montreal.

Du Luth, Tonty, and Durantaye arrived at Niagara on the 27th of June, 1687, with one hundred and seventy French voyageurs, besides Indians, and on the 10th of July joined the army of Denonville at the mouth of the Genesee River, and on the 13th Du Luth and his associates had a skirmish near a Seneca village, now the site of the town of Victor, twenty miles southeast of the city of Rochester, New York. Governor Denonville, in a report, writes: "On the 13th, about 4 o'clock in the afternoon, having passed through two dangerous defiles, we arrived at the third, where we were vigorously attacked by eight hundred Senecas, two hundred of whom fired, wishing to attack our rear, while the rest would attack our front, but the resistance, made produced such a great consternation that they soon resolved to fly. * * * We witnessed the painful sight of the usual cruelties of the savages, who cut the dead into quarters, as is done in slaughter houses, in order to put them into the kettle. The greater number were opened while still warm, that the blood might be drunk. Our rascally Otaoas distinguished themselves particularly by these barbarities. * * * We had five or six men killed on the spot, French and Indians, and about twenty wounded, among the first of whom was the Rev. Father Angelran, superior of all the Otaoan Missions, by a very severe gun-shot. It is a great misfortune that this wound will prevent him going back again, for he is a man of capacity."

In the order to Du Luth assigning him to duty at the post on the site of the modern Fort Gratiot, above the city of Detroit, the Governor of Canada said: "If you can so arrange your affairs that your brother can be near you in the Spring. I shall be very glad. He is an intelligent lad, and might be a great assistance to you; he might also be very serviceable to us."

This lad, Greysolon de la Tourette, during the winter of 1686-7 was trading among the Assinaboines and other tribes at the west end of Lake Superior, but, upon receiving a dispatch, hastened to his brother, journeying in a canoe without any escort from Mackinaw. He did not arrive until after the battle with the Senecas. Governor Denonville, on the 25th of August, 1687, wrote:

"Du Luth's brother, who has recently arrived from the rivers above the Lake of the Allempigons [Nipegon], assures me that he saw more than fifteen hundred persons come to trade with him, and they were very sorry he had not goods sufficient to satisfy them. They are of the tribes accustomed to resort to the English at Port Nelson and River Bourbon, where, they say, they did not go this year, through Sieur Du Lhu's influence."

After the battle in the vicinity of Rochester, New York, Du Luth, with his celebrated cousin, Henry Tonty, returned together as far as the post above the present city of Detroit, Michigan, but this point, after 1688, was not again occupied.

From this period Du Luth becomes less prominent. At the time when the Jesuits attempted to exclude brandy from the Indian country a bitter controversy arose between them and the traders. Cadillac, a Gascon by birth, commanding Fort Buade, at Mackinaw, on August 3, 1695, wrote to Count Frontenac: "Now, what reason can we assign that the savages should not drink brandy bought with their own money as well as we? Is it prohibited to prevent them from becoming intoxicated? Or is it because the use of brandy reduces them to extreme misery, placing it out of their power to make war by depriving them of clothing and arms? If such representations in regard to the Indians have been made to the Count, they are very false, as every one knows who is acquainted with the ways of the savages. * * * It is bad faith to represent to the Count that the sale of brandy reduces the savage to a state of nudity, and by that means places it out of his power to make war, since he never goes to war in any other condition. * * * Perhaps it will be said that the sale of brandy makes the labors of the missionaries unfruitful. It is necessary to examine this proposition. If the missionaries care for only the extension of commerce, pursuing the course they have hitherto, I agree to it; but if it is the use of brandy that hinders the advancement of the cause of God, I deny it, for it is a fact which no one can deny that there are a great number of savages who never drink brandy, yet who are not, for that, better Christians.

"All the Sioux, the most numerous of all the tribes, who inhabit the region along the shore of Lake Superior, do not even like the smell of brandy. Are they more advanced in religion for that? They do not wish to have the subject mentioned, and when the missionaries address them they only laugh at the foolishness of preaching. Yet these priests boldly fling before the eyes of Europeans, whole volumes filled with glowing descriptions of the conversion of souls by thousands in this country, causing the poor missionaries from Europe, to run to martyrdom as flies to sugar and honey."

Du Luth, or Du Lhut, as he wrote his name, during this discussion, was found upon the side of order and good morals. His attestation is as follows: "I certify that at different periods I have lived about ten years among the Ottawa nation, from the time that I made an exploration to the Nadouecioux people until Fort Saint Joseph was established by order of the Monsieur Marquis Denonville, Governor General, at the head of the Detroit of Lake Erie, which is in the Iroquois country, and which I had the honor to command. During this period, I have seen that the trade in eau-de-vie (brandy) produced great disorder, the father killing the son, and the son throwing his mother into the fire; and I maintain that, morally speaking, it is impossible to export brandy to the woods and distant missions, without danger of its leading to misery."

Governor Frontenac, in an expedition against the Oneidas of New York, arrived at Fort Frontenac, on the 19th of July, 1695, and Captain Du Luth was left in command with forty soldiers, and masons and carpenters, with orders to erect new buildings. In about four weeks he erected a building one hundred and twenty feet in length, containing officers' quarters, store-rooms, a bakery and a chapel. Early in 1697 he was still in command of the post, and in a report it is mentioned that "everybody was then in good health, except Captain Dulhut the commander, who was unwell of the gout."

It was just before this period, that as a member of the Roman Catholic Church, he was firmly impressed that he had been helped by prayers which he addressed to a deceased Iroquois girl, who had died in the odor of sanctity, and, as a thank offering, signed the following certificate: "I, the subscriber, certify to all whom it may concern, that having been tormented by the gout, for the space of twenty-three years, and with such severe pains, that it gave me no rest for the spac of three months at a time, I addressed myself to Catherine Tegahkouita, an Iroquois virgin deceased at the Sault Saint Louis, in the reputation of sanctity, and I promised her to visit her tomb, if God should give me health, through her intercession. I have been as perfectly cured at the end of one novena, which I made in her honor, that after five months, I have not perceived the slightest touch of my gout. Given at Fort Frontenac, this 18th day of August, 1696."

As soon as cold weather returned, his old malady again appeared. He died early in A. D. 1710. Marquis de Vaudreuil, Governor of Canada, under date of first of May of that year, wrote to Count Pontchartrain, Colonial Minister at Paris, "Captain Du Lud died this winter. He was a very honest man."

CHAPTER IV.

FIRST WHITE MEN AT FALLS OF SAINT ANTHONY OF PADUA.

Falls of St. Anthony Visited by White Men.—La Salle Gives the First Description of Upper Mississippi Valley. Accault, the Leader, Accompanied by Augelle and Hennepin, at Falls of Saint Anthony.—Hennepin Declared Unreliable by La Salle. His Early Life.—His First Book Criticised by Abbe Bernou and Tronson.—Deceptive Map.—First Meeting with Sioux!—Astonishment at Reading His Breviary, Sioux Name for Guns.—Accault and Hennepin at Lake Pepin.—Leave the River Below Saint Paul.—At Mille Lacs.—A Sweating Cabin.—Sioux Wonder at Mariner's Compass.—Fears of an Iron Pot.—Making a Dictionary.—Infant Baptised.—Route to the Pacific.—Hennepin Descends Rum River.—First Visit to Falls of Saint Anthony.—On a Buffalo Hunt.—Meets Du Luth.—Returns to Mille Lacs.—With Du Luth at Falls of St. Anthony.—Returns to France.—Subsequent Life.—His Books Examined.—Denies in First Book His Descent to the Gulf of Mexico.—Dispute with Du Luth at Falls of St, Anthony.—Patronage of Du Luth.—Tribute to Du Luth.—Hennepin's Answer to Criticisms.—Denounced by D'Iberville and Father Gravier.—Residence in Rome.

In the summer of 1680, Michael Accault (Ako), Hennepin, the Franciscan missionary, Augelle, Du Luth, and Faffart all visited the Falls of Saint Anthony.

The first description of the valley of the upper Mississippi was written by La Salle, at Fort Frontenac, on Lake Ontario, on the 22d of August, 1682, a month before Hennepin, in Paris, obtained a license to print, and some time before the Franciscan's first work, was issued from the press.

La Salle's knowledge must have been received from Michael Accault, the leader of the expedition, Augelle, his comrade, or the clerical attache, the Franciscan, Hennepin.

It differs from Hennepin's narrative in its freedom from bombast, and if its statements are to be credited, the Franciscan must be looked on as one given to exaggeration. The careful student, however, soon learns to be cautious in receiving the statement of any of the early explorers and ecclesiastics of the Northwest. The Franciscan depreciated the Jesuit missionary, and La Salle did not hesitate to misrepresent Du Luth and others for his own exaltation. La Salle makes statements which we deem to be wide of the truth when his prejudices are aroused.

At the very time that the Intendant of Justice in Canada is complaining that Governor Frontenac is a friend and correspondent of Du Luth, La Salle writes to his friends in Paris, that Du Luth is looked upon as an outlaw by the governor.

While official documents prove that Du Luth was in Minnesota a year before Accault and associates, yet La Salle writes: "Moreover, the Nadonesioux is not a region which he has discovered. It is known that it was discovered a long time before, and that the Rev. Father Hennepin and Michael Accault were there before him."

La Salle in this communication describes Accault as one well acquainted with the language and names of the Indians of the Illinois region, and also "cool, brave, and prudent," and the head of the party of exploration.

We now proceed with the first description of the country above the Wisconsin, to which is given, for the first and only time, by any writer, the Sioux name, Meschetz Odeba, perhaps intended for Meshdeke Wakpa, River of the Foxes.

He describes the Upper Mississippi in these words: "Following the windings of the Mississippi, they found the river Ouisconsing, Wisconsing, or Meschetz Odeba, which flows between Bay of Puans and the Grand river. * * * About twenty-three or twenty-four leagues to the north or northwest of the mouth of the Ouisconsing, * * * they found the Black river, called by the Nadouesioux, Chabadeba [Chapa Wakpa, Beaver river] not very large, the mouth of which is bordered on the two shores by alders.

"Ascending about thirty leagues, almost at the same point of the compass, is the Buffalo river [Chippewa], as large at its mouth as that of the Illinois. They follow it ten or twelve leagues, where it is deep, small and without rapids, bordered by hills which widen out from time to time to form prairies."

About three o'clock in the afternoon of the 11th of April, 1680, the travelers were met by a war party of one hundred Sioux in thirty-three birch bark canoes. "Michael Accault, who was the leader," says La Salle, "presented the Calumet." The Indians were presented by Accault with twenty knives and a fathom and a half of tobacco and some goods. Proceeding with the Indians ten days, on the 22d of April the isles in the Mississippi were reached, where the Sioux had killed some Maskoutens, and they halted to weep over the death of two of their own number; and to assuage their grief, Accault gave them in trade a box of goods and twenty-four hatchets.

When they were eight leagues below the Falls of Saint Anthony, they resolved to go by land to their village, sixty leagues distant. They were well received; the only strife among the villages was that which resulted from the desire to have a Frenchman in their midst. La Salle also states that it was not correct to give the impression that Du Luth had rescued his men from captivity, for they could not be properly called prisoners.

He continues: "In going up the Mississippi again, twenty leagues above that river [Saint Croix] is found the falls, which those I sent, and who passing there first, named Saint Anthony. It is thirty or forty feet high, and the river is narrower here than elsewhere. There is a small island in the midst of the chute, and the two banks of the river are not bordered by high hills, which gradually diminish at this point, but the country on each side is covered with thin woods, such as oaks and other hard woods, scattered wide apart.

"The canoes were carried three or four hundred steps, and eight leagues above was found the west [east?] bank of the river of the Nadouesioux, ending in a lake named Issati, which expands into a great marsh, where the wild rice grows toward the mouth."

In the latter part of his letter La Salle uses the following language relative to his old chaplain:

"I believed that it was appropriate to make for you the narrative of the adventures of this canoe, because I doubt not that they will speak of it, and if you wish to confer with the Father Louis Hennepin, Recollect, who has returned to France, you must know him a little, because he will not fail to exaggerate all things; it is his character, and to me he has written as if he were about to be burned when he was not even in danger, but he believes that it is honorable to act in this manner, and he speaks more conformably to that which he wishes than to that which he knows."

Hennepin was born in Ath, an inland town of the Netherlands. From boyhood he longed to visit foreign lands, and it is not to be wondered at that he assumed the priest's garb, for next to the soldier's life, it suited one of wandering propensities.

At one time he is on a begging expedition to some of the towns on the sea coast. In a few months he occupies the post of chaplain at an hospital, where he shrives the dying and administers extreme unction. From the quiet of the hospital he proceeds to the camp, and is present at the battle of Seneffe, which occurred in the year 1674.

His whole mind, from the time that he became a priest, appears to have been on "things seen and temporal," rather than on those that are "unseen and eternal." While on duty at some of the ports of the Straits of Dover, he exhibited the characteristic of an ancient Athenian more than that of a professed successor of the Apostles. He sought out the society of strangers "who spent their time in nothing else but either to tell or to hear some new thing." With perfect nonchalance he confesses that notwithstanding the nauseating fumes of tobacco, he used to slip behind the doors of sailors' taverns, and spend days, without regard to the loss of his meals, listening to the adventures and hair-breadth escapes of the mariners in lands beyond the sea.

In the year 1676, he received a welcome order from his Superior, requiring him to embark for Canada. Unaccustomed to the world, and arbitrary in his disposition, he rendered the cabin of the ship in which he sailed any thing but heavenly. As in modern days, the passengers in a vessel to the new world were composed of heterogeneous materials. There were young women going out in search for brothers or husbands, ecclesiastics, and those engaged in the then new, but profitable, commerce in furs. One of his fellow passengers was the talented and enterprising, though unfortunate, La Salle, with whom he was afterwards associated. If he is to be credited, his intercourse with La Salle was not very pleasant on ship-board. The young women, tired of being cooped up in the narrow accommodations of the ship, when the evening was fair sought the deck, and engaged in the rude dances of the French peasantry of that age. Hennepin, feeling that it was improper, began to assume the air of the priest, and forbade the sport. La Salle, feeling that his interference was uncalled for, called him a pedant, and took the side of the girls, and during the voyage there were stormy discussions.

Good humor appears to have been restored when they left the ship, for Hennepin would otherwise have not been the companion of La Salle in his great western journey.

Sojourning for a short period at Quebec, the adventure-loving Franciscan is permitted to go to a mission station on or near the site of the present town of Kingston, Canada West.

Here there was much to gratify his love of novelty, and he passed considerable time in rambling among the Iroquois of New York. In 1678 he returned to Quebec, and was ordered to join the expedition of Robert La Salle.

On the 6th of December Father Hennepin and a portion of the exploring party had entered the Niagara river. In the vicinity of the Falls, the winter was passed, and while the artisans were preparing a ship above the Falls, to navigate the great lakes, the Recollect whiled away the hours, in studying the manners and customs of the Seneca Indians, and in admiring the sublimest handiwork of God on the globe.

On the 7th of August, 1679, the ship being completely rigged, unfurled its sails to the breezes of Lake Erie. The vessel was named the "Griffin," in honor of the arms of Frontenac, Governor of Canada, the first ship of European construction that had ever ploughed the waters of the great inland seas of North America.

After encountering a violent and dangerous storm on one of the lakes, during which they had given up all hope of escaping shipwreck, on the 27th of the month, they were safely moored in the harbor of "Missilimackinack." From thence the party proceeded to Green Bay, where they left the ship, procured canoes, and continued along the coast of Lake Michigan. By the middle of January, 1680, La Salle had conducted his expedition to the Illinois River, and, on an eminence near Lake Peoria, he commenced, with much heaviness of heart, the erection of a fort, which he called Crevecœur, on account of the many disappointments he had experienced.

On the last of February, Accault, Augelle, and Hennepin left to ascend the Mississippi.

The first work bearing the name of the Reverend Father Louis Hennepin, Franciscan Missionary of the Recollect order, was entitled, "Description de la Louisiane," and in 1683 published in Paris.

As soon as the book appeared it was criticised. Abbe Bernou, on the 29th of February, 1684, writes from Rome about the "paltry book" (meschant livre) of Father Hennepin. About a year before the pious Tronson, under date of March 13, 1683, wrote to a friend: "I have interviewed the P. Recollect, who *pretends* to have descended the Mississippi river to the Gulf of Mexico. I do not know that one *will believe what he speaks* any more than that which is in the *printed relation* of P. Louis, which I send you that you may make your own reflections."

On the map accompanying his first book, he boldly marks a Recollect Mission many miles north of the point he had visited. In the Utrecht edition of 1697 this deliberate fraud is erased.

Throughout the work he assumes, that he was the leader of the expedition, and magnifies trifles into tragedies. For instance, Mr. La Salle writes that Michael Accault, also written Ako, who was the leader, presented the Sioux with the calumet;" but Hennepin makes the occurrence more formidable.

He writes: "Our prayers were heard, when on the 11th of April, 1680, about two o'clock in the afternoon, we suddenly perceived thirty-three bark canoes manned by a hundred and twenty Indians coming down with very great speed, on a war party, against the Miamis, Illinois and Maroas. These Indians surrounded us, and while at a distance, discharged some arrows at us, but as they approached our canoe, the old men seeing us with the calumet of peace in our hands, prevented the young men from killing us. These savages leaping from their canoes, some on land, others into the water, with frightful cries and yells approached us, and as we made no resistance, being only three against so great a number, one of them wrenched our calumet from our hands, while our canoe and theirs were tied to the shore. We first presented to them a piece of

French tobacco, better for smoking than theirs' and the eldest among them uttered the words' "Miamiha, Miamiha."

"As we did not understand their language, we took a little stick, and by signs which we made on the sand, showed them that their enemies, the Miamis, whom they sought, had fled across the river Colbert [Mississippi] to join the Islinois; when they saw themselves discovered and unable to surprise their enemies, three or four old men laying their hands on my head, wept in a mournful tone.

"With a spare handkerchief I had left I wiped away their tears, but they would not smoke our Calumet. They made us cross the river with great cries, while all shouted with tears in their eyes; they made us row before them, and we heard yells capable of striking the most resolute with terror. After landing our canoe and goods, part of which had already been taken, we made a fire to boil our kettle, and we gave them two large wild turkeys which we had killed. These Indians having called an assembly to deliberate what they were to do with us, the two head chiefs of the party approaching, showed us by signs that the warriors wished to tomahawk us. This compelled me to go to the war chiefs with one young man, leaving the other by our property, and throw into their midst six axes, fifteen knives and six fathom of our black tobacco; and then bringing down my head, I showed them with an axe that they might kill me, if they thought proper. This present appeased many individual members, who gave us some beaver to eat, putting the three first morsels into our mouths, according to the custom of the country, and blowing on the meat, which was too hot, before putting the bark dish before us to let us eat as we liked. We spent the night in anxiety, because, before retiring at night, they had returned us our peace calumet.

"Our two boatmen were resolved to sell their lives dearly, and to resist if attacked; their arms and swords were ready. As for my own part, I determined to allow myself to be killed without any resistance; as I was going to announce to them a God who had been foully accused, unjustly condemned, and cruelly crucified, without showing the least aversion to those who put him to death. We watched in turn, in our anxiety, so as not to be surprised asleep. The next morning, a chief named Narrhetoba asked for the peace calumet, filled it with willow bark, and all smoked. It was then signified that the white men were to return with them to their villages."

In his narrative the Franciscan remarks, "I found it difficult to say my office before these Indians. Many seeing me move my lips, said in a fierce tone, 'Ouakanche.' Michael, all out of countenance, told me, that if I continued to say my breviary, we should all three be killed, and the Picard begged me at least to pray apart, so as not to provoke them. I followed the latter's advice, but the more I concealed myself the more I had the Indians at my heels; for when I entered the wood, they thought I was going to hide some goods under ground, so that I knew not on what side to turn to pray, for they never let me out of sight. This obliged me to beg pardon of my canoe-men, assuring them I could not dispense with saying my office. By the word, 'Ouakanche,' the Indians meant that the book I was reading was a spirit, but by their gesture they nevertheless showed a kind of aversion, so that to accustom them to it, I chanted the litany of the Blessed Virgin in the canoe, with my book opened. They thought that the breviary was a spirit which taught me to sing for their diversion; for these people are naturally fond of singing."

This is the first mention of a Dahkotah word in a European book. The savages were annoyed rather than enraged, at seeing the white man reading a book, and exclaimed, "Wakan-de!" this is wonderful or supernatural. The war party was composed of several bands of the M'dewahkantonwan Dahkotahs, and there was a diversity of opinion in relation to the disposition that should be made of the white men. The relatives of those who had been killed by the Miamis, were in favor of taking their scalps, but others were anxious to retain the favor of the French, and open a trading intercourse.

Perceiving one of the canoe-men shoot a wild turkey, they called the gun, "Manza Ouackange," iron that has understanding; more correctly, "Maza Wakande," this is the supernatural metal.

Aquipaguetin, one of the head men, resorted to the following device to obtain merchandise. Says the Father, "This wily savage had the bones of some distinguished relative, which he preserved with great care in some skins dressed and adorned with several rows of black and red porcupine quills. From time to time he assembled his men to give it a smoke, and made us come several days to cover the bones with goods, and by a present wipe away the tears he had shed for him, and for his own son killed by the Miamis. To appease this captious man, we threw on the bones several fathoms of tobacco, axes, knives, beads, and some black and white wampum bracelets. * * * We slept at the point of the Lake of Tears [Lake Pepin], which we so called from the tears which this chief shed all night long, or by one of his sons whom he caused to weep when he grew tired."

The next day, after four or five leagues' sail, a chief came, and telling them to leave their canoes, he pulled up three piles of grass for seats. Then taking a piece of cedar full of little holes, he placed a stick into one, which he revolved between the palms of his hands, until he kindled a fire, and informed the Frenchmen that they would be at Mille Lac in six days. On the nineteenth day after their captivity, they arrived in the vicinity of Saint Paul, not far, it is probable, from the marshy ground on which the Kaposia band once lived, and now called Pig's Eye.

The journal remarks, "Having arrived on the nineteenth day of our navigation, five leagues below St. Anthony's Falls, these Indians landed us in a bay, broke our canoe to pieces, and secreted their own in the reeds."

They then followed the trail to Mille Lac, sixty leagues distant. As they approached their villages, the various bands began to show their spoils. The tobacco was highly prized, and led to some contention. The chalice of the Father, which glistened in the sun, they were afraid to touch, supposing it was "wakan." After five days' walk they reached the Issati [Dahkotah] settlements in the valley of the Rum or Knife river. The different bands each conducted a Frenchman to their village, the chief Aquipaguetin taking charge of Hennepin. After marching through the marshes towards the sources of Rum river, five wives of the chief, in three bark canoes, met them and took them a short league to an island where their cabins were.

An aged Indian kindly rubbed down the way-worn Franciscan; placing him on a bear-skin near the fire, he anointed his legs and the soles of his feet with wildcat oil.

The son of the chief took great pleasure in carrying upon his bare back the priest's robe with dead men's bones enveloped. It was called Pere Louis Chinnen. In the Dahkotah language Shinna or Shinnan signifies a buffalo robe.

Hennepin's description of his life on the island is in these words:

"The day after our arrival, Aquipaguetin, who was the head of a large family, covered me with a robe made of ten large dressed beaver skins, trimmed with porcupine quills. This Indian showed me five or six of his wives, telling them, as I afterwards learned, that they should in future regard me as one of their children.

"He set before me a bark dish full of fish, and seeing that I could not rise from the ground, he had a small sweating-cabin made, in which he made me enter with four Indians. This cabin he covered with buffalo skins, and inside he put stones red-hot. He made me a sign to do as the others before beginning to sweat, but I merely concealed my nakedness with a handkerchief. As soon as these Indians had several times breathed out quite violently, he began to sing vociferously, the others putting their hands on me and rubbing me while they wept bitterly. I began to faint, but I came out and could scarcely take my habit to put on. When he made me sweat thus three times a week, I felt as strong as ever."

The mariner's compass was a constant source of wonder and amazement. Aquipaguetin having assembled the braves, would ask Hennepin to show his compass. Perceiving that the needle turned, the chief harangued his men, and told them that the Europeans were spirits, capable of doing any thing.

In the Franciscan's possession was an iron pot with feet like lions', which the Indians would not touch unless their hands were wrapped in buffalo skins. The women looked upon it as "wakan," and would not enter the cabin where it was.

"The chiefs of these savages, seeing that I was desirous to learn, frequently made me write, naming all the parts of the human body; and as I would not put on paper certain indelicate words, at which they do not blush, they were heartily amused."

They often asked the Franciscan questions, to answer which it was necessary to refer to his lexicon. This appeared very strange, and, as they had no word for paper, they said, "That white thing must be a spirit which tells Pere Louis all we say."

Hennepin remarks: "These Indians often asked me how many wives and children I had, and how old I was, that is, how many winters; for so these natives always count. Never illumined by the light of faith, they were surprised at my answer. Pointing to our two Frenchmen, whom I was then visiting, at a point three leagues from our village, I told them that a man among us could only have one wife; that as for me, I had promised the Master of life to live as they saw me, and to come and live with them to teach them to be like the French.

"But that gross people, till then lawless and faithless, turned all I said into ridicule. 'How,' said they, 'would you have these two men with thee have wives? Ours would not live with them, for they have hair all over their face, and we have none there or elsewhere.' In fact, they were never better pleased with me than when I was shaved, and from a complaisance, certainly not criminal, I shaved every week.

"As often as I went to visit the cabins, I found a sick child, whose father's name was Mamenisi. Michael Ako would not accompany me; the Picard du Gay alone followed me to act as sponsor, or, rather, to witness the baptism.

"I christened the child Antoinette, in honor of St. Anthony of Padua, as well as for the Picard's name, which was Anthony Auguelle. He was a native of Amiens, and nephew of the Procurator-General of the Premonstratensians both now at Paris. Having poured natural water on the head and uttered these words: 'Creature of God, I baptize thee in the name of the Father, and of the Son, and of the Holy Ghost,' I took half an altar cloth which I had wrested from the hands of an Indian who had stolen it from me, and put it on the body of the baptized child; for as I could not say mass for want of wine and vestments, this piece of linen could not be put to better use than to enshroud the first Christian child among these tribes. I do not know whether the softness of the linen had refreshed her, but she was the next day smiling in her mother's arms, who believed that I had cured the child; but she died soon after, to my great consolation.

"During my stay among them, there arrived four savages, who said they were come alone five hundred leagues from the west, and had been four months upon the way. They assured us there was no such place as the Straits of Anian, and that they had traveled without resting, except to sleep, and had not seen or passed over any great lake, by which phrase they always mean the sea.

"They further informed us that the nation of the Assenipoulacs [Assiniboines] who lie northeast of Issati, was not above six or seven days' journey; that none of the nations, within their knowledge, who lie to the east or northwest, had any great lake about their countries, which were very large, but only rivers, which came from the north. They further assured us that there were very few forests in the countries through which they passed, insomuch that now and then they were forced to make fires of buffaloes' dung to boil their food. All these circumstances make it appear that there is no such place as the Straits of Anian, as we usually see them set down on the maps. And whatever efforts have been made for many years past by the English and Dutch, to find out a passage to the Frozen Sea, they have not yet been able to effect it. But by the help of my discovery and the assistance of God, I doubt not but a passage may still be found, and that an easy one too.

"For example, we may be transported into the Pacific Sea by rivers which are large and capable of carrying great vessels, *and from thence it is very easy to go to China and Japan, without crossing the equinoctial line; and, in all probability, Japan is on the same continent as America.*"

Hennepin in his first book, thus describes his first visit to the Falls of St. Anthony: "In the beginning of July, 1680, we descended the [Rum] River in a canoe southward, with the great chief Ouasicoude [Wauzeekootay] that is to say Pierced Pine, with about eighty cabins composed of more than a hundred and thirty families and about two hundred and fifty warriors. Scarcely would the Indians give me a place in their little flotilla, for they had only old canoes. They went four leagues lower down, to get birch bark to make some more. Having made a hole in the ground, to hide our silver chalice and our papers, till our return from the hunt, and keeping only our breviary, so as not to be loaded, I stood on the bank of the lake formed by the river we had called St. Francis [now Rum] and stretched out my hand to the canoes as they rapidly passed in succession.

"Our Frenchmen also had one for themselves, which the Indians had given them. They would not take me in, Michael Ako saying that he had taken me long enough to satisfy him. I was hurt at this answer, seeing myself thus abandoned by Christians, to whom I had always done good, as they both often acknowledged; but God never having abandoned me on that painful voyage, inspired two Indians to take me in their little canoe, where I had no other employment than to bale out with a little bark tray, the water which entered by little holes. This I did not do without getting all wet. This boat might, indeed, be called a death box, for its lightness and fragility. These canoes do not generally weigh over fifty pounds, the least motion of the body upsets them, unless you are long accustomed to that kind of navigation.

"On disembarking in the evening, the Picard, as an excuse, told me that their canoe was half-rotten, and that had we been three in it, we should have run a great risk of remaining on the way. * * * Four days after our departure for the buffalo hunt, we halted eight leagues above St. Anthony of Padua's Falls, on an eminence opposite the mouth of the River St. Francis [Rum] * * * The Picard and myself went to look for haws, gooseberries, and little wild fruit, which often did us more harm than good. This obliged us to go alone, as Michael Ako refused, in a wretched canoe, to Ouisconsin river, which was more than a hundred leagues off, to see whether the Sieur de la Salle had sent to that place a reinforcement of men, with powder, lead, and other munitions, as he had promised us.

"The Indians would not have suffered this voyage had not one of the three remained with them. They wished me to stay, but Michael Ako absolutely refused. As we were making the portage of our canoe at St. Anthony of Padua's Falls, we perceived five or six of our Indians who had taken the start; one of them was up in an oak opposite the great fall, weeping bitterly, with a rich dressed beaver robe, whitened inside, and trimmed with porcupine quills, which he was offering as a sacrifice to the falls; which is, in itself, admirable and frightful. I heard him while shedding copious tears, say as he spoke to the great cataract, 'Thou who art a spirit, grant that our nation may pass here quietly, without accident; may kill buffalo in abundance; conquer our enemies, and bring in slaves, some of whom we will put to death before thee. The Messenecqz (so they call the tribe named by the French Outagamis) have killed our kindred; grant that we may avenge them.' This robe offered in sacrifice, served one of our Frenchmen, who took it as we returned."

It is certainly wonderful, that Hennepin, who knew nothing of the Sioux language a few weeks before, should understand the prayer offered at the Falls without the aid of an interpreter.

The narrator continues: "A league beyond St. Anthony of Padua's Falls, the Picard was obliged to land and get his powder horn, which he had left at the Falls. * * * As we descended the river Colbert [Mississippi] we found some of our Indians on the islands loaded with buffalo meat, some of which they gave us. Two hours after landing, fifteen or sixteen warriors whom we had left above St. Anthony of Padua's Falls, entered, tomakawk in hand, upset the cabin of those who had invited us, took all the meat and bear oil they found, and greased themselves from head to foot,"

This was done because the others had violated the rules for the buffalo hunt. With the Indians Hennepin went down the river sixty leagues, and then went up the river again, and met buffalo. He continues:

"While seeking the Ouisconsin River, that savage father, Aquipaguetin, whom I had left, and who I believed more than two hundred leagues off, on the 11th of July, 1680, appeared with the warriors." After this, Hennepin and Picard continued to go up the river almost eighty leagues.

There is great confusion here, as the reader will see. When at the mouth of the Rum River, he speaks of the Wisconsin as more than a hundred leagues off. He floats down the river sixty leagues; then he ascended, but does not state the distance; then he ascends eighty leagues.

He continues: "The Indians whom he had left with Michael Ako at Buffalo [Chippeway] River, with the flotilla of canoes loaded with meat, came down. * * * All the Indian women had their stock of meat at the mouth of Buffalo River and on the islands, and again we went down the Colbert [Mississippi] about eighty leagues. * * * We had another alarm in our camp: the old men on duty on the top of the mountains announced that they saw two warriors in the distance; all the bowmen hastened there with speed, each trying to outstrip the others; but they brought back only two of their enemies, who came to tell them that a party of their people were hunting at the extremity of Lake Conde [Superior] and had found four Spirits (so they call the French) who, by means of a slave, had expressed a wish to come on, knowing us to be among them. * * * On the 25th of July, 1680, as we were ascending the river Colbert, after the buffalo hunt, to the Indian villages, we met Sieur du Luth, who came to the Nadouessions with five French soldiers. They joined us about two hundred and twenty leagues distant from the country of the Indians who had taken us. As we had some knowledge of the language, they begged us to accompany them to the villages of these tribes, to which I readily agreed, knowing that these two Frenchmen had not approached the sacrament for two years."

Here again the number of leagues is confusing, and it is impossible to believe that Du Luth and his interpreter Faffart, who had been trading with the Sioux for more than a year, needed the help of Hennepin, who had been about three months with these people.

We are not told by what route Hennepin and Du Luth reached Lake Issati or Mille Lacs, but Hennepin says they arrived there on the 11th of August, 1680, and he adds, "Toward the end of September, having no implements to begin an establishment, we resolved to tell these people, that for their benefit, we would have to return to the French settlements. The grand Chief of the Issati or Nadouessiouz consented, and traced in pencil on paper I gave him, the route I should take for four hundred leagues. With this chart, we set out, eight Frenchmen, in two canoes, and descended the river St. Francis and Colbert [Rum and Mississippi]. Two of our men took two beaver robes at St. Anthony of Padua's Falls, which the Indians had hung in sacrifice on the trees."

The second work of Hennepin, an enlargement of the first, appeared at Utrecht in the year 1697, ten years after La Salle's death. During the interval between the publication of the first and second book, he had passed three years as Superintendent of the Recollects at Reny in the province of Artois, when Father Hyacinth Lefevre, a friend of La Salle, and Commissary Provincial of Recollects at Paris, wished him to return to Canada. He refused, and was ordered to go to Rome, and upon his coming back was sent to a convent at St. Omer, and there received a dispatch from the Minister of State in France to return to the countries of the King of Spain, of which he was a subject. This order, he asserts, he afterwards learned was forged.

In the preface to the English edition of the New Discovery, published in 1698, in London, he writes:

"The pretended reason of that violent order was because I refused to return into America, where I had been already eleven years; though the particular laws of our Order oblige none of us to go beyond sea against his will. I would have, however, returned very willingly had I not known the malice of M. La Salle, who would have exposed me to perish, as he did one of the men who accompanied me in my discovery. God knows that I am sorry for his unfortunate death; but the judgments of the Almighty are always just, for the gentleman was killed by one of his own men, who were at last sensible that he exposed them to visible dangers without any necessity and for his private designs."

After this he was for about five years at Gosselies, in Brabant, as Confessor in a convent, and from thence removed to his native place, Ath, in Belgium, where, according to his narrative in the preface to the "Nouveau Decouverte," he was again persecuted. Then Father Payez, Grand Commissary of Recollects at Louvain, being informed that the King of Spain and the Elector of Bavaria recommended the step, consented that he should enter the service of William the Third of Great Britain, who had been very kind to the Roman Catholics of Netherlands. By order of Payez he was sent to Antwerp to take the lay habit in the convent there, and subsequently went to Utrecht, where he finished his second book known as the New Discovery.

His first volume, printed in 1683, contains 312 pages, with an appendix of 107 pages, on the Customs of the Savages, while the Utrecht book of 1697 contains 509 pages without an appendix.

On page 249 of the New Discovery, he begins an account of a voyage alleged to have been made to the mouth of the Mississippi, and occupies over sixty pages in the narrative. The opening sentences give as a reason for concealing to this time his discovery, that La Salle would have reported him to his Superiors for presuming to go down instead of ascending the stream toward the north, as had been agreed; and that the two with him threatened that if he did not consent to descend the river, they would leave him on shore during the night, and pursue their own course.

He asserts that he left the Gulf of Mexico, to return, on the 1st of April, and on the 24th left the Arkansas; but a week after this, he declares he landed with the Sioux at the marsh about two miles below the city of Saint Paul.

The account has been and is still a puzzle to the historical student. In our review of his first book we have noticed that as early as 1683, he claimed to have descended the Mississippi. In the Utrecht publication he declares that while at Quebec, upon his return to France, he gave to Father Valentine Roux, Commissary of Recollects, his journal, upon the promise that it would be kept secret, and that this Father made a copy of his whole voyage, including the visit to the Gulf of Mexico; but in his Description of Louisiana, Hennepin wrote, "We had some design of going to the mouth of the river Colbert, which more probably empties into the Gulf of Mexico than into the Red Sea, but the tribes that seized us gave us no time to sail up and down the river."

The additions in his Utrecht book to magnify his importance and detract from others, are many. As Sparks and Parkman have pointed out the plagiarisms of this edition, a reference here is unnecessary.

Du Luth, who left Quebec in 1678, and had been in northern Minnesota, with an interpreter, for a year, after he met Ako and Hennepin, becomes of secondary importance, in the eyes of the Franciscan.

In the Description of Louisiana, on page 289, Hennepin speaks of passing the Falls of Saint Anthony, upon his return to Canada, in these few words: "Two of our men seized two beaver robes at the Falls of St. Anthony of Padua, which the Indians had in sacrifice, fastened to trees." But in the Utrecht edition, commencing on page 416, there is much added concerning Du Luth. After using the language of the edition of 1683, already quoted it adds: "Herenpon there arose a dispute between Sieur du Luth and myself. I commended what they had done, saying, 'The savages might judge by it that they disliked the superstition of these people.' The Sieur du Luth, on the contrary, said that they ought to have left the robes where the savages placed them, for they would not fail to avenge the insult we had put upon them by this action, and that it was feared that they would attack us on this journey. I confessed he had some foundation for what he said, and that he spoke according to the rules of prudence. But one of the two men flatly replied, the two robes suited them, and they cared nothing for the savages and their superstitions. The Sieur du Luth at these words was so greatly enraged that he nearly struck the one who uttered them, but I intervened and settled the dispute. The Picard and Michael Ako ranged themselves on the side of those who had taken the robes in question, which might have resulted badly.

"I argued with Sieur du Luth that the savages would not attack us, because I was persuaded that their great chief Ouasicoude would have our interests at heart, and he had great credit with his nation. The matter terminated pleasantly.

"When we arrived near the river Ouisconsin, we halted to smoke the meat of the buffalo we had killed on the journey. During our stay, three savages of the nation we had left, came by the side of our canoe to tell us that their great chief Ouasicoude, having learned that another chief of these people wished to pursue and kill us, and that he entered the cabin where he was consulting, and had struck him on the head with such violence as to scatter his brains upon his associates; thus preventing the executing of this injurious project.

"We regaled the three savages, having a great abundance of food at that time. The Sieur du Luth, after the savages had left, was as enraged as before, and feared that they would pursue and attack us on our voyage. He would have pushed the matter further, but seeing that one man would resist, and was not in the humor to be imposed upon, he moderated, and I appeased them in the end with the assurance that God would not abandon us in distress, and, provided we confided in Him, he would deliver us from our foes, because He is the protector of men and angels."

After describing a conference with the Sioux, he adds, "Thus the savages were very kind, without mentioning the beaver robes. The chief Ouasicoude told me to offer a fathom of Martinico tobacco to the chief Aquipaguetin, who had adopted me as a son. This had an admirable effect upon the barbarians, who went off shouting several times the word 'Louis,' [Ouis or We] which, as he said, means the sun. Without vanity, I must say that my name will be for a long time among these people.

"The savages having left us, to go to war against the Messorites, the Maroha, the Illinois, and other nations which live toward the lower part of the Mississippi, and are irreconcilable foes of the people of the North, the Sieur du Luth, who upon many occasions gave me marks of his friendship, could not forbear to tell our men that I had all the reason in the world to believe that the Viceroy of Canada would give me a favorable reception, should we arrive before winter, and that he wished with all his heart that he had been among as many natives as myself."

The style of Louis Hennepin is unmistakable in this extract, and it is amusing to read his patronage of one of the fearless explorers of the Northwest, a cousin of Tonty, favored by Frontenac, and who was in Minnesota a year before his arrival.

In 1691, six years before the Utrecht edition of Hennepin, another Recollect Franciscan had published a book at Paris, called "The First Establishment of the Faith in New France," in which is the following tribute to Du Luth, whom Hennepin strives to make a subordinate: "In the last years of M. de Frontenac's administration, Sieur Du Luth, a man of talent and experience, opened a way to the missionary and the Gospel in many different nations, turning toward the north of that lake [Superior] where he even built a fort, he advanced as far as the Lake of the Issati, called Lake Buade, from the family name of M. de Frontenac, planting the arms of his Majesty in several nations on the right and left."

In the second volume of his last book, which is called "A Continuance of the New Discovery of a vast Country in America," etc., Hennepin noticed some criticisms.

To the objection that his work was dedicated to William the Third of Great Britain, he replies: "My King, his most Catholic Majesty, his Electoral Highness of Bavaria, the consent in writing of the Superior of my order, the integrity of my faith, and the regular observance of my vows, which his Britannic Majesty allows me, are the best warrants of the uprightness of my intentions."

To the query, how he could travel so far upon the Mississippi in so little time, he answers with a bold face, "That we may, with a canoe and a pair of oars, go twenty, twenty-five, or thirty leagues every day, and more too, if there be occasion. And though we had gone but ten leagues a day, yet in thirty days we might easily have gone three hundred leagues. If during the time we spent from the river of the Illinois to the mouth of the Meschasipi, in the Gulf of Mexico, we had used a little more haste, we might have gone the same twice over."

To the objection, that he said, he nad passed eleven years in America, when he had been there but about four, he evasively replies, that "reckoning from the year 1674, when I first set out, to the year 1688, when I printed the second edition of my 'Louisiana,' it appears that I have spent fifteen years either in travels or printing my Discoveries."

To those who objected to the statement in his first book, in the dedication to Louis the Fourteenth, that the Sioux always call the sun Louis, he writes: "I repeat what I have said before, that being among the Issati and Nadouessans, by whom I was made a slave in America, I never heard them call the sun any other than Louis. It is true these savages call also the moon Louis, but with this distinction, that they give the moon the name of Louis Bastache, which in their language signifies, the sun that shines in the night."

The Utrecht edition called forth much censure, and no one in France doubted that Hennepin was the author. D'Iberville, Governor of Louisiana, while in Paris, wrote on July 3d 1699, to the Minister of Marine and Colonies of France, in these words: "Very much vexed at the Recollect, whose false narratives had deceived every one, and caused our suffering and total failure of our enterprise, by the time consumed in the search of things which alone existed in his imagination."

The Rev. Father James Gravier, in a letter from a fort on the Gulf of Mexico, near the Mississippi, dated February 16th, 1701, expressed the sentiment of his times when he speaks of Hennepin "who presented to King William, the Relation of the Mississippi, where he never was, and after a thousand falsehoods and ridiculous boasts, * * * he makes Mr. de la Salle appear in his Relation, wounded with two balls in the head, turn toward the Recollect Father Anastase, to ask him for absolution, having been killed instantly, without uttering a word; and other like false stories."

Hennepin gradually faded out of sight. Brunet mentions a letter written by J. B. Dubos, from Rome, dated March 1st, 1701, which mentions that Hennepin was living on the Capitoline Hill, in the celebrated convent of Ara Cœli, and was a favorite of Cardinal Spada. The time and place of his death has not been ascertained.

CHAPTER V.

NICHOLAS PERROT, FOUNDER OF FIRST POST ON LAKE PEPIN.

Early Life.—Searches for Copper.—Interpreter at Sault St. Marie, Employed by La Salle.—Builds Stockade at Lake Pepin.—Hostile Indians Rebuked.—A Silver Ostensorium Given to a Jesuit Chapel.—Perrot in the Battle against Senecas, in New York.—Second Visit to Sioux Country.—Taking Possession by "Proces Verbal."—Discovery of Lead Mines.—Attends Council at Montreal.—Establishes a Post near Detroit, in Michigan.—Perrot's Death, and his Wife.

Nicholas Perrot, sometimes written Pere, was one of the most energetic of the class in Canada known as "coureurs des bois," or forest rangers. Born in 1644, at an early age he was identified with the fur trade of the great inland lakes. As early as 1665, he was among the Outagamies [Foxes], and in 1667 was at Green Bay. In 1669, he was appointed by Talon to go to the lake region in search of copper mines. At the formal taking possession of that country in the name of the King of France, at Sault St. Marie, on the 14th of May, 1671, he acted as interpreter. In 1677, he seems to have been employed at Fort Frontenac. La Salle was made very sick the next year, from eating a salad, and one Nicholas Perrot, called Joly Cœur (Jolly Soul) was suspected of having mingled poison with the food. After this he was associated with Du Luth in the execution of two Indians, as we have seen. In 1684, he was appointed by De la Barre, the Governor of Canada, as Commandant for the West, and left Montreal with twenty men. Arriving at Green Bay in Wisconsin, some Indians told him that they had visited countries toward the setting sun, where they obtained the blue and green stones suspended from their ears and noses, and that they saw horses and men like Frenchmen, probably the Spaniards of New Mexico; and others said that they had obtained hatchets from persons who lived in a house that walked on the water, near the mouth of the river of the Assiniboines, alluding to the English established at Hudson's Bay. Proceeding to the portage between the Fox and Wisconsin, thirteen Hurons were met, who were bitterly opposed to the establishment of a post near the Sioux. After the Mississippi was reached, a party of Winnebagoes was employed to notify the tribes of Northern Iowa that the French had ascended the river, and wished to meet them. It was further agreed that prairie fires would be kindled from time to time, so that the Indians could follow the French.

After entering Lake Pepin, near its mouth, on the east side, Perrot found a place suitable for a post, where there was wood. The stockade was built at the foot of a bluff beyond which was a large prairie. La Potherie makes this statement, which is repeated by Penicaut, who writes of Lake Pepin: "To the right and left of its shores there are also prairies. In that on the right on the bank of the lake, there is a fort, which was built by Nicholas Perrot, whose name it yet [1700] bears."

Soon after he was established, it was announced that a band of Aiouez [Ioways] was encamped above, and on the way to visit the post. The French ascended in canoes to meet them, but as they drew nigh, the Indian women ran up the bluffs, and hid in the woods; but twenty of the braves mustered courage to advance and greet Perrot, and bore him to the chief's lodge. The chief, bending over Perrot, began to weep, and allowed the moisture to fall upon his visitor. After he had exhausted himself, the principal men of the party repeated the slabbering process. Then buffalo tongues were boiled in an earthen pot, and after being cut into small pieces, the chief took a piece, and, as a mark of respect, placed it in Perrot's mouth.

During the winter of 1684–85, the French traded in Minnesota.

At the end of the beaver hunt, the Ayoes [Ioways] came to the post, but Perrot was absent visiting the Nadouaissioux, and they sent a chief to notify him of their arrival. Four Illinois met him on the way, and were anxious for the return of four children held by the French. When the

Sioux, who were at war with the Illinois, perceived them, they wished to seize their canoes, but the French voyageurs who were guarding them, pushed into the middle of the river, and the French at the post coming to their assistance, a reconciliation was effected, and four of the Sioux took the Illinois upon their shoulders, and bore them to the shore.

An order having been received from Denonville, Governor of Canada, to bring the Miamis, and other tribes, to the rendezvous at Niagara, to go on an expedition against the Senecas, Perrot entrusting the post at Lake Pepin to a few Frenchmen, visited the Miamis, who were dwelling below on the Mississippi, and with no guide but Indian camp fires, went sixty miles into the country beyond the river.

Upon his return, he perceived a great smoke, and at first thought that it was a war party proceeding to the Sioux country. Fortunately he met a Maskouten chief, who had been at the post to see him, and he gave the intelligence, that the Outagamies [Foxes], Kikapous [Kickapoos], and Mascoutechs [Maskoutens], and others, from the region of Green Bay, had determined to pillage the post, kill the French, and then go to war against the Sioux. Hurrying on, he reached the fort, and learned that on that very day three spies had been there and seen that there were only six Frenchmen in charge.

The next day two more spies appeared, but Perrot had taken the precaution to put loaded guns at the door of each hut, and caused his men frequently to change their clothes. To the query, "How many French were there?" the reply was given, "Forty, and that more were daily expected, who had been on a buffalo hunt, and that the guns were well loaded and knives well sharpened." They were then told to go back to their camp and bring a chief of each nation represented, and that if Indians, in large numbers, came near, they would be fired at. In accordance with this message six chiefs presented themselves, After their bows and arrows were taken away they were invited to Perrot's cabin, who gave something to eat and tobacco to smoke. Looking at Perrot's loaded guns they asked, "If he was afraid of his children?" He replied, he was not. They continued, "You are displeased." He answered, "I have good reason to be. The Spirit has warned me of your designs; you will take my things away and put me in the kettle, and proceed against the Nadouaissioux. The Spirit told me to be on my guard, and he would help me." At this they were astonished, and confessed that an attack was meditated. That night the chiefs slept in the stockade, and early the next morning a part of the hostile force was encamped in the vicinity, and wished to trade. Perrot had now only a force of fifteen men, and seizing the chiefs, he told them he would break their heads if they did not disperse the Indians. One of the chiefs then stood up on the gate of the fort and said to the warriors, "Do not advance, young men, or you are dead. The Spirit has warned Metaminens [Perrot] of your designs." They followed the advice, and afterwards Perrot presented them with two guns, two kettles, and some tobacco, to close the door of war against the Nadouaissioux, and the chiefs were all permitted to make a brief visit to the post.

Returning to Green Bay in 1686, he passed much time in collecting allies for the expedition against the Iroquois in New York. During this year he gave to the Jesuit chapel at Depere, five miles above Green Bay, a church utensil of silver, fifteen inches high, still in existence. The standard, nine inches in height, supports a radiated circlet closed with glass on both sides and surmounted with a cross. This vessel, weighing about twenty ounces, was intended to show the consecrated wafer of the mass, and is called a soleil, moustrance, or ostensorium.

Around the oval base of the rim is the following inscription:

CE SOLEIL ESTE DONNE PAR MR NICHOLAS PERROT A LA MISSION
DE ST. FRANÇOIS XAVIER EN LA BAYE DES PVANTS . 1686.

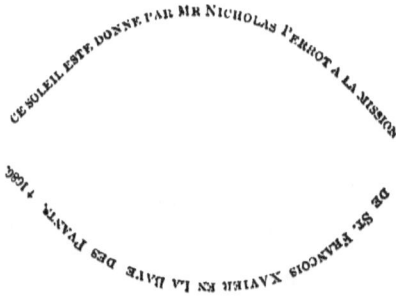

In 1802 some workmen in digging at Green Bay, Wisconsin, on the old Langlade estate discovered this relic, which is now kept in the vault of the Roman Catholic bishop of that diocese.

During the spring of 1687 Perrot, with De Luth and Tonty, was with the Indian allies and the French in the expedition against the Senecas of the Genessee Valley in New York.

The next year Denonville, Governor of Canada, again sent Perrot with forty Frenchmen to the Sioux who, says Potherie, "were very distant, and who would not trade with us as easily as the other tribes, the Outagamis [Foxes] having boasted of having cut off the passage thereto."

When Perrot arrived at Mackinaw. the tribes of that region were much excited at the hostility of the Outagamis [Foxes] toward the Santeurs [Chippeways]. As soon as Perrot and his party reached Green Bay a deputation of the Foxes sought an interview. He told them that he had nothing to do with this quarrel with the Chippeways. In justification, they said that a party of their young men, in going to war against the Nadouaissioux, had found a young man and three Chippeway girls.

Perrot was silent, and continued his journey towards the Nadouaissioux. Soon he was met by five chiefs of the Foxes in a canoe, who begged him to go to their village. Perrot consented, and when he went into a chief's lodge they placed before him broiled venison, and raw meat for the rest of the French. He refused to eat because, said he, "that meat did not give him any spirit, but he would take some when the Outagamis [Foxes] were more reasonable." He then chided them for not having gone, as requested by the Governor of Canada, to the Detroit of Lake Erie, and during the absence of the French fighting with the Chippeways. Having ordered them to go on their beaver hunt and only fight against the Iroquois, he left a few Frenchmen to trade and proceeded on his journey to the Sioux country. Arriving at the portage between the Fox and Wisconsin Rivers they were impeded by ice, but with the aid of some Pottawattomies they transported their goods to the Wisconsin, which they found no longer frozen. The Chippeways were informed that their daughters had been taken from the Foxes, and a deputation came to take them back, but being attacked by the Foxes, who did not know their errand, they fled without securing the three girls. Perrot then ascended the Mississippi to the post which in 1684 he had erected, just above the mouth, and on the east side of Lake Pepin.

As soon as the rivers were navigable, the Nadouaissioux came down and escorted Perrot to one of their villages, where he was welcomed with much enthusiasm. He was carried upon a beaver robe, followed by a long line of warriors, each bearing a pipe, and singing. After taking him around the village, he was borne to the chief's lodge, when several came in to weep over his head, with the same tenderness that the Ayoes (Ioways) did, when Perrot several years before arrived at Lake Pepin. "These weepings," says an old chronicler "do not weaken their souls. They are very good warriors, and reported the bravest in that region. They are at war with all the tribes at present except the Saulteurs [Chippeways] and Ayoes [Ioways], and even with these they have quarrels. At the break of day the Nadouaissioux bathe, even to the youngest. They have very fine forms, but the women are not comely, and they look upon them as slaves. They are jealous and suspicious about them, and they are the cause of quarrels and blood-shedding.

"The Sioux are very dextrous with their canoes, and they fight unto death if surrounded, Their country is full of swamps, which shelter them in summer from being molested. One must be a Nadouaissioux, to find the way to their villages."

While Perrot was absent in New York, fighting the Senecas, a Sioux chief knowing that few Frenchmen were left at Lake Pepin, came with one hundred warriors, and endeavored to pillage it. Of this complaint was made, and the guilty leader was near being put to death by his associates. Amicable relations having been formed, preparations were made by Perrot to return to his post. As they were going away, one of the Frenchmen complained that a box of his goods had been stolen. Perrot ordered a voyageur to bring a cup of water, and into it he poured some brandy. He then addressed the Indians and told them he would dry up their marshes if the goods were not restored; and then he set on fire the brandy in the cup, The savages were astonished and terrified, and supposed that he possessed supernatural powers; and in a little while the goods were found and restored to the owner, and the French descended to their stockade.

The Foxes, while Perrot was in the Sioux country, changed their village, and settled on the Mississippi. Coming up to visit Perrot, they asked him to establish friendly relations between them and the Sioux. At the time some Sioux were at the post trading furs, and at first they supposed the French were plotting with the Foxes. Perrot, however, eased them by presenting the calumet and saying that the French considered the Outagamis [Foxes] as brothers, and then adding: "Smoke in my pipe; this is the manner with which Onontio [Governor of Canada] feeds his children." The Sioux replied that they wished the Foxes to smoke first. This was reluctantly done, and the Sioux smoked, but would not conclude a definite peace until they consulted their chiefs. This was not concluded, because Perrot, before the chiefs came down, received orders to return to Canada.

About this time, in the presence of Father Joseph James Marest, a Jesuit missionary, Boisguillot, a trader on the Wisconsin and Mississippi, Le Sueur, who afterward built a post below the Saint Croix River, about nine miles from Hastings, the following document was prepared:

"Nicholas Perrot, commanding for the King at the post of the Nadouessioux, commissioned by the Marquis Denonville, Governor and Lieutenant Governor of all New France, to manage the interests of commerce among all the Indian tribes and people of the Bay des Puants [Green Bay], Nadouessioux, Mascoutens, and other western nations of the Upper Mississippi, and to take possession in the King's name of all the places where he has heretofore been and whither he will go:

"We this day, the eighth of May, one thousand six hundred and eighty-nine, do, in the presence of the Reverend Father Marest, of the Society of Jesus, Missionary among the Nadouessioux, of Monsieur de Boisguillot, commanding the French in the neighborhood of the Ouiskonche, on the Mississippi, Augustin Legardeur, Esquire, Sieur de Caumont, and of Messieurs Le Sueur, Hebert, Lemire and Blein.

"Declare to all whom it may concern, that, being come from the Bay des Puants, and to the Lake of the Ouiskonches, we did transport ourselves to the country of the Nadouessioux, on the border of the river St. Croix, and at the mouth of the river St. Pierre, on the bank of which were the Mantantans, and further up to the interior, as far as the Menchokatonx [Med-ay-wah-kawn-twawn], with whom dwell the majority of the Songeskitons [Se-see-twawns] and other Nadouessioux who are to the northwest of the Mississippi, to take possession, for and in the name of the King, of the countries and rivers inhabited by the said tribes, and of which they are proprietors. The present act done in our presence, signed with our hand, and subscribed."

The three Chippeway girls of whom mention has been made were still with the Foxes, and Perrot took them with him to Mackinaw, upon his return to Canada.

While there, the Ottawas held some prisoners upon an island not far from the mainland. The Jesuit Fathers went over and tried to save the captives from harsh treatment, but were unsuccessful. The canoes appeared at length near each other, one man paddling in each, while the warriors were answering the shouts of the prisoners, who each held a white stick in his hand. As they neared the shore the chief of the party made a speech to the Indians who lived on the shore, and giving a history of the campaign, told them that they were masters of the prisoners. The warriors then came on land, and, according to custom, abandoned the spoils. An old man then ordered nine men to conduct the prisoners to a separate place. The women and the young men formed a line with big sticks. The young prisoners soon found their feet, but the old men were so badly used they spat blood, and they were condemned to be burned at the Mamilion.

The Jesuit Fathers and the French officers were much embarrassed, and feared that the Iroquois would complain of the little care which had been used to prevent cruelty.

Perrot, in this emergency, walked to the place where the prisoners were singing the death dirge, in expectation of being burned, and told them to sit down and be silent. A few Ottauwaws rudely told them to sing on, but Perrot forbade. He then went back to the Council, where the old men had rendered judgment, and ordered one prisoner to be burned at Mackinaw, one at Sault St. Marie and another at Green Bay. Undaunted he spoke as follows: "I come to cut the strings of the dogs. I will not suffer them to be eaten. I have pity on them, since my Father, Onontio, has commanded me. You Outaouaks [Ottawaws] are like tame bears, who will not recognize them who has brought them up. You have forgotten Onontio's protection. When he asks your obedience, you want to rule over him, and eat the flesh of those children he does not wish to give to you. Take care, that, if oyu swallow them, Onontio will tear them with violence from between your teeth. I speak as a brother, and I think I am showing pity to your children, by cutting the bonds of your prisoners."

His boldness had the desired effect. The prisoners were released, and two of them were sent with him to Montreal, to be returned to the Iroquois.

On the 22nd of May, 1690, with one hundred and forty-three voyageurs and six Indians, Perrot left Montreal as an escort of Sieur de Louvigny La Porte, a half-pay captain, appointed to succeed Durantaye at Mackinaw, by Frontenac, the new Governor of Canada, who in October of the previous year had arrived, to take the place of Denonville.

Perrot, as he approached Mackinaw, went in advance to notify the French of the coming of the commander of the post. As he came in sight of the settlement, he hoisted the white flag with the fleur de lis and the voyageurs shouted, "Long live the king!" Louvigny soon appeared and was received by one hundred "coureur des bois" under arms.

From Mackinaw, Perrot proceeded to Green Bay, and a party of Miamis there begged him to make a trading establishment on the Mississippi towards the Ouiskonsing (Wisconsin.) The chief made him a present of a piece of lead from a mine which he had found in a small stream which flows into the Mississippi. Perrot promised to visit him within twenty days, and the chief then returned to his village below the d'Ouiskonche (iWsconsin) River.

Having at length reached his post on Lake Pepin, he was informed that the Sioux were forming a large war party against the Outagamis (Foxes) and other allies of the French. He gave notice of his arrival to a party of about four hundred Sioux who were on the Mississippi. They arrested the messengers and came to the post for the purpose of plunder. Perrot asked them why they acted in this manner, and said that the Foxes, Miamis, Kickapoos, Illinois, and Maskoutens had united in a war party against them, but that he had persuaded them to give it up, and now he wished them to return to their families and to their beaver. The Sioux declared that they had started on the war-path, and that they were ready to die. After they had traded their furs, they sent for Perrot to come to their camp, and begged that he would not hinder them from searching for their foes. Perrot tried to dissuade them, but they insisted that the Spirit had given them men to eat, at three days' journey from the post Then more powerful influences were used. After giving them two kettles and some merchandise, Poerrt spoke thus: "I love your life, and I am sure you will be defeated. Your Evil Spirit has deceived you. If you kill the Outagamis, or their allies, you must strike me first; if you kill them, you kill me just the same, for I hold them under one wing and you under the other." After this he extended the calumet, which they at first refused; but at length a chief said he was right, and, making invocations to the sun, wished Perrot to take him back to his arms. This was granted, on condition that he would give up his weapons of war. The chief then tied them to a pole in the centre of the fort, turning them toward the sun. He then persuaded the other chiefs to give up the expedition, and, sending for Perrot, he placed the calumet before him, one end in the earth and the other on a small forked twig to hold it firm. Then he took from his own sack a pair of his cleanest moccasins, and taking off Perrot's shoes, put on these. After he had made him eat, presenting the calumet, he said: "We listen to you now. Do for us as you do for our enemies, and prevent them from killing us, and we will separate for the beaver hunt. The sun is the witness of our obedience."

After this, Perrot descended the Mississippi and revealed to the Maskoutens, who had come to meet him, how he had pacified the Sioux. He, about this period, in accordance with his promise, visited the lead mines. He found the ore abundant "but the lead hard to work because it lay between rocks which required blowing up. It had very little dross and was easily melted."

Penicaut, who ascended the Mississippi in 1700, wrote that twenty leagues below the Wisconsin, on both sides of the Mississippi, were mines of lead called "Nicolas Perrot's." Early French maps indicate as the locality of lead mines the site of modern towns, Galena, in Illinois, and Dubuque, in Iowa.

In August, 1693, about two hundred Frenchmen from Mackinaw, with delegates from the tribes of the West, arrived at Montreal to attend a grand council called by Governor Frontenac, and among these was Perrot.

On the first Sunday in September the governor gave the Indians a great feast, after which they and the traders began to return to the wilderness. Perrot was ordered by Frontenac to establish a new post for the Miamis in Michigan, in the neighborhood of the Kalamazoo River.

Two years later he is present again, in August, at a council in Montreal, then returned to the West, and in 1699 is recalled from Green Bay. In 1701 he was at Montreal acting as interpreter, and appears to have died before 1718: his wife was Madeline Raclos, and his residence was in the Seigneury of Becancourt, not far from Three Rivers, on the St. Lawrence.

CHAPTER VI.

BARON LA HONTAN'S FABULOUS VOYAGE.

La Hontan, a Gascon by Birth.—Early Life.—Description of Fox and Wisconsin Rivers. Indian Feast.—Alleged Ascent of Long River.—Bobe Exposes the Deception.—Route to the Pacific.

The "Travels" of Baron La Hontan appeared in A. D. 1703, both at London and at Hague, and were as saleable and readable as those of Hennepin, which were on the counters of booksellers at the same time.

La Hontan, a Gascon by birth, and in style of writing, when about seventeen years of age, arrived in Canada, in 1683, as a private soldier, and was with Gov. De la Barre in his expedition of 1684, toward Niagara, and was also in the battle near Rochester, New York, in 1687, at which Du Luth and Perrot, explorers of Minnesota, were present.

In 1688 he appears to have been sent to Fort St. Joseph, which was built by Du Luth, on the St. Clare River, near the site of Fort Gratiot, Michigan. It is possible that he may have accompanied Perrot to Lake Pepin, who came about this time to reoccupy his old post.

From the following extracts it will be seen that his style is graphic, and that he probably had been in 1688 in the valley of the Wisconsin. At Mackinaw, after his return from his pretended voyage of the Long River, he writes:

"I left here on the 24th September, with my men and five Outaouas, good hunters, whom I have before mentioned to you as having been of good service to me. All my brave men being provided with good canoes, filled with provisions and ammunition, together with goods for the Indian trade, I took advantage of a north wind, and in three days entered the Bay of the Ponteouatamis, distant from here about forty leagues. The entrance to the bay is full of islands. It is ten leagues wide and twenty-five in length.

"On the 29th we entered a river, which is quite deep, whose waters are so affected by the lake that they often rise and fall three feet in twelve hours. This is an observation that I made during these three or four days that I passed here. The Sakis, the Poutouatamis, and a few of the Malominis have their villages on the border of this river, and the Jesuits have a house there. In the place there is carried on quite a commerce in furs and Indian corn, which the Indians traffic with the 'coureurs des bois' that go and come, for it is their nearest and most convenient passage to the Mississippi.

"The lands here are very fertile, and produce, almost without culture, the wheat of our Europe, peas, beans, and any quantity of fruit unknown in France.

"The moment I landed, the warriors of three nations came by turns to my cabin to entertain me with the pipe and chief dance; the first in proof of peace and friendship, the second to indicate their esteem and consideration for me. In return, I gave them several yards of tobacco, and beads, with which they trimmed their capots. The next morning, I was asked as a guest, to one of the feasts of this nation, and after having sent my dishes, which is the custom, I went towards noon. They began to compliment me of my arrival, and after hearing them, they all, one after the other, began to sing and dance, in a manner that I will detail to you when I have more leisure. These songs and dances lasted two hours, and were seasoned with whoops of joy, and quibbles that they have woven into their ridiculous musique. Then the captives waited upon us. The whole troop were seated in the Oriental custom. Each one had his portion before him, like our monks in their refectories. They commenced by placing four dishes before me. The first consisted of two white fish simply boiled in water. The second was chopped meats with the boiled tongue of a bear; the third a beaver's tail, all roasted. They made me drink also of a syrup, mixed with water, made out of the maple tree. The feast lasted two hours, after which, I requested a chief of the nation to sing for me; for it is the custom, when we have business with them, to employ an inferior for self in all the ceremonies they perform. I gave him several pieces of tobacco, to oblige him to keep the party till dark. The next day and the day following, I attended the feasts of the other nations, where I observed the same formalities."

He alleges that, on the 23d of October, he reached the Mississippi River, and, ascending, on the 3d of November he entered into a river, a tributary from the west, that was almost without a current, and at its mouth filled with rushes. He then describes a journey of five hundred miles up this stream. He declares he found upon its banks three great nations, the Eokoros, Essanapes, and Guacsitares, and because he ascended it for sixty days, he named it Long River.

For years his wondrous story was believed, and geographers hastened to trace it upon their maps. But in time the voyage up the Long River was discovered to be a fabrication. There is extant a letter of Bobe, a Priest of the Congregation of the Mission, dated Versailles, March 15, 1716, and addressed to De L'Isle, the geographer of the Academy of Sciences at Paris, which exposes the deception.

He writes: "It seems to me that you might give the name of Bourbonia to these vast countries which are between the Missouri, Mississippi, and the Western Ocean. Would it not be well to efface that great river which La Hontan says he discovered?

"All the Canadians, and even the Governor General, have told me that this river is unknown. If it existed, the French, who are on the Illinois, and at Ouabache, would know of it. The last volume of the 'Lettres Edifiantes' of the Jesuits, in which there is a very fine relation of the Illinois Country, does not speak of it, any more than the letters which I received this year, which tell wonders of the beauty and goodness of the country. They send me some quite pretty work, made by the wife of one of the principal chiefs.

"They tell me, that among the Scioux, of the Mississippi, there are always Frenchmen trading; that the course of the Mississippi is from north to west, and from west to south; that it is known that toward the source of the Mississippi there is a river in the highlands that leads to the western ocean; that the Indians say that they have seen bearded men with caps, who gather gold-dust on the seashore, but that it is very far from this country, and that they pass through many nations unknown to the French.

"I have a memoir of La Motte Cadillac, formerly Governor of Missilimackinack, who says that if St. Peters [Minnesota] River is ascended to its source they will, according to all appearance, find in the highland another river leading to the Western Ocean.

"For the last two years I have tormented exceedingly the Governor-General, M. Raudot, and M. Duché, to move them to discover this ocean. If I succeed, as I hope, we shall hear tidings before three years, and I shall have the pleasure and the consolation of having rendered a good service to Geography, to Religion and to the State."

Charlevoix, in his History of New France, alluding to La Hontan's voyage, writes: "The voyage up the Long River is as fabulous as the Island of Barrataria, of which Sancho Panza was governor. Nevertheless, in France and elsewhere, most people have received these memoirs as the fruits of the travels of a gentleman who wrote badly, although quite lightly, and who had no religion, but who described pretty sincerely what he had seen. The consequence is that the compilers of historical and geographical dictionaries have almost always followed and cited them in preference to more faithful records."

Even in modern times, Nicollet, employed by the United States to explore the Upper Mississippi, has the following in his report:

"Having procured a copy of La Hontan's book, in which there is a roughly made map of his Long River, I was struck with the resemblance of its course as laid down with that of Cannon River, which I had previously sketched in my own field-book. I soon convinced myself that the principal statements of the Baron in reference to the country and the few details he gives of the physical character of the the river, coincide remarkably with what I had laid down as belonging to Cannon River. Then the lakes and swamps corresponded; traces of Indian villages mentioned by him might be found by a growth of wild grass that propagates itself around all old Indian settlements."

CHAPTER VII.

LE SUEUR, EXPLORER OF THE MINNESOTA RIVER.

Le Sueur Visits Lake Pepin.—Stationed at La Pointe.—Establishes a Post on an Island Above Lake Pepin.—Island Described by Penicaut.—First Sioux Chief at Montreal.—Ojibway Chiefs' Speeches.—Speech of Sioux Chief.—Teeoskahtay's Death.—Le Sueur Goes to France.—Posts West of Mackinaw Abandoned.—Le Sueur's License Revoked.—Second Visit to France.—Arrives in Gulf of Mexico with D'Iberville.—Ascends the Mississippi.—Lead Mines.—Canadians Fleeing from the Sioux.—At the Mouth of the Wisconsin. Sioux Robbers.—Elk Hunting.—Lake Pepin Described.—Rattlesnakes.—La Place Killed.—St. Croix River Named After a Frenchman.—Le Sueur Reaches St. Pierre, now Minnesota River.—Enters Mankahto, or Blue Earth, River.—Sioux of the Plains.—Fort L'Huillier Completed.—Conferences with Sioux Bands.—Assinaboines a Separated Sioux Band.—An Indian Feast.—Names of the Sioux Bands. Charlevoix's Account.—Le Sueur Goes with D'Iberville to France.—D'Iberville's Memorial.—Early Census of Indian Tribes.—Penicaut's Account of Fort L'Huillier.—Le Sueur's Departure from the Fort.—D'Evaqe Left in Charge.—Return to Mobile.—Juchereau at Mouth of Wisconsin.—Bondor a Montreal Merchant.—Sioux Attack Miamis.—Boudor Robbed by the Sioux.

Le Sueur was a native of Canada, and a relative of D'Iberville, the early Governor of Louisiana. He came to Lake Pepin in 1683, with Nicholas Perrot, and his name also appears attached to the document prepared in May, 1689, after Perrot had re-occupied his post just above the entrance of the lake, on the east side.

In 1692, he was sent by Governor Frontenac of Canada, to La Pointe, on Lake Superior, and in a dispatch of 1693, to the French Government, is the following: "Le Sueur, another voyageur, is to remain at Chagouamagon [La Pointe] to endeavor to maintain the peace lately concluded between the Saulteurs [Chippeways] and Sioux. This is of the greatest consequence, as it is now the sole pass by which access can be had to the latter nation, whose trade is very profitable; the country to the south being occupied by the Foxes and Maskoutens, who several times plundered the French, on the ground they were carrying ammunition to the Sioux, their ancient enemies."

Entering the Sioux country in 1694, he established a post upon a prairie island in the Mississippi, about nine miles below the present town of Hastings, according to Bellin and others. Penicaut, who accompanied him in the exploration of the Minnesota, writes, "At the extremity of the lake [Pepin] you come to the Isle Pelee, so called because there are no trees on it. It is on this island that the French from Canada established their fort and storehouse, and they also winter here, because game is very abundant. In the month of September they bring their store of meat, obtained by hunting, and after having skinned and cleaned it, hang it upon a crib of raised scaffolding, in order that the extreme cold, which lasts from September to March, may preserve it from spoiling. During the whole winter they do not go out except for water, when they have to break the ice every day, and the cabin is generally built upon the bank, so as not to have far to go. When spring arrives, the savages come to the island, bringing their merchandize."

On the fifteenth of July, 1695, Le Sueur arrived at Montreal with a party of Ojibways, and the *first Dakotah brave* that had ever visited Canada. The Indians were much impressed with the power of France by the marching of a detachment of seven hundred picked men, under Chevalier Cresafi, who were on their way to La Chine.

On the eighteenth, Frontenac, in the presence of Callieres and other persons of distinction, gave them an audience.

The first speaker was the chief of the Ojibway band at La Pointe, Shingowahbay, who said:

"That he was come to pay his respects to Onontio [the title given the Governor of Canada] in the name of the young warriors of Point Chagouamigon, and to thank him for having given them some Frenchmen to dwell with them; to testify their sorrow for one Jobin, a Frenchman, who was killed at a feast, accidentally, and not maliciously. We come to ask a favor of you, which is to let us act. We are allies of the Sciou. Some Outagamies, or Mascoutins, have been killed. The Sciou came to mourn with us. Let us act, Father; let us take revenge.

"Le Sueur alone, who is acquainted with the language of the one and the other, can serve us. We ask that he return with us."

Another speaker of the Ojibways was Le Brochet.

Teeoskahtay, the Dahkotah chief, before he spoke, spread out a beaver robe, and, laying another with a tobacco pouch and otter skin, began to weep bitterly. After drying his tears, he said:

"All of the nations had a father, who afforded them protection; all of them have iron. But he was a bastard in quest of a father; he was come to see him, and hopes that he will take pity on him."

He then placed upon the beaver robe twenty-two arrows, at each arrow naming a Dahkotah village that desired Frontenac's protection. Resuming his speech, he remarked:

"It is not on account of what I bring that I hope him who rules the earth will have pity on me. I learned from the Sauteurs that he wanted nothing; that he was the Master of the Iron; that he had a big heart, into which he could receive all the nations. This has induced me to abandon my people and come to seek his protection, and to beseech him to receive me among the number of his children. Take courage, Great Captain, and reject me not; despise me not, though I appear poor in your eyes. All the nations here present know that I am rich, and the little they offer here is taken from my lands."

Count Frontenac in reply told the chief that he would receive the Dahkotahs as his children, on condition that they would be obedient, and that he would send back Le Sueur with him.

Teeoskahtay, taking hold of the governor's knees, wept, and said: "Take pity on us; we are well aware that we are not able to speak, being children; but Le Sueur, who understands our language, and has seen all our villages, will next year inform you what will have been achieved by the Sioux nations represented by those arrows before you."

Having finished, a Dahkotah woman, the wife of a great chief whom Le Sueur had purchased from captivity at Mackinaw, approached those in authority, and, with downcast eyes, embraced their knees, weeping and saying:

"I thank thee, Father; it is by thy means I have been liberated, and am no longer captive."

Then Teeoskahtay resumed:

"I speak like a man penetrated with joy. The Great Captain; he who is the Master of Iron, assures me of his protection, and I promise him that if he condescends to restore my children, now prisoners among the Foxes, Ottawas and Hurons, I will return hither, and bring with me the twenty-two villages whom he has just restored to life by promising to send them Iron."

On the 14th of August, two weeks after the Ojibway chief left for his home on Lake Superior, Nicholas Perrot arrived with a deputation of Sauks, Foxes, Menomonees, Miamis of Maramek and Pottowatomies.

Two days after, they had a council with the governor, who thus spoke to a Fox brave:

"I see that you are a young man; your nation has quite turned away from my wishes; it has pillaged some of my young men, whom it has treated as slaves. I know that your father, who loved the French, had no hand in the indignity. You only imitate the example of your father, who had sense, when you do not co-operate with those of your tribe who are wishing to go over to my enemies, after they grossly insulted me and defeated the Sioux, whom I now consider my son. I pity the Sioux; I pity the dead whose loss I deplore. Perrot goes up there, and he will speak to your nation from me for the release of their prisoners; let them attend to him."

Teeoshkahtay never returned to his native land. While in Montreal he was taken sick, and in thirty-three days he ceased to breathe; and, followed by white men, his body was interred in the white man's grave.

Le Sueur instead of going back to Minnesota that year, as was expected, went to France and received a license, in 1697, to open certain mines supposed to exist in Minnesota. The ship in which he was returning was captured by the English, and he was taken to England. After his release he went back to France, and, in 1698, obtained a new commission for mining.

While Le Sueur was in Europe, the Dahkotas waged war against the Foxes and Miamis. In retaliation, the latter raised a war party and entered the land of the Dahkotahs. Finding their foes intrenched, and assisted by "coureurs des bois," they were indignant; and on their return they had a skirmish with some Frenchmen, who were carrying goods to the Dahkotahs.

Shortly after, they met Perrot, and were about to burn him to death, when prevented by some friendly Foxes. The Miamis, after this, were disposed to be friendly to the Iroquois. In 1696, the year previous, the authorities at Quebec decided that it was expedient to abandon all the posts west of Mackinaw, and withdraw the French from Wisconsin and Minnesota.

The voyageurs were not disposed to leave the country, and the governor wrote to Pontchartrain for instructions, in October, 1698. In his dispatch he remarks:

"In this conjuncture, and under all these circumstances, we consider it our duty to postpone, until new instructions from the court, the execution of Sieur Le Sueur's enterprise for the mines, though the promise had already been given him to send two canoes in advance to Missilimackinac, for the purpose of purchasing there some provisions and other necessaries for his voyage, and that he would be permitted to go and join them early in the spring with the rest of his hands. What led us to adopt this resolution has been, that the French who remained to trade off with the Five Nations the remainder of their merchandise, might, on seeing entirely new comers arriving there, consider themselves entitled to dispense with coming down, and perhaps adopt the resolution to settle there; whilst, seeing no arrival there, with permission to do what is forbidden, the reflection they will be able to make during the winter, and the apprehension of being guilty of crime, may oblige them to return in the spring.

"This would be very desirable, in consequence of the great difficulty there will be in constraining them to it, should they be inclined to lift the mask altogether and become buccaneers; or should Sieur Le Sueur, as he easily could do, furnish them with goods for their beaver and smaller peltry, which he might send down by the return of other Frenchmen, whose sole desire is to obey, and who have remained only because of the impossibility of getting their effects down. This would rather induce those who would continue to lead a vagabond life to remain there, as the goods they would receive from Le Sueur's people would afford them the means of doing so."

In reply to this communication, Louis XIV. answered that—

"His majesty has approved that the late Sieur de Frontenac and De Champigny suspended the execution of the license granted to the man named Le Sueur to proceed, with fifty men, to explore some mines on the banks of the Mississippi. He has revoked said license, and desires that the said Le Sueur, or any other person, be prevented from leaving the colony on pretence of going in search of mines, without his majesty's express permission."

Le Sueur, undaunted by these drawbacks to the prosecution of a favorite project, again visited France.

Fortunately for Le Sueur, D'Iberville, who was a friend, and closely connected by marriage, was appointed governor of the new territory of Louisiana. In the month of December he arrived from France, with thirty workmen, to proceed to the supposed mines in Minnesota.

On the thirteenth of July, 1700, with a felucca, two canoes, and nineteen men, having ascended the Mississippi, he had reached the mouth of the Missouri, and six leagues above this he passed the Illinois. He there met three Canadians, who came to join him, with a letter from Father Marest, who had once attempted a mission among the Dahkotahs, dated July 13, Mission Immaculate Conception of the Holy Virgin, in Illinois.

"I have the honor to write, in order to inform you that the Saugiestas have been defeated by the Scioux and Ayavois [Iowas]. The people have formed an alliance with the Quincapous [Kickapoos], some of the Mecoutins, Renards [Foxes], and Metesigamias, and gone to revenge themselves, not on the Scioux, for they are too much afraid of them, but perhaps on the Ayavois, or very likely upon the Paoutees, or more probably upon the Osages, for these suspect nothing, and the others are on their guard.

"As you will probably meet these allied nations, you ought to take precaution against their plans, and not allow them to board your vessel, since *they are traitors, and utterly faithless*. I pray God to accompany you in all your designs."

Twenty-two leagues above the Illinois, he passed a small stream which he called the River of Oxen, and nine leagues beyond this he passed a small river on the west side, where he met four Canadians descending the Mississippi, on their way to the Illinois. On the 30th of July, nine leagues above the last-named river, he met seventeen Scioux, in seven canoes, who were going to revenge the death of three Sciouх, one of whom had been burned, and the others killed, at Tamarois, a few days before his arrival in that village. As he had promised the chief of the Illinois to appease the Sciouх who should go to war against his nation, he made a present to the chief of the party to engage him to turn back. He told them the King of France did not wish them to make this river more bloody, and that he was sent to tell them that, if they obeyed the king's word, they would receive in future all things necessary for them. The chief answered that he accepted the present, that is to say, that he would do as had been told him.

From the 30th of July to the 25th of August, Le Sueur advanced fifty-three and one-fourth leagues to a small river which he called the River of the Mine. At the mouth it runs from the north, but it turns to the northeast. On the right seven leagues, there is a lead mine in a prairie, one and a half leagues. The river is only navigable in high water, that is to say, from early spring till the month of June.

From the 25th to the 27th he made ten leagues, passed two small rivers, and made himself acquainted with a mine of lead, from which he took a supply. From the 27th to the 30th he made eleven and a half leagues, and met five Canadians, one of whom had been dangerously wounded in the head. They were naked, and had no ammunition except a miserable gun, with five or six loads of powder and balls. They said they were descending from the Sciouх to go to Tamarois, and, when seventy leagues above, they perceived nine canoes in the Mississippi, in which were ninety savages, who robbed and cruelly beat them. This party were going to war against the Sciouх, and were composed of four different nations, the Outagamies [Foxes], Poutouwatamis [Pottowattamies], and Puans [Winnebagoes], who dwell in a country eighty leagues east of the Mississippi from where Le Sueur then was.

The Canadians determined to follow the detachment, which was composed of twenty-eight men. This day they made seven and a half leagues. On the 1st of September he passed the Wisconsin river. It runs into the Mississippi from the northeast. It is nearly one and a half miles wide. At about seventy-five leagues up this river, on the right, ascending, there is a portage of more than a league. The half of this portage is shaking ground, and at the end of it is a small river which descends into a bay called Winnebago Bay. It is inhabited by a great number of nations who carry their furs to Canada. Monsieur Le Sueur came by the Wisconsin river to the Mississippi, for the first time, in 1683, on his way to the Sciouх country, where he had already passed seven years at different periods. The Mississippi, opposite the mouth of the Wisconsin, is less than half a mile wide. From the 1st of September to the 5th, our voyageur advanced fourteen leagues. He passed the river "Aux Canots," which comes from the northeast, and then the Quincapous, named from a nation which once dwelt upon its banks.

From the 5th to the 9th he made ten and a half leagues, and passed the rivers Cachee and Aux Ailes. The same day he perceived canoes, filled with savages, descending the river, and the five Canadians recognized them as the party who had robbed them. They placed sentinels in the wood, for fear of being surprised by land, and when they had approached within hearing, they cried to them that if they approached farther they would fire. They then drew up by an island, at half the distance of a gun shot. Soon, four of the principal men of the band approached in a canoe, and asked if it was forgotten that they were our brethren, and with what design we had taken arms when we perceived them. Le Sueur replied that he had cause to distrust them, since they had robbed five of his party. Nevertheless, for the surety of his trade, being forced to be at peace with all the tribes, he demanded no redress for the robbery, but added merely that the king, their master and his, wished that his subjects should navigate that river without insult, and that they had better beware how they acted.

The Indian who had spoken was silent, but another said they had been attacked by the Sciouх, and that if they did not have pity on them, and give them a little powder, they should not be able to reach their villages. The consideration of a missionary, who was to go up among the Sciouх, and whom these savages might meet, induced them to give two pounds of powder.

M. Le Sueur made the same day three leagues; passed a stream on the west, and afterward another river on the east, which is navigable at all times, and which the Indians call Red River.

On the 10th, at daybreak, they heard an elk whistle, on the other side of the river. A Canadian crossed in a small Scioux canoe, which they had found, and shortly returned with the body of the animal, which was very easily killed, "quand il est en rut," that is, from the beginning of September until the end of October. The hunters at this time made a whistle of a piece of wood, or reed, and when they hear an elk whistle they answer it. The animal, believing it to be another elk, approaches, and is killed with ease.

From the 10th to the 14th, M. Le Sueur made seventeen and a half leagues, passing the rivers Raisin and Paquilenettes (perhaps the Wazi Ozu and Buffalo.) The same day he left, on the east side of the Mississippi, a beautiful and large river, which descends from the very far north, and called Bon Secours (Chippeway), on account of the great quantity of buffalo, elk, bears and deers which are found there. Three leagues up this river there is a mine of lead, and seven leagues above, on the same side, they found another long river, in the vicinity of which there is a copper mine, from which he had taken a lump of sixty pounds in a former voyage. In order to make these mines of any account, peace must be obtained between the Scioux and Ouatagamis (Foxes), because the latter, who dwell on the east side of the Mississippi, pass this road continually when going to war against the Sioux.

Penicaut, in his journal, gives a brief description of the Mississippi between the Wisconsin and Lake Pepin. He writes: "Above the Wisconsin, and ten leagues higher on the same side, begins a great prairie extending for sixty leagues along the bank; this prairie is called Aux Ailes. Opposite to Aux Ailes, on the left, there is another prairie facing it called Paquilanet which is not so long by a great deal. Twenty leagues above these prairies is found Lake Bon Secours" [Good Help, now Pepin.]

In this region, at one and a half leagues on the northwest side, commenced a lake, which is six leagues long and more than one broad, called Lake Pepin. It is bounded on the west by a chain of mountains; on the east is seen a prairie; and on the northwest of the lake there is another prairie two leagues long and one wide. In the neighborhood is a chain of mountains quite two hundred feet high, and more than one and a half miles long. In these are found several caves, to which the bears retire in winter. Most of the caverns are more than seventy feet in extent, and two hundred feet high. There are several of which the entrance is very narrow, and quite closed up with saltpetre, It would be dangerous to enter them in summer, for they are filled with rattlesnakes, the bite of which is very dangerous. Le Sueur saw some of these snakes which were six feet in length, but generally they are about four feet. They have teeth resembling those of the pike, and their gums are full of small vessels, in which their poison is placed. The Scioux say they take it every mornin ;, and cast it away at night. They have at the tail a kind of scale which makes a noise, and this is called the rattle.

Le Sueur made on this day seven and a half leagues, and passed another river, called Hiambouxecate Ouataba, or the River of Flat Rock. [The Sioux call the Cannon river Inyanbosndata.]

On the 15th he crossed a small river, and saw in the neighborhood several canoes, filled with Indians, descending the Mississippi. He supposed they were Scioux, because he could not distinguish whether the canoes were large or small. The arms were placed in readiness, and soon they heard the cry of the savages, which they are accustomed to raise when they rush upon their enemies. He caused them to be answered in the same manner; and after having placed all the men behind the trees, he ordered them not to fire until they were commanded. He remained on shore to see what movement the savages would make, and perceiving that they placed two on shore, on the other side, where from an eminence they could ascertain the strength of his forces, he caused the men to pass and repass from the shore to the wood, in order to make them believe that they were numerous. This ruse succeeded, for as soon as the two descended from the eminence the chief of the party came, bearing the calumet, which is a signal of peace among the Indians. They said that having never seen the French navigate the river with boats like the felucca, they had supposed them to be English, and for that reason they had raised the war cry, and arranged themselves on the other side of the Mississippi; but having recognized their flag, they had come without fear to inform them, that one of their number, who was crazy, had accidentally killed a

Frenchman, and that they would go and bring his comrade, who would tell how the mischief had happened.

The Frenchman they brought was Denis, a Canadian, and he reported that his companion was accidentally killed. His name was Laplace, a deserting soldier from Canada, who had taken refuge in this country.

Le Sueur replied, that Onontio (the name they give to all the governors of Canada), being their father and his, they ought not to seek justification elsewhere than before him; and he advised them to go and see him as soon as possible, and beg him to wipe off the blood of this Frenchman from their faces.

The party was composed of forty-seven men of different nations, who dwell far to the east, about the forty-fourth degree of latitude. Le Sueur, discovering who the chiefs were, said the king whom they had spoken of in Canada, had sent him to take possession of the north of the river; and that he wished the nations who dwell on it, as well as those under his protection, to live in peace.

He made this day three and three-fourths leagues; and on the 16th of September, he left a large river on the east side, *named St. Croix, because a Frenchman of that name was shipwrecked at its mouth*. It comes from the north-northwest. Four leagues higher, in going up, is found a small lake, at the mouth of which is a very large mass of copper. It is on the edge of the water, in a small ridge of sandy earth, on the west of this lake. [One of La Salle's men was named St. Croix.]

From the 16th to the 19th, he advanced thirteen and three-fourths leagues. After having made from Tamarois two hundred and nine and a half leagues, he left the navigation of the Mississippi, to enter the river St. Pierre, on the west side. By the 1st of October, he had made in this river forty-four and one-fourth leagues. After he entered Blue river, thus named on account of the mines of blue earth found at its mouth, he founded his post, situated in forty-four degrees, thirteen minutes north latitude. He met at this place nine Scioux, who told him that the river belonged to the Scioux of the west, the Ayavois (Iowas) and Otoctatas (Ottoes), who lived a little farther off; that it was not their custom to hunt on ground belonging to others, unless invited to do so by the owners, and that when they would come to the fort to obtain provisions, they would be in danger of being killed in ascending or descending the rivers, which were narrow, and that if they would show their pity, *he must establish himself on the Mississippi, near the mouth of the St. Pierre*, where the Ayavois, the Otoctatas, and the other Scioux could go as well as they.

Having finished their speech, they leaned over the head of Le Sueur, according to their custom, crying out, "Ouaechissou ouaepanimanabo," that is to say, "Have pity upon us." Le Sueur had foreseen that the establishment of Blue Earth river would not please the Scioux of the East, who were, so to speak, *masters of the other Scioux* and of the nations which will be hereafter mentioned, *because they were the first with whom trade was commenced*, and in consequence of which they had already quite a number of guns.

As he had commenced his operations not only with a view to the trade of beaver but also to gain a knowledge of the mines which he had previously discovered, he told them that he was sorry that he had not known their intentions sooner, and that it was just, since he came expressly for them, that he should establish himself on their land, but that the season was too far advanced for him to return. He then made them a present of powder, balls and knives, and an armful of tobacco, to entice them to assemble, as soon as possible, near the fort he was about to construct, that when they should be all assembled he might tell them the intention of the king, their and his sovereign.

The Scioux of the West, according to the statement of the Eastern Scioux, have more than a thousand lodges. They do not use canoes, nor cultivate the earth, nor gather wild rice. They remain generally on the prairies which are between the Upper Mississippi and Missouri rivers, and live entirely by the chase. The Scioux generally say they have three souls, and that after death, that which has done well goes to the warm country, that which has done evil to the cold regions, and the other guards the body. Polygamy is common among them. They are very jealous, and sometimes fight in duel for their wives. They manage the bow admirably, and have been seen several times to kill ducks on the wing. They make their lodges of a number of buffalo skins interlaced and sewed, and carry them wherever they go. They are all great smokers, but their manner of smoking differs from that of other Indians. There are some Scioux who swallow all the smoke of the tobacco, and others who, after having kept it some time in their mouth, cause it to issue from the nose. In each lodge there are usually two or three men with their families.

On the third of October, they received at the fort several Scioux, among whom was Wahkantape, chief of the village. Soon two Canadians arrived who had been hunting, and who had been robbed by the Scioux of the East, who had raised their guns against the establishment which M. Le Sueur had made on Blue Earth river.

On the fourteenth the fort was finished and named Fort L'Huillier, and on the twenty-second two Canadians were sent out to invite the Ayavois and Otoctatas to come and establish a village near the fort, because these Indians are industrious and accustomed to cultivate the earth, and they hoped to get provisions from them, and to make them work in the mines.

On the twenty-fourth, six Scioux Oujalespoitons wished to go into the fort, but were told that they did not receive men who had killed Frenchmen. This is the term used when they have insulted them. The next day they came to the lodge of Le Sueur to beg him to have pity on them. They wished, according to custom, to weep over his head and make him a present of packs of beavers, which he refused. He told them he was surprised that people who had robbed should come to him; to which they replied that they had heard it said that two Frenchmen had been robbed, but none from their village had been present at that wicked action.

Le Sueur answered, that he knew it was the Mendeoucantons and not the Oujalespoitons; "but," continued he, "you are Scioux; it is the Scioux who have robbed me, and if I were to follow your manner of acting I should break your heads; for is it not true, that when a stranger (it is thus they call the Indians who are not Scioux) has insulted a Scioux, Mendeoucanton, Oujalespoitons, or others all the villages revenge upon the first one they meet?"

As they had nothing to answer to what he said to them, they wept and repeated, according to custom, "Ouaechissou! ouaepanimanabo!" Le Sueur told them to cease crying, and added that the French had good hearts, and that they had come into the country to have pity on them. At the same time he made them a present, saying to them, "Carry back your beavers and say to all the Scioux, that they will have from me no more powder or lead, and they will no longer smoke any long pipe until they have made satisfaction for robbing the Frenchman.

The same day the Canadians, who had been sent off on the 22d, arrived without having found the road which led to the Ayavois and Otoctatas. On the 25th, Le Sueur went to the river with three canoes, which he filled with green and blue earth. It is taken from the hills near which are very abundant mines of copper, some of which was worked at Paris in 1696, by L'Huillier, one of the chief collectors of the king. Stones were also found there which would be curious, if worked.

On the ninth of November, eight Mantanton Scioux arrived, who had been sent by their chiefs to say that the *Mendeoucantons were still at their lake on the east of the Mississippi*, and they could not come for a long time; and that for a single village which had no good sense, the others ought not to bear the punishment; and that they were willing to make reparation if they knew how. Le Sueur replied that he was glad that they had a disposition to do so.

On the 15th the two Mantanton Scioux, who had been sent expressly to say that all of the Scioux of the east, and part of those of the west, were joined together to come to the French, because they had heard that the Christianaux and the Assinipoils were making war on them. These two nations dwell above the fort on the east side, more than eighty leagues on the Upper Mississippi.

The Assinipoils speak Scioux, and are certainly of that nation. It is only a few years since that they became enemies. The enmity thus originated: The Christianaux, having the use of arms before the Scioux, through the English at Hudson's Bay, they constantly warred upon the Assinipoils, who were their nearest neighbors. The latter, being weak, sued for peace, and to render it more lasting, married the Christianaux women. The other Scioux, who had not made the compact, continued the war; and, seeing some Christianaux with the Assinipoils, broke their heads. The Christianaux furnished the Assinipoils with arms and merchandise.

On the 16th the Scioux returned to their village, and it was reported that the Ayavois and Otoctatas were gone to establish themselves towards the Missouri River, near the Maha, who dwell in that region. On the 26th the Mantantons and Oujalespoitons arrived at the fort; and, after they had encamped in the woods, Wahkantape came to beg Le Sueur to go to his lodge. He there found sixteen men with women and children, with their faces daubed with black. In the middle of the lodge were several buffalo skins which were sewed for a carpet. After motioning him to sit down, they wept for the fourth of an hour, and the chief gave him some wild rice to eat (as was their custom), putting the first three spoonsful to his mouth. After which, he said all present were relatives of Tioscate, whom Le Sueur took to Canada in 1695, and who died there in 1696.

At the mention of Tioscate they began to weep again, and wipe their tears and heads upon the shoulders of Le Sueur. Then Wahkantape again spoke, and said that Tioscate begged him to forget the insult done to the Frenchmen by the Mendeoucantons, and take pity on his brethren by giving them powder and balls whereby they could defend themselves, and gain a living for their wives and children, who languish in a country full of game, because they had not the means of killing them. "Look," added the chief, "Behold thy children, thy brethren, and thy sisters; it is to thee to see whether thou wishest them to die. They will live if thou givest them powder and ball; they will die if thou refusest."

Le Sueur granted them their request, but as the Scioux never answer on the spot, especially in matters of importance, and as he had to speak to them about his establishment he went out of the lodge without saying a word. The chief and all those within followed him as far as the door of the fort; and when he had gone in, they went around it three times, crying with all their strength, "Atheouanan!" that is to say, "Father, have pity on us." [Ate unyanpi, means Our Father.]

The next day, he assembled in the fort the principal men of both villages; and as it is not possible to subdue the Scioux or to hinder them from going to war, unless it be by inducing them to cultivate the earth, he said to them that if they wished to render themselves worthy of the protection of the king, they must abandon their erring life, and form a village near his dwelling, where they would be shielded from the insults of of their enemies; and that they might be happy and not hungry, he would give them all the corn necessary to plant a large piece of ground; that the king, their and his chief, in sending him, had forbidden him to purchase beaver skins, knowing that this kind of hunting separates them and exposes them to their enemies; and that in consequence of this he had come to establish himself on Blue River and vicinity, where they had many times assured him were many kinds of beasts, for the skins of which he would give them all things necessary; that they ought to reflect that they could not do without French goods, and that the only way not to want them was, not to go to war with our allied nations.

As it is customary with the Indians to accompany their word with a present proportioned to the affair treated of, he gave them fifty pounds of powder, as many balls, six guns, ten axes, twelve armsful of tobacco, and a hatchet pipe.

On the first of December, the Mantantons invited Le Sueur to a great feast. Of four of their lodges they had made one, in which were one hundred men seated around, and every one his dish before him. After the meal, Wahkantape, the chief, made them all smoke, one after another, in the hatchet pipe which had been given them. He then made a present to Le Sueur of a slave and a sack of wild rice, and said to him, showing him his men: "Behold the remains of this great village, which thou hast aforetimes seen so numerous! All the others have been killed in war; and the few men whom thou seest in this lodge, accept the present thou hast made them, and are resolved to obey the great chief of all nations, of whom thou hast spoken to us. Thou oughtest not to regard us as Scioux, but as French, and instead of saying the Scioux are miserable, and have no mind, and are fit for nothing but to rob and steal from the French, thou shalt say my brethren are miserable and have no mind, and we must try to procure some for them. They rob us, but I will take care that they do not lack iron, that is to say, all kinds of goods. If thou dost this, I assure thee that in a little time the Mantantons will become Frenchmen, and they will have none of those vices, with which thou reproachest us."

Having finished his speech, he covered his face with his garment, and the others imitated him. They wept over their companions who had died in war, and chanted an adieu to their country in a tone so gloomy, that one could not keep from partaking of their sorrow.

Wahkantape then made them smoke again, and distributed the presents, and said that he was going to the Mendeoucantons, to inform them of the resolution, and invite them to do the same.

On the twelfth, three Mendeoucanton chiefs, and a large number of Indians of the same village, arrived at the fort, and the next day gave satisfaction for robbing the Frenchmen. They brought four hundred pounds of beaver skins, and promised that the summer following, after their canoes were built and they had gathered their wild rice, that they would come and establish themselves near the French. The same day they returned to their village east of the Mississippi.

NAMES OF THE BANDS OF SCIOUX OF THE EAST, WITH THEIR SIGNIFICATION.

MANTANTONS—That is to say, Village of the Great Lake which empties into a small one.

MENDEOUACANTONS—Village of Spirit Lake.

QUIOPETONS—Village of the Lake with one River.

PSIOUMANITONS—Village of Wild Rice Gatherers.

OUADEBATONS—The River Village.

OUAETEMANETONS—Village of the Tribe who dwell on the Point of the Lake.

SONGASQUITONS—The Brave Village,

THE SCIOUX OF THE WEST.

TOUCHOUAESINTONS—The Village of the Pole.

PSINCHATONS—Village of the Red Wild Rice.

OUJALESPOITONS—Village divided into many small Bands.

PSINOUTANHINHINTONS — The Great Wild Rice Village.

TINTANGAOUGHIATONS — The Grand Lodge Village.

OUAEPETONS—Village of the Leaf.

OUGHETGEODATONS — Dung Village.

OUAPEONTETONS—Village of those who shoot in the Large Pine.

HINHANETONS — Village of the Red Stone Quarry.

The above catalogue of villages concludes the extract that La Harpe has made from Le Sueur's journal.

In the narrative of Major Long's second expedition, there are just as many villages of the Gens du Lac, or M'dewakantonwan Scioux mentioned, though the names are different. After leaving the Mille Lac region, the divisions evidently were different, and the villages known by new names.

Charlevoix, who visited the valley of the Lower Mississippi in 1722, says that Le Sueur spent a winter in his fort on the banks of the Blue Earth, and that in the following April he went up to the mine, about a mile above. In twenty-two days they obtained more than thirty thousand pounds of the substance, four thousand of which were selected and sent to France.

On the tenth of February, 1702, Le Sueur came back to the post on the Gulf of Mexico, and found D'Iberville absent, who, however, arrived on the eighteenth of the next month, with a ship from France, loaded with supplies. After a few weeks, the Governor of Louisiana sailed again for the old country, Le Sueur being a fellow passenger.

On board of the ship, D'Iberville wrote a memorial upon the Mississippi valley, with suggestions for carrying on commerce therein, which contains many facts furnished by Le Sueur. A copy of the manuscript was in possession of the Historical Society of Minnesota, from which are the following extracts:

"If the Sioux remain in their own country, they are useless to us, being too distant. We could have no commerce with them except that of the beaver. *M. Le Sueur, who goes to France to give an account of this country*, is the proper person to make these movements. He estimates the Sioux at four thousand families, who could settle upon the Missouri.

"He has spoken to me of another which he calls the Mahas, composed of more than twelve hundred families. The Ayoones (Ioways) and the Octoctatas, their neighbors, are about three hundred families. They occupy the lands between the Mississippi and the Missouri, about one hundred leagues from the Illinois. These savages do not know the use of arms, and a descent might be made upon them in a river, which is beyond the Wabash on the west. * * *

"The Assinibouel, Quenistinos, and people of the north, who are upon the rivers which fall into the Mississippi, and trade at Fort Nelson (Hudson Bay), are about four hundred. We could prevent them from going there if we wish."

"In four or five years we can establish a commerce with these savages of sixty or eighty thousand buffalo skins; more than one hundred deer skins, which will produce, delivered in France, more than two million four hundred thousand livres yearly. One might obtain for a buffalo skin four or five pounds of wool, which sells for twenty sous, two pounds of coarse hair at ten sous.

"Besides, from smaller peltries, two hundred thousand livres can be made yearly."

In the third volume of the "History and Statistics of the Indian Tribes," prepared under the direction of the Commissioner of Indian affairs, by Mr. Schoolcraft, a manuscript, a copy of which was in possession of General Cass, is referred to as containing the first enumeration of the Indians of the Mississippi Valley. The following was made thirty-four years earlier by D'Iberville:

"The Sioux,	Families,	4,000
Mahas,		12,000
Octata and Ayoues,		300
Canses [Kansas],		1,500
Missouri,		1,500
Akansas, &c.,		200
Manton [Mandan],		100
Panis [Pawnee],		2,000
Illinois, of the great village and Camaroua [Tamaroa],		800
Meosigamea [Metchigamias],		200
Kikapous and Mascoutens,		450
Miamis,		500
Chaetas,		4,000
Chicachas,		2,000
Mobiliens and Chohomes,		350
Concaques [Conchas],		2,000
Ouma [Houmas],		150
Colapissa,		250
Bayogoula,		100
People of the Fork,		200
Counica, &c. [Tonicas],		300
Nadeches,		1,500
Belochy, [Biloxi] Pascoboula,		100
Total,		23,850

"The savage tribes located in the places I have marked out, make it necessary to establish three posts on the Mississippi, one at the Arkansas, another at the Wabash (Ohio), and the third at the Missouri. At each post it would be proper to have an officer with a detachment of ten soldiers with a sergeant and corporal. All Frenchmen should be allowed to settle there with their families, and trade with the Indians, and they might establish tanneries for properly dressing the buffalo and deer skins for transportation.

"No Frenchman *shall be allowed to follow the Indians on their hunts, as it tends to keep them hunters*, as is seen in Canada, and when they are in the woods, they do not desire to become *tillers of the soil.* * * * * * * *

"I have said nothing in this memoir of which I have not personal knowledge or the most reliable sources. The most of what I propose is founded upon personal reflection in relation to what might be done for the defence and advancement of the colony. * * * * * * * * It will be absolutely necessary that the king should define the limits of this country in relation to the government of Canada. It is important that the commandant of the Mississippi should have a report of those who inhabit the rivers that fall into the Mississippi, and principally those of the river Illinois.

"The Canadians intimate to the savages that they ought not to listen to us but to the governor of Canada, who always speaks to them with large presents, that the governor of Mississippi is mean and never sends them any thing. This is true, and what I cannot do. It is imprudent to accustom the savages to be spoken to by presents, for, with so many, it would cost the king more than the revenue derived from the trade. When they come to us, it will be necessary to bring them in subjection, make them no presents, and *compel* them to do what we wish, *as if they were Frenchmen.*

"The Spaniards have divided the Indians into parties on this point, and we can do the same. When one nation does wrong, we can cease to trade with them, and threaten to draw down the hostility of other Indians. We rectify the difficulty by having missionaries, who will bring them into obedience *secretly*.

"The Illinois and Mascoutens have detained the French canoes they find upon the Mississippi, saying that the governors of Canada have given them permission. I do not know whether this is so, but if true, it follows that we have not the liberty to send any one on the Mississippi.

"M. Le Sueur would have been taken if he had not been the strongest. Only one of the canoes he sent to the Sioux was plundered." * * *

Penicaut's account varies in some particulars from that of La Harpe's. He calls the Mahkahto Green River instead of Blue and writes: "We took our route by its mouth and ascended it forty leagues, when we found another river falling into the Saint Pierre, which we entered. We called this the Green River because it is of that color by reason of a green earth which loosening itself from from the copper mines, becomes dissolved and makes it green.

"A league up this river, we found a point of land a quarter of a league distant from the woods, and it was upon this point that M. Le Sueur resolved to build his fort, because we could not go any higher on account of the ice, it being the last day of September. Half of our people went hunting whilst the others worked on the fort. We killed four hundred buffaloes, which were our provisions for the winter, and which we placed upon scaffolds in our fort, after having skinned and cleaned and quartered them. We also made cabins in the fort, and a magazine to keep our goods. After having drawn up our shallop within the inclosure of the fort, we spent the winter in our cabins.

"When we were working in our fort in the beginning seven French traders from Canada took refuge there. They had been pillaged and stripped naked by the Sioux, a wandering nation living only by hunting and plundering. Among these seven persons there was a Canadian gentleman of Le Sueur's acquaintance, whom he recognized at once, and gave him some clothes, as he did also to all the rest, and whatever else was necessary for them. They remained with us during the entire winter at our fort, where we had not food enough for all, except buffalo meat which we had not even salt to eat with. We had a good deal of trouble the first two weeks in accustoming ourselves to it, having fever and diarrhœa and becoming so tired of it as to hate the smell. But by degrees our bodies became adapted to it so well that at the end of six weeks there was not one of us who could not eat six pounds of meat a day, and drink four bowls of broth. As soon as we were accustomed to this kind of living it made us very fat, and then there was no more sickness.

"When spring arrived we went to work in the copper mine. This was the beginning of April of this year [1701.] We took with us twelve laborers and four hunters. This mine was situated about three-quarters of a league from our post. We took from the mine in twenty days more than twenty thousand pounds weight of ore, of which we only selected four thousand pounds of the finest, which M. Le Sueur, who was a very good judge of it, had carried to the fort, and which has since been sent to France, though I have not learned the result.

"This mine is situated at the beginning of a very long mountain, which is upon the bank of the river, so that boats can go right to the mouth of the mine itself. At this place is the green earth, which is a foot and a half in thickness, and above it is a layer of earth as firm and hard as stone, and black and burnt like coal by the exhalation from the mine. The copper is scratched out with a knife. There are no trees upon this mountain. * * * After twenty-two days' work, we returned to our fort. When the Sioux, who belong to the nation of savages who pillaged the Canadians, came they brought us merchandize of furs.

"They had more than four hundred beaver robes, each robe made of nine skins sewed together. M. Le Sueur purchased these and many other skins which he bargained for, in the week he traded with the savages. * * * * We sell in return wares which come very dear to the buyers, especially tobacco from Brazil, in the proportion of a hundred crowns the pound; two little horn-handled knives, and four leaden bullets are equal to ten crowns in exchange for skins; and so with the rest.

"In the beginning of May, we launched our shallop in the water, and loaded it with green earth that had been taken out of the river, and with the furs we had traded for, of which we had three canoes full. M. Le Sueur before going held council with M. D'Evaque [or Eraque] the Canadian gentleman, and the three great chiefs of the Sioux, three brothers, and told them that as he had to return to the sea, he desired them to live in peace with M. D'Evaque, whom he left in command at Fort L'Huillier, with twelve Frenchmen. M. Le Sueur made a considerable present to the three brothers, chiefs of the savages, desiring them to never abandon the French. Afterward we the twelve men whom he had chosen to go down to the sea with him embarked. In setting out, M. Le Sueur promised to M. D'Evaque and the twelve Frenchmen who remained with him to guard the fort, to send up munitions of war from the Illinois country as soon as he should arrive there; which he did, for on getting there he sent off to him a canoe loaded with two thousand pounds of lead and powder, with three of our people in charge."

Le Sueur arrived at the French fort on the Gulf of Mexico in safety, and in a few weeks, in the spring of 1701, sailed for France, with his kinsman, D'Iberville, the first governor of Louisiana.

In the spring of the next year (1702) D'Evaque came to Mobile and reported to D'Iberville, who had come back from France, that he had been attacked by the Foxes and Maskoutens, who killed three Frenchmen who were working near Fort L'Huillier, and that, being out of powder and lead, he had been obliged to conceal the goods which were left and abandon the post. At the Wisconsin River he had met Juchereau, formerly criminal judge in Montreal, with thirty-five men, on his way to establish a tannery for buffalo skins at the Wabash, and that at the Illinois he met the canoe of supplies sent by Bienville, D'Iberville's brother.

La Motte Cadillac, in command at Detroit, in a letter written on August 31st, 1703, alludes to Le Sueur's expedition in these words: "Last year they sent Mr. Boudor, a Montreal merchant, into the country of the Sioux to join Le Sueur. He succeeded so well in that journey he transported thither twenty-five or thirty thousand pounds of merchandize with which to trade in all the country of the Outawas. This proved to him an unfortunate investment, as he has been robbed of a part of the goods by the Outagamies. The occasion of the robbery by one of our own allies was as follows. I speak with a full knowledge of the facts as they occurred while I was at Michillimackinac. From time immemorial our allies have been at war with the Sioux, and on my arrival there in conformity to the order of M. Frontenac, the most able man who has ever come into Canada, I attempted to negotiate a truce between the Sioux and all our allies. Succeeding in this negotiation I took the occasion to turn their arms against the Iroquois with whom we were then at war, and soon after I effected a treaty of peace between the Sioux and the French and their allies which lasted two years.

"At the end of tha time the Sioux came, in great numbers, to the villages of the Miamis, under pretense of ratifying the treaty. They were well received by the Miamis, and, after spending several days in their villages, departed, apparently perfectly satisfied with their good reception, as they certainly had every reason to be.

"The Miamis, believing them already far distant, slept quietly; but the Sioux, who had premeditated the attack, returned the same night to the principal village of the Miamis, where most of the tribe were congregated, and, taking them by surprise, slaughtered nearly three thousand(?) and put the rest to flight.. •

"This perfectly infuriated all the nations. They came with their complaints, begging me to join with them and exterminate the Sioux. But the war we then had on our hands did not permit it, so it became necessary to play the orator in a long harangue. In conclusion I advised them to 'weep their dead, and wrap them up, and leave them to sleep coldly till the day of vengeance should come;' telling them we must sweep the land on this side of the Iroquois, as it was necessary to extinguish even their memory, after which the allied tribes could more easily avenge the atrocious deed that the Sioux had just committed upon them. In short, I managed them so well that the affair was settled in the manner that I proposed.

"But the twenty-five permits still existed, and the cupidity of the French induced them to go among the Sioux to trade for beaver. Our allies complained bitterly of this, saying it was injustice to them, as they had taken up arms in our quarrel against the Iroquois, while the French traders were carrying munitions of war to the Sioux to enable them to kill the rest of our allies as they had the Miamis.

"I immediately informed M. Frontenac, and M. Champigny having read the communication, and commanded that an ordinance be published at Montreal forbidding the traders to go into the country of the Sioux for the purpose of traffic under penalty of a thousand francs fine, the confiscation of the goods, and other arbitrary penalties. The ordinance was sent to me and faithfully executed. The same year [1699] I descended to Quebec, having asked to be relieved. Since that time, in spite of this prohibition, the French have continued to trade with the Sioux, but not without being subject to affronts and indignities from our allies themselves which bring dishonor on the French name. * * * I do not consider it best any longer to allow the traders to carry on commerce with the Sioux, under any pretext whatever, especially as M. Boudor has just been robbed by the Fox nation, and M. Jucheraux has given a thousand crowns, in goods, for the right of passage through the country of the allies to his habitation.

"The allies say that Le Sueur has gone to the Sioux on the Mississippi; that they are resolved to oppose him, and if he offers any resistance they will not be answerable for the consequences. It would be well, therefore, to give Le Sueur warning by the Governor of Mississippi.

"The Sauteurs [Chippeways] being friendly with the Sioux wished to give passage through their country to M. Boudor and others, permitting them to carry arms and other munitions of war to this nation; but the other nations being opposed to it, differences have arisen between them which have resulted in the robbery of M. Boudor. This has given occasion to the Sauteurs to make an outbreak upon the Sacs and Foxes, killing thirty or forty of them. So there is war among the people."

CHAPTER VIII.

EVENTS WHICH LED TO BUILDING FORT BEAUHARNOIS ON LAKE PEPIN.

Re-Establishment of Mackinaw.—Sieur de Louvigny at Mackinaw.—De Lignery at Mackinaw.—Louvigny Attacks the Foxes.—Du Luth's Post Reoccupied.—Saint Pierre at La Pointe on Lake Superior.—Preparations for a Jesuit Mission among the Sioux.—La Perriere Boucher's Expedition to Lake Pepin.—De Gonor and Guignas, Jesuit Missionaries.—Visit to Foxes and Winnebagoes.—Wisconsin River Described.—Fort Beauharnois Built.—Fireworks Displayed.—High Water at Lake Pepin.—De Gonor Visits Mackinaw.—Boucherville, Montbrun and Guignas Captured by Indians.—Montbrun's Escape.—Boucherville's Presents to Indians.—Exaggerated Account of Father Guignas' Capture.—Dispatches Concerning Fort Beauharnois.—Sieur de la Jemeraye.—Saint Pierre at Fort Beauharnois.—Trouble between Sioux and Foxes.—Sioux Visit Quebec.—De Lusignan Visits the Sioux Country.—Saint Pierre Noticed in the Travels of Jonathan Carver and Lieutenant Pike.

After the Fox Indians drove away Le Sueur's men, in 1702, from the Makahto, or Blue Earth river, the merchants of Montreal and Quebec did not encourage trade with the tribes beyond Mackinaw.

D'Aigremont, a French officer, sent to inspect that post, in the summer of 1708, reported that he arrived there, on the 19th of August, and found there but fourteen or fifteen Frenchmen. He also wrote: "Since there are now only a few wanderers at Michilimackinack, the greater part of the furs of the savages of the north goes to the English trading posts on Hudson's Bay. The Outawas are unable to make this trade by themselves, because the northern savages are timid, and will not come near them, as they have often been plundered. It is, therefore, necessary that the French be allowed to seek these northern tribes at the mouth of their own river, which empties into Lake Superior."

Louis de la Porte, the Sieur De Louvigny, in 1690, accompanied by Nicholas Perrot, with a detachment of one hundred and seventy Canadians and Indians, came to Mackinaw, and until 1694 was in command, when he was recalled.

In 1712, Father Joseph J. Marest the Jesuit missionary wrote, "If this country ever needs M. Louvigny it is now; the savages say it is absolutely necessary that he should come for the safety of the country, to unite the tribes and to defend those whom the war has caused to return to Michilimackinac. * * * * * * * I do not know what course the Pottawatomies will take, nor even what course they will pursue who are here, if M. Louvigny does not come, especially if the Foxes were to attack them or us."

The next July, M. Lignery urged upon the authorities the establishment of a garrison of trained soldiers at Mackinaw, and the Intendant of Canada wrote to the King of France:

"Michilimackinac might be re-established, without expense to his Majesty, either by surrendering the trade of the post to such individuals as will obligate themselves to pay all the expenses of twenty-two soldiers and two officers; to furnish munitions of war for the defense of the fort, and to make presents to the savages.

"Or the expenses of the post might be paid by the sale of permits, if the King should not think proper to grant an exclusive commerce. It is absolutely necessary to know the wishes of the King concerning these two propositions; and as M. Lignery is at Michilimackinac, it will not be any greater injury to the colony to defer the re-establment of this post, than it has been for eight or ten years past."

The war with England ensued, and in April, 1713, the treaty of Utrecht was ratified. France had now more leisure to attend to the Indian tribes of the West.

Early in 1714, Mackinaw was re-occupied, and on the fourteenth of March, 1716, an expedition under Lieutenant Louvigny, left Quebec. His arrival at Mackinaw, where he had been long expected, gave confidence to the voyageurs, and friendly Indians, and with a force of eight hundred men, he proceeded against the Foxes in Wisconsin. He brought with him two pieces of cannon and a grenade mortar, and besieged the fort of the Foxes, which he stated contained five hundred warriors, and three thousand men, a declaration which can scarcely be credited. After three days of skirmishing, he prepared to mine the fort, when the Foxes capitulated.

The paddles of the birch bark canoes and the gay songs of the voyageurs now began to be heard once more on the waters of Lake Superior and its tributaries. In 1717, the post erected by Du Luth, on Lake Superior near the northern boundary of Minnesota, was re-occupied by Lt. Robertel de la Noue.

In view of the troubles among the tribes of the northwest, in the month of September, 1718, Captain St. Pierre, who had great influence with the Indians of Wisconsin and Minnesota, was sent with Ensign Linctot and some soldiers to re-occupy La Pointe on Lake Supérior, now Bayfield, in the northwestern part of Wisconsin. The chiefs of the band there, and at Keweenaw, had threatened war against the Foxes, who had killed some of their number.

When the Jesuit Charlevoix returned to France after an examination of the resources of Canada and Louisiana, he urged that an attempt should be made to reach the Pacific Ocean by an inland route, and suggested that an expedition should proceed from the mouth of the Missouri and follow that stream, or that a post should be established among the Sioux which should be the point of departure. The latter was accepted, and in 1722 an allowance was made by the French Government, of twelve hundred livres, for two Jesuit missionaries to accompany those who should establish the new post. D'Avagour, Superintendent of Missions, in May, 1723, requested the authorities to grant a separate canoe for the conveyance of the goods of the proposed mission, and as it was necessary to send a commandant to persuade the Indians to receive the missionaries, he recommended Sieur Pachot, an officer of experience.

A dispatch from Canada to the French government, dated October 14, 1723, announced that Father de la Chasse, Superior of the Jesuits, expected that, the next spring, Father Guymoneau, and another missionary from Paris, would go to the Sioux, but that they had been hindered by the Sioux a few months before killing seven Frenchmen, on their way to Louisiana. The aged Jesuit, Joseph J. Marest, who had been on Lake Pepin in 1689 with Perrot, and was now in Montreal, said that it was the wandering Sioux who had killed the French, but he thought the stationary Sioux would receive Christian instruction.

The hostility of the Foxes had also prevented the establishment of a fort and mission among the Sioux.

On the seventh of June, 1726, peace was concluded by De Lignery with the Sauks, Foxes, and Winnebagoes at Green Bay; and Linctot, who had succeeded Saint Pierre in command at La Pointe, was ordered, by presents and the promise of a missionary, to endeavor to detach the Dahkotahs from their alliance with the Foxes. At this time Linctot made arrangements for peace between the Ojibways and Dahkotas, and sent two Frenchmen to dwell in the villages of the latter, with a promise that, if they ceased to fight the Ojibways, they should have regular trade, and a "black robe" reside in their country.

Traders and missionaries now began to prepare for visiting the Sioux, and in the spring of 1727 the Governor of Canada wrote that the fathers, appointed for the Sioux mission, desired a case of mathematical instruments, a universal astronomic dial, a spirit level, chain and stakes, and a telescope of six or seven feet tube.

On the sixteenth of June, 1727, the expedition for the Sioux country left Montreal in charge of the Sieur de la Perriere who was son of the distinguished and respected Canadian, Pierre Boucher, the Governor of Three Rivers.

La Perriere had served in Newfoundland and been associated with Hertel de Rouville in raids into New England, and gained an unenviable notoriety as the leader of the savages, while Rouville led the French in attacks upon towns like Haverhill, Massachusetts, where the Indians exultingly killed the Puritan pastor, scalped his loving wife, and dashed out his infant's brains against a rock. He was accompanied by his brother and other relatives. Two Jesuit fathers, De Gonor and Pierre Michel Guignas, were also of the party.

In Shea's "Early French Voyages" there was printed, for the first time, a letter from Father Guignas, from the Brevoort manuscripts, written on May 29, 1728, at Fort Beauharnois, on Lake Pepin, which contains facts of much interest.

He writes: "The Scioux convoy left the end of Montreal Island on the 16th of the month of June last year, at 11 A. M., and reached Michilimackinac the 22d of the month of July. This post is two hundred and fifty-one leagues from Montreal, almost due west, at 45 degrees 46 minutes north latitude.

"We spent the rest of the month at this post, in the hope of receiving from day to day some news from Montreal, and in the design of strengthening ourselves against the alleged extreme difficulties of getting a free passage through the Foxes. At last, seeing nothing, we set out on our march, the first of the month of August, and, after seventy-three leagues quite pleasant sail along the northerly side of Lake Michigan, running to the southeast, we reached the Bay [Green] on the 8th of the same month, at 5:30 P. M. This post is at 44 degrees 43 minutes north latitude.

"We stopped there two days, and on the 11th in the morning, we embarked, in a very great impatience to reach the Foxes. On the third day after our departure from the bay, quite late in the afternoon, in fact somewhat in the night, the chiefs of the Puans [Winnebagoes] came out three leagues from their village to meet the French, with their peace calumets and some bear meat as a refreshment, and the next day we were received by that small nation, amid several discharges of a few guns, and with great demonstrations.

"They asked us with so good a grace to do them the honor to stay some time with them that we granted them the rest of the day from noon, and the following day. There may be in all the village, sixty to eighty men, but all the men and women of very tall stature, and well made. They are on the bank of a very pretty little lake, in a most agreeable spot for its situation and the goodness of the soil, nineteen leagues from the bay and eight leagues from the Foxes.

"Early the next morning, the 15th of the month of August, the convoy preferred to continue its route, with quite pleasant weather, but a storm coming on in the afternoon, we arrived quite wet, still in the rain, at the cabins of the Foxes, a nation so much dreaded, and really so little to be dreaded. From all that we could see, it is composed of two hundred men at most, but there is a perfect hive of children, especially boys from ten to fourteen years old, well formed.

"They are cabined on a little eminence on the bank of a small river that bears their name, extremely tortuous or winding, so that you are constantly boxing the compass. Yet it is apparently quite wide, with a chain of hills on both sides, but there is only one miserable little channel amid this extent of apparent bed, which is a kind of marsh full of rushes and wild rice of almost impenetrable thickness. They have nothing but mere bark cabins, without any kind of palisade or other fortification. As soon as the French canoes touched their shore they ran down with their peace calumets, lighted in spite of the rain, and all smoked.

"We stayed among them the rest of this day, and all the next, to know what were their designs and ideas as to the French post among the Sioux. The Sieur Reaume, interpreter of Indian languages at the Bay, acted efficiently there, and with devotion to the King's service. Even if my testimony, Sir, should be deemed not impartial, I must have the honor to tell you that Rev. Father Chardon, an old missionary, was of very great assistance there, and the presence of three missionaries reassured these cut-throats and assassins of the French more than all the speeches of the best orators could have done.

"A general council was convened in one of the cabins, they were addressed in decided friendly terms, and they replied in the same way. A small present was made to them. On their side they gave some quite handsome dishes, lined with dry meat.

On the following Sunday, 17th of the month of August, very early in the morning, Father Chardon set out, with Sieur Reaume, to return to the Bay, and the Sioux expedition, greatly rejoiced to have so easily got over this difficulty, which had everywhere been represented as so insurmountable, got under way to endeavor to reach its journey's end.

"Never was navigation more tedious than what we subsequently made from uncertainty as to our course. No one knew it, and we got astray every moment on water and on land for want of a guide and pilots. We kept on, as it were feeling our way for eight days, for it was only on the ninth, about three o'clock p. m., that we arrived, by accident, believing ourselves still far off, at the portage of the Ouisconsin, which is forty-five leagues from the Foxes, counting all the twists and turns of this abominable river.

This portage is half a league in length, and half of that is a kind of marsh full of mud,

"The Ouisconsin is quite a handsome river, but far below what we had been told, apparently, as those who gave the description of it in Canada saw it only in the high waters of spring. It is a shallow river on a bed of quicksand, which forms bars almost everywhere, and these often change place. Its shores are either steep, bare mountains or low points with sandy base. Its course is from northeast to southwest. From the portage to its mouth in the Mississippi, I estimated thirty-eight leagues. The portage is at 43 deg. 24 min. north latitude.

"The Mississippi from the mouth of the Ouisconsin ascending, goes northwest. This beautiful river extends between two chains of high, bare and very sterile mountains, constantly a league, three-quarters of a league, or where it is narrowest, half a league apart. Its centre is occupied by a chain of well wooded islands, so that regarding from the heights above, you would think you saw an endless valley watered on the right and left by two large rivers; sometimes, too, you could discern no river. These islands are overflowed every year, and would be adapted to raising rice. Fifty-eight leagues from the mouth of the Ouisconsin, according to my calculation, ascending the Mississippi, is Lake Pepin, which is nothing else but the river itself, destitute of islands at that point, where it may be half a league wide. This river, in what I traversed of it, is shallow, and has shoals in several places, because its bed is moving sands, like that of the Ouisconsin.

"On the 17th of September, 1727, at noon, we reached this lake, which had been chosen as the bourne of our voyage. We planted ourselves on the shore about the middle of the north side, on a low point, where the soil is excellent. The wood is very dense there, but is already thinned in consequence of the rigor and length of the winter, which has been severe for the climate, for we are here on the parallel of 43 deg. 41 min. It is true that the difference of the winter is great compared to that of Quebec and Montreal, for all that some poor judges say.

"From the day after our landing we put our axes to the wood: on the fourth day following the fort was entirely finished. It is a square plat of one hundred feet, surrounded by pickets twelve feet long, with two good bastions. For so small a space there are large buildings quite distinct and not huddled together, each thirty, thirty-eight, and twenty-five feet long by sixteen feet wide.

"All would go well there if the spot were not inundated, but this year [1728], on the 15th of the month of April, we were obliged to camp out, and the water ascended to the height of two feet and eight inches in the houses, and it is idle to say that it was the quantity of snow that fell this year. The snow in the vicinity had melted long before, and there was only a foot and a half from the 8th of February to the 15th of March; you could not use snow-shoes.

"I have great reason to think that this spot is inundated more or less every year; I have always thought so, but they were not obliged to believe me, as old people who said that they had lived in this region fifteen or twenty years declared that it was never overflowed. We could not enter our much-devastated houses until the 30th of April, and the disorder is even now scarcely repaired.

"Before the end of October [1727] all the houses were finished and furnished, and each one found himself tranquilly lodged at home. They then thought only of going out to explore the hills and rivers and to see those herds of all kinds of deer of which they tell such stories in Canada. They must have retired, or diminished greatly, since the time the *old voyageurs* left the country; they are no longer in such great numbers, and are killed with difficulty.

"After beating the field, for some time, all reassembled at the fort, and thought of enjoying a little the fruit of their labors. On the 4th of November we did not forget it was the General's birthday. Mass was said for him [Beauharnois, Governor-General of Canada] in the morning, and they were well disposed to celebrate the day in the evening, but the tardiness of the pyrotechnists and the inconstancy of the weather caused them to postpone the celebration to the 14th of the same month, when they set off some very fine rockets and made the air ring with an hundred shouts of *Vive le Roy!* and *Vive Charles de Beauharnois!* It was on this occasion that the wine of the Sioux was broached; it was *par ex-*

cellence, although there are no wines here finer than in Canada.

"What contributed much to the amusement, was the terror of some cabins of Indians, who were at the time around the fort. When these poor people saw the fireworks in the air, and the stars fall from heaven, the women and children began to take flight, and the most courageous of the men to cry mercy, and implore us very earnestly to stop the surprising play of that wonderful medicine.

"As soon as we arrived among them, they assembled, in a few days, around the French fort to the number of ninety-five cabins, which might make in all one hundred and fifty men; for there are at most two men in their portable cabins of dressed skins, and in many there is only one. This is all we have seen except a band of about sixty men, who came on the 26th of the month of February, who were of those nations called Sioux of the Prairies.

"At the end of November, the Indians set out for their winter quarters. They do not, indeed, go far, and we saw some of them all through the winter; but from the second of the month of April last, when some cabins repassed here to go in search of them, [he] sought them in vain, during a week, for more than sixty leagues of the Mississippi. He [La Perriere?] arrived yesterday without any tidings of them.

"Although I said above, that the Sioux were alarmed at the rockets, which they took for new phenomena, it must not be supposed from that they were less intelligent than other Indians we know. They seem to me more so; at least they are much gayer and open, apparently, and far more dextrous thieves, great dancers, and great medicine men. The men are almost all large and well made, but the women are very ugly and disgusting, which does not, however, check debauchery among them, and is perhaps an effect of it."

In the summer of 1728 the Jesuit De Gonor left the fort on Lake Pepin, and, by way of Mackinaw, returned to Canada. The Foxes had now become very troublesome, and De Lignery and Beaujeu marched against their stronghold, to find they had retreated to the Mississippi River.

On the 12th of October, Boucherville, his brother Montbrun, a young cadet of enterprising spirit, the Jesuit Guignas, and other Frenchmen, eleven in all, left Fort Pepin to go to Canada, by way of the Illinois River. They were captured by the Mascoutens and Kickapoos, and detained at the river "Au Bœuf," which stream was probably the one mentioned by Le Sueur as twenty-two leagues above the Illinois River, although the same name was given by Hennepin to the Chippewa River, just below Lake Pepin. They were held as prisoners, with the view of delivering them to the Foxes. The night before the delivery the Sieur Montbrun and his brother and another Frenchman escaped. Montbrun, leaving his sick brother in the Illinois country, journeyed to Canada and informed the authorities.

Boucherville and Guignas remained prisoners for several months, and the former did not reach Detroit until June, 1729. The account of expenditures made during his captivity is interesting as showing the value of merchandize at that time. It reads as follows:

"Memorandum of the goods that Monsieur de Boucherville was obliged to furnish in the service of the King, from the time of his detention among the Kickapoos, on the 12th of October, 1728, until his return to Detroit, in the year 1729, in the month of June. On arriving at the Kickapoo village, he made a present to the young men to secure their opposition to some evil minded old warriors—

Two barrels of powder, each fifty pounds at Montreal price, valued at the sum of	150 liv.
One hundred pounds of lead and balls making the sum of..................	50 liv.
Four pounds of vermillion, at 12 francs the pound.........................	48 fr.
Four coats, braided, at twenty francs...	80 fr.
Six dozen knives at four francs the dozen	24 fr.
Four hundred flints, one hundred gun-worms, two hundred ramrods and one hundred and fifty files, the total at the maker's prices.....................	90 liv.

After the Kickapoos refused to deliver them to the Renards [Foxes] they wished some favors, and I was obliged to give them the following which would allow them to weep over and cover their dead:

Two braided coats @ 20 fr. each.......	40fr.
Two woolen blankets @ 15 fr...........	30
One hundred pounds of powder @ 30 sous	75
One hundred pounds of lead @ 10 sous..	25

Two pounds of vermillion @ 12 fr......	24fr.
Moreover, given to the Renards to cover their dead and prepare them for peace, fifty pounds of powder, making......	75
One hundred pounds of lead @ 10 sous.	50
Two pounds of vermillion @ 12 fr......	24

During the winter a considerable party was sent to strike hands with the Illinois. Given at that time:

Two blue blankets @ 15 fr............	30
Four men's shirts @ 6 fr..............	24
Four pairs of long-necked bottles @ 6 fr	24
Four dozen of knives @ 4 fr...........	16
Gun-worms, files, ramrods, and flints, estimated............................	40

Given to engage the Kickapoos to establish themselves upon a neighboring isle, to protect from the treachery of the Renards—

Four blankets, @ 15f..................	60f
Two pairs of bottles, 6f...............	24
Two pounds of vermillion, 12f.........	24
Four dozen butcher knives, 6f.........	24
Two woolen blankets, @ 15f...........	30
Four pairs of bottles, @ 6f...........	24
Four shirts, @ 6f.....................	24
Four dozen of knives, @ 4f...........	16

The Renards having betrayed and killed their brothers, the Kickapoos, I seized the favorable opportunity, and to encourage the latter to avenge themselves, I gave—

Twenty-five pounds of powder, @ 30sous	37f.10s.
Twenty-five pounds of lead, @ 10s.....	12f.10s.
Two guns at 30 livres each.............	60f
One half pound of vermillion..........	6f
Flints, guns, worms and knives........	20f
The Illinois coming to the Kikapoos village, I supported them at my expense, and gave them powder, balls and shirts valued at...........................	50f
In departing from the Kikapoos village, I gave them the rest of the goods for their good treatment, estimated at....	80f

In a letter, written by a priest, at New Orleans, on July 12, 1730, is the following exaggerated account of the capture of Father Guignas: "We always felt a distrust of the Fox Indians, although they did not longer dare to undertake anything, since Father Guignas has detached from their alliance the tribes of the Kikapous and Maskoutins. You know, my Reverend Father, that, being in Canada, he had the courage to penetrate even to the Sioux near the sources of the Mississippi, at the distance of eight hundred leagues from New Orleans and five hundred from Quebec. Obliged to abandon this important mission by the unfortunate result of the enterprise against the Foxes, he descended the river to repair to the Illinois. On the 15th of October in the year 1728 he was arrested when half way by the Kickapous and Maskoutins. For four months he was a captive among the Indians, where he had much to suffer and everything to fear. The time at last came when he was to be burned alive, when he was adopted by an old man whose family saved his life and procured his liberty.

"Our missionaries who are among the Illinois were no sooner acquainted with the situation than they procured him all the alleviation they were able. Everything which he received he employed to conciliate the Indians, and succeeded to the extent of engaging them to conduct him to the Illinois to make peace with the French and Indians of this region. Seven or eight months after this peace was concluded, the Maskoutins and Kikapous returned again to the Illinois country, and took back Father Guignas to spend the winter, from whence, in all probability, he will return to Canada."

In dispatches sent to France, in October, 1729, by the Canadian government, the following reference is made to Fort Beauharnois: "They agree that the fort built among the Scioux, on the border of Lake Pepin, appears to be badly situated on account of the freshets, but the Indians assure that the waters rose higher in 1728 than it ever did before. When Sieur de Laperriere located it at that place it was on the assurance of the Indians that the waters did not rise so high." In reference to the absence of Indians, is the following:

"It is very true that these Indians did leave shortly after on a hunting excursion, as they are in the habit of doing, for their own support and that of their families, who have only that means of livelihood, as they do not cultivate the soil at all. M. de Beauharnois has just been informed that their absence was occasioned only by having fallen in while hunting with a number of prairie Scioux, by whom they were invited to accompany them on a war expedition against the Mahas, which invitation they accepted, and returned only in the month of July following.

"The interests of religion, of the service, and of the colony, are involved in the maintenance of this establishment, which has been the more necessary as there is no doubt but the Foxes, when routed, would have found an asylum among the Sciaux had not the French been settled there, and the docility and submission manifested by the Foxes can not be attributed to any cause except the attention entertained by the Scioux for the French, and the offers which the former made the latter, of which the Foxes were fully cognisant.

"It is necessary to retain the Scioux in these favorable dispositions, in order to keep the Foxes in check and counteract the measures they might adopt to gain over the Scioux, who will invariably reject their propositions so long as the French remain in the country, and their trading post shall continue there. But, despite all these advantages and the importance of preserving that establishment, M. de Beauharnois cannot take any steps until he has news of the French who asked his permission this summer to go up there with a canoe load of goods, and until assured that those who wintered there have not dismantled the fort, and that the Scioux continue in the same sentiments. Besides, it does not seem very easy, in the present conjuncture, to maintain that post unless there is a solid peace with the Foxes; on the other hand, the greatest portion of the traders, who applied in 1727 for the establishment of that post, have withdrawn, and will not send thither any more, as the rupture with the Foxes, through whose country it is necessary to pass in order to reach the Scioux in canoe, has led them to abandon the idea. But the one and the other case might be remedied. The Foxes will, in all probability, come or send next year to sue for peace; therefore, if it be granted to them on advantageous conditions, there need be no apprehension when going to the Sioux, and another company could be formed, less numerous than the first, through whom, or some responsible merchants able to afford the outfit, a new treaty could be made, whereby these difficulties would be soon obviated. One only trouble remains, and that is, to send a commanding and sub-officer, and some soldiers, up there, which are absolutely necessary for the maintenance of good order at that post; the missionaries would not go there without a commandant. This article, which regards the service, and the expense of which must be on his majesty's account, obliges them to apply for orders. They will, as far as lies in their power, induce the traders to meet that expense, which will possibly amount to 1000 livres or 1500 livres a year for the commandant, and in proportion for the officer under him; but, as in the beginning of an establishment the expenses exceed the profits, it is improbable that any company of merchants will assume the outlay, and in this case they demand orders on this point, as well as his majesty's opinion as to the necessity of preserving so useful a post, and a nation which has already afforded proofs of its fidelity and attachment.

"These orders could be sent them by the way of Ile Royale, or by the first merchantmen that will sail for Quebec. The time required to receive intelligence of the occurrences in the Scioux country, will admit of their waiting for these orders before doing anything."

Sieur de la Jemeraye, a relative of Sieur de la Perriere Boucher, with a few French, during the troubles remained in the Sioux country. After peace was established with the Foxes, Legardeur Saint Pierre was in command at Fort Beauharnois, and Father Guignas again attempted to establish a Sioux mission. In a communication dated 12th of October, 1736, by the Canadian authorities is the following: "In regard to the Scioux, Saint Pierre, who commanded at that post, and Father Guignas, the missionary, have written to Sieur de Beauharnois on the tenth and eleventh of last April, that these Indians appeared well intentioned toward the French, and had no other fear than that of being abandoned by them. Sieur de Beauharnois annexes an extract of these letters, and although the Scioux seem very friendly, the result only can tell whether this fidelity is to be absolutely depended upon, for the unrestrained and inconsistent spirit which composes the Indian character may easily change it. They have not come over this summer as yet, but M. de la St. Pierre is to get them to do so next year, and to have an eye on their proceedings."

The reply to this communication from Louis

XV. dated Versailles, May 10th, 1737, was in these words: "As respects the Scioux, according to what the commandant and missionary at that post have written to Sieur de Beauharnois relative to the disposition of these Indians, nothing appears to be wanting on that point.

"But their delay in coming down to Montreal since the time they have promised to do so, must render their sentiments somewhat suspected, and nothing but facts can determine whether their fidelity can be absolutely relied on. But what must still further increase the uneasiness to be entertained in their regard is the attack on the convoy of M. de Verandrie, especially if this officer has adopted the course he had informed the Marquis de Beauharnois he should take to have revenge therefor."

The particulars of the attack alluded to will be found in the next chapter. Soon after this the Foxes again became troublesome, and the post on Lake Pepin was for a time abandoned by the French. A dispatch in 1741 uses this language: "The Marquis de Beauharnois' opinion respecting the war against the Foxes, has been the more readily approved by the Baron de Longeuil, Messieurs De la Chassaigne, La Corne, de Lignery, La Noue, and Duplessis-Fabert, whom he had assembled at his house, as it appears from all the letters that the Count has written for several years, that he has nothing so much at heart as the destruction of that Indian nation, which can not be prevailed on by the presents and the good treatment of the French, to live in peace, notwithstanding all its promises.

"Besides, it is notorious that the Foxes have a secret understanding with the Iroquois, to secure a retreat among the latter, in case they be obliged to abandon their villages. They have one already secured among the Sioux of the prairies, with whom they are allied; so that, should they be advised beforehand of the design of the French to wage war against them, it would be easy for them to retire to the one or the other before their passage could be intersected or themselves attacked in their villages."

In the summer of 1743, a deputation of the Sioux came down to Quebec, to ask that trade might be resumed. Three years after this, four Sioux chiefs came to Quebec, and asked that a commandant might be sent to Fort Beauharnois; which was not granted.

During the winter of 1745-6, De Lusignan visited the Sioux country, ordered by the government to hunt up the "coureurs des bois," and withdraw them from the country. They started to return with him, but learning that they would be arrested at Mackinaw, for violation of law, they ran away. While at the villages of the Sioux of the lakes and plains, the chiefs brought to this officer nineteen of their young men, bound with cords, who had killed three Frenchmen, at the Illinois. While he remained with them, they made peace with the Ojibways of La Pointe, with whom they had been at war for some time. On his return, four chiefs accompanied him to Montreal, to solicit pardon for their young braves.

The lessees of the trading-post lost many of their peltries that winter in consequence of a fire.

Reminiscences of St. Pierre's residence at Lake Pepin were long preserved. Carver, in 1766, "observed the ruins of a French factory, where, it is said, Captain St. Pierre resided, and carried on a great trade with the Nadouessies before the reduction of Canada."

Pike, in 1805, wrote in his journal: "Just below Pt. Le Sable, the French, who had driven the Renards [Foxes] from Wisconsin, and chased them up the Mississippi, built a stockade on this lake, as a barrier against the savages. It became a noted factory for the Sioux."

CHAPTER IX.

VERENDRYE, THE EXPLORER OF NORTHERN MINNESOTA, AND DISCOVERER OF THE ROCKY MOUNTAINS.

Conversation of Verendrye with Father De Gonor.—Parentage and Early Life.—Old Indian Map Preserved.—Verendrye's Son and Nephew Explore Pigeon River and Reach Rainy Lake.—Father Messayer a Companion.—Fort St. Pierre Established.—Lake of the Woods Reached and Fort St. Charles Built.—De la Jemeraye's Map.—Fort on the Assinaboine River.—Verendrye's Son, Father Ouneau and Associates Killed by Sioux, on Massacre Isle, in Lake of the Woods.—Fort La Reine.—Verendrye's Eldest Son, with Others, Reaches the Missouri River.—Discovers the Rocky Mountains.—Returns to Lake of the Woods.—Exploration of Saskatchewan River.—Sieur de la Verendrye Jr.—Verendrye the Father, made Captain of the Order of St. Louis.—His Death.—The Swedish Traveler, Kalm, Notices Verendrye.—Bougainville Describes Verendrye's Explorations.—Legardeur de St. Pierre at Fort La Reine.—Fort Jonquiere Established.—De la Corne Succeeds St. Pierre.—St. Pierre Meets Washington at French Creek, in Pennsylvania.—Killed in Battle, near Lake George.

Early in the year 1728, two travelers met at the secluded post of Mackinaw, one was named De Gonor, a Jesuit Father, who with Guignas, had gone with the expedition, that the September before had built Fort Beauharnois on the shores of Lake Pepin, the other was Pierre Gualtier Varennes, the Sieur de la Verendrye the commander of the post on Lake Nepigon of the north shore of Lake Superior, and a relative of the Sieur de la Perriere, the commander at Lake Pepin.

Verendrye was the son of Rene Gualtier Varennes who for twenty-two years was the chief magistrate at Three Rivers, whose wife was Marie Boucher, the daughter of his predecessor whom he had married when she was twelve years of age. He became a cadet in 1697, and in 1704 accompanied an expedition to New England. The next year he was in Newfoundland and the year following he went to France, joined a regiment of Brittany and was in the conflict at Malplaquet when the French troops were defeated by the Duke of Marlborough. When he returned to Canada he was obliged to accept the position of ensign notwithstanding the gallant manner in which he had behaved. In time he became identified with the Lake Superior region. While at Lake Nepigon the Indians assured him that there was a communication largely by water to the Pacific Ocean. One, named Ochagachs, drew a rude map of the country, which is still preserved among the French archives. Pigeon River is marked thereon Mantohavagane, and the River St. Louis is marked R. fond du L. Superior, and the Indians appear to have passed from its headwaters to Rainy Lake. Upon the western extremity is marked the River of the West.

De Gonor conversed much upon the route to the Pacific with Verendrye, and promised to use his influence with the Canadian authorities to advance the project of exploration.

Charles De Beauharnois, the Governor of Canada, gave Verendrye a respectful hearing, and carefully examined the map of the region west of the great lakes, which had been drawn by Ochagachs (Otchaga), the Indian guide. Orders were soon given to fit out an expedition of fifty men. It left Montreal in 1731, under the conduct of his sons and nephew De la Jemeraye, he not joining the party till 1733, in consequence of the detentions of business.

In the autumn of 1731, the party reached Rainy Lake, by the Nantouagan, or Groselliers river, now called Pigeon. Father Messayer, who had been stationed on Lake Superior, at the Groselliers river, was taken as a spiritual guide. At the foot of Rainy Lake a post was erected and called Fort St. Pierre, and the next year, having crossed Minittie, or Lake of the Woods, they established Fort St. Charles on its southwestern bank. Five leagues from Lake Winnipeg they established a post on the Assinaboine. An unpublished map of these discoveries by De la Jemeraye still exists at Paris. The river Winnipeg, called by them Maurepas, in honor of the minister of France in 1734, was protected by a fort of the same name.

About this time their advance was stopped by the exhaustion of supplies, but on the 12th of April, 1735, an arrangement was made for a second equipment, and a fourth son joined the expedition.

In June, 1736, while twenty-one of the expedition were camped upon an isle in the Lake of the Woods, they were surprised by a band of Sioux hostile to the French allies, the Cristinaux, and all killed. The island, upon this account, is called Massacre Island. A few days after, a party of five Canadian voyageurs discovered their dead bodies and scalped heads. Father Onneau, the missionary, was found upon one knee, an arrow in his head, his breast bare, his left hand touching the ground, and the right hand raised.

Among the slaughtered was also a son of Verendrye, who had a tomahawk in his back, and his body adorned with garters and bracelets of porcupine. The father was at the foot of the Lake of the Woods when he received the news of his son's murder, and about the same time heard of the death of his enterprising nephew, Dufrost de la Jemeraye, the son of his sister Marie Reine de Varennes, and brother of Madame Youville, the foundress of the Hospitaliers at Montreal.

It was under the guidance of the latter that the party had, in 1731, mastered the difficulties of the Nantaonagon, or Groselliers river.

On the 3d of October, 1738, they built an advanced post, Fort La Reine, on the river Assiniboels, now Assinaboine, which they called St Charles, and beyond was a branch called St. Pierre. These two rivers received the baptismal name of Verendrye, which was Pierre, and Governor Beauharnois, which was Charles. The post became the centre of trade and point of departure for explorations, either north or south.

It was by ascending the Assinaboine, and by the present trail from its tributary, Mouse river, they reached the country of the Mantanes, and in 1741, came to the upper Missouri, passed the Yellow Stone, and at length arrived at the Rocky Mountains. The party was led by the eldest son and his brother, the chevalier. They left the Lake of the Woods on the 29th of April, 1742, came in sight of the Rocky Mountains on the 1st of January, 1743, and on the 12th ascended them. On the route they fell in with the Beaux Hommes, Pioya, Petits Renards, and Arc tribes, and stopped among the Snake tribe, but could go no farther in a southerly direction, owing to a war between the Arcs and Snakes.

On the 19th of May, 1744, they had returned to the upper Missouri, and, in the country of the Petite Cerise tribe, they planted on an eminence a leaden plate of the arms of France, and raised a monument of stones, which they called Beauharnois. They returned to the Lake of the Woods on the 2d of July.

North of the Assiniboine they proceeded to Lake Dauphin, Swan's Lake, explored the river "Des Biches," and ascended even to the fork of the Saskatchewan, which they called Poskoiac. Two forts were subsequently established, one near Lake Dauphin and the other on the river "des Biches," called Fort Bourbon. The northern route, by the Saskatchewan, was thought to have some advantage over the Missouri, because there was no danger of meeting with the Spaniards.

Governor Beauharnois having been prejudiced against Verendrye by envious persons, De Noyelles was appointed to take command of the posts. During these difficulties, we find Sieur de la Verendrye, Jr., engaged in other duties. In August, 1747, he arrives from Mackinaw at Montreal, and in the autumn of that year he accompanies St. Pierre to Mackinaw, and brings back the convoy to Montreal. In February, 1748, with five Canadians, five Cristenaux, two Ottawas, and one Sauteur, he attacked the Mohawks near Schenectady, and returned to Montreal with two scalps, one that of a chief. On June 20th, 1748, it is recorded that Chevalier de la Verendrye departed from Montreal for the head of Lake Superior. Margry states that he perished at sea in November, 1764, by the wreck of the "Auguste."

Fortunately, Galissioniere the successor of Beauharnois, although deformed and insignificant in appearance, was fair minded, a lover of science, especially botany, and anxious to push discoveries toward the Pacific. Verendrye the father was restored to favor, and made Captain of the Order of St. Louis, and ordered to resume explorations, but he died on December 6th, 1749, while planning a tour up the Saskatchewan.

The Swedish Professor, Kalm, met him in Canada, not long before his decease, and had interesting conversations with him about the furrows on the plains of the Missouri, which he erroneously conjectured indicated the former abode of an agricultural people. These ruts are familiar to modern travelers, and may be only buffalo trails.

Father Coquard, who had been associated with

Verendrye, says that they first met the Mantanes, and next the Brochets. After these were the Gros Ventres, the Crows, the Flat Heads, the Black Feet, and Dog Feet, who were established on the Missouri, even up to the falls, and that about thirty leagues beyond they found a narrow pass in the mountains.

Bougainville gives a more full account: he says: "He who most advanced this discovery was the Sieur de la Veranderie. He went from Fort la Reine to the Missouri. He met on the banks of this river the Mandans, or White Beards, who had seven villages with pine stockades, strengthened by a ditch. Next to these were the Kinongewiniris, or the Brochets, in three villages, and toward the upper part of the river were three villages of the Mahantas. All along the mouth of the Wabeik, or Shell River, were situated twenty-three villages of the Panis. To the southwest of this river, on the banks of the Ouanaradeba, or La Graisse, are the Hectanes or Snake tribe. They extend to the base of a chain of mountains which runs north northeast. South of this is the river Karoskiou, or Cerise Pelee, which is supposed to flow to California.

"He found in the immense region watered by the Missouri, and in the vicinity of forty leagues, the Mahantas, the Owilinioek, or Beaux Hommes, four villages; opposite the Brochets the Black Feet, three villages of a hundred lodges each; opposite the Mandans are the Ospekakaerenousques, or Flat Heads, four villages; opposite the Panis are the Arcs of Cristinaux, and Utasibaoutchatas of Assiniboel, three villages; following these the Makesch, or Little Foxes, two villages; the Piwassa, or great talkers, three villages; the Kakokoschena, or Gens de la Pie, five villages; the Kiskipisounouini,. or the Garter tribe, seven villages."

Galassoniere was succeeded by Jonquiere in the governorship of Canada, who proved to be a grasping, peevish, and very miserly person. For the sons of Verendrye he had no sympathy, and forming a clique to profit by their father's toils, he determined to send two expeditions toward the Pacific Ocean, one by the Missouri and the other by the Saskatchewan.

Father Coquard, one of the companions of Verendrye, was consulted as to the probability of finding a pass in the Rocky Mountains, through which they might, in canoes, reach the great lake of salt water, perhaps Puget's Sound.

The enterprise was at length confided to two experienced officers, Lamarque de Marin and Jacques Legardeur de Saint Pierre. The former was assigned the way, by the Missouri, and to the latter was given the more northern route; but Saint Pierre in some way excited the hostility of the Cristinaux, who attempted to kill him, and burned Fort la Reine. His lieutenant, Boucher de Niverville, who had been sent to establish a post toward the source of the Saskatchewan, failed on account of sickness. Some of his men, however, pushed on to the Rocky Mountains, and in 1753 established Fort Jonquiere. Henry says St. Pierre established Fort Bourbon.

In 1753, Saint Pierre was succeeded in the command of the posts of the West, by de la Corne, and sent to French Creek, in Pennsylvania. He had been but a few days there when he received a visit from Washington, just entering upon manhood, bearing a letter from Governor Dinwiddie of Virginia, complaining of the encroachments of the French.

Soon the clash of arms between France and England began, and Saint Pierre, at the head of the Indian allies, fell near Lake George, in September, 1755, in a battle with the English. After the seven years' war was concluded, by the treaty of Paris, the French relinquished all their posts in the Northwest, and the work begun by Verendrye, was, in 1805, completed by Lewis and Clarke; and the Northern Pacific Railway is fast approaching the passes of the Rocky Mountains, through the valley of the Yellow Stone, and from thence to the great land-locked bay of the ocean, Puget's Sound.

CHAPTER X.

EFFECT OF THE ENGLISH AND FRENCH WAR.

English Influence Increasing.—Le Duc Robbed at Lake Superior.—St. Pierre at Mackinaw.—Escape of Indian Prisoners.—La Ronde and Verendrye. Influence of Sieur Marin.—St. Pierre Recalled from Winnipeg Region.—Interview with Washington.—Langlade Urges Attack Upon Troops of Braddock.—Saint Pierre Killed in Battle.—Marin's Boldness.—Rogers, a Partisan Ranger, Commands at Mackinaw.—At Ticonderoga.—French Deliver up the Posts in Canada.—Capt Balfour Takes Possession of Mackinaw and Green Bay.—Lieut. Gorrell in Command at Green Bay.—Sioux Visit Green Bay.—Pennensha a French Trader Among the Sioux.—Treaty of Paris.

English influence produced increasing dissatisfaction among the Indians that were beyond Mackinaw. Not only were the voyageurs robbed and maltreated at Sault St. Marie and other points on Lake Superior, but even the commandant at Mackinaw was exposed to insolence, and there was no security anywhere.

On the twenty-third of August, 1747, Philip Le Duc arrived at Mackinaw from Lake Superior, stating that he had been robbed of his goods at Kamanistigoya, and that the Ojibways of the lake were favorably disposed toward the English. The Dahkotahs were also becoming unruly in the absence of French officers.

In a few weeks after Le Duc's robbery, St. Pierre left Montreal to become commandant at Mackinaw, and Vercheres was appointed for the post at Green Bay. In the language of a document of the day, St. Pierre was "a very good officer, much esteemed among all the nations of those parts; none more loved and feared." On his arrival, the savages were so cross, that he advised that no Frenchman should come to trade.

By promptness and boldness, he secured the Indians who had murdered some Frenchmen, and obtained the respect of the tribes. While the three murderers were being conveyed in a canoe down the St. Lawrence to Quebec, in charge of a sergeant and seven soldiers, the savages, with characteristic cunning, though manacled, succeeded in killing or drowning the guard. Cutting their irons with an axe, they sought the woods, and escaped to their own country. "Thus," writes Galassoniere, in 1748, to Count Maurepas, was lost in a great measure the fruit of Sieur St. Pierre's good management, and of all the fatigue I endured to get the nations who surrendered these rascals to listen to reason."

On the twenty-first of June of the next year, La Ronde started to La Pointe, and Verendrye for West Sea, or Fon du Lac, Minnesota.

Under the influence of Sieur Marin, who was in command at Green Bay in 1753, peaceful relations were in a measure restored between the French and Indians.

As the war between England and France deepened, the officers of the distant French posts were called in and stationed nearer the enemy. Legardeur St. Pierre, was brought from the Lake Winnipeg region, and, in December, 1753, was in command of a rude post near Erie, Pennsylvania. Langlade, of Green Bay, Wisconsin, arrived early in July, 1755, at Fort Duquesne. With Beauyeu and De Lignery, who had been engaged in fighting the Fox Indians, he left that fort, at nine o'clock of the morning of the 9th of July, and, a little after noon, came near the English, who had halted on the south shore of the Monongahela, and were at dinner, with their arms stacked. By the urgent entreaty of Langlade, the western half-breed, Beauyeu, the officer in command ordered an attack, and Braddock was overwhelmed, and Washington was obliged to say, "We have been beaten, shamefully beaten, by a handful of Frenchmen."

Under Baron Dieskau, St. Pierre commanded the Indians, in September, 1755, during the campaign near Lake George, where he fell gallantly fighting the English, as did his commander. The Rev. Claude Coquard, alluding to the French defeat, in a letter to his brother, remarks:

"We lost, on that occasion, a brave officer, M. de St. Pierre, and had his advice, as well as that of several other Canadian officers, been followed, Jonckson [Johnson] was irretrievably destroyed, and we should have been spared the trouble we have had this year."

Other officers who had been stationed on the borders of Minnesota also distinguished themselves during the French war. The Marquis Montcalm, in camp at Ticonderoga, on the twenty-seventh of July, 1757, writes to Vaudreuil, Governor of Canada:

"Lieutenant Marin, of the Colonial troops, who has exhibited a rare audacity, did not consider himself bound to halt, although his detachment of about four hundred men was reduced to about two hundred, the balance having been sent back on account of inability to follow. He carried off a patrol of ten men, and swept away an ordinary guard of fifty like a wafer; went up to the enemy's camp, under Fort Lydias (Edward), where he was exposed to a severe fire, and retreated like a warrior. He was unwilling to amuse himself making prisoners; he brought in only one, and thirty-two scalps, and must have killed many men of the enemy, in the midst of whose ranks it was neither wise nor prudent to go in search of scalps. The Indians generally all behaved well. * * * The Outaouais, who arrived with me, and whom I designed to go on a scouting party towards the lake, had conceived a project of administering a corrective to the English barges. * * * On the day before yesterday, your brother formed a detachment to accompany them. I arrived at his camp on the evening of the same day. Lieutenant de Corbiere, of the Colonial troops, was returning, in consequence of a misunderstanding, and as I knew the zeal and intelligence of that officer, I made him set out with a new instruction to join Messrs de Langlade and Hertel de Chantly. They remained in ambush all day and night yesterday; at break of day the English appeared on Lake St. Sacrament, to the number of twenty-two barges, under the command of Sieur Parker. The whoops of our Indians impressed them with such terror that they made but feeble resistance, and only two barges escaped."

After De Corbiere's victory on Lake Champlain, a large French army was collected at Ticonderoga, with which there were many Indians from the tribes of the Northwest, and the Ioways appeared for the first time in the east.

It is an interesting fact that the English officers who were in frequent engagements with St. Pierre, Lusignan, Marin, Langlade, and others, became the pioneers of the British, a few years afterwards, in the occupation of the outposts of the lakes, and in the exploration of Minnesota.

Rogers, the celebrated captain of rangers, subsequently commander of Mackinaw, and Jonathan Carver, the first British explorer of Minnesota, were both on duty near Lake Champlain, the latter narrowly escaping at the battle of Fort George.

On Christmas eve, 1757, Rogers approached Fort Ticonderoga, to fire the outhouses, but was prevented by discharge of the cannons of the French.

He contented himself with killing fifteen beeves, on the horns of one of which he left this laconic and amusing note, addressed to the commander of the post:

"I am obliged to you, Sir, for the repose you have allowed me to take; *I thank you for the fresh meat you have sent me.* I request you to present my compliments to the Marquis du Montcalm."

On the thirteenth of March, 1758, Durantaye, formerly at Mackinaw, had a skirmish with Rogers. Both had been trained on the frontier, and they met "as Greek met Greek." The conflict was fierce, and the French victorious. The Indian allies, finding a scalp of a chief underneath an officer's jacket, were furious, and took one hundred and fourteen scalps in return. When the French returned, they supposed that Captain Rogers was among the killed.

At Quebec, when Montcalm and Wolfe fell, there were Ojibways present assisting the French

The Indians, returning from the expeditions against the English, were attacked with small-pox, and many died at Mackinaw.

On the eighth of September, 1760, the French delivered up all their posts in Canada. A few days after the capitulation at Montreal, Major Rogers was sent with English troops, to garrison the posts of the distant Northwest.

On the eighth of September, 1761, a year after the surrender, Captain Balfour, of the eightieth regiment of the British army, left Detroit, with a detachment to take possession of the French forts at Mackinaw and Green Bay. Twenty-five soldiers were left at Mackinaw, in command of Lieutenant Leslie, and the rest sailed to Green Bay, under Lieutenant Gorrell of the Royal

Americans, where they arrived on the twelfth of October. The fort had been abandoned for several years, and was in a dilapidated condition. In charge of it there was left a lieutenant, a corporal, and fifteen soldiers. Two English traders arrived at the same time, McKay from Albany, and Goddard from Montreal.

Gorrell in his journal alludes to the Minnesota Sioux. He writes—

"On March I. 1763, twelve warriors of the Sous came here. It is certainly the greatest nation of Indians ever yet found. Not above two thousand of them were ever armed with firearms; the rest depending entirely on bows and arrows, which they use with more skill than any other Indian nation in America. They can shoot the wildest and largest beasts in the woods at seventy or one hundred yards distant. They are remarkable for their dancing, and the other nations take the fashions from them. * * * * * This nation is always at war with the Chippewas, those who destroyed Mishamakinak. They told me with warmth that if ever the Chippewas or any other Indians wished to obstruct the passage of the traders coming up, to send them word, and they would come and cut them off from the face of the earth; as all Indians were their slaves or dogs. I told them I was glad to see them, and hoped to have a lasting peace with them. They then gave me a letter wrote in French, and two belts of wampum from their king, in which he expressed great joy on hearing of there being English at his post. The letter was written by a French trader whom I had allowed to go among them last fall, with a promise of his behaving well: which he did, better than any Canadian I ever knew. * * * * * With regard to traders, I would not allow any to go amongst them, as I then understood they lay out of the government of Canada, but made no doubt they would have traders from the Mississippi in the spring. They went away extremely well pleased. June 14th, 1763, the traders came down from the Sack country, and confirmed the news of Landsing and his son being killed by the French. There came with the traders some Puans, and four young men with one chief of the Avoy [Ioway] nation, to demand traders. * * * * *

"On the nineteenth, a deputation of Winnebagoes, Sacs, Foxes and Menominees arrived with a Frenchman named Pennensha. This Pennensha is the same man who wrote the letter the Sous brought with them in French, and at the same time held council with that great nation in favour of the English, by which he much promoted the interest of the latter, as appeared by the behaviour of the Sous. He brought with him a pipe from the Sous, desiring that as the road is now clear, they would by no means allow the Chippewas to obstruct it, or give the English any disturbance, or prevent the traders from coming up to them. If they did so they would send all their warriors and cut them off."

In July, 1763, there arrived at Green Bay, Bruce, Fisher; and Roseboom of Albany, to engage in the Indian trade.

By the treaty of Paris of 1763, France ceded to Great Britain all of the country east of the Mississippi, and to Spain the whole of Louisiana, so that the latter power for a time held the whole region between the Mississippi River and the Pacific Ocean, and that portion of the city of Minneapolis known as the East Division was then governed by the British, while the West Division was subject to the Spanish code.

CHAPTER XI.

JONATHAN CARVER, THE FIRST BRITISH TRAVELER AT FALLS OF SAINT ANTHONY.

Carver's Early Life.—In the Battle near Lake George.—Arrives at Mackinaw.—Old Fort at Green Bay.—Winnebago Village.—Description of Prairie du Chien.—Earthworks on Banks of Lake Pepin.—Sioux Bands Described.—Cave and Burial Place in Suburbs of St. Paul.—The Falls of Saint Anthony.—Burial Rites of the Sioux.—Speech of a Sioux Chief.—Schiller's Poem of the Death Song.—Sir John Herschel's Translation.—Sir E. Bulwer Lytton's Version.—Correspondence of Sir William Johnson.—Carver's Project for Opening a Route to the Pacific.—Supposed Origin of the Sioux.—Carver's Claim to Lands Examined.—Alleged Deed.—Testimony of Rev. Samuel Peters.—Communication from Gen. Leavenworth.—Report of U. S. Senate Committee.

Jonathan Carver was a native of Connecticut. His grandfather, William Carver, was a native of Wigan, Lancashire, England, and a captain in King William's army during the campaign in Ireland, and for meritorious services received an appointment as an officer of the colony of Connecticut.

His father was a justice of the peace in the new world, and in 1732, the subject of this sketch was born. At the early age of fifteen he was called to mourn the death of his father. He then commenced the study of medicine, but his roving disposition could not bear the confines of a doctor's office, and feeling, perhaps, that his genius would be cramped by pestle and mortar, at the age of eighteen he purchased an ensign's commission in one of the regiments raised during the French war. He was of medium stature, and of strong mind and quick perceptions.

In the year 1757, he was captain under Colonel Williams in the battle near Lake George, where Saint Pierre was killed, and narrowly escaped with his life.

After the peace of 1763, between France and England was declared, Carver conceived the project of exploring the Northwest. Leaving Boston in the month of June, 1766, he arrived at Mackinaw, then the most distant British post, in the month of August. Having obtained a credit on some French and English traders from Major Rogers, the officer in command, he started with them on the third day of September. Pursuing the usual route to Green Bay, they arrived there on the eighteenth.

The French fort at that time was standing, though much decayed. It was, some years previous to his arrival, garrisoned for a short time by an officer and thirty English soldiers, but they having been captured by the Menominees, it was abandoned.

In company with the traders, he left Green Bay on the twentieth, and ascending Fox river, arrived on the twenty-fifth at an island at the east end of Lake Winnebago, containing about fifty acres.

Here he found a Winnebago village of fifty houses. He asserts that a woman was in authority. In the month of October the party was at the portage of the Wisconsin, and descending that stream, they arrived, on the ninth at a town of the Sauks. While here he visited some lead mines about fifteen miles distant. An abundance of lead was also seen in the village, that had been brought from the mines.

On the tenth they arrived at the first village of the "Ottigaumies" [Foxes] about five miles before the Wisconsin joins the Mississippi, he perceived the remnants of another village, and learned that it had been deserted about thirty years before, and that the inhabitants soon after their removal, built a town on the Mississippi, near the mouth of the "Ouisconsin," at a place called by the French La Prairie les Chiens, which signified the Dog Plains. It was a large town, and contained about three hundred families. The houses were built after the Indian manner, and pleasantly situated on a dry rich soil.

He saw here many houses of a good size and shape. This town was the great mart where all the adjacent tribes, and where those who inhabit the most remote branches of the Mississippi, annually assemble about the latter end of May, bringing with them their furs to dispose of to the traders. But it is not always that they conclude their sale here. This was determined by a gen eral council of the chiefs, who consulted whether it would be more conducive to their interest to sell their goods at this place, or to carry them on to Louisiana or Mackinaw.

At a small stream called Yellow River, opposite Prairie du Chien, the traders who had thus far accompanied Carver took up their residence for the winter.

From this point he proceeded in a canoe, with a Canadian voyageur and a Mohawk Indian as companions. Just before reaching Lake Pepin, while his attendants were one day preparing dinner, he walked out and was struck with the peculiar appearance of the surface of the country, and thought it was the site of some vast artificial earth-work. It is a fact worthy of remembrance, that he was the first to call the attention of the civilized world to the existence of ancient monuments in the Mississippi valley. We give his own description :

"On the first of November I reached Lake Pepin, a few miles below which I landed, and, whilst the servants were preparing my dinner, I ascended the bank to view the country. I had not proceeded far before I came to a fine, level, open plain, on which I perceived, at a little distance, a partial elevation that had the appearance of entrenchment. On a nearer inspection I had greater reason to suppose that it had really been intended for this many centuries ago. Notwithstanding it was now covered with grass, I could plainly see that it had once been a breastwork of about four feet in height, extending the best part of a mile, and sufficiently capacious to cover five thousand men. Its form was somewhat circular and its flanks reached to the river.

"Though much defaced by time, every angle was distinguishable, and appeared as regular and fashioned with as much military skill as if planned by Vauban himself. The ditch was not visible, but I thought, on examining more curiously, that I could perceive there certainly had been one. From its situation, also, I am convinced that it must have been designed for that purpose. It fronted the country, and the rear was covered by the river, nor was there any rising ground for a considerable way that commanded it; a few straggling lakes were alone to be seen near it. In many places small tracks were worn across it by the feet of the elks or deer, and from the depth of the bed of earth by which it was covered, I was able to draw certain conclusions of its great antiquity. I examined all the angles, and every part with great attention, and have often blamed myself since, for not encamping on the spot, and drawing an exact plan of it. To show that this description is not the offspring of a heated imagination, or the chimerical tale of a mistaken traveler, I find, on inquiry since my return, that Mons. St. Pierre, and several traders have at different times, taken notice of similar appearances, upon which they have formed the same conjectures, but without examining them so minutely as I did. How a work of this kind could exist in a country that has hitherto (according to the generally received opinion) been the seat of war to untutored Indians alone, whose whole stock of military knowledge has only, till within two centuries, amounted to drawing the bow, and whose only breastwork even at present is the thicket, I know not. I have given as exact an account as possible of this singular appearance, and leave to future explorers of those distant regions, to discover whether it is a production of nature or art. Perhaps the hints I have here given might lead to a more perfect investigation of it, and give us very different ideas of the ancient state of realms that we at present believe to have been, from the earliest period, only the habitations of savages."

Lake Pepin excited his admiration, as it has that of every traveler since his day, and here he remarks: "I observed the ruins of a French factory, where it is said Captain St. Pierre resided, and carried on a very great trade with the Naudowessies, before the reduction of Canada."

Carver's first acquaintance with the Dahkotahs commenced near the river St. Croix. It would seem that the erection of trading posts on Lake Pepin had enticed them from their old residence on Rum river and Mille Lacs.

He says: "Near the river St. Croix reside bands of the Naudowessie Indians, called the River Bands. This nation is composed at present of eleven bands. They were originally twelve, but the Assinipoils, some years ago, revolting and separating themselves from the others, there remain at this time eleven. Those I met here are termed the River Bands, because they chiefly dwell near the banks of this river; the other eight are generally distinguished by the title of Nadowessies of the Plains, and inhabit a country more to the westward. The names of the former are Nehogatawonahs, the Mawtawbauntowahs, and Shashweentowahs.

Arriving at what is now a suburb of the capital of Minnesota, he continues: "About thirteen miles below the Falls of St. Anthony, at which I arrived the tenth day after I left Lake Pepin, is a remarkable cave, of an amazing depth. The Indians term it Wakon-teebe [Wakan-tipi]. The entrance into it is about ten feet wide, the height of it five feet. The arch within is fifteen feet high and about thirty feet broad; the bottom consists of fine, clear sand. About thirty feet from the entrance begins a lake, the water of which is transparent, and extends to an unsearchable distance, for the darkness of the cave prevents all attempts to acquire a knowledge of it.] I threw a small pebble towards the nterior part of it with my utmost strength. I could hear that it fell into the water, and, notwithstanding it was of a small size, it caused an astonishing and terrible noise, that reverberated through all those gloomy regions. I found in this cave many Indian hieroglyphics, which appeared very ancient, for time had nearly covered them with moss, so that it was with difficulty I could trace them. They were cut in a rude manner upon the inside of the wall, which was composed of a stone so extremely soft that it might be easily penetrated with a knife; a stone everywhere to be found near the Mississippi.

"At a little distance from this dreary cavern, is the burying-place of several bands of the Naudowessie Indians. Though these people have no fixed residence, being in tents, and seldom but a few months in one spot, yet they always bring the bones of the dead to this place.

"Ten miles below the Falls of St. Anthony, the river St. Pierre, called by the natives Wadapaw Menesotor, falls into the Mississippi from the west. It is not mentioned by Father Hennepin, though a large, fair river. This omission, I consider, must have proceeded from a small island [Pike's] that is situated exactly in its entrance."

When he reached the Minnesota river, the ice became so troublesome that he left his canoe in the neighborhood of what is now St. Anthony, and walked to St. Anthony, in company with a young Winnebago chief, who had never seen the curling waters. The chief, on reaching the eminence some distance below Cheever's, began to invoke his gods, and offer oblations to the spirit in the waters.

"In the middle of the Falls stands a small island, about *forty feet* broad and somewhat longer, on which grow a few cragged hemlock and spruce trees, and about half way between this island and the eastern shore is a rock, lying at the very edge of the Falls, in an oblique position that appeared to be about five or six feet broad, and thirty or forty long. At a little distance below the Falls stands a small island of about an acre and a half, on which grow a great number of oak trees."

From this description, it would appear that the little island, now some distance below the Falls, was once in the very midst, and shows that a constant recession has been going on, and that in ages long past they were not far from the Minnesota river.

No description is more glowing than Carver's of the country adjacent:

"The country around them is extremely beautiful. It is not an uninterrupted plain, where the eye finds no relief, but composed of many gentle ascents, which in the summer are covered with the finest verdure, and interspersed with little groves that give a pleasing variety to the prospect. On the whole, when the Falls are included, which may be seen at a distance of four miles, a more pleasing and picturesque view, I believe, cannot be found throughout the universe."

"He arrived at the Falls on the seventeenth of November, 1766, and appears to have ascended as far as Elk river.

On the twenty-fifth of November, he had returned to the place opposite the Minnesota, where he had left his canoe, and this stream as yet not being obstructed with ice, he commenced its ascent, with the colors of Great Britain flying at the stern of his canoe. There is no doubt that he entered this river, but how far he explored it cannot be ascertained. He speaks of the Rapids near Shakopay, and asserts that he went as far as two hundred miles beyond Mendota. He remarks:

"On the seventh of December, I arrived at the utmost of my travels towards the West, where I met a large party of the Naudowessie Indians, among whom I resided some months."

After speaking of the upper bands of the Dahkotahs and their allies, he adds that he "left the habitations of the hospitable Indians the latter end of April, 1767, but did not part from them for several days, as I was accompanied on my journey by near three hundred of them to the mouth of the river St. Pierre. At this season these bands annually go to the great cave (Dayton's Bluff) before mentioned.

When he arrived at the great cave, and the Indians had deposited the remains of their deceased friends in the burial-place that stands adjacent to it, they held their great council to which he was admitted.

When the Naudowessies brought their dead for interment to the great cave (St. Paul), I attempted to get an insight into the remaining burial rites, but whether it was on account of the stench which arose from so many dead bodies, or whether they chose to keep this part of their custom secret from me, I could not discover. I found, however, that they considered my curiosity as ill-timed, and therefore I withdrew. * *

One formality among the Naudowessies in mourning for the dead is very different from any mode I observed in the other nations through which I passed. The men, to show how great their sorrow is, pierce the flesh of their arms above the elbows with arrows, and the women cut and gash their legs with broken flints till the blood flows very plentifully. * *

After the breath is departed, the body is dressed in the same attire it usually wore, his face is painted, and he is seated in an erect posture on a mat or skin, placed in the middle of the hut, with his weapons by his side. His relatives seated around, each in turn harangues the deceased; and if he has been a great warrior, recounts his heroic actions, nearly to the following purport, which in the Indian language is extremely poetical and pleasing

"You still sit among us, brother, your person retains its usual resemblance, and continues similar to ours, without any visible deficiency, except it has lost the power of action! But whither is that breath flown, which a few hours ago sent up smoke to the Great Spirit? Why are those lips silent, that lately delivered to us expressions and pleasing language? Why are those feet motionless, that a few hours ago were fleeter than the deer on yonder mountains? Why useless hang those arms, that could climb the tallest tree or draw the toughest bow? Alas, every part of that frame which we lately beheld with admiration and wonder has now become as inanimate as it was three hundred years ago! We will not, however, bemoan thee as if thou wast forever lost to us, or that thy name would be buried in oblivion; thy soul yet lives in the great country of spirits, with those of thy nation that have gone before thee; and though we are left behind to perpetuate thy fame, we will one day join thee.

"Actuated by the respect we bore thee whilst living, we now come to tender thee the last act of kindness in our power; that thy body might not lie neglected on the plain, and become a prey to the beasts of the field or fowls of the air, and we will take care to lay it with those of thy predecessors that have gone before thee; hoping at the same time that thy spirit will feed with their spirits, and be ready to receive ours when we shall also arrive at the great country of souls."

For this speech Carver is principally indebted to his imagination, but it is well conceived, and suggested one of Schiller's poems, which Gœthe considered one of his best, and wished "he had made a dozen such."

Sir E. Lytton Bulwer the distinguished novelist, and Sir John Herschel the eminent astronomer, have each given a translation of Schiller's "Song of the Nadowessee Chief."

SIR E. L. BULWER'S TRANSLATION.

See on his mat—as if of yore,
  All life-like sits he here!
With that same aspect which he wore
  When light to him was dear

But where the right hand's strength? and where
  The breath that loved to breathe
To the Great Spirit, aloft in air,
  The peace pipe's lusty wreath?

And where the hawk-like eye, alas!
  That wont the deer pursue,
Along the waves of rippling grass,
  Or fields that shone with dew?

Are these the limber, bounding feet
That swept the winter's snows?
What stateliest stag so fast and fleet?
Their speed outstripped the roe's!

These arms, that then the steady bow
Could supple from it's pride,
How stark and helpless hang they now
Adown the stiffened side!

Yet weal to him—at peace he stays
Wherever fall the snows;
Where o'er the meadows springs the maize
That mortal never sows.

Where birds are blithe on every brake—
Where orests teem with deer—
Where glide the fish through every lake—
One chase from year to year!

With spirits now he feasts above;
All left us to revere
The deeds we honor with our love,
The dust we bury here.

Here bring the last gift; loud and shrill
Wail death dirge for the brave;
What pleased him most in life, may still
Give pleasure in the grave.

We lay the axe beneath his head
He swung when strength was strong—
The bear on which his banquets fed,
The way from earth is long.

And here, new sharpened, place the knife
That severed from the clay,
From which the axe had spoiled the life,
The conquered scalp away.

The paints that deck the dead, bestow;
Yes, place them in his hand,
That red the kingly shade may glow
Amid the spirit land.

SIR JOHN HERSCHEL'S TRANSLATION.

See, where upon the mat he sits
Erect, before his door,
With just the same majestic air
That once in life he wore.

But where is fled his strength of limb,
The whirlwind of his breath,
To the Great Spirit, when he sent
The peace pipe's mounting wreath?

Where are those falcon eyes, which late
Along the plain could trace,
Along the grass's dewy waves
The reindeer's printed pace?

Those legs, which once with matchless speed,
Flew through the drifted snow,
Surpassed the stag's unwearied course,
Outran the mountain roe?

Those arms, once used with might and main,
The stubborn bow to twang?
See, see, their nerves are slack at last,
All motionless they hang.

'Tis well with him, for he is gone
Where snow no more is found,
Where the gay thorn's perpetual bloom
Decks all the field around.

Where wild birds sing from every spray,
Where deer come sweeping by,
Where fish from every lake afford
A plentiful supply.

With spirits now he feasts above,
And leaves us here alone,
To celebrate his valiant deeds,
And round his grave to moan.

Sound the death song, bring forth the gifts,
The last gifts of the dead,—
Let all which yet may yield him joy
Within his grave be laid.

The hatchet place beneath his head
Still red with hostile blood;
And add, because the way is long,
The bear's fat limbs for food.

The scalping-knife beside him lay,
With paints of gorgeous dye,
That in the land of souls his form
May shine triumphantly.

It appears from other sources that Carvér's visit to the Dahkotahs was of some effect in bringing about friendly intercourse between them and the commander of the English force at Mackinaw.

The earliest mention of the Dahkotahs, in any public British documents that we know of, is in the correspondence between Sir William Johnson, Superintendent of Indian Affairs for the Colony of New York, and General Gage, in command of the forces.

On the eleventh of September, less than six months after Carver's speech at Dayton's Bluff, and the departure of a number of chiefs to the English fort at Mackinaw, Johnson writes to General Gage: "Though I wrote to you some days ago, yet I would not mind saying something again on the score of the vast expenses incurred, and, as I understand, still incurring at Michilimackinac, chiefly on pretense of making a peace between the Sioux and Chippeweighs, with which I think we have very little to do, in good policy or otherwise."

Sir William Johnson, in a letter to Lord Hillsborough, one of his Majesty's ministers, dated August seventeenth, 1768, again refers to the subject:

"Much greater part of those who go a trading are men of such circumstances and disposition as to venture their persons everywhere for extravagant gains, yet the consequences to the public are not to be slighted, as we may be led into a general quarrel through their means. The Indians in the part adjacent to Michillmackinac have been treated with at a very great expense for some time previous.

"Major Rodgers brings a considerable charge against the former for mediating a peace between some tribes of the Sioux and some of the Chippeweighs, which, had it been attended with success, would only have been interesting to a very few French, and others that had goods in that part of the Indian country, but the contrary has happened, and they are now more violent, and war against one another."

Though a wilderness of over one thousand miles intervened between the Falls of St. Anthony and the white settlements of the English, Carver was fully impressed with the idea that the State now organized under the name of Minnesota, on account of its beauty and fertility, would attract settlers.

Speaking of the advantages of the country, he says that the future population will be "able to convey their produce to the seaports with great facility, the current of the river from its source to its entrance into the Gulf of Mexico being extremely favorable for doing this in small craft. *This might also in time be facilitated by canals or shorter cuts, and a communication opened by water with New York by way of the Lakes.*"

The subject of this sketch was also confident that a route would be discovered by way of the Minnesota river, which would open a passage to China and the English settlements in the East Indies."

Carver having returned to England, interested Whitworth, a member of parliament, in the northern route. Had not the American Revolution commenced, they proposed to have built a fort at Lake Pepin, to have proceeded up the Minnesota until they found, as they supposed they could, a branch of the Missouri, and from thence, journeying over the summit of lands until they came to a river which they called Oregon, they expected to descend to the Pacific.

Carver, in common with other travelers, had his theory in relation to the origin of the Dahkotahs. He supposed that they came from Asia. He remarks: "But this might have been at different times and from various parts—from Tartary, China, Japan, for the inhabitants of these places resemble each other. * * *

"It is very evident that some of the names and customs of the American Indians resemble those of the Tartars, and I make no doubt but that in some future era, and this not far distant, it will be reduced to certainty that during some of the wars between the Tartars and Chinese a part of the inhabitants of the northern provinces were driven from their native country, and took refuge in some of the isles before mentioned, and from thence found their way into America. * * *

"Many words are used both by the Chinese and the Indians which have a resemblance to each other, not only in their sound, but in their signification. The Chinese call a slave Shungo; and the Noudowessie Indians, whose language, from their little intercourse with the Europeans, is least corrupted, term a dog Shungush [Shoankah.] The former denominate one species of their tea Shoushong; the latter call their tobacco Shousas-sau [Chanshasha.] Many other of the words used by the Indians contain the syllables *che*, *chaw*, and *chu*, after the dialect of the Chinese."

The comparison of languages has become a rich source of historical knowledge, yet many of the analogies traced are fanciful. The remark of Humbolt in "Cosmos" is worthy of remembrance. "As the structure of American idioms appears remarkably strange to nations speaking the modern languages of Western Europe, and who readily suffer themselves to be led away by some accidental analogies of sound, theologians have generally believed that they could trace an affinity with the Hebrew, Spanish colonists with the Basque and the English, or French settlers with Gaelic, Erse, or the Bas Breton. I one day met on the coast of Peru, a Spanish naval officer and an English whaling captain, the former of whom declared that he had heard Basque spoken at Tahiti; the other, Gaelic or Erse at the Sandwich Islands."

Carver became very poor while in England, and was a clerk in a lottery-office. He died in 1780, and left a widow, two sons, and five daughters, in New England, and also a child by another wife that he had married in Great Britain

After his death a claim was urged for the land upon which the capital of Minnesota now stands and for many miles adjacent. As there are still many persons who believe that they have some right through certain deeds purporting to be from the heirs of Carver, it is a matter worthy of an investigation.

Carver says nothing in his book of travels in relation to a grant from the Dahkotahs, but after he was buried, it was asserted that there was a deed belonging to him in existence, conveying valuable lands, and that said deed was executed at the cave now in the eastern suburbs of Saint Paul.

DEED PURPORTING TO HAVE BEEN GIVEN AT THE CAVE IN THE BLUFF BELOW ST. PAUL.

"To Jonathan Carver, a chief under the most mighty and potent George the Third, King of the English and other nations, the fame of whose warriors has reached our ears, and has now been fully told us by our *good brother Jonathan*, aforesaid, whom we rejoice to have come among us, and bring us good news from his country.

"We, chiefs of the Naudowessies, who have hereunto set our seals, do by these presents, for ourselves and heirs forever, in return for the aid and other good services done by the said Jonathan to ourselves and allies, give grant and convey to him, the said Jonathan, and to his heirs and assigns forever, the whole of a certain tract or territory of land, bounded as follows, viz: from the Falls of St. Anthony, running on the east bank of the Mississippi, nearly southeast, as far as Lake Pepin, where the Chippewa joins the Mississippi, and from thence eastward five days travel, accounting twenty English miles per day; and from thence again to the Falls of St. Anthony, on a direct straight line. We do for ourselves, heirs, and assigns, forever give unto the said Jonathan, his heirs and assigns, with all the trees, rocks, and rivers therein, reserving the sole liberty of hunting and fishing on land not planted or improved by the said Jonathan, his heirs and assigns, to which we have affixed our respective seals.

"At the Great Cave, May 1st, 1767.

"Signed, HAWNOPAWJATIN.
OTOHTONGOOMLISHEAW."

The original deed was never exhibited by the assignees of the heirs. By his English wife Carver had one child, a daughter Martha, who was cared for by Sir Richard and Lady Pearson. In time she eloped and married a sailor. A mercantile firm in London, thinking that money could be made, induced the newly married couple, the day after the wedding, to convey th grant to them, with the understanding that they were to have a tenth of the profits.

The merchants despatched an agent by the name of Clarke to go to the Dahkotahs, and obtain a new deed; but on his way he was murdered in the state of New York.

In the year 1794, the heirs of Carver's American wife, in consideration of fifty thousand pounds sterling, conveyed their interest in the Carver grant to Edward Houghton of Vermont. In the year 1806, Samuel Peters, who had been a tory and an Episcopal minister during the Revolutionary war, alleges, in a petition to Congress, that he had also purchased of the heirs of Carver their rights to the grant.

Before the Senate committee, the same year, he testified as follows:

"In the year 1774, I arrived there (London), and met Captain Carver. In 1775, Carver had a hearing before the king, praying his majesty's approval of a deed of land dated May first, 1767, and sold and granted to him by the Naudowissies. The result was his majesty approved of the exertions and bravery of Captain Carver among the Indian nations, near the Falls of St. Anthony, in the Mississippi, gave to said Carver 1371*l*. 13*s*. 8*d*. sterling, and ordered a frigate to be prepared, and a transport ship to carry one hundred and fifty men, under command of Captain Carver, with four others as a committee, to sail the next June to New Orleans, and then to ascend the Mississippi, to take possession of said territory conveyed to Captain Carver; but the battle of Bunker Hill prevented."

In 1821, General Leavenworth, having made inquiries of the Dahkotahs, in relation to the alleged claim, addressed the following to the commissioner of the land office:

"Sir:—Agreeably to your request, I have the honour to inform you what I have understood from the Indians of the Sioux Nation, as well as some facts within my own knowledge, as to what is commonly termed Carver's Grant. The grant purports to be made by the chiefs of the Sioux of the Plains, and one of the chiefs uses the sign of a serpent, and the other of a turtle, purporting that their names are derived from those animals.

"The land lies on the east side of the Mississippi. The Indians do not recognize or acknowledge the grant to be valid, and they among others assign the following reasons:

"1. The Sioux of the Plains never owned a foot of land on the east side of the Mississippi. The Sioux Nation is divided into two grand divisions, viz: The Sioux of the Lake; or perhaps more literally Sioux of the River, and Sioux of the Plain. The former subsists by hunting and fishing, and usually move from place to place by water, in canoes, during the summer season, and travel on the ice in the winter, when not on their hunting excursions. The latter subsist entirely by hunting, and have no canoes, nor do they know but little about the use of them. They reside in the large prairies west of the Mississippi, and follow the buffalo, upon which they entirely subsist; these are called Sioux of the Plain, and never owned land east of the Mississippi.

"2. The Indians say they have no knowledge of any such chiefs as those who have signed the grant to Carver, either amongst the Sioux of the River or the Sioux of the Plain. They say that if Captain Carver did ever obtain a deed or grant, it was signed by some foolish young men who were not chiefs and who were not authorized to make a grant. Among the Sioux of the River there are no such names.

"3. They say the Indians never received anything for the land, and they have no intention to part with it without a consideration. From my knowledge of the Indians, I am induced to think they would not make so considerable a grant, and have it to go into full effect without receiving a substantial consideration.

"4. They have, and ever have had, the possession of the land, and intend to keep it. I know that they are very particular in making every person who wishes to cut timber on that tract obtain their permission to do so, and to obtain payment for it. In the month of May last, some Frenchmen brought a large raft of red cedar timber out of the Chippewa River, which timber was cut on the tract before mentioned. The Indians at one of the villages on the Mississippi, where the principal chief resided, compelled the Frenchmen to land the raft, and would not permit them to pass until they had received pay for the timber, and the Frenchmen were compelled to leave their raft with the Indians until they went to Prairie du Chien, and obtained the necessary articles, and made the payment required."

On the twenty-third of January, 1823, the Committee of Public Lands made a report on the claim to the Senate, which, to every disinterested person, is entirely satisfactory. After stating the facts of the petition, the report continues:

"The Rev. Samuel Peters, in his petition, further states that Lefei, the present Emperor of the Sioux and Naudowessies, and Red Wing, a sachem, the heirs and successors of the two grand chiefs who signed the said deed to Captain Carver, have given satisfactory and positive proof that they allowed their ancestors' deed to be genuine, good, and valid, and that Captain Carver's heirs and assigns are the owners of said territory, and may occupy it free of all molestation.

The committee have examined and considered the claims thus exhibited by the petitioners, and remark that the original deed is not produced, nor any competent legal evidence offered of its execution; nor is there any proof that the persons, who it is alleged made the deed, were the chiefs of said tribe, nor that (if chiefs) they had authority to grant and give away the land belonging to their tribe. The paper annexed to the petition, as a copy of said deed, has no subscribing witnesses; and it would seem impossible, at this remote period, to ascertain the important fact, that the persons who signed the deed comprehended and understood the meaning and effect of their act.

"The want of proof as to these facts, would interpose in the way of the claimants insuperable difficulties. But, in the opinion of the committee, the claim is not such as the United States are under any obligation to allow, even if the deed were proved in legal form.

"The British government, before the time when the alleged deed bears date, had deemed it prudent and necessary for the preservation of peace with the Indian tribes under their sovereignty, protection and dominion, to prevent British subjects from purchasing lands from the Indians, and this rule of policy was made known and enforced by the proclamation of the king of Great Britain, of seventh October, 1763, which contains an express prohibition.

"Captain Carver, aware of the law, and knowing that such a contract could not vest the legal title in him, applied to the British government to ratify and confirm the Indian grant, and, though it was competent for that government then to confirm the grant, and vest the title of said land in him, yet, from some cause, that government did not think proper to do it.

"The territory has since become the property of the United States, and an Indian grant not good against the British government, would appear to be not binding upon the United States government.

"What benefit the British government derived from the services of Captain Carver, by his travels and residence among the Indians, that government alone could determine, and alone could judge what remuneration those services deserved.

"One fact appears from the declaration of Mr. Peters, in his statement in writing, among the papers exhibited, namely, that the British government did give Captain Carver the sum of one thousand three hundred and seventy-five pounds six shillings and eight pence sterling. To the United States, however, Captain Carver rendered no services which could be assumed as any equitable ground for the support of the petitioners' claim.

"The committee being of opinion that the United States are not bound in law and equity to confirm the said alleged Indian grant, recommend the adoption of the resolution:

"'*Resolved*, That the prayer of the petitioners ought not to be granted."'

Lord Palmerston stated in 1839, that no trace could be found in the records of the British office of state papers, showing any ratification of the Carver grant.

CHAPTER XII.

EXPLORATION BY THE FIRST UNITED STATES ARMY OFFICER, LIEUTENANT Z. M. PIKE.

Trading Posts at the beginning of Nineteenth Century.—Sandy Lake Fort.—Leech Lake Fort.—William Morrison, before Schoolcraft at Itasca Lake.—Division of Northwest Territory.—Organization of Indiana, Michigan and Upper Louisiana.—Notices of Wood, Frazer, Fisher, Cameron, Faribault.—Early Traders.—Pike's Council at Mouth of Minnesota River.—Grant for Military Posts.—Encampment at Falls of St. Anthony.—Block House near Swan River.—Visit to Sandy and Leech Lakes.—British Flag Shot at and Lowered.—Thompson, Topographer of Northwest Company.—Pike at Dickson's Trading Post.—Returns to Mendota. Fails to find Carver's Cave.—Conference with Little Crow.—Cameron sells Liquor to Indians.

At the beginning of the present century, the region now known as Minnesota, contained no white men, except a few engaged in the fur trade. In the treaty effected by Hon. John Jay, Great Britain agreed to withdraw her troops from all posts and places within certain boundary lines, on or before the first of June, 1796, but all British settlers and traders might remain for one year, and enjoy all their former privileges, without being obliged to be citizens of the United States of America.

In the year 1800, the trading posts of Minnesota were chiefly held by the Northwest Company, and their chief traders resided at Sandy Lake, Leech Lake, and Fon du Lac, on St. Louis River. In the year 1794, this company built a stockade one hundred feet square, on the southeast end of Sandy Lake. There were bastions pierced for small arms, in the southeast and in the northwest corner. The pickets which surrounded the post were thirteen feet high. On the north side there was a gate ten by nine feet; on the west side, one six by five feet, and on the east side a third gate six by five feet. Travelers entering the main gate, saw on the left a one story building twenty feet square, the residence of the superintendent, and on the left of the east gate, a building twenty-five by fifteen, the quarters of the voyageurs. Entering the western gate, on the left was a stone house, twenty by thirty feet, and a house twenty by forty feet, used as a store, and a workshop, and a residence for clerks. On the south shore of Leech Lake there was another establishment, a little larger. The stockade was one hundred and fifty feet square. The main building was sixty by twenty-five feet, and one and a half story in height, where resided the Director of the fur trade of the Fond du Lac department of the Northwest Company. In the centre was a small store, twelve and a half feet square, and near the main gate was flagstaff fifty feet in height, from which used to float the flag of Great Britain.

William Morrison was, in 1802, the trader at Leech Lake, and in 1804 he was at Elk Lake, the source of the Mississippi, thirty-two years afterwards named by Schoolcraft, Lake Itasca.

The entire force of the Northwest Company, west of Lake Superior, in 1805, consisted of three accountants, nineteen clerks, two interpreters, eighty-five canoe men, and with them were twenty-nine Indian or half-breed women, and about fifty children.

On the seventh of May, 1800, the Northwest Territory, which included all of the western country east of the Mississippi, was divided. The portion not designated as Ohio, was organized as the Territory of Indiana.

On the twentieth of December, 1803, the province of Louisiana, of which that portion of Minnesota west of the Mississippi was a part, was officially delivered up by the French, who had just obtained it from the Spaniards, according to treaty stipulations.

To the transfer of Louisiana by France, after twenty days' possession, Spain at first objected; but in 1804 withdrew all opposition.

President Jefferson now deemed it an object of paramount importance for the United States to explore the country so recently acquired, and make the acquaintance of the tribes residing therein; and steps were taken for an expedition to the upper Mississippi.

Early in March, 1804, Captain Stoddard, of the United States army, arrived at St. Louis, the agent of the French Republic, to receive from the Spanish authorities the possession of the country, which he immediately transferred to the United States.

As the old settlers, on the tenth of March, saw the ancient flag of Spain displaced by that of the United States, the tears coursed down their cheeks.

On the twentieth of the same month, the territory of Upper Louisiana was constituted. comprising the present states of Arkansas, Missouri, Iowa, and a large portion of Minnesota.

On the eleventh of January, 1805, the territory of Michigan was organized.

The first American officer who visited Minnesota, on business of a public nature, was one who was an ornament to his profession, and in energy and endurance a true representative of the citizens of the United States. We refer to the gallant Zebulon Montgomery Pike, a native of New Jersey, who afterwards fell in battle at York, Upper Canada, and whose loss was justly mourned by the whole nation.

When a young lieutenant, he was ordered by General Wilkinson to visit the region now known as Minnesota, and expel the British traders who were found violating the laws of the United States, and form alliances with the Indians. With only a few common soldiers, he was obliged to do the work of several men. At times he would precede his party for miles to reconnoitre, and then he would do the duty of hunter.

During the day he would perform the part of surveyor, geologist, and astronomer, and at night, though hungry and fatigued, his lofty enthusiasm kept him awake until he copied the notes, and plotted the courses of the day.

On the 4th day of September, 1805, Pike arrived at Prairie du Chien, from St. Louis. and was politely treated by three traders, all born under the flag of the United States. One was named Wood, another Frazer, a native of Vermont, who, when a young man became a clerk of one Blakely, of Montreal, and thus became a fur trader. The third was Henry Fisher, a captain of the Militia, and Justice of the Peace, whose wife was a daughter of Goutier de Verville. Fisher was said to have been a nephew of President Monroe, and later in life traded at the sources of the Minnesota. One of his daughters was the mother of Joseph Rolette, Jr., a member of the early Minnesota Legislative assemblies. On the eighth of the month Lieutenant Pike left Prairie du Chien, in two batteaux, with Sergeant Henry Kennerman, Corporals William E. Mack and Samuel Bradley, and ten privates.

At La Crosse, Frazer, of Prairie du Chien, overtook him, and at Sandy point of Lake Pepin he found a trader, a Scotchman by the name of Murdoch Cameron, with his son, and a young man named John Rudsdell. On the twenty-first he breakfasted with the Kaposia band of Sioux, who then dwelt at the marsh below Dayton's Bluff, a few miles below St. Paul. The same day he passed three miles from Mendota the encampment of J. B. Faribault, a trader and native of Lower Canada, then about thirty years of age, in which vicinity he continued for more than fifty years. He married Pelagie the daughter of Francis Kinnie by an Indian woman, and his eldest son, Alexander, born soon after Pike's visit, was the founder of the town of Faribault.

Arriving at the confluence of the Minnosota and the Mississippi Rivers, Pike and his soldiers encamped on the Northeast point of the island which still bears his name. The next day was Sunday, and he visited Cameron, at his trading post on the Minnesota River, a short distance above Mendota.

On Monday, the 23d of September, at noon, he held a Council with the Sioux, under a covering made by suspending sails, and gave an admirable talk, a portion of which was as follows:

"Brothers, I am happy to meet you here, at this council fire which your father has sent me to kindle, and to take you by the hands, as our children. We having but lately acquired from the Spanish, the extensive territory of Louisiana, our general has thought proper to send out a number of his warriors to visit all his red children; to tell them his will, and to hear what request they may have to make of their father. I am happy the choice fell on me to come this road, as I find my brothers, the Sioux, ready to listen to my words.

"Brothers, it is the wish of our government to establish military posts on the Upper Mississippi, at such places as might be thought expedient. I have, therefore, examined the country, and have pitched on the mouth of the river St. Croix, this place, and the Falls of St. Anthony; I therefore wish you to grant to the United States, nine miles square, at St. Croix, and at this place, from a league below the confluence of the St. Peter's and Mississippi, to a league above St. Anthony, extending three leagues on each side of the river: and as we are a people who are accustomed to have all our acts written down, in order to have them handed to our children, I have drawn up a form of an agreement, which we will both sign, in the presence of the traders now present. After we know the terms, we will fill it up, and have it read and interpreted to you.

"Brothers, those posts are intended as a benefit to you. The old chiefs now present must see that their situation improves by a communication with the whites. It is the intention of the United States to establish at those posts factories, in which the Indians may procure all their things at a cheaper and better rate than they do now, or than your traders can afford to sell them to you, as they are single men, who come from far in small boats; but your fathers are many and strong, and will come with a strong arm, in large boats. There will also be chiefs here, who can attend to the wants of their brothers, without their sending or going all the way to St. Louis, and will see the traders that go up your rivers, and know that they are good men. * * *

"Brothers, I now present you with some of your father's tobacco, and some other trifling things, as a memorandum of my good will, and before my departure I will give you some liquor to clear your throats."

The traders, Cameron and Frazer, sat with Pike. His interpreter was Pierre Rosseau. Among the Chiefs present were Le Petit Corbeau (Little Crow), and Way-ago Enagee, and L'Orignal Leve or Rising Moose. It was with difficulty that the chiefs signed the following agreement; not that they objected to the language, but because they thought their word should be taken, without any mark; but Pike overcame their objection, by saying that he wished them to sign it on his account.

"Whereas, at a conference held between the United States of America and the Sioux nation of Indians, Lieutenant Z. M. Pike, of the army of the United States, and the chiefs and warriors of said tribe, have agreed to the following articles, which, when ratified and approved of by the proper authority, shall be binding on both parties:

ART. 1. That the Sioux nation grant unto the United States, for the purpose of establishment of military posts, nine miles square, at the mouth of the St. Croix, also from below the confluence of the Mississippi and St. Peter's, up the Mississippi to include the Falls of St. Anthony, extending nine miles on each side of the river; that the Sioux Nation grants to the United States the full sovereignty and power over said district forever.

ART. 2. That in consideration of the above grants, the United States shall pay [filled up by the Senate with 2,000 dollars].

ART. 3. The United States promise, on their part, to permit the Sioux to pass and repass, hunt, or make other use of the said districts, as they have formerly done, without any other exception than those specified in article first.

In testimony whereof, we, the undersigned, have hereunto set our hands and seals, at the mouth of the river St. Peter's, on the 23d day of September, 1805.

Z. M. PIKE, [L. S.]
1st Lieutenant and agent at the above conference.

his
LE PETIT CORBEAU, ✗ [L. S.]
mark

his
WAY-AGO ENAGEE, ✗ [L. S.]
mark"

The following entries from Pike's Journal, descriptive of the region around the city of Minneapolis, seventy-five years ago, are worthy of preservation:

"SEPT. 26th, *Thursday.*—Embarked at the usual hour, and after much labor in passing through the rapids, arrived at the foot of the Falls about three or four o'clock; unloaded my boat, and had the principal part of her cargo carried over the portage. With the other boat, however, full loaded, they were not able to get over the last shoot, and encamped about six yards below. I pitched my tent and encamped above the shoot. The rapids mentioned in this day's march, might properly be called a continuation of the Falls of St. Anthony, for they are equally entitled to this appellation, with the Falls of the Delaware and

Susquehanna. Killed one deer. Distance nine miles

SEPT. 27th. *Friday.* Brought over the residue of my loading this morning. Two men arrived from Mr. Frazer, on St. Peters, for my dispatches. This business, closing and sealing, appeared like a last adieu to the civilized world. Sent a large packet to the General, and a letter to Mrs. Pike, with a short note to Mr. Frazer. Two young Indians brought my flag across by land, who arrived yesterday, just as we came in sight of the Fall. I made them a present for their punctuality and expedition, and the danger they were exposed to from the journey. Carried our boats out of the river, as far as the bottom of the hill.

SEPT. 28th, *Saturday.*—Brought my barge over, and put her in the river above the Falls. While we were engaged with her three-fourths miles from camp, seven Indians painted black, appeared on the heights. We had left our guns at the camp and were entirely defenceless. It occurred to me that they were the small party of Sioux who were obstinate, and would go to war, when the other part of the bands came in; these they proved to be; they were better armed than any I had ever seen; having guns, bows, arrows, clubs, spears, and some of them even a case of pistols. I was at that time giving my men a dram; and giving the cup of liquor to the first, he drank it off; but I was more cautious with the remainder. I sent my interpreter to camp with them, to wait my coming; wishing to purchase one of their war clubs, it being made of elk horn, and decorated with inlaid work. This and a set of bows and arrows I wished to get as a curiosity. But the liquor I had given him began to operate, he came back for me, but refusing to go till I brought my boat, he returned, and (I suppose being offended) borrowed a canoe and crossed the river. In the afternoon got the other boat near the top of the hill, when the props gave way, and she slid all the way down to the bottom, but fortunately without injuring any person. It raining very hard, we left her. Killed one goose and a racoon.

SEPT. 29th. *Sunday.*—I killed a remarkably large racoon. Got our large boat over the portage, and put her in the river, at the upper landing; this night the men gave sufficient proof of their fatigue, by all throwing themselves down to sleep, preferring rest to supper. This day I had but fifteen men out of twenty-two; the others were sick. This voyage could have been performed with great convenience, if we had taken our departure in June. But the proper time would be to leave the Illinois as soon as the ice would permit, when the river would be of a good height.

SEPT. 30th, *Monday.*—Loaded my boat, moved over and encamped on the Island. The large boats loading likewise, we went over and put on board. In the mean time, I took a survey of the Falls, Portage, etc. If it be possible to pass the Falls in high water, of which I am doubtful, it must be on the East side, about thirty yards from shore; as there are three layers of rocks, one below the other. The pitch off of either, is not more than five feet; but of this I can say more on my return.

On the tenth of October, the expedition reached some large island below Sauk Rapids, where in 1797, Porlier and Joseph Renville had wintered. Six days after this, he reached the Rapids in Morrison county, which still bears his name, and he writes: "When we arose in the morning, found that snow had fallen during the night, the ground was covered and it continued to snow. This, indeed, was but poor encouragement for attacking the Rapids, in which we were certain to wade to our necks. I was determined, however, if possible to make la riviere de Corbeau, [Crow Wing River], the highest point was made by traders in their bark canoes. We embarked, and after four hours work, became so benumbed with cold that our limbs were perfectly useless. We put to shore on the opposite side of the river, about two-thirds of the way up the rapids. Built a large fire; and then discovered that our boats were nearly half full of water; both having sprung large leaks so as to oblige me to keep three hands bailing. My sergeant (Kennerman) one of the stoutest men I ever knew, broke a blood-vessel and vomited nearly two quarts of blood. One of my corporals (Bradley) also evacuated nearly a pint of blood, when he attempted to void his urine. These unhappy circumstances, in addition to the inability of four other men whom we were obliged to leave on shore, convinced me, that if I had no regard for my own health and constitution, I should have some for those poor fellows, who were killing themselves to obey my orders. After we had breakfast and refreshed ourselves, we went down to our boats on the rocks, where I was obliged to leave them. I then informed my men that we would return to the camp and there leave some of the party and our large boats. This information was pleasing, and the attempt to reach the camp soon accomplished. My reasons for this step have partly been already stated. The necessity of unloading and refitting my boats, the beauty and convenience of the spot for building huts, the fine pine trees for peroques, and the quantity of game, were additional inducements. We immediately unloaded our boats and secured their cargoes. In the evening I went out upon a small, but beautiful creek, which emptied into the Falls, for the purpose of selecting pine trees to make canoes. Saw five deer, and killed one buck weighing one hundred and thirty-seven pounds. By my leaving men at this place, and from the great quantities of game in its vicinity, I was ensured plenty of provision for my return voyage. In the party left behind was one hunter, to be continually employed, who would keep our stock of salt provisions good. Distance two hundred and thirty-three and a half miles above the Falls of St. Anthony.

Having left his large boats and some soldiers at this point, he proceeded to the vicinity of Swan River where be erected a block house, and on the thirty-first of October he writes: "Enclosed my little work completely with pickets. Hauled up my two boats and turned them over on each side of the gateways; by which means a defence was made to the river, and had it not been for various political reasons, I would have laughed at the attack of eight hundred or a thousand savages, if all my party were within. For, except accidents, it would only have afforded amusement, the Indians having no idea of taking a place by storm. Found myself powerfully attacked with the fantastics of the brain, called ennui, at the mention of which I had hitherto scoffed; but my books being packed up, I was like a person entranced, and could easily conceive why so many persons who have been confined to remote places, acquire the habit of drinking to excess, and many other vicious practices, which have been adopted merely to pass time.

During the next month he hunted the buffalo which were then in that vicinity. On the third of December he received a visit from Robert Dickson, afterwards noted in the history of the country, who was then trading about sixty miles below, on the Mississippi.

On the tenth of December with some sleds he continued his journey northward, and on the last day of the year passed Pine River. On the third of January, 1806, he reached the trading post at Red Cedar, now Cass Lake, and was quite indignant at finding the British flag floating from the staff. The night after this his tent caught on fire, and he lost some valuable and necessary clothing. On the evening of the eighth he reached Sandy Lake and was hospitably received by Grant, the trader in charge. He writes.

"JAN. 9th, *Thursday.*—Marched the corporal early, in order that our men should receive assurance of our safety and success. He carried with him a small keg of spirits, a present from Mr. Grant. The establishment of this place was formed twelve years since, by the North-west Company, and was formerly under the charge of a Mr. Charles Brusky. It has attained at present such regularity, as to permit the superintendent to live tolerably comfortable. They have horses they procured from Red River, of the Indians; raise plenty of Irish potatoes, catch pike, suckers, pickerel, and white fish in abundance. They have also beaver, deer, and moose; but the provision they chiefly depend upon is wild oats, of which they purchase great quantities from the savages, giving at the rate of about one dollar and a half per bushel. But flour, pork, and salt, are almost interdicted to persons not principals in the trade. Flour sells at half a dollar; salt a dollar; pork eighty cents; sugar half a dollar; and tea four dollars and fifty cents per pound. The sugar is obtained from the Indians, and is made from the maple tree."

He remained at Sandy Lake ten days, and on the last day two men of the Northwest Company arrived with letters from Fon du Lac Superior, one of which was from Athapuscow, and had been since May on the route.

On the twentieth of January began his journey to Leech Lake, which he reached on the first of February, and was hospitably received by Hugh

McGillis, the head of the Northwest Company at this post.

A Mr. Anderson, in the employ of Robert Dickson, was residing at the west end of the lake. While here he hoisted the American flag in the fort. The English yacht still flying at the top of the flagstaff, he directed the Indians and his soldiers to shoot at it. They soon broke the iron pin to which it was fastened, and it fell to the ground. He was informed by a venerable old Ojibway chief, called Sweet, that the Sioux dwelt there when he was a youth. On the tenth of February, at ten o'clock, he left Leech Lake with Corporal Bradley, the trader McGillis and two of his men, and at sunset arrived at Red Cedar, now Cass Lake. At this place, in 1798, Thompson, employed by the Northwest Company for three years, in topographical surveys, made some observations. He believed that a line from the Lake of the Woods would touch the sources of the Mississippi. Pike, at this point, was very kindly treated by a Canadian named Roy, and his Ojibway squaw. On his return home, he reached Clear River on the seventh of April, where he found his canoe and men, and at night was at Grand Rapids, Dickson's trading post. He talked until four o'clock the next morning with this person and another trader named Porlier. He forbade while there, the traders Greignor [Grignon] and La Jennesse, to sell any more liquor to Indians, who had become very drunken and unruly. On the tenth he again reached the Falls of Saint Anthony. He writes in his journal as follows:

APRIL 11th, *Friday*.—Although it snowed very hard we brought over both boats, and descended the river to the island at the entrance of the St. Peter's. I sent to the chiefs and informed them I had something to communicate to them. The Fils de Pincho immediately waited on me, and informed me that he would provide a place for the purpose. About sundown I was sent for and introduced into the council-house, where I found a great many chiefs of the Sussitongs, Gens de Feuilles, and the Gens du Lac. The Yanctongs had not yet come down. They were all awaiting for my arrival. There were about one hundred lodges, or six hundred people; we were saluted on our crossing the river with ball as usual. The council-house was two large lodges, capable of containing three hundred men. In the upper were forty chiefs, and as many pipes set against the poles, alongside of which I had the Santeur's pipes arranged. I then informed them in short detail, of my transactions with the Santeurs; but my interpreters were not capable of making themselves understood. I was therefore obliged to omit mentioning every particular relative to the rascal who fired on my sentinel, and of the scoundrel who broke the Fols Avoins' canoes, and threatened my life; the interpreters, however, informed them that I wanted some of their principal chiefs to go to St. Louis; and that those who thought proper might descend to the prairie, where we would give them more explicit in‑formation. They all smoked out of the Santear's pipe, excepting three, who were painted black, and were some of those who lost their relations last winter. I invited the Fils de Pinchow, and the son of the Killeur Rouge, to come over and sup with me; when Mr. Dickson and myself endeavored to explain what I intended to have said to them, could I have made myself understood; that at the prairie we would have all things explained; that I was desirous of making a better report of them than Captain Lewis could do from their treatment of him. The former of those savages was the person who remained around my post all last winter, and treated my men so well; they endeavored to excuse their people.

"APRIL 12th, *Saturday*. Embarked early. Although my interpreter had been frequently up the river, he could not tell me where the cave (spoken of by Carver) could be found; we carefully sought for it, but in vain. At the Indian village, a few miles below St. Peter's, we were about to pass a few lodges, but on receiving a very particular invitation to come on shore, we landed, and were received in a lodge kindly; they presented us sugar. I gave the proprietor a dram, and was about to depart when he demanded a kettle of liquor; on being refused, and after I had left the shore, he told me he did not like the arrangements, and that he would go to war this summer. I directed the interpreter to tell him that if I returned to St. Peter's with the troops, I would settle that affair with him. On our arrival at the St. Croix, I found the Pettit Corbeau with his people, and Messrs. Frazer and Wood. We had a conference, when the Pettit Corbeau made many apologies for the misconduct of his people; he represented to us the different manners in which the young warriors had been inducing him to go to war; that he had been much blamed for dismissing his party last fall; but that he was determined to adhere as far as lay in his power to our instructions; that he thought it most prudent to remain here and restrain the warriors. He then presented me with a beaver robe and pipe. and his message to the general. That he was determined to preserve peace, and make the road clear; also a remembrance of his promised medal. I made a reply, calculated to confirm him in his good intentions, and assured him that he should not be the less remembered by his father, although not present. I was informed that, notwithstanding the instruction of his license, and my particular request, Murdoch Cameron had taken liquor and sold it to the Indians on the river St. Peter's, and that his partner below had been equally imprudent. I pledged myself to prosecute them according to law; for they have been the occasion of great confusion, and of much injury to the other traders. This day met a canoe of Mr. Dickson's loaded with provisions, under the charge of Mr. Anderson, brother of the Mr. Anderson at Leech Lake. He politely offered me any provision he had on board (for which Mr. Dickson had given me an order), but not now being in want, I did not accept of any. This day, for the first time, I observed the trees beginning to bud, and indeed the climate seemed to have changed very materially since we passed the Falls of St. Anthony."

The strife of political parties growing out of the French Revolution, and the declaration of war against Great Britain in the year 1812, postponed the military occupation of the Upper Mississippi by the United States of America, for several years.

CHAPTER XIII.

THE VALLEY OF THE UPPER MISSISSIPPI DURING SECOND WAR WITH GREAT BRITAIN.

Dickson and other traders hostile—American stockade at Prairie du Chien—Fort Shelby surrenders to Lt. Col. William McKay—Loyal traders Provencalle and Faribault—Rising Moose or One-eyed Sioux—Capt. Bulger evacuates Fort McKay—Intelligence of Peace.

Notwithstanding the professions of friendship made to Pike, in the second war with Great Britain, Dickson and others were found bearing arms against the Republic.

A year after Pike left Prairie du Chien, it was evident, that under some secret influence, the Indian tribes were combining against the United States. In the year 1809, Nicholas Jarrot declared that the British traders were furnishing the savages with guns for hostile purposes. On the first of May, 1812, two Indians were apprehended at Chicago, who were on their way to meet Dickson at Green Bay. They had taken the precaution to hide letters in their moccasins, and bury them in the ground, and were allowed to proceed after a brief detention. Frazer, of Prairie du Chien, who had been with Pike at the Council at the mouth of the Minnesota River, was at the portage of the Wisconsin when the Indians delivered these letters, which stated that the British flag would soon be flying again at Mackinaw. At Green Bay, the celebrated warrior, Black Hawk, was placed in charge of the Indians who were to aid the British. The American troops at Mackinaw were obliged, on the seventeenth of July, 1812, to capitulate without firing a single gun. One who was made prisoner, writes from Detroit to the Secretary of War:

"The persons who commanded the Indians are Robert Dickson, Indian trader, and John Askin, Jr., Indian agent, and his son. The latter two were painted and dressed after the manner of the Indians. Those who commanded the Canadians are John Johnson, Crawford, Pothier, Armitinger, La Croix, Rolette, Franks, Livingston, and other traders, some of whom were lately concerned in smuggling British goods into the Indian country, and, in conjunction with others, have been using their utmost efforts, several months before the declaration of war, to excite the Indians to take up arms. The least resistance from the fort would have been attended with the destruction of all the persons who fell into the hands of the British, as I have been assured by some of the British traders."

On the first of May, 1814, Governor Clark, with two hundred men, left St. Louis, to build a fort at the junction of the Wisconsin and Mississippi. Twenty days before he arrived at Prairie du Chien, Dickson had started for Mackinaw with a band of Dahkotahs and Winnebagoes. The place was left in command of Captain Deace and the Mackinaw Fencibles. The Dahkotahs refusing to co-operate, when the Americans made their appearance they fled. The Americans took possession of the old Mackinaw house, in which they found nine or ten trunks of papers belonging to Dickson. From one they took the following extract:

"'Arrived, from below, a few Winnebagoes with scalps. Gave them tobacco, six pounds powder and six pounds ball.'"

A fort was immediately commenced on the site of the old residence of the late H. L. Dousman, which was composed of two block-houses in the angles, and another on the bank of the river, with a subterranean communication. In honor of the governor of Kentucky it was named "Shelby."

The fort was in charge of Lieutenant Perkins, and sixty rank and file, and two gunboats, each of which carried a six-pounder; and several howitzers were commanded by Captains Yeiser, Sullivan, and Aid-de-camp Kennerly.

The traders at Mackinaw, learning that the Americans had built a fort at the Prairie, and knowing that as long as they held possession they would be cut off from the trade with the

Dahkotahs, immediately raised an expedition to capture the garrison.

The captain was an old trader by the name of McKay, and under him was a sergeant of artillery, with a brass six-pounder, and three or four volunteer companies of Canadian voyageurs, officered by Captains Grignon, Rolette and Anderson, with Lieutenants Brisbois and Duncan Graham, all dressed in red coats, with a number of Indians.

The Americans had scarcely completed their rude fortification, before the British force, guided by Joseph Rolette, Sr., descended in canoes to a point on the Wisconsin, several miles from the Prairie, to which they marched in battle array. McKay sent a flag to the Fort demanding a surrender. Lieutenant Perkins replied that he would defend it to the last.

A fierce encounter took place, in which the Americans were worsted. The officer was wounded, several men were killed and one of their boats captured, so that it became necessary to retreat to St. Louis. Fort Shelby after its capture, was called Fort McKay.

Among the traders a few remained loyal, especially Provencalle and J. B. Faribault, traders among the Sioux. Faribault was a prisoner among the British at the time Lieut. Col. Wm. McKay was preparing to attack Fort Shelby, and he refused to perform any service, Faribault's wife, who was at Prairie du Chien, not knowing that her husband was a prisoner in the hands of the advancing foe, fled with others to the Sioux village, where is now the city of Winona. Faribault was at length released on parole and returned to his trading post.

Pike writes of his flag, that "being in doubt whether it had been stolen by the Indians, or had fallen overboard and floated away, I sent for my friend the Orignal Leve." He also calls the Chief, Rising Moose, and gives his Sioux name Tahamie. He was one of those, who in 1805, signed the agreement, to surrender land at the junction of the Minnesota and Mississippi Rivers to the United States. He had but one eye, having lost the other when a boy, belonged to the Wapasha band of the Sioux, and proved true to the flag which had waved on the day he sat in council with Pike.

In the fall of 1814, with another of the same nation, he ascended the Missouri under the protection of the distinguished trader, Manual Lisa, as far as the Au Jacques or James River, and from thence struck across the country, enlisting the Sioux in favour of the United States, and at length arrived at Prairie du Chien. On his arrival, Dickson accosted him, and inquired from whence he came, and what was his business; at the same time rudely snatching his bundle from his shoulder, and searching for letters, The "one-eyed warrior" told him that he was from St. Louis, and that he had promised the white chiefs there that he would go to Prairie du Chien, and that he had kept his promise

Dickson then placed him in confinement in Fort McKay, as the garrison was called by the British, and ordered him to divulge what information he possessed, or he would put him to death. But the faithful fellow said he would impart nothing, and that he was ready for death if he wished to kill him. Finding that confinement had no effect, Dickson at last liberated him. He then left, and visited the bands of Sioux on the Upper Mississippi, with which he passed the winter. When he returned in the spring, Dickson had gone to Mackinaw, and Capt. A. Bulger, of the Royal New Foundland Regiment, was in command of the fort.

On the twenty-third ot May, 1815, Capt. Bulger, wrote from Fort McKay to Gov. Clark at St. Louis: "Official intelligence of peace reached me yesterday. I propose evacuating the fort, taking with me the guns captured in the fort. * * * * I have not the smallest hesitation in declaring my decided opinion, that the presence of a detachment of British and United States troops at the same time, would be the means of embroiling one party or the other in a fresh rupture with the Indians, which I presume it is the wish of both governments to avoid."

The next month the "One-Eyed Sioux," with three other Indians and a squaw, visited St. Louis, and he informed Gov. Clark, that the British commander left the cannons in the fort when he evacuated, but in a day or two came back, took the cannons, and fired the fort with the American flag flying, but that he rushed in and saved it from being burned. From this time, the British flag ceased to float in the Valley of the Mississippi.

CHAPTER XIV.

LONG'S EXPEDITION, A. D. 1817, IN A SIX-OARED SKIFF, TO THE FALLS OF SAINT ANTHONY.

Carver's Grandsons.—Roque, Sioux Interpreter.—Wapashaw's Village and its Vicinity.—A Sacred Dance.—Indian Village Below Dayton's Bluff.—Carver's Cave.—Fountain Cave.—Falls of St. Anthony Described.—Site of a Fort.

Major Stephen H. Long, of the Engineer Corps of the United States Army, learning that there was little or no danger to be apprehended from the Indians, determined to ascend to the Falls of Saint Anthony, in a six-oared skiff presented to him by Governor Clark, of Saint Louis. His party consisted of a Mr. Hempstead, a native of New London, Connecticut, who had been living at Prairie du Chien, seven soldiers, and a half-breed interpreter, named Roque. A bark canoe accompanied them, containing Messrs. Gun and King, grandsons of the celebrated traveler, Jonathan Carver.

On the ninth of July, 1817, the expedition left Prairie du Chien, and on the twelfth arrived at "Trempe a l'eau." He writes:

"When we stopped for breakfast, Mr. Hempstead and myself ascended a high peak to take a view of the country. It is known by the name of the Kettle Hill, having obtained this appellation from the circumstance of its having numerous piles of stone on its top, most of them fragments of the rocky stratifications which constitute the principal part of the hill, but some of them small piles made by the Indians. These at a distance have some similitude of kettles arranged along upon the ridge and sides of the hill. From this, or almost any other eminence in its neighborhood, the beauty and grandeur of the prospect would baffle the skill of the most ingenious pencil to depict, and that of the most accomplished pen to describe. Hills marshaled into a variety of agreeable shapes, some of them towering into lofty peaks, while others present broad summits embellished with contours and slopes in the most pleasing manner; champaigns and waving valleys; forests, lawns, and parks alternating with each other; the humble Mississippi meandering far below, and occasionally losing itself in numberless islands, give variety and beauty to the picture, while rugged cliffs and stupendous precipices here and there present themselves as if to add boldness and majesty to the scene. In the midst of this beautiful scenery is situated a village of the Sioux Indians, on an extensive lawn called the Aux Aisle Prairie; at which we lay by for a short time. On our arrival the Indians hoisted two American flags, and we returned the compliment by discharging our blunderbuss and pistols. They then fired several guns ahead of us by way of a salute, after which we landed and were received with much friendship. The name of their chief is Wauppaushaw, or the Leaf, commonly called by a name of the same import in French, La Feuille, or La Fye, as it is pronounced in English. He is considered one of the most honest and honorable of any of the Indians, and endeavors to inculcate into the minds of his people the sentiments and principles adopted by himself. He was not at home at the time I called, and I had no opportunity of seeing him. The Indians, as I suppose, with the expectation that I had something to communicate to them, assembled themselves at the place where I landed and seated themselves upon the grass. I inquired if their chief was at home, and was answered in the negative. I then told them I should be very glad to see him, but as he was absent I would call on him again in a few days when I should return. I further told them that our father, the new President, wished to obtain some more information relative to his red children, and that I was on a tour to acquire any intelligence he might stand in need of. With this they appeared well satisfied, and permitted Mr. Hempstead and myself to go through their village. While I was in the wigwam, one of the subordinate chiefs, whose name was Wazzecoota, or Shooter from the Pine Tree, volunteered to accompany me up the river. I accepted of his services, and he was ready to attend me on the tour in a very short time. When we hove in sight the Indians were engaged in a ceremony called the *Bear Dance;* a ceremony which they are in the habit of performing when any young man is desirous of bringing himself into particular notice, and is considered a kind of initiation into the state of manhood. I went on to the ground where they had their performances, which were ended sooner than usual on account of our arrival. There was a kind of a flag made of fawn skin dressed with the hair on, suspended on a pole. Upon the flesh side of it were drawn certain rude figures indicative of the dream which it is necessary the young man should have dreamed, before he can be considered a proper candidate for this kind of initiation; with this a pipe was suspended by way of sacrifice. Two arrows were stuck up at the foot of the pole, and fragments of painted feathers, etc., were strewed about the ground near to it. These pertained to the religious rites attending the ceremony, which consists in bewailing and self-mortification, that the Good Spirit may be induced to pity them and succor their undertaking.

"At the distance of two or three hundred yards from the flag, is an excavation which they call the bear's hole, prepared for the occasion. It is about two feet deep, and has two ditches, about one foot deep, leading across it at right angles. The young hero of the farce places himself in this hole, to be hunted by the rest of the young men, all of whom on this occasion are dressed in their best attire and painted in their neatest style. The hunters approach the hole in the direction of one of the ditches, and discharge their guns, which were previously loaded for the purpose with blank cartridges, at the one who acts the part of the bear; whereupon he leaps from his den, having a hoop in each hand, and a wooden lance; the hoops serving as forefeet to aid him in characterizing his part, and his lance to defend him from his assailants. Thus accoutred he dances round the place, exhibiting various feats of activity, while the other Indians pursue him and endeavor to trap him as he attempts to return to his den, to effect which he is privileged to use any violence he pleases with impunity against his assailants, even to taking the life of any of them.

"This part of the ceremony is performed three times, that the bear may escape from his den and return to it again through three of the avenues communicating with it. On being hunted from the fourth or last avenue, the bear must make his escape through all his pursuers, if possible, and flee to the woods, where he is to remain through the day. This, however, is seldom or never accomplished, as all the young men exert themselves to the utmost in order to trap him. When caught, he must retire to a lodge erected for his reception in the field, where he is to be secluded from all society through the day, except one of his particular friends whom he is allowed to take with him as an attendant. Here he smokes and performs various other rites which superstition has led the Indians to believe are sacred. After this ceremony is ended, the young Indian is considered qualified to act any part as an efficient member of their community. The Indian, who has the good fortune to catch the bear and overcome him when endeavoring to make his escape to the wood, is considered a candidate for preferment, and is, on the first suitable occasion, appointed the leader of a small war party, in order that he may further have an opportunity to test his prowess and perform more essential service in behalf of his nation. It is accordingly expected that he will kill some of their enemies and return with their scalps. I regretted very much that I had missed the opportunity of witnessing this ceremony, which is never performed except when prompted by the particular dreams of one or other of the young men, who is never complimented twice in the same manner on account of his dreams."

On the sixteenth he approached the vicinity of where is now the capital of Minnesota, and writes: "Set sail at half past four this morning with a favorable breeze. Pased an Indian burying ground on our left, the first that I have seen surrounded by a fence. In the center a pole is erected, at the foot of which religious rites are performed at the burial of an Indian, by the particular friends and relatives of the deceased. Upon the pole a flag is suspended when any person of extraordinary merit, or one who is very much beloved, is buried. In the inclosure were two scaffolds erected also, about six feet high and six feet square. Upon one of them were two coffins containing dead bodies. Passed a Sioux village on our right containing fourteen cabins. The name of the chief is the Petit Corbeau, or Little Raven. The Indians were all absent on a hunting party up the River St. Croix, which is but a little distance across the country from the village. Of this we were very glad, as this band are said to be the most notorious beggars of all the Sioux on the Mississippi. One of their cabins is furnished with loop holes, and is situated so near the water that the opposite side of the river is within musket-shot range from the building. By this means the Petit Corbeau is enabled to exercise a command over the passage of the river and has in some instances compelled traders to land with their goods, and induced them, probably through fear of offending him, to bestow presents to a considerable amount, before he would suffer them to pass. The cabins are a kind of stockade buildings, and of a better appearance than any Indian dwellings I have before met with.

"Two miles above the village, on the same side of the river, is Carver's Cave, at which we stopped to breakfast. However interesting it may have been, it does not possess that character in a very high degree at present. We descended it with lighted candles to its lower extremity. The entrance is very low and about eight feet broad, so that a man in order to enter it must be completely prostrate. The angle of descent within the cave is about 25 deg. The flooring is an inclined plane of quicksand, formed of the rock in which the cavern is formed. The distance from its entrance to its inner extremity is twenty-four paces, and the width in the broadest part about nine, and its greatest height about seven feet. In shape it resembles a bakers's oven. The cavern was once probably much more extensive. My interpreter informed me that, since his remembrance, the entrance was not less than ten feet high and its length far greater than at present. The rock in which it is formed is a very white sandstone, so friable that the fragments of it will almost crumble to sand when taken into the hand. A few yards below the mouth of the cavern is a very copious spring of fine water issuing from the bottom of the cliff.

"Five miles above this is the Fountain Cave, on the same side of the river, formed in the same kind of sandstone but of a more pure and fine quality. It is far more curious and interesting than the former. The entrance of the cave is a large winding hall about one hundred and fifty feet in length, fifteen feet in width, and from eight to sixteen feet in height, finely arched overhead, and nearly perpendicular. Next succeeds a narrow passage and difficult of entrance, which opens into a most beautiful circular room, finely arched above, and about forty feet in diameter. The cavern then continues a meandering course, expanding occasionally into small rooms of a circular form. We penetrated about one hundred and fifty yards, till our candles began to fail us, when we returned. To beautify and embellish the scene, a fine crystal stream flows through the cavern, and cheers the lonesome dark retreat with its enlivening murmurs. The temperature of the water in the cave was 46 deg., and that of the air 60 deg. Entering this cold retreat from an atmosphere of 89 deg., I thought it not prudent to remain in it long enough to take its several dimensions and meander its courses; particularly as we had to wade in water to our knees in many places in order to penetrate as far as we went. The fountain supplies an abundance of water as fine as I ever drank. This cavern I was informed by my interpreter, has been discovered but a few years. That the Indians formerly living in its neighborhood knew nothing of it till within six years past. That it is not the same as that described by Carver is evident, not only from this circumstance, but also from the circumstance that instead of a stagnant pool, and only one accessible room of a very different form, this cavern has a brook running through it, and at least four rooms in succession, one after the other. Carver's Cave is fast filling up with sand, so that no water is now found in it, whereas this, from the very nature of the place, must be enlarging as the fountain will carry along with its current all the sand that falls into it from the roof and sides of the cavern."

On the night of the sixteenth, he arrived at the Falls of Saint Anthony and encamped on the east shore just below the cataract. He writes in his journal:

"The place where we encamped last night needed no embellishment to render it romantic in the highest degree. The banks on both sides of the river are about one hundred feet high, decorated with trees and shrubbery of various kinds. The post oak, hickory, walnut, linden, sugar tree, white birch, and the American box; also various evergreens, such as the pine, cedar, juniper, etc., added their embellishments to the scene. Amongst the shrubery were the prickly ash, plum, and cherry tree, the gooseberry, the black and red raspberry, the chokeberry, grape vine, etc. There were also various kinds of herbage and flowers, among which were the wild parsley, rue, spikenard, etc., red and white roses, morning glory and various other handsome flowers. A few yards below us was a beautiful cascade of fine spring water, pouring down from a projecting precipice about one hundred feet hight. On our left was the Mississippi hurrying through its channel with great velocity, and about three quarters of a mile above us, in plain view, was the majestic cataract of the Falls of St. Anthony. The murmuring of the cascade, the roaring of the river, and the thunder of the cataract, all contributed to render the scene the most interesting and magnificient of any I ever before witnessed."

"The perpendicular fall of the water at the cataract, was stated by Pike in his journal, as sixteen and a half feet, which I found to be true by actual measurement. To this height, however, four or five feet may be added for the rapid descent which immediately succeeds to the perpendicular fall within a few yards below. Immediately at the cataract the river is divided into two parts by an island which extends considerably above and below the cataract, and is about five hundred yards long. The channel on the right side of the Island is about three times the width of that on the left. The quanity of water passins through them is not, however, in the same proportion, as about one-third part of the whole passes through the left channel. In the broadest channel, just below the cataract, is a small island also, about fifty yards in length and thirty in breadth. Both of these islands contain the same kind of rocky formation as the banks of the river, and are nearly as high. Besides these, there are immediately at the foot of the cataract, two islands of very inconsiderable size, situated in the right channel also. The rapids commence several hundred yards above the cataract and continue about eight miles below. The fall of the water, beginning at the head of the rapids, and extending two hundred and sixty rods down the river to where the portage road commences, below the cataract is, according to Pike, fifty-eight feet. If this estimate be correct the whole fall from the head to the foot of the rapids, is not probably much less than one hundred feet. But as I had no instrument sufficiently accurate to level, where the view must necessarily be pretty extensive, I took no pains to ascertain the extent of the fall. The mode I adopted to ascertain the height of a cataract, was to suspend a line and plummet from the table rock on the south side of the river, which at the same time had very little water passing over it as the river was unusually low. The rocky formations at this place were arranged in the following order, from the surface downward. A coarse kind of limestone in thin strata containing considerable silex; a kind of soft friable stone of a greenish color and slaty fracture, probably containing lime, aluminum and silex: a very beautiful satratification of shell limestone, in thin plates, extremely regular in its formation and containing a vast number of shells, all apparently of the same kind. This formation constitutes the Table Rock of the cataract. The next in order is a white or yellowish sandstone, so easily crumbled that it deserves the name of a sandbank rather than that of a rock. It is of various depths, from ten to fifty or seventy-five feet, and is of the same character with that found at the caves before described. The next in order is a soft friable sandstone, of a greenish color, similar to that resting upon the shell limestone. These stratifications occupied the whole space from the low water mark nearly to the top of the bluffs. On the east, or rather north side of the river, at the Falls, are high grounds, at the distance of half a mile from the river, considerably more elevated than the bluffs, and of a hilly aspect.

Speaking of the bluff at the confluence o. the Mississippi and Minnesota, he writes: "A military work of considerable magnitude might be constructed on the point, and might be rendered sufficiently secure by occupying the commanding height in the rear in a suitable manner, as the latter would control not only the point, but all the neighboring heights, to the full extent of a twelve pounder's range. The work on the point would be necessary to control the navigation of the two rivers. But without the commanding work in the rear, would be liable to be greatly annoyed from a height situated directly opposite on the other side of the Mississippi, which is here no more than about two hundred and fifty yards wide. This latter height, however, would not be eligible for a permanent post, on account of the numerous ridges and ravines situated immediately in its rear."

CHAPTER XV.

THOMAS DOUGLAS, EARL OF SELKIRK, AND THE RED RIVER VALLEY.

Early travelers to Lake Winnipeg—Earliest Map by the Indian Otchaga—Bellin's allusion to it—Verendrye's Map—De la Jemeraye's Map—Fort La Reine—Fort on Red River abandoned—Origin of name Red Lake—Earl of Selkirk—Ossiniboia described—Scotch immigrants at Pembina—Strife of trading companies—Earl of Selkirk visits America—Governor Semple Killed—Romantic life of John Tanner, and his son James—Letter relative to Selkirk's tour through Minnesota.

The valley of the Red River of the North is not only an important portion of Minnesota, but has a most interesting history.

While there is no evidence that Grosellier, the first white man who explored Minnesota, ever visited Lake Winnipeg and the Red River, yet he met the Assineboines at the head of Lake Superior and at Lake Nepigon, while on his way by a northeasterly trail to Hudson's Bay, and learned something of this region from them.

The first person, of whom we have an account, who visited the region, was an Englishman, who came in 1692, by way of York River, to Winnipeg.

Ochagachs, or Otchaga, an intelligent Indian, in 1728, assured Pierre Gualtier de Varenne, known in history as the Sieur Verendrye, while he was stationed at Lake Nepigon, that there was a communication, largely by water, west of Lake Superior, to the Great Sea or Pacific Ocean. The rude map, drawn by this Indian, was sent to France, and is still preserved. Upon it is marked Kamanistigonia, the fort first established by Du Luth. Pigeon River is called Mantohavagane. Lac Sasakanaga is marked, and Rainy Lake is named Tecamemiouen. The river St. Louis, of Minnesota, is R. fond du L. Superior. The French geographer, Bellin, in his "Remarks upon the map of North America," published in 1755, at Paris, alludes to this sketch of Ochagachs, and says it is the earliest drawing of the region west of Lake Superior, in the Depot de la Marine.

After this Verendrye, in 1737, drew a map, which remains unpublished, which shows Red Lake in Northern Minnesota, and the point of the Big Woods in the Red River Valley. There is another sketch in the archives of France, drawn by De la Jemeraye. He was a nephew of Verendrye, and, under his uncle's orders, he was in 1731, the first to advance from the Grand Portage of Lake Superior, by way of the Nalaonagan or Grosselliers, now Pigeon River, to Rainy Lake. On this appears Fort Rouge, on the south bank of the Assineboine at its junction with the Red River, and on the Assineboine, a post established on October 3, 1738, and called Fort La Reine. Bellin describes the fort on Red River, but asserts that it was abandoned because of its vicinity to Fort La Reine, on the north side of the Assinneboine, and only about nine miles by a portage, from Swan Lake. Red Lake and Red River were so called by the early French explorers, on account of the reddish tint of the waters after a storm.

Thomas Douglas, Earl of Selkirk, a wealthy, kind-hearted but visionary Scotch nobleman, at the commencement of the present century formed the design of planting a colony of agriculturists west of Lake Superior. In the year 1811 he obtained a grant of land from the Hudson Bay Company called Ossiniboia, which it seems strange has been given up by the people of Manitoba. In the autumn of 1812 a few Scotchmen with their families arrived at Pembina, in the Red River Valley, by way of Hudson Bay, where they passed the winter. In the winter of 1813-14 they were again at Fort Daer or Pembina. The colonists of Red River were rendered very unhappy by the strife of rival trading companies.

In the spring of 1815, McKenzie and Morrison, traders of the Northwest company, at Sandy Lake, told the Ojibway chief there, that they would give him and his band all the goods and rum at Leech or Sandy Lakes, if they would annoy the Red River settlers.

The Earl of Selkirk hearing of the distressed condition of his colony, sailed for America, and in the fall of 1815, arrived at New York City. Proceeding to Montreal he found a messenger who had traveled on foot in mid-winter from the Red River by way of Red Lake and Fon du Lac, of Lake Superior. He sent back by this man, kind messages to the dispirited settlers, but one night he was way-laid near Fon du Lac, and robbed of his canoe and dispatches. An Ojibway chief at Sandy Lake, afterwards testified that a trader named Grant offered him rum and tobacco, to send persons to intercept a bearer of dispatches to Red River, and soon the messenger was brought in by a negro and some Indians.

Failing to obtain military aid from the British authorities in Canada, Selkirk made an engagement with four officers and eighty privates, of the discharged Meuron regiment, twenty of the De Watteville, and a few of the Glengary Fencibles, which had served in the late war with the United States, to accompany him to Red River. They were to receive monthly wages for navigating the boats to Red River, to have lands assigned them, and a free passage if they wished to return.

When he reached Sault St. Marie, he received the intelligence that the colony had again been destroyed, and that Semple, a mild, amiable, but not altogether judicious man, the chief governor of the factories and territories of the Hudson Bay company, residing at Red River, had been killed.

Schoolcraft, in 1832, says he saw at Leech Lake, Majegabowi, the man who had killed Gov. Semple, after he fell wounded from his horse.

Before he heard of the death of Semple, the Earl of Selkirk had made arrangements to visit his colony by way of Fon du Lac, on the St. Louis River, and Red Lake of Minnesota, but he now changed his mind, and proceeded with his force to Fort William, the chief trading post of the Northwest Company on Lake Superior; and apprehending the principal partners, warrants of commitment were issued, and they were forwarded to the Attorney-General of Upper Canada.

While Selkirk was engaged at Fort William, a party of emigrants in charge of Miles McDonnel, Governor, and Captain D'Orsomen, went forward to reinforce the colony. At Rainy Lake they obtained the guidance of a man who had all the characteristics of an Indian, and yet had a bearing which suggested a different origin. By his efficiency and temperate habits, he had secured the respect of his employers, and on the Earl of Selkirk's arrival at Red River, his attention was called to him, and in his welfare he became deeply interested. By repeated conversations with him, memories of a different kind of existence were aroused, and the light of other days began to brighten. Though he had forgotten his father's name, he furnished sufficient data for Selkirk to proceed with a search for his relatives. Visiting the United States in 1817, he published a circular in the papers of the Western States, which led to the identification of the man.

It appeared from his own statement, and those of his friends, that his name was John Tanner, the son of a minister of the gospel, who, about the year 1790, lived on the Ohio river, near the Miami. Shortly after his location there, a band of roving Indians passed near the house, and found John Tanner, then a little boy, filling his hat with walnuts from under a tree. They seized him and fled. The party was led by an Ottawa whose wife had lost a son. To compensate for his death, the mother begged that a boy of the same age might be captured.

Adopted by the band, Tanner grew up an Indian in his tastes and habits, and was noted for bravery. Selkirk was successful in finding his relatives. After twenty-eight years of separation, John Tanner in 1818, met his brother Edward near Detroit, and went with him to his home in Missouri. He soon left his brother, and went back to the Indians. For a time he was interpreter for Henry R. Schoolcraft, but became lazy and ill-natured, and in 1836, skulking behind some bushes, he shot and killed Schoolcraft's brother, and fled to the wilderness, where, in 1847, he died. His son, James, was kindly treated by the missionaries to the Ojibways of Minnesota; but he walked in the footsteps of his father. In the year 1851, he attempted to impose upon the Presbyterian minister in Saint Paul, and, when detected, called upon the Baptist minister, who, believing him a penitent, cut a hole in the ice, and received him into the church by immersion. In time, the Baptists found him out, when he became an Unitarian missionary, and, at last, it is said, met a death by violence.

Lord Selkirk was in the Red River Valley

during the summer of 1817, and on the eighteenth of July concluded a treaty with the Crees and Saulteaux, for a tract of land beginning at the mouth of the Red River, and extending along the same as far as the Great Forks (now Grand Forks) at the mouth of Red Lake River, and along the Assiniboine River as far as Musk Rat River, and extending to the distance of six miles from Fort Douglas on every side, and likewise from Fort Daer (Pembina) and also from the Great Forks, and in other parts extending to the distance of two miles from the banks of the said rivers.

Having restored order and confidence, attended by three or four persons he crossed the plains to the Minnesota River, and from thence proceeded to St. Louis. The Indian agent at Prairie du Chien was not pleased with Selkirk's trip through Minnesota; and on the sixth of February, 1818, wrote the Governor of Illinois under excitement, some groundless suspicions:

"What do you suppose, sir, has been the result of the passage through my agency of this British nobleman? Two entire bands, and part of a third, all Sioux, have deserted us and joined Dickson, who has distributed to them large quantities of Indian presents, together with flags, medals, etc. Knowing this, what must have been my feelings on hearing that his lordship had met with a favourable reception at St. Louis. The newspapers announcing *his arrival, and general Scottish* appearance, all tend to discompose me; believing as I do, that he is plotting with his friend Dickson our destruction—sharpening the savage scalping knife, and colonizing a tract of country, so remote as that of the Red River, for the purpose, no doubt, of monopolizing the fur and peltry trade of this river, the Missouri and their waters; a trade of the first importance to our Western States and Territories. A courier who had arrived a few days since, confirms the belief that Dickson is endeavouring to undo what I have done, and secure to the British government the affections of the Sioux, and subject the Northwest Company to his lordship. * * * Dickson, as I have before observed, is situated near the head of the St. Peter's, to which place he transports his goods from Selkirk's Red River establishment, in carts made for the purpose. The trip is performed in five days, sometimes less. He is directed to build a fort on the highest land between Lac du Traverse and Red River, which he supposes will be the established lines. This fort will be defended by twenty men, with two small pieces of artillery."

In the year 1820, at Berne, Switzerland, a circular was issued, signed, R. May D'Uzistorf, Captain, in his Britannic Majesty's service, and agent Plenipotentiary to Lord Selkirk. Like many documents to induce emigration, it was so highly colored as to prove a delusion and a snare. The climate was represented as "mild and healthy." "Wood either for building or fuel in the greatest plenty," and the country supplying "in profusion, whatever can be required for the convenience, pleasure or comfort of life." Remarkable statements considering that every green thing had been devoured the year before by grasshoppers.

Under the influence of these statements, a number were induced to embark. In the spring of 1821, about two hundred persons assembled on the banks of the Rhine to proceed to the region west of Lake Superior. Having descended the Rhine to the vicinity of Rotterdam, they went aboard the ship "Lord Wellington," and after a voyage across the Atlantic, and amid the ice-floes of Hudson's Bay, they reached York Fort. Here they debarked, and entering batteaux, ascended Nelson River for twenty days, when they came to Lake Winnipeg, and coasting along the west shore they reached the Red River of the North, to feel that they had been deluded, and to long for a milder clime. If they did not sing the Switzer's Song of Home, they appreciated its sentiments, and gradually these immigrants removed to the banks of the Mississippi River. Some settled in Minnesota, and were the first to raise cattle, and till the soil.

CHAPTER XVI.

FORT SNELLING DURING ITS OCCUPANCY BY COMPANIES OF THE FIFTH REGIMENT U. S. INFANTRY. A. D. 1819, TO A. D. 1827.

Orders for military occupation of Upper Mississippi—Leavenworth and Forsyth at Prairie du Chien—Birth in Camp—Troops arrive at Mendota—Cantonment Established—Wheat carried to Pembina—Notice of Devotion, Prescott, and Major Taliaferro—Camp Cold Water Established—Col. Snelling takes command—Impressive Scene—Officers in 1820—Condition of the Fort in 1821—Saint Anthony Mill—Alexis Bailly takes cattle to Pembina—Notice of Beltrami—Arrival of first Steamboat—Major Long's Expedition to Northern Boundary—Beltrami visits the northern sources of the Mississippi—First flour mill—First Sunday School—Great flood in 1826. African slaves at the Fort—Steamboat Arrivals—Duels—Notice of William Joseph Snelling—Indian fight at the Fort—Attack upon keel boats—General Gaines' report—Removal of Fifth Regiment—Death of Colonel Snelling.

The rumor that Lord Selkirk was founding a colony on the borders of the United States, and that the British trading companies within the boundaries of what became the territory of Minnesota, convinced the authorities at Washington of the importance of a military occupation of the valley of the Upper Mississippi.

By direction of Major General Brown, the following order, on the tenth of February, 1819, was issued:

"Major General Macomb, commander of the Fifth Military department, will without delay, concentrate at Detroit the Fifth Regiment of Infantry, excepting the recruits otherwise directed by the general order herewith transmitted. As soon as the navigation of the lakes will admit, he will cause the regiment to be transported to Fort Howard; from thence, by the way of the Fox and Wisconsin Rivers, to Prairie du Chien, and, after detaching a sufficient number of companies to garrison Forts Crawford and Armstrong, the remainder will proceed to the mouth of the River St. Peter's, where they will establish a post, at which the headquarters of the regiment will be located. The regiment, previous to its departure, will receive the necessary supplies of clothing, provisions, arms, and ammunition. Immediate application will be made to Brigadier General Jesup, Quartermaster General, for funds necessary to execute the movements required by this order."

On the thirteenth of April, this additional order was issued, at Detroit:

"The season having now arrived when the lakes may be navigated with safety, a detachment of the Fifth Regiment, to consist of Major Marston's and Captain Fowle's companies, under the command of Major Muhlenburg, will proceed to Green Bay. Surgeon's Mate, R. M. Byrne, of the Fifth Regiment, will accompany the detachment. The Assistant Deputy Quartermaster General will furnish the necessary transport, and will send by the same opportunity two hundred barrels of provisions, which he will draw from the contractor at this post. The provisions must be examined and inspected, and properly put up for transportation. Colonel Leavenworth will, without delay, prepare his regiment to move to the post on the Mississippi, agreeable to the Division order of the tenth of February. The Assistant Deputy Quartermaster General will furnish the necessary transportation, to be ready by the first of May next. The Colonel will make requisition for such stores, ammunition, tools and implements as may be required, and he be able to take with him on the expedition. Particular instructions will be given to the Colonel, explaining the objects of his expedition."

EVENTS OF THE YEAR 1819.

On Wednesday, the last day of June, Col. Leavenworth and troops arrived from Green Bay, at Prairie du Chien. Scarcely had they reached this point when Charlotte Seymour, the wife of Lt. Nathan Clark, a native of Hartford, Ct., gave birth to a daughter, whose first baptismal name was Charlotte, after her mother, and the second Ouisconsin, given by the officers in view of the fact that she was born at the junction of that stream with the Mississippi.

In time Charlotte Ouisconsin married a young Lieutenant, a native of Princeton, New Jersey, and a graduate of West Point, and still resides with her husband, General H. P. Van Cleve, in the city of Minneapolis, living to do good as she has opportunity.

In June, under instructions from the War Department, Major Thomas Forsyth, connected with the office of Indian affairs, left St. Louis with two thousand dollars worth of goods to be distributed among the Sioux Indians, in accordance with the agreement of 1805, already referred to, by the late General Pike.

About nine o'clock of the morning of the fifth of July, he joined Leavenworth and his command at Prairie du Chien. Some time was occupied by Leavenworth awaiting the arrival of ordnance, provisions and recruits, but on Sunday morning, the eighth of August, about eight o'clock, the expedition set out for the point now known as Mendota. The flotilla was quite imposing; there were the Colonel's barge, fourteen batteaux with ninety-eight soldiers and officers, two large canal or Mackinaw boats, filled with various stores, and Forsyth's keel boat, containing goods and presents for the Indians. On the twenty-third of August, Forsyth reached the mouth of the Minnesota with his boat, and the next morning Col. Leavenworth arrived, and selecting a place at Mendota, near the present railroad bridge, he ordered the soldiers to cut down trees and make a clearing. On the next Saturday Col. Leavenworth, Major Vose, Surgeon Purcell, Lieutenant Clark and the wife of Captain Gooding visited the Falls of Saint Anthony with Forsyth, in his keel boat.

Early in September two more boats and a batteaux, with officers and one hundred and twenty recruits, arrived.

During the winter of 1820, Laidlow and others, in behalf of Lord Selkirk's Scotch settlers at Pembina, whose crops had been destroyed by grasshoppers, passed the Cantonment, on their way to Prairie du Chien, to purchase wheat. Upon the fifteenth of April they began their return with their Mackinaw boats, each loaded with two hundred bushels of wheat, one hundred of oats, and thirty of peas, and reached the mouth of the Minnesota early in May. Ascending this stream to Big Stone Lake, the boats were drawn on rollers a mile and a half to Lake Traverse, and on the third of June arrived at Pembina and cheered the desponding and needy settlers of the Selkirk colony.

The first sutler of the post was a Mr. Devotion. He brought with him a young man named Philander Prescott, who was born in 1801, at Phelpstown, Ontario county, New York. At first they stopped at Mud Hen Island, in the Mississippi below the mouth of the St. Croix River. Coming up late in the year 1819, at the site of the present town of Hastings they found a keel-boat loaded with supplies for the cantonment, in charge of Lieut. Oliver, detained by the ice.

Amid all the changes of the troops, Mr. Prescott remained nearly all his life in the vicinity of the post, to which he came when a mere lad, and was at length killed in the Sioux Massacre.

EVENTS OF THE YEAR 1820

In the spring of 1820, Jean Baptiste Faribault brought up Leavenworth's horses from Prairie du Chien.

The first Indian Agent at the post was a former army officer, Lawrence Taliaferro, pronounced Toliver. As he had the confidence of the Government for twenty-one successive years, he is deserving of notice.

His family was of Italian origin, and among the early settlers of Virginia. He was born in 1794, in King William county in that State, and when, in 1812, war was declared against Great Britain, with four brothers, he entered the army, and was commissioned as Lieutenant of the Thirty-fifth Infantry. He behaved gallantly at Fort Erie and Sackett's Harbor, and after peace was declared, he was retained as a First Lieutenant of the Third Infantry. In 1816 he was stationed at Fort Dearborn, now the site of Chicago. While on a furlough, he called one day upon President Monroe, who told him that a fort would be built near the Falls of Saint Anthony, and an Indian Agency established, to which he offered to appoint him. His commission was dated March 27th, 1819, and he proceeded in due time to his post.

On the fifth day of May, 1820, Leavenworth left his winter quarters at Mendota, crossed the stream and made a summer camp near the present military grave yard, which in consequence of a fine spring has been called "Camp Cold Water." The Indian agency, under Taliaferro, remained for a time at the old cantonment.

The commanding officer established a fine

garden in the bottom lands of the Minnesota, and on the fifteenth of June the earliest garden peas were eaten. The first distinguished visitors at the new encampment were Governor Lewis Cass, of Michigan, and Henry Schoolcraft, who arrived in July, by way of Lake Superior and Sandy Lake.

The relations between Col. Leavenworth and Indian Agent Taliaferro were not entirely harmonious, growing out of a disagreement of views relative to the treatment of the Indians, and on the day of the arrival of Governor Cass, Teliaferro writes to Leavenworth:

"As it is now understood that I am agent for Indian affairs in this country, and you are about to leave the upper Mississippi, in all probability in the course of a month or two, I beg leave to suggest, for the sake of a general understanding with the Indian tribes in this country, that any medals, you may possess, would by being turned over to me, cease to be a topic of remark among the different Indian tribes under my direction. I will pass to you any voucher that may be required, and I beg leave to observe that any progress in influence is much impeded in consequence of this frequent intercourse with the garrison."

In a few days, the disastrous effect of Indians mingling with the soldiers was exhibited. On the third of August, the agent wrote to Leavenworth:

"His Excellency Governor Cass during his visit to this post remarked to me that the Indians in this quarter were spoiled, and at the same time said they should not be permitted to enter the camp. An unpleasant affair has lately taken place; I mean the stabbing of the old chief Mahgossau by his comrade. This was caused, doubtless, by an anxiety to obtain the chief's whiskey. I beg, therefore, that no whiskey whatever be given to any Indians, unless it be through their proper agent. While an overplus of whiskey thwarts the benificent and humane policy of the government, it entails misery upon the Indians, and endangers their lives."

A few days after this note was written Josiah Snelling, who had been recently promoted to the Colonelcy of the Fifth Regiment, arrived with his family, relieved Leavenworth, and infused new life and energy. A little while before his arrival, the daughter of Captain Gooding was married to Lieutenant Green, the Adjutant of the regiment, the first marriage of white persons in Minnesota. Mrs. Snelling, a few days after her arrival, gave birth to a daughter, the first white child born in Minnesota, and after a brief existence of thirteen months, she died and was the first interred in the military grave yard, and for years the stone which marked its resting place, was visible.

The earliest manuscript in Minnesota, written at the Cantonment, is dated October 4, 1820, and is in the handwriting of Colonel Snelling. It reads: "In justice to Lawrence Taliaferro, Esq., Indian Agent at this post, we, the undersigned, officers of the Fifth Regiment here stationed, have presented him this paper, as a token, not only of our individual respect and esteem, but as an entire approval of his conduct and deportment as a public agent in this quarter. Given at St. Peter, this 4th day of October, 1820.

J. SNELLING, Col. 5th Inf.	N. CLARK, Lieutenant.
S. BURBANK, Br. Major.	JOS. HARE, Lieutenant.
DAVID PERRY, Captain.	ED. PURCELL, Surgeon,
D. GOODING, Brevet Captain.	P. R. GREEN, Lieut. and Adjt.
J. PLYMPTON, Lieutenant.	W. G. CAMP, Lt. and Q. M.
R. A. MCCABE, Lieutenant.	H. WILKINS, Lieutenant."

During the summer of 1820, a party of the Sisseton Sioux killed on the Missouri, Isadore Poupon, a half-breed, and Joseph Andrews, a Canadian engaged in the fur trade. The Indian Agent, through Colin Campbell, as interpreter, notified the Sissetons that trade would cease with them, until the murderers were delivered. At a council held at Big Stone Lake, one of the murderers, and the aged father of another, agreed to surrender themselves to the commanding officer.

On the twelfth of November, accompanied by their friends, they approached the encampment in solemn procession, and marched to the centre of the parade. First appeared a Sisseton bearing a British flag; then the murderer and the devoted father of another, their arms pinioned, and large wooden splinters thrust through the flesh above the elbows indicating their contempt for pain and death; in the rear followed friends and relatives, with them chanting the death dirge. Having arrived in front of the guard, fire was kindled, and the British flag burned; then the murderer delivered up his medal, and both prisoners were surrounded. Col. Snelling detained the old chief, while the murderer was sent to St. Louis for trial.

EVENTS OF THE YEAR 1821.

Col. Snelling built the fort in the shape of a lozenge, in view of the projection between the two rivers. The first row of barracks was of hewn logs, obtained from the pine forests of Rum River, but the other buildings were of stone. Mrs. Van Cleve, the daughter of Lieutenant, afterwards Captain Clark, writes:

"In 1821 the fort, although not complete, was fit for occupancy. My father had assigned to him the quarters next beyond the steps leading to the Commissary's stores, and during the year my little sister Juliet was born there. At a later period my father and Major Garland obtained permission to build more commodious quarters outside the walls, and the result was the two stone houses afterwards occupied by the Indian Agent and interpreter, lately destroyed."

Early in August, a young and intelligent mixed blood, Alexis Bailly, in after years a member of the legislature of Minnesota, left the cantonment with the first drove of cattle for the Selkirk Settlement, and the next winter returned with Col. Robert Dickson and Messrs. Laidlow and Mackenzie.

The next month, a party of Sissetons visited the Indian Agent, and told him that they had started with another of the murderers, to which reference has been made, but that on the way he had, through fear of being hung, killed himself.

This fall, a mill was constructed for the use of the garrison, on the west side of St. Anthony Falls, under the supervision of Lieutenant McCabe. During the fall, George Gooding, Captain by brevet, resigned, and became Sutler at Prairie du Chien. He was a native of Massachusetts, and entered the army as ensign in 1808. In 1810 he became a Second Lieutenant, and the next year was wounded at Tippecanoe.

In the middle of October, there embarked on the keel-boat "Saucy Jack," for Prairie du Chien, Col. Snelling, Lieut. Baxley, Major Taliaferro, and Mrs. Gooding.

EVENTS OF 1822 AND 1823.

Early in January, 1822, there came to the Fort from the Red River of the North, Col. Robert Dickson, Laidlow, a Scotch farmer, the superintendent of Lord Selkirk's experimental farm, and one Mackenzie, on their way to Prairie du Chien. Dickson returned with a drove of cattle, but owing to the hostility of the Sioux his cattle were scattered, and never reached Pembina.

During the winter of 1823, Agent Taliaferro was in Washington. While returning in March, he was at a hotel in Pittsburg, when he received a note signed G. C. Beltrami, who was an Italian exile, asking permission to accompany him to the Indian territory. He was tall and commanding in appearance, and gentlemanly in bearing, and Taliaferro was so forcibly impressed as to accede to the request. After reaching St. Louis they embarked on the first steamboat for the Upper Mississippi.

It was named the Virginia, and was built in Pittsburg, twenty-two feet in width, and one hundred and eighteen feet in length, in charge of a Captain Crawford. It reached the Fort on the tenth of May, and was saluted by the discharge of cannon. Among the passengers, besides the Agent and the Italian, were Major Biddle, Lieut. Russell, and others.

The arrival of the Virginia is an era in the history of the Dahkotah nation, and will probably be transmitted to their posterity as long as they exist as a people. They say their sacred men, the night before, dreamed of seeing some monster of the waters, which frightened them very much.

As the boat neared the shore, men, women, and children beheld with silent astonishment, supposing that it was some enormous water-spirit, coughing, puffing out hot breath, and splashing water in every direction. When it touched the landing their fears prevailed, and they retreated some distance; but when the blowing off of steam commenced they were completely unnerved: mothers forgetting their children, with streaming hair, sought hiding-places; chiefs, renouncing their stoicism, scampered away like affrighted animals.

The peace agreement beteen the Ojibways and Dahkotahs, made through the influence of Governor Cass, was of brief duration, the latter being the first to violate the provisions.

On the fourth of June, Taliaferro, the Indian agent among the Dahkotahs, took advantage of the presence of a large number of Ojibways to renew the agreement for the cessation of hostilities. The council hall of the agent was a large room of logs, in which waved conspicuously the flag of the United States, surrounded by British colors and medals that had been delivered up from time to time by Indian chiefs.

Among the Dahkotah chiefs present were Wapashaw, Little Crow, and Penneshaw; of the Ojibways there were Kendouswa, Moshomene, and Pasheskonoepe. After mutual accusations and excuses concerning the infraction of the previous treaty, the Dahkotahs lighted the calumet, they having been the first to infringe upon the agreement of 1820. After smoking and passing the pipe of peace to the Ojibways, who passed through the same formalities, they all shook hands as a pledge of renewed amity.

The morning after the council, Flat Mouth, the distinguished Ojibway chief, arrived, who had left his lodge vowing that he would never be at peace with the Dahkotahs. As he stepped from his canoe, Penneshaw held out his hand, but was repulsed with scorn. The Dahkotah warrior immediately gave the alarm, and in a moment runners were on their way to the neighboring villages to raise a war party.

On the sixth of June, the Dahkotahs had assembled, stripped for a fight, and surrounded the Ojibways. The latter, fearing the worst, concealed their women and children behind the old barracks which had been used by the troops while the fort was being erected. At the solicitation of the agent and commander of the fort, the Dahkotahs desisted from an attack and retired.

On the seventh, the Ojibways left for their homes; but, in a few hours, while they were making a portage at Falls of St. Anthony, they were again approached by the Dahkotahs, who would have attacked them, if a detachment of troops had not arrived from the fort.

A rumor reaching Penneshaw's village that he had been killed at the falls, his mother seized an Ojibway maiden, who had been a captive from infancy, and, with a tomahawk, cut her in two. Upon the return of the son in safety he was much gratified at what he considered the prowess of his parent.

On the third of July, 1823, Major Long, of the engineers, arrived at the fort in command of an expedition to explore the Minnesota River, and the region along the northern boundary line of the United States. Beltrami, at the request of Col. Snelling, was permitted to be of the party, and Major Taliaferro kindly gave him a horse and equipments.

The relations of the Italian to Major Long were not pleasant, and at Pembina Beltrami left the expedition, and with a "bois brule", and two Ojibways proceeded and discovered the northern sources of the Mississippi, and suggested where the western sources would be found; which was verified by Schoolcraft nine years later. About the second week in September Beltrami returned to the fort by way of the Mississippi, escorted by forty or fifty Ojibways, and on the 25th departed for New Orleans, where he published his discoveries in the French language.

The mill which was constructed in 1821, for sawing lumber, at the Falls of St. Anthony, stood upon the site of the Holmes and Sidle Mill, in Minneapolis, and in 1823 was fitted up for grinding flour. The following extracts from correspondence addressed to Lieut. Clark, Commissary at Fort Snelling, will be read with interest.

Under the date of August 5th, 1823, General Gibson writes: "From a letter addressed by Col. Snelling to the Quartermaster General, dated the 2d of April, I learn that a large quantity of wheat would be raised this summer. The assistant Commissary of Subsistence at St. Louis has been instructed to forward sickles and a pair of millstones to St. Peters. If any flour is manufactured from the wheat raised, be pleased to let me know as early as practicable, that I may deduct the quantity manufactured at the post from the quantity advertised to be contracted for."

In another letter, General Gibson writes: "Below you will find the amount charged on the books against the garrison at Ft. St. Anthony, for certain articles, and forwarded for the use of the troops at that post, which you will deduct from the payments to be made for flour raised and turned over to you for issue:

One pair buhr millstones	$250 11
337 pounds plaster of Paris	20 22
Two dozen sickles	18 00
Total	$288 33

Upon the 19th of January, 1824, the General writes: "The mode suggested by Col. Snelling, of fixing the price to be paid to the troops for the flour furnished by them is deemed equitable and just. You will accordingly pay for the flour $3.33 per barrel."

Charlotte Ouisconsin Van Cleve, now the oldest person living who was connected with the cantonment in 1819, in a paper read before the Department of American History of the Minnesota Historical Society in January, 1880, wrote:

"In 1823, Mrs. Snelling and my mother established the first Sunday School in the Northwest. It was held in the basement of the commanding officer's quarters, and was productive of much good. Many of the soldiers, with their families, attended. Joe. Brown, since so well know in this country, then a drummer boy, was one of the pupils. A Bible class, for the officers and their wives, was formed, and all became so interested in the history of the patriarchs, that it furnished topics of conversation for the week. One day after the Sunday School lesson on the death of Moses, a member of the class meeting my mother on the parade, after exchanging the usual greetings, said, in saddened tones, 'But don't you feel sorry that Moses is dead?'

Early in the spring of 1824, the Tully boys were rescued from the Sioux and brought to the fort. They were children of one of the settlers of Lord Selkirk's colony, and with their parents and others, were on their way from Red River Valley to settle near Fort Snelling.

The party was attacked by Indians, and the parents of these children murdered, and the boys captured. Through the influence of Col. Snelling the children were ransomed and brought to the fort. Col. Snelling took John and my father Andrew, the younger of the two. Everyone became interested in the orphans, and we loved Andrew as if he had been our own little brother. John died some two years after his arrival at the fort, and Mrs. Snelling asked me when I last saw her if a tomb stone had been placed at his grave, she as requested, during a visit to the old home some years ago. She said she received a promise that it should be done, and seemed quite disappointed when I told her it had not been attended to."

Andrew Tully, after being educated at an Orphan Asylum in New York City, became a carriage maker, and died a few years ago in that vicinity.

EVENTS OF THE YEAR A. D. 1824.

In the year 1824 the Fort was visited by Gen. Scott, on a tour of inspection, and at his suggestion, its name was changed from Fort St. Anthony to Fort Snelling. The following is an extract from his report to the War Department:

"This work, of which the War Department is in possession of a plan, reflects the highest credit on Col. Snelling, his officers and men. The defenses, and for the most part, the public storehouses, shops and quarters being constructed of stone, the whole is likely to endure as long as the post shall remain a frontier one. The cost of erection to the government has been the amount paid for tools and iron, and the per diem paid to soldiers employed as mechanics. I wish to suggest to the General in Chief, and through him to the War Department, the propriety of calling this work Fort Snelling, as a just compliment to the meritorious officer under whom it has been erected. The present name, (Fort St. Anthony), is foreign to all our associations, and is, besides, geographically incorrect, as the work stands at the junction of the Mississippi and St. Peter's [Minnesota] Rivers, eight miles below the great falls of the Mississippi, called after St. Anthony."

In 1824, Major Taliaferro proceeded to Washington with a delegation of Chippeways and Dahkotahs, headed by Little Crow, the grand father of the chief of the same name, who was engaged in the late horrible massacre of defenceless women and children. The object of the visit, was to secure a convocation of all the tribes of the Upper Mississippi, at Prairie du Chein, to define their boundary lines and establish friendly relations. When they reached Prairie du Chein, Wahnatah, a Yankton chief, and also Wapashaw, by the whisperings of mean traders, became disaffected, and wished to turn back. Little Crow, perceiving this, stopped all hesitancy by the following speech: "My friends, you can do as you please. I am no coward, nor can my ears be pulled about by evil counsels. We are here and should go on, and do some good for our nation. I have taken our Father here (Taliaferro) by the coat tail, and will follow him until I take by the hand, our great American Father."

While on board of a steamer on the Ohio River, Marcpee or the Cloud, in consequence of a bad dream, jumped from the stern of the boat, and was supposed to be drowned, but he swam ashore and made his way to St. Charles, Mo., there to be murdered by some Sacs. The remainder safely arrived in Washington and accomplished the object of the visit. The Dahkotahs returned by way of New York, and while there were anxious to pay a visit to certain parties with Wm. Dickson, a half-breed son of Col Robert Dickson, the trader, who in the war of 1812-15 led the Indians of the Northwest against the United States.

After this visit Little Crow carried a new double-barreled gun, and said that a medicine man by the name of Peters gave it to him for signing a certain paper, and that he also promised he would send a keel-boat full of goods to them. The medicine man referred to was the Rev. Samuel Peters, an Episcopal clergyman, who had made himself obnoxious during the Revolution by his tory sentiments, and was subsequently nominated as Bishop of Vermont.

Peters asserted that in 1806 he had purchased of the heirs of Jonathan Carver the right to a tract of land on the upper Mississippi, embracing St. Paul, alleged to have been given to Carver by the Dahkotahs, in 1767.

The next year there arrived, in one of the keel-boats from Prairie du Chien, at Fort Snelling a box marked Col. Robert Dickson. On opening, it was found to contain a few presents from Peters to Dickson's Indian wife, a long letter, and a copy of Carver's alleged grant, written on parchment.

EVENTS OF THE YEARS 1825 AND 1826.

On the 30th of October, 1825, seven Indian women in canoes, were drawn into the rapids above the Falls of St. Anthony. All were saved but a lame girl, who was dashed over the cataract, and a month later her body was found at Pike's Island in front of the fort.

Forty years ago, the means of communication between Fort Snelling and the civilized world were very limited. The mail in winter was usually carried by soldiers to Prairie du Chien. On the 26th of January, 1826, there was great joy in the fort, caused by the return from furlough of Lieutenants Baxley and Russell, who brought with them the first mail received for five months. About this period there was also another excitement, cause by the seizure of liquors in the trading house of Alexis Bailey, at New Hope, now Mendota.

During the months of February and March, in this year, snow fell to the depth of two or three feet, and there was great suffering among the Indians. On one occasion, thirty lodges of Sisseton and other Sioux were overtaken by a snow storm on a large prairie. The storm continued for three days, and provisions grew scarce, for the party were seventy in number. At last, the stronger men, with the few pairs of snow-shoes in their possession, started for a trading post one hundred miles distant. They reached their destination half alive, and the traders sympathizing sent four Canadians with supplies for those left behind. After great toil they reached the scene of distress, and found many dead, and, what was more horrible, the living feeding on the corpses of their relatives. A mother had eaten her dead child and a portion of her own father's arms. The shock to her nervous system was so great that she lost her reason. Her name was Pashuno-ta, and she was both young and good looking. One day in September, while at Fort Snelling, she asked Captain Jouett if he knew which was the best portion of a man to eat, at the same time taking him by the collar of his coat. He replied with great astonishment, "No!" and she then said, "The arms." She then asked for a piece of his servant to eat, as she was nice and fat. A few days after this she dashed herself from the bluffs near Fort Snelling, into the river. Her body was found just above the mouth of the Minnesota, and decently interred by the agent.

The spring of 1826 was very backward. On the 20th of March snow fell to the depth of one or one and a half feet on a level, and drifted in heaps from six to fifteen feet in height. On the 5th of April, early in the day, there was a violent storm, and the ice was still thick in the river. During the storm flashes of lightning were seen and thunder heard. On the 10th, the thermometer was four degrees above zero. On the 14th there was rain, and on the next day the St. Peter river broke up, but the ice on the Mississippi remained firm. On the 21st, at noon, the ice began to move, and carried away Mr. Faribault's houses on the east side of the river. For several days the river was twenty feet above low water mark, and all the houses on low lands were swept off. On the second of May, the steamboat Lawrence, Captain Reeder, arrived.

Major Taliaferro had inherited several slaves, which he used to hire to officers of the garrison. On the 31st of March, his negro boy, William, was employed by Col. Snelling, the latter agreeing to clothe him. About this time, William attempted to shoot a hawk, but instead shot a small boy, named Henry Cullum, and nearly killed him. In May, Captain Plympton, of the Fifth Infantry, wished to purchase his negro woman, Eliza, but he refused, as it was his intention, ultimately, to free his slaves. Another of his negro girls, Harriet, was married at the fort, the Major performing the ceremony, to the now historic Dred Scott, who was then a slave of Surgeon Emerson. The only person that ever purchased a slave, to retain in slavery, was Alexis Bailly, who bought a man of Major Garland. The Sioux, at first, had no prejudices against negroes. They called them "Black Frenchmen," and placing their hands on their woolly heads would laugh heartily.

The following is a list of the steamboats that had arrived at Fort Snelling, up to May 26, 1826:

1 Virginia, May 10, 1823; 2 Neville; 3 Putnam, April 2, 1825; 3 Mandan; 5 Indiana; 6 Lawrence, May 2, 1826; 7 Sciota; 8 Eclipse; 9 Josephine; 10 Fulton; 11 Red Rover; 12 Black Rover; 13 Warrior; 14 Enterprise; 15 Volant.

Life within the walls of a fort is sometimes the exact contrast of a paradise. In the year 1826 a Pandora box was opened, among the officers, and dissensions began to prevail. One young officer, a graduate of West Point, whose father had been a professor in Princeton College, fought a duel with, and slightly wounded, William Joseph, the talented son of Colonel Snelling, who was then twenty-two years of age, and had been three years at West Point. At a Court Martial convened to try the officer for violating the Articles of War, the accused objected to the testimony of Lieut. William Alexander, a Tennesseean, not a graduate of the Military Academy, on the ground that he was an infidel. Alexander, hurt by this allusion, challenged the objector, and another duel was fought, resulting only in slight injuries to the clothing of the combatants. Inspector General E. P. Gaines, after this, visited the fort, and in his report of the inspection he wrote: "A defect in the discipline of this regiment has appeared in the character of certain personal controversies, between the Colonel and several of his young officers, the particulars of which I forbear to enter into, assured as I am that they will be developed in the proceedings of a general court martial ordered for the trial of Lieutenant Hunter and other officers at Jefferson Barracks.

"From a conversation with the Colonel I can have no doubt that he has erred in the course pursued by him in reference to some of the controversies, inasmuch as he has intimated to his officers his willingness to sanction in certain cases, and even to participate in personal conflicts, contrary to the twenty-fifth, Article of War."

The Colonel's son, William Joseph, after this passed several years among traders and Indians, and became distinguished as a poet and brilliant author.

His "Tales of the Northwest," published in Boston in 1820, by Hilliard, Gray, Little & Wilkins, is a work of great literary ability, and Catlin thought the book was the most faithful picture of Indian life he had read. Some of his poems were also of a high order. One of his pieces, deficient in dignity, was a caustic satire upon modern American poets, and was published under the title of "Truth, a Gift for Scribblers."

Nathaniel P. Willis, who had winced under the last, wrote the following lampoon:

"Oh, smelling Joseph! Thou art like a cur.
I'm told thou once did live by hunting fur:
Of bigger dogs thou smellest, and, in sooth,
Of one extreme, perhaps, can tell the truth.
'Tis a wise shift, and shows thou know'st thy powers,
To leave the 'North West tales,' and take to smelling ours."

In 1832 a second edition of "Truth" appeared with additions and emendations. In this appeared the following pasquinade upon Willis:

"I live by hunting fur, thou say'st, so let it be.
But tell me, Natty! Had I hunted thee,
Had not my time been thrown away, young sir,
And eke my powder? Puppies have no fur.

Our tails? Thou ownest thee to a tail,
I've scanned thee o'er and o'er
But, though I guessed the species right,
I was not sure before.

Our savages, authentic travelers say,
To natural fools, religious homage pay,
Hadst thou been born in wigwam's smoke, and
died in,
Nat! thine apotheosis had been certain."

Snelling died at Chelsea, Mass., December sixteenth, 1848, a victim to the appetite which enslaved Robert Burns.

In the year 1828, a small party of Ojibways (Chippeways came to see the Indian Agent, and three of them ventured to visit the Columbia Fur Company's trading house, two miles from the Fort. While there, they became aware of their danger, and desired two of the white men attached to the establishment to accompany them back, thinking that their presence might be some protection. They were in error. As they passed a little copse, three Dahkotahs sprang from behind a log with the speed of light, fired their pieces into the face of the foremost, and then fled. The guns must have been double loaded, for the man's head was literally blown from his shoulders, and his white companions were spattered with brains and blood. The survivors gained the Fort without further molestation. Their comrade was buried on the spot where he fell. A staff was set up on his grave, which became a landmark, and received the name of The Murder Pole. The murderers boasted of their achievement and with impunity. They and their tribe thought that they had struck a fair blow on their ancient enemies, in a becoming manner. It was only said, that Toopunkah Zeze of the village of the *Barre aux Fievres*, and two others, had each acquired a right to wear skunk skins on their heels and war-eagles' feathers on their heads.

EVENTS OF A. D. 1827.

On the twenty-eighth of May, 1827, the Ojibway chief at Sandy Lake, Kee-wee-zais-hish called by the English, Flat Mouth with seven warriors and some women and children, in all amounting to twenty-four, arrived about sunrise at Fort Snelling. Walking to the gates of the garrison, they asked the protection of Colonel Snelling and Taliaferro, the Indian agent. They were told, that as long as they remained under the United States flag, they were secure, and were ordered to encamp within musket shot of the high stone walls of the fort.

During the afternoon, a Dahkotah, Toopunkah Zeze, from a village near the first rapids of the Minnesota, visited the Ojibway camp. They were cordially received, and a feast of meat and corn and sugar, was soon made ready. The wooden plates emptied of their contents, they engaged in conversation, and whiffed the peace pipe.

That night, some officers and their friends were spending a pleasant evening at the head-quarters of Captain Clark, which was in one of the stone houses which used to stand outside of the walls of the fort. As Captain Cruger was walking on the porch, a bullet whizzed by, and rapid firing was heard.

As the Dahkotahs, or Sioux, left the Ojibway camp, notwithstanding their friendly talk, they turned and discharged their guns with deadly aim upon their entertainers, and ran off with a shout of satisfaction. The report was heard by the sentinel of the fort, and he cried, repeatedly, "Corporal of the guard!" and soon at the gates were the Ojibways, with their women and the wounded, telling their tale of woe in wild and incoherent language. Two had been killed and six wounded. Among others, was a little girl about seven years old, who was pierced through both thighs with a bullet. Surgeon McMahon made every effort to save her life, but without avail.

Flat Mouth, the chief, reminded Colonel Snelling that he had been attacked while under the protection of the United States flag, and early the next morning, Captain Clark, with one hundred soldiers, proceeded towards Land's End, a trading-post of the Columbia Fur Company, on the Minnesota, a mile above the former residence of

Franklin Steele, where the Dahkotahs were supposed to be. The soldiers had just left the large gate of the fort, when a party of Dahkotahs, in battle array, appeared on one of the prairie hills. After some parleying they turned their backs, and being pursued, thirty-two were captured near the trading-post.

Colonel Snelling ordered the prisoners to be brought before the Ojibways, and two being pointed out as participants in the slaughter of the preceding night, they were delivered to the aggrieved party to deal with in accordance with their customs. They were led out to the plain in front of the gate of the fort, and when placed nearly without the range of the Ojibway guns, they were told to run *for* their lives. With the rapidity of deer they bounded away, but the Ojibway bullet flew faster, and after a few steps, they fell gasping on the ground, and were soon lifeless. Then the savage nature displayed itself in all its hideousness. Women and children danced for joy, and placing their fingers in the bullet holes, from which the blood oozed, they licked them with delight. The men tore the scalps from the dead, and seemed to luxuriate in the privilege of plunging their knives through the corpses. After the execution, the Ojibways returned to the fort, and were met by the Colonel. He had prevented all over whom his authority extended from witnessing the scene, and had done his best to confine the excitement to the Indians. The same day a deputation of Dahkotah warriors received audience, regretting the violence that had been done by their young men, and agreeing to deliver up the ringleaders.

At the time appointed, a son of Flat Mouth, with those of the Ojibwa party that were not wounded, escorted by United States troops, marched forth to meet the Dahkotah deputation, on the prairie just beyond the old residence of the Indian agent. With much solemnity two more of the guilty were handed over to the assaulted. One was fearless, and with firmness stripped himself of his clothing and ornaments, and distributed them. The other could not face death with composure. He was not d for a hideous hare-lip, and had a bad reputation among his fellows. In the spirit of a coward he prayed for life, to the mortification of his tribe. The same opportunity was presented to them as to the first, of running for their lives. At the first fire the coward fell a corpse; but his brave companion, though wounded, ran on, and had nearly reached the goal of safety, when a second bullet killed him. The body of the coward now became a common object of loathing for both Dahkotahs and Ojibways.

Colonel Snelling told the Ojibways that the bodies must be removed, and then they took the scalped Dahkotahs, and dragging them by the heels, threw them off the bluff into the river, a hundred and fifty feet beneath. The dreadful scene was now over; and a detachment of troops was sent with the old chief Flat Mouth, to escort him out of the reach of Dahkotah vengeance.

An eyewitness wrote: "After this catastrophe, all the Dahkotahs quitted the vicinity of Fort Snelling, and did not return to it for some months. It was said that they formed a conspiracy to demand a council, and kill the Indian Agent and the commanding officer. If this was a fact, they had no opportunity, or wanted the spirit, to execute their purpose.

"The Flat Mouth's band lingered in the fort till their wounded comrade died. He was sensible of his condition, and bore his pains with great fortitude. When he felt his end approach, he desired that his horse might be gaily caparisoned, and brought to the hospital window, so that he might touch the animal. He then took from his medicine bag a large cake of maple sugar, and held it forth. It may seem strange, but it is true, that the beast ate it from his hand. His features were radiant with delight as he fell back on the pillow exhausted. His horse had eaten the sugar, he said, and he was sure of a favorable reception and comfortable quarters in the other world. Half an hour after, he breathed his last. We tried to discover the details of his superstition, but could not succeed. It is a subject on which Indians unwillingly discourse."

In the fall of 1826, all the troops at Prairie du Chien had been removed to Fort Snelling, the commander taking with him two Winnebagoes that had been confined in Fort Crawford. After the soldiers left the Prairie, the Indians in the vicinity were quite insolent.

In June, 1827, two keel-boats passed Prairie du Chien on the way to Fort Snelling with provisions. When they reached Wapashaw village, on the site of the present town of Winona, the crew were ordered to come ashore by the Dahkotahs. Complying, they found themselves surrounded by Indians with hostile intentions. The boatmen had no fire-arms, but assuming a bold mien and a defiant voice, the captain of the keel-boats ordered the savages to leave the decks; which was successful. The boats pushed on, and at Red Wing and Kaposia the Indians showed that they were not friendly, though they did not molest the boats. Before they started on their return from Fort Snelling, the men on board, amounting to thirty-two, were all provided with muskets and a barrel of ball cartridges.

When the descending keel-boats passed Wapashaw, the Dahkotas were engaged in the war dance, and menaced them, but made no attack. Below this point one of the boats moved in advance of the other, and when near the mouth of the Bad Axe, the half-breeds on board descried hostile Indians on the banks. As the channel neared the shore, the sixteen men on the first boat were greeted with the war whoop and a volley of rifle balls from the excited Winnebagoes, killing two of the crew. Rushing into their canoes, the Indians made the attempt to board the boat, and two were successful. One of these stationed himself at the bow of the boat, and fired with killing effect on the men below deck. An old soldier of the last war with Great Britain, called Saucy Jack, at last despatched him, and began to rally the fainting spirits on board. During the fight the boat had stuck on a sand-bar. With four companions, amid a shower of balls from the savages, he plunged into the water and pushed off the boat, and thus moved out of reach of the galling shots of the Winnebagoes. As they floated down the river during the night, they heard a wail in a canoe behind them, the voice of a father mourning the death of the son who had scaled the deck, and was now a corpse in possession of the white men. The rear boat passed the Bad Axe river late in the night, and escaped an attack.

The first keel-boat arrived at Prairie du Chein, with two of their crew dead, four wounded, and the Indian that had been killed on the boat. The two dead men had been residents of the Prairie, and now the panic was increased. On the morning of the twenty-eighth of June the second keel-boat appeared, and among her passengers was Joseph Snelling, the talented son of the colonel, who wrote a story of deep interest, based on the facts narrated.

At a meeting of the citizens it was resolved to repair old Fort Crawford, and Thomas McNair was appointed captain. Dirt was thrown around the bottom logs of the fortification to prevent its being fired, and young Snelling was put in command of one of the block-houses. On the next day a voyageur named Loyer, and the well-known trader Duncan Graham, started through the interior, west of the Mississippi, with intelligence of the murders, to Fort Snelling. Intelligence of this attack was received at the fort, on the evening of the ninth of July, and Col. Snelling started in keel boats with four companies to Fort Crawford, and on the seventeenth four more companies left under Major Fowle. After an absence of six weeks, the soldiers, without firing a gun at the enemy, returned.

A few weeks after the attack upon the keel boats General Gaines inspected the Fort, and, subsequently in a communication to the War Department wrote as follows;

"The main points of defence against an enemy appear to have been in some respects sacrificed, in the effort to secure the comfort and convenience of troops in peace. These are important considerations, but on an exposed frontier the primary object ought to be security against the attack of an enemy.

"The buildings are too large, too numerous, and extending over a space entirely too great, enclosing a large parade, five times greater than is at all desireable in that climate. The buildings for the most part seem well constructed, of good stone and other materials, and they contain every desirable convenience, comfort and security as barracks and store houses.

"The work may be rendered very strong and adapted to a garrison of two hundred men by removing one-half the buildings, and with the materials of which they are constructed, building a tower sufficiently high to command the hill between the Mississippi and St. Peter's [Minnesota], and by a block house on the extreme point, or brow of the cliff, near the commandant's quarters, to secure most effectually the banks of the river, and the boats at the landing.

"Much credit is due to Colonel Snelling, his officers and men, for their immense labors and excellent workmanship exhibited in the construction of these barracks and store houses, but this has been effected too much at the expense of the discipline of the regiment."

From reports made from 1823 to 1826, the health of the troops was good. In the year ending September thirty, 1823, there were but two deaths; in 1824 only six, and in 1825 but seven.

In 1823 there were three desertions, in 1824 twenty-two, and in 1825 twenty-nine. Most of the deserters were fresh recruits and natives of America, Ten of the deserters were foreigners, and five of these were born in Ireland. In 1826 there were eight companies numbering two hundred and fourteen soldiers quartered in the Fort.

During the fall of 1827 the Fifth Regiment was relieved by a part of the First, and the next year Colonel Snelling proceeded to Washington on business, where he died with inflammation of the brain. Major General Macomb announcing his death in an order, wrote:

"Colonel Snelling joined the army in early youth. In the battle of Tippecanoe, he was distinguished for gallantry and good conduct. Subsequently and during the whole late war with Great Britain, from the battle of Brownstown to the termination of the contest, he was actively employed in the field, with credit to himself, and honor to his country."

CHAPTER XVII.

OCCURRENCES IN THE VICINITY OF FORT SNELLING, CONTINUED.

Arrival of J. N. Nicollet—Marriage of James Wells—Nicollet's letter from Falls of St. Anthony—Perils of Martin McLeod—Chippeway treachery—Sioux Revenge—Rum River and Stillwater battles—Grog shops near the Fort.

On the second of July 1836, the steamboat Saint Peter landed supplies, and among its passengers was the distinguished French astronomer, Jean N. Nicollet (Nicolay). Major Taliaferro on the twelfth of July, wrote: "Mr. Nicollet, on a visit to the post for scientific research, and at present in my family, has shown me the late work of Henry R. Schoolcraft on the discovery of the source of the Mississippi; which claim is ridiculous in the extreme." On the twenty-seventh, Nicollet ascended the Mississippi on a tour of observation.

James Wells, a trader, who afterwards was a member of the legislature, at the house of Oliver Cratte, near the fort, was married on the twelfth of September, by Agent Taliaferro, to Jane, a daughter of Duncan Graham. Wells was killed in 1862, by the Sioux, at the time of the massacre in the Minnesota Valley.

Nicollet in September returned from his trip to Leech Lake, and on the twenty-seventh wrote the following to Major Taliaferro the Indian Agent at the fort, which is supposed to be the earliest letter extant written from the site of the city of Minneapolis. As the principal hotel and one of the finest avenues of that city bears his name it is worthy of preservation. He spelled his name sometimes Nicoley, and the pronunciation in English, would be Nicolay, the same as if written Nicollet in French. The letter shows that he had not mastered the English language: "St. Anthony's Falls, 27th September, 1836.

Dear Friend:—I arrived last evening about dark; all well, nothing lost, nothing broken, happy and a very successful journey. But I done exhausted, and nothing can relieve me, but the pleasure of meeting you again under your hospitable roof, and to see all the friends of the garrison who have been so kind to me.

"This letter is more particularly to give you a very extraordinary tide. Flat Mouth, the chief of Leech Lake and suite, ten in number are with me. The day before yesterday I met them again at Swan river where they detained me one day. I had to hear a new harangue and gave answer. All terminated by their own resolution that they ought to give you the hand, as well as to the Guinas of the Fort (Colonel Davenport.) I thought it my duty to acquaint you with it beforehand. Peace or war are at stake of the visit they pay you. Please give them a good welcome until I have reported to you and Colonel Davenport all that has taken place during my stay among the Pillagers. But be assured I have not trespassed and that I have behaved as would have done a good citizen of the U. S. As to Schoolcraft's statement alluding to you, you will have full and complete satisfaction from Flat Mouth himself. In haste, your friend, J. N. Nicoley."

EVENTS OF A. D. 1837.

On the seventeenth of March, 1837, there arrived Martin McLeod, who became a prominent citizen of Minnesota, and the legislature has given his name to a county.

He left the Red River country on snow shoes, with two companions, one a Polander and the other an Irishman named Hays, and Pierre Bottineau as interpreter. Being lost in a violent snow storm the Pole and Irishman perished. He and his guide, Bottineau, lived for a time on the flesh of one of their dogs. After being twenty-six days without seeing any one, the survivors reached the trading post of Joseph R. Brown, at Lake Traverse, and from thence they came to the fort.

EVENTS OF A. D. 1838.

In the month of April, eleven Sioux were slain in a dastardly manner, by a party of Ojibways, under the noted and elder Hole-in-the-Day. The Chippeways feigned the warmest friendship, and at dark lay down in the tents by the side of the Sioux, and in the night silently arose and killed them. The occurrence took place at the Chippeway River, about thirty miles from Lac qui Parle, and the next day the Rev. G. H. Pond, the Indian missionary, accompanied by a Sioux, went out and buried the mutilated and scalpless bodies.

On the second of August old Hole-in-the-Day, and some Ojibways, came to the fort. They stopped first at the cabin of Peter Quinn, whose wife was a half-breed Chippeway, about a mile from the fort.

The missionary, Samuel W. Pond, told the agent that the Sioux, of Lake Calhoun were aroused, and on their way to attack the Chippeways. The agent quieted them for a time, but two of the relatives of those slain at Lac qui Parle in April, hid themselves near Quinn's house, and as Hole-in-the-Day and his associates were passing, they fired and killed one Chippeway and wounded another. Obequette, a Chippeway from Red Lake, succeded, however, in shooting a Sioux while he was in the act of scalping his comrade. The Chippeways were brought within the fort as soon as possible, and at nine o'clock a Sioux was confined in the guard-house as a hostage.

Notwithstanding the murdered Chippeway had been buried in the graveyard of the fort for safety, an attempt was made on the part of some of the Sioux, to dig it up. On the evening of the sixth, Major Plympton sent the Chippeways across the river to the east side, and ordered them to go home as soon as possible.

EVENTS OF A. D. 1839.

On the twentieth day of June the elder Hole-in-the-Day arrived from the Upper Mississippi with several hundred Chippeways. Upon their return homeward the Mississippi and Mille Lacs band encamped the first night at the Falls of Saint Anthony, and some of the Sioux visited them and smoked the pipe of peace.

On the second of July, about sunrise, a son-in-law of the chief of the Sioux band, at Lake Calhoun, named Meekaw or Badger, was killed and scalped by two Chippeways of the Pillager band, relatives of him who lost his life near Patrick Quinn's the year before. The excitement was intense among the Sioux, and immediately war parties started in pursuit. Hole-in-the-Day's band was not sought, but the Mille Lacs and Saint Croix Chippeways. The Lake Calhoun Sioux, with those from the villages on the Minnesota, assembled at the Falls of Saint Anthony, and on the morning of the fourth of July, came up with the Mille Lacs Chippeways on Rum River, before sunrise. Not long after the war whoop was raised and the Sioux attacked, killing and wounding ninety.

The Kaposia band of Sioux pursued the Saint Croix Chippeways, and on the third of July found them in the Penitentiary ravine at Stillwater, under the influence of whisky. Aitkin, the old trader, was with them. The sight of the Sioux tended to make them sober, but in the fight twenty-one were killed and twenty-nine were wounded.

Whisky, during the year 1839, was freely introduced, in the face of the law prohibiting it. The first boat of the season, the Ariel, came to the fort on the fourteenth of April, and brought twenty barrels of whisky for Joseph R. Brown, and on the twenty-first of May, the Glaucus brought six barrels of liquor for David Faribault. On the thirtieth of June, some soldiers went to Joseph R. Brown's groggery on the opposite side of the Mississippi, and that night forty-seven were in the guard-house for drunkenness. The demoralization then existing, led to a letter by Surgeon Emerson on duty at the fort, to the Surgeon General of the United States army, in which he writes:

"The whisky is brought here by citizens who are pouring in upon us and settling themselves on the opposite shore of the Mississippi river, in defiance of our worthy commanding officer, Major J. Plympton, whose authority they set at naught. At this moment there is a citizen named Brown, once a soldier in the Fifth Infantry, who was discharged at this post, while Colonel Snelling commanded, and who has been since employed by the American Fur Company, actually building on the land marked out by the land officers as the reserve, and within gunshot distance of the fort, a very expensive whisky shop."

CHAPTER XVIII.

INDIAN TRIBES IN MINNESOTA AT THE TIME OF ITS ORGANIZATION.

Sioux or Dahkotah people—Meaning of words Sioux and Dahkotah—Early villages—Residence of Sioux in 1849—The Winnebagoes—The Ojibways or Chippeways.

The three Indian nations who dwelt in this region after the organization of Minnesota, were the Sioux or Dahkotahs; the Ojibways or Chippeways; and the Ho-tchun-graws or Winnebagoes.

SIOUX OR DAHKOTAHS.

They are an entirely different group from the Algonquin and Iroquois. who were found by the early settlers of the Atlantic States, on the banks of the Connecticut, Mohawk, and Susquehanna Rivers.

When the Dahkotahs were first noticed by the European adventurers, large numbers were occupying the Mille Lacs region of country, and appropriately called by the voyageur, "People of the Lake," "Gens du Lac." And tradition asserts that here was the ancient centre of this tribe. Though we have traces of their warring and hunting on the shores of Lake Superior, there is no satisfactory evidence of their residence, east of the Mille Lacs region, as they have no name for Lake Superior.

The word Dahkotah, by which they love to be designated, signifies allied or joined together in friendly compact, and is equivalent to "E pluribus unum," the motto on the seal of the United States.

In the history of the mission at La Pointe, Wisconsin, published nearly two centuries ago, a a writer, referring to the Dahkotahs, remarks:

"For sixty leagues from the extremity of the Upper Lake, toward sunset; and, as it were in the centre of the western nations, they have all *united their force by a general league*."

The Dahkotahs in the earliest documents, and even until the present day, are called Sioux, Scioux, or Soos. The name originated with the early voyageurs. For centuries the Ojibways of Lake Superior waged war against the Dahkotahs; and, whenever they spoke of them, called them Nadowaysioux, which signifies enemies.

The French traders, to avoid exciting the attention of Indians, while conversing in their presence, were accustomed to designate them by names, which would not be recognized.

The Dahkotahs were nicknamed Sioux, a word composed of the two last syllables of the Ojibway word for foes

Under the influence of the French traders, the eastern Sioux began to wander from the Mille Lacs region. A trading post at O-ton-we-kpa-dan, or Rice Creek, above the Falls of Saint Anthony, induced some to erect their summer dwellings and plant corn there, which took the place of wild rice. Those who dwelt here were called Wa-kpa-a-ton-we-dan Those who dwell on the creek. Another division was known as the Ma-tan-ton-wan.

Less than a hundred years ago, it is said that the eastern Sioux, pressed by the Chippeways, and influenced by traders, moved seven miles above Fort Snelling on the Minnesota River.

MED-DAY-WAH-KAWN-TWAWNS.

In 1849 there were seven villages of Med-day-wah-kawn-twawn Sioux. (1) Below Lake Pepin, where the city of Winona is, was the village of Wapashaw. This band was called Kee-yu-ksa, because with them blood, relations intermarried. Bounding or Whipping Wind was the chief. (2) At the head of Lake Pepin, under a lofty bluff, was the Red Wing village, called Ghay-mni-chan Hill, wood and water. Shooter was the name of the chief. (3) Opposite, and a little below the Pig's Eye Marsh, was the Kaposia band. The word, Kapoja means light, given because these people are quick travelers. His Scarlet People, better known as Little Crow, was the chief, and is notorious as the leader in the massacre of 1862.

On the Minnesota River, on the south side,

a few miles above Fort Snelling, was Black Dog village. The inhabitants were called, Ma-ga-yu-tay-shnee. People who do not a geese, because they found it profitable to sell game at Fort Snelling. Grey Iron was the chief, also known as Pa-ma-ya-yaw, My head aches.

At Oak Grove, on the north side of the river, eight miles above the fort, was (5) Hay-ya-ta-o-ton-wan, or Inland Village, so called because they formerly lived at Lake Calkoun. Contiguous was (6) O-ya-tay-shee-ka, or Bad People. Known as Good Roads Band and (7) the largest village was Tin-ta-ton-wan, Prairie Village: Shokpay, or Six, was the chief, and is now the site of the town of Shakopee.

West of this division of the Sioux were—

WAR-PAY-KU-TAY.

The War-pay-ku-tay, or leaf shooters, who occupied the country south of the Minnesota around the sources of the Cannon and Blue Earth Rivers.

WAR-PAY-TWAWNS.

North and west of the last were the War-pay-twawns, or People of the Leaf, and their principal village was Lac qui Parle. They numbered about fifteen hundred.

SE-SEE-TWAWNS.

To the west and southwest of these bands of Sioux were the Se-see-twawns (Sissetoans), or Swamp Dwellers. This band claimed the land west of the Blue Earth to the James River, and the guardianship of the Sacred Red Pipestone Quarry. Their principal village was at Traverse, and the number of the band was estimated at thirty-eight hundred.

HO-TCHUN-GRAWS, OR WINNEBAGOES.

The Ho-tchun-graws, or Winnebagoes, belong to the Dahkotah family of aborigines. Champlain, although he never visited them, mentions them. Nicollet, who had been in his employ, visited Green Bay about the year 1635, and an early Relation mentions that he saw the Ouinipegous, a people called so, because they came from a distant sea, which some French erroneously called Puants. Another writer speaking of these people says: "This people are called 'Les Puants' not because of any bad odor peculiar to them, but because they claim to have come from the shores of a far distant lake, towards the north, whose waters are salt. They call themselves the people 'de l'eau puants,' of the putrid or bad water."

By the treaty of 1837 they were removed to Iowa, and by another treaty in October, 1846, they came to Minnesota in the spring of 1848, to the country between the Long Prairie, and Crow Wing Rivers. The agency was located on Long Prairie River, forty miles from the Mississippi, and in 1849 the tribe numbered about twenty-five hundred souls.

In February 1855, another treaty was made with them, and that spring they removed to lands on the Blue Earth River. Owing to the panic caused by the outbreak of the Sioux in 1862, Congress, by a special act, without consulting them, in 1863, removed them from their fields in Minnesota to the Missouri River, and in the words of a missionary, "they were, like the Sioux, dumped in the desert, one hundred miles above Fort Randall"

OJIBWAY OR CHIPPEWAY NATION.

The Ojibways or Leapers, when the French came to Lake Superior, had their chief settlement at Sault St. Marie, and were called by the French Saulteurs, and by the Sioux, Hah-ha-tonwan, Dwellers at the Falls or Leaping Waters.

When Du Luth erected his trading post at the western extremity of Lake Superior, they had not obtained any foothold in Minnesota, and were constantly at war with their hereditary enemies, the Nadouaysioux. By the middle of the eighteenth century, they had pushed in and occupied Sandy, Leech, Mille Lacs and other points between Lake Superior and the Mississippi, which had been dwelling places of the Sioux. In 1820 the principal villages of Ojibways in Minnesota were at Fond du Lac, Leech Lake and Sandy Lake. In 1837 they ceded most of their lands. Since then, other treaties have been made, until in the year 1881, they are confined to a few reservations, in northern Minnesota and vicinity.

CHAPTER XIX.

EARLY MISSIONS AMONG THE OJIBWAYS AND DAHKOTAHS OF MINNESOTA.

Jesuit Missions not permanent—Presbyterian Mission at Mackinaw—Visit of Rev. A. Coe and J. D. Stevens to Fort Snelling—Notice of Ayers, Hall, and Boutwell—Formation of the word Itasca—The Brothers Pond—Arrival of Dr. Williamson—Presbyterian Church at Fort Snelling—Mission at Lake Harriet—Mourning for the Dead—Church at Lac-qui parle—Father Ravoux—Mission at Lake Pokeguma—Attack by the Sioux—Chippeway attack at Pig's Eye—Death of Rev. Sherman Hall—Methodist Missions—Rev. S. W. Pond prepares a Sioux Grammar and Dictionary—Swiss Presbyterian Mission.

Bancroft the distinguished historian, catching the enthusiasm of the narratives of the early Jesuits, depicts, in language which glows, their missions to the Northwest; yet it is erroneous to suppose that the Jesuits exercised any permanent influence on the Aborigines.

Shea, a devoted member of the Roman Catholic Church, in his History of American Catholic Missions writes: "In 1680 Father Engalran was apparently alone at Green Bay, and Pierson at Mackinaw. Of the other missions neither LeClerq nor Hennepin, the Recollect writers of the West at this time, make any mention, or in any way allude to their existence." He also says that "Father Menard had projected a Sioux mission; Marquette, Allouez, Druilletes, all entertained hopes of realizing it, and had some intercourse with that nation, but none of them ever succeeded in establishing a mission."

Father Hennepin wrote: "Can it be possible, that, that pretended prodigious amount of savage converts could escape the sight of a multitude of French Canadians who travel every year? * * * * How comes it to pass that these churches so devout and so numerous, should be invisible, when I passed through so many countries and nations?"

After the American Fur Company was formed, the island of Mackinaw became the residence of the principal agent for the Northwest, Robert Stuart a Scotchman, and devoted Presbyterian.

In the month of June, 1820, the Rev. Dr. Morse, father of the distinguished inventor of the telegraph, visited and preached at Mackinaw, and in consequence of statements published by him, upon his return, a Presbyterian Missionary Society in the state of New York sent a graduate of Union College, the Rev. W. M. Ferry, father of the present United States Senator from Michigan, to explore the field. In 1823 he had established a large boarding school composed of children of various tribes, and here some were educated who became wives of men of intelligence and influence at the capital of Minnesota. After a few years, it was determined by the Mission Board to modify its plans, and in the place of a great central station, to send missionaries among the several tribes to teach and to preach.

In pursuance of this policy, the Rev. Alvan Coe, and J. D. Stevens, then a licentiate who had been engaged in the Mackinaw Mission, made a tour of exploration, and arrived on September 1, 1829, at Fort Snelling. In the journal of Major Lawrence Taliaferro, which is in possession of the Minnesota Historical Society, is the following entry: "The Rev. Mr. Coe and Stevens reported to be on their way to this post, members of the Presbyterian church looking out for suitable places to make missionary establishment for the Sioux and Chippeways, found schools, and instruct in the arts and agriculture."

The agent, although not at that time a communicant of the Church, welcomed these visitors, and afforded them every facility in visiting the Indians. On Sunday, the 6th of September, the Rev. Mr. Coe preached twice in the fort, and the next night held a prayer meeting at the quarters of the commanding officer. On the next Sunday he preached again, and on the 14th, with Mr. Stevens and a hired guide, returned to Mackinaw by way of the St. Croix river. During this visit the agent offered for a Presbyterian mission the mill which then stood on the site of Minneapolis, and had been erected by the government, as well as the farm at Lake Calhoun, which was begun to teach the Sioux agriculture.

CHIPPEWAY MISSIONS.

In 1830, F. Ayer, one of the teachers at Mackinaw, made an exploration as far as La Pointe, and returned.

Upon the 30th day of August, 1831, a Mackinaw boat about forty feet long arrived at La Pointe, bringing from Mackinaw the principal trader, Mr. Warren, Rev. Sherman Hall and wife, and Mr. Frederick Ayer, a catechist and teacher.

Mrs. Hall attracted great attention, as she was the first white woman who had visited that region. Sherman Hall was born on April 30, 1801, at Wethersfield, Vermont, and in 1828 graduated at Dartmouth College, and completed his theological studies at Andover, Massachusetts, a few weeks before he journeyed to the Indian country.

His classmate at Dartmouth and Andover, the Rev W. T. Boutwell still living near Stillwater, became his yoke-fellow, but remained for a time at Mackinaw, which they reached about the middle of July. In June, 1832, Henry R. Schoolcraft, the head of an exploring expedition, invited Mr. Boutwell to accompany him to the sources of the Mississippi.

When the expedition reached Lac la Biche or Elk Lake, on July 13, 1832, Mr. Schoolcraft, who was not a Latin scholar, asked the Latin word for truth, and was told "veritas." He then wanted the word which signified head, and was told "caput." To the astonishment of many, Schoolcraft struck off the first sylable, of the word ver-i-tas and the last sylable of ca-put, and thus coined the word Itasca, which he gave to the lake, and which some modern writers, with all gravity, tell us was the name of a maiden who once dwelt on its banks. Upon Mr. Boutwell's return from this expedition he was at first associated with Mr. Hall in the mission at La Pointe.

In 1833 the mission band which had centered at La Pointe diffused their influence. In October Rev. Mr. Boutwell went to Leech Lake, Mr. Ayer opened a school at Yellow Lake, Wisconsin, and Mr. E. F. Ely, now in California, became a teacher at Aitkin's trading post at Sandy Lake.

SIOUX MISSIONARIES.

Mr. Boutwell, of Leech Lake Station, on the sixth of May, 1834, happened to be on a visit to Fort Snelling. While there a steamboat arrived, and among the passengers were two young men, brothers, natives of Washington, Connecticut, Samuel W. and Gideon H. Pond, who had come, constrained by the love of Christ, and without conferring with flesh and blood, to try to improve the Sioux.

Samuel, the older brother, the year before, had talked with a liquor seller in Galena, Illinois, who had come from the Red River country, and the desire was awakened to help the Sioux; and he wrote to his brother to go with him.

The Rev. Samuel W. Pond still lives at Shakopee, in the old mission house, the first building of sawed lumber erected in the valley of the Minnesota, above Fort Snelling.

MISSIONS AMONG THE SIOUX A. D. 1835.

About this period, a native of South Carolina, a graduate of Jefferson College, Pennsylvania, the Rev. T. S. Williamson, M. D., who previous to his ordination had been a respectable physician in Ohio, was appointed by the American Board of Foreign Missions to visit the Dahkotahs with the view of ascertaining what could be done to introduce Christian instruction. Having made inquiries at Prairie du Chien and Fort Snelling, he reported the field was favorable.

The Presbyterian and Congregational Churches, through their joint Missionary Society, appointed the following persons to labor in Minnesota: Rev. Thomas S. Williamson, M. D., missionary and physician; Rev. J. D. Stevens, missionary; Alexander Huggins, farmer; and their wives; Miss Sarah Poage, and Lucy Stevens, teachers; who were prevented during the year 1834, by the state of navigation, from entering upon their work.

During the winter of 1834-35, a pious officer of the army exercised a good influence on his fellow officers and soldiers under his command. In the absence of a chaplain of ordained minister, he, like General Havelock, of the British army in India, was accustomed not only to drill the soldiers, but to meet them in his own quarters, and reason with them "of righteousness, temperance, and judgment to come."

In the month of May, 1835, Dr. Williamson and mission band arrived at Fort Snelling, and were hospitably received by the officers of the garrison, the Indian Agent, and Mr. Sibley, Agent of the Company at Mendota, who had been in the country a few months.

On the twenty-seventh of this month the Rev. Dr. Williamson united in marriage at the Fort Lieutenant Edward A. Ogden to Eliza Edna, the daughter of Captain G. A. Loomis, the first marriage service in which a clergyman officiated in the present State of Minnesota.

On the eleventh of June a meeting was held at the Fort to organize a Presbyterian Church, sixteen persons who had been communicants, and six who made a profession of faith, one of whom was Lieutenant Ogden, were enrolled as members.

Four elders were elected, among whom were Capt. Gustavus Loomis and Samuel W. Pond. The next day a lecture preparatory to administering the communion, was delivered, and on Sunday, the 14th, the first organized church in the Valley of the Upper Mississippi assembled for the first time in one of the Company rooms of the Fort. The services in the morning were conducted by Dr. Williamson. The afternoon service commenced at 2 o'clock. The sermon of Mr. Stevens was upon a most appropriate text, 1st Peter, ii:25; "For ye were as sheep going astray, but are now returned unto the Shepherd and Bishop of your souls." After the discourse, the sacrament of the Lord's supper was administered.

At a meeting of the Session on the thirty-first of July, Rev. J. D. Stevens, missionary, was invited to preach to the church, "so long as the duties of his mission will permit, and also to preside at all the meetings of the Session." Captain Gustavus Loomis was elected Stated Clerk of the Session, and they resolved to observe the monthly concert of prayer on the first Monday of each month, for the conversion of the world.

Two points were selected by the missionaries as proper spheres of labor. Mr. Stevens and family proceeded to Lake Harriet, and Dr. Williamson and family, in June, proceeded to Lac qui Parle.

As there had never been a chaplain at Fort Snelling, the Rev. J. D. Stevens, the missionary at Lake Harriet, preached on Sundays to the Presbyterian church, there, recently organized. Writing on January twenty-seventh, 1836, he says, in relation to his field of labor:

"Yesterday a portion of this band of Indians, who had been some time absent from this village, returned. One of the number (a woman) was informed that a brother of hers had died during her absence. He was not at this village, but with another band, and the information had just reached here. In the evening they set up a most piteous crying, or rather wailing, which continued, with some little cessations, during the night. The sister of the deceased brother would repeat, times without number, words which may be thus translated into English: 'Come, my brother, I shall see you no more for ever.' The night was extremely cold, the thermometer standing from ten to twenty below zero. About sunrise, next morning, preparation was made for performing the ceremony of cutting their flesh, in order to give relief to their grief of mind. The snow was removed from the frozen ground over about as large a space as would be required to place a small Indian lodge or wigwam. In the centre a very small fire was kindled up, not to give warmth, apparently, but to cause a smoke. The sister of the deceased, who was the chief mourner, came out of her lodge followed by three other women, who repaired to the place prepared. They were all barefooted, and nearly naked. Here they set up a most bitter lamentation and crying, mingling their wailings with the words before mentioned. The principal mourner commenced gashing or cutting her ankles and legs up to the knees with a sharp stone, until her legs were covered with gore and flowing blood; then in like manner her arms, shoulders, and breast. The others cut themselves in the same way, but not so severely. On this poor infatuated woman I presume there were more than a hundred long deep gashes in the flesh. I saw the operation, and the blood instantly followed the instrument, and flowed down upon the flesh. She appeared frantic with grief. Through the pain of her wounds, the loss of blood, exhaustion of strength by fasting, loud and long-continued and bitter groans, or the extreme cold upon her almost naked and lacerated body, she soon sunk upon the frozen ground, shaking as with a violent fit of the ague, and writhing in apparent agony. 'Surely,' I exclaimed, as I beheld the bloody scene, 'the tender mercies of the heathen are cruelty!'

"The little church at the fort begins to manifest something of a missionary spirit Their contributions are considerable for so small a number. I hope they will not only be willing to contribute liberally of their substance, but will give themselves, at least some of them, to the missionary work.

"The surgeon of the military post, Dr. Jarvis, has been very assiduous in his attentions to us in our sickness, and has very generously made a donation to our board of twenty-five dollars, being the amount of his medical services in our family.

"On the nineteenth instant we commenced a school with six full Indian children, at least so in all their habits, dress, etc.; not one could speak a word of any language but Sioux. The school has since increased to the number of twenty-five. I am now collecting and arranging words for a dictionary. Mr. Pond is assiduously employed in preparing a small spelling-book, which we may forward next mail for printing.

On the fifteenth of September, 1836, a Presbyterian church was organized at Lac-qui-Parle, a branch of that in and near Fort Snelling, and Joseph Renville, a mixed blood of great influence, became a communicant. He had been trained in Canada by a Roman Catholic priest, but claimed the right of private judgment. Mr. Renville's wife was the first pure Dahkotah of whom we have any record that ever joined the Church of Christ. This church has never become extinct, although its members have been necessarily nomadic. After the treaty of Traverse des Sioux, it was removed to Hazlewood. Driven from thence by the outbreak of 1862, it has became the parent of other churches, in the valley of the upper Missouri, over one of which John Renville, a descendant of the elder at Lac-qui-Parle, is the pastor.

ROMAN CATHOLIC MISSION ATTEMPTED.

Father Ravoux, recently from France, a sincere and earnest priest of the Church of Rome, came to Mendota in the autumn of 1841, and after a brief sojourn with the Rev. L. Galtier, who had erected Saint Paul's chapel, which has given the name of Saint Paul to the capital of Minnesota, he ascended the Minnesota River, and visited Lac-qui-Parle.

Bishop Loras, of Dubuque, wrote the next year of his visit as follows: "Our young missionary, M. Ravoux, passed the winter on the banks of Lac-qui-Parle, without any other support than Providence, without any other means of conversion than a burning zeal, he has wrought in the space of six months, a happy revolution among the Sioux. From the time of his arrival he has been occupied night and day in the study of their language. * * * * * When he instructs the savages, he speaks to them with so much fire whilst showing them a large copper crucifix which he carries on his breast, that he makes the strongest impression upon them."

The impression, however was evanescent, and he soon retired from the field, and no more efforts were made in this direction by the Church of Rome. This young Mr. Ravoux is now the highly respected vicar of the Roman Catholic diocese of Minnesota, and justly esteemed for his simplicity and unobtrusiveness.

CHIPPEWAY MISSIONS AT POKEGUMA.

Pokeguma is one of the "Mille Lacs," or thousand beautiful lakes for which Minnesota is remarkable. It is about four or five miles in extent, and a mile or more in width.

This lake is situated on Snake River, about twenty miles above the junction of that stream with the St. Croix.

In the year 1836, missionaries came to reside among the Ojibways and Pokeguma, to promote their temporal and spiritual welfare. Their mission house was built on the east side of the lake; but the Indian village was on an island not far from the shore.

In a letter written in 1837, we find the following: "The young women and girls now make, mend, wash, and iron after our manner. The men have learned to build log houses, drive team, plough, hoe, and handle an American axe with some skill in cutting large trees, the size of which, two years ago, would have afforded them a sufficient reason why they should not meddle with them."

In May, 1841, Jeremiah Russell, who was Indian farmer, sent two Chippeways, accompanied by Elam Greeley, of Stillwater, to the Falls of Saint Croix for supplies. On Saturday, the fifteenth of the month they arrived there, and the next day a steamboat came up with the goods. The captain said a war party of Sioux, headed by Little Crow, was advancing, and the two Chippeways prepared to go back and were their friends.

They had hardly left the Falls, on their return, before they saw a party of Dahkotahs. The sentinel of the enemy had not noticed the approach of the young men. In the twinkling of an eye, these two young Ojibways raised their guns, fired, and killed two of Little Crow's sons. The discharge of the guns revealed to a sentinel, that an enemy was near, and as the Ojibways were retreating, he fired, and mortally wounded one of the two.

According to custom, the corpses of the chief's sons were dressed, and then set up with their faces towards the country of their ancient enemies. The wounded Ojibway was horribly mangled by the infuriated party, and his limbs strewn about in every direction. His scalped head was placed in a kettle, and suspended in front of the two Dahkotah corpses.

Little Crow, disheartened by the loss of his two boys, returned with his party to Kaposia. But other parties were in the field.

It was not till Friday, the twenty-first of May, that the death of one of the young Ojibways sent by Mr. Russell, to the Falls of Saint Croix, was known at Pokeguma.

Mr. Russell on the next Sunday, accompanied by Captain William Holcomb and a half-breed, went to the mission station to attend a religious service, and while crossing the lake in returning, the half-breed said that it was rumored that the Sioux were approaching. On Monday, the twenty-fourth, three young men left in a canoe to go to the west shore of the lake, and from thence to Mille Lacs, to give intelligence to the Ojibways there, of the skirmish that had already occurred. They took with them two Indian girls, about twelve years of age, who were pupils of the mission school, for the purpose of bringing the canoe back to the island. Just as the three were landing, twenty or thirty Dahkotah warriors, with a war whoop emerged from their concealment behind the trees, and fired into the canoe. The young men instantly sprang into the water, which was shallow, returned the fire, and ran into the woods, escaping without material injury.

The little girls, in their fright, waded into the lake; but were pursued. Their parents upon the island, heard the death cries of their children. Some of the Indians around the mission-house jumped into their canoes and gained the island. Others went into some fortified log huts. The attack upon the canoe, it was afterwards learned, was premature. The party upon that side of the lake were ordered not to fire, until the party stationed in the woods near the mission began.

There were in all one hundred and eleven Dahkotah warriors, and all the fight was in the vicinity of the mission-house, and the Ojibways mostly engaged in it were those who had been under religious instruction. The rest were upon the island.

The fathers of the murdered girls, burning for revenge, left the island in a canoe, and drawing it up on the shore, hid behind it, and fired upon the Dahkotahs and killed one. The Dahkotahs advancing upon them, they were obliged to escape. The canoe was now launched. One lay on his back in the bottom: the other plunged into the water, and, holding the canoe with one hand, and swimming with the other, he towed his friend out of danger. The Dahkotahs, infuriated at their escape, fired volley after volley at the swimmer, but he escaped the balls by putting his head under water whenever he saw them take aim, and waiting till he heard the discharge, he would then look up and breathe.

After a fight of two hours, the Dahkotahs retreated, with a loss of two men. At the request of the parents, Mr. E. F. Ely, from whose notes the writer has obtained these facts, being at that time a teacher at the mission, went across the lake, with two of his friends, to gather the remains of his murdered pupils. He found the corpses on the shore. The heads cut off and scalped, with a tomahawk buried in the brains of each, were set up in the sand near the bodies. The bodies were pierced in the breast, and the right arm of one was taken away. Removing the tomahawks, the bodies were brought back to the island, and in the afternoon were buried in accordance with the simple but solemn rites of the Church of Christ, by members of the mission.

The sequel to this story is soon told. The Indians of Pokeguma, after the fight, deserted their village, and went to reside with their countrymen near Lake Superior.

In July of the following year, 1842, a war party was formed at Fond du Lac, about forty in number, and proceeded towards the Dahkotah country. Sneaking, as none but Indians can, they arrived unnoticed at the little settlement below Saint Paul, commonly called "Pig's Eye," which is opposite to what was Kaposia, or Little Crow's village. Finding an Indian woman at work in the garden of her husband, a Canadian, by the name of Gamelle, they killed her; also another woman, with her infant, whose head was cut off. The Dahkotahs, on the opposite side, were mostly intoxicated; and, flying across in their canoes but half prepared, they were worsted in the encounter. They lost thirteen warriors, and one of their number, known as the Dancer, the Ojibways are said to have skinned.

Soon after this the Chippeway missions of the St. Croix Valley were abandoned.

In a little while Rev. Mr. Boutwell removed to the vicinity of Stillwater, and the missionaries. Ayer and Spencer, went to Red Lake and other points in Minnesota.

In 1853 the Rev. Sherman Hall left the Indians and became pastor of a Congregational church at Sauk Rapids, where he recently died.

METHODIST MISSIONS.

In 1837 the Rev. A. Brunson commenced a Methodist mission at Kaposia, about four miles below, and opposite Saint Paul. It was afterwards removed across the river to Red Rock. He was assisted by the Rev. Thomas W. Pope, and the latter was succeeded by the Rev. J. Holton.

The Rev. Mr. Spates and others also labored for a brief period among the Ojibways.

PRESBYTERIAN MISSIONS CONTINUED.

At the stations the Dahkotah language was diligently studied. Rev. S. W. Pond had prepared a dictionary of three thousand words, and also a small grammar. The Rev. S. R. Riggs, who joined the mission in 1837, in a letter dated February 24, 1841, writes: "Last summer, after returning from Fort Snelling, I spent five weeks in copying again the Sioux vocabulary which we had collected and arranged at this station. It contained then about 5500 words, not including the various forms of the verbs. Since that time, the words collected by Dr. Williamson and myself, have, I presume, increased the number to six thousand. * * * * * In this connection, I may mention that during the winter of 1839–40, Mrs. Riggs, with some assistance, wrote an English and Sioux vocabulary containing about three thousand words. One of Mr. Renville's sons and three of his daughters are engaged in copying. In committing the grammatical principles of the language to writing, we have done something at this station, but more has been done by Mr. S. W. Pond."

Steadily the number of Indian missionaries increased, and in 1851, before the lands of the Dahkotahs west of the Mississippi were ceded to the whites, they were disposed as follows by the Dahkotah Presbytery.

Lac-qui-parle, Rev. S. R. Riggs, Rev. M. N. Adams, *Missionaries*, Jonas Pettijohn. Mrs. Fanny Pettijohn, Mrs. Mary Ann Riggs, Mrs. Mary A. M. Adams, Miss Sarah Rankin, *Assistants*.

Traverse des Sioux, Rev. Robert Hopkins, *Missionary;* Mrs. Agnes Hopkins, Alexander G. Huggins, Mrs. Lydia P. Huggins, *Assistants*.

Shakpay, or *Shokpay*, Rev. Samuel W. Pond, *Missionary;* Mrs. Sarah P. Pond, *Assistant*.

Oak Grove, Rev. Gideon H. Pond and wife.

Kaposia, Rev. Thomas Williamson, M. D., *Missionary and Physician;* Mrs. Margaret P. Williamson, Miss Jane S. Williamson, *Assistants*.

Red Wing, Rev. John F. Aiton, Rev. Joseph W. Hancock, *Missionaries;* Mrs. Nancy H. Aiton, Mrs. Hancock, *Assistants*.

The Rev. Daniel Gavin, the Swiss Presbyterian Missionary, spent the winter of 1839 in Lac-qui-Parle and was afterwards married to a niece of the Rev. J. D. Stevens, of the Lake Harriet Mission. Mr. Stevens became the farmer and teacher of the Wapashaw band, and the first white man who lived where the city of Winona has been built. Another missionary from Switzerland, the Rev. Mr. Denton, married a Miss Skinner, formerly of the Mackinaw mission. During a portion of the year 1839 these Swiss missionaries lived with the American missionaries at camp Cold Water near Fort Snelling, but their chief field of labor was at Red Wing.

CHAPTER XX.

TREAD OF PIONEERS IN THE SAINT CROIX VALLEY AND ELSEWHERE.

Origin of the name Saint Croix—Du Luth, first Explorer—French Post on the St. Croix—Pitt, an early pioneer—Early settlers at Saint Croix Falls—First women there—Marine Settlement—Joseph R. Brown's town site—Saint Croix County organized—Proprietors of Stillwater—A dead Negro woman—Pig's Eye, origin of name—Rise of Saint Paul—Dr. Williamson secures first school teacher for Saint Paul—Description of first school room—Saint Croix County re-organized—Rev. W. T. Boutwell, pioneer clergyman.

The Saint Croix river, according to Le Sueur, named after a Frenchman who was drowned at its mouth, was one of the earliest throughfares from Lake Superior to the Mississippi. The first white man who directed canoes upon its waters was Du Luth, who had in 1679 explored Minnesota. He thus describes his tour in a letter, first published by Harrisse: "In June, 1680, not being satisfied, with having made my discovery by land, I took two canoes, with an Indian who was my interpreter, and four Frenchmen, to seek means to make it by water. With this view I entered a river which empties eight leagues from the extremity of Lake Superior, on the south side, where, after having cut some trees and broken about a hundred beaver dams, I reached the upper waters of the said river, and then I made a portage of half a league to reach a lake, the outlet which fell into a very fine river, which took me down into the Mississippi. There I learned from eight cabins of Nadouecioux that the Rev. Father Louis Hennepin, Recollect, now at the convent of Saint Germain, with two other Frenchmen had been robbed, and carried off as slaves for more than three hundred leagues by the Nadouecioux themselves."

He then relates how he left two Frenchmen with his goods, and went with his interpreter and two Frenchmen in a canoe down the Mississippi, and after two days and two nights, found Hennepin, Accault and Augelle. He told Hennepin that he must return with him through the country of the Fox tribe, and writes: "I preferred to retrace my steps, manifesting to them [the Sioux] the just indignation I felt against them, rather than to remain after the violence they had done to the Rev. Father and the other two Frenchmen with him, whom I put in my canoes and brought them to Michilimackinack."

After this, the Saint Croix river became a channel for commerce, and Bellin writes, that before 1755, the French had erected a fort forty leagues from its mouth and twenty from Lake Superior.

The pine forests between the Saint Croix and Minnesota had been for several years a temptation to energetic men. As early as November, 1836, a Mr. Pitt went with a boat and a party of men to the Falls of Saint Croix to cut pine timber, with the consent of the Chippeways but the dissent of the United States authorities.

In 1837 while the treaty was being made by Commissioners Dodge and Smith at Fort Snelling, on one Sunday Franklin Steele, Dr. Fitch, Jeremiah Russell, and a Mr. Maginnis left Fort Snelling for the Falls of Saint Croix in a birch bark canoe paddled by eight men, and reached that point about noon on Monday and commenced a log cabin. Steele and Maginnis remained here, while the others, dividing into two parties, one under Fitch, and the other under Russell, searched for pine land. The first stopped at Sun Rise, while Russel went on to the Snake River. About the same time Robbinet and Jesse B. Taylor came to the Falls in the interest of B. F. Baker who had a stone trading house near Fort Snelling, since destroyed by fire. On the fifteenth of July, 1838, the Palmyra, Capt. Holland, arrived at the Fort, with the official notice of the ratification of the treaties ceding the lands between the Saint Croix and Mississippi.

She had on board C. A. Tuttle, L. W. Stratton and others, with the machinery for the projected mills of the Northwest Lumber Company at the Falls of Saint Croix, and reached that point on the seventeenth, the first steamboat to disturb the waters above Lake Saint Croix. The steamer Gypsy came to the fort on the twenty-first of

October, with goods for the Chippeways, and was chartered for four hundred and fifty dollars, to carry them up to the Falls of Saint Croix. In passing through the lake, the boat grounded near a projected town called Stambaughville, after S. C. Stambaugh, the sutler at the fort. On the afternoon of the 26th, the goods were landed, as stipulated.

The agent of the Improvement Company at the falls was Washington Libbey, who left in the fall of 1838, and was succeeded by Jeremiah Russell, Stratton acting as millwright in place of Calvin Tuttle. On the twelfth of December, Russell and Stratton walked down the river, cut the first tree and built a cabin at Marine, and sold their claim.

The first women at the Falls of Saint Croix were a Mrs. Orr, Mrs. Sackett, and the daughter of a Mr. Young. During the winter of 1838 9, Jeremiah Russell married a daughter of a respectable and gentlemanly trader, Charles H. Oakes.

Among the first preachers were the Rev. W. T. Boutwell and Mr. Seymour, of the Chippeway Mission at Pokeguma. The Rev. A. Brunson, of Prairie du Chien, who visited this region in 1838, wrote that at the mouth of Snake River he found Franklin Steele, with twenty-five or thirty men. cutting timber for a mill, and when he offered to preach Mr. Steele gave a cordial assent.

On the sixteenth of August, Mr. Steele, Livingston, and others, left the Falls of Saint Croix in a barge, and went around to Fort Snelling.

The steamboat Fayette about the middle of May, 1839, landed sutlers' stores at Fort Snelling and then proceeded with several persons of intelligence to the Saint Croix river, who settled at Marine.

The place was called after Marine in Madison county, Illinois, where the company, consisting of Judd, Hone and others, was formed to build a saw mill in the Saint Croix Valley. The mill at Marine commenced to saw lumber, on August 24, 1839, the first in Minnesota.

Joseph R. Brown, who since 1838, had lived at Chan Wakan, on the west side of Grey Cloud Island, this year made a claim near the upper end of the city of Stillwater, which he called Dahkotah, and was the first to raft lumber down the Saint Croix, as well as the first to represent the citizens of the valley in the legislature of Wisconsin.

8

Until the year 1841, the jurisdiction of Crawford county, Wisconsin, extended over the delta of country between the Saint Croix and Mississippi. Joseph R. Brown having been elected as representative of the county, in the territorial legislature of Wisconsin, succeeded in obtaining the passage of an act on November twentieth, 1841, organizing the county of Saint Croix, with Dahkotah designated as the county seat.

At the time prescribed for holding a court in the new county, it is said that the judge of the district arrived, and to his surprise, found a claim cabin occupied by a Frenchman. Speedily retreating, he never came again, and judicial proceedings for Saint Croix county ended for several years. Phineas Lawrence was the first sheriff of this county.

On the tenth of October, 1843, was commenced a settlement which has become the town of Stillwater. The names of the proprietors were John McKusick from Maine, Calvin Leach from Vermont, Elam Greeley from Maine, and Elias McKean from Pennsylvania. They immediately commenced the erection of a sawmill.

John H. Fonda, elected on the twenty-second of September, as coroner of Crawford county, Wisconsin, asserts that he was once notified that a dead body was lying in the water opposite Pig's Eye slough, and immediately proceeded to the spot, and on taking it out, recognized it as the body of a negro woman belonging to a certain captain of the United States army then at Fort Crawford. The body was cruelly cut and bruised, but no one appearing to recognise it, a verdict of "Found dead," was rendered, and the corpse was buried. Soon after, it came to light that the woman was whipped to death, and thrown into the river during the night.

The year that the Dahkotahs ceded their lands east of the Mississippi, a Canadian Frenchman by the name of Parrant, the ideal of an Indian whisky seller, erected a shanty in what is now the city of Saint Paul. Ignorant and overbearing he loved money more than his own soul. Destitute of one eye, and the other resembling that of a pig, he was a good representative of Caliban. Some one writing from his groggery designated it as "Pig's Eye." The reply to the letter was directed in good faith to "Pig's Eye"

Some years ago the editor of the Saint Paul Press described the occasion in these words:

"Edmund Brisette, a clerkly Frenchman for those days, who lives, or did live a little while ago, on Lake Harriet, was one day seated at a table in Parrant's cabin, with pen and paper about to write a letter for Parrant (for Parrant, like Charlemagne, could not write) to a friend' of the latter in Canada. The question of geography puzzled Brissette at the outset of the epistle; where should he date a letter from a place without a name? He looked up inquiringly to Parrant, and met the dead, cold glare of the Pig's Eye fixed upon him, with an irresistible suggestiveness that was inspiration to Brisette."

In 1842, the late Henry Jackson, of Mahkahto, settled at the same spot, and erected the first store on the height just above the lower landing, Roberts and Simpson followed, and opened small Indian trading shops. In 1846, the site of Saint Paul was chiefly occupied by a few shanties owned by "certain lewd fellows of the baser sort," who sold rum to the soldier and Indian. It was despised by all decent white men, and known to the Dahkotahs by an expression in their tongue which means, the place where they sell minne-wakan [supernatural water].

The chief of the Kaposia band in 1846, was shot by his own brother in a drunken revel, but surviving the wound, and apparently alarmed at the deterioration under the influence of the modern harpies at Saint Paul, went to Mr. Bruce, Indian Agent, at Fort Snelling, and requested a missionary. The Indian Agent in his report to government, says:

"The chief of the Little Crow's band, who resides below this place (Fort Snelling) about nine miles, in the immediate neighbourhood of the whiskey dealers, has requested to have a school established at his village. He says they are determined to reform, and for the future, will try to do better. I wrote to Doctor Williamson soon after the request was made, desiring him to take charge of the school. He has had charge of the mission school at Lac qui Parle for some years; is well qualified, and is an excellent physician."

In November, 1846, Dr. Williamson came from Lac qui Parle, as requested, and became a resident of Kaposia. While disapproving of their practices, he felt a kindly interest in the whites of Pig's Eye, which place was now beginning to be called, after a little log chapel which had been erected at the suggestion of Rev. L. Galtier, and called Saint Paul's. Though a missionary among the Dahkotahs, he was the first to take steps to promote the education of the whites and half-breeds of Minnesota. In the year 1847, he wrote to ex-Governor Slade, President of the National Popular Education Society, in relation to the condition of what has subsequently become the capital of the state.

In accordance with his request, Miss H. E. Bishop came to his mission-house at Kaposia, and, after a short time, was introduced by him to the citizens of Saint Paul. The first school-house in Minnesota besides those connected with the Indian missions, stood near the site of the old Brick Presbyterian church, corner of Saint Peter and Third street, and is thus described by the teacher:

"The school was commenced in a little log hovel, covered with bark, and chinked with mud, previously used as a blacksmith shop. On three sides of the interior of this humble log cabin, pegs were driven into the logs, upon which boards were laid for seats. Another seat was made by placing one end of a plank between the cracks of the logs, and the other upon a chair. This was for visitors. A rickety cross-legged table in the centre, and a hen's nest in one corner, completed the furniture."

Saint Croix county, in the year 1847, was detached from Crawford county, Wisconsin, and reorganized for judicial purposes, and Stillwater made the county seat. In the month of June the United States District Court held its session in the store-room of Mr. John McKusick; Judge Charles Dunn presiding. A large number of lumbermen had been attracted by the pineries in the upper portion of the valley of Saint Croix, and Stillwater was looked upon as the center of the lumbering interest.

The Rev. Mr. Boutwell, feeling that he could be more useful, left the Ojibways, and took up his residence near Stillwater, preaching to the lumbermen at the Falls of Saint Croix, Marine Mills, Stillwater, and Cottage Grove. In a letter speaking of Stillwater, he says, "Here is a little village sprung up like a gourd, but whether it is to perish as soon, God only knows."

CHAPTER XXI.

EVENTS PRELIMINARY TO THE ORGANIZATION OF THE MINNESOTA TERRITORY.

Wisconsin State Boundaries—First Bill for the Organization of Minnesota Territory, A. D. 1846—Change of Wisconsin Boundary—Memorial of Saint Croix Valley citizens—Various names proposed for the New Territory—Convention at Stillwater—H. H. Sibley elected Delegate to Congress.—Derivation of word Minnesota.

Three years elapsed from the time that the territory of Minnesota was proposed in Congress, to the final passage of the organic act. On the sixth of August, 1846, an act was passed by Congress authorizing the citizens of Wisconsin Territory to frame a constitution and form a state government. The act fixed the Saint Louis river to the rapids, from thence south to the Saint Croix, and thence down that river to its junction with the Mississippi, as the western boundary.

On the twenty-third of December, 1846, the delegate from Wisconsin, Morgan L. Martin, introduced a bill in Congress for the organization of a territory of Minnesota. This bill made its western boundary the Sioux and Red River of the North. On the third of March, 1847, permission was granted to Wisconsin to change her boundary, so that the western limit would proceed due south from the first rapids of the Saint Louis river, and fifteen miles east of the most easterly point of Lake Saint Croix, thence to the Mississippi.

A number in the constitutional convention of Wisconsin, were anxious that Rum river should be a part of her western boundary, while citizens of the valley of the Saint Croix were desirous that the Chippeway river should be the limit of Wisconsin. The citizens of Wisconsin Territory, in the valley of the Saint Croix, and about Fort Snelling, wished to be included in the projected new territory, and on the twenty-eighth of March, 1848, a memorial signed by H. H. Sibley, Henry M. Rice, Franklin Steele, William R. Marshall, and others, was presented to Congress, remonstrating against the proposition before the convention to make Rum river a part of the boundary line of the contemplated state of Wisconsin.

On the twenty-ninth of May, 1848, the act to admit Wisconsin changed the boundary line to the present, and as first defined in the enabling act of 1846. After the bill of Mr. Martin was introduced into the House of Representatives in 1846 it was referred to the Committee on Territories, of which Mr. Douglas was chairman. On the twentieth of January, 1847, he reported in favor of the proposed territory with the name of Itasca. On the seventeenth of February, before the bill passed the House, a discussion arose in relation to the proposed name. Mr. Winthrop of Massachusetts proposed Chippewa as a substitute, alleging that this tribe was the principal in the proposed territory, which was not correct. Mr. J. Thompson of Mississippi disliked all Indian names, and hoped the territory would be called Jackson. Mr. Houston of Delaware thought that there ought to be one territory named after the "Father of his country," and proposed Washington. All of the names proposed were rejected, and the name in the original bill inserted. On the last day of the session, March third, the bill was called up in the Senate and laid on the table.

When Wisconsin became a state the query arose whether the old territorial government did not continue in force west of the Saint Croix river. The first meeting on the subject of claiming territorial privileges was held in the building at Saint Paul, known as Jackson's store, near the corner of Bench and Jackson streets, on the bluff. This meeting was held in July, and a convention was proposed to consider their position. The first public meeting was held at Stillwater on August fourth, and Messrs. Steele and Sibley were the only persons present from the west side of the Mississippi. This meeting issued a call for a general convention to take steps to secure an early territorial organization, to assemble on the twenty-sixth of the month at the same place. Sixty-two delegates answered the call, and among those present, were W. D. Phillips, J. W. Bass, A. Larpenteur, J. M. Boal, and others from Saint Paul. To the convention a letter was presented from Mr. Catlin, who claimed to be acting governor, giving his opinion that the Wisconsin territorial organization was still in force. The meeting also appointed Mr. Sibley to visit Washington and represent their views; but the Hon. John H. Tweedy having resigned his office of delegate to Congress on September eighteenth, 1848, Mr. Catlin, who had made Stillwater a temporary residence, on the ninth of October issued a proclamation ordering a special election at Stillwater on the thirtieth, to fill a vacancy occasioned by the resignation. At this election Henry H. Sibley was elected as delegate of the citizens of the remaining portion of Wisconsin Territory. His credentials were presented to the House of Representatives, and the committee to whom the matter was referred presented a majority and minority report; but the resolution introduced by the majority passed and Mr. Sibley took his seat as a delegate from Wisconsin Territory on the fifteenth of January, 1849.

Mr. H. M. Rice, and other gentlemen, visited Washington during the winter, and, uniting with Mr. Sibley, used all their energies to obtain the organization of a new territory.

Mr. Sibley, in an interesting communication to the Minnesota Historical Society, writes: "When my credentials as Delegate, were presented by Hon. James Wilson, of New Hampshire, to the House of Representatives, there was some curiosity manifested among the members, to see what kind of a person had been elected to represent the distant and wild territory claiming representation in Congress. I was told by a New England member with whom I became subsequently quite intimate, that there was some disappointment when I made my appearance, for it was expected that the delegate from this remote region would make his debut, if not in full Indian costume, at least, with some peculiarities of dress and manners, characteristic of the rude and semi-civilized people who had sent him to the Capitol."

The territory of Minnesota was named after the largest tributary of the Mississippi within its limits. The Sioux call the Missouri Minnesho-shay, muddy water, but the stream after which this region is named, Minne-sota. Some say that Sota means clear; others, turbid; Schoolcraft, bluish green. Nicollet wrote, "The adjective Sotah is of difficult translation. The Canadians translated it by a pretty equivalent word, brouillé, perhaps more properly rendered into English by blear. I have entered upon this explanation because the word really means neither clear nor turbid, as some authors have asserted, its true meaning being found in the Sioux expression Ishtah-sotah, blear-eyed." From the fact that the word signifies neither blue nor white, but the peculiar appearance of the sky at certain times, by some, Minnesota has been defined to mean the sky tinted water, which is certainly poetic, and the late Rev. Gideon H. Pond thought quite correct.

CHAPTER XXII.

MINNESOTA FROM ITS ORGANIZATION AS A TERRITORY, A. D. 1849, TO A. D. 1854.

Appearance of the Country, A. D. 1849—Arrival of first Editor—Governor Ramsey arrives—Guest of H. H. Sibley—Proclamation issued—Governor Ramsey and H. M. Rice move to Saint Paul—Fourth of July Celebration—First election—Early newspapers—First Courts—First Legislature—Pioneer News Carrier's Address—Wedding at Fort Snelling—Territorial Seal—Scalp Dance at Stillwater—First Steamboat at Falls of Saint Anthony—Presbyterian Chapel burned—Indian council at Fort Snelling—First Steamboat above Saint Anthony—First boat at the Blue Earth River—Congressional election—Visit of Fredrika Bremer—Indian newspaper—Other newspapers—Second Legislature—University of Minnesota—Teamster killed by Indians—Sioux Treaties—Third Legislature—Land slide at Stillwater—Death of first Editor—Fourth Legislature—Baldwin School, now Macalester College—Indian fight in Saint Paul.

On the third of March, 1849, the bill was passed by Congress for organizing the territory of Minnesota, whose boundary on the west, extended to the Missouri River. At this time, the region was little more than a wilderness. The west bank of the Mississippi, from the Iowa line to Lake Itasca, was unceded by the Indians.

At Wapashaw, was a trading post in charge of Alexis Bailly, and here also resided the ancient voyageur, of fourscore years, A. Rocque.

At the foot of Lake Pepin was a store house kept by Mr. F. S. Richards. On the west shore of the lake lived the eccentric Wells, whose wife was a bois brule, a daughter of the deceased trader, Duncan Graham.

The two unfinished buildings of stone, on the beautiful bank opposite the renowned Maiden's Rock, and the surrounding skin lodges of his wife's relatives and friends, presented a rude but picturesque scene. Above the lake was a cluster of bark wigwams, the Dahkotah village of Raymneecha, now Red Wing, at which was a Presbyterian mission house.

The next settlement was Kaposia, also an Indian village, and the residence of a Presbyterian missionary, the Rev. T. S. Williamson, M. D. On the east side of the Mississippi, the first settlement, at the mouth of the St. Croix, was Point Douglas, then as now, a small hamlet.

At Red Rock, the site of a former Methodist mission station, there were a few farmers. Saint Paul was just emerging from a collection of Indian whisky shops and birch roofed cabins of half-breed voyageurs. Here and there a frame tenement was erected, and, under the auspices of the Hon. H. M. Rice, who had obtained an interest in the town, some warehouses were constructed, and the foundations of the American House, a frame hotel, which stood at Third and Exchange street, were laid. In 1849, the population had increased to two hundred and fifty or three hundred inhabitants, for rumors had gone abroad that it might be mentioned in the act, creating the territory, as the capital of Minnesota. More than a month after the adjournment of Congress, just at eve, on the ninth of April, amid terrific peals of thunder and torrents of rain, the weekly steam packet, the first to force its way through the icy barrier of Lake Pepin, rounded the rocky point whistling loud and long, as if the bearer of glad tidings. Before she was safely moored to the landing, the shouts of the excited villagers were heard announcing that there was a territory of Minnesota, and that Saint Paul was the seat of government.

Every successive steamboat arrival poured out on the landing men big with hope, and anxious to do something to mould the future of the new state.

Nine days after the news of the existence of the territory of Minnesota was received, there arrived James M. Goodhue with press, type, and printing apparatus. A graduate of Amherst college, and a lawyer by profession, he wielded a sharp pen, and wrote editorials, which, more than anything else, perhaps, induced immigration. Though a man of some faults, one of the counties properly bears his name. On the twenty-eighth of April, he issued from his press the first number of the Pioneer.

On the twenty-seventh of May, Alexander Ramsey, the Governor, and family, arrived at Saint Paul, but owing to the crowded state of public houses, immediately proceeded in the steamer to the establishment of the Fur Company, known as Mendota, at the junction of the Minnesota and Mississippi, and became the guest of the Hon. H. H. Sibley.

On the first of June, Governor Ramsey, by proclamation, declared the territory duly organized, with the following officers: Alexander Ramsey, of Pennsylvania, Governor: C. K. Smith, of Ohio, Secretary: A. Goodrich, of Tennessee, Chief Justice: D. Cooper, of Pennsylvania, and B. B. Meeker, of Kentucky, Associate Judges; Joshua L. Taylor, Marshal; H. L. Moss, attorney of the United States.

On the eleventh of June, a second proclamation was issued, dividing the territory into three temporary judicial districts. The first comprised the county of St. Croix; the county of La Pointe and the region north and west of the Mississippi, and north of the Minnesota and of a line running due west from the headwaters of the Minnesota to the Missouri river, constituted the second: and the country west of the Mississippi and south of the Minnesota, formed the third district. Judge Goodrich was assigned to the first, Meeker to the second, and Cooper to the third. A court was ordered to be held at Stillwater on the second Monday, at the Falls of St. Anthony on the third, and at Mendota on the fourth Monday of August.

Until the twenty-sixth of June, Governor Ramsey and family had been guests of Hon. H. H. Sibley, at Mendota. On the afternoon of that day they arrived at St. Paul, in a birch-bark canoe, and became permanent residents at the capital. The house first occupied as a gubernatorial mansion, was a small frame building that stood on Third, between Robert and Jackson streets, formerly known as the New England House.

A few days after, the Hon. H. M. Rice and family moved from Mendota to St. Paul, and occupied the house he had erected on St. Anthony street, near the corner of Market.

On the first of July, a land office was established at Stillwater, and A. Van Vorhes, after a few weeks, became the register.

The anniversary of our National Independence was celebrated in a becoming manner at the capital. The place selected for the address, was a grove that stood on the sites of the City Hall and the Baldwin School building, and the late Franklin Steele was the marshal of the day.

On the seventh of July, a proclamation was issued, dividing the territory into seven council districts, and ordering an election to be held on the first day of August, for one delegate to represent the people in the House of Representatives of the United States, for nine councillors and eighteen representatives, to constitute the Legislative Assembly of Minnesota.

In this month, the Hon. H. M. Rice despatched a boat laded with Indian goods from the the Falls of St. Anthony to Crow Wing, which was towed by horses after the manner of a canal boat.

The election on the first of August, passed off with little excitement, Hon. H. H. Sibley being elected delegate to Congress without opposition. David Lambert, on what might, perhaps, be termed the old settlers' ticket, was defeated in St. Paul, by James M. Boal. The latter, on the night of the election, was honored with a ride through town on the axle and fore-wheels of an old wagon, which was drawn by his admiring but somewhat undisciplined friends.

J. L. Taylor having declined the office of United States Marshal; A. M. Mitchell, of Ohio, a graduate of West Point, and colonel of a regiment of Ohio volunteers in the Mexican war, was appointed and arrived at the capital early in August.

There were three papers published in the territory soon after its organization. The first was the Pioneer, issued on April twenty-eighth, 1849, under most discouraging circumstances. It was at first the intention of the witty and reckless editor to have called his paper "The Epistle of St. Paul." About the same time there was issued in Cincinnati, under the auspices of the late Dr. A. Randall, of California, the first number of the Register. The second number of the paper was printed at St. Paul, in July, and the office was on St. Anthony, between Washington and Market Streets. About the first of June, James Hughes, afterward of Hudson, Wisconsin, arrived with a press and materials, and established the Minnesota Chronicle. After an existence of a few weeks two papers were discontinued; and, in their place, was issued the "Chronicle and

Register," edited by Nathaiel McLean and John P. Owens.

The first courts, pursuant to proclamation of the governor, were held in the month of August. At Stillwater, the court was organized on the thirteenth of the month, Judge Goodrich presiding, and Judge Cooper by courtesy, sitting on the bench. On the twentieth, the second judicial district held a court. The room used was the old government mill at Minneapolis. The presiding judge was B. B. Meeker; the foreman of the grand jury, Franklin Steele. On the last Monday of the month, the court for the third judicial district was organized in the large stone warehouse of the fur company at Mendota. The presiding judge was David Cooper. Governor Ramsey sat on the right, and Judge Goodrich on the left. Hon. H. H. Sibley was the foreman of the grand jury. As some of the jurors could not speak the English language, W. H. Forbes acted as interpreter. The charge of Judge Cooper was lucid, scho'arly, and dignified. At the request of the grand jury it was afterwards published.

On Monday, the third of September, the first Legislative Assembly convened in the "Central House," in Saint Paul, a building at the corner of Minnesota and Bench streets, facing the Mississippi river which answered the double purpose of capitol and hotel. On the first floor of the main building was the Secretary's office and Representative chamber, and in the second story was the library and Council chamber. As the flag was run up the staff in front of the house, a number of Indians sat on a rocky bluff in the vicinity, and gazed at what to them was a novel and perhaps saddening scene; for if the tide of immigration sweeps in from the Pacific as it has from the Atlantic coast, they must soon dwindle.

The legislature having organized, elected the following permanent officers: David Olmsted, President of Council; Joseph R. Brown, Secretary; H. A. Lambert, Assistant. In the House of Representatives, Joseph W. Furber was elected Speaker: W. D. Phillips, Clerk; L. B. Wait, Assistant.

On Tuesday afternoon, both houses assembled in the dining hall of the hotel, and after prayer was offered by Rev. E. D. Neill, Governor Ramsey delivered his message. The message was ably written, and its perusal afforded satisfaction at home and abroad.

The first session of the legislature adjourned on the first of November. Among other proceedings of interest, was the creation of the following counties: Itasca, Wapashaw, Dahkotah, Wahnahtah, Mahkahto, Pembina, Washington, Ramsey and Benton. The three latter counties comprised the country that up to that time had been ceded by the Indians on the east side of the Mississippi. Stillwater was declared the county seat of Washington, Saint Paul, of Ramsey, and "the seat of justice of the county of Benton was to be within one-quarter of a mile of a point on the east side of the Mississippi, directly opposite the mouth of Sauk river."

EVENTS OF A. D 1850.

By the active exertions of the secretary of the territory, C. K. Smith, Esq., the Historical Society of Minnesota was incorporated at the first session of the legislature. The opening annual address was delivered in the then Methodist (now Swedenborgian) church at Saint Paul, on the first of January, 1850.

The following account of the proceedings is from the Chronicle and Register. "The first public exercises of the Minnesota Historical Society, took place at the Methodist church, Saint Paul, on the first inst., and passed off highly creditable to all concerned. The day was pleasant and the attendance large. At the appointed hour, the President and both Vice-Presidents of the society being absent; on motion of Hon. C. K. Smith, Hon. Chief Justice Goodrich was called to the chair. The same gentleman then moved that a committee, consisting of Messrs. Parsons K. Johnson, John A. Wakefield, and B. W. Brunson, be appointed to wait upon the Orator of the day, Rev. Mr. Neill, and inform him that the audience was waiting to hear his address.

"Mr. Neill was shortly conducted to the pulpit; and after an eloquent and approriate prayer by the Rev. Mr. Parsons, and music by the band, he proceeded to deliver his discourse upon the early French missionaries and Voyageurs into Minnesota. We hope the society will provide for its publication at an early day.

"After some brief remarks by Rev. Mr

Hobart, upon the objects and ends of history, the ceremonies were concluded with a prayer by that gentleman. The audience dispersed highly delighted with all that occurred.'

At this early period the Minnesota Pioneer issued a Carrier's New Year's Address, which was amusing doggerel. The reference to the future greatness and ignoble origin of the capital of Minnesota was as follows:—

The cities on this river must be three,
Two that *are* but and one that is to be.
One, is the mart of all the tropics yield,
The cane, the orange, and the cotton-field,
And sends her ships abroad and boasts
Her trade extended to a thousand coasts;
The *other*, central for the temperate zone,
Garners the stores that on the plains are grown,
A place where steamboats from all quarters range,
To meet and speculate, as 'twere on 'change.
The *third will be*, where rivers confluent flow
From the wide spreading north through plains of snow;
The mart of all that boundless forests give
To make mankind more comfortably live,
The land of manufacturing industry,
The workshop of the nation it shall be.
Propelled by *this* wide stream, you'll see
A thousand factories at Saint Anthony:
And the Saint Croix a hundred mills shall drive,
And all its smiling villages shall thrive;
But then *my* town remember that high bench
With cabins scattered over it, of French?
A man named Henry Jackson's living there,
Also a man—why every one knows L. Robair.
Below Fort Snelling, seven miles or so,
And three above the village of Old Crow?
Pig's Eye? Yes; Pig's Eye! That's the spot!
A very funny name; is't not?
Pig's Eye's the spot, to plant my city on,
To be remembered by, when I am gone.
Pig's Eye converted thou shalt be, like Saul:
Thy name henceforth *shall* be Saint Paul.

On the evening of New Year's day, at Fort Snelling, there was an assemblage which is only seen on the outposts of civilization. In one of the stone edifices, outside of the wall, belonging to the United States, there resided a gentleman who had dwelt in Minnesota since the year 1819, and for many years had been in the employ of the government, as Indian interpreter. In youth he had been a member of the Columbia Fur Company, and conforming to the habits of traders, had purchased a Dahkotah wife who was wholly ignorant of the English language. As a family of children gathered around him he recognised the relation of husband and father, and conscientiously discharged his duties as a parent. His daughter at a proper age was sent to a boarding school of some celebrity, and on the night referred to was married to an intelligent young American farmer. Among the guests present were the officers of the garrison in full uniform, with their wives, the United States Agent for the Dahkotahs, and family, the bois brules of the neighborhood, and the Indian relatives of the mother. The mother did not make her appearance, but, as the minister proceeded with the ceremony, the Dahkotah relatives, wrapped in their blankets, gathered in the hall and looked in through the door.

The marriage feast was worthy of the occasion. In consequence of the numbers, the officers and those of European extraction partook first; then the bois brules of Ojibway and Dahkotah descent; and, finally, the native Americans, who did ample justice to the plentiful supply spread before them.

Governor Ramsey, Hon. H. H. Sibley, and the delegate to Congress devised at Washington, this winter, the territorial seal. The design was Falls of St. Anthony in the distance. An immigrant ploughing the land on the borders of the Indian country, full of hope, and looking forward to the possession of the hunting grounds beyond. An Indian amazed at the sight of the plough, and fleeing on horseback towards the setting sun.

The motto of the Earl of Dunraven, "Quæ sursum volo videre" (I wish to see what is above) was most appropriately selected by Mr. Sibley, but by the blunder of an engraver it appeared on the territorial seal, "Quo sursum velo videre," which no scholar could translate. At length was substituted, "L' Etoile du Nord," "Star of the North," while the device of the setting sun remained, and this is objectionable, as the State of Maine had already placed the North Star on her escutcheon, with the motto "Dirigo," "I guide." Perhaps some future legislature may direct the first motto to be restored and correctly engraved.

In the month of April, there was a renewal of hostilities between the Dahkotahs and Ojibways, on lands that had been ceded to the United States. A war prophet at Red Wing, dreamed that he ought to raise a war party. Announcing the fact, a number expressed their willingness to go on such an expedition. Several from the Kaposia village also joined the party, under the leadership of a worthless Indian, who had been confined in the guard-house at Fort Snelling, the year previous, for scalping his wife.

Passing up the valley of the St. Croix, a few miles above Stillwater the party discovered on the snow the marks of a keg and footprints.' These told them that a man and woman of the Ojibways had been to some whisky dealer's, and were returning. Following their trail, they found on Apple river, about twenty miles from Stillwater, a band of Ojibways encamped in one lodge. Waiting till daybreak of Wednesday, April second, the Dahkotahs commenced firing on the unsuspecting inmates, some of whom were drinking from the contents of the whisky keg. The camp was composed of fifteen, and all were murdered and scalped, with the exception of a lad, who was made a captive.

On Thursday, the victors came to Stillwater, and danced the scalp dance around the captive boy, in the heat of excitement, striking him in the face with the scarcely cold and bloody scalps of his relatives. The child was then taken to Kaposia, and adopted by the chief. Governor Ramsey immediately took measures to send the boy to his friends. At a conference held at the Governor's mansion, the boy was delivered up, and, on being led out to the kitchen by a little son of the Governor, since deceased, to receive refreshments, he cried bitterly, seemingly more alarmed at being left with the whites than he had been while a captive at Kaposia.

From the first of April the waters of the Mississippi began to rise, and on the thirteenth, the lower floor of the warehouse, then occupied by William Constans, at the foot of Jackson street, St. Paul, was submerged. Taking advantage of the freshet, the steamboat Anthony Wayne, for a purse of two hundred dollars, ventured through the swift current above Fort Snelling, and reached the Falls of St. Anthony. The boat left the fort after dinner, with Governor Ramsey and other guests, also the band of the Sixth Regiment on board, and reached the falls between three and four o'clock in the afternoon. The whole town, men, women and children, lined the shore as the boat approached, and welcomed this first arrival, with shouts and waving handkerchiefs.

On the afternoon of May fifteenth, there might have been seen, hurrying through the streets of Saint Paul, a number of naked and painted braves of the Kaposia band of Dahkotahs, ornamented with all the attire of war, and panting for the scalps of their enemies. A few hours before, the warlike head chief of the Ojibways, young Hole-in-the-Day, having secreted his canoe in the retired gorge which leads to the cave in the upper suburbs, with two or three associates had crossed the river, and, almost in sight of the citizens of the town, had attacked a small party of Dahkotahs, and murdered and scalped one man. On receipt of the news, Governor Ramsey granted a parole to the thirteen Dahkotahs confined in Fort Snelling, for participating in the Apple river massacre.

On the morning of the sixteenth of May, the first Protestant church edifice completed in the white settlements, a small frame building, built for the Presbyterian church, at Saint Paul, was destroyed by fire, it being the first conflagration that had occurred since the organization of the territory.

One of the most interesting events of the year 1850, was the Indian council, at Fort Snelling. Governor Ramsey had sent runners to the different bands of the Ojibways and Dahkotahs, to meet him at the fort, for the purpose of endeavouring to adjust their difficulties.

On Wednesday, the twelfth of June, after much talking, as is customary at Indian councils, the two tribes agreed as they had frequently done before, to be friendly, and Governor Ramsey presenting to each party an ox, the council was dissolved.

On Thursday, the Ojibways visited St. Paul for the first time, young Hole-in-the-Day being dressed in a coat of a captain of United States infantry, which had been presented to him at the fort. On Friday, they left in the steamer Governor Ramsey, which had been built at St. Anthony, and just commenced running between that point and Sauk Rapids, for their homes in the wilderness of the Upper Mississippi.

The summer of 1850 was the commencement of the navigation of the Minnesota River by steamboats. With the exception of a steamer that made a pleasure excursion as far as Shokpay, in 1841, no large vessels had ever disturbed the waters of this stream. In June, the "Anthony Wayne," which a few weeks before had ascended to the Falls of St. Anthony, made a trip. On the eighteenth of July she made a second trip, going almost to Mahkahto. The "Nominee" also navigated the stream for some distance.

On the twenty-second of July the officers of the "Yankee," taking advantage of the high water, determined to navigate the stream as far as possible. The boat ascended to near the Cottonwood river.

As the time for the general election in September approached, considerable excitement was manifested. As there were no political issues before the people, parties were formed based on personal preferences. Among those nominated for delegate to Congress, by various meetings, were H. H. Sibley, the former delegate to Congress, David Olmsted, at that time engaged in the Indian trade, and A. M. Mitchell, the United States marshal. Mr. Olmsted withdrew his name before election day, and the contest was between those interested in Sibley and Mitchell. The friends of each betrayed the greatest zeal, and neither pains nor money were spared to insure success. Mr. Sibley was elected by a small majority. For the first time in the territory, soldiers at the garrisons voted at this election, and there was considerable discussion as to the propriety of such a course.

Miss Fredrika Bremer, the well known Swedish novelist, visited Minnesota in the month of October, and was the guest of Governor Ramsey.

During November, the Dahkotah Tawaxitku Kin, or the Dahkotah Friend, a monthly paper, was commenced, one-half in the Dahkotah and one-half in the English language. Its editor was the Rev. Gideon H. Pond, a Presbyterian missionary, and its place of publication at Saint Paul. It was published for nearly two years, and, though it failed to attract the attention of the Indian mind, it conveyed to the English reader much correct information in relation to the habits, the belief, and superstitions, of the Dahkotahs.

On the tenth of December, a new paper, owned and edited by Daniel A. Robertson, late United States marshal, of Ohio, and called the Minnesota Democrat, made its appearance.

During the summer there had been changes in the editorial supervision of the "Chronicle and Register." For a brief period it was edited by L. A. Babcock, Esq., who was succeeded by W. G. Le Duc.

About the time of the issuing of the Democrat, C. J. Henniss, formerly reporter for the United States Gazette, Philadelphia, became the editor of the Chronicle.

The first proclamation for a thanksgiving day was issued in 1850 by the governor, and the twenty-sixth of December was the time appointed and it was generally observed.

EVENTS OF A. D. 1851.

On Wednesday, January first, 1851, the second Legislative Assembly assembled in a three-story brick building, since destroyed by fire, that stood on St. Anthony street, between Washington and Franklin. D. B. Loomis was chosen Speaker of the Council, and M. E. Ames Speaker of the House. This assembly was characterized by more bitterness of feeling than any that has since convened. The preceding delegate election had been based on personal preferences, and cliques and factions manifested themselves at an early period of the session.

The locating of the penitentiary at Stillwater, and the capitol building at St. Paul gave some dissatisfaction. By the efforts of J. W. North, Esq., a bill creating the University of Minnesota at or near the Falls of St. Anthony, was passed, and signed by the Governor. This institution, by the State Constitution, is now the State University.

During the session of this Legislature, the publication of the "Chronicle and Register" ceased.

About the middle of May, a war party of Dahkotahs discovered near Swan River, an Ojibway with a keg of whisky. The latter escaped, with the loss of his keg. The war party, drinking the contents, became intoxicated, and, firing upon some teamsters they met driving their wagons with goods to the Indian Agency, killed one of them. Andrew Swartz, a resident of St. Paul. The news was conveyed to Fort Ripley, and a party of soldiers, with Hole-in-the-day as a guide, started in pursuit of the murderers, but did not succeed in capturing them. Through the influence of Little Six, the Dahkotah chief, whose village was at (and named after him) Shokpay, five of the offenders were arrested and placed in the guard house at Fort Snelling. On Monday, June ninth, they left the fort in a wagon, guarded by twenty-five dragoons, destined for Sauk Rapids for trial. As they departed they all sang their death song, and the coarse soldiers amused themselves by making signs that they were going to be hung. On the first evening of the journey the five culprits encamped with the twenty-five dragoons. Handcuffed, they were placed in the tent, and yet at midnight they all escaped, only one being wounded by the guard. What was more remarkable, the wounded man was the first to bring the news to St. Paul. Proceeding to Koposia, his wound was examined by the missionary and physician, Dr. Williamson; and then, fearing an arrest, he took a canoe and paddled up the Minnesota. The excuses offered by the dragoons was, that all the guard but one fell asleep.

The first paper published in Minnesota, beyond the capital, was the St. Anthony Express, which made its appearance during the last week of April or May.

The most important event of the year 1851 was the treaty with the Dahkotahs, by which the west side of the Mississippi and the valley of the Minnesota River were opened to the hardy immigrant. The commissioners on the part of the United States were Luke Lea, Commissioner of Indian Affairs, and Governor Ramsey. The place of meeting for the upper bands was Traverse des Sioux. The commission arrived there on the last of June, but were obliged to wait many days for the assembling of the various bands of Dahkotahs.

On the eighteenth of July, all those expected having arrived, the Sissetons and Wahpayton Dahkotahs assembled in grand council with the United States commissioners. After the usual feastings and speeches, a treaty was concluded on Wednesday, July twenty-third. The pipe having been smoked by the commissioners, Lea and Ramsey, it was passed to the chiefs. The paper containing the treaty was then read in English and translated into the Dahkotah by the Rev. S. R. Riggs, Presbyterian Missionary among this people. This finished, the chiefs came up to the secretary's table and touched the pen; the white men present then witnessed the document, and nothing remained but the ratification of the United States Senate to open that vast country for the residence of the hardy immigrant.

During the first week in August, a treaty was also concluded beneath an oak bower, on Pilot Knob, Mendota, with the M'dewakantonwan and Wa'paykootay bands of Dahkotahs. About sixty of the chiefs and principal men touched the pen, and Little Crow, who had been in the mission-school at Lac qui Parle, signed his own name. Before they separated Colonel Lea and Governor Ramsey gave them a few words of advice on various subjects connected with their future well-being, but particularly on the subject of education and temperance. The treaty was interpreted to them by the Rev. G. H. Pond, a gentleman who was conceded to be a most correct speaker of the Dahkotah tongue.

The day after the treaty these lower bands received thirty thousand dollars, which, by the treaty of 1837, was set apart for education; but, by the misrepresentations of interested half-breeds, the Indians were made to believe that it ought to be given to them to be employed as they pleased.

The next week, with their sacks filled with money, they thronged the streets of St. Paul, purchasing whatever pleased their fancy.

On the seventeenth of September, a new paper was commenced in St. Paul, under the auspices of the "Whigs," and John P. Owens became editor, which relation he sustained until the fall of 1857.

The election for members of the Legislature and county officers occurred on the fourteenth of October; and, for the first time, a regular Democratic ticket was placed before the people. The parties called themselves Democratic and Anti-organization, or Coalition.

In the month of November Jerome Fuller arrived, and took the place of Judge Goodrich as Chief Justice of Minnesota, who was removed; and, about the same time, Alexander Wilkin was appointed secretary of the territory in place of C. K. Smith.

The eighteenth of December, pursuant to proclamation, was observed as a day of Thanksgiving.

EVENTS OF A. D. 1852.

The third Legislative Assembly commenced its sessions in one of the edifices on Third below Jackson street, which became a portion of the Merchants' Hotel, on the seventh of January, 1852.

This session, compared with the previous, formed a contrast as great as that between a boisterous day in March and a calm June morning. The minds of the population were more deeply interested in the ratification of the treaties made with the Dahkotahs, than in political discussions. Among other legislation of interest was the creation of Hennepin county.

On Saturday, the fourteenth of February, a dog-train arrived at St. Paul from the north, with the distinguished Arctic explorer, Dr. Rae. He had been in search of the long-missing Sir John Franklin, by way of the Mackenzie river, and was now on his way to Europe.

On the fourteenth of May, an interesting lusus naturæ occurred at Stillwater. On the prairies, beyond the elevated bluffs which encircle the business portion of the town, there is a lake which discharges its waters through a ravine, and supplied McKusick's mill. Owing to heavy rains, the hills became saturated with water, and the lake very full. Before daylight the citizens heard the "voice of many waters," and looking out, saw rushing down through the ravine, trees, gravel and diluvium. Nothing impeded its course, and as it issued from the ravine it spread over the town site, covering up barns and small tenements, and, continuing to the lake shore, it materially improved the landing, by a deposit of many tons of earth. One of the editors of the day, alluding to the fact, quaintly remarked, that "it was a very extraordinary movement of real estate."

During the summer, Elijah Terry, a young man who had left St. Paul the previous March, and went to Pembina, to act as teacher to the mixed bloods in that vicinity, was murdered under distressing circumstances. With a bois brule he had started to the woods on the morning of his death, to hew timber. While there he was fired upon by a small party of Dahkotahs; a ball broke his arm, and he was pierced with arrows. His scalp was wrenched from his head, and was afterwards seen among Sisseton Dahkotahs, near Big Stone Lake.

About the last of August, the pioneer editor of Minnesota, James M. Goodhue, died.

At the November Term of the United States District Court, of Ramsey county, a Dahkotah, named Yu-ha-zee, was tried for the murder of a German woman. With others she was traveling above Shokpay, when a party of Indians, of whom the prisoner was one, met them; and, gathering about the wagon, were much excited. The prisoner punched the woman first with his gun, and, being threatened by one of the party, loaded and fired, killing the woman and wounding one of the men.

On the day of his trial he was escorted from Fort Snelling by a company of mounted dragoons in full dress. It was an impressive scene to witness the poor Indian half hid in his blanket, in a buggy with the civil officer, surrounded with all the pomp and circumstance of war. The jury found him guilty. On being asked if he had anything to say why sentence of death should not be passed, he replied, through the interpreter, that the band to which he belonged would remit their annuities if he could be released. To this Judge Hayner, the successor of Judge Fuller, replied, that he had no authority to release him; and, ordering him to rise, after some appropriate and impressive remarks, he pronounced the first sentence of death ever pronounced by a judicial officer in Minnesota. The prisoner trembled while the judge spoke, and was a piteous spectacle. By the statute of Minnesota, then, one convicted of murder could not be executed until twelve months had elapsed, and he was confined until the governor of the territory should by warrant order his execution.

EVENTS OF A. D. 1853.

The fourth Legislative Assembly convened on the fifth of January, 1853, in the two story brick edifice at the corner of Third and Minnesota streets. The Council chose Martin McLeod as presiding officer, and the House Dr. David Day.

Speaker. Governor Ramsey's message was an interesting document.

The Baldwin school, now known as Macalester College, was incorporated at this session of the legislature, and was opened the following June.

On the ninth of April, a party of Ojibways killed a Dahkotah, at the village of Shokpay. A war party, from Kaposia, then proceeded up the valley of the St. Croix, and killed an Ojibway. On the morning of the twenty-seventh, a band of Ojibway warriors, naked, decked, and fiercely gesticulating, might have been seen in the busiest street of the capital, in search of their enemies. Just at that time a small party of women, and one man, who had lost a leg in the battle of Stillwater, arrived in a canoe from Kaposia, at the Jackson street landing. Perceiving the Ojibways, they retreated to the building then known as the "Pioneer" office, and the Ojibways discharging a volley through the windows, wounded a Dahkotah woman who soon died. For a short time, the infant capital presented a sight similar to that witnessed in ancient days in Hadley or Deerfield, the then frontier towns of Massachusetts. Messengers were despatched to Fort Snelling for the dragoons, and a party of citizens mounted on horseback, were quickly in pursuit of those who with so much boldness had sought the streets of St. Paul, as a place to avenge their wrongs. The dragoons soon followed, with Indian guides scenting the track of the Ojibways, like bloodhounds. The next day they discovered the transgressors, near the Falls of St. Croix. The Ojibways manifesting what was supposed to be an insolent spirit, the order was given by the lieutenant in command, to fire, and he whose scalp was afterwards daguerreotyped, and which was engraved for Graham's Magazine, wallowed in gore.

During the summer, the passenger, as he stood on the hurricane deck of any of the steamboats, might have seen, on a scaffold on the bluffs in the rear of Kaposia, a square box covered with a coarsely fringed red cloth. Above it was suspended a piece of the Ojibway's scalp, whose death had caused the affray in the streets of St. Paul. Within, was the body of the woman who had been shot in the "Pioneer" building, while seeking refuge. A scalp suspended over the corpse is supposed to be a consolation to the soul, and a great protection in the journey to the spirit land.

On the accession of Pierce to the presidency of the United States, the officers appointed under the Taylor and Fillmore administrations were removed, and the following gentlemen substituted: Governor, W. A. Gorman, of Indiana; Secretary, J. T. Rosser, of Virginia; Chief Justice, W. H. Welch, of Minnesota; Associates, Moses Sherburne, of Maine, and A. G. Chatfield, of Wisconsin. One of the first official acts of the second Governor, was the making of a treaty with the Winnebago Indians at Watab, Benton county, for an exchange of country.

On the twenty-ninth of June, D. A. Robertson, who by his enthusiasm and earnest advocacy of its principles had done much to organize the Democratic party of Minnesota, retired from the editorial chair and was succeeded by David Olmsted.

At the election held in October, Henry M. Rice and Alexander Wilkin were candidates for deligate to Congress. The former was elected by a decisive majority.

CHAPTER XXIII.

EVENTS FROM A. D. 1854 TO THE ADMISSION OF MINNESOTA TO THE UNION.

Fifth Legislature—Execution of Yuhazee—Sixth Legislature—First bridge over the Mississippi—Arctic Explorer—Seventh Legislature—Indian girl killed near Bloomington Ferry—Eighth Legislature—Attempt to Remove the Capital—Special Session of the Legislature—Convention to frame a State Constitution—Admission of Minnesota to the Union.

The fifth session of the legislature was commenced in the building just completed as the Capitol, on January fourth, 1854. The President of the Council was S. B. Olmstead, and the Speaker of the House of Representatives was N. C. D. Taylor.

Governor Gorman delivered his first annual message on the tenth, and as his predecessor, urged the importance of railway communications, and dwelt upon the necessity of fostering the interests of education, and of the lumbermen.

The exciting bill of the session was the act incorporating the Minnesota and Northwestern Railroad Company, introduced by Joseph R. Brown. It was passed after the hour of midnight on the last day of the session. Contrary to the expectation of his friends, the Governor signed the bill.

On the afternoon of December twenty-seventh, the first public execution in Minnesota, in accordance with the forms of law, took place. Yu-ha-zee, the Dahkotah who had been convicted in November, 1852, for the murder of a German woman, above Shokpay, was the individual. The scaffold was erected on the open space between an inn called the Franklin House and the rear of the late Mr. J. W. Selby's enclosure in St. Paul. About two o'clock, the prisoner, dressed in a white shroud, left the old log prison, near the court house, and entered a carriage with the officers of the law. Being assisted up the steps that led to the scaffold, he made a few remarks in his own language, and was then executed. Numerous ladies sent in a petition to the governor, asking the pardon of the Indian, to which that officer in declining made an appropriate reply.

EVENTS OF A. D. 1855.

The sixth session of the legislature convened on the third of January, 1855. W. P. Murray was elected President of the Council, and James S. Norris Speaker of the House.

About the last of January, the two houses adjourned one day, to attend the exercises occasioned by the opening of the first bridge of any kind, over the mighty Mississippi, from Lake Itasca to the Gulf of Mexico. It was at Falls of Saint Anthony, and made of wire, and at the time of its opening, the patent for the land on which the west piers were built, had not been issued from the Land Office, a striking evidence of the rapidity with which the city of Minneapolis, which now surrounds the Falls, has developed.

On the twenty-ninth of March, a convention was held at Saint Anthony, which led to the formation of the Republican party of Minnesota. This body took measures for the holding of a territorial convention at St. Paul, which convened on the twenty-fifth of July, and William R. Marshall was nominated as delegate to Congress. Shortly after the friends of Mr. Sibley nominated David Olmsted and Henry M. Rice, the former delegate was also a candidate. The contest was animated, and resulted in the election of Mr. Rice.

About noon of December twelfth, 1855, a four-horse vehicle was seen driving rapidly through St. Paul, and deep was the interest when it was announced that one of the Arctic exploring party, Mr. James Stewart, was on his way to Canada with relics of the world-renowned and world-mourned Sir John Franklin. Gathering together the precious fragments found on Montreal Island and vicinity, the party had left the region of icebergs on the ninth of August, and after a continued land journey from that time, had reached

Saint Paul on that day, *en route* to the Hudson Bay Company's quarters in Canada.

EVENTS OF A. D. 1856.

The seventh session of the Legislative Assembly was begun on the second of January, 1856, and again the exciting question was the Minnesota and Northwestern Railroad Company.

John B. Brisbin was elected President of the Council, and Charles Gardner, Speaker of the House.

This year was comparatively devoid of interest. The citizens of the territory were busily engaged in making claims in newly organized counties, and in enlarging the area of civilization.

On the twelfth of June, several Ojibways entered the farm house of Mr. Whallon, who resided in Hennepin county, on the banks of the Minnesota, a mile below the Bloomington ferry. The wife of the farmer, a friend, and three children, besides a little Dahkotah girl, who had been brought up in the mission-house at Kaposia, and so changed in manners that her origin was scarcely perceptible, were sitting in the room when the Indians came in. Instantly seizing the little Indian maiden, they threw her out of the door, killed and scalped her, and fled before the men who were near by, in the field, could reach the house.

EVENTS OF A. D. 1857.

The procurement of a state organization, and a grant of lands for railroad purposes, were the topics of political interest during the year 1857.

The eighth Legislative Assembly convened at the capitol on the seventh of January, and J. B. Brisbin was elected President of the Council, and J. W. Furber, Speaker of the House.

A bill changing the seat of government to Saint Peter, on the Minnesota River, caused much discussion.

On Saturday, February twenty-eighth, Mr. Balcombe offered a resolution to report the bill for the removal of the seat of government, and should Mr. Rolette, chairman of the committee, fail, that W. W. Wales, of said committee, report a copy of said bill.

Mr. Setzer, after the reading of the resolution, moved a call of the Council, and Mr. Rolette was found to be absent. The chair ordered the sergeant at arms to report Mr Rolette in his seat. Mr. Balcombe moved that further proceedings under the call be dispensed with; which did not prevail. From that time until the next Thursday afternoon, March the fifth, a period of one hundred and twenty-three hours, the Council remained in their chamber without recess. At that time a motion to adjourn prevailed. On Friday another motion was made to dispense with the call of the Council, which did not prevail. On Saturday, the Council met, the president declared the call still pending. At seven and a half p. m., a committee of the House was announced. The chair ruled, that no communication from the House could be received while a call of the Council was pending, and the committee withdrew. A motion was again made during the last night of the session, to dispense with all further proceedings under the call, which prevailed, with one vote only in the negative.

Mr. Ludden then moved that a committee be appointed to wait on the Governor. and inquire if he had any further communication to make to the Council.

Mr. Lowry moved a call of the Council, which was ordered, and the roll being called. Messrs. Rolette, Thompson and Tillotson were absent.

At twelve o'clock at night the president resumed the chair, and announced that the time limited by law for the continuation of the session of the territorial legislature had expired, and he therefore declared the Council adjourned and the seat of government remained at Saint Paul.

The excitement on the capital question was intense, and it was a strange scene to see members of the Council, eating and sleeping in the hall of legislation for days, waiting for the sergeant-at-arms to report an absent member in his seat.

On the twenty-third of February, 1857, an act passed the United States Senate, to authorize the people of Minnesota to form a constitution, preparatory to their admission into the Union on an equal footing with the original states.

Governor Gorman called a special session of the legislature, to take into consideration measures that would give efficiency to the act. The extra session convened on April twenty-seventh, and a message was transmitted by Samuel Medary, who had been appointed governor in place of W. A. Gorman, whose term of office had expired. The extra session adjourned on the twenty-third of May; and in accordance with the provisions of the enabling act of Congress, an election was held on the first Monday in June, for delegates to a convention which was to assemble at the capitol on the second Monday in July. The election resulted, as was thought, in giving a majority of delegates to the Republican party.

At midnight previous to the day fixed for the meeting of the convention, the Republicans proceeded to the capitol, because the enabling act had not fixed at what hour on the second Monday the convention should assemble, and fearing that the Democratic delegates might anticipate them, and elect the officers of the body. A little before twelve, A. M., on Monday, the secretary of the territory entered the speaker's rostrum, and began to call the body to order; and at the same time a delegate, J. W. North, who had in his possession a written request from the majority of the delegates present, proceeded to do the same thing. The secretary of the territory put a motion to adjourn, and the Democratic members present voting in the affirmative, they left the hall. The Republicans, feeling that they were in the majority, remained, and in due time organized, and proceeded with the business specified in the enabling act, to form a constitution, and take all necessary steps for the establishment of a state government, in conformity with the Federal Constitution, subject to the approval and ratification of the people of the proposed state.

After several days the Democratic wing also organized in the Senate chamber at the capitol, and, claiming to be the true body, also proceeded to form a constitution. Both parties were remarkably orderly and intelligent, and everything was marked by perfect decorum. After they had been in session some weeks, moderate counsels prevailed, and a committee of conference was appointed from each body, which resulted in both adopting the constitution framed by the Democratic wing, on the twenty-ninth of August. According to the provision of the constitution, an election was held for state officers and the adoption of the constitution, on the second Tuesday, the thirteenth of October. The constitution was adopted by almost a unanimous vote. It provided that the territorial officers should retain their offices until the state was admitted into the Union, not anticipating the long delay which was experienced.

The first session of the state legislature commenced on the first Wednesday of December, at the capitol, in the city of Saint Paul; and during the month elected Henry M. Rice and James Shields as their Representatives in the United States Senate.

EVENTS OF A. D. 1858.

On the twenty-ninth of January, 1858, Mr. Douglas submitted a bill to the United States Senate, for the admission of Minnesota into the Union. On the first of February, a discussion arose on the bill, in which Senators Douglas, Wilson, Gwin, Hale, Mason, Green, Brown, and Crittenden participated. Brown, of Mississippi, was opposed to the admission of Minnesota, until the Kansas question was settled. Mr. Crittenden, as a Southern man, could not endorse all that was said by the Senator from Mississippi; and his words of wisdom and moderation during this day's discussion, were worthy of remembrance. On April the seventh, the bill passed the Senate with only three dissenting votes; and in a short time the House of Representatives concurred, and on May the eleventh, the President approved, and Minnesota was fully recognized as one of the United States of America.

OUTLINE HISTORY

OF THE

STATE OF MINNESOTA.

CHAPTER XXIV.

FIRST STATE LEGISLATURE—STATE RAILWAY BONDS—MINNESOTA DURING THE CIVIL WAR—REGIMENTS—THE SIOUX OUTBREAK.

The transition of Minnesota from a territorial to a state organization occurred at the period when the whole republic was suffering from financial embarrassments.

By an act of congress approved by the president on the 5th of March, 1857, lands had been granted to Minnesota to aid in the construction of railways. During an extra session of the legislature of Minnesota, an act was passed in May, 1857, giving the congressional grant to certain corporations to build railroads.

A few months after, it was discovered that the corporators had neither the money nor the credit to begin and complete these internal improvements. In the winter of 1858 the legislature again listened to the siren voices of the railway corporations, until their words to some members seemed like "apples of gold in pictures of silver," and an additional act was passed submitting to the people an amendment to the constitution which provided for the loan of the public credit to the land grant railroad companies to the amount of $5,000,000, upon condition that a certain amount of labor on the roads was performed.

Some of the citizens saw in the proposed measure "a cloud no larger than a man's hand," which would lead to a terrific storm, and a large public meeting was convened at the capitol in St. Paul, and addressed by ex-Governor Gorman, D. A. Robertson, William R. Marshall and others deprecating the engrafting of such a peculiar amendment into the constitution; but the people were poor and needy and deluded and would not listen; their hopes and happiness seemed to depend upon the plighted faith of railway corporators, and on April the 15th, the appointed election day, 25,023 votes were deposited for, while only 6,733 votes were cast against the amendment.

FIRST STATE LEGISLATURE.

The election of October, 1857, was carried on with much partisan feeling by democrats and republicans. The returns from wilderness precincts were unusually large, and in the counting of votes for governor, Alexander Ramsey appeared to have received 17,550, and Henry H. Sibley 17,796 ballots. Governor Sibley was declared elected by a majority of 246, and duly recognized. The first legislature assembled on the 2d of December, 1857, before the formal admission of Minnesota into the Union, and on the 25th of March, 1858, adjourned until June the 2d, when it again met. The next day Governor Sibley delivered his message. His term of office was arduous. On the 4th of August, 1858, he expressed his determination not to deliver any state bonds to the railway companies unless they would give first mortgages, with priority of lien, upon their lands, roads and franchises, in favor of the state. One of the companies applied for a mandamus from the supreme court of the state, to compel the issue of the bonds without the restrictions demanded by the governor.

In November the court, Judge Flandrau dissenting, directed the governor to issue state bonds as soon as a railway company delivered their first mortgage bonds, as provided by the amendment to the constitution. But, as was to be expected, bonds sent out under such peculiar circumstances were not sought after by capitalists. Moreover, after over two million dollars in bonds had been issued, not an iron rail had been laid, and only about two hundred and fifty miles of grading had been completed.

In his last message Governor Sibley in reference to the law in regard to state credit to railways, says: "I regret to be obliged to state that the measure has proved a failure, and has by no means accomplished what was hoped from it, either in providing means for the issue of a safe currency or of aiding the companies in the completion of the work upon the roads."

ACT FOR NORMAL SCHOOLS.

Notwithstanding the pecuniary complications of the state, during Governor Sibley's administration, the legislature did not entirely forget that there were some interests of more importance than railway construction, and on the 2d of August, 1858, largely through the influence of the late John D. Ford, M. D., a public spirited citizen of Winona, an act was passed for the establishment of three training schools for teachers.

FIRST STEAMBOAT ON THE RED RIVER OF THE NORTH.

In the month of June, 1859 an important route was opened between the Mississippi and the Red River of the North. The then enterprising firm of J. C. Burbank & Co., of St. Paul, having secured from the Hudson Bay Company the transportation of their supplies by way of the Mississippi, in place of the tedious and treacherous routes through Hudson's Bay or Lake Superior, they purchased a little steamboat on the Red River of the North which had been built by Anson Northrup, and commenced the carrying of freight and passengers by land to Breckenridge and by water to Pembina.

This boat had been the first steamboat which moved on the Mississippi above the falls of St. Anthony, to which there is a reference made upon the 121st page.

Mr. Northrup, after he purchased the boat, with a large number of wagons carried the boat and machinery from Crow Wing on the Mississippi and on the 8th of April, 1859, reached the Red River not far from the site of Fargo.

SECOND STATE LEGISLATURE.

At an election held in October, 21,335 votes were deposited for Alexander Ramsey as governor, and 17,532 for George L. Becker. Governor Ramsey, in an inaugural delivered on the second of January, 1860, devoted a large space to the discussion of the difficulties arising from the issue of the railroad bonds. He said: "It is extremely desirable to remove as speedily as possible so vexing a question from our state politics, and not allow it to remain for years to disturb our elections, possibly to divide our people into bond and anti-bond parties, and introduce, annually, into our legislative halls an element of discord and possibly of corruption, all to end just as similar complications in other states have ended. The men who will have gradually engrossed the posession of all the bonds, at the cost of a few cents on the dollar, will knock year after year at the door of the legislature for their payment in full, the press will be subsidized; the cry of repudiation will be raised; all the ordinary and extraordinary means of procuring legislation in doubtful cases will be freely resorted to, until finally the bondholders will pile up almost fabulous fortunes. * * * * It is assuredly true that the present time is, of all others, alike for the present bondholder and the people of the state, the very time to arrange, adjust and settle these unfortunate and deplorable railroad and loan complications."

The legislature of this year passed a law submitting an amendment to the constitution which would prevent the issue of any more railroad bonds. At an election in November, 1860, it was voted on, and reads as follows: "The credit of the state shall never be given on bonds in aid of any individual, association or corporation; nor shall there be any further issue of bonds denominated Minnesota state railroad bonds, under what purports to be an amendment to section ten, of article nine, of the constitution, adopted April 14, 1858, which is hereby expunged from the constitution, saving, excepting, and reserving to the state, nevertheless, all rights, remedies and forfeitures accruing under said amendment."

FIRST WHITE PERSON EXECUTED.

On page 126 there is a notice of the first Indian hung under the laws of Minnesota. On March 23, 1860 the first white person was executed and attracted considerable attention from the fact, the one who suffered the penalty of the law was a woman.

Michael Bilansky died on the 11th of March, 1859, and upon examination, he was found to have been poisoned. Anna, his fourth wife, was tried for the offence, found guilty, and on the 3d of December, 1859, sentenced to be hung. The opponents to capital punishment secured the passage of an act, by the legislature, to meet her case, but it was vetoed by the governor, as unconstitutional. Two days before the execution, the unhappy woman asked her spiritual adviser to write to her parents in North Carolina, but not to state the cause of her death. Her scaffold was erected within the square of the Ramsey county jail.

THIRD STATE LEGISLATURE.

The third state legislature assembled on the 8th of January, 1861, and adjourned on the 8th of March. As Minnesota was the first state which received 1,280 acres of land in each township, for school purposes, Governor Ramsey in his annual message occupied several pages, in an able and elaborate argument as to the best methods of guarding and selling the school lands, and of protecting the school fund.

His predecessor in office, while a member of the convention to frame the constitution, had spoken in favor of dividing the school funds among the townships of the state, subject to the control of the local officers.

MINNESOTA DURING THE CIVIL WAR.

The people of Minnesota had not been as excited as the citizens of the Atlantic states on the question which was discussed before the presidential election of November, 1860, and a majority had calmly declared their preference for Abraham Lincoln, as president of the republic.

But the blood of her quiet and intelligent population was stirred on the morning of April 14, 1861, by the intelligence in the daily newspapers that the day before, the insurgents of South Carolina had bombarded Fort Sumter, and that after a gallant resistance of thirty-four hours General Robert Anderson and the few soldiers of his command had evacuated the fort.

Governor Ramsey was in Washington at this period, and called upon the president of the republic with two other citizens from Minnesota, and was the first of the state governors to tender the services of his fellow citizens. The offer of a regiment was accepted. The first company raised under the call of Minnesota was composed of energetic young men of St. Paul, and its captain was the esteemed William H. Acker, who afterwards fell in battle.

On the last Monday of April a camp for the First regiment was opened at Fort Snelling. More companies having offered than were necessary on the 30th of May Governor Ramsey sent a telegram to the secretary of war, offering another regiment.

THE FIRST REGIMENT.

On the 14th of June the First regiment was ordered to Washington, and on the 21st it embarked at St. Paul on the steamboats War Eagle and Northern Belle, with the following officers:

Willis A. Gorman, *Colonel*—Promoted to be brigadier general October 7, 1861, by the advice of Major General Winfield Scott.

Stephen Miller, *Lt. Colonel*—Made colonel of 7th regiment August, 1862.

William H. Dike, *Major*—Resigned October 22, 1861.

William B. Leach, *Adjutant*—Made captain and A. A. G. February 23, 1862.

Mark W. Downie, *Quartermaster*— Captain Company B, July 16, 1861.

Jacob H. Stewart, *Surgeon*—Prisoner at Bull Run, July 21, 1861. Paroled at Richmond, Virginia.

Charles W. Le Boutillier, *Assistant Surgeon*—Prisoner at Bull Run. Surgeon 9th regiment. Died April, 1863.

Edward D. Neill, *Chaplain*—Commissioned July 13, 1862, hospital chaplain U. S. A., resigned in 1864, and appointed by President Lincoln, one of his secretaries.

After a few days in Washington, the regiment was sent to Alexandria, Virginia, where until the 16th of July it remained. On the morning of that day it began with other troops of Franklin's brigade to move toward the enemy, and that night encamped in the valley of Pohick creek, and the next day marched to Sangster's station on the Orange & Alexandria railroad. The third day Centreville was reached. Before daylight on Sunday, the 21st of July, the soldiers of the First regiment rose for a march to battle. About three o'clock in the morning they left camp, and after passing through the hamlet of Centreville, halted for General Hunter's column to pass. At daylight the regiment again began to move, and after crossing a bridge on the Warrenton turnpike, turned into the woods, from which at about ten o'clock it emerged into an open country, from which could be seen an artillery engagement on the left between the Union troops under Hunter, and the insurgents commanded by Evans.

An hour after this the regiment reached a branch of Bull Run, and, as the men were thirsty, began to fill their empty canteens. While thus occupied, and as the St. Paul company under Captain Wilkins was crossing the creek, an order came for Colonel Gorman to hurry up the regiment.

The men now moved rapidly through the woodland of a hillside, stepping over some of the dead of Burnside's command, and hearing the cheers of victory caused by the pressing back of the insurgent troops. At length the regiment, passing Sudley church, reached a clearing in the woods, and halted, while other troops of Franklin's brigade passed up the Sudley church road. Next they passed through a narrow strip of woods and occupied the cultivated field from which Evans and Bee of the rebel army had been driven by the troops of Burnside, Sykes and others of Hunter's division.

Crossing the Sudley road, Rickett's battery unlimbered and began to fire at the enemy, whose batteries were between the Robinson and Henry house on the south side of the Warrenton turnpike, while the First Minnesota passed to the right. After firing about twenty minutes the battery was ordered to go down the Sudley road nearer the enemy, where it was soon disabled. The First Minnesota was soon met by rebel troops advancing under cover of the woods, who supposed the regiment was a part of the confederate army.

Javan B. Irvine, then a private citizen of St. Paul, on a visit to the regiment, now a captain in the United States army, wrote to his wife: "We had just formed when we were ordered to kneel and fire upon the rebels who were advancing under the cover of the woods. We fired two volleys through the woods, when we were ordered to rally in the woods in our rear, which all did except the first platoon of our own company, which did not hear the order and stood their ground. The rebels soon came out from their shelter between us and their battery. Colonel Gorman mistook them for friends and told the men to cease firing upon them, although they had three secession flags directly in front of their advancing columns. This threw our men into confusion, some declaring they are friends; others that they are enemies. I called to our boys to give it to them, and fired away myself as rapidly as possible. The rebels themselves mistook us for Georgia troops, and waved their hands at us to cease firing. I had just loaded to give them another charge, when a lieutenant-colonel of a Mississippi regiment rode out between us, waving his hand for us to stop firing. I rushed up to him and asked 'If he was a secessionist?' He said 'He was a Mississippian.' I presented my bayonet to his breast and commanded him to surrender, which he did after some hesitation. I ordered him to dismount, and led him and his horse from the field, in the meantime disarming him of his sword and pistols. I led him off about two miles and placed him in charge of a lieutenant with an escort of cavalry, to be taken to General McDowell. He requested the officer to allow me to accompany him, as he desired my protection. The officer assured him that he would be safe in their hands, and he rode off. I retained his pistol, but sent his sword with him." In another letter, dated the 25th of July, Mr. Irvine writes from Washington: "I have just returned from a visit to Lieutenant-Colonel Boone, who is confined in the old Capitol. I found him in a pleasant room on the third story, surrounded by several southern gentlemen, among whom was Senator Breckenridge. He was glad to see me, and appeared quite well after the fatigue of the battle of Sunday. There were with me Chaplain Neill, Captains Wilkin and Colville, and Lieutenant Coates, who were introduced."

The mistake of several regiments of the Union troops in supposing that the rebels were friendly regiments led to confusion and disaster, which was followed by panic.

SECOND REGIMENT.

The Second Minnesota Regiment which had been organized in July, 1861, left Fort Snelling on the eleventh of October, and proceeding to Louisville, was incorporated with the Army of the Ohio. Its officers were: Horatio P. Van Cleve, *Colonel.* Promoted Brigadier General March 21, 1862. James George, *Lt. Colonel.* Promoted Colonel; resigned June 29, 1864. Simeon Smith, *Major.* Appointed Paymaster U. S. A., September, 1861. Alexander Wilkin, *Major.* Colonel 9th Minnesota, August, 1862. Reginald Bingham, *Surgeon.* Dismissed May 27, 1862. M. C. Tollman, *Ass't Surgeon.* Promoted Surgeon. Timothy Cressey, *Chaplain.* Resigned October, 10, 1863. Daniel D. Heaney, *Adjutant.* Promoted Captain Company C. William S. Grow, *Quarter Master.* Resigned, January, 1863.

SHARP SHOOTERS.

A company of Sharp Shooters under Captain F. Peteler, proceeding to Washington, on the 11th.

of October was assigned as Co., A, 2d Regiment U. S. Sharp Shooters.

THIRD REGIMENT.

On the 16th of November, 1861, the Third Regiment left the State and went to Tennessee. Its officers were: Henry C. Lester, *Colonel*. Dismissed December 1, 1862. Benjamin F. Smith, *Lt. Colonel*. Resigned May 9, 1862. John A. Hadley, *Major*. Resigned May 1, 1862. R. C. Olin, *Adjutant*.—Resigned. C. H. Blakely, *Adjutant*. Levi Butler. *Surgeon*.—Resigned September 30, 1863. Francis Millipan, *Ass't Surgeon*.—Resigned April 8, 1862. Chauncey Hobart, *Chaplain*. — Resigned June 2, 1863.

ARTILLERY.

In December, the First Battery of Light Artillery left the State, and reported for duty at St. Louis, Missouri

CAVALRY.

During the fall, three companies of cavalry were organized, and proceeded to Benton Barracks, Missouri. Ultimately they were incorporated with the Fifth Iowa Cavalry.

MOVEMENTS OF MINNESOTA TROOPS IN 1862.

On Sunday the 19th of January, 1862, not far from Somerset and about forty miles from Danville, Kentucky, about 7 o'clock in the morning, Col. Van Cleve was ordered to meet the enemy, In ten minutes the Second Minnesota regiment was in line of battle. After supporting a battery for some time it continued the march, and proceeding half a mile found the enemy behind the fences, and a hand to hand fight of thirty minutes ensued, resulting in the flight of the rebels. Gen. Zollicoffer and Lieut. Peyton, of the insurgents were of the killed.

BATTLE OF PITTSBURG LANDING.

On Sunday, the 6th of April occurred the battle of Pittsburg Landing, in Tennessee. Minnesota was there represented by the First Minnesota battery, Captain Emil Munch, which was attached to the division of General Prentiss. Captain Munch was severely wounded. One of the soldiers of his command wrote as follows: "Sunday morning, just after breakfast, an officer rode up to our Captain's tent and told him to prepare for action. * * * * * We wheeled into battery and opened upon them. * * * The first time we wheeled one of our drivers was killed; his name was Colby Stinson. Haywood's horse was shot at almost the same time. The second time we came into battery, the captain was wounded in the leg, and his horse shot under him. They charged on our guns and on the sixth platoon howitzer, but they got hold of the wrong end of the gun. We then limbered up and retreated within the line of battle. While we were retreating they shot one of our horses, when we had to stop and take him out, which let the rebels come up rather close. When within about six rods they fired and wounded Corporal Davis, breaking his leg above the ankle."

As the artillery driver was picked up, after being fatally wounded, at the beginning of the fight he said, 'Don't stop with me. Stand to your guns like men,' and expired.

FIRST REGIMENT AT YORKTOWN SIEGE.

Early in April the First regiment as a part of Sedgwick's division of the Army of the Potomac arrived near Yorktown, Virginia, and was stationed between the Warwick and York rivers, near Wynnes' mill. During the night of the 30th of May, there was a continual discharge of cannon by the enemy, but just before daylight the next day, which was Sunday, it ceased and the pickets cautiously approaching discovered that the rebels had abandoned their works. The next day the regiment was encamped on the field where Cornwallis surrendered to Washington.

BATTLE OF FAIR OAKS.

While Gorman's brigade was encamped at Goodly Hole creek, Hanover county, Virginia, an order came about three o'clock of the afternoon of Saturday, the thirty-first day of May to to cross the Chicahominy and engage in the battle which had been going on for a few hours. In a few minutes the First Minnesota was on the march, by a road which had been cut through the swamp, and crossed the Chicahominy by a rude bridge of logs, with both ends completely submerged by the stream swollen by recent rains, and rising every hour.

About 5 o'clock in the afternoon the First Minnesota as the advance of Gorman's brigade reached the scene of action, and soon the whole brigade with Kirby's battery held the enemy in check at that point.

The next day they were in line of battle but not attacked. Upon the field around a country farm house they encamped.

BATTLE OF SAVAGE STATION.

Just before daylight on Sunday, June the 29th, Sedgwick's, to which the First Minnesota belonged, left the position that had been held since the battle of Fair Oaks, and had not proceeded more than two miles before they met the enemy in a peach orchard, and after a sharp conflict compelled them to retire. At about 5 o'clock the afternoon of the same day they again met the enemy at Savage Station, and a battle lasted till dark. Burgess, the color sergeant who brought off the flag from the Bull Run battle, a man much respected, was killed instantly.

On Monday, between White Oak swamp and Willis' church, the regiment had a skirmish, and Captain Colville was slightly wounded. Tuesday was the 1st of July, and the regiment was drawn up at the dividing line of Henrico and Charles City county, in sight of James river, and although much exposed to the enemy's batteries, was not actually engaged. At midnight the order was given to move, and on the morning of the 2d of July they tramped upon the wheat fields at Harrison's Landing, and in a violent rain encamped.

MOVEMENTS OF OTHER TROOPS.

The Fourth regiment left Fort Snelling for Benton barracks, Missouri, on the 21st of April, 1862, with the following officers:

John B. Sanborn, *Colonel*—Promoted brigadier general.

Minor T. Thomas, *Lt. Colonel*—Made colonel of 8th regiment August 24, 1862.

A. Edward Welch, *Major*—Died at Nashville February 1, 1864.

John M. Thompson, *Adjutant*—Captain Company E, November 20, 1862.

Thomas B. Hunt, *Quartermaster*—Made captain and A. Q. M. April 9, 1863.

John H. Murphy, *Surgeon*—Resigned July 9, 1863.

Elisha W. Cross, *Assistant Surgeon*—Promoted July 9, 1863.

Asa S. Fiske, *Chaplain*—Resigned Oct. 3, 1864.

FIFTH REGIMENT.

The Second Minnesota Battery, Captain W. A. Hotchkiss, left the same day as the Fourth regiment. On the 13th of May the Fifth regiment departed from Fort Snelling with the following officers: Rudolph Borgesrode, colonel, resigned August 31, 1862; Lucius F. Hubbard, lieutenant-colonel, promoted colonel August 31, 1862, elected governor of Minnesota 1881; William B. Gere, major, promoted lieutenant-colonel; Alpheus R. French, adjutant, resigned March 19, 1863; W. B. McGrorty, quartermaster, resigned September 15, 1864; F. B. Etheridge, surgeon, resigned September 3, 1862; V. B. Kennedy, assistant surgeon, promoted surgeon; J. F. Chaffee, chaplain, resigned June 23, 1862; John Ireland, chaplain, resigned April, 1863.

Before the close of May the Second, Fourth and Fifth regiments were in conflict with the insurgents, near Corinth, Mississippi.

BATTLE OF IUKA.

On the 18th of September, Colonel Sanborn, acting as brigade commander in the Third division of the Army of the Mississippi, moved his troops, including the Fourth Minnesota regiment, to a position on the Tuscumbia road, and formed a line of battle.

BATTLE OF CORINTH.

In a few days the contest began at Iuka, culminated at Corinth, and the Fourth and Fifth regiments and First Minnesota battery were engaged.

On the 3d of October, about five o'clock, Colonel Sanborn advanced his troops and received a severe fire from the enemy. Captain Mowers beckoned with his sword during the firing, as if he wished to make an important communication, but before Colonel Sanborn reached his side he fell, having been shot through the head. Before daylight on the 4th of October the Fifth regiment, under command of Colonel L. F. Hubbard, was aroused by the discharge of artillery. Later in the day it became engaged with the enemy, and drove the rebels out of the streets of Corinth. A private writes: "When we charged on the enemy General Rosecrans asked what little regiment that was, and on being told said 'The Fifth Minnesota had saved the town.' Major Coleman, General Stanley's assistant adjutant-general, was with us when he received his bullet-wound, and his last words were, "Tell the general that the Fifth Minnesota fought nobly. God bless the Fifth.'"

OTHER MOVEMENTS.

A few days after the fight at Corinth the Second Minnesota battery, Captain Hotchkiss, did good service with Buell's army at Perryville, Ky.

In the battle of Fredericksburg, Va., on the 13th of December, the First Minnesota regiment supported Kirbey's battery as it had done at Fair Oaks.

THIRD REGIMENT HUMILIATED.

On the morning of the 13th of July, near Murfreesboro, Ky.; the Third regiment was in the presence of the enemy. The colonel called a council of officers to decide whether they should fight, and the first vote was in the affirmative, but another vote being taken it was decided to surrender. Lieutenant-Colonel C. W. Griggs, Captains Andrews and Hoyt voted each time to fight. In September the regiment returned to Minnesota, humiliated by the want of good judgment upon the part of their colonel, and was assigned to duty in the Indian country.

THE SIOUX OUTBREAK.

The year 1862 will always be remembered as the period of the uprising of the Sioux, and the slaughter of the unsuspecting inhabitants of the scattered settlements in the Minnesota valley. Elsewhere in this work will be found a detailed account of the savage cruelties. In this place we only give the narrative of the events as related by Alexander Ramsey, then the governor of Minnesota.

"My surprise may therefore be judged, when, on August 19th, while busy in my office, Mr. Wm. H. Shelley, one of our citizens who had been at the agency just before the outbreak, came in, dusty and exhausted with a fifteen hours' ride on horseback, bearing dispatches to me of the most startling character from Agent Galbraith, dated August 18th, stating that the same day the Sioux at the lower agency had risen, murdered the settlers, and were plundering and burning all the buildings in that vicinity. As I believe no particulars regarding the manner in which the news were first conveyed to me has been published, it might be mentioned here. Mr. Shelley had been at Redwood agency, and other places in that vicinity, with the concurrence of the agent, recruiting men for a company, which was afterwards mustered into the Tenth regiment under Captain James O'Gorman, formerly a clerk of Nathan Myrick, Esq., a trader at Redwood, and known as the Renville Rangers. He (Shelley) left Redwood, he states, on Saturday, August 16th, with forty-five men, bound for Fort Snelling. Everything was quiet there then. It may be well to note here that one of the supposed causes of the outbreak was the fact that the Indians had been told that the government needed soldiers very badly, that many white men had been killed, and that all those in that locality were to be marched south, leaving the state unprotected. Seeing the men leave on Saturday may have strengthened this belief. Stopping at Fort Ridgely that night, the Renville Rangers the next day continued their march, and on Monday afternoon arrived at St. Peter. Galbraith was with them. Here he was overtaken by a messenger who had ridden down from Redwood that day, bearing the news of the terrible occurrences of that morning. This messenger was Mr. — Dickinson, who formerly kept a hotel at Henderson, but was living on the reservation at that time. He was in great distress about the safety of his family, and returning at once was killed by the Indians.

"When Agent Galbraith received the news, Mr. Shelley states, no one would at first believe it, as such rumors are frequent in the Indian country. Mr. Dickinson assured him of the truth with such earnestness, however, that his account was finally credited and the Renville Rangers were at once armed and sent back to Fort Ridgely, where they did good service in protecting the post.

"Agent Galbraith at once prepared the dispatches to me, giving the terrible news and calling for aid. No one could be found who would volunteer to carry the message, and Mr. Shelley offered to come himself. He had great difficulty in getting a horse; but finally secured one, and started for St. Paul, a distance of about ninety miles, about dark. He had not ridden a horse for some years, and as may be well supposed by those who have had experience in amateur horseback-riding, suffered very much from soreness; but rode all night at as fast a gate as his horse could carry him, spreading the startling news as he went down the Minnesota valley. Reaching St. Paul about 9 A. M., much exhausted he made his way to the capitol, and laid before me his message. The news soon spread through the city and created intense excitement.

"At that time, of course, the full extent and threatening nature of the outbreak could not be determined. It seemed serious, it is true, but in view of the riotous conduct of the Indians at Yellow Medicine a few days before, was deemed a repetition of the *emeute*, which would be simply local in its character, and easily quelled by a small force and good management on the part of the authorities at the agency.

"But these hopes, (that the outbreak was a local one) were soon rudely dispelled by the arrival, an hour or two later, of another courier, George C. Whitcomb, of Forest City, bearing the news of the murders at Acton. Mr. Whitcomb had ridden to Chaska or Carver on Monday, and came down from there on the small steamer Antelope, reaching the city an hour or two after Mr. Shelley.

"It now became evident that the outbreak was

more general than had at first been credited, and that prompt and vigorous measures would be required for its suppression and the protection of the inhabitants on the frontier. I at once proceeded to Fort Snelling and consulted with the authorities there (who had already received dispatches from Fort Ridgely) regarding the outbreak and the best means to be used to meet the danger.

"A serious difficulty met us at the outstart. The only troops at Fort Snelling were the raw recruits who had been hastily gathered for the five regiments. Most of them were without arms or suitable clothing as yet; some not mustered in or properly officered, and those who had arms had no fixed ammunition of the proper calibre. We were without transportation, quartermaster's or commissary stores, and, in fact, devoid of anything with which to commence a campaign against two or three thousand Indians, well mounted and armed, with an abundance of ammunition and provisions captured at the agency, and flushed with the easy victories they had just won over the unarmed settlers. Finally four companies were fully organized, armed and uniformed, and late at night were got off on two small steamers, the Antelope and Pomeroy, for Shakopee, from which point they would proceed overland. It was arranged that others should follow as fast as they could be got ready.

"This expedition was placed under the management of H. H. Sibley, whose long residence in the country of the Sioux had given him great influence with that people, and it was hoped that the chiefs and older men were still sensible to reason, and that with his diplomatic ability he could bring the powers of these to check the mad and reckless disposition of the "young men," and that if an opportunity for this failed that his knowledge of Indian war and tactics would enable him to overcome them in battle. And I think the result indicated the wisdom of my choice.

"I at once telegraphed all the facts to President Lincoln, and also telegraphed to Governor Solomon, of Wisconsin, for one hundred thousand cartridges, of a calibre to fit our rifles, and the requisition was kindly honored by that patriotic officer, and the ammunition was on its way next day. The governors of Iowa, Illinois and Michigan were also asked for arms and ammunition.

During the day other messengers arrived from Fort Ridgely, St. Peter and other points on the upper Minnesota, with intelligence of the most painful character, regarding the extent and ferocity of the massacre. The messages all pleaded earnestly for aid, and intimated that without speedy reinforcements or a supply of arms, Fort Ridgely, New Ulm, St. Peter and other points would undoubtedly fall into the hands of the savages, and thousands of persons be butchered The principal danger seemed to be to the settlements in that region, as they were in the vicinity of the main body of Indians congregated to await the payments. Comers arrived from various points every few hours, and I spent the whole night answering their calls as I could.

"Late that night, probably after midnight, Mr. J. Y. Branham, Sr., arrived from Forest City, after a forced ride on horseback of 100 miles, bearing the following message:

* * * * * * * *

"FOREST CITY, Aug. 20, 1862, 6 o'clock a. m.

His Excellency, Alexander Ramsey, Governor, etc.—Sir: In advance of the news from the Minnesota river, the Indians have opened on us in Meeker. It is war! A few propose to make a stand here. Send us, forthwith, some good guns and ammunition to match. Yours truly,

A. C. SMITH.

Seventy-five stands of Springfield rifles and several thousand rounds of ball cartridges were at once issued to George C. Whitcomb, to be used in arming a company which I directed to be raised and enrolled to use these arms; and Gen. Sibley gave Mr. Whitcomb a captain's commission for the company. Transportation was furnished him, and the rifles were in Forest City by the morning of the 23d, a portion having been issued to a company at Hutchinson on the way up. A company was organized and the arms placed in their hands, and I am glad to say they did good service in defending the towns of Forest City and Hutchinson on more than one occasion, and many of the Indians are known to have been killed with them. The conduct and bravery of the courageous men who guarded those towns, and resisted the assaults of the red savages, are worthy of being commemorated on the pages of our state history."

MOVEMENT OF MINNESOTA REGIMENTS 1863.

On the 3d of April, 1863, the Fourth regiment was opposite Grand Gulf, Mississippi, and in a few days they entered Port Gibson, and here Col. Sanborn resumed the command of a brigade. On the 14th of May the regiment was at the battle of Raymond, and on the 14th participated in the battle of Jackson. A newspaper correspondent writes: "Captain L. B. Martin, of the Fourth Minnesota, A. A. G. to Colonel Sanborn, seized the flag of the 59th Indiana infantry, rode rapidly beyond the skirmishers, (Co. H, Fourth Minnesota, Lt. Geo. A. Clark) and raised it over the dome of the capitol" of Mississippi. On the 16th the regiment was in the battle of Champion Hill, and four days later in the siege of Vicksburg.

FIFTH REGIMENT.

The Fifth regiment reached Grand Gulf on the 7th of May and was in the battles of Raymond and Jackson, and at the rear of Vicksburg.

BATTLE OF GETTYSBURG.

The First regiment reached Gettysburg, Pa., on the 1st of July, and the next morning Hancock's corps, to which it was attached, moved to a ridge, the right resting on Cemetery Hill, the left near Sugar Loaf Mountain. The line of battle was a semi-ellipse, and Gibbon's division, to which the regiment belonged occupied the center of the curve nearest the enemy. On the 2d of July, about 5 o'clock in the afternoon, General Hancock rode up to Colonel Colville, and ordered him to charge upon the advancing foe. The muzzles of the opposing muskets were not far distant and the conflict was terrific. When the sun set Captain Muller and Lieutenant Farrer were killed; Captain Periam mortally wounded; Colonel Colville, Lieut-Colonel Adams, Major Downie, Adjutant Peller, Lieutenants Sinclair, Demerest, DeGray and Boyd, severely wounded.

On the 3d of July, about 10 o'clock in the morning, the rebels opened a terrible artillery fire, which lasted until 3 o'clock in the afternoon, and then the infantry was suddenly advanced, and there was a fearful conflict, resulting in the defeat of the enemy. The loss on this day was also very severe. Captain Messick, in command of the First regiment, after the wounding of Colville, and Adams and Downie, was killed. Captain Farrell was mortally wounded, and Lieutenants Harmon, Heffelfinger, and May were wounded. Color-Sergeant E. P. Perkins was wounded on the 2d of July. On the 3d of July Corporal Dehn, of the color guard was shot through the hand and the flag staff cut in two. Corporal H. D. O'Brien seized the flag with the broken staff and waving it over his head rushed up to the muzzles of the enemy's muskets and was wounded in the hand, but Corporal W. N. Irvine instantly grasped the flag and held it up. Marshall Sherman of company E, captured the flag of the 28th Virginia regiment.

THE SECOND REGIMENT.

The Second regiment, under Colonel George, on the 19th of September fought at Chicamauga, and in the first day's fight, eight were killed and forty-one wounded. On the 25th of November, Lieutenant-Colonel Bishop in command, it moved against the enemy at Mission Ridge, and of the seven non-commissioned officers in the color guard, six were killed or wounded.

The Fourth regiment was also in the vicinity of Chattanooga, but did not suffer any loss.

EVENTS OF 1864.

The Third regiment, which after the Indian expedition had been ordered to Little Rock, Arkansas, on the 30th of March, 1864, had an engagement near Augusta, at Fitzhugh's Woods. Seven men were killed and sixteen wounded. General C. C. Andrews, in command of the force, had his horse killed by a bullet.

FIRST REGIMENT.

The First regiment after three year's service was mustered out at Fort Snelling, and on the 28th of April, 1864, held its last dress parade, in the presence of Governor Miller, who had once been their lieutenant-colonel and commander. In May some of its members re-enlisted as a battalion, and again joined the Army of the Potomac.

SIXTH, SEVENTH, NINTH AND TENTH REGIMENTS.

The Sixth regiment, which had been in the expedition against the Sioux, in June, 1864, was assigned to the 16th army corps, as was the Seventh, Ninth and Tenth, and on the 13th of July, near Tupelo, Mississippi, the Seventh, Ninth and Tenth, with portions of the Fifth, were in battle. During the first day's fight Surgeon Smith, of the Seventh, was fatally wounded through the neck. On the morning of the 14th the battle began in earnest, and the Seventh, under Colonel W. R. Marshall, made a successful charge. Colonel Alexander Wilkin, of the Ninth, was shot, and fell dead from his horse.

THE FOURTH REGIMENT.

On the 15th of October the Fourth regiment were engaged near Altoona, Georgia.

THE EIGHTH REGIMENT.

On the 7th of December the Eighth was in battle near Murfreesboro, Tennessee, and fourteen were killed and seventy-six wounded.

BATTLE OF NASHVILLE.

During the month of December the Fifth, Seventh, Ninth and Tenth regiments did good service before Nashville. Colonel L. F. Hubbard, of the Fifth, commanding a brigade, after he had been knocked off his horse by a ball, rose, and on foot led his command over the enemy's works. Colonel W. R. Marshall, of the Seventh, in command of a brigade, made a gallant charge, and Lieutenant-colonel S. P. Jennison, of the Tenth, one of the first on the enemy's parapet, received a severe wound.

MINNESOTA TROOPS IN 1865.

In the spring of 1865 the Fifth, Sixth, Seventh, Ninth and Tenth regiments were engaged in the siege of Mobile. The Second and Fourth regiments and First battery were with General Sherman in his wonderful campaign, and the Eighth in the month of March was ordered to North Carolina. The battalion, the remnant of the First, was with the Army of the Potomac until Lee's surrender.

Arrangements were soon perfected for disbanding the Union army, and before the close of the summer all the Minnesota regiments that had been on duty were discharged.

LIST OF MINNESOTA REGIMENTS AND TROOPS.

First,	Organized	April, 1861,	Discharged	May 5,	1864.
Second	"	July "	"	July 11,	1865.
Third	"	Oct. "	"	Sept.	"
Fourth	"	Dec. "	"	Aug.	"
Fifth	"	May, 1862,	"	Sept.	"
Sixth	"	Aug. "	"	Aug.	"
Seventh	"	" "	"	"	"
Eighth	"	" "	"	"	"
Ninth	"	" "	"	"	"
Tenth	"	" "	"	"	"
Eleventh	"	" 1861	"	"	"

ARTILLERY.

First Regiment, Heavy, May, 1864. Discharged Sept. 1865.

BATTERIES.

First, October, 1861.	Discharged	June,	1865.
Second, Dec. "	"	July	"
Third, Feb. 1863	"	Feb.	1866.

CAVALRY.

Rangers,	March, 1863.	Discharged	Dec.	1863.
Brackett's,	Oct. 1861.	"	June	1866.
2d Reg't,	July, 1863.	"	"	"

SHARPSHOOTERS.

Company A, organized in 1861.
" B, " " 1862.

CHAPTER XXV.

STATE AFFAIRS FROM A. D. 1862 to A. D. 1882.

In consequence of the Sioux outbreak, Governor Ramsey called an extra session of the legislature, which on the 9th of September, 1862, assembled.

As long as Indian hostilities continued, the flow of immigration was checked, and the agricultural interests suffered; but notwithstanding the disturbed condition of affairs, the St. Paul & Pacific Railroad Company laid ten miles of rail, to the Falls of St. Anthony.

FIFTH STATE LEGISLATURE.

During the fall of 1862 Alexander Ramsey had again been elected governor, and on the 7th of January, 1863, delivered the annual message before the Fifth state legislature. During this session he was elected to fill the vacancy that would take place in the United States senate by the expiration of the term of Henry M. Rice, who had been a senator from the time that Minnesota was organized as a state. After Alexander Ramsey became a senator, the lieutenant-governor, Henry A. Swift, became governor by constitutional provision.

GOVERNOR STEPHEN A. MILLER

At the election during the fall of 1863, Stephen A. Miller, colonel of the Seventh regiment, was elected governor by a majority of about seven thousand votes, Henry T. Welles being his competitor, and representative of the democratic party. During Governor Miller's administration, on the 10th of November, 1865, two Sioux chiefs, Little Six and Medicine Bottle, were hung at Fort Snelling, for participation in the 1862 massacre.

GOVERNOR W. R. MARSHALL.

In the fall of 1865 William R. Marshall, who had succeeded his predecessor as colonel of the Seventh regiment, was nominated by the republican party for governor, and Henry M. Rice by the democratic party. The former was elected by about five thousand majority. In 1867 Governor Marshall was again nominated for the office, and Charles E. Flandrau was the democratic candidate, and he was again elected by about the same majority as before.

GOVERNOR HORACE AUSTIN.

Horace Austin, the judge of the Sixth judicial district, was in 1869 the republican candidate for governor, and received 27,238 votes, and George L. Otis, the democratic candidate, 25,401 votes. In 1871 Governor Austin was again nominated, and received 45,883 votes, while 30,092 ballots were cast for Winthrop Young, the democratic candidate. The important event of his administration was the veto of an act of the legislature giving the internal improvement lands to certain railway corporations.

Toward the close of Governor Austin's administration, William Seeger, the state treasurer, was impeached for a wrong use of public funds. He plead guilty and was disqualified from holding any office of honor, trust or profit in the state.

GOVERNOR CUSHMAN K. DAVIS.

The republicans in the fall of 1873 nominated Cushman K. Davis for governor, who received 40,741 votes, while 35,245 ballots were thrown for the democratic candidate, Ara Barton.

The summer that he was elected the locust made its appearance in the land, and in certain regions devoured every green thing. One of the first acts of Governor Davis was to relieve the farmers who had suffered from the visitation of locusts. The legislature of 1874 voted relief, and the people of the state voluntarily contributed clothing and provisions.

During the administration of Governor Davis the principle was settled that there was nothing in the charter of a railroad company limiting the power of Minnesota to regulate the charges for freight and travel.

WOMEN ALLOWED TO VOTE FOR SCHOOL OFFICERS.

At the election in November, 1875, the people sanctioned the following amendment to the constitution: "The legislature may, notwithstanding anything in this article, [Article 7, section 8] provide by law that any woman at the age of twenty-one years and upwards, may vote at any election held for the purpose of chosing any officer of schools, or upon any measure relating to schools, and may also provide that any such woman shall be eligible to hold any office solely pertaining to the management of schools."

GOVERNOR J. S. PILLSBURY.

John S. Pillsbury, the republican nominee, at the election of November, 1875, received 47,073 for governor while his democratic competitor, D. L. Buell obtained 35,275 votes. Governor Pillsbury in his inaugural message, delivered on the 7th of January, 1876, urged upon the legislature, as his predecessors had done, the importance of providing for the payment of the state railroad bonds.

RAID ON NORTHFIELD BANK.

On the 6th of September, 1876, the quiet citizens of Minnesota were excited by a telegraphic announcement that a band of outlaws from Missouri had, at mid-day, ridden into the town of Northfield, recklessly discharging firearms, and proceeding to the bank, killed the acting cashier in an attempt to secure its funds. Two of the desperadoes were shot in the streets, by firm residents, and in a brief period, parties from the neighboring towns were in pursuit of the assassins. After a long and weary search four were surrounded in a swamp in Watonwan county, and one was killed, and the others captured.

At the November term of the fifth district court held at Faribault, the criminals were arraigned, and under an objebtionable statute, by pleading guilty, received an imprisonment for life, instead of the merrited death of the gallows.

THE ROCKY MOUNTAIN LOCUST.

As early as 1874 in some of the counties of Minnesota, the Rocky Mountain locust, of the same genus, but a different species from the Europe and Arctic locust, driven eastward by the failure of the succulent grasses of the upper Missouri valley appeared as a short, stout-legged, devouring army, and in 1875 the myriad of eggs deposited were hatched out, and the insects born within the state, flew to new camping grounds, to begin their devastations.

In the spring the locust appeared in some counties, but by an ingenious contrivance of sheet iron, covered with tar, their numbers were speedily reduced. It was soon discovered that usually but one hatching of eggs took place in the same district, and it was evident that the crop of 1877 would be remunerative. When the national Thanksgiving was observed on the 26th of November nearly 40,000,000 bushels of wheat had been garnered, and many who had sown in tears, devoutly thanked Him who had given plenty, and meditated upon the words of the Hebrew Psalmist, "He maketh peace within thy borders and filleth thee with the finest of the wheat."

GOVERNOR PILLSBURY'S SECOND TERM.

At the election in November, 1877, Governor Pillsbury was elected a second time, receiving 59,701, while 39,247 votes were cast for William L. Banning, the nominee of the democratic party. At this election the people voted to adopt two important amendments to the constitution.

BIENNIAL SESSION OF THE LEGISLATURE.

One provided for a biennial, in place of the annual session of the legislature, in these words:

"The legislature of the state shall consist of a senate and house of representatives, who shall meet biennially, at the seat of government of the state, at such time as shall be prescribed by law, but no session shall exceed the term of sixty days."

CHRISTIAN INSTRUCTION EXCLUDED FROM SCHOOLS.

The other amendment excludes Christian and other religious instructions from all of the educational institutions of Minnesota in these words: "But in no case, shall the moneys derived as aforesaid, or any portion thereof, or any public moneys, or property be appropriated or used for the support of schools wherein the distinctive doctrines, or creeds or tenets of any particular Christian or other religious sect, are promulgated or taught."

IMPEACHMENT OF JUDGE PAGE.

The personal unpopularity of Sherman Page, judge of the Tenth judicial district, culminated by the house of representatives of the legislature of 1878, presenting articles, impeaching him, for conduct unbecoming a judge: the senate sitting as a court, examined the charges, and on the 22d of June, he was acquitted.

GOVERNOR PILLSBURY'S THIRD TERM.

The republican party nominated John S. Pillsbury for a third term as governor, and at the election in November, 1879, he received 57,471 votes, while 42,444 were given for Edmund Rice, the representative of the democrats.

With a persistence which won the respect of the opponents of the measure, Governor Pillsbury continued to advocate the payment of the state railroad bonds. The legislature of 1870 submitted an amendment to the constitution, by which the "internal improvement lands" were to be sold and the proceeds to be used in cancelling the bonds, by the bondholders agreeing to purchase the lands at a certain sum per acre. The amendment was adopted by a vote of the people, but few of the bondholders accepted the provisions, and it failed to effect the proposed end. The legislature of 1871 passed an act for a commission to make an equitable adjustment of the bonds, but at a special election in May it was rejected.

The legislature of 1877 passed an act for calling in the railroad bonds, and issuing new bonds, which was submitted to the people at a special election on the 12th of June, and not accepted.

The legislature of 1878 proposed a constitutional amendment offering the internal improvement lands in exchange for railroad bonds, and the people at the November election disapproved of the proposition. Against the proposed amendment 45,669 votes were given, and only 26,311 in favor.

FIRST BIENNIAL SESSION.

The first biennial session of the legislature convened in January, 1881, and Governor Pillsbury again, in his message of the 6th of January, held up to the view of the legislators the dishonored railroad bonds, and the duty of providing for their settlement. In his argument he said:

"The liability having been voluntarily incurred, whether it was wisely created or not is foreign to the present question. It is certain that the obligations were fairly given for which consideration was fairly received; and the state having chosen foreclosure as her remedy, and disposed of the property thus acquired unconditionally as her own, the conclusion seems to me irresistible that she assumed the payment of the debt resting upon such property by every principle of law and equity. And, moreover, as the state promptly siezed the railroad property and franchises, expressly to indemnify her for payment of the bonds, it is difficult to see what possible justification there can be for her refusal to make that payment."

The legislature in March passed an act for the adjustment of these bonds, which being brought before the supreme court of the state was declared void. The court at the same time declared the amendment to the state constitution, which prohibited the settlement of these bonds, without the assent of a popular vote, to be a violation of the clause in the constitution of the United States of America prohibiting the impairment of the obligation of contracts. This decision cleared the way for final action. Governor Pillsbury called an extra session of the legislature in October, 1881, which accepted the offer of the bondholders, to be satisfied with a partial payment, and made provisions for cancelling bonds, the existence of which for more than twenty years had been a humiliation to a large majority of the thoughtful and intelligent citizens of Minnesota, and a blot upon the otherwise fair name of the commonwealth.

GOVERNOR HUBBARD.

Lucius F. Hubbard, who had been colonel of the Fifth Regiment, was nominated by the republican party, and elected in November, 1881, by a large majority over the democratic nominee, R. W. Johnson. He entered upon his duties in January, 1882, about the time of the present chapter going to press.

CHAPTER XXVI.

CAPITOL—PENITENTIARY—UNIVERSITY—DEAF AND DUMB INSTITUTION—SCHOOL FOR BLIND AND IMBECILES—INSANE ASYLUMS—STATE REFORM SCHOOL—NORMAL SCHOOLS.

Among the public buildings of Minnesota, the capitol is entitled to priority of notice.

TEMPORARY CAPITOLS.

In the absence of a capitol the first legislature of the territory of Minnesota convened on Monday, the 3d of September, 1849, at St. Paul, in a log building covered with pine boards painted white, two stories high, which was at the time a public inn, afterward known as the Central House, and kept by Robert Kennedy. It was situated on the high bank of the river. The main portion of the building was used for the library, secretary's office, council chamber and house of representatives' hall, while the annex was occupied as the dining-room of the hotel, with rooms for travelers in the story above. Both houses of the legislature met in the dining-hall to listen to the first message of Governor Ramsey.

The permanent location of the capital was not settled by the first legislature, and nothing could be done toward the erection of a capitol with the $20,000 appropriated by congress, as the permanent seat of government had not been designated.

William R. Marshall, since governor, at that time a member of the house of representatives from St. Anthony, with others, wished that point to be designated as the capital.

Twenty years after, in some remarks before the Old Settlers' Association of Hennepin county, Ex-Governor Marshall alluded to this desire. He said: "The original act [of congress] made St. Paul the temporary capital, but provided that the legislature might determine the permanent capital. A bill was introduced by the St. Paul delegation to fix the permanent capital there. I opposed it, endeavoring to have St. Anthony made the seat of government. We succeeded in defeating the bill which sought to make St. Paul the permanent capital, but we could not get through the bill fixing it at St. Anthony. So the question remained open in regard to the permanent capital until the next session in 1851, when a compromise was effected by which the capitol was to be at St. Paul, the State University at St. Anthony, and the Penitentiary at Stillwater. At an early day, as well as now, caricatures and burlesques were in vogue. Young William Randall, of St. Paul, now deceased, who had some talent in the graphic line, drew a picture of the efforts at capitol removal. It was a building on wheels, with ropes attached, at which I was pictured tugging, while Brunson, Jackson, and the other St. Paul members, were holding and checking the wheels, to prevent my moving it, with humorous speeches proceeding from the mouths of the parties to the contest."

The second territorial legislature assembled on the 2d of January, 1871, in a brick building three stories in height, which stood on Third street in St. Paul, on a portion of the site now occupied by the Metropolitan Hotel, and before the session closed it was enacted that St. Paul should be the permanent capital, and commissioners were appointed to expend the congressional appropriation for a capitol.

When the Third legislature assembled, in January, 1852, it was still necessary to occupy a hired building known as Goodrich's block, which stood on Third street just below the entrance of the Merchants' Hotel. In 1853, the capitol not being finished, the fourth legislature was obliged to meet in a two-story brick building at the corner of Third and Minnesota streets, and directly in the rear of the wooden edifice where the first legislature in 1849 had met.

THE CAPITOL.

After it was decided, in 1851, that St. Paul was to be the capital of the territory, Charles Bazille gave the square bounded by Tenth, Eleventh, Wabasha, and Cedar streets for the capitol. A plan was adopted by the building commissioners, and the contract was taken by Joseph Daniels, a builder, who now resides in Washington as a lawyer and claim agent. The building was of brick, and at first had a front portico, supported by four Ionic columns. It was two stories above the basement, 139 feet long and nearly 54 feet in width, with an extension in the rear 44x52 feet. In July, 1853, it was so far completed as to allow the governor to occupy the executive office.

SPEECHES OF EX-PRESIDENT FILLMORE AND GEORGE BANCROFT.

Before the war it was used not only by the legislature, and for the offices of state, but was granted for important meetings. On the 8th of June a large excursion party, under the auspices of the builders of the Chicago & Rock Island railway, arrived at St. Paul from the latter point, in five large steamboats, and among the passengers were some of the most distinguished scholars, statesmen and divines of the republic. At night the population of St. Paul filled the capitol, and the more sedate listened in the senate chamber to the stirring speeches of Ex-President Fillmore, and the historian, George Bancroft, who had been secretary of the navy, and minister plenipotentiary to Great Britain, while at a later period of the night the youthful portion of the throng danced in the room then used by the supreme court.

The "Pioneer" of the next day thus alludes to the occasion: "The ball in honor of the guests of the excursion came off, in fine style. At an early hour, the assembly having been called to order, by the Hon. H. H. Sibley, a welcoming speech was delivered by Governor Gorman, and replies were made by Ex-President Fillmore and the learned historian Bancroft. * * * * * * The dancing then commenced and was kept up till a late hour, when the party broke up, the guests returning to the steamers, and our town's people to their homes, all delighted with the rare entertainment."

HON. W. H. SEWARD'S SPEECH.

On the 8th of September, 1860, the capitol was visited by Hon. William H. Seward. At mid-day he met by invitation the members of the Historical Society in their rooms at the Capitol, and an address of welcome was made by the Rt. Rev. Bishop Anderson, of Rupert's Land, to which he made a brief response.

In the afternoon, crowds assembled in the grounds to listen to an expected speech, and every window of the capitol was occupied with eager faces. Standing upon the front steps, he addressed the audience in the language of a patriot and a statesman, and among his eloquent utterances, was the following prediction.

"Every step of my progress since I reached the northern Mississippi has been attended by a great and agreeable surprise. I had, early, read the works in which the geographers had described the scenes upon which I was entering, and I had studied them in the finest productions of art, but still the grandeur and luxuriance of this region had not been conceived. Those sentinel walls that look down upon the Mississippi, seen as I beheld them, in their abundant verdure, just when the earliest tinge of the fall gave luxuriance to the forests, made me think how much of taste and genius had been wasted in celebrating the highlands of Scotland, before the civilized man had reached the banks of the Mississippi; and the beautiful Lake Pepin, seen at sunset, when the autumnal green of the hills was lost in the deep blue, and the genial atmosphere reflected the rays of the sun, and the skies above seemed to move down and spread their gorgeous drapery on the scene, was a piece of upholstery, such as none but the hand of nature could have made, and it was but the vestibule of the capitol of the state of Minnesota. * * * * * * * * * * * * * Here is the place, the central place where the agriculture of the richest region of North America must pour its tribute. On the east, all along the shore of Lake Superior, and west, stretching in one broad plain, in a belt quite across the continent, is a country where State after State is to arise, and where the productions for the support of humanity, in old and crowded States, must be brought forth.

"This is then a commanding field, but it is as commanding in regard to the destiny of this country and of this continent, as it is, in regard to the commercial future, for power is not permanently to reside on the eastern slope of the Alleghany Mountains, nor in the sea-ports. Sea-ports have always been overrun and controlled by the people of the interior, and the power that shall communicate and express the will of men on this continent is to be located in the Mississippi valley and at the sources of the Mississippi and Saint Lawrence.

"In our day, studying, perhaps what might seem to others trifling or visionary, I had cast about for the future and ultimate central seat of power of North American people. I had looked at Quebec, New Orleans, Washington, Cincinnati, St. Louis, and San Francisco, and it had been the result of my last conjecture, that the seat of power in North America could be found in the valley of Mexico, and that the glories of the Aztec capital would be surrendered, at its becoming at last the capital of the United States of America, but I have corrected that view. I now believe that the ultimate seat of government in this great Continent, will be found somewhere within the circle or radius not very far from the spot where I now stand."

FLAG PRESENTATION.

In a few months after this speech, Mr. Seward was chosen by President Lincoln, inaugurated March 4, 1861, as secretary of state, and the next great crowd in front of the capitol was collected by the presentation of a flag by the ladies of St. Paul to the First Minnesota regiment which had been raised for the suppression of the slave-holders rebellion. On May the 25th, 1861, the regiment came down from their rendezvous at Fort Snelling, and marched to the capital grounds. The wife of Governor Ramsey, with the flag in hand, appeared on the front steps, surrounded by a committee of ladies, and presenting it to Colonel Gorman, made a brief address in which she said: "From this capitol, to the most remote frontier cottage, no heart but shall send up a prayer for your safety; no eye but shall follow with affection the flutterings of your banner, and no one but shall feel pride, when you crown the banner as you will crown it, with glory."

As the State increased in population it was necessary to alter and enlarge the building, and in 1873, a wing was added fronting on Exchange street, and the cupola was improved. The legislature of 1878 provided for the erection of another wing, at an expense of $14,000, fronting on Wabasha street. The building, by successive additions, was in length 204 feet, and in width 150 feet, and the top of the dome was more than 100 feet from the ground.

THE CAPITOL IN FLAMES.

On the morning of the 1st of March, 1881, it was destroyed by fire. About 9 o'clock in the the evening two gentlemen, who lived opposite, discovered the capitol was on fire, and immediately, by the telegraph, an alarm notified the firemen of the city, and the occupants of the capitol.

The flames rapidly covered the cupola and licked the flag flying from the staff on top. One of the reporters of the Pioneer Press, who was in the senate chamber at the time, graphically describes the scene within.

He writes: "The senate was at work on third reading of house bills; Lieutenant Governor Gilman in his seat, and Secretary Jennison reading something about restraining cattle in Rice county; the senators were lying back listening carelessly, when the door opened and Hon. Michael Doran announced that the building was on fire. All eyes were at once turned in that direction, and the flash of the flames was visible from the top of the gallery, as well as from the hall, which is on a level with the floor of the senate. The panic that ensued had a different effect upon the different persons, and those occupying places nearest the entrance, pushing open the door, and rushing pell mell through the blinding smoke. Two or three ladies happened to be in the vicinity of the doors, and happily escaped uninjured. But the opening of the door produced a draft which drew into the senate chamber clouds of smoke, the fire in the meantime having made its appearance over the center and rear of the gallery. All this occurred so suddenly that senators standing near the reporter's table and the secretary's desk, which were on the opposite side of the chamber from the entrance, stood as if paralyzed, gazing in mute astonishment at the smoke that passed in through the open doors, at the flames over the gallery, and the rushing crowd that blocked the door-ways. The senate suddenly and formally adjourned. President Gilman, however stood in his place, gavel in hand, and as he rapped his desk, loud and often he yelled: "Shut that door! Shut that door!"

"The cry was taken up by Colonel Crooks and other senators, and the order was finally obeyed, after which, the smoke clearing away, the senators were enabled to collect their senses and decide what was best to be done. President Gilman, still standing up in his place, calm and collected as if nothing unusual had happened, was encouraging the senators to keep cool. Colonel Crooks was giving orders as if a battle was raging around him.

"Other senators were giving such advice as occurred to them, but unfortunately no advice was pertinent except to keep cool and that was all. Some were importuning the secretary and his assistants to save the records, and General Jennison, his hands full of papers, was waiting a chance to walk out with them. But that chance looked remote, indeed, for there, locked in the senate chamber, were at least fifty men walking around, some looking at each other in a dazed sort of a way; others at the windows looking out at the snow-covered yard, now illuminated from the flames, that were heard roaring and crackling overhead.

From some windows men were yelling to the limited crowd below: "Get some ladders! Send for ladders!" Other windows were occupied. About this time terror actually siezed the members, when Senator Buck remarked that the fire was raging overhead, and at the same moment burning brands began to drop through the large ventilators upon the desks and floor beneath.

"Then, for a moment, it seemed as if all hopes of escape were cut off. * * * * * But happily the flames having made their way through the dome, a draught was created strong enough to clear the halls of smoke. The dome was almost directly over the entrance of the senate chamber, and burning brands and timbers had fallen down through the glass ceiling in front of the door, rendering escape in that director impossible.

"But a small window leading from the cloak room of the senate chamber to the first landing of the main stairway furnished an avenue of escape, and through this little opening every man in the senate chamber managed to get out.

"The windows were about ten feet high, but Mr. Michael Doran and several other gentlemen stood at the bottom, and nobly rendered assistance to those who came tumbling out, some headlong, some sideways and some feet foremost.

"As the reporter of the Pioneer-Press came out and landed on his feet, he paused for a moment to survey the scene overhead, where the flames were lashing themselves into fury as they played underneath the dome, and saw the flag-staff burning, and coals dropping down like fiery hail.

"It took but a few minutes for the senators to get out, after which they assembled on the outside, and they had no sooner gained the street than the ceiling of the senate chamber fell in, and in ten minutes that whole wing was a mass of flames."

Similar scenes took place in the hall of the house of representatives. A young lawyer, with a friend, as soon as the fire was noticed, ran into the law library and began to throw books out of the windows, but in a few minutes the density of the smoke and the approach of the flames compelled them to desist, and a large portion of the library was burned. The portraits of Generals Sherman and Thomas which were hung over the stairway were saved. The books of the Historical Society, in the basement, were removed, but were considerably damaged. In three hours the bare walls alone remained of the capitol which for nearly thirty years had been familiar to the law-makers and public men of Minnesota.

Steps were immediately taken to remove the debris and build a new capitol, upon the old site. The foundation walls have been laid, and in the course of a year the superstructure will be completed.

THE PENITENTIARY.

Before the penitentiary was built, those charged or convicted of crime were placed in charge of the commandants of Fort Snelling or Ripley, and kept at useful employment under military supervision. At the same time it was decided to erect a capitol at St. Paul, it was also determined that the territorial prison should be built at or within half a mile of Stillwater. A small lot was secured in 1851 in what was called the Battle ravine, in consequence of the conflict between the Sioux and Chippeways described on the 103d page. Within a stone wall was erected offices of the prison, with an annex containing six cells. A warden's house was built on the outside of the wall. In 1853, an addition of six cells was made and on the 5th of March, 1853, F. R. Delano entered upon his duties as warden. His reports to the legislature show that for several years there was little use for the cells. The prison was opened for criminals on the 1st of September, 1853, and until January, 1858 there had been received only five convicts, and forty-one county and thirty city prisoners awaiting trial. The use of the prison by the counties and city as a temporary place of confinement led to some misunderstanding between the warden and Washington county, and the grand jury of that county in November, 1857, complained that the warden was careless in discharge of his duties. The jury, among other complaints sent the following ironical statement: "It was also found in such examination that one Maria Roffin, committed on charge of selling spirituous liquors to the Indians within the territory of the United States escaped in the words of the record, 'by leaving the prison' and it is a matter of astonishment to this grand jury that she so magnanimously consented to leave the penitentiary behind her."

Francis O. J. Smith acted as warden for a brief period after Delano, and then H. N. Setzer. In 1859, the number of cells had increased to sixteen, and among the inmates was a hitherto respectable citizen sentenced for fifteen years for robbing a post-office.

In 1860 John S. Proctor became warden, and after eight years of efficient service, was succeeded by Joshua L. Taylor. By successive additions in 1869 nearly ten acres were enclosed by prison walls, and during this year extensive shops were built. The State in 1870 erected a costly prison at an expense of about $80,000, which, besides a chapel and necessary offices, contained two hundred and ninety-nine cells.

A. C. Webber succeeded Taylor as Warden in March, 1870, and the following October, Henry A. Jackman took his place, and continued in office until August, 1874, when the present incumbent, J. A. Reed, was appointed.

It has been the policy of the State to hire the convicts to labor for contractors, in workshops within the walls. At present the inmates are largely engaged in the making of agricultural machines for the firm of Seymour, Sabin & Co.

THE UNIVERSITY OF MINNESOTA.

The Territorial Legislature of 1851, passed an act establishing the University of Minnesota at or near the Falls of St. Anthony, and memorialized Congress for a grant of lands for the Institution. Soon after, Congress ordered seventy-two sections of land to be selected and reserved for the use of said University.

As the Regents had no funds, Franklin Steele gave the site now the public square, on Second Street in the East Division, opposite the Minnesota Medical College. Mr. Steele and others at their own expense erected a wooden building thereon, for a Preparatory Department, and the Rev. E. W. Merrill was engaged as Principal. At the close of the year 1853, the Regents reported that there was ninety-four students in attendance, but that the site selected being too near the Falls, they had purchased of Joshua L. Taylor and Paul B. George about twenty-five acres, a mile eastward, on the heigth overlooking the Falls of St. Anthony.

Governor Gorman, in his message in 1854 to the Legislature said: "The University of Minnesota exists as yet only in name, but the time has come when a substantial reality may and should be created." But the Regents could not find any patent which would compress a myth into reality, for not an acre of the land grant of Congress was available. The Governor in his message therefore added: "It would not embarrass our resources, in my judgment, if a small loan was effected to erect a building, and establish one or two professorships, and a preparatory department, such loan to be based upon the townships of land appropriated for the sole use of the University."

While it was pleasing to local pride to have a building in prospect which could be seen from afar, the friends of education shook their heads, and declared the prospect of borrowing money to build a University building before the common school system was organized was visionary, and would be unsuccessful. The idea, however, continued to be agitated, and the Regents at length were authorized by the Legislature of 1856, to issue bonds in the name of the University, under its corporate seal, for fifteen thousand dollars, to be secured by the mortgage of the University building which had been erected on the new site, and forty thousand dollars more were authorized to be issued by the Legislature of 1858, to be secured by a lien on the lands devoted for a Territorial University. With the aid of these loans a costly and inconvenient stone edifice was constructed, but when finished there was no demand for it, and no means for the payment of interest or professors.

In the fall of 1858, in the hope that the University might be saved from its desperate condition, the Regents elected the Rev. Edward D. Neill as Chancellor. He accepted the position without any salary being pledged, and insisted that a University must necessarily be of slow development, and must succeed, not precede, the common schools, and contended that five years might elapse before anything could be done for a University which would be tangible and visible. He also expressed the belief that in time, with strict watchfulness, the heavy load of debt could be lifted.

The Legislature of 1860 abolished the old board of Regents of the Territorial University by passing an act for a State University, which had been prepared by the Chancellor, and met the approval of Chancellor Tappan, of Michigan University. Its first section declared "that the object of the State University established by the Constitution of the State, at or near the Falls of St. Anthony, shall be to provide the best and most efficient means of imparting to the youth of the State an education more advanced than that given in the public schools, and a thorough knowledge of the branches of literature, the arts and sciences, with their various applications."

This charter also provided for the appointment of five Regents, to be appointed by the Governor, and confirmed by the Senate, in place of the twelve who had before been elected by the Legislature. The Legislature of 1860 also enacted that the Chancellor should be ex-officio State Superintendent of Public Instruction.

The first meeting of the Regents of the State University was held on the fifth of April, 1860, and steps were taken to secure the then useless edifice from further dilapidation. The Chancellor urged at this meeting that a large portion of the territorial land grant would be absorbed in payment of the moneys used in the erection of a building in advance of the times, and that the only way to secure the existence of a State University was by asking Congress for an additional two townships, or seventy-two sections of land, which he contended could be done under the phraseology of the enabling act, which said: "That seventy-two sections of land shall be set apart and reserved for the use and support of a *State* University to be selected by the *Governor of said State*," etc.

The Regents requested the Governor to suggest to the authorities that it was not the intention of Congress to turn over the debts and prospectively encumbered lands of an old and badly managed Territorial institution, but to give the State that was to be, a grant for a State University, free from all connection with the Territorial organization. The Governor communicated these views to the authorities at Washington, but it was not till after years of patient waiting that the land was obtained by an act of Congress.

At the breaking out of the civil war in 1861, the Chancellor became Chaplain of the First Regiment of Minnesota Volunteers, and went to the seat of war, and the University affairs continued to grow worse, and the University building was a by-word and hissing among the passers by. During the year 1863, some of the citizens of St. Anthony determined to make another effort to extricate the institution from its difficulties, and the legislature of 1864 passed an act abolishing the board of Regents, and creating three persons sole regents, with power to liquidate the debts of the institution. The Regents under this law were John S. Pillsbury and O. C. Merriman, of St. Anthony, and John Nicols, of St. Paul.

The increased demand for pine lands, of which the University owned many acres, and the sound discretion of these gentlemen co-operated in procuring happy results. In two years Governor Marshall, in his message to the legislature, was able to say: "The very able and successful management of the affairs of the institution, under the present board of Regents, relieving it of over one hundred thousand dollars of debt, and saving over thirty thousand acres of land that was at one time supposed to be lost, entitles Messrs. Pillsbury, Merriman, and Nicols to the lasting gratitude of the State."

The legislature of 1867 appropriated $5,000 for a preparatory and Normal department, and the Regents this year chose as principal of the school, the Rev. W. W. Washburn, a graduate of the University of Michigan, and Gabriel Campbell, of the same institution, and Ira Moore as assistants. The legislature of 1868 passed an act to reorganize the University, and to establish an Agricultural College therein.

Departing from the policy of the University of Michigan, it established what the Regents wished, a department of Elementary instruction. It also provided for a College of Science, Literature and the Arts; a College of Agriculture and Mechanics with Military Tactics; a college of Law, and a College of Medicine.

The provision of the act of 1860, for the appointment of Regents was retained, and the number to be confirmed by the Senate, was increased from five to seven.

The new board of Regents was organized in March, 1868. John S. Pillsbury, of St. Anthony, President; O. C. Merriman, of St. Anthony, Secretary, and John Nicols, of St. Paul, Treasurer.

At a meeting of the Regents in August, 1869, arrangements were made for collegiate work by electing as President and Professor of mathematics William W. Folwell.

President Folwell was born in 1835, in Seneca county, New York, and graduated with distinction in 1827, at Hobart College in Geneva, New York. For two years he was a tutor at Hobart, and then went to Europe. Upon his return the civil war was raging, and he entered the 50th New York Volunteers. After the army was disbanded he engaged in business in Ohio, but at the time of his election to the presidency of the University, was Professor of mathematics, astronomy, and German at Kenyon College.

THE FACULTY.

The present faculty of the institution is as follows:

William W. Folwell, instructor, political science.

Jabez Brooks, D. D., professor, Greek, and in charge of Latin.

Newton H. Winchell, professor, State geologist, C. N. Hewitt, M. D., professor, Public Health.

John G. Moore, professor, German.

Moses Marston, Ph. D., professor, English literature.

C. W. Hall, professor, geology and biology.

John C. Hutchinson, assistant professor, Greek and mathematics.

John S. Clark, assistant professor, Latin.

Matilda J. Campbell, instructor, German and English.

Maria L. Sanford, professor, rhetoric, and elocution.

William A. Pike, C. E., professor, engineering and physics.

John F. Downey, professor, mathematics and astronomy.

James A. Dodge, Ph. D., professor, chemistry.

Alexander T. Ormond, professor, mental and moral philosophy and history.

Charles W. Benton, professor, French.

Edward D. Porter, professor, agriculture.

William H. Leib, instructor, vocal music.

William F. Decker, instructor, shop work and drawing.

Edgar C. Brown, U. S. A., professor, military science.

James Bowen, instructor, practical horticulture.

THE CAMPUS AND BUILDINGS.

The campus of the university since it was originally acquired, has been somewhat enlarged, and now consists of about fifty acres in extent, undulating in surface, and well wooded with native trees. The buildings are thus far but two in number, the plan of the original building, which in outline was not unlike the insane asylum building at St. Peter, having been changed by the erection in 1876, of a large four-story structure built of stone and surmounted by a tower. This building is 186 feet in length and ninety in breadth, exclusive of porches, having three stories above the basement in the old part. The walls are of blue limestone and the roof of tin. The rooms, fifty-three in number, as well as all the corridors are heated by an efficient steam apparatus, and are thoroughly ventilated. Water is supplied from the city mains, and there is a standpipe running from the basement through the roof with hose attached on all the floors for protection against fire. The assembly hall, in the third story, is 87x55 feet, 24 feet high, and will seat with comfort 700 people, and 1,200 can be accommodated.

THE AGRICULTURAL BUILDING

is the first of the special buildings for the separate colleges, and was built in 1876. It is of brick, on a basement of blue stone, 146x54 feet. The central portion is two stories in height. The south wing, 46x25 feet, is a plant house of double sash and glass. The north wing contains the chemical laboratory. There are class rooms for chemistry, physics and agriculture, and private laboratories for the professors. A large room in the second story is occupied by the museum of technology and agriculture, and the basement is filled up with a carpenter shop, a room with vises and tools at which eight can work. and another room fitted with eight forges and a blower—the commencement of the facilities for practical instruction.

DEAF AND DUMB INSTITUTION.

Of all the public institutions of Minnesota, no one has had a more pleasing history, and more symmetrical development than the Institution for the education of the deaf and dumb and the blind at Faribault.

The legislature of 1858, passed an act for the establishment of "The Minnesota State Institute for the Education of the Deaf and Dumb," within two miles of Faribault, in Rice county, upon condition that the town or county, should within one year from the passage of the law give forty acres of land for its use. The condition was complied with, but the financial condition of the country and the breaking out of the civil war, with other causes retarded the progress of the Institution for five years.

The legislature of 1863 made the first appropriation of fifteen hundred dollars for the opening of the Institution. Mr. R. A. Mott, of Faribault, who has to this time been an efficient director, at the request of the other two directors, visited the East for teachers, and secured Prof. Kinney and wife of Columbus, Ohio. A store on Front Street was then rented, and adapted for the temporary use of the Institution, which opened on the 9th of September, 1863, with five pupils, which soon increased to ten.

On February 13th, 1864, the State appropriated about four thousand dollars for the support of the Institution, and the directors expended about one thousand dollars in the erection of small additional building, eighteen by twenty feet in dimensions, as a boys' dormitory.

After laboring faithfully for three years and securing the respect of his associates, on July 1st, 1866, Prof. Kinney resigned on account of ill health.

The directors the next month elected as Superintendent Jonathan L. Noyes, A. M. On the 7th of September Professor Noyes arrived at Faribault with Miss A. L. Steele as an assistant teacher and Henrietta Watson as matron.

NORTH WING OF EDIFICE COMPLETED.

Upon the 17th of March, 1868, the Institution was removed to a wing of the new building upon a site of fifty-two acres beautifully situated upon the brow of the hills east of Faribault. The edifice of the French louvre style, and was designed by Monroe Sheire, a St. Paul architect, and cost about fifty-three thousand dollars, and water was introduced from springs in the vicinity.

WORK SHOPS.

In 1869, the Superintendent was cheered by the completion of the first work shop, and soon eight mutes under the direction of a mute foreman began to make flour barrels, and in less than a year had sent out more than one thousand, and in 1873 4,051 barrels were made.

SOUTH WING BEGAN.

The completed wing was not intended to accommodate more than sixty pupils and soon there was a demand for more room. During the year 1869 the foundation of the south wing was completed, and on the 10th of September 1873 the building was occupied by boys, the other wing being used for the girls. By the time the building was ready students were waiting to occupy.

MAIN BUILDING COMPLETED.

In 1879 the design was completed by the finishing of the centre building. The whole edifice is thus described by the architect, Monroe Sheire: "The plan of the building is rectangular, and consists of a central portion one hundred feet north and south, and one hundred and eight feet east and west, exclusive of piazzas, and two wings, one on the north, and the other on the south side, each of these being eighty by forty-five. This makes the extreme length two hundred and sixty feet, and the width one hundred and eight feet. The entire building is four stories above the basement."

The exterior walls are built of blue lime stone from this vicinity, and the style Franco Romanesque. Over the center is a graceful cupola, and the top of the same is one hundred and fifty feet above the ground.

The entire cost to the State of all the improvements was about $175,000, and the building will accommodate about two hundred pupils. The rooms are lighted by gas from the Faribault Gas Works.

INDUSTRIAL SCHOOLS.

The first shop opened was for making barrels. To this cooper shop has been added a shoe shop, a tailor shop and a printing office.

MAGAZINE.

The pupils established in March, 1876, a little paper called the Gopher. It was printed on a small press, and second-hand type was used.

In June, 1877, it was more than doubled in size, and changed its name to "The Mutes' Companion." Printed with good type, and filled with pleasant articles it still exists, and adds to the interest in the institution.

EDUCATION OF THE BLIND.

In 1863 a law was passed by the legislature requiring blind children to be educated under the supervision of the Deaf and Dumb Institution. Early in July, 1866, a school for the blind was opened in a separate building, rented for the purpose, under the care of Miss H. N. Tucker. During the first term there were three pupils. In May, 1868, the blind pupils were brought into the deaf and dumb institution, but the experiment of instructing these two classes together was not satisfactory, and in 1874 the blind were removed to the old Faribault House, half a mile south of the Deaf and Dumb Institution, which had been fitted up for their accommodation, and where a large new brick building, for the use of the blind, has since been erected. In 1875, Professor James J. Dow was made principal of the school.

SCHOOL FOR THE FEEBLE MINDED.

From time to time, in his report to the Legislature, Superintendent Noyes alluded to the fact that some children appeared deaf and dumb because of their feeble mental development, and in 1879, the state appropriated $5,000 for a school for imbecile children.

The institution was started in July of that year by Dr. Henry M. Knight, now deceased, then Superintendent and founder of the Connecticut school of the same description, who was on a visit to Faribault. He superintended the school until the arrival, in September, of his son, Dr. George H. Knight, who had been trained under his father.

For the use of the school the Fairview House was rented, and fourteen feeble children were sent from the Insane Asylum at St. Peter. In eighteen months the number had increased to twenty-five.

The site of the new building for the school is about forty rods south of the Blind School. The dimensions are 44x80 feet, with a tower projection 20x18 feet. It is of limestone, and three stories above the basement, covered with an iron hip-roof, and cost about $25,000.

SUPERINTENDENT J. L. NOYES.

The growth of the Minnesota institution for the education of the deaf and dumb and the blind, has been so symmetrical, and indicative of one moulding mind, that a sketch of the institution would be incomplete without some notice of the Superintendent, who has guided it for the last sixteen years.

On the 13th of June, 1827, Jonathan Lovejoy Noyes was born in Windham, Rockingham county, New Hampshire. At the age of fourteen years he was sent to Phillips Academy, Andover. Massachusetts, not only one of the oldest, but among the best schools in the United States. At Andover he had the advantage of the instruction of the thorough Greek scholar, Dr. Samuel H. Taylor, the eminent author, Lyman H. Coleman, D. D., afterwards Professor of Latin in Lafayette College, Pennsylvania, and William H. Wells, whose English grammar has been used in many institutions.

After completing his preparatory studies, in 1848, he entered Yale College, and in four years received the diploma of Bachelor of Arts. After graduation he received an appointment in the Pennsylvania Institution of the Deaf and Dumb, on Broad Street, Philadelphia, and found instructing deaf mutes was a pleasant occupation. After six years of important work in Philadelphia, he was employed two years in a similar institution at Baton Rouge, Louisiana, and then received an appointment in the well known American Asylum so long presided over by Thomas H. Gallaudet, at Hartford, Connecticut. While laboring here he was invited to take charge of the "Minnesota Institution for the Education of the Deaf and Dumb and the Blind," and in September, 1866, he arrived at Faribault. With wisdom and patience, gentleness and energy, and an unfaltering trust in a superintending Providence, he has there continued his work with the approbation of his fellow citizens, and the affection of the pupils of the institution.

At the time that he was relieved of the care of the blind and imbecile, the directors entered upon their minutes the following testimonial:

"*Resolved*, That upon the retirement of Prof. J. L. Noyes from the superintendency of the departments of the blind and imbecile, the board of Directors, of the Minnesota Institution for the Deaf and Dumb, and Blind and Idiots, and Imbeciles, desire to testify to his deep interest in these several departments; his efficient and timely services in their establishment; and his wise direction of their early progress, until they have become full-fledged and independent departments of our noble State charitable institutions.

"For his cordial and courteous co-operation with the directors in their work, and for his timely counsel and advice, never withheld when needed, the board by this testimonial, render to him their hearty recognition and warm acknowledgement."

On the 21st of July, 1862, Professor Noyes married Eliza H. Wadsworth, of Hartford, Connecticut, a descendent of the Colonel Wadsworth, who in the old colony time, hid the charter of Connecticut in an oak, which for generations has been known in history as the "Charter Oak." They have but one child, a daughter.

INSANE HOSPITAL AT ST. PETER.

Until the year 1866, the insane of Minnesota were sent to the Iowa Asylum for treatment, but in January of that year the Legislature passed an act appointing Wm. R. Marshall, John M. Berry, Thomas Wilson, Charles McIlrath, and S. J. R. McMillan to select a proper place for the Minnesota Hospital for the Insane. The vicinity of St. Peter was chosen, the citizens presenting to the State two hundred and ten acres one mile south of the city, and on the Minnesota River, directly opposite to Kasota.

In October, 1866, temporary buildings were erected, and the Trustees elected Samuel E. Shantz, of Utica, N. Y., as the Superintendent. A plan submitted by Samuel Sloan, a Philadelphia architect, consisting of a central building, with sections and wings for the accommodation of at least five hundred patients, in 1867, was adopted, and in 1876 the great structure was completed.

It is built of Kasota limestone, the walls lined with brick, and the roof covered with slates. The central building is four stories in height, surmounted with a fine cupola, and therein are the chapel and offices. Each wing is three stories high, with nine separate halls.

The expenses of construction of the Asylum, with the outbuildings, has been more than half a million of dollars. Dr. Shantz having died, Cyrus K. Bartlett, M. D., of Northampton, Massachusetts, was appointed Superintedent.

In January, 1880, in the old temporary buildings and in the Asylum proper there were six hundred and sixty patients. On the 15th of November, 1880, about half past eight in the evening, the Superintendent and assistants were shocked by the announcement that the north wing was on fire. It began in the northwest corner of the basement, and is supposed to have been kindled by a patient employed about the kitchen who was not violent. The flames rapidly ascended to the different stories, through the holes for the hot air pipes, and the openings for the dumb waiters.

The wing at the time contained two hundred and seventy patients, and as they were liberated by their nurses and told to make their escape, exhibited various emotions. Some clapped their hands with glee, others trembled with fear. Many, barefooted and with bare heads, rushed for the neighboring hills and sat on the cold snow. A few remained inside. One patient was noticed in a window of the third story, with his knees drawn up to his chin, and his face in his hands, a cool and interested looker on, and with an expression of cynical contempt for the flames as they approached his seat. When a tongue of fire would shoot toward him, he would lower his head, and after it passed would resume his position with more than the indifference of a stoic. At last the brick work beneath him gave way with a loud crash, and as he was precipitated into the cauldron of fire soon to be burned to ashes, his maniacal laugh was heard above the roar of the flames.

The remains of eighteen patients were found in the ruins, and seven died in a few days after the fire, in consequence of injuries and exposure.

Immediate steps were taken by the Governor to repair the damages by the fire.

INSANE HOSPITAL AT ROCHESTER.

In 1878, the Legislature enacted a law by which an inebriate asylum commenced at Rochester could be used for an Insane Asylum. With the appropriation, alterations and additions were made, Dr. J. E. Bowers elected Superintendent, and on the 1st of January, 1879, it was opened for patients.

Twenty thousand dollars have since been appropriated for a wing for female patients.

STATE REFORM SCHOOL.

During the year 1865, I. V. D. Heard, Esq., a lawyer of Saint Paul, and at that time City Attorney sent a communication to one of the daily papers urging the importance of separating children arrested for petty crimes, from the depraved adults found in the station house or county jail, and also called the attention of the City Council to the need for a Reform School.

The next Legislature, in 1866, under the influence created by the discussion passed a law creating a House of Refuge, and appropriated $5,000 for its use on condition that the city of Saint Paul would give the same amount.

In November, 1867, the managers purchased thirty acres with a stone farm house and barn thereon, for $10,000, situated in Rose township, in Saint Anthony near Snelling Avenue, in the western suburbs of Saint Paul.

In 1868 the House of Refuge was ready to receive wayward youths, and this year the Legislature changed the name to the Minnesota State Reform School, and accepted it as a state institution. The Rev. J. G. Riheldaffer D. D., who had for years been pastor of one of the Saint Paul Presbyterian churches was elected superintendent.

In 1869 the main building of light colored brick, 40x60 feet was erected, and occupied in December.

In February, 1879, the laundry, a separate building was burned, and an appropriation of the

Legislature was made soon after of $15,000 for the rebuilding of the laundry and the erection of a work shop. This shop is 50x100 and three stories high. The boys besides receiving a good English education, are taught to be tailors, tinners, carpenters and gardeners. The sale of bouquets from the green house, of sleds and toys, and of tin ware has been one of the sources of revenue.

Doctor Riheldaffer continues as superintendent and by his judicious management has prepared many of the inmates to lead useful and honorable lives, after their discharge from the Institution.

STATE NORMAL SCHOOL.

By the influence of Lieut. Gov. Holcomb and others the first State Legislature in 1858 passed an Act by which three Normal schools might be erected, but made no proper provision for their support.

WINONA NORMAL SCHOOL.

Dr. Ford, a graduate of Dartmouth college, and a respectable physician in Winona, with several residents of the same place secured to the amount of $5,512 subscriptions for the establishment of a Normal School at that point, and a small appropriation was secured in 1880 from the Legislature.

John Ogden, af Ohio, was elected Principal, and in September, 1860, the school was opened in a temporary building. Soon after the civil war began the school was suspended, and Mr. Ogden entered the army.

In 1864 the Legislature made an appropriation of $3,000, and and William F. Phelps, who had been in charge of the New Jersey Normal School at Trenton, was chosen principal. In 1865 the State appropriated $5,000 annually for the school and the citizens of Winona gave over $20,000 toward the securing of a site and the erection of a permanent edifice.

One of the best and most ornamental educational buildings in the Northwest was commenced and in September, 1869, was so far finished as to accommodate pupils. To complete it nearly $150,000 was given by the State.

In 1876 Prof. W. F. Phelps resigned and was succeeded by Charles A. Morey who in May, 1879 retired. The present principal is Irwin Shepard.

MANKATO NORMAL SCHOOL.

In 1866, Mankato having offered a site for a second Normal School, the Legislature give $5,000 for its support. George M. Gage was elected Principal and on the 1st of September, 1868 the school was opered, It occupied the basement of, the Methodist church for a few weeks, and then moved into a room over a store at the corner of Front and Main streets. In April 1870, the State building was first occupied.

Prof. Gage resgned in June, 1872, and his successor was Miss J. A. Sears who remained one year. In July 1873, the Rev. D. C. John was elected principal, and in the spring of 1880, he retired.

The present Principal is Professor Edward Searing, formerly State Superintendent of Public Instruction in Wisconsin, a fine Latin scholar, and editor of an edition of Virgil.

ST. CLOUD NORMAL SCHOOL.

In 1869, the citizens of St. Cloud gave $5,000 for the establishment in that city of the third Normal School, and a building was fitted up for its use. The legislature in 1869, appropriated $3,000 for current expenses. In 1870, a new building was begun, the legislature having appropriated $10,000, and in 1873, $30,000; this building in 1875 was first occupied. In 1875, the Rev. D. L. Kiehle was elected Principal, Prof. Ira Moore, the first Principal having resigned. In 1881, Prof. Kiehle was appointed State Superintendent of Public Instruction, and Jerome Allen, late of New York, was elected his successor.

CHAPTER XXVII.

MINNESOTA GOVERNORS—UNITED STATES SENATORS—MEMBERS OF UNITED STATES HOUSE OF REPRESENTATIVES.

GOVERNOR RAMSEY—A. D. 1849 TO A. D. 1853.

Alexander Ramsey, the first Governor of the Territory of Minnesota, was born on the 8th of September, 1815, near Harrisburg, in Dauphin county, Pennsylvania. His grandfather was a descendent of one of the many colonists who came from the north of Ireland before the war of the Revolution, and his father about the time of the first treaty of peace with Great Britain, was born in York county, Pennsylvania. His mother Elizabeth Kelker, was of German descent, a woman of energy, industry and religious principle.

His father dying, when the subject of this sketch

was ten years of age, he went into the store of his maternal uncle in Harrisburg, and remained two years. Then he was employed as a copyist in the office of Register of Deeds. For several years he was engaged in such business as would give support. Thoughtful, persevering and studious, at the age of eighteen he was able to enter Lafayette College, at Easton, Pennsylvania. After he left college he entered a lawyer's office in Harrisburg, and subsequently attended lectures at the Law School at Carlisle, Pennsylvania.

At the age of twenty-four, in 1839, he was admitted to the bar of Dauphin county. His executive ability was immediately noticed, and the next year he took an active part in the political campaign, advocating the claims of William H. Harrison. and he was complimented by being made Secretary of the Pennsylvania Presidential Electors. After the electoral vote was delivered in Washington, in a few weeks, in January 1841, he was elected chief clerk of the House of Representatives of Pennsylvania. Here his ability in dispatching business, and his great discretion made a most favorable impression, and in 1843, the Whigs of Dauphin, Lebanon and Schuylkill counties nominated him, as their candidate for Congress. Popular among the young men of Harrisburg, that city which had hitherto given a democratic majority, voted for the Whig ticket which he represented, and the whole district gave him a majority of votes. At the expiration of his term, in 1845 he was again elected to Congress.

Strong in his political preferences, without manifesting political rancor, and of large perceptive power, he was in 1848 chosen by the Whig party Pensylvania, as the secretary of the Central Committee, and he directed the movements in his native State, which led to the electoral votes being thrown for General Zachary Taylor for President.

On the 4th of March, 1849, President Taylor took the oath of office, and in less than a month he signed the commission of Alexander Ramsey as Governor of the Territory of Minnesota, which had been created by a law approved the day before his inauguration.

By the way of Buffalo, and from thence by lake to Chicago, and from thence to Galena, where he took a steamboat, he traveled to Minnesota and arrived at St. Paul early in the morning of the 27th of May, with his wife, children and nurse, but went with the boat up to Mendota, where he was cordially met by the Territorial delegate, Hon. H. H. Sibley, and with his family was his guest for several weeks. He then came to St. Paul, occupied a small house on Third street near the corner of Robert.

On the 1st of June he issued his first proclamation declaring the organization of the Territorial government, and on the 11th, he issued another creating judicial districts and providing for the election of members of a legislature to assemble in September. To his duties as Governor was added the superintendency of Indian affairs and during the first summer he held frequent conferences with the Indians, and his first report to the Commissioner of Indian Affairs is still valuable for its information relative to the Indian tribes at that time hunting in the valleys of the Minnesota and the Mississippi.

During the Governor's term of office he visited the Indians at their villages, and made himself familiar with their needs, and in the summer of 1851, made treaties with the Sioux by which the country between the Mississippi Rivers, north of the State of Iowa, was opened for occupation by the whites. His term of office as Governor expired in April, 1853, and in 1855 his fellow townsmen elected him Mayor of St. Paul. In 1857, after Minnesota had adopted a State Constitution, the Republican party nominated Alexander Ramsey for Governor, and the Democrats nominated Henry H. Sibley. The election in October was close and exciting, and Mr. Sibley was at length declared Governor by a majority of about two hundred votes. The Republicans were dissatisfied with the result, and contended that more Democratic votes were thrown in the Otter Tail Lake region than there were citizens residing in the northern district.

In 1859, Mr. Ramsey was again nominated by the Republicans for Governor, and elected by four thousand majority. Before the expiration of his term of office, the Republic was darkened by civil war. Governor Ramsey happened to be in Washington when the news of the firing upon Fort Sumter was received, and was among the first of the State Governors to call upon the President and tender a regiment of volunteers in defense of the Republic. Returning to the State, he displayed energy and wisdom in the organization of regiments.

In the fall of 1861, he was again nominated and elected as Governor, but before the expiration of this term, on July 10th, 1863, he was elected by the Legislature, United States Senator. Upon entering the Senate, he was placed on the Committees on Naval Affairs, Post-offices, Patents, Pacific Railroad, and Chairman of the Committee on Revolutionary Pensions and Revolutionary Claims. He was also one of the Committee appointed by Congress to accompany the remains of President Lincoln to Springfield Cemetery, Illinois.

The Legislature of 1869 re-elected him for the term ending in March, 1875. In 1880, he was appointed Secretary of War by President Hayes, and for a time also acted as Secretary of the Navy.

He was married in 1845 to Anna Earl, daughter of Michael H. Jenks, a member of Congress from Bucks county. He has had three children; his two sons died in early youth; his daughter Marion, the wife of Charles Eliot Furness, resides with her family, with her parents in St. Paul.

GOVERNOR GORMAN A. D. 1853 TO A. D. 1857.

At the expiration of Governor Ramsey's term of office, President Pierce appointed Willis Arnold Gorman as his successor. Governor Gorman was the only son of David L. Gorman and born in January, 1866 near Flemingsburgh, Kentucky. After receiving a good academic education he went to Bloomington, Indiana, and in 1836 graduated in the law department of the State University. He imediately entered upon the practice of law with few friends and no money, in Bloomington, and in a year was called upon to defend a man charged with murder, and obtained his acquittal.

That one so young should have engaged in such a case excited the attention of the public, and two years afterwards was elected a member of the Indiana legislature. His popularity was so great that he was re-elected a number of times. When war was declared against Mexico he enlisted as a private in a company of volunteers, which with others at New Albany was mustered into the service for one year, as the Third Regiment of Indiana Volunteers, with James H. Lane, afterwards U. S. Senator for Kansas, as Colonel, while he was commissioned as Major. It is said that under the orders of General Taylor with a detachment of riflemen he opened the battle of Buena Vista. In this engagement his horse was shot and fell into a deep ravine carrying the Major with, him and severely bruising him.

In August, 1847, he returned to Indiana and by his enthusiasm helped to raise the Fourth Regiment and was elected its Colonel, and went back to the seat of war, and was present in several battles, and when peace was declared returned with the reputation of being a dashing officer.

Resuming the practice of law, in the fall of 1848 he was elected to Congress and served two terms, his last expiring on the 4th of March, 1853, the day when his fellow officer in the Mexican War, Gen. Franklin Pierce took the oath of office as President of the United States. With a commission bearing the signature of President Pierce he arrived in Saint Paul, in May, 1853, as the second Territorial Governor of Minnesota.

His term of Governor expired in the spring of 1857, and he was elected a member of the Committee to frame a State Constitution, which on the second Monday in July of that year, convened at the Capitol. After the committee adjourned he again entered upon the practice of law but when the news of the firing of Fort Sumter reached Saint Paul he realized that the nation's life was endangered, and that there would be a civil war. He offered his services to Governor Ramsey and when the First Regiment of Minnesota volunteers was organized he was commissioned as Colonel. He entered with ardor upon his work of drilling the raw troops in camp at Fort Snelling, and the privates soon caught his enthusiasm.

No officer ever had more pride in his regiment and his soldiers were faithful to his orders. His regiment was the advance regiment of Franklin's Brigade, in Heintzelman's Division at the first Battle of Bull Run, and there made a reputation which it increased at every battle, especially at Gettysburg. Upon the recommendation of General Winfield Scott who had known him in Mexico after the battle of Bull Run he was appointed Brigadier General by President Lincoln,

After three years of service as Brigadier General he was mustered out and returning to St. Paul resumed his profession. From that time he held several positions under the city government. He died on the afternoon of the 25th of May, 1876.

GOVERNOR SIBLEY, A. D. 1858 to A. D. 1860.

No one is more intimately assocciated with the development of the Northwest than Henry Hastings Sibley, the first Governor of Minnesota under the State constitution.

By the treaty of Peace of 1783, Great Britain recognized the independence of the United States of America, and the land east of the Mississippi, and northwest of the Ohio river was open to settlement by American citizens.

In 1786, while Congress was in session in New York City, Dr. Manasseh Cutler, a graduate of Yale, a Puritan divine of a considerable scientific attainments, visited that place, and had frequent conferences with Dane of Massachusetts, and Jefferson, of Virginia, relative to the colonization of the Ohio valley, and he secured certain provisions in the celebrated "ordinance of 1787," among others, the grant of land in each township for the support of common schools, and also two townships for the use of a University.

Under the auspices of Dr. Cutler, and a few others, the first colony, in December, 1787, left Massachusetts, and after a wearisome journey, on April 7, 1788, reached Marietta, at the mouth of the Muskingum River.

Among the families of this settlement was the maternal grandfather of Governor Sibley, Colonel Ebenezer Sproat, a gallant officer of Rhode Island, in the war of the Rebellion, and a friend of Kosciusko.

Governor Sibley's mother, Sarah Sproat, was sent to school to the then celebrated Moravian Seminary at Bethlehem, Pennsylvania, and subsequently finished her education at Philadelphia. In 1797 she returned to her wilderness home and her father purchased for her pleasure a piano, said to have been the first transported over the Alleghany Mountains. Soon after this Solomon Sibley, a young lawyer, a native of Sutton, Massachusetts, visited Marietta, and become acquainted and attached to Sarah Sproat, and in 1802, they were married. The next year Mrs. Sibley went to Detroit where her husband had settled, and she commenced housekeeping opposite where the Biddle House is situated in that city. In 1799, Governor Sibley's father was a representative from the region now known as Michigan, in the first Territorial Legislature of Northwest, which met at Cincinnati. From 1820 to 1823 he was delegate to Congress from Michigan, and in 1824 he became judge of the supreme court, and in 1836 resigned. Respected by all, on the 4th of April he died.

His son, Henry Hastings Sibley, was born in February, 1811, in the city of Detroit. At the age of seventeen, relinquishing the study of law, he became a clerk at Sault St. Marie and then was employed by Robert Stuart, of the American Fur Company at Mackinaw. In 1834 he was placed in charge of the Indian trade above Lake Pepin with his new quarters at the mouth of the Minnesota River.

In 1836, he built the first stone residence in Minnesota, without the military reservation, at Mendota, and here he was given to hospitality. The missionary of the cross, and the man of science, the officer of the army, and the tourist from a foreign land, were received with a friendliness that caused them to forget while under his roof that they were strangers in a strange land.

In 1843, he was married to Sarah J. Steele, the sister of Franklin Steele, at Fort Snelling.

On August 6th, 1846, Congress authorized the people of Wisconsin to organize a State government with the St. Croix River as a part of its western boundary, thus leaving that portion of Wisconsin territory between the St. Croix and Mississippi Rivers still under the direct supervison of Congress, and the Hon. M. L. Martin, the delegate of Wisconsin territory in Congress, introduced a bill to organize the territory of Minnesota including portions of Wisconsin and Iowa.

It was not until the 29th of May, 1848, however, that Wisconsin territory east of the Saint Croix, was reorganized as a State. On the 30th of October, Mr. Sibley, who was a resident of Iowa territory, was elected delegate to Congress, and after encountering many difficulties, was at length admitted to a seat.

On the 3d of March, 1849, a law was approved by the President for the organization of Minnesota teritory, and in the fall of that year he was elected the first delegate of the new Territory, as his father had been at an early period elected a delegate from the then new Michigan territory. In 1851, he was elected for another term of two years.

In 1857, he was a member of the convention to frame a State constitution for Minnesota, and was elected presiding officer by the democrats. By the same party he was nominated for Governor and elected by a small majority over the republican candidate, Alexander Ramsey.

Minnesota was admitted as a State on the 11th of May, 1858, and on the 28th Governor Sibley delivered his inaugural message.

After a residence of twenty-eight years at Mendota, in 1862, he became a resident of Saint Paul. At the beginning of the Sioux outbreak, Governor Ramsey appointed him Colonel, and placed him at the head of the forces employed against the Indians. On the 23d of September, 1862, he fought the severe and decisive battle of Wood Lake. In March, 1863, he was confirmed by the senate as Brigadier General, and on the 29th of November, 1865, he was appointed Brevet Major General for efficient and meritorious services.

Since the war he has taken an active interest in every enterprise formed for the advancement of Minnesota, and for the benefit of St. Paul, the city of his residence. His sympathetic nature leads him to open his ear, and also his purse to those in distress, and among his chief mourners when he leaves this world will be the many poor he has befriended, and the faint-hearted who took courage from his words of kindness. His beloved wife, in May, 1869, departed this life, leaving four children, two daughters and two sons.

GOVERNOR RAMSEY, JANUARY 1860 TO APRIL 1863.

Alexander Ramsey, the first Territorial Governor, was elected the second State Governor, as has already been mentioned on another page. Before his last term of office expired he was elected United States Senator by the Legislature, and Lieutenant Governor Swift became Governor, for the unexpired term.

GOVERNOR SWIFT, APRIL, 1863 TO JANUARY, 1864.

Henry A. Swift was the son of a physician, Dr. John Swift, and on the 23d of March, 1823, was born at Ravenna, Ohio. In 1842, he graduated at Western Reserve College, at Hudson, in the same State, and in 1845 was admitted to the practice of the law. During the winter of 1846-7, he was an assistant clerk of the lower house of the Ohio Legislature, and his quiet manner and methodic method of business made a favorable impression. The next year he was elected the Chief Clerk, and continued in office for two years. For two or three years he was Secretary of the Portage Farmers' Insurance Company. In April, 1853, he came to St. Paul, and engaged in merchandise and other occupations, and in 1856, became one of the founders of St. Peter. At the election of 1861, he was elected a State Senator for two years. In March, 1863, by the resignation of Lieutenant Governor Donnelly, who had been elected to the United States House of Representatives, he was chosen temporary President of the Senate, and when Governor Ramsey, in April, 1863, left the gubernatorial chair, for a seat in the United States Senate he became the acting Governor. When he ceased to act as Governor, he was again elected to the State Senate, and served during the years 1864 and 1865, and was then appointed by the President, Register of the Land Office at St. Peter. On the 25th of February, 1869 he died.

GOVERNOR MILLER—A. D. 1864 TO A. D. 1866.

Stephen A. Miller was the grandson of a German immigrant who about the year 1785 settled in Pennsylvania. His parents were David and Rosanna Miller, and on the 7th of January, 1816, he was born in what is now Perry county in that State.

He was like many of our best citizens, obliged to bear the yoke in his youth. At one time he was a canal boy and when quite a youth was in charge of a canal boat. Fond of reading he acquired much information, and of pleasing address he made friends, so that in 1837 he became a forwarding and commission merchant in Harrisburg.

He always felt an interest in public affairs, and was an efficient speaker at political meetings. In 1849 he was elected Prothonatary of Dauphin county, Pa., and from 1853 to 1855 was editor of the Harrisburg Telegraph; then Governor Pollock, of Pennsylvania, appointed him Flour Inspector for Philadelphia, which office he held until 1858, when he removed to Minnesota on account of his health, and opened a store at Saint Cloud.

In 1861, Governor Ramsey who had known him in Pennsylvania, appointed him Lieutenant Colonel of the First Regiment of Minnesota Volunteers, and was present with his regiment on July 21st of that year in the eventful battle of Bull Run. Gorman in his report of the return of the First Minnesota Regiment on that occasion wrote: "Before leaving the field, a portion of the right wing, owing to the configuration of the ground and intervening woods, became detached, under the command of Lt. Col. Miller whose gallantry was conspicuous throughout the entire battle, and who contended every inch of the ground with his forces thrown out as skirmishers in the woods, and succeeded in occupying the original ground on the right, after the repulse of a body of cavalry."

After this engagement, his friend Simon Cameron, the Secretary of War, tendered him a position in the regular army which he declined.

Although in ill health he continued with the regiment, and was present at Fair Oaks and Malvern Hill.

In September, 1862, he was made Colonel of the Seventh Regiment, and proceeded against the

Sioux Indians who had massacred so many settlers in the Upper Minnesota Valley, and in December he was the Colonel commanding at Mankato, and under his supervision, thirty-eight Siox, condemned for participation in the killing of white persons, on the 26th of February, 1863, were executed by hanging from gallows, upon one scaffold, at the same time. This year he was made Brigadier General, and also nominated by the republicans for Governor, to which office he was elected for two years, and in January, 1864, enentered upon its duties.

In 1873, he was elected to the Legislature for a district in the southwestern portion of the State, and in 1876, was a Presidential elector, and bore the electoral vote to Washington.

During the latter years of his life he was employed as a land agent by the St. Paul & Sioux City Railroad Company. In 1881 he died. He was married in 1839 to Margaret Funk, and they had three sons, and a daughter who died in early childhood. His son Wesley, a Lieutenant in the United States Army, fell in battle at Gettysburg; his second son was a Commissary of Subsistence, but is now a private; and his youngest son is in the service of a Pennsylvania railroad.

GOVERNOR MARSHAL, A. D. 1866 to A. D. 1870.

William Rainey Marshall is the son of Joseph Marshall, a farmer and native of Bourbon county, Kentucky, whose wife was Abigail Shaw, of Pennsylvania. He was born on the 17th of October, 1825, in Boone county, Missouri. His boyhood was passed in Quincy, Illinois, and before he attained to manhood he went to the lead mine district of Wisconsin, and engaged in mining and surveying.

In September, 1847. when twenty-two years of age, he came to the Falls of St. Croix, and in a few months visited the Falls of St. Anthony, staked out a claim and returned. In the spring of 1848, he was elected to the Wisconsin legislature, but his seat was contested on the ground that he lived beyond the boundaries of the state of Wisconsin. In 1849, he again visited the Falls of St. Anthony, perfected his claim, opened a store, and represented that district in the lower house of the first Territorial legislature. In 1851, he came to St. Paul and established an iron and heavy hardware business.

In 1852, he held the office of County Surveyor, and the next year, with his brother Joseph and N. P. Langford, he went into the banking business. In January, 1861, he became the editor of the Daily Press, which succeeded the Daily Times.

In August, 1862, he was commissioned Lieut. Colonel of the Seventh Minnesota Regiment of Infantry and proceeded to meet the Sioux who had been engaged in the massacre of the settlers of the Minnesota valley. In a few weeks, on the 23d of September, 1862, he was in the battle of Wood Lake, and led a charge of five companies of his own regiment, and two of the Sixth, which routed the Sioux, sheltered in a ravine.

In November, 1863, he became Colonel of the Seventh Regiment. After the campaign in the Indian country the regiment was ordered south, and he gallantly led his command, on the 14th of July, 1864, at the battle near Tupelo, Mississippi. In the conflict before Nashville, in December, he acted as a Brigade commander, and in April, 1865, he was present at the surrender of Mobile.

In 1865, he was nominated by the Republican party, and elected Governor of Minnesota, and in 1867, he was again nominated and elected. He entered upon his duties as Governor, in January, 1866, and retired in 1870, after four years of service.

In 1870, he became vice-president of the bank which was known as the Marine National, which has ceased to exist, and was engaged in other enterprises.

In 1874, he was appointed one of the board of Railroad Commissioners, and in 1875, by a change of the law, he was elected Railroad Commissioner, and until January, 1882, discharged its duties.

He has always been ready to help in any movement which would tend to promote the happiness and intelligence of humanity.

On the 22d of March, 1854, he was married to Abby Langford, of Utica, and has had one child, a son.

GOVERNOR AUSTIN—A. D. 1870 TO A. D. 1874.

Horace Austin, about the year 1831, was born in Connecticut. His father was a blacksmith, and for a time he was engaged in the same occupation. Determined to be something in the world, for several years, during the winter, he taught school. He then entered the office of a well known law firm at Augusta, Maine, and in 1854 came west. For a brief period he had charge of a school at the Falls of Saint Anthony.

In 1856, he became a resident of St. Peter, on

the Minnesota River. In 1863, in the expedition against the Sioux Indians, he served as captain in the volunteer cavalry. In 1869, he was elected Governor, and in 1871 he was re-elected. Soon after the termination of his second gubernatorial term, he was appointed Auditor of the United States Treasury at Washington. He has since been a United States Land Officer in Dakota territory, but at present is residing at Fergus Falls, Minnesota.

GOVERNOR DAVIS A. D. 1874 TO A. D. 1876.

Cushman Kellog Davis, the son of Horatio N. and Clarissa F. Davis, on the 16th of June, 1838, was born at Henderson, Jefferson county, New York. When he was a babe but a few months old, his father moved to Waukesha, Wisconsin, and opened a farm. At Waukesha, Carroll College had been commenced, and in this institution Governor Davis was partly educated, but in 1857 graduated at the University of Michigan.

He read law at Waukesha with Alexander Randall, who was Governor of Wisconsin, and at a later period Postmaster General of the United States, and in 1859 was admitted to the bar.

In 1862, he was commissioned as first lieutenant of the 28th Wisconsin Infantry, and in time became the adjutant general of Brigadier General Willis A. Gorman, ex-Governor of Minnesota, but in 1864, owing to ill health he left the army.

Coming to Saint Paul in August, 1864, he entered upon the practice of his profession, and formed a partnership with ex-Governor Gorman. Gifted with a vigorous mind, a fine voice, and an impressive speaker, he soon took high rank in his profession.

In 1867, he was elected to the lower house of the legislature, and the next year was commisioned United States District Attorney, which position he occupied for five years.

In 1863, he was nominated by the republicans, and elected Governor. Entering upon the duties of the office in 1874, he served two years.

Since his retirement he has had a large legal practice, and is frequently asked to lecture upon literary subjects, always interesting the audience.

GOVERNOR PILLSBURY—A. D. 1876 TO 1882.

John Sargent Pillsbury is of Puritan ancestry. He is the son of John and Susan Pillsbury, and on the 29th of July, 1828, was born at Sutton, New Hampshire, where his father and grandfather lived.

Like the sons of many New Hampshire farmers, he was obliged, at an early age, to work for a support. He commenced to learn house painting, but at the age of sixteen was a boy in a country store. When he was twenty-one years of age, he formed a partnership with Walter Harriman, subsequently Governor of New Hampshire. After two years he removed to Concord, and for four years was a tailor and dealer in cloths. In 1853, he came to Michigan, and in 1855, visited Minnesota, and was so pleased that he settled at St. Anthony, now the East Division of the city of Minneapolis, and opened a hardware store. Soon a fire destroyed his store and stock upon which there was no insurance, but by perseverance and hopefulness, he in time recovered from the loss, with the increased confidence of his fellow men. For six years he was an efficient member of the St. Anthony council.

In 1863, he was one of three appointed sole Regents of the University of Minnesota, with power to liquidate a large indebtedness which had been unwisely created in Territorial days. By his carefulness, after two or three years the debt was canceled, and a large partion of the land granted to the University saved.

In 1863, he was elected a State Senator, and served for seven terms. In 1875, he was nominated by the republicans and elected Governor; in 1877, he was again elected, and in 1879 for the third time he was chosen, the only person who has served three successive terms as the Governor of Minnesota.

By his courage and persistence he succeeded in obtaining the settlement of the railroad bonds which had been issued under the seal of the State, and had for years been ignored, and thus injured the credit of the State.

In 1872, with his nephew he engaged in the manufacture of flour, and the firm owns several mills. Lately they have erected a mill in the East Division, one of the best and largest in the world.

GOVERNOR HUBBARD, A. D. 1882.

Lucius Frederick Hubbard was born on the 26th of January, 1836, at Troy, New York. His father, Charles Frederick, at the time of his death was Sheriff of Rensselaer county. At the age of sixteen, Governor Hubbard left the North Granville Academy, New York, and went to Poultney, Verment, to learn the tinner's trade, and after a short period he moved to Chicago, where he worked for four years.

In 1857, he came to Minnesota, and established a paper called the "Republican," which he conducted until 1861, when in December of that year he enlisted as a private in the Fifth Minnesota Regiment, and by his efficiency so commended himself that in less than one year he became its Colonel. At the battle of Nashville, after he had been knocked off his horse by a ball, he rose, and on foot led his command over the enemy's works. "For gallant and meritorious service in the battle of Nashville, Tennessee, on the 15th and 16th of December, 1864," he received the brevet rank of Brigadier General.

After the war he returned to Red Wing, and has been engaged in the grain and flour business. He was State Senator from 1871 to 1875, and in 1881 was elected Governor. He married in May, 1868, Amelia Thomas, of Red Wing, and has three children.

MINNESOTA'S REPRESENTATIVES IN CONGRESS OF THE UNITED STATES OF AMERICA.

From March, 1849, to May, 1858, Minnesota was a Territory, and entitled to send to the congress of the United States, one delegate, with the privilege of representing the interests of his constituents, but not allowed to vote.

TERRITORIAL DELEGATES.

Before the recognition of Minnesota as a separate Territory, Henry H. Sibley sat in Congress, from January, 1849, as a delegate of the portion Wisconsin territory which was beyond the boundaries of the state of Wisconsin, in 1848 admitted to the Union. In September, 1850 he was elected delegate by the citizens of Minnesota territory, to Congress.

Henry M. Rice succeeded Mr. Sibley as delegate, and took his seat in the thirty-third congress, which convened on December 5th 1853, at Washington. He was re-elected to the thirty-fourth Congress, which assembled on the 3d of March, 1857. During his term of office Congress passed an act extending the pre-emption laws over the unsurveyed lands of Minnesota, and Mr. Rice obtained valuable land grants for the construction of railroads.

William W. Kingsbury was the last Territorial delegate. He took his seat in the thirty-fifth congress, which convened on the 7th of December, 1857, and the next May his seat was vacated by Minnesota becoming a State.

UNITED STATES SENATORS.

Henry M. Rice, who had been for four years delegate to the House of Representatives, was on the 19th of December, 1857, elected one of two United States Senators. During his term the civil war began, and he rendered efficient service to the Union and the State he represented. He is still living, an honored citizen in St. Paul.

James Shields, elected at the same time as Mr. Rice, to the United States Senate, drew the short term of two years.

Morton S. Wilkinson was chosen by a joint convention of the Legislature, on December 15th, 1859, to succeed General Shields. During the rebellion of the Slave States he was a firm supporter of the Union.

Alexander Ramsey was elected by the Legislature, on the 14th of January, 1863, as the successor of Henry M. Rice. The Legislature of 1869 re elected Mr. Ramsey for a second term of six years, ending March 1875. For a full notice see the 138th page.

Daniel S. Norton was, on January 10th, 1865, elected to the United States Senate as the successor of Mr. Wilkinson. Mr. Norton, who had been in feeble health for years, died in June, 1870.

O. P. Stearns was elected on January 17th, 1871, for the few weeks of the unexpired term of Mr. Norton.

William Windom, so long a member of the United States House of Representatives, was elected United States Senator for a term of six years, ending March 4th, 1877, and was re-elected for a second term ending March 4th, 1883, but resigned, having been appointed Secretary of the Treasury by President Garfield.

A. J. Edgerton, of Kasson, was appointed by the Governor to fill the vacancy. President Garfield having been assassinated, and Mr. Edgerton having been appointed Chief Justice of Dakota territory, Mr. Windom, at a special session of the Legislature in October, 1881, was re-elected United States Senator.

S. J. R. McMillan, of St. Paul, on the 19th of February, 1875, was elected United States Senator for the term expiring March 4th, 1881, and has since been re-elected for a second term, which, in March, 1887, will expire.

REPRESENTATIVES IN THE U. S. HOUSE OF REPRESENTATIVES.

William W. Phelps was one of the first members of the United States House of Representatives from Minnesota. Born in Michigan in 1826, he graduated in 1846, at its State University. In 1854, he came to Minnesota as Register of the Land Office at Red Wing, and in 1857, was elected a representative to Congress.

James M. Cavanaugh was of Irish parentage, and came from Massachusetts. He was elected to the same Congress as Mr. Phelps, and subsequently removed to Colorado, where he died.

William Windom was born on May 10th, 1827, in Belmont, county, Ohio. He was admitted to the bar in 1850, and was, in 1853, elected Prosecuting Attorney for Knox county, Ohio. The next year he came to Minnesota, and has represented the State in Congress ever since.

Cyrus Aldrich, of Minneapolis, Hennepin county, was elected a member of the Thirty-sixth Congress, which convened December 5th, 1859, and was re-elected to the Thirty-seventh Congress.

Ignatius Donnelly was born in Philadelphia in 1831. Graduated at the High School of that city, and in 1853 was admitted to the bar. In 1857, he came to Minnesota, and in 1859 was elected Lt. Governor, and re-elected in 1861. He became a representative of Minnesota in the United States Congress which convened on December 7th, 1863, and was re-elected to the Thirty-ninth Congress which convened on December 4th, 1865. He was also elected to the Fortieth congress, which convened in December, 1867. Since 1873 he has been an active State Senator from Dakota county, in which he has been a resident, and Harper Brothers have recently published a book from his pen of wide research called "Atlantis."

Eugene M. Wilson, of Minneapolis, was elected to the the Forty-first Congress, which assembled in December, 1869. He was born December 25th, 1833, at Morgantown, Virginia, and graduated at Jefferson College, Pennsylvania. From 1857 to 1861, he was United States District Attorney for Minnesota. During the civil war he was captain in the First Minnesota Cavalry.

Mr. Wilson's father, grandfather, and maternal grandfather were members of Congress.

M. S. Wilkinson, of whom mention has been made as U. S. Senator, was elected in 1868 a representative to the congress which convened in December, 1869, and served one term.

Mark H. Dunnell of Owatonna, in the fall of 1870, was elected from the First District to fill the seat in the House of Representatives so long occupied by Wm. Windom.

Mr. Dunnell, in July, 1823, was born at Buxton, Maine. He graduated at the college established at Waterville, in that State, in 1849. From 1855 to 1859 he was State Superintendent of schools, and in 1860 commenced the practice of law. For a short period he was Colonel of the 5th Maine regiment but resigned in 1862, and was appointed U. S. Consul at Vera Cruz, Mexico. In 1865, he came to Minnesota, and was State Superintendent of Public Instruction from April, 1867 to August, 1870. Mr. Dunnell still represents his district.

John T. Averill was elected in November, 1870, from the Second District, to succeed Eugene M. Wilson.

Mr. Averill was born at Alma, Maine, and completed his studies at the Maine Wesleyan University. He was a member of the Minnesota Senate in 1858 and 1859, and during the rebellion was Lieut. Colonel of the 6th Minnesota regiment. He is a member of the enterprising firm of paper manufacturers, Averill, Russell and Carpenter. In the fall of 1872 he was re-elected as a member of the Forty-second Congress, which convened in December, 1873.

Horace B. Strait was elected to Forty-third and Forty-fourth Congress, and is still a representative.

William S. King, of Minneapolis, was born December 16, 1828, at Malone, New York. He has been one of the most active citizens of Minnesota in developing its commercial and agriculutral interests. For several years he was Postmaster of the United States House of Representatives, and was elected to the Forty-fourth Congress, which convened in 1875.

Jacob H. Stewart, M. D., was elected to the Forty-fifth Congress, which convened in December, 1877. He was born January 15th, 1829, in Columbia county, New York, and in 1851, graduated at the University of New York. For several years he practiced medicine at Peekskill, New York, and in 1855, removed to St. Paul. In 1859, he was elected to the State Senate, and was Chairman of the Railroad Committee. In 1864, he was Mayor of St. Paul. He was Surgeon of the First

Minnesota, and taken prisoner at the first battle of Bull Run. From 1869 to 1873, he was again Mayor of St. Paul, and is at the present time United States Surveyor General of the Minnesota land office.

Henry Poehler was the successor of Horace B. Strait for the term ending March 4, 1881, when Mr. Strait was again elected.

William Drew Washburn on the 14th of January, 1831, was born at Livermore, Maine, and in 1854, graduated at Bowdoin College. In 1857, he came to Minnesota, and in 1861, was appointed by the President, Surveyor General of U. S. Lands, for this region. He has been one of the most active among the business men of Minneapolis. In November, 1878, he was elected to represent the 3d district in the U. S. House of Representatives, and in 1880, re-elected. He is a brother of C. C., late Governor of Wisconsin, and of E. B., the Minister Plenipotentiary of U. S. of America, to France, and resident in Paris during the late Franco-German war.

RECAPITULATION — TERRITORIAL GOVERNORS OF MINNESOTA.

Alexander Ramsey	1849 1853
Willis A. Gorman	1853-1857
Samuel Medary	1857

STATE GOVERNORS.

Henry H. Sibley	1858 1860
Alexander Ramsey	1860-1863
H. A. Swift, Acting Gov.	1863-1864
Stephen Miller	1864-1866
W. R. Marshall	1866-1870
Horace Austin	1870-1874
C. K. Davis	1874-1876
John S. Pillsbury	1876-1882
L. F. Hubbard	1882

TERRITORIAL DELEGATES TO CONGRESS.

Henry H. Sibley	1849-1853
Henry M. Rice	1853-1857
W. W. Kingsbury	1857-1858

UNITED STATES SENATORS.

Henry M. Rice	1857-1863
James Shields	1857-1859
M. S. Wilkinson	1859-1865
Alexander Ramsey	1863-1875
Daniel S. Norton	1865-1870
O. P. Stearns	1871
William Windom	1871
A. J. Edgerton	1881
S. J. R. McMillan	1875

MEMBERS UNITED STATES HOUSE OF REPRESENTATIVES.

W. W. Phelps	1857-1859
J. M. Cavanaugh	1857-1859
William Windom	1859-1871
Cyrus Aldrich	1859-1863
Ignatius Donnelly	1863-1869
Eugene M. Wilson	1869-1871
M. S. Wilkinson	1869-1771
M. H. Dunnell	1871
J. T. Averill	1871-1875
H. B. Strait	1875-1879
" "	1881
Henry Poehler	1879-1881
W. S. King	1875-1877
J. H. Stewart	1877-1879
W. D. Washburn	1879

STATE EDUCATION.

BY CHARLES S. BRYANT, A. M.

CHAPTER XXVIII.

EDUCATION DEFINITION OF THE WORD—CHURCH AND STATE SEPARATED—COLONIAL PERIOD—HOWARD COLLEGE—WILLIAM PENN'S GREAT LAW—WILLIAM AND MARY COLLEGE—STATE EDUCATION UNDER THE CONFEDERATION—AID GIVEN TO STATES IN THE NORTHWEST.

As a word, education is of wide application and may convey but an indefinite idea. Broadly, it means to draw out, to lead forth, to train up, to foster, to enable the individual to properly use the faculties, mental or corporal, with which he is endowed; and to use them in a way that will accomplish the desired result in all relations and in any department of industry, whether in the domain of intellectual research, or confined to the fields of physical labor.

State Education points at once to a definite field of investigation; an organization which is to have extensive direction and control of the subject matter embraced in the terms chosen. It at once excludes the conclusion that any other species of education than secular education is intended. It excludes all other kinds of education not included in this term, without the slightest reflection upon parochial, sectarian, denominational or individual schools; independent or corporate educational organizations. State Education, then, may embrace whatever is required by the State, in the due execution of its mission in the protection of individual rights and the proper advancement of the citizen in material prosperity; in short whatever may contribute in any way to the honor, dignity, and fair fame of a State; whose sovereign will directs, and, to a very great extent, controls the destiny of its subjects.

A reason may be given for this special department of education, without ignoring any others arising from the necessity of civil government, and its necessary separation from ecclesiastical control. It must be observed by every reasoning mind, that in the advancement and growth of social elements from savagery through families and tribes to civilization, and the better forms of government, that in the increasing growth multiplied industries continually lead to a resistless demand for devision of labor, both intellectual and physical. This division must eventually lead, in every form of government, to a separation of what may be termed Church and State: and, of course, in such division every separate organization must control the elements necessary to sustain its own perpetuity; for otherwise its identity would be lost, and it would cease to have any recognized existence.

In these divisions of labor, severally organized for different and entirely distinct objects, mutual benefits must result, not from any invasion of the separate rights of the one or the other, by hostile aggression, but by reason of the greatest harmony of elements, and hence greater perfection in the labors of each, when limited to the promotion of each separate and peculiar work. In the division, one would be directed towards the temporal, the other toward the spiritual advancement of man, in any and all relations which he sustains, not only to his fellow men, but to the material or immaterial universe. These departments of labor are sufficiently broad, although intimately related, to require the best directed energies of each, to properly cultivate their separate fields. And an evidence of the real harmony existing between these organizations, the Church and State, relative to the present investigation, is found in the admitted fact that education, both temporal and spiritual, secular and sectarian, was a principal of the original organization, and not in conflict with its highest duty, or its most vigorous growth. In the division of the original organization, that department of education, which was only spiritual, was retained with its necessary adjuncts, while that which was only temporal was relegated to a new organization, the temporal organization, the State. The separate elements are still of the same quality, although wielded by two instead of one organization. In this respect education may be compared to the diamond, which when broken and subdivided into most minute particles, each separate particle retains not only the form and number of facets, but the brilliancy of the original diamond. So in the case before us, though education has suffered division, and has been appropriated by different organisms, it is nevertheless the same in nature, and retains the same quality and luster of the parent original.

The laws of growth in these separate organizations, the Church composed of every creed, and the State in every form of government, must determine the extent to which their special education shall be carried. If it shall be determined by the church, that her teachers, leaders, and followers in any stage of its growth, shall be limited in their acquisitions to the simple elements of knowledge, reading, writing, and arithmetic, it may be determined that the State should limit education to the same simple elements. But as the Church, conscious of its immature growth, has never restricted her leaders, teachers, or followers, to these simple elements of knowledge; neither has the State seen fit to limit, nor can it ever limit education to any standard short of the extreme limits of its growth, the fullest development of its resources, and the demands of its citizens. State Education and Church Education are alike in their infancy, and no one is able to prescribe limits to the one or the other. The separation of Church and State, in matters of government only, is yet of very narrow limits, and is of very recent origin. And the separation of Church and State, in matters of education, has not yet clearly dawned upon the minds of the accredited leaders of these clearly distinct organizations.

It is rational, however, to conclude, that among reasonable men, it would be quite as easy to determine the final triumph of State Education, as to determine the final success of the Christian faith over Buddhism, or the final triumph of man in the subjugation of the earth to his control. The decree has gone forth, that man shall subdue the earth; so that, guided by the higher law, Education, under the direction or protection of the State, must prove a final success, for only by organic, scientific, and human instrumentality can the purpose of the Creator be possibly accomplished on earth.

If we have found greater perfection in quality, and better adaptation of methods in the work done by these organizations since the separation, we must conclude that the triumphs of each will be in proportion to the completeness of the separation; and that the countries the least shackled by entangling alliances in this regard, must, other things being equal, lead the van, both in the advancement of science and in the triumphs of an enlightened faith. And we can, by a very slight comparison of the present with the past, determine for ourselves, that the scientific curriculum of State schools has been greatly widened and enriched, and its methods better adapted to proposed ends. We can as easily ascertain the important fact that those countries are in advance, where the two great organizations, Church and State, are least in conflict. We know also, that from the nature of the human movement westward, that the best defined conditions of these organizations should be found in the van of this movement. On this continent, then, the highest development of these organizations should be found, at least, when time shall have matured its natural results in the growth and polish of our institutions. Even now, in our infancy, what country on earth can show equal results in either the growth of general knowledge, the advance of education, or the triumphs of Christian labor at home and abroad? These are the legitimate fruits of the wonderful energy given to the mind of man in the separate labors of these organizations, on the principle of the division of labor, and consequently better directed energies in every department of industry. This movement is onward, across the continent, and thence around the globe. Its force is irresistible, and all efforts to reunite these happily divided powers, and to return to the culture of past times, and the governments and laws of past ages, must be as unavailing as an attempt to reverse the laws of nature. In their separation and friendly rivalry, exists the hope of man's temporal and spiritual elevation.

State Education is natural in its application. In the beginning God created the heavens and the earth, and every organism after its own kind. Now, in pursuance of this well known law of nature, that everything created is made after its own order and its own likeness, it follows that the new comers on this continent brought with them the germ of national and spiritual life. If we are right in this interpretation of the laws of life relating to living organisms, we shall expect to find its proper manifestation in the early institutions they created for their own special purposes immediately after their arrival here. We look into their history, and we find that by authority of the General Court of Massachusetts, in 1636, sixteen years after the landing of the Pilgrim Fathers, Harvard College was established, as an existing identity; that in 1638, it was endowed by John Harvard, and named after him. But the Common School was not overlooked. At a public meeting in Boston, April 13th 1636, it was "generally agreed that one Philemon Pormont be entreated to become schoolmaster for teaching and nourtering children."

After the date above, matters of education ran through the civil authority, and is forcibly expressed in the acts of 1642 and 1647, passed by the General Court of the Massachusetts Bay Colony. By the act of 1642, the select men of every town are required to have vigilant eye over their brothers and neighbors, to see, first, that none of them shall suffer so much barbarism in any of their families, as not to endeavor to teach, by themselves or others, their children and apprentices so much learning as shall enable them perfectly to read the English tongue, and knowledge of the Capital laws, under penalty of twenty shillings for each offence. By the act of 1647, support of schools was made compulsory, and their blessings universal. By this law "every town containing fifty house-holders was required to appoint a teacher, to teach all children as shall resort to him to write and read;" and every town containing one hundred families or house-holders was required to "set up grammar schools. the master thereof being able to instruct youths so far as they may be fitted for the University."

In New Amsterdam, among the Reformed Protestant Dutch, the conception of a school system guaranteed and protected by the State, seems to have been entertained by the colonists from Holland, although circumstances hindered its practical development. The same general statement is true of the mixed settlements along the Delaware; Menonites, Catholics, Dutch, and Swedes, in connection with their churches, established little schools in their early settlements. In 1682, the legislative assembly met at Chester. William Penn made provision for the education of youth of the province, and enacted, that the Governor and provincial Council should erect and order all public schools. One section of Penn's "Great law" is in the words following:

"Be it enacted by authority aforesaid, that all persons within the province and territories thereof, having children, and all the guardians and trustees of orphans, shall cause such to be instructed in reading and writing, so that they may be able to read the scriptures and to write by the time that they attain the age of 12 years, and that they then be taught some useful trade or skill, that the poor may work to live, and the rich, if they become poor, may not want; of which every county shall take care. And in case such parents, guardians, or overseers shall be found deficient in this respect, every such parent, guardian, or overseer, shall pay for every such child five pounds, except there should appear incapacity of body or understanding to hinder it."

And this "Great law" of William Penn, of 1682, will not suffer in comparison with the English statute on State Education, passed in 1870, and amended in 1877, one hundred and ninety-five years later. In this respect, America is two hundred years in advance of Great Britain in State education. But our present limits will not allow us to compare American and English State school systems.

In 1693, the assembly of Pennsylvania passed a second school law providing for the education of youth in every county. These elementary schools were free for boys and girls. In 1755, Pennsylvania College was endowed, and became a University in 1779.

In Virginia, William and Mary College was famous even in colonial times. It was supported by direct State aid. In 1726, a tax was levied on liquors for its benefit by the House of Burgesses;

in 1759, a tax on peddlers was given this college by law, and from various revenues it was, in 1776, the richest college in North America.

These extracts from the early history of State Education in pre-Colonial and Colonial times give abundant evidence of the nature of the organisms planted in American soil by the Pilgrim Fathers and their successors, as well as other early settlers on our Atlantic coast. The inner life has kept pace with the requirements of the external organizations, as the body assumes still greater and more national proportions. The inner life grew with the exterior demands.

On the 9th of July, 1787, it was proclaimed to the world, that on the 15th of November, 1778, in the second year of the independence of America, the several colonies of New Hampshire, Massachusetts Bay, Rhode Island, Providence Plantations, Connecticut, New York, New Jersey, Pennsylvania, Delaware, Maryland, Virginia, North Carolina, South Carolina, and Georgia had entered into a Confederate Union.

This Confederate Union, thus organized as a Government, was able to receive grants of land and to hold the same for such purposes as it saw proper. To the new government cessions were made by several of the States, from 1781 to 1802, of which the Virginia grant was the most important.

The Confederate Government, on the 13th of July, 1787, and within less than four years after the reception of the Virginia Land Grant, known as the Northwest Territory, passed the ever memorable ordinance of 1787. This was the first real estate to which the Confederation had acquired the absolute title in its own right. The legal government had its origin September 17th, 1787, while the ordinance for the government of the Northwest Territory was passed two months and four days before. Article Third of the renowned ordinance reads as follows:

"Religion, morality, and knowledge being necessary to good government and the happiness of mankind, schools and the means of education shall forever be encouraged."

What is the territory embraced by this authoritative enunciation of the Confederate Government? The extent of the land embraced is almost if not quite equal to the area of the original thirteen colonies. Out of this munificent possession added to the infant American Union, have since been carved, by the authority of the United States government, the princely states of Ohio, Indiana, Illinois, Michigan, Wisconsin, and in part Minnesota. In this vast region at least, the Government has said that education "shall be forever encouraged." Encouraged how and by whom? Encouraged by the Government, by the legal State, by the supreme power of the land. This announcement of governmental aid to State schools was no idle boast, made for the encouragement of a delusive hope, but the enunciation of a great truth, inspired by the spirit of a higher life, now kindled in this new American temple, in which the Creator intended man should worship him according to the dictates of an enlightened conscience, "where none should molest or make him afraid."

The early Confederation passed away, but the spirit that animated the organism was immortal, and immediately manifested itself in the new Government, under our present constitution. On the 17th of September, 1787, two months and four days from the date of the ordinance erecting the Northwest Territory was adopted, the new Constitution was inaugurated. The first State government erected in the new territory was the state of Ohio, in 1802. The enabling act, passed by Congress on this accession of the first new State, a part of the new acquisition, contains this substantial evidence that State aid was faithfully remembered and readily offered to the cause of education:

Sec. 3: "That the following proposition be and the same is hereby offered to the convention of the eastern States of said territory, when formed, for their free acceptance or rejection, which if accepted by the convention shall be obligatory upon the United States:

"That section number sixteen in every township, and where such section has been sold, granted or disposed of, other lands equivalent thereto, and most contiguous to the same, shall be granted to the inhabitants of such township for the use of schools."

The proposition of course was duly accepted by the vote of the people in the adoption of their constitution prior to their admission to the Union, and on March 3d, 1803, Congress granted to Ohio, in addition to section sixteen, an additional grant of one complete township for the purpose of establishing any higher institutions of learning. This was the beginning of substantial national recognition of State aid to schools by grants of land out of the national domain, but the government aid did not end in this first effort. The next State, Indiana, admitted in 1816, was granted the same section, number sixteen in each township; and in addition thereto, two townships of land were expressly granted for a seminary of learning. In the admission of Illinois, in 1818, the section numbered sixteen in each township, and two entire townships in addition thereto, for a seminary of learning and the title thereto vested in the legislature. In the admission of Michigan in 1836, the same section sixteen, and seventy-two sections in addition thereto, were set apart to said State for the purpose of a State University. In the admission of Wisconsin, in 1848, the same provision was made as was made to the other States previously formed out of the new territory. This was the commencement.

These five States completed the list of States which could exist in the territory northwest of the Ohio River. Minnesota, the next State, in part lying east of the Mississippi, and in part west, takes its territory from two different sources; that east of the Father of Waters, from Virginia, which was embraced in the Northwest Territory, and that lying west of the same from the "Louisiana Purchase," bought of France by treaty of April 30, 1803, including also the territory west of the Missisippi, which Napoleon had previously acquired from Spain. The greater portion of Minnesota, therefore lies outside the first territorial acquisition of the Government of the United States; and yet the living spirit that inspired the early grants out of the first acquisition, had lost nothing of its fervor in the grant made to the New Northwest. When the Territory of Minnesota was organized, Hon. Stephen A. Douglas, then a Senator in Congress from the state of Illinois, nobly advocated the claims of Minnesota to an increased amount of Government aid for the support of schools, extending from the Common school to the University. By Mr. Douglas' very able, disinterested and generous assistance and support in Congress, aided by Hon. H. M. Rice, then Delegate from Minnesota, our enabling act was made still more liberal in relation to State Education, than that of any State or Territory yet admitted or organized in the amount of lands granted to schools generally.

Section eighteen of the enabling act, passed on the 3d of March, 1849, is as follows:

"And be it further enacted, That when the lands in said Territory shall be surveyed under the direction of the Government of the United States, preparatory to bringing the same into market, sections numbered sixteen and thirty-six in each township in said Territory, shall be, and the same are hereby reserved for the purpose of being applied to schools in said Territory, and in the States and Territories hereafter to be created out of the same."

As the additions to the family of States increase westward, the national domain is still more freely contributed to the use of schools; and the character of the education demanded by the people made more and more definite. In 1851, while Oregon and Minnesota were yet territories of the United States, Congress passed the following act:

"Be it enacted by the Senate and House of Representatives of America, in Congress assembled: That the Governors and legislative assemblies of the territories of Oregon and Minnesota, be, and they are hereby authorized to make such laws and needful regulations as they shall deem most expedient to protect from injury and waste, sections numbered sixteen and thirty-six in said Territories reserved in each township for the support of schools therein.

(2.) "And be it further enacted, That the Secretary of the Interior be, and he is hereby authorized and directed to set apart and reserve from sale, out of any of the public lands within the territory of Minnesota, to which the Indian title has been or may be extinguished, and not otherwise appropriated, a quantity of land not exceeding two entire townships, for the use and support of a University in said Territory, and for no other purpose whatever, to be located by legal subdivisions of not less than one entire section."

[Approved February 19, 1851.]

CHAPTER XXIX.

STATE EDUCATION IN MINNESOTA—BOARD OF REGENTS - UNIVERSITY GRANT—AID OF CONGRESS IN 1862—VALUE OF SCHOOLHOUSES—LOCAL TAXATION IN DIFFERENT STATES—STATE SCHOOL SYSTEM KNOWS NO SECT—IGNORANCE INHERITED, THE COMMON FOE OF MANKIND—CONCLUSION.

When Minnesota was prepared by her population for application to Congress for admission as a State, Congress, in an act authorizing her to form a State government, makes the following provision for schools:

(1) "That sections numbered sixteen and thirty-six in every township of public lands in said State, and where either of said sections, or any part thereof, has been sold or otherwise disposed of, other lands equivalent thereto, and as contiguous as may be, shall be granted to said State for the use of schools.

(2) "That seventy-two sections of land shall be set apart and reserved for the use and support of a State University to be selected by the Governor of said State, subject to the approval of the commissioner at the general land office, and be appropriated and applied in such manner as the legislature of said State may prescribe for the purposes aforesaid, but for no other purpose." [Passed February 26, 1857.]

But that there might be no misapprehension that the American Government not only had the inclination to aid in the proper education of the citizen, but that in cases requiring direct control, the government would not hesitate to exercise its authority, in matters of education as well as in any and all other questions affecting its sovereignty. To this end, on the second of July, 1862, Congress passed the "act donating public lands to the several States and Territories which may provide colleges for the benefit of agriculture and the mechanic arts."

"Be it enacted, &c., that there be granted to the several States for the purposes hereinafter mentioned, an amount of public land to be apportioned to each State (except States in rebellion), a quantity equal to thirty thousand acres for each senator and representative in Congress to which the States are respectively entitled by the apportionment under the census of 1860."

Section four of said act is in substance as follows:

"That all moneys derived from the sale of these lands, directly or indirectly, shall be invested in stocks yielding not less than five per cent. upon the par value of such stocks. That the money so invested shall constitute a perpetual fund, the capital of which shall remain forever undiminished, and the interest thereof shall be inviolably appropriated by each State which may claim the benefit of the act to the endowment, support, and maintenance of at least one college, where the leading object shall be, without excluding other scientific and classical studies, and including military tactics, to teach such branches of learning as are related to agriculture and the mechanic arts, in such manner as the legislatures of the States may respectively prescribe, in order to promote the liberal and practical education of the industrial classes in the several pursuits and professions of life.

Section five, second clause of said act, provides "That no portion of said fund, nor the interest thereon, shall be applied, directly or indirectly, under any pretence whatever, to the purchase, erection, preservation, or repair of any building or buildings."

Section five, third clause, "That any State which may take and claim the benefit of the provisions of this act shall provide, within five years, at least not less than one college, as described in the fourth section of this act, or the grant to such State shall cease; and the said State shall be bound to pay the United States the amount received of any lands previously sold."

Section five, fourth clause, "An annual report shall be made regarding the progress of each college, recording any improvements and experiments made, with their costs and results, and such other matters, including State industrial and economical statistics, as may be supposed useful; one copy of which shall be transmitted by mail free, by each, to all the other colleges which may be endowed under the provisions of this act, and also one copy to the Secretary of the Interior."

Under this act Minnesota is entitled to select 150,000 acres to aid in teaching the branches in the act named in the State University, making the endowment fund of the Government to the state of Minnesota for educational purposes as follows:

1. For common schools, in acres......	3,000,000
2. For State University, four townships	208,360
Total apportionment............	3,208,360

All these lands have not been selected. Under the agricultural college grant, only 94,439 acres have been selected, and only 72.708 acres under the two University grants, leaving only 167,147 acres realized for University purposes, out of the 208,360, a possible loss of 41,203 acres.

The permanent school fund derived from the national domain by the state of Minnesota, at a reasonable estimate of the value of the lands secured out of those granted to her, cannot vary far from the results below, considering the prices already obtained:

1. Common school lands in acres, 3,000,000, valued at............	$18,000,000
2. University grants, in all, in acres, 223,000, valued at.............	1,115,000
Amount in acres, 3,223,000....	$19,115,000

Out of this permanent school fund may be realized an annual fund, when lands are all sold:

1. For common schools............	$1,000,000
2. University instruction...........	60,000

These several grants, ample as they seem to be, are, however, not a tithe of the means required from the State itself for the free education of the children of the State. We shall see further on what the State has already done in her free school system.

Minnesota, a State first distinguished by an extra grant of government land, has something to unite it to great national interest Its position in the sisterhood of States gives it a prominence that none other can occupy. A State lying on both sides of the great Father of waters, in a continental valley midway between two vast oceans, encircling the Western Hemisphere, with a soil of superior fertility, a climate unequalled for health, and bright with skies the most inspiring, such a State, it may be said, must ever hold a prominent position in the Great American Union.

In the acts of the early settlements on the Atlantic coast, in the Colonial Government, and the National Congress, we have the evidence of a determined intention "that schools and the means of education shall forever be encouraged" by the people who have the destinies of the Western Hemisphere in their hands. That the external organism of the system capable of accomplishing this heavy task, and of carrying forward this responsible duty, rests with the people themselves, and is as extensive as the government they have established for the protection of their rights and the growth of their physical industries, and the free development of their intellectual powers. The people, organized as a Nation, in assuming this duty, have in advance proclaimed to the world that "Religion, Morality, and Knowledge" are alike essential "to good government." And in organizing a government free from sectarian control or alliance, America made an advance hitherto unknown, both in its temporal and spiritual power; for hitherto the work of the one had hindered the others, and the labors and unities of the two were inconsistent with the proper functions of either. The triumph, therefore, of either, for the control of both, was certain ruin, while separation of each, the one from the other, was the true life of both. Such a victory, therefore, was never before known on earth, as the entire separation, and yet the friendly rivalry of Church and State, first inaugurated in the free States of America. This idea was crystalized and at once stamped on the fore-front of the Nation's life in the aphorism, "Religion, morality, and knowledge are alike essential to good government." And the deduction from this national aphorism necessarily follows: "That schools and the means of education should forever be encouraged." We assume, then, without further illustration drawn from the acts of the Nation, that the means of education have not and will not be withheld. We have seen two great acquisitions, the Northwest Territory, and the Louisiana Purchase, parceled out in greater and greater profusion for educational uses, till the climax is reached in the Mississippi Valley, the future great center of national power. At the head of this valley sits as regnant queen the state of Minnesota, endowed with the means of education unsurpassed by any of her compeers in the sisterhood of States. Let us now inquire, as pertinent to this discussion,

WHAT HAS MINNESOTA DONE FOR STATE EDUCATION?

The answer is in part made up from her constitution and the laws enacted in pursuance thereof: First, then, article VIII. of her constitution reads thus:

SECTION 1. The stability of a republican form of government depending mainly upon the intelligence of the people, it shall be the duty of the Legislature to establish a general and uniform system of public schools.

SECTION 2. The proceeds of such lands as are, or hereafter may be granted by the United States, for the use of schools in each township in this State, shall remain a perpetual school fund to the State. * * * * The principal of all funds arising from sales or other disposition of lands or other property, granted or entrusted to this State, shall forever be preserved inviolate and undiminished; and the income arising from the lease or sale of said school land shall be distributed to the different townships throughout the State in proportion to the number of scholars in each township, between the ages of five and twenty-one years; and shall be faithfully applied to the specific object of the original grant or appropriation."

SECTION 3. The legislature shall make such provision by taxation or otherwise, as, with the income arising from the school fund, will secure a thorough and efficient system of public schools in each township in the State.

But in no case shall the moneys derived as aforesaid, or any portion thereof, or any public moneys or property, be appropriated or used for the support of schools wherein the destinctive doctrines, creeds, or tenets of any particular Christian or other religious sect are promulgated or taught."

THE UNIVERSITY.

"SECTION 4. The location of the University of Minnesota, as established by existing laws, [Sept. 1851] is hereby confirmed, and said institution is hereby declared to be the University of Minnesota. All the rights, immunities, franchises, and endowments heretofore granted or conferred, are hereby perpetuated unto the said University; and all lands which may be granted hereafter by Congress, or other donations for said University purposes, shall rest in the institution referred to in this section.

The State constitution is in full harmony with the National government in the distinctive outlines laid down in the extracts above made. And the Territorial and State governments, within these limits, have consecutively appropriated by legislation, sufficient to carry forward the State school system. In the Territorial act, establishing the University, the people of the State announced in advance of the establishment of a State government, "that the proceeds of the land that may hereafter be granted by the United States to the Territory for the support of the University, shall be and remain a perpetual fund, to be called "the University Fund," the interest of which shall be appropriated to the support of a University, and no sectarian instruction shall be allowed in such University!" This organization of the University was confirmed by the State constitution, and the congressional land grants severally passed to that corporation, and the use of the funds arising therefrom were subjected to the restrictions named. So that both the common school and University were dedicated to State school purposes, and expressly excluded from sectarian control or sectarian instruction.

In this respect the State organization corresponds with the demands of the general government; and has organized the school system reaching from the common school to the university, so that it may be said, the State student may, if he choose, in the state of Minnesota pass from grade to grade, through common school, high school, and State University free of charge for tuition. Without referring specially to the progressive legislative enactments, the united system may be referred to as made up of units of different orders, and successively in its ascending grades, governed by separate boards, rising in the scale of importance from the local trustee, directors, and treasurer, in common school, to the higher board of education, of six members in the independent school district, and more or less than that number in districts and large cities under special charter, until we reach the climax in the dignified Board of Regents; a board created by law and known as the Regents of the State University. This honorable body consists of seven men nominated by the Governor and confirmed by the senate of the State legislature, each holding his office for three years; and besides these there are three ex-officio members, consisting of the President of the State University, the Superintendent of Public Instruction, and the Governor of the State. This body of ten men are in reality the legal head of the State University, and indirectly the effective head of the State school system of Minnesota, and are themselves subject only to the control of the State Legislature. These various officers, throughout this series, are severally trustees of legal duties which cannot be delegated. They fall under the legal maxim "that a trustee cannot make a trustee." These are the legal bodies to whom the several series of employes and servitors owe obedience. These various trustees determine the course of study and the rules of transfer from grade to grade until the last grade is reached at the head of the State system, or the scholar has perhaps completed a post-graduate course in a polytechnic school, inaugurated by the State for greater perfection, it may be in chemistry, agriculture, the mechanic arts, or other specialty, required by the State or national government.

This system, let it be understood, differs from all private, parochial, denominational, or sectarian schools. The State organism and all the sectarian elements of the church are, in this department of labor, entirely distinct. The State protects and encourages, but does not control either the schools or the faith of the church. The church supports and approves, but does not yield its tenets or its creed to the curriculum of the schools of the State. The State and the Church are in this respect entirely distinct and different organizations. State education, however, and the education of the adherents of the church are in harmony throughout a great portion of the State curriculum. Indeed, there seems to be no reason why the greater portion of denominational teaching, so far as the same is in harmony with the schools of the State, should not be relegated to the State, that the church throughout all its sectarian element might be the better able to direct its energies and economize its benevolence in the cultivation of its own fields of chosen labor. But, however this may be, and wherever these two organizations choose to divide their labors, they are still harmonious even in their rivalry.

The organism as a State system has, in Minnesota, so matured that through all the grades to the University, the steps are defined and the gradients passed without any conflict of authority. The only check to the regular order of ascending grades was first met in the State University. These schools, in older countries, had at one time an independent position, and in their origin had their own scholars of all grades, from the preparatory department to the Senior Class in the finished course; but in our State system, when the common schools became graded, and the High School had grown up as a part of the organism of a completed system, the University naturally took its place at the head of the State system, having the same relation to the High School as the High School has to the Common School. There was no longer any reason why the same rule should not apply in the transfer from the High School to the University, that applied in the transfer from the Common School to the High School, and to this conclusion the people of the State have already fully arrived. The rules of the board of Regents of the State University now allow students, with the Principal's certificate of qualification, to enter the Freshman class, on examination in sub-Freshman studies only. But even this is not satisfactory to the friends of the State school system. They demand for High School graduates an entrance into the University, when the grade below is passed, on the examination of the school below for graduation therein. If, on the one hand, the High schools of the State, under the law for the encouragement of higher education, are required to prepare students so that they shall be qualified to enter some one of the classes of the University, on the other hand the University should be required to admit the students thus qualified without further examination. The rule should work in either direction. The rights of students under the law are as sacred, and should be as inalienable, as the rights of teachers or faculties in State institutions. The day of unlimited, irresponsible discretion, a relic of absolute autocracy, a despotic power, has no place in systems of free schools under constitutional and statutory limitations, and these presidents and faculties who continue to exercise this power in the absence of right, should be reminded by Boards of Regents at the head of American State systems that their resignation would be acceptable. They belong to an antiquated system, outgrown by the age in which we live.

The spirit of the people of our State was fully intimated in the legislature of 1881, in the House bill introduced as an amendment to the law of 1878-79, for the encouragement of higher education, but finally laid aside for the law then in force, slightly amended, and quite in harmony with the House bill. Sections two and five alluded to read as follows:

"Any public, graded or high school in any city or incorporated village or township organized into a district under the so-called township system, which shall have regular classes and courses of study, articulating with some course of study, optional or required, in the State University, and shall raise annually for the expense of said school double the amount of State aid allowed by this act, and shall admit students of either sex into the higher classes thereof from any part of the State, without charge for tuition, shall receive State aid, as specified in section four of this act. Provided, that non-resident pupils shall in all cases be qualified to enter the highest department of said school at the entrance examination for resident pupils."

"The High School Board shall have power, and it is hereby made their duty to provide uniform questions to test the qualifications of the scholars of said graded or high schools for entrance and graduation, and especially conduct the examinations of scholars in said schools, when desired and notified, and award diplomas to graduates who shall upon examination be found to have completed any course of study, either optional or required, entitling the holder to enter any class in the University of Minnesota named therein, any time within one year from the date thereof, without further examination; said diploma to be executed by the several members of the High School Board."

THE RELATED SYSTEM.

We have now seen the position of the University in our system of public schools. In its position only at the head of the series it differs from the grades below. The rights of the scholar follow him throughout the series. When he has completed and received the certificate or diploma in the prescribed course in the High School, articulating with any course, optional or required, in the University, he has the same right, unconditioned, to pass to the higher class in that course, as he had to pass on examination, from one class to the other in any of the grades below. So it follows, that the University faculty or teacher who assumes the right to reject, condition, or re-examine such student, would exercise an abuse of power, unwarranted in law, arbitrary in spirit, and not republican in character. This rule is better and better understood in all State Universities, as free State educational organisms are more crystalized into forms, analogous to our State and national governments. The arbitrary will of the intermediate, or head master, no longer prevails. His will must yield to more certain legal rights, as the learner passes on, under prescribed rules, from infancy to manhood through all the grades of school life. And no legislation framed on any other theory of educational promotion in republican States can stand against this American consciousness of equality existing between all the members of the body politic. In this consciousness is embraced the inalienable rights of the child or the youth to an education free in all our public schools. In Minnesota it is guaranteed in the constitution that the legislature shall make such provisions, by taxation or otherwise, as, with the income arising from the school fund, will secure a thorough and efficient system of public schools in each township in the State. Who shall say that the people have no right to secure such thorough and efficient system, even should that "thorough and efficient system" extend to direct taxation for a course extending to graduation from a University? Should such a course exceed the constitutional limitation of a thorough and efficient system of public schools?

INTERPRETATION OF THE CONSTITUTION.

The people, through the medium of the lawmaking power, have given on three several occasions, in 1878, 1879, and 1881, an intimation of the scope and measuring of our State constitution on educational extension to higher education than the common school. In the first section of the act of 1881, the legislature created a High School Board, consisting of the Governor of the State, Superintendent of Public Instruction, and the President of the University of Minnesota, who are charged with certain duties and granted certain powers contained in the act. And this High School Board are required to grant State aid to the amount of $400 during the school year to any public graded school, in any city or incorporated village, or township organized into a district, which shall give preparatory instruction, extending to and articulating with the University course in some one of its classes, and shall admit students of either sex, from any part of the State, without charge for tuition. Provided only that non-resident pupils shall be qualified to enter some one of the organized classes of such graded or high school. To carry out this act, giving State aid directly out of the State treasury to a course of education reaching upward from the common school, through the high school to the University, the legislature appropriated the entire sum of $20,000. In this manner we have the interpretation of the people of Minnesota as to the meaning of "a thorough and efficient system of public schools, operative alike in each township in the State." And this interpretation of our legislature is in harmony with the several acts of Congress, and particularly the act of July the second, 1862, granting lands to the several States of the Union, known as the Agricultural College Grant. The States receiving said lands are required, in their colleges or universities, to "teach such branches of learning as are related to Agriculture and the Mechanic arts, without excluding other scientific and classical studies, and including military tactics, in such manner as the legislatures of the States may respectively prescribe, in order to promote the liberal and practical education of the industrial classes in the several pursuits and professions of life."

And the Legislature of Minnesota has already established in its University, optional or required courses of study fully meeting the limitations in the congressional act of 1862. In its elementary department it has three courses, known as classical, scientific, and modern. In the College of Science, Literature, and the Arts, the courses of study are an extension of those of the elementary departments, and lead directly to the degrees of Bachelor of Arts, Bachelor of Science, and Bachelor of Literature. In the College of Mechanic Arts the several courses of studies are principally limited to Civil Engineering, Mechanical Engineering, and Architecture. In the College of Agriculture are: (1) The regular University course, leading to the degree of Bachelor of Agriculture. (2) The elementary course, in part coinciding with the Scientific course of the Elementary Department. (3) A Farmers' Lecture course. (4) Three special courses for the year 1880-81. Law and Medicine have not yet been opened in the State University for want of means to carry forward these departments, now so much needed.

Our State constitution has therefore been practically interpreted by the people, by a test that cannot be misconstrued. They have fortified their opinion by the payment of the necessary tax to insure the success of a thorough and efficient system of public schools throughout the State. This proof of the people's interest in these schools appears in the amounts paid for expenses and instruction. From the school fund the State of Minnesota received, in 1879, the full sum of $232,187.43 The State paid out the same year, the sum of $394,737.71. The difference is $162,-550.28, which was paid out by the State more than was derived from the government endowment fund. And it is not at all likely that the endowment fund, generous as it is, will ever produce an amount equal to the cost of instruction. The ratio of the increase of scholars it is believed will always be in advance of the endowment fund. The cost of instruction cannot fall much below an average, for all grades of scholars, of eight dollars per annum to each pupil. Our present 180,000 scholars enrolled would, at this rate require $1,440,000, and in ten years and long before the sale of the school lands of the State shall have been made, this 180,-000 will have increased a hundred per cent., amounting to 360,000 scholars. These, at $8.00 per scholar for tuition, would equal $2,880,000 per annum, while the interest from the school fund in the same time cannot exceed $2,000,000, even should the land average the price of $6.00 per acre, and the interest realized be always equal to 6 per cent.

SOME OF THE RESULTS

In these infant steps taken by our State, we can discern the tendency of our organism towards a completed State system, as an element of a still wider union embracing the nation. To know what is yet to be done in this direction we must know what has already been done. We have, in the twenty years of our State history, built 3,693 schoolhouses, varying in cost from $400 to $90,-000; total value of all, $3,156,210; three Normal school buildings at a cost of (1872) $215,231.52; a State University at an expenditure for buildings alone of $70,000, and an allowance by a late act of the legislature of an additional $100,000, in three yearly appropriations, for additional buildings to be erected, in all $170,000, allowed by the State for the University. Add these to the cost of common school structures, and we have already expended in school buildings over $4,800,000 for the simple purpose of housing the infant organism, our common school system here planted. We have seen a movement in cities like St. Paul, Minneapolis, Stillwater, and Winona, towards the local organization of a completed system of home schools, carrying instruction free to the University course, with a total enrollment of 13,500 scholars and 265 teachers, daily seated in buildings, all in the modern style of school architecture and school furniture, costing to these cities the sum of $850,000 for buildings, and for instruction the sum of $118,000 annually.

We have, in addition to these schools in the cities named, other home and fitting schools, to whom have been paid $400 each, under the law for the "Encouragement of Higher Education," passed in 1878, and amended in 1879, as follows: Anoka, Austin, Blue Earth City, Chatfield, Cannon Falls, Crookston, Duluth, Detroit, Eyota, Faribault, Garden City, Glencoe, Howard Lake, Hastings, Henderson, Kasson, Litchfield, Lanesboro, Le Sueur, Lake City, Monticello, Moorhead, Mankato, Northfield, Owatonna, Osseo, Plainview, Red Wing, Rushford, Rochester, St. Cloud, St. Peter, Sauk Centre, Spring Valley, Wells, Waterville, Waseca, Wabasha, Wilmar, Winnebago City, Zumbrota, and Mantorville.

These forty-two State aid schools have paid in all for buildings and furniture the gross sum of $642,700; some of these buildings are superior in all that constitutes superiority in school architecture. The Rochester buildings and grounds cost the sum of $90,000. Several others, such as the Austin, Owatonna, Faribault, Hastings, Red Wing, Rushford, St. Cloud, and St. Peter schoolhouses, exceed in value the sum of $25,000; and others of these buildings are estimated at $6,000, $8,000, $10,000, and $15,000. In all they have an enrollment of scholars in attendance on classes graded up to the University course, numbering 13,000, under 301 teachers, at an annual salary amounting in all to $123,569, and having in their A, B, C, D classes 1704 scholars, of whom 126 were prepared to enter the sub-freshman class of the State University in 1880, and the number entering these grades in the year 1879-80 was 934, of whom 400 were non-residents of the districts. And in all these forty-two home schools of the people, the fitting schools of the State University, one uniform course of study, articulating with some course in the University, was observed. As many other courses as the local boards desired were also carried on in these schools. This, in short, is a part of what we have done.

The organic elements that regularly combine to form governments, are similar to those organic elements that combine to form systems of mental culture. The primitive type of government is the family. This is the lowest organic form. If no improvement is ever made upon this primitive element, by other combinations of an artificial nature, human governments would never rise higher than the family. If society is to advance, this organism widens into the clan, and in like manner the clan into the village, and the village into the more dignified province, and the province into the State. All these artificial conditions above the family are the evidences of growth in pursuance of the laws of artificial life. In like manner the growth of intellectual organisms proceeds from the family instruction to the common school. Here the artificial organism would cease to advance, and would remain stationary, as the clan in the organism of government, unless the common school should pass on to the wider and still higher unit of a graded system reaching upward to the high school. Now this was the condition of the common school in America during the Colonial state, and even down to the national organization. Soon after this period, the intellectual life of the nation began to be aroused, and within the last fifty years the State common school has culminated in the higher organism of the high school, and it is of very recent date that the high school has reached up to and articulated in any State with the State University. On this continent, both government and State schools started into life, freed from the domination of institutions grown effete from age and loss of vital energy. Here, both entered into wider combinations, reaching higher results than the ages of the past. And yet, in educational organization we are far below the standard of perfection we shall attain in the rapidly advancing future. Not until our system of education has attained a national character as complete in its related articulation as the civil organization of towns, counties, and States in the national Union, can our educational institutions do the work required of this age. And in Minnesota, one of the leading States in connected school organic relations, we have, as yet, some 4,000 common school districts, with an enrollment of some 100,000 scholars of different ages, from five to twenty-one years; no higher in the scale than the common school, prior to the first high school on the American continent. These chaotic elements, outside of the system of graded schools now aided by the State, must be reduced to the same organized graded system as those that now articulate in their course with the State University.

Our complete organization as a State system for

educational purposes, equal to the demands of the State, and required by the spirit of the age, will not be consummated until our four thousand school districts shall reap the full benefits of a graded system reaching to the high school course, articulating with some course in the State University and a course in commen with every other high school in the State. The system thus organized might be required to report to the Board of Regents, as the legal head of the organization of the State School system, not only the numerical statistics, but the number and standing of the classes in each of the high schools in the several studies of the uniform course, established by the Board of Regents, under the direction of the State Legislature. To this system must finally belong the certificate of standing and graduation, entitling the holder to enter the designated class in any grade of the State schools named therein, whether High School or University. But this system is not and can never be a skeleton merely, made up of lifeless materials, as an anatomical specimen in the office of the student of the practice of the healing art. Within this organism there must preside the living teacher, bringing into this organic structure, not the debris of the effete systems of the past, not the mental exuvia of dwarfed intellectual powers of this or any former age, but the teacher inspired by nature to feel and appreciate her methods, and ever moved by her divine afflatus.

Every living organism has its own laws of growth; and the one we have under consideration may, in its most important feature, be compared to the growth of the forest tree. In its earlier years the forest tree strikes its roots deep into the earth and matures its growing rootlets, the support of its future trunk, to stand against the storms and winds to which it is at all times exposed. When fully rooted in the ground, with a trunk matured by the growth of years, it puts forth its infant branches and leaflets, suited to its immature but maturing nature; finally it gives evidence of stalwart powers, and now its widespreading top towers aloft among its compeers rearing its head high among the loftiest denizens of the woods. In like manner is the growth of the maturing State school organism. In the common school, the foundation is laid for the rising structure, but here are no branches, no fruitage. It seems in its earliest infancy to put forth no branches, but is simply taking hold of the elements below on which its inner life and growth depend. As the system rises, the underlaying laws of life come forth in the principles of invention, manufacturing, engraving, and designing, enriching every branch of intellectual and professional industry, and beautifying every field of human culture. These varied results are all in the law of growth in the organism of State schools carried on above the common schools to the University course. The higher the course the more beneficial the results to the industries of the world, whether those industries are intellectual or purely physical, cater only to the demands of wealth, or tend to subserve the mod st demands of the humblest citizen.

The only criticism that can reach the question now under consideration, is whether the graded organization tends to produce the results to which we have referred. The law relating to the division of labor has especially operated in the graded system of State schools. Under its operation, it is claimed, by good judges, that eight years of school life, from five to twenty-one, has been saved to the pupils of the present generation, over those of the ungraded schools ante-dating the last fifty years. By the operation of this law, in one generation, the saving of time, on the enrollments of State schools in the graded systems of the northern States of the American Union, would be enormous. For the State of Minnesota alone, on the enrollment of 180,000, the aggregate years of time saved would exceed a million! The time saved on the enrollment of the schools of the different States, under the operation of this law would exceed over twenty million years!

To the division of labor is due the wonderful facility with which modern business associations have laid their hands upon every branch of industrial pursuits, and bestowed upon the world the comforts of life. Introduced into our system of education it produces results as astonishing as the advent of the Spinning Jenny in the manufacture of cloth. As the raw material from the cotton field of the planter, passing, by gradation, through the unskilled hands of the ordinary laborer to the more perfect process of improved machinery, secure additional value in a constantly increasing ratio; so the graded system of intellectual culture, from the Primary to the High school, and thence to the University, adds increased lustre and value to the mental development in a ratio commensurate with the increased skill of the mental operator.

The law of growth in State schools was clearly announced by Horace Mann, when he applied to this system the law governing hydraulics, that no stream could rise above its fountain. The common school could not produce a scholarship above its own curriculum. The high school was a grade above, and as important in the State system as the elevated fountain head of the living stream. This law of growth makes the system at once the most natural, the most economical, and certainly the most popular. These several elements might be illustrated, but the reader can easily imagine them at his leisure. As to the last, however, suffer an illustration. In Minnesota, for the school year ending August 21st, 1880, according to the report of the Superintendent of Public Instruction, there were enrolled, one hundred and eighty thousand, two hundred and fifty-eight scholars in the State schools, while all others, embracing kindergartens, private schools, parochial schools, of all sects and all denominations, had an attendance at the same time of only two thousand four hundred and twenty-eight; and to meet all possible omissions, if we allow double this number, there is less than three per cent. of the enrollment in the State school. This ratio will be found to hold good, at least throughout all the Northern States of the American Union. These State schools, then, are not unpopular in comparison with the schools of a private and opposite character. Nor is it owing altogether to the important fact, that State schools are free, that they are more popular than schools of an opposite character; for these State schools are a tax upon the property of the people, and yet a tax most cheerfully borne, in consequence of their superior excellence and importance.

The State school, if not already, can be so graded that each scholar can have the advantage of superior special instruction far better adapted to the studies through which he desires to pass, than similar instruction can be had in ungraded schools of any character whatever. In this respect the State system is without a rival. It has the power to introduce such changes as may meet all the demands of the State and all the claims of the learner.

The State school knows no sect, no party, no privileged class, and no special favorites; the high, the low, the rich, and the poor, the home and foreign-born, black or white, are all equal at this altar. The child of the ruler and the ruled are here equal. The son of the Governor, the wood-sawyer, and the hod-carrier, here meet on one level, and alike contend for ranks, and alike expect the honors due to superior merit, the reward of intellectual culture. But, aside from the republican character of the State school system, the system is a State necessity. Without the required State culture under its control, the State must cease to exist as an organism for the promotion of human happiness or the protection of human rights, and its people, though once cultured and refined, must certainly return to barbarism and savage life. There can be no compromise in the warfare against inherited ignorance. Under all governments the statute of limitations closes over the subject at twenty-one years; so that during the minority of the race must this warfare be waged by the government without truce. No peace can ever be proclaimed in this war, until the child shall inherit the matured wisdom, instead of the primal ignorance of the ancestor.

The State school system, in our government, is from the necessity of the case, national. No State can enforce its system beyond the limits of its own territory. And unless the nation enforce its own uniform system, the conflict between jurisdictions could never be determined. No homogeneous system could ever be enforced. As the graded system of State schools has now reached the period in its history which corresponds to the colonial history of the national organization, it must here fail, as did the colonial system of government, to fully meet the demands of the people. And what was it, let us consider, that led the people in the organization of the national government "to form a more perfect union?" Had it then become necessary to take this step, that "justice" might be established, domestic tranquility insured, the common defense made more efficient, the general welfare promoted, and the blessings of liberty better secured to themselves and their posterity, that the fathers of the government should think it necessary to form a more perfect union?" Why the necessity of a more perfect union? Were our fathers in fear of a domestic or foreign foe, that had manifested his power in their immediate presence, threatening to jeopardize or destroy their domestic tranquility? Was this foe an hereditary enemy, who might at long intervals of time invade their territory, and endanger the liberties of this people? And for this reason did they demand a more perfect union? And does not this reason now exist in still greater force for the formation of a still more perfect union in our system of State schools? Our fathers were moved by the most natural of all reasons, by this law of self-defense. They were attacked by a power too great to be successfully resisted in their colonial or unorganized state. The fear of a destruction of the several colonies without a more perfect union drove them to this alternative. It was union and the hope of freedom, against disunion and the fear of death, that cemented the national government. And this was an external organism, the temple in which the spirit of freedom should preside, and in which her worshippers should enjoy not only domestic but national tranquility. Now, should it be manifested to the world that the soul and spirit, the very life of this temple, erected to freedom, is similarly threatened, should not be the same cause that operated in the erection of the temple itself, operate in the protection of its sacred fires, its soul and spirit? It would seem to require no admonition to move a nation in the direction of its highest hopes, the protection of its inner life.

And what is this enemy, and where is the power able to destroy both the temple and the spirit of freedom? And why should State Education take upon itself any advanced position other than its present independent organic elements? In the face of what enemy should it now be claimed we should attempt to change front, and "form a more perfect union to insure domestic tranquility, and promote the general welfare," to the end that we may the better secure the blessings of liberty to ourselves and our posterity? That potent foe to our free institutions, to which we are now brought face to face, is human ignorance, the natural hereditary foe to every form of enlightened free government. This hereditary enemy is now homesteaded upon our soil. This enemy, in the language of the declaration made by the colonies against their hereditary foe, this enemy to our government, has kept among us a standing army of illiterates, who can neither read nor write, but are armed with the ballot, more powerful than the sword, ready to strike the most deadly blow at human freedom; he has cut off and almost entirely destroyed our trade between States of the same government; has imposed a tax upon us without our consent, most grievous to be borne; he has quite abolished the free system of United States laws in several of our States; he has established, in many sections, arbitrary tribunals, excluding the subject from the right of trial by jury, and enlarged the powers of his despotic rule, endangered the lives of peaceable citizens; he has alienated government of one section, by declaring the inhabitants aliens and enemies to his supposed hereditary right; he has excited domestic insurrections amongst us; he has endeavored to destroy the peace and harmony of our people by bringing his despotic ignorance of our institutions into conflict with the freedom and purity of our elections; he has raised up advocates to his cause who have openly declared that our system of State Education, on which our government rests, is a failure;* he has spared no age, no sex, no portion of our country, but has, with his ignominious minions, afflicted the North and the South, the East and the West, the rich and the poor, the black and the white; an enemy alike to the people of every section of the government, from Maine to California, from Minnesota to Louisiana. Such an inexorable enemy to government and the domestic tranquility of all good citizens deserves the opprobrium due only to the Prince of Darkness, against whom eternal war should be waged; and for the support of this declaration, with a firm reliance on the protection of Divine Providence, we should, as did our fathers, mutually pledge to each other, as citizens of the free States of America, our lives, our fortunes, and our sacred honor.

We have thus far considered the State school system in some of its organic elements, and the nature, tendency, and necessary union of these elements; first in States, and finally for the formation of a more perfect union, that they may be united in one national organization under the control of one sovereign will. The mode in which these unorganized elements shall come into union and harmony with themselves, and constitute the true inner life and soul of the American Union, is left for the consideration of those whose special duty it is to devote their best energies to the promotion of the welfare of the Nation, and by statesman-like forethought provide for the domestic, social, civil, intellectual, and industrial progress of the rapidly accumulating millions who

*Richard Grant White in North American Review

are soon to swarm upon the American continent. We see truly that

"The rudiments of empire here
Are plastic yet and warm;
The chaos of a mighty world
Is rounding into form!

"Each rude and jostling fragment soon
Its fitting place shall find—
The raw material of a State,
Its muscle and its mind."

But we must be allowed, in a word, to state the results which we hope to see accomplished, before the jostling fragments which are yet plastic and warm, shall have attained a temperament not easily fused and "rounded" into one homogenous national system, rising in the several States from the kindergarten to the University, and from the State Universities through all orders of specialties demanded by the widening industries and growing demands of a progressive age. And in this direction we cannot fail to see that the national government must so mould its intellectual systems that the State and national *curricula* shall be uniform throughout the States and territories, so that a class standing of every pupil, properly certified, shall be equally good for a like class standing in every portion of the government to which he may desire to remove. America will then be ready to celebrate her final independence, the inalienable right of American youth, as having a standing limited by law in her State and national systems of education, entitling them to rank everywhere with associates and compeers on the same plain; when in no case, shall these rights be denied or abridged by the United States, or by any State or authority thereof, on account of race, color, or previous condition of scholarship, secular or sectarian, till the same shall forever find the most ample protection under the broad banner of NATIONAL and NATURAL rights, common alike to all in the ever widening REPUBLIC of LETTERS.

HISTORY

OF THE

SIOUX MASSACRE OF 1862.

CHAPTER XXX.

LOUIS HENNEPIN'S VISIT TO THE UPPER MISSISSIPPI IN 1680—CAPTAIN JONATHAN CARVER VISITS THE COUNTRY IN 1766—THE NAMES OF THE TRIBES—TREATIES WITH SIOUX INDIANS FROM 1812 TO 1859—THEIR RESERVATIONS—CIVILIZATION EFFORTS—SETTLEMENTS OF THE WHITES CONTIGUOUS TO THE RESERVATIONS.

The first authentic knowledge of the country upon the waters of the Upper Mississippi and its tributaries, was given to the world by Louis Hennepin, a native of France. In 1680 he visited the Falls of St. Anthony, and gave them the name of his patron saint, the name they still bear.

Hennepin found the country occupied by wild tribes of Indians, by whom he and his companions were detained as prisoners, but kindly treated, and finally released.

In 1766, this same country was again visited by a white man, this time by Jonathan Carver, a British subject, and an officer in the British army. Jonathan Carver spent some three years among different tribes of Indians in the Upper Mississippi country. He knew the Sioux or Dakota Indians as the Naudowessies, who were then occupying the country along the Mississippi, from Iowa to the Falls of St. Anthony, and along the Minnesota river, then called St. Peter's, from its source to its mouth at Mendota. To the north of these tribes the country was then occupied by the Ojibwas, commonly called Chippewas, the hereditary enemies of the Sioux.

Carver found these Indian nations at war, and by his commanding influence finally succeeded in making peace between them. As a reward for his good offices in this regard, it is claimed that two chiefs of the Naudowessies, acting for their nation, at a council held with Carver, at the great cave, now in the corporate limits of St. Paul, deeded to Carver a vast tract of land on the Mississippi river, extending from the Falls of St. Anthony to the foot of Lake Pepin, on the Mississippi; thence east one hundred English miles; thence north one hundred and twenty miles; thence west to the place of beginning. But this *pretended* grant has been examined by our government and entirely ignored as a pure invention of parties in interest, after Carver's death, to profit by his Indian service in Minnesota.

There can be no doubt that these same Indians, known to Captain Carver as the Naudowessies, in 1767, were the same who inhabited the country upon the Upper Mississippi and its tributaries when the treaty of Traverse des Sioux was made, in 1851, between the United States and the Sisseton and Wapaton bands of Dakota or Sioux Indians. The name Sioux is said to have been bestowed upon these tribes by the French; and that it is a corruption of the last syllable of their more ancient name, which in the peculiar guttural of the Dakota tongue, has the sound of the last syllable of the old name Naudowes*sies*, Sioux.

The tribes inhabiting the Territory of Minnesota at the date of the massacre, 1862, were the following: Medawakontons (or Village of the Spirit Lake); Wapatons (or Village of the Leaves); Sissetons (or Village of the Marsh); and Wapakutas (or Leaf Shooters). All these were Sioux Indians, connected intimately with other wild bands scattered over a vast region of country, including Dakota Territory, and the country west of the Missouri, even to the base of the Rocky Mountains. Over all this vast region roamed these wild bands of Dakotas, a powerful and warlike nation, holding by their tenure the country north to the British Possessions.

The Sissetons had a hereditary chief, Ta-tanka Mazin, or Standing Buffalo; and at the date of the massacre his father, "Star Face," or the "Orphan," was yet alive, but superannuated, and all the duties of the chief were vested in the son, Standing Buffalo, who remained friendly to the whites and took no part in the terrible massacre on our border in 1862.

The four tribes named, the Medawakontons, Wapatons, Sissetons and Wapakutas, comprised the entire "*annuity* Sioux" of Minnesota; and in 1862 these tribes numbered about six thousand and two hundred persons. All these Indians had from time to time, from the 19th day of July, 1815, to the date of the massacre of 1862, received presents from the Government, by virtue of various treaties of amity and friendship between us and their accredited chiefs and heads of tribes.

Soon after the close of the last war with Great Britain, on the first day of June, 1816, a treaty was concluded at St. Louis between the United States and the chiefs and warriors representing eight bands of the Sioux, composing the three tribes then called the "Sioux of the Leaf," the "Sioux of the Broad Leaf," and the "Sioux who Shoot in the Pine Tops," by the terms of which these tribes confirmed to the United States all cessions or grants of lands previously made by them to the British, French, or Spanish governments, within the limits of the United States or its Territories. For these cessions no annuities were paid, for the reason that they were mere confirmations of grants made by them to powers from whom we had acquired the territory.

From the treaty of St. Louis, in 1816, to the treaty ratified by the United States Senate in 1859, these tribes had remained friendly to the whites, and had by treaty stipulations parted with all the lands to which they claimed title in Iowa; all on the east side of the Mississippi river, and all on the Minnesota river, in Minnesota Territory, except certain reservations. One of these reservations lay upon both sides of the Minnesota, ten miles on either side of that stream, from Hawk river on the north, and Yellow Medicine river on the south side, thence westerly to the head of Big Stone Lake and Lake Traverse, a distance of about one hundred miles. Another of these reservations commenced at Little Rock river on the east, and a line running due south from opposite its mouth, and extending up the river westerly to the easterly line of the first-named reservation, at the Hawk and Yellow Medicine rivers. This last reservation had also a width of ten miles on each side of the Minnesota river.

The Indians west of the Missouri, in referring to those of their nation east of the river, called them Isantics, which seems to have been applied to them from the fact that, at some remote period, they had lived at Isantamde, or "Knife Lake," one of the Mille Lacs, in Minnesota.

These Indian treaties inaugurated and contributed greatly to strengthen a custom of granting, to the pretended owners of lands occupied for purposes of hunting the wild game thereon, and living upon the natural products thereof, a consideration for the cession of their lands to the Government of the United States. This custom culminated in a vast annuity fund, in the aggregate to over three million dollars, owing to these tribes, before named, in Minnesota. This annuity system was one of the causes of the massacre of 1862.

INDIAN LIFE.—Before the whites came in contact with the natives, they dressed in the skins of animals which they killed for food, such as the buffalo, wolf, elk, deer, beaver, otter, as well as the small fur-bearing animals, which they trapped on lakes and streams. In later years, as the settlements of the white race approached their borders, they exchanged these peltries and furs for blankets, cloths, and other articles of necessity or ornament. The Sioux of the plains, those who inhabited the Coteau and beyond, and, indeed, some of the Sisseton tribes, dress in skins to this day. Even among those who are now called "CIVILIZED," the style of costume is often unique. It is no picture of the imagination to portray to the reader a "STALWART INDIAN" in breech-cloth and leggins, with a calico shirt, all "fluttering in the wind," and his head surmounted with a stove-pipe hat of most surprising altitude, carrying in his hand a pipe of exquisite workmanship, on a stem not unlike a cane, sported as an ornament by some city dandy. His appearance is somewhat varied, as the seasons come and go. He may be seen in summer or in winter dressed in a heavy cloth coat of coarse fabric, often turned *inside out* with all his civilized and savage toggery, from head to foot, in the most bewildering juxtaposition. On beholding him, the dullest imagination cannot refrain from the poetic exclamtion of Alexander Pope,

"Lo! the poor Indian, whose untutored mind!"

EFFORTS TO CIVILIZE THESE ANNUITY INDIANS.—The treaty of 1858, made at Washington, elaborated a scheme for the civilization of these annuity Indians. A civilization fund was provided, to be taken from their annuities, and expended in improvements on the lands of such of them as should abandon their tribal relations, and adopt the habits and modes of life of the white race. To all such, lands were to be assigned in severalty, eighty acres to each head of a family. On these farms were to be erected the necessary farm-buildings, and farming implements and cattle were to be furnished them.

In addition to these favors the government offered them pay for such labors of value as were performed, in addition to the crops they raised. Indian farmers now augmented rapidily, until the appalling outbreak in 1862, at which time about one hundred and sixty had taken advantage of the munificent provisions of the treaty. A number of farms, some 160, had good, snug brick houses erected upon them. Among these *civilized* savages was Little Crow, and many of these farmer-Indians belonged to his own band.

The Indians disliked the idea of taking any portion of the general fund belonging to the tribe for the purpose of carrying out the civilization scheme. Those Indians who retained the "blanket," and hence called "blanket Indians," denounced the measure as a fraud upon their rights. The chase was then a God-given right; this scheme forfeited that ancient natural right, as it pointed unmistakably to the destruction of the chase.

But to the friends of Indian races, the course inaugurated seemed to be, step by step, lifting these rude children of the plains to a higher level. This scheme, however, was to a great degree thwarted by the helpless condition of the "blanket Indians" during a great portion of the year, and their persistent determination to remain followers of the chase, and a desire to continue on the war-path.

When the chase fails, the "blanket Indians" resort to their relatives, the farmers, pitch their tepees around their houses, and then commence the process of eating them out of house and home. When the ruin is complete, the farmer Indians, driven by the law of self-preservation, with their wives and children, leave their homes to seek such subsistence as the uncertain fortunes of the chase may yield.

In the absence of the family from the house and fields, thus deserted, the wandering "blanket Indians" commit whatever destruction of fences or tenements their desires or necessities may suggest. This perennial process goes on; so that in the spring when the disheartened farmer Indian returns to his desolate home, to prepare again for another crop, he looks forward with no different results for the coming winter.

It will be seen, from this one illustration, drawn from the actual results of the civilizing process, how hopeless was the prospect of elevating one class of related savages without at the same time protecting them from the incursions of their own relatives, against whom the class attempted to be favored, had no redress. In this attempt to civilize these Dakota Indians the forty years, less or more, of missionary and other efforts have been measurably lost, and the money spent in that direction, if not wasted, sadly misapplied.

The treaty of 1858 had opened for settlement a vast frontier country of the most attractive character, in the Valley of the Minnesota, and the streams putting into the Minnesota, on either side, such as Beaver creek, Sacred Heart, Hawk and Chippewa rivers and some other small streams, were flourishing settlements of white families. Within this ceded tract, ten miles wide, were the scattered settlements of Birch Coolie, Patterson Rapids, on the Sacred Heart, and others as far up as the Upper Agency at Yellow Medicine, in Renville county. The county of Brown adjoined the reservation, and was, at the time of which we are now writing, settled mostly by Germans. In this county was the flourishing town of New Ulm, and a thriving settlement on the Big Cottonwood and Watonwan, consisting of German and American pioneers, who had selected this lovely and fertile valley for their future homes.

Other counties, Blue Earth, Nicollet, Sibley, Meeker, McLeod, Kandiyohi, Monongalia and Murray, were all situated in the finest portions of the state. Some of the valleys along the streams, such as Butternut valley and others of similar character, were lovely as Wyoming and as fertile as the Garden of Eden. These counties, with others somewhat removed from the direct attack of the Indians in the massacre, as Wright, Stearns and Jackson, and even reaching on the north to Fort Abercrombie, thus extending from Iowa to the Valley of the Red River of the North, were severally involved in the consequences of the warfare of 1862. This extended area had at the time a population of over fifty thousand people, principally in the pursuit of agriculture; and although the settlements were in their infancy, the people were happy and contented, and as prosperous as any similar community in any new country on the American continent, since the landing of the Pilgrim Fathers.

We have in short, traced the Dakota tribes of Minnesota from an early day, when the white man first visited and explored these then unknown regions, to the time of the massacre. We have also given a synopsis of all the most important treaties between them and the government, with an allusion to the country adjacent to the reservations, and the probable number of people residing in the portions of the state ravaged by the savages.

CHAPTER XXXI.

COMPLAINTS OF THE INDIANS—TREATIES OF TRAVERSE DES SIOUX AND MENDOTA—OBJECTIONS TO THE MODE OF PAYMENT—INKPADUTA MASSACRE AT SPIRIT LAKE—PROOF OF CONSPIRACY—INDIAN COUNCILS.

In a former chapter the reader has had some account of the location of the several bands of Sioux Indians in Minnesota, and their relation to the white settlements on the western border of the state. It is now proposed to state in brief some of the antecedents of the massacre.

PROMINENT CAUSES.

1. By the treaty of Traverse des Sioux, dated July 23, 1851, between the United States and the Sissetons and Wapatons, $275,000 were to be paid their chiefs, and a further sum of $30,000 was to be expended for their benefit in Indian improvements. By the treaty of Mendota, dated August 5, 1851, the Medawakantons and Wapakutas were to receive the sum of $200,000, to be paid to their chief, and for an improvement fund the further sum of $30,000. These several sums, amounting in the aggregate to $555,000, these Indians, to whom they were payable, claim they were never paid, except, perhaps, a small portion expended in improvements on the reservations. They became dissatisfied, and expressed their views in council freely with the agent of the government.

In 1857, the Indian department at Washington sent out Major Kintzing Prichette, a man of great experience, to inquire into the cause of this disaffection towards the government. In his report of that year, made to the Indian department, Major Prichette says:

"The complaint which runs through all their councils points to the imperfect performance, or non-fulfillment of treaty stipulations. Whether these were well or ill founded, it is not my promise to discuss. That such a belief prevails among them, impairing their confidence and good faith in the government, cannot be questioned."

In one of these councils Jagmani said: "The Indians sold their lands at Traverse des Sioux. I say what we were told. For fifty years they were to be paid $50,000 per annum. We were also promised $300,000, and *that* we have not seen."

Mapipa Wicasta (Cloud Man), second chief of Jagmani's band, said:

"At the treaty of Traverse des Sioux, $275,000 were to be paid them when they came upon their reservation; they desired to know what had become of it. Every white man knows that they have been five years upon their reservation, and have yet heard nothing of it."

In this abridged form we can only refer in brief to these complaints; but the history would seem to lack completeness without the presentation of this feature. As the fact of the dissatisfaction existed, the government thought it worth while to appoint Judge Young to investigate the charges made against the governor, of the then Minnesota territory, then acting, *ex-officio*, as superintendent of Indian affairs for that locality. Some short extracts from Judge Young's report are here presented:

"The governor is next charged with having paid over the greater part of the money, appropriated under the fourth article of the treaty of July 23 and August 5, 1851, to one Hugh Tyler, for payment or distribution to the 'traders' and 'half-breeds,' contrary to the wishes and remonstrances of the Indians, and in violation of law and the stipulations contained in said treaties; and also in violation of his own solemn pledges, personally made to them, in regard to said payments.

"Of $275,000 stipulated to be paid under the *first* clause of the *fourth* article of the treaty of Traverse des Sioux, of July 21, 1851, the sum of $250,000, was delivered over to Hugh Tyler, by the governor, for distribution among the 'traders' and 'half-breeds,' according to the arrangement made by the schedule of the *Traders' Paper*, dated at Traverse des Sioux, July 23, 1851."

"For this large sum of money, Hugh Tyler executed two receipts to the Governor, as the attorney for the 'traders' and 'half breeds;' the one for $210,000 on account of the 'traders,' and the other for $40,000 on account of the 'half-breeds;' the first dated at St. Paul, December 8, 1852, and the second at Mendota, December 11, 1852."

"And of the sum of $110,000, stipulated to be paid to the Medawakantons, under the fourth article of the treaty of August 5, 1851, the sum of $70,000 was in like manner paid over to the said Tyler, on a power of attorney executed to him by the traders and claimants, under the said treaty, on December 11, 1852. The receipts of the said Tyler to the Governor for this money, $70,000, is dated at St. Paul, December 13, 1852, making together the sum of $320,000. This has been shown to have been contrary to the wishes and remonstrances of a large majority of the Indians." And Judge Young adds: "It is also believed to be in violation of the treaty stipulations, as well as the law making the appropriations under them."

These several sums of money were to be paid to these Indians in open council, and soon after they were on their reservations provided for them by the treaties. In these matters the report shows they were not consulted at all, in open council; but on the contrary, that arbitrary divisions and distributions were made of the entire fund, and their right denied to direct the manner in which they should be appropriated. See *Acts of Congress, August* 30, 1852.

The Indians claimed, also, that the third section of the act was violated, as by that section the appropriations therein referred to, should, in every instance, be paid directly to the Indians themselves, to whom it should be due, or to the tribe, or part of the tribe, *per capita*, "unless otherwise the imperious interest of the Indians or some treaty stipulation should require the payment to be made otherwise, under the direction of the president." This money was never so paid. The report further states that a large sum, "$55,000, was deducted by Hugh Tyler by way of discount and percentage on gross amount of payments, and that these exactions were made both from traders and half-breeds, without any previous agreement, in many instances, and in such a way, in some, as to make the impression that unless they were submitted to, no payments would be made to such claimants at all."

And, finally the report says, that from the testimony it was evident that the money was not paid to the chiefs, either to the Sisseton, Wapaton, or Medawakanton bands, as they in open council requested; but that they were compelled to submit to this mode of payment to the traders, otherwise no payment would be made, and the money would be returned to Washington; so that in violation of law they were compelled to comply with the Governor's terms of payment, according to Hugh Tyler's power of attorney.

The examination of this complaint, on the part of the Indians, by the Senate of the United States, resulted in exculpating the Governor of Minnesota (Governor Ramsey) from any censure, yet the Indians were not satisfied with the treatment they had received in this matter by the accredited agents of the Government.

2. Another cause of irritation among these Indians arose out of the massacre of 1857, at Spirit Lake, known as the Inkpaduta massacre. Inkpaduta was an outlaw of the Wapakuta band of Sioux Indians, and his acts in the murders at Spirit Lake were entirely disclaimed by the "annuity Sioux." He had slain Tasagi, a Wapakuta chief, and several of his relatives, some twenty years previous, and had thereafter led a wandering and marauding life about the head waters of the Des Moines river.

Inkpaduta was connected with several of the bands of annuity Sioux Indians, and similar relations with other bands existed among his followers. These ties extended even to the Yanktons west of the James river, and even over the Missouri. He was himself an outlaw for the murder of Tasagi and others as stated, and followed a predatory and lawless life in the neighborhood of his related tribes, for which the Sioux were themselves blamed.

The depredations of these Indians becoming insufferable, and the settlers finding themselves sufficiently strong, deprived them of their guns and drove them from the neighborhood. Recovering some of their guns, or, by other accounts, digging up a few old ones which they had buried, they proceeded to the settlement of Spirit Lake and demanded food. This appears to have been given to a portion of the band which had first arrived, to the extent of the means of those applied to. Soon after, Inkpaduta, with the remainder of his followers, who, in all, numbered twelve men and two boys, with some women who had lingered behind, came in and demanded food also. The settler gave him to understand that he had no more to give; whereupon Inkpaduta spoke to his eldest son to the effect that it was disgraceful to ask these people for food which they ought to take themselves, and not to have it thrown to them like dogs. Thus assured, the son immediately shot the man, and the murder of the whole family followed. From thence they proceeded from house to house, until every family in the settlement, without warning of those previously slain, were all massacred, except four women, whom they bore away prisoners, and afterward violated, with circumstances of brutality so abhorrent as to find no parallel in the annals of savage barbarity, unless we except the massacre of 1862, which occurred a few years later.

From Spirit Lake the murderers proceeded to Springfield, at the outlet of Shetek, or Pelican lake, near the head waters of the Des Moines river; where they remained encamped for some days, trading with Mr. William Wood from Mankato, and his brothers. Here they succeeded in killing seventeen, including the Woods, making, in all, forty-seven persons, when the men rallied, and firing upon them, they retreated and deserted that part of the country. Of the four women taken captives by Inkpaduta, Mrs. Stevens and Mrs. Noble were killed by the Indians, and Mrs. Marble and Miss Gardner were rescued by the Wapaton Sioux, under a promise of reward from the Government, and for which the three Indians who brought in these captives received each one thousand dollars.

The Government had required of the Sioux the delivery of Inkpaduta and his band as the condition for the payment of their annuities. This was regarded by certain of the bands as a great wrong visited upon the innocent for the crimes of the guilty. One of their speakers (Mazakuti Mani), in a council held with the Sissetons and Wapatons, August 10, 1857, at Yellow Medicine, said:

"The soldiers have appointed me to speak for them. The men who killed the white people did not belong to us, and we did not expect to be called upon to account for the deeds of another band. We have always tried to do as our Great Father tells us. One of our young men brought in a captive woman. I went out and brought in the other. The soldiers came up here and our men assisted to kill one of Inkpaduta's sons at this place. The lower Indians did not get up the war-party for you; it was our Indians, the Wapatons and Sissetons. The soldiers here say that they were told by you that a thousand dollars would be paid for killing each of the murderers. We, with the men who went out, want to be paid for what we have done. Three men were killed, as we know. * * * * * All of us want our money very much. A man of another band has done wrong, and we are to suffer for it. Our old women and children are hungry for this. I have seen $10,000 sent here to pay for our going out. I wish our soldiers were paid for it. I suppose our Great Father has more money than this."

Major Pritchette, the special government agent, thought it necessary to answer some points made by Mazakuti Mani, and spoke, in council, as follows:

"Your Great Father has sent me to see Superintendent Cullen, and to say to him he was well satisfied with his conduct, because he had acted according to his instructions. Your Great Father had heard that some of his white children had been cruelly and brutally murdered by some of the Sioux nation. The news was sent on the wings of the lightning, from the extreme north to the land of eternal summer, throughout which his children dwell. His young men wished to make war on the whole Sioux nation, and revenge the deaths of their brethren. But your Great Father is a just father and wishes to treat all his children alike with justice. He wants no innocent man punished for the guilty. He punishes the guilty alone. He expects that those missionaries who have been here teaching you the laws of the Great Spirit had taught you this. Whenever a Sioux is injured by a white man your Great Father will punish him, and expects from the chiefs and warriors of the great Sioux nation that they will punish these Indians who injure the whites. He considers the Sioux as a part of his family; and as friends and brothers he expects them to do as the whites do to them. He knows that the Sioux nation is divided into bands; but he knows also how they can all band together for common protection. He expects the nation to punish these murderers, or to deliver them up. He expects this because they are his friends. As long as these murderers remain unpunished or not delivered up, they are not acting as friends of their Great Father. It is for this reason that he has witheld the annuity. Your Great Father will have his white children protected; and all who have told you that your Great Father is not able to punish those who injure them will find themselves bitterly mistaken. Your

Great Father desires to do good to all his children and will do all in his power to accomplish it; but he is firmly resolved to punish all who do wrong."

After this, another similar council, September 1, 1857, was held with the Sisseton and Wapaton band of Upper Sioux at Yellow Medicine. Agent Flandrau, in the meantime, had succeeded in organizing a band of warriors, made up of all the "annuity" bands, under Little Crow. This expedition numbered altogether one hundred and six, besides four half-breeds. This party went out after Inkpaduta on the 22d of July, 1857, starting from Yellow Medicine.

On the 5th of August Major Pritchette reported to the Commissioner of Indian Affairs, "That the party of Indians, representing the entire Sioux nation, under the nominal head of Little Crow, returned yesterday from the expedition in search of Inkpaduta and his band," after an absence of thirteen days.

As this outlaw, Inkpaduta, has achieved an immortality of infamy, it may be allowable in the historian to record the names of his followers. Inkpaduta (Scarlet Point) heads the list, and the names of the eleven men are given by the wife of Tatoyahe, who was killed by the party of Sioux under Little Crow, thus: Tatoyahe (Shifting Wind); Makpeahoteman (Roaring Cloud), son of Inkpaduta, killed at Yellow Medicine; Makpiopeta (Fire Cloud), twin brother of Makpeohotomau; Tawachshawakan (His Mysterious Feather), killed in the late expedition; Bahata (Old Man); Kechomon (Putting on as He Walks); Huhsau (One Leg); Kahadai (Rattling), son-in-law of Inkpaduta; Fetoa-tanka (Big Face); Tatelidashinkshamani (One who Makes Crooked Wind as He Walks); Tachanchogahota (His Great Gun), and the two boys, children of Inkpaduta, not named.

After the band had been pursued by Little Crow into Lake Chouptijatanka (Big Dry Wood), distant twenty miles in a northwestern direction from Skunk Lake, and three of them killed outright, wounding one, taking two women and a little child prisoners, the Indians argued that they had done sufficient to merit the payment of their annuities; and on the 18th of August, 1854, Maj. Cullen telegraphed the following to the Hon. J. W. Denver, commissioner of Indian affairs:

"If the department concurs, I am of the opinion that the Sioux of the Mississippi, having done all in their power to punish or surrender Inkpaduta and his band, their annuities may with propriety be paid, as a signal to the military movements from Forts Ridgely and Randall. The special agent from the department waits an answer to this dispatch at Dunleith, and for instructions in the premises."

In this opinion Major Pritchette, in a letter of the same date, concurred, for reasons therein stated, and transmitted to the department. In this letter, among other things, the writer says:

"No encouragement was given to them that such a request would be granted. It is the opinion, however, of Superintendent Cullen, the late agent, Judge Flandrau, Governor Medary, and the general intelligent sentiment, that the annuities may now with propriety, be paid, without a violation of the spirit of the expressed determination of the department to withhold them until the murderers of Spirit Lake should be surrendered or punished. It is argued that the present friendly disposition of the Indians is manifest, and should not be endangered by subjecting them to the wants incident to their condition during the coming winter, and the consequent temptation to depredation, to which the withholding their money would leave them exposed."

The major yielded this point for the reasons stated, yet he continued:

"If not improper for me to express an opinion, I am satisfied that, without chastising the whole Sioux nation, it is impossible to enforce the surrender of Inkpaduta and the remainder of his band." * * * "Nothing less than the entire extirpation of Inkpaduta's murderous outlaws will satisfy the justice and dignity of the government, and vindicate outraged humanity."

We here leave the Inkpaduta massacre, remarking only that the government paid the Indians their annuities, and made no further effort to bring to condign punishment the remnant who had escaped alive from the pursuit of Little Crow and his soldiers. This was a great error on the part of our government. The Indians construed it either as an evidence of weakness, or that the whites were afraid to pursue the matter further, lest it might terminate in still more disastrous results to the infant settlement of the state bordering upon the Indian country. The result was, the Indians became more insolent than ever before. Little Crow and his adherents had found capital out of which to foment future difficulties in which the two races should become involved. And it is now believed, and subsequent circumstances have greatly strengthened that belief, that Little Crow, from the time the government ceased its efforts to punish Inkpaduta, began to agitate his great scheme of driving the whites from the state of Minnesota; a scheme which finally culminated in the ever-to-be-remembered massacre of August, A. D. 1862.

The antecedent exciting causes of this massacre are numerous. The displaced agents and traders find the cause in the erroneous action of the Government, resulting in their removal from office. The statesman and the philosopher may unite in tracing the cause to improper theories as to the mode of acquiring the right to Indian lands. The former may locate the evil in our system of treaties, and the latter in our theories of government. The philanthropist may find the cause in the absence of justice which we exhibit in all our intercourse with the Indian races. The poet and the lovers of romance in human character find the true cause, as they believe, in the total absence of all appreciation of the noble, generous, confiding traits peculiar to the native Indian. The Christian teacher finds apologies for acts of Indian atrocities in the deficient systems of mental and moral culture. Each of these different classes are satisfied that the great massacre of August, 1862, had its origin in some way intimately connected with his favorite theory.

Let us, for a moment, look at the facts, in relation to the two races who had come into close contact with each other, and in the light of these facts, judge of the probable cause of this fearful collision. The white race, some two hundred years ago, had entered upon the material conquest of the American continent, armed with all the appliances for its complete subjugation. On the shores of this prolific continent these new elements came in contact with a race of savages with many of the traits peculiar to a common humanity, yet, with these, exhibiting all, or nearly all, the vices of the most barbarous of savage races. The period of occupancy of this broad, fertile land was lost in the depths of a remote antiquity. The culture of the soil, if ever understood, had been long neglected by this race, and the chase was their principal mode of gaining a scanty subsistence. It had lost all that ennobled man, and was alive only to all his degradations. The white man was at once acknowledged, the Indian being judge, superior to the savage race with which he had come in contact.

Here, then, is the first cause, in accordance with a universal principle, in which the conflict of the two races had its origin. It was a conflict of knowledge with ignorance, of right with wrong. If this conflict were only mental, and the weapons of death had never been resorted to in a single instance, the result would have been the same. The inferior race must either recede before the superior, or sink into the common mass, and, like the raindrops falling upon the bosom of the ocean, lose all traces of distinction. This warfare takes place the world over, on the principle of mental and material progress. The presence of the superior light eclipses the inferior, and causes it to retire. Mind makes aggression upon mind, and the superior, sooner or later, overwhelms the inferior. This process may go on, with or without the conflict of physical organisms. The final result will be the same.

Again, we come to the great law of right. The white race stood upon this undeveloped continent ready and willing to execute the Divine injunction, to replenish the earth and *subdue* it. On the one side stood the white race armed with his law; on the other the savage, resisting the execution of that law. The result could not be evaded by any human device. In the case before us, the Indian races were in the wrongful possession of a continent required by the superior right of the white man. This right, founded in the wisdom of God, eliminated by the ever-operative laws of progress, will continue to assert its dominion, with varying success, contingent on the use of means employed, until all opposition is hushed in the perfect reign of the superior aggressive principle.

With these seemingly necessary reflections, we introduce the remarks of the Sioux agent touching the antecedents of the great massacre, unparalleled in the history of the conflict of the races. The agent gives his peculiar views, and they are worthy of careful consideration.

Major Thomas Galbraith, Sioux Agent, says:

"The radical, moving cause of the outbreak is, I am satisfied, the ingrained and fixed hostility of the savage barbarian to reform and civilization. As in all barbarous communities, in the history of the world, the same people have, for the most part, resisted the encroachments of civilization upon their ancient customs; so it is in the case before us. Nor does it matter materially in what shape civilization makes its attack. Hostile, opposing forces meet in conflict, and a war of social elements is the result—civilization is aggressive, and barbarism stubbornly resistant. Sometimes, indeed, civilization has achieved a bloodless victory, but generally it has been otherwise. Christianity, itself, the true basis of civilization, has, in most instances, waded to success through seas of blood. * * * Having stated thus much, I state as a settled fact in my mind, that the encroachments of Christianity, and its handmaid, civilization, upon the habits and customs of the Sioux Indians, is the cause of the late terrible Sioux outbreak. There were, it is true, many immediate inciting causes, which will be alluded to and stated hereafter, but they are subsidiary to, and developments of, or incident to, the great cause set forth. * * * But that the recent Sioux outbreak would have happened at any rate, as a result, a fair consequence of the cause here stated, I have no more doubt than I doubt that the great rebellion to overthrow our Government would have occurred had Mr. Lincoln never been elected President of the United States.

"Now as to the existing or immediate causes of the outbreak: By my predecessor a new and radical system was inaugurated, practically, and, in its inauguration, he was aided by the Christian missionaries and by the Government. The treaties of 1858 were ostensibly made to carry this new system into effect. The theory, in substance, was to break up the community-system which prevailed among the Sioux; weaken and destroy their tribal relations, and individualize them, by giving them each a separate home. * * * On the 1st day of June, A. D. 1861, when I entered upon the duties of my office, I found that the system had just been inaugurated. Some hundred families of the Annuity Sioux had become novitiates, and their relatives and friends seemed to be favorably disposed to the new order of things. But I also found that, against these, were arrayed over five thousand "Annuity Sioux," besides at least three thousand Yanktonais, all inflamed by the most bitter, relentless, and devilish hostility.

"I saw, to some extent, the difficulty of the situation, but I determined to continue, if in my power, the civilization system. To favor it, to aid and build it up by every fair means, I advised, encouraged, and assisted the farmer novitiates; in short, I sustained the policy inaugurated by my predecessor, and sustained and recommended by the Government. I soon discovered that the system could not be successful without a sufficient force to protect the "farmer" from the hostility of the "blanket Indians."

"During my term, and up to the time of the outbreak, about one hundred and seventy-five had their hair cut and had adopted the habits and customs of white men.

"For a time, indeed, my hopes were strong that civilization would soon be in the ascendant. But the increase of the civilization party and their evident prosperity, only tended to exasperate the Indians of the 'ancient customs,' and to widen the breach. But while these are to be enumerated, it may be permitted me to hope that the radical cause will not be forgotten or overlooked; and I am bold to express this desire, because, ever since the outbreak, the public journals of the country, religious and secular, have teemed with editorials by and communications from 'reliable individuals,' politicians, philanthropists, philosophers and hired 'penny-a-liners,' mostly mistaken and sometimes willfully and grossly false, giving the cause of the Indian raid."

Major Galbraith enumerates a variety of other exciting causes of the massacre, which our limit will not allow us to insert in this volume. Among other causes, * * that the United States was itself at war, and that Washington was taken by the negroes. * * But none of these were, in his opinion, the cause of the outbreak,

The Major then adds:

"Grievances such as have been related, and numberless others akin to them, were spoken of, recited, and chanted at their councils, dances, and feasts, to such an extent that, in their excitement, in June, 1862, a secret organization known as the 'Soldier's Lodge,' was founded by the young men and soldiers of the Lower Sioux, with the object, as far as I was able to learn through spies and informers, of preventing the 'traders' from going to the pay-tables, as had been their custom. Since the outbreak I have become satisfied that the real object of this 'Lodge' was to adopt measures to 'clean out' all the white people at the end of the payment."

Whatever may have been the cause of the fearful and bloody tragedy, it is certain that the manner of the execution of the infernal deed was a deep-laid *conspiracy*, long cherished by Little Crow, taking form under the guise of the "Soldiers' Lodge," and matured in secret Indian councils. In all these secret movements Little Crow was the moving spirit.

Now the opportune moment seemed to have come. Only thirty soldiers were stationed at Fort Ridgely. Some thirty were all that Fort Ripley could muster, and at Fort Abercrombie one company, under Captain Van Der Hork, was all the whites could depend upon to repel any attack in that quarter. The whole effective force for the defense of the entire frontier, from Pembina to the Iowa line, did not exceed two hundred men. The annuity money was daily expected, and no troops except about one hundred men at Yellow Medicine, had been detailed, as usual, to attend the anticipated payment. Here was a glittering prize to be paraded before the minds of the excited savages. The whites were weak; they were engaged in a terrible war among themselves; their attention was now directed toward the great struggle in the South. At such a time, offering so many chances for rapine and plunder, it would be easy to unite, at least, all the annuity Indians in one common movement. Little Crow knew full well that the Indians could easily be made to believe that now was a favorable time to make a grand attack upon the border settlements. In view of all the favorable auspices now concurring, a famous Indian council was called, which was fully attended by the "Soldiers' Lodge." Rev. S. R. Riggs, in his late work, 1880, ("Mary and I"), referring to the outbreak, says:

"On August 17th, the outbreak was commenced in the border white settlements at Acton, Minnesota. That night the news was carried to the Lower Sioux Agency, and a council of war was called." * * * "Something of the kind had been meditated and talked of, and prepared for undoubtedly. Some time before this, they had formed the Tee-yo-tee-pee, or Soldiers' Lodge."

A memorable council, convened at Little Crow's village, near the Lower Agency, on Sunday night previous to the attack on Fort Ridgely, and precisely two weeks before the first massacres at Acton. Little Crow was at this council, and he was not wanting in ability to meet the greatness of the occasion. The proceedings of this council, of course, were secret. Some of the results arrived at, however, have since come to the writer of these pages. The council matured the details of a conspiracy, which for atrocity has hitherto never found a place in recorded history, not excepting that of Cawnpore.

The evidence of that conspiracy comes to us, in part, from the relation of one who was present at the infamous council. Comparing the statement of the narrative with the known occurrences of the times, that council preceded the attack on the Government stores at the Upper Agency, and was convened on Sunday night; the attack on the Upper Agency took place the next day, Monday, the 4th of August; and on the same day, an attempt was made to take Fort Ridgely by strategy. Not the slightest danger was anticipated. Only thirty soldiers occupied the post at Fort Ridgely and this was deemed amply sufficient in times of peace. But we will not longer detain the reader from the denouement of this horrible plot.

Our informant states the evidences of the decrees of the council of the 3d of August, thus:

"I was looking toward the Agency and saw a large body of men coming toward the fort, and supposed them soldiers returning from the payment at Yellow Medicine. On a second look, I observed they were mounted, and knowing, at this time, that they must be Indians, was surprised at seeing so large a body, as they were not expected. I resolved to go into the garrison to see what it meant, having, at the time, not the least suspicion that the Indians intended any hostile demonstration. When I arrived at the garrison, I found Sergeant Jones at the entrance with a mounted howitzer, charged with shell and canister-shot, pointed towards the Indians, who were removed but a short distance from the guard house. I inquired of the sergeant what it meant? whether any danger was apprehended? He replied indifferently, "No, but that he thought it a good rule to observe that a soldier should always be ready for any emergency."

These Indians had requested the privilege to dance in the inclosure surrounding the fort. On this occasion that request was refused them. But I saw that, about sixty yards west of the guard house, the Indians were making the necessary preparations for a dance. I thought nothing of it as they had frequently done the same thing, but a little further removed from the fort, under somewhat different circumstances. I considered it a singular exhibition of Indian foolishness, and, at the solicitation of a few ladies, went out and was myself a spectator of the dance.

"When the dance was concluded, the Indians sought and obtained permission to encamp on some rising ground about a quarter of a mile west of the garrison. To this ground they soon repaired, and encamped for the night. The next morning, by 10 o'clock, all had left the vicinity of the garrison, departing in the direction of the Lower Agency. This whole matter of the dance was so conducted as to lead most, if not all, the residents of the garrison to believe that the Indians had paid them that visit for the purpose of dancing and obtaining provisions for a feast.

"Some things were observable that were unusual. The visitors were all warriors, ninety-six in number, all in undress, except a very few who wore calico shirts; and, in addition to this, they all carried arms, guns and tomahawks, with ammunition pouches suspended around their shoulders. Previous to the dance, the war implements were deposited some two hundred yards distant, where they had left their ponies. But even this circumstance, so far as it was then known, excited no suspicion of danger or hostilities in the minds of the residents of the garrison. These residents were thirty-five men; thirty soldiers and five citizens, with a few women and children. The guard that day consisted of three soldiers; one was walking leisurely to and fro in front of the guard-house; the other two were off duty, passing about and taking their rest; and all entirely without apprehension of danger from Indians or any other foe. As the Indians left the garrison without doing any mischief, most of us supposed that no evil was meditated by them. But there was one man who acted on the supposition that there was always danger surrounding a garrison when visited by savages; that man was Sergeant Jones. From the time he took his position at the gun he never left it, but acted as he said he believed it best to do, that was to be always ready. He not only remained at the gun himself, but retained two other men, whom he had previously trained as assistants to work the piece.

"Shortly before dark, without disclosing his intentions, Sergeant Jones said to his wife: 'I have a little business to attend to to-night; at bed-time I wish you to retire, and not to wait for me.' As he had frequently done this before, to discharge some official duty at the quartermaster's office, she thought it not singular, but did as he had requested, and retired at the usual hour. On awakening in the morning, however, she was surprised at finding that he was not there, and had not been in bed. In truth, this faithful soldier had stood by his gun throughout the entire night, ready to fire, if occasion required, at any moment during that time; nor could he be persuaded to leave that gun until all this party of Indians had entirely disappeared from the vicinity of the garrison.

"Some two weeks after this time, those same Indians, with others, attacked Fort Ridgely and, after some ten days' siege, the garrison was relieved by the arrival of soldiers under Colonel H. H. Sibley. The second day after Colonel Sibley arrived, a Frenchman of pure or mixed blood appeared before Sergeant Jones, in a very agitated manner, and intimated that he had some disclosures to make to him; but no sooner had he made this intimation than he became extremely and violently agitated, and seemed to be in a perfect agony of mental perturbation. Sergeant Jones said to him, 'If you have anything to disclose, you ought, at once, to make it known.' The man repeated that he had disclosures to make, but that he did not dare to make them; and although Sergeant Jones urged him by every consideration in his power to tell what he knew, the man seemed to be so completely under the dominion of terror, that he was unable to divulge the great secret. 'Why,' said he, 'they will kill me: they will kill my wife and children.' Saying which he turned and walked away.

"Shortly after the first interview, this man returned to Sergeant Jones, when again the Sergeant urged him to disclose what he knew; and promised him that if he would do so, he would keep his name a profound secret forever; that if the information which he should disclose should lead to the detection and punishment of the guilty, the name of the informant should never be made known. Being thus assured, the Frenchman soon became more calm. Hesitating a moment, he inquired of Sergeant Jones if he remembered that, some two weeks ago, a party of Indians came down to the fort to have a dance? Sergeant Jones replied that he did. 'Why,' said the Frenchman, 'do you know that these Indians were all warriors of Little Crow, or some of the other lower bands? Sir, these Indians had all been selected for the purpose, and came down to Fort Ridgely by the express command of Little Crow and the other chiefs, to get permission to dance; and when all suspicion should be completely lulled, in the midst of the dance, to seize their weapons, kill every person in the fort, seize the big guns, open the magazine, and secure the ammunition, when they should be joined by all the remaining warriors of the lower bands. Thus armed, and increased by numbers, they were to proceed together down the valley of the Minnesota. With this force and these weapons they were assured they could drive every white man beyond the Mississippi.'

"All this, the Frenchman informed Sergeant Jones, he had learned by being present at a council, and from conversations had with other Indians, who had told him that they had gone to the garrison for that very purpose. When he had concluded this revelation, Sergeant Jones inquired, 'Why did they not execute their purpose? Why did they not take the fort?' The Frenchman replied: 'Because they saw, during all their dance, and then stay at the fort, that big gun constantly pointed at them.'"

Interpreter Quinn, now dead, told the narrator of the foregoing incidents that Little Crow had said, repeatedly, in their councils, that the Indians could kill all the white men in the Minnesota Valley. In this way, he said, we can get all our lands back; that the whites would again want these lands, and that they could get double annuities. Some of the councils at which these suggestions of Little Crow were made, dated, he said, as far back as the summer of 1857, immediately after the Inkpaduta war.

On the 17th day of August, 1862, Little Crow, Inkpaduta, and Little Priest, the latter one of the Winnebago chiefs, attended church at the Lower Agency, and seemed to listen attentively to the services, conducted by the Rev. J. D. Hinman. On the afternoon of that day Little Crow invited these Indians to his house, a short distance above the Agency. On the same day an Indian council was held at Rice Creek, sixteen miles above the Lower Agency, attended by the Soldiers' Lodge. Inkpaduta, it is believed, and Little Priest, with some thirteen Winnebago warriors, attended this council. Why this council was held, and what was its object, can easily be imagined. The decrees of the one held two weeks before had not been executed. The reason why the fort was not taken has been narrated. The other part of the same scheme, the taking of the agency at the Yellow Medicine, on the same day the fort was to have fallen, will be alluded to in another chapter. It then became necessary for the conspirators to hold another council, to devise new plans for the execution of their nefarious designs upon the whites.

The Acton tragedy, forty miles distant, had taken place but a few hours before this council was convened. On Monday, the 18th of August, these Acton murderers were seen at the mill on Crow river, six miles from Hutchinson, with the team taken from Acton; so that these Indians did not go to the Lower Agency, but remained in the country about Hutchinson. One of the number only returned to the Agency by the next morning after the council at Rice Creek had been held. All that followed in the bloody drama, originated at this council of Death, over which Little Crow presided, on Sunday afternoon, the 17th day of August, 1862, on the evening of the same day of the Acton murders. The general massacre of all white men was by order of this council, to commence at the Agency, on the morning of the 18th, and at as many other points, simultaneously, as could be reached by the dawn of day, radiating from that point as a center. The advantage gained by the suddenness of the attack, and the known panic that would result, was to be followed up until every settlement was massacred, Fort Ridgely taken, both Agencies burned, New Ulm, Mankato, St. Peter, and all the towns on the river destroyed, the whole country plundered and devastated, and as many of the inhabitants as were left alive were to be driven beyond the Mississippi river. The decree of this savage council, matured on a Christian Sabbath, by Indians, who were supposed to be civilized, so immediately after attentively listening to the gospel of peace, filled the measure of the long-cherished conspiracy matured by Little Crow, until it was full of the most hopeful results to his polluted and brutal nature. "Once an Indian, always an Indian," seems in this instance to have been horribly demonstrated.

CHAPTER XXXII.

CHANGE OF INDIAN OFFICIALS—PAYMENT OF 1861—REPORT OF AGENT GALBRAITH—UPPER AND LOWER BANDS—SUPPLIES—ATTACK ON THE WAREHOUSE—RENVILLE RANGERS—RETURN TO FORT RIDGELY.

The change in the administration of the Government in 1861, resulting, as it did, in a general change in the minor offices throughout the country, carried into retirement Major William J. Cullen, Superintendent of Indian Affairs for the Northern Superintendency, and Major Joseph R. Brown, Agent for the Sioux, whose places were filled respectively by Colonel Clark W. Thompson and Major Thomas J. Galbraith. Colonel

Thompson entered upon the duties of his office in May of that year, and Major Galbraith on the first day of June. In that month the new agent and many of the new employes, with their families, took up their residence on the reservations.

These employes, save a few young men who were employed as laborers, were, with two exceptions, men of families, it being the policy of the agent to employ among the Indians as few unmarried men as possible.

During that year nothing occurred on the reservations of an unusual character more than the trouble with which the Agents had always to deal at every semi-annual gathering at the Agencies. We say "semi-annual," because they came in the summer to draw their annuities, and again in the autumn for their winter supply of goods.

It has been usual at the payment of annuities to have a small force of troops to guard against any untoward event which might otherwise occur. The payment to the lower bands, in 1861, was made in the latter part of June, and to the upper bands about the middle of July. These payments were made by Superintendent Thompson in person.

The Sisseton bands came down to the Agency at a very early day, as had always been their habit, long before the arrival of the money, bringing with them a large body of Yanktonais (not annuity Sioux), who always came to the payments, claiming a right to a share of the annuities issued to the Indians.

These wild hunters of the plains were an unfailing element of trouble at the payments to the upper bands. At this last payment they were in force, and by their troublesome conduct, caused a delay of some days in the making of the payments. This was, however, no unusual occurrence, as they always came with a budget of grievances, upon which they were wont to dilate in council. This remark is equally true of the annuity Indians. Indeed, it would be very strange if a payment could be made without a demand, on the part of the "young men," for three or four times the amount of their annual dues.

These demands were usually accompanied by overt acts of violence; yet the payment was made; and this time, after the payment, all departed to their village at Big Stone Lake. They came again in the fall, drew their supply of goods, and went quietly away.

It so turned out, however, that the new agent, Galbraith, came into office too late to insure a large crop that year. He says:

"The autumn of 1861 closed upon us rather unfavorably. The crops were light; especially was this the case with the Upper Sioux; they had little or nothing. As heretofore communicated to the Department, the cut-worms destroyed all the Sisetons, and greatly injured the crop of the Wapatons, Medawakantons, Wapakutas. For these latter I purchased on credit, in anticipation of the Agricultural and Civilization Funds, large quantities of pork and flour, at current rates, to support them during the winter.

"Early in the autumn, in view of the necessitous situation of the Sisetons, I made a requisition on the department for the sum of $5,000, out of the special fund for the relief of 'poor and destitute Indians;' and, in anticipation of receiving this money, made arrangements to fe d the old and infirm men, and the women and children of these people. I directed the Rev. S. R. Riggs to make the selection, and furnish me a list.

"He carefully did this, and we fed, in an economical, yea, even parsimonious way, about 1,500 of these people from the middle of December until nearly the first of April. We had hoped to get them off on their spring hunt earlier, but a tremendous and unprecedented snow-storm during the last days of February prevented.

"In response to my requisition, I received $3,000, and expended very nearly $5,000, leaving a deficiency not properly chargable to the regular funds, of about $2,000.

"These people, it is believed, must have perished had it not been for this scanty assistance. In addition to this, the regular issues were made to the farmer Indians in payment for their labor.

* * * * * * * * *

"In the month of August, 1861, the superintendents of farms were directed to have ploughed 'in the fall,' in the old public and neglected private fields, a sufficient quantity of land to provide 'plantings' for such Indians as could not be provided with oxen and implements. In pursuance of this direction, there were ploughed, at rates ranging from $1.50 to $2,00 per acre, according to the nature of the work, by teams and men hired for the purpose, for the Lower Sioux, about 500 acres, and for the Upper Sioux, about 475 acres. There were, also, at the same time, ploughed by the farmer Indians and the department teams, about 250 acres for the Lower, and about 325 acres for the Upper Sioux. This fall ploughing was continued until the frost prevented its further prosecution. It was done to facilitate the work of the agricultural department, and to kill the worms which had proved so injurious the previous year. * * *

"The carpenter-shops at both Agencies were supplied with lumber for the manufacture and repair of sleds, wagons, and other farming utensils. Sheds were erected for the protection of the cattle and utensils of the department, and the farmer Indians, assisted by the department carpenters, erected stables, pens, and out-houses for the protection of their cattle, horses and utensils. * Hay, grain, and other supplies were provided, and, in short, every thing was done which the means at command of the agent would justify.

"The work of the autumn being thus closed, I set about making preparations for the work of the next spring and summer, and in directing the work of the winter. I made calculations to erect, during the summer and autumn of 1862, at least fifty dwelling-houses for Indian families, at an estimated average cost of $300 each; and also to aid the farmer Indians in erecting as many additional dwellings as possible, not to exceed thirty or forty; and to have planted for the Lower Sioux, at least 1,200 acres, and for the Upper Sioux, at least 1,300 acres of crops, and to have all the land planted, except that at Big Stone Lake, inclosed by a fence.

"To carry out these calculations, early in the the winter the superintendents of farms, the blacksmiths, the carpenters, and the superintendents of schools were directed to furnish estimates for the amount of agricultural implements, horses, oxen, wagons, carts, building material, iron, steel, tools, and supplies needed to carry on successfully their several departments for one year from the opening of navigation in the spring of 1862.

"These estimates were prepared and furnished me about the 1st of February. In accordance with these estimates, I proceeded to purchase, in *open market*, the articles and supplies recommended.

"I made the estimates for one year, and purchases accordingly, in order to secure the benefit of transportation by water in the spring, and thus avoid the delays, vexations, and extra expense of transportation by land in the fall. The bulk of purchases were made with the distinct understanding that payment would be made out of the funds belonging to the quarter in which the goods, implements, or supplies, were expended."

"Thus it will be seen that, in the spring of 1862, there was on hand supplies and material sufficient to carry us through the coming year. * * * Thus, to all appearance, the spring season opened propitiously. * * * To carry out my original design of having as much as possible planted for the Indians at Big Stone Lake and Lac qui Parle as early in the month of May, 1862, as the condition of the swollen streams would permit, I visited Lac qui Parle and Big Stone Lake, going as far as North Island, in Lake Traverse, having with me Antoine Freniere, United States Interpreter, Dr. J. L. Wakefield, physician of the Upper Sioux, and Nelson Givens, assistant Agent. At Lac qui Parle I found the Indians willing and anxious to plant. I inquired into their condition and wants, and made arrangements to have them supplied with seeds and implements, and directed Amos W. Huggins, the school teacher there, to aid and instruct them in their work, and to make proper distribution of the seeds and implements furnished, and placed at his disposal an ox-team and wagon and two breaking-teams, with instructions to devote his whole time and attention to the superintendence and instruction of the resident Indians during the planting season, and until the crops were cultivated and safely harvested.

"I also found the Indians at Big Stone Lake and Lake Traverse very anxious to plant, but without any means whatever so to do. I looked over their fields in order to see what could be done. After having inquired into the whole matter, I instructed Mr. Givens to remain at Big Stone Lake and superintend and direct the agricultural operations of the season, and to remain there until it was too late to plant any more. I placed at his disposal ten double plough teams, with men to operate them, and ordered forward at once one hundred bushels of seed corn and five hundred bushels of seed potatoes, with pumpkin, squash, turnip, and other seeds, in reasonable proportion, together with a sufficient supply of ploughs, hoes, and other implements for the Indians, and a blacksmith to repair breakages; and directed him to see that every Indian, and every Indian horse or pony, did as much work as was possible. * *

"On my way down to the agency, I visited the plantings of Tahampih'da, (Rattling Moccasin), Mazasha, (Red Iron), Mahpiya Wicasta, (Cloud Man), and Rattling Cloud, and found that the

Superintendent of Farms for the Upper Sioux had, in accordance with my instructions, been faithfully attending to the wants of these bands. He had supplied them with implements and seeds, and I left them at work. On my arrival at the Agency, I found that the farmer Indians residing thereabouts had, in my absence, been industriously at work, and had not only completed their plowing, but had planted very extensively. The next day after my arrival at the Agency, I visited each farmer Indian at the Yellow Medicine, and congratulated him on his prospect for a good crop, and spoke to him such words of encouragement as occurred to me.

"The next day I proceeded to the Lower Agency, and then taking with me Mr. A. H. Wagner, the Superintendent of Farms for the Lower Sioux, I went around each planting. and, for the second time, visited each farmer Indian, and found that, in general, my instructions had been carried out. The plowing was generally completed in good order, and the planting nearly all done, and many of the farmer Indians were engaged in repairing old and making new fences. I was pleased and gratified, and so told the Indians—the prospect was so encouraging.

"About the first of July I visited all the plantings of both the Upper and Lower Sioux, except those at Big Stone Lake, and found, in nearly every instance, the prospects for good crops very hopeful indeed. The superintendents of farms, the male school teachers, and all the employes assisting them, had done their duty. About this time Mr. Givens returned from Big Stone Lake, and reported to me his success there. From all I knew and all I thus learned, I was led to believe that we would have no 'starving Indians' to feed the next winter, and little did I dream of the unfortunate and terrible outbreak which, in a short time, burst upon us, * * *

"In the fall of 1861, a good and substantial school-room and dwelling, a store-house and blacksmith-shop, were completed at Lac qui Parle, and, about the first of November, Mr. Amos W. Huggins and his family occupied the dwelling, and, assisted by Miss Julia LaFrambois, prepared the school-room, and devoted their whole time to teaching such Indian children as they could induce to attend the school.

"The storehouse was supplied with provisions, which Mr. Huggins was instructed to issue to the children and their parents at his discretion. Here it may be permitted me to remark to Mr. Huggins, who was born and raised among the Sioux, and Miss LaFrambois, who was a Sioux mixed-blood, were two persons entirely capable and in every respect qualified for the discharge of the duties of their situation, than whom the Indians had no more devoted friends. They lived among the Indians of choice, because they thought they could be beneficial to them. Mr. Huggins exercised nothing but kindness toward them. He fed them when hungry, clothed them when naked, attended them when sick, and advised and cheered them in all their difficulties. He was intelligent, energetic, industrious, and good, and yet he was one of the first victims of the outbreak, shot down like a dog by the very Indians whom he had so long and so well served. * * * * * * *

"In the month of June, 1862, being well aware of the influence exerted by Little Crow over the blanket Indians, and, by his plausibility, led to believe that he intended to act in good faith, I promised to build him a good brick house provided that he would agree to aid me in bringing around the idle young men to habits of industry and civilization, and that he would abandon the leadership of the blanket Indians and become a 'white man.'

"This being well understood, as I thought, I directed Mr. Nairn, the carpenter of the Lower Sioux, to make out the plan and estimates for Crow's house, and to proceed at once to make the window and door frames, and to prepare the lumber necessary for the building, and ordered the teamsters to deliver the necessary amount of brick as soon as possible. Little Crow agreed to dig the cellar and haul the necessary lumber, both of which he had commenced. The carpenter had nearly completed his part of the work, and the brick was being promptly delivered at the time of the outbreak.

"On the 15th of August, only three days previous to the outbreak, I had an interview with Little Crow, and he seemed to be well pleased and satisfied. Little indeed did I suspect, at that time, that he would be the leader in the terrible outbreak of the 18th."

There were planted, according to the statement of Agent Galbraith in his report, on the lower reservation, one thousand and twenty-five acres of corn, two hundred and sixty acres of potatoes, sixty acres of turnips and ruta-bagas, and twelve acres of wheat, besides a large quantity of field and garden vegetables. These crops, at a low estimate, would have harvested, in the fall, 74,865 bushels. There were, on the lower reservation, less than three thousand Indians, all told. This crop, therefore, would have yielded full twenty-five bushels to each man, woman and child, including the blanket as well as the farmer Indians

There were, also, of growing crops, in fine condition, on the upper reservation, one thousand one hundred and ten acres of corn, three hundred acres of potatoes, ninety acres of turnips and ruta-bagas, and twelve acres of wheat, and field and garden vegetables in due proportion. These, at a low estimate, would have harvested 85,740 bushels. There were, on the upper reservation, a little over four thousand annuity Sioux. This crop, therefore, would have harvested them about twenty-one bushels for each man, woman and child, including, also, the blanket Indians.

Thus, under the beneficent workings of the humane policy of the Government inaugurated in 1858, they were fast becoming an independent people. Let it be borne in mind, however, that these results, so beneficial to the Indian, were accomplished only through the sleepless vigilance and untiring energy of those who had the welfare of these rude, savage beings in their care.

Major Galbraith, after giving these statistics of the crops on the reservations, and the arrangements made for gathering hay, by the Indians, for their winter's use, says:

"I need hardly say that our hopes were high at the prospects before us, nor need I relate my chagrin and mortification when, in a moment, I found these high hopes blasted forever."

Such, then, was the condition, present and prospective, of the "Annuity Sioux Indians," in the summer of 1862. No equal number of pioneer settlers on the border could, at that time, make a better showing than was exhibited on these reservations. They had in fair prospect a *surplus* over and above the wants of the entire tribes for the coming year. This had never before occurred in their history.

The sagacity and wise forethought of their agent, and the unusually favorable season, had amply provided against the possibility of recurring want. The coming winter would have found their granaries full to overflowing. Add to this the fact that they had a large cash annuity coming to them from the Government, as well as large amounts of goods, consisting of blankets, cloths, groceries, flour and meats, powder, shot, lead, etc., and we confidently submit to the enlightened reader the whole question of their alleged grievances, confident that there can be but one verdict at their hands, and that the paternal care of the Government over them was good and just; nay, generous, and that those having the immediate supervision of their interests were performing their whole duty, honestly and nobly.

The hopes of the philanthropist and Christian beat high. They believed the day was not far distant when it could be said that the Sioux Indians, *as a race*, not only *could be* civilized, but that here were whole tribes who *were* civilized, and had abandoned the chase and the war-path for the cultivation of the soil and the arts of peace, and that the juggleries and sorcery of the medicine-men had been abandoned for the milder teachings of the missionaries of the Cross.

How these high hopes were dashed to the earth, extinguished in an ocean of blood, and their own bright prospects utterly destroyed, by their horrible and monstrous perfidy and unheard of atrocities, it will be our work, in these pages, to show.

We are now rapidly approaching the fatal and bloody *denouement*, the terrible 18th of August, the memory of which will linger in the minds of the survivors of its tragic scenes, and the succeeding days and weeks of horror and blood, till reason kindly ceases to perform its office, and blots out the fearful record in the oblivion of the grave.

Again we quote from the able report of Major Galbraith:

"About the 25th of June, 1862, a number of the chiefs and head men of the Sissetons and Wapatons visited the Agency and inquired about the payments; whether they were going to *get any* (as they had been told, as they alleged, that they would not be paid,) and if so, how much, and when? I answered them that they would certainly be paid; exactly how much I could not say, but that it would be nearly, if not quite, a full payment; that I did not know when the payment would be made, but that I felt sure it could not be made before the 20th of July. I advised them to go home, and admonished them not to come back again until I sent for them. I issued provisions, powder and shot and tobacco to them, and they departed.

"In a few days after I went to the Lower Agency, and spoke to the lower Indians in regard to their payments. As they all lived within a few miles of the Agency, little was said, as, when the money came, they could be called together in a day. I remained about one week there, visiting the farms and plantings, and issued to the Indians a good supply of pork, flour, powder, shot, and tobacco, and urged upon them the necessity of cutting and securing hay for the winter, and of watching and keeping the birds from their corn.

"I left them apparently satisfied, and arrived at Yellow Medicine on the 14th of July, and found, to my surprise, that nearly all the Upper Indians had arrived, and were encamped about the Agency. I inquired of them why they had come, and they answered, that they were afraid something was wrong; they feared they would not get their money, because *white men* had been telling them so.

"Being in daily expectation of the arrival of the money, I determined to make the best of it, and notified the Superintendent of Indian Affairs accordingly.

"How were over 4,000 Annuity, and over 1,000 Yanktonais Sioux, with nothing to eat, and entirely dependent on me for supplies, to be provided for? I supplied them as best I could. Our stock was nearly used up, and still, on the 1st day of August, no money had come.

"The Indians complained of starvation. I held back, in order to save the provisions to the last moment. On the 4th of August, early in the morning, the young men and soldiers, to the number of not less than four hundred mounted, and one hundred and fifty on foot, surprised and deceived the commander of the troops on guard, and surrounded the camp, and proceeded to the warehouse in a boisterous manner, and in sight of, and within one hundred and fifty yards of one hundred armed men, with two twelve-pound mountain howitzers, cut down the door of the warehouse, shot down the American flag, and entered the building, and before they could be stopped had carried over one hundred sacks of flour from the warehouse, and were evidently bent on a general 'clearing out.'

"The soldiers, now recovered from their panic, came gallantly to our aid, entered the warehouse and took possession. The Indians all stood around with their guns loaded, cocked and leveled. I spoke to them, and they consented to a talk. The result was, that they agreed, if I would give them plenty of pork and flour, and issue to them the annuity *goods* the next day, they would go away. I told them to go away with enough to eat for *two days*, and to send the chiefs and head men for a council the next day, unarmed and peaceably and I would answer them. They assented and went to their camp. In the meantime I had sent for Captain Marsh, the commandant of Fort Ridgely, who promptly arrived early in the morning of the next day.

"I laid the whole case before him, and stated my plan. He agreed with me, and, in the afternoon, the Indians, unarmed, and apparently peaceably disposed, came in, and we had a 'talk,' and, in the presence of Captain Marsh, Rev. Mr. Riggs and others, I agreed to issue the annuity goods and a fixed amount of provisions, provided the Indians would go home and watch their corn, and wait for the payment until they were sent for. They assented. I made, on the 6th, 7th and 8th of August the issues as agreed upon, assisted by Captain Marsh, and, on the 9th of August the Indians were all gone, and on the 12th I had definite information that the Sissetons, who had started on the 7th, had all arrived at Big Stone Lake, and that the men were preparing to go on a buffalo hunt, and that the women and children were to stay and guard the crops. Thus this threatening and disagreeable event passed off, but, as usual, without the punishment of a single Indian who had been engaged in the attack on the warehouse. They should have been punished, but they were not, and simply because we had not the power to punish them. And hence we had to adopt the same 'sugar-plum' policy which had been so often adopted before with the Indians, and especially at the time of the Spirit Lake massacre, in 1857."

On the 12th day of August, thirty men enlisted at Yellow Medicine; and, on the 13th, accompanied by the agent, proceeded to the Lower Agency, where, on the 14th, they were joined by twenty more, making about fifty in all. On the afternoon of the 15th they proceeded to Fort Ridgely, where they remained until the morning of the 17th, when, having been furnished by Captain Marsh with transportation, accompanied by Lieutenant N. K. Culver, Sergeant McGrew, and four men of Company B, Fifth Minnesota Volunteers, they started for Fort Snelling by the way of New Ulm and St. Peter, little dreaming of the terrible message, the news of which would reach them at the latter place next day, and turn them back to the defense of that post and the border.

On Monday morning, the 18th, at about 8 o'clock, they left New Ulm, and reached St. Peter at about 4 o'clock P. M. About 6 o'clock, Mr. J. C. Dickinson arrived from the Lower Agency, bringing the startling news that the Indians had broken out, and, before he left, had commenced murdering the whites.

They at once set about making preparations to return. There were in St. Peter some fifty old Harper's Ferry muskets; these they obtained, and, procuring ammunition, set about preparing cartridges, at which many of them worked all night, and, at sunrise on Tuesday morning were on their way back, with heavy hearts and dark forebodings, toward the scene of trouble.

In the night Sergeant Sturgis, of Captain Marsh's company, had arrived, on his way to St. Paul, with dispatches to Governor Ramsey, from Lieutenant Thomas Gere, then in command of Fort Ridgely, bringing the sad news of the destruction of Captain Marsh and the most of his command at the ferry, at the Lower Agency, on Monday afternoon. They had but a slender chance of reaching the fort in safety, and still less of saving it from destruction, for they knew that there were not over twenty-five men left in it, Lieutenant Sheehan, with his company, having left for Fort Ripley on the 17th, at the same time that the "Renville Rangers" (the company from the Agencies) left for Fort Snelling. Their friends, too, were in the very heart of the Indian country. Some of them had left their wives and little ones at Yellow Medicine, midway between the Lower Agency and the wild bands of the Sissetons and Yanktonais, who made the attack upon the warehouse at that Agency only two weeks before. Their hearts almost died within them as they thought of the dreadful fate awaiting them at the hands of those savage and blood-thirsty monsters. But they turned their faces toward the West, determined, if Fort Ridgely was yet untaken, to enter it, or die in the attempt, and at about sundown entered the fort, and found all within it as yet safe.

A messenger had been sent to Lieutenant Sheehan, who immediately turned back and had entered the fort a few hours before them. There were in the fort, on their arrival, over two hundred and fifty refugees, principally women and children, and they continued to come in, until there were nearly three hundred.

Here they remained on duty, night and day, until the morning of the 28th, when reinforcements, under Colonel McPhail and Captain Anson Northrup and R. H. Chittenden arrived.

The annuity money by Superintendent Thompson had been dispatched to the Agency in charge of his clerk, accompanied by E. A. C. Hatch, J. C. Ramsey, M. A. Daily, and two or three others.

On their arrival at the fort, on Tuesday night, Major Galbraith found these gentlemen there, they having arrived at the post Monday noon, the very day of the outbreak. Had they been one day sooner they would have been at the Lower Agency, and their names would have been added, in all probability, to the long roll of the victims, at that devoted point of Indian barbarity, and about $10,000 in gold would have fallen into the hands of the savages.

These gentlemen were in the fort during the siege which followed, and were among the bravest of its brave defenders. Major Hatch, afterwards of "Hatch's Battalion" (cavalry), was particulary conspicuous for his cool courage and undaunted bravery.

Thus it will be seen how utterly false was the information which the Indians said they had received that they were to get no money.

And notwithstanding all that has been said as to the cause of the outbreak, it may be remarked that the removal of the agent from Yellow Medicine, with the troops raised by him for the Southern Rebellion, at the critical period when the Indians were exasperated and excited, and ready at any moment to arm for warfare upon the whites, was one of the causes acting directly upon the Indians to precipitate the blow that afterwards fell upon the border settlements of Minnesota on the 18th of August, 1862. Had he remained with his family at Yellow Medicine, as did the Winnebago agent, with his family, at the agency, the strong probability is that the attack at Yellow Medicine might have been delayed, if not entirely prevented.

CHAPTER XXXIII.

MURDER AT ACTON—MASSACRE AT THE LOWER AGENCY—CAPTURE OF MATTIE WILLIAMS, MARY ANDERSON AND MARY SCHWANDT—MURDER OF GEORGE GLEASON—CAPTURE OF MRS. WAKEFIELD AND CHILDREN.

We come now to the massacre itself, the terrible blow which fell, like a thunderbolt from a clear sky, with such appalling force and suddenness, upon the unarmed and defenceless border, crimsoning its fair fields with the blood of its murdered people, and lighting up the midnight sky with the lurid blaze of burning dwellings, by the light of which the affrighted survivors fled from the nameless terrors that beset their path, before the advancing gleam of the uplifted tomahawk, many of them only to fall victims to the Indian bullet, while vainly seeking a place of security.

The first blow fell upon the town of Acton, thirty-five miles north-east of the Lower Sioux agency, in the county of Meeker. On Sunday, August 17, 1862, at 1 o'clock P. M., six Sioux Indians, said to be of Shakopee's band of Lower Annuity Sioux, came to the house of Jones and demanded food. It was refused them, as Mrs. Jones was away from home, at the house of Mr. Howard Baker, a son-in-law, three fourths of a mile distant. They became angry and boisterous, and fearing violence at their hands, Mr. Jones took his children, a boy and a girl, and went himself to Baker's, leaving at the house a girl from fourteen to sixteen years of age, and a boy of twelve—brother and sister—who lived with him. The Indians soon followed on to Baker's. At Howard Baker's were a Mr. Webster and his wife, Baker and wife and infant child, and Jones and his wife and two children.

Soon after reaching the house, the Indians proposed to the three men to join them in target-shooting. They consented, and all discharged their guns at the target. Mr. Baker then traded guns with an Indian, the savage giving him $3 as the difference in the value of the guns. Then all commenced loading again. The Indians got the charges into their guns first, and immediately turned and shot Jones. Mrs. Jones and Mrs. Baker were standing in the door. When one of the savages leveled his gun at Mrs. Baker, her husband saw the movement, and sprang between them, receiving the bullet intended for his wife in his own body. At the same time they shot Webster and Mrs. Jones. Mrs. Baker, who had her infant in her arms, seeing her husband fall, fainted, and fell backward into the cellar (a trap-door being open), and thus escaped. Mrs. Webster was lying in their wagon, from which the goods were not yet unloaded, and escaped unhurt. The children of Mr. Jones were in the house, and were not molested. They then returned to the house of Mr. Jones, and killed and scalped the girl. The boy was lying on the bed and was undiscovered, but was a silent witness of the tragic fate of his sister.

After killing the girl the savages left without disturbing anything, and going directly to the house of a settler, took from his stable a span of horses already in the harness, and while the family was at dinner, hitched them to a wagon standing near, and without molesting any one, drove off in the direction of Beaver Creek settlement and the Lower Agency, leaving Acton at about 3 o'clock in the afternoon. This span of horses, harness and wagon were the only property taken from the neighborhood by them.

The boy at Jones's who escaped massacre at their hands, and who was at the house during the entire time that they were there, avers that they obtained no liquor there that day, but even that when they came back and murdered his sister, the bottles upon the shelf were untouched by them. They had obtained none on their first visit before going over to Baker's. It would seem, therefore, that the very general belief that these first murders at Acton, on the 17th, were the result of drunkenness, is a mistake.

Mrs. Baker, who was unhurt by the fall, remained in the cellar until after the Indians were gone, when, taking the children, she started for a neighboring settlement, to give the alarm. Before she left, an Irishman, calling himself Cox, came to the house, whom she asked to go with her, and carry her child. Cox laughed, saying, "the men were not dead, but drunk, and that, falling down, they had hurt their noses and made them bleed," and refusing to go with Mrs. Baker, went off in the direction taken by the Indians. This man Cox had frequently been seen at the Lower Agency, and was generally supposed to be an insane man, wandering friendless over the country. It has been supposed by many that he was in league with the Indians. We have only to say, if he was, he counterfeited insanity remarkably well.

Mrs. Baker reached the settlement in safety, and on the next day (Monday) a company of citizens of Forest City, the county seat of Meeker county, went out to Acton to bury the dead. Forest City is twelve miles north of that place. The party who went out on Monday saw Indians on horseback, and chased them, but failed to get near enough to get a shot, and they escaped.

As related in a preceding chapter, a council was held at Rice Creek on Sunday, at which it was decided that the fearful tragedy should commence on the next morning. It is doubtful whether the Acton murders were then known to these conspirators, as this council assembled in the afternoon, and the savages who committed those murders had some forty miles to travel, after 3 o'clock in the afternoon, to reach the place of this council. It would seem, therefore, that those murders could have had no influence in precipitating this council, as they could not, at that time, have been known to Little Crow and his conspirators.

The final decision of these fiends must have been made as early as sundown; for by early dawn almost the entire force of warriors, of the Lower tribes, were ready for the work of slaughter. They were already armed and painted, and dispersed through the scattered settlements, over a region at least forty miles in extent, and were rapidly gathering in the vicinity of the Lower Agency, until some 250 were collected at that point, and surrounded the houses and stores of the traders, while yet the inmates were at their morning meal, or asleep in their beds in fancied security, all unconscious of the dreadful fate that awaited them. The action was concerted, and the time fixed. The blow was unexpected, and unparalleled! In the language af Adjutent-General Malmros:

"Since the formation of our general Government, no State or Territory of the Republic has received so severe a blow at the hands of the savages, or witnessed within its borders a parallel scene of murder, butchery, and rapine."

Philander Prescott, the aged Government Interpreter at that Agency, who had resided among the Sioux for forty-five years, having a wife and children allied to them by ties of blood, and who knew their language and spoke it better than any man of their own race, and who seemed to understand every Indian impulse, had not the slightest intimation or conception of such a catastrophe as was about to fall upon the country. The Rev. S. R. Riggs, in a letter to a St. Paul paper, under date of August 13, writes that "all is quiet and orderly at the place of the forthcoming payment." This gentleman had been a missionary among these people for over a quarter of a century. His intimate acquaintance with their character and language were of such a nature as to enable him to know and detect the first symptoms of any intention of committing any depredations upon the whites, and had not the greatest secrecy been observed by them, the knowledge of their designs would undoubtedly have been communicated to either Mr. Prescott, Mr. Riggs, or Dr. Williamson, who had also been among them almost thirty years. Such was the position of these gentlemen that, had they discovered or suspected any lurking signs of a conspiracy, such as after developments satisfy us actually existed, and had failed to communicate it to the authorities and the people, they would have laid themselves open to the horrible charge of complicity with the murderers. But whatever may be the public judgement upon the course afterward pursued by the two last-named gentlemen, in their efforts to shield the guilty wretches from that punishment their awful crimes so justly merited, no one who knows them would for a moment harbor a belief that they had any suspicion of the coming storm until it burst upon them.

A still stronger proof of the feeling of security of these upon the reservation, and the belief that the recent demonstrations were only such as were of yearly occurrence, and that all danger was passed, is to be found in the fact that, as late as the 15th of August, the substance of a dispatch was published in the daily papers of St. Paul, from Major Galbraith, agreeing fully with the views of Mr. Riggs, as to the quiet and orderly conduct of the Indians. This opinion is accompanied by the very highest evidence of human sincerity. Under the belief of their peaceable disposition, he had, on the 16th day of August, sent his wife and children from Fort Ridgely to Yellow Medicine, where they arrived on Sunday, the 17th, the very day of the murders at Acton, and on the very day, also, that the council at Rice Creek had decided that the white race in Minnesota must either perish or be driven back east of the Mississippi. But early on this fatal Monday morning Mr. Prescott and Rev. J. D. Hinman learned from Little Crow that the storm of savage wrath was gathering, and about to break upon their devoted heads, and that their only safety was in instant flight.

The first crack of the Indian guns that fell on his ear, a moment afterward, found Prescott and Hinman, and his household fleeing for their lives,

> "While on the billowy bosom of the air
> Rolled the dread notes of anguish and despair."

Mrs. Hinman was, fortunately, then at Faribault. All the other members of the family escaped with Mr. Hinman to Fort Ridgely. The slaughter at the Agency now commenced. John Lamb, a teamster, was shot down, near the house of Mr. Hinman, just as that gentleman and his family were starting on their perilous journey of escape. At the same time some Indians entered the stable, and were taking therefrom the horses belonging to the Government. Mr. A. H. Wagner, Superintendent of Farms at that Agency, entered the stable to prevent them, and was, by order of Little Crow, instantly shot down. Mr. Hinman waited to see and hear no more, but fled toward the ferry, and soon put the Minnesota river between himself and the terrible tragedy enacting behind him.

At about the same time, Mr. J. C. Dickinson, who kept the Government boarding-house, with all his family, including several girls who were working for him, also succeeded in crossing the river with a span of horses and a wagon; these, with some others, mostly women and children, who had reached the ferry, escaped to the fort.

Very soon after, Dr. Philander P. Humphrey, physician to the Lower Sioux, with his sick wife, and three children, also succeeded in crossing the river, but never reached the fort. All but one, the eldest, a boy of about twelve years of age, were killed upon the road. They had gone about four miles, when Mrs. Humphrey became so much exhausted as to be unable to proceed further, and they went into the house of a Mr. Magner, deserted by its inmates. Mrs. Humphrey was placed on the bed; the son was sent to the spring for water for his mother. * * The boy heard the wild war-whoop of the savage break upon the stillness of the air, and, in the next moment, the ominous crack of their guns, which told the fate of his family, and left him its sole survivor. Fleeing hastily toward Fort Ridgely, about eight miles distant, he met the command of Captain Marsh on their way toward the Agency. The young hero turned back with them to the ferry. As they passed Magner's house, they saw the Doctor lying near the door, dead, but the house itself was a heap of smouldering ruins; and this brave boy was thus compelled to look upon the funeral pyre of his mother, and his little brother and sister. A burial party afterward found their charred remains amid the blackened ruins, and gave them Christian sepulture. In the charred hands of the little girl was found her china doll, with which she refused to part even in death. The boy went on to the ferry, and in that disastrous conflict escaped unharmed, and finally made his way into the fort.

In the mean time the work of death went on. The whites, taken by surprise, were utterly defenseless, and so great had been the feeling of security, that many of them were actually unarmed, although living in the very midst of the savages. At the store of Nathan Myrick, Hon. James W. Lynd, formerly a member of the State Senate, Andrew J. Myrick, and G. W. Divoll were among the first victims. * * * In the store of William H. Forbes were some five or six persons, among them Mr. George H. Spencer, jr. Hearing the yelling of the savages outside, these men ran to the door to ascertain its cause, when they were instantly fired upon, killing four of their number, and severely wounding Mr. Spencer. Spencer and his uninjured companion hastily sought a temporary place of safety in the chamber of the building.

Mr. Spencer, in giving an account of this opening scene of the awful tragedy, says:

"When I reached the foot of the stairs, I turned and beheld the store filling with Indians. One had followed me nearly to the stairs, when he took deliberate aim at my body, but, providentially, both barrels of his gun missed fire, and I succeeded in getting above without further injury. Not expecting to live a great while, I threw myself upon a bed, and, while lying there, could hear them opening cases of goods, and carrying them out, and threatening to burn the building. I did not relish the idea of being burned to death very well, so I arose very quietly, and taking a bed-cord, I made fast one end to the bed-post, and carried the other to a window, which I raised. I intended, in case they fired the building, to let myself down from the window, and take the chances of being shot again, rather than to remain where I was and burn. The man who went up-stairs with me, seeing a good opportunity to escape, rushed down through the crowd and ran for life; he was fired upon, and two charges of buckshot struck him, but he succeeded in making his escape. I had been up-stairs probably an hour, when I heard the voice of an Indian inquiring for me. I recognized his voice, and felt that I was safe. Upon being told that I was up-stairs, he rushed up, followed by ten or a dozen others, and approaching my bed, asked if I was mortally wounded. I told him that I did not know, but that I was badly hurt. Some of the others came up and took me by the hand, and appeared to be sorry that I had been hurt. They then asked me where the guns were. I pointed to them, when my comrade assisted me in getting down stairs.

"The name of this Indian is Wakinyatawa, or, in English, 'His Thunder.' He was, up to the time of the outbreak, the head soldier of Little Crow, and, some four or five years ago, went to Washington with that chief to see their Great Father. He is a fine-looking Indian, and has always been noted for his bravery in fighting the Chippewas. When we reached the foot of the stairs, some of the Indians cried out, 'Kill him!' 'Spare no Americans!' 'Show mercy to none!' My friend, who was unarmed, seized a hatchet that was lying near by, and declared that he would cut down the first one that should attempt to do me any further harm. Said he, 'If you had killed him before I saw him, it would have been all right; but we have been friends and comrades for ten years, and now that I have seen him, I will protect him or die with him.' They then made way for us, and we passed out; he procured a wagon, and gave me over to a couple of squaws to take me to his lodge. On the way we were stopped two or three times by armed Indians on horseback, who inquired of the squaws 'What that meant?' Upon being answered that 'This is Wakinyatawa's friend, and he has saved his life,' they suffered us to pass on. His lodge was about four miles above the Agency, at Little Crow's village. My friend soon came home and washed me, and dressed my wounds with roots. Some few white men succeeded in making their escape to the fort. There were no other white men taken prisoners."

The relation of "comrade," which existed between Mr. Spencer and this Indian, is a species of Freemasonry which is in existence among the Sioux, and is probably also common to other Indian tribes.

The store of Louis Robert was, in like manner, attacked. Patrick McClellan, one of the clerks in charge of the store, was killed. There were at the store several other persons; some of them were killed and some made their escape. Mr. John Nairn, the Government carpenter at the Lower Sioux Agency, seeing the attack upon the stores and other places, seized his children, four in number, and, with his wife, started out on the prairie, making their way toward the fort. They were accompanied by Mr. Alexander Hunter, an attached personal friend, and his young wife. Mr. Nairn had been among them in the employ of the Government, some eight years, and had, by his urbane manners and strict attention to their interests, secured the personal friendship of many of the tribe. Mr. Nairn and his family reached the fort in safety that afternoon. Mr. Hunter had, some years before, frozen his feet so badly as to lose the toes, and, being lame, walked with great difficulty. When near an Indian village below the Agency, they were met by an Indian, who urged Hunter to go to the village, promising to get them a horse and wagon with which to make their escape. Mr. Hunter and his wife went to the Indian village, believing their Indian friend would redeem his promises, but from inability, or some other reason, he did not do so. They went to the woods, where they remained all night, and in the morning started for Fort Ridgely on foot. They had gone but a short distance, however, when they met an Indian, who, without a word of warning, shot poor Hunter dead, and led his distracted young wife away into captivity.

We now return once more to the scene of blood and conflagration at the Agency. The white-haired interpreter, Philander Prescott (now verging upon seventy years of age), hastily left his house soon after his meeting with Little Crow, and fled toward Fort Ridgely. The other members of his family remained behind, knowing that their relation to the tribe would save them. Mr. Prescott had gone several miles, when he was overtaken. His murderers came and talked with him. He reasoned with them, saying: "I am an old man: I have lived with you now forty-five years, almost half a century. My wife and children are among you, of your own blood; I have never done you any harm, and have been your true friend in all your troubles; why should you wish to kill me?" Their only reply was: "We would save your life if we could, but the *white man must die;* we cannot spare your life; our orders are to kill all white men; we cannot spare you."

Seeing that all remonstrance was vain and hopeless, and that his time had come, the aged man with a firm step and noble bearing, sadly turned away from the deaf ear and iron heart of the savage, and with dignity and composure received the fatal messenger.

Thus perished Philander Prescott, the true, tried, and faithful friend of the Indian, by the hands of that perfidious race, whom he had so long and so faithfully labored to benefit to so little purpose.

The number of persons who reached Fort Ridgely from the agency was forty-one. Some are

known to have reached other places of safety. All suffered incredible hardships; many hiding by day in the tall prairie grass, in bogs and sloughs, or under the trunks of prostrate trees, crawling stealthily by night to avoid the lurking and wily foe, who, with the keen scent of the blood-hound and ferocity of the tiger, followed on their trail, thirsting for blood.

Among those who escaped into the fort were Mr. J. C. Whipple, of Faribault; Mr. Charles B. Hewitt, of New Jersey. The services of Mr. Whipple were recognized and rewarded by the Government with a first lieutenant's commission in the volunteer artillery service.

James Powell, a young man residing at St. Peter, was at the Agency herding cattle. He had just turned the cattle out of the yard, saddled and mounted his mule, as the work of death commenced. Seeing Lamb and Wagner shot down near him he turned to flee, when Lamb called to him for help; but, at that moment two shots were fired at him, and, putting spurs to his mule he turned toward the ferry, passing close to an Indian who leveled his gun to fire at him; but the caps exploded, when the savage, evidently surprised that he had failed to kill him, waved his hand toward the river, and exclaimed, "Puckachee! Puckachee!" Powell did not wait for a second warning, which might come in a more unwelcome form, but slipped at once from the back of his animal, dashed down the bluff through the brush, and reached the ferry just as the boat was leaving the shore. Looking over his shoulder as he ran, he saw an Indian in full pursuit on the very mule he had a moment before abandoned.

All that day the work of sack and plunder went on; and when the stores and dwellings and the warehouses of the Government had been emptied of their contents, the torch was applied to the various buildings, and the little village was soon a heap of smouldering ruins.

The bodies of their slain victims were left to fester in the sun where they fell, or were consumed in the buildings from which they had been unable to effect their escape.

So complete was the surprise, and so sudden and unexpected the terrible blow, that not a single one of all that host of naked savages was slain. In thirty minutes from the time the first gun was fired, not a white person was left alive. All were either weltering in their gore or had fled in fear and terror from that place of death.

REDWOOD RIVER.

At the Redwood river, ten miles above the Agency, on the road to Yellow Medicine, resided Mr. Joseph B. Reynolds, in the employment of the Government as a teacher. His house was within one mile of Shakopee's village. His family consisted of his wife, a niece—Miss Mattie Williams, of Painesville, Ohio—Mary Anderson and Mary Schwandt, hired girls. William Landmeier, a hired man, and Legrand Davis, a young man from Shakopee, was also stopping with them temporarily.

On the morning of the 18th of August, at about 6 o'clock, John Moore, a half-breed trader, residing near them, came to the house and informed them that there was an outbreak among the Indians, and that they had better leave at once. Mr. Reynolds immediately got out his buggy, and, taking his wife, started off across the prairie in such a direction as to avoid the Agency. At the same time Davis and the three girls got into the wagon of a Mr. Patoile, a trader at Yellow Medicine, who had just arrived there on his way to New Ulm, and they also started out on the prairie. William, the hired man, would not leave until he had been twice warned by Moore that his life was in danger. He then went down to the river bottom, and following the Minnesota river, started for the fort. When some distance on his way he came upon some Indians who were gathering up cattle. They saw him and there was no way of escape. They came to him and told him that if he would assist them in driving the cattle they would not kill him. Making a merit of necessity he complied, and went on with them till they were near the Lower Agency, when the Indians, hearing the firing at the ferry, suddenly left him and hastened on to take part in the battle then progressing between Captain Marsh and their friends. William fled in an opposite direction, and that night entered Fort Ridgely.

We return now to Patoile and his party. After crossing the Redwood near its mouth, he drove some distance up that stream, and, turning to the left, struck across the prairie toward New Ulm, keeping behind a swell in the prairie which ran parallel with the Minnesota, some three miles south of that stream.

They had, unpursued, and apparently unobserved, reached a point within about ten miles of New Ulm, and nearly opposite Fort Ridgely, when they were suddenly assailed by Indians, who killed Patoile and Davis, and severely wounded Mary Anderson. Miss Williams and Mary Schwandt were captured unhurt, and were taken back to Wauconta's village.

The poor, injured young woman survived her wounds and the brutal and fiendish violation of her person to which she was subjected by these *devils incarnate*, but a few days, when death, in mercy, came to her relief and ended her sufferings in the quiet of the grave!

Mattie Williams and Mary Schwandt were afterwards restored to their friends by General Sibley's expedition, at Camp Release. We say, restored to their friends; this was hardly true of Mary Schwandt, who, when release came, found alive, of all her father's family, only one, a little brother; and he had witnessed the fiendish slaughter of all the rest, accompanied by circumstances of infernal barbarity, without a parallel in the history of savage brutality.

On Sunday, the 17th, George Gleason, Government store-keeper at the Lower Agency, accompanied by the family of Agent Galbraith, to Yellow Medicine, and on Monday afternoon, ignorant of the terrible tragedy enacted below, started to return. He had with him the wife and two children of Dr. J. S. Wakefield, physician to the Upper Sioux. When about two miles above the mouth of the Redwood, they met two armed Indians on the road. Gleason greeted them with the usual salutation of "Ho!" accompanied with the inquiry, in Sioux, as he passed, "Where are you going?" They returned the salutation, but Gleason had gone but a very short distance, when the sharp crack of a gun behind him bore to his ear the first intimation of the death in store for him. The bullet passed through his body and he fell to the ground. At the same moment Chaska, the Indian who had not fired, sprang into the wagon, by the side of Mrs. Wakefield, and driving a short distance, returned. Poor Gleason was lying upon the ground, still alive, writhing in mortal agony, when the savage monster completed his hellish work, by placing his gun at his breast, and shooting him again. Such was the sad end of the life of George Gleason; gay, jocund, genial and generous, he was the life of every circle. His pleasant face was seen, and his mellow voice was heard in song, at almost every social gathering on that rude frontier. He had a smile and pleasant word for all; and yet he fell, in his manly strength, by the hands of these bloody monsters, whom he had never wronged in word or deed. Some weeks afterward, his mutilated remains were found by the troops under Colonel Sibley, and buried where he fell. They were subsequently removed by his friends to Shakopee, where they received the rites of Christian sepulture.

Mrs. Wakefield and children were held as prisoners, and were reclaimed with the other captives at Camp Release.

CHAPTER XXXIV.

MASSACRE ON THE NORTH SIDE OF THE MINNESOTA—BURNING OF MRS. HENDERSON AND TWO CHILDREN—ESCAPE OF J. W. EARLE AND OTHERS—THE SETTLERS ENDEAVOR TO ESCAPE—MURDER OF THE SCHWANDT FAMILY—WHOLESALE MASSACRE—UPPER AGENCY—THE PEOPLE WARNED BY JOSEPH LAFRAMBOIS AND OTHER DAY—ESCAPE OF THE WHITES FROM YELLOW MEDICINE—SETTLEMENT ON THE CHIPPEWA—MURDER OF JAMES W. LINDSAY AND HIS COMRADE.

Early on the morning of the 18th, the settlers on the north side of the Minnesota river, adjoining the reservation, were surprised to see a large number of Indians in their immediate neighborhood. They were seen soon after the people arose, simultaneously, all along the river from Birch Coolie to Beaver Creek, and beyond, on the west, apparently intent on gathering up the horses and cattle. When interrogated, they said they were after Chippewas. At about 6 or 7 o'clock they suddenly began to repair to the various houses of the settlers, and then the flight of the inhabitants and the work of death began.

In the immediate vicinity of Beaver Creek, the neighbors, to the number of about twenty-eight, men, women, and children, assembled at the house of Jonathan W. Earle, and, with several teams, started for Fort Ridgely, having with them the sick wife of S. R. Henderson, her children, and the family of N. D. White, and the wife and two children of James Carrothers.

There were, also, David Carrothers and family, Earle and family, Henderson, and a German named Wedge, besides four sons of White and Earle; the rest were women and children. They had gone but a short distance when they were surrounded by Indians. When asked, by some of the party who could speak their language, what they wanted, the Indians answered, "We are going to kill you."

When asked why they were to be killed, the Indians consented to let them go, with one team and the buggy with Mrs. Henderson, on giving up the rest. They had gone but a short distance when they were again stopped by the savages, and the remaining team taken. Again they moved on, drawing the buggy and the sick woman by hand but had gone but a few rods further, when the Indians began to fire upon them. The men were with the buggy; the women and children had gone on ahead, as well as the boys and Carrothers.

Mr. Earle, seeing the savages were determined to kill them, and knowing that they could not now save Mrs. Henderson, hastened on and came up with the fleeing fugitives ahead. Mr. Henderson waved a white cloth as a flag of truce, when they shot off his fingers, and, at the same time, killed Wedge. Henderson then ran, seeing that he could not save his wife and children, and made his escape. They came up with his buggy, and, taking out the helpless woman and children, threw them on the prairie, and placing the bed over them, set it on fire, and hastened on after the fleeing fugitives.

The burned and blackened remains of both the mother and her two children were afterward found by a burial party, and interred.

Coming up with the escaping women and children, they were all captured but two children of David Carrothers. These they had shot in the chase after Carrothers, Earle, and the sons of Earle and White. They killed, also, during this chase and running fight, Eugene White, a son of N. D. White, and Radner, son of Jonathan W. Earle.

Carrothers escaped to Crow River, and thence to St. Paul. Mr. Earle and two of his sons, and one son of Mr. White, after incredible hardships, escaped to Cedar City, and subsequently made their way back to St. Peter and Fort Ridgely. All the captives taken at this time were carried to Crow's village, and, with the exception of Mrs. James Carrothers and her children, were recovered at Camp Release.

After they had captured the women and children, they returned to the houses of the settlers, and plundered them of their contents, carrying off what they could, and breaking up and destroying the balance. They then gathered up the stock and drove it to their village, taking their captives with them.

Some two or three miles above the neighborhood of Earle and White was a settlement of German emigrants, numbering some forty persons, quiet, industrious, and enterprising. Early on the morning of the 18th these had all assembled at the house of John Meyer. Very soon after they had assembled here, some fifty Indians, led by Shakopee, appeared in sight. The people all fled, except Meyer and his family, going into the grass and bushes. Peter Bjorkman ran toward his own house. Shakopee, whom he knew, saw him, and exclaimed, "There is Bjorkman; kill him!" but, keeping the building between him and the savages, he plunged into a slough and concealed himself, even removing his shirt, fearing it might be the means of revealing his whereabouts to the lurking savages. Here he lay from early morning until the darkness of night enabled him to leave with safety—suffering unutterable torments, mosquitoes literally *swarming* upon his naked person, and the hot sun scorching him to the bone.

They immediately attacked the house of Meyer, killing his wife and all his children. Seeing his family butchered, and having no means of defense, Meyer effected his escape, and reached Fort Ridgely. In the meantime the affrighted people had got together again at the house of a Mr. Sitzton, near Bjorkman's, to the number of about thirty, men, women, and children. In the afternoon the savages returned to the house of Sitzton, killing every person there but one woman, Mrs. Wilhelmina Eindenfield, and her child. These were captured, and afterward found at Camp Release, but the husband and father was among the slain. From his place of concealment Mr. Bjorkman witnessed this attack and wholesale massacre of almost an entire neighborhood. After dark he came out of the slough, and, going to his house, obtained some food and a bundle of clothing, as his house was not yet plundered; fed his dog and calf, and went over to the house of Meyer; here he found the windows all broken in, but did not enter the house. He then went to the house of Sitzton; his nerves were not equal to the task of entering that charnel-house of death. As he passed the yard, he turned out some cattle that the Indians had not taken away, and hastened toward Fort Ridgely. On the road he overtook a woman and two children, one an infant of six months, the wife and children of John Sateau, who had been killed. Taking one of the children in his arms, these companions in misfortune and suffering hurried on together. Mrs. Sateau was nearly naked, and without either shoes or stockings.

The rough prairie grass lacerated her naked feet and limbs terribly, and she was about giving out in despair. Bjorkman took from his bundle a shirt, and tearing it in parts, she wound it about her feet, and proceeded on.

At daylight they came in sight of the house of Magner, eight miles above the fort. Here they saw some eight or ten Indians, and, turning aside from the road, dropped down into the grass, where they remained until noon, when the Indians disappeared. They again moved toward the fort, but slowly and cautiously, as they did not reach it until about midnight. Upon reaching the fort Mrs. Sateau found two sons, aged ten and twelve years respectively, who had effected their escape and reached there before her.

Mrs. Mary, widow of Patrick Hayden, who resided about one and a half miles from the house of J. W. Earle, near Beaver Creek, in Renville county, says:

"On the morning of the 18th of August, Mr. Hayden started to go over to the house of Mr. J. B. Reynolds, at the Redwood river, on the reservation, and met Thomas Robinson, a half-breed, who told him to go home, get his family, and leave as soon as possible, for the Indians were coming over to kill all the whites. He came immediately home, and we commenced to make preparations to leave, but in a few minutes we saw some three or four Indians coming on horseback. We then went over to the house of a neighbor, Benedict June, and found them all ready to leave. I started off with June's people, and my husband went back home, still thinking the Indians would not kill any one, and intending to give them some provisions if they wanted them. I never saw him again.

"We had gone about four miles, when we saw a man lying dead in the road and his faithful dog watching by his side.

"We drove on till we came to the house of David Faribault, at the foot of the hill, about one and a half miles from the Agency ferry. When we got here two Indians came out of Faribault's house, and stopping the teams, shot Mr. Zimmerman, who was driving, and his two boys. I sprang out of the wagon, and, with my child, one year old, in my arms, ran into the bushes, and went up the hill toward the fort. When I came near the house of Mr. Magner, I saw Indians throwing furniture out of the door, and I went down into the bushes again, on the lower side of the road, and staid there until sundown.

"While I lay here concealed, I saw the Indians taking the roof off the warehouse, and saw the buildings burning at the Agency. I also heard the firing during the battle at the ferry, when Marsh and his men were killed.

"I then went up near the fort road, and sitting down under a tree, waited till dark, and then started for Fort Ridgely, carrying my child all the way. I arrived at the fort at about 1 o'clock A. M. The distance from our place to Ridgley was seventeen miles.

"On Tuesday morning I saw John Magner, who told me that, when the soldiers went up to the Agency the day before, he saw my husband lying in the road, near David Faribault's house, *dead.* John Hayden, his brother, who lived with us, was found dead near La Croix creek. They had got up the oxen, and were bringing the family of Mr. Eisenrich to the fort, when they were overtaken by Indians. Eisenrich was killed and his wife and five children were taken prisoners.

"Mrs. Zimmerman, who was blind, and her remaining children, and Mrs. June and her children, five in number, were captured and taken to the house of David Faribault, where they were kept till night, the savages torturing them by telling them that they were going to fasten them in the house and burn them alive, but for some inexplicable reason let them go, and they, too, reached the fort in safety. Mr. June, who with one of his boys, eleven years old, remained behind to drive in his cattle, was met by them on the road and killed. The boy was captured, and, with the other prisoners, recovered at Camp Release."

The neighborhoods in the vicinity of La Croix creek, and between that and Fort Ridgely, were visited on Monday forenoon, and the people either massacred, driven away or made prisoners. Edward Magner, living eight miles above the fort, was killed. His wife and children had gone to the fort. He had returned to look after his cattle when he was shot. Patrick Kelley and David O'Connor, both single men, were killed near Magner's.

Kearn Horan makes the following statement.

"I lived four miles from the Lower Sioux Agency, on the fort road. On the 18th of August Patrick Horan, my brother, came early from the Agency and told us that the Indians were murdering the whites. He had escaped alone and crossed the ferry, and with some Frenchmen was on his way to the fort. My brothers and William and Thomas Smith went with me. We saw Indians in the road near Magner's. Thomas Smith went to them, thinking they were white men, and I saw them kill him. We then turned to flee, and saw men escaping with teams along the road. All fled towards the fort together, the Indians firing upon us as we ran. The teams were oxen, and the Indians were gaining upon us, when one of men in his excitement dropped his gun. The savages came up to it and picked it up. All stopped to examine it, and the men in the wagons whipped the oxen into a run. This delay enabled us to elude them.

"As we passed the house of Ole Sampson, Mrs. Sampson was crying at the door for help. Her three children were with her. We told her to go into the bush and hide, for we could not help her. We ran into a ravine and hid in the grass. After the Indians had hunted some time for us, they came along the side of the ravine, and called to us in good English, saying, 'Come out, boys; what are you afraid of? We don't want to hurt you.' After they left us we crawled out and made our way to the fort, where we arrived at about 4 o'clock P. M. My family had gone there before me. Mrs. Sampson did not go to the bush, but hid in the wagon from which they had recently come from Waseca county. It was what we call a prairie schooner, covered with cloth, a genuine emigrant wagon. They took her babe from her, and throwing it down upon the grass, put hay under the wagon, set fire to it and went away. Mrs. Sampson got out of the wagon, badly burned, and taking her infant from the ground made he w y to the fort. Two of her children were burned to death in the wagon. Mr. Sampson had been previously killed about eighty rods from the house.

In the neighborhood of La Croix creek, or Birch Coolie, Peter Pereau, Frederick Closen, ——— Pignar, Andrew Bahlke, Henry Keartner, old Mr. Closen and Mrs. William Vitt, and several others were killed. Mrs. Maria Frorip, an aged German woman, was wounded four different times with small shot, but escaped to the fort. The wife of Henry Keartner also escaped and reached the fort. The wife and child of a Mr. Cardenelle were taken prisoners, as were also the wife and child of Frederick Closen.

William Vitt came into Fort Ridgely, but not until he had, with his own hands, buried his murdered wife and also a Mr. Piguar.

A flourishing German settlement had sprung up near Patterson's Rapids, on the Sacred Heart, twelve miles below Yellow Medicine.

Word came to this neighborhood about sundown of the 18th, that the Indians were murdering the whites. This news was brought to them by two men who had started from the Lower Agency, and had seen the lifeless and mutilated remains of the murdered victims lying upon the road and in their plundered dwellings towards Beaver Creek. The whole neighborhood, with the exception of one family, that of Mr. Schwandt, soon assembled at the house of Paul Kitzman, with their oxen and wagons, and prepared to start for Fort Ridgely.

A messenger was sent to the house of Schwandt but the Indian rifle and the tomahawk had done their fearful work. Of all that family but two survived; one a boy, a witness of the awful scene of butchery, and he then on his way, covered with blood, towards Fort Ridgely. The other, a young girl of about seventeen years of age, then residing at Redwood, who was captured as previously stated.

This boy saw his sister, a young married woman, ripped open, while alive, and her unborn babe taken, yet struggling, from her person and nailed to a tree before the eyes of the dying mother.

This party started in the evening to make their escape, going so as to avoid the settlements and the traveled roads, striking across the country toward the head of Beaver creek.

They traveled this way all night, and in the morning changed their course towards Fort Ridgely. They continued in this direction until the sun was some two hours high, when they were met by eight Sioux Indians, who told them that the murders were committed by Chippewas, and that they had come over to protect them and punish the murderers; and thus induced them to turn back toward their homes. One of the savages spoke English well. He was acquainted with some of the company, having often hunted with Paul Kitzman. He kissed Kitzman, telling him he was a good man; and they shook hands with all of the party. The simple hearted Germans believed them, gave them food, distributed money among them, and, gratefully receiving their assurances of friendship and protection, turned back.

They traveled on toward their deserted homes till noon, when they again halted, and gave their pretended protectors food. The Indians went away by themselves to eat. The suspicions of the fugitives were now somewhat aroused, but they felt that they were, to a great extent, in the power of the wretches. They soon came back, and ordered them to go on, taking their position on each side of the train. Soon after they went on and disappeared. The train kept on toward home; and when within a few rods of a house, where they thought they could defend themselves, as they had guns with them, they were suddenly surrounded by fourteen Indians, who instantly fired upon them, killing eight (all but three of the men) at the first discharge. At the next fire they killed two of the remaining men and six of the women, leaving only one man, Frederick Kreiger, alive. His wife was also, as yet, unhurt. They soon dispatched Kreiger, and, at the same time, began beating out the brains of the screaming children with the butts of their guns. Mrs. Kreiger was standing in the wagon, and, when her husband fell, attempted to spring from it to the ground, but was shot from behind, and fell back in the wagon-box, although not dead, or entirely unconscious. She was roughly seized and dragged to the ground, and the teams were driven off. She now became insensible. A few of the children, during this awful scene, escaped to the timber near by; and a few also, maimed and mangled by these horrible monsters, and left for dead, survived, and, after enduring incredible hardships, got to Fort Ridgely. Mrs. Zable, and five children, were horribly mangled, and almost naked, entered the fort eleven days afterward. Mrs. Kreiger also survived her unheard-of sufferings.

Some forty odd bodies were afterward found and buried on that fatal field of slaughter. Thus perished, by the hands of these terrible scourges of the border, almost an entire neighborhood. Quiet, sober, and industrious, they had come hither from the vine-clad hills of their fatherland, by the green shores and gliding waters of the enchanting Rhine, and had built for themselves homes, where they had fondly hoped, in peace and quiet, to spend yet long years, under the fair, blue sky, and in the sunny clime of Minnesota, when suddenly, and in one short hour, by the hand of the savage, they were doomed to one common annihilation.

During all the fatal 18th of August, the people at the Upper Agency pursued their usual avocations. As night approached, however, an unusual gathering of Indians was observed on the hill just west of the Agency, and between it and the house of John Other Day. Judge Givens and Charles Crawford, then acting as interpreters in the absence of Freniere, went out to them, and sought to learn why they were there in council, but could get no satisfactory reply. Soon after this, Other Day came to them with the news of the outbreak below, as did also Joseph Laframbois, a half-breed Sioux. The families there were soon all gathered together in the warehouse and dwelling of the agent, who resided in the same building, and with the guns they had, prepared themselves as best they could, and awaited the attack, determined to sell their lives as dearly as possible. There were gathered here sixty-two persons, men, women, and children.

Other Day, and several other Indians, who came to them, told them they would stand by them to the last. These men visited the council outside, several times during the night; but when they were most needed, one only, the noble and heroic Other Day, remained faithful. All the others disappeared, one after another, during the night. About one or two o'clock in the morning, Stewart B. Garvie, connected with the traders' store, known as Myrick's, came to the warehouse, and was admitted, badly wounded, a charge of buckshot having entered his bowels. Garvie was standing in the door or his store when he was fired upon and wounded. He ran up stairs, and jumping from the window into the garden, crawled away, and reached the Agency without further molestation. At about this time Joseph Laframbois went to the store of Daily & Pratt, and awakened the two men in charge there, Duncan R. Kennedy and J. D. Boardman, and told them to flee for their lives. They hastily dressed and left the store, but had not gone ten rods when they saw in the path before them three Indians. They stepped down from the path, which ran along the edge of a rise in the ground of some feet, and crouching in the grass, the Indians passed within eight feet of them. Kennedy went on toward Fort Ridgely, determined to reach that post if possible, and Boardman went to the warehouse. At the store of William H. Forbes, Constans, book-keeper, a native of France, was killed. At the store of Patoile, Peter Patoile, clerk, and a nephew of the proprietor, was shot just outside the store, the ball entering at the back and coming out near the nipple, passing through his lungs. An Indian came to him after he fell, turned him over, and saying, "He is dead," left him.

They then turned their attention to the stores. The clerks in the store of Louis Robert had effected their escape, so that there were now no white men left, and when they had become absorbed in the work of plunder, Patoile crawled off into the bushes on the banks of the Yellow Medicine, and secreted himself. Here he remained all day. After dark he got up and started for a place of safety; ascending the bluff, out of the Yellow Medicine bottom, he dragged himself a mile and a half further, to the Minnesota, at the mouth of the Yellow Medicine. Wading the Minnesota, he entered the house of Louis Labelle, on the opposite side, at the ford. It was deserted. Finding a bed in the house he lay down upon it and was soon fast asleep, and did not awake until morning. Joseph Laframbois and Narces Freniere, and an Indian, Makacago, entered the house, and finding him there, awoke him, telling him there were hostile Indians about; that he must hide. They gave him a blanket to disguise himself, and going with him to the ravine, concealed him in the grass and left him, promising to return, as soon as it was safe to do so, to bring him food, and guide him away to the prairie. He lay in this ravine until toward night, when his friends, true to their promise, returned, bringing some crackers, tripe, and onions. They went with him some distance out on the prairie, and enjoined upon him not to attempt to go to Fort Ridgely, and giving him the best directions they could as to the course he should take, shook hands with him and left him. Their names should be inscribed upon tablets more enduring than brass. That night he slept on the prairie, and the next day resumed his wanderings, over an unknown region, without an inhabitant. After wandering for days without food or drink, his little stock of crackers and tripe being exhausted, he came to a deserted house, which he did not know. Here he remained all night, and obtained two raw potatoes and three ears of green corn. These he ate raw. It was all the food he had for eight days. Wandering, and unknowing whither to go, on the twelfth day out from Labelle's house, he heard the barking of dogs, and creeping nearer to them, still fearing there might be Indians about, he was overjoyed at seeing white men. Soon making himself and his condition known, he was taken and kindly cared for by these men, who had some days before deserted their farms, and had now returned to look after their crops and cattle. He now learned for the first time where he was. He had struck a settlement far up the Sauk Valley, some forty miles above St. Cloud. He must have wandered, in these twelve days of suffering, not less than two hundred miles, including deviations from a direct course.

He was taken by these men, in a wagon, to St. Cloud, where his wound was dressed for the first time. From St. Cloud the stage took him to St. Anthony, where he took the cars to St. Paul. A case of equal suffering and equal endurance is scarcely to be found on record. With a bullet wound through the lungs, he walked twelve days, not over a smooth and easy road, but across a trackless prairie, covered with rank grass, wading sloughs and streams on his way, almost without food, and for days without water, before he saw the face of a man; and traveled by wagon, stage, and cars, over one hundred miles.

His recovery was rapid, and he soon enlisted in the First Regiment Minnesota Mounted Rangers under General Sibley, in the expedition against the Sioux. Patoile was in the battles on the Missouri in the summer of 1863, where his company, that of Captain Joseph Anderson, is mentioned as having fought with great bravery.

We now return to the warehouse at Yellow Medicine, which we left to follow the strange fortunes of young Patoile. Matters began to wear a serious aspect, when Garvie came to them mortally wounded. Other Day was constantly on the watch outside, and reported the progress of affairs to those within. Toward daylight every friendly Indian had deserted save Other Day; the yells of the savages came distinctly to their ears from the trading-post, half a mile distant. They were absorbed in the work of plunder. The chances of escape were sadly against them, yet they decided to make the attempt. Other Day knew every foot of the country over which they must pass, and would be their guide.

The wagons were driven to the door. A bed was placed in one of them; Garvie was laid upon it. The women and children provided a few loaves of bread, and just as day dawned, the cortege started on its perilous way. This party consisted of the family of Major Galbraith, wife and three children; Nelson Givens, wife, and wife's mother, and three children; Noah Sinks, wife, and two children; Henry Eschelle, wife, and five children; John

Fadden, wife, and three children; Mr. German and wife; Frederick Patoile, wife, and two children; Mrs. Jane K. Murch, Miss Mary Charles, Miss Lizzie Sawyer, Miss Mary Daly, Miss Mary Hays, Mrs. Eleanor Warner, Mrs. John Other Day and one child, Mrs. Haurahan, N. A. Miller, Edward Cramsie, Z. Hawkins, Oscar Canfil, Mr. Hill, an artist from St. Paul, J. D. Boardman, Parker Pierce, Dr. J. L. Wakefield, and several others.

They crossed the Minnesota at Labelle's farm, and soon turned into the timber on the Hawk river, crossed that stream at some distance above its mouth, and ascended from the narrow valley through which it runs to the open prairie beyond, and followed down the Minnesota, keeping back on the prairie as far as the farm of Major J. R. Brown, eight miles below the Yellow Medicine. Mr. Fadden and Other Day visited the house and found it deserted. A consultation then took place, for the purpose of deciding where they should go. Some of them wished to go to Fort Ridgely; others to some town away from the frontier. Other Day told them that if they attempted to go to the fort they would all be killed, as the Indians would either be lying in ambush on that road for them, or would follow them, believing they would attempt to go there. His counsel prevailed, and they turned to the left, across the prairie, in the direction of Kandiyohi Lakes and Glencoe. At night one of the party mounted a horse and rode forward, and found a house about a mile ahead. They hastened forward and reached it in time to escape a furious storm. They were kindly received by the only person about the premises, a man, whose family were away. The next morning, soon after crossing Hawk river, they were joined by Louis Labelle and Gertong, his son-in-law, who remained with them all that day.

On Wednesday morning they left the house of the friendly settler, and that night reached Cedar City, eleven miles from Hutchinson, in the county of McLeod. The inhabitants had deserted the town, and gone to an island, in Cedar Lake, and had erected a rude shelter. From the main land the island was reached through shallow water. Through this water our escaping party drove, guided by one of the citizens of Cedar City, and were cordially welcomed by the people assembled there.

That night it rained, and all were drenched to the skin. Poor Garvie was laid under a rude shed, upon his bed, and all was done for him that man could do; but, in the morning, it was evident that he could go no further, and he was taken to the house of a Mr. Peck, and left. He died there, a day or two afterward. Some of the company, who were so worn out as to be unable to go on beyond Hutchinson, returned to Cedar City and saw that he was decently interred.

On Thursday they went on, by way of Hutchinson and Glencoe, to Carver, and thence to Shakopee and St. Paul. Major Galbraith, in a report to the department, says of this escape:

"Led by the Noble Other Day, they struck out on the naked prairie, literally placing their lives in this faithful creature's hands, and guided by him, and *him alone*. After intense suffering and privation, they reached Shakopee, on Friday, the 22d of August, Other Day never leaving them for an instant; and this Other Day is a *pure, full-blooded Indian*, and was, not long since, one of the wildest and fiercest of his race. Poor, noble fellow! must he, too, be ostracized for the sins of his nation? I commend him to the care of a just God and a liberal government; and not only him, but all others who did likewise."

[Government gave John Other Day a farm in Minnesota. He died several years since universally esteemed by the white people.]

After a knowledge of the designs of the Indians reached the people at the Agency, it was impossible for them to more than merely communicate with the two families at the saw-mill, three miles above, and with the families at the Mission. They were, therefore, reluctantly left to their fate. Early in the evening of Monday, two civilized Indians, Chaskada and Tankanxaceye, went to the house of Dr. Williamson, and warned them of their danger, informing them of what had occurred below; and two half-breeds, Michael and Gabriel Renville, and two Christian Indians, Paul Maxakuta Mani and Simon Anaga Mani, went to the house of Mr. Riggs, the missionary, at Hazelwood, and gave them warning of the danger impending over them.

There were at this place, at that time, the family of the Rev. Stephen R. Riggs, Mr. H. D. Cunningham and family, Mr. D. W. Moore and his wife (who reside in New Jersey), and Jonas Pettijohn and family. Mr. Pettijohn and wife were in charge of the Government school at Red Iron's village, and were now at Mr. Riggs'. They got up a team, and these friendly Indians went with them to an Island in the Minnesota, about three miles from the Mission. Here they remained till Tuesday evening. In the afternoon of Tuesday, Andrew Hunter, a son-in-law of Dr. Williamson, came to him with the information that the family of himself and the Doctor were secreted below. The families at the saw-mill had been informed by the Renvilles, and were with the party of Dr. Williamson. At night they formed a junction on the north side of the Minnesota, and commenced their perilous journey. A thunder-storm effectually obliterated their tracks, so that the savages could not follow them. They started out on the prairie in a northeasterly direction, and, on Wednesday morning, changed their course south-easterly, till they struck the Lac qui Parle road, and then made directly for Fort Ridgely. On Wednesday they were joined by three Germans, who had escaped from Yellow Medicine. On Wednesday night they found themselves in the vicinity of the Upper Agency, and turned to the north again, keeping out on the prairie. On Friday they were in the neighborhood of Beaver Creek, when Dr. Williamson, who, with his wife and sister, had remained behind, overtook them in an ox-cart, having left about twenty-four hours later. They now determined to go to Fort Ridgely. When within a few miles of that post, just at night, they were discovered by two Indians on horseback, who rode along parallel with the train for awhile, and then turned and galloped away, and the fugitives hastened on, momentarily expecting an attack. Near the Three-Mile creek they passed a dead body lying by the road-side. They drove on, passing the creek, and, turning to the left, passed out on to the prairie, and halted a mile and a half from the fort. It was now late at night; they had heard firing, and had seen Indians in the vicinity. They were in doubt what to do. It was at length decided that Andrew Hunter should endeavor to enter the fort and ascertain its condition, and learn, if possible, whether they could get in. Hunter went, and, although it was well-nigh surrounded by savages (they had been besieging it all the afternoon), succeeded in crawling by on his hands and knees. He was told that it would be impossible for so large a party, forty-odd, to get through the Indian lines, and that he had better return and tell them to push on toward the towns below. He left as he had entered, crawling out into the prairie, and reached his friends in safety. It seemed very hard, to be so near a place of fancied security, and obliged to turn away from it, and, weary and hungry, press on. Perils beset their path on every hand; dangers, seen and unseen, were around them; but commending themselves to the care of Him who "suffereth not a sparrow to fall to the ground without His notice," they resumed their weary march. They knew that all around them the work of death and desolation was going on, for the midnight sky, on every side, was red with the lurid flame of burning habitations. They heard from out the gloom the tramp of horses' feet, hurrying past them in the darkness; but they still pressed on. Soon their wearied animals gave out, and again they encamped for the night. With the early dawn they were upon the move, some eight miles from the fort, in the direction of Henderson. Here, four men, the three Germans who had joined them on Wednesday, and a young man named Gilligan, left them, and went off in the direction of New Ulm. The bodies of these unfortunate men were afterward found, scarcely a mile from the place where they had left the guidance of Other Day.

They traveled on in the direction of Henderson, slowly and painfully, for their teams, as well as themselves, were nearly exhausted. That day the savages were beleaguering New Ulm, and the sounds of the conflict were borne faintly to their ears upon the breeze. They had flour with them, but no means of cooking it, and were, consequently, much of the time without proper food. On the afternoon of this day they came to a deserted house, on the road from Fort Ridgley to Henderson, the house of Michael Cummings, where they found a stove, cooking utensils, and a jar of cream. Obtaining some ears of corn from the field or garden near by, and "confiscating" the cream, they prepared themselves the first good meal they had had since leaving their homes so hastily on Monday night.

After refreshing themselves and their worn animals at this place for some hours, their journey was again resumed. That night they slept in a forsaken house on the prairie, and, on Sabbath morning early, were again on their way. As they proceeded, they met some of the settlers returning to their deserted farms, and calling a halt at a deserted house, where they found a large company of people, they concluded to remain until Monday, and recuperate themselves and teams, as well as to observe in a proper manner the holy Sabbath. On Monday morning they separated, part going to Henderson and part to St. Peter, all feeling that the All-seeing Eye that never slumbers or sleeps had watched over them, and that the loving hand of God had guided them safely through the dangers, seen and unseen, that had beset their path.

In the region of the State above the Upper Agency there were but few white inhabitants. Of all those residing on the Chippewa river, near its mouth, we can hear of but one who escaped, and he was wounded, while his comrade, who lived with him was killed. This man joined the party of the missionaries, and got away with them.

On the Yellow Medicine, above the Agency about twelve miles, was a settler named James W. Lindsay. He was unmarried, and another single man was "baching it" with him. They were both killed. Their nearest white neighbors were at the Agency, and they could not be warned of their danger, and knew nothing of it until the savages were upon them.

CHAPTER XXXV.

LEOPOLD WOHLER AND WIFE—LEAVENWORTH—STATEMENT OF MRS. MARY J. COVILL—STORY OF MRS. LAURA WHITON—MILFORD—NICOLLET COUNTY—WEST NEWTON—LAFAYETTE—COURTLAND—SWAN LAKE—PARTIAL LIST OF THE KILLED IN NICOLLET COUNTY—INDIANS SCOURING THE COUNTRY—A SCOUTING PARTY SEEN AT ST. PETER.

The news of the murders below reached Leopold Wohler at the "lime-kiln," three miles below Yellow Medicine, on Monday afternoon. Taking his wife, he crossed the Minnesota river, and went to the house of Major Joseph R. Brown.

Major Brown's family consisted of his wife and nine children; Angus Brown and wife, and Charles Blair, a son-in-law, his wife, and two children. The Major himself was away from home. Including Wohler and his wife, there were then at their house, on the evening of the 18th of August, eighteen persons.

They started, early on the morning of the 19th, to make their escape, with one or two others of their neighbors, Charles Holmes, a single man, residing on the claim above them, being of the party. They were overtaken near Beaver Creek by Indians, and all of the Browns, Mr. Blair and family, and Mrs. Wohler, were captured, and taken at once to Little Crow's village. Messrs. Wohler and Holmes escaped. Major Brown's family were of mixed Indian blood. This fact, probably, accounts for their saving the life of Blair, who was a white man.

Crow told him to go away, as his young men were going to kill him; and he made his escape to Fort Ridgely, being out some five days and nights without food. Mr. Blair was in poor health. The hardships he endured were too much for his already shattered constitution; and although he escaped the tomahawk and scalping-knife, he was soon numbered among the victims of the massacre.

J. H. Ingalls, a Scotchman, who resided in this neighborhood, and his wife, were killed, and their four children were taken into captivity. Two of them, young girls, aged twelve and fourteen years, were rescued at Camp Release, and the two little boys were taken away by Little Crow. Poor little fellows! their fate is still shrouded in mystery. A Mr. Frace, residing near Brown's place, was also killed. His wife and two children were found at Camp Release.

The town of Leavenworth was situated on the Cottonwood, in the county of Brown. Word was brought to some of the settlers in that town, on Monday afternoon, that the Indians had broken out and were killing the inhabitants on the Minnesota. They immediately began to make preparations to leave. Mr. William Carroll started at once for New Ulm alone, to learn the facts of the rumored outbreak. The most of the inhabitants, alarmed by these rumors, fled that night toward New Ulm. Some of them reached that town in safety, and others were waylaid and massacred upon the road.

The family of a Mr. Blum, a worthy German citizen, were all, except a small boy, killed while endeavoring to escape. On Tuesday morning, Mr. Philetus Jackson was killed, while on the way to town with his wife and son. Mrs. Jackson and the young man escaped.

We insert here the statements of two ladies, who escaped from this neighborhood, as they detail very fully the events of several days in that locality. Mrs. Mary J. Covill, wife of George W. Covill, says:

"On Monday, the 18th of August, messengers came to the house of Luther Whiton, from both above and below, with a report of an outbreak of the Indians. My husband was at Mr. Whiton's, stacking grain. He came home about four o'clock P. M., and told me about it, and then went back to Whiton's, about half a mile away, to get a Mr. Riant, who had recently come there from the State of Maine, to take his team and escape. I packed a trunk with clothing, and hid it in the grass, and then went myself to Whiton's, as I was afraid to remain at home. Mr. Riant got up his team, and taking his two trunks—one of them containing over two thousand dollars in gold —took us all with him. There was a family at Mr. Whiton's from Tennessee, and a young child of theirs had died that day. The poor woman took her dead child in her arms, and we all started across the prairie, avoiding the road, for Mankato. We camped that night about three miles from home, on the prairie; and seeing no fires, as of burning buildings, returned to the house of our neighbor, Van Guilder, and found that the settlers had nearly all left. Mr. Van Guilder and family, Edward Allen and wife, Charles Smith and family and Mrs. Carroll, were all we knew of that remained.

"We started on, thinking that we would overtake the Leavenworth party, who had been gone about an hour. We had gone about two and a half miles, when we saw, ahead of us, a team, with two men in the wagon, who drove toward us until they got into a hollow, and then got out and went behind a knoll. We drove quite near them, when Mr. Covill discovered them to be Indians. Riant turned his horses round and fled, when they jumped up out of the grass, whooped, and fired at us. They then jumped into their wagon and followed. Mr. Covill had the only gun in the party that could be used, and kept it pointed at the Indians as we retreated. They fired at us some half-dozen times, but, fortunately, without injuring any one.

"We drove hastily back to the house of Van Guilder, and entered it as quickly as possible, the savages firing upon us all the time. Mr. Van Guilder had just started away, with his family, as we came back, and returned to the house with us. A shot from the Indians broke the arm of his mother, an aged lady, soon after we got into the house, as she was passing a window. In our haste, we had not stopped to hitch the horses, and they soon started off, and the Indians followed. As they were going over a hill near the house, they shook a white cloth at us, and, whooping, disappeared. There were in this company—after Riant was gone, who left us, and hid in a slough—fifteen persons. We immediately started out on the prairie again. We had now only the ox-team of Van Guilder, and the most of us were compelled to walk. His mother, some small children, and some trunks, made a wagon-load. The dead child, which the mother had brought back to the house with her, was left lying upon the table. It was afterward found, *with its head severed from its body* by the fiends. S. L. Wait and Luther Whiton, who had concealed themselves in the grass when they saw the Indians coming, joined us. Mrs. A. B. Hough and infant child were with the family of Van Guilder. These made our number up to fifteen. We traveled across the prairie all day without seeing any Indians, and, at night, camped on the Little Cottonwood. We waded the stream, and made our camp on the opposite side, in the tall grass and reeds. We reached this spot on Tuesday night, and remained there till Friday afternoon, without food, save a little raw flour, which we did not dare to cook, for fear the smoke would reveal our whereabouts to the savages, when a company from New Ulm rescued us.

"On Wednesday night, after dark, Covill and Wait started for New Ulm, to get a party to come out to our aid, saying they would be back the next day. That night, and nearly all the next day, it rained. At about daylight the next day, when just across the Big Cottonwood, five miles from New Ulm, they heard an Indian whooping in their rear, and turned aside into some hazel-bushes, where they lay all day. At the place where they crossed the river they found a fish-rack in the water, and in it caught a fish. Part of this they ate raw that day. It was now Thursday, and they had eaten nothing since Monday noon. They started again at dark for New Ulm. When near the graveyard, two miles from the town, an Indian, with grass tied about his head, arose from the ground and attempted to head them off. They succeeded in evading him, and got in about ten o'clock. When about entering the place, they were fired upon by the pickets, which alarmed the town, and when they got in, all was in commotion, to meet an expected attack.

"The next morning, one hundred and fifty men, under Captain Tousley, of Le Sueur, and S. A. Buell, of St. Peter, started to our relief, reaching our place of concealment about two o'clock. They brought us food, of which our famished party eagerly partook. They were accompanied by Dr. A. W. Daniels, of St. Peter, and Dr. Mayo, of Le Sueur. They went on toward Leavenworth, intending to remain there all night, bury the dead, should any be found, the next day, rescue any who might remain alive, and then return. They buried the Blum family of six persons that afternoon, and then concluded to return that night. We reached New Ulm before midnight. Mr. Van Guilder's mother died soon after we got into town from the effects of her wound and the exposure to which she had been subjected.

"At about the same time that we returned to the house of Mr. Van Guilder, on Tuesday, Charles Smith and family, Edward Allen and wife, and Mrs. Carroll had left it, and reached New Ulm without seeing Indians, about half an hour before the place was attacked. The same day, William Carroll, with a party of men, came to the house for us, found Mr. Riant, who was concealed in a slough, and started back toward New Ulm. But few of them reached the town alive."

An account of the adventures of this company, and its fate, will be found elsewhere, in the statement of Ralph Thomas, one of the party.

On Monday, the 18th of August, two women, Mrs. Harrington and Mrs. Hill, residing on the Cottonwood, below Leavenworth, heard of the outbreak, and prevailed upon a Mr. Henshaw, a single man, living near them, to harness up his team and take them away, as their husbands were away from home. Mrs. Harrington had two children; Mrs. Hill none. They had gone but a short distance when they were overtaken by Indians. Mr. Henshaw was killed, and Mrs. Harrington was badly wounded, the ball passing through her shoulder. She had just sprung to the ground with her youngest child in her arms; one of its arms was thrown over her shoulder, and the ball passed through its little hand, lacerating it dreadfully. The Indians were intent upon securing the team, and the women were not followed, and escaped. Securing the horses, they drove away in an opposite direction.

Mrs. Harrington soon became faint from the loss of blood; and Mrs. Hill, concealing her near a slough, took the eldest child and started for New Ulm. Before reaching that place she met John Jackson and William Carroll, who resided on the Cottonwood, above them; and, telling them what had happened, they put her on one of their horses and turned back with her to the town.

On the next day, Tuesday, Mr. Jackson was one of the party with Carroll, heretofore mentioned, that went out to Leavenworth, and visited the house of Van Guilder, in search of their families. When that party turned back to New Ulm, Jackson did not go with them, but went to his own house to look for his wife, who had already left. He visited the houses of most of his neighbors, and finding no one, started back alone. When near the house of Mr. Hill, between Leavenworth and New Ulm, on the river, he saw what he supposed were white men at the house, but when within a few rods of them, discovered they were Indians. The moment he made this discovery he turned to flee to the woods near by. They fired upon him, and gave chase, but he outran them, and reached the timber unharmed. Here he remained concealed until late at night, when he made his way back to town, where he found his wife, who, with others of their neighbors, had fled on the first alarm, and reached the village in safety. Mrs. Laura Whiton, widow of Elijah Whiton, of Leavenworth, Brown county, makes the following statement:

"We had resided on our claim, at Leavenworth, a little over four years. There were in our family, on the 18th of August, 1862, four persons—Mr. Whiton, myself, and two children—a son of sixteen years, and a daughter nine years of age. On Monday evening, the 18th of August, a neighbor, Mr. Jackson, and his son, a young boy, who resided three miles from our place, came to our house in search of their horses, and told us that the Indians had murdered a family on the Minnesota river, and went away. We saw no one, and heard nothing more until Thursday afternoon following, about 4 o'clock, when about a dozen Indians were seen coming from the direction of the house of a neighbor named Heydrick, whom they were chasing. Heydrick jumped off a bridge across a ravine, and, running down the ravine, concealed himself under a log, where he remained until 8 o'clock, when he came out, and made his escape into New Ulm.

"The savages had already slain all his family, consisting of his wife and two children. Mr. Whiton, who was at work near the door at the time, came into the house, but even then did not believe there was any thing serious, supposing Heydrick was unnecessarily frightened. But when he saw them leveling their guns at him, he came to the conclusion that we had better leave. He loaded his double-barreled gun, and we all started for the timber. After reaching the woods, Mr. Whiton left us to go to the house of his brother, Luther, a single man, to see what had become of him, telling us to remain where we were until he came back. We never saw him again. After he left us, not daring to remain where we were, we forded the river (Cottonwood), and hid in the timber, on the opposite side, where we remained until about 8 o'clock, when we started for New Ulm.

"While we lay concealed in the woods, we heard the Indians driving up our oxen, and yoking them up. They hitched them to our wagon, loaded it up with our trunks, bedding, etc., and drove away. we went out on the prairie, and walked all night and all next day, arriving at New Ulm at about dark on Friday, the 22d. About midnight, on Thursday night, as we were fleeing along the road, we passed the bodies of the family of our neighbor, Blum, lying dead by the road-side. They had started to make their escape to town, but were overtaken by the savages upon the road, and all but a little boy most brutally murdered.

"Mr. Whiton returned home, from his visit to the house of his brother, which he found deserted, and found that our house had already been plundered. He then went to the woods to search for us. He remained in the timber, prosecuting his search, until Saturday, without food; and, failing to find us, he came to the conclusion that we were either dead or in captivity, and then himself started for New Ulm. On Saturday night, when traveling across the prairie, he came suddenly upon a camp of Indians, but they did not see him, and he beat as hasty a retreat as possible from their vicinity.

"When near the Lone Cottonwood Tree, on Sunday morning, he fell in with William J. Duly, who had made his escape from Lake Shetek. They traveled along together till they came to the house of Mr. Henry Thomas, six miles from our farm, in the town of Milford. This house had evidently been deserted by the family in great haste, for the table was spread for a meal, and the food remained untouched upon it. Here they sat down to eat, neither of them having had any food for a long time. While seated at the table, two Indians came to the house; and, as Mr. Whiton arose and stepped to the stove for some water, they came into the door, one of them saying, '*Da mea tepee.*' [This is my house.] There was no way of escape, and Mr. Whiton, thinking to propitiate him, said 'Come in.' Mr. Duly was sitting partly behind the door, and was, probably, unobserved. The savage made no answer, but instantly raised his gun, and shot him through the heart. they then both went into the corn. Duly was unarmed; and, when Mr. Whiton was killed, took his gun and ran out of the house, and concealed himself in the bushes near by.

"While lying here he could hear the Indians yelling and firing their guns in close proximity to his place of concealment. After awhile he ventured out. Being too much exhausted to carry it, he threw away the gun, and that night arrived at New Ulm, without again encountering Indians."

We now return to Mrs. Harrington, whom, the reader will remember, we left badly wounded, concealed near a slough. We regret our inability to obtain a full narrative of her wanderings during the eight succeeding days and nights she spent alone upon the prairie, carrying her wounded child. We can only state in general terms, that after wandering for eight weary days and nights, without food or shelter, unknowing whither, early on the morning of Tuesday, the 26th, before daylight, she found herself at Crisp's farm, midway between New Ulm and Mankato. As she approached the pickets she mistook them for Indians, and, when hailed by them, was so frightened as not to recognize the English language, and intent only on saving her life, told them she was a Sioux. Two guns were instantly leveled at her, but, providentially, both missed fire, when an exclamation from her led them to think she was *white*, and a woman, and they went out to her. She was taken into camp and all done for her by Judge Flandrau and his men that could be done. They took her to Mankato, and soon after she was joined by her husband, who was below at the time of the outbreak, and also found the child which Mrs. Hill took with her to New Ulm.

Six miles from New Ulm there lived, on the Cottonwood, in the county of Brown, a German family of the name of Heyers, consisting of the father, mother and two sons, both young men. A burial party that went out from New Ulm on Friday, the 22d, found them all murdered, and buried them near where they were killed.

The town of Milford, Brown county, adjoining New Ulm on the west and contiguous to the reservation, was a farming community, composed entirely of Germans. A quiet, sober, industrious, and enterprising class of emigrants had here made their homes, and the prairie wilderness around them began to "bud and blossom like the rose." Industry and thrift had brought their sure reward, and peace, contentment and happiness filled the hearts of this simple-hearted people. The noble and classic Rhine and the vine-clad hills of Fatherland were almost forgotten, or, if not forgotten, were now remembered without regret, in these fair prairie homes, beneath the glowing and genial sky of Minnesota.

When the sun arose on the morning of the 18th of August, 1862, it looked down upon this scene in all its glowing beauty; but its declining rays fell upon a field of carnage and horror too fearful to describe. The council at Rice Creek, on Sunday night, had decided upon the details of the work of death, and the warriors of the lower bands were early on the trail, thirsting for blood. Early in the forenoon of Monday they appeared in large numbers in this neighborhood, and the work of slaughter began. The first house visited was that of Wilson Massipost, a prominent and influential citizen, a widower. Mr. Massipost had two daughters, intelligent and accomplished. These the savages murdered most brutally. The head of one of them was afterward found, severed from the body, attached to a fish hook, and hung upon a nail. His son, a young man of twenty-four years, was also killed. Mr. Massipost and a son of eight years escaped to New Ulm. The house of Anton Hanley was likewise visited. Mr. Hanley was absent. The children, four in number, were beaten with tomahawks on the head and person, inflicting fearful wounds. Two of them were killed outright, and one, an infant, recovered; the other, a young boy, was taken by the parents, at night, to New Ulm, thence to St. Paul, where he died of his wounds. After killing these children, they proceeded to the field near by, where Mrs. Hanley, her father, Anton Mesmer, his wife, son Joseph, and daughter, were at work harvesting wheat. All these they instantly shot, except Mrs. Hanley, who escaped to the woods and secreted herself till night, when, her husband coming home, they took their two wounded children and made their escape. At the house of Agrenatz Hanley all the children were killed. The parents escaped.

Bastian Mey, wife, and two children were massacred in their house, and three children were terribly mutilated, who afterward recovered.

Adolph Shilling and his daughter were killed; his son badly wounded, escaped with his mother. Two families, those of a Mr. Zeller and a Mr. Zettle, were completely annihilated; not a soul was left to tell the tale of their sudden destruction. Jacob Keck, Max Fink, and a Mr. Belzer were also victims of savage barbarity at this place. After killing the inhabitants, they plundered and sacked the houses, destroying all the property they could not carry away, driving away all the horses and cattle, and when night closed over the dreadful scene, desolation and death reigned supreme.

There resided, on the Big Cottonwood, between New Ulm and Lake Shetek, a German, named Charles Zierke, familiarly known throughout all that region as "Dutch Charley." On the same road resided an old gentleman, and his son and daughter, named Brown. These adventurous pioneers lived many miles from any other human habitation, and kept houses of entertainment on that lonely road. This last-named house was known as "Brown's place." It is not known to us when the savages came to those isolated dwellings. We only know that the mutilated bodies of all three of the Brown family were found, and buried, some miles from their house. Zierke and his family made their escape toward New Ulm, and, when near the town, were pursued and overtaken by the Indians on the prairie. By sharp running, Zierke escaped to the town, but his wife and children, together with his team, were taken by them. Returning afterward with a party of men, the savages abandoned the captured team, woman, and children, and they were recovered and all taken into New Ulm in safety.

The frontier of Nicollet county contiguous to the reservation was not generally visited by the savages until Tuesday, the 19th, and the succeeding days of that week. The people had, generally in the meantime, sought safety in flight, and were principally in the town of St. Peter. A few, however, remained at their homes, in isolated localities, where the news of the awful scenes enacting around them did not reach them; or, who having removed their families to places of safety, returned to look after their property. These generally fell victims to the rifle and tomahawk of the savages. The destruction of life in this county, was, however, trifling, compared with her sister counties of Brown and Renville; but the loss of property was immense. The entire west half of the county was, of necessity, abandoned and completely desolated. The ripened grain crop was much of it uncut, and wasted in the field, while horses and cattle and sheep and hogs roamed unrestrained at will over the unharvested fields. And, to render the ruin complete the savage hordes swept over this portion of the county, gathering up horses and cattle shooting swine and sheep, and all other stock that they could not catch; finishing the work of ruin by applying the torch to the stacks of hay and grain, and in some instances to the dwellings of the settlers.

William Mills kept a public house in the town of West Newton, four miles from Fort Ridgely, on the St. Peter road. Mr. Mills heard of the outbreak of the Sioux on Monday, and at once took the necessary steps to secure the safety of his family, by sending them across the prairie to a secluded spot, at a slough some three miles from the house. Leaving a span of horses and a wagon with them, he instructed them, if it should seem necessary to their safety, to drive as rapidly as possible to Henderson. He then went to Fort Ridgely to possess himself, if possible, of the exact state of affairs. At night he visited his house, to obtain some articles of clothing for his family, and carried them out to their place of concealment, and went again to the fort, where he remained until Tuesday morning, when he started out to his family, thinking he would send them to Henderson, and return and assist in the defense of that post. Soon after leaving the fort he met Lieutenant T. J. Sheehan and his company, on their way back to that post. Sheehan roughly demanded of him where he was going. He replied he was going to send his family to a place of safety, and return. The lieutenant, with an oath, wrested from him his gun, the only weapon of defense he had, thus leaving him defenseless. Left thus unarmed and powerless, he took his family and hastened to Henderson, arriving there that day in safety.

A few Indians were seen in the neighborhood of West Newton on Monday afternoon on horseback, but at a distance on the prairie. The most of the inhabitants fled to the fort on that day; a few remained at their homes and some fled to St. Peter and Henderson. The town of Lafayette was, in like manner, deserted on Monday and Monday night, the inhabitants chiefly making for St. Peter. Courtland township, lying near New Ulm, caught the contagion, and her people too fled—the women and children going to St. Peter, while many of her brave sons rushed to the defense of New Ulm, and in that terrible siege bore a conspicuous and honorable part.

As the cortege of panic stricken fugitives poured along the various roads leading to the towns below, on Monday night and Tuesday, indescribable terror seized the inhabitants; and the rapidly accumulating human tide, gathering force and numbers as it moved across the prairie, rolled an overwhelming flood into the towns along the river.

The entire county of Nicollet, outside of St. Peter, was depopulated, and their crops and herds left by the inhabitants to destruction.

On the arrival of a force of mounted men, under Captains Anson Northrup, of Minneapolis, and R. H. Chittenden, of the First Wisconsin Cavalry, at Henderson, on the way to Fort Ridgely, they met Charles Nelson, and, on consultation, decided to go to St. Peter, where they were to report to Colonel Sibley, by way of Norwegian Grove. Securing the services of Nelson, John Fadden, and one or two others, familiar to the country, they set out for the Grove.

Captain Chittenden, in a letter to the "New Haven Palladium," written soon after, says:

"The prairie was magnificent, but quite deserted. Sometimes a dog stared at us as we passed; but even the brutes seemed conscious of a terrible calamity. At 2 o'clock we reached the Grove, which surrounded a lake. The farms were in a fine state of cultivation; and, strange to say, although the houses were in ruins, the grain stacks were untouched. Reapers stood in the field as the men had left them. Cows wandered over the prairies in search of their masters. Nelson led the way to the spot where he had been overtaken in attempting to escape with his wife and children. We found his wagon; the ground was strewn with articles of apparel, his wife's bonnet, boxes, yarn, in fact everything they had hastily gathered up. But the wife and boys were gone. Her he had seen them murder, but the children had run into the corn-field. He had also secreted a woman and child und r a hay-stack. We went and turned it over; they were gone. I then so arranged the troops that, by marching abreast, we made a thorough search of the corn-field. No clue to his boys could be found. Passing the still burning embers of his neighbor's dwellings, we came to Nelson's own, the only one still standing. * * * The heart-broken man closed the gate, and turned away without a tear; then simply asked Sergeant Thompson when he thought it would be safe to return. I must confess that, accustomed as I am to scenes of horror, the tears would come."

The troops, taking Nelson with them, proceeded to St. Peter, where he found the dead body of his wife, which had been carried there by some of his neighbors, and his children, *alive*. They had fled through the corn, and escaped from their savage pursuers.

Jacob Mauerle had taken his family down to St. Peter, and returned on Friday to his house, in West Newton. He had tied some clothing in a bundle, and started for the fort, when he was shot and scalped, some eighty rods from the house.

The two Applebaum's were evidently fleeing to St. Peter, when overtaken by the Indians and killed.

Felix Smith had escaped to Fort Ridgely, and on Wednesday forenoon went out to his house, some three miles away. The Indians attacked the fort that afternoon, and he was killed in endeavoring to get back into that post.

Small parties of Indians scoured the country between Fort Ridgely, St. Peter, and Henderson, during the first week of the massacre, driving away cattle and burning buildings, within twelve miles of the first-named place. The Swan Lake House was laid in ashes. A scouting party of six savages was seen by General M. B. Stone, upon the bluff, in sight of the town of St. Peter, on Friday, the 22d day of August, the very day they were making their most furious and determined assault upon Fort Ridgely.

This scouting party had, doubtless, been detached from the main force besieging that post, and sent forward, under the delusion that the fort must fall into their hands, to reconnoiter, and report to Little Crow the condition of the place, and the ability of the people to defend themselves. But they failed to take Fort Ridgely, and, on the 22d, their scouts saw a large body of troops, under Colonel Sibley, enter St. Peter.

CHAPTER XXXVI.

BIG STONE LAKE—WHITES KILLED—LAKE SHETEK—NAMES OF SETTLERS—MRS. ALOMINA HURD ESCAPES WITH HER TWO CHILDREN—THE BATTLE OF SPIRIT LAKE—WARFARE IN JACKSON COUNTY—DAKOTA TERRITORY—MURDERS AT SIOUX FALLS—DESTRUCTION OF PROPERTY—KILLING OF AMOS HUGGINS.

At Big Stone Lake, in what is now Big Stone county, were four trading houses, Wm. H. Forbes, Daily, Pratt & Co., and Nathan Myrick. The *habitues* of these Indian trading houses, as usual, were mostly half-breeds, natives of the country. The store of Daily, Pratt & Co. was in charge of Mr. Ryder of St. Paul. On the 21st of August, four of these men at work cutting hay, unsuspicious of danger, were suddenly attacked and all murdered, except Anton Manderfield; while one half-breed, at the store, Baptiste Gubeau, was taken prisoner, and was informed that he would be killed that night. But Gubeau succeeded in escaping from their grasp, and making his way to the lake. His escape was a wonderful feat, bound as he was, as to his hands, pursued by yelling demons determined on his death. But, ahead of all his pursuers, he reached the lake, and dashing into the reeds on the margin, was hid from the sight of his disappointed pursuers. Wading noiselessly into the water, until his head alone was above the water, he remained perfectly still for some time. The water soon loosened the rawhide on his wrists, so that they were easily removed. The Indians sought for him in vain; and as the shades of night gathered around him, he came out of his hiding place, crossed the foot of the lake and struck out for the Upper Mississippi. He finally reached St. Cloud. Here he was mistaken for an Indian spy, and threatened with death, but was finally saved by the interposition of a gentleman who knew him.

The other employes at the lake were all killed except Manderfield, who secreted himself while his comrades were being murdered. Manderfield, in his escape, when near Lac qui Parle, was met by Joseph Laframboise, who had gone thither to obtain his sister Julia, then a captive there. Manderfield received from Laframboise proper directions, and finally reached Fort Ridgely in safety.

Lake Shetek.—This beautiful lake of quiet water, some six miles long and two broad, is situated about seventy miles west of New Ulm, in the county of Murray. Here a little community of some fifty persons were residing far out on our frontier, the nearest settlement being the Big Cottonwood. The families and persons located here were: John Eastlick and wife, Charles Hatch, Phineas B. Hurd and wife, John Wright, Wm. J. Duly and wife, H. W. Smith, Aaron Myers, Mr. Everett and wife, Thomas Ireland and wife, Koch and wife; these with their several families, and six single men, Wm. James, Edgar Bently, John Voight, E. G. Cook, and John F. and Daniel Burns, the latter residing alone on a claim at Walnut Grove, some distance from the lake, constituted the entire population of Lake Shetek settlement, in Murray county.

On the 20th of August some twenty Sioux Indians rode up to the house of Mr. Hurd. Mr. Hurd himself had left home for the Missouri river on the 2d day of June previous. Ten of these Indians entered the house, talked and smoked their pipes while Mrs. Hurd was getting breakfast. Mr. Voight, the work-hand, while waiting for breakfast, took up the babe, as it awoke and cried, and walked with it out in the yard in front of the door. No sooner had he left the house than an Indian took his gun and deliberately shot him dead near the door. Mrs. Hurd was amazed at the infernal deed, as these Indians had always been kindly treated, and often fed at her table. She ran to the fallen man to raise him up and look after the safety of her child. To her utter horror, one of the miscreants intercepted her, telling her to leave at once and go to the settlements across the prairie. She was refused the privilege of dressing her naked children, and was compelled to turn away from her ruined home, to commence her wandering over an almost trackless waste, without food, and almost without raiment, for either herself or little ones.

These Indians proceeded from the house of Mr. Hurd to that of Mr. Andrew Koch, whom they shot, and plundered the house of its contents. Mrs. Koch was compelled to get up the oxen and hitch them to the wagon, and drive them, at the direction of her captors, into the Indian country. In this way she traveled ten days. She was the captive of White Lodge, an old and ugly chief of one of the upper bands. As the course was towards the Missouri river, Mrs. Koch refused to go farther in that direction. The old chief threatened to shoot her if she did not drive on. Making a virtue of necessity she reluctantly obeyed. Soon after she was required to carry the vagabond's gun. Watching her opportunity she destroyed the explosive quality of the cap, and dampened the powder in the tube, leaving the gun to appearance all right. Soon afterward she again refused to go any farther in that direction. Again the old scoundrel threatened her with death. She instantly bared her bosom and dared him to fire. He aimed his gun at her breast and essayed to fire, but the gun refused to take part in the work of death. The superstitious savage, supposing she bore a charmed life, lowered his gun, and asked which way she wished to go. She pointed toward the settlements. In this direction the teams were turned. They reached the neighborhood of the Upper Agency in ten days after leaving Lake Shetek, about the time of the arrival of the troops under Colonel Sibley in the vicinity of Wood Lake and Yellow Medicine. White Lodge did not like the looks of things around Wood Lake, and left, moving off in an opposite direction for greater safety. Mrs. Koch was finally rescued at Camp Release, after wading or swimming the Minnesota river ten times in company with a friendly squaw.

At Lake Shetek, the settlers were soon all gathered at the house of John Wright, prepared for defense. They were, however, induced by the apparently friendly persuasion of the Indians to abandon the house, and move towards the slough for better safety. The Indians commenced firing upon the retreating party. The whites returned the fire as they ran. Mrs. Eastlick was wounded in the heel, Mr. Duly's oldest son and daughter were shot through the shoulder, and Mrs. Ireland's youngest child was shot through the leg, while running to the slough. Mr. Hatch, Mr. Everett, Mr. Eastlick, Mrs. Eastlick, Mrs. Everett, and several children were shot. The Indians now told the women to come out of the slough, and they would not kill them or the children, if they would come out. They *went out to them* with the children, when they shot Mrs. Everett, Mrs. Smith, and Mrs. Ireland dead, and killed some of the children. Mrs. Eastlick was shot and left on the field, supposed to be dead, but she finally escaped, and two of her children, Merton and Johnny. Her interesting narrative will be found in the large work, from which this abridgment is made up. Mrs. Julia A. Wright, and Mrs. Duly, and the two children of Mrs. Wright, and two of the children of Mrs. Duly were taken captive. Some of these were taken by the followers of Little Crow to the Missouri river, and were subsequently ransomed at Fort Pierre, by Major Galpin. All the men except Mr. Eastlick, being only wounded, escaped to the settlements. The brothers Burns remained on their claim, and were not molested. One sneaking Indian coming near them paid the forfeit with his life.

Spirit Lake.—On or about the 25th day of August, 1862, the "Annuity Sioux Indians" made their appearance at Spirit Lake, the scene of the terrible Inkpaduta massacre of 1857. The inhabitants fled in dismay from their homes; and the savages, after plundering the dwellings of the settlers, completed their fiendish work by setting fire to the country.

DAKOTA TERRITORY.—Portions of Dakota Territory were visited by the Sioux in 1862. At Sioux Falls City the following murders were committed by the Sioux Indians on the 25th of August: Mr. Joseph B. and Mr. M. Amidon, father and son, were found dead in a corn-field, near which they had been making hay. The son was shot with both balls and arrows, the father with balls only. Their bodies lay some ten rods apart. On the morning of the 26th, about fifteen Indians, supposed to be Sioux, attacked the camp of soldiers at that place. They were followed, but eluded the vigilant pursuit of our soldiers and escaped. The families, some ten in number, were removed to Yankton, the capital, sixty-five miles distant. This removal took place before the murders at Lake Shetek were known at Sioux Falls City. The mail carrier who carried the news from New Ulm had not yet arrived at Sioux Falls, on his return trip. He had, on his outward trip, found Mrs. Eastlick on the prairie, near Shetek, and carried her to the house of Mr. Brown, on the Cottonwood.

In one week after the murders at the Falls, one-half of the inhabitants of the Missouri slope had fled to Sioux City, Iowa, six miles below the mouth of the Big Sioux.

THE MURDER OF AMOS HUGGINS.—Amos Huggins (in the language of Rev. S. R. Riggs, in his late work, 1880, entitled "Mary and I,") "was the eldest child of Alexander G. Huggins, who had accompanied Dr. Williamson to the Sioux country in 1835. Amos was born in Ohio, and was at this time (1862) over thirty years old. He was married, and two children blessed their home, which for some time before the outbreak had been at Lac qui Parle, near where the town of that name now stands. It was then an Indian village and planting place, the principal man being Wakanmane—Spirit Walker, or Walking Spirit. If the people of the village had been at home Mr. Huggins and his family, which included Miss Julia Laframboise, who was also a teacher in the employ of the Government, would have been safe. But in the absence of Spirit Walker's people three Indian men came—two of them from the Lower Sioux Agency—and killed Mr. Huggins, and took from the house such things as they wanted." pp. 169-170.

This apology for the conduct of Christian Indians towards the missionaries and their assistants, who had labored among them since 1835 up to 1862, a period of twenty-seven years, shows a truly Christian spirit on the part of the Rev. S. R. Riggs: but it is scarcely satisfactory to the general reader that the Christian Indians were entirely innocent of all blame in the great massacre of 1862.

CHAPTER XXXVII.

OCCURRENCES PREVIOUS TO THE ATTACK ON THE TOWN OF NEW ULM—THE ATTACK BY INDIANS—JUDGE FLANDRAU ARRIVES WITH REINFORCEMENTS—EVACUATION OF NEW ULM.

On the 18th of August, the day of the outbreak, a volunteer recruiting party for the Union army went out from New Ulm. Some eight miles west of that place several dead bodies were found on the road. The party turned back toward the town, and, to the surprise of all, were fired upon by Indians in ambush, killing several of their party. Another party leaving New Ulm for the Lower Agency, when seven miles above the town some fifty Indians near the road fired upon them, killing three of these men. This party returned to town. One of these parties had seen, near the Cottonwood, Indians kill a man on a stack of grain, and some others in the field. The people of the surrounding country fled for their lives into the town, leaving, some of them, portions of their families killed at their homes or on the way to some place of safety.

During the 18th and 19th of August the Indians overran the country, burning buildings and driving off the stock from the farms.

The people had no arms fit for use, and were perfectly panic-stricken and helpless. But the news of the outbreak had reached St. Peter, and at about one o'clock of August 19th, T. B. Thompson, James Hughes, Charles Wetherell, Samuel Coffin, Merrick Dickinson, H. Caywood, A. M. Bean, James Parker, Andrew Friend, Henry and Frederick Otto, C. A. Stein, E. G. Covey, Frank Kennedy, Thomas and Griffin Williams, and the Hon. Henry A. Swift, afterwards made Governor of Minnesota, by operation of the organic law, and William G. Hayden, organized themselves into a company, by the election of A. M. Bean, Captain, and Samuel Coffin, Lieutenant, and took up position at New Ulm, in the defense of that beleaguered place. They at once advanced upon the Indians, who were posted behind the houses in the outer portions of the place. By this opportune arrival the savage foe were held in check. These were soon joined by another arrival from St. Peter: L. M. Bordman, J. B. Trogdon, J. K. Moore, Horace Austin (since Governor), P. M. Bean, James Homer, Jacob and Philip Stetzer, William Wilkinson, Lewis Patch, S. A. Buell, and Henry Snyder, all mounted, as well as a few from the surrounding country.

By the time these several parties had arrived, the savages had retired, after burning five buildings on the outskirts of the town. In the first battle several were killed, one Miss Paule of the place, standing on the sidewalk opposite the Dakota House. The enemy's loss is not known.

On the same evening Hon. Charles E. Flandrau, at the head of about one hundred and twenty-five men, volunteers from St. Peter and vicinity, entered the town; and reinforcements continued to arrive from Mankato, Le Sueur, and other points, until Thursday, the 21st, when about three hundred and twenty-five armed men were in New Ulm, under the command of Judge Flandrau. Captain Bierbauer, at the head of one hundred men, from Mankato, arrived and participated in the defense of the place.

Some rude barricades around a few of the houses in the center of the village, fitted up by means of wagons, boxes and waste lumber, partially protected the volunteer soldiery operating now under a chosen leader.

On Saturday, the 22d, the commandant sent across the river seventy-five of his men to dislodge some Indians intent on burning buildings and grain and hay stacks. First Lieutenant William Huey, of Traverse des Sioux, commanded this force. This officer, on reaching the opposite shore, discovered a large body of Indians in advance of him; and in attempting to return was completely intercepted by large bodies of Indians on each side of the river. There was but one way of escape, and that was to retreat to the company of E. St. Julien Cox, known to be approaching from the direction of St. Peter. This force, thus cut off, returned with the command of Captain E. St. Julien Cox; and with this increased force of one hundred and seventy-five, Captain Cox soon after entered the town to the relief of both citizens and soldiers.

The Indians at the siege of New Ulm, at the time of the principal attack before the arrival of Captain Cox, were estimated at about five hun[illegible]

coming from the direction of the Lower Agency. The movement is thus described by Judge Flandrau:

"Their advance upon the sloping prairie in the bright sunlight was a very fine spectacle, and to such inexperienced soldiers as we all were, intensely exciting. When within about one mile of us the mass began to expand like a fan, and increasing in the velocity of its approach, continued this movement until within about double rifle-shot, when it covered our entire front. Then the savages uttered a terrific yell and came down upon us like the wind. I had stationed myself at a point in the rear where communication could be had with me easily, and awaited the first discharge with great anxiety, as it seemed to me that to yield was certain destruction, as the enemies would rush into the town and drive all before them. The yell unsettled the men a little, and just before the rifles began to crack they fell back along the whole line, and committed the error of passing the outer houses without taking possession of them, a mistake which the Indians immediately took advantage of by themselves occupying them in squads of two, three and up to ten. They poured into us a sharp and rapid fire as we fell back, and opened from the houses in every direction. Several of us rode up to the hill, endeavoring to rally the men, and with good effect, as they gave three cheers and sallied out of the various houses they had retreated to, and checked the advance effectually. The firing from both sides then became general, sharp and rapid, and it got to be a regular Indian skirmish, in which every man did his own work after his own fashion. The Indians had now got into the rear of our men, and nearly on all sides of them, and the fire of the enemy was becoming very galling, as they had possession of a large number of buildings."

FIGHT AT THE WIND-MILL.—Rev. B. G. Coffin, of Mankato, George B. Stewart, of Le Sueur, and J. B. Trogdon, of Nicollet, and thirteen others, fought their way to the wind-mill. This they held during the battle, their unerring shots telling fearfully upon the savages, and finally forcing them to retire. At night these brave men set fire to the building, and then retreated within the barricades, in the vicinity of the Dakota House. During the firing from this mill a most determined and [illegible] fight was kept up from the brick [illegible] ere Governor Swift was stationed, [illegible] most fatally upon the foe, and from this point many an Indian fell before the deadly aim of the true men stationed there.

CAPTAIN WILLIAM B. DODD.—When the attack was made upon the place the Indians had succeeded in reaching the Lower Town. The wind was favoring them, as the smoke of burning buildings was carried into the main portion of the town, behind which they were advancing. "Captain William B. Dodd, of St. Peter, seeing the movement from that quarter, supposed the expected reinforcements were in from that direction. He made at once a superhuman effort, almost, to encourage the coming troops to force the Indian line and gain admittance into the town. He had gone about seventy-five yards outside the lines, when the Indians from buildings on either side of the street poured a full volley into the horse and rider. The Captain received three balls near his heart, wheeled his horse, and riding within twenty-five yards of our lines fell from his horse, and was assisted to walk into a house, where in a few moments he died, 'the noblest Roman of them all.' He dictated a short message to his wife, and remarked that he had discharged his duty and was ready to die. No man fought more courageously, or died more nobly. Let his virtues be forever remembered. He was a hero of the truest type!" --St. Peter Statesman.

At the stage of the battle in which Captain Dodd was killed, several others also were either killed or wounded. Captain Saunders, a Baptist minister of Le Sueur, was wounded, with many others. Howell Houghton, an old settler, was killed. The contest was continued until dark, when the enemy began to carry off their dead and wounded. In the morning of the next day (Sunday) a feeble firing was kept up for several hours by the sullen and retiring foe. The battle of New Ulm had been fought, and the whites were masters of the field; but at what a fearful price! The dead and dying and wounded filled the buildings left standing, and this beautiful and enterprising German town, which on Monday morning contained over two hundred buildings, had been laid in ashes, only some twenty-five houses remaining to mark the spot where New Ulm once stood.

On Sunday afternoon, Captain Cox's command, one hundred and fifty volunteers from Nicollet, Sibley and Le Sueur, armed with Austrian rifles, shot-guns and hunting rifles arrived. The Indians retreated, and returned no more to make battle with the forces at New Ulm.

But strange battle field. The Indians deserted it on Sunday, and on Monday the successful defenders also retire from a place they dare not attempt to hold! The town was evacuated. All the women and children, and wounded men, making one hundred and fifty-three wagon loads, while a considerable number composed the company on foot. All these moved with the command of Judge Flandrau towards Mankato.

The loss to our forces in this engagement was ten killed, and about fifty wounded. The loss of the enemy is unknown, but must have been heavy, as ten of their dead were found on the field of battle, which they had been unable to remove.

We might fill volumes with incidents, and miraculous escapes from death, but our limits absolutely forbid their introduction in this abridgement. The reader must consult the larger work for these details. The escape of Governor Swift, Flandrau and Bird, and J. B. Trogdon and D. G. Shellack and others from perilous positions, are among the many exciting incidents of the siege of New Ulm.

Omitting the story of John W. Young, of wonderful interest, we refer briefly to the weightier matters of this sad chapter, and conclude the same by the relation of one short chapter.

THE EXPEDITION TO LEAVENWORTH.

During the siege of New Ulm, two expeditions were sent out from that place toward the settlements on the Big Cottonwood, and although not really forming a part of the operations of a defensive character at that place, are yet so connected with them that we give them here.

On Thursday morning, the 21st of August, a party went out on the road to Leavenworth for the purpose of burying the dead, aiding the wounded and bringing them in, should they find any, and to act as a scouting party. They went out some eight miles, found and buried several bodies, and returned to New Ulm, at night, without seeing any Indians.

On Friday, the 22d, another party of one hundred and forty men, under command of Captain George M. Tousley, started for the purpose of rescuing a party of eleven persons, women and children, who, a refugee informed the commandant, were hiding in a ravine out toward Leavenworth. Accompanying this party were Drs. A. W. Daniels, of St. Peter, and Ayer, of Le Sueur.

On the way out, the cannonading at Fort Ridgely was distinctly heard by them, and then

Dr. Daniels, who had resided among the Sioux several years as a physician to the lower bands, had, for the first time, some conception of the extent and magnitude of the outbreak.

As the main object of the expedition had already been accomplished—*i. e.*, the rescue of the women and children—Dr. Daniels urged a return to New Ulm. The question was submitted to the company, and they decided to go on, and proceeded to within four miles of Leavenworth, the design being to go to that place, remain there all night, bury the dead next day, and return.

It was now nearly night; the cannonading at the fort could still be heard; Indian spies were, undoubtedly, watching them; only about one hundred armed men were left in the town, and from his intimate knowledge of the Indian character, Dr. Daniels was convinced that the safety of their force, as well as New Ulm itself, required their immediate return.

A halt was called, and this view of the case was presented to the men by Drs. Daniels, Ayer, and Mayo. A vote was again taken, and it was decided to return. The return march commenced at about sundown, and at one o'clock A. M. they re-entered the village.

Ralph Thomas, who resided on the Big Cottonwood, in the county of Brown, had gone with many of his neighbors, on Monday, the 18th of August, into New Ulm for safety, while William Carroll and some others residing further up the river, in Leavenworth, had gone to the same place to ascertain whether the rumors they had heard of an uprising among the Sioux were true. Mr. Thomas makes the following statement of the doings of this little party, and its subsequent fate:

"There were eight of us on horseback, and the balance of the party were in three wagons. We had gone about a mile when we met a German going into New Ulm, who said he saw Indians at my place skinning a heifer, and that they drove him off, chasing him with spears. He had come from near Leavenworth. We kept on to my place, near which we met John Thomas and Almon Parker, who had remained the night before in a grove of timber, one and a half miles from my place. About eight o'clock the evening before, they had seen a party of ten or twelve Indians, mounted on ponies, coming toward them, who chased them into the grōve, the savages passing on to the right, leaving them alone. They stated to us that they had seen Indians that morning traveling over the prairie southward. We stopped at my place and fed our horses. While the horses were eating, I called for three or four men to go with me to the nearest houses, to see what had become of the people. We went first to the house of Mr. Mey, where we found him and his family lying around the house, to all appearance dead. We also found here Joseph Emery and a Mr. Heuyer, also apparently dead. We had been here some five minutes viewing the scene, when one of the children, a girl of seven years, rose up from the ground and commenced crying piteously. I took her in my arms, and told the other men to examine the other bodies and see if there were not more of them alive. They found two others, a twin boy and girl about two years old; all the rest were dead.

"We next proceeded to the house of Mr. George Raeser, and found the bodies of himself and wife lying near the house by a stack of grain. We went into the house and found their child, eighteen months old, alive, trying to get water out of the pail. We then went back to my place, and sent John Thomas and Mr. Parker with an ox-team to New Ulm with these children. Mr. Mey's three children were wounded with blows of a tomahawk on the head; the other child was uninjured. We then went on toward Leavenworth, seeing neither Indians nor whites, until we arrived at the house of Mr. Seaman, near which we found an old gentleman named Riant concealed in a slough among the tall grass. He stated to us that a party of whites with him had been chased and fired upon by a party of Indians. It consisted of himself, Luther Whiton, George W. Covill and wife, Mrs. Covill's son, Mrs. Hough and child, Mr. Van Guilder and wife and two children, and Mr. Van Guilder's mother. All these Mr. Riant said had scattered over the prairie. We remained about two hours, hunting for the party, and not finding them, turned back toward New Ulm, taking Mr. Riant with us. We proceeded down opposite my place, where we separated, eleven going down on one side of the Big Cottonwood, to Mr. Tuttle's place, and seven of us proceeded down on the other, or north side of the stream. The design was to meet again at Mr. Tuttle's house, and all go back to New Ulm together; but when we arrived at Tuttle's, they had gone on to town without waiting for us, and we followed. When near Mr. Hibbard's place we met Mr. Jakes going west. He said that he had been within a mile of New Ulm, and saw the other men of our party. He further informed us that he saw grain-stacks and sheds on fire at that distance from the place.

"When we came to the burning stacks we halted to look for Indians. Our comrades were half an hour ahead of us. When they got in sight of the town, one of them, Mr. Hinton, rode up on an elevation, where he could overlook the place, and saw Indians, and the town on fire in several places. He went back and told them that the Indians had attacked the town, and that he did not consider it safe for them to try to get in, and proposed crossing the Cottonwood, and going toward the Mankato road, and entering town on that side. His proposition was opposed by several of the party, who thought him frightened at the sight of half a dozen Indians. They asked him how many he had seen. He said some forty. They came up and looked, but could see but three or four Indians. Mr. Carroll told them they had better go on, and, if opposed, cut their way through. He told Hinton to lead, and they would follow. They passed down the hill, and met with no opposition until they came to a slough, half a mile from the town. Here two Indians, standing on a large stone by the side of the road, leveled their double-barreled guns at Mr. Hinton. He drew his revolver, placed it between his horse's ears, and made for them. The balance of the company followed. The Indians retired to cover without firing a shot, and the company kept on until they had crossed the slough, when the savages, who were lying in ambush, arose from the grass, and firing upon them, killed five of their number, viz.: William Carroll, Almond Loomis, Mr. Lamb, Mr. Riant, and a Norwegian, and chased the balance into the town.

"We came on about half an hour afterward, and passing down the hill, crossed the same slough, and unconscious of danger, approached the fatal spot, when about one hundred and fifty savages sprang up out of the grass and fired upon us, killing five horses and six men. My own horse was shot through the body, close to my leg, killing him instantly. My feet were out of the stirrups in a moment, and I sprang to the ground, striking on my hands and feet. I dropped my gun, jumped up, and ran. An Indian, close behind, discharged the contents of both barrels of a shot-gun at me. The charge tore up the ground at my feet, throwing dirt all around me as I ran. I made my way into town on foot as fast as I could go. No other of our party escaped; all the rest were killed. Reinforcements from St. Peter came to the relief of the place in about half an hour after I got in, and the Indians soon after retired."

CHAPTER XXXVIII.

BATTLE AT LOWER AGENCY FERRY—SIEGE OF FORT RIDGELY—BATTLE OF WEDNESDAY—JACK FRAZER—BATTLE OF FRIDAY—REINFORCEMENTS ARRIVE.

On Monday morning, the 18th of August, 1862, at about 9 o'clock, a messenger arrived at Fort Ridgely, from the Lower Sioux Agency, bringing the startling news that the Indians were massacreing the whites at that place. Captain John S. Marsh, of Company B, Fifth Regiment Minnesota Volunteer Infantry, then in command, immediately dispatched messengers after Lieutenant Sheehan, of Company C, of the same regiment, who had left that post on the morning before, with a detachment of his company, for Fort Ripley, on the Upper Mississipi, and Major T. J. Galbraith, Sioux Agent, who had also left the fort at the same time with fifty men, afterwards known as the Renville Rangers, for Fort Snelling, urging them to return to Fort Ridgely with all possible dispatch, as there were then in the fort only Company B, numbering about seventy-five or eighty men. The gallant captain then took a detachment of forty-six men, and accompanied by Interpreter Quinn, immediately started for the scene of blood, distant twelve miles. They made a very rapid march. When within about four miles of the ferry, opposite the Agency, they met the ferryman, Mr. Martelle, who informed Captain Marsh that the Indians were in considerable force, and were murdering all the people, and advised him to return. He replied that he was there to protect and defend the frontier, and he should do so if it was in his power, and gave the order "Forward!" Between this point and the river they passed nine dead bodies on or near the road. Arriving near the ferry the company was halted, and Corporal Ezekiel Rose was sent forward to examine the ferry, and see if all was right. The captain and interpreter were mounted on mules, the men were on foot, and formed in two ranks in the road, near the ferry-house, a few rods from the banks of the river. The corporal had taken a pail with him to the river, and returned, reporting the ferry all right, bringing with him water for the exhausted and thirsty men.

In the meantime an Indian had made his appearance on the opposite bank, and calling to Quinn, urged them to come across, telling him all was right on that side. The suspicions of the captain were at once aroused, and he ordered the men to remain in their places, and not to move on to the boat until he could ascertain whether the Indians were in ambush in the ravines on the opposite shore. The men were in the act of drinking, when the savage on the opposite side, seeing they were not going to cross at once, fired his gun, as a signal, when instantly there arose out of the grass and brush, all around them, some four or five hundred warriors, who poured a terrific volley upon the devoted band. The aged interpreter fell from his mule, pierced by over twenty balls. The captain's mule fell dead, but he himself sprang to the ground unharmed. Several of the men fell at this first fire. The testimony of the survivors of this sanguinary engagement is, that their brave commander was as cool and collected as if on dress parade. They retreated down the stream about a mile and a half, fighting their way inch by inch, when it was discovered that a body of Indians, taking advantage of the fact that there was a bend in the river, had gone across and gained the bank below them.

The heroic little band was already reduced to about one-half its original number. To cut their way through this large number of Indians was impossible. Their only hope now was to cross the river to the reservation, as there appeared to be no Indians on that shore, retreat down that side and recross at the fort. The river was supposed to be fordable where they were, and, accordingly, Capt. Marsh gave the order to cross. Taking his sword in one hand and his revolver in the other, accompanied by his men, he waded out into the stream. It was very soon ascertained that they must swim, when those who could not do so returned to the shore and hid in the grass as best they could, while those who could, dropped their arms and struck out for the opposite side. Among these latter was Capt. Marsh. When near the opposite shore he was struck by a ball, and immediately sank, but arose again to the surface, and grasped the shoulder of a man at his side, but the garment gave way in his grasp, and he again sank, this time to rise no more.

Thirteen of the men reached the bank in safety, and returned to the fort that night. Those of them who were unable to cross remained in the grass and bushes until night, when they made their way, also, to the fort or settlements. Some of them were badly wounded, and were out two or three days before they got in. Two weeks afterward, Josiah F. Marsh, brother of the captain, with a mounted escort of thirty men—his old neighbors from Fillmore county—made search for his body, but without success. On the day before and the day after this search, as was subsequently ascertained, two hundred Indians were scouting along the river, upon the the very ground over which these thirty men passed, in their fruitless search for the remains of their dead brother and friend. Two weeks later another search was made with boats along the river, and this time the search was successful. His body was discovered a mile and a half below where he was killed, under the roots of a tree standing at the water's edge. His remains were borne by his sorrowing companions to Fort Ridgely, and deposited in the military burial-ground at that place.

This gallant officer demands more than a passing notice. When the Southern rebellion broke out, in 1861, John S. Marsh was residing in Fillmore county, Minnesota. A company was recruited in his neighborhood, designed for the gallant 1st Minnesota, of which he was made first lieutenant. Before, however, this company reached Fort Snelling, the place of rendezvous, the regiment was full, and it was disbanded. The patriotic fire still burned in the soul of young Marsh. Going to La Crosse, he volunteered as a *private* in the 2d Wisconsin regiment, and served some ten months in the ranks. In the following winter his brother, J. F. Marsh, assisted in raising a company in Fillmore county, of which John S. was elected first lieutenant, and he was therefore transferred, by order of the Secretary of War, to his company, and arrived at St. Paul about the 12th of March, 1862. In the meantime, Captain Gere was promoted to major, and on the 24th Lieutenant Marsh was promoted to the captaincy of his company, and ordered to report at Fort Ridgely and take command of that important frontier post. Captain Marsh at once repaired to his post of duty, where he remained in command until the fatal encounter of the 18th terminated both his usefulness and life. He was a brave and accomplished soldier, and a noble man,

"None knew him but to love him,
None named him but to praise."

SIEGE OF FORT RIDGELY.

Foiled in their attack on New Ulm by the timely arrival of reinforcements under Flandrau, the Indians turned their attention toward Fort Ridgely, eighteen miles north-west. On Wednesday, at three o'clock P. M., the 20th of August, they suddenly appeared in great force at that post, and at once commenced a furious assault upon it. The fort is situated on the edge of the prairie, about half a mile from the Minnesota river, a timbered bottom intervening, and a wooded ravine running up out of the bottom around two sides of the fort, and within about twenty rods of the buildings, affording shelter for an enemy on three sides, within easy rifle or musket range.

The first knowledge the garrison had of the presence of the foe was given by a volley from the ravine, which drove in the pickets. The men were instantly formed, by order of Lieutenant Sheehan, in line of battle, on the parade-ground inside the works. Two men, Mark M. Grear, of Company C, and William Goode, of Company B, fell at the first fire of the concealed foe, after the line was formed; the former was instantly killed, the latter badly wounded, both being shot in the head. Robert Baker, a citizen, who had escaped from the massacre at the Lower Agency, was shot through the head and instantly killed, while standing at a window in the barracks, at about the same time. The men soon broke for shelter, and from behind boxes, from windows, from the shelter of the buildings, and from every spot where concealment was possible, watched their opportunities, wasted no ammunition, but poured their shots with deadly effect upon the wily and savage foe whenever he suffered himself to be seen.

The forces in the fort at this time were the remnant of Company B, 5th Regiment M. V., Lieutenant Culver, thirty men; about fifty men of Company C, same regiment, Lieutenant T. J. Sheehan; the Renville Rangers, Lieutenant James Gorman, numbering fifty men, all under command of Lieutenant T. J. Sheehan.

Sergeant John Jones, of the regular army, a brave and skillful man, was stationed at this fort as post-sergeant, in charge of the ordnance, and took immediate command of the artillery, of which there were in the fort six pieces. Three only, however, were used—two six-pounder howitzers and one twenty-four-pounder field-piece. A sufficient number of men had been detailed to work these guns, and at the instant of the first alarm were promptly at their posts. One of the guns was placed in charge of a citizen named J. C. Whipple, an old artillerist, who had seen service in the Mexican war, and in the United States navy, and had made his escape from the massacre at the Lower Agency, and one in charge of Sergeant McGrew, of Company C; the other in charge of Sergeant Jones in person. In this assault there were, probably, not less than five hundred warriors, led by their renowned chief, Little Crow.

So sudden had been the outbreak, and so weak was the garrison that there had been no time to construct any defensive works whatever, or to remove or destroy the wooden structures and hay-stacks, behind which the enemy could take position and shelter. The magazine was situated some twenty rods outside the main works on the open prairie. Men were at once detailed to take the ammunition into the fort. Theirs was the post of danger; but they passed through the leaden storm unscathed.

In the rear of the barracks was a ravine up which the St. Peter road passed. The enemy had possession of this ravine and road, while others were posted in the buildings, at the windows, and in sheltered portions in the sheds in the rear of the officer's quarters. Here they fought from 3 o'clock until dark, the artillery all the while shelling the ravine at short range, and the rifles and muskets of the men dropping the yelling demons like autumn leaves. In the meantime the Indians had got into some of the old out-buildings, and had crawled up behind the hay-stacks, from which they poured heavy volleys into the fort. A few well-directed shells from the howitzers set them on fire, and when night closed over the scene the lurid light of the burning buildings shot up with a fitful glare, and served the purpose of revealing to the wary sentinel the lurking foe should he again appear.

The Indians retired with the closing day, and were seen in large numbers on their ponies, making their way rapidly toward the Agency. The great danger feared by all was, that, under cover of the darkness, the savages might creep up to the buildings and with fire-arrows ignite the dry roofs of the wooden structures. But about midnight the heavens opened and the earth was deluged with rain, effectually preventing the consummation of such a design, if it was intended. As the first great drops fell on the faces upturned to the gathering heavens the glad shout of "Rain! rain! thank God! thank God!" went round the beleaguered garrison. Stout-hearted, strong-armed men breathed free again; and weary, frightened women and children slept once more in comparative safety.

In this engagement there were two men killed, and nine wounded, and all the government mules were stampeded by the Indians. Jack Frazer, an old resident in the Indian country, volunteered as a bearer of dispatches to Governor Ramsey, and availing himself of the darkness and the furious storm, made his way safely out of the fort, and reached St. Peter, where he met Colonel Sibley and his command on their way to the relief of the fort.

Rain continued to fall until nearly night of Thursday, when it ceased, and that night the stars looked down upon the weary, but still wakeful and vigilant watchers in Fort Ridgely. On that night a large quantity of oats, in sacks, stored in the granary near the stable, and a quantity of cordwood piled near the fort, were disposed about the works in such a manner as to afford protection to the men, in case of another attack. The roof of the commissary building was covered with earth, as a protection against fire-arrows. The water in the fort had given out, and as there was neither well nor cistern in the works, the garrison were dependent upon a spring some sixty rods distant in the ravine, for a supply of that indispensable element. Their only resource now was to *dig* for water, which they did at another and less exposed point, and by noon had a supply sufficient for two or three days secured inside the fort.

In the meantime the small arm's ammunition having become nearly exhausted in the battle of Wednesday, the balls were removed from some of the spherical case-shot, and a party of men and women made them up into cartridges, which were greatly needed. Small parties of Indians had been seen about the fort, out of range, during Thursday and Friday forenoon, watching the fort, to report if reinforcements had reached it. At about 1 o'clock in the afternoon of Friday, the 22d, they appeared again in force, their numbers greatly augmented, and commenced a furious and most determined assault. They came apparently from the Lower Agency, passing down the Minnesota bottom, and round into the ravine surrounding the fort. As they passed near the beautiful residence of R. H. Randall, post sutler, they applied the torch and it was soon wrapped in flames. On came the painted savages yelling like so many demons let loose from the bottomless pit; but the brave men in that sore pressed garrison, knowing full well that to be taken alive was certain death to themselves and all within the doomed fort, each man was promptly at his post.

The main attack was directed against that side of the works next to the river, the buildings here being frame structures, and the most vulnerable part of the fort. This side was covered by the stable, granary, and one or two old buildings, besides the sutler's store on the west side, yet standing, as well as the buildings named above. Made bold by their augmented numbers, and the non-arrival of reinforcements to the garrison, the Indians pressed on, seemingly determined to rush at once into the works, but were met as they reached the end of the timber, and swept round up the ravine with such a deadly fire of musketry poured upon them from behind the barracks and the windows of the quarters, and of grape, canister and shell from the guns of the brave and heroic Jones, Whipple, and McGrew, that they beat a hasty retreat to the friendly shelter of the bottom, out of musket range. But the shells continued to scream wildly through the air, and burst around and among them. They soon rallied and took possession of the stable and other out-buildings on the south side of the fort, from which they poured terrific volleys upon the frail wooden buildings on that side, the bullets actually passing through their sides, and through the partitions inside of them. Here Joseph Vanosse, a citizen, was shot through the body by a ball which came through the side of the building. They were soon driven from these buildings by the artillery, which shelled them out, setting the buildings on fire. The sutler's store was in like manner shelled and set on fire. The scene now became grand and terrific. The flames and smoke of the burning buildings, the wild and demoniac yells of the savage besiegers, the roaring of cannon, the screaming of shells as they hurtled through the air, the sharp crack of the rifle, and the unceasing rattle of musketry presented an exhibition never to be forgotten by those who witnessed it.

The Indians retired hastily from the burning buildings, the men in the fort sending a shower of bullets among them as they disappeared over the bluffs toward the bottom. With wild yells they now circled round into the ravine, and from the tall grass, lying on their faces, and from the shelter of the timber, continued the battle till night, their leader, Little Crow, vainly ordering them to charge on the guns. They formed once for that purpose, about sundown, but a shell and round of canister sent into their midst closed the contest, when, with an unearthly yell of rage and disappointment, they left. These shots, as was afterwards ascertained, killed and wounded seventeen of their number. Jones continued to shell the ravine and timber around the fort until after dark, when the firing ceased, and then, as had been done on each night before, since the investment of the fort, the men all went to their several posts to wait and watch for the coming of the wily foe. The night waned slowly; but they must not sleep; their foe is sleepless, and that wide area of dry shingled roof must be closely scanned, and the approaches be vigilantly guarded, by which he may, under cover of the darkness, creep upon them unawares.

Morning broke at last, the sun rode up a clear and cloudless sky, but the foe came not. The day passed away, and no attack; the night again, and then another day; and yet other days and nights of weary, sleepless watching, but neither friend nor foe approached the fort, until about daylight on Wednesday morning, the 27th, when the cry was heard from the look-out on the roof, "There are horsemen coming on the St. Peter road, across the ravine!" Are they friends or foes? was the question on the tongues of all. By their cautious movements they were evidently reconnoitering, and it was yet too dark for those in the fort to be able to tell, at that distance, friends from foes. But as daylight advanced, one hundred and fifty mounted men were seen dashing through the ravine; and amidst the wild hurras of the assembled garrison, Colonel Samuel McPhail, at the head of two companies of citizen-cavalry, rode into the fort. In command of a company of these men were Anson Northrup, from Minneapolis, an old frontiers-man, and R. H. Chittenden, of the First Wisconsin Cavalry. This force had ridden all night, having left St. Peter, forty-five miles distant, at 6 o'clock the night before. From them the garrison learned that heavy reinforcements were on their way to their relief, under Colonel (now Brigadier-General) H. H. Sibley. The worn-out and exhausted garrison could now sleep with a feeling of comparative security. The number of killed and wounded of the enemy is not known, but must have been considerable, as, at the close of each battle, they were seen carrying away their dead and wounded. Our own fallen heroes were buried on the edge of the prairie near the fort; and the injuries of the wounded men were carefully attended to by the skillful and excellent post-surgeon, Dr. Alfred Muller.

We close our account of this protracted siege by a slight tribute on behalf of the sick and wounded in that garrison, to one whose name will ever be mentioned by them with love and respect. The hospitals of Sebastopol had their Florence Nightingale, and over every blood-stained field of the South, in our own struggle for national life, hovered angels of mercy, cheering and soothing the sick and wounded, smoothing the pillows and closing the eyes of our fallen braves. And when, in after years, the brave men who fell, sorely wounded, in the battles of Fort Ridgely, Birch Coolie, and Wood Lake, fighting against the savage hordes who overran the borders of our beautiful State, in August and September, 1862, carrying the flaming torch, the gleaming tomahawk, and bloody scalping-knife to hundreds of peaceful homes, shall tell to their children and children's children the story of the "dark and bloody ground" of Minnesota, and shall exhibit to them the scars those wounds have left; they will tell, with moistened cheek and swelling hearts of the noble, womanly deeds of Mrs. Eliza Muller, the "Florence Nightingale" of Fort Ridgely. [Mrs. Muller several years since died at the asylum at St. Peter.]

SERGEANT JOHN JONES.

We feel that the truth of history will not be fully vindicated should we fail to bestow upon a brave and gallant officer that meed of praise so justly due. The only officer of experience left in the fort by the death of its brave commandant was Sergeant John Jones, of the regular artillery; and it is but just to that gallant officer that we should say that but for the cool courage and discretion of Sergeant Jones, Fort Ridgely would, in the first day's battle have become a funeral pyre for all within its doomed walls. And it gives us more than ordinary pleasure to record the fact, that the services he then rendered the Government, in the defense of the frontier were fully recognized and rewarded with the commission of Captain of the Second Minnesota Battery.

CHAPTER XXXIX.

CAPTAIN WHITCOMB'S ARRIVAL AT ST. PAUL—PASSES THROUGH MEEKER COUNTY—A FORT CONSTRUCTED—ENGAGEMENT WITH INDIANS—ATTACK ON FOREST CITY—CONDITION OF THE COUNTRY—CAPTAIN STROUT AT GLENCOE—ATTACKED NEAR ACTON BY ONE HUNDRED AND FIFTY INDIANS—ATTACK ON HUTCHINSON.

This chapter will be devoted to the upper portion of the state, and the movements of troops for the relief of the frontier, not immediately connected with the main expedition under Colonel Sibley; and to avoid repetition, the prominent incidents of the massacre in this portion of the state will be given in connection with the movements of the troops. We quote from the Adjutant-General's Report:

The 19th day of August the first news of the outbreak at Redwood was received at St. Paul. On the same day a messenger arrived from Meeker county, with news of murders committed in that county by the Indians, and an earnest demand for assistance. The murders were committed at Acton, about twelve miles from Forest City, on Sunday, the 17th day of the month. The circumstances under which these murders were committed are fully detailed in a previous chapter.

George C. Whitcomb, commander of the state forces raised in the county of Meeker, was stationed at Forest City. On the 19th of August, Mr. Whitcomb arrived at St. Paul, and received from the state seventy-five stand of arms and a small quantity of ammunition, for the purpose of enabling the settlers of Meeker county to stand on the defensive, until other assistance could be sent to their aid. With these in his possession, he started on his return, and, on the following day he met Col. Sibley at Shakopee, by whom he was ordered to raise a company of troops and report with command to the Colonel, at Fort Ridgely. On arriving at Hutchinson, in McLeod county, he found the whole country on a general stampede, and small bands of Indians lurking in the border of Meeker county.

Captain Richard Strout was ordered, under date of August 24, to proceed with a company of men to Forest City, in the county of Meeker, for the protection of that locality.

In the meantime Captain Whitcomb arrived at Forest City with the arms furnished him by the state, with the exception of those left by him at Hutchinson. Upon his arrival he speedily enlisted, for temporary service, a company of fifty-three men, twenty-five of whom were mounted, and the remainder were to act as infantry.

Captain Whitcomb, with the mounted portion of his company, made a rapid march into the county of Monongalia, to a point about thirty miles from Forest City, where he found the bodies of two men who had been shot by the Indians, who had mutilated the corpses by cutting their throats and scalping them. In the same vicinity he found the ruins of three houses that had been burned, and the carcasses of a large number of cattle that had been wantonly killed and devoted to destruction.

Owing to rumors received at this point, he proceeded in a north-westerly direction, to the distance of ten miles further, and found on the route the remains of five more of the settlers, all of whom had been shot and scalped, and some of them were otherwise mutilated by having their hands cut off and gashes cut in their faces, done apparently with hatchets.

On the return to camp at Forest City, when within about four miles of Acton, he came to a point on the road where a train of wagons had been attacked on the 23d., He here found two more dead bodies of white men, mutilated in a shocking manner by having their hands cut off, being disemboweled and otherwise disfigured, having knives still remaining in their abdomens, where they had been left by the savages. The road at this place was, for three miles, lined with the carcasses of dead cattle, a great portion of which belonged to the train upon which the attack had been made. On this excursion the company were about four days, during which time they traveled over one hundred miles, and buried the bodies of nine persons who had been murdered.

On the next day after having returned to the camp, being the 28th of the month, the same party made a circuit through the western portion of Meeker county, and buried the bodies of three more men that were found mutilated and disfigured in a similar manner to those previously mentioned. In addition to the other services rendered by the company thus far, they had discovered and removed to the camp several persons found wounded and disabled in the vicinity, and two, who had been very severely wounded, had been sent by them to St. Cloud for the purpose of receiving surgical attention.

The company, in addition to their other labors, were employed in the construction of a stockade fort, to be used if necessary for defensive purposes, and for the protection of those who were not capable of bearing arms. It was formed by inserting the ends of pieces of rough timber into the earth to the depth of three feet, and leaving them from ten to twelve feet above the surface of the ground. In this way an area was inclosed of one hundred and forty feet in length and one hundred and thirty in width. Within the fortification was included one frame dwelling-house and a well of water. At diagonal corners of the inclosure were erected two wings or bastions provided with port-holes, from each of which two sides of the main work could be guarded and raked by the rifles of the company.

Information was received by Captain Whitcomb that a family at Green Lake, in Monongalia county, near the scenes visited by him in his expedition to that county, had made their escape from the Indians, and taken refuge upon an island in the lake. In attempting to rescue this family Captain Whitcomb had a severe encounter with Indians found in ambush near the line of Meeker county, and after much skirmishing and a brisk engagement, which proved very much to the disadvantage of the Indians, they succeeded in effecting their escape to the thickly-timbered region in the rear of their first position. The members of the company were nearly all experienced marksmen, and the Springfield rifles in their hands proved very galling to the enemy. So anxious was the latter to effect his retreat, that he left three of his dead upon the ground. No loss was sustained on the part of our troops, except a flesh-wound in the leg received by one of the company. As it was deemed unadvisable to pursue the Indians into the heavy timber with the small force at command, the detachment fell back to their camp, arriving the same evening.

On the following day, Captain Whitcomb, taking with him twenty men from his company, and twenty citizens who volunteered for the occasion, proceeded on the same route taken the day previous. With the increase in his forces he expected to be able, without much difficulty, to overcome the Indians previously encountered. After proceeding about ten miles from the camp, their further progress was again disputed by the Indians, who had likewise been reinforced since their last encounter. Owing to the great superiority of the enemy's forces, the Captain withdrew his men. They fell gradually back, fighting steadily on the retreat, and were pursued to within four miles of the encampment. In this contest, one Indian is known to have been killed. On the part of the whites one horse and wagon got mired in a slough, and had to be abandoned. No other injury was suffered from the enemy; but two men were wounded by the accidental discharge of a gun in their own ranks.

A fortification was prepared, and the citizens, with their families, were removed within the inclosure. Captain Whitcomb quartered his company in the principal hotel of the place, and guards were stationed for the night, while all the men were directed to be prepared for any contingency that might arise, and be in readiness for using their arms at any moment.

Between 2 and 3 o'clock the following morning, the guards discovered the approach of Indians, and gave the alarm. As soon as the savages perceived that they were discovered, they uttered the war-whoop, and poured a volley into the hotel where the troops were quartered. The latter immediately retired to the stockade, taking with them all the ammunition and equipments in their possession. They had scarcely effected an entrance when fire was opened upon it from forty or fifty Indian rifles. Owing to the darkness of the morning, no distinct view could be obtained of the enemy, and, in consequence, no very effective fire could be opened upon him.

While one party of the Indians remained to keep up a fire upon the fort and harass the garrison, another portion was engaged in setting fire to buildings and haystacks, while others, at the same time, were engaged in collecting horses and cattle found in the place, and driving them off. Occasional glimpses could be obtained of those near the fires, but as soon as a shot was fired at them they would disappear in the darkness. Most of the buildings burned, however, were such a distance from the fort as to be out of range of the guns of the garrison. The fire kept up from that point prevented the near approach of the incendiary party, and by that means the principal part of the town was saved from destruction. On one occasion an effort was made to carry the flames into a more central part of the town, and the torches in the hands of the party were seen approaching the office of A. C. Smith, Esq. Directed by the light of the torches, a volley was poured into their midst from the fort, whereupon the braves hastily abandoned their incendiary implements and retreated from that quarter of the village. From signs of blood afterward found upon the ground, some of the Indians were supposed to have met the fate intended for them, but no dead were left behind.

The fight continued, without other decided results, until about daylight, at which time the principal part of the forces retired. As the light increased, so that objects became discernible, a small party of savages were observed engaged in driving off a number of cattle. A portion of the garrison, volunteering for the purpose, sallied out to recover the stock, which they accomplished, with the loss of two men wounded, one of them severely.

This company had no further encounters with the Indians, but afterward engaged in securing the grain and other property belonging to the settlers who had abandoned, or been driven from, their farms and homes. Nearly every settlement between Forest City and the western frontier had, by this time, been deserted, and the whole country was in the hands of the savages. In speaking of his endeavors to save a portion of the property thus abandoned, Captain Whitcomb, on the 7th of September, wrote as follows:

"It is only in their property that the inhabitants can now be injured; the people have all fled. The country is totally abandoned. Not an inhabitant remains in Meeker county, west of this place. No white person (unless a captive) is now living in Kandiyohi or Monongalia county."

On the 1st of September, Captain Strout, who had previously arrived at Glencoe, made preparations for a further advance. Owing to the vigorous measures adopted by General John H. Stevens, of the State militia, it was thought unnecessary that any additional forces should be retained at this point. Under his directions no able-bodied man having deserted the country further to the westward, had been permitted to leave the neighborhood, or pass through. All such were required to desist from further flight, and assist in making a stand, in order to check the further advance of the destroyers of their homes. The town of Glencoe had been fortified to a certain extent, and a military company of seventy-three members had been organized, and armed with such guns as were in possession of the settlers. With Glencoe thus provided for, General Stevens did not hesitate to advise, nor Captain Strout to attempt a further advance into the overrun and threatened territory.

The company of the latter, by this time, had been increased by persons, principally from Wright county, who volunteered their services for the expedition, until it numbered about seventy-five men. With this force he marched, as already stated, on the 1st day of September.

Passing through Hutchinson on his way, no opposition was encountered until the morning of the 3d of September. On the night previous, he had arrived at and encamped near Acton, on the western border of Meeker county.

At about half-past five o'clock the next morning his camp was attacked by a force comprising about one hundred and fifty Indians. The onset was made from the direction of Hutchinson, with the design, most probably, of cutting off the retreat of the company, and of precluding the possibility of sending a messenger after reinforcements. They fought with a spirit and zeal that seemed determined to annihilate our little force, at whatever cost it might require.

For the first half hour Captain Strout formed his company into four sections, in open order, and pressed against them as skirmishers. Finding their forces so much superior to his own, he concentrated the force of his company, and hurled them against the main body of the enemy. In this manner the fight was kept up for another hour and a half, the Indians falling slowly back as they were pressed, in the direction of Hutchinson, but maintaining all the while their order and line of battle. At length the force in front of the company gave way, and falling upon the rear, continued to harrass it in its retreat.

About one-half of the savages were mounted, partly on large, fine horses, of which they had plundered the settlements, and partly on regular Indian ponies. These latter were so well trained for the business in which they were now engaged, that their riders would drive them at a rapid rate to within any desirable distance of our men, when pony and rider would both instantly lie down in the tall grass, and thus become concealed from the aim of the sharp-shooters of the company.

With the intention, most likely, of creating a panic in our ranks, and causing the force to scatter, and become separately an easy prey to the pursuers, the Indians would at times, uttering the most terrific and unearthly yells of which their lungs and skill were capable, charge in a mass upon the little band. On none of these occasions, however, did a single man falter or attempt a flight; and, after approaching within one hundred yards of the retreating force, and perceiving that they still remained firm, the Indians would halt the charge, and seek concealment in the grass or elsewhere, from which places they would continue their fire.

After having thus hung upon and harrassed the rear of the retreating force for about half an hour, at the end of which time the column had arrived within a short distance of Cedar City, in the extreme north-west corner of McLeod county, the pursuit was given up, and the company continued the retreat without further opposition to Hutchinson, at which place it arrived at an early hour in the same afternoon.

The loss of the company in the encounter was three men killed and fifteen wounded, some of them severely. All were, however, brought from the field.

In addition to this they lost most of their rations, cooking utensils, tents, and a portion of their ammunition and arms. Some of their horses became unmanageable and ran away. Some were mired and abandoned, making, with those killed by the enemy, an aggregate loss of nine. The loss inflicted upon the enemy could not be determined with any degree of certainty, but Captain Strout was of the opinion that their killed and wounded were two or three times as great as ours.

At Hutchinson a military company, consisting of about sixty members, had been organized for the purpose of defending the place against any attacks from the Indians. Of this company Lewis Harrington was elected captain. On the first apprehension of danger a house was barricaded as a last retreat in case of necessity. The members of the company, aided by the citizens, afterward constructed a small stockade fort of one hundred feet square. It was built after the same style as that at Forest City, with bastions in the same position, and a wall composed of double timbers rising to the height of eight feet above the ground. The work was provided with loop-holes, from which a musketry fire could be kept up, and was of sufficient strength to resist any projectiles that the savages had the means of throwing. At this place Captain Strout halted his company, to await further developments.

At about nine o'clock on the next morning, the 4th of September, the Indians approached the town thus garrisoned and commenced the attack. They were replied to from the fortification; but as they were careful not to come within close range, and used every means to conceal their persons, but little punishment was inflicted upon them. They bent their energies more in attempts to burn the town than to inflict any serious injury upon the military. In these endeavors they were so far successful as to burn all the buildings situated on the bluff in the rear of the town, including the college building, which was here located. They at one time succeeded in reaching almost the heart of the village, and applying the incendiary torch to two of the dwelling-houses there situated, which were consumed.

Our forces marched out of the fort and engaged them in the open field; but, owing to the superior numbers of the enemy, and their scattered and hidden positions, it was thought that no advantage could be gained in this way, and, after driving them out of the town, the soldiers were recalled to the fort. The day was spent in this manner, the Indians making a succession of skirmishes, but at the same time endeavoring to maintain a sufficient distance between them and the soldiers to insure an almost certain impunity from the fire of their muskets. At about five o'clock in the evening their forces were withdrawn, and our troops rested on their arms, in expectation of a renewal of the fight in a more desperate form.

As soon as General Stevens was informed of the attack made upon Captain Strout, near Acton, and his being compelled to fall back to Hutchinson, he directed Captain Davis to proceed to the command of Lieutenant Weinmann, then stationed near Lake Addie, in the same county, to form a junction of the two commands, and proceed to Hutchinson and reinforce the command of Captain Strout.

On the morning of the 4th of September the pickets belonging to Lieutenant Weinmann's command reported having heard firing in the direction of Hutchinson. The Lieutenant immediately ascended an eminence in the vicinity of his camp, and from that point could distinguish the smoke from six different fires in the same direction. Being satisfied from these indications that an attack had been made upon Hutchinson, he determined at once to march to the assistance of the place. Leaving behind him six men to collect the teams and follow with the wagons, he started with the remainder of his force in the direction indicated.

Some time after he had commenced his march the company of Captain Davis arrived at the camp he had just left.

Upon learning the state of affairs, the mounted company followed in the same direction, and, in a short time, came up with Lieutenant Weinmann. A junction of their forces was immediately effected, and they proceeded in a body to Hutchinson, at which place they arrived about 6 o'clock in the evening. No Indians had been encountered on the march, and the battle, so long and so diligently kept up during most of the day, had just been terminated, and the assailing forces withdrawn. A reconnoissance, in the immediate vicinity, was made from the fort on the same evening, but none of the Indians, who, a few hours before, seemed to be everywhere, could be seen; but the bodies of three of their victims, being those of one woman and two children, were found and brought to the village.

On the following morning, six persons arrived at the fortification, who had been in the midst of and surrounded by the Indians during the greater part of the day before, and had succeeded in concealing themselves until they retired from before the town, and finally effected their escape to the place.

The companies of Captain Davis and Lieutenant Weinmann made a tour of examination in the direction that the Indians were supposed to have taken. All signs discovered seemed to indicate that they had left the vicinity. Their trail, indicating that a large force had passed, and that a number of horses and cattle had been taken along, was discovered, leading in the direction of Redwood. As the battle of Birch Coolie had been fought two or three days previous, at which time the Indians first learned the great strength of the column threatening them in that quarter, it is most likely that the party attacking Hutchinson had been called in to assist in the endeavor to repel the forces under Colonel Sibley.

On the 23d of September the Indians suddenly reappeared in the neighborhood. About 3 o'clock in the afternoon a messenger arrived, with dispatches from Lieutenant Weinmann, informing Captain Strout that Samuel White and family, residing at Lake Addie, had that day been brutally murdered by savages.

At about 11 o'clock P. M., the scouts from the direction of Cedar City came in, having been attacked near Greenleaf, and one of their number, a member of Captain Harrington's company, killed and left upon the ground. They reported having seen about twenty Indians, having killed one, and their belief that more were in the party. The scouts from nearly every direction reported having seen Indians, some of them in considerable numbers, and the country all around seemed at once to have become infested with them.

On the 5th of September, Lieutenant William Byrnes, of the Tenth Regiment Minnesota Volunteers, with a command of forty-seven men, started from Minneapolis, where his men were recruited, for service in Meeker and McLeod counties. Upon his arrival in the country designated, he was finally stationed at Kingston, in the county of Meeker, for the purpose of affording protection to that place and vicinity. He quartered his men in the storehouse of Hall & Co., which had been previously put in a state of defense by the citizens of the place. He afterward strengthened the place by means of earth-works, and made daily examinations of the surrounding country by means of scouts.

Capt. Pettit, of the Eighth Regiment Minnesota Volunteers, was, about the same time, sent to reinforce Captain Whitcomb, of Forest City, at which place he was stationed at the time of the sudden reappearance of the Indians in the country. On the 22d of September word was brought to Forest City that the Indians were committing depredations at Lake Ripley, a point some twelve miles to the westward of that place. Captain Pettit thereupon sent a messenger to Lieutenant Byrnes, requesting his co-operation, with as many of his command as could leave their post in safety, for the purpose of marching into the invaded neighborhood.

In pursuance of orders, Lieutenant Byrnes, with thirty-six men, joined the command of Capt Pettit on the same evening. On the next morning, the 23d of September, the same day that Captain Strout's scouting party was attacked at Greenleaf, Captain Pettit, with the command of Lieutenant Byrnes and eighty-seven men, from the post at Forest City, marched in the direction in which the Indians had been reported as committing depredations on the previous day. Four mounted men of Captain Whitcomb's force accompanied the party as guides.

On arriving at the locality of reported depredations, they found the mutilated corpse of a citizen by the name of Oleson. He had received three shots through the body and one through the hand. Not even satisfied with the death thus inflicted, the savages had removed his scalp, beaten out his brains, cut his throat from ear to ear, and cut out his tongue by the roots. Leaving a detachment to bury the dead, the main body of expedition continued the march by way of Long Lake, and encamped near Acton, where Captain Strout's command was first attacked, and at no great distance from the place where his scouts were attacked.

Scouts were sent out by Captain Pettit, all of whom returned without having seen any Indians. Two dwelling-houses had been visited that had been set on fire by the Indians, but the flames had made so little progress as to be capable of being extinguished by the scouts, which was done accordingly. Three other houses on the east side of Long Lake had been fired and consumed during the same day. Three women were found, who had been lying in the woods for a number of days, seeking concealment from the savages. They were sent to Forest City for safety. During the early part of the night, Indians were heard driving or collecting cattle, on the opposite side of Long Lake from the encampment.

During the 24th of September the march was continued to Diamond Lake, in Monongalia county. All the houses on the route were found to be tenantless, all the farms were deserted, and every thing of value, of a destructible nature, belonging to the settlers, had been destroyed by the savages. Only one Indian was seen during the day, and he being mounted, soon made his escape into the big woods. The carcasses of cattle, belonging to the citizens, were found in all directions upon the prairie, where they had been wantonly slaughtered and their flesh abandoned to the natural process of decomposition.

At break of day, on the morning of the 25th, an Indian was seen by one of the sentinels to rise from the grass and attempt to take a survey of the encampment. He was immediately fired upon when he uttered a yell and disappeared. Captain Pettit thereupon formed his command in order of battle and sent out skirmishers to reconnoiter; but the Indians had decamped, and nothing further could be ascertained concerning them.

At seven o'clock the return march to Forest City was commenced, by a route different from that followed in the outward march. About ten o'clock the expedition came upon a herd, comprising sixty-five head of cattle, which the Indians had collected, and were in the act of driving off, when they were surprised by the near approach of volunteers. As the latter could be seen advancing at a distance of three miles, the Indians had no difficulty in making their escape to the timber, and in this way eluding pursuit from the expedition by abandoning their plunder. The cattle were driven by the party to Forest City, where a great portion of the herd was found to belong to persons who were then doing military duty, or taking refuge from their enemies.

At Rockford, on the Crow river, a considerable force of citizens congregated for the purpose of mutual protection, and making a stand against the savages in case they should advance thus far. A substantial fortification was erected at the place, affording ample means of shelter and protection to those there collected; but we are not aware that it ever became necessary as a place of last resort to the people, nor are we aware that the Indians committed any act of hostilities within the county of Wright.

On the 24th of August rumors reached St. Cloud that murders and other depredations had been committed by the Indians near Paynesville, on the border of Stearns county, and near the dividing line between Meeker and Monongalia counties. A public meeting of the citizens was called at four o'clock in the afternoon, at which, among other measures adopted, a squad, well armed and equipped, was instructed to proceed to Paynesville, and ascertain whether danger was to be apprehended in that direction. This party immediately entered upon the discharge of their duty, and started to Paynesville the same evening.

On the evening of the following day they returned, and reported that they met at Paynesville the fugitives from Norway Lake, which latter place is situated in Monongalia county, and about seventeen miles in a south-west direction from the former. That, on Wednesday, the 20th day of August, as a family of Swedes, by the name of Lomberg, were returning from church, they were attacked by a party of Indians, and three brothers killed, and another one, a boy, wounded. The father had fourteen shots fired at him, but succeeded in making his escape. One of his sons, John, succeeded in bearing off his wounded brother, and making their escape to Paynesville.

On the 24th, a party went out from Paynesville for the purpose of burying the dead at Norway Lake, where they found, in addition to those of the Lomberg family, two other entire families murdered—not a member of either left to tell the tale. The clothes had all been burned from their bodies, while from each had been cut either the nose, an ear or a finger, or some other act of mutilation had been committed upon it.

The party, having buried the dead, thirteen in number, were met by a little boy, who informed them that his father had that day been killed by the savages while engaged in cutting hay in a swamp. They proceeded with the intention of burying the body, but discovered the Indians to be in considerable force around the marsh, and they were compelled to abandon the design.

The party beheld the savages in the act of driving off forty-four head of cattle, a span of horses, and two wagons; but the paucity of their numbers compelled them to refrain from any attempt to recover the property, or to inflict any punishment upon the robbers and murderers having it in their possession. A scouting party had been sent to Johanna Lake, about ten miles from Norway Lake, where about twenty persons had been living. Not a single person, dead or alive, could there be found. Whether they had been killed, escaped by hasty flight, or been carried off as prisoners, could not be determined from the surrounding circumstances. As the party were returning, they observed a man making earnest endeavors to escape their notice, and avoid them by flight, under the impression that they were Indians, refusing to be convinced to the contrary by any demonstrations they could make. Upon their attempting to overtake him, he plunged into a lake and swam to an island, from which he could not be induced to return. His family were discovered and brought to Paynesville, but no information could be derived from them respecting the fate of their neighbors.

When this report had been made to the citizens of St. Cloud by the returned party, a mounted company, consisting of twenty-five members, was immediately formed, for the purpose of co-operating with any forces from Paynesville in efforts to recover and rescue any citizens of the ravaged district. Of this company Ambrose Freeman was elected captain, and they proceeded in the direction of Paynesville the next morning at 8 o'clock.

At Maine Prairie, a point to the south-west of St. Cloud, and about fifteen miles distant from that place, a determined band of farmers united together with a determination never to leave until driven, and not to be driven by an inferior force. Their locality was a small prairie, entirely surrounded by timber and dense thickets, a circumstance that seemed to favor the near approach of the stealthy savage.

By concerted action they soon erected a substantial fortification, constructed of a double row of timbers, set vertically, and inserted firmly in the ground. The building was made two stories in height. The upper story was fitted up for the women and children, and the lower was intended for purposes of a more strictly military character. Some of their number were dispatched to the State Capital to obtain such arms and supplies as could be furnished them. Provisions were laid in, and they soon expressed their confidence to hold the place against five hundred savages, and to stand a siege, if necessary. Their determination was not to be thus tested, however. The Indians came into their neighborhood, and committed some small depredations, but, so far as reported, never exhibited themselves within gunshot of the fort.

At Paynesville, the citizens and such others as sought refuge in the town constructed a fortification for the purpose of protecting themselves and defending the village; but no description of the work has ever been received at this office, and, I believe, it was soon abandoned.

At St. Joseph, in the Watab Valley, the citizens there collected erected three substantial fortifications. These block-houses were built of solid green timber, of one foot in thickness. The structure was a pentagon, and each side was fifty feet in length. They were located at different points of the town, and completely commanded the entrance in all directions. In case the savages had attacked the town, they must have suffered a very heavy loss before a passage could be effected, and even after an entry had been made, they would have become fair targets for the riflemen of the forts. Beyond them, to the westward, every house is said to have become deserted, and a great portion of the country ravaged, thus placing them upon the extreme frontier in that direction; but, owing, no doubt, to their activity in preparing the means for effective resistance, they were permitted to remain almost undisturbed.

Sauk Center, near the north-western corner of

the county, and situated on the head-waters of the Sauk river, is, perhaps, the most extreme point in this direction at which a stand was made by the settlers. Early measures were taken to perfect a military organization, which was effected on the 25th of August, by the election of Sylvester Ramsdell as captain. The company consisted of over fifty members, and labored under discouraging circumstances at the outset. The affrighted and panic-stricken settlers, from all places located still further to the north and west, came pouring past the settlement, almost communicating the same feeling to the inhabitants. From Holmes City, Chippewa Lake, Alexandria, Osakis, and West Union, the trains of settlers swept by, seeking safety only in flight, and apparently willing to receive it in no other manner.

Assistance was received from the valley of the Ashley river, from Grove Lake, and from Westport, in Pope county.

A small stockade fort was constructed, and within it were crowded the women and children. The haste with which it was constructed, and the necessity for its early completion, prevented its either being so extensive or so strongly built as the interest and comfort of the people seemed to require.

Upon being informed of the exposed situation of the place, and the determination of the settlers to make a united effort to repel the destroyers from their homes, orders were, on the 30th day of August, issued to the commandant at Fort Snelling, directing him, with all due speed, to detail from his command two companies of troops, with instructions to proceed to Sauk Center, for the purpose of protecting the inhabitants of the Sauk Valley from any attack of hostile Indians, and to co-operate as far as possible with the troops stationed at Fort Abercrombie.

In obedience to these orders, the companies under command respectively of Captains George G. McCoy, of the Eighth Regiment Minnesota Volunteers, and Theodore H. Barrett, of the Ninth Regiment, were sent forward. Their arrival at the stockade created a thrill of joy in the place, especially among the women and children, and all, even the most timid, took courage and rejoiced in their security. Captain Barrett was, shortly afterward, sent with his command in the expedition for the relief of Fort Abercrombie, and a short time afterward Captain McCoy, in obedience to orders from General Pope, fell back to St. Cloud.

Upon the departure of these troops, many of the more timid were again almost on the verge of despair, and would willingly have retreated from the position they so long held. More courageous councils prevailed, and the same spirit of firmness that refused safety by flight in the first instance, was still unbroken, and prompted the company to further action, and to the performance of other duties in behalf of themselves and those who had accepted their proffers of protection. Disease was beginning to make its appearance within the stockade, where no other enemy had attempted to penetrate, and this fact admonished the company that more extensive and better quarters were required in order to maintain the health of the people.

Several plans were submitted for a new stockade, from which one was selected, as calculated to secure the best means of defense, and at the same time, to afford the most ample and comfortable quarters for the women, children, and invalids, besides permitting the horses and cattle to be secured within the works. In a few days the new fort was completed, inclosing an area of about one acre in extent, the walls of which were constructed of a double row of timbers, principally tamarack poles, inserted firmly in the ground, and rising eleven feet above the surface. These were properly prepared with loopholes and other means of protection to those within, and for the repulsion of an attacking party.

When the people had removed their stock and other property within the new fortification, and had been assigned to their new quarters, they for the first time felt really secure and at ease in mind. Had any vigorous attack been made upon the party in their old stockade, they might have saved the lives of the people, but their horses and cattle would most certainly have been driven off or destroyed. Now they felt that there was a chance of safety for their property as well as themselves.

A short time after this work had been completed Captain McCoy, after having rendered services in other parts of the country, was ordered back to Sauk Center. A company from the Twenty-fifth Wisconsin Regiment was sent to the same place upon its arrival in the state, and remained there until about the first of December.

Two days after the citizens from Grove Lake—a point some twelve miles to the south-west of Sauk Center—had cast their lot with the people of the latter place, the night sentinels of Captain Ramsdell's company discovered fires to the southwest. Fearing that all was not right in the vicinity of Grove Lake, a party was sent out the next morning to reconnoiter in that neighborhood. They found one dwelling-house burned, and others plundered of such things as had attracted the fancy of the savages, while all furniture was left broken and destroyed. A number of the cattle which had not been taken with the settlers when they left, were found killed.

A Mr. Van Eaton, who resided at that place, about the same time, started from Sauk Center, with the intention of revisiting his farm. He is supposed to have fallen into the hands of the savages, as he never returned to the fort. Several parties were sent in search of him, but no positive trace could ever be found.

At St. Cloud, in the upper part of the town, a small but substantial fortification was erected, and "Broker's Block" of buildings was surrounded with a breastwork, to be used in case the citizens should be compelled to seek safety in this manner. In Lower Town a small work was constructed, called Fort Holes. It was located upon a ridge overlooking the "flat" and the lower landing on the river. It was circular in form, and was forty-five feet in diameter. The walls were formed by two rows of posts, deeply and firmly set in the ground, with a space of four feet between the rows. Boards were then nailed upon the sides of the posts facing the opposite row, and the interspace filled and packed with earth, thus forming an earthen wall of four feet in thickness. The structure was then covered with two-inch plank, supported by heavy timbers, and this again with sods, in order to render it fire-proof. In the center, and above all, was erected a bullet-proof tower, of the "monitor" style, but without the means of causing it to revolve, prepared with loop-holes for twelve sharp-shooters. This entire structure was inclosed with a breastwork or wall similar to that of the main building, two feet in thickness and ten in height, with a projection outward so as to render it difficult to be scaled. It was pierced for loop-holes at the distance of every five feet. Within this fortification it was intended that the inhabitants of Lower Town should take refuge in case the Indians should make an attack in any considerable force, and where they expected to be able to stand a siege until reinforcements would be able to reach them. They were not put to this test, however; but the construction of the fort served to give confidence to the citizens, and prevented some from leaving the place that otherwise would have gone, and were engaged in the preparation at the time the work was commenced.

On the 22d of September a messenger arrived at St. Cloud from Richmond, in the same county, who reported that, at four o'clock the same morning, the Indians had appeared within a mile of the last-mentioned town, and had attacked the house of one of the settlers, killing two children and wounding one woman. Upon the receipt of this intelligence Captain McCoy, who was then stationed at St. Cloud with forty men of his command, got under way for the reported scene of disturbance at ten o'clock A. M., and was followed early in the afternoon by a mounted company of home-guards, under command of Captain Cramer. Upon arriving at Richmond the troops took the trail of the Indians in the direction of Paynesville, and all along the road found the dwellings of the settlers in smouldering ruins, and the stock of their farms, even to the poultry, killed and lying in all directions. Seven of the farm-houses between these two towns were entirely consumed, and one or two others had been fired, but were reached before the flames had made such progress as to be incapable of being extinguished, and these were saved, in a damaged condition, through the exertions of the troops. On arriving at Paynesville they found eight dwelling-houses either consumed or so far advanced in burning as to preclude the hope of saving them, and all the outbuildings of every description had been committed to the flames and reduced to ruins. Only two dwelling-houses were left standing in the village.

At Clear Water, on the Mississippi river, below St. Cloud, and in the county of Wright, the citizens formed a home guard and built a fortification for their own protection, which is said to have been a good, substantial structure, but no report has been received in regard either to their military force or preparations for defense.

Morrison county, which occupies the extreme frontier in this direction, there being no organized county beyond it, we believe, was deserted by but few of its inhabitants. They collected, however, from the various portions of the county, and took position in the town of Little Falls, its capital, where they fortified the court-house, by strengthening its walls and digging entrenchments around it. During the night the women and children occupied the inside of the building, while the men remained in quarters or on guard on the outside. In the morning the citizens of the town would return to their habitations, taking with them such of their neighbors as they could accommodate, and detachments of the men would proceed to the farms of some of the settlers and exert themselves in securing the produce of the soil. Indians were seen on several occasions, and some of the people were fired upon by them, but so far as information has been communicated, no lives were lost among the settlers of the county.

CHAPTER XL.

HOSTILITIES IN THE VALLEY OF THE RED RIVER OF THE NORTH—CAPTAINS FREEMAN AND DAVIS ORDERED TO GO TO THE RELIEF OF ABERCROMBIE—INDIANS APPEAR NEAR THE FORT IN LARGE NUMBERS—THE ATTACK—INDIANS RETIRE—SECOND ATTACK ON THE FORT—UNION OF FORCES—ANOTHER ATTACK UPON THE FORT—EFFECT OF THE HOWITZER—RETURN OF CAPTAIN FREEMAN TO ST. CLOUD.

On the 23d of August the Indians commenced hostilities in the valley of the Red River of the North. This region of country was protected by the post of Fort Abercrombie, situated on the west bank of the river, in Dakota Territory. The troops that had formerly garrisoned the forts had been removed, and sent to aid in suppressing the Southern rebellion, and their place was supplied, as were all the posts within our state, by a detachment from the Fifth Regiment Minnesota Volunteers. But one company had been assigned to this point, which was under the command of Captain John Van der Horck. About one-half of the company was stationed at Georgetown, some fifty miles below, for the purpose of overawing the Indians in that vicinity, who had threatened some opposition to the navigation of the river, and to destroy the property of the Transportation Company. The force was thus divided at the commencement of the outbreak.

The interpreter at the post, who had gone to Yellow Medicine for the purpose of attending the Indian payment, returned about the 20th of August, and reported that the Indians were becoming exasperated and that he expected hostilities to be immediately commenced. Upon the receipt of this intelligence the guards were doubled, and every method adopted that was likely to insure protection against surprises.

The Congress of the United States had authorized a treaty to be made with the Red Lake Indians, (Chippewas,) and the officers were already on their way for the purpose of consummating such treaty. A train of some thirty wagons, loaded with goods, and a herd of some two hundred head of cattle, to be used at the treaty by the United States Agent, was likewise on the way, and was then at no great distance from the fort.

Early in the morning of the 23d a messenger arrived, and informed the commandant that a band of nearly five hundred Indians had already crossed the Otter Tail river, with the intention of cutting off and capturing the train of goods and cattle intended for the treaty. Word was immediately sent to those having the goods in charge, and requesting them to take refuge in the fort, which was speedily complied with. Messengers were likewise sent to Breckenridge, Old Crossing, Graham's Point, and all the principal settlements, urging the inhabitants to flee to the fort for safety, as from the weakness of the garrison, it was not possible that protection could be afforded them elsewhere.

The great majority of the people from the settlements arrived in safety on the same day, and were assigned to quarters within the fortification. Three men, however, upon arriving at Breckenridge, refused to go any further, and took possession of the hotel of the place, where they declared they would defend themselves and their property without aid from any source. On the evening of the same day a detachment of six men was sent out in that direction, in order to learn, if possible, the movements of the Indians. Upon their arriving in sight of Breckenridge they discovered the place to be occupied by a large force of the savages. They were likewise seen by the latter, who attempted to surround them, but being mounted, and the Indians on foot, they were enabled to make their escape, and returned to the fort.

The division of the company at Georgetown was immediately ordered in; and, on the morning of the 24th, a detachment was sent to Breckenridge, when they found the place deserted by the Indians, but discovered the bodies of the three men who had there determined to brave the violence of the war party by themselves. They had been brutally murdered, and, when found, had chains bound around their ankles, by which it appeared, from signs upon the floor of the hotel, their bodies at least had been dragged around in the savage war-dance of their murderers, and, perhaps, in that very mode of torture they had suffered a lingering death. The mail-coach for St. Paul, which left the fort on the evening of the 22d, had fallen into the hands of the Indians, the driver killed, and the contents of the mail scattered over the prairie, as was discovered by the detachment on the 24th.

Over fifty citizens capable of bearing arms had taken refuge with the garrison, and willingly became soldiers for the time being; but many of them were destitute of arms, and none could be furnished them from the number in the possession of the commandant. There was need, however, to strengthen the position with outside intrenchments, and all that could be spared from other duties were employed in labor of that character.

On the morning of the 25th of August, messengers were dispatched from the post to head-quarters, stating the circumstances under which the garrison was placed, and the danger of a severe attack; but, as all troops that could be raised, and were not indispensable at other points, had been sent to Colonel Sibley, then on the march for the relief of Fort Ridgely, it was impossible at once to reinforce Fort Abercrombie with any troops already reported ready for the field. Authority had been given, and it was expected that a considerable force of mounted infantry for the State service had been raised, or soon would be, at St. Cloud.

As the place was directly upon the route to Abercrombie, it was deemed advisable to send any troops that could be raised there to the assistance of Captain Van der Horck, relying upon our ability to have their places shortly filled with troops, then being raised in other parts of the State. Accordingly, Captain Freeman, with his company, of about sixty in number, started upon the march; but upon arriving at Sauk Center, he became convinced, from information there received, that it would be extremely dangerous, if not utterly impossible, to make the march to the fort with so small a number of men. He then requested Captain Ramsdell, in command of the troops at Sauk Center, to detail thirty men from his command, to be united with his own company, and, with his force so strengthened, he proposed to make the attempt to reach the fort. Captain Ramsdell thought that, by complying with this request, he would so weaken his own force that he would be unable to hold position at Sauk Center, and that the region of country around would become overrun by the enemy, and he refused his consent. Captain Freeman then deemed it necessary to await reinforcements before proceeding any further on his perilous journey.

On the same day that orders were issued to the mounted men then assembling at St. Cloud, similar orders were issued to those likewise assembling in Goodhue county, under the command of Captain David L. Davis, directing them to complete their organization with all speed, and then to proceed forthwith to the town of Carver, on the Minnesota river, and thence through the counties of McLeod, Meeker, and Stearns, until an intersection was made with the stage-route from St. Cloud to Fort Abercrombie, and thence along such stage-route to the fort, unless the officers in command became convinced that their services were more greatly needed in some other quarter, in which case they had authority to use discretionary powers. This company, likewise, marched pursuant to orders; but, in consequence of the attacks then being made upon Forest City, Acton, and Hutchinson, they deemed it their duty to render assistance to the forces then acting in that part of the country.

The first efforts to reinforce the garrison on the Red River had failed. Upon the fact becoming known at this office, there were strong hopes that two more companies of infantry could be put into the field in a very short time, and, therefore, on the 30th day of August, orders were issued to the commandant of Fort Snelling, directing him to detail two companies, as soon as they could be had, to proceed to Sauk Center, and thence to proceed to Fort Abercrombie, in case their services were not urgently demanded in the Sauk Valley. These companies were, soon after, dispatched accordingly, and it was hoped that, by means of this increased force on the north-western frontier, a sufficiently strong expedition might be formed to effect the reinforcement of Abercrombie.

Upon the arrival of these troops at the rendezvous, however, they still considered the forces in that vicinity inadequate to the execution of the task proposed. Of this fact we first had notice on the 6th day of September. Two days previously, the effective forces of the state had been strengthened by the arrival of the Third Regiment Minnesota Volunteers, without any commissioned officers and being but a wreck of that once noble regiment. Three hundred of the men had already been ordered to the field, under the command of Major Welch. It was now determined to send forward the remaining available force of the regiment, to endeavor to effect the project so long delayed, of reinforcing the command of Captain Van der Horck, on the Red River of the North. Orders were accordingly issued to the commandant at Fort Snelling, on the 6th day of September, directing him to fit out an expedition for that purpose, to be composed, as far as possible, of the troops belonging to the Third Regiment; and Colonel Smith, the commandant at the post, immediately entered upon the discharge of the duties assigned him in the order.

During the time that these efforts had been making for their relief, the garrison at Fort Abercrombie was kept in a state of siege by the savages, who had taken possession of the surrounding country in large numbers. On the 25th of August, the same day that the first messengers were sent from that post, Captain Van der Horck detailed a squad, composed of six men from his company and six of the citizens then in the fort, to proceed to Breckenridge and recover the bodies of the men who had there been murdered. They proceeded, without meeting with any opposition, to the point designated, where they found the bodies, and consigned them to boxes or rough coffins, prepared for the purpose, and were about starting on the return, when they observed what they supposed to be an Indian in the saw-mill, at that place. A further examination revealed the fact that the object mistaken for an Indian was an old lady by the name of Scott, from Old Crossing, on the Otter Tail, a point distant fifteen miles from Breckenridge.

When discovered, she had three wounds on the breast, which she had received from the Indians, at her residence, on the morning of the previous day. Notwithstanding the severity of her wounds, and the fact that she was sixty-five years of age, she made her way on foot and alone, by walking or crawling along the banks of the river, until she arrived, in a worn-out, exhausted, and almost dying condition, at the place where she was found. She stated that, on the 24th of August, a party of Indians came to her residence, where they were met by her son, a young man, whom they instantly shot dead, and immediately fired upon her, inflicting the wounds upon her person which she still bore. That then a teamster in the employment of Burbank & Co. appeared in sight, driving a wagon loaded with oats, and they went to attack him, taking with them her grandchild, a boy about eight years of age. That they fired upon the teamster, wounding him in the arm, after which he succeeded in making his escape for that time, and they left her, no doubt believing her to be dead, or, at least, in a dying condition. She was conveyed to the fort, where her wounds were dressed, after which she gradually recovered. A party was sent out, on the 27th of August, to the Old Crossing, for the purpose of burying the body of her son, which was accomplished, and on their way to that point they discovered the body of another man who had been murdered, as was supposed, on the 24th.

On Saturday, the 30th of August, another small party were sent out, with the intention of going to the Old Crossing for reconnoitering purposes, and to collect and drive to the fort such cattle and other live stock as could there be found. They had proceeded ten miles on their way, when they came upon a party of Indians, in ambush, by whom they were fired upon, and one of their party killed. The remainder of the squad made their escape unhurt, but with the loss of their baggage wagon, five mules, and their camp equipage.

At about two o'clock in the afternoon of the same day, the Indians appeared in large numbers in sight of the fort. At this time nearly all the live stock belonging to the post, as well as that belonging to the citizens then quartered within the work, together with the cattle that had been intended for the treaty in contemplation with the Red Lake Indians, were all grazing upon the prairie in rear of the fort, over a range extending from about one-half mile to three miles from it. The Indians approached boldly within this distance, and drove off the entire herd, about fifty head of which afterward escaped. They succeeded, however, in taking between one hundred and seventy and two hundred head of cattle, and about one hundred horses and mules. They made no demonstration against the fort, except their apparently bold acts of defiance; but, from the weakness of the garrison in men and arms, no force was sent out to dispute with them the possession of the property. It was mortifying in the extreme, especially to the citizens, to be compelled to look thus quietly on, while they were being robbed of their property, and dare not attempt its rescue, lest the fort should be filled with their enemies in their absence.

On the 2d day of September, another reconnoitering party of eight were sent out in the direction of Breckenridge, who returned, at four o'clock P. M. without having encountered any opposition from the Indians, or without having even seen any; but brought with them the cattle above spoken of as having escaped from their captors, which were found running at large during their march.

At daybreak on the following morning, the 3d of September, the garrison was suddenly called to arms by the report of alarm-shots fired by the sentinels in the vicinity of the stock-yard belonging to the post. The firing soon became sharp and rapid in that direction, showing that the enemy were advancing upon that point with considerable force. The command was shortly after given for all those stationed outside to fall back within the fortification. About the same time, two of the haystacks were discovered to be on fire, which greatly emboldened and inflamed the spirits of the citizens, whose remaining stock they considered to be in extreme jeopardy. They rushed with great eagerness and hardihood to the stables, and as the first two of them entered on one side, two of the savages had just entered from the other. The foremost of these men killed one of the Indians and captured his gun. The other Indian fired upon the second man, wounding him severely in the shoulder, notwithstanding which, he afterward shot the Indian and finished him with the bayonet. By this time two of the horses had been taken away and two killed.

The fight was kept up for about two hours and a half, during which time three of the inmates of the fort were seriously wounded (one of whom afterward died from the wound) by shots from the enemy; and the commandant received a severe wound in the right arm from an accidental shot, fired by one of his own men. The Indians then retired without having been able to effect an entrance into the fort, and without having been able to succeed in capturing the stock of horses and cattle, which, most probably, had been the principal object of their attack.

Active measures were taken to strengthen the outworks of the fort. The principal materials at hand were cord-wood and hewn timber, but of this there was a considerable abundance. By means of these the barracks were surrounded with a breastwork of cord-wood, well filled in with earth to the height of eight feet, and this capped with hewn oak timbers, eight inches square, and having port-holes between them, from which a fire could be opened on the advancing foe. This was designed both as a means of protection, in case of attack, and a place of final retreat in case the main fort should by any means be burned or destroyed, or the garrison should in any manner be driven from it.

On Saturday, the 6th day of September, the same day that an expedition to that point was ordered from the Third Regiment, the fort was a second time attacked. Immediately after daybreak on that morning, the Indians, to the number of about fifty, mounted on horseback, made their appearance on the open prairie in the rear of the fort. Their intention evidently was, by this bold and defiant challenge, with so small a force, to induce the garrison to leave their fortifications and advance against them, to punish their audacity.

In becoming satisfied that our troops could not be seduced from their intrenchments, the Indians soon displayed themselves in different directions, and in large numbers. Their principal object of attack in this instance, as on the former occasion, seemed to be the Government stables, seeming determined to get possession of the remaining horses and cattle at almost any sacrifice, even if they should make no other acquisition.

The stables were upon the edge of the prairie, with a grove of heavy timber lying between them and the river. The savages were not slow in perceiving the advantage of making their approach upon that point from this latter direction. The shores of the river, on both sides, were lined with Indians for a considerable distance, as their war-whoops, when they concluded to commence the onset, soon gave evidence. They seemed determined to frighten the garrison into a cowardly submission, or, at least, to drive them from the outposts, by the amount and unearthliness of their whoops and yells. They, in turn, however, were saluted and partially quieted by the opening upon them of a six-pounder, and the explosion of a shell in the midst of their ranks.

A large force was led by one of their chiefs from the river through the timber until they had gained a close proximity to the stables, still under cover of large trees in the grove. When no nearer position could be gained without presenting themselves in the open ground, they were urged by their leader to make a charge upon the point thus sought to be gained, and take the place by storm. They appeared slow in rendering obedience to his command, whereby they were to expose themselves in an open space intervening between them and the stables. When at length he succeeded in creating a stir among them (for it assuredly did not approach the grandeur of a charge), they were met by such a volley from the direction in which they were desired to march that they suddenly reversed their advance, and each sought the body of a tree, behind which to screen himself from the threatened storm of flying bullets.

As an instance of the manner in which the fight was now conducted, we would mention a part of the personal adventures of Mr. Walter P. Hills, a citizen, who three times came as a messenger from the fort during the time it was in a state of siege. He had just returned to the post with dispatches the evening before the attack was made. He took part in the engagement, and killed his Indian in the early portion of the fight before the enemy was driven across the river.

He afterward took position at one of the portholes, where he paired off with a particular Sioux warrior, posted behind a tree of his own selection. He, being acquainted with the language to a considerable extent, saluted and conversed with his antagonist, and as the opportunity was presented, each would fire at the other. This was kept up for about an hour without damage to either party, when the Indian attempted to change his position, so as to open fire from the opposite side of his tree from that which he had been using hitherto. In this maneuver he made an unfortunate exposure of his person in the direction of the upper bastion of the fort. The report of a rifle from that point was heard, and the Indian was seen to make a sudden start backward, when a second and third shot followed in rapid succession, and Mr. Hills beheld his polite opponent stretched a corpse upon the ground. He expressed himself as experiencing a feeling of dissatisfaction at beholding the death of his enemy thus inflicted by other hands than his own, after he had endeavored so long to accomplish the same object.

Several of the enemy at this point were killed while in the act of skulking from one tree to another. The artillery of the post was used with considerable effect during the engagement. At one time a number of the enemy's horsemen were observed collecting upon a knoll on the prairie, at the distance of about half a mile from the fort, with the apparent intention of making a charge. A howitzer was brought to bear upon them, and a shell was planted in their midst, which immediately afterward exploded, filling the air with dust, sand, and other fragments. When this had sufficiently cleared away to permit the knoll to be again seen, the whole troop, horses and riders, had vanished, and could nowhere be discovered.

The fight lasted until near noon, when the enemy withdrew, taking with him nearly all his dead. The loss which he sustained could not be fully ascertained, but from the number killed in plain view of the works, and the marks of blood, broken guns, old rags, and other signs discovered where the men had fallen or been dragged away by their companions, it must have been very severe. Our loss was one man killed and two wounded, one of them mortally.

Mr. Hills left the fort the same evening as bearer of dispatches to headquarters at St. Paul, where he arrived in safety on the evening of the 8th of September.

Captain Emil A. Buerger was appointed, by special order from headquarters, to take command of the expedition for the relief of Fort Abercrombie. He had served with some distinction in the Prussian army for a period of ten years. He afterward emigrated to the United States, and became a resident of the state of Minnesota, taking the oath of allegiance to the Government of the United States, and making a declaration of his intention to become a citizen. He enlisted in the second company of Minnesota Sharp-Shooters, and was with the company in the battle of Fair Oaks, in Virginia, where he was severely wounded and left upon the field. He was there found by the enemy, and carried to Richmond as a prisoner of war. After having in a great measure recovered from his wounds, he was paroled and sent to Benton Barracks, in the state of Missouri, where he was sojourning at the time the 3d Regiment was ordered to this state. As the regiment at that time was utterly destitute of commissioned officers, Captain Buerger was designated to take charge and command during the passage from St. Louis, and to report the command at headquarters in this state.

From his known experience and bravery, he was selected to lead the expedition to the Red River of the North, for the relief of the garrison at

Fort Abercrombie. On the 9th of September he was informed, by the commandant at Fort Snelling, that the companies commanded respectively by Captains George Atkinson and Rolla Banks, together with about sixty men of the Third Regiment, under command of Sergeant Dearborne, had been assigned to his command, constituting an aggregate force of about 250 men.

The next day (September 10) arms and accoutrements were issued to the men, and, before noon of the 11th of September, Captain Atkinson's company and the company formed from the members of the Third Regiment were ready for the march. With these Captain Buerger at once set out, leaving Captain Bank's company to receive their clothing, but with orders to follow after and overtake the others as soon as possible, which they did, arriving at camp and reporting about 3 o'clock the next morning.

It was also deemed expedient to send the only remaining field-piece belonging to the state along with the expedition, and Lieutenant Robert J. McHenry was, accordingly, appointed to take command of the piece, and was sent after the expedition, which he succeeded in overtaking, near Clear Water, on the 13th of September, and immediately reported for further orders to the captain commanding the expedition.

Being detained by heavy rains and muddy roads, the expedition was considerably delayed upon its march, but arrived at Richmond, in Stearns county, on the 16th of September, and encamped in a fortification erected at that point by the citizens of the place. Upon his arrival, Captain Buerger was informed that the night previous an attack had been made upon the neighboring village of Paynesville, and a church and schoolhouse had been burned, and that, on the day of his arrival, a party of thirty Sioux warriors, well mounted, had been seen by some of the Richmond home-guards, about three miles beyond the Sauk river at that point.

Captain Buerger thereupon detailed a party of twenty men to proceed to Richmond, to patrol up and down the bank of the river as far as the town site extended, and, in case of an attack being made, to render all possible or necessary assistance and aid to the home militia; at the same time he held the remainder of his command in readiness to meet any emergency that might arise. No Indians appeared during the night, and, on the morning following, the march was resumed.

On the 19th of September the expedition reached Wyman's Station, at the point where the road enters the "Alexandria Woods." At the setting out of the expedition it was next to impossible to obtain means of transportation for the baggage and supplies necessary for the force. The fitting out of so many other expeditions and detachments about the same time had drawn so heavily upon the resources of the country, that scarcely a horse or wagon could be obtained, either by contract or impressment. Although Mr. Kimball, the quartermaster of the expedition, had been assiduously engaged from the 8th of September in endeavoring to obtain such transportation, yet, on the 11th, he had but partially succeeded in his endeavors.

Captain Buerger had refused longer to delay, and started at once with the means then at hand, leaving directions for others to be sent forward as rapidly as circumstances would allow. The march was much less rapid, for want of this part of the train. These, fortunately, arrived while the command was encamped at Wyman's Station, just before the commencement of what was considered the dangerous part of the march.

On the 14th of September, Captains Barrett and Freeman, having united their commands, determined to make the attempt to relieve Fort Abercrombie, in obedience to previous orders. They broke up camp on the evening of that day, and by evening of the 15th, had reached Lake Amelia, near the old trail to Red River, where they encamped. During the night a messenger arrived at their camp, bearing dispatches from Captain McCoy, advising them of the advance of the expedition under command of Captain Buerger, by whom they were directed to await further orders.

On the 18th they received orders directly from Captain Buerger, directing them to proceed to Wyman's Station, on the Alexandria road, and join his command at that point on the 19th, which was promptly executed. Captain Buerger expressed himself as being highly pleased with these companies, both officers and men. He had been directed to assume command over these companies, and believing the country in his rear to be then sufficiently guarded, and being so well pleased with both companies that he disliked to part with either, he ordered them to join the expedition during the remainder of the march.

By the accession of these companies the strength of the expedition was increased to something over four hundred effective men. This whole force, with the entire train, marched on the 20th of September, and passed through the "Alexandria Woods" without seeing any Indians. After passing Sauk Center, however, there was not an inhabitant to be seen, and the whole country had been laid waste. The houses were generally burned, and those that remained had been plundered of their contents and broken up, until they were mere wrecks, while the stock and produce of the farms had been all carried off or destroyed.

On the 21st they passed the spot where a Mr. Andrew Austin had been murdered by the Indians a short time previous. His body was found, terribly mutilated, the head having been severed from the body, and lying about forty rods distant from it, with the scalp torn off. It was buried by the expedition in the best style that circumstances would admit. Pomme de Terre river was reached in the evening.

On the 22d they arrived at the Old Crossing, on the Otter Tail river, between Dayton and Breckenridge, about fifteen miles from the latter place.

On the 23d the march was resumed, and nothing worthy of remark occurred until the expedition had approached within about a mile of the Red River, and almost within sight of Fort Abercrombie. At this point a dense smoke was observed in the direction of the fort, and the impression created among the troops was, that the post had already fallen, and was now being reduced to ashes by the victorious savages, through the means of their favorite element of war.

Upon ascending an eminence where a better view could be obtained, a much better state of affairs was discovered to be existing. There stood the little fort, yet monarch of the prairie, and the flag of the Union was still waving above its battlements. The fire from which the smoke was arising was between the command and the post, and was occasioned by the burning of the prairie, which had been set on fire by the Indians, with the evident design of cutting off the expedition from the crossing of the river. After they had advanced a short distance further toward the river, a party of thirteen Indians appeared on the opposite bank, rushing in wild haste from a piece of woods. They hastily fired a few shots at our men from a distance of about fifteen hundred yards, inflicting no injuries on any one of the command, after which they disappeared in great trepidation, behind some bushes on the river shore.

A detachment comprising twenty mounted men of Captain Freeman's company, under command of Lieutenant Taylor, and twenty from the members of the Third Regiment, the latter to act as skirmishers in the woods, was directed to cross the river with all possible celerity, and follow the retreating enemy. The men entered upon the duty assigned them with the greatest zeal, crossed the river, and followed in the direction taken by the Indians.

Captain Buerger took with him the remaining force of the Third Regiment and the field-piece, and proceeded up the river to a point where he suspected the Indians would pass in their retreat, and where he was able to conceal his men from their sight until within a very short distance.

He soon discovered, however, that the savag.s were retreating, under cover of the woods, across the prairie, in the direction of the Wild Rice river. The whole expedition was then ordered to cross the river, which was effected in less than an hour, the men not awaiting to be carried over in wagons, but plunging into the water, breast-deep, and wading to the opposite shore.

By this time the savages had retreated some three miles, and were about entering the heavy timber beyond the prairie, and further pursuit was considered useless. The march was continued to the fort, at which place the expedition arrived about 4 o'clock of the same day, to the great joy of the imprisoned garrison and citizens, who welcomed their deliverers with unbounded cheers and demonstrations of delight.

When the moving columns of the expedition were first descried from the ramparts of the fort, they were taken to be Indians advancing to another attack. All was excitement and alarm. The following description of the after-part of the scene is from the pen of a lady who was an inmate of the fort during the long weeks that they were besieged, and could not dare to venture beyond half cannon-shot from the post without being in imminent peril of her life:

"About 5 o'clock the report came to quarters that the Indians were again coming from up toward Bridges. With a telescope we soon discovered four white men, our messengers, riding at full speed, who, upon reaching here informed us that in one half hour we would be reinforced by three hundred and fifty men. Language can never express the delight of all. Some wept, some laughed, others hallooed and cheered. The soldiers and citizens here formed in a line and went out to meet them. It was quite dark before all got in. We all cheered so that the next day more than half of us could hardly speak aloud. The ladies all went out, and as they passed, cheered them. They were so dusty I did not know one of them."

* * * * * * * *

On the same day that the expedition reached the fort, but at an early hour, it had been determined to dispatch a messenger to St. Paul, with reports of the situation of the garrison, and a request for assistance. The messenger was escorted a considerable distance by a force of twenty men, composed of soldiers and partly of the citizens quartered at the post. When returning, and within about a mile of the fort, they were fired upon by Indians in ambush, and two of the number, one citizen and one soldier, were killed, and fell into the hands of the enemy. The others, by extraordinary exertions, succeeded in making their escape, and returned to the garrison.

The next morning, about two-thirds of the mounted company, under command of Captain Freeman, escorted by a strong infantry force, went out to search for the bodies of those slain on the day before. After scouring the woods for a considerable distance, the bodies were found upon the prairie, some sixty or eighty rods apart, mangled and mutilated to such a degree as to be almost deprived of human form. The body of the citizen was found ripped open from the center of the abdomen to the throat. The heart and liver were entirely removed, while the lungs were torn out and left upon the outside of the chest. The head was cut off, scalped, and thrust within the cavity of the abdomen, with the face toward the feet. The hands were cut off and laid side by side, with the palms downward, a short distance from the main portion of the body. The body of the soldier had been pierced by two balls, one of which must have occasioned almost instant death. When found, it was lying upon the face, with the upper part of the head completely smashed and beaten in with clubs while the brains were scattered around upon the grass. It exhibited eighteen bayonet wounds in the back, and one of the legs had received a gash almost, or quite, to the bone, extending from the calf to the junction with the body.

The citizen had lived in the vicinity for years. The Indians had been in the habit of visiting his father's house, sharing the hospitalities of the dwelling, and receiving alms of the family. He must have been well known to the savages who inflicted such barbarities upon his lifeless form; neither could they have had aught against him, except his belonging to a different race, and his being found in a country over which they wished to re-establish their supremacy.

That his body had been treated with still greater indignity and cruelty than that of the soldier was in accordance with feelings previously expressed to some of the garrison. In conversation with some of the Sioux, previous to the commencement of hostilities, they declared a very strong hatred against the settlers in the country, as they frightened away the game, and thus interfered with their hunting. They objected, in similar terms, to having United States troops quartered so near them, but said they did not blame the soldiers, as they had to obey orders, and go wherever they were directed, but the settlers had encroached upon them, of their own free will, and as a matter of choice; for this reason the citizens should be severely dealt with.

No more Indians were seen around the fort until the 26th of September. At about 7 o'clock of that day, as Captain Freeman's company were watering their horses at the river, a volley was fired upon them by a party of Sioux, who had placed themselves in ambush for the purpose. One man, who had gone as teamster with the expedition, was mortally wounded, so that he died the succeeding night; the others were unarmed. From behind the log-buildings and breastworks the fire was soon returned with considerable effect, as a number of the enemy were seen to fall and be carried off by their comrades. At one time two Indians were observed skulking near the river. They were fired upon by three men from the fortification, and both fell, when they were dragged away by their companions.

On another occasion, during the fight, one of the enemy was discovered perched on a tree, where he had stationed himself, either for the purpose of obtaining a view of the movements inside of the fort, or to gain a more favorable position for firing upon our men. He was fired upon by a member of Captain Barret's company, when he released his hold upon the tree and fell heavily into a fork near the ground, from which he was removed and borne off by his comrades. In a very short time a howitzer was brought into position, and a few shells (which the Indians designate as rotten bullets) were thrown among them, silencing their fire and causing them to withdraw.

A detachment, comprising Captain Freeman's company, fifty men of the 3d Regiment, and a squad in charge of a howitzer, were ordered in pursuit, and started over the prairie, up the river. At the distance of about two miles they came upon the Sioux camp, but the warriors fled in the greatest haste and consternation upon their approach. A few shots were fired at them in their flight, to which they replied by yells, but were in too great haste to return the fire. The howitzer was again opened upon them, whereupon their yelling suddenly ceased, and they rushed, if possible, with still greater celerity through the brush and across the river.

Their camp was taken possession of, and was found to contain a considerable quantity of plunder, composed of a variety of articles, a stock of liquors being part of the assortment. Everything of value was carried to the fort, and the remainder was burned upon the ground.

On the evening of September 29th a light skirmish was had with a small party of Sioux, who attempted to gain an ambush in order to fire upon the troops while watering their horses, as on a previous occasion. Fire was first opened upon them, which they returned, wounding one man. They were immediately routed and driven off, but with what loss, if any, was unknown.

On the 30th of September Captain Freeman's company and the members of the 3d Regiment, together with a number of citizens and families, started on their return from Fort Abercrombie to St. Cloud. They passed by where the town of Dayton had formerly stood, scarcely a vestige of which was then found remaining. The dead body of one of the citizens, who had been murdered, was there found, and buried in the best manner possible under the circumstances. The whole train arrived in safety at St. Cloud, on the 5th of October, without having experienced any considerable adventures on the journey.

CHAPTER XLI.

SOUTH-WESTERN DEPARTMENT—HON. CHARLES E. FLANDRAU—FEARS OF WINNEBAGOES AND SIOUX—MANKATO RAISES A COMPANY FOR THE DEFENSE OF NEW ULM—HEADQUARTERS AT SOUTH BEND—WAKEFIELD—SIOUX RAID IN WATONWAN COUNTY—PURSUIT OF INDIANS—STATE TROOPS RELIEVED FROM DUTY—COLONEL SIBLEY ADVANCED FROM ST. PETER—CONCLUSION.

That portion of the State lying between the Minnesota river and the Iowa line, supposed in the early part of the military movement to occupy a position of extreme danger, was placed under the control of Hon. Charles E. Flandrau. In the division was the Winnebago Reservation. And it was reasonably supposed that the Winnebagoes would more readily unite with the Sioux than with the Ojibwas [Chippewas] in the northern part of the State, the former tribe being on good terms with the Sioux, while the latter held the Sioux as hereditary enemies, with whom an alliance offensive or defensive would hardly take place, unless under extraordinary conditions, such as a general war of the Indian tribes upon the white race. This peculiar condition did not mark the present outbreak.

In this portion of the State were distributed the following forces, subject to special duty as circumstances required: a company of sixty-three members under the command of Captain Cornelius F. Buck, marched from Winona, Sept. 1, 1861; on the 26th of August, six days previous, Captain A. J. Edgerton, of the 10th Regiment, with one hundred and nine men, arrived at the Winnebago Agency, where the inhabitants were in great terror. After the evacuation of New Ulm, by Colonel Flandrau, he encamped at Crisp's farm, half way between New Ulm and Mankato. On the 31st of August, a company of forty-four members, from Mankato, took up position at South Bend, at which place Colonel Flandrau had established his headquarters. On the 23d of August a company of fifty-eight members, from Winnebago City, under command of Captain H. W. Holly, was raised for special services in the counties of Blue Earth, Faribault, Martin, Watonwan, and Jackson. This command, on the 7th of September, was relieved at Winnebago City by the Fillmore County Rangers, under the command of Captain Colburn. At Blue Earth City, a company of forty-two members, under command of Captain J. B. Wakefield, by order of Colonel Flandrau, remained at that point and erected fortifications, and adopted means for subsisting his men there during the term of their service. Major Charles R. Read, of the State militia, with a squad of men from south-eastern Minnesota, also reported to Colonel Flandrau at South Bend. Captain Dane, of the 9th Regiment, was by order of the Colonel in command, stationed at New Ulm. Captain Post, and Colonel John R. Jones, of the State militia, reported a company of mounted men from the county of Fillmore, and were assigned a position at Garden City. Captain Aldrich, of the 8th Regiment, reported his company at South Bend, and was placed in position at New Ulm. Captain Ambler, of the 10th Regiment, reported his company, and was stationed at Mankato. Captain Sanders, of the 10th, also reported, and was stationed at Le Sueur. Captain Meagher likewise was assigned a position with his company at Mankato, where the company was raised. Captain Cleary, with a company, was stationed at Marysburg, near the Winnebago Reserve, and a similar company, under Captain Potter, was raised, and remained at camp near home. Captain E. St. Julien Cox, with a command composed of detachments from different companies, was stationed at Madelia. He here erected a fort commanding the country for some twenty miles. It was octagonal in form, two stories in height, with thirty feet between the walls. This was inclosed by a breastwork and ditch six feet deep, and four feet wide at the bottom, with projecting squares of similar thickness on the corners, from which the ditch could be swept through its entire length. This structure was named Fort Cox, in honor of its projector.

From this disposition of forces in the department commanded by Colonel Flandrau, it will be seen that the south-western portion of the State was provided with the most ample means of defense against any attack from any open enemy in any ordinary warfare; and yet on the 10th of September, the wily Indian made an attack upon Butternut Valley, near the line of Blue Earth and Brown counties and fired upon the whites, wounded a Mr. Lewis in the hand, killed James Edwards, and still further on killed Thomas J. Davis, a Mr. Mohr, and wounded Mr. John W. Task and left him for dead. Mr. Task, however, survived. And again on the 21st of September, a party of Sioux came into Watonwan county, killed John Armstrong, two children of a Mr. Patterson, and a Mr. Peterson.

The consequences of the massacre we have detailed in these pages to some extent can be easily imagined, and the task of the historian might here be transferred to the reader. But even the reader of fiction, much more the reader of history, requires some aid to direct the imagination in arriving at proper conclusions. A few words in connection with the facts already presented will suffice to exhibit this tragic epoch in our State's history in its proper light.

Minnesota, the first State in the North-west, bounded on the east by the Great Father of Waters, had taken her place in the fair sisterhood of states with prospects as flattering as any that ever entered the American Union. The tide of hardy, vigorous, intelligent emigrants had come hither from the older states, as well as from England, Ireland, and the different countries on the European continent, until a thriving population of 200,000 had taken up their abode upon her virgin soil, and were in the quiet and peaceable enjoyment of her salubrious climate. Her crystal lakes, her wooded streams, her bewitching water-falls, her island groves, her lovely prairies, would have added gems to an earthly paradise. Her Lake Superior, her Mississippi, her Red River of the North, and her Minnesota, were inviting adjuncts to the commerce of the world. Her abundant harvests and her fertile and enduring soil gave to the husbandman the highest hopes of certain wealth. Her position in the track of the tidal human current sweeping across the continent to the Pacific coast, and thence around the globe, placed her forever on the highway of the nations.

Minnesota, thus situated, thus lovely in her virgin youth, had one dark spot resting on the horizon of her otherwise cloudless sky. The dusky savage, as we have seen, dwelt in the land. And, when all was peace, without a note of warning, that one dark spot, moved by the winds of savage hate, suddenly obscured the whole sky, and poured out, to the bitter dregs, the vials of its wrath, without mixture of mercy. The blow fell like a storm of thunderbolts from the clear, bright heavens. The storm of fierce, savage murder, in its most horrid and frightful forms, rolled on. Day passed and night came;

> "Down sank the sun, nor ceased the carnage there—
> Tumultuous horrors rent the midnight air,"

until the sad catalogue reached the fearful number of *two thousand* human victims, from the gray-haired sire to the helpless infant of a day, who lay mangled and dead on the ensanguined field! The dead were left to bury the dead; for

> "The dead reigned there alone."

In two days the whole work of murder was done, with here and there exceptional cases in different settlements. And during these two days a population of *thirty* thousand, scattered over some eighteen counties, on the western border of the state, on foot, on horseback, with teams of oxen and horses, under the momentum of the panic thus created, were rushing wildly and frantically over the prairies to places of safety, either to Fort Ridgely or to the yet remaining towns on the Minnesota and Mississippi rivers. Flight from an invading army of civilized foes is awful; but flight from the uplifted tomahawk, in the hands of savage fiends in pursuit of unarmed men, women and children, is a scene too horrible for the stoutest heart. The unarmed men of the settlements offered no defense, and could offer none, but fled before the savage horde, each in his own way, to such places as the dictates of self preservation gave the slightest hope of safety. Some sought the protection of the nearest slough; others crawled into the tall grass, hiding, in many instances, in sight of the lurking foe. Children of tender years, hacked and beaten and bleeding, fled from their natural protectors, now dead or disabled, and, by the aid of some trail of blood, or by the instincts of our common nature, fled away from fields of slaughter, cautiously crawling by night from the line of fire and smoke in the rear, either toward Fort Ridgely or to some distant town on the Minnesota or the Mississippi. Over the entire border of the State, and even near the populous towns on the river, an eye looking down from above could have seen a human avalanche of thirty thousand, of all ages, and in all possible plight, the rear ranks maimed and bleeding, and faint from starvation and the loss of blood, continually falling into the hands of inhuman savages, keen and fierce, on the trail of the white man. An eye thus situated, if human, could not endure a scene so terrible. And angels from the realms of peace, if ever touched with human woe, over such a scene might have shed tears of blood; and, passing the empyreal sphere into the Eternal presence, we might see

* * * * * "God lament,
And draw a cloud of mourning round his throne."

Who will say, looking on this picture, that the human imagination can color it at all equal to the sad reality? Reality here has outdone the highest flights to which fancy ever goes! The sober-minded Governor Sibley, not unused to the most horrible phases of savage life, seeing only a tithe of the wide field of ruin, giving utterance to his thoughts in official form, says: "Unless some crushing blow can be dealt at once upon these too successful murderers, the state is ruined, and some of its fairest portions will revert, for years, into the possession of these miserable wretches, who, of all devils in human shape, are among the most cruel and ferocious. To appreciate this, one must see, as I have, the mutilated bodies of their victims. My heart is steeled against them, and if I have the means, and can catch them, I will sweep them with the besom of death." Again, alluding to the narrations of those who have escaped from the scenes of the brutal carnage, he says: "Don't think there is an exaggeration in the horrible pictures given by individuals—they fall far short of the dreadful reality."

The Adjutant-General of the State, in an official document, has attempted, by words of carefully-measured meaning, to draw a picture of the scenes we are feebly attempting to present on paper. But this picture is cold and stately compared with the vivid coloring of living reality. "During the time that this force was being marshaled and engaged in the march to this point (St. Peter), the greater portion of the country above was being laid waste by murder, fire, and robbery. The inhabitants that could make their escape were fleeing like affrighted deer before the advancing gleam of the tomahawk. Towns were deserted by the residents, and their places gladly taken by those who had fled from more sparsely-settled portions of the regions. A stream of fugitives, far outnumbering the army that was marching to their relief, came pouring down the valley. The arrivals from more distant points communicated terror to the settlements, and the inhabitants there fled to points still further in the interior, to communicate in turn the alarm to others still further removed from the scene of hostilities. This rushing tide of humanity, on foot, on horse, and in all manner of vehicles, came meeting the advancing columns of our army. Even this sign of protection failed to arrest their progress. On they came, spreading panic in their course, and many never halted till they had reached the capital city of the state; while others again felt no security even here, and hurriedly and rashly sacrificed their property, and fled from the state of their adoption to seek an asylum of safety in some of our sister states further removed from the sound of the war-whoop."

Thirty thousand panic-stricken inhabitants at once desert their homes in the midst of an indiscriminate slaughter of men, women, and children. All this distracted multitude, from the wide area of eighteen counties, are on the highways and byways, hiding now in the sloughs, and now in the grass of the open prairie; some famishing for water, and some dying for want of food; some barefooted, some in torn garments, and some entirely denuded of clothing; some, by reason of wounds, crawling on their hands, and dragging their torn limbs after them, were all making their way over a country in which no white man could offer succor or administer consolation. The varied emotions that struggled for utterance in that fragmentary mass of humanity cannot be even faintly set forth in words. The imagination, faint and aghast, turns from the picture in dismay and horror! What indelible images are burned in upon the tablets of the souls of thousands of mothers bereft of their children by savage barbarity! What unavailing tears fall unseen to the ground from the scattered army of almost helpless infancy, now reduced by cruel hands to a life of cheerless orphanage! How many yet linger around the homes they loved, hiding from the keen-eyed savage, awaiting the return of father, mother, brother, or friend, who can never come again to their relief! We leave the reader to his own contemplations, standing in view of this mournful picture, the narration of which the heart sickens to pursue, and turns away with more becoming silence!

The scene of the panic extended to other counties and portions of the State remote from all actual danger. The Territory of Dakota was depopulated, except in a few towns on the western border. Eastward from the Minnesota river to the Mississippi, the inhabitants fled from their homes to the towns of Red Wing, Hastings, Wabasha, and Winona; and thousands again from these places to Wisconsin, Illinois, Indiana, Ohio, and some to distant New England friends.

Thirty thousand human beings, suddenly forced from their homes, destitute of all the necessaries of life, coming suddenly upon the towns in the Minnesota Valley, can easily be supposed to have been a burden of onerous and crushing weight. It came like an Alpine avalanche, sweeping down, in the wildness of its fury, upon the plain. No wisdom could direct it; no force could resist it. No power of description is equal to the task of presenting it in fitting words. It was horribly "grand, gloomy, and peculiar." One faint picture must here suffice.

St. Peter, on the morning of the 19th of August, 1862, manifested some unwonted commotion. Couriers arrived before the dawn of that day, announcing the alarming news that the neighboring town of New Ulm was on fire, and its inhabitants were being massacred by the savages, led by Little Crow. At the same time, or a little previous, came the tidings that Fort Ridgely was in imminent danger; that Captain Marsh had been killed, and his command almost, if not entirely, cut off, in attempting to give succor to the Lower Agency, which had been attacked on the morning of the 18th, the day previous, and was then in ashes. By nine o'clock the news of these events began to meet a response from the surrounding country. Horsemen and footmen, from different parts of Nicollet and Le Sueur counties, came hurrying into town, some with guns and ammunition, but more without arms. Men were hurrying through the streets in search of guns and ammunition; some were running bullets, while others were fitting up teams, horses, and provisions. Busiest among the agitated mass were Hon. Charles E. Flandrau and Captain William B. Dodd, giving directions for a hasty organization for the purpose of defending New Ulm, or, if that was impossible, to hold the savages in check, outside of St. Peter, sufficiently long to give the men, women, and children some chance to save their lives by hasty flight, if necessary. Every man, woman, and child seemed to catch the spirit of the alarming moment. Now, at about ten o'clock, Judge Flandrau, as captain, with quick words of command, aided by proper subalterns in rank, with one hundred and thirty-five men, armed as best they could be, with shot-guns, muskets, rifles, swords, and revolvers, took up the line of march for New Ulm. At an earlier hour, fifty volunteers, known as the Renville Rangers, on their way to Fort Snelling, had turned their course toward Fort Ridgely, taking with them all the Government arms at St. Peter.

With the departure of these noble bands went not only the wishes and prayers of wives, mothers, brothers, sisters, and children for success, but with them all, or nearly all, the able-bodied citizens capable of bearing arms, together with all the guns and ammunition St. Peter could muster. For one moment we follow these little bands of soldiers, the hope of the Minnesota Valley. Their march is rapid. To one of these parties thirty weary miles intervened between them and the burning town of New Ulm. Expecting to meet the savage foe on their route, flushed with their successful massacre at New Ulm, the skirmishers—a few men on horseback—were kept in advance of the hurrying footmen. Before dark, the entire force destined for New Ulm reached the crossing of the Minnesota at the Red Stone Ferry. Here, for a moment, a halt was ordered: the field of ruin lay in full view before them. The smoke of the burning buildings was seen ascending over the town. No signs of life were visible. Some might yet be alive. There was no wavering in that little army of relief. The ferry was manned, the river was crossed, and soon New Ulm was frantic with the mingled shouts of the delivered and their deliverers. An account of the hard-fought battle which terminated the siege is to be found in another chapter of this work. Such expedition has seldom, if ever, been chronicled, as was exhibited by the deliverers of New Ulm. Thirty miles had been made in a little over half a day, traveling all the time in the face of a motley crowd of panic-stricken refugees, pouring in through every avenue toward St. Peter.

The other party, by dusk, had reached Fort Ridgely, traveling about forty-five miles, crossing the ravine near the fort at the precise point where one hundred and fifty Indians had lain in ambush awaiting their approach until a few moments before they came up, and had only retired for the night; and, when too late to intercept them, the disappointed savages saw the Renville Rangers enter the fort.

But let us now return to St. Peter. What a night and a day have brought forth! The quiet village of a thousand inhabitants thus increased by thousands, had become full to overflowing. Every private house, every public house, every church, school-house, warehouse, shed, or saloon, and every vacant structure is full. The crowd throng the public highways; a line of cooking-stoves smoke along the streets; the vacant lots are occupied, for there is no room in the houses. All is clatter, rattle, and din. Wagons, ponies, mules, oxen, cows and calves are promiscuously distributed among groups of men, women and children. The live stock from thousands of deserted farms surround the outskirts of the town; the lowing of strange cattle, the neighing of restless horses, the crying of lost and hungry children, the tales of horror, the tomahawk wounds undressed, the bleeding feet, the cries for food, and the loud wailing for missing friends, all combine to burn into the soul the dreadful reality that some terrible calamity was upon the country.

But the news of the rapid approach of the savages, the bodies of the recently-murdered, the burning of houses, the admitted danger of a sudden attack upon St. Peter, agitated and moved that vast multitude as if some volcano was ready to engulf them. The overflowing streets were crowded into the already overflowing houses. The stone buildings were barricaded, and the women and children were huddled into every conceivable place of safety. Between hope and fear, and prayer for succor, several weary days and nights passed away, when, on the 22d day of August, the force under Colonel Sibley, fourteen hundred strong, arrived at St. Peter.

Now, as the dread of immediate massacre was past, they were siezed with a fear of a character entirely different. How shall this multitude be fed, clothed and nursed? The grain was unthreshed in the field, and the flour in the only mill left standing on the Minnesota, above Belle Plaine, was almost gone. The flouring mill at Mankato, twelve miles above, in the midst of the panic, had been burned, and fears were entertained that the mill at St. Peter would share the same fate. Nor had this multitude any means within themselves to support life a single day. Every scheme known to human ingenuity was canvassed. Every device was suggested, and every expedient tried. The multitude was fearfully clamoring for food, raiment, and shelter. The sick and wounded were in need of medicine and skillful attention. Between six and seven thousand persons, besides the citizens of the place, were already crowding the town; and some thousand or fifteen hundred more daily expected, as a proper quota from the two thousand now compelled to abandon New Ulm. The gathering troops, regular and irregular, were moving, in large numbers, upon St. Peter, now a frontier town of the State, bordering on the country under the full dominion of the Annuity Sioux Indians, with torch and tomahawk, burning and murdering in their train.

A committee, aided by expert clerks, opened an office for the distribution of such articles of food, clothing and medical stores as the town could furnish, on their orders, trusting to the State or General Government for pay at some future day. So great was the crowd pressing for relief, that much of the exhausting labor was performed while bayonets guarded the entrance to the building in which the office of distribution was held. A bakery was established, furnishing two thousand loaves of bread per day, while many private houses were put under requisition for the same purpose, and, aided by individual benevolence throughout the town, the hungry began to be scantily fed. A butcher-shop was pressed into the needed service, capable of supplying ten thousand rations a day over and above the citizens' ordinary demand. Still, there was a vast moving class, single persons, women, and children, not yet reached by these well-directed efforts. The committee, feeling every impulse of the citizens, to satisfy the demand for food fitted up a capacious soup-house, where as high as twelve hundred meals were supplied daily. This institution was a great success, and met the entire approval of the citizens, while it suited the conditions of the peculiar population better than any other mode in which relief could be administered. Soup was always ready; and its quality was superior. The aged and the young could here find relief, singly or in families; the well relished it, and the sick found it a grateful beverage. In this way the committee, aided by the extreme efforts of private charity, ever active and vigilant, continued for weeks to feed the refugees at St. Peter, taxing every energy of body and mind from twelve to sixteen hours per day. The census of the population was never taken; but it is believed that, after the arrival of the refugees from New Ulm, and a portion of the inhabitants from Le Sueur county, east of the town, excluding the fourteen hundred troops under Colonel H. H. Sibley, who were here a part of the time, the population of St. Peter was at least nine thousand. This was an estimate made by the committee of supplies, who issued eight thousand rations of beef each day to refugees alone, estimating one ration to a person. The ration was from a half-pound to a pound, varied to meet the condition of persons and families.

But the task of feeding the living did not stop with the human element. The live stock, horses and oxen, with an innumerable herd of cattle from a thousand prairies, ruly and unruly, furious from fright, so determined on food that in a few days not a green spot could be protected from their voracious demands. Fences offered no obstruction. Some bold leader laid waste the field or garden, and total destruction followed, until St. Peter was as barren of herbage, with scarce an exception, as the Great American desert. The committee could not meet successfully this new demand. The sixty tons of hay cut by their order was only an aggravation to the teams of the Government and the necessary demands of the gathering cavalry. Some military power seemed needed to regulate the collection and distribution of food in this department. This soon came in an official order from Col. H. H. Sibley to a member of the committee, assigning him to the separate duty of collecting food for Government use at St. Peter. A wider range of country was now brought under contribution, and such of the live stock as was required for constant use was amply supplied. The cattle not required by the butchers were forced to a still wider extent of country.

Not only food, such as the mill, the bakery, the butcher-shop, and the soup-house could furnish was required among this heterogeneous multitude, but the infirm, the aged and the sick needed other articles, which the merchant and druggist alone could furnish. Tea, coffee, sugar, salt, soap, candles, wine, brandy, and apothecaries' drugs, as well as shoes, boots, hats, and wear for men, women and children, and articles of bedding and hospital stores, were demanded as being absolutely necessary. The merchants and druggists of the town honored the orders of the committee, and this demand was partially supplied. In all these efforts of the town to meet the wants of the refugees, it was discovered that the limit of supply would soon be reached. But the demand still continued inexorable. The fearful crisis was approaching! Public exertion had found its limit; private benevolence was exhausted; the requisite stores of the merchant and the druggist were well-nigh expended. It was not yet safe to send the multitude to their homes in the country. The fierce savage was yet in the land, thirsting for blood. What shall be done? Shall this vast crowd be sent to other towns, to St. Paul, or still further, to other States, to seek relief from public charity? or shall they be suffered to perish here, when all means of relief shall have failed?

On the 13th of September, 1862, after a month had nearly expired, a relief committee, consisting of Rev. A. H. Kerr and F. Lange, issued an appeal, approved by M. B. Stone, Provost Marshal of St. Peter, from which we make a few extracts, showing the condition of things at the time it bears date. Previous to this, however, a vast number had left for other places, principally for St. Paul, crowding the steamboats on the Minnesota river to their utmost capacity. The appeal says:

"FRIENDS! BRETHREN! In behalf of the suffering, the destitute, and homeless—in behalf of the widow, the fatherless, and the houseless, we make this appeal for help. A terrible blow has fallen upon this frontier, by the uprising of the Sioux or Dakota Indians. All the horrors of an Indian war; the massacre of families, the aged and the young; the burning of houses and the wanton destruction of property; all, indeed that makes an Indian war so fearful and terribly appalling, are upon the settlements immediately west and northwest of us.

"In some cases the whole family have been murdered; in others the husband has fallen; in others the wife and children have been taken captive; in others only one child has escaped to tell the sad story. Stealthily the Indians came upon the settlements, or overtook families flying for refuge. Unprotected, alarm and terror siezed the people, and to escape with life was the great struggle. Mothers clasped their little ones in their arms and fled; if any lagged behind they were overtaken by a shot or the hatchet. Many, many thus left their homes, taking neither food nor clothing with them. The Indians immediately commenced the work of pillaging, taking clothing and bedding, and, in many instances giving the house and all it contained to the flames. Some have lost their all, and many, from comparative comfort, are left utterly destitute. A great number of cattle have been driven back into the Indian country, and where a few weeks ago plenty abounded, desolation now reigns. * * * * * *

"Friends of humanity—Christians, brethren, in your homes of safety, can you do something for the destitute and homeless? We ask for cast-off clothing for men, women and children—for shoes and stockings; caps for boys, anything for the little girls and infants; woolen underclothing, blankets, comfortables; anything, indeed, to alleviate their sufferings. Can not a church or town collect such articles, fill a box and send it to the committee? It should be done speedily."

Circulars, containing the appeal from which we have made the above quotations, were sent to churches in Illinois, Indiana, Ohio, Pennsylvania, New York, and throughout the towns and cities of New England. And similar appeals, from other places, were made, and met with universal response, worthy of men and women who honor the Christian profession. By these efforts, the refugees throughout the state were greatly relieved. In reply to these circulars about $20,000 were received, to which was added $25,000 by the state, for general distribution.

Other places on the frontier, such as Henderson, Chaska, Carver, and even Belle Plaine, Shakopee, and St. Paul, felt, more or less, the crushing weight of the army of refugees, as they poured across the country and down the Minnesota Valley; but no place felt this burden so heavily as the frontier town of St. Peter.

One reflection should here be made. Had New Ulm and Fort Ridgely fallen on the first attack, Mankato and St. Peter would have been taken before the state troops could have offered the proper assistance. Had New Ulm fallen on the 19th, when it was attacked, and Fort Ridgely on the 20th, when the attack was made on that place, Mankato and St. Peter could easily have been reached by the 21st, when the state troops were below, on their way to St. Peter. The successful defense of these places, New Ulm and Fort Ridgely, was accomplished by the volunteer citizens of Nicollet, Le Sueur, and Blue Earth counties, who reached New Ulm by the 19th of August, and the Renville Rangers, who timely succored Fort Ridgely, by a forced march of forty-five miles in one day, reaching the fort previous to the attack on that post. Whatever credit is due to the state troops, for the successful defense of the frontier and the rescue of the white captives, should be gratefully acknowledged by the citizens of Minnesota. Such acts are worthy of lasting honor to all who were participants in those glorious deeds. But to the brave men who first advanced to the defense of New Ulm and Fort Ridgely, higher honor and a more lasting debt of gratitude are due from the inhabitants of the valley of the Minnesota. Let their names be honored among men. Let them stand side by side with the heroes of other days. Let them rank with veteran brethren who, on Southern battle-fields, have fought nobly for constitutional freedom and the perpetuity of the Union of these states. These are all of them worthy men, who like

"Patriots have toiled, and in their country's cause
Bled nobly, and their deeds, as they deserve,
Receive proud recompense. We give in charge
Their names to the sweet lyre. The Historic Muse,
Proud of her treasure, marches with it down
To latest times; and Sculpture, in her turn,
Gives bond, in stone and ever-during brass,
To guard them, and immortalize her trust."

CHAPTER XLII.

BATTLE OF BIRCH COOLIE—BATTLE OF WOOD LAKE —CAMP RELEASE—MILITARY COMPANIES—SUCCESS OF THE EXPEDITION UNDER GENERAL SIBLEY.

The massacre being the main design of this history, the movement of the troops, in the pursuit and punishment of the Indians connected with the atrocious murders initiated on the 18th of August, 1862, must especially, in this abridgement, be exceedingly brief.

On the day after the outbreak, August 19th, 1862, an order was issued by the commander-in-chief to Colonel H. H. Sibley, to proceed, with four companies, then at Fort Snelling, and such other forces as might join his command, to the protection of the frontier counties of the State. The entire force, increased by the separate commands of Colonels Marshall and McPhail, reached Fort Ridgely, August 28th, 1862. A detachment made up of Company A, 6th Regiment Minnesota Volunteers, under Captain H. P. Grant, some seventy mounted men under Captain Joseph Anderson, and a fatigue party, aggregating in all a force of over one hundred and fifty men, were sent in advance of the main army, to protect the settlements from further devastation, and at the same time collect and bury the dead yet lying on the field of the recent slaughter. On the first of September, near the Beaver Creek, Captain Grant's party found Justina Krieger, who had escaped alive from the murders committed near Sacred Heart. Mrs Krieger had been shot and dreadfully butchered. During this day this detachment buried fifty-five victims of savage barbarity, and in the evening went into camp at Birch Coolie. The usual precautions were taken, and no immediate fears of Indians were apprehended; yet at half-past four o'clock on the morning of the second of September, one of the guards shouted "Indians!" Instantly thereafter a shower of bullets was poured into the encampment. A most fearful and terrible battle ensued, and for the numbers engaged, the most bloody of any in which our forces had been engaged during the war. The loss of men, in proportion to those engaged, was extremely large; twenty-three were killed outright, or mortally wounded, and forty-five so severely wounded as to require surgical aid, while scarce a man remained whose dress had not been pierced by the enemies' bullets. On the evening of the 3d of September the besieged camp was relieved by an advance movement of Colonel Sibley's forces at Fort Ridgely.

This battle, in all probability, saved the towns of Mankato and St. Peter from the destruction intended by the savages. They had left Yellow Medicine with the avowed object of attacking these towns on the Minnesota. The signal defeat of the forces of Little Crow at Birch Coolie, not only saved the towns of Mankato and St. Peter, but in effect ended his efforts in subduing the whites on the borders.

After the battle of Birch Coolie all the marauding forces under the direction of Little Crow were called in, and a retreat was ordered up the valley of the Minnesota toward Yellow Medicine; and on the 16th day of September Colonel Sibley ordered an advance of his whole column in pursuit of the fleeing foe; his forces now increased by the 3d Minnesota Volunteers, paroled prisoners returned from Murfreesboro, Tennessee, under command of Major Abraham E. Welch.

On the evening of the 22d Colonel Sibley arrived at Wood Lake. On the morning of the 23d, at about seven o'clock, a force of three hundred Indians suddenly appeared before his camp, yelling as savages only can yell, and firing with great rapidity. The troops under Colonel Sibley were cool and determined, and the 3d Regiment needed no urging by officers. All our forces engaged the enemy with a will that betokened quick work with savages who had outraged every sentiment of humanity, and earned for themselves an immortality of infamy never before achieved by the Dakota nation. The fight lasted about two hours. We lost in killed four, and about fifty wounded. The enemy's loss was much larger; fourteen of their dead were left on the field, and an unknown number were carried off the field, as the Indians are accustomed to do.

The battle of Wood Lake put an end to all the hopes of the renowned chief. His warriors were in open rebellion against his schemes of warfare against the whites. He had gained nothing. Fort Ridgely was not taken. New Ulm was not in his possession. St. Peter and Mankato were intact, and at Birch Coolie and Wood Lake he had suffered defeat. No warrior would longer follow his fortunes in a war so disastrous. On the same day of the battle at Wood Lake a deputation from the Wapeton band appeared under a flag of truce, asking terms of peace. The response of Colonel Sibley was a demand for the delivery of all the white captives in the possession of these savages. Wabasha, at the head of fifty lodges, immediately parted company with Little Crow, and established a camp near Lac qui Parle, with a view of surrendering his men on the most favorable terms. A flag of truce announced his action to Colonel Sibley, who soon after, under proper military guard, visited Wabasha's camp. After the formalities of the occasion were over, Colonel Sibley received the captives, in all, then and thereafter, to the number of 107 pure whites, and about 162 half-breeds, and conducted them to his headquarters. The different emotions of these captives at their release can easily be imagined by the reader. This place well deserved the name given it, "Camp Release."

A Military Commission was soon after inaugurated to try the parties charged with the murder of white persons. The labors of this commission continued until about the 5th of November, 1862. Three hundred and twenty-one of the savages and their allies had been found guilty of the charges preferred against them; three hundred and three of whom were recommended for capital punishment, the others to suffer imprisonment. These were immediately removed, under a guard of 1,500 men, to South Bend, on the Minnesota river, to await further orders from the United States Government.

Pursuit of the Deserters.—After the disaster met with at Wood Lake, Little Crow retreated, with those who remained with him, in the direction of Big Stone Lake, some sixty miles to the westward. On the 5th of October, Colonel Sibley had sent a messenger to the principal camp of the deserters, to inform them that he expected to be able to pursue and overtake all who remained in arms against the Government; and that the only hope of mercy that they need expect, even for their wives and children, would be their early return and surrender at discretion. By the 8th of October the prisoners who had come in and surrendered amounted to upwards of 2,000. On the 14th of October, Lieutenant Colonel Marshall, with 252 men, was ordered to go out upon the frontier as a scouting party, to ascertain whether there were any hostile camps of savages located within probable striking distance, from which they might be able, by sudden marches, to fall upon the settlements before the opening of the campaign in the coming spring. About this time, Colonel Sibley, hitherto acting under State authority, received the commission of Brigadier General of Volunteers from the United States.

The scouting party under Lieutenant-Colonel Marshall followed up the line of retreat of the fugitives, and near the edge of the Coteau de Prairie, about forty-five miles from Camp Release, found two lodges of straggling Indians. The males of these camps, three young men, were made prisoners, and the women and children and an old man were directed to deliver themselves up at Camp Release. From these Indians here captured they received information of twenty-seven lodges encamped near Chanopa (Two Wood) lakes. At these lakes they found no Indians; they had left, but the trail was followed to the north-west, towards the Big Sioux river. At noon of the 16th, Lieutenant-Colonel Marshall took with him fifty mounted men and the howitzer and started in pursuit, without tents or supplies of any kind, but leaving the infantry and supply wagons to follow after. They crossed the Big Sioux river, passing near and on the north side of Lake Kampeska.

By following closely the Indian trail, they arrived at dark at the east end of a lake some six or eight miles long, and about eight miles in a northwestwardly direction from Lake Kampeska. Here they halted, without tents, fire or food, until near daylight, when reconnoitering commenced, and at an early hour in the morning they succeeded in surprising and capturing a camp composed of ten lodges, and thirteen Indians and their families. From those captured at this place information was received of another camp of some twelve or fifteen lodges, located at the distance of about one day's march in the direction of James river.

Placing a guard over the captured camp, the remaining portion of the force pressed on in the direction indicated, and at the distance of about ten miles from the first camp, and about midway between the Big Sioux and James rivers they came in sight of the second party, just as they were moving out of camp. The Indians attempted to make their escape by flight, but after an exciting chase for some distance they were overtaken and captured, without any armed resistance. Twenty-one men were taken at this place. Some of them had separated from the camp previous to the capture, and were engaged in hunting at the time. On the return march, which was shortly after commenced, six of these followed the detachment, and, after making ineffectual efforts to recover their families, came forward and surrendered themselves into our hands The infantry and wagons were met by the returning party about ten miles west of the Big Sioux.

The men of this detachment, officers and privates, evinced to a large degree the bravery and endurance that characterizes the true soldier. They willingly and cheerfully pressed on after the savages, a part of them without food, fire or shelter, and all of them knowing that they were thereby prolonging the period of their absence beyond the estimated time, and subjecting themselves to the certain necessity of being at least one or two days without rations of any kind before the return to Camp Release could be effected.

On the 7th of November, Lieutenant-Colonel Marshall, with a guard of some fifteen hundred men, started for Fort Snelling in charge of other captured Indians, comprising the women and children, and such of the men as were not found guilty of any heinous crime by the Military Commission, and arrived safely at their destination on the 13th.

From the commencement of hostilities until the 16th day of September the war was carried on almost entirely from the resources of the State alone, and some little assistance from our sister States in the way of arms and ammunition. On this latter date Major-General John Pope, who had been appointed by the President of the United States to take command of the Department of the North-west, arrived and established his headquarters in the city of St. Paul, in this state. The principal part of the active service of the season's campaign had previously been gone through with; but the forces previously under the command of of the State authorities were immediately turned over to his command, and the after-movements were entirely under his control and direction.

He brought to the aid of the troops raised in the State the 25th Wisconsin and the 27th Iowa Regiments, both infantry. These forces were speedily distributed at different points along the frontier, and assisted in guarding the settlements during the autumn, but they were recalled and sent out of the State before the closing in of the winter.

It was contemplated to send the 6th and 7th Regiments Minnesota Volunteers to take part in the war against the rebels in the Southern States, and orders to this effect had already been issued. but on the 6th of November, in obedience to the expressed wish of a large portion of the inhabitants of the State, these orders were countermanded. They were directed to remain in the state, and the 3d Regiment was ordered off instead.

All the forces then remaining in the state were assigned to winter quarters at such points as it was thought expedient to keep guarded during the winter, and on the 25th of November Major-General Pope removed his headquarters to Madison, in the State of Wisconsin. Brigadier-General Sibley then remained in the immediate command of the troops retained in service against the Indians, and established his headquarters in the city of St. Paul.

On the 9th of October the "Mankato Record" thus speaks of this expedition:

"Considering the many serious disadvantages under which General Sibley has labored—a deficiency of arms and ammunition, scarcity of provisions, and the total absence of cavalry at a time when he could have successfully pursued and captured Little Crow and his followers—the expedition has been successful beyond the most sanguine anticipations. Of the three hundred white captives in the hands of the Indians at the commencement of the war, all, or nearly all, have been retaken and returned to their friends. Much private property has been secured, and some fifteen hundred Indians, engaged directly or indirectly in the massacres, have been captured; and those who have actually stained their hands in the blood of our frontier settlers are condemned to suffer death. Their sentence will be carried into execution, unless countermanded by authorities at Washington."

CHAPTER XLIII.

INDIAN SYMPATHIZERS—MEMORIAL TO THE PRESIDENT—THE HANGING OF THIRTY-EIGHT—ANNULLING THE TREATIES WITH CERTAIN SIOUX—REMOVAL OF WINNEBAGOES AND SIOUX TO THE UPPER MISSOURI.

After the campaign of 1862, and the guilty parties were confined at Camp Lincoln, near Mendota, the idea of executing capitally, three hundred Indians, aroused the sympathy of those far removed from the scenes of their inhuman butcheries. President Lincoln was importuned, principally by parties in the East, for the release of these savages. The voice of the blood of innocence crying from the ground, the wailings of mothers bereft of their children was hushed in the tender cry of sympathy for the condemned. Even the Christian ministers, stern in the belief that, "Whosoever sheddeth man's blood by man shall his blood be shed," seemed now the most zealous for the pardon of these merciless outlaws, who, without cause had shed the blood of innocent women and children in a time of peace.

Senator M. S. Wilkinson and Congressmen C. Aldrich and William Windom, made an urgent appeal to the President for the proper execution of the sentence in the case of these Indians. From this appeal the following extract will be sufficient to indicate its character:

"The people of Minnesota, Mr. President, have stood firmly by you and your Administration. They have given both you and it their cordial support. They have not violated any law. They have borne these sufferings with patience, such as few people have ever exhibited under extreme trials. These Indians now are at their mercy; but our people have not risen to slaughter, because they believed their President would deal with them justly.

"We are told, Mr. President, that the committee from Pennsylvania, whose families are living happily in their pleasant homes in that state, have called upon you to pardon these Indians. We protest against the pardon of these Indians; because if it is done, the Indians will become more insolent and cruel than they ever were before, believing, as they certainly will, that their Great Father at Washington either justifies their acts or is afraid to punish them for their crimes.

"We protest against it, because, if the President does not permit the execution to take place under the forms of law, the outraged people of Minnesota will dispose of these wretches without law. These two people cannot live together. We do not wish to see mob law inaugurated in Minnesota, as it certainly will be, if you force the people to it. We tremble at the approach of such a condition of things in our state.

"You can give us peace, or you can give us lawless violence. We pray you, as in view of all we have suffered, and of the danger which still awaits us, let the law be executed. Let justice be done to our people."

The press of Minnesota, without a single exception, insisted that the condemned Indians should expiate their dreadful crime upon the gallows, while the Eastern press, with some few exceptions, gave vent to the deep sympathy of the sentimental philosophers and the fanciful strains of the imaginative poets. It seemed to our Eastern neighbors that Minnesotians, in their contact with savage life, had ceased to appreciate the

> * * * "Poor Indian, whose untutored mind
> Sees God in clouds, and hears HIM in the wind;"

that they had looked upon the modern race of savages in their criminal degradation until they had well-nigh forgotten the renoun of Massasoit, and his noble sons Alexander and Philip.

But two hundred years never fails to change somewhat the character and sentiments of a great people, and blot from its memory something of its accredited history. This may have happened in the case of our fellow-kinsmen in the Eastern and Middle States. They may not now fully enter into the views and sentiments of those who witnessed the outrages of Philip and his cruel warriors in their conspiracies against the infant colonies; in their attacks upon Springfield, Hatfield, Lancaster, Medfield, Seekong, Groton, Warwick, Marlborough, Plymouth, Taunton, Scituate, Bridgewater, and Northfield. They seem not fully now to appreciate the atrocities of the savages of these olden times. The historian of the times of Philip was not so sentimental as some of later days.

"The town of Springfield received great injury from their attacks, more than thirty houses being burned; among the rest one containing a 'brave library,' the finest in that part of the country, which belonged to the Rev. Pelatiah Glover."

"This," says Hubbard, "did, more than any other, discover the said actors to be the children of the devil, full of all subtilty and malice." And we of the present can not perceive why the massacre of innocent women and children should not as readily *discover* these Minnesota savages, under Little Crow, to be children of the devil as the burning of a minister's library two hundred years ago. Minnesotians lost by these Indians SPLENDID, not to say *brave* libraries; but of this minor evil they did not complain, in their demand for the execution of the condemned murderers.

Indians are the same in all times. Two hundred years have wrought no change upon Indian character. Had King Philip been powerful enough, he would have killed all the white men inhabiting the New England Colonies. "Once an Indian, always an Indian," is fully borne out by their history during two hundred years' contact with the white race.

Eastern writers of the early history of the country spoke and felt in regard to Indians very much as Minnesotians now speak and feel. When Weetamore, queen of Pocasset, and widow of Alexander, Philip's eldest brother, in attempting to escape from the pursuit of Captain Church, had lost her life, her head was cut off by those who discovered her, and fixed upon a pole at Taunton! Here, being discovered by some of her loving subjects, then in captivity, their unrestrained grief at the shocking sight is characterized by Mather as "a most horrid and diabolical lamentation!" Have Minnesotians exhibited a more unfeeling sentiment than this, even against condemned murderers? Mather lived, it is true, amid scenes of Indian barbarity. Had he lived in the present day and witnessed these revolting cruelties, he would have said with Colonel H. H. Sibley, "My heart is steeled against them." But those who witnessed the late massacre could truly say, in the language of an Eastern poet,

> "All died—the wailing babe—the shrieking maid—
> And in the flood of fire that scathed the glade,
> The roofs went down!"

Early in December, 1862, while the final decision of the President was delayed, the valley towns of Minnesota, led off by the city of St. Paul, held primary meetings, addressed by the most intelligent speakers of the different localities. An extract from a memorial of one of the assemblages of the people is given as a sample of others of similar import. The extract quoted is from the St. Paul meeting, drawn up by George A. Nourse, United States District Attorney for the District of Minnesota:

"To the President of the United States: We, the citizens of St. Paul, in the State of Minnesota, respectfully represent that we have heard, with regret and alarm, through the public press, reports of an intention on the part of the United States Government to dismiss without punishment the Sioux warriors captured by our soldiers; and further, to allow the several tribes of Indians lately located upon reservations within this State to remain upon the reservations.

"Against any such policy we respectfully but firmly protest. The history of this continent presents no event that can compare with the late Sioux outbreak in wanton, unprovoked, and fiendish cruelty. All that we have heard of Indian warfare in the early history of this country is tame in contrast with the atrocities of this late massacre. Without warning, in cold blood, beginning with the murder of their best friends, the whole body of the Annuity Sioux commenced a deliberate scheme to exterminate every white person upon the land once occupied by them, and by them long since sold to the United States. In carrying out this bloody scheme they have spared neither age nor sex, only reserving, for the gratification of their brutal lust, the few white women whom the rifle, the tomahawk and the scalping-knife spared. Nor did their fiendish barbarities cease with death, as the mutilated corpses of their victims, disemboweled, cut limb from limb, or chopped into fragments, will testify. These cruelties, too, were in many cases preceded by a pretense of friendship; and in many instances the victims of these more than murderers were shot down in cold blood as soon as their backs were turned, after a cordial shaking of the hand and loud professions of friendship on the part of the murderers.

"We ask that the same judgment should be passed and executed upon these deliberate murderers, these ravishers, these mutilators of their murdered victims, that would be passed upon white men guilty of the same offense. The blood of hundreds of our murdered and mangled fellow-citizens cries from the ground for vengeance. 'Vengeance is mine; I will repay, saith the Lord;' and the authorities of the United States are, we believe, the chosen instruments to execute that vengeance. Let them not neglect their plain duty.

"Nor do we ask alone for vengeance. We demand security for the future. There can be no safety for us or for our families unless an example shall be made of those who have committed the horrible murders and barbarities we have recited. Let it be once understood that these Indians can commit such crimes, and be pardoned upon surrendering themselves, and there is henceforth a torch for every white man's dwelling, a knife for every white man's heart upon our frontier.

"Nor will even the most rigorous punishment give perfect security against these Indians so long as any of them are left among, or in the vicinity of our border settlements. The Indian's nature can no more be trusted than the wolf's. Tame him, cultivate him, strive to Christianize him as you will, and the sight of blood will in an instant call out the savage, wolfish, devilish instincts of the race. It is notorious that among the earliest and most murderous of the Sioux, in perpetrating their late massacre, were many of the 'civilized Indians,' so called, with their hair cut short, wearing white men's clothes, and dwelling in brick houses built for them by the Government.

"We respectfully ask, we demand that the captive Indians now in the hands of our military forces, proved before a military commission to be guilty of murder, and even worse crimes, shall receive the punishment due those crimes. This, too, not merely as a matter of vengeance, but much more as a matter of future security for our border settlers.

"We ask, further, that these savages, proved to be treacherous, unreliable, and dangerous beyond example, may be removed from close proximity to our settlements, to such distance and such isolation as shall make the people of this State safe from their future attacks."

DISAPPOINTMENT OF THE PEOPLE IN MINNESOTA.

The final decision of the President, on the 17th of December, 1862, ordering the execution of thirty-nine of the three hundred condemned murderers, disappointed the people of Minnesota. These thirty-nine were to be hung on Friday, the 26th of December.

It was not strange that the people of Minnesota were disappointed. How had New England looked upon her Indian captives in her early history? Her history says:

"King Philip was hunted like a wild beast, his body quartered and set on poles, his head exposed as a trophy for tw[e]n[t]y years on a gibbet, in Plymouth, and one of his hands sent to Boston: then the ministers returned thanks, and one said that they had *prayed* a bullet into Philip's heart. In 1677, on a Sunday, in Marblehead, the women, as they came out of the meeting-house, fell upon two Indians that had been brought in as captives, and, in a very tumultuous way, murdered them, in revenge for the death of some fishermen."

These Puritan ideas have greatly relaxed in the descendants of the primitive stock. But, as the sepulchers of the fathers are garnished by their children as an indorsement of their deeds, shall we not hope that those who ha[v]e in this way given evidence of their paternity will find some palliation for a people who have sinned in the similitude of their fathers?

On the 21th of December, at the request of the citizens of Mankato of a previous date, Colonel Miller, (Ex-Governor Stephen Miller, whose death at Worthington, Minn., took place in August, 1881), in order to secure the public peace, declared martial law over all the territory within a circle of ten miles of the place of the intended execution.

On Monday, the 21st, the thirty-nine had been removed to apartments separate and distinct from the other Indians, and the death-warrant was made known to them through an interpreter—the Rev. Mr. Riggs, one of the Sioux missionaries. Through the interpreter, Colonel Miller addressed the prisoners in substance, as follows:

"The commanding officer at this place has called to speak to you upon a very serious subject this afternoon. Your Great Father at Washington, after carefully reading what the witnesses have testified in your several trials, has come to the conclusion that you have each been guilty of wantonly and wickedly murdering his white children; and, for this reason, he has directed that you each be hanged by the neck until you are dead, on next Friday, and that order will be carried into effect on that day at ten o'clock in the forenoon.

"Good ministers, both Catholic and Protestant, are here, from among whom each of you can select your spiritual adviser, who will be permitted to commune with you constantly during the few days that you are yet to live."

Adjutant Arnold was then instructed to read to them in English the letter of President Lincoln, which, in substance, stated the number and names of those condemned for execution, which letter was also read by Rev. S. R. Riggs, in Dakota.

The Colonel further instructed Mr. Riggs to tell them that they had so sinned against their fellow-men that there is no hope of clemency except in the mercy of God through the merits of the Blessed Redeemer, and that he earnestly exhorted them to apply to Him as their only remaining source of consolation.

The number condemned was forty, but one died before the day fixed for the execution, and one, Henry Milord, a half breed, had his sentence commuted to imprisonment for life in the penitentiary; so that thirty-eight only were hung.

On the 16th of February, 1863, the treaties before that time existing between the United States and these annuity Indians were abrogated and annulled, and all lands and rights of occupancy within the state of Minnesota, and all annuities and claims then existing in favor of said Indians were declared forfeited to the United States.

These Indians, in the language of the act, had, in the year 1862, "made unprovoked aggression and most savage war upon the United States, and massacred a large number of men, women and children within the state of Minnesota;" and as in this war and massacre they had "destroyed and damaged a large amount of property, and thereby forfeited all just claims" to their "monies and annuities to the United States," the act provides that "two-thirds of the balance remaining unexpended" of their annuities for the fiscal year, not exceeding one hundred thousand dollars, and the further sum of one hundred thousand dollars, being two-thirds of the annuities becoming due, and payable during the next fiscal year, should be appropriated and paid over to three commissioners appointed by the President, to be by them apportioned among the heads of families, or their survivors, who suffered damage by the depredations of said Indians, or the troops of the United States in the war against them, not exceeding the sum of two hundred dollars to any one family, nor more than actual damage sustained. All claims for damages were required, by the act, to be presented at certain times, and according to the rules prescribed by the commissioners, who should hold their first session at St. Peter, in the state of Minnesota, on or before the first Monday of April, and make and return their finding, and all the papers relating thereto, on or before the first Monday in December, 1863.

The President appointed for this duty, and with the advice and consent of the Senate, the Hons. Albert S. White, of the state of Indiana, Eli R. Chase, of Wisconsin, and Cyrus Aldrich, of Minnesota.

The duties of this board were so vigorously prosecuted, that, by the 1st of November following their appointment, some twenty thousand sheets of legal cap paper had been consumed in reducing to writing the testimony under the law requiring the commissioners to report the testimony in writing, and proper decisions made requisite to the payment of the two hundred dollars to that class of sufferers designated by the act of Congress. Such dispatch in Government agents gives abundant evidence of national vigor and integrity.

It was, no doubt, the object of this act of Congress to make such an appropriation as would relieve the sufferings of those who had lost all present means of support, and for the further purpose of ascertaining the whole amount of claims for damages as a necessary pre-requisite to future legislation. Regarded in this light, the act is one of wisdom and economy.

On the 21st of February following the annulling of the treaty with the Sioux above named, Congress passed "An act for the removal of the Winnebago Indians, and the sale of their reservation in Minnesota for their benefit." The money arising from the sale of their lands, after paying their indebtedness, is to be paid into the treasury of the United States, and expended, as the same is received, under the direction of the Secretary of the Interior, in necessary improvements upon their new reservation. The lands in the new reservation are to be allotted in severalty, not exceeding eighty acres to each head of a family, except to the chiefs, to whom larger allottments may be made, to be vested by patent in the Indian and his heirs, without the right of alienation.

These several acts of the General Government moderated to some extent the demand of the people for the execution of the condemned Sioux yet in the military prison at Mankato awaiting the final decision of the President. The removal of the Indians from the borders of Minnesota, and the opening up for settlement of over a million of acres of superior land, was a prospective benefit to the State of immense value, both in its domestic quiet and its rapid advancement in material wealth.

In pursuance of the acts of Congress, on the 22d of April, and for the purpose of carrying them into execution, the condemned Indians were first taken from the State, on board the steamboat Favorite, carried down the Mississippi, and confined at Davenport, in the state of Iowa, where they remained, with only such privileges as are allowed to convicts in the penitentiary.

On the 4th of May, A. D. 1863, at six o'clock in the afternoon, certain others of the Sioux Indians, squaws and pappooses, in all about seventeen hundred, left Fort Snelling, on board the steamboat Davenport, for their new reservation on the Upper Missouri, above Fort Randall, accompanied by a strong guard of soldiers, and attended by certain of the missionaries and employes, the whole being under the general direction of Superintendent Clark W. Thompson. By these two shipments, some two thousand Sioux had been taken from the State and removed far from the borders of Minnesota. The expedition of 1863, fitted out against the scattered bands of the Sioux yet remaining on the borders of the State, or still further removed into the Dakota Territory, gave to the border settlements some assurance of protection and security against any further disturbance from these particular bands of Indians.

DEATH OF LITTLE CROW.

On Friday evening, July 3, 1863, Mr. Lampson and his son Chauncey, while traveling along the road, about six miles north of Hutchinson, discovered two Indians in a little prairie opening in the woods, interspersed with clumps of bushes and vines and a few scattering poplars, picking berries. These two Indians were Little Crow and his son Wowinapa.

STATEMENT BY HIS SON.

"I am the son of Little Crow; my name is Wowinapa; I am sixteen years old; my father had two wives before he took my mother; the first one had one son, the second one a son and daughter; the third wife was my mother. After taking my mother he put away the first two; he had seven children by my mother—six are dead; I am the only one living now; the fourth wife had four children born; do not know whether any died or not; two were boys and three were girls; the fifth wife had five children—three of them are dead, two are living; the sixth wife had three children; all of them are dead; the oldest was a boy, the other two were girls; the last four wives were sisters.

"Father went to St. Joseph last spring. When we were coming back he said he could not fight the white men, but would go below and steal horses from them, and give them to his children, so that they could be comfortable, and then he would go away off.

"Father also told me that he was getting old, and wanted me to go with him to carry his bundles. He left his wives and his other children behind. There were sixteen men and one squaw in the party that went below with us. We had no horses, but walked all the way down to the settlements. Father and I were picking red-berries, near Scattered Lake, at the time he was shot. It was near night. He was hit the first time in the side, just above the hip. His gun and mine were lying on the ground. He took up my gun and fired it first, and then fired his own. He was shot the second time when he was firing his own gun. The ball struck the stock of his gun, and then hit him in the side, near the shoulder. This was the shot that killed him. He told me that he was killed, and asked me for water, which I gave him. He died immediately after. When I heard the first shot fired I laid down, and the man did not see me before father was killed.

"A short time before father was killed an Indian named Hinka, who married the daughter of my father's second wife, came to him. He had a horse with him—also a gray-colored coat that he had taken from a man that he had killed to the north of where father was killed. He gave the coat to father, telling him he might need it when it rained, as he had no coat with him. Hinka said he had a horse now, and was going back to the Indian country.

"The Indians that went down with us separated. Eight of them and the squaw went north; the other eight went further down. I have not seen any of them since. After father was killed I took both guns and the ammunition and started to go to Devil's Lake, where I expected to find some of my friends. When I got to Beaver creek I saw the tracks of two Indians, and at Standing Buffalo's village saw where the eight Indians that had gone north had crossed.

"I carried both guns as far as the Sheyenne river, where I saw two men. I was scared, and threw my gun and the ammunition down. After that I traveled only in the night; and, as I had no ammunition to kill anything to eat, I had not strength enough to travel fast. I went on until I arrived near Devil's Lake, when I staid in one place three days, being so weak and hungry that I could go no further. I had picked up a cartridge near Big Stone Lake, which I still had with me, and loaded father's gun with it, cutting the ball into slugs. With this charge I shot a wolf, ate some of it, which gave me strength to travel, and went on up the lake until the day I was captured, which was twenty-six days from the day my father was killed."

Here ends this wonderful episode in our contact with the Indian race in Minnesota. It commenced with Little Crow, in this instance, and it is proper that it should end with his inglorious life. With the best means for becoming an exponent of Indian civilization on this continent, he has driven the missionaries from his people and become a standing example of the assertion: "Once an Indian always an Indian."

Little Crow has indeed given emphasis to the aphorism of Ferdousi, "For that which is unclean by nature, thou cans't entertain no hope; no washing will make the gypsy white."

CHRONOLOGY.

CHAPTER XLIV.

PRINCIPAL EVENTS CHRONOLOGICALLY ARRANGED.

1659. Groselliers (Gro-zay-yay) and Radisson visit Minnesota.

1661. Menard, a Jesuit missionary, ascends the Mississippi, according to Herrot, twelve years before Marquette saw this river.

1665. Allouez, a Jesuit, visited the Minnesota shore of Lake Superior.

1679. Du Luth planted the arms of France, one hundred and twenty leagues beyond Mille Lacs.

1680. Du Luth, the first to travel in a canoe from Lake Superior, by way of the St. Croix river, to the Mississippi. Descending the Mississippi, he writes to Signelay, 1683: "I proceeded in a canoe two days and two nights, and the next day, at ten o'clock in the morning, found Accoult, Augelle, and Father Hennepin, with a hunting party of Sioux." He writes: "The want of respect which they showed to the said Reverend Father provoked me, and this I showed them, telling them he was my brother, and I had placed him in my canoe to come with me into the villages of said Nadouecioux." In September, Du Luth and Hennepin were at the Falls of St. Anthony on their way to Mackinaw.

1683. Perrot and Le Sueur visit Lake Pepin. Perrot, with twenty men, builds a stockade at the base of a bluff, upon the east bank, just above the entrance of Lake Pepin.

1688. Perrot re-occupies the post on Lake Pepin.

1689. Perrot, at Green Bay, makes a formal record of taking possession of the Sioux country in the name of the king of France

1693. Le Sueur at the extremity of Lake Superior.

1694. Le Sueur builds a post, on a prairie island in the Mississippi, about nine miles below Hastings.

1695. Le Sueur brings the first Sioux chiefs who visit Canada.

1700. Le Sueur ascends the Minnesota River. Fort L'Huillier built on a tributary of the Blue Earth River.

1702. Fort L'Huillier abandoned.

1727. Fort Beauharnois, in the fall of this year, erected in sight of Maiden's Rock, Lake Pepin, by La Perriere du Boucher.

1728. Verendrye stationed at Lake Nepigon.

1731. Verendrye's sons reach Rainy Lake. Fort St. Pierre erected at Rainy Lake.

1732. Fort St. Charles erected at the southwest corner of the Lake of the Woods.

1734. Fort Maurepas established on Winnipeg River.

1736. Verendrye's sons and others massacred by the Sioux on an isle in the Lake of the Woods.

1738. Lort La Reine on the Red River established.

1743. Verendrye's sons reach the Rocky Mountains.

1766. Jonathan Carver, on November 17th, reaches the Falls of St. Anthony.

1794. Sandy Lake occupied by the Northwest Company.

1802. William Morrison trades at Leach Lake.

1804. William Morrison trades at Elk Lake, now Itasca.

1805. Lieutenant Z. M. Pike purchases the site since occupied by Fort Snelling.

1817. Earl of Selkirk passes through Minnesota for Lake Winnipeg.

Major Stephen H. Long, U. S. A., visits Falls of St. Anthony.

1818. Dakotah war party under Black Dog attack Ojibways on the Pomme de Terre River.

1819. Col. Leavenworth arrives on the 24th of August, with troops at Mendota.

1820. J. B. Faribault brings up to Mendota, horses for Col. Leavenworth.

Laidlow, superintendent of farming for Earl Selkirk, passes from Pembina to Prairie du Chien to purchase seed wheat. Upon the 15th of April, left Prairie du Chien with Mackinaw boats and ascended the Minnesota to Big Stone Lake, where the boats were placed on rollers and dragged a short distance to Lake Traverse, and on the 3d of June reached Pembina.

On the 5th of May, Col. Leavenworth established summer quarters at Camp Coldwater, Hennepin county.

In July, Governor Cass, of Michigan, visits the camp.

In August, Col. Snelling succeeds Leavenworth.

September 20th, corner-stone laid under command of Col. Snelling.

First white marriage in Minnesota, Lieutenant Green to daughter of Captain Gooding.

First white child born in Minnesota, daughter to Col. Snelling; died following year.

1821. Fort St. Anthony was sufficiently completed to be occupied by troops.

Mill at St. Anthony Falls constructed for the use of garrison, under the supervision of Lieutenant McCabe.

1822. Col. Dickson attempted to take a drove of cattle to Pembina.

1823. The first steamboat, the Virginia, on May 10th, arrived at the mouth of the Minnesota river.

Mill stones for grinding flour sent to St. Anthony Falls.

Major Long, U. S. A., visits the northern boundary by way of the Minnesota and Red River.

Beltrami, the Italian traveler, explores the northernmost source of the Mississippi.

1824. General Winfield Scott inspects Fort St. Anthony, and at his suggestion the War Department changed the name to Fort Snelling.

1825. April 5th, steamboat Rufus Putnam reaches the Fort. May, steamboat Rufus Putnam arrives again and delivers freight at Land's End trading post on the Minnesota, about a mile above the Fort.

1826. January 26th, first mail in five months received at the Fort.

Deep snow during February and March.

March 20th, snow from twelve to eighteen inches.

April 5th, snow-storm with flashes of lightning.

April 10th, thermometer four degrees above zero.

April 21st, ice began to move in the river at the Fort, and with twenty feet above low water mark.

May 2d, first steamboat of the season, the Lawrence, Captain Reeder, took a pleasure party to within three miles of the Falls of St. Anthony.

1826. Dakotahs kill an Ojibway near Fort Snelling.

1827. Flat Mouth's party of Ojibways attacked at Fort Snelling, and Sioux delivered by Colonel Snelling to be killed by Ojibways, and their bodies thrown over the bluff into the river.

General Gaines inspects Fort Snelling.

Troops of the Fifth Regiment relieved by those of the First.

1828. Colonel Snelling dies in Washington.

1829. Rev. Alvin Coe and J. D. Stevens, Presbyterian missionaries, visit the Indians around Fort Snelling.

Major Taliaferro, Indian agent, establishes a farm for the benefit of the Indians at Lake Calhoun, which he called Eatonville, after the Secretary of War.

Winter, Spring and Summer very dry. One inch was the average monthly fall of rain or snow for ten months. Vegetation more backward than it had been for ten years.

1830. August 14th, a sentinel at Fort Snelling, just before daylight, discovered the Indian council house on fire. Wa-pa-sha's son-in-law was the incendiary.

1831. August 17th, an old trader Rocque, and his son arrived at Fort Snelling from Prairie du Chien, having been twenty-six days on the journey. Under the influence of whisky or stupidity, they ascended the St. Croix by mistake, and were lost for fifteen days.

1832. May 12th, steamboat Versailles arrives at Fort Snelling.

June 16th, William Carr arrives from Missouri at Fort Snelling, with a drove of cattle and horses.

Henry R. Schoolcraft explores the sources of the Mississippi.

1833. Rev. W. T. Boutwell establishes a mission among the Ojibways at Leech Lake.

E. F. Ely opens a mission school for Ojibways at Aitkin's trading post, Sandy Lake.

1834. May. Samuel W. and Gideon H. Pond arrive at Lake Calhoun as missionaries among the Sioux.

November. Henry H. Sibley arrives at Mendota as agent of Fur Company.

1835. May. Rev. T. S. Williamson and J. D. Stevens arrive as Sioux missionaries, with Alexander G. Huggins as lay-assistant.

June. Presbyterian Church at Fort Snelling organized.

July 31st. A Red River train arrives at Fort Snelling with fifty or sixty head of cattle, and about twenty-five horses.

Major J. L. Bean surveys the Sioux and Chippeway boundary line under treaty of 1825, as far as Otter Tail Lake.

November. Col. S. C. Stambaugh arrives; is sutler at Fort Snelling.

1836. May 6th, "Missouri Fulton," first steamboat, arrives at Fort Snelling.

May 29th. "Frontier," Capt. Harris, arrives.

June 1st. "Palmyra" arrives.

July 2d. "Saint Peters" arrives with J. N. Nicollet as passenger.

July 30. Sacs and Foxes kill twenty-four Winnebagoes on Root River.

1837. Rev. Stephen R. Riggs and wife join Lake Harriet Mission.

Rev. A. Brunson and David King establish Kaposia Mission.

Commissioners Dodge and Smith at Fort Snelling make a treaty with the Chippeways to cede lands east of the Mississippi.

Franklin Steele and others make claims at Falls of St. Croix and St. Anthony.

September 29th. Sioux chiefs at Washington sign a treaty.

November 10th. Steamboat Rolla arrives at Fort Snelling with the Sioux on their return from Washington.

December 12th. Jeremiah Russell and L. W. Stratton make the first claim at Marine, in St. Croix valley.

1838. April, Hole-in-the-Day and party kill thirteen of the Lac-qui-parle Sioux. Martin McLeod from Pembina, after twenty-eight days of exposure to snow, reaches Lake Traverse.

May 25th, Steamboat Burlington arrives at Fort Snelling with J. N. Nicollet and J. C. Fremont on a scientific expedition.

June 14th, Marryat, the British novelist, Franklin Steele and others rode from the Fort to view Falls of St. Anthony.

July 12th, steamboat Palmyra arrives at Fort Snelling with an official notice of the ratification of treaty. Men arrived to develop the St. Croix Valley.

August 2d, Hole-in the-Day encamped with a party of Chippeways near Fort Snelling, and was attacked by Sioux from Mud Lake, and one killed and another wounded.

August 27th, Steamboat Ariel arrives with commissioners Pease and Ewing to examine half-breed claims.

September 30th, steamboat Ariel makes the first trip up the St. Croix river.

October 26th, steamboat Gypsy first to arrive at Falls of St. Croix with annuity goods for the Chippeways. In passing through Lake St. Croix grounded near the townsite laid out by S. C. Stambaugh and called Stambaughville.

1839. April 14th, the first steamboat at Fort Snelling, the Ariel, Capt. Lyon.

Henry M. Rice arrives at Fort Snelling.

May 2d, Rev. E. G. Gear, of the Protestant Episcopal church, recently appointed chaplain, arrived at Fort Snelling in the steamboat Gipsy.

May 12th, steamboat Fayette arrives on the St Croix, having been at Fort Snelling, with members of Marine Mill Company.

May 21st, the Glaucus, Gapt. Atchinson, arrives at Fort Snelling.

June 1st, the Pennsylvania, Capt. Stone, arrives at Fort Snelling.

June 5th, the Glaucus arrives again.

June 6th, the Ariel arrives.

June 12th, at Lake Harriet mission, Rev. D. Gavin, Swiss missionary among the Sioux at Red Wing, was married to Cordelia Stevens, teacher at Lake Harriet mission.

June 25th, steamboat "Knickerbocker," arrived at Fort Snelling.

June 26th, steamboat Ariel, on third trip.

June 27th, a train of Red River carts, under Mr. Sinclair, with emigrants, who encamped near the fort.

July 2d, Chippeways killed a Sioux of Lake Calhoun band.

July 3d, Sioux attack Chippeways in ravine above Stillwater.

1840. April, Rev. Lucian Galtier, of the Roman Catholic church, arrives at Mendota.

May 6th, squatters removed on military reservation.

June 15th, Thomas Simpson, Artic explorer, shoots himself near Turtle River, under aberration of the mind.

June 17th, four Chippeways kill and scalp a Sioux man and woman.

1841. March 6th, wild geese appeared at the fort.

March 20th, Mississippi opened.

April 6th, steamboat Otter, Capt. Harris, arrived. Kaboka, an old chief of Lake Calhoun band, killed by Chippeways.

May 24th, Sioux attack Chippeways at Lake Pokeguma, of Snake river. Methodist mission moved from Kaposia to Red Rock, Rev. B. F. Kavenaugh, superintendent.

November 1st, Father Galtier completes the log chapel of St. Paul, which gave the name to the capital of Minnesota. Rev. Augustin Ravoux arrives.

1842. July, the Chippeways attack the Kaposia Sioux.

1843. Stillwater laid out. Ayer, Spencer and Ely establish a Chippeway mission at Red lake.

July 15th, Thomas Longly, brother-in-law of Rev. S. R. Riggs, drowned at Traverse des Sioux mission station.

1844. August, Captain Allen with fifty dragoons marches from Fort Des Moines through southwestern Minnesota, and on the 10th of September reaches the Big Sioux River. Sisseton war party kill an American named Watson, driving cattle to Fort Snelling.

1845. June 25th, Captain Sumner reaches Traverse des Sioux, and proceeding northward arrested three of the murderers of Watson.

1846. Dr. Williamson, Sioux missionary, moves from Lac-qui-parle to Kaposia. March 31st, steamboat Lynx, Capt. Atchinson, arrives at Fort Snelling.

1847. St. Croix county, Wisconsin, organized. Stillwater the county seat. Harriet E. Bishop establishes a school at St. Paul. Saw-mills begun at St. Anthony Falls.

August, Commissioner Verplanck and Henry M. Rice make treaties with the Chippeways at Fond du Lac and Leech Lake. The town of St. Paul surveyed, platted, and recorded in the St. Croix county Register of Deeds office.

1848. Henry H. Sibley Delegate to Congress from Wisconsin territory.

May 29th, Wisconsin admitted, leaving Minnesota (with its present boundaries) without a government.

August 26th, "Stillwater convention" held to take measures for a separate territorial organization.

October 30th, H. H. Sibley, elected Delegate to Congress.

1849. March, act of Congress creating Minnesota Territory.

April 9th, Highland Mary, Capt. Atchinson, arrives at St. Paul.

April 18th, James M. Goodhue arrives at St. Paul with first newspaper press.

May 27th, Gov. Alexander Ramsey arrives at Mendota.

June 1st, Gov. Ramsey issues proclamation declaring the territory duly organized.

August 1st, H. H. Sibley elected Delegate to Congress from Minnesota.

September 3d, first Legislature convened.

November, First Presbyterian church, St. Paul, organized.

December, first literary address at Falls of St. Anthony.

1850. January 1st, Historical Society meeting.

June 11th, Indian council at Fort Snelling.

June 14th, steamer Governor Ramsey makes first trip above Falls of St. Anthony.

June 26th, the Anthony Wayne reaches the Falls of St. Anthony.

July 18th, steamboat Anthony Wayne ascends the Minnesota to the vicinity of Traverse des Sioux.

July 25th, steamboat Yankee goes beyond Blue Earth River.

September, H. H. Sibley elected Delegate to Congress.

October, Fredrika Bremer, Swedish novelist visits Minnesota.

November, the Dakotah Friend, a monthly paper appeared.

December, Colonel D. A. Robertson establishes Minnesota Democrat.

December 26th, first public Thanksgiving Day.

1851. May, St. Anthony Express newspaper begins its career.

July, treaty concluded with the Sioux at Traverse des Sioux.

July, Rev. Robert Hopkins, Sioux missionary drowned.

August, treaty concluded with the Sioux at Maukato.

September 19th, the Minnesotian, of St. Paul, edited by J. P. Owens, appeared.

November, Jerome Fuller, Chief Justice in place of Aaron Goodrich, arrives.

December 18th, Thanksgiving Day.

1852. Hennepin county created.

February 14th, Dr. Rae, Arctic explorer, arrives at St. Paul with dog train.

May 14th, land slide at Stillwater.

August, James M. Goodhue, pioneer editor, dies.

November, Yuhazee, an Indian, convicted of murder.

1853. April 27th, Chippewas and Sioux fight in streets of St. Paul. Governor Willis A. Gorman succeeds Governor Ramsey.

October, Henry M. Rice elected delegate to congress. The capitol building completed.

1854. March 3d, Presbyterian mission house near Lac-qui-parle burned.

June 8th, great excursion from Chicago to St. Paul and St. Anthony Falls.

December 27th, Yuhazee, the Indian, hung at St. Paul.

1855. January, first bridge over Mississippi completed at Falls of St. Anthony.

October, H. M. Rice re-elected to Congress.

December 12, James Stewart arrives in St. Paul direct from Arctic regions, with relics of Sir John Franklin.

1856. Erection of State University building was begun.

1857. Congress passes an act authorizing people of Minnesota to vote for a constitution.

March. Inkpadootah slaughters settlers in southwest Minnesota.

Governor Samuel Medary succeeds Governor W. A. Gorman.

March 5th. Land-grant by congress for railways.

April 27th. Special session of legislature convenes.

July. On second Monday convention to form a constitution assembles at Capitol.

October 13th. Election for State officers, and ratifying of the constitution.

H. H. Sibley first governor under the State constitution.

December. On first Wednesday, first State legislature assembles.

December. Henry M. Rice and James Shields elected United States senators.

1858, April 15th. People approve act of legislature loaning the public credit for five millions of dollars to certain railway companies.

May 11th. Minnesota becomes one of the United States of America.

June 2d. Adjourned meeting of legislature held.

November. Supreme court of State orders Governor Sibley to issue Railroad bonds.

1859. Normal school law passed.

June. Burbank and Company place the first steamboart on Red River of the North.

August. Bishop T. L. Grace arrived in St. Paul.

1859. October 11th, State election, Alexander Ramsey chosen governor.

1860. March 23d, Anna Bilanski hung at St. Paul for the murder of her husband, the first white person executed in Minnesota.

1861. April 14th, Governor Ramsey calls upon President in Washington and offers a regiment of volunteers.

June 21st, First Minnesota Regiment, Col. W. A. Gorman, leaves for Washington.

July 21st, First Minnesota in battle of Bull Run.

October 13th, Second Minnesota Infantry, Col. H. P. Van Cleve, leaves Fort Snelling.

November 16th, Third Minnesota Infantry, H. C. Lester, go to seat of war.

1862. January 19th, Second Minnesota in battle at Mill Spring, Kentucky.

April 6th. First Minnesota Battery, Captain Munch, at Pittsburg Landing.

April 21st, Second Minnesota Battery goes to seat of war.

April 21st, Fourth Minnesota Infantry Volunteers. Col. J. B Sanborn, leaves Fort Snelling.

May 13th, Fifth Regiment Volunteers, Col. Borgensrode, leaves for the seat of war.

May 28th, Second, Fourth, and Fifth in battle near Corinth, Mississippi.

May 31st, First Minnesota in battle at Fair Oaks, Virginia.

June 29th, First Minnesota in battle at Savage Station.

June 30th, First Minnesota in battle near Willis' Church.

July 1st, First Minnesota in battle at Malvern Hill.

August, Sixth Regiment, Col. Crooks, organized.

August, Seventh Regiment, Col. Miller, organized.

August, Eighth Regiment, Col, Thomas, organized.

August, Ninth Regiment, Col. Wilkin, organized.

August 18th, Sioux attack whites at lower Sioux Agency.

September 23d, Col. Sibley defeats Sioux at Mud Lake.

December 26th, Thirty-eight Sioux executed on the same scaffold at Mankato.

1863. January, Alexander Ramsey elected United States Senator.

May 14th, Fourth and Fifth Regiment in battle near Jackson, Mississippi.

July 2d, First Minnesota Infantry in battle at Gettysburg, Pennsylvania.

September 19th, Second Minnesota Infantry engaged at Chickamauga, Tennessee.

November 23d, Second Minnesota Infantry engaged at Mission Ridge.

1864. January. Col. Stephen Miller inaugurated Governor of Minnesota.

March 30th; Third Minnesota Infantry engaged at Fitzhugh's Wcoods.

June 6th, Fifth Minnesota Infantry engaged at Lake Chicot, Arkansas.

July 13th, Seventh, Ninth, and Tenth, with portion of the Fifth Minnesota Infantry, engaged at Tupelo, Mississippi.

July 14th, Col. Alex. Wilkin, of the Ninth, killed.

October 15th, Fourth Regiment engaged near Altoona, Georgia.

December 7th, Eighth Regiment engaged near Murfreesboro, Tennessee.

Fifth, Seventh, Ninth, and Tenth Regiments at Nashville, Tennessee.

1865. January 10th, Daniel S. Norton, elected United States Senator.

April 9th, Fifth, Sixth, Seventh, Ninth, and Tenth at the siege of Mobile.

November 10th, Shakpedan, Sioux chief, and Medicine Bottle executed at Fort Snelling.

1866. January 8th, Col. William R. Marshall inaugurated Governor of Minnesota.

1867. Preparatory department of the State University opened.

1868. January, Governor Marshall enters upon second term.

1869. Bill passed by legislature, removing sea of Government to spot near Big Kandiyohi Lake —vetoed by Governor Marshall.

1870. January 7th, Horace Austin inaugurated as Governor.

1871. January, Wm. Windom elected United States Senator. In the fall destructive fires, occasioned by high winds, swept over frontier counties.

1872. January, Governor Austin enters upon a second term.

1873. January 7th, 8th, and 9th, polar wave sweeps over the State, seventy persons perishing.

May 22d, the senate of Minnesota convicts State Treasurer of corruption in office.

September, grasshopper raid began, and continued five seasons. Jay Cooke failure occasions a financial panic.

1874. January 9th, Cushman K. Davis inaugurated Governor. William S. King elected to congress.

1875. February 19th, S. J. R. McMillan elected United States senator.

November, amendment to State constitution, allowing any women twenty-one years of age to vote for school officers, and to be eligible for school offices. Rocky Mountain locusts destroy crops in southwestern Minnesota.

1876. January 7th, John S. Pillsbury inaugurated Governor.

September, 6th, outlaws from Missouri kill the cashier of the Northfield Bank.

1879. November. State constitution amended forbidding public moneys to be used for the support of schools wherein the distinctive creeds or tenets of any particular Christian or other religious sect are taught. J. H. Stewart, M. D., elected to congress. Biennial sessions of the legislature adopted.

1878. January, Governor Pillsbury enters upon a second term.

May 2d, explosion in the Washburn and other flour mills at Minneapolis. One hundred and fifty thousand dollars appropriated to purchase seed grain for destitute settlers.

1880. November 15th, a portion of the Insane Asylum at St. Peter was destroyed by fire. and twenty-seven inmates lost their lives.

1881. March 1st, Capitol at St. Paul destroyed by fire.

November. Lucius F. Hubbard elected Governor.

HISTORY

OF

FREEBORN COUNTY.

CHAPTER XLV.

LOCATION—TOPOGRAPHICAL AND PHYSICAL FEATURES——GEOLOGICAL—COAL MINING.

Freeborn is on the southern tier of Minnesota counties, the fourth from the Mississippi, and next to Mower county; on the south it has Winnebago and Worth counties in Iowa; on the west it is the sixth from the Dakota line, and next to Faribault; and Steele and Waseca are the northern neighbors.

There are thirty or more lakes in its territory, the most prominent among which are Lake Albert Lea, Geneva Lake, Rice Lake, Freeborn Lake, Twin Lakes, and Pickerel Lake. It is well watered, being really on a divide, with waters flowing north and south. Among the more noted streams are the Shell Rock River, Cobb River, Goose Creek, Turtle Creek, Deer Creek, Bancroft Creek, Stewart's Creek, and State Line Creek, with several others. These, with the lakes and other topographical features, receive special mention in the geological sketch and in the town histories. The twenty townships all coincide with the government survey, and have corresponding political organizations.

The following geological description is taken from the very able report of Prof. N. H. Winchell, State Geologist:

SITUATION AND AREA.

Freeborn county borders on the state of Iowa, and is very near the center of the southern boundary line of Minnesota. It has the form of a rectangle, having a length, east and west, of five government towns, and north and south, a width of four, making an area of 720 square miles, or 449,235.63 acres, after deducting the areas covered by water.

NATURAL DRAINAGE.

With the exception of Freeborn, Hartland, and Carlston townships, the surface drainage is towards the south and southeast. The county embraces the headwaters of the Shell Rock and Cedar Rivers of Iowa, and those of the Cobb River which joins the Minnesota toward the north. Hence it lies on the watershed between two great drainage slopes. For the same reason none of its streams are large; the Shell Rock, where it leaves the State, being its largest. The streams have not much fall, but afford some water-power, which has been improved in the construction of flouring mills. Such are found at Albert Lea and Twin Lakes. In these cases the body of water confined in the upper lake serves as the water-head and the reservoir, mills being constructed near their outlets. There is also an available water-power at Shell Rock village, but its use would cause the flooding of a large body of land adjoining the river.

SURFACE FEATURES.

The surface of the county, although having no remarkable and sudden changes of level, yet is considerably diversified as a rolling prairie, more or less covered with sparse oaks and oak bushes. The plats of the United States surveyors, on file in the Register's office at Albert Lea, indicate considerably more area covered with timber, or as "oak openings," when the county was surveyed by them (1854), than is now the case. The following minutes are based on an examination of their plats, and will give a pretty correct idea of the distribution of the oak openings and the prairie tracts throughout the county.

LONDON.—The most of this township is prairie, a belt of oak openings and timber entering it from the north, about three miles wide, in the center of the town, and extending to the center, bearing off to the southeast, and terminating in section twenty-four. The magnetic variation throughout the town was, when surveyed, from 8 deg. 20 min. to 10 deg. 42 min., the greatest being in sections thirty-three and thirty-four.

OAKLAND.—A little more than a half of this township consists of oak openings, an area in the eastern half only being prairie, with a small patch also in section thirty-one. Two large sloughs cross the town, one through sections thirty, thirty-one, and thirty-two, and the other through sections four, five, eight, seven, and eighteen. Magnetic variation about 9 deg., varying from 8 deg. 12 min. to 10 deg. 8 min.

MOSCOW.—Nearly the whole of this township is taken up with oak openings and marshes. Turtle Creek crosses it from northwest to southeast. A large portion of the northern half of the town is a floating marsh, containing a great quantity of peat. Magnetic variation 8 deg. 20 min. to 10 deg. 20 min.

NEWRY.—There is a small patch of prairie in the north-east part of this town, in sections one, twelve, thirteen, and twenty-four, and a small area in sections twenty and twenty-one. There is another in the northwest corner, embracing sections six and seven and parts of five, thirteen, and eighteen. The rest is openings and marsh, particularly in the northwest corner. Magnetic variation, 8 deg. 20 min. to 9 deg. 40 min.

SHELLROCK.—A belt about one and one-half miles wide along the west side of this town, accompanying the Shellrock River, constitutes the only openings occuring in sections three, ten, and fifteen. The northwest part of the township is rolling, and the southeast is level and wet with marshes. Magnetic variation, 11 deg. 30 min. to 13 deg. 40 min.

ALDEN.—This town is all prairie, with scattered small marshes. Magnetic variation, 11 deg. 27 min. to 13 deg. 15 min.

CARLSTON.—This town is all prairie, except a narrow belt of sparse timber about Freeborn Lake. Long narrow marshes spread irregularly over the central and eastern portions of the town. In the southeast quarter of section thirty-six there is also a small area of sparse timber. Magnetic variation, 11 deg. 13 min. to 13 deg.

FREEBORN.—In this town there is a little sparse timber about the north part. Magnetic variation, 8 deg. 50 min. to 10 deg. 15 min.

BATH.—An area of openings comprising about half of this town, in the central and eastern portion, is nearly surrounded by a belt of prairie. Small marshes are scattered through the town. Magnetic variation, 8 deg. 45 min. to 10 deg. 35 min.

NUNDA.—This town is also mostly openings, but an area of prairie occurs in sections four, five, nine, and three, and another lies southwest of Bear Lake. Considerable marsh land is embraced within the area of openings. Magnetic variation, 10 deg. 5 min. to 12 deg. 15 min., the latter in section thirty-one.

PICKEREL LAKE.—The west half of this township is prairie, and the eastern is devoted to openings with lakes and marshes. Magnetic variation, 9 deg. 45 min. to 11 deg. 50 min.

MANCHESTER.—About one-half of this town is prairie, the remainder being oak openings. The prairie lies in the northwestern and southern portions. Small marshes occur both in the prairie and openings. Magnetic variations, 10 deg. to 12 deg. 15 min.

HARTLAND.—This town is almost entirely composed of prairie, the only timber being about Lake Mule, and in the southern portions of sections thirty-four, thirty-five, and thirty-six. There is not much marsh in the town. Magnetic variation, 9 deg. 45 min. to 12 deg. 25 min.

MANSFIELD.—This town is nearly all prairie. Magnetic variation, 8 deg. 45 min. to 10 deg. 15 min.

HAYWARD.—A wide belt of prairie occupies about two-thirds of this town, running north and south through the center. On the west of this is a rolling tract embracing a portion of Lake Albert Lea and some tributary marshes, while on the east a large marsh covers sections twelve and fourteen, and portions of thirteen, eleven, fifteen, twenty-two, and twenty-three. There is also a prairie tract in section one.

RICELAND.—This township is about equally divided between prairie, openings, and marsh, the first being in the south central portion, the second in the northwest and central, bordering on Rice Lake, and the marsh in the northeastern part of the town. Magnetic variation, from 8 deg. 45 min. to 10 deg. 30 min.

GENEVA.—There is but little prairie in this town, the southern portion being comprised in a large marsh which is crossed by Turtle Creek, the outlet of Walnut Lake. The central portion is occupied by oak openings which also extend to the northwest and west boundaries. The prairie is in the northern and eastern portions. Magnetic variation, 9 deg. 10 min. to 10 deg. 23 min.

FREEMAN.—This township contains no prairie. It is mostly devoted to oak openings, but a series of marshes, drained by the tributaries of the Shell Rock that crosses it toward the southeast, take up a considerable area in the central and eastern portion. Magnetic variation 9 deg. to 10 deg. 40 min., the greatest being in section thirty-one.

ALBERT LEA.—This township is nearly all taken up with oak openings, but a few small marshes, trending northwest and southeast., are found in different portions. There is also a small patch of prairie in section six, and another in the south east corner of the county. The western arm of Albert Lea Lake, through which the Shell Rock River runs, is in the central and eastern part of this town, and adds greatly to the variety and beauty of its natural scenery. Pickerel Lake is also partly in this township. Magnetic variation 8 deg. 46 min. to 10 deg. 8 min.

BANCROFT.—A little more than one-fourth of this township is prairie, situated in the center and southwestern portions. The rest of the town is covered with oak openings. The source of the Shell Rock is in the northwestern ends of Freeborn and Spicer Lakes, and a little adjoining Spicer Lake on the east. There are also some openings in section twenty-six, where the arms of the marsh protect the timber from the prairie fires. The rest is of prairie with spreading marshes. Magneitc variation 11 deg. 55 min. to 12 deg. 50 min. North and west of Albert Lea is a very broken and rolling surface of sparse timber. This tract consists of bold hills and deep valleys wrought in the common drift of the country. On some of these hills are granitic boulders, but the country generally does not show many boulders. The drift is generally, in this broken tract, a gravel-clay. In some of the street-cuts for grading, a gravel is found, containing a good deal of limestone.

A great many of the marshes of the county are surrounded with tracts of oak openings, a fact which indicates that the marshes serve as barriers to the prairie fires. Such marshes are really filled with water, and quake with a heavy peat deposit on being trod on. They are very different from those of counties further west, as in Nobles county, which, in the summer, are apt to become dried, and are annually clothed with a growth of coarse grass, which feeds the fires that pass over the country in the fall. As a general rule, but little or no grass grows on a good peat marsh.

The county contains some of the highest land in the State. Some of the counties farther west, particularly Nobles and Mower counties on the east, rise from one to two hundred feet higher. There is also a high and rolling tract in the north central portion of the State, covering Otter Tail county, which rises to about the same level, as shown by railroad profiles. The greater portion of the State, however, lies several hundred feet lower than Freeborn county.

SOIL AND TIMBER.

Throughout the county the soil depends on the nature of the drift, combined with the various modifying local circumstances. There is nothing in the county that can properly be designated a limestone or a sandstone soil. The materials of which it is composed have been transported, perhaps, several hundred miles, and are so abundantly and universally spread over the underlying rock that they receive no influence from it. The subsoil is a gravelly clay, and in much of the county that also constitutes the surface soil. In low ground this, of course, is disguised by a wash from the higher ground, causing sometimes a loam and sometimes a tough fine clay; the latter is particularly in those tracts that are subject to inundation by standing water. On an undulating prairie, with a close clay, or clayey sub-soil, such low spots are apt to leave a black, rich loam or clayey loam, the colored being derived from the annual prairie fires that leave charred grass and other vegetation to mingle with the soil. The same takes place on wide tracts of flat prairie. In these may be, but rarely, a stone of any kind—indeed that is usually the case—but below the immediate surface, a foot or eighteen inches, a gravelly clay is always met with. This at first doubtless formed the soil, the disintegrating forces of frost, rain, and wind, combined with the calcining effects of the prairie fires, having reduced the stones and gravel to powder, leaving a finely pulverized substance for a surface soil.

In a rolling tract of country, while the low ground is being filled slowly with the wash from the hills, and furnished with a fine soil, the hills are left covered with a coarse and stony surface soil. For that reason a great many boulders are sometimes seen on the tops of drift knolls. Along streams and about the shores of lakes, the action of the water has carried away the clay of the soil and often eaten into the original drift, letting the stones and boulders tumble down to the bottom of the bank, where they are often very numerous. Along streams they are sometimes again covered with alluvium—indeed are apt to be - but along the shores of lakes they are kept near the beach line by the action of the winter ice. After a lapse of time sufficient, the banks themselves become rounded off and finally turfed over or covered with trees. These lakes sometimes extend their limits laterally, but slowly become shallower. This county is furnished with a number of beautiful lakes. These are generally in the midst of a rolling country, and some of their banks are high.

In the survey of the county the following species of trees and shrubs are noticed growing native:

Burr Oak. Quercus macrocarpa. *Michx.*
Red Oak. Quercus rubra. *L.* (This species is not satisfactorily indentified.)
Aspen. Populus tremuloides. *Michx.*
Elm. Ulmus Americana, (*Pl. Clayt.*) *Willd.*
Black cherry. Prunus serotina. *Ehr.*
American Crab. Pyrus coronaria. *L.*
Bitternut. Carya amara. *Nutt.*
Black Walnut. Juglans nigra. *L.*
Wild Plum. Prunus Amecicana. *Marsh.*
White Ash. Fraximus Americana. *L.*
Butternut. Juglans cinerea. *L.*
Hazlenut. Corylus Americana. *Walt.*
Forest Grape. Vitis cordifolia. *Michx.*
Bittersweet. Celastrus scandens. *L.*
Smooth Sumach. Rhus glabra. *L.*
Red Raspberry. Rubus strigosus. *Michx.*
Rose. Rosa blanda. *Ait.*
Wolfberry. Symphoricarpus occidentalis. *R. Br.*
Bass. Tilia Americana. *L.*
Prickley Ash. Zanthoxylum Americanum. *Mill.*
Cornel. (Different species.)
Willow. (Different species.)
Gooseberry (prickley.) Ribes cynosbati. *L.*
Thorn. Crataegus coccinea. *L.*
Hackberry. Celtis occidentalis. *L.*
Sugar Maple. Acer saccharinum. *Wang.*
Cottonwood. Populus monilifera. *Ait.*
Soft Maple. Acer rubrum. *L.*
Cockspur Thorn. Cretaegus Crus-galli. *L.*
Slippery Elm. Ulmus fulva. *Michx.*
Black Ash. Fraximus sambucifolia. *Lam.*
High-bush Cranberry. Niburnum Opuvus. *L.*
Choke Cherry. Prunus Virginiana. *L.*
Shagbark Hickory. Crrya alba. *Nutt.* On M. L. Bullis' land in Moscow township, near the county line.—*A. A. Harwood.*)

Besides the foregoing, the following list embraces trees that are frequently seen in cultivation in Freeborn county:

Spruce.
Red Cedar. Juniperus Virginiana. *L.*
Mountain Ash. Pyrus Americana. *D. C.*
Balsam Poplar. Populus balsamifera. *L. Var.* candicans.
Lombardy Poplar. ditatata. *Ait.*
Locust. Robinia Pseudacacia. *L.* [The Locust dies out in Freeborn county.]
Hackmatack. Larix Americana. *Michx.*
Arbor Vitæ. Thuja occidentalis.

THE GEOLOGICAL STRUCTURE.

There is not a naturrl exposure of the underlying rock in Freeborn county. Hence the details of its geological structure are wholly unknown. It is only by an examination of outcrops in Mower county and in the adjoining counties of Iowa, together with a knowledge of the general geology of that portion of the State, that anything can be known of the geology of Freeborn county. In the absence of actual outcrops of rock within the county, there are still some evidences of the character of rock that underlies the county, in the nature and position of the drift materials. There is, besides, a shaft that has struck the Cretaceous in the northwestern portion of the county, in exploration of coal.

Although the drift is heavy it lies in such positions that it shows some changes in the surface of the bed rock. It is a principle pretty well established that any sudden great alternation in the rock from hardness to softness, as from a heavy limestone layer to a layer of erosible shales, or from shales to more enduring sandstone, each stratum having a considerable thickness, is expressed on the drift by changes from a rough and rolling, more or less stony surface, to a flat and nearly smooth surface, or *vise versa*. It sometimes happens that the non-outcropping line of superposition of one important formation with another, either above or below, can be traced across a wide tract of drift covered country by following up a series of gravel knolls or ridges that accompany it, or by some similar feature of the topography. Again, the unusual frequency of any kind of rock in the drift at a certain place, especially if it be one not capable of bearing long transportation, is pretty good evidence of the proximity of the parent rock to that locality.

Applying these principles to Freeborn county, we find throughout the county a great many boulders of a hard, white, compact magnesian limestone, that have been extensively burned for quicklime. These attracted the attention of early settlers, and before the construction of the Southern Minnesota railroad,supplied all the lime used in the county. Although these boulders are capable of being transported a great distance, their great abundance points to the existence of the source of supply in the underlying bed-rock. In the drift also are frequently found pieces of lignite or Cretaceous coal, which cannot be far transported by glacier agencies. This also indicates the existence of the Cretaceous lignites in Freeborn county. In regard to changes in the character of the natural surface, we see an evenly flat and prairie surface in the western tier of towns, and in the southeastern part of the county, and a hilly and gravelly tract of irregular shape in the central portion. There are two ridges or divides, formed superficially of drift, that occur in the central part of the county, one north of Albert Lea, and the other south of it, separated about eleven miles, as shown by a series of elevations from a preliminary railroad survey by Mr. William Morin. What may be their directions at points further removed from Albert Lea it is not possible to state with certainty, but on one side they seem to trend toward the northwest. Indeed there seems to be a northwest and southeast trend to the surface features of Freeborn county generally. Such rough surfaces, and especially the ridges of drift, are more stony and gravelly than the flat portions of the county. They mark the location of great inequalities in the upper surface of the underlying rock, the exact nature of which cannot be known.

In addition to these general indications of the character of the rock of the county, the shaft sunk for coal at Freeborn, reveals the presence of the Cretaceous in that portion of the county, and examinations of the nearest exposures in the neighboring county of Iowa, discloses the Hamilton limestone of the Devonian age. This limestone is exactly like that found so abundantly in the form of boulders in Freeborn county. As the general direction of the drift forces was toward the south, and as the trend of the Hamilton in Iowa, according to Dr. C. A. White (see his map of the geology of Iowa, final Report, 1870,) is toward the northwest, there is abundant reason for concluding that that formation also extends under Freeborn county. The preliminary geological map of the state of Minnesota, published in 1872, indicates Freeborn county almost entirely underlain by the Devonian, the only exception being in the northwestern corner. How much farther toward the northwest these limestone boulders can be traced with equal abundance, the explorations of the survey have not yet revealed.

The northwestern corner of Freeborn county has been regarded as underlain by a limestone of the age of Niagara, belonging to the Upper Silurian, that formation in the northwest coming directly below the limestones of the Devonian. That may be correct; but it is certain that there is in the neighborhood of Freeborn an area of the Cretaceous, which must, in that case, overlie the Silurian limestones. This Cretaceous area is believed to extend north and south across the west end of the county, and to be roughly coincident with the flat and prairie portion in the western part, in which case it overlaps the Devonian.

EXPLORATIONS OF COAL.

In common with many other places in Southern Minnesota, Freeborn township, in the northwestern corner of the county, has furnished from the drift pieces of cretaceous lignite that resemble coal. These have, in a number of instances, incited ardent expectations of coal, and led to the outlay of money in explorations. Such pieces are taken out in digging wells. The opinion seems to grow in a community where such fragments are found, that coal of the Carboniferous age exists in the rocks below. In sinking a drill for an artesian well at Freeborn village, very general attention was directed to the reported occurrence of this coal in a regular bed, in connection with slate rock. This locality was carefully examined, and all the information gathered bearing on the subject that could be found. The record of the first well drilled is given below, as reported by the gentleman who did the work:

	feet	inches
1. Soil and subsoil, clay	15	....
2. Blue clay	35	....
3. "Conglomerated rock" (hard to drill)	....	2
4. Sand with water	5	....
5. Fine clay, tough, hard to drill, with gravel and limestone pebbles	60	....
6. Sand with water		4
7. "Slate rock," probably cretaceous	7	....
8. "Coal," " "	5	4
Total depth	127	10

This indication of coal induced the drilling of another well, situated 100 feet distant, toward the northeast. In this the record was as follows, given by the same authority:

	feet	inches
1. Soil and subsoil, clay	15	....
1. Blue clay	33	....
3. "Conglomerated rock"		2
4. Sand with water, and pieces of coal	12	....
Total depth	60	2

When the drill here reached the "conglomerated rock," it was supposed to have reached the "slate rock," No. 7 of the previous section. The amount of coal in the sand of No. 4 was also enough to cause it to be taken for No. 8 of the previous section. Hence the boring was stopped; and having thus demonstrated the existence of a coal-bed, to the satisfaction of the proprietors, the enterprise was pushed further in the sinking of a shaft. In sinking this shaft the water troubled the workmen so that at thirty-five it had to be abandoned.

Three-quarters of a mile north of these drills a shaft was sunk 57 feet, but not finding the coal as expected, according to the developments of the last section above given, the explorers stopped here. In this shaft the overseer reports the same strata passed through in the drift as met with in the first well drilled, but the so called "conglomerated rock" was met at a depth of 45 feet. The sand below the "conglomerated rock" here held no water, but was full of fine pieces of coal. Before sinking a shaft at this place a drill was made to test the strata. These being found "all right" the shaft was begun. In that drill gas was first met. It rose up in the drill hole, and being ignited it flamed up eight or ten feet with a roaring sound. The shaft was so near the drill hole that it drew off the gas gradually, allowing the intermixture of more air, thus preventing rapid burning. From this place the exploration was redirected to the first situation, where another shaft was begun. This was in search for the "lower rock," so called, or the "slate rock," supposed to overlie the "coal." Here they went through the same materials, shutting off the water in the five foot sand-bed, and 60 feet of fine clay, when water rose so copiously from the second sand-bed (No. 6 of the first section given) as to compell a cessation of the work. In this shaft were found small pieces of the same coal, all the way. These pieces had sharp corners and fresh surfaces. The total depth here was 106 feet, and the water seems to have been impregnated with the same gas as that which arose in the drill at the point three-fourths of a mile distant. Such water is also found in the well at the hotel in Freeborn. With sugar of lead it does not present the reactions for sulphurated hydrogen, and the gas is presumed to be carbonated hydrogen. This account of explorations for coal is but a repetition of what has taken place in numerous instances in Minnesota. The cretaceous lignites have deceived a great many, and considerable expense has been needlessly incurred in fruitless search for good coal.

In the early discovery of these lignites, some exploration and experimentation within the limits of the State, were justifiable, but after the tests that have already been made it can pretty confidently be stated that these lignites are at present of no economical value. This, not in ignorance of the fact that they will burn, or that they contain, in some proportion, all the valuable ingredients that characterize coal and carbonaceous shales, but in the light of the competing prices of other fuels, the cost of mining them, and the comparative inferiority of the lignites themselves. If they were situated in Greenland they would probably be pretty thoroughly explored, and extensively mined, and even then they would havea powerful competitor in the oil in use there.

THE DRIFT.

This deposit covers the entire county and conceals the rock from sight. It consists of the usual ingredients, but varies with the general character of the surface. In rolling tracts it is very stony and has much more gravel. In flat tracts it is clayey. It everywhere contains a great many boulders, and these are shown abundantly along the beaches of the numerous lakes of the county. The frequency of limestone boulders, and their significancy, have already been mentioned. Thousands of bushels of lime have been made from such loose boulder masses, mainly gathered about the shores of the lakes. In general the drift of Freeborn county consists of a glacier hard-pan, or unmodified drift. Yet, in some places, the upper portion is of gravel and sand that show all the effects of running water in violent currents. The beds here are oblique, and subject to sudden transitions from one material to another. At Albert Lea the following section was observed. It occurs just west of the center of the town. It covers eight feet perpendicular, and eight feet east and west.

1. Earth and soil gravelly,below twenty inches.
2. Gravel, unstratified, with considerable limestone, six inches.
3. Stratified gravel, eighteen inches.
4. Regular strata of coarse gravel, two feet.
5. Unstratified.
6. Fine sand seen two feet.

In a gravel bank at Albert Lea, according to Mr. Wiliam Morin, the jaw bone of a Mastodon was found a number of years ago. It was sent to St. Paul and is supposed to be preserved.

The average thickness of the drift in Freeborn county would not vary much, probably, from one hundred feet. In the survey of the county, considerable attention was paid to the phenomena of common wells, with a view to learn the nature and thickness of this deposit, and the following list is the result of notes made.

WELLS OF FREEBORN COUNTY.—Good water is generally found throughout the county, in the drift, at depths less than eighty feet; but some deep wells that occur within the Cretaceous belt, in the western part of the county, are spoiled by carburetted hydrogen. This must rise from carbonaceous shales in the Cretaceous, and indicates the extent of that formation. Much of the information contained in the following tabulated list of wells was obtained of W. A. Higgins, well borer, of Albert Lea:

OWNER'S NAME.	Location.	Depth Feet.	Kind of Water	Remarks.
W. P. Sargent	Sec. 29 Albert Lea	28	Good	One-half bushel of coal at 26 feet
Geo. Stevens	Freeborn	47	Carburetted	Pieces of coal in the blue clay,
T. A. Southwick	"	46	Soft	44 ft. of water. [26ft water.
Ezra Sterns	½m w. of Freeborn	30	Good	Found pieces of coal.
Ezra Sterns	" "	42	"	" " "
James Hanson	1m nw. of Freeborn	50	Carburetted	" " "
F. D. Drake	Sec. 13, Freeborn	90	"	Water stands 5 feet from the top.
O. U. Wescott	Byron, Waseca	94	Soft	[and gravel.
L. C. Taylor	6ms nw. Freeborn	96	Good	Artesian: at first bringing stones
Geo. Snyder, Jr.	2ms nw. Freeborn	61	Carburetted	
A. M. Trigg	Alden	37	"	Found pieces of coal in clay.
H. M. Foot	"	50	Good	" " "
John Meleuder	"	50	"	" " "
L. C. Taylor	6ms nw. Freeborn	96	Carburetted	Artesian.
Wm. Comstock	3ms ne Alden	48	"	Nearly artesian.
Chas. Ayers	Nw. cor. Freeborn	125		Bore for coal.
John Ayers	Trenton	142		" " lost tools.
T. A. Southwick	Freeborn	35	Carburetted	Blue clay—water in sand&gravel
J. F. Jones	Geneva	20	Good	Water in quicksand.
Nelson Kengsley	"	12	Soft	" " "

OWNER'S NAME.	Location.	Depth feet.	Kind of Water	Remarks
John Farrell........	Geneva.................	12	Soft..........	Water in quicksand.
A. Chamberlain.....	"	12	"	" " "
D. G. Parker........	Albert Lea............	72	Good	Struck gravel below the blue clay
Dr. C. W. Ballard...	"	38	"	In gravel.
James Barker.......	"	52	"	Small bed of gravel in blue clay
C. W. Levens.......	"	25	"	In gravel.
H. Rowell..........	"	72	"	In gravel below the blue clay.
W. W. Cargill	"	85	Not good	St'k bl'k clay, no sticks nor grit.
Chas. Ostrou.......	"	30	Good.........	In very fine blue sandy clay.
Lewis Gaul.........	"	28	"	"Yellow clay" all the way.
H. Rowell..........	"	72	"	Yellow and blue clay, then gravel
Col. S. A. Hatch....	Sec. 4, Albert Lea......	42	"	Gravel and sand, water in quick-
Ole Knutson........	Albert Lea.............	34	"	" " " " [sand
W. W. Cargill	Sec. 28, Albert Lea	28	"	Water in gravel. [rock.
Geo. Topon........	Sec. 29, "	65	No water.....	Gravelly clay, fine sandy clay, on
And. Palmer........	" "	28	Good.........	Water in green sand.
Dr. A. C. Wedge....	Sec. 8 "	28	"	" " "
W. C. Lincoln......	Albert Lea.............	32	"	Gravel in sand, then quicksand.
Frank Hall.........	"	65	"	" " " "
Town well..........	Alden	44	"	In gravel.
A. W. Johnson.....	Albert Lea.............	80	Not Good....	Drift clay, water in gravel.
Rev. G. W. Prescott		80	"	"Tastes like kerosene."
Town well..........	Twin Lakes	75	"	Clay only.
	Alden	40	"	
A. Palmer, Jr.......	Sec. 29, Albert Lea......	30	"	Lump of coal at 27 feet.

In some wells at Albert Lea a muck is struck, and such wells afford a water that is unfit for use. This muck is reported to contain sticks, and is about thirty-eight or forty feet below the surface. It may indicate a former bed of the river, or an interglacial marsh, as Mr. James Geikie has explained in Scotland. (See "The Great Ice Age.") It is by some called *slush*, and seems not to uniformly hold sticks and leaves, but to be rather a fine sand of a dark color. The well-diggers call it quicksand. This indicates that it is either a bed of Cretaceous black clay, arenaceous, or Cretaceous debris. Dr. Wedge, of Albert Lea, thinks the site of the city was once covered by a lake, and that this *slush* was its sediment; and that the overlying gravel, which is about thirty-eight feet thick, has since been thrown onto it by a later force, perhaps by currents. There is no doubt that the overlying gravel was thus deposited, those currents being derived from the ice of a retiring glacier.

Wells at Geneva are generally not over twenty feet in depth. They also pass through a gravel that overlies a quicksand. This village is situated with reference to Geneva Lake as Albert Lea is with Albert Lea Lake, both being at the northern extremities of those lakes. The phenomena of wells at the two places are noticeably similar, and in the same way different from the usual phenomena of wells throughout the county,

At Albert Lea, gravel, about thirty feet, quicksand with water, sometimes black and mucky.

At Geneva, gravel, twelve to fifteen feet, quicksand and water.

It would seem that the history of the drift at Albert Lea was repeated at Geneva. These villages being both situated at the northern end of lake basins, are probably located where pre-glacial lakes existed. On all sides, both about Albert Lea and Geneva, the usual drift clay, hard and blue, is met in wells and has a thickness of about one hundred feet.

MATERIAL RESOURCES.

In addition to the soil, Freeborn county has very little to depend on as a source of material prosperity. As already stated, there is not a single exposure of the bed-rock in the county. All building stone and quicklime have to be imported. The former comes by the Southern Minnesota railroad from Lanesboro and Fountain in Fillmore county, though it is very likely that the Shakopee stone from Mankato will also be introduced. The latter comes from Iowa largely (Mason City and Mitchell), and from kilns at Mankato and Shakopee. Some building stone is also introduced into the eastern part of the county from the Cretaceous quarries at Austin.

LIME.—At Twin Lakes three or four thousand bushels of lime have been burned by Mr. Carter from boulders picked up around the lake shores. This lime sold for seventy-five cents per bushel. It was a very fine lime, purely white. The construction of railroads put a stop to his profits, as the Shakopee lime could then be introduced and sold cheaper. The boulders burned were almost entirely of the same kind as those that are so numerous in McLeod county. They are fine, close grained, nearly white, on old weathered surfaces, and of a dirty cream color on the fractured surfaces. They very rarely show a little granular or rougher texture, like a magnesian limestone, though this grain is intermixed with the closer grain. They hold but few fossils. There are a few impressions of shells, and by some effort a globular mass of a course Favositoid coral was obtained.

Besides the above, which are distinguished as "white limestone," there are also a few bluish green limestone boulders. One of these, which now lies near Twin Lakes, is about seven feet long, by five or six feet broad, its thickness being at least two and one-half feet. It has been blasted into smaller pieces for making quicklime; but nearly all of it yet lies in its old bed, the fragments being too large to be moved. This stone is also very close-grained. It is heavier than the other and more evidently crystalline. It holds small particles of pyrites. It is not porous, nor apparently bedded. On its outer surface it looks like a withered diorite, and it would be taken, at a glance, for a boulder of that kind. It is said to make a very fine lime. Several hundred bushels of lime were formerly burned at Geneva.

The clay used, which is about five feet below the surface, is fine and of a yellowish ashy color. It is underlain by gravel. The clay itself locally passes into a sand that looks like "the bluff." At other places it is a common, fine clay-loam, with a few gravel-stones. There is but little deleterious to the brick in the clay, although some of the brick are, on fractured surfaces, somewhat spotted with poor mixing, and with masses of what appear like concretions. The clay itself is apparently massive, but it is really indistinctly bedded, rarely showing a horizontal or oblique, thin layer of yellow sand. In other places the clay shows to better advantage, and is plainly bedded. It contains sticks, the largest observed being a little over half an inch in diameter. These sticks are plainly endogenous in cellular structure, but have a bark. They are not oxydized so as to be brittle, but are flexible still, with small branches like rootlets hanging to them. It is uncertain whether they belong to the deposit, or are the roots of vegetation that grew on surface since the drift. There are no boulders of any size in the drift; but a few granitoid gravel-stones.

Brick was formerly made at Geneva, and at a point two and one-half miles east of that place. At Geneva the clay was taken from the bank of Allen Creek, about eighteen inches below the surface. It was a drift clay, with small pebbles. That used two and one-half miles east of Geneva was of the same kind. In both places sand had to be mixed with the clay. About Geneva sand is abundant, taken from the gravel and sand knolls, and from the banks of the creek.

Peat.—In Freeborn county there is an abundance of peat. The most of the marshes, of which some are large, are peat-bearing. In this respect the county differs very remarkably from those in the western portion of the same tier of counties which were specially examined for peat in the season of 1873, and which, being entirely destitute of native trees, are most in need of peat for domestic fuel.

The peat of the county is generally formed entirely of herbaceous plants, though the marshes are often in the midst of oak-openings. The peat-moss constitutes by far the larger portion.

There is no observed difference in peat-producing qualities between the marshes of the prairie districts and those of the more rolling woodland tracts of the county.

At Alden village, in the midst of the open prairie, the peat of a large marsh rose to the surface and floated, when, for certain purposes, the marsh was flooded. The water now stands ten feet deep below the floating peat, which is about three feet thick.

At Freeborn, peat has been taken out on John Scovill's land. Here it is eight feet thick, two rods from the edge, and it is probably much thicker toward the center of the marsh. That below the surface of the water now standing in the drain is too pulpy to shovel out; and after being dipped out and dried on boards, it is cut into blocks and hauled to town. That above the water is more fibrous, and can be taken out with a spade and cut into convenient blocks. Yet the level of the water varies, and that datum is not constant. It appears as if there were here a stratum of more fibrous peat that separates from the lower, about twenty inches thick, and floats above it at certain times In the peat at this place a sound Elk horn was taken out at the depth of six feet.

There is a large peat marsh in section eleven, Hayward, owned by non-residents.

COAL MINING.

As a kind of supplement to this account of the natural history and the geology of the county, an account of the "Freeborn Consolidated Coal and Mining Company" is added, for, notwithstanding the discouraging opinion of the State geologist, who, of course, deals with facts as he knows and sees them, with few conjectures as to what is not potent, there are men of discrimination, intelligence, and means, who believe there is valuable mineral there, and propose to test the question.

In November, 1879, Mr. E. B. Clark commenced prospecting for coal, and employed F. D. Drake to put down a four inch mining pipe. Mr. Drake had been prospecting more or less at Freeborn for five years. At one time, in connection with L. T. Scott and E. D. Rogers, he had partially organized a coal company and taken leases of several hundred acres of land in that vicinity for coal purposes. This company bored in several places as far down as the second vein of water, about 100 feet, where they struck quicksand, and not having any tubing could go no farther; consequently, when they bored the last time they knew no more about the existence of coal than when they bored at first.

A man named A. Short, from La Crosse, Wisconsin, came to Freeborn and leased about 2,000 acres of land for prospecting purposes, worked a short time to make his leases hold good, and left. This was in 1875. After it became evident that he would do no more towards developing what coal or other substances might be there, Mr. E. B. Clark bought his interest in the leases, and in the fall of 1879, together with E. G. Perkins and W. W. Cargill of La Crosse, commenced prospecting, and hired Mr. Drake to put down the pipe. He not having had any experience in sinking such wells did not start the bore plumb, and after expending a large amount of labor, first by Drake and then by Mr. P. Morse, of Wells, and Geo. Cross, of Freeborn, the work in that well had to be abandoned in consequence of trouble in the fall of 1880. In April, 1881, Mr. E. B. Clark, together with E. G. Perkins and W. W. Cargill, organized the Freeborn Consolidated Coal and Mining Company, and in July following held its first meeting for election of officers, since which time there has been developed a vein of gypsum, eight feet thick, which is considered by experts to be a sure indication of coal. The company will soon sink a shaft to the gypsum, and mine the same while they sink the shaft on down. The gypsum is 115 feet below the surface in the present well, as well as in the well put down in 1881; in the former well they went through a vein of mineral, supposed to be Galena, which lies about 130 feet below the surface. Experts who have been there generally concede that with the many indications found in the locality there must be large quantities of lead deposits underlaying the gypsum. The company held its annual meeting at Alden, where the general office is located, on the 31st of July, 1882, at which time the following officers were elected:

President, L. T. Walker; Secretary, E. B. Clark; Treasurer, O. S. Gilmore; Superintendent, E. B. Clark.

Directors: L. T. Walker, J. Goward, O. S. Gilmore, N. P. Jacobson, E. B. Clark, A. R. Walker, C. K. Clark.

Great credit is due, and universally conceded to Mr. E. B. Clark, whose zeal and untiring energy and perseverance is the moving power through which all the present developments have been made, and in all future operations he will, in all probability, be prominently identified with what we hope will be the successful termination of further efforts.

When prospecting, blue clay is found about fifteen feet from the surface, interspersed with pieces of coal and soapstone, slate, sulphur balls, and gas in abundance, as well as oil. When a distance of forty-five to fifty feet from the surface is reached, a vein of water is found in all places except one, in which dry sand was found, and a vein of gas came in so strong that it raised the rods being used for boring several feet. The men at work supposed they had struck a flowing vein of water by the noise down in the well, a roaring, gurgling sound being heard. Mr. E. D. Rogers, who smokes occasionally, remarked that he would take a smoke, and scratched a match upon the bowl of his pipe; this ignited the gas which was the cause of all the noise, and it was thought by those present that a blaze the full size of the tube, which was six inches, shot up in the air about fifteen feet and gradually settled down to about six feet. It burned for an hour or two when it was smothered out by placing a sod over the hole. For several weeks afterward it was visited by people from the surrounding country, who would remove the sod and apply a match to see it burn. This vein of gas was found at the same depth that a vein of water is usually found in other localities where boring has been done, and water thus found is strongly impregnated with gas; in some places so much so that it is not fit for use. A tin pail was lost in one well and taken out in a few days after covered with a black greasy substance that could not be removed until subjected to a hard scouring with soap and sand. Coal has been found in every bore put down far enough to reach the blue clay. Mr. L. T. Scott says he found in a well put down on his place a piece of coal the length of a spade and handle, and about as large square as his spade blade was wide, which is the largest piece yet found. All those indications, with the gypsum found, are supposed to point to coal when a sufficient depth is reached.

CHAPTER XLVI.

EARLY EXPLORATIONS—COL. ALBERT LEA—EARLIEST SETTLEMENT—EARLY INCIDENTS—RUBLE'S LETTER FROM LOOKOUT MOUNTAIN—GENERAL REMARKS.

In March, 1857, a letter was written to Samuel M. Thompson by Col. Albert M. Lea, in relation to the Black Hawk purchase, and so much of this autogram, as relates to the early history of Freeborn county, will be transcribed here:

KNOXVILLE, Tenn., March 6th, 1857.

DEAR SIR—Your favor of the 26th of January reached me a few days since, and I may as well confess that I was both surprised and gratified by it. You ask for information about "Lake Albert Lea." In the year 1835, being a Lieutenant in the Twelfth Regiment, U. S. Dragoons, stationed at Fort Des Moines, now Montrose, on the Iowa side of the Mississippi, I accompanied an expedition from that part of the Sioux country, composed of three companies of troops under Lieut. Col. Kearney, afterwards a General and killed at Chantilly, Sept. 1st, 1862. The detachment marched up the tablelands laying east of the Des Moines River to the "neutral grounds," and then turning more eastwardly crossed the Iowa and Cedar Rivers and struck the Mississippi at Wabasha's village, below Lake Pepin, and thence, taking a west course, touched some of the tributaries of the St. Peter's River, struck the Des Moines above the upper forks, and then followed the general course of the stream back to the fort.

Although during this long march I was the only officer attached to the command, I sketched the whole route topographically, taking the courses with a pocket compass, and computing the distances by the time and rate of marching. On the return to quarters I made out a map of the country traversed, accompanied by a memoir which was sent by Col. Kearney to the Adjutant General, and the next year, having obtained additional material, I made a more full map, and wrote an extended description of the country, which was published by H. S. Tanner, of Philadelphia, in 18 mo. form, under the title of "Notes on the Iowa District of Wisconsin Territory." I have one copy of this work that I will send you.

On our march westward from Wabasha's village we passed through that beautiful region of lakes, open woods, and prairie, in which the head waters of the Blue Earth and Cedar Rivers intertwine, and having passed one breezy day across a deep creek, connecting, as we supposed, two of these lakes, we came out upon an elevated promontory descending rather abruptly to the edge of the most beautiful sheet of water that we had ever seen. We stopped for an hour on that exquisite spot, and took a sketch of the lake as I could from that point. In making out my map, the form I gave the lake, but which the lithographer did not preserve, suggested to me the idea of a military chapeau, and I gave it that name.

In 1841, when Nicollet was making out his map of the region between the Mississippi and the Missouri rivers, he filled in a large part of it by copying mine, and in acknowledgement to me for such material, gave my name to the pretty piece of water I had called "Lake Chapeau" and which I had described to him somewhat enthusiastically. Several years since a friend sent me a slip from a newspaper containing an extract from a letter written by some one in Iowa,stating that the writer had been all over where Lake Albert Lea ought to be, but found no sign of such water, and I concluded that either I had failed to give it the proper position on the map, or it had been so misplaced in the transfer to Nicollet's map, that the original would never again be recognized. Hence my surprise and gratification on the receipt of your letter giving me the first information that my pet lake was not lost. * * * *

Very respectfully your obedient servant,

ALBERT MILLER LEA.

On referring to the map of Lieut. Lea, it is found that the Lake now called Albert Lea was originally Fox Lake, and is not the one originally called Albert Lea by Nicollet. The lake Lieut. Lea named Lake Chapeau, and changed by Nicollet, is that beautiful sheet of water, a short distance west of the village, known as White's Lake, near the residence of A. W. White.

The early settlers found, when they arrived at the camping spot of Lieut. Lea and his command near White's Lake, an inscription cut on a tree which was deciphered as "Lake Anllolin." By whom this was cut, is very uncertain, as it could hardly have been done by Lea, or any of his party, because he gave the name of Lake Chapeau to this charming sheet of water, and the name Albert Lea was proposed some years afterwards by Nicollet, as already mentioned.

EARLY SETTLEMENT.

Up to the spring of 1853, as far as known, no white man had planted a home in this county, now so well filled with a thriving population. The expansive prairies and beautiful groves bordering the placid lakes and beautiful streams, up to that time were in a state of repose, and only occupied by animal life and perhaps a few of the aboriginal race, which was in a condition of senility, ready to depart and give place to a superior race.

At the time above mentioned, Ole Gulbrandson, whose name reveals his nationality, with his family, entered in and took possession of a moderate portion of this goodly land in section thirty-three in the township of Shell Rock, and rolled up some logs in the form of a cabin, which still stands on the farm of P. J. Miller, who is himself a well known old settler. Mr. Gulbrandson went to work, and when the next settler came along, two years afterwards, he had provided for himself and family, and could also supply his neighbors with the necessities of life. A passing notice should be made of the courage of this man, to thus plant himself so far beyond the confines of civilization, where, for aught he knew, they were liable to be devoured by wild beasts, and where the savages might have blotted him and his amily from the face of the earth, with no one to follow on the avenging trail. And some credit is also due the Indians themselves, that they did not molest him as they certainly were aware of his presence. In the fall of 1854, a daughter was born in their little log house, which must have been the very first, whatever rival claims may be put in.

In the early spring of 1855, Mr. William Rice came straggling along and secured a place in section eight in the same township, near where Joseph Landis now resides. In June Mr. Rice was followed by his family and his wife's relatives with families, and they placed their claims where Shell Rock City now is, and during that summer settlements were made in various parts of the county.

LyBrand and Thompson located within the township of Albert Lea and laid out as a town site the village of St Nicholas, which was the first of this brood that was soon hatched out in such rapid succession. Here the first store was opened with a large stock of goods, a hotel, a saw-mill, a blacksmith shop, and other improvements rapidly followed, and the impression went out that this was be the great metropolis of this section, the energy of its founders, with the wealth of Mr. Ly Brand, encouraging this idea. But to-day not a vestige of its greatness remains, not a relic can be picked up as a remainder of its improvement. Oblivion has marked it for its own, and it remains only as a recollection.

In the fall of 1855, Lorenzo Merry and George S. Ruble located and founded Albert Lea, the shire town of the county. Geneva was also settled this year, and also Freeborn Lake and Moscow.

In September Mrs. Fanny Andrews, the wife of William Andrews, a prominent old settler, died, and this must have been the first death in the county, which was after a brief two months' residence.

In November Willie Andrews, son of Oliver and Mary Andrews, was ushered into the light of this world, in the township of Hayward, his parents having come the July previous. This was the first son born, and the second child.

We have thus rapidly sketched the earliest settlements in the county, and a continuation of when the various locations were peopled, will be found in the several town histories.

Hon. A. H. Bartlett, in his old settlers' address, thus speaks of events at this period:

"The Territory of Minnesota had been organized, and its delegate to the National congress, Hon. H. H. Sibley, had been admitted to a seat in the National halls of legislation, and Freeborn county had been organized into a voting precinct, for the election of Territorial officers, and on the 3d day of November, A. D. 1856, the first election in the county was held at the house of Oliver Andrews, situated on the town line, between the townships of Hayward and Shell Rock. Said spot being the established voting place in this precinct. At this election the entire voting population of the county turned out, and a total of forty-four votes were polled. Post-offices were now established in various parts of the county, mail facilities being supplied by private enterprise from Mitchell, in Mitchell county, Iowa. On the 3d day of December, A. D. 1856, William Rice (the second settler in Freeborn county), while carrying the mail across the broad and bleak prairie, lying between the Cedar and Shell Rock rivers, was caught in a severe snow storm and lost his way. He wandered around over the trackless prairie, without shelter or protection from the storm, until he froze to that extent that he died of his injuries some three or four days afterwards. This calamity was followed in quick succession, on the 20th day of the same month, by Byron Packard and Charles Walker (a part of the company who laid out and founded Shell Rock City) being caught in a terrific storm on the same broad prairie, while hauling a steam boiler to its destination at Shell Rock, and both perished from the severity of the storm and the extreme cold. Their bodies, frozen stiff and cold in death, were found four days afterwards, lying upon the frozen crust of the deep snow. Their bodies were carried to Shell Rock, and there buried upon the town site they had so lately helped to lay out and form. No relatives were there to attend their funeral obsequeis and mourn their sad fate, yet sorrowing and bereaved friends and brother pioneers, composing the then entire community, assisted in performing the last duty to the untimely departed. No preacher of the Gospel could be found in the county to speak words of consolation to sorrowing and bereaved friends and associates, and our friend Jacob Hostetter, one of Freeborn county's earliest pioneers, feelingly and eloquently addressed the early pioneers there gathered, upon the sadness and suddenness of their bereavement, upon the mysterious and inscrutable ways of an overshadowing providence, in which no one could tell why, in the prime of vigorous manhood, when hope, the ministry of life is most buoyant, and future expectations in the coming life of usefulness is most prominent, that a mysterious providence should step in with its dread mandates, and the brightest and most promising life should be consigned to oblivion and the grave. These sad bereavments and others which happened in the county about that time, caused by the unparalleled severity of the memorable winter of A. D. 1856, cast a sad and sorrowing gloom over the young settlement of Freeborn county. Some few of the settlers became disheartened and discouraged, and early the following spring returned to their former eastern homes."

About the first judicial proceedings in the county were in January, 1857, in which Henry Boulton was plaintiff, and C. T. Knapp, defendant, and the case came before William Andrews, who must have been the first Justice of the Peace. Mr. Bartlett was counsel for both parties, who were beaten by the decision of the court.

At Shell Rock City the first schoolhouse in the county was built and finished in the style of civilization, on the 18th of August, 1857, and immediately thereafter a common school therein was put in full blast, with Miss Emily Streeter as teacher, being the first school put in operation in the county. Great interest was taken by the early settlers in everything pertaining to a civilized life. Churches were organized and religious services held in the schoolhouses and private dwellings of the inhabitants. Thus the nucleus was formed from which our present proud position in the arts and sciences, moral and religious intelligence, and in short everything that pertains to a civilized and intelligent people, has emanated.

The first permanent bridge built in the county was at Shell Rock, by subscription, the document bearing date on the 9th of June, 1857. The sums given were from two to twenty-five dollars, each designating as to whether it was to be paid in money, work, or material. The men who signed the paper were: Edward P. Skinner, A. M. Burnham, A. H. Bartlett, F. L. Cutler, G. Cottrell, J. W. Smith, C. W. Phillips, Lars Severson, David L. Phillips, Almon M. Cottrell, C. T. Knapp, James Laff, I. S. Horning, George Gardner, William Andrews, Robert Budlong, Thomas Budlong, C. Tarbell, E. S. Anderson, William C. Ellsworth, Elijah Young, James Andrews, George P. Holmes, J. M. Sannes, R. I. Frank, —— Swarthout, J. Hostetter, Jacob LyBrand, and S. M. Thompson.

Bids were received until June 15th, when it was begun and built by Dr. Burnham in nine days. The whole sum subscribed was $277. There can be no question as to these men being old settlers. Some of them are still living in the county, and some are in other counties or States, and many of them are well situated. In relation to the name of the founder of St. Nicholas, while it is said that he subsequently wrote it differently, his signature here is "Jacob LyBrand."

At an early day there was considerable trouble to have legal documents executed. Magistrates were often scores of miles apart, and getting married involved difficulties we can hardly comprehend in these days. The first trouble arose from the scarcity of marriagable women, but having secured that indespensible pre-requisite, the trouble of finding a minister or a justice to legalize the union was often most exasperating to the victims of "loves young dream."

Mr. McReynolds had not been ordained, and therefore was not vested by the prospective State of Minnesota with authority to pronounce single ladies and gentlemen, husbands and wives, with the admonition that no man should put them asunder. But he was not unfrequently called upon to perform this service, and on one occasion he was hailed as he passed a log house, on the way to fill an appointment, and requested to step as he came back and "join two hearts that beat as one." Several men were then just starting out to shoot some ducks for the wedding feast. This was near Bear Lake, and Mr. McReynolds on his return brought a Justice, and the happy pair were duly and legally started in the journey of life hand in hand; and so the society papers the next week might have read, "Marriage in high life. On the 7th inst., at the home of the bride's parents, by Frederick McCall, Esquire, assisted by Rev. Isaac W. McReynolds, Mr. J. H. Bluberson to Miss Mary Jane Clark, no cards.

A great many strories are told about securing timber by borrowing it when the owner was away, and while the stories that are told are for the most part fabrications, a large number of instances might be related that will never see the light. Dr. Burnham says that he owned thirteen acres of land near Albert Lea, and cut a lot of logs and hauled them out on the flat, and every one mysteriously disappeared. His idea was that the business men of Albert Lea thought it would be a good joke, after beating him for the county seat, to compel him involuntarily to furnish timber for the county buildings.

After the saw-mill was in operation, Mr. Sheehan, who was a robust young man, was told by Mr. Ruble that he had a fine yoke of cattle, and if Sheehan would take them and haul in logs from where ever he could find them, they would go shares on the lumber after it was sawed out. So the young man went to work and did a good business, and when the settlement came in the spring, Sheehan was not quite satisfied with the lumber turned over to his share, and entered a mild protest at the inequality of the division; but Ruble politely invited him to take that or nothing. Seeing no method of redress he accepted his allotment, which having secured, he got even by remarking "well Mr. Ruble you are not so far ahead as you may think, for I got every one of those logs off of your own land." This incident is related on account of its intrinsic merit, for both "George" and "Tim" declare that nothing of the kind ever happened.

George S. Ruble was one of the settlers of 1855. The first time he visited Freeborn county was in June, 1854, and slept under a tree near one of the little lakes in Albert Lea. At that time there was not a house in the county. The few people here lived in wagons, happy and contented, at least for a time.

At the sixth annual reunion of the old settlers, a letter was received from Mr. Ruble, who was then at Lookout Mountain, Tennessee, and as it relates to the early history, some portion of it will be printed here.

"When, for the first time, I saw the country, I loved it well enough to make it my future home, with a few others to devote the energies of my life, to redeem it from its wild state, and help to lay the stepping stones into the garden spot of the Northwest. As I look around upon the general improvements, in both city and country, I conclude that I have never seen them equalled, and can scarcely realize that the days of my absence have witnessed it all. Those who have read "The Mysteries of Metropolisville" will understand my feelings in 1855, for I, of course, like hundreds of others, had sought the West to find a city destined in the future to be the "great business center." You certainly will remember the little towns that sprung up all around, and that in a few years, like Metropolisville, in Rice county, were compelled to yield to the force of circumstances, for they could not all be County Seats, and in this vitality alone seemed centered. I had come with my head full of towns, and with this all absorbing idea began hunting immediately for desirable locations. With such material at hand, it took me but a short time to find just what I wanted. Having made all arrangements I left, and in the fall returned with my family and a gang of men, and began at once the erection of the old saw-mill, which was, by the way, when completed, the finest frame building ever erected in Minnesota. About this time St. Nicholas was founded, under the chief auspices of Jacob Ly Brand, as doubtless many will remember. One day I went and looked over the position, and came to the conclusion that the situation of St. Nicholas was in every way equal to Albert Lea, and the mill power was ever so much better than the one I was improving. I therefore made a proposition to LyBrand to unite town interests and influences, build the mill, procure the County Seat, and make the future metropolis at St. Nicholas, instead of Albert Lea. My proposition was received with indignation by that confident individual, who informed me that I might abandon my town if I chose to do so, at any rate he proposed to have both mill and County Seat at his place, and did not propose to have any partnership about it, either. So I left him and went my way. The intervening years tell the story with its results. Some may remember the dances and very good entertainments we enjoyed for a short time at this point, at the hotel, which, like the one at Itasca, the old settlers will all remember, has long since been removed. In relation to Itasca, it should be remembered that it was the strongest opponent in the County Seat contest, and it was at one time hard to tell what the result would be.

So the saw-mill progressed. I still have in my possession the old day book used in the transaction of this business, and I prize it as a choice relic. The first entry is as follows:

ALBERT LEA, Oct. 27, 1855.

Lewis Osgood,	Dr.
To cash given him by Willford in advance for work on mill	$30.00
Saxon C. Roberts,	Dr.
To cash for work	$6.00
One half pound tobacco	20
One box caps	12½
One comb	12½
	$6.45

These were the first book entries of business done here. Two years later this entry appears:

Oct. 28, 1857.

I. T. Adrianne,	Dr.
To goods bought of A. B. Webber, as per bill	$1.50

Webber was our first Attorney, and poor Adrianne came to a sad end. Under the same date was a charge to the printing office for seventeen and one half pounds of nails at 10 cents per pound, $1.75. The book runs up to May, 1859, and almost the last charge is:

Town of Albert Lea,	Dr.
To 60 feet of plank	$1.75

Now, as I fail to find any credit, I think that the town still owes me that bill, but I might be induced to sign a receipt.

On the fly leaf I find this memorandum: "Swineford and Gray arrived in Albert Lea on the 28th of March, 1857." Albert Lea was named not long after I arrived. Merry, Willford, myself, and others were sitting in a tent one evening, and then and there the present name was decided upon, and the handsome little city with its peculiarly odd name has attained as wide-spread popularity as any place of its size in the country, and it is justly entitled to it. The principal object of the meeting in the tent was to make application for a Post-office, and the name for it was arrived at after considerable discussion, when at my suggestion, Albert Lea was finally chosen, with Mr. Merry as Postmaster. How many of us will remember our first dance in the old log house, with Charley Colby for our musician, and how we all enjoyed it. Calico was in demand then, and I venture to say that not a single lady complained of some awkward booby's treading on her train. It is true the old roughly hewn plank floor was not as smooth as the waxed affairs over which the dancers of the present day now glide, but it was the best the country afforded, and all participating had the good sense to appreciate the situation and find hearty enjoyment in the affairs, as they then existed.

So also we remember the first fourth of July celebration, followed by the dance at the log house now standing on lot four, block twelve. In this same house old Uncle McReynolds, in his plain, earnest manner would expound to us the gospel, and always found an attentive and appreciative audience. In this house also was taught our first school, and I doubt not that many persons who have come to man's estate in these later years, have children as old as they themselves were when they attended our first school with Lucy Parker for a teacher. So will many remember the school that followed, taught in Clark's old log store room on Clark street. Certain I am, that the teacher of that school, if present, will remember it. * * *

On the occasion of our first celebration, our first liberty pole was raised near where Brown's bank now is, and a view of it was obstructed in no direction by buildings at that time. During those times we had a few old-fashioned camp-meetings over on what is now known as Ballard's Point, and the number that attended satisfied the faithful that our country was fast peopling. * *

Long years of plenty and prosperity could never obliterate from the minds of the old settlers of Freeborn county the days when hunger and want were daily in sight. No money to buy with and nothing to buy if money was plenty. Our only possessions were health and energy, with a determination to find in the end better days.

How we all looked forward to the completion of the saw-mill, with a longing intensified by inadequate house accommodations and the excitement on the day of starting was intense. After that got in operation it was found necessary to have a grinding apparatus also, and the old iron corn cracker was then added. How quickly the mill sprung into popularity. Grists from all parts of the country came pouring in, and what grists they were, ranging from four quarts to two bushels, and usually far from first quality, not unfrequently being half rotten. I well remember one man who came on foot fifteen miles with a little less than a peck of corn in his grist; to this, instead of taking toll, was added two quarts extra. On his return home some one remarked about the smallness of his grist, whereupon they were informed that Ruble had stolen three-fourths of it while grinding. There is no doubt that the old corn cracker is entitled to membership in the old settlers' association.

Not a few will remember the big seine knitted by the old man Ward, and the mighty hauls, we made with it below the dam. I well remember one haul made by us that filled a common wagon box. Suckers were largely in the majority sandwiched thinly with pickerel. Suckers and milk were the staples, with a scanty allowance of corn bread for desert. Hard fare it seems now, but providence gave us an appetite to enjoy even that, and I think I am safe in saying that those days witnessed some of the happiest ones in the history of Freeborn county.

The years '58 and '59 might be called the "sucker period." When I came, in July, 1855, there was no house in the county. Bill Rice, Cottrell, Gardner, and Hostetter were living in their wagons. While at Freeborn Lake I found Miller and Bickford camping out. When I started for St. Paul, in the winter of 1856-57, to do some County Seat log rolling, which was not altogether useless, I found it necessary to go down to Merry's Ford in Iowa, on the Cedar River, then strike the Austin road. From Austin I went toChatfield, thence up to Red Wing,thence up the Mississippi River on the ice to St. Paul. The same circuitous route was followed in March, on my return. A few days later, with my wife and son C. N., then a lad of five years, I went to Geneva around by the Iowa route, and brought in E. C. Stacy, S. N. Frisbie, and Wm. Andrews, the three Commissioners appointed by Governor Gorman to organize Freeborn county. They met in the old log house situated on what was known for years as the "Island" and performed the work for which they had been appointed, and the county was organized with your humble servant as the first sheriff and tax collector. The bill to organize the county was rolled through in opposition to Morton S. Wilkinson, Ramsey, Emmett Smith, Brisbin, and others, and perhaps to its early passage Freeborn owes much of its advancement and prosperity.

Upon my arrival last month, as the train passed behind the woods into full view of our little city, I could scarcely realize, as I looked upon the church spires rising above the town, and the other many evidences of a healthy growth and prosperity, that this was the same place I had visited twenty-five years before, and found without even a wagon road to mark a degree in civilization. But though I did not then exactly locate a railroad, shortly after, when our town had been located, with a Post-office and a hotel, I began to feel the necessity of a railroad, and the idea settled into conviction, that at some future day not so far distant, we would have it, and I am going to do myself the credit to say that in that position I was nearly alone, for when I consulted A. B. Webber, for whose opinions we entertained much respect, he laughed and said, "Why Ruble, you are crazy on the subject of Albert Lea, and are constantly imagining all sorts of impossible things about it; you will never live to see a railroad in Albert Lea. But you see Webber was mistaken, as well as the others who, becoming dissatisfied, sold their property at a sacrifice and left, or what was worse, went away at a period when they should have stayed, leaving property here to the tender manipulation of those left behind."

After some general reflections Mr. Ruble closed his admirable letter with the hope that the meeting of the old settlers might be a source of pleasure and a harbinger of many more equally enjoyable in the years to come.

GENERAL REMARKS.

To any one who has lived in an old community, there is something of surprise and admiration in the remarkable transition from an expanse of wildness, solitude, and natural helplessness, to a living civilization; from barbarism to enlightenment, as presented in this region, which, within the remembrance of the present generation has sprung from an unproductive domain into towns and cities equipped and enriched with all that makes life desirable. This wonderful change has been simply marvelous.

The pioneers of this whole region were particularly fortunate in their contact with the Indians.

The scenes of the massacre, which began with the planting of the English colonies in Virginia and Massachusetts, and moved with the advancing civilization in a crimson line along the frontier with the most heart-rendering atrocities, seem to have stopped at the Mississippi, although the terrible Sioux were reputed second to no others in bloodthirstiness, leaving this section in peace and quietness, to crop out, however, in all its original fierceness to the west of us in 1862, at that terrible Sioux massacre so forcibly depicted in the preceeding pages of this work.

Although the tomahawk and scalping-knife were not a constant menace to the early comers, it must not be imagined that there was not toil, privation, cold, and hunger to undergo, for there was absolutely nothing in these wilds of Minnesota, except the intrinsic merit of the location, to attract people from their more or less comfortable homes in the East, or on the other continent, from whence so many came. Those who first arrived were inspired with hope, which indeed "springs enternal in the human heart;" but they were regarded by their friends, who were left behind, as adventurers, soldiers of fortune, who, if they got through alive would certainly never be able to return, as they would surely be anxious to do, unless they were particularly fortunate. They were a sturdy race, who realized the inequalities of the struggles in the old States or Countries, where humanity on the one hand, claiming "the inaleinable right to life, liberty, and the pursuit of happiness;" and on the other hand the accumulations of labor in vast aggregations, in sordidly avaricious clutches, hedged in with traditional precedents and barriers, with every facility for receiving and gathering in, but with few and small outlets for distribution, and they resolved to establish themselves where merit would not be discarded and supplanted by the antiquated, but still protent relics of feudalism.

The men who come here to establish homes for themselves, their families, and their posterity, were as a rule, hard-working, open-hearted, clear-headed, and sympathizing. They were good neighbors, and so good neighborhoods were created, and they made a practical illustration of the great doctrine of the brotherhood of man, by actual example rather than by quoting creeds, or conforming to outward observances, which may or may not spring from motives of purity. With a bearing that never blanched in the presence of misfortune or danger, however appalling, they were nevertheless tender, kind, and considerate, when confronted by disaster and adversity, and it is certain that their deficiencies in the outward manifestations of piety, were more than compensated for by their love and regard for the claims of humanity.

We who enjoy the blessings resulting from the efforts of these hardy pioneers, many of whom are around us in actual life, would be less than human if we were not filled with gratitude to these early settlers, who paved the way and made the condition of things we find a reality. The value of what they accomplished cannot be overestimated, and it should be constantly remembered that whatever of romance attended the early colonists, was more than compensated for by hard work.

If this meed of praise is justly due the men, as it assuredly is, what shall be said in commendation of the heroic women, who learned the vicissitudes of frontier life, endured the absence from home, friends, and old associations, whose tender ties, that only a woman's heart can feel, must have wrung all hearts as they were severed. The devotion that would lead to such a breaking away to follow a father, a husband, or a son, into the trackless waste beyond the Mississippi, where dark and gloomy apprehensions must have overshadowed the mind, is above all praise. The nature of the part taken by the noble women who first came to this uninhabited region cannot be fully appreciated. Although by nature and education, liberal if not lavish, they practiced the most rigid economy, and secured comforts from the most meager means. They often at crtical times preserved order, reclaiming the men from utter despair during gloomy periods; and their constant example of frugal industry and cheerfulness, continually admonished them to renewed exertions; the instincts of womanhood intermittingly encouraging integrity and manhood.

As to the effects of frontier life, socially and morally, upon those who have secured homes here in the West, a few observations may not be inappropriate. During the past generation a noted divine in the East, Dr. Bushnell, who will be remembered by those who came from there in the fifties, preached a sermon on the "barbarous tendencies of civilization in the West," and on this theme the reverend gentleman predicated an urgent and almost frantic appeal to Christianity to put forth renewed and strenuous exertions to save this region from a relapse into barbarism. This tendency, it was urged, must result from the disruption of social and religious ties, the mingling of heterogeneous elements, and the removal of the external restraints so common, and supposed to be so potent in older communities. It is evident, however, that Dr. Bushnell did not have a sufficiently broad and extended view of the subject; for the arbitrament of time has shown that his apprehensions were entirely groundless, for if he had even carefully surveyed the history of the past, he would have seen that in a nomadic condition, which emigration temporarily involves, there is never any real progress in civilization or refinement. Institutions for the improvement and elevation of the race must be planted deep in the soil before they can raise their battlements in grandeur and majesty toward heaven, and bear fruit for the enlightenment of the nations. The evils of which Dr. Bushnell was so alarmed were without a lasting impression, because merely temporary in character. The planting of a new colony where so much labor is imperative, where everything has to be constructed, involves an obvious increase of human freedom, which is sometimes taken advantage of, and the conventionalities of society are necessarily disregarded to a great extent. But the elements composing a sincere regard for the feelings and welfare of others, and of self government, everywhere largely predominates; and the fusion of the races modifies the asperities and the idiosyncrasies of each, and certainly will in due time create a composite nationality, in which it is hoped in conformity with the spirit of this remarkable age, will produce a nationality or a race, as unlike as it must be superior to those that have preceded it. Even now, before the first generation has passed away, society here has outgrown the irritation of the transplanting, and there are not more vicious elements in it, if as many, as there are in the old communities, as the criminal statistics abundantly show.

In a large majority of cases the men and women coming here had at first to struggle to meet the physical wants of themselves and little ones, and they had no time, even if they had an inclination, to make protestations involving postulates of doctrinal faith, but the results of whatever teaching they had received was materialized in honest labor for the good of the whole community, and in special acts of beneficence whenever occasion presented. It is no exaggeration to say that what has been accomplished here in thirty years, in the planting of educational and moral institutions, has been almost equal to what has been realized in New England in two hundred and fifty years.

To one who has not been actually engaged in reclaiming a farm from a state of nature, and bringing it to a condition that will yield a comfortable support for a family, it is difficult to conceive the amount of toil required, which is often not represented by the difference between the government price of the land and its market value to-day. And as time goes on the estimation in which the settlers who formed the management of this northwestern civilization will be held, will be higher and higher; and the generation now so rapidly taking their places should appreciate the presence of those who remain, and endeavor to strew with flowers the pathways that are shortening so certainly, and must all terminate at no distant day. Let kindness and consideration wait upon them while they are still with us, and not heedlessly postpone our substantial appreciation of their merits, and between our remembrances of the toil, the privations, and the suffering they endured which has redounded to our benefit, until they are all gone, and then erect cold and passionless monuments to their memory.

"Be grateful, children, to your sires:
Light up affection's fervent fires,
And fan them with your love and care,
Until their aged hearts grow warm,
Close sheltered from want's chilling storm,
And heads are bowed in thankful prayer."

CHAPTER XLVII.

CENTENNIAL HISTORY.

The centenial history of the county is printed entire on account of the intrinsic value of the material it contains and because it is in itself a historical document. Without doubt there are some recapitulations of events in the part of the work recently compiled, and it is possible there may be discrepancy, as there always is between eye witnesses of any event, even when under oath in a court of justice. In the lists of county officers, they all are extended to the present time, to prevent repetition, otherwise the article is intact.

CENTENNIAL HISTORY OF FREEBORN COUNTY.

PREPARED BY D. G. PARKER AT THE REQUEST OF THE COMMITTEE OF ARRANGEMENTS, FOR DELIVERY AT THE CELEBRATION IN ALBERT LEA, JULY 4, 1876.

Mr. President and Fellow Citizens of Freeborn County:—A recommendation having been adopted by Congress, that the people make this Centenial Anniversary one of historic interest, the committee to whom was referred the general management of your local celebration, have extended to me the very flattering compliment of entrusting to my hands the delicate duty of compiling a brief record of Freeborn county. While appreciating the courtesy, and feeling grateful for the confidence thus reposed, I enter upon the work with hesitancy, fully conscious of the responsibility which it entails, and not unmindful of the criticism which the historian is likely to provoke.

The task is the more embarrassing from the fact that all history is dry, and he who looks for flower of romance or the poetry of song in the musty volumes of public records, has read history to no purpose.

Nevertheless, it is fitting and proper that the 100th anniversary of our National Independence should be invested with marks of special recognition, to the end that the people may retrospect the past; post their growth and doings to the present, and so, like a reckoning upon the broad sea of life, take from this a new departure.

EARLY EXPLORATIONS.

Until the year 1835, the region now embracing Freeborn county, was comparatively unknown. In the summer of that year, the Government fitted out an exploring party, consisting of 164 men, under the command of Lieut. Albert Miller Lea, with instructions to make a triangular march, from Fort Des Moines, northwest to Lake Pepin, thence southwesterly to the Des Moines river, thence following the stream southward to the place of departure. On the 31st of July, of that year, Lieut. Lea crossed the Turtle River, at Moscow, and on the following day passed beyond the western line of our county, within the limits of Alden township.

On this march he encamped for the night in Hayward, rested his command the next afternoon on the east bank of what is known as White's Lake, and made copious notes of the country along the entire route.

The solitude of this untrodden waste, impressed itself upon him. Sparkling lakes encircled by gently sloping woodlands, suggested the romance of nature. Smooth prairies, interspersed with shady groves, rich with the melody of feathered songsters, was a charm to his poetic spirit. Ever has he referred to this locality, as one of the most beautiful he has ever witnessed. Afterwards one Nicollet mapped out this section of country, using Lt. Lea's notes freely, and in the acknowledgement of the favor, gave the name of that brilliant officer to one of these Elysian gems.

We can learn of no other white man visiting these parts, until 1841, when Henry M. Rice, conconducting a party of trappers, encamped upon the shores of these enchanting waters, spending here a part of four consecutive years, in a life of daring bravery, startling adventures, and rude associations. That this was then, as now, the paradise of the sportsman, is attested by Mr. R., who affirms that in the summer of 1842 he saw over 300 elk in one day, while making his peregrinations around these lakes, and that in 1843 he killed two of these fleet-footed animals, one morning before breakfast.

This tract of country was embraced within a neutral strip of territory, lying between two hostile bands of Indians, and was frequently made the scalping ground of both; nor were they particular as to whose hair was lifted, provided they could exhibit some trophy of their savage propensity. Mr. Rice speaks of many a hair-breadth escape on the part of himself and company, during his hazardous adventures in this wild and unfrequented region.

TERRITORIAL ACTION.

By an act of the Territorial Legislature approved February 20th, 1855, the county limits were designated by boundary lines and the name chosen. It covers a territory of 30 miles from east to west, and 24 from north to south, embracing 20 townships, 13 lakes, more or less important, and a tillable area of about 400,000 acres. A reasonably temperate climate, and an unsurpassed richness of soil, combine to make it one of the most productive regions on the inhabitable globe.

It was named in honor of Wm. Freeborn, one of the pioneers of Goodhue county, and a worthy member of the early Territorial Legislature.

By a subsequent act of the same year, the county was attached to Dodge and Goodhue for Legislative purposes, which constituted the Fourth Council District.

According to the Land Office abstracts, the first entry of land was made in January 1855, by Nelson Everest, and thirty-four of the first conveyances, by deed, were recorded in Dodge county, between April '56 and March '57, though I find nothing in the general laws to indicate by what authority this was done. In February of 1859, however, these records were transcribed and brought home to their own county.

POLITICAL HISTORY.

Although the county limits were defined at so early a date, it had no political organization until March, 1857, when the Territorial Legislature made provision for its independent government, authorizing Gov. Gorman to carry the act into effect, which he did by appointing E. C. Stacy, S. N. Frisbie, and Wm. Andrews, as temporary Commissioners.

It may be here stated that the county was organized into one general election precinct, by authority of the State Department, in the fall previous, and forty-four votes polled in the election of that year; the same being held at the house o Wm. Andrews, in Shell Rock.

The Commissioners referred to assembled on the 3d of March, 1857, and proceeded te appoint the various County Officers, as follows:

Register of Deeds, Samuel M. Thompson; Treasurer, Thomas C. Thorne; Sheriff, Geo. S. Ruble; Probate Judge, E. C. Stacy; Coroner, A. H. Bartlett; Co. Attorney, J. W. Heath; Surveyor, E. P. Skinner; Justices, Geo. Watson, I. P. Linde, Elias Stanton, Patrick Fitzsimmons.

These appointments took effect on the 20th of the same month, except that of Fitzsimmons, who received his authority afterwards. In April following, Wm Morin was appointed Register of Deeds in place of Mr. Thompson, who declined to qualify. The Coroner's office also went begging, and was tendered in succession to Geo. Watson and C.

S. Tarbell, after Mr. Bartlett had signified his unwillingness to serve.

At the April session, the Commissioners authorized the clerk to procure all necessary books and the Surveyor's field notes of the public surveys; but as there were no taxes assessed, or other public revenue to draw upon, we have yet to learn which one of these generous officers donated the money. It is fair to presume that neither of them were in a hurry to lay his purse upon the public altar, for we find that the minutes of the Board were long kept upon sheets of foolscap, stitched together, and that field notes were not obtained until years afterward. It may also be presumed that the Commissioners felt the weight of their great responsibility, for it appears that no less than seven sessions were held between March, 1857, and November of the same year.

I do not refer to this sluringly. Everything was in a chaotic state, out of which they were expected to bring regularity and order. There were assessments to be made, districts to organize, towns to officer, precincts to form, roads to survey—in short, everything to be done, and the obligation resting upon themselves. Between the various meetings of the Board, during the spring and summer of 1857, there were eleven voting precincts organized and the judges duly appointed.

The first general election was held in October, 1857, at which 646 votes were polled in the county, and the following officers chosen: Register of Deeds, Wm. Morin; Treasurer, Henry King; Sheriff, J. W. Heath; Probate Judge, A. W. White; Clerk of Court, E. P. Skinner; Surveyor, H. D. Brown; Coroner, A. M. Burnham; Commissioners, S. N. Frisbie, Joseph Rickard, Peter Clauson.

The Legislature of 1857-58 changed the County Governments, and provided for what is known as the Supervisor system, by which each organized town was represented on the County Board, through its chairman. Several of the towns in this county being either unorganized or attached to others for township purposes, necessarily limited the representation, so that the first Board under the Supervisor system, which met in June, 1858, was composed of ten delegates, as follows:

Shell Rock, William Andrews; Moscow, Theop. Lowry; Geneva, E. C. Stacy; Riceland, Isaac Baker; Hartland, B. J. Boardman; Freeborn, C. D. Giddings; Albert Lea, A. C. Wedge; Pickerel Lake, A. W. White; Manchester, H. W. Allen; Nunda, Patrick Fitzsimmons.

Of this Board, E. C. Stacy was elected Chairman.

The Supervisor system continued until the winter of 1860, when its complicated and expensive character induced a return to the Commissioner plan, and in June following, the Board elected under this law, consisting of Wm. N. Goslee, G. W. Skinner, and Asa Walker, met and organized with the latter as Chairman.

COUNTY OFFICERS.

The county offices, other than the Commissioners, have been filled as follows:

Auditor.—Wm. Morin, from 1859 to 1861; E. C. Stacy, from 1861 to 1865; C. C. Colby, from 1865 to 1867; E. C. Stacy, from 1867 to 1869; Samuel Bachelder, from 1869 to 1877; then William Lincoln and Giles Q. Slocum, to the present time.

Register of Deeds.—Wm. Morin, from 1857 to 1862; John Wood, from 1862 to 1872; August Peterson, from 1872 to ——; then Ole Simonson and Gurs Hanson, to the present time.

It will be seen from this, that from 1859 to 1861, Mr. Morin performed the double duty of Register of Deeds and Auditor.

Treasurer.—T. C. Thorne, from March, 1857 to 1858; Henry King, from 1858 to 1860; Ole I. Ellingson, from 1860 to 1862; J. E. Smith, from 1862 to 1866; D. G. Parker, from 1866 to 1868; Charles Kittleson, from 1868 to 1877; since then, Frank W. Barlow.

Probate Judge.—E. C. Stacy, from March, 1857 to 1858; A. W. White, from 1858 to 1860; B. J. House, from 1860 to 1862; A. H. Bartlett, from 1862 to 1866; B. J. House, from 1866 to 1870; A. M. Tyrer, from 1870 to 1872; G. Gulbrandson, from 1872 to ——; and then James H. Parker, and now Ira W. Towne.

Sheriff.—Geo. S. Ruble, from March, 1857 to 1858; John W. Heath, from 1858 to 1860; J. A. Robson, from 1860 to 1862; R. K. Crum, from 1862 to 1864; Leander Cooley, from 1864 to 1866; A. W. St. John, from 1866 to October, 1867; John Brownsill from October, 1867 to 1868; E. D. Porter from 1868 to 1872; T. J. Sheehan, from 1872 to the present time.

Clerk of the Court.—A. Armstrong, from August, 1857 to 1858; E. P. Skinner, from 1858 to 1862; H. D. Brown, from 1862 to October, 1871; John Weed from October, 1871 to 1873; A. W. White, from 1873 to ——; and George T. Gardner to the present time.

COUNTY ATTORNEY.—J. W. Heath, from March, 1857 to 1858.

From that time until 1860 the office was not known to the law, it having been abolished by the adoption of the State Constitution, and a District Prosecuting Attorney substituted, which office was held by Mr. Perkins, of Faribault.

In 1860, the office having again been provided for, J. U. Perry held, by appointment, from March until December of that year. D. G. Parker, from December, 1860 to December, 1862; A. Armstrong, from 1862 to 1865; H. B. Collins, from 1865 to 1869; J. A. Lovely, from 1869 to 1873; A. G. Wedge, from 1873 to the election of John A. Lovely, who is the present incumbent.

COURT COMMISSIONER. A. W. White held this in connection with the Probate office, from August, 1858 to 1861; J. M. Drake, from 1861 to 1862; Samuel Eaton, from 1862 to 1874; B. H. Carter, from 1874 to 1876; R. B. Spicer, from January, 1876 to 1878; then John Anderson, and now Herman Blackmer.

Much of this time, the office existed more in name than in fact.

CORONER.—C. S. Tarbell, from April, 1857 to 1858. At the general election of 1857, Dr. A. M. Burnham was chosen to this office, but he did not qualify, and it stood vacant for a period of ten years. Geo. S. Ruble was elected in 1861, but did not serve; Samuel Eaton, from 1868 to 1872; W. W. Cargill, from 1872 to 1874; N. H. Ellickson, from 1874 to 1876; Dr. John Froshaug, from 1876 to the present time.

SCHOOL SUPERINTENDENT.—Up to July, 1865, no well defined management of schools existed. In speculating upon the best system, the Legislature created first a town Superintendcy, then an Examiner for each Commissioner district, and lastly the present plan of one general Superintendent for each county. Under this, S. Batchelder was appointed July, 1865, and served until 1869. E. C. Stacy, from 1869 to 1870; H. Thurston, from 1870 to the election of Charles W. Levens, the present official.

SURVEYOR.—E. P. Skinner, from March, 1857 to 1858; H. D. Brown, from 1858 to 1860; C. C. Colby was elected to this office in the fall of 1859, and for the two subsequent terms, holding until 1865. From this time nobody seems to have aspired to the place until the fall of 1867, when Levi Pierce was invested with that honor and held until 1872. W. G. Kellar, from 1872 to 1874; H. C. Lacy, from 1874 to 1876; W. G. Kellar, from 1876 to to the present time.

STATE REPRESENTATION.

Passing from our county politics, I will next refer to our legislative representation and the various changes of district boundary. Your attention has already been called to the connection of our county under the Territorial Government, and it is unnecessary to refer to it again.

In the early part of 1857, Congress passed an act authorizing the people to form a State Constitution, and in July a convention was held at Mantorville, to nominate delegates to the district and to agree upon a division of them among the three counties. From some cause, Freeborn was not represented in that convention, and the other two magnanimously awarded to her one out of the six delegates to be elected; but ever true to her local interest, she threw off on Dodge, defeating Isaac Turtlott, of that county, thereby securing two representatives in the constitutional convention, viz: Geo. Watson and E. C. Stacy.

By the provision of the Constitution that year adopted, our representative boundary was changed, and we became attached to Faribault county, the two being known as the Fourteenth Senatorial District, entitled to one Senator and three Representatives, and of these Freeborn elected the Senator, Dr. Watson, and one Representative, A. H. Bartlett, as the first delegation under this apportionment.

In 1860, another change was made, connecting the county with Steele and Waseca, entitled the Sixteenth Senatorial District, which was awarded one Senator and two Representatives. Under this apportionment, Geo. Watson was sent to the Senate while J. E. Child, of Waseca, and W. F. Pettit, of Steele, were honored with seats in the House, as the first Representatives.

In 1871, the representation of the State was enlarged, Freeborn county made an independent district numbered Five, and awarded one Senator and two Representatives, which still continues to be the status of the county.

A view of our representation in the Legislature shows the following:

SENATORS.—Dr. Geo. Watson, from 1858 to 1862; A. B. Webber, from 1862 to 1863; M. A. Daley, of Steele, from 1863 to 1864. This latter filling the vacancy occasioned by Mr. Webber's enlistment in the army, as a commissary officer. F. J. Stevens, of Steele, from 1864 to 1865; B. A. Lowell, of Waseca, from 1865 to 1867; Aug. Armstrong, from 1867 to 1869; J. B. Crooker, of Steele, from 1869 to 1871; W. C. Young, of Waseca, from 1871 to 1872; H. D. Brown, from 1872 to 1873; T. G. Jonsrud, from 1873 to 1875; T. H. Armstrong, from 1875 to the present time. It will be noticed that a number of these served only one year, which is accounted for by entries into the Government service during the war, or by vacancies occasioned through a change of district. I give the names of the Senators of the counties with which we have been connected, because we had an equal interest in their representation, and therefore the record would not be complete without them.

REPRESENTATIVES.—A. H. Bartlett, from 1858 to 1859; T. H. Purdie, from 1859 to 1860; A. B. Webber, from 1860 to 1861. It may be remarked that Mr. Webber's election was a bestowment of cheap honor, as there was no session of the Legislature during his term. J. E. Child, of Waseca, and F. W. Pettit, of Steele, from 1861 to 1862; H. C. Magoon, of Steele, and P. C. Bailey, of Waseca, from 1862 to 1863; Asa Walker, from 1863 to 1864; J. L. Gibbs, from 1864 to 1866; Aug. Armstrong, from 1866 to 1867; J. E. Smith, from 1867 to 1869; Aug. Armstrong, from 1869 to 1870; A. C. Wedge, from 1870 to 1872; E. D. Rogers and Wm. Wilson, from 1872 to 1873; J. W. Devereaux and E. D. Rogers; from 1873 to 1874; Even Morgan and Warren Buel, from 1874 to 1875; H. Tunell and R. Fitzgerald, from 1875 to 1876; H. Tunell and J. L. Gibbs ,from 1876 to the present time. This covers substantially our political history. We might revive the memory of some stormy conventions, but that would be productive of no good, and the animosities there engendered may well be allowed to die with the issues which inspired them.

FIVE MILLION LOAN.

We would not be doing justice to our people, did we not refer to their noble act in unitedly opposing what was known as the Five Million Loan Bill, under which the State, in 1858, unwisely pledged its credit to the railroad companies, and entailed a debt which, just or unjust, threatens a burdensome taxation, or the stigma of repudiation. To the credit of Freeborn county, be it said that she saw the danger, and opposed the measure by a negative vote of 455 to 18.

We have yet to learn what became of those *eighteen*. If, indeed, they still survive, there are none among them who now refer with any degree of pride to that ill conceived ballot, and long before this would gladly have obliterated the record.

We will next call in review our

COUNTY SEAT CONTESTS.

The act of March, 1857, organizing the county, authorized the commissioners appointed by the Governor, to select a temporary county seat until the question should be determined by a vote of the people. Under this authority, the Board, on the second day of its session, March 4th, 1857, called up the question, and Mr. Frisbie moved to make Bancroft the seat of honor. Mr. Stacy proposed an amendment striking out Bancroft and inserting St. Nicholas ; lost. He then moved to insert Geneva, which was also defeated. Mr. Andrews then moved to insert Albert Lea in place of Bancroft, and this carried unanimously. In this, we are free to say that we think the Commissioners acted wisely and well; but it will always remain a mystery, what inspiring light concentrated them so suddenly upon a point which seems to have escaped their notice in the first instance.

On the 19th of May following, a special session of the Legislature passed an act incorporating Bancroft, and a proviso was sandwiched into the bill making that town the county seat. The bill passed in this shape, apparently without being understood by a majority of those who voted for it; for it appears that the members having been apprised of what they had done, recalled their their votes and expunged the objectionable proviso on the same day.

At the general election in October of that year the question was submitted to the people. Four towns entered the contest, viz: Shell Rock, Bancroft, St. Nicholas, and Albert Lea, which resulted in favor of the later, by a majority of 165 over all, on a total vote of 642.

The next contest was in 1860. In September of that year, a petition was presented to the

County Board, asking for another vote. A. S. Everest appeared for the petitioners, and Aug. Armstrong opposed their prayer. The decision was postponed until the 22d of October, at which meeting the petition was granted, and a vote of the people followed. Itasca alone entered the arena with Albert Lea, resulting again in favor of the latter, by 198 majority, on a total vote of 770.

Passing from this, we will next notice our

JUDICIAL RECORD.

Under the Territorial Government, Freeborn county, with fifteen others, constituted the Third Judicial District, and Judge Flandreau, after appointing Aug. Armstrong clerk, which he did in the summer of 1857, advertised to hold court at Albert Lea in October following; but as there was no business at that time, the announcement was only formal, and no court was in fact called.

By the constitution of 1857, the district was changed in form and size, so that Freeborn, with eight other counties, became the Fifth Judicial District, and Hon. N. M. Donaldson, of Owatonna, was elected in the fall of that year, presiding Judge. In the fall of 1871, the Hon. Samuel Lord, of Mantorville, was elected Judge in place of Donaldson, but his association with our people was of short duration, for in 1872 the Legislature created a new district called the Tenth, composed of Freeborn and all the counties in the southern tier, east of it. Over this District, Hon. Sherman Page, of Austin, was called to preside, and then J. Q. Farmer, who still holds that position.

Under those organizations, courts have been held twice a year regularly, with one or two exceptions.

Among the important cases disposed of, was that of Henry Kregler, who was charged with the murder of Nelson Boughton, near the State line, in September, 1859, and tried in Steele county, under change of venue, in January, 1861. He was convicted, brought back to this county and executed at Albert Lea, in March following, being about one and a half years after the offense was committed.

LOYALTY AND PATRIOTISM.

No county in the State, if indeed in the country, has displayed a greater loyalty, or a truer patriotism. In the first year of its organization, when settlement was in disorder, weakness, and poverty, the people, though few in number, did not forget the noble example of their ancestry, and on the first return of this Anniversary of their National holiday, the 4th of July, 1857, they assembled *en masse*, at Shell Rock, to celebrate this time-honored event. At that celebration, Samuel Batchelder delivered the address, being the first oration ever made in the county. From that year to the present, nearly every return of the day has been marked by some appropriate honor.

At the first call for troops when war broke out, men left their farms, their shops, their stores, and their offices, to engage in the defense of their common country, leaving scarcely any but old men and boys to care for and defend their homes against the Indian outbreak, which threatened the entire State.

Two companies, made up almost entirely from this county, constituted some of the best fighting stock of the 4th and 5th Regiments of Infantry, while the third, in their zeal to get into service, accepted the first opening and joined a Wisconsin brigade.

Other detachments of men connected themselves with commands in this, or in other States, as duty dictated or fancy led them. Although this scattering of individuals or squads renders it difficult to determine the number exactly, a reasonably correct approximation will fix it about 400 persons, which, as an act of patriotism, to fully appreciate, it is necessary to bear in mind our sparse settlement and limited population.

To place the matter in a still clearer light, it is only necessary to state that the quota assigned to the county at the last call for troops by the Adjutant General in 1864, was 273, and that we had already furnished and received credit for 292, being an excess over all demands upon us, of 19 men, besides an estimate of 100 who are known to have gone into commands of other States, for which the enlistment officers gave us no credit. I submit that a fairer or more creditable record cannot be produced by any county, sharing the fortunes of the late war. Nor were the ladies less true to the interests of their country. On every occasion which presented itself, they encouraged enlistments, and cheered their brothers on to the conflict. The silken banner carried by company F, of the 4th Regiment throughout their long and faithful services, upon which is inscribed the memorable name of many a bloody battle field, was presented by these noble women, as the appropriate offering of anxious and sympathizing mothers, wives, and sisters, and will ever be sacredly preserved and treasured as a lasting memorial of their patriotic devotion.

SCHOOLS AND CHURCHES.

This county has shared its full benefit of the liberal public provision made for fostering the common school system. Nor have the people been less enterprising in their efforts to encourage public education. In fact, the greater part of our taxation has been for the erection of new schoolhouses, and the employment of qualified teachers. In 1858 there were but two schoolhouses of any character in the county. There are now 100 districts, 74 of which can boast of fine frame or brick houses, while in nearly all, the buildings are good and substantial. In Albert Lea there is a graded school which ranks among the best in the State, while a seminary of learning at this place and at Alden are also mantained a part of the time by private contributions. In addition to this, there is a charter which was early granted by the Legislature, creating a College Board at Albert Lea, and which will doubtless be revived in due time. The first enumeration was made in January, 1858, and showed a total of 222 scholars. The last, taken in the fall of 1875, gives 5,136, being an increase, in 17 years, of 4,914, or at the rate of about eight per cent. per annum.

The churches are well represented and liberally sustained, nearly every town in the county having one or more organizations for public worship. These societies do a creditable mission work, and sustain 23 Sabbath Schools through the summer months, while about half of them are continued the year through.

SECRET SOCIETIES.

A Masonic Lodge, nearly as old as the county, is established at Albert Lea, which enjoys a membership in good standing of 74 persons. Growing out of this is a Royal Arch Chapter of 15 members.

Twenty-four Granges, with a membership of about 960.

One division of the Sons of Temperance, having about 30 members.

There are eight Good Templar's lodges in the county, with an aggregate membership of over 700.

NEWSPAPERS.

The history of our newspaper interest is a checkered one, and has often been referred to. Of the five that have had an existence, two, the first and the last, remain, apparently well supported, and offer their weekly budgets to an appreciative public.

TAXATION.

In March, 1857, the first board of Commissioners divided the county into three assessment districts, as follows:

The first was composed of Newry, Geneva, Bath, Hartland, Freeborn, and Carlston, over which J. M. Drake was appointed assessor.

Second, Moscow, Riceland, Bancroft, Manchester, Oakland, London, under the charge of John Dunning, as assessor.

The third was composed of Hayward, Shell Rock, Freeman, Pickerel Lake, Nunda, Alden, Mansfield, and Albert Lea, with Walter Scott, as assessor.

In July following these officers completed and returned their rolls, the aggregate of which footed up, $212,088. Upon this was levied a tax for school, county, and Territorial purposes of $4,449, or 20½ mills on each dollar valuation.

A year or two after that, each organized town became a district, and has steadily shown an increase of wealth. The last assessment reported, that of 1875, aggregated a valuation, of $3,183,822, with a tax for all purposes of $65,602, showing an increase of property at the rate of about 16 per cent. per annum, and a marked decrease in the rate of taxation, when we consider that railroads, bridges, and other matters, have increased the objects for which we are taxed.

RAILROADS.

In 1859, the Southern Minnesota railroad was built through the county, in a westerly direction, touching the towns of Moscow, Oakland, Hayward, Albert Lea, Pickerel Lake, Alden, and Carlston, and establishing, then and subsequently, four stations, viz: Oakland, Hayward, Albert Lea, and Alden. This enterprise has had a marked influence upon the property and growth of the county, and while its management has been generally satisfactory to our people, that of the present period is so in the highest degree.

Crossing this line at Albert Lea, is another survey, termed the North and South Road, which is designed to connect Minneapolis with St. Louis, and when built will touch Shell Rock, Albert Lea, Manchester, and Hartland. Still a third company, under the auspices of the Central Railroad of Minnesota, acting in connection with the Burlington & Cedar Rapids Line, have already graded from Albert Lea to a point near the State line, and it is only a question of time, when the iron will be laid thereon.

COMMERCE.

Another evidence of our prosperity as a county, may be seen in its rapidly increasing productions.

The first three years of settlement, say from 1857 to 1860, was an era of importation of food, and marked the most trying times. From 1860 to the close of the war, little, if anything was raised beyond home needs; so that really the last ten years cover the period of prosperity. How rapidly that has been, is seen in the reports of last year, which show that, in addition to feeding our population, we exported 1,099,986 bushels of wheat, besides a fair proportion of other products. The freight reports of our station agents show that these exportations are increasing at the rate of about 20 per cent. per annum.

The richness of this, as a grazing county, was early recognized and is now duly appreciated. The area and luxuriance of our nutritious grasses have encouraged our people to deversify their industry, and to make stock growing not only one of the leading, but a very profitable branch. A number of buyers make this a purchasing point, and thousands of cattle are driven to the Chicago and other markets spring and fall. Nor do our people show less sagacity in the improvement of of quality, many of the growers already dealing in none but the finest strains of blood,

Wool is becoming a highly important article of export, while in the matter of dairying, some estimate may be formed of its value from the fact that one shipper, at Albert Lea, alone sends off about 200,000 pounds of butter per annum.

POPULATION.

A census of the county taken in November, 1857, showed the population to be 2,486. That of 1875, the last wheih has been taken, aggregates our population at 13,171, showing a gain of about 47 per cent. in every five years.

TOWNSHIP RECORDS.

We have spent too much time in reviewing matters pertaining to the county at large, to justify a critical examination of township organization and early settlement. The record, however, incomplete at best, could not be satisfactorily closed, without presenting a few of the prominent facts connected with their history.

At the January session of the County Board, in 1858, London, Moscow, Newry, Carlston, Riceland, Bath, and Manchester, were organized, though most of them under other names. Whether any official action was ever taken in regard to Albert Lea, Nunda, Shell Rock, and Geneva, is not clear, but it seems that their political status as towns was recognized even previous to this, and their representatives occupied prominent places in the councils of the County Board. Various changes were made, and towns organized from this time until January, 1866, when the last one, Mansfield, assumed an independent government.

London was organized under the name of Asher, thus conferring an honor upon one of her citizens of that name, now deceased. In June, 1858, the town was attached to Shell Rock for township purposes. In October following, it again assumed an independent organizstion, and changed its name to London, The first election was held at the house of H. B. Riggs.

Shell Rock occupies a high post of honor in many of the events of our early settlement. One of the first Commissioners, Wm. Andrews, was appointed from this town, and he became the first chairman of the County Board. It was here that the first schoolhouse was erected, June, 1857, in the district now known as 49. The building was a frame, also the first of the kind put up. Although the records do not support it, it is nevertheless believed that the first title to land was acquired in this town, by Clark Andrews, which occurred November 3, 1855. We have already mentioned the fact that here the first patriotic demonstration was made, as early as 1857, and we may add, that here also, the first suit was tried, being a case of one Boulton against C. T. Knapp, before justice Andrews, in the spring of 1857, in which A. H. Bartlett appeared as attorney for both parties, and, as he admits, was beaten at last.

As already noticed, Shell Rock was the scene

of the first election, November 4th, 1856, when the whole county constituted but one precinct, and 44 votes indicated nearly the total strength of our adult male population. George Gardner, William and Madison Rice, and Gardner Cottrell, were the first settlers and date their entry on the 9th of June, 1855.

Freeman, after its organization, was divided: the east half being attached to Shell Rock, and the west half to Nunda, for township purposes. It was named in honour of the Freeman family, who were the first to move into the central portion of the town. In December, 1860, it was granted a separate organization, and the name changed to Green, but it nevertheless continued to be called by its first title and has ever been known as Freeman. This town is supposed to have received the first settler of the county, in the person of Ole Olenhouse, as early as the summer of 1854, who, also, is claimed to have erected the first house, in the same season.

Nunda was first known as Bear Lake, but was afterwards changed at the suggestion of Patrick Fitzsimmons, who was anxious to honor a favorite town in McHenry county, Ill. This town is watered by three important lakes. The first settler was Anthony Bright, who made his claim in the spring of 1856.

Twin Lake village, in the northern part, is a thriving town, having a mill, store, Post-office, hotel, etc. It was surveyed into lots as early as 1857. The long legal controversy between Wm. Banning and a Mr. Forbes, growing out of claims of each upon the millsite, will long be remembered by some of the old settlers.

Mansfield was early attached to Nunda for township purposes, and was the last in the county to ask for a separate organization. Its name was suggested by Geo. S. Ruble, now of Chattanooga, Tenn. John and Henry Tunell entered upon their claims in June, 1856, and were the first settlers.

Oakland was divided in Jan., 1858, and the north half attached to Moscow, while the south half was assigned to London for township purposes. In June following, when London became attached to Shell Rock, the County Board ordered that the whole of Oakland be attached to Moscow, then known as Guildford. In September, 1858, the town was granted an independent organization. Its large area of oak openings suggested the name.

Hayward, so called in compliment to one of her citizens of that name, was, in January, 1858, divided into three parts. The northeast quarter of the town being assigned to Riceland, then known as Beardsley; the northwest to Albert Lea, and the south half to Shell Rock. In September following, the town was granted a separate organization. At a subsequent session of the County Board, the name was changed to Douglass, in honor of the distinguished Illinois Senator, of that period. At the same meeting the southern tier of sections was set off to Shell Rock for township purposes.

In September, 1859, these sections were set back to the control of the town, and the name again changed from Douglass to Hayward. The first settler was Wm. Andrews, who located in the summer of 1855, but afterwards moved across the line into Shell Rock.

Albert Lea is the shire and central town. It is located between two picturesque lakes, and was named in honor of the distinguished explorer previously mentioned. It was first settled in July, 1855, by Lorenzo Merry, who took the first claim, did the first breaking, erected the first house, and opened the first hotel. St. Nicholas, in the southern part of the town, was at one time a village of considerable importance, and aspired to the county seat. Nothing now remains of the village, and the land has been converted into a stock farm.

The report of the Southern Minnesota Railroad Company for 1875, shows that the revenue of this station, as well as the amount of freight received and forwarded, is largely in excess of any other town upon the entire line of the road.

Pickerel Lake was attached to Albert Lea for township purposes, in 1858. In the following year, it was voted a separate organization. In October, 1860, it was attached to Manchester for election purposes, but afterwards became a part of Albert Lea, and remained so until September, 1865, when the citizens petitioned for an independent government, which was granted. The name of the fine lake within its borders, first suggested that of the town. Charles and William Wilder and A. D. Pinkerton located in the summer of 1855, and were the first settlers.

Alden was attached to Pickerel Lake for township purposes, in Jan. 1858, but in October, 1860, it was detached, and made a part of Carlston. In September following a singular entry appears upon the record, showing that the Board granted a petition to detach Alden from Albert Lea, and attach it to Carlston. How it became separated from Carlston, after its connection of the previous year, or how it became part of Albert Lea, with Pickerel Lake intervening, the record is silent. In the absence of further light, we presume it to be an error. In March, 1866, the town was granted a separate organization.

The village of Alden is located upon the Southern Minnesota Railroad, ten miles west of Albert Lea, and is second in size in the county. The station reports show, also, that it is second in importance in the receipt and shipment of freights.

Moscow is one of the towns of distinguished prominence in the settlement, organization, and early political history of the county. S. N. Frisbie was one of the three first Commissioners. Dr. Watson, also a citizen of this town, was not only one of the delegates to the Constitutional Convention in 1857, but enjoyed the honor of a seat in the State Senate for the first three terms. The Rev. S. G. Lowry, also of this town, may be regarded as the pioneer clergyman, and for years answered calls, picking his trackless way to all parts of the county.

A heavy body of timber, on section seventeen, was long previous known as the Moscow woods, and this suggested to the early settlers the name of the town, which so continued until its organization, when it took the name of Guildford, but in June, 1858, it was again changed to its original title. A colony, consisting of Thomas R. Morgan, Nathan Hunt, Robt. Spear, and Thos. Ellis, made the first settlement, on the 30th of May, 1855.

Riceland was organized under the name of Beardsley, in honor of Sam. Beardsley, one of the first settlers; but in October, 1858, it was changed to its present name, at the suggestion of Isaac Baker, who was then on the County Board. Shortly after settlement, a small tract was surveyed into town lots, under the name of Fairfield, but it never acquired the dignity of a village. Ole C. Oleson and Ole Hanson located in August, 1856, and were the first settlers.

Bancroft village had its origin in what was known as the St. Paul Land Company, of which W. N. Oliver was agent. Afterwards, by general consent, the name was applied to the whole township. To far as we can learn, this town has the honor of having erected the second schoolhouse in the county, which was done in the fall of 1857, by the district now known as No. 20.

The village of Bancroft was a sharp rival for the county seat in 1857, and at that time a place of considerable importance, having a newspaper, store, saw-mill, and other evidences of busy life, all of which has since disappeared.

Manchester was first known by the name of Oldburg, but was christened Buckeye at its organization. In May, 1858, it was changed to Liberty. Finally, in October fallowing, at the suggestion of Mathias Anderson, it was changed to Manchester, in honor of a place of the same name in Illinois, where Mr. A. had previously lived. S. S. Skiff entered this town in June, 1856 as the first settler.

Carlston was organized in January, 1858, under the name of Stanton, out of respect to Elias Stanton, who had already suffered amputation on account of frost-bitten feet, and who died of the same in the spring following. After its organization it was attached to Freeborn for township purposes. In June, 1858, the name was changed to Springfield, and in October following to Groton. In September, 1859, the citizens asked for a seperate organization, which was granted, and the name changed to Carlston. This name was finally agreed upon, in respect to the memory of a distinguished Swede of that name, who settled in that town in an early day, and who was drowned in Freeborn lake. Robert H. Miller was the first settler, and located in August, 1855.

Newry was first named Seward, as a mark of respect to the distinguished Senator from New York, and at the same time, January, 1858, was attached to Geneva for township purposes. In October following, the name was changed to Union, and the town granted a separate organization. In the early part of 1859, the name was again changed to Dover, but from some cause this proved to be unsatisfactory to the State Auditor, and upon his recommendation another change took place, which resulted in adopting the present name.

Geneva was among the prominent towns in organizing the early affairs of the county. E. C. Stacy, one of her citizens, was among the three first County Commissioners, and by them was appointed the first Probate Judge. He was also elected a delegate to the Constitutional Convention, to which we have already referred. It was also upon his suggestion that the town was named Geneva, in remembrance of Geneva, N. Y., for which pleasant recollections were entertained. The village of Geneva, situated upon the bank of a beautiful lake of that name, is a town of considerable prominence. Milton Morey was the first settler, locating in the fall of 1855.

Bath was first organized under the name of Porter, in honor of E. D. Porter, who settled near Clark's Grove. The east half of the town was attached to Geneva, and the the west half to Hartland for township purposes, but in September, 1858, assumed an independent organization, and the name changed to Bath, at the instance of F. W. Calkins, who was desirous of perpetuating the memory of the town in which he was born. Mr. Calkins was the first settler of Bath, and made his entry in the spring or early summer of 1857.

While the town of Hartland is one of the best agricultural districts in the county, it yields but few facts concerning early history. It is understood to have been named after a town in Windsor county, Vermont, and was first settled by two brothers by the name of Boardman, in the fall of 1856. One of these, B. J. Boardman, erected the first house, and at one time represented the town on the County Board.

Freeborn was among the early towns organized, and the first election held in May, 1858. The township and village, as well as the lake upon the bank of which the village is located, all seem to have followed, in name, that of the county. T. K. Page and Wm. Montgomery were the first settlers, and entered upon their claims in July, 1856. The village of Freeborn is handsomely located and is a town of considerable importance. It is in this town that the first entry of land appears on record, by Nelson Everet, as previously mentioned, though the correctness of this is doubted.

ORIGIN OF NAMES OF LAKES, RIVERS, AND TIMBER.

A word will also be in place regarding the origin of names as applied to lakes, rivers, etc. Bear Lake should be properly known as Pickerel Lake. The story is this: Buffalo being found in this section as late as 1853, a party consisting of Joseph Hewitt, Joshua Jackson, and Joseph Kelley, visited the region of Nunda, in quest of that game, in the summer of that year. Their hunt was rewarded by one or two buffalo calves, and some fine pickerel taken from that lake, which suggested the name, as mentioned.

On the other hand Pickerel Lake should be known as Bear Lake. Some years previous to settlement, the Indians killed a large bear near that body of water, and ever afterwards called it Bear Lake. In 1854, one Austin Nichols, who had previously obtained from the three buffalo hunters glowing accounts of their beautiful Pickerel Lake, made a tour through from the Cedar to the Blue Earth River, and struck Bear Lake in his route, of which he knew nothing. Supposing it to be the Pickerel Lake of which he had been told of, he so called it, and his acquaintances settling in soon after, accepted his impression without further inquiry. A year later, the pioneers who settled Nunda, knowing that their northern neighbors had got the *Pickerel*, supposed of course that the *Bear* belonged to them, and so the accidental change became a fixed fact.

Lake Albert Lea was originally known as Fox Lake. In 1835, when the exploring command of Lieut. Lea approached this body of water a white fox ran past the head of the column, and thus unconsciously had his memory perpetuated.

White Lake was first known as Lake Chapeau. From the bank of this, where Lieut. Lea rested his command a few hours, the lake presents the shape of a French military hat, and this suggested the name. When this section of country was afterwards mapped out, Chapeau was dropped and Albert Lea applied. The early settlers knew but little about these lakes, and took it for granted that the large one bore the name of the distinguished explorer, and thus the *Fox* was finally allowed to escape. In the meantime, Capt. A. W. White settled upon the bank of the original Chapeau, and by common consent his name has become associated with that lake.

Turtle Creek is said to have been so named in 1854. A party crossing the same was stepping from one stone to another, when one of the number suddenly lost his footing—the stone as he supposed gracefully sliding from under him. It proved to be a huge turtle, with which the river then abounded, and the stream was ever afterwards called Turtle River. It is noted in Lieut. Lea's minutes as Iowa River.

Mule Lake was discovered by the Boardman brothers, who, as we have already said, first settled in Hartland. Their entry into that town was with a mule team, driven across the country from Geneva. On their return they related their observations, and the mules were at once dignified in the naming of the lake.

Some years previous to settlement, the heavy body of timber which covered section seventeen, in Moscow, was set on fire in a dry season, creating such a conflagration as to suggest scenes in Russia under the great Napoleon. From that time it was known as the Moscow timber, and thus the name of the town had its origin.

I have now passed in review the salient points in the history of our county, and although that review has been necessarily brief, it shows a record and a growth of which any people may feel justly proud, and calculated to inspire high hopes for future prosperity. Few agricultural regions have ever witnessed a more rapid advancement in population, growth of products, educational endowments, and general material wealth ; and I may add, that seldom has it fallen to the lot of man to have his destiny fixed in such an Eden of natural beauty.

Looking back over the period of the last twenty years, we have little to regret. From a trackless and uninhabited region, we have sprung into a community of 15,000 souls, teaming with a busy life. Vineyards and groves rise up everywhere to please the eye and gratify the taste, while thousands of laughing grain fields wave their golden treasures to triumph to make glad the hearts of the husbandmen. Log cabins yield to the advancing progress of wealth and civilization, and in their places rise up the homes of greater material comfort, and domestic enjoyment; the rail pens have given away to substantial granaries, and straw stables are fast making room for spacious and costly barns.

Schoolhouses afford educational facilities at convenient intervals, while the green foliage, beneath which they are embowered, offer their inviting shade to thousands of promising children.

Sloughs, inlets, and streams have been substantially bridged, while long rows of shade trees mark the line of the well-beaten turnpikes.

Railroads and grain stations remind us that we have already passed the period of pioneer life, and that we are entering upon an area full of inspiring hope for the future.

Looking upon our material prosperity for the twenty years past, we may well enquire what will be the condition of Freeborn county one hundred years hence. I will not undertake the speculation. None of us will be living, but remember that the present is always the parent of the future. As the twig is bent, so it will grow. Our influence does not end with our lives. The uncounted generations to come, hold us largely responsible for their intellectual, moral, and religious character : for, be it known, that whether we will it or not, the broad or restricted philanthrophy of our own lives will impress itself upon all the distant future.

CHAPTER XLVIII.

THE OLD SETTLERS' ASSOCIATION.

As a continuation of the early history of the county, quite a full account of the meetings of the Old Settlers' Association is given here, with very full reports of some of the speeches or addresses, which are rich in reminiscences and so well presented that a rewriting could not improve them. Coming in this form, it slightly interferes with the continuity of the plan of the work, but this is fully compensated for by a disruption of the monotony which might otherwise become tedious in the perusal.

The old settlers of Freeborn county who were desirous of perpetuating the memory of the hardships, the trials, troubles, and privations on the one hand, and the pleasures and triumphs on the other, of pioneer times and frontier life, joined in a call to all those who came previous to 1860, to meet on the 12th of July, 1875, for the purpose of organizing an Old Settlers' Association.

In response to this call a meeting was held at the Court House on the day mentioned, at two o'clock. The assembly was called to order by D. G. Parker, who read the call that had been issued. On motion of John L. Melder, Mr. Parker was made temporary chairman. On motion of F. McCall, H. D. Brown was appointed secretary. On motion of Isaac Botsford, the following committee on resolutions was appointed : Henry Thurston, F. McCall, and H. G. Emmons; on nominations, Isaac Botsford, John L. Melder, and Jason Goward. While waiting for the reports of committees Mr. Melder, who was the original mover in the matter, was called upon for a speech, and responded in a facetious vein, relating amusing anecdotes. Remarks were made by Father Lowry and others.

The committee appointed for the purpose reported a constitution which, after discussion and amendment, was adopted. Its provisions were that any old settler could join by paying a nominal sum, who was here previous to January 1st, 1859, and the limitation is advanced each year so that any one who has been a resident sixteen years can then join the association.

The officers elected under this constitution were: President, D. G. Parker; vice-Presidents, J. L. Melder, H. Bickford, and O. C. Goodnature; Secretary, Henry Thurston; Treasurer, H. D. Brown; Chaplain, Rev. S. H. Lowry; Financial Committee, Ole Peterson, J. W. Ayers, and the President, Secretary, and Treasurer, ex-officios. The constitution was then signed by thirty-nine persons; the President delivered an address which was requested for publication. Previous to adjournment, a cordial invitation was extended to all the ladies and gentlemen of the county who were old settlers to become members.

The second meeting was held on Tuesday, the 2d of June, 1876, at the Court House in Albert Lea. The opportunity was given for joining the society, and sixty-five persons signed the constitution, who had come here previous to January, 1860. Several amendments were presented and adopted, the most important of which was the appointment of a committee on obituary notices.

The officers elected for the year were: President, D. G. Parker; vice-Presidents, William N. Goslee, of London; D. R. Young, Shell Rock; N. I. Lowthian, Freeman; H. G. Emmons, Nunda; Henry Tunell, Mansfield; C. E. Butler, Oakland; Ender Gulbrandson, Hayward; I. Botsford, Albert Lea; J. H. Pace, Moscow; Lewis Bill, Riceland; William H. Long, Bancroft; E. D. Hopkins, Manchester; Asa Walker, Carlston; C. E. Johnson, Newry; J. T. Jones, Geneva; Richard Fitzpatrick, Bath; A. S. Purdie, Hartland; and Jason Goward, Freeborn; Secretary, H. Thurston; Treasurer, H. D. Brown; Chaplain, S. G. Lowry; Finance Committee, Ole Peterson, J. W. Ayers, the President, Secretary, and Treasurer. E. C. Stacy was appointed on the obituaries for the ensuing year.

Judge Cooley, of Minneapolis, delivered the annual address, which was entertaining, instructive, and satisfactory. Judge Stacy read the obituary notices of those who had moved on to an unknown frontier during the year, and also mentioned some of the old settlers who had gone before the association was organized, and depicted the valuable services they had rendered while here. H. D. Brown read a poem prepared in another part of the State, but revised to suit the the conditions here presented.

The question as to the earliest resident arose, and George Gardner and H. Bickford claimed the honor of being the oldest continuous settlers. Various reminiscences were brought out as to early political affairs; how majorities were rolled up; how men got elected delegates to conventions, and became candidates after they got there, with other points of interest. The supper was at the Hall House, and the fare was in striking contrast with the fare in the fifties.

The third meeting was on the 13th of June, 1877. A procession was formed and marched to the picnic ground in Albert Lea. Prayer was offered by Rev. Walter Scott, one of the pioneers of the county. A letter was read from A. P. Swineford regretting his inability to meet his old friends this year. Twenty-seven joined the association.

The officers chosen this year were; President, E. C. Stacy; Treasurer, H. D. Brown; Secretary, Henry Thurston; and a Vice President from each town in the county. The finance committee with the ex-officios were J. L. Melder and J. W. Ayers.

A paper was read from Col. Albert M. Lea, giving an account of his early explorations and relating the incidents which gave his name to one of the lakes in the county and subsequently to the county seat. A large portrait of the Colonel was also shown and he was unanimously elected an honorary member. Walter Scott gave an account of some transactions in his neighborhood in 1856 and '57. Other stories were told, and the basket dinner was eaten with enjoyment by all. Isaac Botsford was appointed to look after the honored dead of next year. D. G. Parker then read the history of the county prepared for this centennial year.

The fourth annual meeting was on the second Friday in June, 1878. A procession headed by the Albert Lea Brass Band marched to the pic-nic ground. President Stacy presided, and the exercises commenced by singing the long Doxology, "Praise God from whom all blessings flow," and a song by the Purdie family. Alfred P. Swineford was then introduced, the oldest printer in the county, who was successful in his attempt to satisfy the high expectations of those who remember the meteor-like scintillations of the "Southern Minnesota Star" during the first county election. It is presented in full:

"If I have any apology to offer for having once failed to keep my engagement with you, and finally having come so far only, I fear, to dissapoint those who may have been led to expect an address worthy of the name and of the occasion, it is that in the first instance unexpected business complications imperatively demanded my personal attention at the time I had fondly hoped to be with you; and I hope and trust that the lingering desire that I have long felt to revisit the "scenes of my youth," will be accepted as a sufficient apology for my presence now. For, though grown to man's estate when, a little more than twenty-one years ago, I came to the then almost absolutely vacant site of your beautiful, thriving young city of Albert Lea, I was, in fact, a mere boy in years as well as in experience of the world and its business affairs. Coming here, as I now have, in a palatial railway coach, borne along in ease and comfort, at the rate of twenty-five or thirty miles an hour, annihilating the distance between here and the Mississippi in less time than used to be required to work up sufficient courage to attempt the trip, I could not avoid, as I came along, a mental contrast between the present coming, and that of twenty-one years agone. Never, while life lasts, shall I forget that first trip!

I had been a journeyman printer out of an uncompleted apprenticeship with the last governor of the Territory of Minnesota, and for a brief period before coming here, was foreman on a St. Paul weekly paper. The Railroad, Real Estate, and Financial Advertiser, was at least a part of its title, of which Charles H. Parker, a banker, was publisher, and Joe Wheelock the editor. Whatever time may have accomplished for him, Joe was then a dyspeptic, peevish, irascible individual, though a most vigorous, caustic writer. The paper invariably came out late on the day of publication or the day after, for the reason that Wheelock always had something of the utmost importance, at the very last moment, which must go in or there would be a row, and there generally was one. Joe laid the blame for the late appearance of the paper on the foreman, and the foreman reciprocated his gentle insinuations in that regard by imputing the whole of it to the editor. Parker thought somebody lied; Wheelock felt sure of it, and the foreman, though an orphan of tender years, was certain of it, and that it wasn't him, and that anybody who said it was, was a horse-thief and a liar, and hadn't truth enough in him to make an ordinary gas meter. Wheelock, in his virtuous wrath, produced an old pepper-box revolver, and with the most horrid oaths, threatened to fill your humble orator on this occasion, as full of holes as the useful article of table ware from which his implement of war took its name; but he didn't, for which forbearence on his part I have mentally thanked him innumerable times, and here and now, in this public manner I most cheerfully and magnanimously forgive him, for if he had shot and hadn't told a whopper about it, he would have saved me all these after years of editorial drudgery, and you this infliction. If I were to meet him now, I really believe I should shake hands with him, and thank him most cordially for the wrong he did me in not shooting, though I doubt much if the pistol was loaded, or if he could have hit the gable end of the capitol at arm's length, if it had been double-shotted. However, we continued together a few weeks longer, eyeing each other askance, instituting and preserving an armed truce, as it were, your humble servant all the time anxious to get away from the near vicinity of that pepper-box revolver, which he knew would shoot in all directions if it went off at all, and I have no doubt Joe was equally anxious to have him do so, when one morning an advertisement appeared in one of the daily papers calling for a printer to go into the south part of the Territory to establish a newspaper in a new town of great promise, and directed applicants to call at a certain room in the then leading hotel of St. Paul. Here was the coveted opportunity. I thirsted more for literary and editorial fame than for a personal encounter with Wheelock and his treacherous pepper-box, which I was assured by those who ought to know, scattered fearfully. I had, by dint of great perseverance and the practice of the most rigid economy, managed to save a whole week's salary, and was ready to venture in search of other fields, "and pastures new." I did not stand on the order of my calling at the avertiser's room, but called at once, and there I met for the first time, the founder of Albert Lea, rotund, jovial, large-hearted George S. Ruble, who had lately succeeded in having the place where he knew there ought to be a town, designated as the county seat of the newly organized county of Freeborn. I had heard the name of the place before. The weekly paper to which I have referred kept standing on its fourth page a large map of the territory, an electrotype plate, into which I would drill a hole large enough to permit the insertion of a small letter o to designate the sight, and close to it chisel through a space large enough to hold the name of any new town the proprietor of which was willing to pay for its insertion. I had only the week before put Albert Lea on the map, and I remember that the lake was not large enough to hold the bold faced letters, for the insertion of which I presume Ruble paid liberally. I think I can claim the honor of having placed Albert Lea on the first map upon which it ever appeared.

I found some difficulty in convincing Ruble that the mole under my right optic was legitimate and not the result of any discretion on my part; but that matter finally settled to his satisfaction, the negotiations were easily concluded. George agreed to endorse notes with which to purchase an outfit, and also advanced funds with which to pay necessary expenses to Chicago. He also agreed to and did, deed to myself and N. T. Gray, who was desirous of embarking with me in the enterprise, a sufficient number of lots in the new town to have made me a richer man than I am to-day, had I remained here and waited patiently for the coming of that era of prosperity which has since dawned upon you. And here let me remark (in a parenthesis, as it were,) that though I came here and went away again as poor as Job's turkey gobbler, I have, through strict integrity, untiring toil and perseverance, and the practice of close economy, managed to hold my own ever since. However, to return to my ower-true narrative, Ruble stipulated as a sort of side agreement, having an eye, I presume, to the more rapid growth of his new town, that I should get married, which stipulation I readily accepted, although I was not certain that "the girl I left behind me" would ratify the arrangement, but she did, came here with me to live, and regrets that she cannot be here with you to-day; the best she could do, under the circumstances, was to send her card in the shape of her daughter, who was born in Minnesota, shortly after we left Freeborn county. But I'm afraid I'm getting the story mixed up. I went to Chicago, traversing the Mississippi most of the way on the ice, from St. Paul to Prairie du Chein, thence by stage to Boscobel, then the western terminus of the Milwaukee & Mississippi Railroad; thence by rail to Janesville, then again by stage to a connection with what is now the Madison division of the Chicago & Northwestern Railway, and of which a former Albert Lea boy is Superintendent. That was in February, 1857. Having purchased a hand press, type enough for a six column paper, and some job type, I then went up to Oshkosh to carry out the stipulation referred to, and early in March, accompanied by my wife, started on the return trip to Minnesota. Portage City was then the terminas of the old La Crosse & Milwaukee Railroad, and from that point we had to travel the entire distance by stage, over the devious route, through Sparta, Black River Falls, Eau Claire, River Falls, to Prescott and Hastings, in doing which a whole week's time was consumed. At Hastings I was joined by my partner, Gray, and leaving Mrs. Swineford with some relatives, we set out by stage for Albert Lea. The route was through Northfield, Faribault, Owatonna, to Austin, where the stage route, so far as it benefitted us was at an end. Stopping here over night, we were fortunate enough to fall in with Dorr Stacy, then a half grown lad, who was there after the Geneva mail, which was carried semi-occasionally by Foot & Walker's line, Dorr being horses, driver, and all hands. Taking the mail upon his back, he piloted us through to his father's, that being recommended to us as the best route, the road to Albert Lea not being open. An all day's walk brought us to the residence of your honorable President, Judge Stacy, and I am postively certain that never before or since have I watched with such an absorbing interest a woman engaged in the arduous task of baking griddle cakes, as I did the Judge's estimable wife that evening.

The next morning, bright and early, we set out for Albert Lea, whose "tall spires and turrets crowned" were vividly pictured in our imaginations. Picture to yourself two lone sailors adrift in an open boat on the trackless sea, with compass or rudder, and you have a true representation of Gray and your humble servant, as they plodded their weary way over the trackless prairies and through the leafless tress of the oak openings in search of their final harbor of refuge. It was about the middle of March. The snow still lay on the ground to the depth of a foot or more, though the weather was mild and the snow was melting, and under it there appeared to be an equal depth of water, which the frost prevented the ground from absorbing. We had started on the road pointed out to us, but it had grown fainter and fainter, and we had not traveled an hour before it entirely disappeared. Gray was a dogged determinnd sort of a fellow, and didn't have any new wife to grieve over his loss in the wilderness, while she set her cap for another fellow, and I was determined, too, that mine should not have a chance to laugh at me, as I knew she would do if we turned back, so we struck out in the direction we thought Albert Lea ought to lie. You who live here now in the enjoyment of all the ease and comfort of civilized life in your cozy and elegant homes, embellished with all the treasures of art, if you came at a later period, can have little appreciation of the feelings, of the hopes and fears, I might almost say, of the sighs and tears, of those two forlorn weary pilgrims, as they plodded their slow way along in search of the spot where now stands the beautiful, prosperous capital of your equally beautiful and prosperous country. Over the hillocks, through the sloughs, which toward nightfall became, to us, veritable "sloughs of despond," the feet sinking at every step through the snow into the water underneath, leg-weary and sore, it was little wonder that when we reached Ruble's the following day, we were not only lame and halt, but blind as well. All day we traveled without meeting a single person or seeing a human habitation of any kind. All was a dreary, barren waste; we were literally afloat on the wide and seemingly boundless prairie, without compass and "nary" a guide-board to direct us to a haven of rest. Just at dusk we came upon the bank, or low marshy shore, rather, of a lake; and were hesitating whether to go around or attempt to cross it, when we heard the welcome report of a gun, apparently not over a dozen rods off and on the other side of a low ridge or hillock. Talk about the music of the bells, or of the horn about dinner time! If that gun had been aimed directly at us by an unseen foe or assassin, its report would have been sweeter music by far, to our ears, than that of the laughter of the bubbling brook, or of a wind instrument under the gentle manipulation of a forty lung power operator of the teutonic persuasion. We were about used up, despaired indeed of ever being able to reach a human habitation, and King Richard the three times, never wanted somebody to bind up his wounds and bring a horse, half as bad as we did. Gray prayed accordingly, and I'm afraid I profaned, and used cuss-words all that memorable afternoon. Gray prayed for guidance to Albert Lea, and I swore I did not believe there was any such place, except on the map, that it was a myth, an *ignus fatuus* luring us on to a worse fate than that of the babes in the woods; only in this case it was babes on the inhospitable prairie, for I was morally certain we had traveled far enough to find a dozen Albert Leas, had they been as big as St. Paul or New York. The fact was we were only about six miles on a straight line from Geneva. With difficulty we dragged our weary limbs along in the direction from whence the report of the gun had come, and shortly encountered a solitary indian who was lying low for wild geese, and by signs and facial gestures made him understand that we were lost, and didn't feel very well ourselves, when, instead of taking our scalps, as he might easily have done, and thus forever extinguished the brilliancy of that luminary, the Southern Minnesota Star, ere yet it had begun to illuminate the darkened earth, led us to a house in a clump of trees not half a mile off, owned and occupied, I believe, by a pioneer named Beardsley. It was a primitive residence in the primeval forest, as it were, to which that primitive child of nature, Lo! the poor Indian, conducted us, but never since, even in the palatial hotels of Chicago or any of the great cities, have I feasted more sumptuously than I did that night in that little log cabin by the lake, on a bill of fare which consisted wholly of bread, salt pork, starch gravy, and a decoction of rye, not the rye that comes from the still, but still it was rye, coffee; nor do I think I ever slumbered more sweetly or peacefully on the costliest spring bed or hair mattress, with snowy sheets and embroidered counterpoint, than I did that night on a straw tick, spread upon the rough floor of that rude log hut. The next day we made our grand entree into Albert Lea, just in time to break bread with its founder at his meridianal meal, and sop it with him in the starch gravy, in the preparation of which, good, kind-hearted, eccentric Mrs. Ruble was a real artist.

You who have come here in later years should have seen Albert Lea then; it was a county seat without buildings, and literally without inhabitants. One solitary little log building, occupied by Clark as a store and bachelor's hall, together with Ruble's log house on the isthmus, and Capt. Thorne's frame shanty on his addition to a town that had no existence save on paper, constituted the whole of the wealth, and contained all of the inhabitants of your now handsome full-fledged city of 2,500 people. Coming from Austin by the shortest route, you passed a single frame house on the way, and in the whole county, six months later, there were not voters enough to elect my respected friend and fellow pioneer, Judge Stacy, and your humble servant to the first State Legislature. It wasn't our fault, however; simply a lack of votes, that was all -for even at this late day I am conscious of the fact that we were both willing, if not anxious, to serve the State in the capacity of law makers; that we were abundantly qualified to do so with credit to ourselves and profit to the then budding young commonwealth, nobody seemed to have a doubt—with the trifling exeption of the people who cast a majority of the ballots. Judge Stacy had been a member of the double barreled Constitutional Convention, in which he had acquitted himself well and ably. I was an editor, and—I was about to say, a lawyer—but that wouldn't be true; I was a member of the bar, but no lawyer- -and what I didn't think I knew about the affairs of State, most certainly has never since been learned by any one. And right here I want to thank any and all old settlers who may be here present, who contributed to the result of that first general election, and especially my old friend and successful competitor for legislative honors, for laying me out on that occasion colder than a wrought iron wedge in January. Had they endorsed my pretensions, I now know that it would have been the worse for me, and most probably for them—for that legislature did the five million loan business, which certainly has not redounded to the credit of the State, and it is quite probable that had I been a member I should have voted for it, or, who knows? I might have gone on from bad to worse until I landed in Congress or the penitentiary, it wouldn't have made much difference which—for, while there may not be any persons in our penitentiaries who ought to be in Congress, it is morally certain that a great many members of Congress are badly lied about, or else they ought to be in the penitentiary. The bare possibility of what might have followed in the wake of a different result in the first general election in Freeborn county, is, even at this distant day, fearful to contemplate. For, I have held not a few offices of trust and responsibility since that time, and have learned to rate the honor which an election or an appointment to official position is supposed to confer, at its real value. I have come to believe that in these degenerate days, with the ballot in the hands of the ignorant, the sordid, and the vicious elements of the country, who are either bought or driven to the polls, when legislators are bought and sold like sheep in the shambles, and offices of the highest trust and importance are made objects of barter and of sale to the highest bidders, when corruption rankles in every vein and has become a festering sore in the body politic, I have come to believe that at such a time and in such a generation the post of highest honor is, indeed, the private station. But were it otherwise, the holding of official position ought to be the highest ambition of the true American citizen. The man who has sufficient ability to discharge with promptness and efficiency, the duties of any office to which he may aspire, ought to be, and in ninety-nine cases out of a hundred is, able to make more money and live more comfortably, in the pursuit of some legitimate business, and if he isn't able to do so, he isn't fit to hold office. The man who seeks an office is, most generally, the one above all others who shouldn't have it; and there is no honor attached to the incumbency of an office which does not come to the holder as the free, unsought offering of an intelligent people. It's a funny thing though, this running for office, almost always. Two years ago I stumped the Congressional district in which I live in behalf of my party candidate for Congress. He was a good, honest fellow, not much of a talker himself, but unfortunately had a nasal protuberance of unusual size and lustre, from the end of which a wart had been amputated by a rebel bullet, giving it the appearance of having been through several dog fights and as many Indian wars. At every meeting I was compelled to explain, first of all, that this black eye of mine was perfectly legitimate, and not the logical result of having called the wrong man a liar, and that my friend, the candidate's olfactory organ hadn't really been mutilated in a dog or barrow fight, but that it had been shorn of a part of its original majesty by a minnie ball while he was leading the advance of a well conducted retreat, in the cause of his country, during the rebellion: and though I pledged my sacred honor, and my inaleinable right to life, liberty, and the pursuit of happiness, for the truth of both statements, those Michiganders gently waved their massive auriculars, smiled a sweet smile of incredulity, and then went to the polls and elected the other candidate. Those of you who know my politics, however, and sympathise with them will appreciate the remark when I say that Michigan has a painful habit of always electing the wrong man. Now, my party want me to stand for Congress, but I won't even "lay" for it; I haven't one-twentieth part the desire to go to Congress, as I once had to represent your county in the State legislature; and I have no more desire to meet and shoot off epithets at those Confederate brigadiers now, than I was anxious to go down and shoot bullets at them in 1863-4.

But I'm afraid I'm getting this story badly mixed up. I wanted to tell you something about the early history of Albert Lea and Freeborn county, but I've wandered so far from the subject and the early history was made so long ago, that it's hard to get back to it. I believe I was telling you what constituted the wealth and population of Albert Lea in March, 1857. It was Yankee Doodle who couldn't see a traditional town because there were so many houses; but that wasn't the case with the founders of your first local newspaper; there wasn't any houses when they came to your town, to obstruct the vision, or mar the great natural beauty of the site upon which it has since been built, and if there had been, it would have made no material difference, for they hadn't been an hour at Ruble's before they were both as blind as herrings—herrings that are red and didn't take any pleasure in viewing the landscape o'er, at least to not any considerable extent, until after a period of four or five days had elapsed. It was what is known as a snow blindness, and just as effectual for the time being as though the eye had been put out by an explosion of nitro-glycerine. Ruble was then busy completing his mill, but when it was about finished, the spring rains united with the melting snow in raising a flood which carried away part of the dam, and he found himself in possession of "a mill by a dam site, but no dam by the mill site," and we all turned out and helped make the necessary repairs. When he finally got the mill started, the first cut of lumber was used for the erection of the printing office, which was, if my memory is not at fault, the first frame building on the original townsite. In the meantime I had gone back to Hastings after my wife, and returning, again commenced the erection of the second frame building, designed for a dwelling. It was a princely mansion, made of rough boards set up on end, and upon which, although I was no carpenter, I did the most of the work. In it my wife and I commenced housekeeping as soon as it was enclosed and roofed over with slabs instead of shingles; well do I remember the primitive cupboard with which we commenced life; it was made out of a large dry goods box set on end, while the graceful festoons in which my wife arranged the quilts and coverlets which were made to do duty as doors and windows, will never be forgotten. At that time, I verily believe that there wasn't such a thing as a carpet in the settlement, nor any but the rudest home made furniture. And right here I desire to relieve the tedious narrative with the relation of an incident which occured about that time. When I went back to Hastings after my wife, Ruble armed me with a well executed plat of the embryo city, and a power of attorney constituting me an agent for the sale of lots. While at Hastings I fell in with a Boston capitalist named Stowell, to whom I sold two or three lots, which, judging from the plat and site designated for the printing office, were quite eligibly located. Stowell was a rather convivial sort of a fellow, and had plenty of money which he was investing in wild lands and town lots in what he considered the best localities. The town plat of Albert Lea had been surveyed in the winter, and in order to preserve the symmetry of form which would be most pleasing to the eye when it was placed on paper, a corner of the lake was taken in. I was not aware of the fact at the time, and the lots I sold to Stowell, happened to be that particular part of the plat. I had been back from Hastings only a few days when Stowell put in an appearance. I had said so much praise of the new town, pictured in glowing colors the great natural beauty of the location, that after buying the lots, he couldn't resist the temptation to come and see for himself. It was a very wet season; the river and lakes had over-flown their banks, every slough was a lake in itself, and how the fellow got here when he did was a mystery. He said he swam most of the way, and I was inclined to believe him, for I remembered that shortly afterwards I went on horse-back to Geneva after a cow I had purchased from Mr. Robson or John Heath, I don't remember which, and I had a terrible time of it. The horse was a blooded animal; I don't remember exactly whether he was sired by old Duroc, Hambletonian, or Lucifer, but I do think he must have been, as Mark Twain would say, damned by everybody who ever rode him. I started to drive the cow home, and whenever I came to a slough, I would drive her in and crack the whip at her till she got across, and then I would get off the horse start him in, and hang on to his tail so as to be ready to pull him out in case he got mired. Sometimes before I could get across, the cow would start back again, higher up or lower down, and then the horse and I would have to follow suit. When I finally got that cow home, she was blind of one eye, and couldn't see out of the other, had lost a horn, and had but a part of a tail to tell the story of her own muley-ishness, and man's inhumanity. But here again I've got two stories mixed. Before I got on the last tangent I was about to say that after Stowell had been here a day or two, he came to me and wanted to know if I had a boat or canoe, I told him my partner had a canoe, and if he wanted to go duck shooting, I would get it and go with him. "Duck shooting be--blessed!" said he, "I want to go out and look at those d-ashed lots you sold me, that's all!" I went with him to Mr. Ruble, who very readily and willingly consented to make a fair exchange with him, gave him the same number of lots on terra firma, and he went away satisfied. I did not see him again till the latter part of summer, and from what then occurred I was led to believe that I was not the only person from whom he had bought water lots. I then met him at the Merchant's Hotel, St. Paul, not exactly in a beastly state of sobriety, but a trifle the worse for liquor. Being obliged to remain over Sunday, myself and a friend or two concluded to attend divine service, just as we were leaving the hotel, Stowell accosted us with an inquiry as to where we were going. He had been imbibing rather freely during the previous night, and had more liquor aboard than one man ought to try to carry—unless he has a jug in which to put at least a part of it. Being told that we were going to church, ne said, "thash all right (hic) boys, gnesh I'll go too," and it was impossible to get away from him, though we walked fast and left him following some distance behind. Reaching the church we entered and were shown a seat well up in front by the usher; just as we were sitting down Stowell stepped inside the door, and the minister began lining out that old familiar hymn:

"There is a land of pure delight
Where saints immortal dwell,"

when he was interrupted and the congregation horrified by the emphatic exclamation from Stowell--"Yes, thash's another Minnesota story, sell wile lan's and water lots!" It is needless to remark that our friend Stowell didn't remain to hear the sermon, but was unceremoniously ushered out, and I have never heard of him from that day to this. The story went the rounds of the papers at the time, and perhaps some of you may remember having read it.

I will not dwell upon the condition of affairs in Albert Lea and Freeborn county at the time I left them, after a two years' residence. The town was a mere hamlet, with no public buildings, churches or schools, and not even a wagon road worthy of the name. I had established a newspaper according to agreement with Mr. Ruble, and did all I could, considering my youth and inexperience, to advertise abroad the great natural advantages and attractions of the town and county; but looking back through the vista of years, I must say that I'm afraid that the Southern Minnesota Star illumined with rather a pale, flickering light the regions round about; certain it was that its little light was soon extinguished, and for a time Freeborn county was plunged into the depths of a literary darkness. A second paper—The Freeborn County Eagle—was started after the lapse of a few months, and soared for a time among the literary clouds, passing into the hands of Mr. Botsford, when I gave it up and left the county; the Standard, I am informed, is the legitimate offspring of the papers I founded upon the sands of the desert, as it were—two dollars a year strictly in advance. I could relate many incidents that occurred during my residence here; among the laughable lawsuits, the fight for the county seat with Bancroft, a mythical town which could then only be found with the aid of a mariner's compass, though it had a larger local paper than Albert Lea—The Bancroft Pioneer—published by D. Blakely, afterwards Secretary of State; of the political squabbles; the congratulations extended to me as the father of the first child born on the original town site; of the first funeral; but I will not weary your patience further than to relate one anecdote which had its beginning when I was an apprentice boy with old Governor Sam. Medary in Columbus, Ohio, and its ending after he came to St Paul as chief executive of the territory. As a boy I was generally credited with being able to concoct and execute more mischief in an hour than I would be able to atone for in a lifetime. As an apprentice with the governor; the order of business consisted principally in being discharged one day and hired over again the next. I owed my frequent dismissals to the pranks I played on the Colonel, as he was then called, and my reinstatement, to the kind interposition of his good wife, with whom, notwithstanding my mischievous propensities, I was something of a favorite. I slept in a room at the office, and took my meals at the Colonel's house, doing the little chores morning and evening, and sometimes hoeing up early corn, cabbages, and potatoes in the garden. I had played many tricks on the Colonel, who was at times, terribly profane, but the one I am about to relate broke the camel's back, and resulted in my coming west. An unruly cow was in the habit of breakfasting on the Colonel's tender young cabbages, and that, coupled with the fact that she could never get out the same way she got in, but had to have the gate opened for her, made him terribly angry. In a room in the printing office building was stored a lot of old flint-lock muskets which belonged to a defunct militia company, and which myself and another apprentice used to fire off, one after another, from the top of the building at an early hour in the morning to the annoyance of the whole town. One fine summer morning, when the cow was taking her regular matutinal meal, the Colonel ordered me to go to the office, load the musket with powder, and carry it to the house, so that, as he remarked, he could "pepper her cabbage for her." I went, not in the best of humor possible, and did as I was ordered. I put into that musket powder enough to load a siege gun, put some dry paper on top of the powder, and rammed upon that some more paper which was not so dry, then put in a handfull of old type from the printers' "hell box" and some more paper on top of that. Going back to the house, I found the Colonel waiting impatiently with a handful of pepper-berries, which I put into the musket with some more paper on top, in the meantime suggesting that the gun kicked, and he had better let me do the shooting, though I wouldn't have been behind that musket when it went off for the best dollar of the daddies that ever came from the mint. He was indignant, and proposed to do his own cow killing—and he did. That cow for the first time went out of the garden the same way she got in—over the fence—with a long drawn out bellow, that would have gone to the heart of a less wicked boy than I now know myself to have been—and she didn't come back again either —but just went out on the commons and died. When the roar of the musket had died away, and the cloud of smoke began to soar heavenward, the Colonel was seen trying to pick himself up from between two rows of potatoes, livid with rage, and—but it is sufficient to say he paid for the cow, and I took Greeley's advice, and came west, after a few years bringing up at Albert Lea. In the fall of 1857, Judge Stacy and myself were delegates to the first Democratic State Convention, and I lost no time after reaching St. Paul to call on the Colonel, who was then governor. I had grown from a boy to man's estate, and was, of course, considerably changed. Without telling my name, I said to him that I was running a little paper in the south part of the territory, a delegate to the convention, and had called to see if he couldn't give me an appointment to help me along, if it was nothing more than that of notary public. He eyed me keenly for a moment and then remarked, 'It seems to me I ought to know you; your face is familiar, and yet I can't exactly place you.' I ventured to say that I thought he ought to remember me, 'don't you remember Colonel'—'Hold on, not another word!' said he, 'I know you now! You're the infernal rascal who loaded that musket! Notary public! Why God bless me Alfred, I'd make you president if I could.' And he grasped my hand and shook it as cordially and heartily as he could have done had his arm never been partially paralyzed by the rebound of a musked loaded with a cannon charge.

Up to the time I left here, not a dollar's worth of farm produce had been exported from the county, and but few if any of the farmers had grown more grain than would suffice for planting the following year. All the breadstuffs consumed by the population at that time were imported. There was no flouring mill, and I do not think there was a single reaper in the county, though there may have been one or two. Salt pork and starch gravy was the regular bill of fare. I remember the first summer I was here I had occasion to go to Chatfield, and returning on foot, a short distance this side of that place I saw some pie-plant growing in a farmer's garden, a package of which I purchased at a fabulous price, and carried all the way home as a rare and not easily obtained luxury. And I so far remember those old pioneer days that sometimes when my wife suggests that there is little variety in our table bill of fare, and she would like a change, I go down town, carry up a piece of salt pork and say to her, 'there my dear; a little salt pork, with starch gravy, *a la* Albert Lea, if you please;' and we enjoy it as much and even more than we would have relished the luxuries which were not attainable in those pioneer days.

Now I am told that Freeborn county, instead of importing its breadstuffs, exports annually wheat to the extent of over a million and a quarter of bushels, and other farm products in proportion. Most heartily do I congratulate you, people of Freeborn county, and the old settlers particularly, upon what you have accomplished. Where twenty years ago was a dreary waste I see now a most beautiful city, with costly buildings, elegant residences, fine hotels, churches, and schools, thriving villages, and on every hand fields of waving grain, lowing herds, and unmistakable evidences of material prosperity and wealth. Your patient perseverance has conquered a signal success, of which you are in every way worthy and deserving. May you continue to prosper, and that Heaven's choicest blessings may continue to fall upon you and yours, is the earnest prayer of one who has oftimes regretted that he did not remain to share the trials and hardships through which you have passed to a final participation in the grand triumph you have achieved. It is a beautiful custom you have inaugurated—this reunion of old settlers every year, when you meet like old soldiers, fight your battles over again, lay aside the cares of business, and forgetful of party strife and personal bickerings, cement anew the bonds of friendship, and that unity of sentiment and endeavor which has enabled you to conquer all obstacles and make yours the garden county of the garden State of the Union.

If I attempted to say to you all I would like to say on this occasion, I know I should tax your patience. I apprehend that my old pioneer friends wanted to see me more than they wanted to hear me talk, and I am certain that I desired to see them once more before joining that memorable caravan that has gone before; and I want to hear some of them talk too. I see about me some faces that were familiar twenty years ago; but alas, I miss from among you many who shared with us the trials and hardships, the hopes and the fears of that early period in the history of Freeborn county. They have passed away to the silent and mysterious future; some died battling in their country's cause, others surrounded by their families in the homes they had builded for themselves in the wilderness, which they and you have made to bloom as a garden and blossom as the rose. Of my old friend and partner I have heard nothing since the war, in which he was a soldier, either from choice or compulsion, on the Confederate side. I miss from among you my old and valued friend, Armstrong, who died in the meridian of a noble manhood; William Andrews, the good Dr. Blackmer, and others I might name, friends of my younger years, are not here to extend, as I know they would, if living, a friendly, cordial greeting. It may be that my old friend and partner still lives; I know not; but it is more than proable that he lies buried in an unknown grave, the unwilling victim of a cruel war. If indeed he be dead, sing, oh ye sirens, your saddest strains, and chant ye winds and birds a requiem over his tomb! Does he rest under a cairn of pebbles in the shadow of some grand old southern sierra, may some grieving Oread come by night to drop a tear of pity and place a garland on his barren sepulchre. Nor do I know where the others sleep. Wherever it be, may the evening dews fall, oh so gently, and the flowers spread sweet perfume around; may the tall trees make mournful music, and the forest songsters chant their evening hymns over the places where they rest. And whether they lie in the vast ocean, or somewhere in the broad bosom of this fair land of ours, may the crimson morning dawn softly, and the first rays of God's golden sunshine rest long and lovingly over the places where they sleep."

Mr. Botsford presented the obituaries, and some touching remarks were made by Father Lowry in relation to those who had passed away during the year. The song "No Night There" was sung. Forty-four joined the association this year. A letter from Rev. C. L Clausen was read and ordered on file. Messrs. Jones, Goward, Swineford, Botsford and others related stories of the olden time. Mr. Parker read some town histories. The assembly was dismissed with the bene diction by Rev. Father McReynolds.

The Fifth annual reunion. This unusually interesting affair took place on Tuesday, the 10th of June, 1879, at the Court House. At half past ten the procession formed, with the right in front of the building, and it is said that there were six hundred teams and not less than three thousand five hundred people present. Headed by the Albert Lea Cornet Band it marched to the pic-nic grounds where ample provision had been made for the exercises. After music by the band, President Stacy made a few remarks expressing his satisfaction at seeing so many familiar faces, and feelingly alluded to those who had gone upon the last journey of this life, and called upon the chaplain to invoke the divine presence in prayer. Mr. Lowry came forward and asked the audience to join in singing, "Praise God from whom all blessings flow." He then offered a fervent prayer, which was followed by the song "Wake the Song of Jubilee," by the Pardie family. Judge Stacy then introduced Lieut Governor Wakefield, who gave a most admirable address, paying a high tribute of respect to the early public men with whom he was associated in the early legislation of the Territory and State, and especial commendations were presented to the memory of Augustus Armstrong. The address was received with great applause. Then came the lunches and laughter, with jest and joke, conversation, cakes, cookies, and confectionery.

It was the largest basket pic-nic, perhaps, ever held in the State, certainly in southern Minnesota. At half past one o'clock the assembly was called to order by the president, who announced that the proudest duty which had devolved upon him since his connection with the association, was the introducing of Colonel Albert Miller Lea, who, forty-four years ago, conducted a military expedition across the territory which now constitutes Freeborn county, and who, without doubt, passed within one hundred feet of the spot where he now stands. The venerable and distinguished man now came forward, and was greeted with most hearty applause, and when it had subsided he made a most admirable address, which is preserved in the archives of the association.

He began as follows: "Mr. President and old settlers of Freeborn county, your worthy president has told you who I am and why I am here. As I am expected to give you personal reminiscences, I must necessarily mingle them with some egotism and so I shall talk with you as familiarly as with old friends. There is not a face in all this large assembly I ever saw before last Saturday, and yet, I venture to flatter myself that there is not a heart among you that does not throb kindly toward the old man whom you have so generously welcomed. After many solicitations, repeated from year to year, and after disappointments not a few, at length, last Thursday morning, still feeble from recent illness, I took a train at my home in Central Taxes, to meet you here to-day in this genial reunion. Traveling continuously over a thousand miles, across eleven degrees of latitude, in sixty-two hours I passed through five States; from green corn and melons to the early ripening berries; from the land of cotton to the land of wheat. The glorious visions of fertility and prosperity have dispelled from my system all traces of disease; and your cordial greetings extended through your committee even beyond the limits of your State, have made my heart, at three score and eleven, beat as warmly as when, in my younger days, it was stirred by the lovely scenes of the fair country which you have since come to possess and enjoy, and still more to beautify and adorn."

Most of the historical part of his address appears in the early history of the county. His description of the incident connected with the giving of his name to the lake is worth transcribing here. "I was brought in contact with J. N. Nicollet, then engaged in mapping the surveys made by him in the northern basin of the Mississippi. He had made free use of my map in filling up his own, and invited me one morning to breakfast with him and to inspect his work. During a pleasant sitting I described the scene of that beautiful lake. He drank in the description enthusiastically, and exclaimed 'Ah zat is magnifique! what you call him?' I replied 'Lake Chapeau' 'Ah, zat is not ze name, it is Lake Albert Lea,' and he thus wrote it on the map. And thus originated the name of the lake, that of the township, and of this beautiful city."

At the conclusion of this address, letters were read from Henry M. Rice, George S. Ruble, then at Lookout Mountain, Tennessee, and from Horace Greene. Thirty three new members joined the association this year. John L. Melder made a proposition looking toward the establishment of an old settlers' home which was referred to the President, Secretary, and Treasurer.

The officers elected for the year were: President, A. C. Wedge; Secretary, Augustus Peterson; Treasurer, Samuel Batchelder; and a Vice-President for each town; Financial Committee, H. D. Brown, Henry Thurston, with the three executive officers.

Committee on obituaries: H. Thurston. This meeting was acknowledged to be a very successfull one.

The sixth annual reunion was on the 8th of July, 1880. The longest procession ever seen in this city started from in front of the Court House at the appointed time. Two brass bands furnished the music, and the concourse proceeded to the grove north of Fountain Lake, where a varied programme was carried out. Twenty-six joined the association this year. Hon. M. S. Wilkinson was the orator of the occasion, and quite a long historical letter was read from George S. Ruble, the substance of which appears in our sketch of the early history of the county.

The following gentlemen were chosen as officers for the year: President, A. C. Wedge: Secretary Augustus Peterson: Treasurer, Samuel Batchelder; and Obituarian, H. Thurston.

Notices of the honored dead were then read. The occasion was one of enjoyment, as they have ever been from the inception of the society.

The seventh annual reunion was held in Albert Lea on the 14th of June, 1881, and its features were not unlike those of previous years. The Fireman's Band furnished the music, and the exercises were on the pic-nic grounds north of Fountain Lake. The Hon. David Blakely, of Minneapolis, delivered the annual address, the locally historic part of which is here given.

The officers for the year were: President, Francis Hall; Secretary, Isaac Botsford; Treasurer, D. G. Parker; Committee on Obituaries, H. Thurston, J. Goward, A. H. Bartlett, J. F. Jones, and S. N. Frisbie.

There was singing by the Glee Club, and short speeches by Judge Stacy and Hon. Mr. Purdie.

No apology is deemed necessary that so much space is given to the Old Settlers' Association, and to the addresses that were made from time to time, because it is from just such sources as this that the present and the future historian must gather his material, and where we have found facts to record in the transactions of the association we have used them without hesitation.

Extracts from the Address of Hon. David Blakely:

Mr. President, Ladies and Gentlemen, Old Settlers and Old Friends:—Twenty-four years ago this coming fall there might have been seen coursing over the prairie a few miles north of this spot, a solitary prairie schooner, inhabited by a brace of gentlemen of whom many of you have heard, but few have ever seen. One of these gentlemen, you will already have anticipated me in guessing, was the pushing and energetic business agent of the town of Bancroft. The other was a young, unsophisticated, confiding companion of his, who, after a somewhat checkered career, of which this was the anticipated golden beginning, to-day, once more stands before you. I say once more, because there are many old settlers of Freeborn county within the sound of my voice, who will recall that twenty-three years, not far from this very spot, they suffered at my hands an affliction akin to that with which they are again to-day threatened. The occasion was the fourth of July, and I was then, as I chance to be now, the honored orator of the day. I say they suffered on that occasion; and say it advisedly, because many of them were good, sound Democrats then, as they are good, sound Democrats now; and I was a red hot Republican then, and, if my good old friends will pardon me for saying it, I still obstinately continue to be. Well, those times were times that tried men's souls, at least in a political sense. They were the times of the Kansas Nebraska struggle, and antedated but a too brief period, the raid of old John Brown into Virginia, and the doom of the infamous institution of slavery consequent upon the mad assault upon Sumter.

But to resume: As the solitary prairie schooner of which I made mention, neared the flourishing town of Bancroft, the unsophisticated but confiding traveller aforesaid, might have been observed by the wayfarers along the road, if there had been any wayfarers along the road, or if indeed there had been any discernable road, earnestly and perseveringly peering into the airy labyrinths for a sight of the town. I say the town, because, having been prevailed upon by the seductive enticements of the energetic and enterprising business agent aforesaid, to join him and publish a newspaper there, and having, by virtue of an exceedingly deficient education in western town sites, taken it for granted that where a big newspaper was to be published, there must necessarily be a big town; he kept straining his eyes through the hazy October atmosphere for a sight of the town. Never did a poor Christian gaze with more intense longing for the sight of the golden gates and the beautiful temples of the everlasting city which was to be the end of his pilgrimage, than I through the curtains of that old prairie schooner for the lofty spires, the imposing edifices, and the smoke of a thousand manufactories that I proudly expected to see ascend to heaven from the noisy and populous mart which I was soon to gratify and surprise by the publication of my new, and as a matter of course, my "able" newspaper.

I have often reflected upon the peculiar vealy character of the verdancy which distinguished this peculiar episode in my career. The limit of my western pioneering had been the city of Chicago, where, fresh from my eastern home and just forsaken text books, I was looking for a very small opening for a large young man. It was at this critical juncture that my friend, the energetic business agent of Bancroft, discovered me. We had been old friends in early years, for he was a Vermonter too, and well knew that I had been educated a printer before I entered the University.

Naturally enough, he convinced me that I was just the talented youth for the opening that a beneficent providence had placed at his disposal. He was, he said, in Chicago to purchase a newspaper outfit for a Minnesota town in which he had settled; and the landed interests of whose proprietors he happened to be agent. Then followed a list of these landed proprietors and a titled list it was.

It contained the names of the Governor of the territory, of the Chief of Justice, of Generals and Colonels, and bankers and capitalists, until my imagination peopled its streets with dignitaries, and its squares with sky reaching edifices; and so much a matter of course did I take this condition of things to be, that it never entered my head to inquire into the actual facts. It is not strange then, that on the memorable day referred to I was still gazing anxiously into the distance for a sight of the spires of my anticipated Arcadia, when the schooner brought up by the side of a freshly built board shanty, and my friend, the agent, announced with a gravity that would have become one of Rip Van Winkle's ghostly mountain boblins, that we had arrived. Shades of Chuzz Crvit! I exclaimed, am I too the victim of a town site demon, and is this the Eden of the conspiracy?

'Oh, no,' replied he with a calmness which would have done honor to the referee of a cock-fight, 'this is no Eden, although if Eden equalled it in loveliness, you will admit it was a sad day for our luckless ancestors when they were expelled from it. No, this not Eden, but Bancroft!'

Bancroft! ejaculated I with mingled scorn and indignation, then where is the town?

'Why this is the town, or rather, the town site!'

Oh, town SITE! town SITE! and sure enough it was a town "site", but in all the wide expanse of prairie and openings there was never a sight of a town.

A single board shanty, a screaming steam saw-mill, and a grass covered prairie stretching away for miles, constituted the sad realization of my pictured spires, my sky-reaching edifices, and my great metropolitan squares peopled with Governors, poets, brave men, and beautiful women!

But the enthusiasm of youth is not easily dampened. My printing establishment was on the way, it had already been loaded upon the meandering ox-cart, which was then the distinguishing avenue of freight transportation between the river and these sequestered parts. My friend, the agent, had a pushing and active spirit; he assured me that out here in the far West, towns and villages sprang up like mushrooms in the night; that the saw-mill which I saw whirring and whizzing before me, was already cutting up and forming the material which was to enter into the construction of my printing office, several stores, dwellings, and buildings of divers and sundry uses, purposes, and ends; and he whispered into my of quickly reassured year as a matter of sacred confidence, but with the air and manner of a man who knew whereof he spoke, that Bancroft was to be the future county seat of the county; that the insignificant collection of board tenements and tumble down mill, known as George Ruble's at Albert Lea, would soon be transformed into rookeries for fowls, while the people would flock to the future metropolis, the procession headed by Morin, the Register of Deeds of this county, and by Swineford, the flamboy and editor of the weekly concern which my able metropolitan journal would very speedily swallow up and supplant. Moreover, while the Governor, the Chief Justice, the Generals, the Colonels, the bankers, and the capitalists were not actual residents of Bancroft, and possibly never would be, they were in a position of influence which would insure for the town a mighty future. Indeed, it was not too sweet to anticipate that the dome of the State Capitol would some day glisten in the sun from the spot where we stood. To cap the climax I was presented with a deed to twenty of the lots of the town, and thus, in the twinkling of an eye, transformed from a seedy stripling in search of an opening, to a bloated town proprietor already entered into the possession of his wealth. My friends, it was enough! From that hour I was a convert to the colossal possibilities of the future town and seat of the county, and the undoubted final Capital of the State. From that hour I was the zealous lieutenant and coadjutor of as sanguine a townsite devotee as ever builded from a rosy imagination a magnificent castle in Spain. From that hour the whirring and whizzing steam mill redoubled its efforts; the lumber for my printing office, for the first store, for the biggest dwelling house in the county, to be occupied by the business agent, his family and guests, was soon on the ground, and by the time the meandering ox-carts arrived from the river laden with my precious newspaper material, the roomiest office in the county awaited its reception. I set to work and put it in order. The election which was to transfer its county seat from Albert Lea to Bancroft was close at hand. At most I could issue but one copy of the new and "able" paper before the voters would decide the argument. I put my whole heart and soul into the event. I wrote nights and put the heated fulmination of my goose-quill in type daytimes, I scarcely ate or slept. I had no experienced help, and feeling that the eyes of the people of the county, if not the whole world were upon me, and that the issue of the appeal was in my keeping, I endeavored to be equal to the crisis. But alas, the fates were against me. For one man to lay the cases, to put up the press, to write editorials, to perambulate the town and record the vast variety of local events, to receive and arrange the news and the commercial departments, and above all, to set up and classify the great crush of advertisements that crowded the columns of a newspaper published in a town of upwards of twenty thousand, or, I should rather say, upwards of twenty inhabitants, was too much! My first paper did not appear until the very dawn of election day, too late to reach the rural districts—too late to influence, to persuade,to electrify the people, too late to frustrate the damnable plot concocted by the Rubles, the Morins, the Wedges, the Armstrongs, of this city, and the wily Staeys, the sly Frisbies, and the festive Bartletts of the county! Too late to secure the fondly anticipated transfer of the county seat from Albert Lea to Bancroft—too late to lay the foundation of a mighty emporium—too late to command the future location of the Capital of the State, and possibly of the nation—too late to establish at the final hub of the Universe, a newspaper that should be read by the inhabitants of the globe.

But the fire of youth is not to be burned out at a single conflagration, and Agent Oliver and I were not long in finding compensations for our sorry disaster. During the progress of the campaign the town had trebled in growth. That is, where at the outset had been but a single board shanty, there were now two or three quite respectable buildings; and it must be admitted that any town whose buildings double and treble in a month, is an amazingly flourishing town. We soon rejoiced in the possession of the largest store and finest private mansion—that of Agent Oliver in the county, and my newspaper—well, modesty forbids my dwelling on the merits of that historical sheet. * * * *

The musical critic of the paper had little to contribute, although the town was really distinguished for its talent in this direction. Agent Oliver and wife were cultured New Englanders—he a superior pianist and organist, and she a soprano whose rare voice has since made her one of the finest concert singers in the country, and long a favored occupant of the first choir in New York. Then Mr. Charles Etheridge, at that time a skilful contracting carpenter, who erected the buildings on the town site, but who afterwards became a St. Paul insurance agent, and acquired sudden wealth by decamping with the money of his companies, and who thus proved the only successful financier ever connected with Bancroft history—was the base, and I the warbling tenor. The organization constituted the only opera the town ever boasted.

The religious editor of the "Bancroft Pioneer" also found his occupation gone. This, I say, was a lamentable fact, because I am satisfied that if there had been religious services at Bancroft and Albert Lea in those days, and Morin and Ruble and Wedge and Stacy—let me never forget Stacy's finger in that unholy pie—and Colby and Lybrand and Bartlett and Frisbie and many other wicked conspirators had attended divine service on the memorable Sabbath before the county seat election was held, instead of being scattered about the county plotting the overthrow of Bancroft, there is not a peg on which to hang the shadow of a doubt that Bancroft would to-day have been the county seat of this beautiful county; and the spot whereon we stand, by an instance of rare poetic justice, would have been the site of the handsomest and most productive poor farm that ever fructified under the rays of a quickening June sun! I do not add, old settlers and old friends, I considerately and purposely do not add, that the wicked conspirators who plotted against Bancroft on that memorable "Sunday" above referred to, would to-day have been tilling the soil on the county's farm on this spot; but there is no law against your drawing whatever inference the circumstances warrant. But, to resume; while the religious editor of the Bancroft Pioneer, owing to circumstances beyond his control, had little to interfere with his main occupation, I will not say of playing poker, the interviewing *fiend*, who had then not become a regular adjunct of the weekly press, had quite as little. The truth is, the streets and offices did not swarm with people to interview. The town was full of office-holders, however. If my memory is not at fault, *every* regular citizen played that beautiful role. Agent Oliver was Postmaster, genial Mose Comfort, the clerk in the store, was his deputy, and I, by a rare instance of misplaced confidence, had become a school trustee. Shortly after, by a promotion, the suddenness of which almost turned my head, I was elected to the office of town Supervisor, and at the first meeting of the Board, demonstrated my utter incapacity for the place by voting for Stacy for Chairman of the County Board. But this was a youthful indiscretion for which I ought not to be held to strict account. Bear in mind the letter by which a depraved son beguiled his father into following him to Minnesota, when he wrote that "mighty mean men get offices out West." Offices were plenty in those days. There was a Supervisor to every town, and it often happened to youthful counties that there were more in the Board than outside of it. Don't wonder, then, that Stacy was honored, but rather accuse yourselves, for you subsequently promoted him to higher trusts, which, it seems, he never betrayed, a fact which, considering the past, he played in destroying the prospects of the town of Bancroft, is a cause of never ending amazement.

It was not long before overtures were made me to abandon the town of my first love and earliest adventures, and cast my fortunes with those of the flushed adventurers who were already enjoying the results of their successful conspiracy. I resisted these bland enticements, however, until resistance ceased longer to be a virtue; I stuck to the town of Bancroft as long as a single subscriber remained upon its site, of the three which it originally contained. But when the store was closed, and Comfort departed, and Agent Oliver struck his colors, and I watched the schooner which bore him and his away from the town, until it disappeared among the oak openings in the distance, I felt

'like one
Who treads above
Some banquet-hall deserted;
Whose garlands dead,
Whose lights are fled,
And all but me departed.'

The eighth annual reunion occurred on the 15th of September, 1882, in the grove north of the lake. The usual procession was formed at half past ten o'clock, made up of country delegations and city residents, with martial music, and proceeded to the pic-nic grounds. The day was most delightful and there was a large concourse of old and young settlers, and it should be said that they made a remarkable good appearance, comparing favorably with any like number that can anywhere be found.

At the meeting Mr. Botsford presided, and the announcement was made that any persons who were here previous to the 1st of January, 1866, were entitled to membership, and quite a list was added.

Hon. A. H. Bartlett delivered the annual address, which was replete with reminiscences relating to the early history of the county, and which has been largely drawn upon to make up our portrayal of the first settlement.

The Purdie family were present, as they have been at every meeting since the organization of the society, and enlivened the occasion with their songs, which were well rendered.

Mr. Frisbie, in an extemporaneous way, gave an account of the organization of the county. Miss Maggie Purdie gave a recitation "A fiend and a man." Col. T. J. Sheehan being called upon made some comparisons between "Now, and then." And gave a list of the men from Freeborn county who defended Fort Ridgely in August, 1862.

So much of his speech as relates to the growth and prosperity of the county is reproduced here: "I will call your attention to the material increase of wealth of Freeborn county during the little over a quartee of a century that it has been organized, and I think you will see that we are the most prosperous county for the number of inhabitants in the State. In 1857, the date of the organization of the county, the amount of real and personal assessments covered only a few thousand dollars; I cannot give the exact sum, but it was less than many of you are worth to-day. Year by year its resources increased, until in the year 1864, I find we had an assessed valuation all told, of $920,687. The county has gradually increased in wealth from that time, and in this year of our Lord, 1882, it reaches the magnificent sum of $5,210,311—assessor's measure, with the possibilities within our reach, during the next quarter of a century, of making it $50,000,000. The increasing population and the consequent occupancy and improvement of new lands, the excellent railroad facilities bringing the northern, southern, eastern, and western markets to our very doors, soliciting your produce for other lands, and your own indomitable perseverance and hard work makes it highly profitable that millions upon millions will be added to its wealth as the succeeding years roll by. The Chicago, Milwaukee & St. Paul, the Minneapolis & St. Louis, the Burlington, Cedar Rapids & Northern, and the Albert Lea and Fort Dodge railways meet here at our county seat and make the heart of our county the third largest railroad center in the State. The population of the city of Albert Lea is about 2,500 and of the entire county over 18,000. The business of the county I believe has always been transacted honorably and uprightly by its officers, and its expenditures have been considerably less than those of its neighbors, as is shown year by year in the annual appropriations for the necessary expenses of its government. I will now allude to a less agreeable history of our county, to show you how willing our people are to pay their debts, when circumstances permit them to do so. For a few years following the war, there was a season of prosperity which stimulated our people with a laudable ambition for great accomplishments, and for a few years they rolled along upon a wave of plenty; but suddenly there swept over the land a cloud of adversity, and many felt the iron chains of debts incurred in the purchase of lands and machinery, pressing hard and close upon them with a tyrant's power, and although they struggled long and honorably to meet its just demands, the continuing hard times, short crops, low prices and accumulating interest, were an army they could not withstand, and they sank beneath its overpowering weight. Honest men they were, and true, but they could not surmount impossibilities. The ravages of the creditor commenced, and the iron hand of the law was called upon to enforce his relentless demands. In 1876 there were 125 executions levied by the sheriff and his deputies; in 1877 there were 98, of which nearly all were paid; in 1878 there were 54; and since that time there has been a gradual decrease until the present year, during which I am sure you will all rejoice with me to learn there has been but four, and two of those have been settled.

The good behavior of our people is attested by the fact that there is not one person confined in the county jail at the present time. 'Tis true at times it is filled to overflowing, but I am gratified to be able to say to you that its occupants are for the most part transient criminals representing a dangerous class of society, and but rarely one of our own citizens. Whoever they are, I say to you proudly as your Sheriff, that they are never the early settlers of Freeborn county, and at the risk of being accused of flattery I will add that it is largely due to the high order of intelligence you possessed, your virtuous teachings, and the excellent examples you set before the new and rising generations."

Dr. Ballard recited a poem, which was inimitable in its way, and described the celebrated horse race, upon the result of which all Bancroft and Albert Lea staked everything movable that they possessed, each with the idea that it was a sure thing; but the Bancroftites were, to use a sporting phrase, "beautifully scooped."

The obituaries were read by several gentlemen, and there were other recitations and remarks. Of course there was a recess of an hour to go through the baskets that were laden with good things. This was voted on all hands as being one of the most interesting reunions yet held, and it is likely that September will in future be the month for the old settler's reunion. The officers for 1883 are: President, I. Botsford; Secretary, H. D. Brown; Treasurer, Gilbert Gulbrandson, and a list of vice-Presidents.

Necrology.—Here is an imperfect list of old settlers who have been transferred to "that bourne from which no traveler returns:" Elias Stanton, L. C. Carlston, William Andrews, Peter Beighley, Rev. Theop. Lowry, James A. Robson, David Southwick, Squire Dunn, Patrick Fitzsimons, Howell Davis, Gardner Cottrell, A. Armstrong, William White, Luther Parker, H. B. Riggs, Pardon Greene, Lydia Barber, John Colby, Mrs. Elizabeth Beighley, Joseph Laug, George Boulton, Harvey B. Earle, Warner Barber, Mr. Baxter, Mrs. T. J. Jordon, Mrs. William Beighley, Mrs. Jennette Smith, Mrs. W. R. Squires, David M. Farr, Emery Davis, Nathan Bullock, Mrs. J. M. Melander, Mrs. M. C. Wallace, B. J. House, Ezra Stearns, Israel N. Pace, Frederick H. White, Geo. Carpenter, Henry Schmidt, Henry Weiser, Mary Knapp, E. S. Smith, Harold Anderson Jr., John S. Corning, J. S. Harris, N. H. Ellikson, Hiram E. Jones, Amanda Woodruff, Eliab Eggleston, Dr. Franklin Blackmer, J. Marvin, J. W. Burdick, Fred. S. Woodward, Thomas Morrison, William Hare, Mrs. William White, Rev. Walter Scott, Mrs. Elizabeth Williams, Jeremiah Ward, Eric Erickson, Ole Oleson Fossum, Hiram J. Rice, William McKune, Hiram Thomas, Mrs. Vanderwalker.

MEMBERS OF THE OLD SETTLERS ASSOCIATION WITH THE RECORDED DATE OF THEIR COMING.

1854. E. C. Stacy, Mrs. E. C. Stacy.

1855.—John Colby, Hanibal Bickford, George Gardner, Margaret Gardner, Mr. and Mrs. Isaac Botsford, Charles Peterson, T. R. Morgan, Christopher Michelson, M. L. Frost, Oliver Andrews, Mrs. Oliver Andrews, Ed. Hostetter, George S. Ruble.

1856.—John L. Melder, Samuel Batchelder, Frank Ross, C. Narveson, J. W. Ayers, Charles C. Ayers, William Beighley, J. E. Simaus, D. R. Young, Mrs. Addie A. Batchelder, J. H. Heath, William Pace, F. McCall, Mrs. F. McCall, William Freeman, Witling Wordsworth, Mrs. Willing Wordsworth, Ole Peterson, Gilbert Gulbrandson, A. W. White, A. M. Burnham, Mrs. J. W. Melder, Mrs. Mary B. Ayers, J. F. Jones, Mrs. J. F. Jones, P. E. Pace, John Murtaugh, John W. Murtough, Mrs. J. W. Murtaugh, Mr. and Mrs. Simaus, Saniel Prescott, M. V. Kellar, Jacob Beighley, Mrs. Jacob Beighley, Ole C. Oleson, Hans Gulbrandson, John G. Godley, H. Peck, R. P. Gibson, N. S. Hardy, Mrs Aug. Peterson, John Freeman, A. C. Trow, Henry Loomis, Mary Loomis, William Morin, Nancy Frost, J. Stage, Mrs. John Stage, E. D. Hopkins, S. P. Beighley, J. B. Gordon, T. J. Gordon D.G. Parker, Charles C. Ayers, E.D. Porter, S. G. Lowry, C. O. Baarness, S. N. Frisbie, Mrs. Sarah Town, Mrs. Mary Vineland, Ed. Skinner, Frank Merchant, Anna Merchant, E. Eggleson, J. M. Boulton, J. C. Frost, Philip Herman, Mary English, Charley Thompson, Hanna O'Connor.

1857.—L. R. Luce, Richard Fitzgerald, N. C. Lowthian, Henry Thurston, C. J. Grandy, Mrs. C. J. Grandy, Herman Blackmer, Frank Barlow, A. C. Wedge, Mrs A. C. Wedge, Mrs. J. W. Heath, William H. Long, H. Eustrin, B. Schodd, James Lair, Mrs. James Lair, H. D. Brown, David Horning, Mrs. D. R. Young, Mrs. N. I. Lowthian, Alfred Lowry; F. W. Purdie; H. C. Lacy, Mathias Anderson, Timothy J. Shehan, John N. Wolhunter, Mrs. S. G. Lowry, A. K. Norton, Charles

Norton, Mrs. Charles Norton, James Long, Mrs. James Long, Joseph France, S. B. Smith, W. J. Horning, John Wood, Daniel Dills, W. H. Long, Mrs. W. H. Long, Michael Sheehan, John A. Schoen, Mrs John A. Schoen, F. A. Blackmer, John Beighley, John Slater, N. H. Ellickson, M. O. Whitney, George Hyatt, E. M. Ellingson, Willard C. Marvin, Mrs. Willard C. Marvin, Reuben Williams, Mrs. Willard Eaton, Samuel Eaton, Henry Emmons, C. Kittleson, A. J. Anderson, Ole Narveson, N. C. Narveson, Samuel W. Horning, George McColley, J. Walaski, William Baker, Mrs. William Baker, H. A. House, William P. Spooner, Jacob Baker, William L. Lowry, Asaph V. Thomas, L. J. Thomas, Lewis Marpie.

1858.—Jason Goward, August Peterson, Ole Narveson, Rebecca A. Dills, Chester Holcomb, Mrs. Chester Holcomb, D. C. Calvin, William English, Francis Hall, Mrs. Jason Goward, B. J. House, O. F. Peck, Mrs. O. F. Peck, N. T. Sanbury, Mrs. N. T. Sanbury, Mrs. C. Boven, H. L. Webster, George B. Chamberlain, Mrs. George B. Chamberlain, Mary J. Horning, David Horning, John Johnson, William Norton, Milton Hewett, Charles Dunbar, Ole J. Jordahl, Mrs. David Colvin, Mrs. Emma Ward.

1859.—W. S. Hand, Mrs. W. S. Hand, Josiah Jones, Mrs. Josiah Jones, Maurice Russenger, Mrs. Eugene Walker, C. M. Hewett, Mrs. C. M. Hewett, Simeon Jones, Mrs. Simeon Jones, Mrs. Martha L. Thurston, Mrs. Sarah W. Edwards, William Fenholt, R. H. Boven, Mrs. E. Wanemaker, Asa Walker, Harriet J. Barden, Ole Narveson, J. Dunbar, John C. Ross, H. N. Ostrander, Freeman Briggs.

1860.—Mrs. Sarah J. Riggs, Charles G. Bickford, F. W. Drake, Gunwold Johnsaud, Jacob Larson.

1861.—E. F. Leonard, G. W. Bark, John Murphy, Mrs. Daniel W. Horning, Charles Mann, Susan Bartlett.

1862.—S. S. Challis, Mrs. A. J. Challis.

1864.—Ira A. Town, Edmund Town, James H. Chamberlain.

It seems unfortunate, and it is a source of annoyance to us, that the record of those who joined in 1880 and in 1881 has not been preserved, and so our list is incomplete. In 1882, the date of the coming of a number was omitted; the names of those who joined are here given:

R. C. Spear, John Smith, G. H. Prescott, Mrs. G. H. Prescott, Mrs. James Whittemore, W. G. Barnes, all of whom came in May, 1857. Miss Grace Prescott, Miss Emma Frost, H. Loomis, Mrs. H. Loomis, Henry Blackmer, Mrs. Henry Blackmer, M. M. Luce, Mrs. M. W. O'Connor, O. C. C. Howe, Mrs. O. C. C. Howe, Fred Fink, Henry Schneider, E. Budlong, Mrs. E. Burlong, R. Tykeson, Alex. Peterson, Mrs. Alex. Peterson, Mrs. J. A. Lovely, Stephen Kelley, Samuel Thompson, A H. Bartlett, Mrs. A. H. Bartlett.

CHAPTER XLIX.

JUDICIAL—COUNTY GOVERNMENT—COUNTY SEAT CONTEST—EDUCATIONAL—PATRONS OF HUSBANDRY RAILROADS—AGRICULTURAL STATISTICS.

Freeborn county was in the fifth judicial district of Minnesota under the first organization. In 1857, the Clerk of the Court having been appointed, business was commenced by him, attending to the regular routine work. The first case recorded was that of J. S. Corning against James M. Young, for the recovery of one hundred and thirty one dollars due on a note. An attachment was made, no answer filed; so judgement was entered. The date of this case was the 27th of November. Up to the time when the first circuit court was opened there were twenty-seven cases.

This court was held on the 27th of September, 1858, and at this session Alfred P. Swineford was admitted to practice at the bar. J. W. Perry was also admitted as an attorney. A committe was also appointed to examine W. D. Chilson and John W. Heath with a view to their admission as attorneys. A. B. Webber, Augustus Armstrong, and J. W. Perry were the committee, who reported favorably, and the candidates were admitted.

The lawyers who appear at this early day were, A. Armstrong, D. G. Parker, A. B. Webber, J. W. Perry, and A. P. Swineford.

The grand jury was called and eighteen answered to their names. Two indictments were found against William L. Gray for "unlawful trafficking in spirituous liquors, and for keeping a gambling house." He was brought in on a bench warrant and pleaded not guilty, and was put under bonds in the sum of one hundred dollars for his appearance.

The calendar being called, the following cases appeared ready for trial: Asa Ballard *versus* John T. Asher; Hagan Mathews *versus* Hans Johnson: Ola Gruberson *versus* Lars Evenson, which were duly disposed of.

The names of the judges who have set on this bench, and that of the clerks, will be found in the Centennial History by Mr. Parker, which has been brought down to 1882.

It seems that no record of the earliest marriages was preserved, until the county was organized. The first mentioned was that of Mr. Henry Snyder and Miss Mary Fink, on the 25th of June, 1857, by William Anderson, Justice of the Peace. The next is that of William Andrews himself to Miss Mary Leonard, by the redoubtable J. Clark, Justice of the Peace. The third and last one this year was Mr. Oscar Miller and Miss Betsey M. Bullock; the magistrate was George Watson, and the witnesses were H. B. Earle and Daniel Gates. These were all those reported in 1857.

The number of cases of record up to the second term of the court was sixty-one. This term commenced on the 25th of September, 1859.

At this session the case of Henry Kreigler, accused of wilful-murder, and which is mentioned elsewhere, was brought up. J. M. Perry was appointed to assist the prosecuting attorney. The case was transferred to Steele county, as it was declared impossible to secure an impartial trial here, on account of prejudice,

E. C. Stacy was admitted to practice in the courts of the State at this term. There were some cases of absorbing interest at the time, in a local way, but none of general importance.

The first deed spread on the records was that of William Rice and wife to Uriah Grover. The second to be recorded was that of Uriah Grover and wife to Elihu C. and Anthony C. Trow, a piece of land in consideration of $100 in township 102, range 20. John S. Corning was the magistrate. The next was William Rice and wife to Uriah Grover, September 1st, 1856. Charles T. Knapp and wife to E. C. and A. C. Trow on the 22d of October, of the same year. This year there were but three recorded, but several came in later which had been executed during the year.

The first recorded in 1857 was that of George W. Beighley and wife, to S. Batchelder and C. C. Colby.

The mortgage book commences on the 9th of November, 1856, and the first one that appears was Welcome S. Bacon, to Elbridge G. Potter, to secure the payment of $3000, a tract of land; and this seems to have been the only one this year. The next year a mortgage was executed and recorded on the 3d of March, by L. T. Carlson to C. A. Lundrone, and was the only one recorded that year.

Since that time the deeds and mortgages have accumulated to fill thirty-two volumns of deeds and twenty-six of mortgages. The books are 640 pages, and average a little less than one deed for a page; so it can be seen that the transfer of real property has been lively in the county since its organization.

The Board of County Commissioners met on the 3d of March, 1857, for the purpose of organization. It consisted of William Andrews, E. C. Stacy, and S. N. Frisbie. William Andrews was chosen Chairman. On motion of Mr. Frisbie, E. C. Stacy was chosen Judge of Probate.

At an adjourned meeting on the 4th, the County Officers were appointed as follows: Sheriff, George S. Ruble, of Albert Lea; Surveyor, Edward P. Skinner, of Shell Rock City; Coroner, A. H. Bartlett, of Shell Rock City; District Attorney, John W. Heath, of Geneva. The county was divided into three assessor's districts, and the following assessors appointed: James M. Drake, John Dunning, and Walter Scott; Justices of the Peace, Isaac P. Lynde and Joseph Watson; Constables, George Doerman, William A. Hoag, and Walter Stoll. At this meeting a county seal was adopted, and the time for entering upon the duties by the several officers appointed was placed on the 20th inst.

The location of the county seat came up for careful consideration. Mr. Frisbie moved that the temporary county seat be Bancroft; Mr. Stacy moved to strike out Bancroft and insert Saint Nicholas, which motion was lost. Mr. Stacy moved to strike out the word Bancroft and insert Geneva, which was not agreed to. Mr. Andrews moved to strike out the word Bancroft and insert Albert Lea, which was carried by a unanimous vote.

A resolution was adopted instructing the Constables, Justices, and School Trustees, to be vigilant in protecting the school lands from trespass.

At an adjourned meeting on the 5th, among other items of business, L. T. Carlson was appointed Justice of the Peace, and Elias Stanton Constable. At these meetings William Morin was deputy clerk.

The next meeting of the Board was on the 6th of April, 1857, and then the interminable road business began. The first road laid out as a county road was described as follows: "Commencing on the section line between thirty-two and thirty-three in town 101, range 20, running north as near said section line as the surface of the the ground will admit, through towns 101, 102, and 103, thence in a northerly direction to the town of Geneva, thence north to the county line."

Clark Andrews, of Shell Rock, and George P. Hoops were appointed viewers of the route.

The next road was in response to a petition, and commenced at St. Nicholas, crossing the Shell Rock River in section thirty and running southeast to the south line of town 102, about 120 rods west of Oliver Andrew's house, then east on said town line about two miles, thence southeasterly to the vicinity of John T. Asher's place, thence down the west bank of Woodbury Creek to the county line. Oliver Andrews, of Shell Rock, and John T. Asher, of Burr Oaks, were viewers of this road. At this meeting the appointments of L. T. Carlson as Justice of the Peace, and Elias Stanton as Constable, was rescinded for non-compliance with the statute; and Elias Stanton was appointed Justice, and Charles Giddings, Constable. Election precincts were arranged, several other roads projected, and school districts were established. About fifteen road districts were disignated. These matters consumed much time but the management of the interests of the county seem to have been judicious. This session of the board continued until the 10th, and among other things done, the surveyor was authorized to procure from the United States Surveyors the field notes relating to the county.

The third session of the board was on the 18th of May, 1857, and continued three days. Welcome S. Bacon was appointed Assessor of the first precinct, vice Erastus D. Porter—not qualified. C. S. Tarbel was appointed Coroner in place of George Watson, who declined to qualify. Lafayette Scott was appointed Justice and Daniel Davis, Constable. At this session the table was loaded with road petitions, which were given respectful consideration.

The fourth session of the board was on the 6th of July, and they proceeded to wrestle with the large number of yeomanry of the county of Freeborn, who considered that the welfare of the country and the perpetuity of republican institutions depended upon their having a road right by their doors.

The assessment rolls were brought in at this meeting, and the footings were as follows:

District No. 1.—Real	$31,295
Personal	20,590
District No. 2.—Real	28,065
Personal	35,840
District No. 3.—Real	53,553
Personal	40,665
	$210,088

A tax of three mills on the dollar was assessed for road purposes, and two and one half mills for school purposes. At this meeting the county orders appear for the first time and they aggregated $549.19. The total county tax for all purposes footed up twenty and one half mills on a dollar, making the sum of $4,347.80, to which ten per cent was added, making $444.65 to be collected.

The fifth session of the county board was on the 9th of September of the same year. The clerk of the district court was instructed to inform Judge Flandreau that it is not the wish of the County Commissioners that a court should be held here in October of this year. Routine business claimed especial attention.

The sixth session was on the 5th of October. Bills by this time got up to $1,556.44, and nothing remarkable was done.

The election as to the location of the county seat was held on the 13th of October, 1857. The result of the balloting, as returned by the board of canvassers, William Andrews, George Watson, and William Morin, was as follows:

	Votes.
Albert Lea	403
Bancroft	199
Saint Nicholas	29
Shell Rock	10
Freeborn	1

So this question was settled with such a round majority that there has been no change since.

William Morin was the first Register of Deeds, and was also clerk of the board of County Commissioners.

1858. The new board convened on the 4th of January, and consisted of S. N. Frisbie, Joseph Reikhard, and Peter Clausen. S. N. Frisbie was elected chairman. Auditing bills was the great business of the board during the first day's session. The next day, among other things, Swineford & Gray were made county printers. J. M. Palmer and Thomas W. Purdie were appointed road commissioners. Grand and pettit jurors were drawn. The report from the schools revealed 222 scholars in the county, in nine districts, but there must have been sixteen at least at that time, as that was the number of one of the districts. The amount of school tax was $5,322, which gave to $2.38 to each scholar. The Territorial tax assessed was $212.08.

At a meeting held on the 1st of February, 1858, the resolution giving the county printing to Swineford & Gray was rescinded, and it was given to David Blakely of the Bancroft Pioneer. The next day an offer was made by the deposed firm to do all the county printing for six months free; but it was not agreed to. At the meeting in April, the board proceeded to organize the county into towns, in accordance with an act of the Legislature, and the following names were proposed: Asher, Oakland, Guildford, Seward, Geneva, Beardsley, Hayward, Shell Rock, Freeman, Albert Lea, Bancroft, Porter, Hartland, Buckeye, Pickerel Lake, Nunda, Mansfield, Alden, Stanton, and Freeborn. A vote of the town on the 11th of May changed Buckeye to Liberty. Most of the towns were coupled together in pairs for township purposes.

On the 9th of June a petition to change the name of Stanton to Springfield was favorably considered, and Guildford was changed to Moscow.

The town meetings for organization and election of officers was held on the 11th of May, and some of the election officers presented their bills to the county, but they were promptly rejected.

In September a communication was received from the State Auditor requiring the name of the town of Liberty to be changed, as there was a township with a prior claim to this cognomen.

In accordance with the provisions of the State law, after the organization of the State, the board of County Commissioners was superseded by a board of Supervisors, and in this county the first board consisted of: Theop. Lowry, William Andrews, A. C. Wedge, D. Blakely, B. S. Boardman, Mathias Anderson, A. W. White, Patrick Fitzsimmons, H. W. Allen, and E. C. Stacy, the latter being chairman.

William Morin was the first County Auditor, and also recorder for the county board.

1859.--The board met in annual session on the 13th of September. The members were as follows: William H. Goslee, Asa Bullock, Theop. Lowry, Michael Brennan, Edwin C. Stacy, Isaac Baker, I. W. Devereux, A. C. Wedge, N. H. Ellickson, Horace Greene, Mathias Anderson, Patrick Fitzsimons, and E. D. Rogers. Edwin C. Stacy was elected temporary chairman, and Theop. Lowry, permanent chairman.

About this time the towns began to be detached from their partners to set up for themselves.

1860.—The bond of the Treasurer was fixed at $13,000. The compensation of the clerks and judges of elections was fixed at $2 a day, and ten cents a mile one way, making returns.

The School fund for the year 1859 footed up $983.10, with 793 children of school age.

Ole S. Ellingson was the Second County Treasurer.

A committe reported the expense of the district court to be as follows:

September term, 1858, ...	$248.48
April, 1859, ...	75.85
September, 1859, ...	199.10

At a meeting in January it was moved that a jail to hold six persons be built, not to exceed a cost of $500, which motion was not agreed to.

The board gave specific instructions to assessors as to their methods of procedure to secure uniformity and accuracy.

On the 5th of September, 1860, the Treasurer had on hand funds to the amount of $4,115.26. The whole amount of county orders issued up to that date was $8,364.18.

At a meeting on the 18th of September a petition was presented to allow the people of the county to vote on the question of removing the county seat to Itaska. But, as a question as to the legality of the election already held on that subject was already in the courts for adjudication, it was laid on the table. Several propositions were received making generous offers to the county in consideration of having the county seat in some specified locality, and the one of Albert Lea was entertained. A more full account is given of this business in the article on the contest for the county seat.

On the 20th of October the petition in relation to the vote on county seat, in obedience to the order of Judge Atwater, was favorably considered and the order issued. At the same meeting the town of Pickerel Lake was attached to Manchester for election purposes, and Alden to Carlston. A petition of citizens of the town of Freeman asking to have township 101, range 21, organized for town purposes under the name of Green, was granted and the 5th of January fixed as the day of holding the first town meeting.

1861.—The Board got together on the 1st of January. James E. Smith was elected chaiaman. At the meeting the next day the bills of D. G. Parker as Attorney for the State in the Kreigler murder case, and of Augustus Armstrong the prisoner's counsel, were allowed at $120 each. Numerous other bills for witness fees in the same case were presented, and the District Attorney was requested to furnish his opinion as to the liability of the county. The bill of James A. Robson, the Sheriff in this case, footed up to $207.50. On the 9th of April the bill of expense in this expensive trial, presented by Steele county was $1,125.09.

The cost of printing the delinquent tax roll was $300, done by A. D. Clark, who agreed to complete the year's printing free.

In April the salary of the Auditor was fixed at $800 per annum, and that of the County Attorney at $150. Up to this time the expense of the Kreigler trial, exclusive of the Steele county bills, was $888.17.

At the September meeting the bill of F. O. Perkins for professional services in defending Henry Kreigler, to the amount of $200, was laid over for further consideration, and at a regular meeting in October the account was allowed at $75.00. Up to the first of January, 1862, the bills audited in the Kreigler case amounted to $1,579.29.

1862.—Asa Bullock was chosen chairman of the board. Nothing of especal note occured this year, routine work taking up most of the time.

1863.—Asa Bullock was chairman this year. At a meeting in July it was resolved that the law licensing dogs and for the protection of sheep be complied with in this county.

The State law requiring the militia to be organized by districts was complied with as far as possible, and elections ordered for the 18th of July. This movement was not a phenomenal success, although it may have served to keep up an interest in military affairs.

In November the question of building fire proof county offices was introduced.

1864.—C. H. McIntyre was chairman. In March a committee consisting of William Morin, Frank Hall, and Augustus Armstrong submitted plans and estimates for the construction of a fire-proof building for offices and court room, as follows:

Brick at $6	$1,320.00
Fire proof roof	300.00
Laying brick and furnishing lime	550.00
Eight thousand feet of lumber at $20	160.00
Doors, nails, sash, glass, and putty	400.00
Carpenter work	300.00
Plastering and lime	300.00
	$3,330.00

Various petitions were presented against the issue of bonds for county buildings. A resolution, however, was adopted to issue and appropriate bonds to the amount of two thousand dollars toward erecting fire-proof buildings for the county offices, with the understanding that Albert Lea shall appropriate one thousand dollars to add a suitable hall for court purposes. Messrs. Hall, Morin, and Armstrong were appointed commissioners to sell the bonds and to erect the building.

Two parties who were reported as selling spirituous liquors without a license, it was ordered should be prosecuted. In July George S. Ruble was appointed Overseer of the poor.

The first bond of $1,500, was issued, and cashed by Joseph Hall. It bore 10 per cent. interest and was dated the 16th of March, 1864. The location of the Court House was agreed upon, provided a strip six rods wide and extending to the next street south could be secured free of cost. On the 6th of September Mr. Asa Bullock, a member of the board, having died, suitable resolutions were engrossed, presented to his family, and spread upon the records.

1865.—The first record with any reference to the war was on the 6th of September, when assistance was voted to several families of soldiers at the front, which will be mentioned more fully in the war history of the county. On the 8th of September the tax on the property of the county was ordered assessed as follows:

State tax,	3½ mills.
Interest on State debt,	1 "
Sinking fund,	1 "
County purposes,	4 "
Poor tax,	1 "
Special for county building,	2½ "

The cost of printing the delinquent tax list audited and allowed at the April meeting was $323.85. In June action was taken in regard to vacating the town site of Bancroft. The lots in the village of Itaska, delinquent since 1863, were ordered sold. On the 22d of June James F. Jones, Asa Walker, and E. P. Skinner were added to the building committee. The Court House was going up, and provisions were made to pay the bills as they occurred.

1866.—The new board organized on the 2d of January. Clark Andrews was chairman. On the 3d of January the town of Mansfield was organized. In March the town of Alden was organized. On the 6th of September the county board appointed Samuel Batchelder as Superintendent of Schools at a compensation of $2.50 per day.

1867.—The annual meeting of the board this year was on the 1st of January. William White was made chairman. The salary of the County Superintendent was adjusted at $300 per year.

On the 14th of March the following appears on the records: Whereas, the two churches holding divine service in Albert Lea have got at loggerheads in relation to occupying the Court House for meetings, and submitted the matter to the board, both churches being ably represented by Capt. Hagaman on the one side and Colonel Eaton on the other, therefore,

Resolved, That the Congregationalists be allowed to use the Court room in the forenoon of the next Sunday, and the Baptists the Sunday following, and so on alternately, reserving the use of the room for other denominations in the afternoon.

In September, 1867, Sheriff St. John having removed from the county, John Brownsill was appointed to fill the vacancy. The county at this time was divided into five commissioner districts.

1868.—The board of County Commissioners met on the 7th of January and consisted of Mons Grinager of the first district; Stephen N. Frisbie, of the second district; Henry N. Ostrander of the third; Jedediah W. Devereux of the fourth, and William H. Moore of the fifth.

J. W. Devereux was elected chairman for the ensuing year.

At this time the license had got up to $100 per annum.

In March the Court House was insured for $2,500.

Nothing of a startling character occured during this year in connection with the board.

1869.—J. W. Devereux was re-elected chairman. The other commissioners were Mons Grinager, S. N. Frisbie, H. N. Ostrander, and W. H Moore.

On the 8th of January a committee was appointed to attend to the planting of trees in the Court House grounds, and otherwise improving the appearance of the location.

The town site of Bancroft village was on the floor this year, and the County Attorney was instructed to perfect the title of the county in the property.

1870.—The board this year consisted of J. W. Devereux, chairman; William H. Moore, Mons Grinager, Adam Christie, and H. N. Ostrander.

This year was uneventful as regards the county government. There were various road matters to receive attention, Sunday School districts to be rearranged, certain railroad lands to be assessed, taxable property to be equalized, bills to be audited, and all the routine work of such a board to receive careful supervision. In the winter of this year the law in relation to agricultural statistics had to be enforced.

1871.—The board this year was made up of J. W. Devereux, Chairman, Henry G. Emmons, H. N. Ostrander, Mons Grinager, and Adam Christie.

On the 6th of January the board considered the advisability of constructing a fire proof vault in the Court House, and in March Mons Grinager and J. W. Devereux were appointed a committee on the subject.

During this year the County Surveyor made a record of the county roads, which were fully described and engrossed on the county records.

1872.—Mr. Devereux was chairman of the board again this year.

The Court House was repaired, including lightning rods, to the extent of $3,140.84. Regular business requiring the consideration of the board took up the time at the various sessions.

1873.—The County Commissioners met on the 7th of January in annual session. The members were: H. G. Emmons, James Thoreson, Hans Christopherson and Halver Thompson. On the organization Mr. Devereux was elected chairman.

1874.—The board met at the regular session in January. The members were: H. G. Emmons, chairman, H. Christopherson, W. C. Lincoln, Halver Thompson, and James Thoreson.

An abstract of the business for the year would read: Bills, school district changed, road petition rejected, poor fund expenditures, change of county road, bills, Sheriff's fees, petition for new district, equalization, taxes abated, bills, &c., &c.

1875.—The board has been of rather a conservative tendency, and have as a rule been continued in office for long terms, and the character of the functions have been more of an executive than of a legislative kind, so it seems unnecessary to go over the ground to furnish a detailed sketch of the transactions from year to year. Items relating to the early period of course have been given in detail.

1876.—The board this centennial year consisted of: H. G. Emmons, chairman, W. C. Lincoln, James Thoreson, W. N. Goslee, and Ole Hanson.

1877.—Two new members appeared this year, the personnel of the board being, William N. Goslee, James Thoreson, John M. Geisler, Ole Hanson, and W. W. Johnson.

In relation to taxation, its collection and disbursement, which embraces the great bulk of county business, it would make this work objectionably statistical to particularize from year to year, but to furnish an insight into the question, which is so interesting, as to "how the money goes," an extract from the minutes of the board will be made.

The board directed the following taxes to be levied to meet the expenses of the year 1878:

State taxes in such sum or rate as the State Auditor may direct.

School tax one mill.

Special county tax for jail, $3000.

County tax of $20,000 based on the following estimate:

Auditor's salary	$1,500
Auditor's clerk	880
Treasurer	1,500
Superintendent	1,000
County Attorney	800
Judge of Probate	800
County Commissioners	400
Jailor fees	480
Sheriff and Deputies	2,500
Coroner's fees	100
Tree bounty	20
Gopher bounty	500
Judge of Probate orders	150
Watching jail	300
Board of prisoners	400
Constable fees	170
Clerk of Court and Justices	1,000
Juror fees Justice Court	100
Witnesses Justice Court	200
Grand Jurors	600
Petit Jurors	1,000
Witness fees	400
Court House repairs, &c	800
Printing blank books, stationery, stenographer, &c	1,500
Articles for jail, express, postage, insurance, &c	600
Births and Deaths	200
Election returns	100
Outstanding orders	2,000
Total	$20,000

1878. J. M. Geisler was chairman of the board this year, with W. W. Johnson, W. N. Goslee, R. Fitzgerald, and J. A. Rodsater.

There was some action taken resulting from the fact that Mr. Batchelder, who had been County Auditor, had drawn his salary from a computation made by the valuation of the property of the county for the current year, instead of the year previous as the law provided. This made a difference of $777.08 in the compensation for three years in which it was so calculated, and he was required to return that amount. It is known that Mr. Batchelder worked night and day, almost, in his office, doing what may be called extra work, and was allowed $1,000 a year for clerk hire, having a clerk at a low price, and a part of this was also demanded, but a decision of Judge Berry was in his interest and the claim was not pushed. The overdraft was, as believed by his friends, the result of an inadvertence, as no one could suppose anything but honesty and integrity would actuate the Auditor.

1879.—This was another uneventful year with the county board, which consisted of John M. Geisler, chairman; W. W. Johnson, W. N. Goslee, R. Fitzgerald, I. A. Rodsater.

Charles Kittleson, the County Treasurer, resigned in December, and Frank W. Barlow was appointed to fill the vacancy.

1880.—This year R. Fitzgerald was chairman of the board, with W. N. Goslee, I. A. Rodsater, J. M. Geissler, and C. W. Ballard.

1881. The board this year was I. A. Rodsater, chairman; J. M. Geissler, W. N. Goslee, D. N. Gates, and E. C. Johnson.

1882.—The present board consists of D. N. Gates, chairman, I. A Rodsater, J. M. Geissler, E. C. Johnson, and Michael O'Leary.

The county tax assessed this year was $22,000, with one mill for school tax.

A few items in this sketch are duplicate statements made by Mr. Parker in his Centennial History, while some things that are omitted here will be found there.

THE COUNTY SEAT CONTEST.

The county seat was fixed by the County Commissioners appointed by the Governor, and in accordance with what has been done all over the State, those interested in keeping the county seat procured the passage of a general act, prohibiting any action looking to a change of location within three years after its establishment. In 1860, the contest here was re-opened, but the County Commissioners declined to order an election. The Itasca people procured a mandamus through Mr. Everett, a lawyer in Austin, requiring an election to be ordered.

Itasca was at this time a flourishing place, with its hotel, blacksmith shop, shoemaker's shop, and twelve or fifteen houses all told, and a newspaper, printed in the octagon house which still stands. Its location was on a beautiful prairie which had been named by the first explorers, "Paradise Prairie," which is on a plateau overlooking the surrounding country, affording a view of Albert Lea City and of the lake beyond.

The adherents to the claims of Itasca declare that they went into the fight on its merits and on the square, but that they were counted out; that a precinct was established with headquarters on a stump in the township of Pickerel Lake, that John Ruble and Charley Norton were judges of the election, and they returned 240 votes, solid for Itasca. It is claimed that compliance with a demand to produce the voting list would have been impossible.

The history of this Court House struggle, if it was told in all its details, would reveal a species of which, while having analagous counterparts in other more important contests, was nevertheless an indigenous production of Freeborn county soil, and displayed some peculiarities of political guerrilla warfare which might might have been disagreeable to the participants, if published and believed at the time. But now, such a length of time having elapsed, and most of the participants having interests in the successful towns in this eventful struggle, they freely talk it over and relate to each other the various methods which were resorted to in securing the several advantages which finally settled the contest. It is not possible, even if it were desirable, to give a detailed account of all the incidents connected with this conflict, but enough will be presented to give a good idea of some of the courses pursued by the contending parties.

In those times the community was manouvering as to whether law and order predominated, or mere force, with a predomination in favor of the latter. The men at Albert Lea had made up their minds to retain the county seat at all hazards, and to-day they claim that whatever might have happened at the polls would not have changed the result. To show the methods employed to destroy Itasca, and blot it out of existence, a single instance will be mentioned. A Presbyterian clergyman, by the name of Mercer, came here and was enthusiastic in his ideas as to building up institutions in his denominational interest in this new country, and so advantage was taken of his propagating spirit, and it was suggested that Itasca would be a fine suburban locality for such a school as he proposed to establish, and he went up and purchased the hotel of Dr. Burnham, who was delighted with the idea and anxious to do what he could to aid in the work. So the transfer was made, the Albert Lea proprietors paying for it, and it was then torn down and removed to the county seat; the scheme having served its purpose, no more money was advanced in the interest of the school, and the poor man who had been used by the ring, was frozen out, and sadly wended his way to some more promising locality.

The newspaper was fitted out by Dr. Burnham and D. F. Blackmer, Dr. Burnham having bought material, including press and fifty-two fonts of type, at Zumbrota. When the county seat business had collapsed, so far as Itasca was concerned, Mr. Botsford and young Blackmer took the material to Blue Earth City, established a paper there, and run it until during the war, when one night Dr. Burnham was called up by a man who had some business with him. It proved to be Botsford, who had come to pay the $600 for the press and type, for which no security had been taken. This act should be particularly emphasized in the history of those times, where even legal obligations were not always observed.

They all worked together in Albert Lea, it only required a suggestion of some plan which would redound to their benefit to have it instantly acted upon. The proprietors of Itasca were equally on the alert in relation to Bancroft, and the Doctor bought up the buildings in that town and removed them to Itasca. The printing office is now a part of the house of E. K. Pickett, which is located on the site of that embryotic city.

While the county seat question was being agitated, in 1860, the leading citizens of Itasca, to secure if possible the county seat there, executed a bond in the penal sum of $6,000, pledging themselves to build a Court House according to certain plans and specifications, within two years, and also to furnish suitable offices for county purposes, including the building then there, 24 x 50 feet, and two stories high. The building was to be of brick, two stories high, in the octagon form, forty-eight feet or more in diameter.

The plan was a good one, giving good, large sized offices, jail room, and a court room twenty-four by twenty-eight feet, with suitable jury rooms. The parties who executed this bond were: A. M. Burnham, C. C. Colby, J. G. Sanborn, R. J. Franklin, E. D. Hopkins, Samuel Batchelder, Charles Dunbar, J. Dunbar, J. Colby, J. D. Adams, and J. S. Longworth.

This was signed in the presence of Isaac Botsford and Hannibal Bickford, and certified to by Ole J. Ellingson, clerk, per Samuel Eaton, deputy.

The citizens of Albert Lea, not to be outdone by the liberality of other aspiring places, agreed to furnish offices for the county officers and a jail for three years, free of cost to the county, and the following named gentlemen executed a bond in the penal sum of five thousand dollars for the faithful execution of this promise: A. B. Webber, George S. Ruble, William Morin, A. C. Wedge, James A. Robson, Samuel Eaton, John Brownsill, A. Armstrong, and H. D. Brown: which proposition was formally accepted.

A brief recapitulation of all the stories told in relation to that contest, which, after considerable legal quibbling, was set for the 6th of November, the day on which Abraham Lincoln was elected president of the United States, and Albert Lea carried off the prize, and to-day there are really few, if any, who regret the result of the struggle. The several horse races which are briefly alluded to in the "events," are connected in the old settlers' mind with this contest, and at the old settlers' reunion in September, 1882, Dr. Ballard, the Mayor of the City, read a humorous poem largely devoted to the details of that memorable race, just a sample of which is spread on these pages.

* * * * * * * *

"So, conning o'er the aspects of the case,
They came unanimously to this conclusion:
That public morals required another race;
Advantage should be taken of the delusion
That Sheriff Heath's Red Tom could always win.
By beating him they'd bring to dire confusion
The folks in Albert Lea; 'twould be no sin,
They said, to cheat those sinners,
Especially if Itasca's men were winners.
They'd buy Old Fly, a mare of reputation,
Whose four white feet for years had earned the fame
Of being the fleetest feet in all creation.
They'd paint those feet, and then they'd change her name.
And shave her tail, and otherwise adorn her
Until she looked like misery's last mourner,
And then they'd challenge Heath's Red Tom to run,
And banter Albert Lea to betting high;
They'd let the country people in the fun,
And take with them all bets against Old Fly.
They'd win that race in just a half mile heat—
They'd bankrupt Albert Lea, and with the money
Buy votes enough to win the county seat.

* * * * * * * * *

"To make a long story short, and the list quite complete,
People bet all they had on this half-mile heat.
People in town and out, and all over the county;
Old soldiers put up the last cent of their bounty,
Boys, women, and girls, they all took a hand,
And tremendous excitement reigned over the land.
The day was appointed, the place had been named.
The hour was set—through the county it flamed
In staring great hand-bills of all colors and sizes,
Inviting the people to come and win prizes."

According to the legend the Albert Lea horse, which had been secretly tested one night with the Itasca animal, won the race and threw confusion into the Itasca camp, won all their money and most of their valuables, and effectually destroyed their ability to carry on the contest for the county seat, because they were thus deprived of the means to buy votes. Of course this is what the exultant ones told, and perhaps believed. But enough has been said to give an idea for all coming time that this was one of the great contests of the period.

"Of all the words of tongue or pen,
The saddest is, it might have been."

EDUCATIONAL.

The school district system of the county, like all other valuable institutions, has been a matter of growth from the smallest beginnings; and while it is proposed to give a local sketch of each school in the county in connection with the town where it is situated, yet, the difficulties, in the absence of record knowledge, in obtaining the dates of the organization and of other events are much greater than would be supposed, when we remember that most of the men who helped create and sustain these schools are still alive.

The date of the organization of most of the districts, especially the earlier ones, will be presented heer.

District No. 1 was organized on the 6th of April, 1857, on the petition of R. K. Creem and others, and embraced thirty-three, thirty-four, thirty-five, twenty-eight, and the southwest quarter of section twenty-seven in township 103, range 19, which is the present town of Moscow. This was in Mr. Frisbie's district, on whose motion the prayer of the petitioners was granted. This was the initial district.

District No. 2. The second district to see itself in form, was organized on the 8th of April, the same year, and was in answer to a petition of George Watson and others, and comprised sections nineteen, twenty, twenty-nine, thirty, thirty-one, and thirty-two in the same township.

District No. 3. The boundaries of this district are elaborately described in the records, but the township is omitted, so that if anyone knows where it is it is all right, and to those who don't know, it does not perhaps matter where it was. This was on the same date as the last one. The petitioner was David M. Farr.

District No. 4 was on the petition of Watson H. Brown, and was constituted a district at that first session of the board. It was at Shell Rock. It is evident that a reiteration of the sectional boundaries of all the districts would be burdensome, as well in the preparation as in the reading so it will be sufficient that the date and the township be indicated.

District No. 5 was formed on the 8th of April on the petition of H. Bartlett, and was in Shell Rock and Hayward.

District No. 6. George P. Hoops asked to have this district set apart, and it embraced some sections in Hayward and in Albert Lea.

District No. 7. A. P. Swineford petitioned for a school district in Bancroft, which was favorably acted upon. These embraced the school districts projected at the first meeting of the county board.

District No. 8. The petition of Isaac Vandermaker and others was favorably considered on the 6th of July. It was located in Newry and Moscow.

District No. 9. On the 7th of Septemer this came into existence, in response to a request from D. Prescott, and was in Bancroft.

District No. 15. This is the next on the list; what became of the missing numbers is among the problems, such as the lost tribes of Israel, but it is quite certain that enough others will turn up before we get through with them, to compensate for their absence. C. C. Colby was the petitioner in this case, with others, and included Albert Lea, Bancroft, and Manchester, each in part. This was on the 9th of September, 1857.

District No. 16 was also brought into existence on the 9th of September. E. C. Dunn headed the petition, and it took in sections of Carlston and Freeborn.

District No. 10. On the 5th of October this district comes in view like a lost child, and was located in Moscow. J. M. Stage was the applicant, with others.

District No. 11 was in Bath and Geneva, with Isaac P. Lynde as the head petitioner.

District No. 12. On the 7th of October this was instituted, and its habitation was in Moscow.

District No. 13. John W. Ayers and others asked for a new school in Freeborn and the prayer was granted.

District No. 14. Daniel Ingraham respectfully requested the honorable body to organize a new district in Oakland, and it was done on the 16th of November, 1857.

District No. 17. Having gathered up the straggling districts the regular sequence will be taken up. David Blakely and others wanted a district in Bancroft, embracing nearly two thirds of the township, and the *fiat* thus went forth on the 1st of Febrnary, 1858.

It appears that during the year 1857 there were sixteen districts formed in the county, some of the townships having several, and others none. But in almost every settlement there were schools sustained in a private way. In April, 1858, school districts from No. 18 to 25 inclusive, were authorized, and they were located as follows: No. 18 in Manchester and Carlston; No. 19 in Pickerel Lake and Nunda; No. 20 in Nunda and Freeman; No. 21 in Nunda. No. 22 in Bancroft; No. 23 in south half of Shell Rock; No. 24 in Riceland and Bancroft; No. 25 in Pickerel Lake.

District No. 26. This was set apart in September, 1858, in the town of Hartland, and included the whole township. Additions were made to district No. 3 in the same month.

District No. 27 was organized in October, and was in Freeborn.

District No. 28 was organized at the same session, and was in Hartland.

District No. 29 was instituted on the same date in Hayward.

District No. 30 started with a like date in London.

District No. 31 was organized at the same time in Geneva.

The School fund available in October, 1858, was as follows:

From the county	$391.43
From fines	7.53
Total	$398.96
To each pupil	$1.70

District No. 32. This was organized in the fall of 1858, in the towns then called Liberty and Springfield.

District No. 33 was organized with others up to and including No. 37, on the 5th of January, 1859, and their locations were in Freeman, Manchester, Carlston, Bancroft ,and Geneva. In September the districts were organized up to 45, which includes the whole number at that time in the county.

An act of the legislature about this time undertook to revolutionize the county school system by making each town a school district to be subdivided according to the requirements of each case. So then each town would begin No. 1, No. 2, and so on. But this was soon repealed and the county schools placed under a superintendent, and the system as it is now firmly established. A new numbering also took place, so that the districts cannot now be identified by their original numbers, but the order in which the schools were started can be seen.

To furnish a complete idea of the schools in this county at this time, it has been concluded that a full copy of the admirable report of Superintendent Levens should be transcribed. That this includes various suggestions as to what ought to be done does not mitigate against its value in a historical work, and it gives the *personnel* of the teachers of the last session of each school, as well as the names of the clerks of the school districts.

REPORT OF THE SCHOOLS OF FREEBORN COUNTY, FOR THE WINTER TERM OF 1881–82. – The following facts, relating chiefly to the important matter of attendance, are compiled from teachers' reports of the winter schools.

Six Districts—29, 58, 69, 85, 86, and 111, had no winter term.

Six Districts—25, 50, 66, 95, 105, and 108, report no tardiness.

Fourteen schools made no report as to tardiness—whether, because, they thought it of no importance, or too much trouble, or because they had too many cases, or had none, is not certain. It is a fact, however, that should be recognized by teachers, that punctuality and regular attendance go together, and that the *habit* of promptness and punctuality acquired and practiced in school is an important element of future success in life.

No. of District.	NAME OF TEACHER.	No. Days School.	Whole No. Enrolled
1	Augus McGinnis	98	36
2	Ellen A. O'Leary	60	17
3	Mrs. J. M. Tracy	60	17
4	John L. Gibbs	70	54
5	Betsey C. Thompson	70	45
6	James McClure	60	25
7	Sarah C. Burke	80	53
8	Ellen M. McClelland	80	26
9	Oluf Hofland	80	40
10	Billia Drake	60	30
11	Jennie E. Harrison	60	8
12	S. J. Fuller	60	28
13	Geo. P. Latin	79	50
14	O. H. Smeby	60	18
15	Maggie E. Purdie	60	20
16	Geo. M. Miller	65	26
17	Z. A. Ransom	60	28
18	H. R. Fossum	60	35
19	L. J. Aga	60	31
20	Eva B. Loomis	80	32

No. of District.	Name of Teacher.	No. days School.	Whole No. Enrolled
21	H. R. Fossum	60	33
22	Charles Horning	60	31
23	Elmer C. Webster	80	44
24	Annie English	60	34
25	Grace Slater	80	53
26	Arthur Trow	60	43
27	O. K. Fiskerback	60	45
28	Mary Jordon	60	15
29	No Winter School	..	..
30	Mary Brown	77	12
31	John J. Morrison	60	37
32	Wm. A. Norris	54	17
33	Charles N. Hatch	79	12
34	Chas. E. Budlong	60	43
35	John W. Gillard	60	26
36	Viola N. Palmer	60	12
37	George Hurd	60	32
38	Albert Lea Reports Annually	..	..
39	Emma Ruble	60	8
40	Lennie Patrick	60	24
41	Mary A. Quinn	80	13
42	Charles J. Dudley	60	37
43	Rosa Sutton	80	26
44	John Siverson	60	26
45	Leda M. Hewitt	60	48
46	Frank H. Palmer	60	23
47	Lizzie Wadsworth	70	22
48	L. T. Lawrence	60	31
49	Glenville, Reports Annually	..	..
50	Mary Fisk	80	46
51	Belle Cheadle	80	38
52	D. S. Palmer	80	42
53	Eva E. Gibson	60	17
54	J. E. Nelson	80	31
55	Cora A. Norton	60	18
56	M. P. Howe	70	22
57	Hannah Daniels	39	15
58	No Winter Term	..	..
59	E. E. Geesey	60	22
60	Ellen Hare	60	23
61	S. E. Walker	78	29
62	Frank E. Phipps	80	40
63	Ida M. Taylor	50	18
64	Emily Wood	80	37
65	John D. Herman	60	22
66	John J. Quam	60	37
67	Emma Allen	80	20
68	Martha Palmer	80	18
69	No Winter Term	..	..
70	Dora E. Chamberlain	65	17
71	John D. Murphy	80	32
72	Emma A. Ames	60	19
73	Mary O'Leary	60	34
74	Viola A. Marvin	60	24
75	John W. Booen	59	45
76	Arthur Budlong	60	38
77	Betsie Miller	80	24
78	Robert H. Graham	79	32
79	T. K. Haugen	80	44
80	J. H. Ransom	59	17
81	Henry A. Davis	80	33
82	Mettie Ostrander	60	37
83	Gordon Mayland	60	20
84	Emil Hanson	60	46
85	No Winter Term	..	
86	No Winter Term	..	..
87	Olive S. Austin	80	23
88	R. E. English	60	41
89	Orpha J. Skinner	60	29
90	Clara Pierce	80	43
91	O. H. Smeby	60	39
92	Annie Fitzgerald	100	26
93	L. W. Bassett	120	57
94	Ellen Meadowcroft	80	23
95	Rose Harris	60	15
96	Lora Vaughn	60	17
97	John M. Tracy	80	21
98	Maggie J. Davis	80	37
99	Olive Skinner	80	18
100	Charles Young	60	15
101	Netta E. Scott	60	16
102	John K. Richards	60	20
103	James St. John	60	16
104	Francis Murphy	80	26
105	Ashley Narvey	40	19
106	Lydia Purcell	57	13
107	Ella Slater	50	29
108	John J. Quam	60	23
109	R. F. Challis	79	50
110	Lettie P. English	40	14
111	No Winter Term	..	..
	Averages	68	29

The average number of visitors to each school —26—so far as it has any significance, would seem to indicate a fair amount of interest on the part of parents, though two schools report only one visitor.

The actual attendance is shown to be only 62 per cent. of the total enrollment. This means that all the scholars enrolled were absent on an average, over one day out of every three, during the term. The figures show a direct loss of 38 per cent. of school. But the real loss was much greater. No scholar absent one day and present two, can get any thing like the full value of these two. Irregular attendance retards the whole work of the school. Hence this 38 per cent of absence greatly lessons the value of the remaining 62 per cent. of attendance. If we also consider the number not enrolled at all, but who might and should have been, there was an actual loss, at the lowest estimate, of more than one-half of the cost of the schools in the matter of attendance alone, to say nothing of the quality of teachers' work or of any other deficiencies. Good attendance is absolutely essential to a good school. Many parents do not appreciate this fact. Teachers who do, and are thoroughly in earnest about it, can make their influence felt among parents as well as scholars. Last week I visited two schools, in each of which only three scholars were present. The most of the absent ones were probably planting corn. Though often convenient, it is not profitable in the end, to interrupt a child's attendance at school for a little work at home, if it can possibly be avoided.

TO TEACHERS.

I respectfully submit to your consideration the following simple outline of a "Course of Study," and "Program of Recitations," in the hope that they may aid in securing more systematic and efficient work in our schools.

Any course of study for country schools must, of necessity, ignore the element of *time;* hence, only the studies themselves and the proper *order* in which they should be taken up by the different grades are here given.

For convenience and simplicity the grades are made and named to correspond to the different numbers of the series of readers: 1st Reader, or 1st Grade; 2d Reader or 2d Grade, up to and including the 5th Reader, making five grades.

The studies of the different grades should be as follows:

1st GRADE—1st Reader and Spelling, Writing, Oral Number Lessons.

2d GRADE—Second Reader and Spelling, Writing, Oral Arithmetic, Oral Geography.

3d GRADE—3d Reader, Spelling, Writing, Primary Arithmetic, Primary Geography.

4th GRADE—4th Reader, Spelling, Writing, Practical Arithmetic, Language Lessons, Intermediate Geography.

4th GRADE—5th Reader or History, Spelling, Writing, Practical Arithmetic, Grammar, Physiology.

(*a*). 1st and 2d Grades spell in connection with each reading exercise the words of the lesson, and and write reading lessons on slates.

(*b.*) "Oral Number Lessons" includes the development of the idea of numbers and their combinations by the use of objects, counting and such simplé exercises in notation, numeration, and such elementary operations as are adapted to the capacity of pupils of the first Grade.

(*c*) "Oral Arithmetic" means such oral instruction and practice in *slate* work as will enable pupils of the 2d Grade completing the 2d Reader, to perform promptly and correctly, simple examples in Addition, Subtraction, Multiplication, and Division, and the knowledge of the tables requisite therefor.

(*d.*) Much extra slate work should be given the 3rd Grade, in connection with the Primary Arithmetic, to prepare them to take the Practical Arithmetic when they take the 4th Reader.

(*e.*) "Language Lessons" for the 4th Grade, means the State text book, so named. But the greatest attention should be given from the first, through all grades, and in connection with all school exercises, to give practical instruction and drill in language. To teach correctly the elements of *reading, talking,* and *writing* the English language, is the most important business of a school.

While it is desirable that all the pupils of each grade be together in all the studies of that grade, yet, owing to irregularity of classification in the past, and to various other causes, this will not in all cases be possible. A 5th Grade pupil in other branches, but who has never studied Geography, will have to be in the 3rd Grade in *that* branch. Similar cases will occur in other branches, But no effort should be spared to secure regular grading when possible, always using common sense and judgment in regard to exceptional cases.

The following "Program of Daily Exercises" is presented, not as the *best* that can be made for all schools, but as one which, with slight changes, can be used to advantage in all schools, and especially in those attempting to conform to this plan of grading:

FORENOON.

Hour	Grade	Exercises	Time
9:00	All...	Opening exercises	05
9:05	1	Oral Number Lesson	10
9:15	2	2d Reader and Spelling	15
9:30	3	3d Reader	15
9:45	4	4th Reader	20
10:05	5	"A" Practical Arithmetic	25
10:30	......	RECESS.	15
10:45	1	1st Reader and Spelling	10
10:55	2	Oral Geography	10
11:05	3	Primary Arithmetic	15
11:20	4	"B" Practical Arithmetic	20
11:40	5	"A" Grammar	20

AFTERNOON.

Hour	Grade	Exercises.	Time
1:00	1	1st Reader and Spelling	10
1:10	2	2d Reader and Spelling	15
1:25	4	"A" Geography	15
1:40	5	History	20
2:00	3&4	"B" Spelling	10
2:10	All	Writing	20
2:30	......	RECESS.	15
2:45	1	1st Reader and Spelling	10
2:55	2	Oral Arithmetic	15
3:10	4	Language Lessons	20
3:30	3	Primary Geography	15
3:45	4&5	"A" Spelling	15

This program is intended to be the best possible arrangement of the greatest possible number of daily exercises—22. The number *should* not and *can* not be increased. If it is absolutely neccessary to introduce additional recitations in other branches, they must take the place of some of these, on alternate days, as Algebra one day and A Arithmetic the next; or the 5th Reader alternate with the 4th Reader; or Physiology with History or A Geography. In many schools, especially during the summer term, all the classes found on this program will not be formed. The time thus gained can be divided among the other classes most needing it.

Thy 3rd grade and the *poorest* in the 4th can form the "B" spelling class; the 5th grade and the *best* in the 4th, the "A" spelling class. In some cases doubtless the 4th and 5th grades can belong to the same class, as in Physiology—a study that should be introduced whenever possible—*always* in preference to Algebra or the 5th Reader. If history is substituted for the 5th Reader, as a reading exercise, it should be *studied* as well as *read*.

In changing this program to adopt it to the circumstances of your school, remember that the objects to be secured are: (1.) The distribution of the recitations of each pupil throughout the entire day, with time for study between—thus making it also a *study* program. (2.) A proper amount of time to each recitation, taking into account the subject, the number in the class, and their age. (3.) Plenty of time for the *little ones* the oldest ones *can* learn without any teacher. (4.) A just division of the time among the different *branches*—Reading, 95 minutes; Writing, 20; Arithmetic, 85; Grammar, 40; Geography, 40; History, 20; Spelling, 25. (5.) As few as 18 daily recitations, if possible.

If, by the approval of school officers and parents and the co-operation of teachers, this attempt at partial grading proves reasonably successful, blanks will be provided in which to record the classification of the school at the close of the term, and showing the progress of each class and pupil. Such a record, left with the register in the care of the clerk of the district, will be of great use to the next teacher in organizing the next term of school.

Teachers should preserve this circular for reference and further use.

C. W. LEVENS.
Co. Supt. of Schools.

SCHOOL DISTRICT CLERKS.

Below is a list of the names of the school district clerks of the 110 districts of Freeborn county, together with the Post-office address of each clerk, as appears on the records in the County Auditor's office:

No. Dis.	*Clerk.*	*P. O. Address.*
1	Ben Benson,	Blooming Prairie.
2	Garrett Barry,	Blooming Prairie.
3	Wm. Lehy,	Geneva.
4	W. H. Twiford,	Geneva.
5	E. C. Johnson,	Albert Lea.
6	John Lightly,	Oakland.
7	R. Fitzgerald,	Albert Lea.
8	F. E. Phipps,	Hartland.
9	Thos. Donovan,	Hartland.
10	John Ingebrigston,	Hartland.
11	C. C. Ayers,	Trenton.
12	S. J. Fuller,	Freeborn.
13	Wilbur Fisk,	Freeborn.
14	C. G. Johnsrud,	Albert Lea.
15	L. W. Gilmore,	Alden.
16	Josiah Jones,	Alden.
17	L. C. Larken,	Alden.
18	Bennett Asleson,	Manchester.
19	Paul J. Spilde,	Manchester.
20	Wm. H. Long,	Albert Lea.
21	H. Christopherson,	Hartland.
22	R. Kelly,	Albert Lea.
23	H. S. Olson,	Clark's Grove.
24	August C. Arneson,	Albert Lea.
25	Ole Henry,	Albert Lea.
26	W. H. Baker,	Albert Lea.
27	Ole A. Lee,	Hayward.
28	Asa Rowley,	Oakland.
29	V. P. Lewis,	Moscow.
30	J. E. Johnson,	Austin.

No. Dist.	Clerk.	P. O. Address.
31	S. N. Frisbie,	Oakland.
32	J. M. Purcell,	Austin.
33	Abram Young,	Oakland.
34	A. P. Hanson,	Hayward.
35	Thos. Wiley,	Glenville.
36	A. L. Jackson,	Hayward.
37	John Murphy,	Albert Lea.
38	W. C. McAdam,	Albert Lea.
39	W. C. Norton,	Albert Lea.
40	J. W. Peck,	Alden.
41	George LaValley,	Alden.
42	R. A. White,	Nunda.
43	Alfred Emery,	Nunda.
44	L. H. Emmons,	Norman, Iowa.
45	P. Kelly,	Nunda.
46	Erick Lee,	Albert Lea.
47	E. K. Flaskerud,	Albert Lea.
48	O. O. Opdahl,	Albert Lea.
49	F. F. Carter,	Glenville.
50	J. W. Abbott,	Gordonsville.
51	J. W. Manning,	London.
52	Wm. Flatt,	Glenville.
53	E. K. Pickett,	Albert Lea.
54	John Murtaugh,	Albert Lea.
55	O. J. Taylor,	Albert Lea.
56	Robert Hanf,	Armstrong.
57	Wm. Schneider,	Albert Lea.
58	A. Bottleson,	Albert Lea.
59	C. A. Conklin,	Gordonsville.
60	H. C. Nelson,	Hayward.
61	J. L. Garlock,	Alden.
62	H. H. Hanson,	Hartland.
63	H. C. Randall,	Freeborn.
64	Andrew Jenson,	Bath.
65	L. J. Hagen,	Glenville.
66	Elling Isaackson,	Albert Lea.
67	J. E. N. Backus,	Alden.
68	J. C. Ross,	Albert Lea.
69	Lewis Yost,	Armstrong.
70	E. A. Skiff,	Alden.
71	H. N. Lane,	Glenville.
72	Ole G. Anderson,	Lansing.
73	Pat Jordan,	Moscow.
74	John Kraushaar,	Mansfield.
75	R. W. Hatch,	Oakland.
76	John Donahue,	Nunda.
77	D. S. Hoyt,	Gordonsville.
78	G. Ryan,	Moscow.
79	O. C. Johnson,	Blooming Prairie.
80	N. R. Norton,	Alden.
81	A. H. Stevens,	Alden.
82	N. P. Peterson,	Bath.
83	O. R. Johnson,	Hayward.
84	Steuer O. Lee,	Norman, Iowa.
85	Wm. Beede,	Hartland.
86	Nels N. Loftus,	Norman, Iowa.
87	Henry Tunell,	Mansfield.
88	Ole Jenson,	Clark's Grove.
89	H. Babbitt,	Alden.
90	John Sheehan,	Hartland.
91	H. O. Foduess,	Hayward.
92	Albert Mattick,	Mansfield.
93	Thos. W. Wilson,	Alden.
94	Edward Thomas,	Austin.
95	A. F. Myatt,	Moscow.
96	Michael Murphy,	Austin.
97	Michael Fenton,	Geneva.
98	R. D. Burdick,	New Richland.
99	Loren Fessenden,	Alden.
100	P. H. Nelson,	Glenville.
101	H. J. Pickard,	Freeborn.
102	George Widman,	Albert Lea.
103	John Sullivan,	Hartland.
104	W. H. Stewart,	Gordonsville.
105	Ole N. Greshen,	Norman, Iowa.
106	Andrew O'Leary,	Blooming Prairie.
107	Ole A. Hammer,	Albert Lea.
108	J. A. Larson,	Norman, Iowa.
109	E. A. Wicks,	Hartland.
110	Ole I. Ellingson.	Albert Lea.

THE PATRONS OF HUSBANDRY.

This is a fraternal order, instituted in the interest of the farmer, with a ritual in some of its particulars bordering on the mythological.

Its origin was in Washington, D. C., in the year 1867, so that it does not, like Masonry, antedate the Christian era by four thousand years, or like the Knights of Carthage, go back nine thousand years before the Christian era. It claimed to be what it was, a modern institution, and it had a rapid growth and swept through the country attaining its growth and maturity in perhaps less than ten years.

In obedience to the great law of growth, maturity, old age, and death, which prevails in all living animated creation, it has already passed into a condition of senility, and while at this point its vitality may be equal to that in any other locality, it must at no distant day reach the final stage depicted by the great English poet:

"To-day he puts forth the tender leaves of hope, to-morrow bears his blushing honors thick upon him, the next day comes a frost, and when he thinks his greatness still aspiring, he falls like autumn leaves to enrich our mother earth."

A man who lives a few brief years on this earth and then passes away, may be of the greatest use if all opportunities are improved, and the world in each case should be the better for anyone's having lived in it. So with the Grange, for while no one could be made over by joining it, the teachings and tendency of the order was in the direction of an enlargement of ideas and an elevation of purposes among those who came under its benign influence. The Grange will be remembered for the good it has done.

FREEBORN COUNTY GRANGE.—This institution was organized on the 1st of February, 1876, the Centennial year, with the following list of officers:

J. F. Hall, Master; George R. Prescott, Overseer; E. K. Pickett, Lecturer; N. L. Laflin, Steward; C. E. Budlong, Assistant: Loren Marlett, Treasurer; William Morin, Secretary; A. J. Luther, Gate-Keeper; Mrs. A. H. Bartlett, Ceres; Mrs. David Gibson, Pomona; Mrs. O. G. Taylor, Flores; Mrs. D. Colman, Lady Assistant Steward.

As a matter of fact there are few counties where the grange has secured a more permanent foothold than in Freeborn county, for here it has not been permitted to lapse.

As revealing the aims and objects of the patrons of husbandry, the following papers are printed:

SUPPLEMENTAL REPORT OF THE COMMITTEE ON REORGANIZATION APPOINTED BY THE FREEBORN COUNTY GRANGE. In addition to those suggestions which relate solely to the reorganization of the Grange, your committee would recommend the establishment of local citizen's associations, whose members shall be pledged to vote only for men who can be relied upon to use the powers conferred upon them in procuring such legislation as will secure to individual shippers of produce, fuel, lumber, or merchandise, the same rates for freight and equal facilities for transportation from railroad companies with those accorded to associations, corporations, and rings, whose present exclusive privileges are detrimental to and often destructive of individual enterprise and healthy competition, and wherever these are destroyed the community is at the mercy of monopolists. This favoritism shown to these corporations and associations by some of the railway companies of the State, in granting them reduction on freights, or special facilities for shipping the commodities in which they deal, is too pernicious in its results to be permitted to go on unchecked; it is rapidly securing to capitalists and monopolists the business of the country, and enables them at their will to depress or inflate prices which should be left only to the natural gradations resulting from the laws of supply and demand.

Nothing can be more detrimental to the development of a new State than a system which creates and fosters monopolies. It crushes out the enterprises of individuals having but limited capital; it prevents that healthy growth of competition which builds up our towns and cities, as well as our agricultural interests, and which constitutes the only safe basis for a rapid and permanent development, and all past experience has taught us that as fast as monopolies are established and individual enterprise is repressed, our farmers, merchants, manufacturers, and citizens generally are too often forced to sell their produce for less than its actual value, and as often compelled to pay more for the necessaries of life than would be the case if freights and facilities for transportation were furnished to all upon equal terms, and a healthy competition thereby established.

The recent heavy losses entailed upon the farmers by the sudden and arbitrary change in the established grades of wheat by a few capitaists acting in the interest, or ostensibly, of the millers of the central portion of the State, is but another evidence of the necessity of compelling, by legal enactment, where such can be safely devised, the adoption of a policy less grasping in its selfishness, and more in accord with the spirit of justice. It is an insult to your intelligence to assert that the grade of wheat cannot be safely and justly estab- by legal enactment, while whisky is, and has been so graded for years. Had the grain producers of the State combined to establish the grade of wheat for their own profit and without regard to the rights or interests of the millers, we may safely conclude that the Millers' Association would not have hesitated long in applying to the law making power for relief and protection from unjust discrimination. The Millers' Association has assumed, arbitrarily, to establish the grade to suit themselves, by combining with foreign buyers; and with the railway companies they have been enabled to enforce their grade upon the farmers. They could not be expected to exercise such a power impartially, representing as they do only one of the parties in interest. They have assumed to exercise it, nevertheless, and the results have been felt by our farmers most oppressively. Having done this once they may be relied upon to do it as often as may suit their convenience, and with the same slight regard for justice or the interests of others, unless checked by the law-making power. We must firmly, though temperately, demand of our law-makers that they exercise their undoubted authority to settle by legal enactment, and in a spirit of equity and justice to all parties in interest, this question which one party without legal authority has assumed to settle with such gross and selfish injustice, and if it should prove necessary to curb the powers of our railway corporations in order to prevent them from aiding and abetting this or similar arbitrary and unjust schemes, then this also must be required.

In bringing your case before the people your committee would most earnestly press upon you the importance of couching your demands in temperate and moderate language. In appealing to the people for justice, see that you are guilty of no injustice. In securing protection, see to it that you do not become oppressors. In placing your own wrongs before the public, endeavor most sedulously to avoid wronging others. Under all circumstances let your conduct and language be such as will convince your opponents that, while you fully appreciate your position as the representatives of the leading industry and interest of Minnesota, you recognize the railroad, milling, and manufacturing interests of the State as only subordinate to the agricultural interests in a pecuniary sense: that your several interests are so inextricably interwoven that one cannot be injured without ultimately reflecting injury upon all, and that your sole purpose is to procure such legislation as will secure to each and every citizen protection against the oppressions that inevitably result from the unjust discriminations of which you complain.

The constitutions of the State and of the United States guarantee to every citizen equal rights before the law. The policy and the management of our corporations, whose chartered existence is by the power of the law, must be made to conform to the principles of the constitution. These principles must be enforced against all who would oppress. The hardships and injustice of the past, forecasting as they do an ominous future, if these abuses are allowed to grow, seem imperatively to demand prompt and determined action in securing our inalienable rights of equality and justice before the law, and from all the creatures of the law.

The combined interests of every right minded citizen demand with a force equally imperative that the forms we would inaugurate should not be dwarfed or restricted by the narrowed interests, or weakened by the advocacy of a single class or calling. "Equal Rights" for the few, too often degenerate into oppression for the many. Demands for "equal rights and exact justice to all," have never yet in this land been successfully resisted, nor will they ever be opposed, save by those whose selfishness or avarice is greater than their patriotism.

The wide-spread corruption and extravagance, and the too common incompetence of public officials, are also common evils which call for immediate remedy, and here also your interests as a class and as individuals are identical with those of every citizen who does not live by dishonest means.

Your committee, while convinced of the necessity of your united action in support of these reforms, is deeply impressed with the importance of your moving in the matter, controlled only by the broadest and most liberal views. In seeking public reform neither class associations nor secret societies can ever hope successfully to lead; it matters not what the class may be, whether farmers, artisans, mechanics, manufacturers, or an aristocracy either of descent or wealth, the legislation moulded by a class will surely end in arrogating to the class in power, privileges or immunities that will be but public robberies or public oppressions.

Bear also in mind that however pure and noble may be the object sought to be attained by a secret association, those who are not admitted to its conclaves are necessarily ignorant of their motives, and ignorance begets distrust and suspicion. The American people are wisely jealous of secret associations when they discover them endeavoring to secure political power or special legislation. A natural good sense, love of liberty and justice, a desire to do what is right and fair for all, characterizes our citizens, both native and foreign, and constitutes them a safe tribunal for appeal where public benefits or reforms are desired. If these premises are correct, it follows that political success through the Patrons of Husbandry cannot be expected, and ought not to be desired. Neither would it be wise to act solely as farmers. These questions appeal to your citizenship for solution, and you can never hope successfully to accomplish their settlement, except by your joint action as citizens, with citizens of all classes and nationalities, using the organizing and harmonizing powers of the order to aid the citizens' organizations in working for the public good.

The members of the Grange should never lose sight of the great fact that the prosperity of a nation must be dependent upon, and indeed consists in the prosperity of her citizens as a whole, and not in the prosperity of a single class, not even when that class constitutes a majority of the people. As a rule, the greater the variety of industries, the greater and more enduring the prosperity. Above all things you especially should bear in mind that the success of the producer is proportioned to the number of consumers, and the nearer the consumers are to the producers the greater the profit. Your financial interests are enhanced by the building up of home markets and local interest, mechanical, manufacturing, and commercial, should be encouraged by you, for these increase the consumption and price of your products, and decrease the cost of your supplies. The ignoring of a wise and generous policy in this direction at a time when the inexperience of the Grange led to its capture by demagogues, arrayed against you all other classes of your fellow-citizens. For the future we must advise with them, act with, and, more important still, for them and their interests, conjointly with our own, ever exercising the greatest prudence and caution in the establishment of our own rights, that we do not trespass upon the rights of others, and trusting implicitly, as we assuredly may, that in working for the general good, we cannot fail to reap our share of the general prosperity. It would be unpatriotic to work for less, it would be extremely selfish to strive for more.

CHAS. W. BALLARD,
W. G. BARNES,
GEO. H. PRESCOTT,
B. W. PRITCHARD,
} Com.

The following song, by Mrs. Mary F. Tucker, of Omro, Wis., received the prize from the National Grange of Patrons of Husbandry, as being the best song for the order. Mrs. Tucker had many able competitors, and the decision in her favor was made by Mr. Alden, of Harper's Magazine. We give the song for the benefit of our many Grange readers:

"'Tis ours to guard a sacred trust,
We shape a heaven-born plan;
The noble purpose, wise and just,
To aid our fellow man.
From Maine to California's slope,
Resounds the reaper's song;
"We come to build the nation's hope,
To slay the giant Wrong."

Too long have Avarice and Greed,
With coffers running o'er,
Brought sorrow, and distress and need
To Labor's humble door.
From Maine to California's slope,
Resounds the reaper's song;
"We come to build the nation's hope,
To slay the giant Wrong."

A royal road to place and power
Have rank and title been;
We herald the auspicious hour,
When honest Worth may win.
From Maine to California's slope,
Resounds the reaper's song;
"We come to build the nation's hope,
To slay the giant Wrong."

Let every heart and hand unite
In the benignant plan;
The noble purpose just and right,
To aid our fellow man.
From Maine to California's slope,
Resounds the reaper's song;
"We come to build the nation's hope,
To slay the giant Wrong." "

Accounts of township Granges appear in their proper places.

In the summer of 1882, a pic-nic was held at Itasca of which here is the newspaper account:

"THE COUNTY GRANGE FEAST.—A very pleasant and enjoyable time was spent at Mr. and Mrs. Dominick's residence—on Dr. Burnham's farm—last Tuesday by the Grangers of the county. Nearly every Grange in the county was represented, even though the weather was thratening and farmers generally busy haying. The session of the county grange was held in the forenoon when the business thereof was transacted. At one o'clock those present sat down to a sumptuous feast, the long table under a lot of magnificent trees, so invitingly spread with good things of this world, which had been prepared by the thrifty wives and daughters of the members of the grange, was greatly relished and enjoyed by the participators.

The merry laugh and cheery conversation of the Patrons as they feasted on the bounties of Providence, was refreshing and did one's soul good to behold.

After dinner speech making was in order. Various subjects having been assigned to a number of enterprising Patrons for discussion. First on the list being "Onion Culture," which was well handled by Mr. Daniel Prescott, of Oak Hill Grange, who has had long experience in raising onions, and the many valuable suggestions of the aged gentleman will no doubt be of profit to his listeners.

"Potatoe Culture," by W. G. Barnes of Shell Rock, was the next subject, which proved an interesting theme for discussion. Mr. Barnes has ten acres of potatoes and related his mode of planting, cultivating, and care of the same. Senator Johnson, G. H. Prescott, and others also spoke on this subject, giving valuable hints.

J. C. Frost, of Oak Hill Grange, handled the subject of "Market Gardening and Strawberry Culture" in a manner that elicited much interest that will be valuable to all his hearers. Mr. Frost has been remarkably successful in both the above branches of agriculture, and spoke from actual experience.

E. K. Pickett, of Itasca, handled the subject of the "Grange on Politics," without gloves, giving his views straight from the shoulder. Above all things, said Mr. Pickett, we should not be bound to any party with such strong ties that should prevent us from voting for the best men—regardless of party Mr. Pickett is an independent thinker and holds radical views on most all subjects, and is disposed to look upon the present management of governmental affairs with distrust. Although we differ with Mr. Pickett in many of his views, yet we give him credit for being honest, admiring his frankness and outspoken sentiments. Dr. Ballard gave a very interesting account of the condition of the agricultural classes in England, and observations of his trip through that country. Judge Bartlett, Rev. Mr. Gowdy, Dr. Burnham, and others made short speeches and everything passed off very pleasantly, the meeting closing with singing, after which the Patrons dispersed and started for their various homes, feeling that it had been good to be there. The next general meeting of the Grange will be held the fore part of October, due notice of which will be given hereafter."

RAILROADS.

The county may be said to be well supplied with railroads, as there is an east and west line, a north and south line, and a line running from Albert Lea in a southwest direction. The Southern Minnesota road, which is so intimately connected with this region in its earlier history, and which was the first to open up the county to steam transportation, will be more fully sketched than the others, which have been constructed since railroad building was much easier than formerly.

THE SOUTHERN MINNESOTA RAILROAD.—This trunk line started as the Root River Valley road, finally assumed its present name, and is now a division of the Chicago, Milwaukee & St. Paul railway company's system of roads, which is said to have the largest number of miles of any road in America under one management.

It has its eastern terminus at La Crosse, and entering Fillmore county at Rushford, follows the Root River as far as Lanesboro. Here it extends toward the west with a southern deflection, and leaves the county near the center of the western boundary. It has stations at convenient distances along the route. The early history of this enterprise is one crowded with vicissitudes.

Soon after Brownsville, in Houston county, was settled, a charter was obtained with the mouth-filling title of "Mississippi & Missouri Railroad Company." That road was to start up the Wild-cat Valley, and it proved to be a "wild cat" scheme, coming into the world in a still-born condition.

The Root River Valley Railroad Company was organized under territorial auspices. Clark W. Thompson, of Hokah, T. B. Twiford, of Chatfield, and T. B. Stoddard, of La Crosse, and their associates, whoever they were, kept the breath of life in this corporation for several years.

On the 3rd of November, 1856, it having got to be the "Root River and Southern Minnesota Company," the officers met at their usual headquarters in Chatfield, and the places of directors whose terms of office had expired were filled; the board then stood as follows: Clark W. Thompson, President; C A Stevens, Vice-President; H. L. Edwards, Secretary; T. B. Twiford, Treasurer, H. W. Holley, Chief Engineer. The Executive Committee were T. B. Twiford, Edward Thompson, T. B. Stoddard, William B. Gere, and T. J. Stafford.

Soon after this a survey was made by the chief engineer, H. W. Holley, from the Mississippi River to Hokah.

On the 8th of December, 1856, a public meeting of those favorable to the construction of the road was held in Chatfield. The meeting was called to order by Wm. B. Gere, who stated the objects of the meeting, and gave a brief history of the enterprise, stating that it was chartered in 1854, and that $50,000 had been subscribed to the stock. G. W. Willis was appointed chairman of the meeting, and Edward Dexter was selected for Secretary. Earnest speeches were made by several gentlemen. A committee was appointed to solicit subscriptions to defray the expenses of an agent to Washington, to secure, if possible, congressional aid in the form of a land grant. It was understood that this committee succeeded in raising about $1,300 in Chatfield, and James M. Cavanaugh, afterwards member of Congress, was appointed to proceed to Washington and look after a land grant. The thanks of the meeting were voted to Col. Thomas B. Stoddard of La Crosse, for his untiring energy in the service of the enterprise.

It will thus be seen what service was done by Chatfield during the struggling infancy and weakness of this corporation, and how remorselessly it was passed by when the company had secured strength and power. Ingratitude is the most despicable sin that exists. The land grant passed Congress, and became a law on the last day of President Pierce's administration, on the 4th of March, 1857, and was among the last bills signed by the New Hampshire President. As there were other similar land grants for roads in various parts of the territory, an extra session of the Legislature was called by Governor Gorman, to meet on the 10th of May, 1857, to pass the appropriate acts on the subject.

On the 3d of April the railroad company had a meeting at La Crescent, and a survey by the Chief Engineer, Mr. Holley, was ordered to be made at once, to begin at or near St. Peter, and to run thence east to LaCrosse. The party accordingly started to make this survey from Chatfield to St. Peter, on the 6th of April, 1857. At the meeting of the Legislature it granted to the Southern Minnesota Railroad Company the land pertaining to the line from LaCrescent to Rochester, also from St. Paul up the Minnesota valley to the Iowa State line.

The survey from St. Peter to LaCrescent was completed early in June, but in the meantime a transfer of the stock of the company had been made by the directors to a Wisconsin company, the Milwaukee and LaCrosse, which continued the survey, but did nothing whatever in the way of grading. And thus it remained, until in 1858. The five million loan bill became a law, and then the company graciously graded twenty miles, from La Crescent to Houston, and there it stopped.

In 1859, there was a kind of a supplementary collapse, and various roads went into bankruptcy, this among the others. About this time there was an atempt to float some railroad currency, but it was not a brilliant success.

In 1869, C. D. Sherwood, Clark W. Thompson, H. W. Holley, Dr. L. Miller, Hiram Walker, and their associates, reorganized the company and obtained from the Legislature of the State the franchises and lands of the old company, upon the condition that ten miles should be completed in one year. But the time elapsed and the ten miles did not materialize, and the next year the Legislature kindly gave the company another year, and this time it succeeded in making the trip, and having the requisite ten miles in running condition by the 25th of December, 1866. During the previous winter an effort had been made to secure an additional grant of land from Houston to the western boundary of the State, which was successful, and this aid was secured on the 4th of July, 1866.

From this time the progress of the road was rapid. As above stated, the road to Houston was opened and running in 1866; to Rushford and Lanesboro in 1868; from Ramsey to Wells in 1869; and from Lanesboro the road was pushed on to Ramsey in 1870, the total distance being 167 miles. It will thus be seen that the road was finally constructed and put in operation by practically the same men who conceived the project in territorial days, and obtained, through their efforts, the donations that made its success possible, and without which it might never have been built. As to the *personnel* of the early and the later management; Col. T. B. Stoddard, of La Crosse; C. W. Thompson, of Hokah, and his brother, Edward Thompson, of the same place;

and Hon. H. W. Holley, the Chief Engineer, of Fillmore county, who were on the board of directors in 1856, stuck to its varying fortunes and destinies through good and evil report till in 1870, the first division from La Crosse to Winnebago City was completed.

As to the last land grant from Congress in 1866, without which the road could not, or would not have been extended west of Houston, perhaps the most credit should be given to Charles D. Sherwood, Dr. Luke Miller, C. G. Wyckoff, and D. B. Sprague, who joined their fortunes with the enterprise at these organization in 1865.

In relation to the route of the road west of Lanesboro, where it leaves the Root River Valley, the inside history would be remarkably rich reading if faithfully portrayed. Chatfield being on the main stream, had no shadow of doubt as to its going there. Preston, the county seat, confidently expected the road. Either way would have avoided the terrible grade west of Lanesboro, which will forever require a "Pusher" to overcome. But in view of "other hearts that would bleed," the story perhaps better be left untold in this volume. It is not unlikely, at some time not very distant, when this road shall become a part of the "Chicago, Milwaukee & St. Paul International line to the Pacific," that the bed of the road may be changed to follow one of the branches of the Root River from Lanesboro.

STATISTICS.

Crop Reports.—The returns made by the Marshals who gathered the statistics from the farmers for the United States census bureau, do not in all respects coincide with those taken by the State. They are, however, as reliable as can be secured. The acreage and crop of the four leading cereals of the county for 1880 was as follows:

	Acreage.	*Bushels.*
Wheat	103,783	1,143,879
Oats	20,445	747,030
Corn	14,587	582,514
Barley	3.015	72,647

Freeborn county is one of the thirteen in Minnesota that produces more than a million bushels of wheat annually, being the second on the list; Goodhue county raising 2,740,962 and Freeborn 1,444,527 bushels. As to the average yield in the several counties, Otter Tail takes the lead with 17.68 bushels to the acre, then Polk with 16.40, Rice 15.25, Stearns 14.73, Waseca, 14.45, Goodhue 14.42, Blue Earth 13.43, and Freeborn 12.96. The lowest on the list being Fillmore county, which has run down to 7.76. In 1881, as compared with the previous year, there was a decrease in acreage of 5,637 acres.

Rye; only 117 acres was given to this crop, and 2,977 bushels produced.

Buckwheat; 32 acres and 372 bushels.

Potatoes; 1,047 acres and 111,111 bushels, or 93.83 buchels per acre.

Beans; 10 acres, 165 bushels.

Sugar cane; 102 acres; 9,874 gallons of syrup; an average of 96.80 per acre. Cultivated hay, 1,479 acres, 2,087 tons.

The above are the principal crops raised in the county.

Whole number of farms of the various sizes, 1,833.

Whole number of acres, 158,038.

Apple trees in Freeborn county. The number growing in 1881 was 28,983, with 6,117 bearing trees, producing about 2,298 bushels.

Grapes. The numbes of grape vines in bearin the county was 442. Showing that little attention is paid to this fruit.

Tobacco. A small amount of this leaf is produced each year, a few hundred pounds.

Honey. The reports give about 3,000 pounds a year.

Milch cows. The number of cows must be constantly increasing; at present there are upwards of 7,000, producing 545,116 pounds of butter and 16,450 pounds of cheese.

Sheep and wool. Number of sheep sheared, 4,652; pounds of wool produced, 17,308.

Horses. All ages, 7,633.

Cows. All ages, 8,100; all other cattle, 631; total cattle, all ages, 16,186,

Mules, 211.

Hogs, 6,896.

Total valuation of personal property in the county, $1,144,666.

County valuation:

1860	$334,729
1861	469,639
1862	423,904
1863	483,781
1864	711,310
1865	780,640
1866	973,831

Productions of Freeborn county during the year 1869:

	Bushels.
Wheat	334,049
Corn	160,698
Oats	200,000
Barley	2,124
Potatoes	72,621
Sorghum, gallons	10,890
Hay, tons	25,859
Wool, pounds	12,140
Butter, pounds	173,370

ASSESSORS' RETURNS FOR 1882.—A glance over the assessors returns of Freeborn county, for the year 1882, gives some interesting figures in regard to the wealth in the different towns in the county, both personal and real. The total valuation for the year named, as returned by the assessors, is as follows:

	Real	Personal
London	$165,682	$34,523
Shell Rock	191,281	75,904
Freeman	108,311	33,930
Nunda	134,846	44,391
Mansfield	141,443	39,866
Oakland	159,717	49,063
Hayward	142,646	39,388
Albert Lea	169,960	50,472
Pickerel Lake	128,912	37,308
Alden	153,460	36,588
Moscow	163,137	36,733
Riceland	153,176	49,772
Bancroft	226,886	67,510
Manchester	168,672	45,807
Carlston	154,125	38,640
Newry	114,871	43,766
Geneva	108,461	30,453
Bath	145,596	32,407
Hartland	131,127	48,371
Freeborn	97,993	38,941
Albert Lea City	408,604	143,291

It will be seen that the town of Shell Rock leads in personal property, while Bancroft surpasses all others in real estate. Freeborn has the lowest valuation on real property, and Geneva would go to the bottom of the column in the worth of its personal property.

From the crop statistics we find the following, which will be of interest to our readers:

	1881	1882
Apple trees, growing	28,540	31,989
Apple trees, bearing	6,902	7,771
Apples, bushels	3,293	....
Grape Vines, No	663	643
Grapes, pounds	1,565	....
Tobacco, pounds	541	....
Sheep, No	3,767	4,267
Wool, pounds	17,866	18,594
Cows, No	7.042	6,623
Butter, pounds	518,329	....
Cheese, pounds	23,780	
Bees, hives	82	....
Honey, pounds	556	....

Those places in the 1882 column in which a dash is placed could not be returned by the assessor, as in most cases the crop is yet growing.

RETURNS FOR 1881-82.

	1881.	1882.
Wheat, acres	72,537	62,727
Wheat, bushels	835,937	......
Oats, acres	16,025	17,427
Oats, bushels	514,591	......
Corn, acres	14,449	22,132
Corn, bushels	522,072	......
Potatoes, acres	1,048	1,438
Potatoes bushels	109,124	......
Barley, acres	2,398	3,992
Barley, bushels	54,765	......
Flax, acres	738	779
Tame hay, acres	1,528	2,502
Total acreage	109,348	110,776
Timothy, bushels	927	......
Clover, bushels	42	......
Apple trees	20,660	31,839
Apples, bushels	3,273	......
Sheep	3,767	4,269
Wool, pounds	17,866	18,594
Cows	7,042	6,023
Butter, pounds	58,339	6,623
Cheese	23,780	......

It will be seen from the above that there is a marked increase in the acreage of all products except wheat, which shows a great falling off.

TAXES.

The following is the amount of county and state taxes, and penalty and interest, collected from March 1st to June 1st, 1882:

County taxes	$13,471 68
Penalty and interest	95 56
State taxes	4,731 71
Total	$18,298 94

AMOUNT DUE EACH TOWN.

London	$ 348 17
Shell Rock	1,125 69
Freeman	423 63
Nunda	361 21
Mansfield	236 50
Oakland	133 60
Hayward	262 34
Albert Lea	1,584 35
Pickerel Lake	677 21
Alden	1,337 75
Moscow	198 42
Riceland	324 31
Bancroft	323 03
Manchester	244 80
Carlston	461 21
Newry	18 89
Geneva	297 53
Bath	215 67
Hartland	658 20
Freeborn	281 92
City of Albert Lea	4,272 36
Total	$13,786 80
Less R. R. interest	4,373 31
Leaves to credit of towns	$9,413 49

POPULATION IN 1880.

Albert Lea City	1,966
Albert Lea Township	878
Alden Township	474
Alden village	235
Bancroft	959
Bath	919
Carlston	500
Freeborn	414
Freeborn village	72
Freeman	772
Geneva	454
Hartland	699
Hayward	659
London	614
Manchester	784
Mansfield	552
Moscow	650
Newry	737
Nunda	776
Oakland	629
Pickerel Lake	530
Riceland	783
Shell Rock	1,013
Total	16,069

The population is thus divided:

Male	8,528
Female	7,542
Natives	10,193
Foreign	5,876
White	16,058
Colored	11

A comparison with other census years makes this showing:

1860	3,369
1865	5,688
1870	10,578
1875	13,189
1880	16,069

The greatest increase in any semi-decade was between the close of the war and 1870. As to the growth of the capital of the county, this is the record:

1860, the whole town had	262
1870	1,167
1875	1,897
1880, including the town	2,844

Albert Lea is the twenty-first city in the State, in point of population. But it may be a consolation to know that there are twenty cities yet smaller, that have a population of not less than 1,000.

Taxes in Freeborn county in 1880:

State tax	$ 9,433.18
School tax	26,142.32
County tax	17,252.96
Town tax	3,481.50
All other taxes	19,837.10
Valuation of the county in 1880	5,229,134.00
Valuation of the county in 1881	5,238,555.00
Valuation of county seat in 1880	494,955.00
Valuation of county seat in 1881	495,021.00

THE INTERNAL REVENUE, collected in the first district, in which Freeborn county is situated. The office is at Albert Lea, and Dr. A. C. Wedge is the collector. The report is for the year 1881:

Collection on lists	$ 7,829.71
Spirit stamps	110.70
Tobacco and cigars	24,183.92
Beer stamps	42,162.64
Special tax stamps	40,342.87
Making a grand total of	$114,729.84

For the year ending June 30, 1882:

Amount collected from the sale of beer stamps	$ 43,854.95

Amount collected from the sale of cigars and tobacco..............	27,669 62
Amount collected from the sale of special tax.....................	11,660.18
Amount collected from banks and bankers..........................	11,419.47
Amount collected from sale of check and adhesive stamps............	765.19
Amount collected from penalties, costs, etc........................	458.18
Total collections for the year....$125,836.59	

This is an increase over the collections for the year ended June 30, 1881, of about $9,000. Of the tax-payers of the district there are: Brewers 29; cigar manufacturers 23, tobacco manufacturers 21, rectifiers 1, wholesale liquor dealers 3, wholesale dealers in malt liquor 3, retail liquor dealers 86, dealers in manufactured tobacco 2,088.

METEOROLOGICAL.—It is difficult to convey an idea of the character of the average weather of any locality without burdening pages with barometrical and theometrical statistics. But a few general points which may serve to give an imperfect impression of what one has to encounter in this section will be presented. The highest range of the thermometer and the lowest in each month for the year 1881 was as follows;

	HIGHEST	LOWEST
January....................	35.	.25
February...................	38.	.09
March......................	51.	9.
April......................	78.	10.
May........................	85.	36.
June.......................	92.	50.
July.......................	91.	55.
August.....................	96.	52.
September..................	91.	40.
October....................	71.	30.
November...................	57.	02.
December...................	52.	00.

This gives an annual mean temperature of 48.08, which, if correct, for a series of years, gives an idea of the temperature of water from the earth a a depth of forty feet, where it is not affected by atmospherical influences. The amount of rainfall for the year was 39.16 inches. The number of days on which rain or snow fell was 167, which was above the average.

The autumn months in Minnesota are described as the most charming months of all the year, "when the golden grain is gathered by the farmer, when his hay in the stack has been heaped high in the sweet scented fields, and the horny-handed granger has nothing to do but sit on the fence in the shade and shake hands with the political candidates as they pass along in a soothingly sweet scented smiling procession."

FREEBORN COUNTY BIBLE SOCIETY.

The annual meeting of the Society was held according to appointment, at the M. E. Church, on the 28th day of May, 1882, at which time the following officers were elected: President, Isaac Botsford; Vice-President, Rev. N. F. Hoyt; Secretary, W. C. McAdams; Treasurer, D. R. P. Hibbs; Executive Committee, R. F. Sulzer, Rev. R. B. Abbott, and Rev. N. F. Hoyt.

A collection of $22.75 was taken during the day for the benefit of the society, of which $15.-60 was given in the Presbyterian church in the forenoon, and $7.15 at the meeting in the evening.

The following is an abstract of the Secretary's report of the affairs of the Society for the year ending May 28th, viz:

The Bibles on hand at date of annual meeting, May 30th, 1881..............	$103,07
Bibles and Testaments since received...	34.70
Total..........................	$137.77
Bibles sold during the year............	$ 35.24
Discount on Testaments "marked down"	2.35
Bibles turned over to Sulzer "damaged" for distribution....................	3.10
Shortage on invoice and lost in money..	8.33
Bibles delivered on life membership certificates..........................	1.60
Bibles on hand.........................	87.15
Total..........................	$137.77
Cash on hand at date of last annual meeting....................................	$ 29.13
Amount collected at anniversary........	20.87
Amount received on sale of Bibles......	35.24
Total	$ 85.24
By donation to American Bible Society per vote of annual meeting..........	$ 20,87
By amount paid American Bible Society June 1..............................	29.13
By amount allowed in exchange of Bibles and for freight on Bibles............	1.12
By amount paid for moving books	35
By commission on sales. ..	3.52

By expenses...	1.25
Cash on hand...	29.00
Total...	$85.24
Account with American Bible Society June 30, 1881. Bibles and Testaments received...	$ 34.70
June 21, 1881. Cash	29.13
Due American Bible Society.	$ 5.57

PRESENT CONDITION.

Books on hand...	$ 87.15
Cash from last year..	29.00
Cash collection...	22.75
Total amount cash....	$51.75
Less indebtedness....	5.57
Balance....	$46.18

CHAPTER L.

FREEBORN COUNTY IN THE WAR OF THE REBELLION —THE INDIAN OUTBREAK.—NAMES OF SOLDIERS WHO PARTICIPATED.

When the war had been actually proclaimed, and the people began to realize that most of the southern States, were actually in rebellion against the government, there was no hesitation in actually starting the work to meet the demand for men with which to create an army. The State at this time was only three years old, and this county had been settled but about five or six years, and few of the people had got out of their primitive shanties, and it will ever be a matter of profound astonishment how so many men were found to thus take their lives in their hands and go to the front to assist in forming the walls of steel to repel the enemies of the American Union.

Many of the people of the county were born in the old world, but they had been educated with faith in the New, and only those who have been through a like ordeal can understand the bitter experience of most of them in procuring means to tear themselves away from old companions to come to this land of the free, and the home of the brave; but having come, and began to taste the fruits of their own labor, with no grasping landlord to secure the usufruct of the land and reap the reward of toil, they were alarmed when these new found rights and privileges were thus jeopardized. And with the true instincts of freedom and manhood, in response to an intelligent interpretation of the laws of self preservation, and in a spirit meriting the highest commendation, they enlisted to protect their adopted country. Their heroism, valor, and devotion, on many a well fought field, attest their title to the proud appellation of American citizens, and as time goes on their names will be more and more tenderly regarded, and their deeds will be recounted with greater and greater reverence, and will be pointed at with pride by coming generations, as worthy of emulation.

That such a young county should be able to fill its quota as against older communities, before the land itself was subjugated, or the people had provided the comforts of home for themselves, will ever excite the liveliest satisfaction in the hearts the people of the nation.

The usual scenes transpiring all over the country were occurring here, in a form of course modified by the circumstances. Knots of men in earnest conversation, men reading aloud the latest news to interested groups, public meetings, and anon, the shrill, ear-piercing fife, and the roll of the martial drum, were heard in these western wilds, and finally, the tramp of the citizen soldiery with the sharp command, giving a realization of war's wrinkled front, was actually abroad in the land.

One of the first meetings called was in Shell Rock on the 1st of May, 1861. Manly C. Isham was chosen chairman, and H. L. Dow was appointed secretary. Rousing speeches were made and war committees appointed, as follows:

Daniel Giffard, Orlando McFall, Manly C. Isham, Luther Phelps, George Gardner, J. A. Knapp and others.

On the 11th of May, the people of Albert Lea met and raised a liberty pole, and then repaired to the Webber House and held a mass meeting. E. K. Pickett was chairman, and William Morin was secretary. It was resolved to form a rifle company, and a committee on resolutions was appointed as follows: E. O. Stacy, E. P. Skinner, and A. W. White. E. K. Pickett, Samuel Eaton, H. D. Brown, Benjamin Frost, D. G. Parker and others, made patriotic addresses, and forty-six persons were enrolled.

"Be but the foe arrayed,
And war's wild trumpet blown,
Cold is the heart that has not made
His country's cause his own,"

was the sentiment aroused at this meeting.

Arrangements were made to hold meetings all over the county, in each prominent place: Shell Rock, Nunda, Freeborn, Moscow, and other points. At these four places two men were to go to each, and for the four men each had two meetings. These speakers were two Democrats and two Republicans, but some of them weakened when the supreme moment came, and as a matter of fact E. C. Stacy went through the campaign without faltering, and did good service in firing up the northern heart. The story is told that at one of these meetings, at a large schoolhouse, he got warmed up and was pacing the floor and gesticulating with frenzied eloquence, when he became conscious of a boisterous uproar in the audience, and on turning he saw a man who had been carried away by the enthusiasm of the moment, following him as he walked, and in frantic imitation of the speaker, reasserting his postulates! And the story may as well be told here, that only a few years ago the judge, who was counsel in a case in town, made an eloquent plea for his client, and a German who was on the jury was visibly affected by it, who, on being questioned about it afterwards, said "Oh yes, he made that same speech when raising troops for the war."

At these war meetings the girls would sing patriotic songs and the recruiting books would be opened. The second meeting in Albert Lea was in the Webber House and was well attended.

Judge Stacy went in person with two companies of the Fourth regiment to Fort Snelling.

Our sketches of war incidents must necessarily be desultory and disconnected, owing to the incompleteness of the record.

Capt. Lewis McKune was killed at Bull Run, and the people began to realize that putting down the rebellion was no holiday affair; and that no three months, as at first supposed, would close, the war.

In the summer of 1861, Sergeant J. E. Hall of Co. K, which was stationed at Fort Snelling, was here on recruiting service.

The quota of the State in September was 3,950.

In December, the ladies of Freeborn County had manufactured in an eastern city, a regulation flag of fine material and best workmanship. A delegation carried it to Fort Snelling, and in their behalf Frank Hall, of Albert Lea, with pertinent and patriotic words, presented it to Co. F, of the Fifth Regiment Minnesota Volunteers, which was composed of Freeborn county men. It was gallantly received in behalf of the company by Captain White, who acknowledged its protecting folds the harbinger of victory, and assured the fair donors that it should ever be borne aloft "until the last armed foe expires," and "that when sad and dispirited, the sight of this banner, and the remembrance of the fair donors, would rally their latent energies, and again their drooping spirits should revive and new courage inspire their hearts." As a matter of history the folds of this flag were never sullied by those who fought under its protecting care.

Lieutenant William F. Wheeler, of Company F, Fourth Regiment was presented with a service, sword, and belt by his fellow citizens.

In addition to those who enlisted in Minnesota Regiments in 1861, there were 46 Norwegians who went to Wisconsin to go into a regiment of their own nationality there. In order to get, if possible, these names, a letter was directed to Chandler P. Chapman, the assistant Adjutant General of Wisconsin, who, in reply submitted the names found in the list of soldiers credited from Freeborn county as far as they were recorded. He mentions that it is not unlikely that others may have gone into other regiments.

Company C was organized by Captain Frank Hall, at Fort Snelling, in March, 1862, and was reorganized as a veteran regiment in March, 1864, at Vicksburg, Mississippi, and mustered out at Demopolis, Alabama, on the 6th of September, 1865, having participated in most, if not all, the battles of the Southwest. Captain Hall was promoted to Major of the Fifth Regiment on the 31st of August, 1862.

The first Company raised in the county of Freeborn was by Captain A. W. White.

Here is a recruiting notice that will be read with interest:

"ATTENTION!

FIVE HUNDRED RECRUITS WANTED

FOR THE

FIFTH REGIMENT, MINNESOTA VOLUNTEERS.

To all Recruits enlisted by recruiting Officers, to serve for three years, or the war, in old regiments now organized, whose term of service expired in 1864 or 1865, there will be paid one month's pay in advance, and in addition a bounty and premium amounting to $302 as follows:

On being mustered into the United States service, under this authority and before leaving the recruiting station or depot to join his company or regiment, shall receive one month's advance pay	$13 00
First installment of bounty.............	60 00
Premium...........................	2 00
Total pay before joining the Regiment...	$70 00
At the first regular pay day, or two months after mustering, an additional installment will be paid..................	40 00
At the first regular pay day, after six months' service, an additional installment of bounty will be paid........	40 00
At the first regular pay day, after the end of the first year's service, an additional installment of bounty will be paid..	40 00
At the first regular pay day after eighteen month's service, an additional installment of bounty will be paid........	40 00
At the first regular pay day after two year's services, an additional installment of bounty will be paid........	40 00
At the expiration of three years' service, or to any soldier enlisting under this authority, who may be honorably discharged after two years' service, the remainder of the bounty will be paid.	40 00

II. If the government shall not require these troops for the full period of three years, and they be mustered honorably out of the service before the expiration of their term of enlistment, they shall receive, on being mustered out, the whole amount of bounty remaining unpaid, the same as if the full term had been served.

III. The legal heirs of soldiers who die in the service shall be entitled to receive the whole bounty remaining unpaid at time of the soldier's death.

To persons desirous of entering the United States' service, this fine Regiment now offers an opportunity. The advantages of entering an old and well drilled regiment, are too well known to be enumerated. The wishes of persons enlisting, who have friends or relatives in the regiment, will be regarded as to the companies to which they wish to be assigned.

The present presents a most favorable opportunity to any man who contemplates joining the service, especially those liable to draft should at once join this brave regiment that has already earned lasting honor by its courage and valor.

CAPT. T. J. SHEEHAN,
Recruiting officer, 5th Minn.

Volunteers will report to me at A. Armstrong's office at Albert Lea, Freeborn Co."

As far as the county was concerned, the government left recruiting affairs to individual exertion and town action. In the county records no mention is made relating to the rebellion until September, when George S. Ruble was authorized to appropriate the sum of fifty-five dollars for the benefit of the family of George Conrad of the Second Minnesota Cavalry, and forty dollars for the benefit of the widow of George W. Gile, late of company F, Fourth Cavalry. Wannemaker's widow, late of company E, Tenth regiment, was also furnished a small sum, and other sums for like purposes were also appropriated at this time.

At the annual meeting in January, 1865, a petition was presented from E. P. Hathaway and others, asking the Board to vote a bounty of $300 to pay volunteers to help fill the quota, but it was rejected. A petition of citizens of Moscow to the same effect met a like fate.

In this war sketch it must be recorded as to how some of the soldiers' families lived during their absence at the front. While Major Hall was in the army Mr. C. M. Hewitt managed his store and did an enormous business. All the soldiers' wives bought their goods there, and those who were in Hall's command would remunerate him at the pay table when the paymaster came around.

On the 1st of February, 1864, the quota of Freeborn county stood as follows: Whole number demanded, 273; number actually furnished, 292; making nineteen more than the regular quota.

In November the impending draft was suspended until the 5th of January, 1864.

The following from a paper at that date will show what occupied the attention of the journals of the day, and how things were accomplished.

"THE DRAFT POSTPONED.

The result of Gov. Swift's visit to Washington was made manifest in the following telegrams received at St. Paul on the 6th, which will be received with general satisfaction throughout the State:

"WASHINGTON, Nov. 7, 11 P. M.

Capt. T. M. Saunders, A. A. P. M.

The quota for Minnesota has been so much reduced by former excess of volunteers since the draft was ordered, that no draft will be made in that State before the fifth day of January, 1864, and only then in case she fails to raise her quota of 300,000 volunteers called for by the President.

(Signed) JAMES B. FRY,
Provost Marshal General."

The following also to Captain Saunders:

"WASHINGTON, Nov. 7, 11:40 A. M.

Capt. T. M. Saunders.—If a State furnishes her full quota of volunteers under the President's call of October 17th, 1863, for three hundred thousand, the draft ordered for the first of January, 1864 will not take place in that State.

JAMES B. FRY."

A few other specimens of the prevailing literature of the day will be appended for the sake of the information they contain.

The detail for men was from the congressional districts and Freeborn was in the first.

THE QUOTAS.

"The Provost Marshal of this District has completed the enumeration of the township sub-district in this Congressional District, carried out the number of men enrolled in the first and second classes respectively, and forwarded the same to the War Department.

In this district there are 243 sub-districts distributed among the counties as follows, and numbered from No. 1, in Houston Co., to No. 243 in Watonwan Co., in the following order:

Houston Co., 17 sub-districts; Fillmore, 24; Mower, 14; Freeborn, 18; Martin, 3; Faribault, 10; Winona, 22; Olmsted, 19; Dodge, 10; Steele, 12; Waseca, 10; Blue Earth, 16; Rice, 15; LeSueur, 15; Nicollet, 9; Brown, 6; Scott, 12; Sibley, 9; Renville, 1; Watonwan, 1.

As we understand the matter, the Provost Marshal General requires 1,425 men from this district, giving the Adjutant General the appointment of these men among these 243 township sub-districts, each of which must raise its quota independent of any other sub-district. The Adjutant General has furnished a table given by us last week, showing the aggregate quotas of the counties in this district. Each township in these counties must furnish the proportionate number of men that the *enrolled militia* of that town bears to the whole number of enrolled militia of the county.

Congress has adjourned until the 5th of January without coming to any definite conclusion on the proposed amendments to the enrollment Act. The Senate Military Committee proposes to strike out the word 300 and insert no amount in its stead, but let each drafted man make the best terms to procure a substitute or appear in person; also, any man enrolled may furnish an acceptable substitute, which will relieve him from military duty during the time his substitute has accepted to serve, The committee are unanimous in recommending that there be but *one* class of militia —the 2d will, without doubt (and very justly, too,) take rank with their juniors, alike improve the present condition of both by arousing the one from apathy, and encourage the other by relieving it of the whole burthen so generously bestowed on it by a Congress composed almost wholly of class No. 2."

It need not be disguised that there were some who were more anxious to fill the quota than to recruit our armies in the field.

"Governor Swift, sometime since, applied for permission to apportion our quota by townships and wards, and on Wednesday receiving the following dispatch, granting his request:

'WASHINGTON, Dec. 22.

To His Excellency H. A. Swift, Governor of Minnesota:

You are authorized to apportion your quota of the three hundred thousand volunteers among the several towns or subdivisions of your State as you may find proper. The whole quota of the State, must, however, be distributed.

JAMES B. FRY, P. M. G.'

"The War Department has notified the Governor that the names of volunteers must be certified to by the mustering officer before they are forwarded to Washington, and in order to assure the credit due wards and townships, this officer must certify the towns, wards, and counties from which the recruits were enlisted. It is therefore not only necessary that our wards should ascertain the number of men they have sent, but they should also see that they are credited to the proper wards on the mustering officer's books."

"MARSHAL'S NOTICE.—We call attention to the notice of Capt. See, Provost Marshal for this Congressional District, which is published in to-day's paper, by which it will be seen that the time for hearing claims for exemption from military duty is extended to the 5th of January next. All wishing to avail themselves of this opportunity can now proceed to the 'Captain's office' at Rochester and have their cases duly passed upon; none need be bashful who have proper cause; the sooner such names are stricken from the rolls the better it will be for all concerned."

"MILITARY APPOINTMENTS.—Col. A. D. Nelson resigned his commission yesterday as Colonel of the Sixth Regiment."

"Lieutenant Colonel Crooks, of the Seventh Regiment, was appointed Colonel of the Sixth, vice Nelson, resigned."

"Captain Samuel McPhail, of Houston county, was appointed Lieutenant Colonel of the Seventh Regiment, vice Crooks, promoted. Lieutenant Colonel McPhail joins the Indian expedition as commander of the irregular cavalry."

"Lieutenant Colonel Averill, of the Sixth Regiment, reported for duty yesterday. He left for Lake City, and will take a volunteer cavalry force to the Indian country from that locality."

"HARDEE REVISED.—Captain Saunders has received a copy of Hardee's Tactics revised and amended, which can be seen and examined by military men on calling at his office. All officers should have a copy before entering the field. Capt. S. is a perfect military scholar, and is willing to give all the necessary instructions concerning the new work to all officers who have had no experience in military matters."

"HELP FROM WISCONSIN.—A dispatch was received yesterday from Governor Solomon, stating that he had shipped several hundred thousand rounds of cartridges to Minnesota, in answer to the request of Governor Ramsey."

"MORE CAVALRY NEEDED.—More mounted men are wanted on the frontier.

Let every man that can obtain a horse, arms and equipments, hasten to the assistance of the settlers on the frontier. There will be work for all to do.

Our people must not think the emergency is past."

"THIRD REGIMENT COMING HOME.—Governor Ramsey has telegraphed to the War Department, asking that the Third Regiment might be sent to Minnesota for the protection of the frontier. Yesterday the Governor received a dispatch from General Halleck, stating that his request would be granted. This regiment may be expected home this week, when it will be reorganized and sent to the frontier."

These items are copied at random from the newspapers of the day, and the war news so filled them that there is no wonder that the little girl should ask her mother after the close of the war what they would fill the papers with now?

With the war came a new form of taxation. Excise duty, or any form of government control of manufacturing or industrial interests were before unknown. Now most kinds of business and professional men were subject to a special tax in the form of a license, and personal incomes beyond a certain sum had to contribute a certain per cent, and notices like this were common.

"INTERNAL REVENUE.—Attention is again called to the notice of the Collector of Internal Revenue, which is published in to-day's paper, all assessments for the current year are requested to be paid before the 31st day of December. If not so paid 2 per cent per month will be added thereto."

On the 15th of April, 1861, President Lincoln called for 75,000 troops, and to keep up the delusion which was generally entertained by the South as to the superiority of Southern over Northern men, Jefferson Davis the next day called for 32,000.

On the 10th of July, 1861, President Lincoln called for 500,000 volunteers, and, according to the Adjutant General's report, the whole number enlisted before the close of the war, including officers, was 2,157,047 white men, and 178,895 colored.

In the winter of 1863-64 it became evident that the war could not be brought to a close before the term of enlistment of the great bulk of the army would expire, and so inducements of an extraordinary character were held out for the members of the various regiments in the field to re-enlist, including bounties of several hundred dollars and a promise of a visit home, and where whole regiments or companies re-enlisted, they came home with their officers in an organized form, and as they returned they were handsomely received.

On the 31st of March, 1864, the members of Co. F, of the 4th Minnesota Regiment Veteran Volunteers were tendered a reception by the citizens of Albert Lea. The affair was a cordial outgrowth of the feeling of gratitude which filled all hearts toward the noble men who had stood between them and desolation. Among the veterans present are remembered: J. Fredenburg, B. J. House, John Cottrell, F. E. Drake, George C. Snyder, Alfred Taylor, Henry McGraw, Phineas Taylor, William Fenholt, Henry Woodruff, A. Wishman, Henry House, O. Perkins, Turner Shaw, Alfred J. Knapp, Jacob Frost, Ira Lovell, Andrew Anderson, W. Peterson, Harrison Bullock, and others. There was a dinner at the Webber House, with 68 plates. Speeches were made by A. Armstrong, J. L. Gibbs, George W. Skinner, and E. C. Stacy. In the evening the festivities were closed by a grand ball.

When this Fourth regiment returned South it stopped several days in La Crosse to consolidate and secure transportation, and the officers and men were highly commended for their soldierly bearing and gentlemanly deportment.

Dr. Wedge, Dr. Burnham, and Captain Ruble used to keep the home papers well supplied with papers from the South when they could get hold of them.

On the 5th of January, 1864, when the draft in the State was ordered, Freeborn county had sent 302 men into the army, and there were seventeen more wanted. The total requisition upon the State had been 2,939; of these, 1,515 belonged to the First Congressional District, and 1,424 to the Second. The draft was to be made up in this way; all the men of military age in each town were enrolled, and each one could appear before a medical board connected with the Provost Marshal's office, and if he could show a disability his name would be stricken from the roll, and the prizes in this lottery, where the blanks were so distressingly few, would be drawn from the reduced list. But the malingering in various parts of the district became so extensive that the exemptions were set aside by a general order from the department.

In May, 1864, the district being behind in its quota, the draft was ordered for certain; but few, however, were required to be taken from the county, as the quota was well nigh filled.

On the 21st of June, 1864, the amount paid in the first congressional district for commutation was by 341 men, who contributed an aggregate of $102,300.

The operation of the draft called forth considerable feeling, as with improper exemptions and various causes, there were great inequalities. Any man who had drawn a prize from the conscription list could hire a substitute, as many did, or pay a commutation of $300.

The Sanitary and Christian commission must not be omitted, but on account of the burning of the Standard office with the files of papers, in the spring of 1882, we are unable to furnish full accounts of the Ladies' Aid Societies and other auxiliaries that were engaged in this work.

Most of the regiments in which were Freeborn men, re-enlisted in the winter of 1864, with a view of seeing the end of the rebellion, and of course receiving the large bounties which were offered. The privilege of wearing chevrons on their arms as veteran badges also might have had some influence.

The Freeborn county men who were in the Fifth Regiment were in the following battles: Fort Ridgely; Jackson, Miss.; Vicksburg; Richmond, La.; Fort DeRussy; Henderson Hill, Campti, La.; Pleasant Hill; Cloutersville, La.; Mansura Bayou; De Glaize; Lake Chicott, Tupelo, Abbeyville; Nashville.

INDIAN OUTBREAK OF 1862.

Although there is a good history of the terrible scenes connected with the Indian outbreak of August, 1862, in the earlier pages of this work, yet, as many of the chief actors, particularly those who defended Fort Ridgely, were and still are residents of Freeborn county. It is deemed proper to present some facts not recorded there, and to indicate the special part taken by these heroic men.

Lieutenant Timothy J. Sheehan, the present Sheriff of Freeborn county, was in command of Company C, Fifth Regiment Minnesota Volunteers, and kept a record of each day's doings, of all the orders received and issued, and from these notes we here present a *resume* of the movements of this Company from the time when it left Fort Ripley, where it was stationed at the time of the outbreak.

"SPECIAL ORDER NO. 30.

H. D., FT. RIDGELY, June 18, 1862.

First Lieut. T. J. Sheehan, of Co. C, Fifth Reg., Minn. Vols., will proceed with 50 men to Fort Ridgely, and there report to Capt. Marsh, commanding post, for further orders.

CAPT. FRANCIS HALL, COMD'G POST."

"The detachment started promptly on the 19th, and marched 18 miles; on the 20th, marched 20 miles; on the 21st, camped at Clear Lake after a march of 18 miles. Reached Elk River on the 22d, after a march of 21 miles, and attended preaching. Marched 21 miles on the 23d, and camped at Industriana. On the 24th, marched 20 miles and camped on the prairie; made 20 miles on the 25th; day warm; all the boys feeling wall, and so cn to the 28th, when they arrived at Fort Ridgely and were warmly welcomed."

The next day, the 29th of June, Lieut. Sheehan was ordered by Captain Marsh, to take fifty men of Co. C, and 51 men of Co. B, and proceed by the most expeditious route to the Yellow Medicine Agency, and report to Maj. Thomas Galbraith, the Sioux agent, to protect the United States property during the annuity payments.

"Arrived on the 2d of July and went into camp on a knoll about 25 rods from the Government warehouse. On the 4th of July they had a celebration ; used up a keg of powder in practice on a howitzer. There were thousands of Indians about, including the Yanktons and Cutheads, who were not entitled to pay, but it was feared would make trouble. They had hideous begging and buffalo dances. On the 14th of July I estimated that there were 6,700 Indians camped near there : they were in a starving condition, and were constantly prowling around, begging. Went with Lieut. Gere to talk with the agent about issuing provisions to the Indians. He said that he would soon count them and issue rations, and send them back to look after their crops, to stay until he could send for them to receive their pay."

"On the 23d of July some Chippewas killed two Sioux belonging to Red Iron's band, within eighteen miles of the whole Sioux Nation. In scalping them their heads were completely skinned. The next day, the Sioux, about 1,500 strong, started for the Chippewas, mounted and on foot, with guns and ammunition, bows and arrows, all in full war paint. About four o'clock in the afternoon they returned, dejected and irritable."

"On the 26th the men were counted and furnished crackers by the barrel, which would be emptied on the ground by the soldiers, and there was a grand scramble for them, men tumbling over each other, but the soldiers kept them within due bounds. It took forty barrels of water to go round, and when their stomachs had become distended, they sat down on the grass in groups, and smoked and enjoyed themselves. The Indians not entitled to rations, were kept out of the ring."

On the 27th of July, Lieut. Sheehan was requested to take a small detachment of his men and go toward the source of the Yellow Medicine, in pursuit of Inkpaduta and his followers, and to capture and bring them in, alive if possible.

On the 28th they started with a party of reliable citizens to assist in the enterprise, and a single Indian guide, Wausue, who was a civilized member of Mr. Riggs' church. Traveled 40 miles that day, as they were all well mounted. On the 29th they made 35 miles and encamped at Ash Creek. The march on the 30th was due west and then north, and they saw "Medicine Sticks" planted along, showing that they were on the trail. The next day, being fatigued and the horses tired, they laid over in camp.

On the 1st of August the command moved toward "Hole in the mountain." On the 2d started on the return march and arrived on the 3d.

On the 4th were the first hostile demonstrations. At seven o'clock in the morning about 1,500 red men surrounded the camp and commenced firing their guns, and a party broke open the warehouse and began take out flour, being protected by about 400 braves. Lieut. Sheehan took 25 soldiers and got into the warehouse, marching through a large body of Indian warriors. Gorman and Fadden, two of the agent's employes came out to assist in quelling the riot.

When quiet was restored, Sheehan got permission of the agent to council with the Indians, and the government interpreter was sent out for that purpose. The leader of the band made this speech : "We are the braves, we have sold our land to the Great Father, and we think he intends to give us what he has promised us, but we can't get it ; we are starving, and must have something to eat."

They were told that they should have asked the agent for food before breaking open the storehouse. That if the Great Father knew what they had done, he would be very angry.

The red man answered, "Almost every day we have asked him, but he gives us nothing. Last night at our council fire we all said, we must have bread. We want you to ask him for us for something to eat. We know that our Great Father would be mad if we kill the soldiers."

They were asked, "if they got a good issue of provisions to-morrow, if they would at once retire?" to which they consented.

Major Galbraith then issued an order to Lieut. Sheehan to direct the interpreter to order the Indians to meet him in council on the morrow, and to accept the food he would distribute. Major Galbraith also ordered the flour to be re-conveyed into the warehouse, but the immense horde of savages prevented this, and a liberal issue was made under the urgent advice of Lieut. Sheehan, and they retired fully satisfied that they had carried their point.

On Tuesday, August 5th, two Indians who were identified as being concerned in the acts of violence the day before, were arrested and locked up by order of the Agent, who started a team off with his family, which was driven back, and the threat made that they could not go off until the men were released, which he directed to be done. Word was sent to Capt. Marsh at Fort Ridgely as to the trouble at Yellow Medicine, and the Captain promptly ordered the provisions and clothing to be issued at once, coming himself on the 6th, and the issue was made the next day.

On the 10th of August, as there was no prospect of an immediate payment of the annuities, the command prepared to return to the Fort, and took up the line of March the next day, going 25 miles and bivouacking at Redwood.

The next day they arrived at Fort Ridgely; halting near the Fort, they were met by music, and marched inside in good order.

They spent a few days in preparation, and on the 17th of August received orders to proceed to Fort Ripley. Started at 7 o'clock in the morning, and marched 23 miles, and went into bivouac at Cumming's Farm. The next day they got as far as a point between New Auburn and Glencoe, and after being in camp half an hour, Corporal McLean of Co. B, dashed into their midst with the following order:

"HEADQUARTERS FORT RIDGELY, }
August 18th, 1862. }

Lieut. Sheehan;

It is absolutely necessary that you should return with your command immediately to this post. The Indians are raising hell at the lower agency. Return as soon as possible.

JOHN S. MARSH,
Captain Commanding Post."

Lieut. Sheehan started to return at once, and on the way met a second dispatch, urging haste: kept up the march and arrived the next morning, having made a forced march of 42 miles in nine and one-half hours. On the way, they came across families fleeing from the murderous tomahawk and scalping knife.

On August 19th, the day of arrival, Lieut. Sheehan took command, Capt. Marsh having been shot, and all the available men who had flocked in from the country around were armed and placed under discipline. The Indians who were seen approaching were shelled and kept from advancing. The siege actually commenced on the 20th, and an account of it will not be repeated here, as it appears in the history of the Sioux Massacre. Among the civilians who were present were Mr. G. C. Wyckoff, Clark W. Thompson's Secretary, who was Superintendent of Indian Affairs at the time; J. C. Ramsey, brother of the Governor; A. J. VanVorhes, editor of the "Stillwater Messenger;" and Maj. E.A.C. Hatch. This party brought $108,-000 in gold, and came in to assist in its payment, and they rendered valuable assistance. It may be mentioned that the gold was turned over to Lieut. Sheehan, and buried within the inclosure, and a dispatch sent to Mr. Thompson, indicating where it was, that in case of the massacre of the inmates of the fort, it could afterward be found. In due time it was turned over to Mr. Thompson and a receipt taken.

On the 2d of September a detachment was sent to reinforce Capt. Grant, under command of Colonel McPhail. About 16 miles from camp they met a large force of Indians, and Lieut. Sheehan was ordered to return to Fort Ridgely to report to Col. Sibley. The Indians saw him start and chased him about seven miles, firing scores of shots, but he got through safely.

Lieut. Sheehan's report continues until the 31st of October, when the companies of the 5th, were ordered to join the regiment. There was rejoicing as these men who had been baptized with blood in the Indian war, were anxious to try their hands in fighting Rebels.

On the 26th of September, 1862, Lieut. Sheehan was promoted to Captain of the company he so gallantly led in the terrible seven days of peril at Fort Ridgely.

To furnish an idea of how completely the public mind was absorbed by these blood-curdling events, an extract from the "Pioneer Democrat" of St. Paul of the 24th of August, 1862, is presented, including the head lines which were displayed in "Chicago Times" style.

"THE INDIAN WAR.

THE LATEST NEWS—DISPATCH FROM LIEUT. SHEEHAN—FORT ATTACKED EVERY HOUR—CANNOT HOLD OUT MUCH LONGER.

THE LITTLE BAND ALMOST EXHAUSTED—INTERESTING ACCOUNT OF THE INDIAN ATTACK ON THE FORT.

GALLANTRY OF LT. SHEEHAN—THE RED SKINS REPULSED—NAMES OF THE KILLED AND WOUNDED.

LATER FROM NEW ULM—DISPATCH FROM JUDGE FLANDRAU—LETTER FROM MR. MYRICK—FROM GOV. SIBLEY'S COMMAND.

LIEUT. SHEEHAN'S DISPATCH.

FORT RIDGLEY, Aug. 21, 2 P. M.
GOV. ALEXANDER RAMSEY:

We can hold this place but little longer, unless reinforced. We are being attacked almost every hour, and unless assistance is rendered we cannot hold out much longer. Our little band is becoming exhausted and decimated. We had hoped to be reinforced to-day, but as yet can hear of none coming.

T. J. SHEEHAN,
Co. C., Fifth Regiment Minnesota Vols.,
Commanding Post.

LETTER FROM A. J. VAN VORHES, ESQ.

FORT RIDGELY, Aug, 21, 1862, A. M.
To the Editors of the Pioneer and Democrat:

On yesterday I sent you by messenger, a full account of affairs at this place and vicinity; but fearing the messenger was cut off, who also bore important dispatches to headquarters, I will briefly recapitulate before proceeding to detail the important events of yesterday afternoon.

I need not detail the horrible butcheries at the Upper and Lower Sioux Agencies, at New Ulm, and throughout this entire region, as you have already been advised of the terrible details.

* * * * *

By his energy, Lieut. Sheehan inspired all with hope and confidence that the possition could be held until reinforced from Fort Snelling. Every thing the hurry and exigencies of the time could suggest, seemed to have been done to meet the emergency. Small squads of Indians continued to prowl about in the distance, but were usually shelled away by the accurate shots of Sergeant Jones, the old and experienced artillerist at this post."

Mr. Van Vorhes describes the events of the siege up to that time. The letters alluded to from Judge Flandrau and others were from the seat of war and of absorbing interest at that time.

In order to obtain a list of the men who were under Col. Sheehan's command, and who are the the heroes of that obstinately defended fort, a letter was sent to him by the compilers of this work, to which he replied as follows:

"ALBERT LEA, MINN., August 4, 1882.

Gentlemen:—Your kind note is received and I at once hasten to comply with your request, and enclose the roster of the men who were in the fort with me on that memorable occasion, and to whom the country is indebted for a successful resistance to the murderous, inhuman savages, who were thirsting for the heart's blood of every inmate of that devoted post.

I have often thought that the difficulties attending the defence of that agency were unappreciated, because calling it a fort was a misnomer. The idea usually conveyed by this word involves a rampart, breastworks, a stockade, with perhaps a ditch, and a *chevaux de frise*, or at least an enclosure, but here there was a mere group of buildings, which, of course, afforded shelter to a certain extent, and it is a fact that if the unnumbered hordes of assailants had displayed one half the courage exhibited by the fearless defenders of the place, they could have carried it at any time during the fight. On one side was a level plateau, on the other sides were deep ravines, most admirably adapted to the skulking habits of the bloodthirsty foe, and when about to make a rush to carry the place, they would mass a lot of warriors on the plain, who, with demoniac yells and frantic gestures, would make a feint of charging from that side, while the real attacking party would skulk up through the ravines and make a desperate rush to get inside of the temporary obstructions we had piled up in the form of forage and provisions. They confidently expected to set the buildings on fire by arrows armed with ignited punk. To prevent this we cut scuttles through the roofs, and with water would extinguish each arrow as it fell, but as the supply of water was sixty rods away, and was cut off by the the wily savages, we foresaw that unless relief came sooner than we had reason to expect, we would be out of water. So at night pieces of scantling were placed on the roofs at suitable intervals, in a longitudinal way, and buckets of sand drawn up and spread to present an incombustible covering.

There was plenty of ammunition for the field pieces, but that for the musketry ran short, and we broke up the case-shot and used the powder to make cartridges, which was done by Mrs. Dr. Muller, Mrs. Reynolds, Mrs. Cummings and others, who worked night and day. It should be stated as a remarkable fact, that among all the sick and wounded who sought shelter in the fort, and who were under Dr. Muller's care, that only died, and that among the other skillful surgical operations, the Doctor disarticulated a rib and removed an arrow from a man's lung, and he recovered.

There were not arms enough to put in the hands of all the able-bodied citizens, but when a man fell his weapon was given to another.

On arriving at the post after that fatiguing march of forty-two hours, which was accomplished by the men taking off their stockings and shoes, and depositing everything except their gun and twenty rounds of ammunition, in the single mule team we had along, and then, to use an unmilitary phrase, striking a "dog trot," over hill and vale with the briefest breathing spells. We found the little garrison surrounded with five hundred men, women, and children, in an alarming condition of panic, weeping and howling as though the scalping-knife was actually in their hair.

The soldiers and citizens saw the necessity for strict subordination, and their co-operation was efficient beyond all praise, and I wish you would particularly emphasize the value of the services rendered by Mr. C. G. Wyckoff, Mr. A. J. Van Vorhes, Mr. J. C. Ramsey, and Major Hatch, whose counsel, advice, and support in that trying time has led me to regard them as God's noblemen.

I should have mentioned above that when it rained, as it did in a copious way during the siege, every available barrel and vessel was used to catch water, and so we were thus providentially saved from perishing of thirst.

The six half-breeds who deserted the night before the principal first attack, had stuffed the cannon with rags, which was not discovered until the attempt was made to discharge them, and this well nigh created a panic which would have been immediately fatal, but prompt and energetic measures soon drew the obstructing charges, and their belching forth of shot and shell was the sweetest kind of music to us, but it was death and dismay to the dastardly devils who were after our scalps.

I need not say that I rejoice at the opportunity to furnish the names of the men who defended those helpless women and children during those seven horrible days and sleepless nights, which, even now, can hardly be recalled without a shudder; for if there had been any blanching in the presence of the overhanging doom, or any faltering in the execution of the commands that every moment made imperative, not a living soul would have remained to tell the tale of the hideous butchery that would have followed.

On the 19th of August the following men were at Fort Ridgely, members of Company B, Fifth Regiment, 2d Lieut. Thomas P. Gere commanding:

Privates Ellis, Pfremer, McAllister, Smith, Culver, Annies, Atkins, Boyer, Chase, Elphee, French, Good, Ives, Lester, Lindsey, Martin, Magill, Pray, Perrington, Rufridge, Robinson, Scripture, Spornity, Farmer, Taylor, Underwood, Williamson, Wilson, Wall, Sergt. Jones, and Sutler Randall; of whom six were sick, and three hospital attendants.

At dark that night the following returned, having escaped from the ambuscade at Lower Agency Ferry, but were not effective that night: Sergt. Bishop, Corporals Winslow, Huntley, and Hawley, Privates Brennan, Carr, Dunn, Hutchinson, McGowan, Rebenski, Steward, Serfling, Svendson (wounded), VanBuren, and Murray.

There came in about midnight, Privates Foster, Parsley, and Gardner.

Detachments of Co. C. of the Fifth Minnesota Infantry who were at Fort Ridgely:

OFFICERS.

T. J. Sheehan,	F. A. Blackmer.
John P. Hicks,	M. A. Chamberlain.

PRIVATES.

J. C. Butler,	John C. Ross,
Dennis Porter,	Edward D. Brooks,
Joel Bullock,	James M. Brown,
S. P. Beighley,	Z. Chute,
S. Cook,	Charles E. Chapel,
Charles H. Dills,	S. W. Dogan,
Daniel Dills,	L. H. Decker.
Lyman A. Eggleston,	Halver Elefson,
Martin Ellingson,	Charles J. Grandy,
Mark M. Greer,	Andrew Gilbrandson,
Jerome P. Green,	A. R. Grout,
Jas Honan,	Philo Henry,
Charles Dills,	D. M. Hunt,
Lyman C. Jones,	A. J. Luther,
F. M. McReynolds,	Dennis Moreau,
Orlando McFall,	J. H. Meade,
John D. Miller,	Peter Nisson,
John McCall,	Andrew Peterson,
Ed Roth,	C. O. Russell,
Charles A. Rose,	B. F. Ross,
Walter S. Russell,	J. M. Rice,
Isaac Shortledge,	Josiah Weckley,
Geo. Wiggins,	James M. T. Bright,
N. J. Lowthian.	

On Tuesday morning I arrived with my command bringing with me 51 men, above named, Corpl. McLean included.

On Tuesday P. M., there joined from detached service at St. Peter: 1st Lieut. N. K. Culver, A. A. Q. M.; Sergt. J. G. McGrew; Wagoner, Hoyt; Privates, Baker, Farrver, Nehrhood, Wait.

Tuesday night there came in wounded from the ferry: Privates Blodget (shot through the bowels,) and Sutherland, (shot through the lungs.

Wednesday morning other men from the ferry arrived. Private Rose escaped across the country to Henderson. Therefore, at the time of the attack on Fort Ridgely on Wedesday, August 20th, my command consisted of Company B, 60 men, 51 effective; Company C, 50 men, all effective; Renville Rangers and citizens, 50 men; Orderly Sergt., 1 man; Sutler, 1 man. Total effective men first days fight, August 20th, 153 men under arms.

Three soldiers were killed and thirteen wounded. Four citizens were killed and twenty-six wounded during the seige from the 20th to the 28th.

Of seven men who volunteered, one after another, to carry dispatches to St. Peter, only John McCall and Antoine Freuien, a half breed, got through alive.

Most respectfully your obedient servant,

LIEUT. T. J. SHEEHAN.

Late Col. 5th Minn. Infantry."

That it may be seen that Mr. Sheehan's services were appreciated after joining his regiment at the front, where he served until the end of the war, being at the close commissioned Lieutenant Colonel. We clip from the Pioneer Press of the 16th of November, 1865, the following item:

"A HANDSOME GIFT.—We had the pleasure of seeing yesterday a beautiful gold badge of the 16th A. C. suspended from a gold shield of a U. S. Double Eagle, to which is attached a handsome gold safety chain and pin.

Upon the polished surface of the shield and badge is engraved the following, which speaks the object of the donors, Col. Houston and others of the 5th Minn. Infantry:

'Presented to Lieut. Col. T. J. Sheehan, Fifth regiment Minnesota V. V. Infantry, for services rendered during the rebellion, from October 13th, 1861, to September 5th, 1865; Fort Ridgely, Minnesota, August 20th and 22d, 1862; Jackson, Mississippi, May 14th, 1863; Siege and assault of Vicksburg, from May 18th to July 4th, 1863; Tupelo, Mississippi, July 14th and 15th, 1864; Abbeyville, Mississippi, August 13th, 1864; Campaign against Price in Arkansas, fall of 1864; Nashville, Tennessee, December 15th and 16th, 1864; Siege and capture of Spanish Fort, Alabama, from March 27th, 1865—captured April 9th, 1865.'

Such a gift is felt by the soldier to be priceless. Colonel Sheehan will wear this with pride, in those halcyon days which we trust will accompany him to a ripe old age."

So far as these gallant men are concerned, whatever they may have been since, or whatever they are now, or however regarded by their fellow citizens, it can be said of them as Daniel Webster said of Massachuetts, "the past at least is secure; there is Concord, Lexington, and Bunker Hill, and there they will remain forever." There is Fort Ripley, Yellow Medicine, and Fort Ridgely, and there they will remain forever; and the deeds of this heroic land shall be inscribed on the indelible roll of fame.

The following are names of Freeborn county men who enlisted in the 15th Wisconsin regiment, which was made up of Norwegians, and which has been kindly furnished us by the Adjutant General of that State:

Captain Mons Grinager,	2d Lt. Olaus Solberg,
1st Lt. Ole Peterson,	Sergt. Tosten Erickson,
2d Lt. Ellend Erickson,	Corp. N. Pederson,
Sergt. Jens Jacobson,	Corp. Ole N. Danenen.

PRIVATES.

Halver Aslakson,	Engrebet Amundson,
Peder Bjuth,	Ole Everson,
Christian Gulbrandson,	Lars Halverson,
Peder Hulgerson,	Ole T. Jenson,
Lars Jargenson,	Jens Jenson,
Christopher Johnson,	Iver Jacobson,
Andreas Madison,	Nils Nilson,
Gullbrand Olson,	Knud Olson,
Helge Olson,	Jacob Olson,
Huagen Pederson,	Lars Sebjornson,
Iver Olson,	Peter Peterson.
Rolof Tykson,	

From the Adjutant General's report we are enabled to obtain the following list of volunteers, who enlisted from Freeborn county during the Rebellion, which will serve to some extent, as a recapitulation of the different lists already presented. There is no doubt that many are excluded from the list by incorrect registering, being credited to other counties, and other causes.

SECOND REGIMENT INFANTRY, COMPANY A. PRIVATE.

Wesley Rogers.

COMPANY K.—PRIVATES.

Charles Gahagen.

Warren Osborne; promoted Corporal and Sergeant.

THIRD REGIMENT INFANTRY.

Albert C. Wedge, Assistant Surgeon; promoted Surgeon.

COMPANY D.

Hendrick Peterson, Corporal; promoted Sergeant.

Hans Enstrom, Second Lieutenant; promoted First Lieutenant and Captain.

COMPANY K.—PRIVATE.

Benjamin H. Langworthy.

FOURTH REGIMENT INFANTRY, COMPANY F.

Asa W. White, Captain.

Adrian K. Norton, First Sergeant; promoted First Lieutenant and Captain.

Osborne J. Wheeler, Sergeant.

Hannibal Bickford, Sergeant.

Reuben Williams, Sergeant.

Frank B. Fobes, Sergeant; promoted Second Lieutenant.

Loren Blackmer, Corporal.

Justice C. Stearns, Corporal.

Enoch Croy, Corporal.

Jeremiah Fredenburg, Corporal.

Richard A. White, Corporal.

Perry H. Jewett, Corporal.

Erastus D. Porter, Corporal.

Henry House, Musician.

John Pease, Musician.

John Cottrell, Wagoner.

PRIVATES.

Charles J. Allen,	Joseph W. Burdick,
Charles Bromwich,	Robert W. Bebee.
Benjamin B. Baker,	Harrison Buckley,
George Callahan,	Jacob Croy,
Almon H. Cottrell,	Frederick L. Cutler,
Horace L. Dow,	Francis E. Drake,
Lucas Eckhart,	Ole J. Ellingson,
John Eichler,	Jacob C. Frost,
Elias B. Farr,	Mohlon Frost,
William Fenholt,	George W. Gile,
William S. Hand,	Benjamin H. Hathaway,
Benjamin J. House,	Barhart Haberceom,
Chester Holcombe,	William Hanson,
John D. Hochstrasser,	Joseph A. Knapp,
Milton M. Luce,	Luther I. Lovell,
William H. Lovell,	Henry R. Loomis,
Hiram M. Luce,	Joseph Meyers,
Alexander Morrell,	Orville F. Peck,
Charles Parvin,	William C. Peck,
Ira O. Russell,	John Ryan,
George C. Snyder,	Martin L. Scoville,
James Shields,	Nicholas J. Sandborg,
Hollis E. Sargent,	Thomas Smith,
Stillman Sanders,	Phineas R. Taylor,
Alfred L. Taylor,	

COMPANY K—PRIVATE.

Nathan Thomas.

FIFTH REGIMENT INFANTRY—COMPANY C.

Francis Hall, Captain; promoted Major.

Timothy J. Sheehan, First Lieut.; promoted Captain.

Frank B. Fobes, Second Lieutenant; promoted First Lieutenant.

Horatio D. Brown, First Sergeant; promoted Second Lieutenant and Adjutant of Eleventh Regiment.

John P. Hicks, Sergeant.

Dorr K. Stacy, Sergeant; promoted First Lieutenant.

Manhard A. Chamberlain, Sergeant.

Dwight E. Brooks, Corporal.

Horace M. Beach, Corporal; promoted Sergeant.

John C. Ross, Corporal; promoted Sergeant.

Wm. Young, Corporal; promoted Sergeant.

John S. Godley, Corporal; promoted Sergeant.

Wm. Thompson, Corporal.

Aaron Canfield, Musician.

Nathan E. Babcock, Musician.

John McCall, Wagoner.

PRIVATES.

David Ames,	Edward D. Brooks,
Leonard R. Beighley,	Joel L. Bullock,
Simeon Beighley,	David Crawford,
Charles H. Dills,	Charles Dills,
Daniel Dills,	Samuel W. Dogan,
Lyman A. Eggleston,	Martin Ellingson,
Charles J. Grandy,	Andrew Gilbrandson,
Jerome P. Green,	James Honan,
Philo Henry.	Nathan A. Hunt,
William J. Horning,	Richard O. Hitchcock,
Lyman C. Jones,	Curtis B. Kellar,
Isaac Kendall,	Wm. F. Lawrence,
Andrew J. Luther,	Nicholas Lowthian,
Frank M. McReynolds,	John Melchy,
Terrence McMahan,	John. B. Miller,
Peter Nillson,	Andrew Peterson,
Loriston C. Roberts,	Charles O. Russell,
Benjamin F. Ross,	Walter S. Russell,
James M. Rice,	Isaac Shodridge,
Ole Oleson Stugo,	Aven Oleson Stugo,
Andrew W. St. John,	John Smith,
Josiah Weakley,	Oliver P. Williams,
George H. Wiggins,	James Youngs, Jr.,
Stephen L. Beardsley,	John Reed,
L. W. Grandy.	

COMPANY D—PRIVATE.

Napoleon Hard.

COMPANY F.

Charles H. Boswick, Wagoner.

TENTH REGIMENT INFANTRY.

Alfred H. Burnham, Assistant Surgeon.

Louis Proebsting, Hospital Steward; promoted Assistant Surgeon.

COMPANY E.

James A. Robson, Captain.

John W. Heath, First Lieutenant; promoted Captain.

Charles Kittleson, Second Lieutenant; promoted First Lieutenant.

Eli Ash, First Sergeant; promoted Second Lieutenant and First Lieutenant Company G.

Eli K. Pickett, Sergeant; promoted Second Lieutenant Company I.

George H. Partridge, Sergeant.

Wm. H. Lowe, Sergeant.

James L. Cook, Sergeant.

George Osborn, Corporal.

John G. Dunning, Corporal.

Henry D. Burlingame, Corporal; promoted Sergeant.

Jedediah W. Devereux, Corporal.

Rufus Kelly, Corporal.

Alva S. Sterns, Corporal.

Christian Alspaugh, Corporal.

Lars Wicks, Corporal.

John L. Scoville, Musician.

Peter E. Olson, Musician.

Asa Hurd, Wagoner.

Daniel Anderson, Private; promoted Corporal.

Andrew Black, Private; promoted Hospital Steward.

Cyrus E. Bullock, Private; promoted Corporal.

Patrick Morin, Private; promoted Corporal.

Loren S. Meeker, Private; promoted Com. Sergeant

Hiram J. Rice, Private; promoted Corporal.

PRIVATES.

Andrew Anderson,	Andrew Anderson,
Stengrew Benson,	Gilbert G. Barden,
Samuel E. Bullock,	James Bowen,
Edwin Brownesville,	Henry C. Bartlett,
Rodney M. Campbell,	W. G. Carpenter,
Dan. E. Cozzen,	Fred. Chamberlain,
George H. Chandler.	Samuel Clark,
Russel B. Davis,	Francis W. Davis,
Matthew L. Dearman,	John Edson,
William E. Everett,	Engeret Erickson,

George W. Gates, Lorenzo Dow Godberg,
Thomas Iverson, Ole Iverson,
Henry Johnson, Erick C. Johnson,
John C. Kaiser, James Lair,
Fritz Maixner, Christopher Mickleson,
Elijah W. Owen, Israel H. Pace,
Benjamin Park, Isaac Perry,
Cyrus S. Prescott, John Peterson,
Charles Peterson, John L. Reynolds,
Robert H. Reynolds, James C. Seely,
Jacob Stewart, James A. Smith,
Peter P. Shoyer, Henry Smith,
Leander J. Thomas, Joseph S. Trigg,
Patrick Tansty, Samuel Wannemaker,
Reuben Wilsey, Asa Ward.

FIRST BATTALION INFANTRY

COMPANY F.

Clark Andrews, Second Lieutenant.

FIRST REGIMENT HEAVY ARTILLERY.

COMPANY B. PRIVATE.

John Blythe.

COMPANY C.

George S. Ruble, Sr. First Lieutenant.
Jonas C. Bane, Sergeant.
Hannibal Bickford, Sergeant.

PRIVATES.

John L. Bliss, John Buckley,
Henry Lawrence, Louis Marpie,
Oliver Andrews.

FIRST REGIMENT MOUNTED RANGERS.

COMPANY H.

George S. Ruble, Captain.
Adolph Walter, Sergeant.
Charles T. D. Marlett, Corporal.
Charles R. Rickercker, Teamster.
John Van Antwerp, Blacksmith.
David T. Colvin, Wagoner.

PRIVATES.

John M. Ames, Pat. Bannon,
Frank D. Hardy, Harvey Hill,
Matthew Hogan, James Morrison,
James F. Nadeau, M. W. Perry,
Michael Sheehan, David Tubbs,
Abram L. Van Asdal, Amherst D. Wait,
Jesse Wheeler, Leroy B. Woodruff,
Ed. A. Wright.

COMPANY M—PRIVATES.

Martin O. Gunderson, Egbert Hanson.
John Johnson.

SECOND REGIMENT, CAVALRY.

COMPANY A—PRIVATE.

Woodworth Lee.

COMPANY B.

Willliam M. Catherwood, Com. Sergeant.

PRIVATES.

Clraence H. Shafner, Julian F. Shafner
James F. Spafford, Alma B. Sija.

COMPANY C.

Frederick L. Cutler, Second Lieutenant.
Adelbert E. Pettingill, Commodore Sergeant.
Charles E. Fitzsimmons, Sergeant.
George P- Conrad, Corporal.
Aaron A. Webster, Corporal.
Robert G. Spear, Blacksmith.
John H. Rich, Wagoner.

PRIVATES.

William H. H. Buckley, Orson Buckley,
Augustus Bremer, Ashbel H. Barnhart,
Frank Barber, William Clark,
David L. Courtier, James E Ford,
Alfred Holland, William R. Herrington,
Jacob Larson, John Levenick,
Joseph F. Parcher, Edwin W. Parshall.
Charles Stocklale, Henry L. Slaven,
John Tracy, Henry Wyent,
Henry Wiseman.

INDEPENDENT BATTALION CAVALRY.

COMPANY B—PRIVATES.

Charles Hutchins, Elias Hoyt.

FIRST BATTERY LIGHT ARTILLERY.

PRIVATE.

Homer W. Dorman,

SECOND BATTERY, LIGHT ARTILLERY.

Henry A. Symonds, Corporal.
Edward D. Rogers, Artificer.

PRIVATES.

Carlos Dimick, William M. Preston.

CHAPTER LI.

EVENTS OF INTEREST, CHRONOLOGICALLY ARRANGED.

These items commence in 1857, at a time when the county was fast filling up, and after the very earliest events, which have elsewhere been recorded, occurred. There is no pretense that everything which it may be valuable to rescue from oblivion has been caught in this gathering seine, but enough to disclose the drift of affairs while this region was filling, and to give an idea of what the people were interested in, and of the vicissitudes to which they were subjected.

THE YEAR 1857.

The school district in Albert Lea was No. 7 at this time, and measures were taken to build a schoolhouse, and a tax of $400 was levied.

Early this year Newcomb & Barnes began merchandizing. Woodruff & Eaton also appeared, as well as Mr. E. Follett.

This summer Mr. H. T. Smith got a shingle machine in operation.

The Albert Lea drug store was started by A. C. Wedge.

Alf. P. Swineford was a dealer in real estate, as well as editor of the newspaper.

Col. Samuel Eaton did an insurance, pension, and bounty land business.

In July, A. B. Webber, of Decorah, came and began the practice of law.

About the third number of the "Southern Minnesota Star," which was started in July, contained the names of sixty-one subscribers who had paid in advance. The list began in this way:

George S. Ruble	$38.50
Thomas C. Thorne	20.00
J. H. Snyder	10.00
David Hurd	10.00

and so on down to $1.00.

At this time there were two mails a week from Red Wing, carried by Hancock & Co.

The building in Albert Lea, was so extensive this year, that all the lumber the saw-mill could turn out was used up, and the supply at St. Nicholas was exhausted.

The "Southern Minnesota Star" was so busy printing election tickets in October, that on one week only a page of a half sheet was sent out.

In October, there were four stage lines running into Albert Lea; from Mankato, Mitchell, Winona, and Red Wing.

In November wheat was selling for forty-five cents a bushel, and flour was nine dollars a barrel.

The grand opening of the Webber House, which had been built by Mr. Webber, was on the 24th of November. A Ball, a Supper, and other festivities marked the occasion.

The total population of the county, enumerated in November, was 2,486, which was disappointing to the sanguine ones; Albert Lea had 285.

Late in November Elias Stanton, of Freeborn City, froze both feet by getting them wet in a slough; his oxen also froze to death, and he subsequently died of his injuries.

Fritz Ewald started a sash and door shop in November.

The "Bancroft Pioneer" flashed upon a bewildered world about this time.

In December, Col. Eaton fitted up the Postoffice with boxes.

On the 26th of December a lyceum was organized in Dr. Wedge's office, under the inspiring name of "Albert Lea Senate."

THE YEAR 1858.

In January the people of the shire town congratulated themselves that they were to have regular preaching every Sunday. Rev. Mr. Lowry and Rev. Mr. McReynolds officiating alternately.

In February the necessity of a bridge across the river at the foot of the lake became apparent, and measures were adopted to have one built.

In February the first funeral procession ever seen at the county seat was that of Elias Stanton.

In the spring of this year civilization had made such progress that a race course was talked of.

On the 15th of April, the question as to issuing the five million bond loan was voted upon, and this county voted against it.

Walker's new line of stages was put on in April, between Hastings and Chatfield, Austin, and Albert Lea.

On the 6th of April a public meeting was held at Albert Lea, to consider the bond question. David Blakely called the meeting to order; E. P. Skinner was called to the chair, and John Wood was appointed secretary. The meeting was addressed by A. H. Bartlett, Mr. Blakely, Dr. Tarbell, and others, and the sentiment of the meeting was unanimous against the proposition. Mr. Bartlett stumped the county in opposition to the scheme, and the only town he did not visit gave seventeen of the twenty-seven votes in the county in its favor.

On the 1st of May the "Star" had a map of Freeborn county on its first page, and it occasionally appeared for some time thereafter.

Albert Lea began to flourish as a sea-port in the spring of this year, when the brig Itasca, Captain Franklin, of Shell Rock, arrived, loaded with shingles. The people began to use nautical terms and to hitch their trousers as though they had just come ashore.

THE YEAR 1859.

On the 6th of May the first and only deliberate murder ever committed in the county, was by Henry Kreigler, causing the death of Nelson Boughton in the town of Nunda. It appears that Kreigler whipped his wife, and she fled to the house of Mr. Boughton with her child, and was protected by him; and Kreigler came over and made an assault, fatally stabbing him in the back with a long knife, penetrating the heart and producing instant death.

The murderer was arrested and sent to Faribault jail for safe keeping. The defence secured a change of venue to Steele county, and he was tried at Owatonna. The prosecution was conducted by D. G. Parker, County Attorney, assisted by Gordon E. Cole, Attorney General; and he was ably defended by Hon. A. Armstrong and Hon. O. F. Perkins.

The trial lasted thirty days, a large number of witnesses were called, and the costs were piled up so that the county was well nigh bankrupt, its orders going for 20 cents on the dollar. The culprit was remanded back to the county for execution, which took place on the first day of March, 1861, at a point just east of Broadway, not far from the place where the railroad crosses the street. Here, in that amphitheatre formed by the surrounding hills, a gibbet had been erected in the form of a post with a projecting arm, from which a pendant rope was connected by pullies to a huge log, as the engine of death. The legal strangulation was witnessed by several thousand people, being conducted by the Sheriff, James Robson. Rev. Mr. Storey, who was then here, asked the condemned man if he desired prayer, to which he replied that he had no money to pay for it; but the minister fervently prayed nevertheless. It seems that the criminal did not realize that he was after all to be actually hung, and when the fatal cord was applied to his neck, and the dismal black cap drawn over his head, he completely broke down, and as the newspapers at the time related, "bawled like a calf." All being ready, the stick of timber was dropped and the victim was jerked from his footing, and in a few minutes his earthly career was thus ingloriously ended. It is said that this was the only white man ever legally executed in Minnesota.

The remains were buried in an old cemetery on the Austin road, but the belief existed rather extensively at the time, that two enterprising physicians who resided here had resurrected the remains for anatomical and physiological purposes. But no one took pains to verify the surmise, or to disprove it. A few years ago, however, the cemetery having been applied to other uses, the bones were disinterred, and fully identified by the manacles which were rusting around the bones of his fleshless wrists.

On the 12th of February Mr. Swineford having gone to LaCrescent to battle against LaCrosse, Mr. Isaac Botsford secured an interest in the "Star."

In September an early frost caught many late crops in its withering embrace.

This was the season when the horse racing mania was upon the community, and one of the first recorded was between a horse owned by F. L. Cutler and one owned by F. Lamb, for $100 a side. Then came a race between Botsford's black gelding, Crazy Frank, and Dr. Wedge's horse Selam, in which Crazy Frank won and Botsford raked in $40.

THE YEAR 1860.

The newspaper, which had become the "Eagle," screamed for the last time on the 17th of March, and the "Standard" was lifted up on the 26th of May by Ruble and Hooker, with the latter as editor.

In July the Webber House was leased to J. A. Robson, of Geneva.

During this summer Morin, Wedge, and Hall got a new steam saw-mill in motion.

Another horse race was run between George S. Ruble's Sleepy Kate, and F. L. Cutler's Bay Lady. Sleepy Kate was declared the winner.

The second fair of the Agricultural Society was held at Albert Lea on the 10th and 11th of October.

In the early fall of this year, a land sale had been ordered by the departmnnt, and the people, who were mostly living on government land, did not feel able to pay for it at that time, so a meeting was held at the cradle of Freeborn county liberty, the Webber House. A. B. Webber was Chairman, and C. H. Bostwick, Secretary. Col. G. W. Skinner, who had been appointed to secure co-operation in procuring the postponement of the land sale, reported what had been accomplished. Stacy, Hoops, Rickard, Ash, Webber, with others, addressed the meeting, and Mr. Skinner was sent to Washington to use his influence in the matter, and a committee was appointed to secure funds to pay the expenses. A meeting had been previously held in Porter, at the house of F. W. Calkins, and J. M. Drake prepared that safety value of American feeling, the resolutions. The county seat election was fixed for the day of the general election, on the 6th of November.

Col. Skinner returned, and on the 25th of October another meeting took place at the Webber House; S. G. Lowry in the chair, and E. C. Stacy as Secretary. The Colonel reported that although there was to be no postponement of the sale, he had obtained concessions which practically gave the settlers what they wanted, it as was provided that no speculators should bid or locate land warrants on lands actually occupied, and the following gentlemen were designated to see the idea carried out: A. B. Webber, of Albert Lea; H. Melder, Carlston; C. Fitzsimmons, Nunda; Eli Ash, Bancroft; J. C. Seeley, Hartland; J. W Burdick, Geneva; E. Croy, Riceland; A. M. Young, Shell Rock; George Callahan, London; C. Bullock, Oakland; and D. Gates, Moscow.

In December of this year, the trial of Kreigler for murder, in Steele county, almost depopulated this region, so many were summoned as witnesses; even the mail carriers' duties were interrupted.

THE YEAR 1861.

Wheat was reported as selling in Milwaukee for 79 cents a bushel.

Henry Kreigler was executed on the first of March, at Albert Lea.

Ruble's mill was wrecked and the dam washed away by a freshet in April. This was the only water privilege in Albert Lea.

In May, the Standard proudly came out with a new dress, as if "bound to dress well if it did not lay up a cent."

In April a military company was formed at the county seat.

On the 1st of August, A. B. Webber having bought the Standard, issued his first number.

In October the butchers in Albert Lea offered two cents a pound for cattle weighing eleven hundred pounds or more.

THE YEAR 1862.

An anti cattle and horse thief society was organized early in 1862, with the following officers: President, Joshua Dunbar; Vice-President, J. M. Drake; Secretary, William Morin; Treasurer, A. Armstrong; Finance Committee, George S. Ruble, E. P. Skinner, and James F. Jones; Vigilance Committee, E. C. Stacy, A. B. Webber, John B. Brownsill, and L. T. Scott.

In 1862, Hannibal Bickford, who was a soldier in the army, lay sick in a hospital in St. Louis, and his death daily expected. His wife started for that city intending to bring back his remains, but on reaching his hospital she found him actually recovering, and as soon as he was considered able to travel, the two started for home on the steamer Denmark, and while she was laying at the wharf their attention was called to a little girl who was in a pitiable condition. An investigation showed tkat the father of the little girl was a union soldier, and having taken sick his wife went to his relief with the little girl. She too sickened and both died, and an old tarmagant of an aunt had her in charge to carry home, and she had shamefully abused the little waif. The indignation of the Captain and all on board was aroused, and they resolved to rescue the motherless little one from her heartless relative. The woman was willing to be relieved of what she considered a burdensome charge, so she was turned over to Mr. and Mrs Bickford, the Captain bestowing the name of Denmark Bickford upon her. She was adopted and came home with them to this country, and grew up to be a fine young woman, and a few years ago was married to Henry White, now living at Jackson, Heron Lake. Since the marriage an advertisement appeared in the "Inter Ocean" of Chicago, relating the occurrence at St.

Louis and seeking to find the lost one. Of course there was back pay, pension, and perhaps other money due. Less romantic incidents than this have furnished the ground work for many a thrilling story.

THE YEAR 1864.

In February a dam was built at Shell Rock by Ruble and Tanner.

The directors of the Southern Minnesota railroad for this year were: E. B. Stoddard, C. D. Sherwood, Luke Miller, H. W. Holley, D. B. Sprague, and William Morin.

In April the contract for making the brick for the Court House was let to H. M. Manley at $6 per thousand.

THE YEAR 1866.

On the 14th of February Mrs Charles Anderson, living in the town of Bancroft, went out to the barn to milk in a blinding snow storm, and notwithstanding the house and barn were in an enclosure which she had to climb over, she lost her way and was found the next morning two miles away from home, stark and cold in the icy embrace of death.

This year a daily mail was ordered through from LaCrosse to Winnebago City. J. C. Burbank & Co. were contractors. The service commenced on the 1st of July.

During the summer there was an average of twenty wagons a day passing through Albert Lea with emigrants.

In the summer of this year there was talk of organizing an agricultural society.

Wheat in July was selling in Milwaukee for $2.04½ per bushel.

On the 10th of July the hotel barn in Albert Lea was burned.

F. Hall started his flouring mill in August, with a single run of stones operated by water under a head of eighteen and one half feet.

In November two persons were drowned in Nunda; Willard Parshall and Thomas J. Stockdale.

On the 15th of December a cemetery association was formed in Albert Lea: Luther Parker was Chairman, and S. S. Luther, H. D. Brown, and D. G. Parker, were trustees.

THE YEAR 1867.

By a general order promulgated on the 1st of March, the merchants of Albert Lea adopted the cash system.

The school fund for the county this year was $646.64.

At the cemetery meeting in April, E. C. Stacy was Chairman; H. D. Brown, Secretary; the Trustees appointed were William Morin, S. S. Luther, and S. Eaton. It was resolved to ask the town to subscribe $500.

During this year there were a large number of railroad projects brought out, with Albert Lea as a focal point.

In May the Albert Lea Musical and Theatrical Association was organized. President and General Manager, F. B. Fobes; Vice-President, P. W. Dickinson; Secretary, S. S. Edwards; Treasurer, A. W. St. John; Musical Director, D. G. Parker. On the 18th of June the Association gave its initial entertainment, "Box & Cox; married and settled."

The 4th of July was celebrated with more than usual display. A basket pic-nic with a barbecued ox as an auxiliary was thrown in. Thirteen guns were fired at sunrise and thirty-eight at noon. The procession made a grand display. Thirty-eight beautiful girls represented the States of the Union, and the various societies marched with martial music to Thomas' Point. Rev. S. G. Lowry was the President of the day. The declaration of independence was read by H. D. Brown. The orator of the day was Hon. A. Armstrong. In the evening there was a grand ball at W. J. Martin's, and a performance at the Court House, which included "Slasher & Crasher," and several tableaux representing the "Gipsey Camp," and "Pocahontas saving the life of Capt. Smith."

Mr. Stage, on the 6th of August, lost a tin and hardware shop in Albert Lea by fire, entailing a loss of $1500.

On the 8th of September, Hon. William F. Stearns, of Chicago, who was stopping at Albert Lea to transact some business, was seized with hallucinations that parties were on his track to torture him, and he committed suicide. He was an attorney, and a man highly respected.

At Twin Lakes, on the 21st of September, Peter Peterson fell from a stack of hay, so injuring him that he died within four hours.

THE YEAR 1868.

In January, Mr. A. B. Davis, an early pioneer

in the staging business, bought an interest in the Austin & Winnebago City line.

Some time in the month of January, James Buchanan, of Shell Rock, shuffled off this mortal coil through the medium of fifty cents worth of morphine. He was about forty-five years of age and had been in Arizona.

In August, Nathaniel Stacy, father of Judge Stacy, died. He had been a Mason for more than sixty years, and was buried with funeral rites, in accordance with the land-marks of that ancient order.

Samuel Wedge, who was 66 years of age, paid the debt of mortality on the 19th of September.

This season Albert Lea became a money order office.

In the fall of this year, Clark W. Thompson, of the Southern Minnesota railroad, proposed to have the towns issue bonds to assist in building the line.

THE YEAR 1869.

Early in 1869, the patrons of husbandry came into notice in Freeborn county.

In April the hopes of the people were carried up several degrees by the statement that the railroad engineers were between Austin and Albert Lea.

During April bonds were issued to the amount of $12,500 to assist in building a schoolhouse in Albert Lea.

The engineers reached Albert Lea on the 17th of April.

In April Albert Lea was honored by the appointment of A. Armstrong as United States Marshal for Minnesota.

In the spring of 1869, pigeons were so plentiful in the region of Albert Lea, that like clouds they darkened the sun.

In the town of Bath on the 7th of May, a Dane by the name of Christen Rassmuson, disappointed in love, and climbing into the branches of a tree, tied a cord around his neck and the other end to a limb, with a razor cut his throat in a ghastly manner, and jumped from his perch, to leave his sanguinary looking corpse to horrify the first person who happened near.

The tide of emigration in May was at its flood. Prairie schooners by the score were floating along through town, and day after day their white canvass might be seen surrounded by herds of cattle, as they wended their way toward the setting sun, which presaged a rising orb to all their hopes.

The surveyors of the railroad, during May, had their headquarters at Albert Lea.

The contractors between Austin and Albert Lea were Allen & Stewart.

The flag, which it will be remembered was presented to Company F, of the Fourth Regiment, and carried through nine battles (which were inscribed on it at a cost of $25) was kept by Sergeant Enoch Croy for several years, and then placed in the hands of the County Treasurer.

The construction of the new schoolhouse in Albert Lea was commenced in August.

On the 22d and 23d of September a regular county fair was held.

In September Col. Albert M. Lea suggested a grand trunk railroad from Galveston, Texas, to St. Paul, Minnesota, saying that the traffic between the North and South should be larger than between the East and West.

The Southern Minnesota railroad reached Albert Lea on Saturday, the 16th of October, and on Monday business began.

In the summer of this year a new brass band was organized.

In November there were two confidence men around through this section, who represented that they were engaged in an extensive manufacture of an article that required old feathers, and that they would exchange new ones for old, paying thirty cents a pound difference between the two; and as they had teams would take them away at once, paying the difference, and that the new ones would be sent in about two weeks. A great many thrifty housewives emptied their feather beds, and put up with the inconvenience of sleeping on straw for a week or two until the new feathers came. The result was, of course, they never saw the new feathers, but had sold their old ones for thirty cents a pound.

THE YEAR 1870.

Wheat in January was selling at from 43 to 46 cents a bushel.

In the summer Mr. Ernst erected a building and started a boarding school in Alden.

A violent tornado swept over the county on the 14th of July; houses were unroofed and much other damage done.

During the month of July a petrified duck was found near Pickerel Lake.

A hook and ladder company was organized on the 22d of November, at the Court House. Col. S. Eaton was called to the chair and Capt. A. W. White was appointed secretary. A committee was appointed to draft By-Laws.

A great railroad excursion took place on the 17th of October to celebrate the completion of the through line to LaCrosse. The train was in holiday trim and had a refreshment car where the liquid samples predominated over the solid comforts. At every station the number kept augmenting, until they crossed the river from LaCrescent to LaCrosse, and at Pomeroy's Hall they were welcomed in a speech by the Mayor, which was responded to by Hon. M. S. Wilkinson. The next day they were entertained at the Opera House, and the company returned after an enjoyable trip.

In the spring of this year a special act was passed enlarging the powers of the officers of Albert Lea in relation to the village, giving authority as to ordinances and licenses.

At the celebration of the Independence of the United States at Albert Lea there were 5,000 people present. The oration was by Rev. R. B. Abbott.

THE YEAR 1871.

A town meeting was held at Albert Lea on the 4th of January, and $1,500 voted in aid of the St. Louis railroad. Shell Rock voted $1,500, and Hartland voted $10,000.

On the 7th of January the Orophilian Lyceum was organized. Miss Minnie Ernst read an essay on the occasion.

A cheese factory was started in Albert Lea in March.

On the 23rd of February there was a great freshet in Southern Minnesota.

Andrew Larson, a Swede, hung himself in the town of Hayward on the 14th of March at the house of Andrew Sanderson. He was an erratic and insane individual.

On the 12th of April the citizens of Albert Lea had a meeting and resolved to secure six Babcock fire extinguishers.

In April the citizens of Albert Lea contributed to pay for the instruments for the cornet band.

The railroad bond question was submitted to a vote of the people; and this county was almost solid against it, the whole number of votes cast being 760: for the payment, 80—against the payment 680. Hayward, Alden Riceland, Bancroft Manchester, and Hartland had no votes for the payment, while Carlston and Newry had one each.

The Albert Lea cheese factory with its appointments cost $6,000, and it was completed in June. William Peck was the foreman of the establishment, which had a six horse-power engine.

In October an elk was seen near the residence of Dr. Blackmer, and was shot at with a bird charge by the Doctor's son. He ran across the railroad track, going south; quite a cavalcade was soon in pursuit, and he was followed as far as the Shell Rock and beyond that he was "lost to sight but to memory deer," to the many weary pilgrims who sadly retraced their steps. It was probably a mournful satisfaction to afterward learn that the royal game was killed in Cresco, Iowa.

When Chiego was burned, in October, the citizens of Albert Lea had relief meetings and sent what they could.

THE YEAR 1872.

James Fitzgerald, a resident of the town of Bath, 50 years of age, was frozen to death on the 1st of February. He was away with a team, and it is supposed had an attack of asthma, and did not survive the cold, which was intense; he was found a few miles from home.

Gardiner Cottrell, an old settler of Shell Rock, died in May.

Martin Sheehan, an old settler who located in Bath in 1857, quietly passed away on the 7th of of August. He had lived an unobtrusive life.

On the second of November, Mr. L. G. Pierce, of Alden, with his wife and four children were struck by the engine of a passing train, while on a wagon loaded with goods, and singularly enough none of them were seriously injured.

In November Hon. Charles McIlrath was appointed receiver of the Southern Minnesota railroad.

Here is a model return on a writ issued in this county. "This cuss is a dead beat; after harvest he will have something; then hand me the writ and I will give him a clatter."

THE YEAR 1873.

In October there was quite an extensive conspiracy to obtain money by selling land not their own, by parties from Cleveland, Ohio. They had obtained descriptions of land owned by Cleveland men, and then came out here with forged deeds, and having had them recorded, proceeded to sell the lots ; but as they were on the point of leaving, they were detected and their plans frustrated. Considerable trouble was caused by the affair which will be related elsewhere.

THE YEAR 1874.

Early in 1874 there was quite a spirited controversy as to the name, Albert Lea. Various suggestions were made pro and con. The objection to the name being because it was unusual and unlike the name of any other place in the wide world, which ought to strike the majority of people as being a most admirable reason why it should be retained.

In February a young man was frozen to death, near Albert Lea, when intoxicated, and a coroner's jury declared that the saloon-keeper who sold him the liquor was responsible.

The Albert Lea Temperance Alliance was organized in February. Fifty-eight persons joined the Society. The first officers were: President, Gilbert Gulbrandson; Vice President, Capt. A. W. White; Treasurer, H. O. Hankness; Secretary, August Peterson.

In March Mr. A. A. Munn, a leading citizen of Freeborn, died.

A library and reading room was organized on the 27th of March at the office of Ballard & Hibbs. Dr. Ballard presided at the first meeting.

There was quite a gale swept across the county on the 25th of July; in Bath, Manchester, and Freeborn it was particularly fierce, unroofing houses, destroying crops, and doing thousands of dollars worth of damage.

Grange Hall in Shell Rock was dedicated on the 6th of November. Among the concomitants of the occasion were a supper and a dance with 62 couples in attendance.

Albert Lea Seminary was opened for pupils on the 9th of December by Miss S. A. Thayer of Boston, a graduate of Mount Holyoke Seminary.

THE YEAR 1875.

At the March meeting in Albert Lea the No-License party carried their point by fifty majority.

23

The spring term of the Albert Lea Seminary was under the charge of Miss Jennette Curtis, of Michigan.

The Congregationalist church bell, weighing 616 pounds, was swung up about the 1st of November, and waked the slumbering echoes of the village with its joyous ringing.

THE YEAR 1876.

Joseph Schorbeck, 14 years of age, was killed by a runaway accident early in January. His body was dragged three miles and mangled beyond all recognition.

In Freeman, Mr. Lea Hughes secured a through ticket to the land of the hereafter, by a shot through a vital part. This was in the winter of this year.

In the year 1874 and 1875 the opponents of license had carried the day at the polls, but in 1876 the order was reversed and the license party were triumphant.

John H. Smith, a venerable man of 86 years, and father-in-law of Mr. T. Walcott, on the 7th of June, while fishing at Albert Lea, near the railroad, became bewildered and stepped in front of an engine and was instantly killed. He was a pensioner of the war of 1812.

At Freeborn, in the early summer of this year, "Dora" a little daughter of Mr. Shoen, six years of age, was lost, and after eleven hours search by the whole neighborhood, was found near midnight on the prairie near a grove, fast asleep, and restored to her distracted parents.

The Centennial Anniversary of the Declaration of Independence by the United States of America was celebrated in Albert Lea in a way and manner befitting the occasion, which was one of rejoicing that the experiment of self government had been in every way so successful, that ten solid decades had passed away since the American people had declared "that they were and by right ought to be free and Independent," and that from a few millions, they were nearly half a hundred millions, occupying, instead of a small strip of country along the Atlantic coast, the wide expanse from ocean to ocean, from the Bay of Fundy to San Diego, and from Vancouver's Island to the Florida Reefs. The citizens of Albert Lea and the surrounding country, were fully alive to the spirit of the occasion, and the display was quite equal to that in Philadelphia, considering the size of the two places. Nothing like it had ever happened here nor will occur again until some remarkable occasion shall call for a duplication of the pageant. There were soldiers on parade keeping time to martial music. Beautiful young ladies representing the States; General Washington and his family represented in the long procession, enthusiasm everywhere, flags, fire-crackers, fire arms, fire works, and in a few words an exaggerated fourth of July.

The procession was made up as follows:

1. Soldiers of the late war.
2. Thirty-nine girls representing the States.
3. General and Lady Washington, son and daughter.
4. President of the day, orator and reader.
5. City and County Officers in carriages.
6. Band.
7. Citizens on foot.
8. Citizens in carriages.

The Hon. Lea Barton was orator of the day.

Various amusements, boat racing and other sports were indulged in and a good example set for the next Centennial when it shall roll around.

Freeborn and Geneva also appropriately celebrated the Centennial 4th.

The grasshoppers appeared in the county in August.

In September the grasshopper plague had proved so disastrous in other places that serious fears were entertained that they would actually depopulate the county, and on the 10th of this month, in accordance with suitable notice, a convention was held, and the speeches that were made reminded one of the dark days of the rebellion when reinforcements were wanted to fight the common enemies of the country. The meeting was at the Court House, all parts of the county being represented. Hon. J. L. Gibbs was called to the chair, and Isaac Botsford was named for Secretary. A committee on resolutions was appointed as follows: A. M. Johnson, Wm. Morin, J. T. Hall, Dr. Ballard, and E. C. Stacy. Mr. J. T. Hall addressed the meeting, and declared that he was not to be destroyed by grasshoppers; that, although the ground was peppered with grasshopper eggs, he proposed next year to put in a full crop and use all the means that should come to his knowledge to exterminate these unwelcome pests. A. M. Burnham had two hundred acres under the plow, and as his soil was sandy, it was said to be the particular breeding ground for these lively insects. A part of his land had been rented to a man who had had experience wieh the "hopper" plague, and his opinion was that the eggs there were spoiled. Mr. S. Smith, of Manchester, had been through all hardships, the privation and toil of pioneer life, and he had faith to believe that providence would help those who helped themselves. William Morin said that he had 1,100 acres under cultivation; most of it was leased to other parties, but he proposed to break up 125 acres of it himself, just for fun, and to keep his hand in. David Calvin had a panacea for the grasshopper plague in the form of large doses of fowls; he had several scores of turkeys and hens, and they worked for nothing and found themselves, and kept his place clear. Mr. Fern, of Hayward, had experience with the pestiferous locusts in Kansas, and he had learned that a wet season was bad for them and good for the farmers, for in such a case most of them would decay. Judge Stacy said that those who were residents of Freeborn county came here to stay, and they proposed to stay, for people who had lived on Johnny-cake and suckers for several years were not to be driven off by such a miserable, insignificant jerky insect as a grasshopper. J. H. Parker had thirty-five acres of new breaking, which he found was completely filled with eggs, and he proposed to cover the knolls and sandy places with hay, and as soon as they hatched out in the spring, make it hot for the little beasts by firing the whole business. Mr. Dominick came to Minnesota to follow the occupation of farming, and he proposed to go on, hoppers or no hoppers. Hannibal Bickford served notice that he would shoot every dog found on his premises, and fifty others shouted "me too!" He preferred chickens to hoppers. Mr. Tilton had experienced a four years siege with the "varmints," but these were of a smaller variety. Among other things, burning prairie grass in the spring instead of the fall was recommended.

The resolutions were submitted, and they stated that it was a deplorable fact that there were grasshoppers in our midst, but not enough to discourage the farmers. That we came to stay and have a prior right to the soil. That a stop should be made to killing birds. The following committee was appointed to arrange concert of action: Dr. A. C. Wedge, Dr. C. W. Ballard, E. C. Stacy, I. Botsford. The meeting was large and enthusiastic, with a predominating spirit of "*carthaginum est delenda*." The meeting adjourned to the last day of the county fair, which would be on the 12th of October.

In November the murder and attempted robbery at Northfield excited considerable interest in the chase and capture of the bandits, and what assistance could be given was rendered.

Early in October two well dressed gentlemen stopped at Martin's Hotel, and while here, after some days, a lady claiming to be the wife of one of the men, and a boy fourteen years of age, came, and remaining a few days, they left. About this time Mr. D. W. Goodrich learned that his trunk had been broken and robbed of $13,000 in notes, bonds, and mortgages. Suspicion at once rested on this party, and they were followed, identified, and arrested at Wells, and lodged in jail here. The property being found, they gave their names as Frank Clifford, William E. Wilson, Mrs. Clifford, and a son by a former husband. In December they were brought up for trial. Wilson was put on the defense as there was the least evidence against him, and he was acquitted. It was then proposed to put him on the stand, where he proved that he was really the guilty man and that the others knew nothing about it. The others were also acquitted. The man Wilson was then re-arrested and afterwards the other, and the next July they were convicted and sent up for five years.

THE YEAR 1877.

At the March meeting in Albert Lea the "No License" vote came out ahead with sixty-five majority. The contest was spirited and active, and settled a great question for twelve months.

A severe snow storm raged for several days near the last of April, and the prediction was universal that it was a distressing time for the infantile "hoppers" who were just warming into life, and who came to an untimely end by the million.

Much ingenuity was displayed in the invention of engines of death for the unwelcome insects. Large numbers of devices were arranged, ditches dug, and various measures adopted. In the town of Alden alone a careful estimate placed the number of bushels caught at one thousand.

A woman mysteriously disappeared in Carlston in June; her name was Martha Sweet, and sometime afterwards her remains were found, she having drowned in ten inches of water, leaving a note that she intended to take an aqueous route for that 'other side."

In 1877, the tramps were so numerous that a military company was organized to look after them. The officers were: Captain, Theodore Tyrer; First Lieutenant, H. D. Brown; Second Lieutenant, Charles Kittleson.

The Burlington, Cedar Rapids & Northern railroad reached Shell Rock on the 15th of August, and created the usual rejoicing.

At Nunda on the 30th of August, the eldest son of Mr. Bessenger was killed by a runaway accident.

The county Bar Association met on the 4th of September at the office of Stacy & Tyrer, to take action on the accusations that had been so pointedly made in the "Pioneer Press" against Sherman Page, the judge of the district court. The feeling was that if true they should be known, and if not true the judge was certainly entitled to a vindication. The following committee was appointed to confer with other members of the bar in the district, and to have the charges investigated: E. C. Stacy, J. A. Lovely, and D. R. P. Hibbs. At a subsequent meeting a district committee which had been appointed reported that the charges were groundless.

The Minneapolis & St. Louis railway reached this point on the 11th of November, and there was a regular opening excursion. The Mayor and counci of Minneapolis, with railroad magnates, invited guests, and citizens, came on a special train, ran down to the State line and returned to partake of a dinner at the Hall House. The welcome speech was made by Judge Stacy, who, it is needless to remark, did ample justice to the occasion, to which Mayor De Laittre responded. Hon. W. D. Washburn, in the course of his remarks, said that this was the happiest day of his life, that this was

"The day he long had sought,"
And mourned because he found it not,"

or words to that effect. It was a day of general rejoicing, beccuse the city of Albert Lea and neighboring towns now had direct communication in the direction of the four cardinal points of the compass.

THE YEAR 1878.

In Bancroft on Sunday, the 24th of February, the friends of Mr. and Mrs. Daniel Prescott met at the house of Henry Loomis to celebrate the semi-centennial of their wedding day. Mr. Prescott appeared to be a well kept gentleman of the old school, still active and full of vivacity. Mrs. Prescott was a lady of rare culture and refinement, and at the age of four score was remarkable for her mental vigor and sprightliness. There were present three children, twenty-three grand-children, and five great grand-children. The presents covered a large center table with beautiful tokens of love and respect for the venerable pair. Two long tables were spread and charmingly ornamented with fruits, flowers, and dainties, and loaded with tempting viands, reflecting great credit upon those who prepared it with such taste.

Daniel Prescott and Miss Elizabeth Masservey were married on the 24th of February, 1828, at Appleton, Waldo county, Maine, from where they removed to Cincinnati, Ohio, in 1831, and from thence came to Bancroft in 1857. They raised seven children, three of whom were at this time living near their aged parents.

The golden ceremony on this occasion was performed by E. K. Pickett, Esq. The groomsman and bridesmaid being Mr. and Mrs. Jerry Ward. The following ritual for this rare event had been prepared by the magistrate:

"With this ring, Betsey, I thee wed,
So fifty years ago I said
While standing at the holy shrine.
I took your troth and plighted mine.
Our love was like a laughing stream,
Or as the morning's gentle beam,
No clouds or shadows hid from view,
The bliss in store for me and you.

The rivulet soon became a river,
Deeper and broader, ever, ever;
No longer skipping like a fawn,
But deep and wide it rolled along,
And so with you and I, dear wife,
These fifty years of wedded life
Have added depth, and strength, and truth,
And replaced joys for fleeting youth.

Faithful we've kept the marriage vow,
Honest and true, and even now,
Though fifty years we've walked together,
We'll now renew our troth forever.
I take thee, Betsey, for my wife,
Another fifty years of life,
Renew the bliss for you and me,
And Betsey says, so mote it be.

Angels attend and witness bear,
I here rejoin this happy pair,
The band now bound shall ever hold
With chains of love and links of gold.
Eternity can never sever
These cords of love thus bound forever;
A husband and a wife again,
And angels say Amen! Amen!"

The company separated after a most joyous time, interspersed with reminiscences and good wishes expressed for the continued health and prosperity of the aged couple. This, the first golden wedding in Bancroft, which was such a success, it is hoped was but the beginning of a long list to follow as time rolls on.

The Farmers' Mutual Fire Insurance Company of Bath was organized on the 1st of January, and commenced business on the 1st of February. H. P. Jenson was president, and Nels P. Peterson, secretary.

In March the question as to city or no city, charter or no charter, was the all absorbing one in Albert Lea. Petitions *pro* and *con* went to the Legislature; the number signing *for* were 132 tax payers; those *against*, 77 tax payers. The arguments were mostly in relation to the relative cost and to the influence of a city charter upon the prospective growth of the city.

It passed the Legislature and was submitted to the people on the 1st of April, and carried by 75 majority.

Mr. and Mrs. J. W. Smith had a surprise Crystal wedding on the 23rd of April. The bride appeared in her original dress, worn fifteen years before. Rev. R. B. Abbott and Rev. J. T. Todd officiated to readjust the marital tie. The occasion was an enjoyable one, the presents being numerous and appropriate.

The first city election was held on the 12th of May. The whole number of votes cast was 380, of which Frank Hall had 369.

Ole Oleson Fossom, who came to Manchester in 1856, and opened a farm which he cultivated till his death, passed on with the great majority on the 9th of June. He was a fine old gentleman.

In the fall W. C. Lincoln, County Auditor, plead guilty to a charge of embezzlement of school funds belonging to District No. 38, and was sent to State Prison for one year and fined $1,273, or double the amount of the misappropriation. It seems that the amount had been returned, and it is regarded by many as a deplorable mistake of Mr. Lincoln to plead guilty under the circumstances.

THE YEAR 1879.

In Hartland, on the 31st of January, Mr. Mads Madson, landlord of the Madson House, hung himself in his barn. The cause assigned for this act was temporary embarrassment.

THE YEAR 1880.

A terrible tragedy occurred on Sunday, October 2d. Ray McMillen, with Henry Johnson and his brother, started on a hunt, going out to White's Lake, where they expected to find sport through the day. They had shot one duck when the trio separated, McMillen being at the foot of the lake and the Johnsons to the north, where a number of ducks were seen. The two were away an hour or so; on returning they found McMillen sitting on a rail, a little benumbed with the cold, and on rising he stumbled and fell over the rail, discharging his gun, which took effect in the right side of the mouth, and entering the brain produced instant death. He was thirty years of age, a native of New York State, and had lived in Albert Lea two and one-half years. He left a wife and many friends.

THE YEAR 1881.

On the 28th of January a Post of the Grand Army was instituted in the city.

A Board of Trade in the city of Albert Lea was organized on the 10th day of February, and the following officers were elected: President, H. D. Brown; Vice President, W. P. Sergeant; Treasurer, C. M. Hewett; Secretary, C. W. Ballard; Executive Committee, D. E. Dwyer, W. W. Johnson, William Morin, D. G. Parker, G. Gulbrandson, and G. A. Patrick.

In June some children in the town of Moscow, who were playing in some clay that had been thrown from a well at a depth of thirty feet, found several copper coins with square holes through the center of them, not unlike the copper coins of the Chinese. If these coins actually came from that depth of undisturbed deposite it is one of the most remarkable discoveries in this line ever made.

THE YEAR 1882.

In January there was some sporadic smallpox in the city, but it was so carefully looked after by the proper authorities that it did not become epidemic.

On the 13th of January, 1882, Mr. and Mrs. David Hurd had their Silver wedding, which was the most noticeable event of the kind yet taking place in the county, because this couple, with Mr. and Mrs. C. C. Colby, were the first couples married in the town of Albert Lea, according to the report. On this occasion the weather was cold, but there was a house full, and a bountiful repast with warmth and geniality. The center table was strewn with silver tokens of love and esteem, and really a day to be long remembered by those who were present.

In June there was a gang of robbers in town who went through the railway station and several residences, getting considerable booty; but they soon left for a healthier climate.

On the 11th of April one of the most extensive conflagrations that ever afflicted Albert Lea occurred. Several buildings were consumed, and among the losses sustained were those of the "Standard" office, to the extent of about $3,000. Mr. L. Lace lost in personal property about $300. Other sufferers were W. Buel, Strauss & Schlesinger, Knatvold Brothers, D. E. Dwyer, Judge Town, Mrs. Pratton, J. P. Colby, W. M. Butler, C. F. Davis, T. J. Wauck and others.

CITY OF ALBERT LEA.

CHAPTER LII.

DESCRIPTIVE—EARLY BEGINNINGS—NECROLOGY—INDUSTRIAL ENTERPRISES—CITY GOVERNMENT—PERIODICALS—ASSOCIATIONS—EDUCATIONAL—RELIGIOUS—CEMETERIES—FRATERNAL ORDERS.

The city of Albert Lea is situated in the township bearing the same name, a full description of which will be found in another chapter. The city is located in sections eight, nine, sixteen, and seventeen. It is laid out in the usual form, in rectangular blocks, with alleys, some running north and south and others east and west. Broadway is a north and south street, one hundred feet wide, the others being eighty. Parallel with Broadway, on the east, is Newton, Elizabeth, and Lake; on the west are the avenues, Washington, Jefferson, Madison, Monroe, Adams, Jackson, Taylor, and Lincoln, with Grove and Park as local streets. South of the railroad the streets are numbered, First, Second, etc. Madison and Court are diagonal streets, converging toward the Southern Minnesota depot. Above the railroad are South, Pearl, and Cottage streets, the latter of which runs by the Court House; then Main, William, and Clark, where the first business place was located; then comes Water and Fountain streets. These are the the principal streets and avenues and give a general idea of the nomenclature associated with the highways.

Spring lake, which was at first not a repulsive body of water is within the city, but it is under going the process of being filled up, and in due time will exist only as a name and a recollection. Fountain Park, a comparatively late addition to the city, is a symetrical projection into Fountain Lake, at a good elevation, and is dotted with fine residences. The buildings in the city are of a good character, especially those lately constructed. Like all western cities, it began in a small way, the business blocks and dwelling houses were mere makeshifts, improvised to supply an emergency, except in rare cases. Now there is the ability and taste to supplement the utilitarian aspect of buildings with elegance, which is shown in the improved architectural pretentions.

Albert Lea is a delightful city in which to live; the natural inducements to purchase suburban residences are here in all their pristine beauty,—a salubrious climate, good society, near schools and churches, and but a few minutes walk from the depot. The environments and concomitants of the place, are such that we must be excused for dwelling upon them.

The surroundings of Albert Lea are fairer than dreamland. On the southeast is Lake Albert Lea with its waving lines of meadow and woodland; and on the north is the charming Fountain Lake, with its graceful, wooded slopes, cheerful headlands, and peaceful bays, half encircling the town; on the west and beyond these bright waters, other lakes lie in the quiet prairie, like islands on the bosom of the sea.

The Shell Rock River takes full volumes of limpid water from these basins, and flows southward along one of the loveliest of valleys.

The city, particularly the residence portions, is embowered in a flowery forest, and the very atmosphere of poetry is upon lake and river, woodland and prairie. Picturesque views are surrounded with overarching trees, embosomed cottages and villas. These placid and unruffled waters are rife with boating, fishing, and of course, love making in the humid summer afternoons and evenings, and no fleet of Venetian gondolas ever bore fairer freightage of beauty, laughter and song, than the many hued pleasure craft of Fountain Lake. As a summer pleasure resort nothing could be more superb.

The lakes and rivers are alive with fish and fowl. People from all over the East and South come here to pass a week or a month; and the angling and shooting leave nothing to be desired. Some take quarters at the hotels, some live in cottages, and others camp out, where the conventionalities of society may be measurably ignored, and communion with nature enjoyed without restraint. The people of Albert Lea should make a specialty of entertaining summer visitors, and transform the whole city into a rural boarding house community, where homelike fare and favor could be obtained without the starched formalities of hotel life at the summer resorts.

Around the lake there is a drive, but if the public-spirited citizens would make a boulevard around the entire lake, close to the shore, following the contour of its winding banks, it would be the finest drive between Long Branch and the Golden Gate.

Poets have sung of many beautiful spots, and painters pictured charming scenes, and here are scenes for both.

Below we copy an article published in the "Turf, Field and Farm" of New York, under date of May 22d, 1874:

"Albert Lea, a beautiful lake about thirteen miles in length and varying in width from a quarter of a mile to three miles, and situated in Freeborn county, Minnesota, is an attractive body of water to the sportsman. A gentleman, whose name is known to the whole country, and who is a thorough sportsman, writes us some interesting facts from that neighborhood. The elevation being great, the air is pure and the climate healthy. People seldom die there. A few years ago the lake was stocked with fish, but we are told that the 'Vandals who follow murder for a living, having no perception or appreciation of sport, have nearly drained it.' In the winter a hole is cut in the ice, and the fish are speared with a pitchfork and hauled away by the wagon-load. From five to twenty-five tons of pickerel have been taken out of the lake each winter for several years. It is gratifying to learn that the sportsmen of the State have been successful in the effort to have the Legislature pass a stringent law for the preservation of fish and game, and also that they are determined to see the law enforced. In the fall of the year ducks and geese visit Albert Lea in myriads, and it is said that no place on the continent affords better sport. Sandhill cranes cover the prairie and grain fields, and snipe, plover, and curlew are, to use an expressive phrase, 'as thick as flies in a country tavern,' and prairie chickens are without number. All this will sound most eloquent to the ear of the sportsman, and doubtless he will dream fond dreams of Albert Lea when he reads this paragraph."

In driving about the various lakes and natural parks, constant surprises are in waiting for those who appreciate nature in her quiet moods. One of the highest authorities as to sporting grounds is the above mentioned journal, and in connection with other pleasant things said about Albert Lea a few years ago, we cull the following:

"Col. S. A. Hatch has returned to the city from his shooting-box on the romantic shores of the lake at Albert Lea, Minnesota. He reports that the duck and geese shooting was never better than this fall. Quite a party of gentlemen from New York gathered at Albert Lea in the last days of September, and remained until the lakes closed on the 29th of October. The majority of them were Wall street magnates, who had shot ducks in various parts of the country, not excepting Maryland and Virginia and the Carolina coast. After a thorough experience they were unanimous in expressing the opinion that they never saw ducks in greater abundance, and of such delicate flavor, as in the bracing altitudes of Minnesota. They voted Albert Lea the center of the sportsman's paradise. It is just far enough removed from the great hatching district, to become the first feeding-ground of the full-grown birds. And the food is so abundant and of such fine quality, that the ducks fairly burst with fatness when stopped short in their flight by a charge of number sixes. Very large bags of canvas backs, mallards, red heads, and teal, were made every day by each member of the party. The goose shooting was also superb in October. In a small body of water, which the gentlemen christened Lake Rosa, rude blinds were made, and one day a well-known shot of the party killed six geese, in addition to a large number of red heads and mallards. Any one who has had experience in wild goose shooting, knows how difficult it is to bring the cautious birds to bag, and therefore he will appreciate the skill of the sportsman who captured six in a hunt lasting but a few hours. The sandhill cranes swarmed the prairies, but no effort was made to bring them to bag. We are surprised at this, for there is a charm in crane shooting, which is only heightened by the wariness of the huge birds. The pinnated grouse had packed early in October, and so not much time was wasted on them. When the "chickens" move in flocks, which number thousands, they will not lie to the dogs, and no pleasure is extracted from the pursuit of them, especially when water fowl swarm by the million right under your nose. The fishing was very fine this fall in the lakes about Albert Lea. One day shortly after the arrival of the party, Col. Hatch entered the house with a splendid string of pickerel in his hand. "What are those?" asked a well-known New Yorker, his eyes blazing with admiration. "Trout," was the laconic reply. "Good heavens! you don't tell me so. Why, they are the biggest trout I ever saw. Where did you catch them?" "They came from the lake which you see before you," said Col. Hatch, with a wave of the hand. "And are there any like those left in the lake?" queried the New Yorker, with the deepest interest in his tones. "Plenty of them," said the host. "Then, boys," almost shouted the enthusiastic disciple of Walton, rising from his chair, "no duck shooting for me to-morrow. I shall try my hand at the trout." When the would be fisherman realized that a joke had been played on him, he put on a grave face, and swore that the pickerel bred in the cool and clear waters of Fountain Lake were equal to the best trout ever taken from a mountain brook in Virginia, or a limpid stream in the Adirondacks. This fish story beats all hollow the little mud-hen narrative which had circulation last year. There seems to be something deceptive in the air of Minnesota. Objects do not always look what they really are. The Storm King swept down from the north earlier than usual this year. On the 29th of October, the ice was an inch and a half thick on the lakes, and the water fowl moved in solid bodies for the South, bringing the shooting to an abrupt close at Albert Lea."

Of course there is no place in the county, so interwoven with its history from the earliest period up to the present time as the county seat, and in respect to many points they are identical, and in giving something of the early settlement several items already alluded to, reappear here, in order not to destroy the connection. As to the town, the village or city, little attempt will be made to separate them here, although the town and the city governments will receive individual mention.

Those who first came here resolved to build a town that should become a city, and although their determination was supplemented by the natural advantages of the location, it is doing but simple justice to the pioneers to express the opinion that equal energy and determination, displayed almost anywhere else, would have accomplished a like result.

When Mr. Ruble made the proposition to LyBrand and Thompson to pool their united energies and means, and make St. Nicholas the metropolis of this region, they made a fatal mistake in spurning the offer, for that city, which so filled their minds as almost to dethrone common sense, now has no shelter, even for the owls and the bats, which are supposed to linger around deserted habitations.

Albert Lea village was platted by Charles C. Colby, and recorded on the 29th of October 1856, in Dodge county, of which it then formed a part. On the 24th of February, 1859, it was duly recorded in the Register's office of this county, and numerous additions have been made since that time, the most important of which will be mentioned.

The first plat recorded had the name of Charles C. Colby as surveyor. Austin T. Clark, as administrator of Lucius P. Wedge, signed the document. A. Armstrong was the Notary Public. John Wood was Register of Deeds, and J. E. Bancroft, Deputy Register. William Morin and George S. Ruble were also proprietors.

E. C. Stacy had a subdivision recorded on the 13th of October, 1877. H. C. Stacy, Surveyor.

Ballard's Addition was recorded on the 22d of March, 1880.

Out-lots of Parker's Addition, surveyed by W. G. Kellar, went on the record on the 22d of June, 1880.

F. A. Blackmer's addition was on the records on the 25th of June, 1880.

Charles W. Ballard's Subdivision to Albert Lea was recorded on the 15th of November, 1880.

Among the earlier additions were Kittleson & Johnson's, recorded as a subdivision on the 16th of June, 1869.

FrancisHall's addition was recorded on the 12th of June, 1859.

D. G. Parker's addition was made on the 28th of November, 1869.

The Railroad Addition, south of the railroad,

was made by William Morin, Francis Hall, H. W. Holley, and A. P. Man, at the time the railroad reached this point.

Augustus Armstrong had an addition recorded on the 31st of August, 1872.

North Point Subdivision was recorded on the 1st of February, 1871.

Francis Hall's Subdivisson was recorded on the 2nd of April, 1872.

It seems that a part of the south part of the city has never been platted, that between the Court House and railroad, but the residents there seem contented and happy.

EARLY EXPLORATION AND SETTLEMENT.

In the State history the reader will perceive the steps by which this quarter of the world was opened up to the Caucasian race, but here we have to record the visit of a single exploring party nearly twenty years before the country began to be actually settled, and this will be done while furnishing a sketch of the life of the Commandant of the expedition, which seems to naturally fit in at this point.

COL. ALBERT MILLER LEA was born in Richland, Grainger County, Tennessee, on the 23rd of July, 1808. His parents were Major Luke Lea and Lavinia Jarnagin. At thirteen years of age he entered college at Knoxville, Tennessee. In 1827 he received an apppointment at West Point, and graduated the fifth in his class in 1831. He was appointed a Lieutenant in the 13th Artillery but shortly afterwards exchanged positions with the since noted John B. Magruder, of the Seventh Infantry, and was stationed at Fort Gibson, then on the extreme frontier.

From thence he was ordered to Washington, there receiving instructions and orders to report to Knoxville, Tennessee, to survey and plan improvements for the Tenessee River and its tributaries. From this time he passed through the usual variations in army life, being detailed for different duties in several parts of the country, and in 1835, was in Fort DesMoines, Iowa, and there received orders to undertake a summer campaign to the St. Peters, now the Minnesota River.

On the seventh of June, 1835, the march was commenced with three detachments of sixty men each, with Captain Nathan Boone, a son of the Daniel Boone, as guide. The route taken was up the divide between the DesMoines and Mississippi Rivers to Lake Pepin, then the column turned west and headed for the source of the Blue Earth River, Kossuth county, in Iowa.

On this march the trip was made through Freeborn county. As near as can now be traced the column entered the county near the schoolhouse in district No. 30, in the town of Moscow. Proceeding thence in a circuitous route across a portion of Moscow, the southern part of Riceland, northwest corner of Hayward, and into Albert Lea township, striking Albert Lea Lake, which they named Fox Lake, and following up to section six, crossed into Pickerel Lake and halted for dinner on the banks of White's Lake. This lake was given the name of Lake Chapeau, from its resemblance to that form of a military hat. They then moved southwesterly to Alden and Mansfield, crossing the county line near the middle of section nineteen, and continued the march down the DesMoines to the place of starting, now the capital of Iowa.

In the latter part of the winter of 1835 36, Mr. Lea resigned his commission in the army, to take effect June 1st, in the mean time having obtained a leave of absence, which he improved by writing up for publication in book form, a sketch of this expedition, including a map of the country, which was published in Philadelphia by H. S. Tanner. In this book the name Iowa was first applied to the territory now composing the State of that name.

In May, 1836, the Colonel was married to Ellen Shoemaker, of Philadelphia. For a time he was located at the mouth of Pine River, below Rock Island, to survey some lands, which being completed he received the appointment of Chief Engineer of the state of Tennessee, with headquarters at Nashville, and for some time he was engaged in prosecuting internal improvements in that State. Soon afterward he was appointed by Martin VanBuren to establish the southern boundary of Iowa, which he did. Afterwards he was in the employ of the Baltimore & Ohio Railroad company as locating engineer. In March, 1841, he was appointed Chief Clerk in the war department, and in September of that year, upon the resignation of President Harrison's cabinet, he became Secretary of War *ad interim*, which he held for six weeks.

About this time, as elsewhere recorded, Jean N. Nicollet, a French *savant*, gave to Lake Chapeau the name of Albert Lea, which has since been transferred to the larger lake below the city.

In 1841, he accepted the appointment of Professor of Mathematics in the East Tennessee University at Knoxville, which position he held until 1851.

In the meantime, having lost his wife, he married Catherine S. D. Heath. He then started a new enterprise, the manufacture of glass in Knoxville, which proved a financial failure.

In railroad interests he afterwards went to Texas, and on the breaking out of the war between the two sections of the country, he offered his services to the Confederacy, and served in various capacities. His son Edward, who adhered to the Union cause, was killed at Galveston, Texas, while acting as chief officer of the steamer Harriet Lane.

After the close of the war, Col. Lea resided for a time in Galveston, but afterwards removed to Corsicana, Texas.

In June, 1879, on a special invitation of the municipality, he visited this city and region, and was given a right royal welcome, delivering an interesting address to the Old Settlers' Association. He was profuse in his expressions of astonishment at the change which had been wrought.

While preparing the history a letter was sent to Col. Albert M. Lea, asking if there was anything connected with his journey across the county, or in relation to his last visit here, to which he wished to add, and his brief reply is herewith published:

"Corsicana, Texas, August 18th, 1882.

Prof. I. H. Stearns, Albert Lea, Minn.

Dear Sir: Referring to your note of the 9th instant, allow me to say that more honor has been done me by the people of Freeborn county than my transient visit at an early day would seem to merit, and that I do not wish to make my name still more conspicuous in that connection by personal communications in your proposed HISTORY OF FREEBORN COUNTY, which you will doubtless fill with more interesting matter.

With thanks for your courteous tender. I am very truly your obedient servant,

ALBERT LEA."

George S. Ruble came here in July, 1855, to find a mill site, and after a careful reconnoissance selected a point at the foot of Lake Albert Lea, where he proposed to build a dam, and by raising the lake a few feet secure a splendid water power. While away for reinforcements, Jacob Lybrand secured that point, and so Mr. Ruble did the next best thing; came here and planted himself and built his mill.

Mr. Lorenzo Merry, from Cedar River, the man who gave his name to Merry's Ford, in Iowa, was here living in his wagon, which he had hauled here with an ox team; and he soon got up a log cabin on block eight between Clark and Water and Broadway and Washington streets, which of course is to be remembered as the location of the first residence of a white man in Albert Lea City. He went to Walnut Lake and built a hotel, and then to the Red River country. The next house was that of George S. Ruble, on what was called the Island. This may be described as a double log house, with magnificent proportions for those times, the size being 18x18 and 14x18 feet. This house still stands, but it has been sided up and measurably modernized.

The first mill was on the corner of the lake, south of its present location, a race having been cut from that point to the river some rods below; and there it stood and did good service until the 12th of April, 1861, when it was undermined by the freshet, and settled four feet at the upper end. It was never repaired, part of the machinery going to Northwood and a part into the new mill. The building of this mill, which was the nucleus of the village and city of Albert Lea, was commenced on the 29th of October, 1855.

The next residence to go up was on block nine, and as an evidence of the metropolitan ideas entertained in those early days by these pushing pioneers, it should be recorded that the next building to go up was a printing office, built by Mr. Ruble, and presented to Swineford and Gray, the first printers to penetrate this region. The next shanty to go up was by Daniel Hard, and Swineferd soon built an office and used the one presented by Ruble as a residence.

Mr. Merry opened the first hotel, although Mr. Ruble, having a house of two rooms, entertained people by the dozen, as his table was an extension one in a certain sense, and his beds were all elastic—that is, there were bunks on three sides of the room.

The Clark building, as it was called, was erected in 1856. The first building on the spot was Mr. Merry's boading house, which was burned in 1865. It was 14x16 feet, and had a few shelves with some goods.

Squire Clark used to hold court here. A ladder extended to a room above, and a trap-door to a hole below. In this room the court would meet, and in a jury case the people would have to be turned out of doors, and would listen through the cracks to the unconfined eloquence within, and know the verdict as soon as it was agreed upon.

The old settlers relate many anecdotes as to the marriages that were performed there; one of them, which is of course told as the first ceremony of the kind in town, if not in the county, and to one who has never looked up such matters, it is astonishing how many of these first events will be discovered. Well, the story is that when the first bridal pair stood up before the 'Squire, and had joined hands, while the crowd, with feverish anxiety, awaited the consummation of their plighted vows, the magistrate nerved himself to the task, with the awful feeling of responsibility resting upon him, and began: "Know all men by these presents", but finding that this did not sound all right, he began again. "To whom it may concern"; this "splurge" created such an impression that he abruptly stopped and called for the statutes or any book that had a marriage form, but on being told that the form was not essential, he ended the ceremony by pronouncing them husband and wife.

In this building it is reported that the first sermon was preached; Rev. Mr. Lowry and Rev. Mr. McReynolds being the early preachers.

On one occasion, a man who lived somewhere near, who had listened to what he considered a powerful discourse, offered publicly to give the minister half a cheese, if he would come over to his house and discuss the matter with "Lucinda," his wife, in whose Biblical knowledge he had the utmost confidence. The Sabbath School Convention at first met here; but the old building finished its own history in the fall of 1872.

The men who came here to work for Mr. Ruble were: Saxon C. Roberts, Joseph Willford, who was afterward frozn to death in Martin county, Charles F. Warren, H. V. Henderson, A. Ableman, L. C. Roberts, John B, Lenox, John Rion, Ed. Murphy, Arthur Boulton, Edward Henderson, and David Irons.

The pay roll for these men commenced on the 2d of November, 1855. Of course these men had to be boarded and lodged by Ruble, and Mr. H. Peck used to say that any one coming within forty miles of Albert Lea would swing round here and get a meal at Ruble's.

The next store in the place was opened by Col. Eaton, opposite where the Post-office now is.

Francis Hall, whom usage has transformed into Frank Hall, was the next man to come and commence general merchandising, and he has been a prominent and public spirited citizen ever since, being frequently mentioned in this work.

G. A. Watrous made the first brick, in 1857.

The land on the site of the city was pre-empted by Mr. Ruble on the east of Broadway, and by Mr. Merry on the west of that street. The latter secured 160 acres, 40 of which he sold to T. C. Thorn, who transferred it to William Morin, and he, being an engineer, surveyed and platted it.

At first the lots were sold fron $25 to $100 each, according to location. The fact that there was no exorbitant prices for lots was one of the elements contributing to the success of the town.

Mr. Ruble laid out 312 acres east of the town, and Thomas Smith, of Red Wing, also had an interest in the town site and sold town lots.

In 1857, during the fall, the hard times that prevailed in every section of the country, most seriously affected the growth and prosperity of the place, and a few of the lots east of the town were sold, and to-day that is Ruble's farm.

When Swineford and Gray, the printers, came, Mr. Ruble made arrangements to have a newspaper started at once, and endorsed their paper to Rounds, of Chicago, to secure press and material. In about a year it was sold to Gray, who finally turned it over to Botsford, but a sketch of the paper appears under the proper head.

Mr. Merry's interest was bought out by L. P. Wedge, a non-resident, who sent his relative, A. C. Wedge, to look after the property. L. P. Wedge subsequently died and his widow married Augustus Armstrong.

Charles Kittleson, a young man, came out west to obtain work, and not finding it, as he had no trade, became discouraged and was about to return to Wisconsin when Ruble offered him fifty cents a day to work in the mill, and afterwards he went to work for Frank Hall in his store. Subsequently some one built a saloon for him, which he kept until the war broke out, and then went into the army, in Captain Heath's company. On his return he was elected County Treasurer, and afterwards re-elected, serving ten years; he is now State Treasurer of Minnesota.

A. B. Webber was a Republican, and among other things he did for the good of the town, was building the Webber House, a part of which is still standing unoccupied next to the Chicago furniture establishment on Broadway. He went into the army, was in the commissary department, and afterwards moved to Kansas, and thence to California.

The first dance was on that first Christmas eve, with C. C. Colby to furnish the music, and it was an enjoyable affair. Mr. Colby is now in New York in the music business.

The first child born in town was a daughter of Mr. Walford and his wife Mary, in March, 1856; her name was Louisa. She is married and now lives in Vinton, Iowa.

Mr. Crowfoot started the first blacksmith shop, and in due time others came in, and the town has always been well supplied with iron working artizans.

The supplies in those times were generally brought from McGregor, Iowa, and the transportation was from two to three dollars for a hundred pounds, depending upon the weather to some extent. Sometimes several weeks would be consumed in a trip, as the country was roadless and bridgeless, and the water in the sloughs would be too deep to ford.

Hall's first store was built by Wedge & Morin. When Hall went into his new store his old place was occupied by Whitten.

One of the early society events was the marriage by Colonel Eaton, who was a Justice of the Peace, of Mr. Heath, the second Sheriff of the county, to Miss Rice. The ritual employed was a striking improvement upon Squire Clark's jerkey impromptu. The magistrate's fee was $2.50, in gold. What the Colonel could possibly do with so much gold in those days no one could conjecture.

The story is told of a devout church member who had a passion for card playing, and who spent most of his evenings in the saloons, engaged in his favorite game, but he was quite regular at the prayer meetings, and he would take part in the exercises, not unfrequently interluding his remarks with such expressions as "at this stage of the game," "go it alone," get euchred," and "playing the best trump," which evidently conveyed quite as much meaning as he intended.

In 1857, the new-comers were numerous; the village of Albert Lea began to assume some proportions, and it is a matter of congratulation that it is still growing, the present season having witnessed the erection of some of the finest buildings in town, as residences and for business purposes

As to what became of the men who came to work for Mr. Ruble: E. W. Murphy is one of the leading merchants of Albert Lea; Roberts and his son Lars went to Kansas: the Hendersons left some years ago; Gertler, Ableman and Willford have climbed the golden stair. Mr. Willford had the general management of the gang.

Lorenzo Merry had been on the ground one month, and the only persons then known to be in the county, according to E. W. Murphy, were Theodore Lilly, Charles C. Colby and two sisters, and Charles Wilder and brother, who were all on the west side of the lake; and on the opposite side were Chris. Mickleson and family, and Charles Peterson.

Mr. Merry remained about two years, when he started for pastures new.

In 1856, a stage line commenced running through Albert Lea, and the people began to feel that they must very soon begin to put on some style, for this brought in settlers in a rapid manner.

In the summer of 1856, the urgent and pressing necessity was felt for an establishmsnt where, to use the characteristic vernacular, the ever festive "bug juice" might be dispensed, and in response to this demand, a man made his appearance on the scene and opened a saloon.

When Frank Hall arrived, he made everything lively; as one of the early settlers remarked, "he was a buster," and at once commenced the erection of a fine store-for those times, and opened a first-class assortment of goods, embracing general merchandise in great variety. This was in 1857. A number of years afterward he built the "old brick store," which was and still is a landmark.

Mr. Wilder, at an early day, opened a small stock of general merchandise and a large stock of whisky, in Hall's old place. At this time the inhabitants of the village were few, but as the tide of emigration in this direction was on the flood-tide, and the country was fast settling up, the streets presented a busy appearance.

Brock Woodruff opened a small store of general merchandise, and as that was the first thing usually called for by the thirsty traveler, he also put in liquid refreshments.

'Squire Clark may be described as an inferior looking man, who had a chronic opthalmia. He had considerable professional pride, and when he was called down to Shell Rock to marry Mr. Andrews senior, and completely broke down, he was a good deal mortified, telling his friends when he returned that he "completely broke down, by gosh!" H. D. Brown was present at that wedding.

At one time there was a man who was on trial for some offense, and he demanded a jury, but the justice decided that he could only have a jury by paying the expenses of such luxury. This startling proposition was shown by the counsel for the defense to be contrary to the statutes, but 'Squire Clark stated that he had once so decided, and he did not propose to reverse his own decision, for a Justice in all things should be consistent.

Affairs were not long in assuming form and coherence in the town; men gravitated to their proper level, a subdivision of labor, the true index of civilization, resulted, and to-day there is a thriving and prosperous community.

NECROLOGICAL.

It has been deemed proper to furnish a brief sketch of some of the most prominent men and women who have drifted into that unseen Sea, which is but a step from our present existence, and ultimately swallows every living soul. It is not unlikely that some names that should appear here have been omitted, for it is a notable thing to see how soon one is disremembered, who, having joined the endless possession, has passed from mortal view,

AUGUSTUS ARMSTRONG.—The thread of his life was snapped asunder on the 18th of August, 1873 at the age of 39 years. He was born in Milan, Ohio, and after the necessary preliminary education, began the study of law in a school in Cincinnati, and after admission to the bar, began practice. In 1857, he came to this county, where as a lawyer, public officer, private citizen, and legislator, he became identified with the growth and prosperity of the rising State. He was the first County Treasurer and the first district Attorney. In 1865, he was elected to the Legislature, returned the next year, was sent to the Senate in 1867, and again to the House in 1869. He was one of the directors of the Southern Minnesota railroad, and was United States Marshal of Minnesota. Stricken down in the meridian of his life's journey, Minnesota lost a son very faithful, loboring for the good of all. His friends mourned a counselor and his family lost the sun that shone o'er their pathway. He was married on the 10th of October, 1861, to Mrs Mary J. Wedge. He left two children; Mary A. and Augustus.

SAMUEL BATCHELDER.—A leading citizen of Freeborn county, was born in Topsham, Orange county, Vermont, on the 28th of April 1825, and after attending the common school went to Norwich University, and there regularly graduated at the age of twenty years. He then studied law under Judge Underwood and was duly admitted to the bar and entered upon the practice of his profession. Symptoms of pulmonary disease appearing he went to Georgia where his condition was materially improved. He had already been married to Miss Susan P. Taplin who went south with him. In 1850, he went to Kemper Springs, Mississippi, and taught and conducted an Academy with eminent success. In 1856, he removed to Philadelphia, and leaving his wife there spent the winter of 1856-57 in Minnesota. At first he took a claim near Mr. Dill's but relinquished that and purchased a farm near Itasca, which is still known by his name. The following season he returned to Philadelphia and took charge of Attleborough Academy, about twenty miles from there. In 1861, his wife died, leaving a child six months old. This little one subsequently died as had two others, also in infancy. Two years later, in 1863, he came here for a permanent residence. In 1867, he was married to Miss Adide Sims of Albert Lea. He was elected Superintendent of Schools for Freeborn county, serving with rare ability for three years, and in 1869, was chosen County Auditor, a position he occupied with credit to himself until 1877. He built a house in this city, where his estimable widow now lives. He was one of the few early members of the Presbyterian church, and was a ripe scholar, with unusual attainments, being especially efficient in mathematics, Latin, and Greek. His character for honesty, integrity, and perfect reliability, was never questioned. It may be truly said that he was unselfish, true, and firm in his convictions of right. He was sadly missed in the secular and church circles.

ASHLEY M. TYRER was a native of Concord, Erie county, New York, and studied law in the office of Judge Hazelton, at Jamestown, Chautauqua county. Sometime after the war he came to Albert Lea, and went into the office of Augustus Armstrong, and afterwards with Judge Stacy. His death was in June, 1880. He was an honorable man, highly respected, a member of the Masonic fraternity, and of the Presbyterian church.

N. H. Ellickson.—Mr. N. H. Ellickson, of Albert Lea, one of the first settlers of this county, had an extensive acquaintance, and was well known as a man of ability and learning. He was the editor of the first Norwegian paper printed in thr United States, and for a number of years was coroner of this county. He died February 1st, aged 58 years, and was buried in the cemetery west of this city, where "Life's fitful fever o'er, he sleepeth well."

Mrs. Minerva Blackmer, widow of Dr. Franklin Blackmer, entered this world in Middlebury, Vermont, on the 9th of January, 1811. At the age of three years, her parents moved to Chautauqua county, New York, where they were the first settlers. She was left motherless at thirteen years of age, and assumed the care of the younger children. At the age age of twenty she was married to Dr. Blackmer, and five years later went to Ohio and lived in the town of Amherst. In the year 1856, they removed to Minnesota and located in Albert Lea. After living here more than twenty years, the Doctor died, in 1877. Most of her life was spent on the frontier, as she removed three times to the border of civilization to help subdue the wilderness. She was remarkably well fitted for success in such an arduous life; possessing, as she did, a strong constitution, with an earnest will she endured hardships beyond the ability of many. She was always happy in making others comfortable. Her departure to an unknown frontier was on the 17th of May, 1882.

"After the shower, the giving sun,
Silver stars when the day is done.
After the snow the emerald leaves,
After the harvest the golden sheaves."

Mrs. Charity Fay.—The wife of L. W. Fay, was born in Otterville, Indiana, and came to this county in 1857. The dial of time struck its last hour for her on the 25th of May, 1882. A husband and three children were left to love and remember a beloved wife and mother.

Mrs. Mary Dow Rowell, wife of Mr. H. Rowell, yielded up her natural life on Sunday morning, the 11th of June, 1876, at three score and eight years. She was a native of Norfolk, England; was married to Mr. Rowell in Chelsea, England, in October, 1831. The next year they came to New York, and lived there two years. Then spent eight years in New Orleans and Vicksburg. In 1840 went up the Mississippi as far as Illinois, and lived near Springfield four years; then pushed on up to Wisconsin. In 1854 they came to Rochester, in this State, and in 1869 came here, where the family became well known. While in New Orleans, Mrs. Rowell had an attack of Yellow fever, from the effects of which she never recovered.

John Colby. At the age of three score and ten, on the 5th day of June, 1876, he was gathered to his fathers. His nativity dated from the 4th of December, 1806, in the Green Mountain State. He was married on the 21st of January, 1829, to Miss Hannah Rowell. In 1835, he removed to Pennsylvania and remained there fifteen years, then came west as far as Wisconsin where he lived six years; then got over on this side of the Mississippi, and pre-empted the farm now in possession of some of the family. He was an honest, upright man, held in great regard by his acquaintances. A wife, one son and seven daughters, all married, survive him. His remains were deposited in the cemetery on part of the land where he first located.

Mrs. Amanda Woodruff came in 1856 with her husband, and found a place in the Burr Oaks in London township, and in 1857 removed to Albert Lea. She was true to all the instincts of womanhood, and was thus an eminently useful woman. On the 28th of May, 1879, the cares of life were quietly laid down for whatever else may be in store for her.

Ole O. Simonson died suddenly on the 21st of February, 1881, of Cerebro-spinal Meningitis, while filling the office of Register of Deeds. He was a very conscientious, careful, painstaking, accurate and reliable man, and his loss was deeply felt throughout the county. Suitable resolutions were passed by the county officers in commemoration of his services. He was born in Normandy, was forty years of age at the time of his death, and left a widow and four children.

B. J. House was formerly a member of the Massachusetts legislature, where he served with great ability. He came west in 1858, locating in

Albert Lea. He was elected three times as Probate Judge, and held other positions of responsibility. He served in the Fourth Minnesota Regiment, from which he was honorably discharged, and remained a respectable private citizen. He was mustered out of earthly service on the 22d of January, 1879.

HIRAM J. JONES, one of the oldest persons in the county, died during the year 1879, much respected.

MRS. ELIZABETH WILLIAMS was born in Onondaga county, New York, and at an early day married Mr. Gideon Marlett. They moved west to Elkhart, Indiana, and while there her husband died. She afterwards married Mr. R. Williams at Chillicothe, Illinois, and they came to Albert Lea in 1857. Mrs. Williams was one of the six who organized the Congregational church in 1858. Her loss was especially felt in the church. Her trials ended on the 18th of June, 1877, at the age of 63 years.

INDUSTRIAL.

Albert Lea is a commercial city. It is true there are a few manufacturing establishments on a moderate scale, and most of them are mentioned in a briefway. No attempt is made togive a business directory of the city; the changes in this respect are so frequent that a correct list of all the business houses might be written to have it very imperfect by the time it gets into print. Among the industrial enterprises may be mentioned the following,which, to save too many headings, includes the Post-office and Banks.

POST-OFFICE.—The office was opened at an early day, as mentioned in the early history, when there was but the house of Mr. Merry, before Mr. Ruble had got out of his tents, and while the bulk of the inhabitants were his workmen. A petition was drawn up, and all signed it, requesting a Post-office, to be called Albert Lea. It was favorably considered, and Lorenzo Merry was appointed Postmaster. The office was at first in his house, but when Clark opened his store he was appointed deputy Postmaster. Mr. A. C. S vineford was afterward appointed to the position, while Clark still held his old place until Col. Eaton was appointed deputy, and removed the office to his boot and shoe store, which was on the Hall House block.

Clark kept the mail on a shelf in his store. Eaton had a case made, with twenty-four call boxes and four lock boxes. But a single one was let for some time, and that was taken by George S. Ruble. Col. Eaton himself was appointed Postmaster in 1861, and continued to keep it for some years. President Johnson appointed D. K. Stacy, Postmaster, and he kept it in his law office. When General Grant became President, the Colonel was re-appointed, and for a time it was held in a building on the corner of Newton and William streets. In 1870, it was placed in a building put up for the purpose on Broadway. G. Johnston was the next Postmaster, appointed in the spring of 1876. Mr. H. A. Hanson received the appointment in November, 1881, and the office was removed to its present location in the Opera House block. It has 730 call boxes and 194 lock boxes, and is roomy and convenient.

It 1868 it was made a Money Order office, the first order sold being dated on the 2d of November. Seven mails are received each day by rail, and a tri-weekly from Owatonna by stage. It is rated as a third-class office. S. H. Cady has been the efficient mailing clerk and assistant for eight years. The salary of the Postmaster is $1,600 per annum. The stamps, &c., sold in 1881 amounted to $5,053.52; and the money order business, $38,101.24.

FREEBORN COUNTY BANK.—Thomas H. Armstrong, President; W. B. Rumsey, Cashier. The correspondents are the Merchants National Bank, at St. Paul; The Security Bank, at Minneapolis; The First National Bank, at Chicago; the American Exchange National Bank, in New York; The Batavian Bank, at LaCrosse; and the First National Bank, in Milwaukee. The deposits average about $80,000. This bank was started on the 1st of September, 1874, by the present proprietor.

H. D. BROWN & CO.'S BANK.—This banking house was started in the fall of 1669, by Frank Hall, who at first had the safe in his store; but he soon built the brick block where the bank now is, on the corner of Broadway and William streets. In the fall of 1871, the business was bought out by H. D. Brown, who was sole proprietor until 1876, when D. R. P. Hibbs became associated with him, and is still interested in the ownership. The correspondents of this bank in the business centers are: First National Bank, Minneapolis; First National Bank, St. Paul; Merchants' Loan and Trust Company, Chicago; Alexander Mitchell's

Bank, Milwaukee; Fourth National Bank, New York; and The LaCrosse National Bank. This institution has deposits to the extent of $75,000.

CITY BANK.—This banking house began business in 1878, on the 1st of September. Gilbert Gulbrandson has been the proprietor from the first; D. W. Dwyer is Cashier, and it does a general banking business, having deposits to the extent of $70,000. The banks with which it transacts business are: Dawson, Smith & Shaffer, St. Paul; The Merchants' National, Chicago; Marshall & Ilsley, Milwaukee; and American Exchange National, New York.

ALBERT LEA FLOURING MILL. This is the only flouring mill in town; it has two run of stones and can grind 125 bushels in ten hours. For power it has Fountain Lake, which may be said to be the headwaters of Shell Rock River, and this is communicated by two turbine wheels, with ten and fifteen horse power respectively. In addition to this there is a steam engine of forty horse-power, manufactured by A. P. Allis, of Milwaukee. A. M. Avery has managed the mill for the past three years. It does custom work.

During the summer of 1882 a feed-mill was added, to be driven by an improved vertical windmill—in which the wind is admitted through slats, to operate upon a drum with buckets not unlike a turbine wheel. This mill is identified with the early history of the town, and is owned at this time jointly by Mr. Ruble and Mr. Ball.

SPRING LAKE CREAMERY.—This establishment is owned and operated by a joint stock company, with a capital of $10,000, and is located at the foot of Broadway, near the lake. Some of the leading business men in the city are interested in the enterprise. The stockholders were John Godley, Frank Hall, F. A. Blackmer, A. C. Wedge, J. W. Smith, Knatvold Brothers, E. S. Prentice, H. A. Colburn, Theodore Tyrer, D. R. P. Hibbs, H. D. Brown, W. P. Sergeant, and William Hazleton.

The officers of the company are: President, A. C. Wedge; Secretary and Treasurer, D. R. P. Hibbs; Superintendent, William Hazleton.

The business was started on Tuesday the 11th of May, 1881, with cream from 200 cows, although 1,000 had been promised. During the first year the number of cows having increased, the average make was between seven and eight hundred pounds a day.

Specific directions are given as to how the milk shall be set by the farmers, in cans of certain size, and the price paid is fifteen cents or more an inch for cream, which is equivalent to a pound of butter. The business being new the farmers are only beginning to learn how to get the best results from their cows; one very desirable point being to lengthen the season as far as possible, and to do this, catttle should be started early on green feed, which is inexpensively accomplished by sowing rye in the fall, to put them on early; and the fall which is apt to be dry should be lengthened out by sowing corn fodder to the extent of one fourth of an acre for each cow.

As to the income from cows where cream is sold to a creamery, the annexed statements are good examples of how the dairy pays:

One man, who had eighteen cows, realized during the season $1,021,68.

Another with sixteen cows, received $882 73.

Twenty cows' cream for one month was sold for $143.54, and six cows for the same length of time nitted $40.74.

Examples might be multiplied but the above items are sufficient to furnish an idea of what the profits on the business actually is.

RULES OF THE ALBERT LEA CREAMERY COMPANY.

"The following rules have been adopted by the Albert Lea Creamery Company, to keep up the high standard of the butter of their manufacture. They are the same as have been adopted by the creameries of Iowa, and have resulted in placing that State at the head of the butter manufacturing interests of the country. These rules will be strictly adhered to:

1. Any patron found selling milk from an unhealthy cow, or from cows still feverish from calving, will be dropped and the case reported to the civil authorities.

2. Cream from milk showing careless and uncleanly milking, or containing insects or dirt of any kind, will not be accepted.

3. Milk should be kept out of vegetable cellars, and its surroundings be kept free from all odors and impurities.

4. No tainted or frozen cream will be received.

5. No collector will, in any case, take cream except what he himself skims from the cans.

6. Any person discovered tampering with cream in any fraudulent way, either by stirring,

pouring in water, or any other substance, will be dropped and subjected to punishment by law.

7. Cream from milk standing in low temperature is thin and will not hold out. Such cream will not be taken unless the proper reduction be made. The proper temperature for milk to stand in is from 50 to 60 degress, and to make honest cream; milk should stand from fourteen to twenty-four hours in summer, and from twenty-four to thirty-six in the winter before skimming.

8. Ice and snow are detrimental to cream, and when used in milk will not be taken.

9. Two different milking must not be put into the same can, nor must the milk or can be disturbed after the milk is set.

10. Milk must stand at least ten hours after straining before the cream can skimmed and then be determined by the collector whether it is in condition to skim or not.

11. It is distinctly understood by all that the word inch is used as the equivalent of a pound or half pound of butter, according to the size of the can, and the creameries reserve the right to pay any patron for the number of pounds his cream will make.

12. Patrons are required to notify their creameries at once of any neglect of the collectors, or any failure on their part to conform with the above rules.

ALBERT LEA CREAMEY CO."

ELEVATORS AND WAREHOUSES.—The produce of the county which is shipped from this city is handled by the following concerns:

Armstrong's elevator, which is 30x50 feet, two stories, and will hold 4,000 bushels. It is owned and operated by T. H. Armstrong. In 1870 this was erected by the farmers of the county, as a company, and managed by them for about four years, when it was sold to the present owner, who put in a two horse-power engine. It is managed by John Heising, who purchases grain and hides.

William W. Cargill put up a small warehouse on the completion of the Southern Minnesota railroad to this point. This building collapsed some time after, and he put up the present building, which has a capacity of about 15,000 bushels and an eight horse-power engine. The firm is now Cargill Brothers, who are large buyers all all along the line, and deal in grain, hogs and hides.

Another ware-house was built just before the railroad was completed, by Bassett and Huntingdon. It is a frame building, and is now simply used as a storehouse for oats and corn by Cargill Brothers.

Vining, Calkins & Co. put up a small warehouse and used it but a few years. They had an engine, the power from which was used mostly in cleaning grain. It would hold about 8,000 bushels; it is owned by L. F. Hodges & Co. and is now laying idle.

An elevator with a capacity of 30,000 bushels was put up by Henry Rowell in 1876. He owned and operated it for about three years, when it was disposed of to Cargill Brothers, who took it to Sherman and it has since been burned. It had a ten horse-power engine.

In 1877, Sergeant and Skinner built an elevator at a cost of $7,500. It is a frame building, with a capacity of about 35,000 bushels, and is operated with an eight horse-power engine. In 1879 Mr. Sargent's interest was purchased by H. D. Brown, amd the firm is now Brown & Skinner, who buy wheat only.

At the same time R. M. Todd & Co. of Rock Falls, Iowa, put up a flat ware-house, for the purpose of buying wheat for their mill.

Kimmer & Lamb put up that same season a small ware-house at a cost of $500. This was at first rented by Todd & Co., but is now owned by that firm.

D. G. Parker subsequently put up his warehouse, a one-story building, and buys wheat and barley.

The Albert Lea Board of Trade built a one-story ware-house in 1881, and began the purchase of wheat. It is now used as a store-house by Ransom Brothers.

It is understood that the prices are well up to the large wheat markets, after deducting the freights.

OLSON & ANDERSON, WAGON-MAKERS AND GENERAL BLACKSMITHING.—This establishment has been in operation since 1869, with Martin Olson as a member of the firm. The shop is on Clark Street. At first general blacksmithing business only was done, but in 1879, the manufacture of wagons and buggies was commenced. In 1882 the firm put in a small steam engine of six horse-power. They do considerable plow repairing and other like kinds of work.

G. A. Hauge & C. Christopherson manufacture wagons and repair plows. They also manufacture C. D. Edwards Ditchers, which cuts a ditch two and one half feet wide and three and one half deep. The power is conveyed by a capstan turned by horses or oxen, and it seems to be a valuable device for the purpose of excavating drainage ditches. Mr. Hauge purchased the establishment in 1875. About seven hands are employed. The shop is a large brick building on Washington street, near Spring Lake, and has a horse-power to drive some of the machinery. Such an establishment is of great value in the midst of an agricultural community.

Albert Lea Carriage Shop.—Charles Drommerhausen is the proprietor, having started the business in 1866, on the corner of Newton and William streets, in a blacksmith shop, where he did repairing and made a few wagons and sleighs. In 1868, he moved to Clark street and built the shop he still occupies, and after a time commenced the manufacture of carriages and a variety of light wagons. The establishment has three buildings and quite an extensive business.

Wagon, Carriage, and Blacksmith Shop, Joseph Peffer, Proprietor.—This wagon shop was started in 1869, and work continued in it until 1878, when a blacksmith shop was added. General repairing, blacksmithing, horse shoeing, and wagon making is carried on, employing four men.

Blacksmithing.—C. P. Johnson oped a shop in May, 1882, and does general repair work and horse shoeing.

A Wagon Shop was opened by Brown & Pratt, in 1867, and after changing hands several times it was bought by A. J. Balch, who added blacksmithing and kept it in operation until August, 1882, when it passed into the hands of F. W. Balch and M. C. Larson. They do general repairing and horse shoeing.

Boat Building.—In 1865, Mr. C. D. Marlett built a shop in which to construct boats. It is still in operation by Mr. Marlett, who also does general repairing.

The city is not noted as a manufacturing place, but it is predicted that in the near future more attention will be paid to the subject; for manufacturing, especially of articles having a general sale, serves as a kind of business balance wheel to steady affairs during crop shortages or other local fluctuations. A flouring mill on a large scale would conduce to the prosperity of the city, and in due time it will no doubt be established.

Cigar Manufactory.—Thomas J. Wanek began manufacturing cigars on the 6th of April, 1878. Cigar manufacturers are still amenable to the revenue tax, started during the war of 1861. The license to start with is $10 per year, and then a stamp tax of $6 per thousand must be affixed to all that are made. About thirty-five or forty thousand are put up each month. Among the various brands made are the "Select," "Henry Clay," "Evening Star," "Happy Dream," "Protector," "Magic Slipper," "Shade," and "La Montana."

Merchandising.—Albert Lea is the trading point for the whole county, for while there are some good stores in the townships, the bulk of the trade is done at the county seat. Here may be found grocery stores, dry goods, hardware, agricultural implements, furniture, drugs and medicines, clothing, millinery, fancy goods, and in fact, all the usual variety of articles required by the present stage of civilization.

Lager Beer Warehouses.—C. and J. Michels have a refrigerating storehouse for their LaCrosse beer. It holds perhaps two hundred barrels, and is stored here to be shipped northwest and south, about a car-load a week being disposed of. Mr. T. Blacklin is the agent at this point.

John Gund Brewing Company has a refrigerating warehouse at the depot, which holds about two hundred barrels of lager beer. It is sold along the line of road to the extent of about three car-loads every two weeks. O. Knudsen is the manager at Albert Lea.

It may be remarked that the growth of the lager beer business has been rather marked, and when we remember that the Anglo-Saxon race is a drinking race, as is also the Scandinavian and the Celtic race, their favorite beverage being spirits, the change in favor of malt liquor is noticeable. What is to be the outcome is a matter that the political and social scientists may speculate upon, as the question is not yet decided whether the use of malt liquor, in contradistinction to spirituous, is really a guard against drunkenness.

HOTELS.

Hall House.—This building was erected for a dwelling by Frank Hall, in 1866 or '67. In about four years he remodeled the house, and it has since been run as a hotel. A man named Foster was the first landlord, but after a year or two Mr. Hall assumed charge, and has conducted it ever since. It is a three-story brick, has 33 guest rooms, is near the central part of the city, and has the reputation of being a good hotel.

GILBERT HOUSE.—This building was erected by Morin, Armstrong, and others, in 1868, for a cheese factory, and run as such a couple of seasons. S. S. Sutton, in the meantime, had come into possession of the property and converted it into a hotel, known as the Lake House. After a year or so it was sold to Warren Gilbert, who is still the owner. The next lessees were Gardner & Hunter, who run it a few years when a dissolution of partnership occurred, the latter continuing as proprietor about one year longer. During this time it had been changed to the Gardner House. The present proprietor, John B. Foote, leased the premises in 1879, and since then the capacity of the house has been doubled, and the standard raised so that it now ranks among the best hotels of the city. Seventy-five guests can be comfortably accommodated at this hotel.

LA CROSSE HOUSE.—This was built by the present proprietor, L. Oentrich, in 1877. It is a two-story frame, and can accommodate about twenty guests. It is located on Clark street, west of Broadway.

CITY HOTEL.—In 1867, William Fenholt erected this hostlery, and still continues its management. It is a two story frame house, and can accommodate about thirty guests. It is located on Clark street, east of Broadway.

NATIONAL HOUSE.—This was built in 1875 by Andrew Rolfson, who conducted it until the first of September, 1882, when H. A. Crandall became proprietor. It is a two story frame house, situated on East Clark street, and can accommodate about thirty-five guests.

WINSLOW HOUSE.—This house was built at the station of the Minneapolis & St. Louis railroad, on the completion of that line to Albert Lea, in 1878. It was run by Mr. Bunker until 1882, and has since been conducted by Frank Hall. It is a two story brick, and contains twenty-six rooms.

ALBERT LEA HOUSE.—This sign appears on the outside of a white frame house, nearly oppothe Winslow House, but as the proprietor did not possess sufficient courtesy to answer the few civil questions propounded to him, no further remarks can be made regarding this place.

There is a hotel and boarding house near the depot on the Southern Minnesota railroad, kept by Mr. Brandon. It is a neat and home-like place, and gives good satisfaction to its patrons.

CITY GOVERNMENT.

In the winter of 1878, the city charter was granted by the State Legislature, in obedience to a numerously signed petition of the tax-payers of the village. And having been accepted by a vote of the people, on the 12th day of May, 1878, the city government was organized, the first officers being: Mayor, Frank Hall; Board of Aldermen, W. P. Sergeant, President, J. W. Smith, R. E. Johnson, John F. Anderson, and E. D. Porter, two from each ward; Clerk, Fred. S. Lincoln.

After the organization, the various details requiring action were attended to. Some of the most important of which will be mentioned.

The city Justices were required to furnish bonds for the faithful discharge of their duties in the sum of $1,000 each. The City Treasurer for $5,000. The license for the sale of beer was fixed at $100, and both malt and spirituous liquors at $250.

The second meeting was on the 15th of the same month, when the Mayor delivered his inaugural address.

A license fee for Cole's circus, which desired to exhibit, was fixed at $25.

The city Assessor's bonds were fixed at $500; the city Attorney's, $500, and various committees were appointed. At a subsequent meeting the order of business was established.

1st. Reading of Minutes.

2d. Reports of Committees.

3d. Action on the reports of Committees.

4th. Unfinished business.

5th. New business.

Meetings of the board were arranged for the 1st and 3d Tuesdays of each month.

The first ordinance was passed on the 1st of May, and related to the sale of intoxicating beverages.

The city printing, after some manouvering, was given to the "Enterprise."

Side walks early received attention.

In June the pay of the police was fixed at $45 per month.

The machinery of the city government was set

in motion and run with little friction considering its newness, and the financial condition at the end of the year presented a good showing, as the expenditures had not been extravagant, and there was a small balance in the treasury.

The exhibit was as follows:

Cash received	$5,549 52
Cash paid out	5,523 11
In the treasury	26 41

1879.—The election was on the 5th of May. There were two candidates for Mayor, H. D. Brown and W. P. Sergeant. Mr. Brown was elected by seven majority, and the officers this year were: Mayor, H. D. Brown; Aldermen, W. P. Sergeant, President, Thomas H. Armstrong, Elland Erickson, J. W. Smith, William Fenholt, and John H. Anderson; Clerk, John Anderson; Attorney, R. M. Palmer; Assessor, D. N. Gates; Street Commissioner, E. D. Porter; Chief of Police, Reuben Williams; City Surveyor, William Morin.

Liquor licenses were fixed at $150, and the one hundred dollar licenses for selling malt liquors were discontinued. The license for a brewery was fixed at $200 a year.

On the 27th of June it was voted to purchase a La France Steam fire engine at a cost of $2,800. This was done after careful investigation. The question as to the location of an engine house was one of the problems the Council had to wrestle with. Several lots were offered, and finally two were accepted which were presented by William Morin and Thomas H. Armstrong. On the 26th of August the engine arrived, and after examination and testing, it was declared satisfactory.

An ordinance, passed to prevent the obstruction of certain streets by forbidding the feeding of teems on them, was vetoed by the Mayor on account of its improver discriminations and because the streets were made for use, and the prosperity of the city largely depended upon the trade brought by the persons who would be thus incommoded.

1880.—The officers this year were: Mayor, R. C. VanVechten, who received 358 votes out of 390; Treasurer, N. H. Shaugh, who received 393 votes; Justice of the Peace, E C Stacy, who received 391 votes, and H A Haukness; Aldermen, Wm Morin chairman, O. F. Nelson, J. A. Anderson, with those holding over; Clerk, John Anderson; Street Commissioner, E. D. Porter; Treasurer, W. A. Higgins; Chief of police, E. D. Patrick; City Engineer, A. Motzfeldt.

Some of the salaries were fixed as follows: Chief of Police, $45 a month, and the night watchman $35. The clerk $250 a year; Street Commissioner $2 a day for actual work; Engineer of steam fire engine, $150 a year, and the fireman $60 a year; the city engineer $100 a year.

On the 21st of June a bell was authorized for the engine house, and the fire limits were fixed.

The public drive around the lake was made in the summer of 1880. The right of way was conveyed by Theodore Tyrer, of Albert Lea, and Washington Lee, of New York, who materially assisted in doing the work. The city gave $269, and received a deed of the property.

In October, the Spring Lake having become so filled as to be obnoxious, exhaling foul emanations, five physicians, A. C. Wedge, M. E. Woodbury, W. H. Smith, G. W. Barch, and M. M. Dodge, presented a petition to the council as to the effects upon the sanitary condition of the city, and recommended that it be filled or drained. Their prayer was supplemented by another from Frank Hall and seventy-one other citizens, and the machinery was set in motion to have it drained and filled.

On the 15th of March, a board of health was established, with Dr. A. M. Burnham, the Mayor, and president of council, as members. J. H. Parker was appointed City Attorney for the balance of the year

1881. The new government was organized on the 3rd of May. The Mayor was Frank Hall. The board of aldermen were: John A. Anderson, President, O. F. Nelson, M. P. Sergeant, Thomas H. Armstrong, William Morin, and Willam Fenholt; Clerk, John Anderson; Assessor, A. W. White; Treasurer, B. H. Skaug; Sinking Fund Commissioner, D. G. Parker; City Attorney, J. H. Parker; Health Officers, A. M. Burnham, M. D., John A. Anderson, and Frank Hall.

The city, on the question of "License" or "No License," voted aye, and the price fixed for a parchment conferring rights and privileges in this respect was fixed at $400.

The Secretary of the State Board of Health, Charles N. Hewitt, inspected Spring Lake, and reported what should be done in the interest of the sanitary condition of the city, and his suggestions were carried into effect, not, however, without considerable friction.

1882.—There was what is called a dead-lock in the Board of Aldermen. It being understood that there was an equal division of parties, and as the President has no vote, except in case of a tie, a compromise was effected by the appointment of a President *pro tem.*

According to the index, there are eighty-two subjects for town ordinances, which are included in thirty-five separate acts. These regulations embrace the matters usually legislated upon by local authorities, and while in such cases there is a constant interference with individual freedom, of course upon the plea of the public good, this has not been of an *unusual* character, and honesty and economy have been the prevailing traits in the administration of city affairs.

Herewith is presented an abstract of the report of the City Clerk and Treasurer for the year ending on the 15th of April, 1882, which will be useful for reference or comparison:

"CITY CLERK'S OFFICE,
CITY OF ALBERT LEA, MINNESOTA,
April 16th, 1882.

To the Common Council:

I herewith submit to you a statement of the city's finances for the fiscal year ending April 15th, 1882:

ABSTRACT OF RECEIPTS.

Cash in treasury April 15, 1881	$ 336 29
Liquor and brewery licenses	3,750 00
Miscellaneous licenses	248 00
Poll tax	18 00
Justice fees	208 80
General tax	1,615 75
Sidewalk	182 77
Roads	789 04
Fire department	778 72
Bridge bonds	2,990 00
	$11,218 37

ABSTRACT OF EXPENDITURES.

Paid outstanding orders and time orders, including engine and hose orders	$2,201 89
Poor	811 68
Salaries	2,592 10
Fire bell, freight and hanging	252 88
Of road funds	1,439 47
A. McNeill on bridge contract	1,250 00
Court and jail expenses	51 60
Brought over to sinking fund	937 50
Books for justice and stationery	24 80
Wood and wood sawing	63 55
Street cleansing, shoveling snow, etc	65 82
Mill dam	225 00
Printing	163 80
Election expenses	73 00
Pound	10 00
Street lamps, oils, etc	58 55
Spring Lake drain and cistern	739 61
Pest house and small-pox patients	736 07
Lumber and hardware	980 84
Miscellaneous	229 11
	$12,007 30

GENERAL BALANCE SHEET.

	Assets.	*Liabilities.*
Taxes for 1881 and previous years	$3,624 76	
Sidewalks (to be levied)	94 52	
Value real and personal city property, as per last annual statement	7,909 00	
Shed by engine house	100 00	
Fire bell	250 00	
Pest house, and furniture, &c., therein	250 00	
Bridge fund	1,740 00	
City Lake Park, owned by city and valued at	1,500 00	
La France Manufacturing Company, non-interest bearing orders		$3,648 00
B. F. Goodrich & Co		1,066 00
Other outstanding orders		3,530 30
Bridge bonds (bearing 7 per cent. interest)		3,000 00
Balance		4,223 98
Total	$15,468 28	$15,468 28

Most respectfully submitted.

JOHN ANDERSON,
City Clerk."

Report of Treasurer of City of Albert Lea, from April 15, 1881, to April 15, 1882:

"*To the Honorable Mayor and Common Council of the City of Albert Lea:*

GENTLEMEN:—Pursuant to section 6, chapter 3, of the charter of the city of Albert Lea, I herewith transmit to you a statement of all monies received as City Treasurer, and all orders paid on the same.

RECEIPTS.

1881.		
April 15.	By cash balance in treasury.	$882 51
	By 9 liquor licenses, $400 each	3,600 00
	By 1 beer license	150 00
	By 14 billiard table licenses, 10 each	140 00
	By concert licenses	43 00
	By circus license	35 00
	By auction licenses	25 00
	By poll tax	19 25
	By fines from city justices	208 80
	By amount from county treasurer	3,666 03
	By sale of bridge bonds	2,990 00
		$11,764 59

DISBURSEMENTS.

	Orders on general fund paid.	$4,547 48
	Orders on road fund paid	1,739 50
	Orders on fire department fund paid	904 38
	Orders on sinking fund paid	456 37
	Orders on bridge fund paid	1,250 00
	Orders on railroad bond interest paid	210 00
April 15, 1882, balance in treasury at at this date		2,656 85
		$11,764 59

BALANCE IN DIFFERENT FUNDS.

1882.		
April 15.	General fund	$37 76
	Road fund	57 63
	Fire department fund	4 11
	Sinking fund	481 13
	Bridge fund	1,740 00
	S. M. R. R. fund	336 22
		$ 2,656 85

Respectfully submitted.

B. H. SKAUG,
City Treasurer."

PERSONAL TAXES IN ALBERT LEA.

In this list is presented those who pay a tax of this character on one thousand dollars and upwards:

T. H. Armstrong	$9,900
M. A. Armstrong	1,100
D. H. Brown & Co	5,550
Brigham & Co	3,500
Brown & Skinner	2,000
C. Burtch	1,712
G. M. Crane	3,654
Conklin, Dwight & Co	2,625
Chicago Furniture Co	1,760
C. L. Coleman	1,750
P. Clauson	1,444
D. E. Dwyer	2,473
Enterprise Printing Co	1,021
Gulbrandson Bros	1,395
I. O. Greene	1,092
Gulbrandson	2,595
C. F. Hedenstad	1,067
C. M. Hewett	4,005
Frank Hall	1,579
W. W. Johnson	2,501
Knatvold Bros	3,150
Ed. Murphy	1,313
McCormick Bros	1,525
William Morin	2,072
Now & Soth	4,625
John Paul	1,442
A. Palmer, Jr	1,095
R. N. Parks	1,821
W. W. Powell & Co	3,500
Ransom Bros	3,625
Raymon Bro. & Prentice	3,535
Strauss & Schlesinger	2,100
G. O. Ludley	5,481
W. P. Sergeant	5,463
Smith & Gassett	3,500
Wedge & Spicer	3,900
Williams & Drake	1,134

There is a large number coming well up toward like amounts.

The following table shows the value of improvements that have been made in Albert Lea since the year 1869, the smallest being in the year 1873, and the largest in 1878:

1869	$59,230
1870	45,842
1871	70,959
1872	48,275

1873	34,310
1874	76,121
1875	84,200
1876	42,201
1877	89,689
1878	99,941
1879	62,700
1880	81,965

On the 18th of July, 1879, a public meeting was held for the purpose of organizing a fire company. Rev. J. R. Chalmers was chosen chairman, and J. K. Richards secretary. An organization was effected, with the subjoined officers: Chief, James Allen; Assistant, Aus. Peck; Chief of Hose, Charles Soth; Assistant, J. J. Bond; Treasurer, N. O. Narveson; Secretary, J. K. Richards. At this meeting a committee to draft a constitutian was appointed.

This is an efficient organization, supplied with modern apparatus. The officers for 1882 are: Chief Engineer, William P. Sergeant; First Assistant, J. J. Bond; Second Assistant, E. W. Murphy; Foreman, James Allen; Assistant Foreman, M. C. Mitchell; Hose Foreman, E. H. Ellickson; Assistant, George Pratt; Secretary, Adam Wiegard; Treasurer, N. O. Narveson; Engineer, George Rutam; Second Engineer, A. Peck; First Fireman, Thomas Carney; Second Fireman, Andrew Peterson; Finance Committee, H. O. Brager, A. M. Anderson; Steward, Axle Brundin.

The department is a compromise between a paid and a volunteer institution. The skilled mechanics on the force receiving a salary.

The city officers for the year ending in May 1883, are as follows: Mayor, Dr. C. W. Ballard; Treasurer, N. O. Narveson; Assessor, Aug. Peterson; Justices of the Peace, E. C. Stacy and H. O. Haukness; Aldermen:

1st Ward, W. P. Sergeant, Martin Olson;

3d Ward, Wm. Morin, T. H. Armstrong,

3rd Ward, Wm. Fenholt, John Thompson.

On the vote regarding the license question, there was 186 majority for license.

PERIODICALS.

Freeborn County Standard.—This paper was first issued on the 11th of July, 1857, by Swineford & Gray, under the name of the Minnesota Star." It was a Democrat paper and, it is said, was encouraged by the Damocratic Central Committee, to the extent of $500 in cash, and many citizens took ten copies, subscribing for them at the rate of $2 a year in advance, but it soon fell the victim of one of those diseases incident to juvenile newspaperdom, and which are so fatal. The press on which it had been printed, after laying idle some months, was sold under a foreclosure, to satisfy a mortgage held by G. S. Ruble, and was bid in by him, who afterwards sold it to Alf. P. Swineford, one of the former proprietors. Mr. Swineford then commenced the publication of the "Freeborn County Eagle."

This paper commenced on the 11th of September, 1858, and went on as a Democratic paper until the 26th of February, 1859, when the publishers retired and Isaac Botsford took the supervision, and from that time it was Republican. On the 19th of May, 1860, the Eagle made its last flight, and George S. Ruble, who held the greatest interest in the establishment, associated with him Joseph Hooker, and on the 20th of the same month came out with the Freeborn County Standard.

This firm had an experience of just twenty-three weeks, when the office was sold at a great discount to A. D. Clark, who on the 21st of October, 1860, assumed the editorial chair and began to use the royal pronoun "we", until the 25th of July, 1861, when he divested himself of the editorial harness, and sold to A. B. Webber.

This gentleman kept distributing ink up to the 10th of October, when the concern passed into the hands of J. C. Ross, who conducted the paper up to the 20th of February, 1862, when he sold to William Morin and enlisted in the army. Mr. Morin kept the paper going until the 4th of July, 1864, and then his foreman and compositors leaving for the war, the paper was suspended.

In March, 1865, Mr. D. G. Parker bought the paper, and on the 6th of April recommenced the publication, which has been kept up ever since.

Mr. Isaac Botsford was again connected with the paper, which has always been a journal with considerable influence.

In April, 1878, George T. Robinson bought out Mr. Botsford's interest, and in May of that year W. W. Williams bought out D. G. Parker, and in February, 1879, T. W. Drake purchased Mr. Robinson's part of the establishment.

In 1878 the the paper was enlarged to its present size and form, a six column folio. This establishment was burned on the 11th of April, 1882, entailing a heavy loss.

BANCROFT BANNER.—This was one of those county seat papers which, having failed in the object for which it was issued, there was no further necessity for its existence, and so died a natural death. But Mr. Bleakely, who had brought it into existence, tells the story in such an admirable way, that it would be a pity to mar its beauty, so the reader is referred to the extract from his speech before the Old Settlers' Association.

THE ALBERT LEA ENTERPRISE—This is a weekly republican newspaper, which first appeared on th 25th of April, 1872, with James C. Hamlin, of Mason City, Iowa, as publisher. It was an eight column folio. At the end of a year, S. H. Cady, of Wisconsin, came and brought a job printing outfit, and the paper then appeared as published by the Enterprise Printing Company. On the 25th of September, 1873, Mr. Hamlin sold his interest to Mr. Cady, and on the 2d of October the paper came out with S. H. Cady as sole proprietor. Thus it remained until the winter of 1874-75, when Fred Cochrane became editor of the sheet. On the 26th of August, 1875, the establishment was purchased by the present proprietor, M. Halverson, who has been the sole owner, except in the spring of 1881, when an interest in the concern was sold to F. D. Pierce and A. E. Ellickson, who retained a share in the paper for nine months, until the present time.

In the spring of 1876, the paper was enlarged to a six column quarto. It is on a sound financial basis, with a local habitation, and a circulation of 1,000 copies. There is a Babcock & Cottrell power press, with three job presses, knife paper cutter, 125 fonts of type, and in all respects a well appointed office. When purchased by Mr. Halverson the paper had a circulation of 400. At present the press work of the other papers is done in this office. The building is 20x50 feet, of brick.

THE ALBERT LEA POSTEN was first issued on the 5th of July, 1882, by the Albert Lea Publishing Company, the officers of which are: H. Erickson, President; H. G. Emmons, Vice-President; J. P. Grnager, Secretary; H. O. Haukness, Treasurer and general manager; and O. J. Hagen, Editor. It is a seven column folio, printed in the Norwegian language, at $1.25 a year, and has a circulation of 864.

This paper is the successor of the "Sanverke," of which N. Nelson was editor, published by the same company. Before this there was the "Sondre Minnesota," by Peterson, Anderson, and Motczfeldt, and then there was the "North Star," by Jac. Elleston, and T. T. Pierce.

There have been several other papers in the city and county, which have had an existence more or less brief, and have passed away from inanition or some other disease. Some of them were precocious, and could not have been reasonably expected to live and thrive in this bleak and inhospitable world.

Among the various buds of promise may be mentioned the "Will of the Wisp," which launched upon the troubled sea of existence, breasted the waves for three months, and sunk forever beneath its waters. T. T. Pierce was at the helm of this well managed sheet.

THE HIGH SCHOOL JOURNAL was a sprightly, well behaved little entity, managed by W. W. Parker, Jerry Sheehan, and Willie Crane, high school students, and during the four months it survived was a credit to all concerned.

THE FREEBORN SPRINGS HERALD.—This was a campaign sheet, evolved by the county seat contest in the interest of Itasca, where it was published, and Dr. Burnham was the *Visa tergo* that furnished the power. Isaac Botsford was the editor and proprietor, and it was a battle ax worthy of a more successful cause. For thirteen weeks the friction of its presence filled the air with electricity so that a good many heads of hair stood on end until after the election. The octagon from which it issued still stands, but the paper itself is a mere recollection.

During the county seat contest there was considerable fierceness between the rival sheets, and each one, of course, estimated the value of its utterances in moulding public opinion quite as high as they would bring in open market, and the Itasca concern, as was claimed at the time, sent a young man down, who purloined the "toggle joint" of the Albert Lea press, hoping thus to prevent the issue of its hated rival until the election was over, but Ruble and the boys were equal to the emergency, and did not propose to let a little thing like that prevent the regular appearance of the paper. So they procured a long scantling for a lever, and, letting one end project out of the door, the form was run under the platen, when a man outside would heave down, and take the impression. Mr. F. W. Drake was a young man in the office at the time, and helped to work off the edition.

If there have been other newspapers or periodicals in the county, they will be mentioned in the towns where they existed.

FREEBORN COUNTY CANE GROWERS' ASSOCIATION.

This association is in the interests of the syrup and sugar manufacture, and the raising of cane generally. Considerable attention has been paid to the cultivation of the amber cane, and there are quite a number of mills and evaporating pans, where small amounts of syrup are made. A mill was started a few years ago to manufacture on quite a liberal scale, but it was this season removed into the country. The President of the association is H. N. Ostrander; Secretary, George H. Prescott.

ANTI HORSE THIEF ASSOCIATION OF FREEBORN COUNTY.

After a preliminary meeting an organization was effected at the Court House, on the afternoon of the 30th of September, 1882. A constitution was adopted, and the following officers elected: President, George S. Ruble; Vice Presidents, A. C. Wedge, T. J. Sheehan, and N. P. Howe; Treasurer, L. B. Spicer; Secretary, C. W. Levens.

The proposition is to appoint active riders, and make it exceedingly uncomfortable for the equine purloiners who visit this section.

THE GREAT ALBERT LEA ROUTE.

The Minneapolis & St. Louis railroad was completed to this point on the 10th of September, 1877. It makes a through route between the twin cities and Chicago, over the Burlington, Cedar Rapids & Northern, and the Rock Island & Pacific. railroads. The line to St. Louis is over the same line to Burlington, and then over the Chicago, Burlington & Quincy road. These lines are called the "Great Albert Lea Route," which receives a large patronage. At this station there are, including the eight passenger trains, about forty arrivals each twenty-four hours.

The southwestern line runs to Angus, Iowa, and there connects with the Des Moines and Fort Dodge line.

An account of the celebration of the arrival of the first train on this route, is given in the chapter on "Events," and need not be repeated here.

Although the difficulties of railroad building, when this road was constructed, were as nothing compared to those attending the construction and equipment of the Southern Minnesota, it must not be supposed that it did not require the highest order of talent and energy, and a liberal exchequer, to get them into running order.

EDUCATIONAL.

The first district school established in Albert Lea was number seven, which was soon after the organization of the county. Before this, however, there had been private schools, which are elsewhere mentioned. The first appropriation was in the form of a district tax to the amount of $400. The schoolhouse built with that money lasted several years, and then another was built which still stands in the corner of the school grounds, which occupy a square west of the public square on Clark street. Messrs. Stacy, Tyrer, and Wedge were on the board when it was built, and Mr. I. J. Fuller, of Oconomowoc, furnished the plans.

On the organization of the district system in 1860, this became the Thirty-eighth, and so continued until the winter of 1881, when an independent district was created by a special act of the Legislature, and the present fine schoolhouse was erected. Messrs. D. R. P. Hibbs, D. N. Gates, and W. P. Sergeant constituted the school board. The plans were furnished by Mr. Jones, of Madison, Wisconsin. The cost of the building, which is of brick, modern in style and well adapted for school purposes, was $20,000, and it was completed on the 1st of January, 1881.

The school system of the county has been fostered here, as it has been all over the country, by "Teachers' Institutes," which, in addition to the knowledge as to the science of school teaching imparted, serve to create and sustain the *esprit du corps*, which is so important in this profession. There have been other schools of a graded character, which did good work, but they are in existence no longer, and the energies of the friends of education are concentrated upon the public schools.

When the new schoolhouse was ready for occupancy, there were some formalities attending the tearing away from the old building, and among the other good things said was a poem by Miss

Lora Levens, which is given entire. It is entitled

FAREWELL TO THE OLD SCHOOL HOUSE.

"When an old friend, tried and true,
We change for one unknown and new,
It seems but meet to leave behind
A tear for the old one, true and kind.
Ten years ago last gone by spring,
When flowers were in bloom and birds on wing,
I entered first this public school,
(For, happily, 'twas free to wit or fool.)
The house then stood upon a spot,
Remote from flower, or tree, or cot;
Just here in front of the "Public Square."
With plenty of gravel, and dirt, and air
But 'twas not built in the ancient way,
As was the Deacon's One Hoss Shay—
"To last a hundred years to a day"
For the builders thought it "wouldn't pay."
Soon the ceiling cracked, and then it fell
And dropped on our heads and laps—pell mell.
And then the windows would rattle and shake,
And the floor beneath would tremble and quake,
And in and out all through its walls,
In closets and entries, and rooms and halls,
The wind would whistle and rush and roar,
And e'en come up through the cracks in the floor.
In vain we've punched and knocked and poked,
But still the old stove has smoked and smoked;
And many an hour have we stood and sat,
With wrap and shawl and cloak and hat,
While tears adown our cheeks would flow—
But not the tears of grief and woe,
But perhaps by these we'll value more
The comforts that now for us are in store!
And everything else in this old room—
From our teacher there to—even the broom,
Has so long been subject to wear and tear
They do with each other, most fitly compare.
But the end has come. Let us take our last view
Ere the old and the dear we change for the new,
For so long they've been with us and each is so old,
Places, like living friends, in our hearts they hold,
Many a year before us has stood
Numbering the hours for bad or good,
The big old clock, with its tick, tick tick,
Keeping time to the pencils' click, click, click.
Full many an hour with listless look,
The idler has sat with eyes off his book,
With many a groan and many a sigh,
Watching how slowly the hours went by.
Upon the wall, with a deep, dark frown,
Our "country's hero" has long looked down,
Inciting us to strive for a station,
Equal to his in affairs of the nation.
Though none may tread the senate hall,
Yet each of us will heed some call;
And we'll all look back now and then with a sigh,
To the happy hours that here passed by.
Before the stove is the low front seat,
With little of room and much of heat,
Where the wicked have got (I've heard some say,)
A taste of the heat of a future day.
We can never forget, though far away,
The old green curtains that, day after day,
Have hung at the windows, slit and torn—
Of all their former beauty shorn.
And ever "green," in memory, will stand
The old ink keg, with bright red band;
And ne'er to be erased from our minds—or the floor
Is that beautiful ink spot we made there of yore;
And as "bright" in memory as e'er it shown
Will that little bell be with its silvery tone;
And 'twill seem, on memory's wall to call
Pictures of school days, gone from us all.
And oh! what tales these walls could tell
Of the sad lots that have us befell—
Of the weary limbs, and aching head,
And real tears that we have shed.
And how, at times, have they echoed and swelled
With cries and groans that could not be quelled,
At the fall of the stick, or wooden rule,
When a culprit has broken a law of the school.
Again, sounds of gay mirth and glee
Are softly brought back on the air to me;
And again the walls all seem to resound
With a sort of stifled, giggling sound.
They could tell of classes that have passed away,
Till now is left the school of to-day.
Of some who have joined the fierce, weary strife,
And are fighting nobly the battle of life,
And of a few who are lying, lying low,
Under the sod and under the snow.
But others come on, and in they pour,
Till now no room is left for more.
So now at last is built, complete,
A new schoolhouse, with comforts replete,
Where all of the rising generation
May be fitted to fill, in life, their station.
So farewell, old schoolhouse! We'll say good bye.
And away to the new we'll each of us hie.
We know all thy faults, they are before us in view,
But even by these you are endeared to us, too.
Soon will thy walls be covered with must,
The stove will be coated with dirt and with rust,
Unmolested, the mice will come out to their play,
But finding no crumbs will soon hasten away.
Around the corners, deserted and lone,
The fierce winter wind will whistle and moan.
In through the cracks the snow will soon sift.
And over the steps, unheeded, 'twill drift.
The spiders will weave their webs overhead,
And all will be silent and still as the dead.
But O! the lessons we've mastered here
Will live with us all for many a year.
Lessons of truth, and honor, and trust,
Lessons that show us we can and we must,
Lessons that will help us to keep our place,
In this great, and hard, and worldly race."

As to the present condition of the schools in the city, a reference to the returns of the work done shows that they are in a healthy condition, and in competent hands.

From the first annual report of Prof. J. C. Alling, the Principal and Superintendent of the schools of Albert Lea, which includes the school year ending on the 1st of July, 1882, the following statistics are gathered:

Whole number of scholars entitled to apportionment	548
Not of school age, or non-residents paying tuition	24
Separate names enrolled during the year	572
Days of school	195
Total attendance, in days, by all scholars	60,559

Average daily attendance	311
Whole number of teachers—one man and seven women	8
Pupils enrolled per teacher	72
Average attendance per teacher	44
Percentage of perfect attendance through the year	55
Number of grades below the High School	8
Cost of supervision and instruction, based on average daily attendance, per capita	$12.34

HIGH SCHOOL.

Whole number of pupils enrolled during the year	76
Greatest number present at any one time	67
Number of days of school	195
Average daily attendance	45
Percentage of perfect attendance on enrollment	59
Number of teachers	2

The curriculum of statistics embraces the higher English branches and Latin.

At the commencement exercises, in June, a wide range of subjects was embraced, and those having parts acquitted themselves in a very creditable manner.

RELIGIOUS.

THE PRESBYTERIAN CHURCH OF ALBERT LEA.—It must have been in April, 1857, when Rev. S. G. Lowry visited this place, and he, in connection with Rev. Isaac McReynolds, a Methodist clergyman, who still lives in the county, were the first to break the bread of the word to the people in this region. For three years Mr. Lowry continued to hold meetings from time to time, but finally his health failed, and Rev. Mr. Cook, a Congregational minister, of Austin, visited the town and was invited to preach, and the result was that a church was organized under the Congregational form, with six members, three of whom had been Presbyterians, and three Congregationalists. This church, which was maintained in this form until the autumn of 1868, is alluded to under its own heading.

At the Fall meeting of the Presbytery of Southern Minnesota, Old School, a petition was presented, subscribed to by the members of the Congregational Church in Albert Lea, and a few other persons, requesting the organization of a Presbyterian Church. The petitioners were eighteen in number, all expressing a desire to become members. In response to this petition, the Presbytery appointed Rev. D. C. Lyon and Rev. A. J. Stead a committee to meet the petitioners, and, if the way should be clear, organize the church. Accordingly, on the 29th of September, 1868, these brethren held a meeting for this purpose in the Court House in Albert Lea. Rev. S. G. Lowry and Rev. Theophus Lowry, of the Presbytery of Mankato, New School, were present by invitation, and assisted in the proceedings. The Church was then formally organized, under the name of the First Presbyterian Church of Albert Lea, with the following members: Benjamin Brownsill, Mrs. Elizabeth Brownsill, Curtis B. Kellar, Samuel Eaton, Mrs. Clarissa Eaton, Mrs. S. M. Robinson, Mrs. Eliza Hunt, Mrs. Harriet J. Barden, Mrs. Mary F. Armstrong, Samuel Thompson, Mrs. Amanda Woodruff, Mrs. Darrow, Mrs Henrietta Ruble, Mrs. C. E. Sheehan, Thomas Sherwood, Clarencé Wedge, Mrs. Mary Buell, Samuel Batchelder, and Wm. J. Squier—19. Samuel Batchelder, Samuel Eaton, and Curtis B. Kellar, were elected Ruling Elders, to serve respectively one, two, and three years. A public service was held in the evening; a sermon was preached by Rev. A. J. Stead, and the elders were ordained—the charge to them was given by Rev. Theophus Lowry. Brief addresses were made by Rev. S. G. Lowry and Rev. D. C. Lyon, and the meeting was dismissed with the Apostolic benediction.

Thus the former Congregational Church of this place was, by the unanimous choice and action of its own members, merged into the Presbyterian Church; and they, with a few others received at the time, constituted the original membership of the present organization.

Rev. Dr. W. M. Paxton, of the First Presbyterian Church of New York City, was here during that summer, on his vacation, and conceived a lively interest in the people and the church, going so far as to offer to build a church, if the people desired it and would contribute what they were able. This proposition was accepted by the people, and the Congregationalists considered that it was the best they could do, under the circumstances, as it involved no sacrifice of any article of belief; the real difference in the two denominations being in their form of church government. In this way, then, the Presbyterian church in Albert Lea came into existence, and was organized as above recorded.

They at once commenced to build, and before the following winter had fairly set in, this house was raised and enclosed. It was completed the following summer, and was dedicated to the worship of God on the 15th day of August, 1869. The Presbytery of Southern Minnesota was in session here at that time, and the dedicatory sermon was preached by Dr. Paxton, from Matt. 26;8. "To What Purpose is This Waste?" The success of the entetprise was largely owing to the liberality and energy of one who has since gone to his rest. Augustus Armstrong, who, though not a communicant, was nevertheless one of the wisest in council and the most efficient in executing all that was needful to the establishment of the church. While he lived he manifested a lively interest in the growth of the church, spiritual as well as material; and was always to the minister a prudent and safe adviser.

Along with the names of Dr. Paxton and Mr. Armstrong, honorable and grateful mention must be made of Miss Mary Gelston, a member of Dr. Paxton's church, from the city of New York, who from first to last has contributed more than half the means necessary to build and complete the church property in its present form. "This excellent christian lady, though an entire stranger to every one of us, became interested in Albert Lea and this church through her Pastor, and sent us $3,000 for the church building and grounds, $2,000 towards building the Manse, and less than two years ago sent us $500 more to assist in the erection of our chapel, besides at one time a handsome donation for our Sabbath School Library. Altogether we have received from her nearly $6,000. It is her munificence which, under God, has raised up and established this church. Let us record her name in our hearts with most affectionate remembrance, and in our prayers let us seek for the blessings of God upon one through whose beneficence so great blessings have come upon us. This church has been raised up and fostered by Mary Gelston: let it be her everlasting memorial. Let it tell to the end of time what well directed giving can accomplish. And may God grant that her unselfish devotion to the cause of Christ, and her liberal spirit in giving to build up the church, a church she has never seen may be imitated by the people she has blessed by all of us upon whom the blessing has come."

Mrs. Armstrong and Clarence Wedge gave the land. The pulpit was presented by Mr. Tuttle, the bell by Mr. Darlington of Pittsburg. The Bible and hymn books, to the value of $100, were presented by Mr Denney of Pittsburg. H. D. Brown presented a three years' policy of insurance on the church for $5,000, at a net cost of $75.

For nine months after the church was organized, it was supplied with preaching by different ministers. Among these were Rev. Charles Thayer, of Farmington, Rev. John L. Gage, of Kasson, and Rev. R. B. Abbott, who first preached on the 21st of March, 1869. He soon received a formal call, and removed here from St. Paul in July. On the 15th of August the church was dedicated in the morning, and the pastor was installed in the evening. The sermon was preached by Rev. W. S. Wilson, of Owatonna, the charge to the Pastor was given by Rev. D. C. Lyon, and the charge to the people by Dr. Paxton.

The resident membership at this time consisted of eighteen persons, as follows:—Mr. and Mrs. Brownsill, Mr. and Mrs. C. B. Kellar, Mr. and Mrs. Eaton, Mrs. Robinson, Mrs. Armstrong, Mrs. Barden, Mr. Samuel Thompson, Mrs. Woodruff, Mrs. Ruble, Mr. and Mrs. Squier, Mr. Batchelder, Mrs. Buell, Mr. Clarence Wedge, and Mr. Sherwood.

Up to the centennial year, when Mr. Abbott preached a historical sermon, from which many of these facts were gathered, there had been a total number received into the church of two hundred and sixty-four.

The Sabbath School was at first commenced as a union one, and although there have been losses by detachments going to make up other schools, it has kept on growing.

There are connected with the Sunday school work, half a dozen mission schools, with an aggregate attendance of two hundred and fifty children.

In 1874, the church undertook the erection of a chapel, which was felt to be a necessity, and here that estimable woman, the fast friend of the church, Miss Gelston, did not fail them, for she sent $500, and, with another $500 added, it was completed.

Rev. Mr. Abbott has been the pastor since his installation. The church may be said to be in a flourishing condition, with a good house of worship, and a commodious Manse adjoining.

THE METHODIST EPISCOPAL CHURCH.—Like the most of the frontier regions, this vicinity early received the attention of the itinerant Methodist preacher. Isaac W. McReynolds, who was a local preacher, but had never been ordained, came here and took a farm, a mile west of the village, in 1856. He was born in North Carolina, in 1806. He came here in the fall of the year, and the next season went back and brought his family, in an ox-team. Mr. McReynolds, it is likely, was the first to hold religious services in the county, which he did in Shell Rock, in the fall of 1856. Rev. Mr. Wilson was also at Shell Rock several times, at the house of brother Scott. Preaching was also done near the State line, at Gordonsville, and a class was formed, with Jacob Beighley as leader; also at Bear Lake and other places, where there was an opportunity. The very first in Albert Lea must have been at the house of George Ruble, near the saw-mill. Mr. Gates, with his family, attended in an ox-team. Mr. McReynolds was one year in the employ of the conference as a supply, which must have been the conference year of 1858. Thomas Kirkpatrick was the Presiding Elder. Classes were formed where it seemed to be feasible, at Bear Lake, Rice Lake, Glendale; and although there was a stated supply at Geneva, no class was organized there. In Albert Lea there was occasional preaching. Several more or less promising organizations were formed, but from various reasons they failed to be sustained. There was a kind of floating population; restive individuals, who would remain a certain time and then push on west. Regular supplies were started several times by the conference. Rev. Mr. Watson, Rev. John Garner, and perhaps one or two more, but the ground was either stony or was preoccupied.

One year, Mr. McReynolds told the conference that if they would send a man who had no family, he would board him for a year without cost, and I. W. W. Wright was sent; but, after a time, finding his affinity, he got married, and went to keeping house. The young man soon preached the schoolhouse, where the meetings were held, empty. A few of the heads of families, as a matter of duty, kept on attending, but it terminated in a collapse of the Methodist interest here. It is told that on one occasion this ecclesiastical luminary announced, among other things, that Abraham was the first one to proclaim that the universe was governed by one God. But to the young man's credit, it should be stated that, having accepted what he considered a call to preach, he also had the good sense to stop preaching in obedience to a like mandate, which is sometimes all unheeded.

Late in the fifties a Sunday School was started; it was a union school, patronized by all denominations.

When Mr. McReynolds had finished his conference work, he took charge of the school in the schoolhouse, and really made a good success of it.

When the Methodist influence waned as above related, the Congregational predominated, and it finally became denominational and was at last merged into the Presbyterian, and is still in existence, one of the largest and most flourishing in town.

Thus matters remained until the year 1878, when the interest was revived and the church reorganized on a firm basis.

In February, 1878, Rev. Robert Fobes, of Waseca, who had been an agent of Hamline University, but at that time had no charge, came down here to look over the situation, and he started out in a business way; went and secured the use of the Court House, and then canvassed the the village for an audience; the result was he got a good hearing, and the next week he went around again drumming up delinquents, telling them to come round and listen to the best sermon they ever heard.

This went on for some time. He did preach good sermons, and at last came to the subject of a regular church organization, and one Sunday, invited those who would join, to rise, and sixteen responded to the invitation. Two weeks from that time was set for the regular organization. When the time came, about half of the number had weakened and the reverend gentlemen was a good deal cast down, and hesitated as to what he should do. He consulted Mr. J. H. Parker, who declined to advise either *pro* or *con*, but Mrs. Parker happened along while they were talking it over. Mr. Fobes asked her what he had better do? She replied: "If there is ever going to be a Methodist Church in Albert Lea, now is the time to start it; you came down for that purpose and you better go on and organize *Jim and I*, if nobody else is present!" That settled it. The church was duly organized with nine members. The list is mislaid, but from memory there were: Mr. J. H. Parker and his wife Mary J. Parker; Mr. and Mrs. Frank Tilton, C. B. Parkinson, Mr. J. W. Abbott, Mr. and Mrs. J. M. Bond, and Peter Nelson. Eddie Nelson had applied to join as a probationer before the church was formed.

While Rev. Robert Fobes was here the Sunday school that is still in existence, was started, and it has kept up to a good state of efficiency ever since.

In October, 1878, Rev. J. W. Klepper was assigned here by the conference, and building operations were soon commenced. A lot was purchased at a cost of $100, about one third of its market value, and the church was built at a cost of $1,700. The business men and citizens generally, took hold and did what they could. The sum of $200 was borrowed from the church extension fund, and a like sum was also donated from that fund. Mr. Klepper remained two years, when Mr. Henry Frank was stationed here and still remains. He came from Kansas in October 1881. He formerly resided in Chicago.

In October, 1881, Mr. Frank started an eight page four column illustrated paper, called the "Church Visitor," intending it for a speciol purpose and continued it up to July, 1882.

Mr. Frank is an advanced thinker, a good worker, and a remarkably fine speaker.

The Sunday school is in a good condition under Mr. J. H. Parker as superintendent, and has an enrollment of more than one hundred, and a large average attendance.

The First Baptist Church of Albert Lea.— The first preaching with any sort of regularity in this place was by Rev. D. H. Palmer, in the schoolhouse. This was before the war. Rev. Amory Gale, the very first State missionary, also held service here, and so much of an interest was manifested that it was resolved to organize a church, and after suitable preliminary meetings, a council of brethren convened on the 29th of September for that purpose. Rev. Gilead Dodge was chosen Moderator, and Rev. D. H. Palmer, Clerk. The customary examination resulting satisfactorily, the church was duly organized and the following named persons admitted to membership: Eunice Jennings, Lydia C. Jennings, Charles Green, Sarah Green, Jeremiah Walker, Mrs. J. Walker, Maggie E. Morin, John Wood, Emeline A. Wood, Reuben C. Cady, Rodah Lowe, Alden G. Douglass, and Winnah Pride, with H. D. Palmer pastor of the church. On the following day Sister D. Stage was baptized and admitted to full fellowship.

At the organization the following services took place: Sermon by Rev. H. I. Parker; hand of fellowship by Rev. A. L. Cole; prayer by Rev. Gilead Dodge; charge by Rev. E. L. Rugg; benediction by the pastor, Rev. D. H. Palmer.

In connection with these services, rich and appropriate discourses were preached by Brothers Cole, Parker, Dodge, and Rugg.

It should be mentioned that the venerable missionary, Rev. M. W. Hopkins, rendered invaluable aid to the society during the preliminary labors incident to the organization.

Elder Cornelius Smith was the next pastor, commencing his duties on the 1st of October, 1868.

After Elder Smith left, the church was for a time pastorless. Elder Weeden was invited to temporarily supply the pulpit.

The church was duly incorporated on the 13th of May, 1871. In October, 1873, Rev. Amos Weaver became pastor. In October, Rev. Norman F. Hoyt became pastor of the church, and remains still at his post.

On the 5th of February, 1874, the subject of building a church was vigorously taken in hand, the parsonage having been previously built. Services at this time were held in Masonic hall. It was rapidly pushed to completion, and dedicated on the 1st of November, 1874, at 10:30 A. M. Amory Weaver was the pastor. Several other ministers were present, among them Rev. S. F. Drew, R. B. Abbott, and George Prescott. The cost of the structure was $3,585.56, and there was a debt upon the property of $2,300, which was reduced by contributions at that time by the sum of $856. The building is a rather severely plain gothic, 28x50 feet, with sixteen foot posts, a recess 4x14 feet in the rear and a tower 10 feet square, with the spire reaching an altitude of 63 feet. The front has a fine large window—6x14 feet of stained glass. It is supplied with patent seats, is carpeted, and is really neat and tasty.

In 1876 this church was without a pastor, and the debt upon it was pressing heavily upon the few members who were struggling to preserve the altar they had erected with such self-sacrificing devotion, so, after much thought and consultation, it was resolved to make an appeal to the denomination generally, for help. Implorations not unlike this have been sent east from every State in the Union, beginning with the Pilgrims—as they planted religious liberty on Plymouth Rock. This circular is printed, that coming generations may see how the early settlers adapted means to ends, and that while the injunction has always been to put religion into business, that here they did not hesitate to put business into religion.

AUSTIN, MINN., March, 30, 1876.

DEAR BROTHER.—Freeborn County, in the Southern tier of counties, in this State, has a population of over 13,000, and is constantly filling up. Its county seat is Albert Lea, a thrifty and important railroad center in a township of 1,900 inhabitants. The little Baptist Church there, of 27 members, mostly females, is in trouble. As one of the nearest Baptist Ministers, I have become deeply interested in the needy condition of this church. I know its members to be earnest and self-sacrificing. They are in danger of losing their neat house of worship, which was recently built, and for which they have worked so hard. After raising, in two years, over $2,500 for religious purposes, they can do little more and are liable to lose all they have thus far gained. On a property, (including a parsonage, built some years ago) valued at over $5,000, they owe about $1,800. The meeting house, costing $3,500, is completely finished and furnished—except an organ. The united testimony of the community is that the expenditure has been very economical, and without many favors received must have been greater. To-day this church is without a pastor or preacher, and burdoned with this debt. There are two other small native churches in the county accessible from Albert Lea, but without preaching, so that there is not a single Baptist Minister in the county to-day, excepting the Swedish. Remove this dept and we can put a pastor in this field and he will find a good support. Let it drag Albert Lea Church down, and Baptist interests in that whole section suffer irreparable injury. Look at the map and see how important a point it is for us to hold. Its possibilities within ten or fifteen years are very great. Now, Baptists can raise this debt and not feel it. We ask of your whole church the specific sum of two dollars. How easy in a few moments to raise so small an amount and thus rescue this church. The only expense in this movement is the printing and sending this circular, so that every dollar you send goes directly to raise the debt. If you respond, the amount required will be raised. Perhaps your Sabbath school would like to own a share in one of God's houses out on these broad prairies. Will you, for the Master's sake, help to make this plan a success? If we had asked a hundred dollars, you might lay this appeal aside as useless, but surely the amount named is not a large one. If you treat this as a small matter and lay it aside unnoticed, of course the plan fails. They need help at once. Three are waiting baptism. Ground can now be occupied, that soon will be out of reach. Contributions may be sent to John Wood, or Mrs. M. E. Morin, Albert Lea, Freeborn County, Minn.; to Rev. W. W. Whitcomb, Owatonna, or to me. Yours fraternally.

C. D. BELDEN,
Minister of the Baptist Church, Austin, Minn.

We, the advisory committee to the State Convention Board, from the Minnesota Central Association, of which body the Baptist Church at Albert Lea is a member, heartily endorse the above movement for the relief of that church, and wish complete success.

W. W. WHITCOMB,
J. D. DENISON,
C. D. BELDEN.

This paper was indorsed by the trustees of the Minnesota Baptist State Convention as certified to by A. A. Russell, Secretary of the Board. It was quite extensively circulated and the result was contributions to the extent of about $500, which relieved their present necessities, and in October 1874, Rev. Norman F. Hoyt located here, and since that time the society has beem moving along in a prosperous way, and now has a good membership and a thriving Sunday school.

ROMAN CATHOLIC.—THE CHURCH OF ST. THEODORE. A beautiful brick church was erected in 1877, and dedicated on the 9th of September, Bishop Ireland, Rev. P. Riordan, and Rev. Theodore Venn, were present and conducted the exercises, the Bishop preaching a sermon on the Rules of Faith. There are sixty families connected with this church. The pastor is Rev. James Fleming, who came in November, 1881. His predecessor was Rev. P. F. Dargnault, and before him was Rev. Theodore Venn. There are several mission churches in the county, with Albert Lea as the mother church. One of these is in Bath, one in Newry, one at Twin Lakes, and another at Alden, which are supplied from here with services at regular intervals. In the whole parish there are 210 families. The connection is with the St. Paul Diocese, under Bishop Grace.

The parochial residence was built in the summer of 1882, at a cost of $1,950. The cost of the church was upward of $4,200, and it is without doubt the finest and most durable edifice for church purposes in town.

THE FIRST UNIVERSALIST SOCIETY OF ALBERT LEA.—There had been religious services in the interest of this form of belief for some time, with more or less regularity, in the Court House, and on the 14th of May, 1870, pursuant to four weeks notice, a meeting was held for the purpose of organizing. Wm. C. Pratt was chosen chairman, and Alonzo Brown was appointed secretary. On motion the meeting adjourned to the house of C. R. Ransom.

On reassembling the Committee on Constitution, which had been previously appointed, reported a Constitution and Articles of Faith, which were unanimously adopted. The document embraced twenty-one articles, including the Declaration of Faith.

The following officers were elected: Moderator, C. R. Ransom; Clerk, E. C. Stacy; Collector and Treasurer, C. R. Ransom; Trustees, E. C. Stacy, A. Brown, and M. M. Luce.

On the 4th of March, 1872, a meeting was held to take into consideration the building of a house of worship, and a committee was appointed to solicit subscriptions, consisting of E. C. Stacy, Charles Levens, Frederick Cochrane, A. H. McMillen, and J. M. Pratt.

Little progress seems to have been made until the fall of 1876, when the following building committee was elected: William C. Pratt, John M. Marty, and G. C. Harper. In the spring of 1877 the edifice was completed, and is an unpretentious building in size and architectural appointments; it was christened "Our Father's Chapel." Articles of incorporation were filed in the office of the Register of Deeds on the 22d of April, 1879.

The first preaching was by Rev. Mr. Woodbridge. Mr. Frederick Cochrane also officiated for quite a time. Rev. A. Vedder was also here.

Rev. G. S. Gowdy came here in April, 1876, and has officiated ever since, also having charge of the church in Glenville.

THE CONGREGATIONAL CHURCH.—The history of this society is, during its early period, identical with the Presbyterian, into which it was transformed, as related in the sketch of that denomination. It will be remembered that when the church was organized there were three Presbyterians and three Congregationalists, and in deference to Mr. Cook, who visited and preached here at an early day, and who was connected with the Congregationalists, that church form was adopted.

The Presbyterian members were Mr. and Mrs. Samuel Eaton and Mrs. Woodruff. Those of the other connection were Mrs. A. Armstrong, and J. U. Perry and wife. Father Lowry was a Presbyterian. At first meetings were held at any place where convenient. When Mr. Lowry, or any minister came round, Col. Eaton, who had a good team, would get Tim Sheehan to take it, with a big sled, and circle about the vicinity of the village and bring them into church.

When the church was turned over two-thirds of them were of Presbyterian antecedents. After a time the Congregationalists, or most of them, in the church, concluded to go back to their first love, and to build a church of their own. Mrs. Reuben Williams took an active part in the work, and considerable aid was obtained from the Home Mission fund, it is believed to the extent of $1,000, and perhaps other sums from the East, and so the church was built, a very neat structure.

Their first pastor was Rev. Mr. Drew, who turned Presbyterian and went to Preston. Rev. Mr. Todd was the next minister, and he too went into a Presbyterian pulpit. The next, and last, was Rev. Chalmers, who went to Dakota, and the church was then sold at quite a sacrifice to the Episcopalians, and most of the members were again merged in the old society.

ALBERT LEA EVANGELICAL LUTHERAN NORWEGIAN CHURCH.—This society has a fine church on Clark street, opposite the Public Park, built in imitation of freestone. There are about fifty families who worship here. The church was got together and the edifice built about 1874. Rev. Mr. Vulpsburg was the pastor at one time, and Rev. Mr. Eiver. The present pastor is Rev. O. H. Smeby. There is a Sunday school, and the church fully administers to the wants of the Lutheran Norwegians in the community.

THE SCANDINAVIAN UNION BAPTIST CHURCH.—This church is usually called the Danish Baptist church, and was organized in 1874, with eleven members. It now has about eighty. Preaching in this interest was commenced at an early day, and kept up with more or less regularity until the organization of the society. Of those who have been here may be mentioned: Rev. Louis Jorjenson, Rev. James Hendrickson, Adolph Carlsen, and others. The erection of the edifice was at a cost of more than $2,500.

The church having been completed, was dedicated on Sunday, the 2d of July, 1876, with services in the Scandinavian language by Rev. Mr. Ostergreen, of St. Paul, and Rev. Mr. Lunde, of Clark Grove. In the evening the service was in English, by Messrs. Abbott, Alden, Lunde, and Wood. The building is a fine appearing building, 28x42 feet, with a tower extending 65 feet. Rev. Carl Carlson, the architect and builder, came here in 1873, and for some years has regularly filled the pulpit. The services are in English.

DANISH EVANGELICAL LUTHERAN CHURCH—INDEPENDENT.—This is a small church located in Parker's Addition, and built in 1881. The pastor is Rev. J. Danielson, who resides in Freeborn and officiates here once every few weeks.

EPISCOPALIAN—THE CHURCH OF THE GOOD SHEPHERD.—There have been occasional services here in this form since an early day. Sometimes it has been quite regular, with some one from the Cathedral in Faribault, and Bishop Whipple has occasionally been here himself, as well as his brother, Rev. George B. Whipple. The church edifice was purchased of the Congregationalists for $2,000, and arranged for the Episcopal service. It was first opened for service on Christmas day, 1879. Rev. Mr. Irwin was the first pastor, who was succeeded by Rev. W. R. Powell, the present incumbent. There are twenty-five families who worship here.

CEMETERIES.

Albert Lea people have, up to this time, paid little attention to the ornamentation of burial places, which is in any case a mere sentiment, as nothing that can be done here for the departed ones, however dear in life and cherished in remembrance, will be of any service to them, although the kind offices we perform in token of our love for those who have gone before, does have a beneficent influence upon us and upon those who take cognizance of this bestowal of such tokens of regard.

About the first burial place was that on the Pickerel Lake road, taken from McReynold's farm. A certain amount of money was appropriated by the town at one time to fence the grounds, but only the side next to the road got so supplied, the money having been used for other purposes. This cemetery has some fine monuments, and is otherwise very highly ornamented with shrubbery and prairie flowers, and if "beauty unadorned is adorned the most," this place is embellished in the highest style of nature.

There is also a small corner, north of Fountain Lake, that is devoted to burial purposes.

In the spring of 1882, the subject of a new cemetery was agitated, and in May a meeting was held to discuss measures to provide a new cemetery. Hon. H. D. Brown was called to the chair. The matter was freely talked over, and it was the almost universal feeling and decision of all present, that a new cemetery ground should be purchased and the old cemetery abandoned. As to the location there were various opinions, although the majority seemed to favor a place north of Fountain Lake. Others favored a location east of the mill. The matter was finally relegated to a committee of nine, consisting of H D. Brown, Chairman; T. H. Armstrong, J. A. Lovely, D. R. P. Hibbs, W. P. Sergeant, W. W. Johnson, J. W. Smith, Dr. Wedge, and George Davies, who were to report to a future meeting of citizens concerning all the matters that pertained to the location of a new cemetery. So that it is likely that at no distant day, Albert Lea will have its "Mount Auburn," "Greenwood," or "Glendale," with its wealth of landscape scenery, and costly marble.

ITASCA CEMETERY.—This was laid out and appropriated as a burial place in 1871. It is owned by a company. A. M. Burnham is President; Isaac Botsford, Secretary; and E. D. Hopkins, Treasurer. It is located to the west of the buried city whose name it bears, commanding a view for quite a distance in several directions, and is just east of the old north and south territorial road, traces of which can yet be seen. Those who repose here have fine marble monuments. The price of the lots is $20.

FRATERNAL ORDERS.

MASONIC. Western Star Lodge No. 26 was instituted in October, 1857, and worked under a dispensation until October 27th, 1858, when a charter was granted.

The first officers were: Asa W. White, W. M.; Charles Norton, S. W.; J. Brownsill, J. W.; A. C. Wedge, Tr.; H. D. Brown, Sec'y; A. B. Webber, S. D.; Aug. Armstrong, J. D.; Isaac Botsford, Tyler.

The present officers of the lodge are; William C. Pratt, W. M.; G. T. Gardner, S. W., J. J. Bond, J. W.; S. S. Edwards, Sec'y; W. P. Sergeant, Tr.; T. E. Schleuder, S. D.; S. S. Mallery, J. D.; Axel Brundeu, Tyler.

The Masters of the lodge have been, from the first until 1882, as follows: Asa W. White, John Brownsell, H. D. Brown, F. B. Fobes, D. N. Gates, W. P. Sergeant, J. F. Reppy, F. S. Lincoln, and William C. Pratt.

The lodge is in a flourishing condition, and has a capacious and well furnished hall. The meetings in the summer are on the second Wednesday in each month, and the rest of the year, on the second and fourth Wednesdays.

ALBERT LEA CHAPTER NO. 30, ROYAL ARCH MASONS.—Instituted on the 30th of March, 1874. The first meeting was on the 17th of April. The first officers were; A. W. White, H. P.; C. L. West, K.; S. Partridge, S.; H. Powell, C. of H.; F. S. Lincoln, P. S.; George Woodward, R. A. C.; William Morin, Tr.; F. S. Sinclair, Sec'y.

The present officers are: H. D. Brown, H. P.; George C. Harper, K.; J. D. Prime, S.; J. F. Reppy, C. of H.; George T. Gardner, P. S.; C. M. Wilkinson, R. A. C.; S. S. Edwards, Sec'y; William P. Sergeant, Tr.

There are 31 members.

APOLLO COMMANDERY, KNIGHTS TEMPLAR, NO. 12.—Instituted on the 1st of October, 1879, with nineteen charter members. The officers were: John Boyce, E. C.; H. R. Wells, Gen.; M. H. Avery, C. of G.

The present officers are: William Morin, E. C.; J. F. Reppy, Gen.; M. H. Avery, C. G.; H. D. Brown, Prel.; G. S. Ruble, S. W.; A. A. Peck, J. W.; W. P. Sergeant, Tr.; George F. Gardner, Recorder.

Meetings are held on the third Wednesday of each month, The membership is 30.

EQUITABLE AID UNION.—At the last regular semi-annual election of officers of Albert Lea Union, No. 390, E. A. U., the following named persons were elected officers for the ensuing term: Ira A. Town, Chancellor; L. D. Smith, Advocate; Theo. Schleuder, Vice President; E. H. Ellickson, Auxiliary; H. O. Haukness, Treasurer; T. K. Ramsey, Secretary; John Doerr, Accountant; A. G. Brundin, Chaplain; Ole Knudson, Jr., Warden; M. P. Johnson, Sentinel; C. O. Barnes, Watchman.

ODD FELLOWS—ALBERT LEA LODGE NO. 61. Instituted on the 27th of August, 1877, with the following officers: G. S. Gowdy, N. G.; E. C. Stacy, V. G.; S S. Edward, R. S.; A. H. Squier, J. S.; T. W. Long, Tr.

There is a membership of 70. Their hall is a good one, over Smith & Gossett's store.

The present officers are: J. P. Colby, N. G.; S. Strauss, V. G.; C. D. Marlett, Sec.; S. S. Edwards, Treas.; D. L. Squier, Mar.; A. H. Squier, Con.; E. S. Wilson, I. G.; L. Stefferson, O. G.; E. C. Stacy, R. S. N. G.; W. H. Long, L. S. N. G.; L. Gahl, R. S. V. G.; H. S. Menifee, L. S. V. G.; A. Noble, R. S. S.; Aug. Peterson, L. S. S.; J. B. Claybourne, O. C.; Rev. G. S. Gowdy, Chaplain; Z. K. Mallery, P. G.

DAUGHTERS OF REBEKAH.—The following are the officers of Albert Lea Degree Lodge No 16, Daughters of Rebekah: E. C. Stacy, N. G.; Mrs. C. D. Marlett, V. G.; Mary Gahl, Rec. Sec.; Katie Tunell, F. Sec.; Mrs. D. L. Squier, Treas.; Mrs. A. H. Squier, I. G.; W. H. Long, O. G.; D. L. Squier, Warden; Eva Long, Con.; Mrs. A. H. McMillan, R. S. N. G.; Mrs. W. O. Rousberry, L. S. N. G.; L. Gahl, R. S. V. G.; S. Strauss, L. S. V. G.; G. S. Gowdy, Chaplain; A. H. Squier, P. G.

ANCIENT ORDER OF UNITED WORKINGMEN.—This fraternal and beneficial society was instituted in Albert Lea on the 10th of March, 1878.

The first officers were: Dr. A. C. Wedge, P. M. W.; W. P. Sergeant, M. W.; T. J. Watt, G. F.; R. C. VanVechten, O.; J. F. Reppy, Rec.; P. M. Wilkinson, F.; August Peterson, Recr.; W. G. Kellar, I. W.; G. C. Harper, O. W.; G. T. Gardiner, G.

Their meetings were held on Tuesday evenings, at Masonic Hall.

GRAND ARMY OF THE REPUBLIC.—Robson Post, No. 5, was instituted in the winter of 1880, and was named in honor of Captain James A. Robson, of Company E, Tenth Minnesota Regiment.

The present officers of the post are: Commander, George S. Ruble; Senior Vice Commander, G. Q. Annis; Adjutant, F. W. Drake; Quartermaster, Jerome P. Greene; Officer of the Day, John Murtaugh; Officer of the Guard, J. B. Frauss; Chaplain, William Lowe; Surgeon, D. M. M. Dodge; Sergeant Major, J. J. Bond; Quartermaster Sergeant, Martin Olson; Sentinel, Ai Rice.

The list of members was burned in the fire of April, 1882, but it is made up of the men who went to the front from wherever they lived when the war broke out.

There have been various other fraternal orders, some of them with insurance features, and others with monopathic reformatory ideas, and they have had an existence more or less extended. Some of them may be in existence now, and while they are of interest, and perhaps use to those who are connected with them, the public, as a rule, are not sufficiently concerned to warrant the occupancy of much space in a work like this.

MILITARY.

From time to time there have been military companies in existence here since the war, which have been more or less creditable Now we have the ALBERT LEA LIGHT GUARDS, which was organized on the 4th of May, 1882. It is Company F, Second Battalion of the Minnesota National Guard. Fifty-two men were mustered in by Major Bobeleter, commanding the Second Battalion. The company is duly armed and equipped, and is a fine body of men.

The commissioned officers are: Captain, George T. Gardner; First Lieutenant, T. K. Ramsey; Second Lieutenant, C. S. Roberdson.

This company took part in the Decoration services on the 30th of May, the same month they were organized, and made a fine appearance. Their uniform is identical with that of the United States regular army, but of finer material.

CHAPTER LIII.

BIOGRAPHICAL.

JAMES CAREY ALLING was born on the 7th of January, 1857, in Chemung, New York. In 1858, the family moved to Greene county in the same State, where his parents still live. His father, Harvey Alling, is a Baptist minister. In 1873, James entered the State Normal School at Oswego, taking a classical course and graduating in 1879. He had meanwhile studied law and had also taught some; and after his graduation went to Alabama where he was engaged as professor of the sciences in the State Normal School, remaining two years. In September, 1881, he came to Minnesota and obtained the position of Principal of Pleasant Grove school at Mankato. Since January 1882, he has been Principal and Superintendent of the Public Schools of Albert Lea, having a present attendence of over four hundred pupils and a corps of nine teachers. Mr. Alling is the founder of the "Albert Lea City Library" and a member of the "American Association for the Advancement of Science."

REV. R. B. ABBOTT is a native of Franklin county, Indiana. The son of a thrifty farmer, he was brought up to habits of manual labor, industry and self reliance. After improving such opportunities for education as the common schools of that time afforded, he prepared himself for college by private study. He entered the Indiana State University and was graduated in the class of '47. Three years later he received the degree of Master of Arts from the same institution. For several years he was engaged in teaching, first in Muncie, then in New Castle, and afterward in the Whitewater Presbyterian Academy. After studying Theology privately several years, he was ordained to the ministry of the gospel by the Presbytery of the latter place in 1857, and very soon after became pastor of the church at Brookville in his native county, continuing seven years with much success. This was followed by a two years' pastorate at Knightstown. From this place, on account of his wife's failing health, he removed to Minnesota and again engaged in teaching, first as Principal of the Public schools of Anoka, and afterward as the Principal of the St. Paul Female Seminary. In 1869, he retired from teaching and accepted the pastorate of the Presbyterian church of Albert Lea, which has since grown to be one of the best and strongest churches in southern Minnesota. In connection with this, he is laboring for the establishment of a college in Albert Lea for the education of young women, in which enterprise there is great hope of abundant success.

His wife, whose failing health brought him to

this State, having died in 1879, he was married again, two years later to Miss Marietta Hunter, a graduate of Ripon College, Wisconsin, and for several years a teacher in Albert Lea.

F. A. BLACKMER, M. D., a native of Ohio, was born in Amherst, Lorain county, on the 16th of January, 1848. His father, Dr. Franklin Blackmer, was one of the first physicians to locate in this town, coming in 1856. They settled on a farm near the city, and in 1862, F. A. enlisted in Company C, of the Fifth Minnesota Volunteer Infantry, and while at Fort Ridgely was wounded, a ball passing through his face, in one cheek and out of the other. After his return from the army he attended school from 1863 to 1868, then entered the Oberlin College, in Ohio, which he attended during the winter months, and in summer continued his studies at the University of Worcester, in Cleveland, Ohio. After graduating from the latter institution he was in the drug business, and also engaged in the practice of his profession, having, since 1872, devoted his entire attention to the latter. He was joined in marriage on the 15th of October, 1872, with Miss Franc E. Wedge. The union has been blessed with one child, Roe C., born on the 17th of October, 1873.

HEMAN BLACKMER, also a son of Dr. Franklin Blackmer, was born in Amherst, Lorain county, Ohio, on the 3d of January, 1850. He came to Albert Lea with his parents when seven years old, attended the public schools until 1865, when he entered the Oberlin College, in Ohio, and remained four years, teaching a portion of each year. He then returned to his home, and in 1870, continued his studies at the Appleton College, in Wisconsin, and after a year there entered the college in Ripon, and in 1872, took a law course in the State University at Madison, graduating in 1873. He was married in October of the latter year to Miss Helen Webster, who has borne him five children, two of whom are living. Mr. Blackmer was admitted to practice in the Supreme Court of Wisconsin; subsequently moved to Kansas, and practiced in Osborne until his return to Albert Lea in 1874. For the past seven years he has held the office of Justice of the Peace, and is also Court Commissioner.

CHARLES W. BALLARD, M. D., Mayor of the city of Albert Lea, and one of its public-spirited and prominent citizens, was born in New York city on the 22d of January, 1826. He attended different boarding schools in New Jersey and New York, and, in 1847, began the studies of medicine and dentistry in the Washington Medical University of Baltimore, and the College of Dental Surgery, graduating from both institutions in 1850. He was united in matrimony on the 4th of February, in the latter year, to Miss Annie E. Harris. Mr. Ballard practiced dentistry in North Carolina two years, then returned to New York, and remained in business there until 1868, living, the latter portion of the time, in Connecticut, and while there was a member of the State Senate two terms, taking a decided stand against slavery. In 1868, he went to Florida for the improvement of his health, remained two years and came to Minnesota, buying the land in Albert Lea now known as Ballard's Point. He is engaged in the real estate business.

F. W. BARLOW was born in Genesee county, New York, on the 27th of November, 1852, and came to this county when a child, his parents being pioneers of Bancroft. He was brought up on a farm, and attended school until eighteen years old, then entered a drug store in this city, remaining seven years. On the 14th of June, 1875, he was joined in wedlock with Miss Emma F. Prescott, and they have had two children, both daughters, only one of whom is living. In the fall of 1879, Mr. Barlow was elected County Treasurer, and has since held the office.

CHANCEY BURTCH, a native of Ohio, was born near Seneca on the 22d of April, 1859. In 1864, his parents moved to Michigan, locating near Adrian, where his father died in 1869. Chancey came with his mother and the family to Osage county, Iowa, in 1871, and there attended school. In April, 1881, he moved to Albert Lea, and started in the drug business, in which he has been successful. He was married in May, 1881, to Miss Ada Cutler, who was born in Osage county, Iowa.

WARREN BUEL was born in Genesee county, New York, on the 4th of December, 1826. When he was twelve years old his parents moved to a farm near Tiffin, Seneca county, Ohio. After finishing school Mr. Buel engaged in teaching for a time. In July, 1852, he was married to Miss Mary Deming, who was born in Livingston county, New York, on the 5th of November, 1829. They resided on a farm in Huron county, Ohio, until 1859, and the following year moved to Ann Arbor, Michigan, and in 1861, to Jackson, where he was engaged in the grocery business during the war. They came from there to Albert Lea in 1877. Mr. Buel was in the grocery business for two years after coming here, but has since been engaged in insurance and real estate, his office being on Broadway. In 1873, he was elected to the State Legislature, and has also held local offices.

H. O. BRAGER, a native of Norway, was born on the 1st of February, 1841. In early life he learned the watchmaker's trade, and since the age of fifteen has been dependent on himself for support. He came to America in 1866, and located in Black Earth, Dane county, Wisconsin, where, in 1873, he married Miss Inger Mathia Gulson, of the town of Vermont, in the latter county. They have had three children, all boys, only one, Joachim, of whom is living. In 1878, Mr. Brayer came to Albert Lea, and opened a jewelry and watchmaking business, to which he has since devoted his time.

HORATIO D. BROWN, one of the early settlers of Freeborn county, was born in Onondaga county, New York, on the 15th of April, 1835. He was brought up on a farm, and at the same time prepared for college; attended the DeRuyter and Cazenovia seminaries, and afterward, in 1852, entered the Union College, from which he graduated as a civil engineer in 1855. He immediately came West, and spent one year teaching in Illinois and Iowa, then came to this county and took a claim about six miles south-east of Albert Lea, in Hayward. He was engaged at surveying, and, in 1857, was elected County Surveyor; was soon after appointed deputy Clerk of the Court, and, in 1861, elected to the office, holding the same ten years. On the 19th of December, 1861, he was married to Miss Mary L. Peck, and they have had four children, three of whom are living. Mr. Brown enlisted in the Fifth Minnesota Volunteer Infantry. Company C; was soon promoted to Second Lieutenant, and, in 1864, was made Adjutant of the Eleventh Minnesota Regiment. After receiving his discharge, he returned to this place, and, in 1871, resigned the office of Clerk of the Conrt, to fill that of State Senator, to which he was elected. In the latter year he engaged in the banking business, which he has since continued. He owns a fine residence on the lake shore.

A. M. BURNHAM, M. D., one of the pioneer physicians, and an early settler of this county, was born in Genesee county, New York, on the 16th of October, 1824. When he was quite young he entered the family of a Mr. Giles; attended the public schools, and assisted Mr. Giles in his dairy. He subsequently attended the Bethany High School, the Springville and Centreville Academies, then studied medicine with Drs. Steward and Farmers, and finally entered the University of Buffalo, from which he was graduated, in 1853, as an M. D. In the meantime, he had established a good practice in the latter city. In 1857, he came to Wisconsin, and the following year to this county, taking land adjoining the town site of Iosca in Waseca county, but spent the winter at Shell Rock, where he built a hotel, and was engaged in other enterprises. In the spring, he returned to his farm, taking a prominent part in the contest in regard to the county seat of the county. During all this time he was engaged in the practice of his profession. In 18—, he went to Wyoming Territory, where he operated a sawmill, and was an extensive contractor for the Union Pacific Railroad, doing a heavy business, and also engaged in mercantile pursuits. In 1871, after visiting New York, he returned to his farm, and has since continued the practice of medicine, Albert Lea has been his home since 1880.

REV. CARL CARLSEN is a native of Denmark, born in the city of Nyborn on the 4th of March, 1842. He attended the common schools, and, while learning the carpenter trade, continued his studies at an evening school. In 1863, he came to America; first to Wisconsin, but soon after located in Chicago, where he was engaged at his trade, and contracting, for ten years. On the 25th of December, 1867, he was joined in marriage with Miss Anna Hansen, a native of Norway. In 1873, they came to Albert Lea, and, besides working at his trade, Mr. Carlsen frequently preaches in the Danish Baptist Church. Mr. and Mrs. Carlsen have had four children, two of whom are living, Olga and Victor.

M. M. DODGE, M. D. was born in New Lime, Ashtabula county, Ohio, on the 28th of October, 1842, and at the age of fifteen years commenced to teach school. In 1859 he studied medicine with Dr. Porter Key, in his native town, and two years later entered the Cincinnati Hospital, and in the winter of 1863 and '64, attended lectures at Ann Arbor, Michigan. The following spring he moved to Wisconsin, immediately enlisted in the

Fortieth Wisconsin Volunteer Infantry, Company D, and was detached as Assistant Surgeon in the Adams Hospital upon the regiment's arrival in Memphis. After the close of the war he located in Chicago, and after the fire, being burned out, he attended lectures in Hahnemann Medical College, from which institution he graduated on the 22d of February, 1872. On the 24th of the same month he was joined in wedlock with Miss Lucy H. Norton, and the same year they came to Lone Rock, Wisconsin. In the spring of 1874 they came to Albert Lea, where Dr. Dodge has an extensive practice. They have one child, Louis, nine years old.

George Drommerhausen, one of the pioneer mechanics of the county and among the earliest settlers of Geneva, is a native of Prussia, born on the 22d day of June, 1832. When young he learned the trade of a wagon and carriage maker, and in 1854, came to America and worked at his trade in Pittsburg, Pennsylvania. He afterward worked in Ohio, Illinois, Wisconsin, and in Red Wing, coming to Geneva in 1857, and started the the first wagon shop in the place. He was married in the latter year to Miss Julia Persig, who has borne him four children, all boys. Mr. Drommerhausen took a farm in Bancroft in 1859, which he still owns, but in 1866, came to this place. He owns one of the largest carriage and general repair shops in the city.

C. C. Dwight, a Vermonter, was born in Vershire, Orange county, and when about twelve years old removed with his parents to Cambridge, Massachusetts, in which State he received an academical education. At the age of eighteen years he came west as traveling salesman for an eastern clothing house, and in 1876 opened a clothing store in Winnebago City, in the southern part of this State. In March, 1880, he married Miss Emma L. Harvey, a native of Cambridge, Massachusetts. The same month they came to Albert Lea, and Mr. Dwight opened a boot and shoe store in company with J. O. Conklin, but is now in the business alone. He is the father of one child, Margaretta, born on the 8th of January, 1881.

S. S. Edwards, one of the early settlers, and the oldest photographer in the city, was born in Watertown, Connecticut, on the 15th of July, 1843. He attended the common schools near his home, and afterward the high school of New Haven. In 1871, he married Miss B. M. Lunde, who is a native of Christiania, Norway. They have two children, Mary E. and Charles G. Mr. Edwards came to Albert Lea in 1863, and immediately started in his present business, at which he has been unusually successful.

Col. Samuel Eaton is a native of New York, born in Onondaga county in 1815. At the early age of seven years his lot was cast with strangers, his parents being unable to provide for and educate him. Having learned the trade, he commenced the manufacture of leather and boots and shoes, at which he was engaged twenty years. Having a taste for military life, he filled all positions from a private to the command of a regiment, holding the latter five years. In 1857 he came to Albert Lea, where he has since resided, and during this time he has been called upon to fill offices of trust, such as Justice of the Peace, Assessor, Treasurer, Coroner, Judge of Probate, and since 1879 has been Postmaster, having retired from all other business. He was also Deputy Clerk of the Court four years and Deputy County Treasurer two years.

John B. Foote is a native of New York, born in the town of Salisbury, Herkimer county, on the 11th day of September, 1823. He completed his studies at the Fairfield Academy, receiving from the Superintendent a certificate to teach in any part of New York State, and for thirteen years availed himself of this privilege. On the 1st of November, 1848, he was joined in wedlock with Miss Eliza Sharp, a native of Fulton County, New York. She died on the 23d of February, 1867, and was buried in Yorkshire, Cattaraugus County. Mr. Foote was again married on the 25th of April, 1871, his bride being Mrs. Louisa Burnette. From 1860 to 1879 he was employed by publishing houses of New York and Philadelphia, and in the latter year came to Albert Lea. He has since been proprietor of the Gilbert House, one of the principal hotels in the city. He had three children by his first marriage; Charles M., Francelia Ann, and Sherwood L., the two latter being dead; and one, Ernest B., by his second wife. The eldest son, Charles M., is of the firm of Warner and Foote, Minneapolis, one of the most extensive publishing houses in the State.

O. B. Fobes was born in St. Lawrence county, New York, on the 30th of July, 1832. He received an academical, education, and in 1854, came to Ripon, Wisconsin. In 1861, he moved to Minnesota, and was engaged in the mercantile business in Winnebago City until 1863, when he enlisted in Company M, of the Fourth Wisconsin Volunteer Infantry, and remaining in service until the close of the war. After receiving his discharge he returned to Ripon, Wisconsin, and was Deputy Postmaster for about six years. He then came to Albert Lea, and in company with his brother opened a hardware store but has recently sold out and is now in the grocery business, the firm name being Fobes & Owen. Mr. Fobes was married in 1876, to Miss Cassie McNeill, a native of Canada. The union has been blessed with one child, Lucile.

WILLIAM FENHOLT, one of the earlier settlers of Freeborn county, was born in Saxony, Germany, on the 12th of May, 1835. He came to America in 1854, first located in Wisconsin, and in 1858, moved to this county, near the head of Freeborn lake, in Carlston township. He was married in 1859 to Miss Emma Killmer, a native of Canada. Soon after the outbreak of the war he enlisted in Company F, of the Fourth Minnesota Volunteer Infantry and participated in many hard fought battles; was hurt at the battle of Chattanooga and Atlanta, and now draws a pension. He came to Albert Lea after the war and opened the City Hotel which he still owns and conducts. Mr. and Mrs. Fenholt have a family of seven children.

REV. HENRY FRANK was born in Lafayette, Indiana, on the 21st of December, 1853. When a child his parents moved to Chicago where he attended the public schools, and after graduating entered the Philip Academy, at Andover, Massachusetts, and later the Harvard University. In 1875, he obtained the position of professor of English Literature and Elocution in the Cornell University, at Mt. Vernon, Iowa. He was united in marriage with Miss Carrie L. Cleveland, daughter of Dr. Cleveland of Chicago, in 1876. The following year he entered the ministry and for several years preached in Kansas, then, in 1880, on account of failing health came to Minnesota and has since had charge of a church in Albert Lea.

JOSEPH A. FULLER is a native of Walworth county, Wisconsin, born on the 17th of March, 1851, near the village of Geneva. When 21 years old he went to Decorah, Iowa, and learned photography, at which business he has since been engaged, coming to Albert Lea soon after finishing the study of his profession. He was married in 1874, to Miss Luella A. Owen, who was born in Wisconsin. They have one child; Mert L., born on the 11th of January, 1875.

P. H. GREEN was born in Otsego county, New York, on the 5th of April, 1818. When he was young his parents moved to Erie county, where he grew to manhood and then farmed for himself. In 1861, he came west to Freeborn county and located in the town of Freeman, where he improved a farm and remained until 1874, during which time he held several of the local offices. In the latter year he came to Albert Lea, which has since been his home, and resides with his sons who carry on the homestead. Mr. Green was married before leaving his native State to Miss Margaret R. Miner, the ceremony taking place on the 17th of August, 1843. Mrs Green died on the 24th of December, 1873, leaving a family of five children.

WALTER GILLETTE was born in the city of Amherst, New Hampshire, on the 22d of February, 1848. In 1855, his parents moved to Milwaukee where Walter received a good business education. His father was a leather dealer in the latter city, for a number of years; in 1872, he moved to Ripon, Wisconsin, in the same business, and remained until coming here in 1878. Walter is associated with him, and besides leather they deal in wool, hides, and furs, theirs being the only enterprise of the kind in the city.

REV. G. S. GOWDY, a native of New York, was born in Rome, Oneida county, on the 19th of May, 1810. When he was young his parents removed to Jefferson county, in the same State, and G. S. attended school and learned of his father the miller's trade. He was married in 1830, to Miss Nancy Allen, who was born in Oswego county, on the 1st of February, 1812. Mr. Gowdy entered upon the ministry at the age of thirty years, and has since continued in that field of labor in the Universalist faith. He had charge of a parish in Yorkshire for a time, and after coming to Minnesota was in Faribault until 1876, then came to Albert Lea as pastor of the church here. Mr. and Mrs. Gowdy have had three children, two of whom are living; Mary Ann, now Mrs. Sylvester Rice, and Nancy M., now Mrs. Franklin Gould.

DANIEL N. GATES, a native of New York, was born in Hopewell, Ontario county, on the 25th of July, 1832. He received an academical education in a Canada college, and in 1853 came west, first to Dubuque, Iowa, and engaged in surveying on the St. Croix river, and a year later began mercantile pursuits in Brownsville, Houston county. On the 9th of October, 1856, he was joined in marriage with Miss Sarah A. Dunbar, and the union has been blessed with three children. In 1858 Mr. Gates moved to St. Paul, where he was Deputy State Auditor three years, and remained until 1869, when he came to Albert Lea and has since been freight and ticket agent for the Chicago, St. Paul & Minneapolis railroad. He is President of the Board of Education for this city and Chairman of the Board of Education for the county.

GEORGE T. GARDNER was born in Albion, Orleans county, New York, on the 18th of August, 1848. He removed with his parents to Buffalo, and in 1856 to Joliet, Illinois, thence to Milwaukee and to Kilbourn City, Wisconsin. In 1861, he returned to Buffalo, New York, and entered a drug store, but in 1870 came to Lone Rock, Wisconsin, and opened a store of his own. On the 28th of November, 1872, he married Miss Hattie H. Hayes, and the next year they removed to this city, Mr. Gardner clerking in a drug store. Later he purchased the business of A. H. Street, and conducted it until 1880, when he was elected Clerk of the District Court, running on a Democratic ticket, and received a majority of 281 in a district which has heretofore given 2,500 Republican majority. Mr. and Mrs. Gardner have had three children, two of whom are living.

M. HALVORSEN was born in Norway on the 24th of February, 1855. In 1863 he came with his father, Richard Halvorsen, who was a Methodist minister, to Chicago, Illinois, but for three years the family was not permanently located. They finally settled in Forest City, Iowa, and when our subject was fourteen years old he commenced to learn the printer's trade in the office of the "Winnebago Press," and in 1871, purchased the enterprise in partnership with W. C. Hayward. In 1873 Mr. Halvorsen became sole proprietor, being the youngest editor in the State, but a few months later again took a partner. The paper proved a financial failure under the new management, and in 1874 he removed to Lake Mills, Iowa, purchasing there a full outfit, and started "The Independent Herald," making it a grand success. In August, 1875, he purchased the "Albert Lea Enterprise," and has succeeded here far beyond his expectations, having the largest office in the county, and a circulation of his paper of nearly 1,000. Mr. Halvorsen was married on the 15th of August, 1876, to Miss Mildred A. Salsich, and they have one child, Alexander Salsich.

OLE J. HAGEN is a native of Norway, born near Christiania, on the 31st of August, 1852. He came with his parents to America and settled on a farm in Winneshiek county, Iowa, remaining until the age of fifteen years, during which time he attended the public schools. In 1867 the family came to this county and located on a farm near Freeman. On the 18th of May, 1872, the subject of this sketch was united in marriage with Miss Anna A. Stovern. The same year he came to Albert Lea, and for eighteen months was in the drug business in company with his brother. He was subsequently engaged in the sale of agricultural implements, and later entered a printing office, remaining in the office in the winter and selling machinery in the summer. In 1880 he again worked in the printing office, and when the "Albert Lea Posten" was started he was appointed its editor, which position he still holds. He has a family of four children.

H. A. HANSON was born in Hurdalen, Norway, on the 26th of August, 1843. When about ten years old he became an apprentice to the tailor trade, and worked at the same six years, when he started in business for himself. On the 6th of November, 1868, he was united in marriage with Miss Bertha M. Nelson. They came to America the following year, directly to this county, and engaged in farming for one summer. In the fall, Mr. Hanson opened a tailor shop in this city, and in 1870 increased his business, thus obtaining the best class of trade in the place. In 1880, he sold out to fill the office of Postmaster, to which he had been appointed. He was the first City Treasurer, and has held other local offices. Mr. and Mrs. Hanson have had eight children, five of whom are living.

REV. NORMAN F. HOYT was born in Saratoga county, New York, in the village of Waterford, near Troy, on the 23rd of May, 1840. At the age of ten years he moved with his parents to Almira, where he received his early education and remained until the breaking out of the war, when he enlisted in Company F, of the 23rd New York Volunteer Infantry. He went South with his regiment, and was in the battles of Bull Run, Fredericksburg, and others. At the expiration of his term of service, (two years,) he returned home, having been promoted to the rank of Sergeant, and in December re-enlisted as a veteran in the the One Hundred and Forty-Eighth Regiment, Company B; was promoted to Brigade Adjutant, and participated in the first and second battles of Petersburg, Cold Harbor, Fort Harrison, and Richmond. After the close of the war he was sent to Texas, and remained in service two years longer, receiving an honorable discharge in February, 1867. He returned to his native State, and the following August came west to Chicago, where for five years he attended the Baptist Theological Seminary, In 1872, he was joined in matrimony with Miss Emma J. Slayson, a native of New York. The following year he took charge of a church at Maquoketa, Iowa, and presided over it three years. Mrs. Hoyt died in October, 1874, leaving a young child, and in January, 1875, he married his present wife, Miss Mary E. Baldwin, who has borne him two children, Mary A. and Mable F. His eldest child is Emma. Mr. Mr. Hoyt came to Albert Lea in 1875, and until the present year conducted services at Northwood and in the Baptist Church here, but now confines his labor to his congregation in this city.

G. A. Hauge was born in Christiania, Norway, on the 19th of December, 1840. When he was ten years old his parents came to America, and located on a farm in Winneshiek county, Iowa. Since the age of sixteen years he has maintained himself, and on the 16th of October, 1861, enlisted in Company G, of the Twelfth Iowa Volunteer Infantry; was in several heavy engagements, the battles of Shiloh, Nashville, etc., and remained in service until the close of the war, when he was honorably discharged. He returned to his home in Iowa, and in 1869, married Miss Nellie Lagon, a native of Norway. In 1870, they came to this county, first settling in Bancroft, but since 1875, have been residents of this city. Mr. Hauge, with Mr. Christopherson as partner, conducts the largest blacksmith shop in Albert Lea. Mr. and Mrs Hauge have two children.

Major Frank Hall, one of the early settlers, and the first Mayor of Albert Lea, was born in Lewis county, New York, on the 28th of July, 1834. In 1854, his parents moved to a farm near Beaver Dam, in Dodge county, Wisconsin, and a few years later to Ripon. There Frank attended college for a few years. In 1858, he married Miss Maggie Foster, and the same year came to Albert Lea, and opened one of the first stores in the place. In the spring of 1862, he raised a company in the Fifth Minnesota Volunteer Infantry, of which he was Captain. He remained in service until the spring of 1863, when he received an honorable discharge and returned home. He is landlord of the Hall House, the leading hotel in the city. He is the father of two children, Ida and Joseph W.

C. P. Hedenstad is a native of Norway, born in Kongsberg, on the 3d of March, 1853. In 1864, he came with his parents to America, and located in Waseca county, Minnesota, where his mother still lives, his father having died there in 1872. C. P. learned the jeweler's trade when quite young, and in 1875, came to Albert Lea and opened a store in which he keeps jewelry, musical instruments, and sewing machines. In 1880, he was married to Miss Sina Wangsnes, who was born in Bergen, Norway. They have one child, a girl.

C. M. Hewitt, one of the early settlers and enterprising merchants of this place, is a native of of New York, born in Oneida county on the 27th of December, 1837. When young his parents moved to Columbus, Warren county, Pennsylvania, where he grew to manhood. In 1859 he came to Minnesota, and located a farm in Bancroft, where he remained eighteen months and, then came to Albert Lea. He was married in 1867, to Miss Lura E. Ash, and they have one daughter, May A. For ten years after coming here Mr. Hewitt clerked for Frank Hall; and in June, 1869, engaged in business for himself on Broadway, at present having a $12,000 stock.

Hans E. Knatvold was born in Drammen, Norway, on the 3d of September, 1848. When he was about fourteen years old his parents came to America and directly to this county, locating in Oakland. In 1862, his father enlisted in Company M, of the First Minnesota Mounted Rangers, and after receiving his discharge moved his family to the town of Hayward, where they still reside. In 1867, Hans came to Albert Lea and clerked in a general mercantile store until 1877, when he, in company with his brother, T. V. Knatvold, started in the hardware business, and they carry the largest stock in the city, their store being located on the west side of Broadway, Mr. Knatvold, the subject of our sketch, also owns a fine residence. He was married in 1879, to Miss Clara McArthur, a native of Port Huron, Michigan. They have one child, Bertha May, born in August, 1880.

William G. Kellar is a native of Grant county, Wisconsin, born on the 17th of August, 1849. His parents are pioneers of this township, coming in 1856, and locating on a farm near the city. William attended the common schools, and in 1865 entered the Oberlin College in Ohio, and since his return has been engaged in surveying for several years, in the employ of the Southern Minnesota railroad. He has been County Surveyor since 1870. In 1874, he was joined in marriage with Miss Ada Green, who was born in Zanesville, Ohio. They have one child, Ira A., born on the 22nd of March, 1878. C. B. Kellar, a brother of the above, was also born in Grant county, Wisconsin, on the 19th of May, 1845. He came with his parents to this place and in 1862, enlisted in Company C, of the Fifth Minnesota Volunteer Infantry, under Major Hall, and after his discharge attended Oberlin College a few years. He has a wife and two children. He is at present in the employ of H. D. Brown as cashier.

Prof. Charles W. Levens was born in Windsor, Windsor county, Vermont, on the 7th of February, 1840. When he was three years old his parents moved to Racine county, Wisconsin. Charles attended the State University, teaching during the vacations, until 1860. In the latter year he married Miss Rebecca B. Teachout, a native of Lorain county, Ohio, and the same year moved to California, remaining one year engaged in school teaching. He returned to Wisconsin, and for two years was County Superintendent of the schools of Racine county; then for four years was Superintendant of the public schools of the city of Racine. In 1876, he moved to Minnesota, and after a residence of two years in Olmsted county, came to Albert Lea, and was employed as Principal of the public schools here, afterwards was elected Superintendent of the same and held both positions until resigning to fill the office of County Superintendant, to which he was elected in 1882. Mr. Levens has been instrumental in building up and giving to the public schools of this city their high reputation for solid worth. He has a family of six children, four daughters and two sons.

William Clifford McAdam, a native of New York, was born near Utica, in Oneida county. He grew to manhood in his native State, preparing for college in the Utica Free Academy, and in 1873, entered the Hamilton College, graduating in the classical course in 1877, and from the law department one year later. He then came to Chicago and continued his legal studies in the office of Higgins and Swett. In 1880, he moved to Albert Lea; was with Judge Whytock for a time, and is now of the firm of Palmer and McAdam.

M. T. Magelssen, A. M., M. D., one of the more recent settlers of Albert Lea, is a native of Norway, born in Christiania on the 5th of April, 1852. His father was Chief of Police of that city until 1859, when the family moved to Bergen, where the latter was made Magistrate, and still holds the position. The subject of this sketch spent his early days at school, attending the Learned Latin College in Bergen, and in 1869 entered the Royal University of Norway, from which he received a diploma as physician and surgeon in 1876. He continued his medical studies in the Royal University at Vienna, Austria, graduating in 1879, and completed his education in France. He then located in London, England, where he had a good practice, still continuing to study. In the fall of 1881, he came to America, to Minnesota, and in January, 1882, located in this city, where he has established a good practice.

E. W. Murphy was born in county Armagh, Ireland, near the seaport village of Dundalk, on the 1st of May, 1832. At an early age he began life for himself, coming to America, and at the age of sixteen years located in Illinois. He came to Albert Lea in November, 1855, but did not remain more than three years; going south he spent three years traveling. In 1861 he returned to this city, and engaged in the milling business, but in 1878 opened a general mercantile store, to which he has since devoted his time. He was joined in marriage on the 20th of November, 1870, to Miss Ann Hoffman, a native of Vermont. They have been blessed with one son, William Henry, born on the 18th of July, 1875.

C. D. Marlett is a native of Cass county, Michigan, where he was born on the 19th of May, 1845. He came with his parents to Albert Lea in 1857; attended school, and in 1863 enlisted in Company H, of the First Minnesota Cavalry, serving two years. After returning from the army he learned the trade of a carpenter and joiner, and is now engaged in building and repairing boats. He was married on the 22d of February, 1864, to Miss Alice Killiner, and the union has been blessed with three children, two of whom are living.

SAMUEL MARSH, a native of England, was born in Northampton on the 16th of October, 1836. After reaching maturity he was employed as a book-keeper in his native town, and in 1855 came to America. He first located in Iowa, and engaged in buying and selling grain. While there he married, in 1864, Miss Michal Bradfield, who was born in La Crosse, Wisconsin. They moved to Albert Lea in 1870, and for about seven years Mr. Marsh continued the business of buying and selling grain, since which time he has been employed as car accountant at the depot. He has four children; William N., Robert S., John B., and Ida M.

WILLIAM MORIN was educated in New York as a civil engineer, and followed the profession for five years in the eastern States. He then came to Minnesota and acquired extensive tracts of land, being at present the largest land holder in Freeborn county. He was married in 1862, to Miss M. E. Wedge, and they have two children at home. Mr. Morin is one of the townsite proprietors, his interest being on the west side of Broadway, and is also largely interested in building enterprises in the city. He is a half owner of the finest business block, and is now erecting a fine residence in the western part of the city, on the site he selected twenty years ago.

RICHARD MILLS, a native of Pennsylvania, was born near the village of Brownsville, in Fayette county, on the 14th of April, 1834. He learned the trade of a saddler and harnessmaker in the latter village, and in 1861 enlisted at New Castle for one year, with the One Hundredth Pennsylvania Roundheads; in 1862, re-enlisted in the United States Navy, and served under Commodore Farragut. After his discharge, in the autumn of of 1865, he came west to Peoria, Illinois, and in 1870, to Albert Lea. Mr. Mills has a wife and three children. His father, Richard Mills, now eighty-seven years old, makes his home with him. He draws a pension for injuries received in the war of 1812.

N. O. NARVESON was born near Christiania, Norway, on the 2d of January, 1850. In 1853, his parents came to America, locating in Winneshiek county, Iowa, and in 1858, came to this county, where they were pioneers in the town of Bancroft. N. O. came to Albert Lea in 1871, and was employed as clerk for Hazelton & Johnson, afterward for Andrew Palmer, Jr., and finally for A. E. Johnson for four years. In 1879, he was married to Miss Anna C. Hanson, a native of Denmark. They have one child, Orine, born on the 15th of June, 1880. In May, 1882, Mr. Narveson commenced business for himself, having a stock of groceries, crockery, glassware, etc.

OSCAR N. OLBERG was born in Christiania, Norway, on the 13th of November, 1848. He attended the Christiania University, and graduated in 1868. The same year he came to America, and, in 1869, to Madison, Wisconsin. In the fall of 1870, he moved to Minnesota, and was engaged in a foreign ticket office, located in Austin, Mower county; also was cashier of the Mower County Bank for several years. In the fall of 1873, he opened a general mercantile store in Adams, Mower county, and two years later built and carried on a double store in Taopi, in the same county. He was married in 1876, to Miss Henrietta Dahl, a native of Waupun, Wisconsin. They have one child, Clara Mable, born on the 7th of November, 1878. In 1881, Mr. Olberg was connected with a wholesale notion house in Chicago, from which place he moved to Albert Lea on the 1st of October, 1882. At present he owns three mercantile stores, located, one in Albert Lea, one in Taopi, and one at Forest City, Iowa, the one here having been started in 1881. He is also still in the foreign ticket business, being general agent for the "Monarch" line of steamers.

MARTIN W. O'CONNER, a native of Ireland, was born in Tipperary on the 7th of October, 1846. When he was an infant his parents came to America, and located in Burlington, Vermont, where his father died a few years later. When he was seven years old his mother moved with her children to Philadelphia, and in 1861, to St. Louis, where he learned the machinist trade. He enlisted at Cincinnati, Ohio, in the One Hundred and Eighty-first Ohio Volunteer Infantry, Company E, but was soon discharged on account of sickness. In 1868, he came to Albert Lea, and worked at his trade for a time, but now has a saloon and billiard hall, located on the corner of Railroad and College avenues. He was married in 1869, to Miss Hannah Melder, a native of

Sweden. The issue of the union is two children Mary and Ellen.

ROBERT MULFORD PALMER was born on the 22d of October, 1855, near Janesville, in Rock county, Wisconsin, where he received a first-class academical education. In October, 1876, he entered the law office of Winans & McElroy, and was duly admitted to the bar of that State in November, 1877. In January of the following year he came to Albert Lea, and in June was admitted to practice law in Minnesota. In June, 1881, he formed a law partnership with William C. McAdam, Esq., under the firm name of Palmer & McAdam. In 1880, he was nominated for County Attorney on the Democratic ticket, but, though running several hundred votes ahead of his ticket at the polls, he was defeated by John A. Lovely, Esq., a regular Republican nominee, and a lawyer of marked ability. In 1879, he was elected City Attorney, and in 1882, received the regular nomination for City Attorney in the Republican convention over John A. Lovely and John Whytock.

DANIEL G PARKER, late editor and proprietor of the "Standard," and a son of Luther and Ann (Gott) Parker, was born in Mount Desert, Hancock county, Maine, on the 2nd of April, 1831. His branch of the Parker family were very early settlers in the Pine Tree State, his father, a mechanic, serving as a waiter boy for the continental troops in the war of 1812, and '15. Daniel received only a common school education, and at the age of fourteen years went to sea, and for seven years served on a number of merchant vessels, either as seaman or mate, sailing the latter part of the time from Portsmouth, New Hampshire. In 1851, he went to Boston and worked one year in a locomotive machine shop, and in 1854, came as far west as Chicago, where he spent three years, at first as a merchant's clerk and afterward in trade for himself. In 1857, he removed to Red Wing, Minnesota; read law with Judge Charles McClure, and the next year was admitted to the bar at Albert Lea. Here he practiced until the commencement of the rebellion, then resigned the office of County Attorney in 1862, to enter the army as Corporal of Company F, of the First Minnesota Engineers, and served a little more that three years, passing through the various grades of promotion, being First Lieutenant when discharged, most of the time he was on detached duty, acting as Provost Marshal, Judge Advocate in military courts and in other capacities. On returning to Albert Lea, Mr. Parker purchased the "Standard," which had been suspended, and conducted it until May, 1878, when, in consequence of declining health, he sold to W. W. Williams, formerly editor of the "Stillwater Lumberman." During his period of journalism, in 1866, and '67, he filled the office of County Treasurer, and for the last five years has been a director in the public school board. Since 1878, he has been engaged in the real estate and grain trade. On the 21st of January, 1861, Mrs. Eliza W. Pickett, daughter of Nathan P. Smith, of New York, became the wife of Mr. Parker, and they have a pleasant home in western part of the city and, a liberal share of the comforts of life.

AUGUST PETERSON, one of the early settlers and influential men of this county, was born in Christiansand, Norway, on the 20th of September, 1843. His father was policeman and warden of the jail of that city until 1854, when he brought his family to America. They came to Wisconsin and first located in Janesville, then in Kilbourn City. In 1858, they came to Freeborn county, and settled on a farm in Hartland township. In 1861, the father enlisted in the Third Minnesota Volunteer Infantry, and a few days later, August ran away from home and joined Company F, of the Fourth Minnesota Regiment. On arriving at Fort Snelling he met his father, who had him transferred to his company. In 1862, he (August) was taken prisoner at Murfreesboro; was afterward paroled and took part in the Indian massacre, remaining in service until the close of the war. After his return he farmed in Manchester until 1872, when he was elected County Register of Deeds and held the office three years. He was appointed by Gov. Pillsbury a member of the State board of immigration for 1879 and 1880. Mr. Peterson is the compiler and owner of a set Freeborn county, "Abstract of Titles;" is also engaged in the real estate and insurance business. His wife was Miss Sarah Peterson, daughter of an early resident of Manchester.

J. H. PARKER, one of the successful attorneys of the city, was born in Orland, Maine, on the 2d, of December, 1835. When quite young, he moved with his parents to Portsmouth, New Hampshire, where he attended school, and in 1851, engaged in clerking, soon after entering the United States postal service. In 1855, he came to Chicago and clerked about a year; then to Red Wing, and was in the County Register's office one year, after which he studied law in the office of Judge Charles McClure. He was admitted to the bar and taken in partnership with Mr. McCluer, and, in 1859, was appointed County Attorney, and afterward elected, holding the office six years. In 1860, he purchased the "Red Wing Sentinel," changed its name to the "Goodhue Volunteer," and conducted it till 1864, when he sold it, and became connected with the "Red Wing Republican." He was joined in wedlock in 1862, with Miss Clarinda H. Sterns, who bore him three children, only one of whom is now living. Mrs. Parker died in 1870, and the following year he moved to this city and opened a law office. He was again married in April, 1874, to Mary J. Lytle, and of five children born to the union, only one is living. Mr. Parker was elected Judge of Probate in 1878, and held the office two years. He has lately given some attention to farming, owning a good farm in this county.

Captain George S. Ruble was born in Mifflin county, Pennsylvania, on the 31st of August, 1822, and is a grandson of Petre Ruble, who emigrated from Germany in 1738, and settled in Codorus township, York county, Pennsylvania, in 1750. He had four sons, Christian, Petre, Abraham, and Mathias. The latter settled in the east end of Kishacoquillas valley several years previous to the Revolution, and he also had four sons; Petre, Michel, John, and Henry. The latter married Mary E. Simons, of Little York, York county, and they also had four sons; Simon, George S., Henry, and John, all born in the above named valley. The family moved to Wayne county, Ohio, in 1829, settling in Green township, where they lived for nearly twenty years. George S., the subject of this sketch, married on the 1st of February, 1849, Elethear Humphrey, and removed to Rock county, Wisconsin, settling on a farm three miles west of the city of Beloit. He engaged in stock raising and the sale of agricultural implements. In 1855, he came to Freeborn county, and laid out the village (now city) of Albert Lea, building and operating both a steam and water saw and grist mill. When the Indian war broke out, in the fall of 1862, he raised and became Captain of Company H, of the First Minnesota Mounted Rangers, and after serving his time and being mustered out, he re-enlisted in the autumn of 1864. He went South as Sen. First Lieutenant of Company C, First Minnesota Heavy Artillery; was stationed at Chattanooga, Tenn.; afterward placed in command of Fort Bishop, at Charleston, East Tennessee. After the close of the war, he located at Chattanooga, and was engaged in the sale of farm implements. He bought property on Lookout Mountain; built, and for twelve years run, the house famous all over the South for good fare and genial hospitality, known as Ruble's Cottage House. Selling out in the spring of 1881, he returned to Albert Lea, and now devotes his time to cultivating the lands he located in 1855. The Captain comes from a hale and vigorous family, the combined weight of the four brothers being, previous to the war, 1265 pounds, and the height of each, exactly six feet two and a half inches. He finds himself able to do his share of the work, although his sixtieth birthday is passed.

Soren P. Sorenson was born in Port Washington, Wisconsin, on the 12th of January, 1855. He removed with his parents to Door county, and resided on a farm there twelve years; thence to Green Bay, Brown county, where he attended the Green Bay Business College. For three years Mr. Sorenson was engaged in an auction store in company with D. M. Whitney, and, in 1876, moved to Northwood, Iowa. On the 13th of January, 1878, he was married to Miss Alice Gunderson, of the town of Freeborn, and the union has been blessed with two children. The following year they came to Albert Lea, and in a few months went to Blue Earth City and opened a sample room and billiard hall, which he conducted until May, 1881, when he returned to this place and opened his present billiard hall and sample room.

Timothy J. Sheehan, Sheriff of Freeborn county since January, 1872, is a native of Ireland, a son of Jeremiah and Ann (McCarthy) Sheehan, and was born on the 21st of December, 1836. He was educated in the national schools of his native country, being kept to his studies most of his time till he was fourteen, at which age he came to this country. He learned a mechanics trade at Glens Falls, New York; worked there till 1855, when he went to Dixon, Illinois; was employed one season there in a saw-mill, and in the autumn of 1856, settled in Albert Lea and engaged in farming till the civil war broke out. In the autumn of 1861. Mr Sheehan enlisted as a private in the fourth Minnesota Infantry, his company being stationed at Fort Snelling. On the 18th of the following February he was commissioned, by Governor Ramsey, First Lieutenant of Company C, Fifth Minnesota Infantry, and on the 18th of June, 1862, was ordered with a detachment of fifty men, to report at Yellow Medicine Agency, for the purpose of preserving order during the time of annuity payments. On the 4th of August, fifteen hundred Sioux broke into the warehouse and seized the goods which were awaiting distribution. Lieutenant Sheehan, with twenty-five men, ordered the Indians to "fall back," under the penalty of instant death if they failed to obey. His good judgment, coupled with decision and courage, thus prevented an immediate outbreak--an outbreak, however, delayed only two weeks. Captain Marsh being killed at Redwood agency, the command of the company devolved on Lieutenant Sheehan: Fort Ridgely being threatened, he marched to that point from Glencoe, a distance of forty miles, in nine hours, many of the men trotting with boots off, while such as could not keep up on foot were put on wagons drawn by mules. Fort Ridgely was then filled with five hundred refugees, men, women and children,—and with one hundred and one men, for ten days from the 18th of August, the Lieutenant gallantly defended them from the savages. On the 18th and 21st his men fought all day and all night. It was a desperate siege and a period of awful suspense on the part of the inmates of the fort, until relief came, at the end of ten days. For his bravery on this occasion Lieutenant Sheehan received a captain's commission. After being in other severe engagements with the murderous Sioux, in November, 1862, Captain Sheehan accompanied his regiment to the South, and joined General Sherman's Corps. They engaged in the siege of Vicksburg; was in General A. J. Smith's division, under General Thomas, at Nashville; was subsequently at Spanish Fort and Mobile, and Captain Sheehan participated in these sieges and battles, being in fifteen or sixteen engagements with his regiment, and strange to say, never received a scar. At Nashville he commanded the color company, and received from the Colonel of the regiment, William B. Gere, in his report, the following commendation: "Captain T. J. Sheehan, commanding Company C, color company, gallantly stood by the colors, and in the last charge on the 16th inst. (December) two color-bearers having been shot, he placed the colors in the hands of the third, a non-commissioned officer of his company, who planted them on the rebel intrenchments." Such intrepidity characterized Captain Sheehan all through the war. He was promoted to Lieutenant-Colonel on the 1st of September, 1865, having made a military record of which the State may be proud. Colonel Houston and others presented him with a gold badge, engraved as follows: "Presented to Lieutenant-Colonel T. J. Sheehan, for services during the Rebellion, from October 13, 1861, to September 5, 1865." On the badge is a list of the engagements in which he participated. It was a well-merited tribute to his bravery and daring.

On returning to Albert Lea Colonel Sheehan was appointed Deputy United States Marshal by United States Marshal Augustus Armstrong, and in 1871, was elected to the office of Sheriff. In this position he has shown great activity, adroitness, and expedition in arresting criminals of various kinds, and is a very popular county official. In politics, he was a Douglas democrat before the war, but he has since acted with the republican party, being an influential and efficient worker in its character. The wife of Colonel Sheehan was Miss Jennie Judge, a native of Ireland. They were married in November, 1866, and have three boys, Jeremiah, George, and Edward. Colonel Sheehan lost both parents when he was two years old; was early thrown upon his own resources, and is emphatically a self-made man. His success in life is owing wholly to his self-reliance, energy, and perseverance.

William Henry Smith, a physician for nearly forty years, and an army surgeon, was born in Denmark, Lewis county, New York, on the 9th of March, 1815. His parents, Selah and Catherine (Tisdale) Smith, were classed among the agriculturalists, the father being one of the first settlers in that part of the Black River country, and died when William was thirteen years old. From that date the son took care of himself. He was educated at common and select schools; commenced teaching winter terms at the age of nineteen years, receiving eight dollars a month and board for the first season, and taught six winters, working on a farm and attending select schools the rest of the time. At twenty-four years of age Mr.

Smith commenced reading medicine with Dr. Elkanes French, of his native town, attending the last course of lectures held at Fairfield, Herkimer county, before the medical college was moved to Geneva. He received from the authorities of Jefferson county a certificate permitting him to practice, and followed his profession four years at Pamelia Four Corners, in that county; in 1846, removed to Beaver Dam, Wisconsin, and was there in practice twenty years, except when in the army. In 1856 he took a course of lectures at Rush Medical College, Chicago, from which he received his diploma.

In 1862 Dr. Smith went south as surgeon of a Wisconsin artillery regiment; at the end of one year was transferred to the same position in the Twenty-eighth Wisconsin Infantry, and served three more years. During nine months of this time he was post surgeon at Pine Bluff, Arkansas. He is a kind-hearted man, and was very attentive to the wants of the sick and wounded.

While at the south the doctor contracted a disease, from which he has suffered more or less for a long time; and in 1866, thinking a change of climate might be beneficial, he went to Fulton, Missouri, practicing when he had sufficient strength; and in 1873, much improved, returned to the north and settled at Albert Lea. Here he has a good run of business, and an excellent standing. He holds the office of County Coroner.

While in Beaver Dam, during the administrations of Presidents Taylor and Fillmore, he held the office of Postmaster. A whig in early life, with free-soil tendencies, he naturally drifted into republican ranks, where he is still found.

For the last twenty-five years he has paid very little attention to politics, except to vote. His leisure time is given mainly to medical studies.

On the 22nd of February, 1843, he received the hand of Miss Louisa M. Stevens, of West Martinsburgh, Lewis county, New York. They have three children living; a son, Selah H., was accidentally killed on the railroad at Cherokee, Kansas, in January, 1874; Mary is the wife of Jasper J. Bond, of Albert Lea; Frances E. and Charles Henry both reside in Albert Lea.

Edwin Clark Stacy is a native of Madison county, New York, born in the town of Hamilton, on the 6th of September, 1815. His parents were Nathaniel and Susan (Clark) Stacy. His grandfather, Rufus Stacy, a native of Gloucester, Massachusetts, was in the battle of Bunker Hill, and at Cherry Valley, when it was ravaged and burned by the combined forces of the Tory, Butler, and the savage, Brant. Nathaniel Stacy, a Universalist minister, was Chaplain of a regiment in 1814, and stationed at Sacket's Harbor. He wrote the memoirs of his own life—a work of more than five hundred pages, published in 1850—and in it gives a pretty full account of the rise and progress of Universalism in the State of New York, a movement in which he was very prominent. The volume is written in an easy, familiar style, veined with humor, and is decidedly readable. The author died ten years ago. Edwin received an academic education at Hamilton, New York, and Erie, Pennsylvania, the family moving to Warren county, Pennsylvania, when he was fourteen years old. He farmed more or less till he was of age; teaching winter schools, and securing his education entirely with his own means. In 1836, he came westward to Ann Arbor, Michigan; read law a while with Miles & Wilson, of that place, and finished with a cousin, Consider A. Stacy, at Tecumseh, Lenawee county. He was admitted to the bar at Adrian, in 1840, and in the autumn of that year returned to Warren county, Pennsylvania, practicing at Columbus and at Erie till 1856. He then came to Minnesota, and located at Geneva, where he was engaged in farming for four years. The year Mr. Stacy settled in this State he was appointed by Governor Gorman one of the commissioners to organize Freeborn county, and was made its first Judge of Probate. He was a member of the Constitutional Convention. In 1860, Mr. Stacy removed to Albert Lea, the county seat, and when not in some county office, has been engaged in the practice of his profession and the real estate business. He does a good deal of collecting for commercial, agricultural, and other houses, being a prompt and reliable man. Several years ago he served as County Auditor three terms, and County Superintendent of Schools one term. No man in Freeborn county is better known than Judge Stacy, the title he has had since Judge of Probate. He is among the leading men of the older class in the county, and greatly esteemed by all who know him. He has always affiliated with the Democratic party; has been quite active and prominent in county and district politics, and was the candidate of his party for Congress in

1876. He is an Odd-Fellow; holds the office of Noble Grand in the Albert Lea Lodge, and is a member of the Universalist Society. Judge Stacy was married on the 22d of February, 1842, to Miss Elizabeth D. Heath, of Erie county, Pennsylvania, and of four children, the fruit of this union, two sons are living. Both are married, and reside in Albert Lea. Dorr is a member of the city police, and Day F. is a printer and surveyor.

J. W. Smith, one of the oldest and most successful merchants of this city, is a native of Connecticut, born in Sharon, Litchfield county, on the 14th of January, 1838. When he was seventeen years old his parents moved to Rock county, Wisconsin, and settled on a farm. J. W. attended the Hamlin University in Red Wing, Minnesota, two years, then returned to Wisconsin and resided several years. On the 23d of April, 1863, he married Olive M. Clifford, and the following year moved to Albert Lea and engaged in the insurance business. In 1866, he opened a general mercantile store at Shell Rock, in company with R. B. Skinner, and in 1867, they removed their stock to this place. Mr. Smith has since been in the business, but has changed partners twice. The firm is now Smith & Garrett, and they keep the largest stock of dry goods in the city.

G. O. Sundby, a native of Norway, was born near the city of Christiania, on the 25th of July, 1845. He was brought up on a farm, and when about fifteen years old went to the city and clerked for one year. In 1861, he came with his parents to America and located on a farm near Winona, in this State. G. O. soon went to the latter city and found employment in a store, where he remained three years, during which time he also attended Eastman's Business College. In 1865, he moved to Owatonna and engaged in business for himself about a year, then sold out, and two months later visited Norway. On his return he opened another store in Owatonna, and in 1869, came to this city, where he has since successfully continued in the mercantile business, building a store in 1870, and in 1879, erected his present fine brick block. He was united in wedlock on the 14th of July, 1873, with Miss Laura Abbott, and they have one child, Cleon, born in April, 1874.

W. P. Sergeant, one of the active business men of the city, was born in Oneida county, New York, on the 24th of May, 1839. His great-grandfather came to that county as a missionary to the Indians about one hundred years ago, and secured Government land, upon which his son, grandson, and the subject of this sketch were all born. Mr. Sergeant's father died when W. P. was quite a small boy, and he lived with an uncle, and assisted him on his farm. He afterward clerked in stores, and, in 1861, enlisted in Company I, of the Eigth New York Cavalry, serving three years. He then was employed in a wholesale fancy dry goods house in Utica, New York, until 1868, when he opened a store in Penn Yan. On the 13th of March, 1867, Mr. Sergeant was united in marriage with Miss Harriet I. Stebens. In 1871, they moved to Cresco, Iowa, but the same year came to Albert Lea and bought out a lumber firm, to which business he has since given his attention, also carrying on a farm. He is a strong Republican, and has been Alderman four years, acting as President of the Council the two latter years. On the 7th of November, 1882, he was elected to the State Senate by 397 majority over Ex-Lieutenant Governor Armstrong.

Rev. O. H. Smeby was born in Rock Prairie, Wisconsin, on the 31st of January, 1851. When he was an infant his parents moved to Allamakee county, Iowa, where he attended school, and later entered the college at Decorah, graduating in 1871, after which he attended the Theological Seminary at St. Louis. After completing his studies in the latter institution, he came to Albert Lea, and has since had charge of the Evangelical Lutheran Church in this place. He was married in 1876, to Miss Marie Carlson, a native of Skien, Norway, her birth dating the 12th of August, 1854. They have had three children, two girls and a boy, the oldest girl being dead.

D. K. Stacy, whose parents were among the early settlers of this county, was born in Columbus, Warren county, Pennsylvania, on the 16th of November, 1842. The family moved to Minnesota when he was fourteen years old; located first in Geneva, and in 1860, came to Albert Lea. In February, 1862, D. K. enlisted in the Fifth Minnesota Volunteer Infantry, Company C. He was on the frontier, and fought against Hole in the Day at the Crow Wing Agency, and was in several of the heavy engagements in the South, remaining in service until after the close of the war. He was promoted to the office of Captain, and received his discharge in October, 1865. Soon after, he was married to Miss Lelia G. Moon, a native of Rock county, Wisconsin. This union has been blessed with three children. It was Mr. Stacy who carried the first mail into the town of Geneva, taking it on his back.

SIMON STRAUSS was born in Kirch Brombach, Germany, on the 22d of March, 1850. He attended the Commercial College at Frankfort on the Main for five years, and after graduating was employed as Assistant Teller in a bank at the same place. In 1876, he emigrated to America, directly to Iowa, where he clerked for his brother, and in September, 1878, came to Albert Lea, and started in business under the firm name of Strauss & Jacoby. His present partner is Mr. Schlesinger, and they keep the largest stock of clothing, gents' furnishing goods, boots, shoes, etc., in the city.

G. O. SLOCUM was born in Rock county, Wisconsin, on the 29th of August, 1840. His early life was devoted to agricultural pursuits and in 1850, the family removed to Menasha, where the father of our subject built the first mill in that place. In 1856, they removed to Stephenson county, Illinois, and in 1858, G. O. attended school at Oberlin, Ohio, remaining there two years. He then returned to Illinois, engaged at farm labor in the summer and taught school during the winter seasons. In 1862, he enlisted in the Seventy-fourth Indiana Volunteer Infantry, served eighteen months in Company H, and was then discharged for disability. During the winter of 1864-65 he attended a business college in Chicago, re-enlisted the next spring, and served till the close of the war in the Twenty-third Illinois Volunteer Infantry, Company K. He was married on the 7th of March, 1865, to Miss Mary A. Carter, and in 1868, they came to Oakland township, going, a year later, to Hayward, where Mr. Slocum purchased a farm, to which he gave his attention in the summer, and taught school in the winter, also filled some local offices. In 1875, they removed to Albert Lea, and he clerked in the Auditor's office until 1878, when he was elected to his present office of County Auditor. Mr. and Mrs. Slocum have been blessed with five children, two of whom are living, both daughters.

IRA A. TOWN was born in Franklin, Franklin county, New York, on the 2d of April, 1848. In 1864, the family removed to Shell Rock in this county, and in 1869 our subject attended the Cedar Valley Seminary in Iowa, graduating as Bachelor of tht Sciences in 1873. He then returned home, but a year later entered the law department of the Iowa State University, graduating in 1875, as Bachelor of the Law, and soon after entered a law office in Albert Lea. In 1878, he began practice by himself and after the organization of the city of Albert Lea, was one of its first City Justices. He was defeated by a small majority as an independent candidate for the office of Judge of Probate in 1877, but was elected two years later, and is now serving his second term. On the 22d of November, 1879, he was married to Mrs. Fannie V. Steele, of Fredericktown, Ohio. They have one child, a daughter.

LEANDER J. THOMAS, an old settler of this State, was born in Springfield, Bradford county, Pennsylvania, on the 24th of October, 1841. When he was an infant his parents moved to Wisconsin and located in Janesville, Rock county, and in 1857, came to Minnesota. Leander attended select school at Owatonna for two years, and afterward learned the printer's trade. In 1862, he enlisted in Company E, of the Tenth Minnesota Volunteer Infantry; was in General Sibley's expedition across the plains, and, in the fall of 1863, sent south, and remained in service until the close of the war, when he was honorably discharged. He was united in marriage on the 25th of December, 1868, to Miss Clara M. Colby, a native of Wisconsin. They have one son, Edwin D., born on the 29th of October, 1871. Mr. Thomas has been practicing veterinary surgery for the past twelve years. He came to this place in 1873, and located just outside the city limits, but is now living in the city, running a feed stable in connection with veterinary business. Mr. Thomas is an honorable man, and respected by all who know him.

TORGER L. TORGERSON was born near the capital of Norway on the 6th of August, 1848. His parents came to America when he was about five years old, and first located in Iowa. In 1861, they came to this county and settled in Manchester, where his mother still lives, his father having died after coming there. In 1867, Mr. Torgerson was married to Miss Anna M. Fossom, also a native of Norway. They have four children: Anna M., Louis P., Aase E., and George A. Mr. Torgerson located on a farm of his own after his marriage, and in 1877 came to Albert Lea, where he is engaged in the sale of agricultural implements.

ANDREW L. TOCKLE is a native of Norway, born in Trondhjem on the 16th of December,

1835. He there learned the tailor trade, and, in 1869, came to America, and directly to Albert Lea. Previous to leaving his native country he was married to Miss Marrette Eunbo. They have one child, Anna M., born on the 23d of October, 1866, who now attends the St. Olaf's school in Northfield. Mr. Tockle opened a merchant tailor establishment on the corner of Broadway, and also deals in agents' furnishing goods and sewing machines.

Dr. Fred A. Twichell is a native of Vermont, born in Stockbridge on the 29th of July, 1854. After attending the common schools he entered the Black River Academy, and was subsequently employed as book-keeper at Lawrence, Massachusetts. Returning to his home in Vermont he began the study of his profession in the office of Dr. R. M. Chase, one of the prominent dentists and physicians of the place, and remained with him three years. He came to Albert Lea in April, 1881, and began the practice of dentistry in company with Dr. Street.

Walter Thompson, one the oldest business men of Albert Lea, was born in Buckingham county, England, on the 5th of April, 1840. His parents came to America in 1854, but he remained in his native country until 1859, and there learned the boot and shoe business. He came to this place in 1863, and opened a boot and shoe store in which he has a good trade. Mrs. Thompson was formerly Martha Slater and they have a family of five children, four sons and one daughter.

John Whytock is a native of Buffalo, New York, born of Scotch parentage on the 14th of November, 1835. He attended the public schools, afterward the Aurora Academy, and when twenty-two years old commenced the study of law which he continued three years. In about 1860, he came to La Crosse, Wisconsin, and the following year enlisted in the Second Wisconsin Cavalry, was enrolled as First Lieutenant and soon promoted Captain of Company B; in 1865, was made Major of the regiment, which position he filled until the close of the war. He then located in Little Rock, Arkansas, and remained ten years, being private secretary of the Governor, and also United States District Attorney two years. He was joined in matrimony on the 6th of August, 1872, with Miss Taylor. In 1875, they came north to Minneapolis, where Mr. Whytock practiced law until 1878, and then came to Albert Lea which has since been his home, doing a successful business in his profession.

W. W. Williams, a son of Rev. John L. and Priscilla D. Williams, was born on the 1st of December, 1840, in Blairsville, Indiana county, Pennsylvania. His father was a noted divine of the Methodist Episcopal church, and an early abolitionist. He was an agent of the "Underground Railroad" and in 1849, removed to Wisconsin. W. W. received a common school education supplemented by several terms at the Monroe (Wisconsin) Institute. He commenced to learn the printer's trade in 1858, and has since been in the newspaper and printing business, except two years spent in the drug business at Spring Valley, Minnesota; two years of which he served as Deputy Warden of the Minnesota State Prison, and a year in the employ of Seymour, Sabin & Co., of Stillwater. In 1864, he came to Minnesota, and the following year purchased the "Preston Republican," which he sold in 1866, and in 1869, started the "Blue Earth City Post." During most of his residence in the latter place he was Postmaster; sold his paper in 1874, and removed to Stillwater. In 1878, he purchased the interest of D. G. Parker in the "Freeborn County Standard" to which he has since devoted his time. Mr. Williams is a clear and fearless writer and has opinions of his own which he does not hesitate to avow and since he has been in this county has exercised a powerful influence in political circles.

ALBERT LEA TOWNSHIP.

CHAPTER LIV.

TOPOGRAPHY AND PHYSICAL FEATURES—EARLY SETTLERS—TOWN GOVERNMENT—EDUCATIONAL —THE FIRST MARRIAGE.

The township bearing this name is the southern of the two center towns of the county, Bancroft being its comrade on the north, with Riceland impinging on the northeast, Hayward on the east, Shell Rock to the southeast, Freeman on the south, Nunda to the southwest, Pickerel Lake on the west, and Manchester to the northwest. It coincides with the original government survey, having thirty-six sections.

It may be said to be a prairie town, with numerous oak groves; and when first visited presented a most inviting prospect, which will be described further on.

The principal river is the Shell Rock, which flows in an average direction toward the southeast, diagonally through the township. Lake Albert Lea is the largest body of water in town, and is a magnificent sheet, with its irregular but gently curving outline and undulating surrounding meadows and hillside. Most of it lays in the town, but its length is about eight miles. Pickerel Lake also laps over into its territory, as does White's Lake, which Col. Lea at first called Lake Chapeau. Goose Lake, a compact little body of water, may be found in section three. Fountain Lake is an artificial pond created by the mill dam erected by Mr. Ruble on his first coming here. It hugs around the northern side of the city in a curvilinear way, and with its graceful foliage, at various points coming down to the water's edge, presents one of the most pleasing views to be found in all Southern Minnesota.

The interest in this town, as well as the whole county, centers in the city which has sprung up here, and retains the same name.

The early settlement of this township has, of necessity, been given in the history of Albert Lea City, so that very little remains to be said here. A few pioneer notes, however, will be given.

Mr. and Mrs. Blackmer were early settlers, but both are dead. Two sons, Loren and Heman, live on the homestead, and other sons reside in Albert Lea and vicinity. Dr. F. Blackmer, residing in the city, is a son.

John G. Godley is an old settler, and still lives in the township.

The Nelsons are among the very first settlers in the south-eastern part of the town, and still live there.

The old town of St. Nicholas, which, at one time, had lofty aspirations, was located in this township, but as its history is fully depicted in the sketch of the city, no further reference to it will be made here.

TOWN GOVERNMENT.

It would be monotonous to furnish the names of the various town officers from year to year, as many of them have been re-elected from time to time. But it will be sufficient to name the various gentlemen who have been prominent in the town government up to the time of the organization of the city government. Among the men who have been town officers we notice: A. C. Wedge, D. G. Parker, John Brownsill, Bernard McCarthy, Luther Parker, H. T. Smith, T. J. Sheehan, F. Blakely, Chauncy Conley, Thomas Smith, Reuben Williams, H. D. Brown, A. B. Webber, Joseph France, E. C. Stacy, F. D. Dudley, John Ruble, L. Eaton, George Thompson, Francis Hall, John Wood, A. Armstrong, Charles T. Knapp, James E. Smith, William Morin, Reuben C. Cady, Reuben Williams, O. P. Kenfield, J. G. Godley, H. M. Manley, W. J. Martin, A. W. St. John, George Whitman, D. K. Stacy, A. M.

Tyrer, John Ross, F. B. Frost, Charles Kittleson, William Hazelton, Ole J. Ellingson, Joseph Green, G. D. Ball,* Lewis Hager, M. M. Luce, A. E. Johnson, W. C. Lincoln, M. W. Greene, D. N. Gates, C. G. Jonsrud, and D. R. P. Hibbs. As to the business of the officers of the town, it was of course mostly of an executive character, but legislative within certain limits.

In 1861, a pound was ordered to be built. In 1863, a petition was considered in relation to a bridge at Ruble's. In 1868, the Southern Minnesota railroad made a proposition to several towns in the county to vote aid to the company. Albert Lea was requested to vote $40,000, while six of the towns were asked for $15,000 each, and seven of them were invited to contribute $10,000 each.

At one time in the history of the town, the powers of the town board were enlarged by the legislature, and numerous ordinances were adopted to be in force in the village.

The government has been in accordance with the wishes of the town, the powers delegated to the Supervisors and other officers never having been abused in any notable instance.

On the 8th of October, 1864, the town voted $25 to each volunteer duly credited, and $225 was paid on that account. During that year thirteen enlistments were credited on the quota of the town.

EDUCATIONAL.

There are five schoolhouses in the township, as follows:

District No. 37 has a house located on the northwest quarter of section twelve.

District No. 14. The juveniles of this district meet for instruction in a neat schoolhouse on the northeast quarter of section fourteen.

District No. 54. The schoolhouse of this district is situated on the northwest quarter of section thirty-five.

District No. 68. This house is on the southwest corner of section twenty-nine.

District No. 110 is the next to the last organized in the county, and has its schoolhouse on the northwest quarter of section twenty-eight.

School is kept in these buildings a great portion of the year, and the standard of both teachers and scholars is up to that of any other portion of Freeborn county.

THE FIRST MARRIAGE.

January 13th, 1857, was an eventful day in Albert Lea, for then occurred the first marriage in the township, and it was none of your time affairs: it was a double wedding, and the people began to feel that the semi-civilization of pioneer life was fast giving way to a condition of enlightment. C. C. Colby and Ellen Frost, David Hard and Mary A. Colby were the especially interested and interesting parties. The event happened at the house of John Colby. Squire Clark was employed to secure the nuptial knot.

The old settlers will remember that the squire was not noted for his literary genius, for his delicacy or polish, but he was the only available authority vested by the infantile commonwealth of Minnesota, to declare the banns indissolubly fixed, and so he consented to do the best he could under the circumstances.

The guests were assembled and the parties stood up in the magisterial presence, to be legally united, as they already were heart to heart, with a single ceremony for both couples.

Here was a perspiration provoking predicament for this lugubrious limb of the law. In his perplexity he glanced over a marriage ceremony he had picked up somewhere, but there was no double attachment, either "back action" or otherwise, and he was totally lacking in the ability to improvise the requisite amendment, or to modify the document to meet the present emergency. So, after reading it over to himself, and seeing no possible way to make the ceremony appear ritualistic, in his desperation he blurted out, "I pronounce you husbands and wives, and you may now go where you please, by Gosh!"

This constituted the nuptial ceremony, no one gave the brides away, no questions were asked, no rings were presented, no prayers were offered, and it may be added, no expensive bridal trosseau was provided in either case.

Of course whatever else was dispensed with, the bridal tour could not be omitted, and so the only pair of horses in town was called into requisition, and the outfit went to Shell Rock where an impromptu dance was got up at George Gardner's, and "they chased the hours with flying feet" until morning, when the jaded party started for home; but a snow storm had so blocked the road that when three miles away, the team had to be abandoned, and the rest of the way was made on foot.

They were a jolly party, and all enjoyed themselves except 'Mrs. B,' whoever she was, whose prodigious weight carried her down through the snow at every step.

Notwithstanding the informality of the technical joining, the marriage "took" as they say about vaccination, and twenty-five years afterwards the silver wedding of one of the couples was celebrated here, as is recorded in the proper place.

BIOGRAPHICAL.

JOHN BURGLAND, one of the prominent men of this county, is a native of Sweden, born on the 29th of November, 1834. He remained at his birth place until 1854, when he married Miss Anna M. Johnson and the same year bought a farm which he carried on until 1862, then engaged in the lumber business. In 1868, they emigrated to America, came directly to Albert Lea and bought a farm in section twenty-seven, which now contains over two hundred acres. He has a family of nine children.

MARTIN CAREY was born in Jefferson county, Wisconsin, on the 28th of August, 1850. When fifteen years old he commenced going to the pineries during winter seasons, and in 1871, came with his parents to this county and settled on a farm in this township. In 1874, he bought land for himself and has since made it his home. He was married on the 30th of June, 1875, to Miss Mary Tracy, who has borne him five children, four of whom are living. Mr. Carey has held several local offices.

OWEN DOYLE, one of the early settlers of Freeborn county, was born in Carlow county, Michigan, on the 1st of March, 1820. His father died when he was eight years old, and when fifteen he emigrated to America, settling near Kingston, in Canada, where he was engaged in farming for eight years. In 1850, he married Miss Bridget Murphy. From 1843 to 1853, he had no settled home, but in the latter year located in Columbus, Ohio, and resided there three years. He then came to Burlington, Iowa, and three years later to this township, having since made his home in section eleven. Mr. and Mrs. Doyle have had eight children, three of whom died in infancy, and five are living.

OGDEN EDWARDS was born in Jefferson county, New York, on the 5th of May, 1826. He assisted his father on the farm until 1854, when he bought land of his own. On the 28th of February, in the latter year, he was married to Miss Prudence Doughkuse. In 1859, Mr. Edwards went to California and engaged in mining two years, then returned to his native State and again carried on a farm. In 1866, he came to this place and bought a farm in section one, where he now lives. Mr. and Mrs. Edwards have had four children; Charles D., John, Frederick J., and Ada. John died at the age of two years and six months.

OLE J. ELLINGSON is a native of Norway, born on the 26th of January, 1825. When twenty-three years of age he enlisted in the Norwegian army; spent one year in Germany, and remained in the service until the 16th of April, 1853. The following day he started for America, having the year before married Miss Engel C. Erickson. They first located in Allamakee county, Iowa, but in 1856, became pioneers of this county, settling in Bancroft. In 1859, Mr. Ellingson was elected County Treasurer and moved to Albert Lea; held the office two years and in 1861, enlisted in the Fourth Minnesota Volunteer Infantry, Company F, serving till 1864. He then returned to this place, and has since devoted his time to agricultural pursuits. He is the father of eight children.

ANDREW O. FROSAGER is a native of Norway, and dates his birth on the 26th of October, 1846. He resided with his parents until the spring of 1871, when he came to America and settled in Lafayette county, Wisconsin. In 1874, he removed to Marquette county, Michigan, where he engaged in mining and railroading one year; thence to Jo Daviess county, Illinois, and in 1876, came to this county. He bought a farm in Albert Lea two years later, and has since devoted his time to its cultivation. He was married on the 24th of December, 1877, to Miss Ellen Torgenson.

JOHN G. GODLEY, one of the early settlers of Freeborn county, was born in Lincolnshire, England, in 1837. He was engaged as book-keeper for two and a half years in his native place, and in 1854 came to America, settling on Long Island. He moved from there to Chemung county, New York, and a year later came to Richland City, Wisconsin. In 1857, he moved to this township, and claimed land in section eighteen, where he "batched" it six months and returned to Wisconsin. In 1860, he came again to his claim, and in February, 1862, enlisted in the Fifth Minnesota Volunteer Infantry; was Chief Clerk in the Quartermaster's department for two years and six months, and returned home in 1866. The same year he sold his former farm and bought his present, which contains two hundred and forty acres. On the 15th of April, 1868, he was married to Miss Maggie Slater, who has borne him one child, Anna M.

S. C. JASPERSON was born in Denmark on the 18th of April, 1838. When he was twenty-one years old he enlisted in the Danish army and served three years, then returned home and engaged in farming. He was married on the 7th of April, 1860, to Miss Johanna M. Jostenson The result of the union is seven children. Mr Jasperson came to America in 1867, settled in Chicago, where he learned the carpenter trade and worked at the same four years. He then went to Tennessee and engaged in the construction of railroads one winter, and in the spring of 1871. came to this county and bought a farm in Bath township. Since 1875, he has been a resident of Albert Lea, his farm being in section ten. He is the father of seven children.

OLE A. JOHNSON is a native of Norway, born on the 17th of December, 1831. He was married before leaving his birthplace, to Miss Elizabeth Goegerson. They emigrated to America in 1859, and settled in Waupaca county, Wisconsin; three years later moved to a farm in Winnebago county, and in 1868, came to this township. They have a family of eight children.

WILLIAM KELLAR, one of the pioneers of this county, was born in Jefferson county, Kentucky, on the 24th of December, 1820. At the age of ten years he removed with his parents to Edgar county, Illinois, where he resided until 1842, when, through public excitement, he was attracted to the lead mines of Wisconsin. In 1844, he returned to his old home in Illinois, where, on the 15th of February, he was married to Miss Elizabeth C. Kies, which union has been blessed with three children. He immediately took up his residence in Grant county, where he remained until the spring of 1856, when he took a claim in section seventeen in this township, erecting a log dwelling. The first religious meeting ever held in this vicinity took place in his house in May, 1857, conducted by Rev. Mr. Phelps, a Methodist. In 1864, Mr. Kellar enlisted in Company C, of the First Minnesota Heavy Artillery, serving until the close of the war.

W. H. LOWE, one of the early settlers of this county, is a native of the Empire State, born in the city of New York on the 16th of October, 1832. When he was four years old he moved with his parents to Huron county, Ohio, and in 1851 went to Lawrence, Kansas. He soon returned to his home, and in a short time came to Hastings, where he learned the carpenter's trade and resided two years. In 1854 he settled in this place and work-at his trade. He was united in marraige on the 4th of November, 1860, to Miss Rhoda A. Baker, and the result of the union is five children. Mr. Lowe enlisted in 1862, in the Tenth Minnesota Volunteer Infantry, Company E, and served three years, the two latter as First Sergeant. After his discharge he returned to Albert Lea, and worked at his trade until 1867, then bought a farm and has since devoted his time to its cultivation.

ISAAC W. MCREYNOLDS, one of the pioneers of the county, is a native of North Carolina, born on the 4th of February, 1806. In 1816 he moved with his parents to Jefferson county, Indiana, where they resided on a farm three years, then went to Bond county, Illinois. In 1827 Isaac came to Grant county, Wisconsin, and was engaged in farming and mining there until coming to this place in 1856. He took a claim in section seven, and has since made it his home. The maiden name of his wife was Nancy Sparks, who has borne him seven children, four of whom are living.

OLE O. STIVE was born in Norway on the 7th of May, 1842. He came with his parents to America in 1850, settled in Dane County, Wisconsin, until 1853, then moved to Winneshiek county, Iowa. They came to this county in 1857, and located in Bancroft, where Ole resided with his parents until 1859, when he returned to Wisconsin and worked in the pineries. On the 13th of May, 1861, he enlisted in the Fifth Wisconsin Volunteer Infantry and served four years and three months. He then returned to his home and lived with his parents until 1868, when he married Miss Ingeborg G. Bottolfson on the 20th of December. They have had seven children, six of whom are living. In 1873 they bought a farm in Albert Lea township, and have since made it their home

ALDEN.

CHAPTER LV.

General Description—Early Settlement—Township Government—Statistical—Post-offices—Educational—Alden Village—Biographical.

This lies in the western tier of Freeborn county's towns, and is separated from Iowa by one town. Its contiguous surroundings are, Carlston on the north; Pickerel Lake on the east; Mansfield on the south, and Faribault county on the west. It is constituted as originally surveyed by the United States officers, of thirty-six square miles, and contains 23,040 acres, of which the greater portion is under a high state of cultivation, being one of the richest farming towns in this part of the State, and containing as much real value.

It is a prairie town, containing little if any timber of any kind within its borders. In the central and southeastern part we find some marsh land, but this is all valuable, if not for tillage purposes, for hay and grazing, while it is all most valuable meadow land. The farmers are so advanced in their modes and procedures of agriculture that those lands, formerly too wet for raising grain, has, by the use of drains and ditches, all been brought under the plow, and is now among the best of farming land. There are but few streams in the town, and no lakes.

The soil, as a rule, and in fact almost throughout the entire town, is a rich dark loam, of from three to four feet deep, which is underlaid with a subsoil of clay. It is very rich and well adapted to the crops of this latitude, such as wheat, corn, oats, barley, and all cereals. The abundant growth of indigneons grasses which covers the broad expanse of prairie, makes stock raising not only an inexpensive but very profitable business, and already many of the farmers are turning their attention from grain, and making stock their principal industry. The creameries, which are springing into existence all through this part of the State, serve to encourage and make this change more universal. It has already been demonstrated, as an article published elsewhere will show, that the hopes and expectations of those who thus change from grain to stock are not unfounded; but that there is a great deal more money made with less risk of capital, and one-half the work in taking care of stock, than is required to raise grain at customary prices.

EARLY SETTLEMENT.

The early development of this sub-division of Freeborn county commenced a little later than the average of towns in this part of Minnesota, but the changes wrought have been equal to any and surpassed by none; for, we find the township, by a glance at the statistical returns, as productive and rich, agriculturally, as the best.

As to who the first settlers were, there is some dispute here, and the means are not easy of access with which to prove any of the statements. A short sketch, purporting to be the history of the township, was published in 1877, which we herewith present. It is as follows:

"John Hauek entered this town in the spring of 1858, and is supposed to have been the first settler. He also erected the first house in the summer of that year. John Tirrel was the first merchant, and commenced business in the winter of 1869-70. Mr. Miller, a blacksmith, was the first mechanic; M. W. Green, the first lawyer, and a Mr. Barber, the first doctor. The first school was taught in the Russell district, but when, or by whom, I have been unable to ascertain. The first religious service is said to have been held at the house of William Humes, but authorities differ regarding the officiating clergyman; the conflict laying between Rev. D. P. Curtis and Rev. A. P. Wolcott. The first schoolhouse was erected in

1867, and in the same year the Free Will Baptists effected the first church organization. A. G. Hall served as Chairman of the first board of Supervisors, and E. P. Clark acted as Clerk."

The above, it is said, was gathered by correspondence, and as stated, errors are liable to creep in, so we do not vouch for it, but give it just as received by us through the newspapers.

It is pretty certain that the first farm settled upon in the town was in section two, by Walter Scott Russell, in the spring of 1858. He was a young man, coming from Wisconsin with a yoke of oxen, and the same summer broke three acres of land and "erected" a dug-out in the side of a hill, in which he took up his abode. In a short time he returned to Wisconsin for his father and family, whom he had left there, and brought them back with him. He remained upon his second trip only a short time, when he sold his claim and removed to parts unknown.

John Hauck (or Houck) was the next arrival, making his appearance in the summer of the same year, and taking a farm in the northern part of the township, in section one, where, it is said, he erected the first house, and opened a farm. He remained a few years and then removed, his whereabouts at present being a mystery, to us at least. Mr. A. G. Hall purchased and still owns the farm.

With this the settlement of the town remained rather *quiescent* for a time, and the next pioneer to make a claim was James Rundel, in October, 1860, in section two, but we cannot find where he came from, as he died not long after his arrival. The place he took is now owned by a Mr. Dunning, of Chicago, Ill.

Elisha Davis came by team from Wisconsin, and arrived here in 1862, building a sod house on the claim which he selected in section five. He remained here until the year 1877, when he sold out and went to Valley county, Nebraska.

Joseph W. Harrington, a native of Illinois, came to Alden in 1863, and in the spring of that year took a homestead in section twelve, where he remained until 1873, when he removed to the village and remained there until the time of his death, which occurred in 1875. He was among the prominent men of this locality.

Moses Cheesebrough, late of Wisconsin, made his appearance in this township in the fall of 1864. He came with teams, driving several head of stock, and went to the big woods, thirty miles away, to get lumber with which to erect a frame dwelling. He remained on the homestead, which he took in section seven, for a number of years, but finally went to Nebraska.

William B. Humes came to Minnesota in 1864, locating first in Pleasant Grove, where he remained for five years; then came to Alden township and homesteaded a place in section one. He was the first Justice of the Peace elected in the township.

James Whitehead was another arrival in 1864, coming from Wisconsin with a yoke of oxen and locating in section three, where, in the spring of that year he erected a sod habitation. He remained until 1866, when he left the county.

George W. Sanders also came in the spring of 1864, from Wisconsin, with a team of horses, and settling in section nine erected a house of two logs and a pile of sod. He remained here for about seventeen years, when he removed to other fields.

A. G. Hall arrived in 1865, in the spring, coming from McGregor, Iowa, to Alden, with horse teams, and being twenty-four days on the road. Shortly after his arrival he bought out the claim of John Houck, in section one, where he remained until the village of Alden was projected, and then went to that place and erected the first building there. He was the first chairman of Supervisors of the town, and is now a prominent man in public affairs.

In 1865, the Rev. O. P. Hull made his arrival from Wisconsin, and secured a home in sections eight and seventeen, where he erected a house and barn and remained a number of years, then returned to Wisconsin, where he lived until within a few years, when the grim messenger of death called him hence.

Russell Maxson, a native of New York, who had for a time been stopping in Wisconsin, came in about 1863, and secured a claim, which he held for several years, when he left.

OFFICIAL RECORD.

In earlier days the township of Alden was connected with adjoining townships for local governmental purposes, and therefore, as a separate organization, its era does not commence until late in the sixties.

The records show that the first town meeting was held at the house of E. P. Clark, in section four, on the 3d of April, 1866. The meeting came to order by the selection of A. G. Hall, chairman, and proceeded to business. It was then resolved, by unanimous consent, that $100 be raised by tax to defray town expenses for the ensuing year. It was also resolved that the sum of $30 be appropriated for the purpose of building a pound, and George W. Sanders was elected poundmaster.

Balloting for town officers came next in the program, and the following officers were declared elected: Supervisors, Albert G. Hall, Chairman, Nathan L. Bassett, and Washington Sanders; Clerk, Edwin P. Clark; Assessor, Russell Maxson; Treasurer, Charles H. Clark; Justices of the Peace, Elisha R. Davis and William B. Humes; Constables, Ebenezer Brown and Henry S. Davis. The number of votes cast was twenty-two.

The official business of the township has been conducted in a frugal and business-like manner, with no jars to disturb the usual tranquility of such matters, and no useless waste or expenditure of public funds. The officers elected and serving in 1882 are as follows: Supervisors, Thomas Dunn, chairman, S. S. Skiff, and A. H. Stevens; Clerk, J. T. Johnson; Assessor, J. W. Peck; Treasurer, T. W. Wilson; Justices of the Peace, H. Babbitt and A. G. Hall; Constables, O. M. Woodruff and W. A. Hart.

STATISTICAL.

We have here grouped together, from various sources, a complete crop cultivation and production report of Alden, together with various other items that will be of interest and value to those who wish to know the extent to which the rich and productive soil of the prairies is utilized; and while it will be undoubtedly dry to those who are reading for pastime rather than information, we hope it will interest a majority sufficient to repay us for the labor incident to collecting such matter.

FOR THE YEAR 1881.—Giving the acreage and the amount produced, of the various crops in the township of Alden:

Wheat—3,659 acres, yielding 38,791 bushels.

Oats—959 acres, yielding 26,497 bushels.

Corn—1,226 acres, yielding 34,530 bushels.

Barley—210 acres, yielding 4,095 bushels.

Rye—3 acres, yielding 35 bushels.

Buckwheat—10 acres, yielding 102 acres.

Potatoes—35 acres, yielding 4,381 bushels.

Beans—3¼ acres, yielding 14 bushels.

Sugar cane—6¾ acres, yielding 699 gallons.

Cultivated hay—32 acres, yielding 29 tons.

Flax—259 acres, yielding 2,359 bushels.

Total acreage cultivated in the town in the year 1881, 6,401.

Wild hay gathered—2,359 tons.

Bushels of timothy seeded, 70.

Apple trees—growing, 1,368; bearing 81, yielding 11 bushels.

Grape vines—3, yielding 40 pounds.

Sheep—205 sheared, yielding 1,198 pounds of wool.

Dairy—259 cows, yielding (about) 23,000 pounds of butter and 4,000 pounds of cheese.

FOR THE YEAR 1882.—It being at this writing too early to get returns as to the amount of productions, we are only able to give the acreage for 1882, with other information, as follows:

Wheat, 2,732 acres; Oats, 1,183; Corn, 2,059; Barley, 298; Buckwheat, 16; Potatoes, 85½; Beans, 2½; Sugar cane, 5¾; Cultivated hay, 81; Flax, 306. Total acreage cultivated in 1882, 6,768¾.

Apple trees—growing, 1,521, bearing, 96.

Grape vines bearing, 3.

Milch cows—296.

Sheep—242 head, yielding 1,261 pounds of wool.

Whole number of farms reported for 1881, 102.

Forest trees—planted in 1882, 10½ acres; number of acres planted and growing, 202½.

POPULATION.—The census taken in 1870 gives the township a population of 381. At the last census, taken in 1880, the village of Alden is reported as having a population of 235, and the town 475; total 710.

POST-OFFICES.

The first Post-office established in the township was called Buckeye. It was originally in the township of Manchester, with James E. Smith as Postmaster, and named in honor of the pet cognomen of the native State of the Postmaster, at whose house, in section thirty, in Manchester, the office was kept. In 1860, S. B. Smith was appointed Postmaster, and the mail came by way of the Mankato and Otronto, Iowa, route, under the supervision of A. L. Davis, who carried the mail by team. In 1866, the office was removed from Manchester to Alden township, and A. G. Hall was made mail handler. In 1870 the office was discontinued, having been removed to the village while Mr. Hall was awaiting the action of the department upon his resignation.

In 1867 Alden Post-office was established with E. P. Clark as Postmaster, and office upon his farm. When the village of Alden commenced building up it was removed to that point, and in 1870, A. G. Hall, who had removed from his farm to the village, was appointed to handle the mails, and continued in this capacity for about four years, when L. S. Crandall was commissioned and held it until 1877, when L. T. Walker received the appointment and is still the incumbent, with the office at "Walker's Store."

EDUCATIONAL.

DISTRICT No. 40.—Effected an organization in 1867, and in 1868 erected a schoolhouse in the southeastern corner of section ten. The first officers were: William Townsend, Clerk; George Larman, Treasurer; and Harrington Austin, Director. The first school was taught by Miss Maxson, for $15 per month, and boarding "round," with eleven scholars present. The last term of school was taught by Miss Lena Patrick, with about twenty-three scholars to answer the roll call; her compensation was $25 per month, and board, the latter to be received among the scholars' parents.

DISTRICT No. 70.—A meeting was held on the 28th of March, 1865, at the house of O. T. Hull, at which the organization of the district was effected by the election of the following officers: Director, N. L. Bassett; Treasurer, O. T. Hull; Clerk, E. F. Clark. The first school in the neighborhood was taught at the house of Mr. Russell Maxson in the fall of 1868, by Ada Bassett, with nine scholars present. The first instruction given in the schoolhouse was by Angelia Langdon, in the spring of 1869, with eighteen scholars present, and for $12 per month. The house was erected in the winter of 1868-69, size 18x26, at a cost of $600, in the northwest corner of section seventeen. The last term of school was taught by Isabella Bickford; attendance, twenty-three pupils.

DISTRICT No. 80.—Embraces as its territory the northeastern part of Alden, and extends over the town line into Carlston. The first and organizing meeting was held at the residence of Ira Russell, on the 24th of August, 1866, and the following were the first officers elected: Director, Ira Russell; Treasurer, William B. Humes; Clerk, James H. Whitehead. In 1869 their schoolhouse was erected at a cost of $600, in the northeastern corner of section two, being a neat frame building, 16x24, with patent seats. The first school in this house was taught by E. J. Russell, with nine scholars present; the last was taught by Emma Allen to an enrollment of twenty-three pupils, for $25 per month.

DISTRICT No. 81.—The first meeting was held at the house of S. T. Brown, on the 26th of March, 1869, at which the district was organized and the following officers elected: A. H. Stevens, Director; I. A. Blackman, Clerk; F. F. Blackman, Treasurer. The sum of $400 was voted for the purpose of constructing a schoolhouse, and the following summer it was erected at a cost of $500, size 22x28 feet, in the southwestern part of section twenty-seven, being equipped with patent seats and all necessary apparatus. The first school was taught in a sod house in section twenty-seven, in the summer of 1869, by Olivia Burdick, and after this there were three terms taught in the same primitive structure.

DISTRICT No. 89.—Embraces the territory in the southeastern part of the town, with its schoolhouse in the southwestern part of section twenty-five. The district effected an organization at a meeting held at the residence of H. Babbitt, in the winter of 1869-'70. In the following spring a house was erected, size 16x20 feet, in which Dette Stillman taught the first term of school as soon as completed, to an attendance of twelve pupils, for $12 per month. In 1874, the school structure now in use was built, at a cost of $250. The last term was taught by Chester Maywood, for $23 per month, and an average attendance of twenty-three juveniles.

DISTRICT No. 93.—This district embraces the territory known as the Alden District, with a schoolhouse in the village of Alden. The schoolhouse was erected in the summer of 1875, size 20x40 feet, two stories high, with two rooms, and cost about $2,300. The first school was taught by George Miller in 1876, for $45 per month, with fifty-seven scholars in attendance. The last term was taught by L. W. Bassett, with forty-one scholars present, and the teacher received $50 per month as compensation for his services.

VILLAGE OF ALDEN.

This is the only village in the town, and is among the prosperous "villas" in the county. It is located in the northern part of the town whose name it bears, on the southern Minnesota branch of the C., M. & St. Paul railroad, about ten miles from Albert Lea, the county seat, and is surrounded by the most valuable farming land in the county. A small body of water covering about five acres of land lies adjoining the town, but there is no stream or, in fact, any water, near the village, as the water mentioned is merely a pond.

EARLY SETTLEMENT.—In this line the village has not a history like the other villages in the county; no fighting or jobbery for the county seat; nor any squabbling for railway connection with the outer world, as it came into existence after the railroad had passed through.

It was laid out and platted by William Morin and H. W. Holley; the former of Albert Lea and the latter of Winnebago City. After a short time Mr. Morin purchased the interest of Mr. Holley, and still retains the greater part of the property. The first business of any kind opened on the village site was the Post-office, which A. G. Hall moved from his place in section one. This was only continued for a short time, while the Post-master was waiting for his resignation to be acted upon by the department.

The first actual business establishment was started about the time of the arrival of the railroad, in 1869, by a Mr. Terrill, who opened a stock of general merchandise, together with hot drinks, beer, etc. He shortly after took into partnership J. H. Sherwood, who, in a few months, purchased the entire establishment, and continued it until he failed, about two years later.

A. G. Hall erected the first residence in the village, just prior to the opening of this store.

The station was commenced by the railroad company, and by the first of January, 1870, the track was completed to the village.

Next came the business house of George Whitman. Holley & Morin erected a store building, which was rented to Mr. Whitman, and he moved a stock of general merchandise in the building and placed the same in charge of Joseph Green and Victor Gilrup. This store was finally moved to Delavan and succumbed to financial difficulties.

Dell Miller fell into the line of progress, and erecting a suitable shop, commenced blowing the bellows and hammering the anvil. He ran the shop for about a year, when he was called away to the eternal shore.' The shop has been used for various purposes, but is now in use as a dwelling house.

Arthur Grigg came about the same time and opened a blacksmith shop, which he continued for some time, and finally it became the property of the present manipulator of the iron, N. S. Cromett.

Soon afterward, L. T. Walker and a Mr. Kenyon started a general merchandise store under the firm name of Walker & Co. Mr. Kenyon died a few years afterward, and Mr. Walker for a time was in partnership with a Mr. Paulson, under the same firm name: but, financial difficulties, in the hard times, involved the firm, and business was finally discontinued. It was, however, afterwards re-opened, and now carries a light stock, with the Post-office in connection.

About the time that the above establishment originated, A. G. Hall, who is mentioned as really having been the first resident of the village, erected a store building in connection with his dwelling house, and opened up a large stock of general merchandise, which he still continues, with a large and increasing trade. A few years after this establishment was started, Mr. Hall took into partnership with him, his son, and in this manner the firm continued until 1877, when the sad death of the young man occurred, and the father continues it alone.

Shortly afterward, H. N. Burnham purchased the old Whitman building and opened a general merchandise store, which he ran for two years and then closed out. Later on Charles Pfeffer started a store in the same building which he still continues.

Armstrong & Wheelock opened a store here, but were finally closed out and they disappeared.

H. B. Collins was the first lawayer in the village, and about one year ago opened a general merchandise store, which he still continues with a good trade add heavy stock.

At an early day a man named R. D. Barber, calling himself a doctor, located in the village and commenced "peddling pills." He remained less than a year, as he was very unpopular, and then left, locating at some point in the southwestern part of the State, where he again made himself odious by transporting an own brother, whom he insisted was crazy, to the Insane Asylum, and then charged an enormous bill for the labor of so doing. The bill was paid but gave him the reputation he deserves. His whereabouts at present is a mystery, to the satisfaction of all who knew him.

ALDEN FLOURING MILL.—This enterprise originated in 1875, having been erected that year by Wm Wilson. The building is 28x50 feet,a story and half high, containing four sets of burrs, which are driven by sufficient force, by steam power, to grind fifty-five barrels of flour per day. The mill is located near the lake and cost about $12,000. The present proprietor is William Wilson, Jr., son of the original owner.

A large grain elevator has been put up at this point by a LaCrosse firm.

PATRONS OF HUSBANDRY.—This Grange was instituted on the 28th of March, 1873. The initial officers were: A. H. Stearns, M. O.; F. Peck, Tr.; E. H. Clark, Sec.; Mrs. S. P. Dromer, Ch.; Mrs. A. W. Clark, G. K.; Mrs. J. A. Burdick, Ceres; Mrs. O. S. Peck, Flora; Mrs. E. A. Hall, Pomona; Mrs. A. W. Clark, L. S.

This is said to have been the first grange in this county.

BIOGRAPHICAL.

ELI B. CLARK is a native of New York, born on the 12th of April, 1818. He resided at home until the age of twenty-one years, then carried on a farm for two years. In 1840, he married Miss Joan A. Strope and in the autumn of that year they went to Ohio, where Mr. Clark was engaged at the blacksmith trade. In 1848, he moved to Portage county, Wisconsin, and in the fall of 1849, was elected Clerk of the Circuit Court; resigned the following year and engaged in the mercantile business at Plover in the same county. In 1858, he sold out and was chosen under Sheriff. In the fall of 1860, he moved to Ohio and engaged in mercantile pursuits until 1864, when he returned to Portage county. Mr. Clark came to Canton, in Fillmore county, in 1865, and while there established a Post-office called Prosper; was appointed its first Postmaster and also dealt in real estate. He subsequently bought and conducted a hotel in Hokah, Houston county, until 1869. In the latter year his wife died. He then sold his hotel and was traveling salesman for three years. In 1872, he married a second time and then purchased a hotel in Freeborn. He also owns an interest in the coal and gypsum mines and is secretary of the company. He has three daughters; Rosaline, the eldest, married L. Rossiter, a Captain in the late war; the second married W. S. Prentiss, now a passenger conductor on the C. R. I. & P. railroad; the youngest married H. L. MaGee, now train master on the central branch of the Missouri Pacific railroad in Kansas.

SEYMOUR F. CARY was born in Michigan in 1850. In 1860, he removed to Vernon, Waushara county, Wisconsin, and remained ten years. He then came to Manchester, in this county, staked out a claim in section nineteen but soon moved to Alden, erected a wagon shop on Main street, and is now of the firm of Cary Bros. He was married in 1875, the ceremony taking place on the 24th of June. His younger brother, Frank R., was born on the 21st of April, 1860, and learned the wheelwright trade in 1879. The older brother has run a thresher in this State for many years.

HENRY B. COLLINS was born in New York, on the 30th of March, 1832, and grew to manhood on a farm. He finished his education at Milton College, and after leaving school taught during the winter seasons. In 1843, the family removed to Rock county, Wisconsin, where our subject continued to teach school. In 1854, he was joined in matrimony with Miss Almeda L. Main, and in 1859, removed to Carlston, Freeborn county, pre-empting land in sections twenty-two and twenty-seven, and buying in section twenty-eight. He commenced the study of law; was admitted to the bar in 1862, and has followed the practice of his profession ever since. He has been Justice of the Peace for eighteen years; Town Clerk twelve years, and District Attorney in 1864, '66, and '68. He is now located in Alden, has a law office and conducts a dry goods store, in which he formerly kept drugs. He is a Notary Public and collection agent; has two hundred acres of land in this State and four hundred in Nebraska. He was appointed Chairman of the Congressional convention held at Rochester in July, 1882.

N. S. CROMETT was born in Sebec, Maine, on the 1st of January, 1823, and when nineteen years old learned the blacksmith trade of John J. Lovejoy, with whom he worked four years. He then purchased the stock, and conducted the business twenty-five years. He was joined in marriage in 1845, with Miss Emily F. Gliden, who has borne him three children. In March, 1865, he removed to Davis, and in a short time to Bangor where he conducted a music store; remaining in his native State until 1866, when he came to Iowa, and engaged at his trade. In 1870, he came to this State, located on a homestead of three hundred acres in Mansfield township, where he was a member of the board of Supervisors during his residence there. After farming there five years, he removed to this place, engaged at his trade on Main street, and in 1875, purchased a house and lot on Washington street, and now has a large shop connected with his business. He also owns a farm of one hundred and sixty acres in section six, the greater part of which is improved. He has been Chairman of the board of Supervisors, and is at present a prominent member of the village council.

Mrs. Floretta Davis was born in New York in 1845. She moved with her father to Illinois, where the family resided seven years, and in 1862, came to Carlston, in this county. Mrs. Davis married her husband, Elmer E. Davis, in 1864, and moved to his farm in section six, Alden township. He came to Wisconsin in an early day, and moved from there to this place in 1863. He died in 1873, of consumption, leaving a family of four small children, the youngest of whom died soon after. Mr. Davis was a member of the Baptist Church, to which she also belongs.

W. S. Fost was born in Germany on the 12th of April, 1852, and learned the blacksmith trade when sixteen years old. In 1870, he emigrated to America, came directly to Albert Lea, and in a short time removed to Mansfield. After working at his trade in that place one year, he went to Winnebago City, engaged in farming and the next fall removed to Wells, working in the railroad shops one year. He then was employed at his trade in different parts of the State until 1874, coming to this village in that year. He has a blacksmith shop on Main street. Miss Mary E. Jonky became his wife on the 18th of May, 1877, and they have three children.

Henry C. Friely is a native of Germany, born in 1841, and when sixteen years old emigrated to America. He came directly to Chicago, Illinois; was conductor on a street car until 1862, when he enlisted in the One hundred and thirteenth Illinois Volunteer Infantry, being Orderly Sergeant two years, then was promoted to First Lieutenant; served till the close of the war and returned to Chicago. He clerked in the retail store of Field, Leiter & Co. eight years, and later took charge of Mandell Bros'. dry goods store one year, at the end of which time he went into business for himself, selling out in 1875 and coming to Alden. In 1876, Mr. Friely removed to Albert Lea, where he clerked for C. M. Hewitt; afterward rented a farm near Pickerel Lake, which he conducted three years and returned to this place. He was married in 1879, to Miss Clara Bethker, and built his present house, in connection with which he has a billiard hall.

A. G. Hall was born in Clinton county, New York, on the 16th of August, 1824, and made his home in that county until 1865, when he came to this place; locating in section one. He was married in his native State in 1849 to Miss Susan A. Goodsell, and they have three children. In the autumn of 1869 they removed to what is now the village of Alden, building the first house in that vicinity, and two years after, an addition to it, which he uses for store purposes, having a stock of dry goods and groceries on Main street. He was chairman of the board of Supervisors three successive terms, and kept the first Post-office in town, known as the Buckeye Post-office.

John A. Hazle was born in Canada on the 22d of February, 1847. His father was a merchant tailor, and John remained at home until 1859, when he came to Michigan. He was Captain of a boat on the lake for some time, then learned tha carpenter trade and moved to Missouri, returning to Michgan in four years. He was married in 1873 to Miss Ella M. Wilbur, and the next year they came to Alden, Mr. Hazle purchasing the Alden House, a large hotel on the corner of Main and Broadway streets, near the depot. He has been a member of the board of Supervisors two years and is at present village marshal. He has a livery stable near his hotel.

William B. Humes was born in New Jersey, on the 25th of May, 1839, and while young removed with his parents to Illinois, and to Minnesota in the fall of 1854. In 1862 he enlisted in the Sixth Minnesota Volunteer Infantry, and was discharged the next year for disability. In 1864 he was joined in marriage with Miss Rachel M. Harrington, a native of Illinois, and they have two children. On the 25th of May, 1864, he removed from Pleasant Grove, where they had first located, to Alden, and erected a log house 14x16 feet. The next spring he assisted in the organization of the town, and was appointed first Town Treasurer; has been Justice of the Peace, and a member of the board of Supervisors one year. He has a farm of one hundred and sixty acres in section one, seventy acres of which is improved, and a three acre grove.

REV. F. M. KRISTENSEN is a native of Denmark, born on the 31st of March, 1846, and graduated from Yelling Seminary, having been a student there three years. After teaching school seven years he attended a high school two years, then, in 1877, came to America. He remained in Michigan two years, and on the 5th of June, 1879, was married to Miss J. Nelson. They removed to Iowa and in the fall he came to Alden, and he preaches for the Danish Lutherans here and in Carlston, having about fifty followers. Mr. and Mrs. Kristensen have two children.

MRS. CLARISA NORTON, deceased, the wife of Nelson R. Norton, and mother of Charles, William, and Adrian Norton, of this county, a lady who was universally beloved and respected. Her maiden name was Derling, and she was born in Woodstock, Vermont. She afterwards lived in Hampton, New York, and there was married, remaining six years. In 1833, they got west as far as Chicago, and remained there six years, and then located in Burlington, Racine county, Wisconsin. In 1872, came to Minnesota and located near Alden, where the remainder of her life of varied experiences was passed. She had been married fifty-four years and had nine children. She was a woman of many virtues. After an experience of seventy-three years in this world, on the 17th of September, 1881, she quietly passed to the other shore.

CORNELIUS N. OSTRANDER was born in Clinton county, New York, on the 26th of September, 1849. He moved with his parents to Fond du Lac county, Wisconsin, and in 1859, came to Minnesota, where he learned the carpenter trade, and for eleven years was engaged in farming and at his trade. In 1870, he removed to Wells, where he was engaged in a machine shop, thence to Minneapolis, returning, in a short time, to Albert Lea, and was employed at his trade and wagon-making. He next located in Alden, where he has a wagon and paint shop in the business portion of the village and also a jewelry store. He was married in 1870, to Miss Jennie Comstock. They have two children.

GUSTAV A. SCHWAUDKE was born in Prussia in 1854. His father kept a hotel and conducted a farm, and when fourteen years old our subject learned the butcher business. In 1876, he came to America and directly to Owatonna, Minnesota, where for sixteen months he was engaged in a meat market, then removed to Minneapolis and eight months later to Alden. In 1879, he opened a meat market and packing house on Broadway, and is doing an excellent business. He was joined in marriage on the 26th of May, 1879, with Miss Matilda Hammell.

JOHN N. WIESSNER is a native of Germany, born on the 25th of July, 1854, and when fifteen years old emigrated to America. In 1869, he came to New Ulm, Minnesota, worked on a farm eight years, then came to Alden and opened a saloon on Main Street. In 1881, he left his business in charge of a clerk and was agent for the John Gund brewery company one year. He now has a billiard hall and is doing a prosperous business. He was married on the 7th of January, 1880, to Miss Barbara Hoffman.

BANCROFT.

CHAPTER LVI.

DESCRIPTIVE — EARLY SETTLEMENT — RELIGIOUS SERVICES—OAK HILL GRANGE—OFFICIAL RECORD—BANCROFT VILLAGE—ITASCA VILLAGE—EDUCATIONAL—BIOGRAPHICAL.

This township is one of the center subdivisions of Freeborn county, being separated by one tier from the north, and an equal distance from east and west county lines. Its contiguous neighbors are, Bath township on the north: Riceland on the east; Albert Lea on the south, and Manchester on the west, embracing the territory of town 103, range 21, containing thirty-six sections, or 23,040 acres, of which there are very few unsuitable for agricultural purposes, and the greater part is already under a high state of cultivation.

The town has no lakes, and no streams of importance. Bancroft Creek is the principal one; rising in the northwestern part of the town it takes a southerly course, and finally enters Fountain Lake. A small body of water, dignified with the appellation of Itaska Lake, covers a few acres of land in the southwestern portion of section thirty-one.

The general make-up of the locality would be called prairie and oak openings. The early settlers say that originally, at least three-fourths of the area of the town was covered with a growth of burr and jack oak and other timber of the smaller varieties, interspersed with natural meadows and prairie. The greater part of the former growth of timber has been removed, and the rich country transformed into beautiful and productive farms. There are, however, a number of groves left, one upon section nineteen, another in section five, and in a number of other localities small groves mark the remains of former miniature forests. A strip of valuable prairie, known as the Paradise Prairie, enters the town in the southwestern corner and extends northeasterly almost across the entire town, gradually disappearing towards Clark's Grove, in the northeast corner.

The locality known as Oak Hill is the most elevated tract of land in the township, taking its name from the variety of timber with which it was formerly covered. It makes itself visible on the surface in the northwestern extremity of the town, and extends easterly across the entire township, embracing the northern tier of sections.

The farmers here, as a rule, are in comfortable circumstances, and the average appearance of the farm buildings indicate their thrift and energy, the town having the reputation of being one of the most valuable farming localities in the county.

The willow hedge is used to a considerable extent for fencing purposes, and is an excellent medium for giving the prairie a picturesque and pleasant appearance. J. C. Frost has four miles of this hedge, and has also cultivated fruit with success, having at this writing an orchard of 400 bearing and thrifty apple trees, of nearly twenty years growth. His brother, M. L. Frost, also has about three miles of this beautiful and useful hedge.

The soil on the prairie is mostly a rich dark loam, underlain with a rich sub-soil of clay; while in the timber, or oak opening, it is of a lighter nature, with a marked tendency, in places, to clayeyness and a sub-soil of sand and gravel.

The township has no railroad through it, and therefore has not been the scene of the usual railroad assistance bond issue. It has had two villages, or hamlets, the rise and decline of each of which will be treated under proper heads.

EARLY SETTLEMENT.

Early in the spring of 1855, a party of Eastern people left Wisconsin, where they had stopped for some time, and headed toward the prairie and timber land of Southern Minnesota. They consisted of Mr. Bethuel Lilly and wife, and the

Colby family, John and his wife Hannah and six children. They arrived at Caledonia, Houston county, on the 18th of May, 1855, and here part of the little colony decided to remain, while the balance should push on toward the West in search of future homes. The lots fell upon Charles C. and Sarah Jane Colby, a son and daughter of John, mentioned above, and Bethuel Lilly and wife. They took the ox teams, and in July pushed on toward the setting sun. They made their way direct to Bancroft, and selected farms in the southwestern part of the town, about the future site of Itasca village. C. C. Colby took the place on which the village was afterwards platted, and also selected a farm for his father, John Colby, who was yet in Caledonia. He remained until after the war, and finally found his way to New York City, where he is agent for the Musical Art Journal. Mr. Lilly remained upon his place for about one year; finally went to Kansas, enlisted and sacrificed his life for his country during the rebellion.

The following spring, in March, of 1856, the balance of the party made their appearance, and settled upon the place which the son had selected, just over the line in Albert Lea township, now occupied by Daniel Gibson. The party consisted of John Colby, his wife, and several children. The old gentleman lived upon his place until June, 1876, when he peacefully yielded up the burdens of life to enter upon eternity, and his widow still lives with her son-in-law, Mr. Leander J. Thomas, of Albert Lea.

Guttorm Bottelson, a native of Norway, who had remained for a time in Wisconsin, arrived a few weeks after John Colby, in 1856, and commenced a sojourn which he still continues, upon a place near Itasca. He came with ox teams, bringing his family and considerable stock.

The Frost family were also among the most prominent and active pioneers, and still remain in the town; but they are treated at length under the head of "Biographical."

Others who were also early pioneers in this part of the town, were Andrew Bottelson, who is yet living upon his place in the southwestern part of the town; John and Andrew Hermanson, Dr. Burnham, and others whose names have been forgotten.

In the meantime the northern part of the town began to receive the attention of the early comers; but ere this claims were getting to be scarce, except second hand, and in the same ratio that they were scarce, so they became valuable. The settlement north of the center of the town is more universally known as the "Oak Hill neighborhood."

A. C. Hall, a native of Maine, was the first to make his appearance, and he selected his domain in sections five and eight, in the middle of September, 1856, where he put up a shanty and made some improvements; but was not really an actual settler, as he soon sold out and removed to Iowa.

Andrew Barlow was the next to arrive, making his appearance in September. He "footed it" all the way from McGregor, leaving his family, and after taking a claim, left for Iowa in search of work. While gone, the weather seemed to be antagonistic to his best interests, as the snow was very deep, and he was consequently unable to return to his proposed home, so his place was jumped; and when he finally returned in the spring of 1859, he purchased the farm back for $20. He still lives upon the place in comfortable circumstances.

H. R. Loomis, from Erie county, Pennsylvania, came by stage from Dubuque to near Merry's Ford, on the Cedar River, Iowa, which is near the southeastern corner of the county, and from there walked to Bancroft, arriving and selecting his place on the first day of November, 1856. He erected a small shanty and made some improvements, and, as it was a lonely sojourn, bought a yoke of oxen, as he says, "to talk to."

At one time during the winter he went four miles for a load of hay, a job which engaged him from early morn till late at night, and upon his return could take the object and fruits of his entire day's labor in his arms and feed it ere another day should dawn. On the 26th of December, he started with his oxen to Delaware county, Iowa, and remained there until February, 1857, when he returned, bringing with him his sister, Louisa Loomis, and Oscar and Fannie Ward, the latter is now Mrs. George H. Prescott. The last two named were aged twenty and fifteen years, respectively. The entire party came in a sleigh, camping out on the way, finally arriving at Benjamin Frost's house, in the southeastern part of the town, where the manager of the party, Mr. Loomis, left them and proceeded to his selected home in section eight; prepared a fire and set matters in shape for his guests. The balance of the party, whom he had left at Frost's, followed on foot, on the top of the snow, there being a heavy crust.

They arrived and got settled in safety, and William Oscar Ward selected a farm for his father. Louisa Loomis is now Mrs. Caswell, living in Iowa. H. R. Loomis still lives upon the farm he first selected, a most prominent and popular man.

Early in the fall of 1857, Jeremiah Ward, a native of New York, father of Oscar and Fannie, arrived and located upon the place selected for him, and lived upon it until 1879, when he was called upon to cross the dark river from earthly to eternal existence, and his loss was severely felt by the many friends who honored him. His widow still lives in the town.

Early in the spring of 1857, Albert Loomis, from Erie county, Pennsylvania, came to the "Hole-in-the-ground" of H. R. Loomis, and immediately took a claim adjoining, in section nine, where he made his home for about ten years, when he went back to Pennsylvania.

About a week later, Cyrus Prescott, a native of Maine, who had made his home from childhood in Ohio, made his appearance in the town, coming by way of Hastings; and making a claim in section five took up his abode with H. R. Loomis' people, while he made improvements sufficient to live upon his place. He resided here until 1876, when he moved to Albert Lea, and now lives in Dakota Territory.

Later in the season Cyrus' father, Daniel, joined his son, and made him a habitation and a home in section four, where he remained until a few years ago, and now, at the ripe old age of eighty, lives upon the farm of H. R. Loomis.

In June, 1857, the next pioneer drifted in, in the person of William H. Long, a native of Newark, New Jersey, and commenced a sojourn upon a farm in sections five and eight, which he still owns; but in the spring of 1882, he removed to city of Albert Lea.

In the spring of 1858, Charles Dills, a native of the Empire State, came and purchased a place in section nine, of Charles E. Teneycke, who had previously secured it. Mr. Dills still lives there.

Ere this time nearly two-thirds of the land in this locality was taken up by actual settlers, and already a stride in the advance of civilization was perceptible. Among those who had arrived, whose names and actions have not been dotted upon the pages of memory, a few more will be chronicled. George H. Prescott, who still lives in section four. G. Thompson, who took land in section eight and is now in the West. Andrew Knudson took land in section nine, and is also in the West. Messrs. Wells and Clark took land, but soon left.

Jeremiah Ward is mentioned elsewhere. He was a carpenter and stone mason by trade; but could do a good job at almost anything, and his famous old "turn keys" are yet remembered as ferocious instruments in his hands, with a shudder, by many of the old pioneers; as they were the means of extracting all the poor teeth in the neighborhood. It is said in the winter of 1857-58, he pulled a tooth for David Blakely, and after the "turnkeys" were set, either head or tooth had to come, and for a time it was doubtful which.

VARIOUS MATTERS OF INTEREST.

The first marriage of parties from this place, occurred on the 13th of January, 1857, and united the destinies of two couples, at the residence of John Colby, just over the line in Albert Lea. An account of this is found in the article on the town of Albert Lea, to which we refer the reader.

The first marriage within the boundaries of Bancroft took place the spring of 1858, the high contracting parties being Mr. John Raiser and Miss Margaret Baker. The event took place in the "old-time" village of Bancroft, where the Poor Farm now is, the ceremony being performed by Rev. S. G. Lowry, a Presbyterian minister. The parties now reside in Austin.

The first death in the township occurred in the spring of 1857, and was a one day old child of Mr. and Mrs. Lewis Mickleson.

The first death of a matured person was the demise of Margaret Horning, in April, 1859. Her remains were deposited in the graveyard at Albert Lea.

Oak Hill Religious Services.—Meetings of various denominations have been held in this locality ever since its early settlement, in private houses and the schoolhouse. In 1858, services were held by an itinerant preacher, Rev. Mr. Adams. Rev. Mr. Lowry, or, as he was usually called, Father Lowry, held services here at an early day also.

Itasca Cemetery.—This burial ground is located in the southwestern part of section thirty-one, on the farm of A. M. Burnham. In 1861, Samuel Henderson, a resident of Pickerel Lake, died, and was the first person buried here. Others' remains were also deposited here, and about the year 1870, the grounds were regularly arranged, platted, and set aside for the purpose. This location was selected by Mrs. Burnham, and the site does justice to her taste, as it is a beautiful spot. She also selected the last resting place that her remains now occupy.

Oak Hill Grange.—This society was instituted on the 7th of July, 1873, with the following charter members:

Messrs. Geo. H. Prescott, M. Frost, J. C. Frost, Asa Ward, William H. Long, D. Prescott, H. R. Loomis, Hans Nelson, J. Ward, Clark H. Dills, Peter Peterson, Charles Peterson; Mesdames Fannie M. Prescott, Nancy Frost, H. E. Prescott, Jenny M. Frost, Helen E. Ward, Eliza Long, E. H. Prescott, Nancy Loomis, Emma Ward, and Maria Dills.

The first officers elected were as follows: Henry Loomis, Master; George H. Prescott, Overseer; William H. Long, Lecturer; Charles Dills, Steward; J. C. Frost, Assistant Steward; Asa Ward, Chaplain; Clark H. Dills, Secretary; Hans Nelson, Treasurer; Harriet E. Prescott, Ceres; Nancy Frost, Flora; Emma Ward, Pomona; C. S. Prescott, Gate Keeper.

The order is now in a flourishing condition, having about twenty-seven members. During the summer months meetings are held the first Saturday in each month, and in the winter once every two weeks, in Frost's hall in section eight.

On the 7th of March, 1876, a corporation was formed and shares of stock issued at $5 each, for the purpose of establishing a grange store. The undertaking was a success, and a store was started with about $500 capital, and continued under the management of directors until 1881, when Daniel Prescott purchased the establishment and still runs it. The dividends declared, while under the managemant of the grange, amounted to 10 per cent. upon the capital invested.

The present officers of the order are as follows: Clark H. Dills, Master; J. C. Frost, Overseer; H. E. Nielson, Lecturer; H. Ward, Steward; Daniel Prescott, Assistant Steward; Fannie Prescott, Chaplain; Charles Dills, Treasurer; George H. Prescott, Secretary; H. Frost, Gate Keeper; Mary Dills, Ceres; Nancy Frost, Pomona; Anna Nielson, Flora; Adella Dills, ———.

OFFICIAL RECORD.

The first meeting in the township for the purpose of effecting the organization of Bancroft, was held on the 11th of May, 1858, at the house of Ole Olson. The meeting came to order by the appointment of N. H. Ellickson, Chairman; W. N. Oliver, Moderator, and J. M. Clark, Clerk. E. D. Porter and Gardner Frost were elected overseers of roads, and a resolution was then adopted declaring that all cattle, mules, and horses, except stallions over two years of age, could run at large.

The election of officers was next taken up, and the following gentlemen for the various positions of trust, were declared elected: Supervisors, D. Blakely, Chairman, J. M. Clark, and C. C. Colby; Clerk, G. M. Frost; Assessor, Daniel Prescott; Treasurer, Ole Ellingson; Overseer of Poor, Henry Loomis; Justices of the Peace, S. Hanson and S. S. Watson; Constables, H. Bedells and R. G. Franklin.

For several years the annual meetings were held at the store in Bancroft (now the county Poor Farm); at present they are held in the residence of Ole Gulbrandson, in section sixteen.

The present officers of the township are as follows: Supervisors, M. E. Hewett, Chairman, Ole Narveson, and Andrew Barlow; Clerk, Erick Johnsrud; Treasurer, N. Sandburg; Assessor, A. O. Moen; Justices of the Peace, E. K. Pickett and C. Nelsen; Constables, C. H. Dills and T. B. English.

EMBRYOTIC VILLAGES.

Bancroft Village.—In the fall of 1856, a village was platted under this name in sections twenty-eight and twenty-nine, which figured high in the contest for the county seat, as narrated elsewhere.

Thomas Edgar erected the first store, in the spring of 1857, and put in a stock of goods. This building was removed to Austin in 1859.

The first building put up on the village site was a shanty erected just previous to the store, in 1857, by W. N. Oleson. He had first lived in a "dug-out," to which he brought his wife, but finally gave up this mode of life and became civilized. Oleson brought his wife from Shell Rock on a hand sled, as the snow was so deep.

A steam saw mill was moved to the village from Hastings by the Town Site Company, which was set up and operated by B. F. Ross and Addison Caswell. The cost of the mill was about $2,500, it occupying a building 20x40, and for two years the mill kept piling up the sawdust of hard wood; but, alas! the entire concern was finally, in 1859, sold for taxes.

The Town Site Company commenced, soon after, the erection of a hotel, by digging a cellar; but this was a failure and was given up.

A saloon was started by a Swede named Peterson, which had a brief existence.

A newspaper was next started by David Blakely, under the flaming banner of the "Bancroft Pioneer," which, for a few short mouths, distributed its newsy wares among its limited number of subscribers. Mr. Blakely is a native of Vermont, and is now the Minneapolis editor of the "Pioneer Press."

A Post-office was also established, which has since been removed to Itasca, although it still bears the name of Bancroft.

When the county seat matter was settled, all hopes of the village amounting to anything vanished, and the lots which were purchased were afterward sold for taxes, and in 1870, Freeborn county bought the entire property, and it is now used as the County Poor Farm.

ITASCA VILLAGE.—The land where this village had its rise and decline was taken under the government laws, in 1855, by C. C. Colby and Samuel Batchelder. In the winter following the idea of a village was conceived and carried out by the platting and recording of Itasca, C. C. Colby being the surveyor. The scene was laid in section thirty-one of Bancroft, about the little body of water called by the same name as the village.

A newspaper was started here by Dr. Burhnam, with a finely equipped office, and the doctor engaged a man to run it for him.

Soon after the preliminary steps were taken, a man named Dunbar, started a store by putting in a very limited stock of goods. A Post-office was established with C. C. Corby as Postmaster, and mail wss received regularly. The name of this office was "Freeborn Springs" and prior to its establishment the citizens were obliged to go as far as Osage, Iowa, for mail matter. After a time the office was changed to Bancroft, and Mr. Josh. Dunbar was made Postmaster. The store was continued for many years.

In 1857 Pres. Hall and James Longworth started a store which they ran for a few years, making a profit, such as buying calico for 11 cents and selling it for 60 cents per yard.

Dr. Burnham arrived at an early day, got a large farm and erected thereon a $7,500 house, hauling the lumber by water from Shell Rock; coming up the Shell Rock river and thence by way of the lake. The energetic doctor had a little brig, called "Itasca," built, which continued to ply up and down the water for a number of years. Through him a number of buildings were erected, and his energy enbued life into the whole locality; but all was of no avail.

As soon as the county seat was settled the interest in the village began to wane, the stores pulled out one by one, for pastures green, and the village now lives only in the memories of those who were connected with it in its brief career.

EDUCATIONAL MEDIUMS.

DISTRICT NO. 20.—Was originally organized in 1857, as a part of District No. 9, and a log house was soon afterwards erected in which Mary Prescott taught the first school to an attendance of about twenty-five pupils. The first officers were Messrs. Ole Stuga, Daniel Prescott, and A. Loomis. In 1859, it was made a part of District No. 2, and three years later, in 1862, it was reorganized under its present number. The schoolhouse now in use was erected in 1875, in the southeast corner of section five, size 24x30, furnished with patent seats, and cost about $1,000. The present officers are: Director, Asa Ward; Treasurer, G. H. Prescott; Clerk, W. H. Long; the latter officer having held that position for twenty years. The last term of school was taught by Miss Eva Loomis, with au an attendance of forty-four scholars.

DISTRICT NO. 24.—Effected an organization in 1862, the first meeting being held at the residence of Knute Tolloftson, on the 19th of April of that year, and the following officers were elected: Director, Lars Johnson; Treasurer, G. J. Johnson; Clerk, Knute Tolloftson. A log house was at once erected, 16x16 feet, at a cost of $150, which lasted until the year 1881 when the present school structure was built, occupying a place in the northwestern part of section twenty-six, size 20x26 feet, at a cost of $600, being supplied with patent seats and improved furniture. The first school was taught in 1863, by Lida Hewitt. it is claimed with thirty pupils in attendance, and she received the sum of $45 for her services for two months.

DISTRICT No. 58 was organized in 1863, and on 10th of April, that year, the first meeting was held, at which officers were elected as follows: Clerk, Andrew Bottelson; Director, B. Frost; Treasurer, John Hermanson. This meeting was held at the residence of Benjamin Frost in section nineteen. The first school commenced on the 9th day of May, 1863, with sixteen scholars present, in the back room of A. Bottelson's house, with Miss Mary Frost teacher, she receiving $1.50 per week. The log shoolhouse was finished in 1864. The present officers are: Director, Erick Attleson; Treasurer, O. G. Bottelson; Clerk, A. Bottelson. The schoolhouse is located in section twenty.

DISTRICT No. 22—The first school in this district was taught by Mrs. Margaret Fitzgerald, in her husband's house in section twenty-six in the summer of 1860, for $1.50 per week. The district was organized at a meeting held in the spring of the year at the same place. The first officers were Ole Narveson, J. Fitzgerald, and D. N. Ostrander. A log schoolhouse was rolled together by subscription, which lasted until 1872, when the present schoolhouse was erected in the northwestern corner of section twenty-six, being a frame building, 20x30 feet, and cost about $700.

DISTRICT No. 23.—Effected an organization in 1861, the first meeting being held at the house of William English, in the fall of 1860. The same gentleman donated a site, and a schoolhouse was secured and moved upon it in 1862. The present schoolhouse was erected in 1874, on the southeast quarter of section two, at a cost of about $1,200, size 18x26 feet, equipped with patent seats for sixty pupils. The last term of school was taught by Anna English for $25 per month, with thirty-five scholars present. The officers at the present writing are Thomas D. English, H. L. Oleson, and O. Nelson.

DISTRICT No. 107.—Is one of the younger districts of the county, having effected an organization in 1878. The first meeting was held at the residence of Daniel Peterson, and officers elected as follows: John Slater, Director; I. Hammer, Clerk; and O. O. Styve, Treasurer. A schoolhouse was soon afterward erected in the southern part of section thirty-three, at a cost of $770. The first school was taught in the winter of 1879, by Ella Slater. The last term was instructed by Grace Slater, with thirty-one scholars present, and her compensation was $25 per month.

BIOGRAPHICAL.

ANDREW BOTTELSON, one of the first settlers in this place, was born in Norway on the 22d of May, 1833. At the age of twenty he emigrated to America, residing in Illinois for one year, and in November, 1855, came to Bancroft, pre-empting one hundred and sixty acres in section twenty-nine. He devotes his entire time to the cultivation of his farm; has been a member of the board of Supervisors four years, and is a member of the Freeborn church. He was united in marriage on the 22d of March, 1860, to Miss Irene Iverson, and they have four children.

EUGENE CHAMBERLAIN is a native of New York, born on the 25th of December, 1857. He came west with his parents when seven years old, and they located in Manchester, where Eugene run a ditching machine for some time after reaching maturity. He was married in 1880, to Miss Fannie Reynolds, and the following spring came to Bancroft, having since devoted his time to agricultural pursuits.

JACOB C. FROST was born in Ohio on the 9th of April, 1841. He removed with his parents to Walworth county, Wisconsin, when six years old, and in 1856, came to Itasca, in this township. Jacob resided with his parents until 1861, when he enlisted in the Fourth Minnesota Volunteer Infantry under Captain White; was with Sherman in his march to the sea, and participated in twenty battles, receiving his discharge after a service of three years and ten months. After his return to this place he purchased a farm in section nine, which contains two hundred and eighteen acres; built a residence, and has since made it his home. He was married on the 17th of March, 1864, to Miss Jennie Gibson, and the issue of the union is five children.

MAHLAN L. FROST, one of the early settlers of this place, is a native of Ohio, born on the 20th of September, 1838. He came with his parents to Bancroft in 1856, and took a claim in section thirty, but resided with his parents until enlisting on the 9th of October, 1861, in Company F, of the Fourth Minnesota Volunteer Infantry. He was in the army three years and three months, coming home on furlough in 1862, and then married Miss Nancy E. Ward, daughter of J. Ward, one of the pioneers of the place, and formerly from Pennsylvania. After Mr. Frost's return from the army he bought land in section eight, and now has a well improved farm of three hundred acres, with good house, barn, etc. He has three children.

PETER FINTON is a native of Ohio, born on the 23d of March, 1830. When young he learned the carpenter trade, and at the age of sixteen years moved with his parents to Indiana, where he was employed at his trade. He was united in marriage to Miss Mary B. Shaul in 1856. She was formerly from Logan county, Ohio. They moved to Olmsted county, Minnesota, in 1861, and in 1874, sold their farm there and went to Nebraska, but after a residence of nine months returned to Minnesota. He is the father of seven children. Mr. Finton was elected to the Legislature from Olmsted county in 1871 and '72; was Justice of the Peace fourteen years, and also a member of the board of Supervisors.

ERICK JOHNSRUD was born in Norway on the 27th of March, 1850, and emigrated with his father to America, locating in Green county, Wisconsin, in 1857. They resided in New Albany township three years and then came to this county, being pioneers of Hayward, where they lived three years and then removed to this township, locating in section thirteen. Erick bought the old homestead in 1879, and his parents live with him. He has held the office of Town Clerk since 1876. His brother, G. Johnsrud, was born on the 31st of March, 1841, and lived with his parents until enlisting in Company H, of the Sixteenth Wisconsin Volunteer Infantry. He served until receiving his discharge on the 3rd of March, 1865, after which he located a farm near his father's. He was married in 1866, to Miss Anna Johnson, who has borne him five children. He was appointed Postmaster at Albert Lea in 1877, and held the office until 1880, since which time he has given his time to agricultural pursuits.

H. P. JENSEN was born in Denmark on the 31st of December, 1828. His father died when H. P. was six years old, and at an early age he assisted in the support of the family. He was converted, and in 1840 joined the Baptist Church. He was married in the fall of 1852, to Miss Christina Olson, who had joined the church in 1847. They have a family of five children. In the autumn of 1862, they came to America, located in Wisconsin and remained until the spring of 1864, when they removed to Freeborn county. Mr. Jensen owns a farm of four hundred and twenty acres, all of which is improved, containing a grove of ornamental trees, and he also owns some very fine cattle and sheep. When the Farmers' Mutual Insurance Company was organized, in 1878, Mr. Jensen was appointed President, and still fills the office.

H. R. LOOMIS, one of the first settlers in the northern part of the township, is a native of Erie county, Pennsylvania, born on the 12th of October, 1828. He attended the district school, after which he was engaged in chopping wood in the Southern States for eight winters, returning home and assisting on the farm summers. In 1854, he visited California and worked in the mines two years with moderate success. In 1856, he came to Bancroft and took a claim of one hundred and sixty acres, which has since been his home, having now a good frame residence and well improved ground. He was married on the 4th of April, 1860, to Miss Mary Prescott. In 1861, he enlisted in the Fourth Minnesota Volunteer Infantry, Company F, and at the expiration of his term, three years, re-enlisted in the same regiment and served till the close of the war, being promoted to the rank of brevet Second Lieutenant. He participated in nineteen engagements, although in the siege of Vicksburg, on the 22d of May, 1863, he was shot, a ball passing through his body. He is the father of five children.

HENRY N. OSTRANDER, one of the early settlers of this county, is a native of New York, born in Plattsburg on the 15th of October, 1824. When he was an infant his parents moved to Upper Canada, and in 1828, his mother died. His father soon after returned to New York, and Henry resided with him until the age of twenty-one years. He then went to Beekmantown and engaged in the coal and lumber business for three years. On the 22d of November, 1846, he was joined in matrimony with Miss Sarah A. Smith, also a native of New York. In June, 1849, they moved to Fond du Lac county, Wisconsin; resided in town about four months and then moved on a farm in the western part of the county. On the 12th of June, 1859, Mr. Ostrander staked out a claim in section twenty-six, Bancroft, and has since made it his home. He came here with four yoke of oxen, meeting with many difficulties. He has been a member of the school board most of the time since his residence here, and was Chairman of the board of Supervisors five years, also was County Commissioner five years. He has had a family of eight children, six of whom are living; Hannah B., the eldest, was born on the 6th of June, 1852, and died on the 3rd of May, 1856; and the second, Eva E., was born on the 9th of May, 1854, and died on the 20th of March, 1878.

Tom Oleson was born in Norway in 1859, and resided in his native country until the age of eighteen years. He then emigrated to America, and came directly to Minnesota; made his home in Houston county two years, and in the spring of 1879, found employment on the railroad in this county. He afterward lived in Albert Lea until the spring of 1882, when he came to this township and has since been engaged in farming.

E. K. Pickett, one of the respected and old settlers of this place, was born in Alexander, Genesee county, New York, on the 27th of September, 1828. When he was four years old his parents movsd to Cattaraugus county, where he was brought up on a farm and received his education. He was married on the 4th of March, 1849, to Miss Philena A. Skiff. In 1850, he came to Wisconsin and settled in Sheboygan county, two years later moved to Waukesha county, where our subject worked at the carpenter trade three years. In 1855, he moved to Walworth county and in 1860, came to this township, settling in section thirty-two, having driven the entire distance, bringing two span of horses and two wagons. In 1862, he enlisted in the Tenth Minnesota Volunteer Infantry, Company E; was soon after promoted Second Lieutenant and assigned to Company C, of the Tenth Regiment and served three years, until the close of the war, being with the company in every march and battle. Since coming here Mr. Pickett has worked at his trade a portion of the time. Of five children born to him, three are living.

George H. Prescott was born in Maine on the 20th of January, 1829. He resided with his parents until the age of twenty-one years, then engaged in the milling business on the Ohio river, owning a saw and grist mill which he conducted five years. In 1851, he was married to Miss Elizabeth Poor, of Utopia, Clermont county, Ohio. In 1856, they came to this township and was one of the first to open a farm in the place. After a residence of one year here he returned to Hastings, and two years later moved to Stearns county where he took a homestead and engaged in farming seven years. In October 1864, his wife died leaving four children, two daughters and two sons. He then returned to Bancroft and bought the farm his father pre-empted. Mr. Prescott was again married, on the 25th of December, 1870, to Mrs Fannie Ward Frost, widow of the late G. M. Frost, and the mother of two children, Emma and Edward. This latter union has been blessed with one son, Gerald, born in April, 1875. Their farm is well improved, having a good orchard, and Mr. Prescott is also interested in a sorghum factory at Albert Lea. He was elected Justice of the Peace in 1871, and held the office two terms.

B. F. Ross is a native of Pennsylvania, born on 27th of June, 1835. When he was three years old his parents moved to New York where he grew to manhood and at the age of twenty married Miss Jane Starks. Immediately after their marriage they came west, resided one year in Iowa, and then, in 1856, moved to Riceland, where they were the third family to locate, and made it their home several years. They have a family of five children. In 1862, Mr. Ross enlisted in Company C, of the Fifth Minnesota Volunteer Infantry and remained in service till the 29th of August, 1865. After his discharge he returned to his farm and in 1870 came to Albert Lea, remaining six years. In 1877, he rented the county poor farm which has since been his home.

Al Rice was born in New York on the 18th of March, 1840. When he was but six years old his father died and he has since maintained himself, working at different occupations. When he was nineteen years old he enlisted in the Eleventh Wisconsin Regiment, Company K, was under Gen. Grant and participated in fifteen battles, receiving an honorable discharge on the 4th of September, 1865. He returned to Wisconsin and engaged in the lumber business four years, then came to Rochester, Minnesota, and in 1877, married Margaret Knapp. The same year he came to Bancroft and has since devoted his time to farming.

Asa Ward was born in Plainsville, Ashtabula county, Ohio, on the 4th of November, 1844. In 1855, the family moved to Iowa, and two years ater to Bancroft, his father taking a claim in section seventeen. Asa enlisted in the Tenth Minnesota Volunteer Infantry, Company I, in 1862, and served three years. After his discharge he returned to his home and remained one year, then spent three years traveling. He returned to this place and on the 9th of April, 1868, married Miss Helen Dills. The same year he purchased his present farm in section four and has it well improved.

REV. JOHAN T. YLVISAKER, a native of Norway, was born on the 10th of November, 1858. His father was a minister and came to America, locating at Red Wing, Minnesota, in 1868. He died in 1877, at the age of forty-four years. Johan attended the Norwegian College in Decorah, Iowa, for six and a half years, graduating in the summer of 1877, and then entered the Concordia Theological Seminary at St. Louis, from which he graduated three years later. He returned to his home and in March, 1881, came to Bancroft; was ordained on the last day of the same month, Rev. Bishop Koren performing the ceremony. He assists the Rev. E. Hulfsbury, having charge of the Norwegian Lutharian Congregation in this place.

BATH.

CHAPTER LVII.

GENERAL DESCRIPTION—EARLY SETTLEMENT—WAR RECORD—OFFICIAL RECORD—STATISTICAL—ASSOCIATIONS—RELIGIOUS—EDUCATIONAL—BIOGRAPHICAL.

The township with this name is the center of the northern tier of towns in Freeborn county. Its contiguous surroundings are as follows: Waseca county on the north; Geneva township on the east; Bancroft township on the south; and Hartland township on the west. It contains thirty-six sections or square miles, comprising the territory of Town 104, Range 21.

In early days the most of the township was covered with a growth of burr oak, much of it large and heavy, enough so to have earned the name of "forest." This was interspersed with meadow or small patches of prairie land. There is a prairie of about 2,560 acres, located in the southwestern part of the township. The timber has now, to a great extent, been removed, and the rich land been converted into valuable farms. The surface is rolling, and in places the undulation is so abrupt as to be called ridges, which are not subject to cultivation. The soil is a dark sandy loam, underlain with a subsoil of clay.

The town is not so well watered as its neighbors, has no stream, and only one lake wholly within its borders. An arm of Geneva Lake extends from the town bearing its name into section twenty-five of Bath, and covers a few acres of land. Lake George is the only body of water wholly within the boundaries, lying in the southern part of section twenty-two. It was named in honor of George Skinner, Jr.

The town has a large portion of its area under a high state of cultivation, and its broad rich looking fields yield a substantial income to the thrifty inhabitants, which are, in majority, Danes, with a scattering of Norwegians, Irish, and Americans.

EARLY SETTLEMENT.

The earliest infringement by settlers, upon the territory of this town, commenced in the spring of 1856. The first parties to arrive and secure permanent homes were the Brooks brothers. The party consisted of Edward D., Dwight E., and Henry L. Brooks, with their sister Augusta, and mother. They were originally from Massachusetts, coming by way of Pennsylvania, and arriving in the spring of 1856, with teams, and all settled in and about section twenty-four, where the brothers joined interests and erected a log cabin 14x26 feet. Edward took a claim just over the line into Geneva township, and remained until 1866, when he went to Faribault county, where he yet lives. Dwight E. remained until 1868, when he followed his brother, and they were subsequently joined by the other brother, Henry L.

These were about all that came and settled this year; of course, a few travelers passed through, and many of them staked out claims, but they were never improved or occupied.

In May of the following year, 1857, John Keily, a native of the old Emerald Isle who had stopped for a time in Iowa, came with his family, in an ox cart, and settled in section eleven or fourteen, where he yet remains. He, soon after his arrival, erected a 14x18 foot log house, which he covered with sod and slabs.

Soon afterward John Harty and Martin Sheehan, of the same nationality, drifted in and secured places. Harty became satisfied with a farm in section four, where he remained until the time of his death, which occurred in the latter part of the sixties, and his family still occupy the old homestead. Sheehan secured a farm in the northeastern part of the town, where he remained until he died in 1875, and his family still remain on the place.

In the summer of 1857, a party of Norwegians, consisting of Hans Peterson, Ingebret Erickson, and Nels Nelson, came with teams, bringing their families, and settled upon claims. The first is still in the town. The second left in 1880 for the Red River country; and the third died during the war, in defense of his country.

About the same time Richard Fitzgerald, a native of Ireland, came and first located at St. Nicholas, where he put in a crop; but soon after made his way to Bath, and yet resides in the town.

George W. Skinner left Corning, New York, on the 24th of August, 1858, and arrived in Bath township on the 7th of September, having spent the preceding night in Geneva, where he found quite an important little settlement. On the 10th of the same month he selected the southeastern quarter of section twenty-two for his future home, and still occupies it. Mr. Skinner has been prominent in all public movements, and has done much to prevent the robbery of the public purse by railroad corporations and political fiends, and stands high in the estimation of his fellow citizens.

Shortly after Mr. Skinner's arrival, John and George Blessing, natives of Germany, made their appearance and selected claims in section twenty-three, where they remained for several years. Joseph Blessing came with his family and located in section thirty-five, remaining four or five years.

Horace Green came about the same time from Wisconsin, and located in section fourteen. From the last advice he now lives in Moscow.

Fred. W. Calkins, a native of New York State, who had for a time sojourned in Iowa, made his appearance in June, 1857, and located in section sixteen, where he remained until he died in 1863.

Jacob Bower, a German, came in the fall of 1858 and planted his stakes in section twenty-seven; but his stay was abruptly terminated by the government officers, as he was discovered selling whisky to the Indians, and he made himself "abundantly scarce."

Mons Grinager came in 1859 and settled. He is at present Register of the U. S. Land office at Worthington, Minnesota.

Elland Ellingson, a Norwegian, came in 1859, and still remains in Bath.

James M. Drake, a native of Massachusetts, came in 1856, and located in Geneva; but has since moved his residence over the line into Bath.

Others came in rapidly and soon all the government land was taken. A few of the most prominent arrivals are treated under the head of "Biographical."

EVENTS AND MATTERS OF INTEREST.

The first birth in the township took place on the 1st of June, 1859, and ushered John Shoalt (or Schad), a son of Mr. and Mrs. Bernhart Schad, living in section fourteen, into existence. The second birth was a child of Mr. and Mrs. George W. Skinner, and occurred two weeks later than the above.

Triple Marriage.—One of these rare events occurred in Bath on the 22d of December, 1864, at the residence of the Brooks brothers, the ceremony being performed by George W. Skinner, Esquire. The parties most interested were joined as follows: Edward D. Brooks to Miss Mary Bliss; Dwight E. Brooks to Mrs. Savanah Calkins, widow of Edward Calkins; Lieut. Loren Meeker, of Company C, Tenth Minnesota Infantry, to Augusta T. Brooks. All of the parties are alive, in various parts of the Northwest.

FIRST DEATH.—This sad affair occurred late in November, 1858, and carried away Edward Calkins, son of F. W. Calkins, aged 21 years.

WAR RECORD.—On the 6th of December, 1864, the sum of $1,000 was voted for the purpose of securing volunteers to fill the quota assigned the town, and to prevent the necessity of a draft. Of this amount $600 was used. The town was somewhat embarrassed in this regard, as Capt. Mons Grinager had taken forty men from this locality, six of them being from this town, and enlisted them in Wisconsin, thus cheating the town and State out of able-bodied men who should have gone to the war under the banner of a Minnesota regiment. The names of the participants in the war from Bath are as follows, fourteen in all: F. Drake, Dwight E. Brooks, Edward D. Brooks, O. Iverson, Ingebret Erickson, Mr. Jacobson, Michael Sheehan, E. Johnson, John Peterson, C. Johnson, Capt. Grinager, Nels Nelson, Tim Keily, and Peter Nason. Of these, Nels Nelson, Ole Iverson, and Mr. Jacobson never returned, finding the graves of martyrs in southern soil.

OFFICIAL RECORD.

When the county of Freeborn came into existence, the present area of the township of Bath was merged into territory taken from Geneva and Hartland, and was known as "Porter Township." What the name originated from, or what suggested it, we are unable to imagine; but we can simply state that all through its early settlement it was known under that caption. Therefore, the township of Bath proper did not come into existence as a separate organization until some time after a majority of Freeborn county's sub-divisions.

Porter township was organized for local government at a meeting held on the 15th of April, 1859, at the residence of Frederick W. Calkins. The meeting came to order and James M. Drake was chosen chairman; F. W. Calkins, moderator; and Harris Green, clerk *pro tem.* The next matter taken up was that of the town name, and finally, a short one being desired, some one suggested "Bath," after the name of the county seat of Steuben county, Ohio, and the name was adopted. It was next voted that the lake near the center of the township should be known as "Lake George," in honor of the oldest son of G. W. Skinner.

The matter of election next came up, and the judges of election were appointed as follows: George W. Skinner, Andrew Black, and B. Renwoiler. The judges were duly sworn before F. W. Calkins, Esq., and the election of officers for the ensuing year began, resulting as follows: Supervisors, Harris Green, Chairman, Joseph Blessing, and E. Erickson; Clerk, Horace Green; Assessor, Joseph Loreman; Collector, E. Erickson; Justices of the Peace, George W. Skinner and Horace Green; Constable, Jack Bower. The elections were held in early days at the residence of John Munsen; and as time went by they were held at various places as the annual meeting directed.

The present condition of town affairs is above criticism; as public trusts have always been in honest and efficient hands, with nothing occurring out of the usual line of such business to disturb the tranquility. The present officers are as follows: Supervisors, A. Erickson, Chairman, Patrick Farry, and J. P. Larson; Clerk, M. P. Peterson; Treasurer, Hans Rasmusson; Assessor, Andrew Jensen; Constables, Mike Sheehan and E. C. Johnson; Justice of the Peace, George W. Skinner.

STATISTICAL.

FOR THE YEAR 1881.—The area included in the following report, takes in the whole town, as follows:

Wheat—3,987 acres; yielding 69,737 bushels.
Oats—794 acres; yielding 25,482 bushels.
Corn—859 acres; yielding 19,646 bushels.
Barley—46 acres; yielding 2,530 bushels.
Rye—2 acres; yielding 53 bushels.
Potatoes—55½ acres; yielding 4,080 bushels.
Sugar cane—10 acres, yielding 237 gallons.
Cultivated hay—17 acres; yielding 30 tons.
Other products—101 acres.
Total acreage cultivated in 1881—5,854¾ acres.
Wild hay—2,515 acres.
Timothy seed—2 bushels.
Clover seed—32 bushels.
Apples: number of trees growing, 1,128; number bearing, 65.
Grapes—10 vines; yielding 100 pounds.
Sheep—152 sheared; yielding 531 pounds of wool.
Dairy—375 cows; yielding 32,550 pounds of butter, and 550 pounds of cheese.

FOR THE YEAR 1882.—It being too early in the season, at this writing, to procure the returns of threshing, we can only give the acreage sown this year:

Wheat, 3,511 acres; oats, 553; corn, 801; barley, 155; potatoes, 52; sugar cane, 3; cultivated hay, 83; other products, 27; total acreage cultivated in 1882, 5,515.

Apple trees: growing, 1,132; bearing, 24.

Milk cows, 416.

Sheep, 644; yielding 2,880 pounds of wool.

Whole number of farms cultivated in 1882, 101.

Forest trees planted and growing, 209.

POPULATION.—The census of 1870 gave Bath a population of 404. The last census, taken in 1880, reports 919 for the town; showing an increase of 515.

ASSOCIATIONS.

FARMERS' MUTUAL FIRE INSURANCE ASSOCIATION OF BATH.—This was organized at a meeting held at the Danish Baptist Church on the first of January, 1878. On the 14th of the same month it was incorporated under the State law, and seven directors were elected, as follows: H. P. Jensen, N. P. Peterson, John Henderson, Peter Johnson, J. P. Larson, C. F. Peterson, and C. Nelson. They met and elected officers of the association as follows: President, H. P. Jensen; Secretary, N. P. Peterson; Treasurer, C. T. Peterson.

The association has license to do business in the townships of Riceland, Bath, Albert Lea, Bancroft, and Geneva.

In the past the corporation has been exceedingly fortunate, having had but two losses, which were small, one $6.66 and the other $69.15, both of which were promptly paid. According to the report of January 1st, 1882, there was $73,150 of insurance in force in the above towns. The same executive officers are yet in the same positions as mentioned above.

GRANGE.—A society under this name was organized in Bath township in 1875, at a meeting called at the old log Baptist church, and the following officers were elected: Master, James Lawson; Treasurer, Peter Jensen; Lecturer, Lewis Jorgerson; Secretary, G. W. Skinner; Gatekeeper, E. Nelson; Pomona, Mrs. N. P. Nelson; Flora, Hattie E. Skinner; Ceres, Mrs. L. Jorgerson. Meetings were held once each month.

BATH POST-OFFICE.

This office was established in 1876, on section thirty six, at the residence of the Postmaster, L. P. Carlson, who was appointed and held the office for about two years when a Dane named Lingby was commissioned to handle the mails. This gentleman proved to be a defaulter, and after some trouble the matter was settled and the present Postmaster, A. H. Peterson, was appointed. Mail now arrives four times each week.

RELIGIOUS.

DANISH BAPTIST CHURCH.—This society was organized in May, 1863, and until 1865, services were held in the houses of Nels Larson and Hans Christianson, with Lewis Jorgerson as pastor, which were the first religious services held in the township. In 1865 a log church was rolled together by subscription, 20x26 feet, and seated to accommodate 100 people, in section thirty-five, which was used until 1875, when it was abandoned and the present church edifice erected. A building committee was appointed, consisting of Peter Johnson and Nels Clauson, which raised funds to the amount of $1,200, and the church was at once erected in the eastern part of section thirty-five, one and a half stories high, size 28x40 feet, and seated to accommodate 200 people. The first preacher was Rev. James Henderson, the elders at the time being H. P. Jenson and Peter Johnson. The present elders are, H. P. Jenson, Peter Johnson, John Anderson, Nels Otterson, and Lars Sorenson. The minister is Rev. J. S. Lunn, assisted by A. Carlson. The society raises annually about $1,000, for all expenses, including missionary fund, minister's salary, etc.,—the pastor only gets from $200 to $300 of this. The first persons married in the church were J. Nelson and Miss Mary Christenson, in 1877.

In connection with this society, and adjoining the church, is a burial ground, containing about one acre, which was laid out in 1875, under the supervision of J. P. Larson and P. C. Christenson. The first person buied here was Nels Otterson, who yielded up the spirit in the spring of 1875. At present there are about sixty-five graves occupied by the last remains of the departed.

NORWEGIAN LUTHERAN CHURCH.—This society was organized years ago in the township of Bancroft, and the membership has continually increased, until the denomination embraces a good share of this town. The church edifice wss erected in 1868, in the southwestern part of section twenty-one, at a cost of $2,000. The pastor who first officiated here was the Rev. Mr. Koren.

CATHOLIC CHURCH.—The catholic society first organized in Bath at the residence of Michael Sheehan, as early as 1865, and soon afterward a small frame building was erected for worship, in ection eight, which was used for the purpose until within the last few years, when they commenced the erection of a new and very fine edifice, which is at present in process of construction. The society is in good financial condition, und has a good membership.

EDUCATIONAL.

DISTRICT NO. 5.—Effected an organization in October, 1863, at a meeting held at the cabin of James M. Drake, in section twenty-five. Several terms of school had been held prior to this, and the whole town had been partially organized as a single district, so that when this was organized it embraced the entire eastern half of the town. The first school within the limits of this district was held in the summer of 1860, and was taught by Miss Lucia Thomas. In 1864, an old log house was purchased of Torkel Ludwigson, in the northeastern part of section twenty-six, and in it school was held for five months of the same year, taught by the same teacher as is mentioned above. In 1871, the present schoolhouse was erected in the eastern part of section twenty-six, at a cost of between $1,000 and $1,200. Since its original organization the district has been divided, and now consists of about four and one-half sections. The last term of school was taught by Miss Julia Whalen.

DISTRICT NO. 7.—This was organized on the 14th of May, 1864, at a meeting held at the residence of R. Fitzgerald, and the following were the first officers: Director, James Fitzgerald; Treasurer, G. Oleson; Clerk, R. Fitzgerald. During the summer a small log schoolhouse was rolled together in the eastern part of section thirty, at a cost of about $100, which did service until 1875, when the present house was completed on the same site, size 18x28 feet, at a cost of $600. The first teacher in the district was Mrs. Reynolds, who received $20 per month. The last term was taught by Miss Anna Oleson to an attendance of forty-four scholars, for $25 per month.

DISTRICT NO. 64.—This is the educational subdivision embracing the territory in the eastern part of the township, and is among the most useful in this locality. The first school held in this neighborhood was at the residence of H. Green, in section fourteen, and was taught by Mrs. Mary Johnson, for $1.50 per week, to an attendance of fifteen pupils. This was in the summer of 1863, and the same teacher instructed the school during another term, held in the fall of the same year. The location of the schoolhouse is near the center of section fourteen, and was erected in 1873, the district having been organized in 1871.

DISTRICT NO. 82.—This is one of the younger districts in the town. It was formerly a part of District No. 5, but in 1874 it was set off, and on the 16th of October legally organized at a meeting held at the Baptist church, at which officers were elected as follows: Nels Larson, Director; Nels Jensen, Clerk; and J. P. Larson, Treasurer. The first school was held in the log church during the summer of 1874, with Miss Susan Kinnear as teacher. In 1875 the present schoolhouse was built near the center of section twenty-five, but it has since been remodeled and greatly improved. There are now forty-five scholars enrolled.

DISTRICT NO. 90.—This embraces the territory just west of the center of the township, with a scoolhouse located on the eastern line of section sixteen. The district, it is claimed, was organized in 1859, at a meeting held at the house of John Sheehan, at which the following officers were elected: Director, M. S. Sheehan; Treasurer, Hans Rasmusson; Clerk, John J. Sheehan. The first school was taught in the old Catholic Church by Miss B. A. Ryan, aged twelve years. The schoolhouse was erected in 1860, size 14x16 feet.

DISTRICT NO. 103.—The organization of this district was effected a number of years ago, at a meeting held at the residence of Michael Sheehan in section eight, and their schoolhouse was erected shortly after in the northwestern corner of the same section. The school is in a flourishing condition and well attended.

BIOGRAPHICAL.

NIELS PETER PETERSON, a native of Denmark, was born on the 28th of April, 1847. His father died when our subject was six years old, and in 1867, his mother sold out and came with her son to America, directly to Minnesota, and located in Winona. In 1871, Niels came to this township and farmed with his brother for three years, then bought land in section twenty-four and has since made it his home. He has been a member of the board of Supervisors, and is serving his second term as Town Clerk. He has been Secretary of the Bath Mutual Fire Insurance Company since its organization.

David A. Peirce was born in Maine on the 2d of October, 1830. His father was a farmer and David lived at home until the age of twenty-one years. He was married in 1856, to Miss Amanda M. Bailey, and the following year moved to Mower county, Minnesota. Five years later they removed to Spring Valley, and in March, 1862, Mr. Peirce enlisted in Company E, of the Seventh Minnesota Volunteer Infantry, and served two years and ten months. After his discharge he returned to Spring Valley and removed his family to Bath, locating in section eighteen, where he has a good home with commodious buildings. His two oldest daughters are school teachers in this county and he has a son editing a Marshall county paper.

Mitchell Slater is a native of England, born on the 29th of April, 1854. His parents emigrated to America when he was six weeks old, and settled in Smithville, Massachusetts. Four years later they came to Minnesota, and Mitchell remained at home until twenty-one years old, then worked in different places until buying a farm in section twelve, Bath township, and has since made it his home. He was united in marriage on the 9th of January, 1880, with Miss Dora E. Heath, and they have two children.

George W. Skinner, one of the early residents and prominent citizens of this county, was born in the city of Warren, Massachusetts, on the 9th of August, 1815. His father was a scythe maker and he learned the same trade, after which he went to Kentucky as salesman for the firm of Blanchard & Co. (for which his father also worked), and traveled one year, then returned, but soon went to St. Louis. While there he met Gen. Marcy, with whom, in 1837, he went to Fort Snelling, thence to the Missouri and up the Yellowstone, and a short time after to Ohio, where he remained one and a half years. He then returned east and entered upon the practice of law until his health failed, when he gave up the profession and accepted a commission from Gov. Briggs, of Massachusetts, as Colonel for the Tenth Massachusetts Regiment; went to Mexico and served till the close of the war, having participated in the battle of the National Bridge, and others. In 1848, he again returned to his native State and entered the office of the Rhode Island & Massachusetts Telegraph Co., and operated the same for one year. In 1849, he was joined in wedlock with Miss Elizabeth A. Brooks, of Oneida county, New York. The same year he went to Mexico and erected a telegraph line between the cities of Vera Cruz and Mexico, after which he returned to Massachusetts and was employed in an office at Narrasburg for the Erie Railroad Company. He subsequently built a line from Elmira, New York, to Philadelphia. Previous to 1857, he had accumulated railroad bonds to the amount of $100,000, all of which he lost in the Ohio Life and Trust Company. Then, after settling up business, he came to Minnesota in September, 1858, and preempted land on section twenty-two, in this township. He came by water to Red Wing, where he hired a team to bring him here, and the same autumn got up a log house. In an early day he was sent to Washington by the settlers of the county, for the purpose of importuning President Buchanan to withdraw the lands from market for the benefit of settlers, and gained an extension of one year for the settlers to raise money to pay back dues on their claims. Mr. Skinner has been a prominent official since the organization of the town, and served as Justice of the Peace seventeen years. He has four children: Hattie, one of the teachers in this county; George W., Henry D., and Maud L.

CARLSTON.

CHAPTER LVIII.

DESCRIPTIVE—EARLY SETTLEMENT—STATISTICAL RELIGIOUS—EDUCATIONAL—BIOGRAPHICAL.

This is a township lying in the western tier of Freeborn county towns, and containing an area of thirty six sections or square miles, making 23,040 acres. Its immediate surroundings are Freeborn on the north; Manchester on the east; Alden on the south; and the county of Faribault on the west. As will of course be imagined, this is a prairie town, the only places in which a show of timber is found being in the northern part, in the vicinity of the lake. The town is watered by a lake and several small streams which bisect the prairie.

Freeborn Lake, taking its name after the same gentleman in whose honor the county received its name, is one of the largest and most beautiful bodies of water in the county, and lies mostly within the limits of this town, only extending into the town north a few rods. It is situated in the northeastern part, and covers about 2,240 to 2,400 acres, or three and a half sections, being about three miles long and, to the utmost, about a mile and a half wide, while its depth will not exceed twelve feet. The water of the lake is soft and of rather a muddy hue. Originally it abounded with fish of all local species, but in the winter of 1868-9, which was very severe, the lake water froze very deep, and remained a solid mass of ice for six months. After the thaw came, thousands of dead fish washed upon the shores, and so thinned the supply that to this day the spawning has failed to replenish the ranks of the finny tribe. The shores are covered with a small growth of timber, mostly burr oak, this constituting the timber land of the town, the balance being prairie of a rolling nature.

The Chicago, Milwaukee, and St. Paul railway line traverses the southwestern corner of the town, entering from the south in section thirty-three and taking a northwesterly direction leaves by way of section thirty, to enter Faribault county.

There are no villages in the town, except to the extent to which the village of Alden extends from the town bearing the same name into section thirty three of this town. This village is located wrong upon the map published by Warner & Foote, in 1878, it being one mile further west than shown on said map.

The town contains many valuable and well improved farms and is among the best agricultural towns of the county, but then this is unnecessary, as its agricultural resources are well shown by the article upon statistics, published in another place. The inhabitants are mostly Swedes and Danish.

EARLY SETTLEMENT.

The following is a sketch of the early matters in this town, published several years ago by the Old Settlers' Association, in the Albert Lea papers. It should be stated that the matter was all gathered by correspondence, and errors may, and probably have crept in.

"CARLSTON was first settled in 1855, by Robert Miller. Miller built of logs the first house, in 1855, and opened the first farm in the same year. John L. Melder, a blacksmith, was the first mechanic. H. B. Collins opened the practice of law in 1860. The first school was taught by Martha Taylor in 1860, and the first schoolhouse was built by District 61, in the fall of the same year. The first religious service was held by Rev. Mr. Marsh, United Brethren Minister, at the schoolhouse in District No. 15 in 1861. The Seventh Day Baptists effected the first church organization, in November, 1863. The first parties married, were David Horning and Mary Jane Elliott, who were united by H. Melder, Esq., on the 24th of December, 1861. In 1856 the first child was born to Mr. and Mrs Melder. The first death was that of Elias Stanton, who froze his feet, suffered several amputations, and finally died in the spring of 1858. The first title to land was acquired by Robert H. Miller, on sections ten and eleven, on the 21st of April, 1856."

But setting this aside we will turn our attention to the earliest comers in the township. The first settler in the township was Robert Riller, who came in the spring of 1855, and settled on a claim in section fifteen on the banks of Feeeborn Lake, where he erected the first house and did the first breaking. He did not remain long, as he was discovered selling liquor to the Indians and was obliged to leave to avoid trouble. The land he took is now owned by John Larson.

Shortly after the arrival of the first, the second settler put in an appearance in the person of Theodore L. Carlston, after whom the town was named. He erected a house in the same spring that he arrived, and "bachelor's hall" until the time of his death in 1858. He was drowned while crossing the lake in a boat in company with three others, one of whom, Mr. Johnson, also found a watery grave. Carlston's body remained in the lake until the following spring.

The next to arrive was Elias Stanton, who also located on the shore of Freeborn lake, in section fourteen; he likewise put up a log house and commenced keeping "bachelor's hall." In 1857, during the winter, he was caught in one of the noted Minnesota snow storms, and frozen so badly that after several amputaions he lost his life. His original place is now occupied by David Horning.

Thomas Ford arrived in 1856, and was another of the first settlers in the town. He located in section fifteen; the land as yet not being in market, and remained until 1859, when he left for parts unknown.

Elias Stanton, upon his arrival, was accompanied by a gentleman named Huyck (Houk,) who also settled in section eleven and remained for a number of years.

L. T. Walker; a native of Vermont, drifted into the township in the spring of 1858, and located in section thirteen, where he opened and commenced cultivating a valuable farm. He remained here for a number of years and then moved to the village of Alden, where he is now running a store. He is Postmaster and a prominent man.

Mr. Henry Collins came to Carlston in 1859, and located in section twenty-seven, where he remained cultivating and improving the farm for about eleven years, when he removed to the village of Alden and engaged in the pursuit of his profession, that of law. He has recently opened a fine store, and is a most public spirited man.

David T. Calvin and family came in the spring of 1861, and settled upon one hundred and sixty acres in this town. He brought with him horses, wagon, and several head of cows, and purchased a corn crib of Mr. Howard, in which he and his family made their home for some time. He now lives on section thirty-six, well located and comfortable.

Charles Sweet was born in Allegany county, New York, in 1828, and in 1863, came to Minnesota, to the township of Carlston, locating in section thirty-two. He came to his death in 1880. He was returning home from the village of Alden with a neighbor, and while crossing the railroad track a train struck the wagon in which they were traveling, inflicting injuries upon Mr. Sweet from which he died shortly after.

SOME WHO HAVE PASSED AWAY.

Hannah Melder, wife of John Melder, was taken from this plane of life on the 12th of January, 1879, at the age of 52. She came to Freeborn county with her husband in the year 1857, thus being one of the pioneers, who was well known and beloved by all as a kind-hearted woman, an affectionate wife, and careful mother.

Mrs. J. M. Melander went to the great hereafter, on the 12th of January, 1879. Her maiden name was Christenson, and she was born in Stockholm, Sweden, on the 17th of July, 1825. Her father was city collector and died when she was nine years old, and her mother two years later. On the 9th of May, 1850, she was married to John S. Melander. She landed in Boston on the 18th of October, 1855, and remained there alone until joined by her husband the following spring, who had been sick in New Orleans. They left Massachusetts for Iowa in June of that year, and remained in the Hawkeye State until this section began to be opened up, when she came here and remained up to the time of death.

Mrs. Mary C. Walker. She was a Bruce, of Scotch descent, born in Townsend, Vermont, on the 13th of October, 1818, and was married to Asa Walker in 1839. They removed to Madison, Wisconsin, and to Minnesota in 1859. She was always first at a sick-bed, and was full of energy and activity: sadly missed and long to be remembered. She died on the 21st of January, 1879.

Mrs. S. Twist, a daughter of Mr. Nathan and Mrs. Sally Pierce, was born in New York State on the 29th of July, 1833. At the age of eleven years her parents moved to Waushara county, in the same State. Her marriage to Mr. Twist was in 1859, when she came with him to Carlston. They lived in Albert Lea for three years before her death, which was on the 1st of January, 1881. Two children preceded her a month. A husband and seven children remained. Her remains were interred in Alden. She was an exemplary woman.

STATISTICAL.

From the report of the County Auditor to the commissioner of statistics of the State, and other sources, we have compiled a few items to show the value and agricultural resources of this township, for the benefit of those who are not liable to see this report as it comes from the State department. The items represent the acreage and yield of the various crops sown, together with other matters of interest.

THE YEAR 1881.—The area included in this report takes in the whole town, as follows:

Wheat—3,569 acres, yielding 32,915 bushels.

Oats—814 acres, yielding 21,197 bushels.

Corn—769 acres, yielding 26,905 bushels.

Barley—110 acres, yielding 2,789 bushels.

Rye—3 acres, yielding 50 bushels.

Potatoes—31 acres, yielding 3,500 bushels.

Beans—1 acre, yielding 43 bushels.

Sugar cane—10 acres, yielding 1,031 gallons.

Cultivated hay—113 acres, yielding 198 tons.

Flax—129 acres, yielding 1,235 bushels.

Total acreage cultivated in 1881—5,558.

Wild hay—2,168 tons. Timothy 269 bushels.

Apples—number of trees growing, 2,044; number bearing, 505, yielding 327 bushels.

Grapes 37 vines, yielding 127 pounds.

Sheep—278 sheared, yielding 1,749 pounds of wool.

Dairy—238 cows, yielding 27,450 pounds of butter and 50 pounds of cheese.

FOR THE YEAR 1882.—It being too early in the season, at this writing, to procure the returns of threshing, we can only give the acreage sown this year in Carlston.

Wheat, 2,933 acres; oats, 923; corn, 1,303; barley, 347; rye, one-half acre; potatoes, 70 acres; beans, 3¼; sugar cane, 6¾; cultivated hay, 186; flax, 139; total acreage cultivated in 1882, 5,952¼.

Apple trees—growing, 2,037; bearing, 476.

Milk cows—239.

Sheep—67, yielding 297 pounds of wool.

Whole number of farms cultivated in 1882—82.

Forest trees planted and growing, 165 acres. Five acres planted this year.

POPULATION.—The census of 1870 gave Carlston a population of 378. The last census, taken in 1880, reports 500 for this town, showing an increase of 122.

RELIGIOUS.

There is not a church edifice in the township. There is one organization, and a number of denominations which occasionally and irregularly hold services in the various schoolhouses.

DANISH LUTHERAN CHURCH.—This society is presumed to have been organized about 1874, as one who has been living there for nearly twenty years says it was organized in 1864, and another who has been there almost as long, says 1874. There are now about fifty families in the society, and services are held in the schoolhouse of District No. 61, in the eastern part of section twenty-two. Rev. F. M. Kristensen is the officiating minister of this denomination.

ALDEN UNION ASSOCIATION CEMETERY.—This burial ground is located near the central part of section thirty-four. The association was organized on the 17th of January, 1877, with the following as their trustees: John A. Hazle, A. T. Briggs, J. E. N. Backus, W. A. Clark, and L. M. Hall. The first burial here was of the remains of Justin, a son of Henry Ernst, who died on the 27th of June, 1871. The grounds now contain the graves of many departed ones, and has been the scene of many sad and sorrowful events of parting and farewell. The cemetery contains three acres.

DANISH LUTHERAN CEMETERY.—This "village of the dead" occupies a few acres in the eastern part of section twenty-two, adjoining the schoolhouse of District No. 61, and it often goes by the name of this district. The association controlling it was organized in 1874, the trustees then being John Rasmusson, Christ. Johnson, and Peter Larson, and they still hold their positions. The first burial here was the interment of the remains of Hans Paulson in 1874.

EDUCATIONAL.

DISTRICT No. 15.—This educational subdivision came into existence by organization late in 1859, and the following summer, 1860, the first school was taught in a log house, by Martha Stane, with nine scholars in attendance, the teacher receiving as compensation the sum of $18 per month. The present schoolhouse was erected in 1877, at a cost of $640, equipped with patent seats for forty scholars. The last term was taught by Lida L. Chester, who instructed the twenty scholars present, and received the salary of $20 per month. The location of the schoolhouse is the western part of section ten, and it is a credit to the district.

DISTRICT No. 16.—Effected an organization in the year 1860, and in the following year the first school in the district was held at the residence of James Cook, taught by Mary J. Trigg, with ten scholars present; the teacher received for services the sum of $1.50 per week, and "boarded around." The school was held here and in other residences until the fall of 1865, when a log house was erected at a cost of $800, size 22x30 feet, equipped with patent seats and the necessary apparatus. The last term of school was taught by Harte E. Jones, with twenty-three scholars present, and wages $20 per month. The schoolhouse is located in the center of section thirteen.

DISTRICT No. 61.—The first school meeting was held at the residence of William W. Coon on the 27th of March, 1874, at which the organization of the district was effected, and on the 30th of the same month again met and elected the following officers: Director, William W. Coon; Clerk, John L. Garlack; Treasurer, David Horning; and soon after the schoolhouse was erected in the eastern part of section twenty-two, at a cost of $600, the size of which is 20x30; supplied with patent seats for forty pupils, and all the necessary apparatus. The first school consisted of eighteen scholars, and was instructed by Chandler Sweet, who received $30 per month for his services. The last term was taught by Miss Walker, with an average attendance of twenty-one.

DISTRICT No. 67.—Effected an organization in 1865, by the election of the following officers: Director, David Clark; Treasurer, Charles Sweet, Clerk, D. T. Clinton. A little shanty was thrown together, with no floor and a board roof, in which the first school was taught by Adelia Bassett, to an attendance of nineteen or twenty, receiving for her services $18 per month. The following year, 1866, the present school edifice was constructed, a short distance from the board shanty, in the eastern part of section thirty, at a cost of $500, size 20x26 feet, equipped with patent seats and the necessary apparatus. The last term of school was taught by Miss Sadie Pratt, who received $20 per month.

ADVENTISTS' ACADEMY.—A select school under this caption was instituted in the village of Alden, over the line in Carlston township, in the upper story or hall of Henry Ernst's house, by the gentleman in whose house it was kept. The school commenced on the 15th of December, 1875, with from forty to fifty students in attendance: the tuition being from $5.00 to $7.00 per term, in accordance with the studies pursued. The teachers were Mr. Henry Ernst and his sister, Miss Minnie Ernst. The school was continued for several years, but was finally discontinued, as this method of education was too advanced to find its entire support in the local neighborhood in which it was founded.

BIOGRAPHICAL.

DAVID T. CALVIN, one of the earliest settlers and the one who cast the first vote in this town, is a native of New York, born on the 29th of April, 1831. The family moved to Ohio when David was three years old, and our subject remained in that State engaged in farming pursuits until 1846. He then removed with his parents to Wisconsin, settling on a farm near Southport, and after a residence of three years went to Chicago, and was employed in a butcher shop until the age of twenty-three years. He was married in 1853, to Miss Hulda Russell, and they have one daughter, Emma Amy, born in Iowa. In 1858, Mr. Calvin came to Freeborn county and settled in the town of Pickerel Lake, but the following spring came to Carlston and selected land in section twenty-five. He enlisted in the First Minnesota Mounted Rangers in 1862, went west and fought the Indians under Gen. Sibley, participating in two battles, in the last of which his horse stumbled and he received injuries which necessitated his discharge, after a service of fourteen months. He returned to his home, and ten years after taking his first land here moved to his present farm in section thirty-six. He has converted this wild prairie into a well cultivated farm, having seven acres planted in timber, some of the trees being now two feet through. He takes great interest in fine stock, having recently sold two of the finest calves raised in this part of the country.

WILLIAM CLARK was born in Indiana, on the the 18th of January, 1833, and his father, who was a cabinet maker, died when William was nine years old. When his mother married again he left home, and at the age of eighteen years learned the carpenter trade. In 1851 he located in Iowa, erected the first building in Postville, and in three years came to Minnesota He was united in marriage in 1855, with Miss Eunice Lampher, a native of New York. They located at Rice Lake, built a house and worked at his trade until 1861, when he enlisted in the Third Minnesota Volunteer Infantry; went south and was under General Buell, but was discharged for disability after a year's service, and now receives a pension. In the latter part of 1862 he returned home, rented a farm for one season, then removed to Carlston, locating in section thirty-one, where he has a large farm, well improved, and a new residence. Mr. Clark has a family of ten children. He has been one of the Supervisors of the town for one term. About two years ago his son met with a very narrow escape while crossing the railroad track, the engine striking the wagon and killing one of the neighbors who was with him, and also one of the horses.

MILES W. DODD was born in New York on the 10th of October, 1824. He remained at home until the age of fourteen years, then engaged with Frink and Walter in stage driving, and remained in the company's employ six years. In 1846 he removed to Wisconsin, settling near Oshkosh, and was engaged in the Wolf River pineries in the winter seasons and on the farm summers for fourteen years. He was married in 1851 to Miss Harriet Lee, daughter of Justin Lee, who was the brother of Gideon Lee, the Mayor of New York City at one time. In 1860 Mr. Dodd came to Minnesota and farmed in Fillmore county six years, then moved to the town of Chatfield, and brought his family on the 15th of October, 1880, to his present farm in section nineteen, Carlston township. He owns over one thousand acres of land, with a good brick house and out buildings, and has some very fine cattle.

CHARLES J. GRANDY, one of the first settlers of this place, is a native of Vermont, born on the 20th of July, 1819. When he was quite young he moved with his parents to New York, where he resided for twenty-five years and in 1846 married Miss Huldah Winters. They removed to Wisconsin in 1854, remained there on a farm for three years, and in June, 1857, came to this township, locating in section twelve and were the first settler on the east of Freeborn Lake. In 1862 Mr. Granby enlisted in the Fifth Minnesota Volunteer Infantry where he served three years as Sergeant, then re-enlisted and served seven months as veteran. Since his return from the army he has devoted his entire time to the cultivation of his farm.

NATHAN JACKMAN was born in New Hampshire in 1829. He left his home at the age of fifteen years and was employed by the month until twenty-five. In 1854, he married Miss Sarah Bumpus, and in July of the following year they came West to Lafayette county, Wisconsin. Early in 1861, they moved to Fillmore county, Minnesota, and the following May came to this township and pre-empted one hundred and sixty acres of land in section nine. Mr. Jackman drove from Wisconsin with a horse team and brought two yoke of oxen. Upon his arrival here he built a plank shanty 10x12, in which they lived thirteen years, then erected a good house and barn which were destroyed by fire in 1874. He owns some good stock and his farm is well improved. Mr. and Mrs. Lambert are members of the Advent Church. They have a family of four children.

DENNIS H. ODAY was born in Ireland on the 25th of March, 1821. He was married in 1845, to Miss Catharine McGrath, and the next year came to America; landed in New York and removed thence to Fox Lake, Wisconsin. He remained there eighteen years, then went to Rochester, Minnesota, and in seven years came to Alden; thence, in 1880, to a homestead in this place in section nineteen. Mr. Oday has a family of ten children.

ASA WALKER, one of the early settlers of Carlston and one of the first members of the board of Supervisors after the organization of the town, was born in Vermont on the 31st of May, 1813. He resided at home until his marriage with Miss Mary C. Bruce in 1840. For ten years they lived on a stock farm at Townsend in his native State, and in 1856, removed to Dane county, Wisconsin. In the spring of 1859, they came to this township and staked out a claim upon which they still reside in sections twenty-four and twenty-five. In 1862 and '63, Mr. Walker was in the Legislature, has also held local offices, and during the war was enrolling officer. His wife died on the 21st of January, 1878, leaving two children. The daughter, S. Emegene, lives at home and keeps house for her father. She taught several of the first schools in different towns in this county, with which money she bought one hundred and sixty acres of land adjoining her father's.

FREEBORN.

CHAPTER LIX.

DESCRIPTIVE—FIRST SETTLEMENT — NECROLOGY—MATTERS OF INTEREST—RELIGIOUS — GOVERNMENTAL — STATISTICS — FREEBORN VILLAGE — SCHOOLS—BIOGRAPHICAL.

This town, with a name identical with that of the county, occupies one of the four most prominent places—the northwestern corner. Its immediate surroundings are, Waseca county on the north; Faribault county on the west; Carlston township on the south, and Hartland on the east. It is constituted, as are all the townships in this county, of a full congressional township, containing 23,040 acres, known in legal parlance as Township 104, Range 23.

Freeborn is principally a prairie town, not so much inclined to be rolling as most of the towns, but level, and in places marshy. The lakes are surrounded by a small growth of the shrubby varieties of timber, which is all in the northwestern and southeastern parts of the town. The soil is a dark and sandy loam, with a sub-soil of clay and gravel, and almost the entire area is well adapted to agricultural purposes, and has a large cultivated acreage, yielding good crops of the cereals and other products of the latitude; and in the low lands hay is a most valuable crop. Fruit culture is more or less successful, although, as yet, but little attention has been paid to this department of agriculture.

The soil and climate is remarkably well adapted to the cultivation of Amber cane, and considerable attention has been paid to this crop, several mills being now in active operation. This industry, being new to most of the settlers, but gradually receives attention, but this very fact ensures its permanency, and with the large and ever increasing demand for "sweetening" this must in time take its place in the front rank of crops raised here.

The township is well watered by numerous lakes and streams, which diversify the scenery and help make the land valuable for agricultural purposes. First in order should be mentioned the lake bearing the name of Freeborn, which extends from Carlston township, in which a greater part of the lake lies, northward, and covers a few acres of land in section thirty-five, just south of the village of Freeborn. Lake George lies about one mile to the north, in sections twenty-six and twenty-seven. Still farther north, in sections eleven and fourteen, is located another small body of water, known as Spicer Lake. Trenton Lake covers quite an area in sections two and three, and extends northward into Waseca county. Another body of water known as Prairie Lake, is located in the extreme southwestern part of the town.

Two rivers known as the Big and Little Cobb Rivers, traverse the town from the southeast to the northwest, almost parallel, within about two miles of each other, and enter Faribault county.

The population of the town is mostly American, with a scattering of foreign element, less in number than almost any town in Freeborn county.

EARLY SETTLEMENT.

There is a preponderance of testimony that the first settlers in this township were T. K. Page and William Montgomery, who came from Dodge county, Wisconsin, and in July, 1856, located in section twenty-six and commenced improvements; the former erecting the first house, of logs. They remained several years, when they returned to their former homes.

About the same time, or possibly a little later in 1856, the next settlers, John W. Ayers and E. S. Dunn, made their appearance and secured farms in the northern part of the township, in sections two, three, and four. Mr. Ayers still resides upon his place, in prosperous circumstances, and Mr. Dunn remained upon his until 1857, when he removed to the southern part of the town, and in June took 320 acres of land in sections thirty-four and thirty-five, under the provisions of the law allowing it for town site purposes. He lived here until within the last year, when he removed to Missouri.

A little later in 1856, came Charles Giddings, Parker Page, and L. T. Scott, from Dodge county, Wisconsin, who all settled upon sections twenty-five and twenty-six. Mr. Giddings remained about six years, when he removed to Faribault, and from there to Blooming Prairie, Steele county, where he now lives. Mr. Page remained about eight years, when he went to his present home in Saline county, Nebraska, *via* Wisconsin. Mr. Scott still lives in the township, and is one of the most successful, as well as most prominent men. This party came with ox teams, bringing also a few cows.

Early in the summer of 1856, H. T. Sims and D. C. Davis had made their way into the town and secured homes. Sims located upon a tract of land in section ten, and lived there for a number of years; finally, in 1881, he quietly passed away, in the city of Albert Lea. Davis located upon a place in section two, which he improved and occupied for a time, and then removed to Waseca county.

October of 1856 witnessed the ingress of John Bostwick and William Purdie, from La Crosse county, Wisconsin, who took claims and settled to pioneer life. But two weeks of it, however, seemed to be sufficient, as they sold their provisions to the other settlers and left in disgust, for Wisconsin.

These are about all the pioneers who arrived and wintered this year. A few others had come, but they were merely transient, who staked a claim, now and then, and moved on to find their ideal spot elsewhere. The winter following, 1856-57, was very severe, and the settlers, not having had sufficient time to prepare for it, even had they imagined what they should have to pass through, necessarily fared badly. They were obliged to haul their provisions on hand sleds from Wilton, eighteen miles distant, through the deep snow and piercing cold, many of them not more than half clad, and slim shelter when the trip was over.

The year, or spring and summer following, witnessed many accessions to the meagerly settled township, and the greater part of the government land was claimed and settled by actual residents.

The winter of 1857-58 was not so severe as the preceding one, and the residents fared very well. Mr. L. T. Scott, on one occasion, about this time, made a trip to St. Nicholas, where he purchased a sack of flour for $5, of the hotel keeper. This season there had been no crops raised, and settlers depended mainly upon people coming in for supplies.

THE HONORED DEAD.

Ezra Stearns.—A settler who came in 1861, and converted a wild waste prairie into a blooming, cultivated, and prolific farm. He was injured two years before his death, which was on the 7th of February, 1879, at the age of 79 years. Mr. Stearns was from the old New England stock, his ancestors having come to Boston on the ship Arbella, with Gov. Winthrop, in 1630.

Squire Dunn, on the 7th of September, 1874, at the mellow age of 80, was at last confronted by by the grim messenger that had already visited almost the last one of his early companions. Claiming New Jersey for his nativity, at an early day he went to Albany, New York, and in 1841, to Wisconsin, and to Minnesota in 1854, making the first halt in Faribault, Rice county, and when this county was opened up came here. He had been married 55 years, and left quite a family, Mrs. George Whitman and Mrs. Dr. Bareck among them.

Nathan McQinney was born in Williston, Vermont, in 1820, and lived in the Green Mountain State until the year 1850, and then pushed on west as far as Dane county, Wisconsin. There he engaged in farming up to the year 1860, when he came to Minnesota and secured a place in Freeborn, but after a time took up his residence in the village and went into business, at one time with O. S. Gilmore. He was a kindhearted man, much respected. His last removal was from his earthly tenement on the 19th of April, 1879.

Mrs Charlotte Goward was born in Easton, Bristol county, Massachusetts, and was a daughter of William and Keziah Dean, who was married to Jason Goward in 1849, and has lived here since 1859. She was highly esteemed and was a woman of fine qualities, a devoted wife and mother, and a sincere friend. A very large concourse of people expressed their devotion by following her remains to their last resting place.

H. T. Sims was called hence on the 26th of February, 1881, at the age of 69. He was born in Salem county, New York, and lived forty-two years in that State. In 1854, he came west and stopped two years in Wisconsin, and then, in 1856, come over the Mississippi and located in the northern part of Freeborn township. After living there sixteen years he went to Itasca, and for a year or two lived in Albert Lea with his daughter, Mrs. Batchelder. At 30 years of age he was married to Miss Anna B. Moore. They had three children, two of whom are still living. He was noted for his purity of character, faithfulness to his engagements, and the generosity of his impulses. His house, in early days, was headquarters for ministers for preaching and religious services.

MATTERS OF INTEREST.

It is claimed that the first birth in the township occurred on the 12th of February, 1857, and ushered into the light of this world, George, a son of Mr. and Mrs. L. T. Scott.

The first marriage took place in August, 1858, and united the destinies of Mr. John Wood and Miss Emily Allen.

Early in the spring of the same year the grim and sorrow laden messenger of death lowered itself in the midst of sparsely settled Freeborn and carried away its first victim in the person of George C. Snyder.

Freeborn Grange No. 206.—The organization of this society took place in the latter part of May, 1874, at the schoolhouse in the village of Freeborn by Deputy F A. Elder, of the State Grange, with twenty-eight charter members. The officers were as foll Master, S. S. Challis; Lecturer, E. D. Rodgers, Overseer, L. T. Scott; Treasurer, P. M. Coon; Secretary, Ole. O. Simonsen; Chaplain, S. P. Purdie; Steward, J. Goward; Assistant Steward, D. A. Scoville; Gate Keeper, John A. Scoville; Lady Assistant Steward, Serena M. Cram; Flora, Caroline Scheen; Ceres, Amanda C. Purdie; and Pomona, Maggie A. Scoville. The Grange met once in two weeks in the schoolhouse until March, 1881, when it consolidated with the Carlston Grange, which is still in existence.

Trenton Post-office.—This office was established as early as 1858 and still continues, supplying quite an area with mail. John W. Ayers was the first and is the present Postmaster, with the office at his house in section three, near Trenton Lake, in the northern part of the township. The mail arrives once each week from Alden, by way of Freeborn.

RELIGIOUS.

Congregational Church—This edifice was erected in 1879, by the Baptist society, at a cost of $1,000, its size being about 26x40 feet. In 1880 the building was purchased by the Congregationalists, who now own it, and moved to its present location, about eighty rods east of the old site. The first pastor here was the Rev. Mr. Luce, the present is Rev. Wilbur Fisk.

Methodist Episcopal Church.—This building was erected in 1878, at a cost of $1,000, its size being 24x36 feet. The first pastor was the Rev. S. B. Smith.

Freeborn Cemetery Association Was originally organized in June, 1872, when the grounds were laid out containing six acres, just north of the village of Freeborn, in section thirty-five, the land being donated to the project by L. G. Pierce; it is well adapted by nature for a "last resting place," and the natural beauty has been enhanced by improvements, fencing, etc. The first buried here was of the remains of Mrs. E. S. Dunn, in 1858, some twelve years prior to the organization of the association.

There is also a cemetery located in the northern part of the town, in section eleven; which was set apart for burial purposes in 1862. The first person buried here was Norman Olin, and since the advent of his remains, a number, who have yielded to the irresistable call of death, have found their last earthly abode by his side, while many gleaming monuments rear their heads in perpetuation of the memory and virtues of the departed ones.

HISTORICAL SKETCH.

As a matter alike interesting to all who are at all concerned in what has, or is to be said of their home, we herewith present a short historical sketch of the township, prepared by D. G. Parker, President of the old settlers' Association, and read by him at their annual re-union in the spring of 1877. It is only proper to state that the matter was obtained by correspondence, and it is not improbable that errors have creptin. The sketch is published in the county papers as follows:

"FREEBORN was settled by T. K. Page and William Montgomery, in July, 1856. The former built a house of logs and opened a farm. The same season, being in advance of any other, Clark and West opened a small store in the winter of 1857-8, in the village, but left in the following spring. E. D. Rogers, a blacksmith, was the first mechanic. J. R. Giddings was the first lawyer, and located in 1860. In 1861 J. K. Moore offered his services as the first doctor. The first school was taught at the village in 'Squire Dunn's log house by Miss Emeline Allen, in the summer of 1857. The first schoolhouse was built by district No. 13, in the fall of 1858. In the same year L. T. Scott opened the ball-room of his hotel to Rev. Isaac Ling for the first religious service. In 1859 the Methodists perfected the first church organization, and in 1867 the Baptists built the first house of worship. The first title to land, according to the land office abstracts, was acquired by Nelson Everest, on section twenty-two, as early as the 9th of January, 1855, but as this was eighteen months before there was any settlement, it is believed to be an error of record. John Wood and Emeline Allen were the first parties married, and the ceremony was performed by E. S. Dunn, Esq., in 1858. The first child born was George F. Scott, February 14th, 1857. The first death was that of Emily Dunn, in the fall of 1858. L. T. Scott opened the first hotel and was the first Postmaster, the latter in the winter of 1857-58. C. D. Giddings, J. W. Ayers, and E. D. Rogers constituted the first board of Supervisors, and were elected, May 25th, 1858. John Wood, Clerk. The first board of school officers were J. S. Rickard, L. T. Scott, and C. D. Giddings."

GOVERNMENTAL.

The township of Freeborn came into existence as an official subdivision of the county, at a meeting held for the purpose of organization at the house of E. S. Dunn on the 11th of May, 1858. The meeting came to order and Charles D. Giddings was chosen moderator, and John Wood, clerk. After the usual preliminaries the polls were declared open for the election of officers for the ensuing year, which election resulted as follows: Supervisors, Charles D. Giddings, Chairman, E. D. Rogers, and John W. Ayers; Clerk, John Wood; Assessor, Thomas W. Purdie; Collector, John B. Purdie; Overseer of the poor, Joseph S. Rickard; Constables, John B. Purdie, and S. B. McGuire; Justices of the Peace, Edward Dunn and Henry Olin.

Public matters have progressed quietly and without interuption, the voters having been sufficiently careful to keep good, honest, and capable officers at the helm of the town affairs, and therefore there has been no useless waste of public money, or extravagance.

In 1865, during the rebellion, a special town meeting was help at which the sum of $1,800 was voted to pay men who should volunteer to enlist in the service and fill the quota assigned the town, the amount to be issued in bonds as directed by a committee for the purpose.

At the twenty-fourth annual town meeting, held in the spring of 1882, the following officers were elected, and are now in charge of the public business: Supervisors, L. T. Scott, Chairman, J. W. Ayers, and H. Stensrud; Clerk, J. Goward; Treasurer, O. S. Gilmore; Justices of the Peace, Geo. Miller and H. S. Olin; Assessor, J. B. Purdie; Constables, A. Andrews and C. Ayers.

It will be observed that some of the present officers were members of the first board elected in the town, at the meeting on the 11th of May, 1858.

STATISTICS.

FOR THE YEAR 1881.—Showing the acreage and

yield in the township of Freeborn, for the year named:

Wheat—3,214 acres, yielding 27,267 bushels.

Oats—595 acres, yielding 19,806 bushels.

Corn—495 acres, yielding 18,394 bushels.

Barley—122 acres, yielding 2,111 bushels.

Buckwheat—4 acres, yielding 35 bushels.

Potatoes—31 acres, yielding 2,856 bushels.

Beans—2 acres, yielding 13 bushels.

Sugar cane—17 acres, yielding 1,943 gallons.

Cultivated hay—18 acres, yielding 28 tons.

Flax-seed—233 acres, yielding 1,611 bushels.

Other produce—34 acres.

Total acreage cultivated in 1881, 4,763.

Wild hay—2,400 tons.

Timothy seed—172 bushels.

Apples—number of trees growing, 1,904; number bearing, 732; yielding 585 bushels.

Grapes—83 vines, yielding 123 younds.

Sheep—189 sheared, yielding 1,009 pounds of wool.

Dairy—202 cows, yielding 15,950 pounds of butter.

Hives of Bees—17, yielding 120 pounds of honey.

For the Year 1882.—It being two early in the season, at this writing, to procure the returns of threshing, we can only give the acreage sown this year in Freeborn:

Wheat, 2,039 acres; oats, 629; corn, 835; barley, 220; buckwheat, 5; potatoes, 33; beans, 14; sugar cane, 41; cultivated hay, 112; flax, 175; other produce, 42.

Total acreage cultivated in 1882, 4,145.

Apple trees growing, 2,076; bearing, 1,037; grave vines bearing, 106; milch cows, 206; sheep, 208, yielding 1,171 pounds of wool.

Farms cultivated in 1881, 69.

Forest trees planted and growing, 22 acres.

Population.—The census of 1870 gave Freeborn a population of 362. The last census, taken in 1880, reports 480 for this town; showing an increase of 118.

FREEBORN VILLAGE.

This is the only village in the township, and may be said to be the only one in this portion of the county; and, although as yet not large, it may, at almost any time, get a railroad which will connect it with the outer world, and commence an expansion which will bring it into prominent notice, as it has an excellent location for a village, and is surrounded by some of the most productive farming lands in the county. It is located in the south-eastern part of the town, in sections thirty-four and thirty-five, on the north bank of Freeborn Lake.

The land upon which the village stands was claimed for town site purposes in June, 1857, by E. S. Dunn, who had arrived in the township the year previous and located in the northern part, and the village was platted the same year.

It is claimed that the first store was started in the winter of 1857-58, by Clark & West, and in the spring following were succeeded by Jason Goward, who may be said to have opened the first substantial store, as he put in a fair stock of general merchandise, which he continued to manage for about ten years. In 1861, another store was opened, by the Southwick Brothers, which is still in active operation.

Freeborn Post-Office.—This office was originally established in 1857, with L. T. Scott as Postmaster, on the site of the village of Freeborn. In 1858, Mr. J. Goward was commissioned Postmaster, and the mail was received once each week, *via* the Mankato and Otronto, Iowa, mail route, Henry Lacy being the mail carrier. In 1867 J. Goward resigned and David Southwick received the appointment, holding the same for about three years, when A. Munn took the mail pouch keys and continued in the capacity of Postmaster until the year 1876 rolled around, when he relieved the usual monotony of affairs by committing suicide. His principal bondsman, J. Goward, took charge of the office, and removed it to the store of T. A. Southwick, who received the appointment of deputy, and in a few weeks was made Postmaster, which position he still occupies. Mail arrives daily from Alden, and supplies the Trenton Post-office with mail matter.

At the present writing a *resume* of what the village contains, would read something like this:—two general stores by M. A. Southwick and O. S. Gillmore; a black-smith shop by D. A. Scoville; a wagon repair shop, by J. H. Clarke; broom factory by L. T. Scott; shoemaking shop by A. Andrews. And a population, it is said, of about one hundred.

MEDIUMS OF EDUCATION.

The territory of Freeborn is divided, for educational purposes, into five school districts, with numbers and locations of houses as follows; No.

11, with schoolhouse in section four; No. 12, in section twenty-three; No. 13, in Freeborn village; No. 98, in section one; No. 101, in section twenty-eight. The districts are all in good condition, and under careful management, having good buildings and moderate attendance. A short sketch of the various districts is herewith presented:

District No. 11.—Effected the first organization in the township in 1857, and school was first held in a house 12x14, in section three, taught by Miss Normand Olin, to an attendance of about twelve scholars. In 1860 a schoolhouse was constructed in section three, size 20x24 feet, at a cost of $350, and in this school is still held, although in 1874 it was removed to the eastern part of section four, remodeled and partly rebuilt at a cost of $400.

District No. 12.—It is claimed that this educational subdivision did not arrive to the dignity of an organization until 1865, and soon afterward a building was purchased for $50 to be used for school purposes. The first school was taught by Miss Minnie Caswell with an attendance of twelve pupils. In 1870, the school edifice now in use was constructed at a cost of about $400, size 16x20 feet. The last term of school was instructed by Miss Nellie Scott, there being an attendance of twenty-eight pupils. The schoolhouse is located in the northeastern corner of section twenty-three.

District No. 13.—This is the district embracing the village of Freeborn and immediately surrounding country. The organization was effected in 1858, and the first term of school was held at the private residence of E. S. Dunn, on the site of the present village, shortly afterward being taught by Mr. Joel Southwick, with an attendance of ten scholars. The school was held in private houses for about two years when a little shanty twelve feet square was erected, costing about $20, and three years later another school building was substituted, size 20x30 feet, at a cost of $700. In 1876, the latter structure was dispensed with and the present neat and commodious schoolhouse was built at a cost of $1,500, size 30x40 feet, two stories high, and the finest schoolhouse in the township. The district has lately been organized into a graded school, employing two teachers, and is one of the most effectual educational mediums in the county. George Latin was the last principal, and the average attendance amounted to about sixty.

District No. 98.—Effected an organization in 1872. The first school was taught by Mrs. Mattie B. Frisby in the residence of R. D. Burdick in section one, with an attendance of twelve pupils. In 1873, the schoolhouse was erected in the south-western part of section one, size 16x24 feet, at a cost of $350. The last term was taught by Miss Ellen Roland.

District No. 101.—This district effected an organization in the spring of 1876, and the same year erected their schoolhouse in section twenty-eight, size 18x22 feet, at a cost of $450. The first teacher was Miss Emily Blighton, with an attendance of ten scholars. The last teacher was Miss Abby Chase, to an attendance of nine.

BIOGRAPHICAL.

Russell D. Burdick was born in New York on the 27th of January, 1830. He attended the common schools near his home, and afterward an academy in Madison county. In 1855, he came West to Dane county, Wisconsin, and two years later married Miss Luransa Champlin, also a native of New York. They have had four children, one of whom died on the 4th of May, 1876. In 1865, Mr. Burdick brought his family to this place and has since made it his home, his farm being located in section one of this township. He was one of the organizers of his school district and has since been one of its officers. In religious belief he is a Seventh Day Baptist.

Alfred Crandall is a native of Rhode Island, born on the 14th of April, 1814. When an infant he removed with his parents to a farm in Madison county, New York, and at the early age of twelve years left home and began working for his own support. When twenty-two years of age he moved to Massachusetts and found employment in wagon shops. In 1840, he married Miss Almira Day, a native of New York. They came to Dane county, Wisconsin, in 1846, and to this place in 1863. For ten years Mr. Crandall had charge of different mail routes from Freeborn, going to Geneva, to Owatonna, to Albert Lea, and from the latter place to Waseca. He is one of the old and respected citizens, and has been instrumental in the organization and growth of the place. His farm contains two hundred acres. Mr. and Mrs. Crandall have a family of eleven children.

Francis D. Drake was born in Cortland county,

New York, on the 2d of November, 1833. When thirteen years old he came with his parents to Dane county, Wisconiin, where they lived on a farm. He was married in 1858, to Miss Alma Richmond, and they have a family of seven children. At the outbreak of the war Mr. Drake enlisted in the Seventh Wisconsin Volunteer Infantry, Company C; in March, 1862, joined the Army of the Potomac under General Grant, and took part in the battles of Pittsburg Landing, Shiloh, and several other important ones. He was honorably discharged in 1864, and returned to his home in Wisconsin. In 1867, he came to this township and bought a farm of two hundred and eighty acres, to which he has since added, and it is now well improved. He is the father of seven children.

CHARLES H. DERBY, another native of the Empire State, was born in Otsego county on the 7th of October, 1832. When ten years old he removed with his parents to Pennsylvania, where they resided until 1854, then came to La Crosse county, Wisconsin, but the same year went to Virginia. In the latter year Mr. Derby was united in wedlock with Miss Harriet E. St. John, a native of New York. They have been blessed with three children. In 1857, he returned with his wife to Wisconsin, and soon after moved to St. Paul. He has been a prominent resident of this place since 1863, owning a well cultivated farm of two hundred and forty acres.

STEPHEN FULLER, one of the pioneers of this place, is a native of Orange county, Vermont, born on the 2d of May, 1828. He attended the common schools in Vershire, his native town, completing his education at the Thetford Academy, and afterward taught school for several years in Vermont and New Hampshire. In 1852 he married Miss Luvia M. Carpenter, also a native of that State, by whom he had three children. They came west in 1859, and located a farm in sections fourteen and twenty-three, where Mr. Fuller has since devoted his time. His wife died in 1861, and he has since married Miss Elizabeth M. Anghenbaugh, of Freeborn. They have a family of four children.

SAMUEL J. FULLER was also born in Vershire, Orange county, Vermont, his birth dating the 15th of July, 1834. He assisted his father on the farm until twenty years old when he entered the academy known as the New London Literary and Scientific Institution, at New London, New Hampshire, where he took a scientific course, learning the theory of surveying and civil engineering, which, however, he never practiced. In the fall of 1856, he emigrated to Keokuk, Iowa; the winter following taught school in the old Mormon town of Nauvoo, Illinois. The following spring he became one of the pioneers of Freeborn, and staked out a claim in sections twenty-three and twenty-four which has since been his home, dividing his attention between farming and school teaching. He was married in 1865, to Miss Sarah A. Turner, a native of New York, and they have been blessed with two children, both boys. Mr. Fuller served three years in the army. He has been a member of the board of Supervisors several terms and Clerk of his school district for the past twelve years.

REV. WILBUR FISK was born in Sharon, Windsor county, Vermont, on the 7th of June, 1839. He is the son of a farmer and arrived at manhood in his native place. In 1861, he enlisted for three years in the Second Regiment Vermont Volunteer Infantry, Company E; went South, joined the army of the Potomac, and re-enlisted as a veteran before his first term had expired; was in active service with that army till the close of the war. In July, 1865, he received an honorable discharge, having served nearly four years, including six months off duty on account of sickness. He was married to Miss Angelina S. Drew, of Tunbridge, Vermont, and in September, 1865, they removed to a farm he had purchased in Kansas. Mr. Fisk was here led to commence ministerial labors in his own and contiguous neighborhoods. In 1875, he received an invitation to come to this place and devote his whole time to the work of the ministry, which call he accepted. He was ordained and installed pastor of the Congregational Church of Freeborn on the 13th of June, 1876. His labor is under the auspices of the American Home Missionary Society of the Congregational denomination, and his field includes, with Freeborn, places in Hartland, New Richland, and Lemond. He has four children living and one buried in Kansas.

ORVILLE S. GILMORE was born in Ripton, Addison county, Vermont, on the 17th of February, 1844. He resided at home until the age of eighteen years, then enlisted in the army and served six months. In the fall of 1865, he came to Dane county, Wisconsin, from whence he soon after came to Freeborn county, and located in Freeborn township. In 1871, he came to the village of Freeborn, and for two years clerked in the store of T. A. Southwick, then bought out the business of A. A. Munn, deceased, and has since conducted it, having a good trade. On the 29th of September, 1874, Mr. Gilmore was married to Miss Jennie E. Leonard, and they have three children. He has held several local offices and is now Treasurer of the town and also of the school district in which he resides. He is a member of the M. E. Church. His father was born in Bristol, Vermont, in 1802, and now resides with him.

JASON GOWARD was born in Croydon, New Hampshire, on the 19th of November, 1820, and lived with and worked for his father on his farms until arriving at the age of twenty-one. He then began for himself, working at different occupations for two years; then went south to Acton, Massachusetts, where he engaged to carry on a sash and blind factory, buying the same after three years. In 1849, he married Miss Charlos Dean, who bore him five children. In 1852, he sold out his business in the latter place and made a trip to California where he engaged in mining two and a half years. He experienced all kinds of luck, at some times being worth several thousand dollars and at other times several hundred worse than nothing, the latter being occasioned by a protracted illness. On his return to his native State, he located on a farm which he purchased previous to going west. In September, 1857, he sold his lands and the following spring came to this section of the country. After a two weeks sojourn at McGregor, Iowa, he started for the northern part of that State and southern Minnesota and while at Brownsdale in Mower county, he made the acquaintance of a Mr. Bigelow and his son-in-law, in company with whom he bought a yoke of oxen and wagon, supplied themselves well with provisions and started west with high hopes of future success. They drove to Freeborn, a distance of thirty miles, in four days, and Mr. Goward staked out a claim in section twenty-five. He immediately erected a small frame dwelling and then returned for his family. In July, 1858, he opened a store which he carried on for ten years, during all of which time he was Postmaster. He now owns about eight hundred acres of farming land in the county and is also interested in the coal and gypsum mines. He was one of the leading men in the organization of the first schools in this place, and has held nearly all the local offices, having for the past eight years filled the office of Town Clerk. Many of the old settlers remember Mr. and Mrs. Goward (the latter of whom is lying in the Freeborn cemetery, having died on the 29th of March, 1882) with gratitude for the aid rendered by them during hard times in 1859.

JOHN G. HARRISON was born in Derbyshire, England, on the 18th of March, 1827. When he was an infant his parents moved to Liverpool and in 1837 came to America and located in Canada West, Durham county, where they were pioneers. They returned to England in 1840, remained four years and then came to this country, settling in Dane county, Wisconsin. In 1851, Mr. Harrison was joined in marriage with Miss Mary J. Pierce and they have six children. He became one of the pioneers of this place in 1857, having been to the State two years previous residing one of the years in Iowa. Immediately after coming here he staked out a claim in section twelve, which has since been his home.

NELS HANSSON, a native of Denmark, was born on the 11th of January, 1845. When twenty-two years old he joined the army and served eighteen months, receiving at the end of time, an honorable discharge. In 1870, he came to America and located in Indianapolis, Indiana, where he was engaged in the blacksmith trade for about ten years. He was married in 1874, to Miss Christina Hanson, also a native of Denmark. The result of the union is two children. They came to this place in 1880, and own a farm in section twenty-six.

JAMES HANSEN, one of the first Danish settlers of this place, dates his birth the 7th of January, 1837. At the age of nineteen years he came to America and resided in Wisconsin until 1862, when he enlisted in the Eighth United States Infantry, Company D, and served three years. He then returned to Wisconsin, and in 1867, came to Minnesota and bought a farm in this township, remaining three years. He returned to Wisconsin and Miss Augusta Dorn, a native of Germany, since which time his farm has been their home. They have a family of five children.

OLE JOHNSSON was born in Norway, near Bergen, on the 4th of October, 1835. He reached his majority in his native country, and in 1849, married Isabelle Johnson and the issue of the union is eleven children. They emigrated to America in 1861, and first settled in Dane county, Wisconsin, where he carried on a farm for ten years. In 1871, he moved to Minnesota and has since been one of the respected and industrious farmers of this place.

HENRY S. OLIN, one of the early settlers of Freeborn, was born in Chenango county, New York, on the 12th of July, 1829. When but twelve years of age he began to learn the carpenter and joiner's trade which he followed in his early life. In 1852, he moved to Illinois, and in November, 1856, to Wisconsin, in both of which places he worked at his trade. He was joined in marriage in 1856, with Miss Annie P. Crandall, who was born in Madison county, New York. They have a family of three children. Mr. Olin came to this place in 1857, and has a good farm of two hundred and sixty acres. He has been Justice of the Peace and held other town and school offices since his residence here.

THOMAS W. PURDIE, a native of Scotland, was born near Glasgow, on the 3d of September, 1828. When he was five years old his parents moved to America and settled in St. Lawrence county, New York, where he reached his majority. In 1848 he came to Wisconsin, and in 1857 to Minnesota, taking a claim in section twenty-five, Freeborn township. He was married in 1860 to Miss Tilley L. Crandall, a native of New York. Mr. Purdie was one of the first County Commissioners, first Town Clerk, and in 1859, and again in 1877, was elected to the State Legislature. He is the father of four children.

JOHN B. PURDIE was also born near Glasgow, Scotland, his birth dating the 24th of March, 1830. He came with his parents to America, resided in St. Lawrence county, New York, and afterward in Wisconsin where he was engaged in agricultural pursuits. In 1855 he made a trip to Kansas, remained a short time, and returned to Wisconsin and two years later came to Minnesota, locating a claim in section twenty-five, in this township. He was married in 1865 to Miss Amanda C. Augtrendaveb, a native of Pennsylvania. The issue of the union is one child. Mr. Purdie was the first constable of this place and has filled other offices of trust.

NOYES P. STILLMAN was born in Cattaraugus county, New York. When he was an infant his parents moved to Michigan, and three years later to Dane county, Wisconsin, where they were engaged in farming. They came to Freeborn township in 1862, where Noyes was engaged with his father on a farm until he became of age, then returned to Wisconsin and entered Albion Academy, from which he graduated in 1869, and afterward taught in the institution. He returned to this place in 1871, and has since taught twenty terms of school, at the same time carrying on his farm, which is in section one. In 1874, Miss Emma Benjamin, of Newport, Vermont, became his wife. She has borne him two children; Gertie Maud and Edith May.

JOHN A. SCHOEN, an early resident of this place is a native of Germany, born on the 2d of January, 1829. He came to America in 1852, and for five years lived in New York City, marrying, in 1856, Miss Caroline Herold, a native of Switzerland. In 1857, they came to Minnesota, and took a claim in this township but after two years returned to New York. He subsequently resided in Wisconsin, and in 1865 enlisted in the army, went south and joined the army of the Potomac, receiving an honorable discharge after a service of six months. Mr. Schoen always takes an active part in school and local matters. He is the father of five children.

GEORGE SEATH, one of the old citizens, is a native of Scotland, and dates his birth the 15th of October, 1833. When he was quite young he came with his parents to America, and for one year lived in New York City. The family then moved to Delaware county, and on the 9th of February, 1858, George married Miss Phœbe Larribee. He came to this township in 1861, taking a claim in section twenty-seven, which has since been his home. Mr. and Mrs. Seath have five children.

FRIETZ TACK was born in northern Prussia, on the 15th of April, 1849, and arrived at manhood's estate in his native country. He was joined in wedlock, in 1867, with Miss Mary Shodenberg. The issue of the marriage is two children. In 1869, Mr. Tack emigrated with his family to America and was a resident of Milwaukee eleven years, engaged in the lumber business. In 1882 he came to this place, where he resides with his widowed mother, his father having died a year previous to their coming. They have a good home, the farm being located in section twenty-six and is well cultivated.

FREEMAN.

CHAPTER LX.

TOPOGRAPHY AND LOCATION—EARLY SETTLEMENT—DECEASED PIONEERS — OFFICIAL RECORDS—STATISTICS — RELIGIOUS —SCHOOLS—BIOGRAPHICAL.

This one of the southern tier towns of Freeborn county, lying contiguous to Iowa on the south; and the townships of Albert Lea, Shell Rock, and Nunda, respectively, on the north, east, and west. It is a full congressional township, the greater part of which is under an admirable state of cultivation, as a glance at the statistics will show.

The surface of the township is considerably broken and inclined, in places, to be very hilly although there are no bluffs, and but few places so abrupt as to be detrimental to agriculture. There are also numerous sloughs dotting the prairie, which form the only obstruction to cultivation to be found, and many of these are valuable for hay and grazing. A good deal of small timber is found, and it might be said the greater part of the area is jack and burr oak opening land, although very open, with prairie and natural meadows interspersed. The main body of timber is in the central part.

The soil is variable, but in the greater portion of the town is of a rich dark loam, although not unfrequently a locality is passed where the sand and clay are visible.

The water courses of this town are all sluggish and small affairs, there being only one which is as yet dignified upon the map with a name. This is Goose Creek, which rises west of the boundary and enters by way of section eighteen, then taking a southeasterly course passes through Grass Lake and leaves for Iowa. Another small stream rises in the northern part and flows southeasterly across the northeast corner of the town. Several small streams flow into Grass Lake, but have no names, and in the low country are liable to change their courses.

Grass Lake is a body of water located in the corners of the four southeastern sections in the township. It is a sloughy concern, and is surrounded by such a low, wet and marshy country, that it is impossible to get to it; in fact, it is said that the entire southeastern part of Freeborn has *never been explored!*

Therere are no villages in the township. The Minneapolis and St. Louis railroad enters and crosses the northeastern corner, and the B. C. & N. railway line crosses the northwestern corner.

EARLY SETTLEMENT.

The early settlement and initiatory steps which led to the founding and subsequent development of this thriving township, in common with the majority of Freeborn county's subdivisions, dates back well into the fifties. Its early pioneers and hardy civilizers were not adventurers who came here merely for speculation, nor were they men who expected or even hoped to accumulate a fortune in a day; but men who knew there would be trials and hardships to endure, while the first few years of their existence here must be almost a hermitage. And they were not mistaken, as those who can retrace the steps of memory to actual experience will testify, while those without having passed through it can never know.

It is claimed that Freeman township had received a settler as early as 1854; this statement is made in a sketch of the history of the township published in the Albert Lea papers in 1877, and prepared by Mr. Parker, president of the Old Settlers' Association, and Mr. Botsford. But for the edification of our readers we will publish the sketch *verbatim*, to-wit:

"The first settler in this town was Ole Olenhouse, who made his claim as early as the summer of 1854, and was probably the first settler in the county.

Jacob Hostetter acquired the first title to land, which occurred on the 19th of June, 1856. He was the first mechanic, and worked as a carpenter.

Sarah White, in 1859, taught the first school, the same being held in the dwelling-house of Joseph Shaw. The first parties married were Louis B. Probetin and Libbie Banning, in 1857, the ceremony being performed by William Andrews, Esq. The first child born was in 1857, and connected with the Olenhouse family. The first death was that of Mrs. Wadsworth, who died in 1860."

Where the above information came from we know not, and, therefore, will make no comment upon it; but will commence the story of early settlement, as we get it from the most reliable and oldest settlers now living.

Among the early settlers, not the first in the township, was John Freeman, in whose honor the town received the name it bears. He was born in Northamptonshire, England, in the year 1805. In 1855, he came to Minnesota, and direct to this township, where he secured, under the pre-emption law, the whole of section fifteen for himself and three sons. After living in a tent for several months he erected the log house in which he now lives, the logs being cut from poplar trees, and covered with what was termed a "shake roof," *i. e.*, clapboards cut from oak timber. The log house is in a good state of preservation, and under the third roofing. Three of Mr. Freeman's sons are yet in the town, and one is on the Pacific coast.

The above statement is disputed by some, as to his being the first, and we give all sides a hearing by producing the statement. John Oldinghouse [or Olenhouse] was a native of Germany, having lately sojourned for a time in Wisconsin, rrrived in Freeman township in the summer of 1855, with his family, and squatted upon section twelve, where he dug a hole in the ground and covering it with poles and hay, spent the winter here. The following year he pulled up stakes and removed to section twenty-four, and this point is probably the hinge leading to the error into which many settlers have fallen in thinking the date of his settlement in section twenty-four was identical with that of his arrival; for in early days, his original place in section twelve was considered in the town east of this, or the Shell Rock settlement.

Olenhouse erected a shanty upon his new farm and made improvements, remaining there about two years, when he with his family removed to Kansas, where he died soon after his arrival, from the effects of an exposure which affected his brain.

In the fall, a man named Mr. Oliver Diamond, arrived and constituted the next settler. He was a native of Vermont, and located in the same section with Oldinghouse (24,) where, among other improvements, he erected a log house, 16x22 feet, which still stands, although rather delapidated and unoccupied, a remembrance of 'ye olden time', Diamond did not remain long and sold to Charles Grim who still lives on the place.

About the same time in 1855, Jacob Hostetter, a Pennsylvania German, who came direct from Ohio, *via* Wisconsin, settled with his wife, four daughters, and two boys, upon section one. He erected a log house and commenced improvements which he continued for fifteen or sixteen years, and then sold to Mr. Nelson who is yet on the place. Mr. Hostetter now resides in the township of Albert Lea.

The spring following the arrival of Hostetter, in March, 1856, Christian Blas, a German, arrived, and being a single man, commenced keeping "batch," upon the claim he secured in section twenty-two, the present Joseph Lang place, and remained here for a couple of years when he returned to Illinois from whence he came.

William Edwards, from England originally, but late from Beaver Dam, Wisconsin, arrived on foot in Freeman township on the 20th of September, 1856, and took a claim in section twenty-four, where he commenced improvements, boarding in the meantime with Oliver Diamond. His claim was jumped shortly afterwards by a Mr. Finch, and he took a place in section twenty-two; but finally, in 1857, sold that and took the place he now occupies in section three.

Just before Christmas, in 1856, a couple of Germans, Charles Bessinger and Phillip Herman, late from Canada, made their appearance and selected homes. Chas. Bessinger selected his domain in section nine and lived there several years, when he sold to his brother, Morris Bessinger, who yet owns the place. Phillip Herman planted his stakes upon a fine track of land in section thirteen where he yet holds forth.

The first of that small but determined army of the natives of Norway, arrived shortly afterward in the person of Lars Nelson, who declared himself at rest upon a farm in section twenty-three, and he has since been joined by enough of his countrymen to declare a majority of the inhabitants of the town.

PIONEERS DECEASED.

JOSEPH LANG was born in Glasgow, Scotland, on the 25th of July, 1799. When 23 he married miss Jeannette Lockhard, and seven years thereafter came to Canada, and in 1856 to Freeborn County, and planted himself in the township of Freeman where he spent the remainder of his life until finally transplanted to the mystic realm on the 11th of April, 1875. He was a member of the Presbyterian Church and left a wife and seven children.

MISS JOSIE LANG came with her parents when they settled in Shell Rock, and afterwards removed to Freeman. She was a dutiful daughter, affectionate sister, and a worthy member of society, and her name should have a place among Freeman's honored dead. The future life, with its hopes, promises, and possibilities, was opened up for her on the 10th of June, 1881.

PARTON GREENE was born in Rhode Island on the 15th of May, 1795. His parents removed to New York State in 1805. In 1817, he located in Erie county, and remained there until 1855, when he came and procured a farm in Freeman where, at the age of four score and three, he, on the 15th of May, 1878, was gathered as a sheaf fully ripe. He never married, but was industrious, sober, and enjoyed uniform good health, always preferring to walk rather than ride, having thus made a journey to Albert Lea a few days before his death.

EARLY EVENTS.

FIRST BIRTHS.—The first event of this kind to transpire occurred in 1857, and ushered into this reputed world of sorrow, Matilda Oldinghouse, whose parents resided in the town. Another early birth was that of a son of Oliver and Emily Diamond, it is claimed late in 1856.

FIRST MARRIAGE.—This took place in March, 1858, and joined by the holy ties of wedlock, Mr. W. Wadsworth and Miss Sarah Freeman.

DEATH.—It is claimed that the first death in the township carried away George W. Wadsworth, a son of the parties who were first married in the town. The child was nine months old.

OFFICIAL RECORDS.

This town effected an organization as a local government at a meeting held on the 2d of April, 1861, at the house now occupied by William Freeman, by the election of the following officers: Supervisors, B. H. Carter, Chairman, William H. Moore, and Lars Nelson; Clerk, W. Wadsworth; Treasurer, Henry Eaton; Assessor, William Eaton; School Superintendent, J. E. Marvin. After this meetings were held for four years in the same house, and then the schoolhouses were brought into requisition.

The present officers are as follows: Supervisors, Ole Opdahl, Chairman, Robert Freeman, and Ole Anderson; Clerk, W. Wadsworth; Treasurer, O. K. Flaskerud; Assessor, E. K. Flaskerud; Justice of the Peace, Andrew Lang. Another Justice was elected, but he stubbornly refused to qualify or have anything to do with it, so, as expressed by a citizen, "his place was easily filled by leaving it vacant."

The matters pertaining to the public welfare have been well and ably managed, nothing having transpired to disturb the usual tranquility of such business.

STATISTICS.

From various reports we have compiled the following statistics, showing the agricultural resources, the values, and the products of the township:

FOR THE YEAR 1881.—Showing acreage and yield in the township of Freeman for the year named:

Wheat—4,090 acres, yielding 48,160 bushels.
Oats—707¾ acres, yielding 23,239 bushels.
Corn—785 acres, yielding 27,409 bushels.
Barley——50 acres, yielding 951 bushels.
Potatoes—55¾ acres, yielding 3,603 bushels.
Sugar cane—1 acre, yielding 117 gallons.
Cultivated hay—37 acres, yielding 38 tons.
Total acreage cultivated in 1881, 5,730 acres.
Wild hay gathered—2,695 tons.
Timothy seed—15 bushels.
Apple trees growing—1,317.
Trees bearing—117.
Apples—179 bushels.
Grape vines bearing—5.
Grapes—50 pounds.
Sheep sheared—107.
Wool—481 pounds.

Milch cows—398, yielding 27,115 pounds of butter.

Hives of bees—5.

FOR THE YEAR 1882.—Wheat, 3,371 acres; oats, 849; corn, 1,219½; barley, 88; potatoes, 58½; beans, 1½; sugar cane, 1¾; cultivated hay, 69½. Total acreage cultivated in 1882, 5,668¾.

Apple trees—growing, 1,198; bearing, 449; grape vines bearing, 53; milch cows, 384; sheep, 124, yielding 457 pounds of wool.

Forest trees planted and growing—3 acres.

POPULATION.—The census of 1870 gave Freeman a population of 604. The last census, taken in 1880, reports 772 for this town. Showing an increase of 168.

RELIGIOUS.

Freeman has two church organizations, each having neat and valuable buildings. The total cost of church buildings in the town amounts to about $2,750. The total number of members of the two organizations is about 350. The churches are about one mile apart.

The first religious services were held on the 8th of October, 1861, by Rev. Walter Scott. It was held at the house of Mr. W. Wadsworth, upon the occasion of the obsequies of his deceased son.

NORWEGIAN LUTHERAN CHURCH.—This is located in the northeastern part of section twenty-one. It was erected in 1874 at a cost of $1,350, but in the summer of 1880, it was reduced to an almost entire wreck by a severe wind storm which did considerable damage throughout this county. It was rebuilt, however, the same year, and now stands on the old site, in good condition, a monument to the public spirit and enterprise of the builders. The first pastor of this temple of worship was Rev. T. A. Torgeson, and through the earnest efforts of this good and sincere gentleman, prosperity shed its bright rays upon the small band of worshipers, until its membership increased to two hundred. After about two years a change of pastors was made and Rev. J. Mosby was installed. The present pastor is Rev. S. B. Hustuet.

There is a cemetery ground in connection with the church of this society, which was laid out about the time the building was erected.

LUTHERAN CHURCH.—Belonging to the Norsk Dansk Conference, is located in the northwestern part of section sixteen. It was erected in 1878 at a cost of $1,400, being a neat and commodious building, equal to any in this part of the county. The church society has been very successful and efficient in its labors, for it now numbers as followers of its faith about one hundred and fifty members. There is also a cemetery ground connected with this church.

SCHOOLS.

Educational facilities in Freeman are at least at par with a majority of the towns, both in numerical strength and in efficiency. The territory of the town for this purpose is divided into five districts, which, if divided equally, would give an area of a little over six square miles to each district. The numbers and location of schoolhouses in the various districts are shown in the short sketch of each which is below presented.

DISTRICT NO 46.—Effected an organization in 1862, and the first term of school was taught by Orfa Skinner at the residence of William Eaton, with seventeen scholars present. Shortly afterward a schoolhouse was constructed in the southern part of section three at a cost of $600, equipped with common furniture and the necessary apparatus. The attendance has grown from the first, and at present, instead of seventeen, the rolls show about thirty.

DISTRICT NO 44.—The first school in this district was taught in 1865, at the residence of Swan Anson, by Miss Altha Young, with eighteen juveniles on the benches. This was about, or shortly after the district effected an organization. School was held in private houses after this until 1873, when a building was decided upon and the schoolhouse now in use was constructed, at a cost of about $125, in which Miss Mary Buchanan first called school to order, with an average attendance of twenty-two. The location of the schoolhouse is the center of section sixteen.

DISTRICT NO. 48.—The first school in this educational locality was taught by Mrs. W. H. Moore with an attendance of thirty scholars. In 1873, a good and substantial school structure was erected, at a cost of $800, being well furnished and well kept. The present attendance of the school is about forty pupils. The district embraces the territory in the southwestern part of the town, with the schoolhouse in the northwestern part of section thirty-two.

DISTRICT NO. 65.—It is claimed that the first school taught in this township was in this district, although at that time it was unorganized. This first school was taught in Charles Grims' house, in the winter of 1862, by Mr. Charles Grim, with an attendance of fifteen pupils. This district effected an organization and continued holding school in private residences until 1870, when a school house 16x20 was erected in the north-eastern part of section twenty-three, which is still in use. The first school in this district was taught by Miss Jemima Blighton, with an attendance of twenty pupils; the average attendance has now increased to thirty.

DISTRICT No. 66.—This district embraces the territory in the northwestern part of Freeman with a schoolhouse located in section six, which was erected in 1867, at a cost of $150. The first school therein was taught by Miss S. Carter, with an attendance of fifteen pupils. The average attendance has gradually increased, and is now about twenty-four.

BIOGRAPHICAL.

OLE A. BERGDOL was born in Norway, and when twenty years old he emigrated to America with his parents, his father dying with lung fever while on the ocean. The remainder of the family located in Dane county, Wisconsin, and after five years experience in farming in that place came here and purchased his present farm of two hundred and forty acres, most of which is now under cultivation. In 1872 he went to Northwood, Iowa, and purchased two hundred and twenty acres of land, and remained there two years. He was married in 1872 to Miss Betsy Johnson, and they have one child, a daughter, aged eight years. Mr. Bergdol's mother was killed by a stroke of lightning, at the age of sixty-nine years. She is buried in the Norwegian Evangelical Lutheran cemetery at this place.

WILLIAM FREEMAN was born in Northampton, England, on the 1st of August, 1832. At the age of thirteen years he was obliged to depend upon his own resources, and for some time he lived with Henry Follett, brother of Sir John Follett, of London. In 1852 he came to America, engaged in farming four years near Rutland, Vermont, and then came to Illinois, thence, in a short time, to Minnesota. He located on his present farm, first living in a tent, but soon after erected his house, which has been improved, and now has the third roof. His farm contains one hundred and sixty acres and is well improved, having a grove of oak timber and a very fine orchard. It is centrally located, convenient to two churches, and altogether is a very desirable home.

ROBERT FREEMAN was born in Northampton, England, on the 18th of March, 1841, and when when fourteen years old came to America and engaged in farming near Castleton, Rutland county, Vermont. In 1857 he came west to Illinois, located in Kaneville, Kane county, where he remained one year, and came to Minnesota, pre-empting his present land in sections eleven and four, Freeman township. In 1862 he returned to Illinois, where he remained twelve years, and in 1874 married Miss Louisa Nelson, coming again to his farm in this place the following year. They have three children, John P., Edna B., and Alice, an infant. Mr. Freeman is a member of the Town and School boards.

OLE K. FLASKERUD was born near Christiania, Norway, on the 29th of August, 1843. In 1866, he came to America, and after spending some time in Calmar, Iowa, removed to this county, locating near Twin Lakes, in Nunda, and purchased forty acres of land, on which he made some improvements. In 1868, he went to Otter Tail county, purchased land near Fergus Falls, but in 1875, came to this place and bought a quarter of section twenty-seven. He was married to Miss Mary Jacobson, who has borne him four children, two of whom are dead. Those living are, Karl Johan and Anna. Mr. Flaskerud has been Town Treasurer three successive years, and has also held other local offices. His father and mother died in Norway, being quite aged.

ERIK K. FLASKERUD was born on the 20th of July, 1841, near Christiania, Norway, and received a good education, learning the shoemaker's trade in his native country. In 1869, he was married to Miss Caroline Stromsod, of Norway, and the same year they emigrated to America, remained for awhile in Iowa, and then came to this State, locating on his present farm of one hundred and sixty acres in this township, section twenty-one. His parents died in the old country at an advanced age. Mr. Flaskerud has always taken an interest in church, school, and town affairs, having been Clerk of his school district ten successive years, assessor three years, and Town Treasurer three years. His children are; Christian, Theodore, Olive, Anna, Inger Mary, and Edward.

CHARLES GRIM is a Prussian, born near Gorlitz

in the province of Saxony, on the 22d of February, 1824, and grew to manhood in his native country. In 1854, he came to America, and for two years was engaged in a sugar factory in Memphis, Tennessee; removed to Davenport, Iowa, and thence to Minnesota, locating on section one in Nunda township. He soon sold his claim there, however, and for three years worked on neighboring farms, then purchased two hundred and forty acres of land in this township, section twenty-four. In 1859, he married Miss Catharine Beighley, of Pennsylvania, and they have had six children, four of whom are living; Ada M., Rosa S., Georgiana B., and George W. Mr. Grim's mother died in Prussia in 1860, aged seventy-two years, and his father, Gottlieb Grim, was in the war of 1812, and continued in service nearly twenty years. He was at one time taken prisoner with five others, and after several days of fasting, they finally made their escape, some one from the outside making an opening in the cellar in which they were confined. After nine days wandering, their only food being sour sorrel, they all died but Mr. Grim, who recovered from his exposure, but only lived a few years, then found an early grave, which is kept green in memory by his son Charles.

GEORGE HYATT was born in Cayuga county, New York, on the 5th of July, 1832, and at an early age removed with his parents to Oswego county, near Hannibal Centre, where he received his education and grew to manhood. In 1855, he removed to Yankee Settlement, Iowa, engaged at the carpenter and joiner trade, and in 1857, came to Shell Rock, Minnesota. He soon after pre-empted land in this township, in section thirteen, and now has a farm of two hundred and eighty acres under a high state of cultivation, with a finely finished house, commodious granaries, barns, etc., and gives his attention to farming and stock raising. He was married in 1863, to Miss Ione Bartlett, and they have six children; Annette, Sherman, Willett L., Frank C., and Edgar and Edna, who are twins.

ALEXANDER JOHNSON was born on the 23d of April, 1823, near Arendahl, Norway, and remained in his native country until thirty-five years old. He came to America, and for some time found employment in the pineries in Michigan and later engaged in fishing on Lake Michigan. In 1862, he removed to Minnesota and staked out a claim, but soon sold and bought a farm in Freeman, section thirty-one, where he still resides. He married Miss Mary Mickleson in 1868, and they have two children: Julius, and Louisa.

ANDREW J. LANG was born in 1834, in Canada, in Dalhousie, province of Ontario, and received a good education. When twenty-two years old, he came to Shell Rock, this county, and purchased his farm of two hundred acres in section twenty-four. He and his brother Robert have lived together for many years in single blessedness. They were the first to own and operate a threshing machine in this place, that being their employment for fifteen summers. They wore out three machines of the J. I. Case make. Their father, mother, and sister have all passed away, and are buried in the Greene cemetery. The sister's name was Jeannette and she died on the 10th of June, 1881. Andrew and Robert, the last of the family, have, through their superior and careful business management, acquired wealth and the sincere respect of all who know them.

OLE O. OPDAHL is a native of Norway and dates his birth on the 25th of July, 1844. He attended school until the age of sixteen years, when he learned the blacksmith trade, and continued his studies at an evening school for two years. In 1869, he emigrated to America, located in Ossian, Iowa, where he was employed at his trade six years, and was married in 1871, to Miss Rachel Christiansen. He went to Forest City, and for two years dealt in agricultural implements, coming to Minnesota in 1875, and purchased his present farm of three hundred and twenty acres, and has conducted it since, also engaging at his trade. He has been Clerk of the board of School trustees most of the time since his residence here, and also a member of the board of Supervisors and afterward Chairman of the same, still holding the latter office. He has had four children, three of whom are living; G. O., Thorston E., and Eliza A. His mother is still living, sixty-seven years of age. His father was drowned, the vessel being wrecked in a trip from Christiania to his home.

WIFFING WADSWORTH was born at Stoke Doyel, Northamptonshire, England, on the 10th of September, 1830, and grew to manhood in that country, receiving such an education as the common schools afforded. In 1854, he came to America, and for some time engaged in farming in Vermont, coming to this State in 1856, and pre-empted a claim. He soon sold that and purchased two hundred acres of school land in section sixteen, where he now resides. In 1858, he married Miss Sarah Freeman, and they had six children; Elizabeth A., Joseph L., Ada J., Agnes, George R., and Mary. In 1864, Mr. Wadsworth enlisted in the army and served till the fall of 1865, when he received an honorable discharge. He has always taken a deep interest in public affairs, and has been kept constantly in office, being Town Clerk at present.

GENEVA.

CHAPTER LXI.

General description—Early settlement—Honored dead—Political—Statistical—Manufacturing—Geneva village—Religious—Schools—Biographical.

This is on the northern tier of towns in the county, the second from Mower county on the east, Newry lying between. Steele county is on the north, Bath on the west, and Riceland on the south. Like all the other towns in the county, the integrity of the original government survey has been maintained. Most of the sections from twenty-five to thirty-six is what may be called slough land, and is covered by college and railroad scrip. The remainder is rolling prairie, with a black sandy loam, which, on some of the ridges is mixed with clay and is very productive, as there is seldom a failure of crops from any cause. Nearly all the timber in town, when first entered for settlement, was on sections seventeen and thirty-six.

Geneva Lake is the only one in town. It is in the western part, and occupies parts of six sections. It has an irregular outline, with an area of perhaps three sections, and is three miles long and a little over a mile wide in its widest part. A small stream finds its way into it from the north, while an exit is obtained toward the east that is deflected to the south as it leaves the town from section thirty-six to join Turtle River. This river, was formerly noted for the abundance of fish it contained, and it is still an eligible point for the disciples of Sir Isaak Walton. The water pond, in their season are still found. There are no streams in the northeast part of the town, but good water is obtained at no great depth.

EARLY SETTLEMENT.

Milton Morey is said to be the first settler in town. He took a claim in 1855, built a cabin and did some breaking that fall. About Christmas his dwelling was unfortunately burned, and as he could not then put up another, he took his family in an ox team and turned his face towards civilization and spent the winter in or near where Austin now is, returning in the spring and putting in some crops. After a time he went to Dakota and now lives near Yankton. There were several settlers in 1856, and to write the truth as though it were fiction, on the 20th of April, on one of those days so characteristic of spring time in Minnesota, there might have been seen a solitary traveler, moving along the Indian trail between Austin and some point beyond this. From his appearance he was a pilgrim in quest of some shrine where he might kneel and pay homage to the home he expected to find, after he had created it. This stranger was looking for Mr. Morey's residence, which he had a confused idea was somewhere near the trail he was following. This man was Elmer Eggleston, and in one hand he carried a grip sack and in the other an umbrella. He was a native of Ohio but had come from Galena, and soon found Mr. Morey, who of course gave him the best the house afforded, and two days later assisted the young adventurer to stake out a farm in section eight which he opened up and cultivated until 1863, when he sold out, but still lives on the same section. In August following, the father reported in person and surmounted some of Uncle Sam's acres in the same section, where he wrought until gathered in by the grim reaper.

In May Robert P. Farr, a native of Missouri, came and placed his sign manual on a spot of land in section fourteen, and he has been bustling around there ever since. Along with him came Joseph W. Burdick, a native of New York, who selected his place in section ten, and there he established a home in which he dwelt until he exchanged worlds on the 24th of April 1877.

Henry King, who was born in Canada, took up his residence in section twenty-three, but he now lives on the town site.

E. C. Stacy, who had been through here in 1854, secured a place in section seven. He was one of the first three County Commissioners appointed by the Governor of the territory. He now resides in Albert Lea.

Isaac Lyon, from Illinois, took a claim in section eight which he soon disposed of to Jones & Robson. He afterwards lived in Steele county, and since that in Warren, Illinois.

Samuel Woodworth came here from the Badger State and planted his boundary stakes in section twenty-six, and there he remained until 1866, when he again set his face toward the setting sun, and sometime in 1881, he left his bones mouldering in Dakota soil.

Nathan Hunt got his real estate in sections fifteen and sixteen, went into the army, on his return marched west and halted in Faribault county, where he settled permanently.

Walter Drake, from the Nutmeg State, procured his slice of Minnesota territory in section thirty, and in 1866 he too sailed in command of a prairie schooner, and found a haven in Faribault county.

John Reed, from Kent county, England, surrounded a piece of free soil in section twenty-two, which he improved and cultivated. In February, 1862, he enlisted in the Union army and went to Fort Snelling, but in one short month he was mustered out, and went to join the legion of whom it is said:

'On fame's eternal camping ground
Their silent tents are spread,
And glory guards with solem around,
The bivouac of the dead.'

His widow and daughter are residents of the town site.

Thomas Cashman, of the Ever Green Isle, came from Iowa, and cast his lot on section thirteen, and there he may still be found.

Alexander Schutt, a native of the province of Quebec, Canada, came here from Ontario, and his choice was in sections eleven and twelve. He is now in section sixteen.

Burdette and Charles, sons of Eliab Eggleston, were early settlers, but both died young.

John Hines was here a short time, but pushed on to Dakota.

O. G. Goodnature, of Canada, arrived in June, and transplanted himself in section fourteen; he still remains a resident of the town.

Late this year, two particularly enterprising men from New York State, with their minds filled with town sites, arrived and secured a beautiful spot, located a town, and soon made it one of the most populous and thriving, in their minds, in the whole Northwest. Mr. Jones still survives, but Mr. Robson, who was Sheriff of the county and a highly respected citizen, when the war broke out joined the army and lost his life.

Hans Enstrom, a native of Sweden, came here from Boston and located in section four. He is now in Kittson county holding the position of Auditor.

Those already mentioned were settlers of 1856. A large settlement came in 1857, but only a few of their names could be obtained, among them the following:

Bernhard Schad, an enterprising German from Red Wing, arrived and at once went into the blacksmith and wagon business, which he still carries on.

John Heath, Sr., took a claim in section seven, but afterwards removed to Albert Lea, where he now lives.

Charles Henion, from New York State, came here from Wisconsin and secured a foothold in section four, which he still holds.

Some of the arrivals of 1858 were:

George Osborne, a native of Ohio, who spent a winter here and afterwards lived in Steele county. In about two years he returned to Geneva. Was in the army, and afterwards for a time Postmaster. He is now dead.

Thomas Hines, of Vermont, settled in section sixteen. He removed to Faribault county in 1864.

and lived there until 1872, when his movements in this world were terminated. His family returned here to reside in section fourteen.

Robert Hill, a native of the Key Stone State, pre-empted a place in section ten, and afterwards lived with his son-in-law. Robert P. Farr, until in 1865 the portals of the other world opened before him.

EARLY BIRTHS.—Anna Geneva, daughter of Bernhard and Anna Schad, was born on the 8th of September, 1857. Arriving at womanhood she married James Harvey Robson on the 16th of February, 1881. They live in Owatonna. He was the son of James A. and Martha Robson, and was ushered into this world in February, 1858.

Ralph Freeborn Drake was born in August, 1856.

Irvin E. Burdick, son of Joseph W. Burdick, was born on the 10th of September, 1856.

THE FIRST DEATHS.—Seymour E., son of Eliab and Esther Eggleston, was removed to the spiritual world on the 24th of December, 1857, in his 14th year.

The wife of W. S. Bacon was overtaken by the angel of immortality in the winter of 1857-58.

Burdette E., son of Eliab and Esther Eggleston, received a summons that could not be disregarded, on the 28th of November, 1857, in his 22d year.

THE HONORED DEAD.

HARVEY PARTRIDGE was born in Canaan, Litchfield county, Connecticut, on the 16th of July, 1786, and in 1834, removed to Genesee county, New York, in 1846 to Rock county, Wisconsin, and in 1864 came to Geneva. About a year before his death he went fo Albert Lea to live with his son, Sidney Partridge. For fifty years he was a Methodist. In 1812, he took the blue lodge degrees in Masonry, and the scarlet degrees in 1813. On the 7th of August, 1875, he was admitted to the "Supreme Lodge above, where the Grand Master of the Universe presides." He was buried with Masonic honors.

DANIEL KINNEAR was born in Schuylkill county, Pennsylvania. He moved to Iowa in 1841 and remained until 1864 when he removed to Freeborn county. He was a Methodist, and his life here was abruptly terminated by a second stroke of paralysis on the 29th of March, 1876, at the age of 75 years. His wife, one son, and five daughters were present at the funeral.

HIRAM R. JONES, one of the oldest persons in the county, died in Geneva where he was much respected, and was mourned by a large number of people with whom he has been associated for many years.

ELIAB EGGLESTON.—At Whitehall, New York, in 1808, the subject of this sketch was born. When quite young he went to Ohio, afterwards to Illinois, and finally to Minnesota, settling in Geneva, where he arrived in the year 1856. He furnished three sons for the war of 1861, only one of whom survived. Mr. Eggleston left his son, Elmer, and his wife with whom he had sojourneyed for forty seven years. On the 10th of June, 1880, he quietly breathed his last.

POST-OFFICE.

In 1856, E. C. Stacy made an application through Hon. Henry M. Rice, the delegate in Congress, for a Post-office, which was secured with E. C. Stacy as Postmaster, and they had a weekly mail, to be procurred at the expense of the town, from Austin. Dorr K. Stacy, who was then a mere lad, used to go over the twenty-two miles for it. The office was put in the store after that was opened, and still continues its good work.

POLITICAL.

The first town meeting was on that noted 11th of May, 1858, when the new constitution went into effect. The Supervisors were: E. C. Stacy, Chairman, W. S. Bacon, and John Brannan; Clerk, Hans Enstrom. The earliest records are lost so there are no particulars as to what was done, or of the names even of the other officers.

At the annual town meeting held in Chamberlain's Hall on the 14th of March, 1882, the followlowing officers were elected: Supervisors, Michael Quinn, Chairman, B. H. Conklin, and J. M. Sawyer; Clerk, A. J. Chamberlain; Treasurer, Bernhard Schad; Assessor, M. J. Fenton; Justice of the Peace, W. H. Twiford; Constable, Octave Goodnature.

Honesty and economy have characterized the management of town affairs from the first.

STATISTICAL.

THE YEAR 1881.—The area included in this report takes in the whole town; as follows:

Wheat—2,885 acres, yielding 36,813 bushels.

Oats—799 acres, yielding 25,640 bushels.

Corn—879 acres, yielding 28,515 bushels.

Barley—144 acres, yielding 3,020 bushels.

Rye—2 acres, yielding 35 bushels.

Buckwheat—2¼ acres, yielding 440 bushels.

Potatoes—339⅛ acres, yielding 4,914 bushels.

Beans—1⅛ acres, yielding 10 bushels.

Sugar cane—2½ acres, yielding 142 gallons.

Cultivated hay—59 acres, yielding 113 tons.

Total acreage cultivated in 1881—477.

Wild hay—12,184 tons.

Timothy seed—11 bushels.

Apples—number of trees growing, 830; number bearing, 330, yielding 134 bushels.

Grapes—7 vines, yielding 6 pounds.

Sheep—255 sheared, yielding 133 pounds of wool.

Dairy—255 cows, yielding 29,250 pounds of butter and 130 pounds of cheese.

Hives of bees—10, yielding 125 pounds of honey.

THE YEAR 1882.—Wheat, 2,530 acres; oats, 944; corn, 1,311; barley, 271; buckwheat, 8; potatoes, 55½; beans, 6¾; sugar cane, 5; cultivated hay, 60; other produce, ½ acre; total acreage cultivated in 1882, 6,376¼.

Apple trees—growing, 781; bearing, 367; grape vines bearing, 3.

Milch cows—234.

Sheep—45, yielding 174 pounds of wool.

Whole number of farms cultivated in 1882, 54.

Forest trees planted and growing, 128 acres.

POPULATION.—The census of 1870 gave Geneva a population of 378. The last census, taken in 1880, reports 454 for this town; showing an increase of 76.

MANUFACTURING.

In 1858, a Mr. Deacon Brant started the manufacture of shingles on section eight. The establishment was a marvel in its way, and displayed a genius that should have been handsomely rewarded, for it was the missing link between hand labor and machinery. The blocks were cut the proper length by a cross-cut saw, and they were then boiled to soften them and then were slashed up into shingles by a knife attached to a lever worked by a man and a woman power, the latter being his wife.

SAW-MILL.—In the fall of 1856, Bacon & Eggleston put up a saw-mill on section thirty-six, and kept it vibrating until the summer of 1857, when it was transferred to section seventeen, where Bacon run it for two years, having, in 1858, added a grist-mill, which did good business. In 1859, this mill was carried off by the western fever, which was epidemic at that time and has been ever since.

PATRONS OF HUSBANDRY.

A Grange was instituted on the 7th of July, 1872, with W. H. Twiford as Master, and Hans Enstrom Sr. and fifteen other charter members, which afterward swelled up to fifty or more. Weekly meetings were held in the Robson House hall. The members went into the fraternal part of the order in a whole-souled way, having a monthly banquet, followed by music and dancing. But in 1877, the banquet halls were deserted, and the life of the institution fled to seek companionship with those who had gone before.

HISTORICAL SKETCH.

The following in regard to this town was published in 1877: "It was first settled by Milton Morey, in the fall of 1855, who immediately constructed a log house, which was burned down on the Christmas following. To him also belongs the honor of opening the first farm, which he did in the spring of 1856. E. C. Stacy, who settled in June, 1856, was the first lawyer, while his wife, who arrived in August following, was the first doctor. Robson and Jones were the first merchants, and commenced the sale of goods in July, 1857. Schad and Drommerhausen, blacksmith and wagon-makers, were the first mechanics. In the same summer of 1857, a Mrs. Clark taught the first school in a log shanty at the village. The first schoolhouse was built by district No. 3, in 1858. In the summer of 1857, Rev. Isaac McReynolds held the first religious service. In 1858 the Catholics organized the first religious society, and built the first church in 1861. The Post-office was established in the winter of 1856-7, which was supplied by special service from Austin. E. C. Stacy was the first Postmaster. The first child born was Ralph Freeborn Drake, on the 30th of July, 1856. William Robson and Atlanta Smith were the first parties married, John Reed performing the ceremony in the summer of 1859. The first death was that of Mrs. Welcome Bacon, which occurred in February, 1859. James A. Robson opened the first hotel in June, 1858, although Judge Stacy had thrown his house open to the public ever since his first settlement. The first title to land was acquired by Welcome L. Bacon, August 16th, 1858, the selection being made on section thirty. The first board of officers was elected May 11, 1858, consisting of E. C. Stacy, W. S. Bacon, and John Brennan; H. Enstrom, Clerk."

GENEVA VILLAGE.

The village of Geneva was platted in the winter of 1856-57 by James F. Jones and James Robson, on section eight, and contained about four hundred acres. This was one of the first crop of villages ever raised in the county, and was very pleasantly situated, and of course calculated and expected to become the Chicago of the new Northwest.

In the spring of 1857, Jones and Robson started business and put up a store and hotel. They soon, however, dissolved partnership, Jones retaining the store which he managed for several years, part of the time in company with C. H. McIntire; but they afterwards sold out to Cabot & Lester, who continued the business but a short time, when they went to Martin county with their goods. The store was then occupied by Mr. Loring, and was soon consumed by fire.

Two Swedes, named Lohyed and Matison, put up a store and placed a stock of goods in it. They soon sold out and it changed hands several times; finally it was purchased by Charles Kittleson, now State Treasurer, and was burned while he owned it.

George and Warren Osborne began merchandising in 1865, and continued one year, when George secured his brother's interest and run it alone one year and then turned over his stock to Charles Kittleson.

The only store in town now is kept by Archibald Chamberlain, which was first opened by Dwight Brooks in 1880.

In 1857 Bernhard Schad and George Drommerhausen started a blacksmith and wagon shop. Wagons and plows, custom work and general repairing were their specialties. In about a year Schad became sole proprietor, and he is still hammering away at the old stand.

The hotel which had been built was leased to Isaac Lyons who opened it with an appropriate flourish in 1858, and managed it for a year or two and then sold to O. A. Jones, of Fillmore county. His father, H. R. Jones, kept it one winter and then his son, James F. Jones, bought and moved into it and is now the proprietor.

In 1857, in deference to a demand, Mr. Graham put up a building and opened a saloon, and as the business increased he erected a larger building, which afterwards changed hands and a store was opened there.

RELIGIOUS.

METHODIST.—The first religious meetings held in the village were in the store of Loyhed & Matison, in 1857, by a Methodist itinerant. Soon after an organization was effected. Elder Towne, a Baptist preacher, also had meetings at Deacon Brant's house, but as far as remembered, no organization was perfected. The Methodist denomination still "holds the fort" with a garrison of twenty members. The meetings are in the schoolhouse, with Rev. W. H. Burkaloo, who lives in Berlin, as pastor.

ROMAN CATHOLIC CHURCH.—The first mass known to have been said in this township, was in May, 1859, by Father Pendergast, in the residence of Thomas Cushman. Services were frequently held in this house, until in 1866 the church edifice was erected. It is a frame building, and was put up under the care of Father McDermott. The congregation is now under the charge of Father Fleming of Albert Lea, of which it is an outlying mission.

UNITED BRETHREN.—Religious meetings were held in John Hime's house in 1858, also in John Brown's house in section twenty-three, that was also used as a schoolhouse. In 1859 a society was accumulated with about a dozen members, by Rev. John Arnold, who also expounded in Geneva village. This society had sufficient attraction of cohesion to hold together for two or three years, when it became disrupted.

THE SEVENTH DAY ADVENTISTS.—The first time this peculiar doctrine was advocated in town was in the summer of 1876. Meetings were held in the schoolhouse by Elder Dimmick. On the 24th of September they organized with ten members, and a Sunday school was also commenced with Lucius Gibbs as Superintendent. Afterwards meetings were held in a tent. Rev. D. T. Curtis came after this and expounded the gospel as he understood it, once a month. Rev. Henry Ellis succeeded him and held the last meeting on the 20th of Janunry, 1882.

UNIVERSALIST.—Elder Wakefield, a pioneer preacher in this faith, had a series of meetings here, and quite a society was gathered. Their meetings are held at stated times in the schoolhouse, with Rev. G. S. Gowdy as pastor, who has good congregations, which is a little remarkable in this western country where, as a rule, the so called liberal denominations do not meet with much encouragement.

SCHOOLS.

District No. 3.—The first school was opened in a private house belonging to John Brown, in section fifteen, in the summer of 1858. Mrs. Henry King wielded the ferule during this term. The next year the citizens succeeded in building a schoolhouse on section fourteen. Miss Lucy Thomas called the first school to order in the new house, which was a log affair, 20x24 feet, which was put up by a regular "Bee," each farmer contributing something. This served until 1877, when the frame building now standing was erected on section twenty-three, at a cost of about $400.

DISTRICT No. 4.—A school was opened in a claim shanty on the town site in 1878. Mrs. Clark was the constituted authority during this term. Afterwards the school was kept in the store of Loyhed & Matison, and then in a building erected for a saloon. The schoolhouse was gotten up in 1865.

DISTRICT No. 97.—This was organized in 1875, having been taken from the third district. That same year the schoolhouse was built on the northwest corner of section fourteen. The initial teacher was Miss Ella Davis.

BIOGRAPHICAL.

HARRISON M. DAVIS, a native of New York, was born in Holland, Erie county, on the 19th of January, 1832. He was married in 1851, to Miss Aurilla Benedict, and four years after they moved to Wisconsin. In the summer of 1858, he came to Minnesota, lived in Steele county until fall, then returned to Wisconsin. They came again to Steele county in 1862, and on the 1st of December of the year following, Mr. Davis enlisted in the Second Minnesota Cavalry, went west on the frontier, and remained in service until November, 1865, when he received an honorable discharge. In 1866, he bought a farm in section six, Geneva, where he has since lived. He is the father of two children: Adelmar F. and Edwin W.

ELIAB EGGLESTON, deceased, one of the pioneers of Geneva, was born in Whitehall, New York, on the 29th of July, 1808. When quite young he learned the carpenter and joiner trade, and afterward was engaged as an architect. When about twenty years old he moved to Ohio, and a few years later to Indiana. On the 4th of November, 1833, he was united in marriage with Miss Esther Chapman. They resided in Galena, Illinois, seven years, and in 1856 came to Minnesota and settled on a farm in this place. He devoted his time to the improvement of his home until his death on the 9th of June, 1880. Mr. and Mrs. Eggleston had six children; Charles, who enlisted in 1862 in the Fourth Minnesota volunteer infantry, Company F, went south and was under Grant at Vicksburg, came home on a furlough and died on the 19th of October, 1863, aged twenty-eight years; Elmer, the only son now living, married on the 22d of October, 1861, Miss Catherine Gross, and they have two children, Burdette and Eliab J.; Burdette, the third son, died on the 28th of November, 1857, in his twenty-second year: Olive Ann died when two and a half years old: Alvanus enlisted in the Fifth Minnesota Regiment, Company C, went south and died near Vicksburg on the 5th of July, 1863; and Seymour E. died on the 24th of December, 1857, aged fourteen years. Mrs. Eggleston lives on the old homestead with her son Elmer.

MICHAEL FENTON, one of the early settlers of this place, is a native of Ireland, born on the 29th of September, 1811. He was brought up in Middlesex county, England, and there learned the trade of a brickmaker. In 1830 he sailed with his parents for America, his father dying on the way. The remainder of the family proceeded from Quebec to Boston, and thence to Waterbury, Vermont, where Michael was engaged at his trade one summer. He then returned to Canada and worked in the lumber business for two years, from thence to Rochester and subsequently to Buffalo, Detroit, and back to Rochester. He was married in 1847 to Miss Mary White. While at Rochester he enlisted in the first United States artillery, went south to Florida, and after a service of three years was honorably discharged. He spent eight months in Georgia and from there went to Newburg, New York, thence to Vermont and worked at his trade. He went to Michigan and settled on a farm about eleven miles from Jackson, and after a residence of five years moved to Ottawa, Illinois. He served in the Mexican war under Gen. Shields, was wounded twice at the battle of Buena Vista, and confined in the hospital four months, after which he received his discharge and returned to Illinois by way of New Orleans and St. Louis. After reaching his home he was laid up two years on account of injuries received while in service. In 1857 he came to Minnesota, resided in Stillwater until 1858, then selected a farm in this place, and the following year moved his family. He is a member of the National Veterans' Association and is a Mexican pensioner, probably, the only one in the county. Mr. and Mrs. Fenton have had three children; Johanna M., Michael J., and William R., the latter of whom died on the 10th of July, 1880, from the effect of injuries received from a falling capstan.

Robert P. Farr, one of the pioneers of this place, is a native of Missouri, born in 1827. When quite young he removed with his parents to Indiana, and at the age of nine years went to live with his grandparents in Pennsylvania. After four years he returned to his home, and four years later removed to Clayton county, Iowa, where he bought a saw-mill and run it until 1856. In the latter year he came to Minnesota, took a claim in section fourteen of this township, and has since made it his home. He has a fine orchard, and his farm contains four hundred acres. In 1861, he was united in marriage with Miss Belle Hill, a native of Pennsylvania. They have had seven children, six of whom are living; Esther, May, Sarah, Robert, Alice, and Charles. George died when eighteen months old.

Lucius Gibbs was born in Pennsylvania on the 17th of February, 1831. He received an academical education, and in 1862, his health failed, which necessitated a change of climate. He went to Illinois, thence to St. Louis up the Missouri river, and west to Montana. After an absence of three years he returned to his native State, where he married Miss Mary A. J. Maynard, and after a few weeks started for Minnesota. He located in Geneva, where he bought a farm and has since made it his home. Mr. and Mrs. Gibbs have had five children, three of whom are living; Lester D., Carrie S., and Willie L. Stephen died on the 16th of January, 1881, aged nine years, and Henry died four days later at the age of four years.

John L. Gibbs was born in Pennsylvania on the 3d of May, 1838. He acquired the fundamental principles of a good education in the common schools of his native State, and afterward attended Le Raysville Academy, and subsequently taught school, using the proceeds for the advancement of his education. After a course at the Susquehanna Collegiate Institute and the Pokeepsie Law School of Indiana, he entered the law department of the university at Ann Arbor, Michigan, graduating one year afterwards. He then taught school in Iowa, and in 1861, came to Albert Lea. The following year he was elected County Attorney, and in 1863, elected to the Legislature and again in '64, '75, and '76. Thus it will be seen by the public positions he has occupied, in what esteem he is held by his fellow citizens. He was married in 1868, to the widow of Capt. James Robson. Mr. Gibbs has always been a careful and methodical student, and by his perseverance has overcome many obstacles that to an ordinary mind would seem insurmountable. As presiding officer of the House his qualifications are marked with that degree of firmness and ability that has so distinguished some of his predecessors. In selecting the standing committees no man could have been more just and impartial, or displayed better judgment than did he.

O. C. Goodnature, one of the pioneers and most successful farmers of Freeborn county, is a native of Canada, born in 1825. When quite young he moved to Clinton county, New York, and was there employed in a saw-mill and in driving a team. He was marrid to Miss Emily De-Marre and the issue of the union is nine children; Octave C., George, Peter, Nicholas, Eli, Emily, Rosalie, Michael, and David. Mr. Goodnature sought a home in Minnesota in 1856, and settled in section fourteen of this township where he has since resided.

Charles Henion, one of the early settlers of Geneva, is a native of Albany county, New York, where he was born on the 17th of September, 1831. In 1854, he removed to Wisconsin, which was his home until coming to this place in 1857. He took a claim in section four and the same year returned to New York and married Clarisa Hubbs. The result of the union is five children; Ophelia, Alva, Cora, Lillie, and Bina. Immediately after marriage Mr. Henion returned to his farm and has since devoted his time to its improvement. Mrs Henion died on the 16th of July, 1872, and in 1876, he married his present wife, whose maiden name was Libbie Clipper. She is a native of Schenectady county, New York, born in 1842, and resided in her native county until coming to Minnesota.

JAMES F. JONES, one of the pioneers of this place, was born in Onondaga county, New York, on the 15th of June, 1822. When quite young he was engaged in a tan yard and subsequently learned the trade of a tanner, currier, and shoe maker. At the age of twenty-one years he was married to Miss Adelpha Moon, and after a few days they started with a team for Milwaukee. Just before reaching their destination Mr. Jones was taken sick with fever, and when able was taken to his brother's house in the city and remained during the winter. In the spring he took some land which, the next year, he sold and moved to Rock county, Wisconsin, where he bought a farm. After a residence of three years there his health failed and they returned to New York where he was engaged in the manufacture of boots and shoes, which he brought to Wisconsin every year and traded for wheat; that he took to Janesville and had made into flour, then to Milwaukee where he shipped it to Buffalo for sale. After continuing in this business for three years he returned to his farm in Rock county, and in 1856 came to this county, and in company with Captain Robson located the town site of Geneva, built a hotel and engaged in mercantile pursuits and farming. He is at present landlord of the hotel here and is also interested in stock raising in the Missouri valley in Dakota. Mr. and Mrs Jones have a family of six children; Hiram, Eugene, Helen, Adelle, Jay, and Mark.

GEORGE OSBORN, deceased, one of the early residents of this place, was born in Erie county, Ohio, on the 6th of September, 1832. He was married in 1857 to Miss Maria J. Gross, a native of New York, and the year following they came to Minnesota and located a farm in this place. They afterward resided for two years in Waseca county and then returned to Geneva. In 1862 Mr. Osborn enlisted in the Tenth Minnesota Regiment, Company E, and served as sergeant. He was in several battles and once was wounded; after a service of three years he received an honorable discharge, having gained the confidence and respect of every officer and soldier who knew him. While in the army he contracted a lung disease which resulted in consumption, and finally terminated his life. In the spring of 1866 he opened a boot and shoe store which he carried on nine years; was also Postmaster a number of years. He was a Universalist, but his house was always open to ministers of any denomination, and no man could be more thoroughly missed, his death occurring on the 23d of February, 1875. He left a wife and two daughters.

RICHARD QUINN was born in Ireland in 1828, and emigrated to America in 1851. He landed in New York on St. Patrick's Day, and after a month went to Indiana, where he was in the employ of the railroad company one year, then went to Dayton, Ohio, and engaged in the livery business. He was afterward employed as porter in a hotel at Cincinnati, and there married, in 1854, Miss Mary Ann Hayes. For a time Mr. Quinn was engaged in the wholesale and retail liquor business at Dubuque, Iowa. He came to Minnesota and settled in the Crow River country, working at Dayton and afterward engaged in farming about four miles from that place. After a residence of four years there he sold and moved to Minneapolis, where he was engaged in the lumber business, and in 1868 came to this township, locating in section fifteen, which has since been his home. Mr. and Mrs. Quinn have had thirteen children, ten of whom are now living; Mary Ann, Edmund J., Michael J., William F., Nora J., Mary F., Johanna A., John R., Philip P., and Monica C. The two eldest died in infancy, and Anne E. died in June, 1882, aged sixteen years.

BERNHARD SCHAD is a native of Germany, born on the 28th of April, 1834. At the age of fourteen years he began to learn the blacksmith trade, and after serving an apprenticeship of three years came to America. He located in Genesee county, New York, and three years later moved to Chicago, then to Red Wing, in this State, where he was married in 1856 to Miss Anna Andrist, who was born in Berne, Switzerland, on the 6th of October, 1834. They remained in Red Wing one year and then moved to this township and opened a blacksmith shop, which he still carries on. Mr. and Mrs. Schad have had seven children, six of whom are living; Anna Geneva, John B., Mary M., Katie Belle, Libbie E., and Frankie E.

MICHAEL QUINN is a native of Ireland, born in 1834, and left his birth place for America, in 1852. He went from New York to Elizabeth, New Jersey, and two months later to Lancaster, Ohio, thence to Cincinnati, and Newport, Kentucky. He came to Debuque, Iowa, to visit friends, and in April, 1856, made a trip to St. Paul, traveled through the big woods to the prairie of

Forest City with the early settlers and after a time went to Chicago and resided one year. He then returned to Minnesota and assisted a Mr. Dayton in laying out a townsite, building a saw and grist mill in the Crow River Valley. Mr. Quinn was united in marriage in Mobile, Alabama, with Miss Margaret O'Shea, on the 10th of April, 1860. In 1862, he enlisted in the First Alabama Mounted Cavalry, and after serving one year was transferred to a gun boat in Mobile bay, remaining till the close of the war. He then opened a grocery store in Mobile, and after running it two years sold out and came again to Minnesota and bought land in section nine, ten, and sixteen of this township and has since made this place his home. He has filled different offices of trust and is at present chairman of the board of Supervisors. He is the father of seven children; Edward, William, Mary A., Catharine A., Margaret, Honora, and John. Mr. Quinn has traveled quite extensively through both the northern and southern States.

CAPTAIN JAMES A. ROBSON, deceased, one of the early settlers of Freeborn county, was born in western New York, on the 23d of May, 1825. His father died when he was an infant, and he lived with his mother until 1847, when he removed to Rock county, Wisconsin, and settled in Magnolia. He was joined in matrimony on the 26th of October, 1848, to Miss Martha Partridge, and the union was blessed with four children. In 1857, Mr. Robson came to Geneva, and in 1859 was elected County Sheriff and moved to Albert Lea, where he also carried on a hotel, the Webber House, during his term of service. In August, 1862, he took an active part in raising Company E, of the Tenth Minnesota Volunteer Infantry and by unanimous voice was chosen its Captain. He was accidently shot by Lieut. McCarty of Company H, and died on the 9th of November, of the same year, two days after the accident. He was a popular man at home and in the army, and his death was a great loss to the community in which he lived.

ALEXANDER SCHUTT, one of the pioneers of Geneva, was born in Quebec, Canada, on the 28th of February, 1833. He remained at his birthplace until twenty-one years old, then was engaged at the carpenter trade for three years in Ontario. In 1866, he married Miss Elizabeth Carson and the same year came to Minnesota. They came directly to this county and first settled in Moscow, but the same year came to this township and took land in sections eleven and twelve. They have a family of eight children: Hiram, Francis, John, James, Albert, Maria, Lillie, and Alexander. Mr. Schutt now owns a fine farm of six hundred acres and good buildings.

DR. WILLIS H. TWIFORD was born on the 12th of May, 1821, in Fayette county, Ohio. His mother died when he was seven years old and left the family of ten children. In early life Willis improved all opportunities afforded him for obtaining an education, attending the Academy of Delaware, Ohio, for two terms. He afterward entered the office of Dr. J. Sidney Skinner at West Canaan, Ohio, and studied medicine three years, taking his degree as M. D. at the Starling Medical College of Columbus. In April, 1846, he was joined in wedlock with Miss Nancy R. Darning, daughter of Jeremiah Darning, Esq., of Madison county, Ohio. Dr. Twiford practiced his profession in Pleasant Valley, now Plain City, until August, 1853, when he removed to Union City, Indiana, and remained there till the war. He entered the Twenty-fifth Indiana Regiment as Assistant Surgeon, and was soon after commissioned Surgeon, being in charge of the hospital on the Antietam battle field. He was appointed by General Hooker, Surgeon in Chief of the First Division of the Twelfth Army Corps and held the same until July, 1864, when he resigned in consequence of an injury of the spine, resulting in partial paralysis. The same year he came to Minnesota, and settled at River Point, in Steele county. He was elected to the ninth Minnesota Legislature, and in 1870, resumed his practice of medicine, coming to Geneva in July, 1873.

CHARLES E. VINTON was born in Hampshire county, Massachusetts, on the 23d of January, 1826. When he was five years old his parents moved to Cattaraugus county, New York, and in 1856, to McHenry county, Illinois, settling on a farm. Charles was married in 1851, to Miss Britana Hurlburt, a native of New York. After a residence of two years in Illinois they came to Minnesota, and took land in Summit, Steele county. In 1875 they removed to Geneva, where Mr. Vinton bought twenty-two lots in the town site, and has since added five more to his purchase. He is the father of three children; Mary, Martinette, and Charles W.

JOHN W. WALASKI, one of the early settlers of

this place, was born at Castle Garden in New York, on the 5th of January, 1834. His father was a Polander and a captain in the Regular Army, being among the ninety-six banished from that country at the fall of the empire. Those banished came to America and took the oath of allegiance to the United States, and were cared for by the Government, each family given one hundred and sixty acres of land in Jo Daviess county, Illinois. Mr. Walaski's parents settled there and remained until the breaking out of the Black Hawk War when they removed to Jefferson Barracks, Missouri. His father joined the army and went to Florida, where he took part in the Seminole War, leaving his famiy at Fort Clark, near St Louis. After a service of four years he returned to Illinois and settled on Government land in Clay County where they resided until 1857, then came to Minnesota to seek a home. The father and son both took land in this county and in 1862, came to Geneva, where the former died on the 30th of November in the same year. His widow died on the 14th of November, 1870, aged fifty-six years. In 1862, John went with a volunteer company, furnished his own horse and equipments, and went west to guard the frontier until relieved by government troops. He was married in 1865, to Miss Amy Baker, and they have one child, Edna G.

HAYWARD.

CHAPTER LXII.

GENERAL DESCRIPTION EARLY SETTLEMENT—POLITICAL—EVENTS OE INTEREST—STATISTICS—SCHOOLS—BIOGRAPHICAL.

This township is the southeast of the six interior towns of the county, and the towns in contact with it are, Riceland on the north; Oakland on the east; Shell Rock on the south; and Albert Lea on the west. It is six miles square, like all the other towns in the county.

An arm of Lake Albert Lea, three miles long and a third of a mile wide, lays near the western boundary, in a north and south direction. A stream called Peter Lund Creek enters the lake in section seven, made up of two branches arising back in the town.

The land may be described as prairie, with oak openings and meadow land interspersed, the prairie predominating; the timber being found mostly in the western part of its territory, in the region of the lake. In the northern part of this region may be found, with the oak, some poplar timber, while southward the wood is red oak and a small growth of poplar. The heaviest timber is in section thirty-one, which is divided into wood lots of five, ten, or twenty acres. The prairie is rolling, and some of it inclined to be low. The northeast part of the township, particularly in sections eleven, twelve, thirteen, and fourteen, has not yet been reclaimed, and is still owned by the State and railroad. A scheme is however contemplated by which the whole tract is to be drained and improved.

The soil, as a rule, is a black loam, productive of all crops in this latitude. The subsoil is clay and gravel. The Southern Minnesota railroad runs through the town from east to west, entering it on section one and leaving it from section seven.

EARLY SETTLEMENT.

The town was named in honor of David Hayward, an early settler, who came from Postville, Iowa, in the summer of 1856, and selected a place in section six, claiming a quarter section, and there he lived until 1858, when he returned to Iowa. His taxes becoming delinquent the place was sold, and it is now owned in part by Charles E. Fisher.

The first two settlers were two Norskmen, Peter Lund and E. Gilbrandson, who came in company from Iowa county, Wisconsin. They left their families in Houston county, and came through to this place and secured claims on sections eight and seventeen, and on the 20th of June, 1856, they went back and brought their families. At first they lived in a tent arranged by poles and wagon covers; in this they lived until fall, when they dug a hole in the ground, and sodding it over existed in that for a year.

The very first breaking done in the town was by a young man named Olson Andrews, on section thirty-two. This was in the summer of 1856.

James Andrews also broke some land on section thirty-two. He lived in the town of Shell Rock before he brought his family.

The next comers were the Pennsylvania Germans, two of whom located in Albert Lea and one here.

William Newcomb, in the fall of 1856, drifted on to section seven with his family and a team of horses, and put up a log house, which he staid in until 1874, when he sold to John Murphy, and took himselt to Council Bluffs, Iowa.

In section eight the first settlement was made by Norwegians.

Section two was settled by Americans.

The southeast corner of the township was first settled by Americans, but is now inhabited by Bohemians.

Lysander R. Luce came to this town in April, 1858, and surrounded a claim on sections seven and eight. He was from Clayton county, Iowa, and pulled through this roadless region with an ox team. He constructed a timber residence, which was all the fashion on the frontier, and here he lived and wrought until on the 16th of June 1882, he drifted across that mystic river of which we talk so much and know so little. He was a native of New York State,

Lysander Raymond Luce, Sen., deceased, This Freeborn county pioneer entered upon the enjoyment of human life on the 21st of July, 1814, at Stowe, Vermont, and at the age of twenty-six was married to Ann Morrison, of his native town. They lived there until 1855, and had five children. At this time he caught the western fever, which was then epidemic in New England, and brought his family to Clayton county, Iowa, and remained two years. Then removed to Albert Lea and staid one year when he went to Hayward. His release from the body was by a lingering method which he bore with great fortitude, and was on the 16th of June, 1882.

POLITICAL.

The first town meeting in response to a legal notice was held on the first Tuesday in April, 1859, at the house of S. H. Ludlow. According to the records there were two moderators, S. H. Ludlow and I. W. Devereux. The officers of the election were H. M. Luce and Charles Bush. On motion the meeting adjourned to meet at the house of Charles Bush, where the following officers were elected: Supervisors, J. W. Devereux, Chairman, Peter Lund, and H. L. Dow; Clerk, Charles Bush; Treasurer, Peter Lund; Assessor, A. T. Butts; Justice of the Peace, Charles Bush; Constable, H. L. Dow.

The whole number of votes cast at this election was nine, and there was no charge of ballot-box stuffing.

A tax of fifty dollars was levied for town expenses. It was voted that the next town meeting be at the house of A. T. Butts, on section seventeen.

Since that time the town has run on in the even tenor of its way, and the expenses of the government have been gradually increasing until it has now got up to the sum of $125, the amount raised for 1882, and yet no motion has been made to have a committee of investigation to see what has become of their money. It is evident that this is a poor town for rings.

At the election held on the 27th of March, 1882, the following officers were elected: Supervisors, H. C. Nelson, Chairman, Ole Anderson, and Peter O. Stensven; Clerk, R. Campbell; Treasurer, Peter Lund; Assessor, E. W. Knatvold.

The whole number of votes cast at this election was eighty, although the number of registered voters is 190. So that less than one-half turned out. The established polling place is the Howard schoolhouse, in District No. 34.

HAYWARD VILLAGE.

A village was platted here in 1869 by H. C. Lacy. Martha P. Gibbs was the proprietor and it was recorded on the 20th of December. Morin & Armstrong, of Albert Lea, took an interest in the village in 1870 and erected a warehouse on the railroad grounds. The next building put up was a store and dwelling by Oliver Nelson in the fall of 1870. In 1877 he sold to R. Campbell and went to Lake Mills, Iowa. In 1870 the depot was built.

It is a mere hamlet, and to-day is made up of a good sized store, kept by Hanson brothers; two blacksmith shops; a boarding house kept by William Hoyt; two warehouses, and two dwelling houses. The population consists of five families. The location is in section nine, and it is six and one half miles east of Albert Lea.

POST-OFFICE.

This perquisite of civilization was established during the war, in 1863. The first man entrusted with the key to unlock the mail pouch was M. W. Campbell, who received and distributed the mail in his house on section four. In 1870 it was transferred to the village, to Oliver Hanson's care, in the store, and after a time it was turned over to H. T. Hanson, who is still entitled to write P. M. after his name. It has a daily mail each way, from the train.

WIND FEED MILL.

There is a feed mill, driven by wind, on the railroad in section eight. It was built by M. M. Luce in 1877, and is 18x32, two stories high, and has a capacity, when there is sufficient wind, to grind two hundred bushels a day. It is one and one fourth miles west of the village.

PATRONS OF HUSBANDRY.

A Grange was instituted on the 9th of December, 1874, in the schoolhouse in district number sixty. The prominent officers were, Luther Phelps, Wm. Bragg, and G. Y. Slocum. At first there were thirty members and meetings were kept up until some time in 1879, when the charter was surrendered. At one time it was flourishing, having seventy members. A hall was built in 1876, 20x40 feet, one story high. It finally passed in the hands of Robert Campbell, Jr., and is now owned by Hanson & Brother who use it for store purposes.

CEMETERY.

The city of the dead, where all mortality finds a home at last, is on section nine, south of the village of Hayward, on a commanding piece of ground. The association was organized in June, 1874, the first officers being Olson Nelson and Andrew Gilbrandson. There are four acres. The first one to leave his earthly remains here was Arne Overby, in the winter of 1874. He was a native of Norway and lived on section twenty-three, being one of the early settlers. At the time of his demise he was about forty years of age. There are now sixteen graves here.

EARLY EVENTS.

Ole P. Lund, son of Peter and Else Lund, as is reported, was the first settler to arrive by birth in this town. It was on the 27th of May, 1858, and he still lives here and is himself a married man.

The first known death was that of an infant child of Philo Butts, in the winter of 1858, who at that time lived in section seventeen, but in 1862 he returned to Wisconsin.

STATISTICS.

THE YEAR 1881.—The area included in this report takes in the whole town, as follows:

Wheat—3,858 acres, yielding 40,132 bushels.
Oats—787 acres, yielding 25,283 bushels.
Corn—612 acres, yielding 25,340 bushels.
Barley—91 acres, yielding 2,055 bushels.
Rye—33 acres, yielding 354 bushels.
Buckwheat—6 acres, yielding 47 bushels.
Potatoes—37 acres, yielding 3,682 bushels.
Sugar cane—2 acres, yielding 420 gallons.
Cultivated hay—66 acres, yielding 98 tons.
Flax—20 acres, yielding 193 bushels.
Other products—5 acres.
Total acreage cultivated in 1881—5,517.
Wild hay—2,075 tons.
Timothy seed—7 bushels.
Apples—number of trees growing, 1,251; number bearing, 307, yielding 124 bushels.
Grapes—242 vines, yielding 210 pounds.
Sheep—117 sheared, yielding 497 pound of wool.
Dairy—282 cows, yielding 24,625 pounds of butter and 200 pounds of cheese.
Hives of bees—9, yielding 100 pounds of honey.

THE YEAR 1882.—Wheat, 2,898 acres; oats, 848; corn, 932; barley, 178; rye, 69; buckwheat, 20; potatoes, 82; beans, 3; sugar cane, 1; cultivated hay, 149; flax, 30; total acreage cultivated in 1882—5,210.

Apple trees growing—1,196; bearing, 489.

Grapes--vines bearing, 245.

Milch cows—243.

Sheep—135, yielding 581 pounds of wool.

Whole number of farms cultivated in 1882 87.

POPULATION.—The census of 1870 gave Hayward a population of 382. The last census, taken in 1880, reports 659 for this town; showing an increase of 277.

SCHOOLS.

The first school taught in this town was in the north part, in section three, in a timber building which was put up for that purpose. Miss Olive Callahan was the first to teach the young idea how to shoot under this roof, and B. Lamb taught here from 1864 until 1875. It was finally removed to the village, and is now District No. 34. The first school here was held at the Grange hall on the 2d of October, 1875 The officers elected were E. A. Campbell, Lars Lund, and Peter Lund. The present building cost about $700, is 24x36 feet, and has seats for about forty scholars. The first school here was managed by W. Cooley in the late autumn of 1875 at $32 per month, with forty pupils.

District No. 35.—This was organized in 1866 at the house of Watson Brown. The first officers were O. Andrews, James Andrews, and Watson Brown. In the summer of that year they succeeded in getting up a log house, 16x20 feet. In 1880, the old house becoming inadequate to the wants of the district, a new one was built, a frame structure, 18x30 feet, with room for eighty scholars, at a cost of $700.

District No. 36.—In 1864 this district assumed form; the meeting for organization being in the house of Peter Lund, on the 12th of April, and a log house was soon rolled together on section eighteen, 16x18 feet. The first school had fourteen pupils. It was called to order and managed by Miss Esther Lowry, for $20 a month. The first school officers were Peter Lund, Andrew Sanderson, and L. R. Luce.

District No. 60.—In 1864 this was taken from No. 35, and created into a new district, the first meeting being held at the house of Daniel Chute, on the 2d of June, 1864. The first officers were Daniel Chute, Luther Phelps, and David Ansley. They proceeded to build a log house without floor, and with a sod roof, and dignified it by calling it a schoolhouse, but it was the best they could do, and here Miss Emma Fenholt got togethes thirteen pupils and taught them ten weeks for $2 per week and boarded herself. The house now there was constructed in 1875 at a cost of $400. It is 20x26 feet and can seat thirty-five. The last school was taught by Miss Hellen Hare, at $22 per month, and there were twenty-three scholars; considerable more difference in the wages than in the number of pupils.

BIOGRAPHICAL.

ROBERT CAMPBELL, SR., one of the pioneers of this county, is a native of Vermont, born in Chester, Windsor county, on the 7th of September; 1795. His father was a revolutionary soldier, and drew a pension until the time of his death. In the spring of 1855, Mr. Campbell came to Wisconsin and resided on a farm in Janesville, Rock county, until coming to this township in 1858. He drove here with an ox team, and staked out a claim in section ten where he has lived ever since. He was appointed Postmaster in 1865, and has held other local offices. The maiden name of his wife was Belinda Woodward and of ten children born of the union, six are living. One son was killed in the army, and had he lived would now be sixty-one years old.

ROBERT CAMPBELL, JR., a son of the subject of our last sketch, was also born in Chester, Windsor county, Vermont, his birth dating the 14th of March, 1836, and at the age of nineteen years came with his parents to Wisconsin. He went from there to California in 1859, and was engaged in the mines and in the lumber business for eight years, then took a trip to Oregon and Washington territories and returned to San Francisco. In 1867 he came to Minnesota and located in section ten, Hayward. The following year he was married to Miss Isadore A. Luce, the ceremony taking place on the 23d of March. After living on his farm some years Mr. Campbell removed to Albert Lea, and started in the machinery business with Gilbrandson and Bro., and remained with them for five years, then returned to this place and in the autumn of 1877 bought Granger's Hall, converted it into a store building and commenced trade. In March, 1880, he sold to Hanson Bros. and moved to section four, where he now lives. His farm contains five hundred and forty acres and he also owns a warehouse and haypress in the village. He was Postmaster from

1877 to 1880, and has been Town Clerk since 1878. He is the father of five children.

NEHEMIAH W. CAMPBELL, deceased, was a native of Vermont, born on the 29th of April, 1823. He married the daughter of Amos Robbins; she was born on the 25th of November, 1825, in Vermont, the marriage ceremony taking place on the 30th of September, 1849. In 1857 Mr. Campbell moved with his family to Wisconsin, and the following year he came to Hayward, located a farm in section four, and brought his family the following year. On the 7th of November, 1864, he enlisted in Company C, of the First Minnesota Heavy Artillery, under Capt. George S. Ruble, and served until the 18th of May, 1865, when he died in the hospital. His widow lives on the old homestead with Elbridge A., the oldest son, who was born on the 18th of February, 1851. He has been Justice of the Peace and school Clerk, each, several years. Mrs. Campbell has another son and two daughters.

JOSEPH FEARN, was born in England on the 20th of June, 1832. He came to America when eighteen years old and remained in Ohio one year, thence to Illinois, and in a year enlisted at Chicago in the regular army for a period of five years. During the time he was in several skirmishes with the Indians, then went to New Mexico and accompanied emigrants across the plains to California. During the Mountain Meadow massacre he was for nine days buried in the snow with nothing to eat but horse flesh. After receiving his discharge on the 15th of August, 1860, he traveled through Kansas to Ohio, and on the 20th of June, 1862, married Miss Sarah McClum, who was born on the 5th of June, 1825. In 1869 Mr. Fearn came to Minnesota, and for some time was engaged in keeping a boarding-house at Armstrong, then removed to Hayward and located a farm in section twenty, which is well improved with a fine orchard. He is the father of one child.

A. P. HANSON is a native of Norway, born on the 6th of May, 1849, and emigrated with his parents to America when twelve years old. They came directly to Minnesota and resided in Bancroft for one year, then came to Hayward and lived on a farm a number of years. In 1870 Mr. Hanson was married to Miss Oleana Hanson, and they have five children. In 1880 they moved to the village and his brother bought the Campbells' store where A. P. has since devoted his time, keeping a line of general merchandise on the corner of Main street. The Post-office is located at their store.

EDWARD W. KNATVOLD was born in Norway on the 11th of April, 1851, and came with his parents to America when eleven years old. They came directly to this township and took a homestead in section eighteen where Edward assisted in the farm labor until twenty-three years old. He then bought a farm of his own, has twice added to it and now owns three hundred and forty acres containing good buildings. He was married on the 16th of November, 1874, to Miss Nettie Barny and the union has been blessed with four children. Mr. Knatvold is a partner of Robert Campbell in a hay press and warehouse in the village of Hayward. His father came from Norway to this country and immediately enlisted in the army, served one year and settled on his present farm. He is now sixty-five years old.

SAMUEL T. KIRKPATRICK is a native of Pennsylvania, born on the 1st of May, 1836. At the age of thirteen years he left home and worked on farms until sixteen years old when he served an apprenticeship of two years in a blacksmith shop. He then moved to Armstrong county, worked three years and in 1856, came to Utica, Crawford county, where he erected a shop and remained several years. On the 17th of December, 1857, he was joined in matrimony with Miss Nancy Davis. In 1864, Mr. Kirpatrick sold his shop, bought a farm and carried it on in connection with another shop for six years. In March, 1870, he came to this place, purchased eighty acres in section thirty-three, and in June returned for his family, settling on the farm the same year. He now owns two hundred and forty acres all improved, with a fine grove all around his house. Mr. and Mrs. Kirkpatrick have a family of five: Mary Ann, twenty-four years old; Martha J., twenty-two; Leonard C., nineteen; Robert T., fourteen; and Frank J., twelve.

MILTON M. LUCE, one of the early settlers of this place, was born in Vermont on the 21st of September, 1843. He resided with his parents on a farm in his native State until 1855, when they moved to Clayton county, Iowa. In the spring of 1857, his father came to Minnesota, left his family in Albert Lea and pre-empted land in Hayward where they have since lived. In 1861, Milton enlisted in the Fourth Minnesota Volunteer Infantry, Company I; at the fall of Vicksburg he was transferred to the Invalid Corps, sent to Rock Island and remained during the winter of 1863 and '64. In October of the latter year, he went to Chicago where he received an honorable discharge and returned home, remaining until March 1st, 1865, when he went to St. Paul as a veteran in Company A, of the Ninth Regiment, Hancock's First Veteran corps; was mustered in on the 10th of March and witnessed the hanging of Lincoln's conspirators. He was sent to Indianapolis, Indiana, where he guarded Government stores till March, 1866, when he was mustered out. The same month he was united in marriage with Miss M. E. Stulty of the latter place. Mr. Luce returned with his wife to his home and remained until 1869, when he moved to Albert Lea where he was constable four years, and also worked at the carpenter trade; was elected City Marshal in 1874; in 1877, he returned to his father's farm where he still resides.

Samuel Landis was born on the 4th of May, 1837, in Ohio, and lived with his father until of age, when he came west. After a residence of two years in Iowa he returned to Ohio and in the fall of 1861, came to Blue Earth, Faribault county, Minnesota. He soon after enlisted in the First Minnesota Mounted Rangers, Company K, went to St. Peter, thence to Missouri River and fought the Indians, participating in eight battles. After receiving his discharge he went to Ohio and re-enlisted in Company H, of the One Hundred and Ninty-seventh Ohio Regiment; was sent south to Virginia and remained in service until the close of the war, receiving an honorable discharge on the 31st of July, 1865. On the 21st of December following he was married to Miss Eva Smith, by whom he has three children. For four years after his marriage he lived in Michigan, then came to Freeborn county and bought a farm in section twenty-six, Hayward, moved his family here in October, 1869, and has since made it his home. He and his wife are members of the United Brethren Church.

Peter Lund, one of the pioneers of this place, was born in Norway on the 13th of June, 1820. He was married in his native place on the 16th of June, 1846, to Miss Elsie Gravli, and they have two children. In 1850, he came to America, located first on Rock Prairie, Wisconsin, and a year later moved to Iowa county in the same State, where he worked in lead mines three years; then moved to Iowa, and a year afterward to Minnesota. He came to this township and selected claims in sections eighteen and eight, returned to Iowa for his family, whom he brought here with an ox team, arriving on the 1st of July, 1856. Mr. Lund now owns three hundred and twenty acres, a large portion of which is cultivated. He was the first Town Treasurer, and held the same several years.

John Park is a native of Huron county, Ohio, born on the 23rd of May, 1833. His mother died when he was nineteen years old, after which he came to Winnebago county, Wisconsin, and after a residence of eight years moved to Waushara county, where he took a claim and remained two years. He was married to Miss Elizabeth Rice, from New York, and they have a family of nine children. In 1861, Mr. Park came to Minnesota, lived on a farm near Albert Lea one year, then moved to Hartland, and the same year came to Hayward, first bought railroad land, and in the spring of 1866, purchased his brother's farm in section twenty-nine, which is well improved and contains a good frame house.

Edmund Town is a native of Vermont, born on the 26th of August, 1822. When twenty-one years old he removed to New York where, on the 12th of December, 1843, he married Miss Betsy E. J. Lyon, formerly from Vermont. In 1854, they came to Minnesota, arriving in Shell Rock on the 2d of May. Mr. Town purchased a hotel, of which he was landlord until 1876, then traded it for a farm in this township, and moved here on the 14th of November of that year. While at Shell Rock he served as Justice of the Peace two years. Mr. and Mrs. Town have a family of five; their oldest son served in the late war, enlisting in Company C, of the One Hundred and Eighteenth New York Regiment in 1863.

Thomas Wiley was born in Boston Massachusetts, on the 21st of November, 1820. At the age of thirteen years he was apprenticed to a manufacturer of printing presses, where he remained several years, subsequently learning the trade of piano forte maker in his native city. In 1840, he engaged with a firm of book publishers and dealers, remaining some six years. He was married in 1846, to Miss Emily A. Johhson, of Worcester, Massachusetts. A few years later they removed to Detroit, Michigan, where he was employed in the Superintendent's office of the M. C. Railroad, subsequently moved to Chicago, Illinois, afterward to Central Illinois, and in 1856, was elected Clerk of the Circuit Court and Recorder of Deeds in McHenry county, which office he held four years. He enlisted in the One Hundred and Twelfth Illinois Volunteer Infantry, but was rejected on account of physical disability. He was engaged in the dry goods business in Chicago for several years. In 1857, his wife died, leaving four children. He was afterward married to Miss Harriet E. Soule in Cambridge, Illinois. Three children survive their mother, who died in Albert Lea in June, 1882. Mr. Wiley moved to this place in 1873, and purchased a farm in section thirty-three. He has been forward in promoting agricultural enterprises, successfully managing the county fairs and introducing improved machinery. In 1874, he was elected Justice of the Peace, and has since filled the office.

HARTLAND.

CHAPTER LXIII.

DESCRIPTIVE—EARLY DAYS—MATTERS OF INTEREST—OFFICIAL RECORD—VILLAGE OF HARTLAND—STATISTICS—SCHOOLS—BIOGRAPHICAL.

The town bearing this name is one of the northern tier of townships in Freeborn county, and in the second tier from the west. It is bounded on the north by Waseca county; on the south by the township of Manchester; on the east by Bath; and on the west by Freeborn. It is constituted as originally surveyed, of thirty-six sections, but the survey correction line passing through it cuts off 278.85 acres, making it so much less than the usual congressional township, and leaving about 22,861.15 acres.

It is almost entirely a prairie town, and the expanse of undulating prairie presents a pleasing and beautiful contrast to the usual broken and sparsely timbered sections throughout this part of Minnesota. There are yet, however, traces of timber in the town, most of it about Mule Lake, in sections thirteen, fourteen, twenty-three, and twenty-four; and in the western part, in and about sections seven and twenty, although the latter has long since been converted into fertile and valuable farms.

The entire area of the town is well adapted to the modes of agriculture and crops of the day, and the farmers are, as a rule, in moderate circumstances, with fair farm buildings and moderate conveniences. The soil is of a dark loam, from eighteen to twenty-four inches in depth, underlaid with a sub-soil of clay. Rocks or stone of any kind are scarce, and there is no limestone whatever. The soil in the burr oak region of Mule Lake is more of a sandy nature.

There are two water courses in the town and one lake. Mule Lake is situated in the four corners of sections thirteen, fourteen, twenty-three and twenty-four, and constitutes the head waters of the LeSueur River, which takes a northward course, bearing a little to the east, until it leaves the township, when it bears westwardly. Boot Creek rises in section ten and flows northwesterly to enter Waseca county.

The Minneapolis & St. Louis railroad crosses the township from north to south, and on it is located the village bearing the same name as the township.

A few words as to the lake will not be out of place. The Indians named it Le Sueur, and it went by this name through the early settlement; but, n 1857, a fine span of mules belonging to B. J. Boardman were drowned in it, and the settlers began designating it as Mule Lake, until it was as generally known under this caption as the other. The lake finally got upon the map as Le Sueur or Mule Lake, and thus both will be perpetuated.

IN EARLY DAYS.

There seems to be a preponderating amount of testimony that the first settlers in this township were the Boardman brothers, who came in the spring of 1857, and located about Le Sueur or Mule Lake, one taking on the south and the other to the east of that body of water. Both had families and at once commenced the erection of houses. They remained for about one year and then left for parts unknown.

About the same time, two others, whose names have been forgotten, made their appearance and took claims on the north and west sides of Mule Lake; thus surrounding it. But little is known of the actions of any of these; as they left shortly for other scenes.

Uncle Charles Sheldon joined this settlement at about the period of its starting, coming from Rochester and taking a place just north of Mule Lake, in section thirteen, where he yet remains.

Levi Jones next put in an appearance, having come from Geneva, and jumped a claim from a Norwegian named Wunj, and during the summer he was joined by a Mr. Montgomery, who took a place just west of Uncle Sheldon's, built a house and remained until the next spring, when he left. Jens Thorson also came early this summer, and took the place he now occupies.

In October, 1857, George McColley, of New York, accompanied by his family and brother-in-law, Charles Morehouse, came with a yoke of cattle, a cow, and his household furniture, and located in section twenty-nine. Mr. McColley still lives on his place, although his estimable wife has passed away. He is one of Freeborn county's most public-spirited men. Charles Morehouse settled in section twenty, but has since moved away.

About the same time came the Motson family, consisting of Mr. and Mrs. Motson, and the five boys, Ole, Erick, Mot, John, and Andrew, who all settled about George McColley's place. They were Norwegians, and all are yet living in the town except the old gentleman, who died several years ago, and Mot Motson, who hung himself in Hartland.

In the fall of 1858, a pair from Wisconsin, in the *personnel* of John P. Duncan and John P. Huggins, drifted in and secured homes. Duncan dropped anchor in section twenty, and remained a citizen of the town until within two years, when matters became too torrid for him and he left between two days, as the saying goes. Huggins was a true man, and settling in section twenty-eight remained until the war broke out, when he enlisted and heroically died in defense of his native land.

The same year witnessed the arrival of Sandy Purdie, William C. Cram, Hat. Pierce, and Jonathan Pickard, who all took places and are yet on them, except the last named, Jonathan Pickard, who now resides in Freeborn township.

In 1859, Seth. S. Challis, of the New England States, made his arrival and commenced a sojourn in section thirty-one, which he still continues.

Speculators, after this, took most of the land, and if early settlers wanted it they must purchase at a good round figure. At this time the town had no name, more than Town 104, Range 22.

MATTERS OF INTEREST.

The first birth in Hartland township was Mary A. McColley, on the 9th of August, 1858. She is now Mrs. Charles Doty, and yet resides in the town. Freeman Beede was another early birth.

The first marriage ceremony performed within the limits of the town, took place in May, 1859, the high contracting parties being Mr. J. Seely and Miss Frances Farris.

Death, that insatiable enemy to immortality, soon hovered over the little community, and took as its first victim, Martha, a daughter of William and Judith Wrangham, aged nine years, on the 18th of June, 1859.

The township was named Hartland by Mrs. O. Sheldon, in 1858, and she also bestowed the same name upon the Post-office, which was established at the same time, with O. Sheldon as Postmaster. What the name was in honor of, or what had suggested it, we are unable to say.

During the late war of the rebellion bonds were

voted to the amount of $1,700, to secure volunteers, but it seems that it was ineffectual, for two drafts were made, notwithstanding nine volunteers were furnished. John McCartney, John McClelland, and Perry Haugen, of this township, never returned, the second named leaving a wife and child to mourn his loss.

Bonds to the amount of $10,000 were voted to the Minneapolis & St. Louis railroad, as bonus.

RELIGIOUS.—The first sermon preached in the township was by the Rev. Mr. McReynolds, an itinerant Methodist preacher, in the fall of 1858, at B. J. Boardman's house in section twenty-four. The Methodist church was organized in 1859, at William Wrangham's house, with Rev. Mr. Corey officiating and six members. The society finally merged with other denominations.

The Congregational society was organized in 1877, at the schoolhouse of district No. 8, by Elder Cobb, with twelve members. A store building was afterward purchased in the village of Hartland and converted into a church. The present pastor is Rev. Wilbur Fisk, with a membership of thirty-five.

The Presbyterian denomination first held services in the old log schoolhouse in 1869, with Rev. William Wrallson as minister, and for several years thereafter services were held regularly once in three weeks.

OFFICIAL RECORD.

The early town records of this township are a curious set of documents, and should be preserved as a curiosity, if not for official purposes. They consist of a small book made of foolscap, containing ten or fifteen pages, and from the center of the document some one has cut about the same number of pages, for some reason best known to the cutter. The school districts, oaths of officers, roads, and all matters pertaining to the town are promiscuously thrown together, and the legal terms such as "to wit," "whereas," "therefore," etc., are indiscriminately mixed in without regard to their appropriateness in connection with the subject; but calculated to inspire the sturdy pioneer officers with the full and fearful responsibility of their positions.

The first town meeting was held at the house of O. Sheldon on the 11th of May, 1858, and the following officers were elected for the ensuing year: Supervisors, B. J. Boardman, Chairman, J. L. Reynolds, and J. C. Seeley: Clerk, E. Boardman; Assessor, T. W. Calkins; Collector, B. J. Boardman; Constables, Alexander Spencer and James Sheehan; Justices of the Peace, T. W. Calkins and O. Sheldon; Overseer of the Poor, Jacob Heath; Overseers of Roads, E. A. Calkins and B. Cromwell.

The first meeting of Supervisors was held at the Town Clerk's office on the 14th of June, 1858, at which the town was divided into three road districts, and the following gentlemen were made overseers of them: First, E. A. Calkins; second, B Cromwell; third, Charles Morehouse.

The officers for 1882 are: Supervisors, Olaf Lee, Chairman, Sandy Purdie, and Peter Mace; Clerk, Peter Grinager; Treasurer, C. Hendrickson; Justices of the Peace, E. Wicks and S. S. Challis; Assessor, Frank Phipps; Constable, Peter Peterson.

VILLAGE OF HARTLAND.

This is the only village in the township. It is located on a fine village site, on a high portion of the town, and at every hand lies a fine view of prairie, dotted with the modest homes of thrifty farmers and artificial groves, and to the north farm houses can be seen at a distance of seven miles. The sight is all that can be desired, except the absence of a water course or lake; as one inhabitant suggested, "it is a boss site in summer but——in winter," as its elevation serves as an "estoppel," so to speak, of the wind. To the stranger the burg presents rather a dreary appearance, with the "butt ends" of the buildings pointed towards the railroad, and the absence of shade trees; but the last objection is fast being remedied by the citizens who are planting trees.

ITS EARLY DAYS.—The land upon which the village was started was originally the property of Torger Samuelson; but in 1877, when the railroad was started, twenty acres in the northwestern corner of section twenty-one, were purchased by A. E. Johnson, then of Albert Lea, and it was at once platted and the sale of lots begun. At this time William Morin platted a few acres of his land east of the railroad track, and for a time considerable strife existed, a few buildings being erected upon both sections. But finally a settlement was arrived at and Mr. Morin platted twenty acres into lots and blocks, just north of Johnson's in the southwest corner of section sixteen, and the whole forty and the small portion east of the track became the village site. This was at the time of the arrival of the railroad.

The first business opened in the town took place in September, 1877. A small frame building was moved from the town of Manchester to this place by Andrew J. Anderson, and opened for a boarding house. In a few months he sold it to Mots Motson, who enlarged and remodeled it, carrying it on for a year or so when he committed suicide by hanging himself, and the building is now occupied as a residence by his widow.

In September of the same year, 1877, J. P. Grinager and C. K. Hovland put up a frame building 20x80, one story high, and in November put in their stock of general merchandise. About two years later Mr. Hovland retired from the firm and Mr. Grinager continues it alone.

About the same time Scarseth and Lee commenced building and opened their $4,000 stock of general merchandise to customers late in October, in a building 50x22 and two stories high. In 1879 Mr. Scarseth died and Mr. Olof Lee has since managed the business.

In a few weeks after the above advent, E. S. Dunn moved a building, 22x50 feet, from Freeborn village to Hartland, and with it brought and opened a limited stock of drugs. Mr. Dunn afterwards sold to Hovland & Nelson, and they in turn rented to the present proprietor, Dr. M. Torkelson.

The same fall, Hoff & Seim moved a small building, 18x24 feet, to the village, bringing also a stock of goods, and locating their building east of the track, opened a general merchandise store. This store was formerly located on the farm of Louis Knudson in section fifteen, where the Post-office was originally established. In July, 1878, the goods were moved to the main part of the village, where the business is still continued, now under the firm of Seim & Hufland.

Thus the growth of the village went on, and new stores and saloons, and various other shops were started, and a number of buildings erected, many of which, however, are now vacant.

In 1881 a building was erected east of the railroad track, size 50x55 feet, for a hay press, by Tunell & Harper, in which the necessary machinery was put into operation by a twelve horse-power steam engine. This is quite an enterprise, and makes a ready market for all the hay put up in the neighborhood, baling it for shipment to the cities and distant markets. Lately W. P. Sergeant purchased Tunell's interest, and the business is continued under the new firm.

WAREHOUSES.—The first warehouse erected in the village was put up about the middle of September, 1877, by C. D. White, being a frame building, one story, size 32x40 feet. This was pretty well filled with grain by the time the railroad got here.

The next warehouse was put up by C. W. Whiton, in November, 1877, size 40x80, one story high, and was run by A. McDermid in the interest of the Millers' Association. The latter gentleman purchased it, and in 1881 it was increased in size and changed into an elevator with a capacity of about 9,000 bushels, using a ten horse-power steam engine. This elevator was entirely destroyed by fire in the winter of 1881-82.

In the winter of 1877 Grinager & Fitzgerald erected a warehouse 30x60 feet, which was operated for three years and then torn down.

P. Olson erected a warehouse, 30x50 feet, one story high, in 1878, which is still on the ground.

HARTLAND POST-OFFICE.

Before the village was thought of this Post-office was established and held in various parts of the township. In December, 1876, J. C. Hoff was appointed Postmaster, and moved the office to his store in section fifteen. In the fall of 1877 it was removed with the store to the village, and in 1879, when he sold out his interest in the store to his partner, Ole A. Seim, the latter gentleman became, and still is, Postmaster, with the office at the store. Mail now arrives daily on the railroad.

STATISTICS.

THE YEAR 1881.—Showing the acreage and yield in the township of Hartland for the year named.

Wheat—4,939 acres, yielding 58,651 bushels.
Oats—1,000 acres, yielding 33,353 bushels.
Corn—735 acres, yielding 29,615 bushels.
Barley—77½ acres, yielding 1,882 bushels.
Buckwheat—7 acres, yielding 90 bushels.
Potatoes—37 acres, yielding 4,494 bushels.
Beans—⅝ of an acre yielding 9 bushels.
Sugarcane,—2⅛ acres, yielding 369 gallons.
Cultivated hay—14 acres, yielding 91 tons.
Total acreage cultivated in 1881,—6,833.
Wild hay—2,799 tons.
Timothy seed—41½ bushels.

Apples—number of trees growing, 1,987, number bearing, 307, yielding 140¾ bushels.

Grapes—23 vines, yielding 285½ pounds.

Sheep—690 sheared, yielding 2,979 pounds of wool.

Dairy—409 cows, yielding 33,955 pounds of butter.

Hives of bees—2, yielding 20 pounds of honey.

THE YEAR 1882—Wheat, 4,434 acres; oats, 1,109; corn, 1,203; barley, 122; buckwheat, 24; potatoes, 43; beans, ⅛; sugar-cane, 2; cultivated hay, 52; flax, 1; other products, 55⅛; total acreage cultivated in 1887,050¼.

Apple trees—growing, 1,881; bearing, 349; grapevines bearing, 31.

Milch cows—416.

Sheep—644, yielding 2,880 pounds of wool.

Farms cultivated in 1881—104.

Forest trees planted and growing—209.

POPULATION.—The census of 1870 gave Hartland a population of 485. The last census, taken in 1880, reports 699 for this town. Showing an increase of 214.

EDUCATIONAL.

DISTRICT No. 8—The organization of this district was effected in the spring of 1863, at a meeting held at the house of Aaron Carr in section ten. The first officers were: Director, W. J. McClelland; Treasurer, William Wrangham; Clerk, William Beede. A log schoolhouse was bought for $9, and located in section eleven. The first school was taught by Miss Mary Bliss with eight scholars enrolled; the last term in this building was taught by Miss Maggie McClelland to an attendance of forty pupils. The present house is located near the center of section eleven, size 18x24, and cost $400. The present officers are Messrs. Hendrickson, Peterson, and Phipps.

DISTRICT No. 9.—This district embraces the territory in the southwestern part of the township, with a schoolhouse located in section thirty-five, and was among the first districts organized in the county, although the records only extend back to 1869, prior to that having, by some means, been lost. The district is in a flourishing condition, fully up to the average schools in attendance and efficiency.

DISTRICT No. 10.—It is claimed that this district was organized in the summer of 1858, and the first school was taught the same year by Mrs. Charles Morehouse at her residence, with six pupils present. The first school meeting was held in the fall of 1858, at the residence of C. Morehouse, six voters present, and the following officers were elected: Clerk, George McColley; Director, J. P. Duncan; Treasurer, Charles Morehouse. In 1863, a schoolhouse was erected near the center of the district, size 26x30, frame, at a cost of $800, which is still in use. The schoolhouse is located in the northern part of section thirty-two.

DISTRICT No. 62.—The first school held within the boundaries of this district was called in the summer of 1860, with twelve pupils present, and Elizabeth Sibley as instructor. In the spring of 1862 the district effected an organization, the officers being L. Knudson, O. Sheldon, and Levi Jones, and the first school after organization was taught by Miss C. Reynolds in a private house. In 1868 the school structure was erected in the center of section fourteen at a cost of $415. The present clerk is Henry Hanson.

DISTRICT No. 109.—This is the Hartland village school, and, as will be inferred from the number, is the youngest school district in the township. Prior to its organization the children attended in, and the territory was annexed to, other districts. At the time of platting the village, or shortly after, the district was brought into existence, and in the fall of 1878 the schoolhouse was erected, being a frame building, size 24x36 feet, two stories, with a belfry, well painted and furnished, and cost about $1,800. The lower story is used for church services, lectures, town meetings, and all public purposes. The school has had as many as fifty-five scholars enrolled and is in a flourishing condition now, having about thirty average attendance.

BIOGRAPHICAL.

WILLIAM BEEDE, one of the pioneers of this place, is a native of Vermont, born on the 9th of April, 1824. He was raised on a farm, and in 1845, married Miss Cynthia Sleeper, who was born in New Hampshire. In 1856, they came west and settled first in Wisconsin and two years later started with an ox team for this place. They pre-empted land in section four, which has since been their home. They have a family of three children. Mr. Beede in an early day took an active part in the organization and support of the schools.

S. S. CHALLIS was born in Corinth, Orange county, Vermont, on the 7th of April, 1822. In 1847 he removed to New Hampshire, and in 1850 to Massachusetts. He was married on the 22d of November, 1852, to Miss N. Julia Orr, who has borne him four children. In 1857 Mr. Challis went to California where he remained three years, then returned to Vermont, and in June, 1862, came to Hartland which has since been his home, his farm being in section thirty-one. He was Chairman of the Board of Supervisors in 1864, and the year following elected Justice of the Peace, which office he now holds. In 1863 he was chosen and served as captain of a military company raised in this county.

GULL GUTTORMSEN, one of the old residents of Hartland, is a native of Norway, born on the 16th of June, 1822. He sailed for America in 1850, landing in New York on the 4th of July, and came directly to Columbia county, Wisconsin. On the 10th of February, 1855, he was united in marriage with Miss Engelburt Tearksendatter, who has borne him two children, only one of whom is living. In 1856 they removed to Minnesota, and resided in Steele county for two years, then came to Hartland. He served in the First Minnesota Volunteer Infantry from the 16th of March, 1865, until the close of the war.

WALTER L. HANSEN, a native of the Empire State, was born in Oswego county on the 25th of May, 1845. When he was ten years old he moved with his parents to Illinois where, on the 1st of August, 1864, he enlisted in the One Hundred and Forty-sixth Illinois Volunteer Infantry, Company E, was on garrison duty all the time until discharged on the 10th of July, 1865. In 1867 he moved to McGregor, Iowa, and a year later to Wisconsin, where he married on the 18th of March, 1870, Miss Margaret Ramsey. She died on the 9th of June, 1872, leaving one child, Margaret Irene. In 1875 Mr. Hansen came to Hartland and purchased a farm in section three, which has since been his home. His present wife was formerly Miss Emma Challis, whom he married on the 26th of October, 1876. This union has been blessed with one child, Maud Lillie.

CARL HENDRICKSON was born in Norway on the 12th of May, 1838, and when ten years old emigrated with his parents to America. They settled in Wisconsin where he married, in 1860, Miss Esther Madison. They have had eleven children, nine of wom are living. He came here in 1865, and purchased his present farm. Since 1877 he has been Town Treasurer, and has held other local and school offices.

OLE T. JOHNSON was born in Norway on the 6th of August, 1856, and when an infant came with his parents to America. The family first located in Columbia county, Wisconsin, until 1867, then came to this township and have since made it their home, their farm being in section two.

LEWIS KNUDSON, one of the early residents here, is a native of Norway, and dates his birth the 5th of August, 1830. He was married in April, 1853, to Miss Isabel Kittleson, and the same year they came to America. In 1858, they moved from Wisconsin to this township, and secured a farm in section fifteen. Mrs. Knudson died on the 28th of April, 1871, having borne seven children, only one of whom is now living. His present wife, Miss Isabel Torgenson, he married on the 20th of May, 1872, and of six children born to this union, four are living.

THOMAS S. LEE was born near Bergen, Norway, on the 3d of January, 1834. When he was twenty-two years of age he came to America and first settled in Racine county, Wisconsin. He was married in 1861, to Miss Sarah Johnson, also a native of Norway. They resided in different parts of the latter State until 1873, when they came to Minnesota and located in Freeborn township until 1880, then came to Hartland. They have a family of ten children.

OLUF LEE was born in Norway, about twenty-five miles from Christiania, on the 21st of April, 1849. His father died when he was twelve years old, and after finishing his schooling he clerked in a store. When he was seventeen years of age he went to sea, and in 1870, spent one summer traveling in England. He emigrated to America in 1871, and located in Oconomowoc, Wisconsin, and clerked in a dry goods store for ten months, thence to LaCrosse in the same occupation. He was subsequently employed as book-keeper for J. C. Easton, of Chatfield, and later filled the same position in the First National Bank in LaCrosse, Wisconsin, also for a lumbering company. In 1877, he came to Hartland and bought an interest in the first store in this place, and is now sole proprietor. He is at present Chairman of the board of Supervisors, and has held other local offices.

George McColley, one of the pioneers of Hartland, was born in Cattaraugus county, New York, on the 24th of March, 1831. When he was young his parents moved to Ohio, and in 1845, to Portage City, Wisconsin. On the 6th of March, 1853, George was joined in wedlock with Miss Electa Morehouse and they have six children. In 1857, Mr. McColley started with an ox team to this place and for two months camped in his wagon, in the meantime putting up a slab house in section twenty-nine which has since been his home. He served for a time in Company E, of the First Minnesota Volunteer Infantry. His wife died on the 19th of July, 1881.

Francis E. Phipps, a native of New Hampshire, was born on the 14th of April, 1833. When young he learned engineering, and in 1854, came to Green Lake county, Wisconsin, where he was engaged in running stationary engines in a steam mill. In 1860, he came to Minnesota and took a claim in this place, sections ten and fifteen, where he has since lived. He was married in 1862, to Miss Mary Samson, a native of Canada. After a lingering illness of several years Mrs. Phipps died in 1881, leaving three children. Mr. Phipps has taken an active part in the support and organization of the schools and has held several local offices.

O. A. Seim was born in Norway on the 25th of December, 1840, and when fifteen years old emigrated to America. He was engaged in farming in Wisconsin until 1857, then came to Steele county, Minnesota, and worked his father's farm until buying one of his own. At the same time he carried on a general mercantile store in the southeastern part of Waseca county. In 1876, he came to Hartland township and opened the first store in the place with John C. Hoff as partner, but a year later moved to the village and is now carrying on a merchandise business in company with Oluf Hufland. Mr. Seim has been Postmaster since 1879, besides holding other offices.

Peter P. Shager, one of the early settlers of this county, is a native of Norway, born on the 16th of January, 1819. He came to America in 1849, and resided in Dane county, Wisconsin, one year, afterward in Columbia county until 1854, then went to Winneshiek county, Iowa. In the spring of 1857, he came to this county and settled in Manchester until enlisting on the 15th of August, 1862, in the Tenth Minnesota Volunteer Infantry, Company E, and served twenty-one months. After his discharge he located on a farm in section thirty-four, Hartland, and has since devoted his time to its cultivation.

LONDON.

CHAPTER LXIV.

Topography and location—Early settlers—Statistics — Mediums of education — Biographical.

This is the southeastern sub-division of Freeborn county, with Mower county bounding it on the east; the state of Iowa on the south; the township of Oakland on the north; and Shell Rock on the west. It is a complete congressional township of 36 sections or square miles, and comprising the territory, technically speaking, of Township 101, Range 19.

The greater part of the township is prairie land, and is well adapted to tillage and profitable agriculture. Toward the central and northern part there is considerable small timber; such as burr, red, and scrub oak, interspersed with natural meadows and small patches of prairie, and is known as "oak-opening land." The general inclination of the surface is rolling, although it may be said to be more level than any township in Freeborn county. In and about sections fifteen and sixteen is the most broken, although not enough so to be impractical for cultivation. The soil is a dark loam, rich and productive, and is underlain with a subsoil of clay. The best farming land in the town is the eastern part, while the balance is moderate or up to the average.

There are few streams and only one lake to water the surface of London. This body of water lies near the center of the town, and is known as Elk Lake, covering the greater part of 160 acres in section twenty-one. Two streams flow across the northeastern part of the town, and one traverses he southwest corner.

EARLY SETTLERS.

The early steps leading to the founding and subsequent development of this thriving township, began at about the same period as did most of the towns in Freeborn county, and in none of them has the growth been more substantial, or progress more marked than in London. The early pioneers of this locatity were not of a class that were indolent; but they were thriving, energetic, and high spirited. They were good neighbors, and so good neighborhoods were created, and this was one of the great comforts, and in fact, blessings, for which the pioneers had cause to be thankful; for without the few good companions to each, which formed neighborhoods, and the unanimity of good fellowship and purpose, pioneeer life on the then barren frontier must have been unendurable.

About the first settlement made in the township was by a party of various nationalities from Wisconsin, who settled in sections eight, nine, and ten, in what was termed the burr oak opening land. This party was made up of Edward F. Budlong, who now lives in Shell Rock township; John T. Asher from Wisconsin, who is now dead; Asa Bullock and family, and a Mr. Carpenter, the last two mentioned, after a year's residence in London, pulled up stakes and removed to Oakland township, where friends and relatives had preceded them. In the article upon that town they are treated more at length. During the ensuing winter the young folks who were matrimonially inclined decided to have the conjugal knot tied in the overlasting and let-no-man-put-asunder way; so the ox teams were "*corraled*" and yoked, and away the parties hied themselves on a rapid ox walk for Osage, Iowa, 25 miles distant, where the ceremony was performed making the *four, two*, and uniting Lemuel Bullock to Miss Carpenter, and Willard L. Carpenter to Miss Bullock.

This was about all who arrived in London in the year 1855, and they passed the winter as best they could, depending upon each other for entertainment and keeping off despondency. During the following year, however, the beauties of this region began to be heralded abroad, and many who had come to realize the inequality of the contest between labor and capital in the older and eastern States, thronged in to find a new home, where, for the first years, at least, equality would reign supreme and merit must be ranked side by with capital. Among those who arrived in 1856, as many of the most prominent ones as can be remembered, will be given.

William N. Goslee, a native of Connecticut, who had stopped for a time in Iowa, came from the latter place with an ox team, and in May, 1856, secured the place he now occupies in section thirteen. Timothy F. Goslee came about the same time; but located just over the line in Mower county.

Benjamin Stanton joined this party by securing a slice from Uncle Sam's domain in section twelve. In October, 1857, while engaged in building a log house his earthly career was abruptly terminated by a stroke of lightning.

Just north of Stanton, in section one, the same year, B. R. P. Gibson, a native of Connecticut, succeeded in making his anchor take firm hold and his moorings still remain intact. H. B. Riggs, late of Michigan, joined this party and made himself a home in section eleven, where he remained for a number of years, and then removed to Shell Rock, where he finally paid the debt of mortality.

These parties had scarcely got nicely settled when the tranquility of their reign was disturbed by the arrival of a native of Wisconsin in the person of D. B. German, who located in section twelve, where he remained until 1880, when he removed to Mower county, and now lives there.

Avery Strong, a native of New York State, was another of the arrivals in 1856, who secured a habitation in this settlement by installing himself in section thirteen. He soon left, however, and is now living in his native State.

Silon Williams came from Vermont at about the same time, and planted his stakes in section eleven, where he still continues to thrive.

Edward Thomas, also about the same time, commenced a sojourn which he still perpetuates in this settlement.

William Davis and a Mr. Lunt also arrived in 1865.

Section twenty-one received a settler this year in the person of Ole Lewis, who remained a year or two and then left the country.

In the spring of 1857 James H. Goslee left his home in Connecticut and pushed toward the setting sun, coming as far as Dubuque by rail, from there taking the stage route to St. Paul, where he was engaged for a couple of weeks, and then came on as far as West Union with a man who had horses for sale. The snow was very deep and he was delayed for several days; but finally found a man who was on a milling trip from Chickasaw county, Iowa, and with him rode to the latter place. Here he was detained for three days by a severe blizzard, and was finally carried on to Otronto, Iowa, from whence he walked to his brother's place in Lyle, Mower county, who is mentioned above as having settled there the year previous. Being favorably impressed by the country, bought a place in sections twelve and thirteen in this township, of Sylvester West, which he still occupies.

In 1858 James H. Stewart, a native of the Empire State, made his appearance in London, and became an inhabitant by placing his sign manual upon papers for a claim in section twenty-four, where he now tills the soil.

The same year Joseph Chmelik and A. Raymond, Bohemians, arrived and took claims in section five where they are still plodding.

After this the immigration was more gradual, yet this is enough to indicate the class with which London began its civilization.

MATTERS OF INTEREST.

The first birth in the township occurred late in the fall of 1856, and brought into existence George Adkins.

The second made its appearance in February, 1857, and this time a child of Horace Lamb became a living creature.

The first death was that of Benjamin F. Stanton, who died by a stroke of lightning on October 6th, 1857. His remains were deposited in their last resting place near Otronto, Iowa.

For political purposes this township was originally merged with Oakland, and subsequently for a time a part of Shell Rock; but finally it was set off from these and is now a separate organization under the head of London.

From the records we learn that the first title to land was acquired by William Clatworthy and W. A. Pierce, on the 15th of August, 1856, these parties taking their claims on sections eight and nine.

LONDON POST-OFFICE.—This office was established in September, 1876, with Henry Lang as Postmaster, and shortly afterward Mrs. Meadowcroft was appointed as deputy, with the office in section fourteen. Mail arrives once each week from Austin, the mail carrier being John Connor. The office remained in section fourteen until April, 1880, when Mr. James Lacy was commissioned Postmaster and Marion Connor deputy, and again, in the spring of 1882 the Postmasters changed, this time John Manning took the mail pouch keys and still fills the position of Postmaster, the office being kept in section fifteen at his residence.

STATISTICS.

THE YEAR 1881.—Showing the acreage and yield in the township of London for the year named:

Wheat—2,365 acres, yielding 25,723 bushels.
Oats—753 acres, yielding 22,321 bushels.
Corn—710 acres, yielding 26,895 bushels.
Barley—169 acres, yielding 4,491 bushels.
Rye—1 acre, yielding 6 bushels.
Buckwheat—5 acres, yielding 22 bushels.
Potatoes—28¼ acres, yielding 3,049 bushels.
Sugar cane—3¼ acres, yielding 300 gallons.
Cultivated hay—56 acres, yielding 42 tons.
Total acreage cultivated in 1881—4,132½.
Wild hay—569 tons.
Apples—number of trees growing, 704; number bearing, 111, yielding 25½ bushels.
Tobacco—19 pounds.
Sheep—31 sheared:
Dairy—129 cows, yielding 5,275 pounds of butter.

THE YEAR 1882.—Wheat, 995 acres; oats, 758; corn, 1,059; barley, 224; rye, 10; buckwheat, 2; potatoes, 34; sugar cane, 2¾; cultivated hay, 99; flax, 3.

Total acreage cultivated in 1882—3,188¾.
Apple trees—growing, 668; bearing, 93.
Grape vines—bearing, 1.
Milch cows—150.
Sheep—31.
Whole number of farms cultivated in 1882—55.
Forest trees planted and growing, 3¼ acres.

POPULATION.—The census of 1870 gave London a population of 311. The last census, taken in 1880, reports 614 for this town; showing an increase of 303.

MEDIUMS OF EDUCATION.

DISTRICT No. 51.—Effected an organization in 1862, and the following year the first term of school was held at the residence of H. B. Riggs, in section eleven, by Miss Orpha Skinner, with an attendance of about twelve scholars. Then, in 1867, the schoolhouse was erected in the western part of section twelve, which has since been greatly improved. The last term of school was taught by Miss Belle Cheadle with an average attendance of twenty-five scholars.

DISTRICT No. 59.—Embraces territory in the southwestern part of the town, and has a schoolhouse located in the northern part of section thirty-two.

DISTRICT No. 71.—This district came into existence by organization in 1865, the first school being held in Morgan Eckert's granary, in section eighteen, taught by Miss Dora Sabin with an attendance of about six pupils. After this school was continued in private houses and granaries until the summer of 1869, when a schoolhouse, 16x20, was completed in section eight at a cost of $220, and Carrie Harrison taught a school with an attendance of eighteen. The house has since been remodeled and improved to the extent of $500. The last teacher was John D. Murphy; attendance thirty-two.

DISTRICT No. 94.—Effected an organization in 1874, and the school building was erected the same year, in the southern part of section twenty-three, size 20x20, with an ante-room 12x16 feet, and cost $1,025. The first teacher was Mr. John Bewick with an attendance of fifteen scholars. Ella Meadowcroft was the last instructor of the young idea and had an average attendance of about twenty pupils.

BIOGRAPHICAL.

PERSONS BUMP was born in Wyoming county, New York, on the 29th of March, 1844. When he was seven years old his parents came west and settled in Wisconsin. Persons enlisted in 1862, in the Twenty-second Wisconsin Volunteer Infantry, Company E, was in considerable active service in the South and spent four months in Libby prison, receiving an honorable discharge in 1865, having attained the rank of Frst Lieutenant. He returned to his home and the same year married Miss Marinette Colson, a native of Ohio. In 1868 they came to London township, and bought a farm of two hundred and forty acres, in sections twenty-two and twenty-seven and have since made it their home. They have five children.

THOMAS BONNALLIE, one of the early settlers of this place, is a native of Scotland, born on the 5th of Apil, 1819, His parents came to America when he was an infant, and located in Canada. He remained with an uncle in Scotland until four years old, then joined his parents in Canada. In 1851 he was united in marriage with Miss Charlotte Philips and two years later they came to Wisconsin. Since 1856 Mr. Bonnallie has been a resident of this place. His first wife died, and in 1873, he married his present, Mrs. Janette Campbell, a native of Philadelphia, Penn. The issue of this union is seven children.

JAMES H. GOSLEE, one of the old and respected citizens of this section of the country, is a native of Connecticut, born in Hartford county, on the 31st of January, 1831. The early part of his life was spent in farming and learning the carpenter trade, and in 1857, he came to this township. His farm now contains over seven hundred acres and is well improved, he devoting his time principally to stock raising. In 1860 he was united in wedlock to Miss Zillah T. Beach, a native of New York. They have had two children; Henry A., born on the 2d of July, 1861; and Dwight W., born on the 8th of April, 1866. The latter died on the 12th of January, 1882.

WILLIAM N. GOSLEE, another pioneer of London township, was born in Hartford county, Connecticut, on the 12th of May, 1826. He was married before leaving his native State, in 1850, to Miss Sarah E. Ellis. They came west in 1855 and located in Iowa, but the following year came to this place, staking out a farm in section thirteen where he has since made his home. Mrs. Goslee died in 1862. His present wife was formerly Mary A. Cheadle, a native of Indiana, and they have two children. Mr. Goslee owns a fine farm, and since his residence here has served the town and county in different capacities.

ROGER P. GIBSON was born in Connecticut on the 17th of August, 1817. He grew to manhood on a farm and in 1840, married Miss Colista Goslee, who died three years later. Some years after he was again married to a Connecticut lady, who came west with him to Iowa in 1855, and to this township the following year. Death again entered his home in 1861, and took away his partner in life, whose remains rest in the cemetery at this place. In 1863, he was wedded to Miss Emma M. Bolton, who was born in Ohio. This union has been blessed with six children. Mr. Gibson's farm has the appearance of a careful and experienced manager. He is one of the pioneers here and has filled offices of trust in the town.

ARTHUR E. JOHNSTON, a New Yorker, was born on the 6th of June, 1850. When he was sixteen years old he came with his parents to Butler county, Iowa. They resided there until 1879, then came to this place and located in section twenty-four, which is still their home. Mr. Johnston is at present Treasurer of the school board.

HENRY LANG, a native of Scotland, was born on the 10th of January, 1842. He came with his parents to America when an infant, first settled in New York City and afterward lived in Missouri. After a residence of five years in the latter place the family came to Wisconsin and in 1862 to this township. Henry was joined in matrimony to Miss Jane Meadowcroft, also a native of Scotland. They have a family of seven children. Mr. Lang owns a well improved farm of two hundred and forty acres.

JOHN W. MANNING, the present Postmaster of London, was born in New Jersey on the 31st of October, 1845. He remained in his native place until twenty years old, then came to Rock county, Wisconsin, and in 1867, married Miss Sylvia Mosher, a Canadian lady. The issue of the union is five children. In 1872, Mr. Manning moved to Iowa and in 1879 came to this place. He has a good farm in section fifteen.

JOHN ROBERTSON was born near Glasgow, Scotland, on the 15th of May, 1836. He came with his parents to America in 1844, and resided for some time in Rock county, Wisconsin. In 1858 he married Miss Margaret Campbell, also a native of Scotland. They came to Minnesota in 1866, and settled in section twelve of this township, which has since been their home, the farm containing three hundred and twenty acres. Mr. and Mrs. Robertson have a family of three children.

JAMES H. STEWART, one of the early settlers of London township, is a native of New York, born on the 19th of August, 1832. In 1853 he came to Wisconsin, where he married, in 1856, Miss Clarissa H. Hubbard, a native of Vermont. The same year they moved to Illinois, and a year later came to this place, taking land in section twenty-four, which is now a well cultivated farm. Mr. Stewart has filled offices of trust since coming here. He is the father of three children.

EDWARD T. THOMAS, a native of Wales, was born in March, 1835, and when very young came with his parents to America. They located in Utica, New York, and several years later moved to Ohio, finally coming west to Rock county, Wisconsin. In 1860 Edward married Anna Thompson, of Ohio. The following year he came to Minnesota and took a claim in London, section twenty-two. Mr. and Mrs. Thomas have a family of three children.

JAMES VAN WINKLE, deceased, was born in Illinois on the 9th of September, 1825. He was married in 1853 to Miss Nancy Sutherland, also a native of Illinois. They came to Minnesota in 1858, but only remained a year and a half, and returned to their native State. In 1861 they came again to this State and bought a farm in London, where Mr. Van Winkle died on the 4th of February, 1876. He left a widow and six children to mourn his loss.

SILON WILLIAMS, one of the pioneers of this place, was born in Derby, Vermont, on the 23d of July, 1832. When twenty-two years old he moved to Osage, Iowa, and a year later came to this place, settling in section eleven. He was joined in wedlock in 1860 with Miss Mary A. Phelps, a Canadian lady. They have ten children. In 1862 Mr. Williams enlisted in the Ninth Minnesota Volunteer Infantry, Company C, spent one year on the frontier, and then went south and participated in considerable active service, receiving his discharge in 1865. He has since made his farm his home.

MANCHESTER.

CHAPTER LXV.

LOCATION AND TOPOGRAPHY—EARLY SETTLEMENT—ORGANIZATION—STATISTICS—EVENTS OF INTEREST—MANCHESTER VILLAGE—SCHOOLS—BIOGRAPHICAL.

Whatever the population of this town, it is certain it bears an English name. It lies in the second tier from the north and also second from the western line of Freeborn county. Its contiguous surroundings are, Hartland on the north; Bancroft on the east; Pickerel Lake on the south; and Carlston on the west. It contains 11,689 acres less than a full congressional township, because of the "correction line" of the survey, and has thirty-six sections, comprising the territory of Town 103, Range 22, in all about 22,923 acres.

Originally the greater part of the town was covered with timber of small varieties, such as burr and black oak, maple, basswood, black walnut, butternut, ash, and elm, interspersed with natural meadows and prairie land. The southwestern part of the town was principally burr oak opening land, except in sections twenty-eight and twenty-nine, where is found the sugar maple which is still, to a considerable extent, intact. The greater part of what was originally timber land is now under a high state of cultivation. The principal parcel of timber now in the town is black and burr oak, the latter being the most plentiful. The entire northwest portion of the town is a rolling prairie, and is among the best of farming land.

The soil, as a rule, is a dark rich loam of from two to three feet in depth, and underlaid with a subsoil of clay; but this is particularly applicable to the timber land, as on the prairie a lighter tendency is apparent, while the subsoil is of clay and sand. All the land is very productive and well adapted to the mode of cultivation and crops of the latitude. The prairie land is made picturesque by groves of domestic poplar, which have been planted and well cared for by the thrifty settlers.

The township is well watered and has its full complement of small lakes and water courses. A cluster of small lakes is found in the southwestern part of the town, and on the map appear the names of Lake Peterson, Sugar Lake, Silver Lake, and Lake Whitney, which are all near together on sections twenty, twenty-one, twenty-eight, twenty-nine, and thirty. The only one of these having an outlet is Lake Peterson, from which a small stream taking a southeasterly course finally leaves the town *via* section thirty-six, and enters Bancroft township. South of this cluster of lakes, in section thirty-two, Spring Lake infringes upon and covers a few acres of land. A small body of water known as Gun Lake is located in the eastern part of section nine. School Section Lake is located in the southeastern portion of the town, in section thirty-six.

There is but one village in the township, Manchester, located in section fifteen, on the Minneapolis & St. Louis Railroad, which crosses the township from north to south, bearing a little southeasterly.

The surface of the town is rolling, and although, in places, inclined to be rather abrupt in its modulations, is not hilly, or in any place broken sufficiently to be detrimental to agriculture. The town is well adapted to agricultural purposes, and has a large cultivated area yielding good crops of the cereals.

EARLY SETTLEMENT.

The earliest attempt at settling this town commenced in 1856, when, on the 6th day of June of that year, S. S. Skiff, a native of New York, came from Wisconsin and took a claim in section twenty-six, where he remained until 1858, and then returned to Wisconsin where he stayed until 1860. This year he again pushed his way back to his newly made habitation and settled down in earnest. He made this his home until 1880, and then removed to the town of Alden, where his light still "holds out to burn." He, it is claimed, was the very first settler, and there is a preponderance of testimony to uphold it. He had been here about one week, when, on the 15th of June, 1856, there arrived a party from Iowa, which soon took the name of Winneshiek county settlement as they came from their Norwegian homes by way of Iowa and had stopped for a time in the county indicated.

Among this party were Gunie Thykeson, who secured a place in sections nine and ten, upon the banks of the miniature lake which received its name after him, and he may still be found upon the place, evidently well satisfied with his venture.

N. N. Wangin, who planted his stakes upon a part of Uncle Sam's domain in section seventeen, where he may still be found.

Rollof, a brother to Gunie Thykeson, made himself at home in section fifteen, where he remained until 1879, when he took up his abode upon a place in sections nine and sixteen.

Stiner Mickelson also settled in section fifteen and remained until 1864, when he disposed of his farm and removed to Blue Earth City, where he still lives.

Ole O. Klappe, who settled in section twenty-two, and remained until 1858, when he went to Bancroft, and in 1864, went to the south.

This comprised the original members of the Wineshiek county settlement. They were all natives of Norway, and they have since been joined by countrymen, who have thronged in until they constitute the greater part of the town's inhabitants.

In the latter part of the same month that the above settlement arrived, in June, 1856, a party known as the Rock county settlement, all natives of Norway, who had sojourned for a short time in Rock county, Wisconsin, came to the town, and their names and movemements are chronicled as follows:

Thor Anderson, Andrew Everson, and Ole Kittleson all took claims in and about section ten, where they still remain.

Peter O. Fossum planted his hopes on a tract in section fourteen, and is still bustling around there.

Ole Peterson commenced a sojourn which he still perpetuates in section fifteen.

Halver Peterson anchored his bark of worldly possessions in section nine, and remained there until August, 1868, when, as matters, evidently, did not progress in a satisfactory manner, tired of the practical problem of world's life, solved the matter by hanging himself; his family still live upon the old place.

O. O. Fossum located on sections twenty-one and twenty-two, and remained there until the time of his death, which occurred in 1878, and his remains were sorrowfully deposited in their last resting place, in the Norwegian Lutheran Cemetery. His family still occupy the old home-stead.

THE HONORED DEAD.

HENRY SCHMIDT came to this county when it was wild and desolate, but lived to see the town settled, filled with farms, and in a flourishing condition. He had been Town Treasurer, and was a thorough American German. The respect in which he was held was attested by the large funeral which took place a few days after his death, which was on the 6th of September, 1878, at the age of 67 years.

OLE OLSON FOSSUM came to Manchester in 1856, took a claim and opened a farm and continued to live on it until the 9th of June, 1878, when he went over the river at the age of 64. He is remembered as a fine old gentleman.

MRS. HARRIET L. JOHNSON was thirty-five years of age when her presence was required in the great beyond, on the 6th of April, 1873. She was a daughter of Dr. Solomon Douglass, of Oswego county, New York. With her husband she came west as far as Winnebago county, Wisconsin, where they remained six years, and then came to Freeborn county. Three children were left. She was a woman who won the esteem of all her acquaintances

OFFICIAL ORGANIZATION.

The first town meeting, at which the organization was effected, was held at the house of Ole Peterson, on the 11th of May, 1858, pursuant to to notice of the Clerk of County Commissioners. After the usual preliminaries the meeting was called to order, and the polls opened for the election of town officers for the ensuing year. Upon counting the ballots the following candidates were found to have the number of votes set opposite their names, as follows:

For Chairman of Supervisors, Matthias Anderson received 25 votes; E. S. Smith, 7. Supervisors, Ole Peterson and Tostin Knutson, unanimously elected, 32 votes each. Clerk, James E. Smith, 32. Assessor, Bennett Asleson, 25; Mattias Anderson, 7. Collector, Thomas Anderson, 32. Overseer of the Poor, John Ellingson, 32. Constables, Charles Oleson and David Ames, each 32 votes. Justices of the Peace, James E. Smith and Thomas Oleson, 32 votes each. Overseer of Roads, Charles Olson, 25; Ole Peterson, 7. There were in all thirty-two votes cast.

TOWN NAME.—The original name of the township was "Olborg," in honor of the Post-office in in Norway from whence Ole Peterson came. After a short reign under this caption it was changed to Buckeye, in a joke upon Stanley and S. B. Smith, who were natives of Ohio, and a Post-office by this name was established. In 1858, at the meeting above mentioned, the matter of the name again came up, and "Liberty" was proposed to take the place of the Ohio caption. The matter was put to a vote and resulted in a unanimous assent to the new name. The town then commenced its career as "Liberty"; but in a short time notice was received from the State Auditor that as there were already two "Libertys" in the State, their name must be changed. In accordance with this, in 1859, the name was again changed, this time, finally, to "Manchester."

Thus the township of Manchester was started on its career as a municipality, and since that time the affairs of the public have been faithfully cared for. It being a farming community there has been but little expenditure of public funds, except for school and highway purposes, and the burdens of local taxation have never been excessive.

The present township officials are as follows: Supervisors, Claus Faudt, Chairman, Rolloff Thykeson, and Thor Anderson; Clerk, I. A. Rodsater; Assessor, D. H. Johnson; Treasurer, Bennett Asleson; Justice of the Peace, L. C. Larken; Constable, M. O. Whitney. The last town meeting was held in the spring of 1882, at the schoolhouse of District No. 18.

STATISTICS.

This article is intended to convey to the reader an idea of the wealth and productiveness of the township, and to what extent the facilities and richness of soil which nature has endowed, have been utilized and improved.

THE YEAR 1881.—Showing the acreage and yield in the township of Manchester for the year named:

Wheat—2,696 acres, yielding 16,937 bushels.

Oats—450 acres, yielding 16,147 bushels.

Corn—521 acres, yielding 17,650 bushels.

Barley—26 acres, yielding 690 bushels.

Rye—10 acres, yielding 200 bushels.

Buckwheat—1 acre, yielding 25 bushels.

Potatoes—68 acres, yielding 2,260 bushels.

Flax seed—42 acres, yielding 350 bushels.

Total acreage cultivated in 1881—3,814.

Wild hay—2,184 tons.

Apples—number of trees growing, 1,453; number bearing 275 yielding 78 bushels.

Sheep—366 sheared, yielding 1,200 pounds of wool.

Dairy—872 cows, yielding 15,700 pounds of butter.

THE YEAR 1882.—Wheat, 2,894 acres; oats, 532; corn, 500; potatoes, 29; other products, 19; total acreage cultivated in 1882—3,974.

Apple trees growing—1,902.

Milch cows—518.

Sheep—67, yielding 631 pounds of wool.

POPULATION.—The census of 1870 gave Manchester a population of 701. The last census, taken in 1880, reports 784 for this town, showing an increase of 83.

MATTERS OF INTEREST.

The first child born in the township was Michael Michaelson, in September, 1856. The boy grew to manhood, was married, and now lives in Blue Earth county.

It is claimed that the first marriage in the township occurred in December, 1858, the high contracting parties being Mads Madson and Miss Opengarden. The ceremony was performed by Thomas Oleson at the residence of John Ellingson, in section sixteen. The groom died in 1880, and the widow now resides in Hartland.

The above, however, was not the first marriage of parties from this town; for on the 2d of October, 1858, a double wedding occurred in Cedar Rapids, Iowa, which united the destinies of Miss Inglebert Peterson to Ole Knudson, and Miss Sarah Kittleson to Lewis Sebertson. The ceremony was performed by Rev. L. Clausen.

The first death occurred in August, 1858, and carried to that mysterious hereafter, Peter Johnson, aged 24 years.

The first religious services in the town were held in June, 1858, at the residence of Ole Peterson, in section fifteen, by the Rev. Mr. Brown, a Lutheran minister. The church organization was not effected until 1876.

The first house in the township was erected in June, 1856, by Gunio Thykeson, on section nine. It was a log building, 12x14 feet, and was afterward used as a stable.

Mickle Mickleson, in July, 1856, the following month, erected the second house of the same material, and this was subsequently used as a blacksmith shop.

At an early day a number of the pioneers in a rude way manufactured sorghum, by using three wooden home-made rollers, propelled by a yoke of oxen, for a press; but this crude machinery has long since been supplanted by the patent process and new machinery.

It is claimed that Mathias Anderson, who came from the town of Manchester, Boone county, Illinois, gave to this township its present name.

Originally town meetings were held in private houses, and anywhere that shelter could be found. At present they are held in the schoolhouse of district No. 18, in section twenty-two.

The first blacksmith shop was erected and operated by a Mr. Mickleson, on the northwest quarter of section fifteen. In 1865 he sold out and went to Blue Earth county, where he now lives. This was erected in 1856.

In 1858, the next shop was erected in section thirteen, size 12x14 feet, and put in operation by Lewis Oleson. It was of logs, with a log and sod roof, and was operated by him until about 1873, when it changed hands: finally, in 1879, becoming the property of Ole O. Olson who now owns it.

Suicide.—In August, 1868, Halver Peterson, an early Norwegian settler living in section ten, disgusted and disheartened by the vicissitudes and uncertainties of this cruel world, departed from it, in spirit, by hanging himself to a tree. He had been sick for eighteen months, and the only excuse offered, was the old one in these cases, "tired of life."

Frozen to Death.—A Mr. Gulbrandson was frozen to death on the evening of the 8th of January, 1873. One of his oxen perished with him.

Manchester's War Record.—It cannot be denied that this town did its full share during the war of the rebellion. Of those who volunteered and went into the service, nine never returned, finding graves in southern soil. Strengen Benson was the only married man of the departed heroes; he left a wife and two children to mourn his loss. The rest were all single men and most of their parents resided in the town at the time. Manchester voted bonds to the amount of $4,000 for the purpose of securing volunteers to fill the quota assigned the town, which amount was duly paid and recruits secured.

Buckeye Post-office.—This was the first office in the township, having been established in 1858, named after the pet cognomen of Ohio, with James E. Smith as Postmaster, and the office at his residence in section thirty, where it remained, there being but little business for it, until 1860, when S. B. Smith was appointed, with a mail route from Mankato to Otronto, Iowa, under the supervision of A. L. Davis, who carried the mail by team. After a time A. G. Hall was appointed, and the office was removed to his residence in section one of Alden, where it was finally discontinued about 1870.

Manchester Post-office was established in the village of this name in 1878, upon a petition gotten up by H. R. Fossum and E. H. Stensrud, and signed by a majority of the citizens. H. R. Fossum was first appointed as the Postmaster, and held the office until 1880, with a business in the meantime amounting to $6 per quarter, when E. H. Stensrud was commissioned and still holds the mail pouch key; the business of the last quarter amounted to $8.89. The office is kept in the store at the village.

Farmers' Mutual Insurance Company of Manchester.—This corporation, instituted for the protection of the farmers from fire and lightning, is growing rapidly each year; and, as there is not visible in this, the band of dishonesty and trickery that is so apparent in the procedures of a great many of the city corporations, it has been, and, with the same capable management in the future that it has had in the past, will continue to be a true benefit and assistance to its patrons. The company was organized at the Central church of the Freeborn Norwegian Lutheran Congregation on the 7th of December, 1876, on which day the following officers were elected; President, O. Peterson; Secretary, I. A. Rodsater; Treasurer, O. Narveson; and Directors, E. C. Johnson, K. Ingebrigtson, A. N. Teslow, I. Hammer, H. Stensrud, and John Madson. It commenced business on the 10th of February, 1877, and consisted at that time of 102 members, and the capital insured was $135,172. During the first year the company had a loss of only $10. Total losses during the first five years, $765. Last year's loss was $200. At the last annual meeting the company consisted of 338 members, with an amount of insurance of $375,000.

Present officers: President, O. Peterson; Secretary, Iver A. Rodsater; Treasurer, O. Narveson; Directors, C. C. Johnson, K. Ingebrigtson, A. Teslow, C. Jonsrud, H. Stensrud, John Madson.

Norwegian Lutheran Church.—This society was organized about 1876, with Rev. V. Koren officiating, and had about nine members. In 1876, the church was erected in section four, Gust. Peterson donating two acres of land for a site. It cost about $5,700, and is 36x82 feet, with a tower, in which an 800 pound bell has been placed which cost $300, and is one of the finest church buildings in the county. The society is very prosperous and strong, and now counts about 400 as its followers. Rev. Ina Woolfsburg is the present minister, and has been upon the circuit for fifteen years. Services are held every other Sunday.

There is also a neat burial ground adjoining the church, which was laid out in 1872. The first burial here was of the remains of an infant child of Andrew Madson and wife, in 1873. The first matured person whose remains were deposited here, was Cornelius Gilbertson, who died at Freeborn at the age of twenty-four.

VILLAGE OF MANCHESTER.

This is the only village in the township, and though as yet nothing metropolitan, it has a prospect of becoming a good center for trade.

It is located in section fifteen, on the Minneapolis & St. Louis railway, about seven miles from Albert Lea, the county seat, and surrounded by an excellent farming country.

The village was platted in 1882 by Ole Peterson, but had already taken a start.

In 1877 Cosgan & White erected an elevator which was moved to section twenty-three soon after its erection, and has since been moved back to the village.

In 1878, Anton Anderson erected a blacksmith shop, 24x28 feet, and commenced blowing the bellows. In the fall of 1881, an addition was erected, 12x28 feet, for a wagon shop, and an engine house 10x12 feet, in which was placed a five horse-power steam engine to run the machinery. The shop employs three men.

In February, 1878, a building was erected by H. R. Fossum and E. H. Stensrud, and a good stock of dry goods, groceries, and general merchandise was placed upon the shelves to the amount of about $400. In May the Post office was established.

MEDIUMS OF EDUCATION.

District No. 18. This district effected an organization in the year 1861. The year previous a schoolhouse of logs was erected by subscription on section fifteen, in which a school of thirty scholars was taught by Emma Walker. After this district was organized they took charge of the school building, and school was continued under their management. The first school officers were: Thorson Knuteson, John Ellingson, and O. O. Fossum, Clerk, Director, and Treasurer. In 1867 the house was moved to the site it now occupies in section twenty-two. The present officers are; Director, Dennis Sipple; Treasurer, Claus Flindt; Clerk, Bennett Asleson. The last term of school was taught by H. B. Fossum, with forty pupils enrolled.

District No. 19. A meeting was held on the 8th of May, 1862, at the residence of Christian Jacobson, at which the organization of this district was effected and made permanent by the election of officers, as follows: Director, Tosten Knutson; Clerk, Clarles Olson; Treasurer, Charles Johnson. The same summer Mr. Henderson taught the first school, a term of three months, in Charles Oleson's house in section thirteen, with seven or eight pupils present. In 1864 Christian Jacobson donated a site, and the schoolhouse was erected in the center of section twelve, by contribution of labor, at a cost of about $50, size 16x20. The present officers are: Director, Ole Knutson; Treasurer, John Johnson; Clerk, P. J. Spilde. The last instructor was L. P. Jensen, and there were forty scholars upon the roll.

District No. 21.—Effected an organization in 1864, the first meeting being held at the house of Erick Olson, in section nine, in the spring, at which the following officers were elected: Director, Carl Gustaveson; Treasurer, Halver Peterson; Clerk, August Peterson. The first school was taught by Miss Emma King in Erick Olson's house, in section nine, with twenty pupils present.

In 1867 a frame house, which is still in use, was erected in the western part of section nine, size 16x22, at a cost of $300. The present officers are: Director, Ed. Mortenson; Treasurer, Hans Christopherson; Clerk, Nels N. Wangin. The last term of school was taught by John C. Quammen, with thirty-five scholars enrolled.

DISTRICT NO. 55.--This educational sub-division embraces the territory in the southeastern part of the town. It was organized in the fall of 1864 in E. D. Hopkins' house, on section thirty-four, and the following officers were elected: Director, O. Kemfield; Treasurer, J. Welcor; Clerk, E. D. Hopkins. The first school was taught by Maggie Colby in 1864, in a log house belonging to A. M. Johnson, on the bank of Lake Albert Lea. The following year a log house, 18x16 feet, was procured, which has since been moved to its present site in the southeast corner of section thirty-four, having cost about $100. The present officers are as follows: Director, A. M. Johnson; Treasurer, J. H. Converse; Clerk, O. J. Taylor. The last teacher, in the summer of 1882, was Miss Eva Gilson, and there were nineteen scholars enrolled.

BIOGRAPHICAL.

MATHIAS ANDERSON, one of the first settlers and organizers of this township, was born in Norway on the 15th of June, 1824. He emigrated with his parents to America in 1851, located in Broome county, Illinois, where his mother and one sister still reside. On the 1st of October, 1854, Mathias was joined in matrimony with Miss Betsey Helga. In 1857, they came to this township and staked out a claim in section two, which is still their home. Mr. Anderson was Chairman of the first board of Supervisors and the first Clerk of School District No. 18. He is the father of five children, three boys and two girls.

ERIK O. AASEN was born in Norway on the 15th of October, 1832, and learned the blacksmith trade in his native country. In 1857, he emigrated to America, came to Iowa and resided one year, then moved to this place and located in section nine which has since been his home. In 1860, he met with an accident, one of his cows hooking him, which resulted in the loss of his eyesight. He was married on the 25th of December, 1870, to Miss Argatta Mark, who has borne him five children, four of whom are living. Mr. Aasen has held town and school offices since his residence here.

LEWIS BEACH was born in New York on the 20th of December, 1830. He was married on the 27th of September, 1857, to Miss Lessie T. Sonmiss and the same fall moved to Michigan. In the spring of 1858, he came to this township and was among the first settlers, staked out a claim in section eighteen and has since made it his home. In 1863, he was elected Town Clerk and held the office five years. Mr. and Mrs. Beach have had nine children, six of whom are living.

CHARLES BICKFORD, a native of Vermont, was born in Richford, Franklin county, on the 29th of September, 1835. He enlisted in Company A, of the Sixth Vermont Volunteer Infantry, in September, 1864, and served till the close of the war, participating in seven battles, and while in the battle of Petersburg was wounded. After his discharge he returned to his home and remained until the spring of 1866, when he came to Minnesota and settled on his present place in this township. He was married on the 25th of December, 1868, to Miss Almira J. Tucker. They have had six children, five of whom are living.

JAMES H. CHAMBERLAIN was born in Ashford, Cattaraugus county, New York, on the 1st of April, 1830, and was never outside of his native State until coming to this State in 1864. He was married on the 10th of March, 1850, to Miss Angeline Margaret Hall. They have had nine children, eight of whom are living. Mr. Chamberlain was drafted in the late war but was not able to serve. He came to Freeborn county and resided in Bancroft until 1868, when he moved to this township and has since made his home in section thirty-four, engaged in the cultivation of his farm.

CARL GUSTAVESEN is a native of Norway, born on the 8th of December, 1828. Having a talent for music he devoted considerable time to its study and for a time was leader of the "Great Norway Military Band." He was married on the 26th of December, 1852, to Miss Annie Mortenson. In 1855, they came to America, resided in Iowa until 1863, and then moved to Manchester in section five where they still make their home. Of seven children born to the union, four are living. When first coming here Mr. Gustavesen taught instrumental music but since 1876 has devoted his time to farming.

PIUS HUBER was born in Germany on the 5th of May, 1849. He emigrated to America in 1867, and first settled in Connecticut; in 1873, came to Houston county, and the following year to this township. In 1876, he purchased land in section twenty-one and has since devoted his time to its cultivation. He was married on the 25th of December, 1877, to Miss Mary Flaelman. They have been blessed with three children.

JOHN JOHNSON, one of the first settlers of Manchester, is a native of Norway, and dates his birth the 14th of February, 1831. He came to America in 1855, and first settled in Walworth county, Wisconsin. On the 7th of February, 1856, he married Miss Esther M. Olson. The following year they removed to this place and located in section one where they have since devoted their time to the cultivation of the farm. They have had six children, four of whom are living. Mr. Johnson is one of the Directors of school district No. 19.

JOHN OLSEN JORDAHL, deceased, was a native of Norway, born on the 14th of February, 1820. In 1857, he emigrated to America, and first settled on Washington prairie, in Winneshiek county, Iowa. In the autumn of 1857, he came to this county and made a pre-emption in sections eleven, fourteen, and fifteen, and in 1858, moved his family on the same. He married in the spring of 1842, Miss Flora Nelson, and of thirteen children born to the union, nine are living. Mr. Jordahl died on the 8th of October, 1871, and his wife followed on the 27th of October, 1881.

OLE J. JORDAHL was born on the 19th of July, 1842, in Norway. He emigrated with his parents to America in 1857, and resided on Washington prairie in Winneshiek county, Iowa, until 1858. He then came to this township with the family, and in 1866 bought his present place, in section two. He was married on the 3d of December, 1865, to Miss Anna Johnson. They have a family of seven children. Mr. Jordahl has been Chairman of the board of Supervisors five successive years and clerk of his school district five years.

CHARLES M. JOHNSON was born in Norway on the 20th of August, 1829. He left his native country in 1841, and came to America with his parents, settling in Boone county, Illinois. In 1852, he went to the gold mines of California, but four years later returned to Boone county, where, on the 20th of March, 1856, he married Miss Adeline Olson. On the 2d of July, 1857, he started for this State, and located a claim in section twelve, Manchester township. He has been road Overseer two years, and Treasurer of his school district two terms. He is the father of six children, two boys and four girls.

SIVERT JOHNSON, one of the pioneers of this place, was born in Norway on the 12th of August, 1807. He was united in matrimony on the 13th of January, 1829, to Miss Anna Peterson, who bore him eight children, three of whom are still living. She died on the 4th of August, 1848, and the following year he came to America with five of his children, two having died since coming here. He married his present wife, formerly Annie Paulson, on the 1st of January, 1849. This union has been blessed with four children, three of whom are living. When first coming to this country Mr. Johnson settled in McHenry county, Illinois; in 1855, moved to Butler county, Iowa, and two years later came to Manchester, taking a farm in section twelve, which has since been his home. His eldest son, Lewis Johnson, was born on the 12th of March, 1838, in Norway, and resided with his father until 1861. He was married on the 8th of May in that year, and moved to his farm in section two. He has been a member of the board of Supervisors several terms. He is the father of six children.

JENS O. JENSON was born in Norway on the 16th of November, 1813. He was married on the 25th of December, 1832, to Miss Martha Olsdatter. In 1851, he came with his family to America, first located in Dodge county, Wisconsin, remaining in that State until coming here, in 1860. He immediately selected his present farm in section twenty-four, to which he has since devoted his time. Mr. and Mrs. Jenson have had ten children, three of whom are living, one girl and two boys; three of their sons were killed in the army.

KNUT KNUTSON MORRUM, a native of Wisconsin, was born in Waukesha county, on the 1st of October, 1844. In 1855 he moved with his parents to Goodhue county where they remained one year, and in 1856, became pioneers of this township. Knute was married on the 25th of December, 1873, to Miss Inglebert Olcson, who has borne him four children. His farm is located in section fourteen and is well cultivated.

OLE K. MORRUM was born in Norway on the 14th of September, 1835. He emigrated to America in 1843, and settled in Wisconsin, thence in 1857, to Manchester, where he married his wife, Miss Ingeborg Peterson, on the 2d of October, 1858. They have had ten children, eight of whom are living. Mr. Morrum's farm is in section thirteen, and he is one of the Directors of school district No. 19.

LEWIS L. OLSON, one of the pioneers of this place, was born in Norway on the 15th of Octobers, 1824. He was drafted and served in the army in his native country for five years. On the 5th of December, 1846, he married Miss Annie Helgunesdatter. In the spring of 1832 they came America, and on the 10th of September of the same year, Mrs. Olson died. Of three children, the result of the union, one is living. Mr. Olson first settled in Racine county, Wisconsin, and there married Miss Rangle Deisledatter on the 4th of July, 1854. In 1857 they removed to this township and located their present farm in section thirteen. While in Wisconsin Mr. Olson learned the blacksmith trade, at which he was engaged until quite recently, he has devoted his entire time to the cultivation of his farm. Mr. and Mrs. Olson have been blessed with seven children.

OLE PETERSON, one of the earliest settlers and a leading man of this township, is a native of Norway, born on the 16th of February, 1832. He emigrated to America in 1851, and settled in Illinois, first in Boone and afterward in Rock county. On the 20th of December, 1852, he married Miss Eliza Gulbrandson, and they have had six children, five of whom are living. In 1856 Mr. Peterson came to this county and selected a home in section fifteen, Manchester. He was a member of the first board of Supervisors, and afterward elected Justice of the Peace, taking an interest in all local matters. He is President of the Farmers' Mutual Insurance Company, of which he was also the organizer. In 1862 Mr. Peterson enlisted in the Fifteenth Wisconsin Volunteer Infantry, Company K, was promoted to First Lieutenant, and served one year when his health failed, on account of which he was discharged and returned to his family, having since made this place his home.

IVER A. RODSATER was born in Norway on the 18th of September, 1845. He received a good education in his native place, and in 1856 emigrated to America, first settling in Wisconsin. In the spring of 1857 he moved to Worth county, Iowa, and the same summer came to this place. He was married on the 27th of October, 1867, to Miss Ingeborg Anderson, and have since made their home in section ten. Mr. Rodsater was elected Town Treasurer in 1869, served till 1871, and was then elected Town Clerk, having since held the offices. He has been a member of the board of County Commissioners since 1877, and has held school offices; has also been Secretary of the Farmers' Mutual Insurance Company of Manchester since its organization. Mr. and Mrs. Rodsater have had seven children, six of whom are living.

S. B. SMITH, more familiarly known as Uncle Sam, is one of the earliest settlers and organizers of Manchester. He was born in Renville, Licking county, Ohio, on the 16th of July, 1818, and moved with his parents to Portage county in the same State in 1832. When twenty-one years old he was united in marriage with Miss Sabra S. Dewey, the ceremony taking place on the 16th of June, 1839. She was born on the 16th of December, 1819, in Westfield, Hampden county, Massachusetts. In 1844 they moved from Ohio to Indiana, and remained until 1850, then resided in Illinois for several years. In the summer of 1857 Mr. Smith came to Manchester, and has since been interested in the improvement of the town and of his own home. His wife died on the 27th of March, 1869. She bore him two children; William A., and Helen J., both of whom are now dead. The son enlisted on the 18th of August, 1862, in the Sixth Minnesota Volunteer Infantry, Company E, and served his country until 1865; and the daughter died on the 12th of November, 1876. On the 27th of August, 1870, Mr. Smith was joined in wedlock to his present wife, Mrs. Sarah J. Gray. This union has been blessed with two children, both girls.

PAUL J. SPILDE, youngest son of Sivert and Annie Johnson, was born in Norway on the 24th of December, 1849. He came with his parents to America at the age of eight months, and has always lived with them, they now making their home on his farm in section twelve. He was joined in matrimony on the 29th of January, 1874, to Syneva Guttormson, who has borne him four children, three boys and one girl. Mr. Spilde is one of the Directors of his school district.

JOHN SIPPEL, deceased, was a native of Germany, born on the 28th of September, 1807. He was married on the 26th of June, 1838, to Miss Margaret Wenzel. The result of the union was ten children, eight of whom are still living. Mr. Sippel brought his family to America in 1855, lived for three years in Wisconsin and in June, 1858, became one of the pioneers of this place, staking out a claim in section twenty-seven. He died on the 27th of May, 1871. His son Dennes Sippel was born in Germany on the 27th of July, 1845, and now resides on the old homestead. He was joined in matrimony on the 4th of May, 1871, to Miss Ida Tida and they have had six children, four of whom are living.

Gunne Thykeson, who built the first log house in this place, was born in Norway on the 22d of March, 1832. He was united in marriage on the 1st of May, 1853, with Miss Siuga Olson, and the same year they came to America. They resided in Winneshiek county, Iowa, until coming to this place in 1856, taking a claim in section nine, which is still their home. They have had eight children, six of whom are living.

Rollof Thykeson, one of the pioneers of this place, was born in Norway on the 27th of February, 1837. In 1852, he came to America and directly to Dane county, Wisconsin, where he remained until 1854, then moved to Winneshick county, Iowa. In 1856, he came to Manchester and staked out a claim in section fifteen upon which he lived several years, then moved to his present home in section sixteen. On the 20th of January, 1862, he enlisted in the Fifteenth Wisconsin Volunteer Infantry, Company K, and served till the close of the war, having participated in four battles. After his discharge he returned to his farm in this place, and on the 25th of July, 1866, married Miss Annie Ellingson. Of nine children born to this union, eight are living. Mr. Thykeson has been a member of the board of Supervisors several times and has held school offices.

O. J. Taylor, a native of New York, was born in Hamburgh, Erie county, on the 21st of March, 1832. In 1845, he moved with his parents to Milwaukee, Wisconsin, where he grew to manhood, and on the 15th of August, 1862, enlisted in the Twenty-second Wisconsin Volunteer Infantry, Company C. He was in several important engagements and returned to his home at the close of the war, without a scratch, having received an honorable discharge. Before entering the army, on the 6th of February, 1860, he was married to Miss Emily A. Gibson and they have been blessed with one child, Ervin O. Mr. Taylor has been a resident of this place several years, his farm being located in section thirty-five.

Severt Thoreson, a native of Norway, was born on the 14th of November, 1849. He came with his parents to America when five years old and settled on Jefferson prairie in Boone county, Illinois. On the 12th of August, 1862, he enlisted in Company M, of the Twelfth Illinois Volunteer Infantry and served till the close of the war, participating in a few small skirmishes. In 1866, he removed to Iowa, which State he made his home two years, then came to Manchester and selected a farm in section nine. He was married on the 30th of May, 1869, to Betsy, widow of Halver Peterson, and the mother of four children. Mr. and Mrs. Thoreson have had six children. He is at present Postmaster and has held other local offices.

MANSFIELD.

CHAPLER LXVI.

DESCRIPTIVE—EARLY SETTLEMENT—EVENTS OF INTEREST — POLITICAL— STATISTICAL—SCHOOLS—BIOGRAPHICAL.

The township bearing this old, time honored name, receiving it, as did so many towns throughout the United Kingdom, in honor of Lord Mansfield, is a full congressional township embracing the territory of Town 101, Range 23. It is the southwestern subdivision of Freeborn county, its contiguous surroundings being, Alden on the north; Nunda on the east; Faribault county on the west; and the state of Iowa on the south.

As to the surface and physical features, not much can be said of this that would not readily apply to almost any other prairie town, and this is one in the full sense of the word. However, there are a few patches of timber here, the most of which is domestic, and located mostly in sections seven, eight, ten, and thirty-six. The northwestern part of the town is high and rolling, furnishing some of the finest farming land immaginable; but, as you go southward and to the east it becomes more level and low, with numerous marshes and sloughs, which makes the locality less valuable for farming and agricultural purposes, although there are many fine farms in this as well as other portions of the town. In the extreme southeastern corner, a ridge of high land abruptly pushes its way through the surface of the prairie, which inaugurates the area of the tableland, commencing here and extending eastward through Nunda and other towns.

The soil is a dark loam, with a subsoil of sand and gravel, as a rule; but this is not invariable, for in places a marked tendency to a lighter nature is visible, with a clayey subsoil.

Mansfield has no lakes within its borders, nor has it any streams of much importance. The largest in the township is Steward's Creek, which rises in Alden and crossing a corner of section two passes through the center of section one and twelve, forming a miniature lake in section one, touches a corner of thirteen and leaves the town on its way to Bear Lake, in Nunda. Lime Creek crosses the southeastern corner of the township. Another small stream, not as yet dignified with a name upon the map, rises in section eight, and flowing northward through section five, leaves the town and enters Alden.

The geological and natural history survey of county of Freeborn, by N. H. Winchell, State Geologist, published in 1875, says of Mansfield:— "This town is nearly all prairie, a small patch of oak openings occuring in sections three, ten, and fifteen. The northwestern part of the township is rolling, and the southeastern is level and wet with marshes.

EARLY SETTLEMENT.

The earliest steps leadings to the founding and subsequent development of this thriving township commenced early in 1856, which was about the time that the Western fever actually set in, and found root in the minds of the eastern people.

The first settlers in Mansfield were the Tunell brothers, John and Henry, who came from Illinois by the way of Iowa, with their families, and with teams, arriving on the 23d of June, 1856, and locating on section eight. Here John remained until 1873, when he went to Oregon, where he now resides with his family; while Henry still occupies the place he originally secured in section eight, and is one of the prominent men of both town and county. These brothers brought with them about one hundred head of cattle, and shortly after their arrival commenced putting up hay, securing enough to carry them safely through the winter; but a prairie fire came rolling along and destroyed all the fruits of their labor. For a time the prospect looked seriously dubious, but they finally managed to purchase enough hay from parties in Iowa to tide them over the winter, without a loss of more than half their stock, as the poor brutes suffered considerable from the severe cold and deep snow.

Shortly after these parties made their appearance, Henry Schmidt and Henry Jahnke arrived and secured tracts of the government domain; Henry Schmidt located on section ten, where he remained until that insatiable enemy of immortality, Death, called him hence. Mr. Jahnke made himself at home in section ten, and still holds forth there, a prosperous and prominent farmer.

After this there were no arrivals for some time, but gradually the attention of incomers was turned this way, and the government land began to disappear. Messrs. Stenvaldson and Kittleson, natives of Norway, came in and located where they still live, on valuable farms in section fifteen. Shortly after this we notice the arrivals of a number of additions to this littlement of Norwegians; H. Knutson, Nels Nelson, John Kraus Haar, and others who are yet occupying their places.

VARIOUS MATTERS OF INTEREST.

It is claimed that the first birth in the township was the minor arrival of Louisa Schmidt, on the 10th of October, 1856.

Among, if not the very first marriages in the township, occurred in 1864, and united August Heintz and Miss Louisa Yost in the holy bonds of matrimony.

The first death of a matured person was the demise of Mrs. Henry Schmidt, who was called away on the 20th day of December, 1862. She was first buried on the farm, but her remains were subsequently removed to the Mansfield cemetery.

The first religious services in the township were held in 1859, by Rev. Mr. Smith, an itinerant preacher from New Ulm.

MANSFIELD POST-OFFICE.

This luxury was established about 1875, the first Postmaster being Mr. James M. Emerson, who held the office until the 8th of March, 1878, when the present Postmaster, Henry J. Smith, was commissioned to handle the mail, and still acts in that capacity. The location of the office is at the Postmaster's house in section ten, and it supplies a good area of country with its postal matter, proving a great convenience to the farmers, who would otherwise be obliged to go out of the township for the news from friends.

Lutheran Church.—This society effected an organization as early as 1874, and in that year they erected a neat and commodious church edifice in the southeastern corner of section thirty-six, at a cost of about $3,300. The denomination belongs to the conference of Minnesota. Their first pastor was Rev. B. B. Gelduger, who was succeeded by Rev. Mr. Nelson, and next came the present officiating clergyman, Rev. Mr. Ostrop. It is one of the strongest societies in Freeborn county, having about three hundred members.

There is a cemetery in connection with this church, located just south of it, on a high spot of land, which contains about thirty graves. This was laid out about the time of the organization of the society, and is one of the most beautiful grounds for the purpose in Mansfield.

Mansfield Cemetery.—This burial ground is located in the northeastern part of section sixteen, containing one acre, which is neatly fenced and well improved. This "village of the dead" contains many members of the earliest settlers in Mansfield, and among the gleaming head boards we see the epitaph of the father of Henry Tunell, one of the first and most honored settlers.

POLITICAL.

In earlier days Mansfield was merged into surrounding towns for local government, and the records of it as a separate organization do not commence until 1866, when they state that the first meeting was held in Henry Schmidt's house.

The first officers elected were: Supervisors, Henry Tunell, Chairman, John Kraus Haar, and John B. Oleson; Clerk, John Tunell; Assessor, Nicholas Stenoldson; Treasurer, John Tunell. At present, meetings are held in the schoolhouses throughout the town.

Mansfield has always been in good hands, so far as its officials are concerned, and public matters have been attended to with a zeal and honesty that is indeed commendable; it is out of debt, has voted $400 for road and bridge fund, and has never voted any railroad bonds to beggar the people and enrich monopolists.

STATISTICAL.

We will say, as an introductory remark to this article, that, as a rule, statistics are rather dry reading to one who is merely perusing a work for pastime, as they go too much into fine detail to suit mere fancy; but to one who is searching for facts concerning a locality which he has in contemplation for a future home, they are everything and all important. They determine for him with accuracy the resources of a country; the class of people with which it is settled, giving the amount of their productions, and they are indisputable. In fact, all vital matters concerning the wealth, prosperity, and welfare of a locality are embodied in a careful summing up of the statistics of values, cultivation, and production. We have, therefore, compiled a statement of such for this township, taken from the County Auditor's report to the commissioner of statistics of Minnesota for 1882, and elsewhere, which we herewith present. It must be remembered that although the report was made in the year 1882, the acreage and number of bushels raised was in the year 1881.

Wheat—1,844 acres, yielding 22,611 bushels; average 12.25 bushels per acre.

Oats—399 acres, yielding 12,162 bushels; about 33 bushels per acre.

Corn—534 acres, yielding 19,480 bushels; 36½ bushels per acre.

Barley—33 acres, yielding 740 bushels; 22½ per acre.

Potatoes—29 acres, yielding 3,075 bushels; 106 per acre.

Sugar cane—5¼ acres, yielding 670 gallons of syrup; 127 gallons per acre. No sugar reported.

Hay—30 acres, yielding 60 tons; per acre, two tons. Wild hay, 1,230 tons.

Other products, about five acres.

Total number of acres cultivated in 1881, 2,879.

Apples—867 growing trees, 141 bearing; yielding 20 bushels.

Sheep—82 sheared, yielding 292 pounds of wool; over three pounds and a half per head.

Dairy—210 cows, yielding 10,800 pounds; averaging over fifty pounds each. No cheese reported.

Bees and honey—3 hives, yielding 12 pounds of honey.

This closes the report for the year 1881. From the report of Assessors, for the present year, 1882, we have gleaned the following which will be of interest:

The Year 1882. Acreage sown to wheat, 1,861; oats, 423; corn, 834; barley, 22; rye, 1; potatoes, 35½; sugar cane, 3¼; cultivated hay, 30; other produce, 3. Total acreage cultivated in 1882—3,213.

Other items for the same year: growing apple trees, 1,162; bearing apple trees, 406; grape vines in bearing, 13; milch cows, 205; sheep, 229; wool, 807; whole number of farms reported, 35.

Population.—In the year 1860, the population of Mansfield may be said to be almost nothing. In 1870, the census report gives it 379, and at the last census, in 1880, we find the population to be 552; showing an increase in ten years of 173.

SCHOOLS.

Educational facilities in Mansfield are up to the average of towns in the county, having six districts, all in good condition and well managed. If the territory were equally divided in the township, this would give an area of six square miles to each educational sub-division. The districts, with numbers and location of schoolhouses, are as follows: No. 41, building in section thirty-two; No. 74, in section two; No. 84, in section twenty-six; No. 86, in section thirty-five; No. 87, in section eight; No. 92, in section ten. Below is given a short sketch of the organization, growth, and present condition of the various districts.

District No. 41.—Embraces the territory lying in the southwestern part of the township. It was organized at an early day, but as to the actual date there are many conflicting reports, and as we have failed in seeing the records we cannot here decide the question; but, it is certain, however, that about the year 1872 their schoolhouse was erected in the northern part of section thirty-two, at a cost of about $100, the size of it being 12x16. The first school was instructed by Miss Hattie Coblett, to nine scholars. The attendance at the present time is sixteen.

District No. 74.—Effected an organization about 1870, and held school in the private residence of John Kraus Haar in section two, with Miss Rhoda Gripman as teacher and twelve pupils to answer the roll call. In 1872 their schoolhouse was erected in the southwestern corner of section two at a cost of $400, the size of which is 18x30. The school has not increased much in numerical strength.

District No. 84.—This district commenced its existence by erecting a school edifice in section twenty-six, the size of which is 16x24 and cost $300. The first teacher was C. H. Emmons with an attendance of about twenty-five, which has increased to about thirty-five pupils. This district embraces the territory southwest of the center of the township.

DISTRICT No. 86.—Effected an organization in 1872, the first school being taught in Mr. Hellek Knudson's house in section thirty-six, the teacher being Miss Jennie L. Romanson, with twenty-five students present. In the year 1874, two years after organization, the school building now in use was erected in the southeastern cornet of section thirty-five, at a cost of about $200, the size being 18x24. This district is really a union one, as it embraces as part of its territory several sections in the state of Iowa.

DISTRICT No 87.—It is claimed by some that this educational subdivision came into existence in the year 1867; and the first school was taught by Miss Ivey Thomas in John Tunnell's residence with fourteen pupils present. The following year their school edifice was erected in the southwestern part of section eight, size 16x24 at a cost of $400. The lumber from 'this house was hauled from Austin.

DISTRICT No. 92.—This district is presumed to have been organized about 1875, for in that year we find their school house was erected in the southwestern part of section ten, at a cost of $400, size 18x24. Mr. Ambrus Morey was the first teacher, to an enrollment of twenty-one scholars. The district is in good condition and now has an attendance of about twenty-five.

BIOGRAPHICAL.

BENJAMIN H. DILLINGHAM was born in Maine on the 27th of December, 1841. He was raised on a farm and attended the Friends' Seminary, located in Providence, Rhode Island. In 1862, he was joined in marriage to Miss Emma J. McCurdy, who was born in his native State. They came to Iowa in 1866, and engaged in farmfng three years, since which time Mansfield has been their home, taking a quarter in section thirty-two. Their children are, Henry E., James S., Charles H., Oliver E., George A., Mary F., Millard F., Lilian, and an infant not named. Mr. Dillingham takes a deep interest in educational matters, was one of the leading men in starting the public schools in this place and has been Clerk of the school board eight successive years.

JOHN KRAUS HAAR, an old settler in this place, is a native of Germany, born in the village of Shlenklfeldt, near Frankfurt-on-the-Main, on the 15th of April, 1817. He received a good education in the public schools of the village, and when fourteen years old began the trade of a cabinet-maker, and after four years at the same was engaged in the manufacture of the celebrated Kraus Haar pianos and organs. In 1842 he came to America, located in Erie county, Ohio, and followed his trade two years, then to Berlin Centre, and afterward to Litchfield, Michigan. In 1844 he was married to Miss Sarah Beck. After some years at his trade in the latter place his health failed and he came to Rock county, Wisconsin, where he resided on a farm five years and then moved to Mitchell county, Iowa. Since 1863, he has been a resident of this place, taking land in section two. He is a respected citizen, has always taken an active part in all school and local matters, and assisted in the organization of the township, having since held a number of the principal town offices. His children are George H., Mary L., Samuel H., Elizabeth C., Isaac N., John C., and Sarah M.

WILLIAM JOST was born in Waldeck, Germany, on the 27th of August, 1842. In 1864, he came with his parents to America, and directly to Minnesota, locating in section nine, Mansfield. He now owns two hundred and eighty-four acres, about half of which is under cultivation, having a good house and barn. In 1870 he was joined in matrimony with Miss Caroline Frese, also a native of Germany. They have five children; Frederic, Fredrica, Mary, Augusta, and Emma. Mr. Jost's father died at the advanced age of eighty-two years, and his mother still lives, aged seventy-two.

HENRY JAHNKE, one of the first settlers in Mansfield, is a native of Mecklinburg, Germany, born on the 1st of August, 1822. He there grew to manhood, attending school, and in 1852 came to America, first locating in Illinois. He was married in 1852 to Miss Mary Miller. Two years later they came to this township, and under the homestead law took one hundred and sixty acres in sections three and ten, which is still their home, having a desirable farm well cultivated. Mr. and Mrs. Jahnke have had six children, five of whom are living, John, Mary, Christ, Mina, and Louisa.

VALENTINE KATZUNG, a native of Germany, was born on the 6th of January, 1844. When eleven years of age he came with his parents to America and located on a farm in Rockford, Ill. From thence they moved to Kilbourn City, Wisconsin. and shortly after came to Minnesota and located in Blue Earth City. In 1864 Valentine enlisted in Company F, of the First Minnesota Volunteer Infantry, was in the service one year and then honorably discharged. In 1867 he married Miss Christiana Yost, who was also born in Germany. They have a family of seven children; August, Edward, William, Ferdinand, Herman, Bertha, and Ernestina. Mr. Katzung's farm is situated in section nine.

David Lavalle, one of the old and substantial citizens of this place, was born near Lake Champlain in Canada in 1839. He grew to manhood in his native place and in 1860, married Miss Louisa Pearmsoll, who was also raised in Canada. In 1865, Mr. Lavalle came west and three years later located in Mansfield, upon the farm which is still his home. He has a family of six children; Elizabeth, David, Milda, Hulda, Eva, and John O. His father, Paul L. Lavalle, lives with him and is a well perserved man of seventy-three years, enjoying the comforts of life with his children's children.

John Niebuhr was born in Hanover, Germany, on the 22d of November, 1828. He received his education there and in 1864, married Miss Catharine King. They emigrated to America in 1872, coming directly to this place and locating in section seventeen which is still their home. Mr. Niebuhr now owns five hundred and seventy acres of land, about half being under cultivation, and has one of the largest dwelling houses in the place. He is an energetic farmer, keeping a fine lot of stock and also raising small grain He has a family of ten children; Dora, Mary, Eliza, Kate, Henry, William, Louisa, Maggie, Minnie, and George.

Rev. P. G. Ostby was born in Trysil, Norway, on the 12th of August, 1836. He received a good education and at the age of twenty commenced teaching school, and after two years entered a high school, similar to our Normal schools, where he remained two years, then returned to teaching. In 1868, he came to America and attended the College at Paxton, Illinois, and afterward at Marshall, Wisconsin, where he passed a theological course and was ordained as a Lutheran minister. He was Chaplain for C. L. Clauson at St Ansgar, Iowa, for one year, then moved to Austin, Minnesota, and was pastor of the Norwegian Lutheran church there for seven years. In 1871, he married Miss Garo B. Thornby, and they have a family of five boys; Johannas G., Bernhard I., Paul I. D., Selmar O., and James O. C. In 1878, Mr. Ostby came to Mansfield as pastor of the Lutheran Church of this place, and through his energy and benevolence it is now in a prosperous condition.

Ole I. Opdahl was born near Bergen, Norway, on the 5th of January, 1853, and came with his his parents to America in 1865. After a residence of a short time in Iowa the family removed to Minnesota and located in Nunda. In 1874, Ole was united in marriage with Miss Betsy Davidson, also a native of Norway, and the same year came to Mansfield, buying land in section eleven which has since been their home. Mr. Opdahl takes an active part in the advancement of education, has held school offices and was a member of the board of Supervisors three years. His farm now contains three hundred and twenty acres and is well improved. He has five children; Louisa, Emma, Gilla, Eva, and David.

Alexander Peterson was born in Uddevalla, Sweden, on the 8th of August, 1829. At the age of fifteen he went to Norway where he received a good education. He was married in 1853, to Miss Enger Serena Norby, a native of Norway. In 1864, they came to America and resided in Iowa for three years, then moved to this place, settling in section twenty-four. His farm now contains two hundred acres of well improved land. Mr. Peterson is always interested in local matters and has held different offices, is at present Town Clerk and also school clerk. His children are; Mary, Hanna, Caroline, Carl, Peter, Otto, and Alphons.

Hiram M. Pettit was born in Crawford county, Pennsylvania, on the 18th of July, 1833. He was raised on a farm, and in 1853, came west to Iowa, where he resided two years, then located in Minnesota, but returned to Iowa in a few years. He was joined in matrimony with Miss Elisif Dibble in 1859. In 1861, he enlisted in the Twenty-seventh Iowa Volunteer Infantry, Company I, and after a campaign through to Mississippi, was taken sick and confined in the hospital at Jackson, Tennessee, five months, after which he was honorably discharged. In 1864, he entered land in section one, Mansfield, and now has it nearly all under cultivation, making a good home. He has filled a number of school and town offices. Mr.

and Mrs. Pettit have four children; Edison, Hudson, Elmer, and Mary.

HIRAM J. STEWARD, a native of Maine, was born near Bangor, on the 21st of September, 1831. At the early age of twelve years he began working by the day, following the lumber business twelve years. In 1855, he was married to Miss Mary E. Steward, who was also born in Maine, and they settled on a farm near Saint Albans. In 1862, Mr. Steward enlisted in the Twenty-second Maine Volunteer Infantry, Company K, went New Orleans and at the battle of Port Hudson, June 13th, 1862, was wounded in the right knee where the buckshot still remains. After a service of eleven months, he received an honorable discharge and returned to his home. In 1866, he came west to Iowa, remained three years and then came to Minnesota, taking land in section twelve where he still resides. He has a fine farm, and the tidy appearance of his home gives evidence of his eastern education and habits. Mr. and Mrs. Steward have three children; Phedora C., Lizzie M., and Hiram H.

HENRY J. SCHMIDT was born near Joliet, Illinois, on the 26th of August, 1853, and when three years old came to Mansfield with his parents who were among the first settlers in this place. Henry was married in 1878, to Miss Caroline Leonhardi, also a native of Illinois. They have had two children; Henry and Arthur, the former having died when one year old, and the latter on the 23d of September, 1882. Their farm contains two hundred and eighty acres with the greater portion under cultivation. Mr. Schmidt has been school Clerk six years, Town Treasurer four years, Postmaster for a time, and is at present Treasurer of the school district. His parents are both dead, his mother having died when thirty-eight years old, and his father at the age of sixty-seven.

HENRY TUNELL was born the 29th of June, 1826, near Hanover, Germany. When seventeen years old he enlisted in the army as a Volunteer, serving seven years and one month. In 1850 he married Miss Dora Olmyer and the same year emigrated to America. They located near Blooming Grove, Illinois, and after farming there six years, came to Minnesota, settling in Mansfield on section eight, where he has a farm of four hundred and twenty acres, all cultivated. He has eight children; William C., Henry J., Charles, George J., Alvina D., Gustavus, Robert, and Edward, all of whom are grown. Mr. Tunell is one of the influential citizens of this place; has been in the Legislature two terms; Chairman of the board of Supervisors fifteen years; school Director ten years, and Clerk of the school board of Trustees. After the Sioux Massacre in 1863, he was commissioned Captain of a Militia company for home protection.

MOSCOW.

CHAPTER LXVII.

LOCATION AND TOPOGRAPHY—EARLY SETTLEMENT—THE HONORED DEAD—STATISTICS—RELIGIOUS—VILLAGE OF MOSCOW—SUMNER VILLAGE—EVENTS OF INTEREST—MANUFACTURING, SOCIETIES, ETC.—BIOGRAPHICAL.

This is one of the eastern towns in Freeborn county; one lying between it and the northern boundary. Its contiguous surroundings are as follows: Mower county on the east; Oakland on the south; Riceland on the west; and Newry on the north. Moscow is a full congressional township of thirty-six sections or square miles, containing 23,040 acres.

The greater part of the township is what is called burr oak opening land, that is, small patches of burr and black oak timber, interspersed with natural meadows and prairies. Along the Turtle Creek, in sections seven, eight, seventeen, eighteen, twenty-one, and twenty-two, considerable heavy timber is found, among the varieties being white, red, and burr oak, white and black ash, bass and elm, and on section twenty-six there was a fine growth of heavy oak timber, where the first claim in the township was taken.

Turtle Creek is the principal water course in the town, entering from Riceland by way of sections seven and eighteen, and taking a southeasterly course, crosses the town and leaves through section thirty-six to enter Mower county. This stream furnishes an excellent water-power in section twenty-two, which has been improved to some extent, and greater improvement is now in contemplation and will probably be carried out. Deer Creek is a small stream whice rises in Newry, and taking a southerly course, makes a conflu ence with the Turtle in section eighteen.

The soil is a clayey loam, dark in places and again of a lighter nature, with a tendency to sandiness in many places. It is well adapted to agricultural purposes, and is productive if properly tilled.

EARLY SETTLEMENT.

There seems to be a preponderance of testimony that the first claim in the township was taken in May, 1855, by a man named Nathan Hunt, who located in section twenty-six, and remained for about one year and sold to Alexander Schutt, who in turn sold to the present proprietor, Henry Fero.

The next to put in an appearance after Hunt, was a party composed of various nationalities: Robert Speer, a native of New York State, Thomas R. Morgan, and Thomas Ellis, natives of Wales, who came from Wisconsin where they had been for a few years, and accomplishing the journey with ox teams by camping on the way, arrived here on the first of June, 1855. It should be chronicled to the credit of the parties, as it is unusual to such journeys, that they did not travel on Sunday, and made the trip in one month.

Mr. Speer took a claim in section twenty-two, where he pitched a tent to live in while he was breaking, and he still holds forth on the same spot.

Mr. Morgan drove his stakes upon a place in section twenty-eight, and lived upon the place until 1881, when he rented and moved to Austin.

Mr. Ellis also took a tract of land in section twenty-eight, where he lived in comfortable circumstances up to the time of his death, which occurred in 1874, and his family are now in Dakota.

James Bush, John G. and James Dunning, soon after arrived, all being natives of New York State, having stopped for a time in in Wisconsin and secured homes. Bush took his farm in section twenty-seven, where he erected a log house covered with bark; but he soon built a better one and still lives upon his place. James Dunning halted in section twenty-seven, where he lived until 1876, and then removed to Kansas, where he now lives. John G. Dunning took a claim in sections twenty-two and twenty-seven, and continued his sojourn here until 1872, when he removed to Oregon.

Evan Morgan was another of the fifty-fivers. He was a native of Wales, having become Americanized in Wisconsin, and after his arrival in Moscow tarried a while in section twenty-one; but soon sold that place and removed to section twenty-two, where he may yet be found.

This is about a complete list of the arrivals in the year 1855. The year following there were a great many to make their appearance upon the progressive scene in Moscow township, and as many of them as can be remembered will be chronicled.

Stephen N. Frisbie,a native of Connecticut, came rom Wisconsin early this year and secured a farm in section thirty-five, where he is yet to be found.

Nathan S. Hardy, a school teacher from the Empire State, arrived and kept Frisbie company by securing a place and erecting a habitation in the same section, where he yet holds forth. William Pace, an Englishman, who had been naturalized in Wisconsin, joined this little settlement by taking a place in section thirty-four, where he remained until the time of his death in September, 1882.

Henry Fero, a native of New York, drifted in and took a slice from Uncle Sam's domain just north of this little settlement, in section twenty-six, where his light still holds out to burn. Two others in the persons of George W. Dearmin and Benjamin Martin, originally from North Carolina, but late of Indiana, extended the neighborhood above treated, westward, by securing and subduing claims in sections twenty-eight and twenty-nine. The former still resides in section twenty-eight, but the latter, after a sojourn of two years returned to Indiana.

Ashabel Barnhart, from the Buckeye State, pushed the neighborhood northward and selected his territory in section twenty-one, where he remained until his death in 1872, and his family now reside in Dakota.

Rufus K. Crum, a native of Pennsylvania, came from Indiana and took a claim in section twenty-eight. He remained for a number of years, laying out a town site, and finally removed to Iowa. With Crum came George W. Davis, of the Buckeye State, who took land in section twenty-eight: but one Minnesota winter was enough for him, and he pulled up stakes and left for Iowa, where he has since died.

A. A. Webster, of the Empire State, drifted in and anchored in section twenty-three, lived there awhile and then sold and removed to section fourteen, where he remained until 1879, and now lives in Dakota Territory.

About the same time David Gates, of the same descent, made his appearance, coming direct from Wisconsin, and located upon a place in section thirty-three, which he still owns; but in 1875 he removed to Austin.

Hiram C. Porter, a native of Vermont, came from Iowa this year, and settled just north of Gates in section twenty-eight, and lived here up to the time of his death, which sad event occurred in 1868. His son now occupies the place; while his widow became the wife of John G. Dunning, and now resides in Oregon.

Another of the arrivals this year was George Watson, a native of Pennsylvania, who selected his portion of Government land in section thirty. He was a member of the State Constitutional Convention; was elected a Senator to the first Minnesota Legislature; was the first Postmaster of the Sumner Post-office, and in 1863, received a Government appointment at St. Paul, where he now resides. He was joined, soon after his arrival to Minnesota, by Josiah W. Hardy, a native of New York State, who came from Iowa, and planted his stakes upon a farm in section twenty-five. He lived here for about one year, when he returned to Iowa, and in May, 1864 gave up his life in St. Louis, in defense of his country.

The Vanderwurkers, father and son, natives of Michigan, arrived this year, and commenced pioneer life upon claims in Moscow, but both have, since 1878, pulled up their claim stakes, and removed; the former to Wisconsin, and the latter to Lyon county, Minnesota.

Robert A. Dearmin was another to arrive this year, locating in section twenty-eight; he may yet be ound upon the original homestead, at this writing, overturning the land for the crop of 1883.

Four Englishmen came in about this time, in the persons of Messrs. Bridle, Prey, Hallenback, and Galpin, who all took claims with the avowed intention of making this their future home; but the severe winter succeeding their arrival apparently satisfied them, as they all soon after pulled up stakes and left for parts unknown.

A. B. Lizer, George Balton, and Leonard Webster were also among the arrivals of 1856, and took farms. Lizer came from Wisconsin and located in section thirty-five, remaining until 1879, when he went to Kansas. Balton established himself in section thirty-three, where he remained until called upon by the angel of death. Webster first settled upon a farm in section twenty-three, and remained in the town until 1880, when he went to Dakota.

Tollef Oleson and Ole Tollefson, whose names indicate their nationality, arrived late in this year, and squatted in section twelve, where they lived for a number of years. The son is now dead, and the father is living in Lansing, it is said, at the age of ninety-seven years.

Michael Murphy, an Irishman, also arrived this year, and took a place in section twenty-five, where his smiling visage is still on exhibition.

In 1857, we note the arrival of several pioneers; among whom were Francis Hardy, father of N. S. and J. W. Hardy; Daniel S. Ingraham; Samuel Degood; Samuel G. Lowry, and soon after, his son, Theophus Lowry; David M. Farr; and Leonard Ware.

THE HONORED DEAD.

David M. Farr was an early settler in Moscow, having dawned upon the western scenes in section twenty-two, in the township of Moscow, in September, 1856, and the next year got his family upon the spot where they lived at the time of his death, which took place on the 8th of July, 1878, in Texas, at the age of 55 years. He was born in Orleans county, New York, on the 2d of December, 1822, and was liberally educated. On the 20th of July, 1843, he was married to Miss Hannah Robbins. His ability was recognized wherever he was known, and he served in almost every local office. Was Justice of the Peace, Town Clerk, Postmaster, Supervisor, and for years was known as the model Assessor of Freeborn county. He was a good, careful, and correct surveyor, and a very useful man in the community. He left a wife and four children to bewail his sudden taking off, which was, as above mentioned, away from home.

Hiram J. Rice moved into this county in 1857, and securing a foothold in section thirty-six in the town of Moscow, remained there up to the year 1876, when he went to Floyd county, Iowa, and there died, in September, 1877. He enlisted in the army, was a faithful soldier, but lost his health and never fully recovered.

Thomas Ellis died in the town of Moscow on the 13th of September, 1874, having fought the good fight and finished his course. He was a native of Wales. On coming to America he stopped a while in Ohio, and then pushed on to Wisconsin where, catching the tide that was setting so strongly into the new territory of Minnesota, he was brought out here in 1855, securing a place where he remained through life. He was in the army during the war, was a kind father and husband, and was sadly missed.

Israel N. Pace.—The year 1840, and Bennington, Wyoming county, New York, claims the subject of this sketch as the time and place of his birth. From the age of two years he lived in Wisconsin, coming to this place in 1856. He was married on the 9th of December, 1867, to Miss Rosanna Farr. For three years he served his country in the Union army, in the Tenth Minnesota Regiment, and was slightly wounded at the battle of Nashville in September, 1864. He was a good citizen, friend and neighbor, and left a wife and five children. The bugle call that sounded the *reveille* for his rising in the other life, was on the 17th of April, 1879, at the age of 38.

Mrs Mary T. Cheadle terminated her earthly journey on Monday evening, the 10th of November, 1879, at the age of 54 years. Entering upon the activities of this life in Rockvale, Indiana, on the 7th of October, 1825, she, at an early day, married Mr. Cheadle, and with him lived and reared her family. During the war her husband volunteered in the army and left his bones to bleach on southern soil. Several years ago she came to this county and located near her relatives in Moscow. She was an exemplary member of the Presbyterian church.

J. S. Harris.—The balance sheet of this life was struck on the 8th of December, 1879. He was born in the Old Dominion, in Augusta county, in 1823, and was one of the seven children who removed to Rockwell, Illinois, in 1844, and about that time he joined the Presbyterian church. Was married to Miss Ella Elsley in 1853, and in 1856, removed with his wife and one child to Iowa. In 1859 he came to Moscow. He was a constant and devout worshipper at the church of his choice.

STATISTICAL.

The year 1881.—The area included in this report takes in the whole town as follows:

Wheat—3,842 acres, yielding 41,525 bushels.

Oats—1,131 acres, yielding 32,700 bushels.

Corn—998 acres, yielding 33,723 bushels.

Barley—380 acres, yielding 7,641 bushels.

Buckwheat—4 acres, yielding 30 bushels.

Potatoes—58½ acres, yielding 5,637 bushels.

Beans—4⅝, yielding 56 bushels.

Sugar cane—3½ acres, yielding 450 gallons.

Cultivated hay—415 acres, yielding 590 tons.

Total acreage cultivated in 1881—6,813¾.

Wild hay—1,235 tons.

Timothy seed—45 bushels.

Clover seed—15½ bushels.

Apples—number of trees bearing, 649, yielding 391 bushels.

Grapes—4 vines, yielding 105 pounds.

Tobacco—70 pounds.

Sheep—150 sheared, yielding 984 pounds of wool.

Dairy—308 cows, yielding 19,830 pounds of butter, and 15,050 pounds of cheese.

Hives of bees—2, yielding 50 pounds of honey.

The year 1882: Wheat, 2,732 acres; oats, 1,183; corn, 2,058; barley, 298; buckwheat, 16; potatoes, 85½; beans, 2½; sugar cane, 5¾; cultivated hay, 81; flax, 306; total acreage cultivated in 1882—6,768¾.

Apple trees—growing, 1,521; bearing, 96; grapes vines bearing, 3.

Milch cows—275

Sheep—226, yielding 1,236 pounds of wool.

Population—The census of 1870 gave Moscow a population of 592. The last census, taken in 1880, reports 650 for this town; showing an increase of 58.

RELIGIOUS.

The earliest settlers of Moscow were mostly Americans, with strong religious tendencies, representing various creeds or denominations, including the Congregationalists, Methodists, Baptists. Campbellites, and Presbyterians, which faiths were held to with a Puritanic tenacity. All felt the need of religious instruction, and when a preacher of the gospel put in an appearance he was hailed with joy. The first to dawn upon the scene was "Elder" Phelps, a young man fresh from the discipline of the theological college, who had located at Austin. He first preached in Rufus K. Crum's house, in section twenty-eight, in 1856, and he occasionally preached in this vicinity until March, 1857; but no society was formed. Later in the same year he preached in Samuel Degood's house in section thirteen, and a class was formed with about fifteen members, with Isaac Vanderwurker, leader. A Sunday school was organized about the same time, which was continued until 1880, Samuel Degood being superintendent a number of years. The last school was held at the schoolhouse in section thirteen. Elder Reynolds was the regular preacher, and as most of the original members of the class have either removed to other localities, or died, it has been discontinued.

During the winter of 1856-57, Daniel Ingraham, an itinerant exhorter not identified with any denomination: but, as he said, "anything to beat the devil," preached in private houses, among them George Bolton's and William Paul's. A class was organized at Bolton's house in 1857, with George Bolton as leader, and the same year Elder Mapes held services in various places, and also held a series of protracted meetings, the result of which was an organization. In 1865, when Elder Tice was preaching here he started the project of building a church, which was accordingly erected in section twenty-two. This was the Methodist Episcopal society, and for a time religious matters prospered and the church grew; but finally, interest began to wane, the members, many of them, moved away, preaching became irregular, and then discontinued, and the organization was declared *moribund*.

PRESBYTERIAN CHURCH.—The first services by this denomination were held during the fall of 1857, at the house of the reverend gentleman who officiated, S. G. Lowry. The society effected an organization soon after, under the name of the Sumner and Moscow Presbyterian church. Mr. Lowry continued to preach at his house and in school buildings for about two years, when the Rev. Mr. Morse, a follower of the Congregational faith, took the religious training of the community in charge, and continued preaching once every two weeks for about one year.

In 1858, Theophus Lowry organized a Sunday school at the schoolhouse in section thirty-one, and acted in the capacity of superintendent. This school continued in active work until 1878.

CONGREGATIONAL CHURCH.—The first minister of the gospel following this faith, to hold services in this township, was Rev. Stephen Cook, of Austin. He preached in the schoolhouse of district No. 31 in 1859, and on the 8th of April, 1860, a society was organized at the same schoolhouse with eleven members. The second preacher was a brother of the first, Rev. Nelson Cook. As most of the original members have either died or moved away, no services have been held since 1875. Rev. A. Morse, of Austin, was the last pastor.

A Union Sunday School was organized at the house of William Pace, in March, 1857, which was about the first school of this kind formed in the township. Money was very liberally subscribed and a good supply of books procured. The organization started its good work under the most favorable auspices, with S. N. Frisbie as superintendent, and continued its efficiency for many years.

FAIRVIEW CEMETERY.—Was platted and recorded on the 4th of June, 1875. It is in the southeast corner of the southeast quarter of section twenty-nine. The trustees were J. S. Harris, T. B. Morgan, S. W. Pitts, N. F. Earle, W. Mann, and N. B. Vansthouse. A. C. Spicer was the surveyor.

VILLAGE OF MOSCOW.

In June, 1857, this little burg was conceived, and was laid out in lots and blocks by Daniel Johnson, surveyor, for the proprietors, Nathan Owens, Benjamin Lindsey, and David M. Farr. It is located near the center of section twenty-two, or, to be technical, the northeast of the southwest of section twenty-two, on the bank of Turtle Creek.

A Post-office under the name of Moscow was established at the village in 1858, with John G. Dunning as Post-master, and office at David Farr's house, in section twenty-two. In 1860 David M. Farr was commissioned, and held the office for two years, when the present incumbent, Evan Morgan, was appointed to handle the mail, which arrives twice each week from Oakland. The office is kept at the house of the Postmaster.

In 1866, Joseph James, John Chandler, and James Dyrlyn, put in machinery and commenced operating a steam saw-mill near the main part of the village. They continued to pile up saw-dust for about four years, when timber began to get scarce and they sold the concern, which was finally removed to Waseca county.

In 1879, Arthur Sanderson and his son, George, erected a two story frame building for a store and tenement, and in January, 1880, put in a good stock of general merchandise, which they still continue to manage. This is what has long been needed by the village and surrounding country, and it is to be hoped the farmers will sufficiently appreciate the enterprise to make it a financial success to the projectors.

SUMNER VILLAGE.

In 1857, a village was laid out into lots in section thirty-one by Rufus K. Crum, and recorded under this caption. A Post-office was also established the same year, with George Watson as Postmaster, which was continued until 1876, Aaron McKune being the last mail-handler. In 1858, Mr. Crum, the projector of the embryo city, erected a house on the village site, and used to entertain travelers. But all of no avail: gradually the interest, even of the town proprietors, weakened, and the village of Sumner became a thing of the past, and the fond hopes for lots, blocks, stores, schools, and Churches, were abandoned, and the surer and more practical plan of making money, by transforming the imaginary lots and blocks into fields of corn and wheat, was resorted to.

VARIOUS MATTERS OF INTEREST.

It is claimed, and upon good authority, that the first birth in the township took place on the 26th of December, 1855, and ushered into existence Sophia Matilda, a daughter of Evan and Sarah Morgan. The little girl grew to womanhood; and on the 12th of May, 1879, married A. M. Lee, and now resides in Sibley, in the northwestern part of Iowa.

About the next minor arrival was the birth of Eva Maria, daughter of Robert and Mary Speer. She was married in 1875 to DeForest Lincoln, and in 1881 died at Alexandria, leaving one child.

Alfred Silas, a son of Henry amd Mary A. Fero, was also among the early births, in Moscow, his natal existence dating back to the 29th of October, 1856. He now lives in Dakota.

The earliest marriage occurring within the lines of Moscow and of residents of the town, took place in October, 1856, and united the future fortunes of George Bridle to Miss Galpin. Rev. Stephen Cook, of Austin, performed the ceremony at the house of the bride's parents in section thirty-two. In 1877 the happy couple returned to Illinois.

Another early marriage took place on the 17th of May, 1859, the high contracting parties being George W. Dearmin and Miss Lucia Campbell, the knot being tied by Rev. Theophus Lowry. The parties still live in section twenty-eight of Moscow.

Nathan S. Hardy and Amelia A. Pace were united in the holy bonds of matrimony on the 10th of August, 1859, by the Rev. Stephen Cook, at the residence of the bride's parents in section thirty-four.

FIRST DEATH.—This sad event made its impress on the minds of the members of the scanty community, and long it will be ere it will be effaced from their memories. A child of an Englishman named Galpin, living in section thirty-two, was the first victim, and quietly passed away in 1856.

Another early event of this kind was the demise of Harriet, wife of James Bush, at the age of thirty-five, on the 25th of December, 1858.

FIRST STORE. In 1856, Elbridge Gerry, a Yankee from the Green Mountain State, opened a general store in section twenty-eight, in a little log house. The building had been erected by the neighbors as an inducement to business men, and during its erection Gerry furnished whisky to keep the *populace* in a good humor. When the store was completed Gerry put in a limited stock of dry goods, boots and shoes, and groceries, and an unlimited stock of poor whisky, which was his staple article. He did a very brisk business for about one year; but finally left and returned to his former home in Vermont. The building he used is now in the village of Hayward, used as a barn, and belongs to Mrs. E. J. Campbell.

FIRST MILL.—In 1857, Messrs. Lindsey & Owens put up a steam saw-mill in section twenty-one, equipping it with a circular saw and power sufficient to cut 3,500 feet per day. In 1858 a burr for the purchase of grinding feed was attached and the mill run for both a saw-mill and feed grinding. Thus the industry continued until about 1866, when the machinery was removed to Wisconsin.

FIRST BLACKSMITH SHOP. This enterprise originated through the energy of Robert Speer, who in the fall of 1855 erected a small shanty, put in tools, and during the winter following did considerable blacksmithing. In 1856 he put up a substantial log building in which to carry on his business, and the pioneers came all the way from Blue Earth county for plow-sharpening. Mr. Speer carried on the business until 1877.

SORGHUM MILL—J. H. McIntire, in 1877, put in machinery and commenced operating a mill of this description for the manufacture of syrup, and since its construction, as regularly as the season rolls round, this mill is found to be in operation. A good article is manufactured and the enterprise is of great benefit to the neighboring community.

WOODLAWN GRANGE.—This society of the Patrons of Husbandry, effected an organization in 1873 or '74, with about twenty charter members, among whom were George King, Samuel Degood, Abijah Webster, and James H. McIntire, and Abner Vanderwurker was chosen Worthy Master. The organization continued in active existence for about two years, and in fact, the charter has never been formerly surrendered; but one by one, the original and enterprising members moved away, or lost interest, until the lodge finally died from inappetency for success. Meetings of the order, while it was in force, were held at the houses of Mr. Vanderwurker and George King.

MOSCOW GRANGE.—This lodge effected an organization a few weeks after the Woodlawn society, and among the charter members we notice the names of Henry Fero, Evan Morgan, James Bush, Robert Speer, John Ruh, Joseph James, and James Dunning. The first Master was Mr. John Ruh. Meetings were held at the schoolhouse in section twenty-two. It is said that this Grange broke up in a quarrel after a brief existence of about two years.

I. O. OF G. T.—This society was organized at Henry Fero's house in April, 1876, with seventeen charter members, among whom were Henry Fero, Evan Morgan, G. W. Edwards, H. C. Lee, Mary Fero, R. G. Speer, William Rogers, and L. M. Fero. The society flourished for a time but is now defunct.

BIOGRAPHICAL.

WILLIAM L. BLISS was born in Montpelier, Vermont, on the 19th of September, 1818. He learned the shoemaker trade and when twenty-two years old moved to Lowell, Massachusetts, where he bought an interest in a restaurant and conducted the same two years. He then went to New York City and engaged in the wholesale and retail liquor traffic. In 1848, he was married to Miss Almina O. Spaulding. They have four children; Gilbert R., Almina O., George S., and Ida May. Previous to his marriage he traveled through New York, Vermont and Canada, selling jewelry and dry goods and afterwards settled in Clinton county, New York; but in 1856, went to California, and engaged in mining, remaining sixteen months. On his return he traveled along the Pacific slope selling honey-bees and introduced the first ones in Oregon and Washington territories. After an absence of two and a half years he returned to New York, and in 1859, again started for California, but upon reaching this county stopped at Moscow and concluded to settle, taking a claim in section thirteen where he still lives.

JAMES BUSH, one of the earliest settlers of this place, was born in New York on the 5th of September, 1828. When young he worked for a time at the shoemaker's trade and before leaving his native State married, in 1844, Miss Harriet Gates. In 1855, they came to Dodge county, Wisconsin, and the following year to Moscow, taking a claim in section twenty-seven. In February, 1857, his wife died at the age of thirty-two years. She bore him four children, two of whom are living. In 1859, he married his second wife, a sister of the former, and she died on the 30th of August, 1881, leaving a family of nine children. In 1874, Mr. Bush built a fine frame residence in which he now lives.

GEORGE W. DEARMIN, one of the pioneers of this place, was born in North Carolina, on the 30th of October, 1828. When he was a small child his parents became pioneers of Indiana, where George resided until 1847, when he enlisted in the Fifth Indiana Volunteer Infantry, Company E, participating in the Mexican war, and serving till its close. After his discharge he came to Indiana, and in 1855 came to Iowa; resided in Mitchell county until the spring of 1856, when he came to this township and took a claim in section eight, but soon after sold and bought in section twenty-eight. In March, 1865, he enlisted in Company F, of the First Minnesota Volunteer Infantry; was sent to Washington and remained in service until the following July. He was united in marriage in May, 1859, with Miss Lucia Campbell. Of eight children born to this union, only three are living: Jessie F., Orra A., and Mary E.

STEPHEN N. FRISBIE, one of the pioneers of this place, was born in Guilford, New Haven county, Connecticut. His mother, Miss Amada Scranton, was a descendant of John Scranton, who came with twenty-five other families from England, and settled in the latter town in 1639. His father was a sea faring man; and when Stephen was ten years of age he went to live with his uncle on a farm, with whom he remained until twenty-one, then removed to Genesee, Waukesha county, Wisconsin. On the 30th of August, 1848, he was married to Miss Theresa M. Castle, formerly of Colesville, New York, and the issue of the union was five children--three sons and two daughters. In 1850, they moved to Beaver Dam, Dodge county, and resided there until 1853, thence to Leeds, Columbia county. In June, 1856, he and his family started with ox teams, and on the 23d of July, arrived in this township and staked out the claim upon which he now lives. Mr. Frisbie enjoys the esteem and confidence of his townsmen in a large degree, having been repeatedly elected to fill offices of trust and honor. In 1857, he was appointed one of the commissioners to organize Freeborn county, and that fall, at the first general election, was made one of the County Commissioners, and again in 1877 elected to the same office. He has been Chairman of the board of Supervisors, Assessor, Town Treasurer, and Justice of the Peace, in which latter capacity he now officiates. In 1878, he was honored with a seat in the House of Representatives. Although his business has been farming, he has engaged to some extent in other occupations; from the fall of 1869 till 1875 he handled grain, first for Bassett, Hunting & Co., and afterwards for other parties; subsequently kept a lumber yard on his own account. In religious views he is a Congregationalist, and when the Union Sabbath School was organized in this place he was appointed its Superintendent. A Congregational church was organized here in 1859, of which he was a member; but meetings in it have since been discontinued, and he joined the church at Austin. He is a staunch Republican, and has always been a zealous advocate of its principles. He was appointed Postmaster in 1858, the office being kept at his house until August, 1877, when it was removed to the railroad station, and its name changed to Oakland. Mr. Frisbie's first wife died on the 25th of June, 1875, after a long and painful illness, and he married his present wife on the 9th of August, 1877. She was formerly Miss Sophie A. Little, of Oberlin, Ohio.

JOHN GUY, a native of Ireland, was born in Donegal in 1845. In 1869, he left his birth place and emigrated to America, landed in New York, and came directly to Minnesota. He resided for a year and a half with his uncle in Oakland, and in 1871 bought land in this place in company with his brother. Mrs. Guy was formerly Miss Mary Taylor. Mr. Guy has been a member of the Presbyterian church since quite young; is a Republican and takes an active interest in politics.

NATHAN S. HARDY, one of the old settlers of Moscow, was born in Essex county, New York, on the 10th of January, 1833. After teaching school for a time in his native State in the spring of 1854, he moved to Illinois, engaged in farming during the summer and in the fall clerked in the store of L. S. Felt, in Galena. In the autumn of 1855, he returned to New York, and in the spring of '56, again started west, locating in this township the 1st of July. He was married on the 10th of August, 1859, to Annette, a daughter of William Pace, and the union has resulted in four children; Lovina S., Adda F., Louis E., and Milton J.

REV. THEOPHUS LOWRY, deceased, the eldest son of Rev. Samuel G. Lowry, was born in Nicholas county, Kentucky, on the 9th of September, 1821. His father, after preaching for some time in Lewis county, Kentucky, moved to New Richmond, Clermont county, Ohio, in 1823, thence, two years later, to Decatur county, Indiana, and afterward, in 1832, to Putnam county. In 1835, he went to Crawfordsville, the location of Wabash College, where Theophus graduated in 1843, and in 1846, graduated from Lane Seminery, in Cincinnati, Ohio. In the latter year he was married to Miss Nancy T. Elsey, of Parker county. He was ordained by the Presbytery of Crawfordsville.

After preaching two years at Danville and other points in Hendricks county, he was compelled to retire to a farm for a year. At the end of that time he took charge of the Bethany church, Owen county, but after a year, was obliged to give up the ministry and engaged in farming for some five or six years. In the spring of 1857, in company with his father and other friends, he came to Minnesota and located a claim in section twenty-nine, Moscow, where he died, on the 23d of April, 1874. For some eight years before his death, he was able to preach again, and supplied the churches of Sumner and Woodbury. His wife survives him and resides on the old homestead, with her adopted son, Eugene Lowry.

EDWARD LUGG, a native of England, was born in the parish of St. Martin, county of Cornwall, on the 14th of August, 1834. He was brought up as a farmer, attended school in his youth, and at the age of nineteen joined the Wesleyan Methodist church. On the 11th of April, 1858, he left his birth place and sailed for America, landed in Quebec, Canada, and came directly to Racine county, Wisconsin. He came to Freeborn county in 1859 and settled on a claim in Bath township which was afterward jumped. In January, 1862, he married Miss Almira Williams. They soon after moved to Riceland and rented a farm for a year, thence to Brush Creek, Fairbault county. In August, 1864, Mr. Lugg enlisted in Company E, Tenth Minnesota Volunteer Infantry, went South and joined the army of the Cumberland at Memphis and remained in service until the close of the war. On his return he settled on railroad land in Riceland. In 1874, he came to Moscow, and rented a farm for three years, then purchased his present in section twenty-eight. Mr. and Mrs. Lugg have had six children, four of whom are living: Charles H., James E., Samuel R., and Laura Z. Maggie, born on the 8th of November, 1863, died on the 6th of October, 1870, and Zelda, born on the 15th of December 1867, died on the 11th of September, 1870.

MICHAEL MCCOURT, one of the early settlers of Mower county, was born in county Down, Ireland, in October, 1830. In 1847, he came to America and settled in Rochester, New York, where he was employed in agricultural pursuits eight years. He married, in 1855, Miss Ellen White, and they spent a short time in Canada, then came to Clinton county, Iowa, and the following spring to Minnesota, locating in Nevada, Mower county. He lived there until 1868, when he sold and came to this place which has since been his home. Mr. McCourt is the largest individual landholder in the place. In the spring of 1881, his stable was burned with six head of horses, a colt, all the harnesses, and considerable farm machinery. He has a family of six children; John, Michael, Thomas, Stephen, Mary, and Daniel.

EVAN MORGAN, one of the pioneers of this county, is a native of Wales, born on the 10th of March, 1805. He was married before leaving Wales to Miss Winifield Reese, and they emigrated to America in 1838. They located on a farm in Portage county, Ohio, and remained until 1848, when they moved to Rock county, Wisconsin. In 1855, they sold their interest in the latter place and came to this township. Mr. Morgan bought land in the town site and also some adjoining, all of which he still owns. His wife died leaving six children, three of whom are now living. His present wife was formerly Sarah L. Thomas and the marriage took place in 1862. Of seven children born to this union, five are living. Mr. Morgan has held offices of trust since his residence here; in 1866, was sent to the State Legislature and is at present Town Clerk.

WILLIAM PACE, deceased, one of the oldest settlers of this place, was born in Sussex county, England, on the 10th of March, 1803. He learned the miller trade in his native place; emigrated to America and for years worked at his trade in New York. He was married in 1831, to Miss Amelia Ridge and they had two children, one of whom is living, a son. Mrs. Pace died in 1834, and in 1836, Mr. Pace married Miss Lavina Castle. In 1842, they came to Waukesha county, Wisconsin, and after a residence of nine years moved to Dodge county. In 1856, Mr. Pace became a pioneer of this county, taking a claim in section thirty-four, Moscow, which was his home until his death which occurred on the 6th of September, 1882. He left a widow and five grown children. He was a member of the Congregational church at Austin; was a good citizen and neighbor and respected by all who knew him.

PHILO PACE, a native of Genesee county, New York, was born on the 2d of August, 1843. When he was thirteen years old his parents moved to this place which Philo has ever since made his home. In 1863, he was engaged in selling farm machinery, afterward in carpentering and now divides his time between mercantile and farming pursuits. He was joined in marriage in 1874, with Miss Mary Scullin and they have four children; Clara Nellie, Hattie Lou, Genevieve, and Ivy B.

ROBERT G. SPEER, one of the pioneers of this county, was born in Seneca county, New York, on the 12th of April, 1826. When he was five years old his parents moved to Washtenaw county, Michigan, where Robert learned the blacksmith trade when quite young. He was married in 1847, to Miss Mary E. Hutchinson. In 1850, they moved to a farm in Dane county, Wisconsin, and five years later settled in this place. Mr. Speer erected a blacksmith shop, the first in the place, and followed that occupation until 1862, when he enlisted in the Second Minnesota Cavalry and served as blacksmith for the regiment eleven months when he was discharged for disability. Mr. and Mrs. Speer have had seven children, five of whom are living; Mary E., Dewitt C., George W., Generva, and Amanda.

NUNDA.

CHAPTER LXVIII.

LOCATION AND DESCRIPTION—EARLY SETTLEMENT—EVENTS OF INTEREST—STATISTICS—BUSINESS AND OTHER MATTERS—RELIGIOUS—TWIN LAKE VILLAGE—MEDIUMS OF EDUCATION—BIOGRAPHICAL.

The sub-division of Freeborn county bearing this name lies in the southern tier of towns, and within one of the western boundary of the county. Its contiguous surroundings are, Pickerel Lake on the north; Freeman on the east; Mansfield on the west, and the state of Iowa on the south. It is constituted as originally surveyed, of 36 sections, or 23,040 acres.

Nunda is, locally speaking, a prairie town: although the eastern part was formerly what is called "oak opening" land, and there were some fine groves of maple, butternut, bass, iron wood, and occasionally walnut, about the lakes; but this has all or nearly all been long since removed. The north and west parts of the town are made up of rolling prairie, with a soil of dark loam, underlaid with a sub-soil of clay. The southern and eastern part of the township is more given to soil of clayey nature, and quite rocky in places. There has been considerable lime-stone, of the variety known as "Floating," picked up and burned to a limited extent by B. H. Carter; but there has never been any ledges discovered.

This town is well watered by numerous brooks, rivers, and lakes, which diversify the scenery, and make of Nunda a picturesque and beautiful township. Bear Lake, the largest in the township, is a beautiful sheet of water, covering about 1,500 acres in the western portion of the town, while a stream known as Lime Creek is its outlet, and takes a southwesterly course to finally empty into the Shell Rock River. Lower Twin Lake is a body of water lying in the northwestern part of the town, containing several islands of a few acres each. This is connected by a stream called "The Inlet," with the Upper Twin Lake, which infringes on this township to the extent of about 220 acres in section two. We suppose the lakes received the names of Upper and Lower Twin Lakes from the fact of their similarity in size. Goose Creek constitutes the outlet of these lakes, and flows through sections twelve and thirteen on its way eastward to Freeman township, eventually to help swell the Shell Rock. State Line Lake, which name was suggested by the fact that the extreme southern point of the lake touches the

Iowa and Minnesota State lines; is the smallest in town, covering about 400 acres of land, mostly in section thirty-three; from this flows a creek bearing the same name and entering Iowa. All of these lakes abound in fish of various species, among which we notice pickerel, sucker, bass, and bullhead, and are much frequented by pleasure seekers in quest of "finny sport."

Almost all of the land in the town is under a high state of cultivation, and as the soil is rich and well adapted to the crops and modes of cultivation of the day, as a natural sequence, the farmers are all in comfortable circumstances, notwithstanding they have had serious drawbacks in the last decade in the way of drought, failure of wheat crop, etc., and they are now turning their attention more toward stock—which exist almost solely on the rich prairie grass—with the most satisfactory results.

EARLY SETTLEMENT.

The early or earliest settlement of Nunda dates back to 1856, and was rapid and constant until all the vacant land was secured and occupied.

As it nearly always gives rise to controversy and contention in a work of this kind, to state that any one of a party, made a claim or secured a farm, *first*, we have adopted the plan, for this township at least, of merely giving the date of arrival of early settlers as given to our interviewers; so that one reading it can come to his own conclusion as to who was first, etc.

Among, if not the first settlers in the township, were James Wright and Anthony Bright, who came in the winter of 1855-56, and commenced what was known as the Bear Lake Settlement. Wright took a claim on section sixteen and remained until 1857 when he sold to John V. Wohlhuter who still occupies it. Anthony Bright took a place in section twenty-one, south of Wright, and in 1857 sold out and left.

Patrick Fitzsimmons, a native of Ireland, made his appearance from Winneshiek county, Iowa, and joined this settlement in May, 1856. He took a claim in section sixteen, where he lived up to the time of his death, which occurred on the 18th of July, 1866. It was he who named the township Nunda, in honor of towns of the same name in which he had lived in New York and Illinois. He was a prominent man in the township and his death was much regretted by all who knew him.

About the same time came Fred McCall, another native of the Emerald Isle, who made himself at home about one mile east of his fellow-countryman, in section fourteen, where he still lives, one of the public-spirited men of this locality, and one of the oldest settlers in Nunda.

Nels Bergeson and Nels Walaker, natives of Norway, came to Minnesota in 1856; the first came direct to this town and took a place in section twenty-eight; the latter did not arrive here until 1860.

It should have been mentioned in connection with the above, that Charles Fitzsimmons and Irvin Elsworth came in the early part of 1856, and it is claimed by some that they were the first. Fitzsimmons placed his signet upon a quarter of section sixteen, where he remained until 1868 and then removed to Martin county, Minnesota. Elsworth enriched himself by pre-empttng a place in section fourteen, where he lived for about one year when he sold, and now sojourns in California, from last accounts.

In the fall of this year, 1856, Harry Brown drifted in and made a habitation in section seven, where he remained until 1858 when he sold out.

Seneca Stockdale was a native of Ohio, having been born on the 26th of March, 1801, and after attaining the age of fifty-five came to the township of Nunda, where he was among the first; arriving on the 14h of July, 1856. He took a farm in section one, where he remained for about thirteen years, and then removed to section three, remaining here until the 7th of February, 1871, when, at the ripe old age of seventy years, he passed peacefully away to that land where the "wicked cease from troubling and the weary are at rest."

A few more came in this year, but they were merely transients, and only remained a short time, and their names have been forgotten.

The following year, 1857, the emigration to this locality seemingly commenced in earnest, and, although to name them all would be almost impossible, as many of them as are remembered will be given. As will be seen, there were already several settlements in the town, and those coming this year were not subjected to that, (as an old settler termed it) "solitary confinement" inevitable to the pioneer times of those who were already in, and waiting for the neighbors whom the arrivals in 1857 furnished.

Nelson Boughton, a native of New York, came this year and took a farm in section thirty-five, where he lived until 1859, when he was murdered by a man named Kreigler, which is mentioned in another place.

Alonzo White, of Vermont, came about the same time and settled in the same section, where he lived until 1859, and then went back to the East.

James Carle, of the same nativity also came at the same time and took land in sections thirty-four and thirty-five, where he lived until 1860 when he sold and followed his friend east.

Lafayette Hall, of New York, came and settled in this vicinity: in 1860 he went to the eastern part of the State, where he now lives.

Michael Donahue had arrived in the spring of 1857, and settled a mile or so north of this little settlement, in section twenty-three, where he still holds forth.

Martin Forbes also came at the same time and settled on the same section.

John Honan, a native of Ireland, came in 1857, an settled on section twenty-four.

John M. Geissler, a native of Germany, and one of the pioneers of Freeborn county, came to Nunda in 1857, and selected the place he now occupies in sections three and ten. He has probably been the most prominent man in the township in public matters and has held many offices of trust and importance.

John V. Wohlhuter, a native of Germany, came to America in 1847, and in the fall of 1857 to this township and purchased the farm he now occupies near Bear Lake.

R. A. White made his appearance in the spring of this year, and settled on section nine, where he still remains. William White came to this country at the same time.

George Hall and Johnson Hall, from the eastern States came to Nunda in the spring of 1857, and took farms in sections three and four, where the latter lived for a time and then went east. Mr. George Hall is still on his farm.

John Donahue, originally from the Emerald Isle, but late from Illinois, arrived in July, 1857, and settled with his parents on section fourteen.

There may have been others who came this year, but this is enough to indicate the rapidity with which the unoccupied land was taken. A few of those who have since arrived will be noted.

In 1858, Mr. Cunningham, a native of the land of the Shamrock, made his appearance and secured land in section twenty-three.

Narve Esleson, of Norway, lost no time in securing a habitation in section thirty-three, where he now lives.

Knudt Oleson, in 1861, had also secured land, and has since been joined by a small army of his countrymen.

John McGuire, a native of Ireland, on the 23d June, 1860, made his appearance, and settled on section fourteen.

B. H. Carter, a native of the eastern States, arrived in Nunda in 1861, and made himself at home in section one, where he still lives, a prominent man in the township.

This quite extended list embraces the most of the early settlers, and many of them who are not found here will be seen under the head of Biographical.

EARLY SETTLERS WHO HAVE PASSED AWAY.

William White, one of the pioneers, was inducted into this life on the 8th of September, 1796, at Bemis Heights, on the battle field where the English, under General Burgoyne, surrendered to General Gates, in the town of Saratoga, New York. When two years of age his father went to Clinton county, in the same State. In the war of 1812 he served as a teamster, and so received a bounty land warrant. In 1814 his father and himself went to Tioga county, and on the Susquehana he was in business for forty-one years. He married Margaret Love, and they had four sons and five daughters, all living when he died on the 17th of January, 1876. He came to Nunda on the 7th of June, 1857, so that he had been a resident of the town for nineteen years. A few days before his death he was seized with a sensation of numbness in his left foot, in which the circulation stopped, and gaugrene supervened with a fatal result. An able and prominent man, he was for six years County Commissioner, a Justice of the Peace, and in other public positions.

Erick Erickson.—Mr. Erickson commenced building in section thirty-three in the town of Nunda, on the 25th of June, 1856, and there he wrought up to the time of his final exit from this sphere of existence, which occurred on the 14th of December, 1877, at the age of 55 years. He hae opened a fine farm and was an honest and upright man.

Thomas Morrison, having nearly filled up the measure of his one hundredth year, was gathered with the innumerable host from whence no tidings come, on the 8th of November, 1876. His birth was in Belfast, Ireland, on the 12th of September, 1777, and came to America in 1811, and was a soldier in the war of 1812. In 1861 he came to Minnesota. He was a member of the Baptist church and had six children. His wife had preceded him but two months.

FREDERICK H. WHITE came with his father in 1857, and captured a farm in Nunda. Himself and two brothers were in the war of the rebellion. He was next to the youngest of thirteen children. While in the service he contracted a cough which finally terminated fatally. His kind disposition and gentle manners had drawn to him large numbers of friends. It was on the 17th of February, 1879, at the age of 32, the recall was sounded for him for the last time.

MRS MARY WALKER, wife of Hon. Asa Walker, aged 60 years, went through the final transposition on the 20th of January, 1869, at Nunda. Mrs. Walker was one of the pioneers, and a faithful member of the Congregational church, and had a firm faith that "it is not all of life to live nor all of death to die."

EVENTS OF INTEREST.

EARLY BIRTHS.—One of the first births in the town was the ushering into existence of Louis H. Emmons, on the 30th of December, 1856, who is still in the land of the living.

On the 24th of February, 1858, a similar instance occurred and brought into existence John David McCall, who grew to manhood and still lives in the town.

EARLY MARRIAGES.—It is reported that the first couple to be joined in wedlock within the limits of the township, were Mr. Louis Proebstein, (or some such name) and Elizabeth Banning, in the fall of 1856. This date is pretty early early; but we give it to our readers just as given to us.

Another early marriage was that of Isaac Kendall to Miss Christina Clark, in April, 1858, by Frederick McCall.

DEATHS.—An early, if not the first death in the township, occured on the 23d of March, 1858, and caried Jacob Zimmerman, age 23, to that land "from whence no traveler returns." He was the first person buried in the Brush Hill Cemetery.

Hulda, wife of Patrick Fitzsimmons, died on the 28th of November, 1858.

TOWNSHIP ORGANIZATION.

Politically speaking, the residents of Nunda first came together in 1857, late in the fall, for the election of a representative in the territorial legislature, and in the spring following, an organization of the township was effected, whereupon, on the 11th day of May, 1857, they again assembled, and made their organization substantial by the election of town officers.

Among the first officials were: Supervisors, Patrick Fitzsimmons, Chairman, J. V. Wohlhuter, and Henry Tunell; Clerk, William B. Spooner. This meeting was held in John Hoffman's house, in section twenty-two.

In government, the township has run along very smoothly, with no jars, embezzlement, or inefficiency to disturb the tranquility of matters, and the management has always been in capable and honest hands.

At the 24th annual meeting, held in the spring of 1882, the following officers were elected: Supervisors, L. Marpe, Chairman, E. T. Yeadon, and John F. Wohlhuter; Clerk, John M. Geissler; Justices of the Peace, H. Rasmusson and R. A. White; Treasurer, John Donahue; Constables, T. Swenson and Hugh Donahue; Assessor, T. Swenson.

STATISTICS.

The object of presenting these few figures is not so much on account of the intrinsic importance of knowing how much was raised this particular year, or the kind of crops cultivated, although this knowledge is valuable, but more as a basis of comparison in future years.

THE YEAR 1881.—Showing the acreage and yield in the township of Nunda for the year named:

Wheat—3,962 acres; yielding 40,698 bushels.

Oats—744 acres; yielding 23,082 bushels.

Corn—912 acres; yielding 30,662 bushels.

Barley—50 acres; yielding 954 bushels.

Potatoes—90 acres; yielding 7,248 bushels.

Total acreage cultivated in 1881, 5,788.

Wild hay—3,086 tons.

Apple trees growing—1,704; trees bearing, 249; apples, 90 bushels.

Grape vines bearing—8.

Tobacco—126 pounds.

Sheep—257 sheared; yielding 1,028 pounds of wool.

Dairy—499 cows; yielding 44,594 pounds of butter.

THE YEAR 1882.—Wheat,3,834 acres; oats, 734; corn, 942; barley, 50; potatoes, 96; total acreage cultivated in 1882, 5,756.

Apple trees growing—1,662; trees bearing, 244; grape vines bearing, 8.

Milch cows—551; sheep, 297, yielding 1,118 pounds of wool.

Whole number of farms in 1881 100.

POPULATION.—The census of 1870 gave Nunda a population of 675. The last census, taken in 1880, reports 777 for this town; showing an increase of 102.

BUSINESS AND OTHER MATTERS.

A manufacturing establishment, in which the man with the anvil and bellows manouvers, was commenced in the spring of 1866 on section four, in a shop 12x16. The proprietor of this was William Pickle, and times have evidently been flourishing with the establishment, as it is still there, now occupying a shop 16x20.

In 1876 a similar institution was started in a building erected for the purpose, in the northeastern part of section thirty, by H. H. Edwin, which is still in full blast.

In September, 1880, a general merchandise store was started by George Emmons, in section thirty-two. This was continued until the 6th of December, 1881, when it was moved to Norman, Iowa.

A blacksmith shop was established in the southwestern part of section nine, by John Bettner, in 1875, and it is still in good running order, with Mr. B. still at the anvil.

In the spring of 1872, Mr. George Reim erected a shop and commenced blacksmithing in section eight. He still continues the business, now being in a shop 16x20 feet, which was erected in 1881.

A sorghum mill was started in section eight in 1873, which is still on the ground, having a capacity of about forty gallons per day.

The first Post-office in the township was established in the spring of 1859, and Patrick Fitzsimmons was appointed Postmaster, with the office at his house in section sixteen, where mail arrived once each week. Here the office remained until the 21st of June, 1866, when Frederick McCall was appointed mail handler, and the office was removed to his residence in section fourteen, mail at this time being carried once each week by Albert Davis. In 1877 it was again removed, this time to Twin Lake in section twelve, and on the first of July, 1881, the name was changed from Nunda to Twin Lake, under which name it is now known. Mail now arrives twice each day. When the office was moved to the village, in 1877, B. H. Carter was appointed Postmaster, and held it several years, when Mr. McCall was again appointed, and is still the incumbent.

State Line Post-office.—The citizens of the southern portion of the town first indulged in this luxury in 1864, on the first of August, in which year this office was established by Congress, and Mr. H. G. Emmons was appointed to handle the mail, with the office at his house in section thirty-two, mail arriving once each week from Albert Lea. In November, 1879, Mr. Emmons resigned his position as Postmaster, and the office was removed to Norman, Iowa, where it is now kept by Mr. Thomas Wangsness.

RELIGIOUS.

GERMAN LUTHERAN CHURCH.—The first services for this Society were held in the summer of 1862, at the residence of Mr. John Wohlhuter, in section sixteen, by Rev. Mr. L. Scheor. The Society was organized in 1866, with John Wohlhuter, John Tunell, and Mr. Fink as Trustees. Services were held in private houses until the schoolhouse of District No. 42 was erected, and this was then used until the summer of 1881, when their present neat church was erected near the center of section four, size 28x40, at a cost of about $2,300. At organization the Society had thirteen members, it now has thirty, the present pastor being the Rev. Ferdinand Tiede. The Trustees are John M. Geissler, August Linderman, and Henry Drommerhausen.

LUTHERAN CEMETERY.—This ground was laid out in December, 1875, by John M. Mertz, near the center of section four, containing 126 lots, 10x15 feet. The first burial here was William White, who died on the 14th of January, 1876.

BRUSH HILL CEMETERY.—The land for this ground was donated as a cemetery ground by Christian Hogen in 1859, the first burial being Jacob Remmermand, in March, 1858. Although the land was given, verbally, no deed was made, and the farm changing hands the new proprietor refused to recognize former arrangements, and in 1879 the land was purchased at a cost of $100.

The ground is located about the center of section fifteen.

Bear Lake Cemetery.—This was platted on the 8th of December, 1875, and recorded on the 8th of March, 1876. The trustees were R. J. White, William P. Pickle, S. F. Foster, William P. Spooner, and John M. Geissler.

State Line Cemetery.—This burial ground is located on the Iowa and Minnesota State line, in section thirty-two, containing about one acre of land surveyed into lots. The ground was platted and laid out in 1861, on the land of Mr. T. Nelson, but did not receive an occupant until February, 1863, when Christina Emmons passed to that unseen world, and her remains were interred in this as her last earthly abode.

Catholic Society Cemetery.—Located in the central part of section twenty-four, was laid out and dedicated to burial purposes on the 29th of August, 1876, land being donated by John Honan; and was divided into 126 lots, 24x25, in all two acres and a half. The first person so unfortunate as to need burial here was John Honan, who passed away on the 9th of September, 1876.

TWIN LAKE VILLAGE.

This is the only village in the township, and is located in the northeastern part of Nunda, at the outlet of the lower lake bearing the name of the village, in section twelve: and although its growth up to this time has been slow, being situated upon a main railroad thoroughfare, it has a chance yet of making a healthy and moderate sized village.

Its Early Days.—The land upon which the village now stands originally belonged to Mr. William Wilson and Mr. Tanner. The first plat came into existence in 1858, at the instigation of Augustus Armstrong, and was laid into lots on the land of William Banning, but as no growth was developed, and no interest in the little burg manifested, the lots and blocks were finally reclaimed as a farm. Matters ran along in this way, nothing being done in regard to it, until 1869, when a surveyor again made his appearance and the lots and blocks of the village were again brought into existence, about eighty rods north of the old plat, on land of Mr. Wilson and Mr. Tanner as above stated, and in the fall of this year John Donahue and William Knudtson erected the first business house and opened a stock of groceries and general merchandise.

A store was opened by Frederick McCall, in March, 1863, at his residence in section fourteen, and the original Twin Lake Post office was also kept here. In 1877, the business was moved to the village; and for a time groceries were kept; but finally all was discontinued except the tin shop. The Post-office is also kept here.

In the fall of 1875, Peter Donahue laid the foundation of his present general merchandise store by placing a stock of groceries upon the shelves.

In 1870, Mr. William Beatty assisted in the growth of the village and erected a hotel which he ran until 1877, and then sold it to Ole Nelson who still continues it as a boarding house.

In 1868, a building was erected and a blacksmith shop put into operation by a Norwegian whose name is forgotten. In a few years it was transferred to the Booth brothers, who ran it for a year and then sold to B. H. Carter and John Donahue, who operated it for several years in partnership, and then Mr. Donahue purchased the entire business and still manages the concern.

A mill was erected at an early day, and later, a schoolhouse. The railroad pushed its way through the village, and a depot and elevator followed, with the accompanying advantages, until the place now contains three general stores, one grist mill, an elevator, depot, schoolhouse, blacksmith shop, a shoe shop, and ten or twelve dwelling houses.

Twin Lake Mill.—In 1857, a saw-mill was erected in the northern part of the southwest quarter of section twelve, where the village was afterwards laid out, by William Banning and a Mr. Forbes, and commenced operations with a forty horse water-power, making a capacity for cutting 1,000 feet per day. Matters got complicated with the managers and the mill remained idle most of the time until 1863, while the proprietors engaged in a long legal controversy out of claims of each upon the mill site. In 1863, David Perry, who owned an interest in the mill, took charge of it, employing B. H. Carter to straighten it up, increasing the capacity to 1,500 feet per day. After running it a short time he transferred it to Augustus Armstrong and J. M. Tanner. After this Mr. Tanner ran it for a time and in 1868 sold one-half interest to Mr. William Wilson, and soon after the other half was also transferred. The latter gentleman at once commenced the erection of a flouring mill which was completed in due time and is now a valuable enterprise in the village; having a capacity for grinding 120 bushels of wheat per day.

The mill is equipped with modern machinery, deriving its power from the Goose Creek, which furnishes a power of forty horse, or 18½ feet of water head. Altogether the mill is the main and principal enterprise in the surrounding country.

MEDIUMS OF EDUCATION.

Realizing that "knowledge is power" the citizens of Nunda have fortified themselves against that curse to civilization, ignorance, by dividing their territory into eight school districts, with numbers and locations of schoolhouses as follows: No. 42, with building on section four; No. 43 on section sixteen; No. 44 on section thirty-two; No. 45 on section twenty-four; No. 76 in Twin Lake village; No. 99 on section six; No. 105 in section thirty-four; No. 108 in section fourteen; a short sketch of each of which is given in connection herewith. It is unnecessary to state, knowing the enterprise of the people here, that the districts are all in good financial condition with neat buildings, and ably managed.

District No. 42.—Embraces the territory in the northern part of the town toward the center. The first school was held by Miss Mary Ann White, in the winter of 1858-59, at the residence of Samuel Clark in section three, with twelve juveniles upon the hard benches. School was continued in the houses of various farmers throughout the district until 1870, when the present frame building was erected at a cost of $550 in section four. Miss Eva Morey first opened school here with thirty-five scholars in attendance. The present officers are: R. A. White, Clerk: August Linderman, Director; and William Lenz, Treasurer.

District No. 43.—The first school held within the territory comprising this district, was at the residence of John Hoffman in section twenty-two, in the spring of 1858, by Joseph White, with an attendance of twenty scholars, and the district effected an organization by the election of the following officers: Clerk, P. Fitzsimmons; Director, John V. Wohlhuter; Treasurer, Michael Donahue. In 1868 the present school edifice was erected in the western part of section sixteen, at a cost of $400, where the first teacher was Isabell Wilson. The present school board consists of: Alfred Emery, Clerk; Christian Yost, Director; and Fred H. Yost, Treasurer.

District No. 44.—It is stated by some that this district effected an organization in 1858, the first clerk being D. G. Emmons, and the same year the first school was taught by Miss Sarah Emery in an empty house belonging to N. Asleson on section thirty-two. After this school was held in private residences until about 1870, when they erected a frame schoolhouse in the northeastern part of section thirty-two, at a cost of $650, in which Miss Robinson first called school to order. The present officers are: Messrs L. Emmons, A. Freemott, Nels Nelson, respectively Clerk, Director, and Treasurer.

District No. 45.—Effected an organization in the fall of 1861, and embraced the territory now included in district No. 76. The first officers were Messrs Rupson, Donahue, and Berry; but as nothing was accomplished by this board, the following year Patrick Kelly and John McQuire took their places, and in the fall of 1862 a log schoolhouse was erected in the northeastern part of section fourteen by contribution of labor, and and school was taught in the following summer by Eliza Eaton with twenty scholars enrolled. This building was used until 1871 - the district having been divided in the meantime—and a new frame house was constructed at a cost of $400 in the western part of section twenty-four. This building served its purpose until the 9th day of June, 1881, when it was destroyed by fire, and in the fall of the same year the present neat frame building was erected on the old site at a cost of $770, in which Miss Leda Hewett first called school to order, with an attendance of forty-six juveniles. Matters have ran along pleasantly and the present school officers are: Patrick Kelly, Martin Forbes, and Patrict Honan, respectively Clerk, Treasurer, and Director.

Since the above was written the Albert Lea Standard of September 7th 1882, says:—"School district 45 held their annual meeting last Saturday and elected M. Conors director, and H. Donahue clerk. Also voted $78 tax for current expenses and also to have seven months school—four in the winter with a man teacher, and three in the summer."

District No. 76.—The territory now comprised under this number was formerly embraced in Dis trict No. 45. In 1863 this district was set off and organized by the election of Mr. B. H. Carter, Clerk; Elof Knudtson, Director; J. M. Tanner, Treasurer. In 1865 a schoolhouse was erected in the village of Twin Lake at a cost of $500, in which the first school was taught by Isabella Wilson to an attendance of forty scholars. This house was used until March, 1881, when a passing engine set it on fire and it was destroyed. The railroad company refused to pay any damages, and upon being sued by the district the courts rendered a judgment in favor of the district of about $450 for the building, and $110 for the lot, making a total of $560 and costs.

In the spring of 1881 a new schoolhouse was erected on a lot purchased of William Wilson, for $60, and is a neat frame building having cost $1,000. The school has at present an attendance of about forty scholars, the officers being John Donahue, Clerk; Henry Eaton, Treasurer; B. H. Carter, Director.

DISTRICT No. 99.—This district effected an organization in 1875, the first officers elected being: Clerk, W. J. Morey; Director, Fernando Fessenden; and Treasurer, E. T. Yeadon. In the spring of 1876 the present neat schoolhouse was erected in the southwestern part of section six, at a cost of $475, in which the first school was instructed by Miss Louisa Rodgers, with eighteen scholars enrolled. At the present time the school officers are: Clerk, Loren Fessenden; Director, William Barnes; Treasurer, F. Reimen.

DISTRICT No. 105.—Effected an organization in 1864, and the first school was taught in the house of Peter Knutson in the spring of this year. In the spring of 1866 a small building was erected in section thirty-five at a cost of about $100, the labor being donated by the residents. This building was used until 1879, when the present house was erected upon the same site at a cost of $300, in which the first school was taught by Priscilla V. Hemon, with an attendance of thirty scholars. The first officers were: Clerk, Silas White; Treasurer, Peter Knutson; Director, Helga Larson. The present officers are: Ole N. Gvephvim, Helga Larson, and J. Sorenson.

DISTRICT No. 108.—This district is really a division of, or it might be called a reorganization of No. 84, coming into existence as a separate organization in 1879 by electing John Larson, Clerk; Knute Hovland, Director, and Hogen Rasmusson, Treasurer. In 1881 a neat school building was erected in the southern part of section nineteen, at a cost of $350, and in which knowledge is still dispensed. The first school in this house was taught by a lady teacher named Eslen Nerverson.

BIOGRAPHICAL.

B. H. CARTER was born in Cayuga county, New York, on the 9th of January, 1823. He resided at home and attended school until 1842, when he began to learn the wheelwright trade, and finished in 1845. On the 22d of October in the latter year, he was married to Miss Helen Eaton. The same year they moved to Cuyahoga county, Ohio, where he was engaged at his trade two years, then came west to Dodge county, Wisconsin. In 1859 they removed to this county, purchased a farm in Freeman, and resided there until 1861, when they came to Nunda, taking a claim in section one. In 1863 Mr. Carter was commissioned Second Lieutenant, and enrolled a large portion of the men of Nunda and Freeman for a draft; he served in the Fifth Minnesota Regiment from 1864 till the close of the war. After his return he engaged in farming three years and then built a wagon shop in the village of Twin Lake, but in 1879 returned to his farm, which has since been his home. He has held several offices of trust, and was Court Commissioner three years. Mr. and Mrs. Carter have had fifteen children, those living are: Henrietta, Eva, Theda, Daisy, Jerome, Clide, Lillis, James, Ada, Anna, and Asa. Three died in infancy.

JERRY CALLAGHAN was born in the North Parish Chapel in the city of Cork, Ireland, in September, 1829. He attended North Manestry School ten years, after which he engaged in delivering milk, and in five years was employed as a waiter. In 1848, he emigrated to America, located in Schenectady county, New York, where he farmed one year, and came to Racine county, Wisconsin. In 1856, he removed to Freeborn county, and purchased a farm near Albert Lea, resided there until 1864, and bought his present farm in Nunda, section twenty-three. He was married on the 14th of October, 1859, to Miss Mary Honan, and in 1864, enlisted in the army, served nine months and returned home. On the 20th of December, 1870, as he was returning home from Albert Lea, he lost his way, was out all night and was so badly frozen as to necessitate the amputation of the left leg six inches above the ankle, the toes from the right foot and the fingers from both hands. Mr. Callaghan has eight children: Joseph, Mary, Ann, Catharine, John, William, Bridget, and Jennie.

H. H. EDWIN was born in Norway on the 7th of January, 1841. When fifteen years old he commenced to learn the blacksmith trade, serving an apprenticeship of three years. He then went to Denmark; two years later to Germany, and in one year returned to Norway, working at his trade in both places. In 1865, he emigrated to America, first located in LaCrosse, Wisconsin, engaged in the blacksmith shop of Devon, Smith & Co. until 1867. On the 6th of October in the latter year, he married Miss Martha Thompson, and they removed to Jackson, where Mr. Edwin was employed at his trade until 1874. He then removed to Nunda and purchased a farm of one hundred and twenty acres on section thirty, where he still resides. He has a family of seven children; Caroline, Theodore, Martinis, Amelia, Dorothy, Nels, and Hannah.

H. G. EMMONS, one of the early settlers of Freeborn county, was born in Norway, on the 16th of October, 1828. He emigrated to America in 1850, directly to Rock county, Wisconsin, where he engaged in farming and railroading. In 1854, he married Miss Christina Larson, and two years later they removed to Minnesota, driving the distance with a yoke of oxen. They located in Nunda, where Mr. Emmons now owns five hundred acres of land. They lived in their wagon two months when a shanty was completed, and in 1861 built a portion of their present dwelling. He has held local offices, being a member of the board of County Commissioners six years, four years of which he was chairman, and in 1877 and 1878, was in the State Legislature. His farm is supplied with good outbuildings, barn, granary, etc. Mr. and Mrs. Emmons have had eight children, five of whom are living. Two children died at the age of two years, and Charles while attending school at Carlton College, on the 12th of April, 1882, at the age of twenty-three years. Mr. Emmons has filled the office of Postmaster fifteen years and Justice of the Peace fourteen years.

ELLEF EVENSON, a native of Norway, was born the 9th of September, 1847, and reared on a farm. When nineteen years old he served an apprenticeship at the carpenter trade, at which he worked until 1868, in his native country. In the latter year he came to America, direct to Watonwan county, this State, and located a claim. In 1872, he sold his farm and engaged on the Winona and St. Peter railroad for one year, and at the end of that time went to Winnebago county, Iowa; followed farming until 1874, then came to this place, and in 1878, purchased his present farm of one hundred and seventy-three acres, in section thirty-three. He was married to Mrs. Sarah Everson, on the 14th of February, 1878.

ALEXANDER FREEMOTT is a native of Germany, born on the 9th of December, 1822. At the age of fifteen years he commenced to learn the trade of carriage painting, serving as an apprentice four years. In August, 1853, he came to America, and on the 31st of January, 1854, was joined in marriage with Miss Minnie Hundredmark, in Chicago, Illinios. In 1865, they moved to Batavia in the latter State, and he was engaged at his trade, as foreman, until 1876. Then he came to Nunda ana purchased his present farm of one hundred and forty acres, and built a large frame dwelling. Mr. and Mrs. Freemott have had eleven children, two of whom died in infancy: those living are; Albert, Amelia, Henry, Edward, Alexander, Lucy, Edith, Anna, and Lena.

GEORGE HALL is a native of Licking county, Ohio, born on the 21st of July, 1837. In 1848, he moved with his parents to Green county, Wisconsin, and thence to Winneshiek county, Iowa. He came to Nunda in the spring of 1857, located a claim in section four and remained one season, then returned to Winneshiek county and settled on a farm. He was married on the 11th of August, 1858, to Miss Eliza A. Stockdale. In 1864, Mr. Hall sold his farm in the latter place, and again came to Nunda,taking land in section three, which is still his home. He has a family of nine children; William, Ruth, James, Lenora, Mary, Rosa, Burt, Flora, and Flossa.

J. R. JONES, a native of England, was born in March, 1824. He resided at home, assisting in the farm labor and attending school until the age of fourteen years, when he began farming for himself. In 1848, he was employed by an English nobleman as groomsman, and remained with him until he emigrated to America in 1852. He was married the previous year to Miss Elizabeth Hughes. They first settled in Green county, Wisconsin, where he carried on a farm a number of years. On the 18th of May, 1854, Mrs. Jones died leaving one son, who is now a doctor living in Iowa. Mr. Jones was married to his second wife in 1857. She was formerly Savilla Kelley, and bore him six children; Charles, David, Lauren, Mary, Clarence, and William. In 1866, they moved to this county, and after residing in Freeman for a short time, came to Nunda in the spring of 1870, and located on his present farm. His wife died on the 25th of September, 1874.

HELGE LARSON is a native of Norway, born on the 9th of June, 1834, and remained at home until twenty years of age. He then engaged in farming on neighboring farms, and in 1860, emigrated to America, coming direct to Nunda and locating in section thirty-six, where he now owns two hundred acres of land. He was married on the 11th of April, 1861, to Miss Barbara Esselson, and in 1874, erected his present frame house, having previously lived in a log shanty. Mr. and Mrs. Larson have been blessed with ten children.

LOUIS MARPE, a pioneer of Freeborn county, was born in Germany in 1832, and after finishing school was engaged in a wholesale grocery house five years. In 1854, he emigrated to America, located on a farm in Genesee county, New York, and in the fall of 1856, removed to this county, settling in Pickerel Lake township. He was married in 1857, to Miss Caroline Yeost, and in 1863 they came to this place, first erecting a log house, but now has a fine frame house in the process of construction. He had eight children, two of whom are dead. His wife also died on the 17th of January, 1875. On the 15th of October 1876, he was again married, his bride being Miss May Fulton, who bore him two children, and died on the 7th of September, 1881.

TOSTEN NELSON was born in Norway in the 26th of November, 1816. When fourteen years old he learned the shoemaker's trade and was engaged at the same four years. He then, in company with his father, started a tan yard and carried it on until the death of his father. Tosten then took charge of the homestead until coming to America. He married when twenty-six years years old Miss Susan Johnson, and in 1850 they emigrated to this country, locating in Columbia county, Wisconsin. They purchased a farm there but in 1858, sold and removed to Mitchell county, Iowa. In 1863, they removed to Nunda, and bought a farm in section thirty-one which is still their home. Mr. and Mrs. Nelson had eight children; Nels, the eldest died in the army in 1863, aged twenty-two years; Martha, the second; Johanes died when two years old; John, Mary, Martin, Carlin, and Andrew. Mrs Nelson died on the 11th of May, 1866, at the age of fifty-one years. On the 2d of June, 1869, Mr. Nelson again married, his bride being Miss Betsey Peterson. He has held numerous offices of trust in the town.

IVER O. OPDAL, a native of Norway, dates his birth the 10th of August, 1825. He spent ten years in the army in his native country, and in November, 1851, married Miss Isabelle Dahlen. In 1864, they emigrated to America, came to Dane county, Wisconsin, and in a short time removed to Winnebago county, Iowa. He came to Nunda in 1865, and purchased land in sections thirty and nineteen which is still his home. Mr. and Mrs. Opdal have had two children.

KNUDT OLSEN was born in Norway, on the 7th of August, 1829. His father died when Knudt was but eight years old, and he remained on the farm with his mother until 1860, when he came to America and directly to this township, buying eighty acres of land in section nineteen, where he now owns one hundred and twenty acres. He was joined in matrimony with Miss O. Thompson in January, 1872, and the issue of the union is two children.

WILLIAM PICKLE was born in New York, on the 31st of December, 1834. His younger days were spent on a farm and in school, finishing his education at a select school in Wisconsin. At the age of eighteen years he was apprenticed to the blacksmith trade in what is now known as the "Upton Manufacturing Works" at Battle Creek, Michigan. In 1855, he was engaged in a shop at Marshall in the same State and in 1857, went to the Rocky Mountains, where he found employment at his trade and mining, remaining until 1859. In that year he came to Freeborn county, locating in Freeman township, and in 1862 enlisted in the Twenty-first Iowa Volunteer Infantry, served three years and two months, being mustered out the 7th of April, 1865, and returned to his farm. He sold his farm in Freeman and purchased one hundred and sixty acres of land in this township on section four, and has his farm supplied with a fine frame dwelling and numerous out-buildings. On the 27th of May, 1865, he was joined in matrimony with Miss Mary Kranshoor, and they five children: Lillian, Walter, Martin, Etta, and Ralph.

HOGAN RASMUSSON, one of the old settlers of this township, was born in Norway, on the 29th of March, 1835, and came to this country with his parents in 1857. They located in Columbia county, Wisconsin, and in 1858, Hogan came to this township and staked out a claim in section thirty, where he now owns two hundred and forty-six acres of land. He was married on the 10th of October, 1858, to Miss Isabelle Anderson, and they had three children. Mrs. Rasmusson died on the 24th of May, 1865, and our subject was again married on the 21st of April, 1867, his bride being Miss Christina Nelson. This latter union has been blessed with seven children, one of whom is dead. Mr. Rasmusson has held many local offices in the place.

OLE TARALDSON is a native of Norway and dates his birth the 8th of May, 1827. He was married in 1859, to Miss Alena Mikkelson, the ceremony taking place the 25th of December. In 1862, he learned the carpenter trade, and in 1867, came to America, directly to Nunda, where he has a farm of one hundred and sixty-six acres. Mr. and Mrs. Taraldson have a family of six children; Theodore, Martin, Alena, Ole, Christinn, and Tena.

ANDREW A. TOMPSON was born in Norway in 1836, and remained at home until eighteen years old, then went to work for himself on a farm. He was married in 1864, to Miss Martha Oleson, and the same year they emigrated to America locating in Spring Prairie, Wisconsin; a year later they removed to Mitchell county, Iowa, being engaged in farming in both States. In 1868, he came to this township, purchased a farm of one hundred and sixty acres in section nineteen, where he still resides. He has four children: Ole, Mary, Amy, and Betta.

N. N. WALAKER is a native of Norway, born on the 16th of April, 1830, and when seventeen years old learned the shoemaker's trade. In November, 1854, he was married to Miss Carrie Lewis, and two years later they came to America. For several years they lived in Dane county, Wisconsin, where he farmed during summer months and worked at his trade in the winter. In 1860, he removed to Nunda, section twenty-nine, building first a log house, and in 1874, erected his present commodious dwelling. He has a family of four children: Anna, George, Nicholas, and Louis. Mr. Walaker has held many offices of trust in the place since his residence here.

JOHN V. WOHLHUTER, a pioneer of this county, was born in France, on the 29th of September, 1827. In the spring of 1847, he emigrated to America, went to Buffalo, New York, where, for seven months, he was engaged on the Erie Canal; from there went to Peru, Indiana, and thence, in 1849, to Chicago, Illinois, and found employment at teaming. On the 28th of February, 1853, he married Miss F. Fortman and the same year removed to Fayette county, Iowa; remained until the fall of 1857, and then came to this place, locating in section sixteen, where he has two hundred and seventeen acres of land. He was one of the first officers here and has held many offices since. He has four children.

R. A. WHITE, one of the oldest settlers of this place, was born in Tioga county, New York, on the 11th of January, 1840. He came here with hif parents in 1857, and on the 11th of October, 1861, he enlisted and was appointed Sergeant of the Fourth Minnesota Volunteer Infantry, Company F, serving until the 22d of December, 1864, when he received an honorable discharge. He returned to Nunda and has since been engaged in farming, owning four hundred and twenty-eight acres of land, which is all well improved. He was married on the 26th of March, 1873, to Miss Jennie M. Rudler, and the result of the union is four children; Belle M., William M., Allen R., and Ferris L.

CHRIST. YOST was born in Germany on the 15th of September, 1837. He attended school seven years, and afterward engaged in teaming until 1857. In the latter year he emigrated to America, located near Chicago on a farm, and in one year removed to that city where he again engaged in teaming. On the 11th of May, 1862, he married Miss Elizabeth Lucas, who was born in Germany on the 17th of July, 1843. Later, Mr. Yost was a street car conductor, and in 1866, purchased a farm in Nunda, and brought his family here. In 1875, he sold his land in section twenty-two, and bought his present farm of one hundred and sixty acres in section sixteen. His children are; Frederick W., Mary L., Katie A., Margaret A., and Louis J.

NEWRY.

CHAPTER LXIX.

DESCRIPTIVE—EARLY SETTLEMENT—TOWN ORGANIZATION—STATISTICAL—MATTERS OF INTEREST—RELIGIOUS—SCHOOLS—BIOGRAPHICAL.

This is the northeast corner township of Freeborn county, and is therefore one of the most prominent towns as to the location. Its boundaries are as follows: Steele county on the north; Mower county on the east; Moscow township on the south; and Geneva on the west. It is a full congressional township of 36 sections or square miles, embracing the territory of township 104, Range 19.

The surface of the town is quite rolling and is made up mostly of oak opening land. The greater part of the prairie land is found in the northern part of the town, while the southern part is chiefly covered with timber of the varieties of black, red, and burr oak, poplar and black walnut, although the latter has now been mostly removed.

The soil is different as you change localities: the west, north, and eastern parts being mostly a dark loam of from two to three feet in thickness, and underlaid with a subsoil of blue clay; and the southern and central part is more of a sandy nature or, as it is called, "black sandy loam," with a subsoil of gravel.

There are not so many water courses or lakes in this town as in a majority of its neighbors, yet it is not altogether devoid of them. A small body of water lying in section two is known as Newry Lake Oak, or Johnson's Lake, lies in section twenty-six, and from it flows a substantial little stream which empties into Deer creek in the northern part of section thirty-four. The population is almost entirely Irish and Norwegian, there being no Americans and only three German families in the township.

EARLY SETTLEMENT.

The early settlement of this township commenced in 1854, and was about the second settlement started in Freeborn county. Ellof Kinetson and family, natives of Norway, were the first to arrive, making their appearance in 1854, and claiming a place in section twenty-five, where they remained until 1874, when Mr. Kinetson died and was buried in Mower county. The family, with the exception of the youngest son, Halver Ellofson, removed in 1876 to Otter Tail county where they yet reside. The young man still remains in the township, living on section twenty-six. These were about the only actual settlers in this year.

In 1855 quite a number of emigrants thronged in. Christian Erick Rukke and family, natives of Norway, who had stopped for a time in Illinois, were among the number to arrive this year, and they took a claim in section thirty-six, where they remained until 1868, when they secured the place they now occupy in section twenty-six. Helge Oleson came at the same time from the same place, and planted his stakes in section ten, where he has since been living.

In the spring of 1856 a colony of Irishmen came from Illinois and secured homes. The party consisted of Thomas Fitzsimmons, William and John Bell, John Brennan, and Patrick Creegan, and all of the party settled on land near the center of the town where they yet remain, with the exception of Thomas Fitzsimmons, who died upon the 11th of April, 1867.

About the same time, or probably a little later than the above arrivals, Ole O. Thorson, a native of Norway, came from Dane county, Wisconsin, and secured a home in section thirty-six, where he remained until 1857, when he removed to Olmsted county and still lives there.

The year following the settlers came in so rapidly that it is impossible to trace them in sequence, and by 1860 all of the government land in the township that was really valuable had been taken, and claims must be purchased according to the amount of improvements that had been made, instead of getting them free from Uncle Sam.

TOWN ORGANIZATION.

When this locality first began to be colonized, by common consent or usage, it took the name of Dover, more as the name of the locality than the township. Thus it was at the time of the first town meeting on the 11th of May, 1858, at the house of William Bell, in section twenty-one, and the first matter upon the program was to take into consideration the propriety of changing the former order of things and give the township a permanent appellation. It had been proposed by some one to call it "Liberty" instead of Dover, and there was quite a following to this idea; but all of this was dispelled by Thomas Fitzsimmons, who stated that he was in favor of the name of Newry, in remembrance of a little town in Ireland from whence a number of the pioneers hailed, and so that name was bestowed by vote.

The first officers elected were as follows: Supervisors, John Brennan, Chairman, Daniel Hollywood, and William Bell; Clerk, Thomas Fitzsimmons; Treasurer, C. E. Johnson; Assessor, Patrick Creegan; Justice of the Peace, Thomas Hollywood.

The present officials of the town, serving in 1882, are as follows: Supervisors, John Herron, Chairman, Peter P. Haugen, and Michael Dowd; Clerk, Thomas A. Helvig; Treasurer, Ole Easton; Assessor, Ole C. Johnson; Justices of the Peace, Thomas Herron and Patrick Creegan; Constable, Andrew O'Leary. Elections are held in schoolhouses.

STATISTICAL.

THE YEAR 1881.—The area included in this report takes in the whole town as follows:

Wheat—4,224 acres, yielding 56,212 bushels.

Oats—1,012½ acres, yielding 31,132 bushels.

Corn—755½ acres, yielding 21,816 bushels.

Barley—116¾ acres, yielding 3,307 bushels.

Potatoes—47¼ acres, yielding 5,113 bushels.

Sugar cane—¼ acre, yielding 50 gallons.

Cultivated hay—123¼ acres, yielding 816 tons.

Total acreage cultivated in 1881, 6,277½ acres

Wild hay—2,703 tons.

Timothy seed—3 bushels.

Apples—Number of trees growing, 319; num bearing, 87; yielding, 36 bushels.

Grapes—10 vines, yielding 100 pounds.

Tobacco—276 pounds.

Sheep sheared 177, yielding 479 pounds of wool.

Dairy—405 cows, yielding 29,250 pounds of butter.

Hives of bees—31.

THE YEAR 1882.—Wheat, 4,035 acres; oats, 909; corn, 1,079¾; barley, 129½; buckwheat, 9; potatoes, 55½; beans, ½; sugar cane, ¼; cultivated hay, 158; other produce, ¼; total acreage cultivated in 1882—6,376½;

Apple trees—growing, 395; bearing, 77; grape vines bearing—8.

Milch cows—383.

Sheep—187, yielding 505 pounds of wool.

Forest trees planted and growing, 10¼ acres.

POPULATION.—The census of 1870 gave Newry a population of 596. The last census, taken in 1880, reports 737 for this town; showing an increase of 141.

MATTERS OF INTEREST.

The first birth in the township occurred at four o'clock a. m., on the 9th of February, 1856, and ushered into existence Tingue, a daughter of Christian E. and Randi N. D. Johnson who resided upon section thirty-six. The child grew to womanhood in the township and on the 6th of February, 1876, was married to John G. Quamm and now resides in Dakota.

The first marriage ceremony was performed by Rev. C. S. Clauson on the 5th of June, 1858, and united the destinies of Halver Elofson and Caroline Fingerson, and, sad to say, the happy bride mentioned, ere six months had elapsed, was called upon by the hand of death and passed to the unknown shore, making the first death in the township.

The first title to land within the boundary of Newry township was acquired by Oliver R. Austin and W. R. Lincoln, who proved upon lands in sections four and five on the 4th of of September, 1856.

NEWRY GRANGE LODGE NO. 99.—This society or order effected an organization on the 9th of December, 1873, at the schoolhouse of District No. 79, under the auspices of Messrs Butler and King, of Albert Lea, with fifteen charter members, and C. E. Johnson was elected Master. The lodge flourished, holding meetings once each week until 1875, when the charter, thirty members, and fifteen dollars which was in the treasury, were merged with the Albert Lea Lodge.

NEWRY POST-OFFICE.—This office was established upon a petition from the citizens in 1874, with John Herron as Postmaster and office at his house in the northwestern part of section nine. Mail arrived by way of the Blooming Prairie and Geneva route, and is yet carried to this point from the former place. The business has amounted to about $3 per quarter. The office, location, and Postmaster are the same at present as when first established.

RELIGIOUS.

The first services held in the township, of a religious character, were in the fall of 1856, at the house of Ole Thorson, in section thirty-six, and Rev. C. L. Clauson and Rev. O. Pierce were the ministers who officiated, both being followers of the Lutheran faith. In 1857 C. L. Clauson organized the Norwegian Lutheran Church at a house in section thirty-six, owned by C. E. Rukke, with thirty-six members, and the society commenced holding services at private residences, which they continued until 1874, when they erected a fine church building just over the county line in Mower county, adjoining section twenty-four, which cost $6,000, and is a credit to the society. The church now has a membership of over two hundred, and is known under the title of Red Oak Grove Norsk Lutheran Church.

EDUCATIONAL.

For educational purposes this township is divided into six school districts, which are all in good financial condition, and have a fair average attendance in each. Their numbers are 1, 2, 73, 79, and 106.

BIOGRAPHICAL.

THOMAS A. HELVIG is a native of Norway, born on the 14th of September, 1845. He emigrated to America in 1861, and settled in Fayette county, Iowa. On the 27th of February, 1864, he enlisted in the Ninth Iowa Volunteer Infantry, and participated in the battles of Kenesaw Mountain, Atlanta, Jonesboro, and several others. In the winter of 1865 he was sick about a month, but afterwards returned to service and was sent to the regiment at Goldsborough, North Carolina, on the 2d of March, 1865. They marched from there to Washington, and after about three weeks was sent to Clinton, Iowa, where he received his discharge, and reached home on the 1st of July, 1865. On the 29th of November, 1867, he came to this place, and just two years after was joined in marriage with Miss Dora Benson. The following December Mr. Helvig purchased a farm in section thirteen, which has since been his home. In 1870 he was chosen a member of the board of Supervisors, and again in 1878; in 1876 was elected Town Clerk, and again in 1880 still filling the office. He is also clerk of his school district.

CHRISTIAN ERICK RUKKE was born in Norway on the 18th of July, 1822. He learned the stonemason trade in his native place, and worked at the same more or less until coming to America. He was married on the 14th of April, 1852, to Miss Randi Nelsdatter Sustegard, who has borne him fifteen children, eleven of whom are living, five boys and six girls. In 1852 Mr. and Mrs. Rukke emigrated to this country, arriving in Rock county, Wisconsin, on the 9th of August. The following year they moved to Stephenson county, Illinois, and in the spring of 1856 once more changed their place of residence, coming this time to Newry, where they were among the first settlers. Mr. Rukke was the organizer of school District No 79, and had control of it a number of years. He was the first Town Treasurer, and has been elected to different offices since but would not accept.

OAKLAND.

CHAPTER LXX.

DESCRIPTIVE — EARLY SETTLEMENT — OFFICIAL RECORD — OAKLAND VILLAGE — STATISTICS — RELIGIOUS — SCHOOLS — BIOGRAPHICAL.

This is one of the eastern towns of Freeborn county, and is bounded as follows: Moscow township on the north, Oakland on the south, Mower county on the east, and Hayward township on the west. It is a full congressional township, the integrity of the original government survey remaining unchanged, as in all the towns of the county.

Unlike all other of Freeborn county's subdivisions, this has no lakes or water courses; but water can be obtained by boring to a reasonable depth. A little brook is marked upon the map as rising in the northern part of section six and flowing northward into Moscow.

The entire western part of the town is made up of what is termed "oak opening" land, or prairie and natural meadows dotted with groves of small growth burr and black oak timber, and there is also considerable moderately heavy timber; although this has been greatly diminished as in comparison with what it was in early days. The eastern part is, as a rule, prairie land with the usual pleasant and beautiful rolling tendency, which, as you go toward the south, becomes rather low and marshy, yet, not sufficiently so to be wholly impractical for agriculture. In section fourteen considerable burr oak timber is found. The soil is a rich dark loam, with a subsoil of clay and gravel, and the entire township is well fitted for the crops and modes of farming of the present day, yielding abundant and profitable crops to the energetic and industrious.

EARLY SETTLEMENT.

An absorbing interest is always manifested in regard to the very first pioneer who ventured into any locality to establish a home, and it would seem that while parties who were cotemporary with the first settlers are still living, it would not be difficult to promptly arrive at the fact, but for various reasons which it may not be necessary to state, this is not the case, and there is much more uncertainty in this respect than would be supposed by those who have not undertaken to gather this kind of information. It is quite certain, that the first settlement in the township of Moscow was made in 1855, by a party from Illinois. This party consisted of G. W. Carpenter and family, and W. L. Carpenter, with Joel Bullock and family and Lemuel Bullock. George W. Carpenter located in section ten; W. L. Carpenter, a young man, secured a piece of land in section three,; Joel Bullock with his family made himself at home in section four, and Lemuel Bullock made a claim in section three.

The next settlement was made near the center of the town by a party of Irishmen, who arrived in July, 1856. Cornelius Kennevan, together with his family, among whom were three sons, came at this time, and located upon a good farm in section twenty-two, where he remained until the time of his death, which occurred in 1880, and his three sons still remain in the town in comfortable and prosperous circumstances. John Murane, a native of the Old Emerald Isle, arrived at the same time and located in section twenty-seven. He remained upon his original homestead until 1874, when he gave up the ghost, and his family still occupy the place.

Within a few weeks after the arrival of these Irishmen, a couple of Norwegian brothers in the *personnel* of Ole and George O. Gunderson, late of Wisconsin, made their appearance upon the scene and took claims just north of the above mentioned parties, in and about section nine. Ole took a claim of 160 acres in this section, brought his family, and erected a log hut among other improvements; he remained here until 1877, when his earthly career was abruptly terminated.

Francis Merchant, Sr., a Frenchman, was also among the arrivals of 1856, and settled in section one. The old homestead is still in the hands of members of his family.

Reuben Babcock was among the arrivals of 1856, coming in November of that year from Illinois, and filed upon 160 acres of Uncle Sam's domain in section fifteen, where he located his family, erected a log house, and remained until 1859, when he sold his place and removed to Albert Lea.

Asa Bullock, Jr., a native of Vermont, arrived in Oakland in the latter part of October, 1856, and pre-empted 160 acres, where he erected a log house and remained until 1864, when he was called upon by the Great Overseer to report upon the other shore of the valley of death. Mr. Bullock was highly esteemed by his neighbors, having held many public positions of trust and responsibility, discharging the duties with credit to himself and satisfaction to his constituents.

Others among the early settlers were A. D. Weight, Jerry Griffin, Henry Hollenshead, James Robinson, and in the southern part of the town a great many Bohemians, whose names have been forgotten.

VARIOUS MATTERS OF INTEREST.

The first birth in the township was that of a child of Samuel Bullock and wife, in February, 1856. The parents of the child had settled in section three in 1855, having come from Wisconsin.

The first marriage of parties living in Oakland took place in the winter of 1855 and '56, and united W. L. Carpenter to Miss Prudence Bullock; and L. E. Bullock to Miss Yuba Carpenter, being a double wedding. As there was no one in the township licensed to marry, the parties went over the line into Mower county, where the ceremony was performed by Squire Beach.

Another early marriage was that of Oscar Miller and Miss Bullock, in September, 1857. This ceremony was performed by George Watson, Esquire, in the township of Moscow.

It is claimed that the first death in Oakland took place in the spring of 1858, and carried to that great unknown shore Asa Bullock, the father of a large family of early pioneers, who had, in 1857, located in section nine.

33

W. L. Carpenter and L. E. Bullock turned the first sod in the way of breaking in the township, in section three, in the spring of 1856. They also put up the first dwelling houses in Oakland, of logs.

From the official records we glean that the first title to land was acquired by George N. Crane, to the northeast quarter of section thirty, on the 15th day of August, 1856.

OFFICIAL RECORD.

The first election or town meeting held within the boundaries of Oakland, and, in fact, at which the town organization was effected, took place on the 5th of April, 1857, at the house of Thomas Riley in the northeastern part of the town. The gentleman, at whose house the meeting was held, was made clerk, and Asa Bullock was chosen moderator. After the usual preliminaries the matter of electing township officials for the ensuing year was turned to, and after the polls were closed it was found there were 31 votes cast, and the following officers were declared elected: Supervisors, Asa Bullock, Chairman, Willard L. Carpenter, and Henry Hollenshead; Clerk, Cornelius Kennevan; Collector, John Murane; Assessor, John Murane; Justice of the Peace, Cornelius Kennevan; Constable, James Robinson; Overseer of the Poor, James Robinson; Pound Master, Asa Bullock, Jr.

Public matters have been attended to with zeal and honesty, and through the capability of the gentlemen who have officiated there has been no waste of public funds; but economy has tempered all expenditures. At the last annual town meeting, held in the spring of 1882, the following gentlemen were made officers for the ensuing year: Supervisors, Frank Merchant, Chairman, D. C. Kennevan, and A. Lesum; Clerk, A. G. Wiseman; Assessor, Edward Cotter; Treasurer, John J. Roylston; Justices of the Peace, E. B. Earl and William Chester. Town meetings are held alternately at the schoolhouses of districts thirty-two and thirty-three. The town now registers 160 voters, although at the last election only 43 votes were polled.

In 1864, bonds were voted to the amount of $1,000 to pay bounty to volunteers to fill the quota assigned the town and thus prevent a draft. In the spring of 1865 another special meeting was held and again bonds were voted.

OAKLAND VILLAGE.

This is located upon the line of the Southern

Minnesota Division of the Chicago, Milwaukee & St. Paul railroad and lies partly in Oakland and Mower [illegible] village being [illegible] in the [illegible] and in the northwestern part of section two. The village has never been platted and is therefore only a village in the same sense [illegible] the railroad company [illegible] the station. The [illegible] belongs to S. N. [illegible] who buys [illegible] and furnishes [illegible] as they are in demand. The village has a population of about [illegible].

STATISTICS.

The Year 1881.—The area cultivated in this report taken in the whole town as follows:

Wheat—4,171 acres, yielding [illegible] bushels.
Oats—[illegible] acres, yielding [illegible] bushels.
Corn—[illegible] acres, yielding [illegible] bushels.
Barley—[illegible] acres, yielding [illegible] bushels.
Rye—[illegible] acres, yielding [illegible] bushels.
Potatoes—[illegible] acres, yielding [illegible] bushels.
Beans—[illegible] acre, yielding [illegible] bushels.
Sugar cane—[illegible] acres, yielding [illegible] gallons.
Cultivated hay—[illegible] acres, yielding [illegible] tons.
Other products—[illegible] acres.
Total acreage cultivated in 1881—[illegible] acres.
Wild hay—[illegible] tons.
Timothy seed—[illegible] bushels.
Apples—number of trees growing [illegible]; number bearing [illegible], yielding [illegible] bushels.
Grapes—vines bearing [illegible].
Sheep—[illegible] sheared, yielding [illegible] pounds of wool.
Dairy—[illegible] cows, yielding [illegible] pounds of butter and [illegible] pounds of cheese.
Hives of bees—3, yielding [illegible] pounds of honey.
Wheat, [illegible] acres; oats, [illegible]; corn, [illegible]; barley, [illegible]; rye, [illegible]; buckwheat, [illegible]; potatoes, [illegible]; beans, [illegible]; cultivated hay, [illegible]; flax, [illegible]; other products, [illegible]; total acreage cultivated in 1890—[illegible].
Apple trees growing—[illegible]; bearing [illegible].
Grape vines bearing—[illegible].
Milch cows—[illegible].
Sheep—[illegible], producing [illegible] pounds of wool.
Whole number of farms cultivated in 1890, [illegible].
Forest trees planted and growing—[illegible] acres.

Population.—The census of [illegible] gave Oakland a population of [illegible]. The last census taken in 1890 reports [illegible] for this town, showing an increase of [illegible].

CHURCHES.

Oakland Evangelical Lutheran Church.—This society first came into existence in this township by organization in [illegible] and the same year a neat church building was erected at a cost of [illegible], size [illegible] feet, and seated to accommodate an audience of [illegible]. The first pastor was the Rev. [illegible] H. [illegible], and he is still officiating. The money was raised by subscription.

In connection with the church the society have laid out a cemetery containing about two acres, or a little less, which now contains twenty graves.

Oakland Presbyterian Church.—This society was organized through the efforts of Elder Lowry, and was first called the [illegible] Presbyterian Church. The first regular officers were Edward [illegible], John Gay, and J. J. [illegible]. The church was erected in [illegible], in the northern part of section two, at a cost of [illegible], size [illegible] feet; [illegible] was donated to this church by Miss Lenox of New York and with this the building was completed. It is seated to accommodate [illegible] persons. The first minister was the Rev. J. D. Todd, who held services in January, [illegible]. The present officiating minister is Rev. N. C. Green, and the membership is thirty-six. Minister's salary [illegible] per annum.

SCHOOLS.

For educational purposes the township of Oakland is divided into five school districts, which would if the territory was equally divided give an area to each district of a fraction over seven square miles. They are all in good financial condition, having a fair average attendance, and on the whole the educational facilities of Oakland are at par with other townships. A short sketch of the various districts is herewith presented.

District No. [illegible].—This embraces the territory in the northeastern part of the township, with a schoolhouse located in the western part of section twelve. This district was organized in [illegible], the first school meeting being held at the house of Mitchell Clark; Clerk, John Lightly; [illegible] Treasurer, James Hand. The schoolhouse was erected soon afterward, size [illegible] feet, frame. The first school was taught by [illegible] Phelps, with eight pupils in attendance. The present officers are James Boylson, James Lightly, and John J. Boylson. The last term was taught by Miss [illegible] Smith, the attendance being twenty.

District No. 32.—Effected an organization in 1866, and their schoolhouse was erected size 16x30, at a cost of $990, in the eastern part of section twenty-two. The first Board of school officers was made up of John Murane, Adam Chista and Peter Young, who employed Miss A. J. Chista to teach the first term of school, the attendance being thirty-five pupils. This term of school was held in a private house in 1861. The present officers are as follows: Director, Patrick Comer; Clerk, J. Purcell; Treasurer, J. Kennevan. The last school taught in this district had an attendance of forty-five pupils.

District No. 33.—This district was set apart from No. 32 not long after the organization of that district, and it is claimed the first school meeting was held at the house of Ira Fuller, in the fall of 1861; yet some contradict this statement by asking the question, "How can it be that District No. 33 held its first meeting in 1861, when No. 32 was not organized until several years afterward?" It is certain, however, that the first school was taught in the fall of 1861, at the house of George Carpenter, by Thomas Parker, with thirteen scholars on the benches. The present schoolhouse was erected of logs in the northeastern part of section nine, early in the summer of 1866, size 16x24 feet. The last school was taught by Eva Pilgrim, to an attendance of sixteen scholars, she receiving for her services $20 per month. The present board of school officers is as follows: Director, C. B. Wiseman; Treasurer, A. T. Wiseman; Clerk, A. Young.

District No. [illegible].—Effected an organization in 1865, embracing the territory in the southwestern part of the township. The first school meeting was held at the house of Daniel Kennevan, on the 27th of March, 1865, at which the following officers were elected: Director, E. B. Earle; Clerk, A. D. Wait, Jr.; Treasurer, A. D. Wait, Sr. The first school was held in the same place as was the meeting, by W. E. Wait, with six scholars present. The schoolhouse now in use was constructed in 1866, being a frame, 16x26 and cost $[illegible], to which a 16 foot addition has been made since. The location of the building is the southwest part of section twenty-nine. The present officers are: Director, Peter Sorenson; Treasurer, Joseph Raymond; Clerk, E. B. Earle. The last term of school was attended by forty-one pupils.

District No. [illegible].—This additional sub-district effected an organization in 18[illegible], and during the same year the house was erected of logs, size 18x[illegible] feet, in the eastern part of section seven, and seated to accommodate twenty-five students. The first officers were S. Ballock, C. [illegible] and [illegible] Ingham. The first school was taught by [illegible] Ingham, in the house of H. Wyant, with thirteen scholars present, she receiving $[illegible] per month for her services. The last term was taught by Carrie T[illegible], with thirteen scholars and wages $[illegible] per month. The present officers are as follows: Director, Henry Wyant; Clerk, [illegible] Johnson; Treasurer, G. O. Sanderson.

BIOGRAPHICAL.

Alfred F. Dunsy was born in England on the 14th of August, 1851. When he was four years old his parents had both died, and he was brought up by an uncle who came to America and settled in Wisconsin. At the age of nineteen years he entered a telegraph office at Winnebago City, and after one year and nine months was sent to this station as telegraph operator and remained with the company seven years. On the 14th of August, 1876, he married Miss Alida C. Evelyn, a native of Canada. After leaving the above company, Mr. Dunsy engaged in business with S. J. Smith, and put up a flouring mill at Moscow, on Turtle Creek, at a cost of $[illegible]; also built a store in the village of Oakland, which they still run, the mill having burned in August, 1880. Mr. Dunsy was appointed Postmaster in 1878, and still holds the office. He was sent to the Legislature in 1879 and again in 1881.

Ephraim E. Earl is a native of Jefferson county, New York, born on the [illegible] of March, 1841. His parents came to this county in 1856, and he resided with them until enlisting in 1862 in Company E, of the Tenth Minnesota Volunteer Infantry, under Capt. E. P. Moore; was sent south and remained in service until December 1863, when he was honorably discharged for disability. He returned to his home and the [illegible] of January, 1864, married Miss Phoebe A. Lindsly. The same year he bought a farm on section twenty-eight, Oakland township, where he now lives, having since added to his first purchase. He has been Justice of the Peace eleven years and Constable three years, at present holding the former office. His wife died on the [illegible] of May, 1881, leaving four children. He married his present wife, formerly Eliza L. Wait, on the [illegible] of March, 1882.

FRANCIS MERCHANT, JR., one of the early setlers of this place, was born in France on the 20th of September, 1842. He came with his parents to America when seven years old, resided in Oneida county, New York, until 1856, when they removed to Wisconsin, and a year later to this place, locating a farm in section one, which is still their home. In 1862, Francis enlisted in Company C, of the Ninth Minnesota Volunteer Infantry; was appointed First Lieutenant, sent south, and at the close of the war, returned to Fort Snelling, where he received a Captain's commission and was honorably discharged. He then returned to his home, and on the 11th of November, 1866, married Miss Annie Lamping, formerly from Illinois. They have five children. Mr. Merchant bought his father's farm in 1877, and now carries on the same, his parents living in Walla Walla, Washington Territory.

ASA ROWLEY is a native of the Empire State, born on the 12th of October, 1830. He moved with his parents to Columbia county, Wisconsin, in 1846, and on the 14th of October, 1856, married Miss Hutchison Smith. They lived on a farm in Adams county, Wisconsin, for three years, then returning resided on a farm adjoining his father's until 1864, when they came to Oakland and homesteaded in section six. He has since added to his farm and makes it his home; he has held town offices, also church offices, being a member of the Presbyterian Church. Hee is the father of four children, two sons and two daughters. His eldest son was graduated from the State University in 1881, and the younger is now in the junior class in the same institution, and his daughters are both prominent teachers in this county.

WILLIAM T. SPILLANE, a native of Pennsylvania, was born in Potter county, on the 22d of January, 1856. When he was sixteen years old he came to Albert Lea, and was employed by H. Rowell in an elevator for three years, then moved to Dubuque, Iowa, and attended school for one year. He subsequently took a trip through Kansas and Missouri, returning to this county in 1877. He was engaged in buying wheat for Cargill & Co., being at different stations on the road until the autumn of 1879, when he took charge of the elevator in this place and has since held the position.

JAMES TORRENS was born in Ireland on the 15th of October, 1831, and when eighteen years old emigrated to America. He lived in New York, then in Michigan, and in 1859, started to Minnesota, but on arriving in Illinois, stopped and remained through the winter. He was married on the 4th of July, 1858, to Miss Charlotte J. Finlon. Early in the spring they came on to this State, and located a farm in this township, which conta ins two hundred and forty acres, and is well improved. Mr. and Mrs. Torrens have a family of ten children, all but two of whom are at home.

ALONZO P. WARREN, a native of the Empire State, was born in Genesee county, on the 2d of September, 1823. When he was fifteen years old he came to Racine, Wisconsin, where he worked at the carpenter trade for two and a half years, then returned to his native State. After a residence of three years he again came to Wisconsin; bought a farm in Dodge county, which he carried on for a few years and then came to Waupun and opened a harness shop. He was married on the 13th of April, 1846, to Miss C. B. Rogers. They conducted a hotel for one year in Algona, Winnebago county. For a time they lived in Alma, where his wife died, on the 14th of September, 1851, leaving a son and a daughter. The son enlisted in the army, and was killed in the battle of Atlanta. Mr. Warren was married to his present wife, formerly Miss C. E. Fuller, on the 9th of October, 1866.

HENRY WYENT, one of the pioneers of this place, was born in Pennsylvania in 1822. His father died when Henry was fifteen years old and he soon after moved with his mother to a different locality in the same State, and worked at various occupations, finally renting a farm which he carried on for four years, He was married in the autumn of 1849, to Miss Eliza Showese and they have four children, three boys and one girl. In the fall of 1845, Mr. Wyent came to this place and took a claim in section six, returning to Pennsylvania for the winter, and in the spring brought his family. At the time of the Indian trouble he sent his family back to their former home, and enlisted in Company C, of the Second Minnesota Cavalry; went west and served till the spring of 1864, when he was mustered out at Fort Snelling. He then went for his family, and has since made this place his home. He owns a good farm of three hundred and twenty acres.

PICKEREL LAKE.

CHAPTER LXXI.

DESCRIPTION—EARLY DEVELOPMENT—ORGANIZATION—ARMSTRONG VILLAGE—RELIGIOUS—SCHOOLS—BIOGRAPHICAL.

The town bearing this appellation is among the center towns of Freeborn county, having as its contiguous surroundings, the township of Manchester on the north; Nunda on the south; Albert Lea on the east; and Alden on the west. It is constituted as originally surveyed by the government officers, of thirty-six sections, or 23,040 acres.

The surface of the town may be said to be diversified, as we find both timber and prairie and. In early days the greater part of the eastern half of the town was timber of divers varieties, among which were burr and black oak, maple, basswood, beach, elm, butternut, and some black walnut, and yet there are many traces of this miniature forest visible in the region of the lakes, some even claiming that at least one-eighth of the township is now covered with timber; but we think that this statement is a little overdrawn. There are, however, many spots of land covered with patches of oak openings and groves, as the town may be said to be, in a limited way, noted for its beautiful landscape which is greatly enhanced by these small groves of timber. The surface is rolling, in places given to abrupt hills called "knolls," which also help to make the scenery picturesque. One of these, known as "Jennings Point" in section two, rises higher than the surrounding country, and is the highest point in the county. It is claimed by a great many, and through Freeborn county generally believed, that this is the highest point of land in the State; but this is a very apparent mistake, for the very report, (Winchell's geological survey report, published in 1876), upon which this theory is based, contradicts it. There are three points in Minnesota which rise to a height of 200 feet above this; one in Nobles, one in Mower, and one in Otter Tail county. It is true, however, that this is the highest point in Freeborn county, it being 1,342 feet above the level of the ocean, and 667 feet above Lake Superior.

The soil, in the eastern part, is a rich dark loam of from two to two and one-half feet in depth; underlaid by a subsoil of yellow clay of about 20 feet, beneath which lies the blue clay. As you go westwardly, to the more open rolling prairie, the soil becomes of a lighter nature, with a tendency to sandiness, the depth of which varies from eight to eighteen inches; having a gravelly loam and sand subsoil of twelve feet, underneath which is the sand bed. There is no lime or sandstone to speak of, but in places there is a profusioh of boulders. The best of water is found at reasonable depth.

The town is well watered by various lakes and streams, which are all teeming with fish, and are much frequented by seekers after sport of this kind. White's Lake lies in the northeastern part of the town, covering about 160 acres in section one; this was originally known as Albert Lea Lake, but since 1856, when A. W. White preempted a claim touching it, the lake has been known under its present name. Pickerel Lake, after which the town was named, derives its appellation from the abundance of fish of this name which are found in its waters. It lies in the eastern part of the town, in sections thirteen and twenty-four, and extends into the town of Albert Lea; a large tract of land northwest of this lake is marked on the map as overflown land and useless for farming purposes. In sections twenty-three and twenty-six are located the Little Oyster Lakes, so called because of their shape, and it is made a joke that on wet occasions they open their mouths in the shape of an inlet to admit fresh water. Next comes the upper Twin Lake, the largest body of water in the township, lying in the southeastern part, mostly in section thirty-five, and extending southward to make connection with its twin, the Lower Lake, which lies in Nunda township. A number of other small bodies of water are scattered through the town, which are sometimes called lakes, but more properly known as ponds. The lakes of this town are the headwater of the Shell Rock River.

FIRST SETTLEMENT.

Charles and William Wilder (or as many spell it, Weilder,) and A. D. Pinkerton, made their appearance and located on and about section twelve in 1855. Charles Wilder at once commenced and completed the first dwelling shanty in the township. They remained on the places for some years but have now all gone to other parts.

In the following spring, 1856, John Ruble, a native of Pennsylvania who had stopped for a time in Rock county, Wisconsin, make his appearance and was the next settler in the township. He brought his family with him and settled upon 160 acres in section twelve, where he opened the first farm in the township and still remains a prominent man in Freeborn county.

In the fall of the same year another settler crowded into this section. This was A. W. White after whom the lake was named. He was a native of the Empire State, and remained upon his farm until 1861, when he removed to the village of Albert Lea, where he still resides. Section twenty-nine received a settler the same fall, in the person of Louis Marplee, of the German Faderland, who settled in the section mentioned and remained there until 1866 when he removed to Nunda. Several of his countrymen came in this fall, and were the vanguard of that determined band which subsequently followed and now about monopolize the township.

Henry Schneider and Frederick Fink, Germans, both came this fall and settled. The former dropped anchor in section fifteen where his moorings still remain fast, and Mr. Fink also placed himself on a place in the same section, where he remained until 1876 and then moved to his present place in section twenty-nine. He is a prominent man in public matters,

Christian Bohle, of the same nationality, came about the same time as Fink and settled in section fifteen where he yet remains. All of these parties had just come from the state of New York, where they had sojourned for a time.

Section eleven ,in the Ruble settlement, received an additional settler also about the same time as the last named, in the fall of 1856, in the person of Frederick Woodward, fresh from the "Badger State," who secured a habitation there and remained until 1861, when he enlisted in the army, and upon his return settled in Iowa, where he lived up to the time of his death.

Early in the following spring, 1857, Charles and A. K. Norton, natives of the "Green Mountain" State, who had been whiling away a short time in Racine county, Wisconsin, drifted into this township. Charles planted his stakes on a pleasant farm in sections thirteen and fourteen, while his brother, A. K. Norton, bought land in sections thirteen and twenty-three, where he remained until 1861 when he enlisted in the army, and upon his return settled in Freeborn township, where he still lives.

Luther Smith also arrived this spring. He was a native of New York and settled in section three, where he lived until the war broke out when he also enlisted, but never returned, finding a lonely grave in the sunny south. His family have gone.

After 1857 the ingress upon the government land of the town was so rapid and incessant that it is impossible to note them all, but we will try and give a few of the most important.

E. Jennings, a native of New York, first made his appearance in this township in the spring of 1862, but returned to Illinois for his family which he had left there, and did not re-arrive here until 1865, when he settled on the place where he now lives, in sections two and three.

The settlement in the western portion of the township did not commence until about 1860, when L. L. Lovell made his appearance and took a farm in or adjoining what was afterwards known as Lovell's grove in section eight. W. G. Bloe came with Lovell from the eastern States and took a place in section eighteen. He remained here until 1872 when he left the county.

In 1863, Mortimer Whitney came and took a a place in section seven where he remained until 1871, when he removed to Owatonna, and still holds forth in the latter place.

N. H. Stone, a native of Pennsylvania, was another early settler, arriving in 1864, and still lives in the town. Also Knudt Knudtson, a native of Norway, arrived during the same year and still remains; it is said he is the only representative of the Norwegian race in the township.

ITEMS OF INTEREST.

The first death to occur in the township, was the demise of Mrs. Christian Bohle in January, 1859; she had been living on section fifteen.

The first marriage in the town took place on the 6th of July, 1859, and united the destinies of Frederick Fink and Miss Frederica Weiser; the ceremony being performed by B. McCarty, Esq. The bridegroom went to Mitchell county, Iowa, and from there brought his bride to John Ruble's place in section twelve, on foot, where the ceremony took place. They still reside in the township.

The first birth within the limits of the town, was on the night of the 14th of September, 1857, and ushered into existence, Amelia, a daughter of John and Harrietta Ruble, in the old log house in section twelve. She still lives with her parents in the township, and at her birth-place.

COUNTY SEAT.—It is claimed that when the matter of where the county seat should be located, was being agitated, a meeting was held in John Ruble's barn yard, for the purpose of feeling the public pulse on the matter, and it was found that there were only *seven legal voters* in the town; but after the election was over, counting the polls disclosed that *forty-five votes had been cast.* We cannot explain.

INDUSTRIAL ENTERPRISES.

Some years ago John Ruble erected a shop on his place in section twelve, and hired a brawny son of vulcan to manipulate the bellows.

In the year 1868, Anson Hauf erected on section eleven, a 16x20 frame shop in which he did blacksmithing until 1876, when he made it a part of his barn, and in 1878 erected the building he now occupies in section eleven, the size 16x18, and does his own work.

Several parties, in the latter part of the sixties, burned lime in section twelve with moderate success.

OFFICIAL RECORD.

Pickerel Lake was first annexed for local government purposes to the township of Manchester, in its organization in 1858, and thus remained until 1860, when the County Commissioners, in answer to a petition, annulled its connection to Manchester and made it a part of Albert Lea township. Finally, at the annual meeting of the board of County Commissioners, held at Albert Lea the 8th of September, 1865, a petition was presented signed by William C. Pentecost and twenty-four other legal voters and residents of Pickerel Lake, asking to be separated from Albert Lea and made a separate political organization. The request was granted, and on motion of Commissioner Andrews, it was ordered by the board that $400 of a special tax of $1,500, voted for roads and bridges, and for finishing the county buildings, be granted Pickerel Lake for roads and bridges. The board then selected the following as township officers until the time of the annual election: Supervisors, John Ruble, Chairman, J. France, and J. H. Converse; Clerk, A.W. White; Treasurer, E. Jennings; Justices of the Peace, R. C. Cady and William Schneider; Constables, O. Kenfield and Peter Lampman. The Clerk refused to qualify, but his place was readily filled by the appointment of R. C. Cady.

The first annual election was held at the house of John Ruble on the 3d of April, 1866, and the following officers were elected: Supervisors, John Ruble, Chairman, Joseph France, and J. H. Converse; Justices of the Peace, R. C. Cady and William Schneider; Assessor, John Ruble; Treasurer, E. Jennings; Constables, William Weiser and O. Kenfield; Clerk, R. C. Cady; Overseer of Highways, A. C. Howe, W. C. Whitney, J. Smith, E. Ames, and A. C. Davis. A couple of these parties also refused to qualify, but their places were filled by the appointment of Peter Lampman.

At the last annual town meeting, held in the spring of 1882, the following officers were elected: Supervisors, J. George Widmann, Chairman, Charles Schneider, and Charles Kreuger; Clerk, Charles H. Ruble; Treasurer, Henry Ruethe; Assessor, H. S. Holt; Justices of the Peace, B. A. Cady and S. A. Foster. The Judges of this election were Charles Martin, George Widmann, and Charles Schneider. The sum of $700 was voted for the roads and bridges.

The public matters pertaining to the town have always been in good hands and ably managed; there never having been any extravagance or useless expenditure of public money.

ARMSTRONG VILLAGE.

This is the only village in the township of Pickerel Lake, and is the youngest village in Freeborn county, if it can be called a village, for probably the name of Station would be more appropriate. It is located in the eastern part of section four, on the Southern Minnesota railroad, about five miles from Albert Lea, the county seat.

It came into existence in 1878, at the instigation of T. H. Armstrong, who that year erected an elevator, and a store building was also built the same spring by Jason T. Goward. A Post-office was established in 1882, and G. H. Kenerson was appointed Postmaster, and still holds the office.

In 1879, a Mr. Dewey erected a blacksmith shop, and commenced hammering the anvil; but he left in 1880.

The railroad company erected the depot in 1879, and it was opened with P. D. Barticus, station agent. The present agent is F. D. Babcock.

This is about all that can be said of the village; it may have a future and it undoubtedly has; but as to what that future will be, time must determine.

STATISTICS.

We have gathered from the report of the County Auditor to the Commissioner of Statistics, and elsewhere, a number of items which we present in this connection, to give an idea of the agricultural resources of the township, and from which the reader can determine the wealth and productiveness of the town.

The Year 1881.—Showing the acreage and yield of the various crops:

Wheat—2,340 acres, yielding 29,550 bushels.

Oats—460 acres, yielding 16,300 bushels.

Corn—517 acres, yielding 18,850 bushels.

Barley—50 acres, yielding 1,300 bushels.

Potatoes—46 acres, yielding 4,925 bushels.

Cultivated Hay—6 acres, yielding 10 tons.

Other products—40 acres.

Total acreage cultivated in the year 1881—3,459.

Wild Hay gathered—2,445 tons.

Apple trees—growing, 300.

Sheep—31 sheared; yielding 489 pounds of wool.

Cows—223, yielding 14,200 pounds of butter.

Bees—Five hives.

The Year 1882.—Wheat, 2,030 acres; oats, 484; corn, 827; barley, 85; potatoes, 50; cultivated hay, 27; flax, 20; total acreage cultivated in 1882, 3,523.

Apple trees growing—300; apple trees bearing, 100.

Milch cows—346.

Sheep—220, yielding 1,440 pounds of wool.

Whole number of farms reported in 1881—50.

Forest trees—Whole number of acres planted and growing, 20.

Population.—The census of 1870 gave Pickerel Lake township a population of 337. The last census, taken in 1880, reports it as having 533.

RELIGIOUS.

The first religious services were held at the residence of Mr. John Ruble, in section twelve, in the year 1861, by a German Lutheran divine, the Rev. Mr. Charles Bucholz. Since that time services have been continued at various places in the township, and two church organizations have come into existence, a sketch of each of which will be given. It is stated that a Rev. Mr. Smith held services in the town at an early day; also in Mr. John Ruble's house.

German Lutheran Church.—This denomination held services at an early day, and in 1874 an organization was effected in the schoolhouse of District No. 57, with fourteen members, Rev. H. Kretzchmer being the officiating minister. In 1878, the need of an edifice in which to worship God became too apparent, and the present church building used by the Society was erected. It is a frame building about 20x30, 12 foot posts, and cost $1,200, being nicely furnished. The present minister is Rev. J. Kettle, and the Society is now composed of about thirty members. The church is located in section eleven.

German M. E. Society.—There are conflicting statements as to the organization of this society, and suffice it to say that it was effected prior to 1873; for, in that year we find the church edifice now in use by this denomination, being erected by subscription on section twenty-tree, size 24x36, with 14 foot posts. The first preaching was done by Rev. A. Bibighausen, with twenty members constituting his audience. The present minister is Rev. A. H. Koemer, of Albert Lea.

In connection with this church the society have laid out a cemetery adjoining, containing four acres, which is neatly fenced, well kept, and splendidly located. The first burial here was Fritz Brantz, in the winter of 1876, and now there are about thirty headstones marking the last resting places of those departed.

MEDIUMS OF EDUCATION.

As to the facilities for the gaining of knowledge, Pickerel Lake township is supplied with five districts, which are all in good running order, with a good attendance of scholars. Their numbers and the location of their buildings are as follows: No. 39, schoolhouse in section 12; No. 56, in section 7; No. 57, in section 22; No. 69, in section 19; No. 102, in section 24. A short sketch of each of the districts is below given, showing the organization, and history of their progress.

DISTRICT NO. 39.—Was the first district to come into official existence in the township, effecting an organization in 1862, with the following as its officers; Director, John Murphy; Clerk, Charles Norton; Treasurer, John Ruble. The first school was taught in John Ruble's log house, by Miss Bassett, with ten scholars present, and school was held here until 1855, when a frame house was erected on land owned by George S. Ruble, in section eleven, at a cost of $700, which is still in use. The last teacher was Miss Norton, with an attendance of twelve scholars. The present officers are: W. C. Norton, Charles H. Ruble, and John Ruble, respectively Clerk, Director, and Treasurer.

DISTRICT NO. 56.—Effected an organization in 1864 by the election of: Director, Frederick Rickard; Clerk, L. L. Lovell; and Treasurer, N. H. Spoon. The next year a school building was constructed, 14x16 feet, at a cost of $150, which occupied a site in section eight until 1868, when it was moved to the present site in the southeastern part of section seven, of which the district as yet has no title. In 1879, the present school structure was erected on the same location, size, 16x22 feet, at a cost of $300. The first school in this district was taught in the fall of 1864, in Mr. Lovell's house, in section eight, by Kate Nichols, with seven scholars present. The present officers are: Clerk, R. Hanf: Director, Benjamin Randall: Treasurer, Knute Knuteson: Malon Howe was the last teacher, with twenty-three pupils.

DISTRICT NO. 57.—Was the next district to effect on organization, which it did in April, 1869, with Messss. Fred Fink, Henry Weisser, and Henry Eberhart, as its officers. The schoolhouse was constructed the same year, in the southeastern part of section twenty-three, Henry Weisser donating the land. The size is 16x20 and cost $300. The first teacher was Miss Nancy Ruble, and there were twelve juveniles upon the hardwood benches. The last board consisted of: Director, H. Drommerhausen; Clerk, William Schneider; Treasurer, William Weisser, (now deceased). The The last teacher was Miss Hannah Daniels. This house has been used a great deal for religious purposes.

DISTRICT NO. 69.—A special meeting was held at August Yost's house in section nineteen, on the 16th of April, 1881, at which bonds were voted to the amount of $300 to build a schoolhouse, and organization was effected by the election of the following officers: Director, Fred Fink; Clerk, August Yost; Treasurer, H. Schulenburg; there were ten votes cast. In the same year the house was erected on land belonging to C. M. McKee, size 16x24, at a cost of $316. The first school was taught by Katie Everhardt, to an attendance of twelve; the last was taught by Miss Ella Ruble, with thirteen. The same officers still manage the affairs of the district.

DISTRICT NO. 102.—The first taught was in the summer of 1876, in a carpenter shop on Mr. Widman's land, by Katie Eberhart, with eighteen or twenty scholars. The following year, 1877, a neat frame house was erected in the southwestern corner of section twenty-four, at a cost of $300. The district was organized by the election of the following officers: Clerk, George Widman; Treasurer, Mr. Jeklin; Director, F. Schneider. The present officers are, Messrs. L. Jeklin, Director; George Widman, Clerk; and John Kaemmer, Treasurer. Miss Carrie Norton was the last instructor, to an attendance of about thirty scholars.

BIOGRAPHICAL.

F. D. BABCOCK, is a native of Iowa, born in Bradford, Chickasaw county. He attended school there until eighteen years old, then removed to Herseyville, Wisconsin, and completed his education, residing with his grand-parents for a year and a half. He returned to his native State, but in a year returned to Wisconsin and remained six years. He then came to Minnesota, resided in Hokah, Houston county, Hayward, and Armstrong, in this county, returned to Whalen, Houston county, and in July, 1882, came again to Armstrong, where he now resides. He is station agent and telegraph operator, having learned telegraphy in Wisconsin. He was married in the latter State, in Herseyville, in December, 1880, to Miss Frankie C. Palmer, a native of Virginia, in that State. Her father was killed in the army and her mother still resides in Wisconsin. Mr. Babcock's father died in South Carolina in 1881, aged fifty years, and his mother resides in Wisconsin, aged forty-nine. He and his wife are members of the M. E. Church.

B. A. CADY, was born in Saratoga county, New York, in 1849, and removed from his native State when two years old, coming to Omro, Wisconsin. He attended school in the latter State and finished his education in Minnesota, having come to Pickerel Lake in 1861. He was married in Albert Lea on the 7th of February, 1875, to Mary A. Richards, a native of New York. When a child she came with her parents to Fox Lake, Dodge county, Wisconsin, and resided until 1872, then moved to Albert Lea, and remained until her marriage. She is a member of the Catholic church. Her parents still live in the latter place. Mr. Cady's father is a native of New York, and now lives in Kansas. His mother was born in Vermont, and died in Pickerel Lake in 1878, aged fifty-nine years. He has a brother living in Albert Lea, who has been employed in the Post-office there for several years.

BARBARA EBERHARDT is a native of Germany, born in 1838, and emigrated with her parents to America when seven years old. They located in Wisconsin where Barbara received a common school education, and at the age of twenty-two years was married to Henry Eberhardt. He was born in Germany in 1838, and came with his parents to America when ten years old. At the age of nineteen years he entered the ministry, preaching for three years in a German Methodist church in Wisconsin. He was then married and moved to Des Moines county, Iowa, where he preached five years and in 1865, returned to Wisconsin: but two years later, his health failing, he came to Pickerel Lake, in section twenty-three, and engaged in farming. After a time his health was restored and he returned to the ministry, removed to Hokah and was pastor of the M. E. church three years when his health again became impaired and he returned to his farm where he died in 1875, aged thirty-seven years, and is buried in the cemetery near his home. He left a widow and five children; Annie K., twenty-one years of age; Edward H., eighteen years; Emma E., fifteen; Amelia, twelve; and Alfred, aged seven years. Mrs. Eberhardt has kept her children all together, educated them and carried on the farm. She is a member of the M. E. church in this place.

ANSON HANF, one of the old settlers of the county and the first to open a blacksmith shop in Albert Lea, was born in Germany on the 5th of June, 1833. When ten years old he came with his parents to America and first resided in Milwaukee, Wisconsin, a short time, then moved to Racine county, and in 1848, to Dodge county. He was married there on the 17th of June, 1856, to Miss Verletti Ferry, and in September following they went to Kansas. That State not suiting them for a home they returned to Dodge county, and in May, 1858, came to Minnesota, locating in Mower county, but in less than a year moved to Oakland in this county. In March, 1860, Mr. Hanf removed to Albert Lea, and as previously stated opened a blacksmith shop where he continued to hammer until 1864, then purchased a farm in section eleven, Pickerel Lake township, moved to it and has since made it his home. In 1870, he was Chairman of the board of Supervisors, but since that has taken no part in politics. He is the father of six children, three boys and three girls.

ROBERT HANF was born in Dodge county, Wisconsin, on the 22d of March, 1852. He resided with his parents until March, 1874, when he made a trip to Nebraska; remained during the summer, and in October came to this township, buying land in section seven. For several years he spent the summers on his farm and in the fall returned to his home in Wisconsin, where, on the 18th of July, 1879, he married Amelia Suenther. They have since made this place their home, and have been blessed with one child, Minnie. Mr. Hanf is Clerk of his school district.

EUMENES JENNINGS was born in Jefferson county, New York, on the 6th of July, 1819. He grew to manhood and was married in his native State to Miss L. C. Haskins, the ceremony dating the 24th of October, 1842. In July, 1858, they removed to Illinois, locating in Antioch, Lake county, where they remained until coming to Minnesota in the spring of 1861. They first lived in Olmsted county one year, then came to Pickerel Lake and settled in section two. The following September they returned to Illinois, but in the spring of 1865 again sought a home in this township where they have since remained. Of a family of nine children, seven are living. Mr.

Jennings was elected Town Treasurer at the first town meeting, which was in the fall of 1865, and re-elected the following year. He now devotes his entire time to the improvement of his home.

G. H. Kenerson was born in New Hampshire in 1841, and lived in his native State, attending school until seven years old. He then removed with his parents to Troy, New York, and six years after to Galesville, Washington county, in both of which places he attended school. In 1859, he came to Fall River, Columbia county, Wisconsin, and completed his education. In the fall of 1860 he removed to Mower county, Minnesota, and followed farming until 1875, then engaged in the grain business, buying and shipping. He was married on the 1st of January, 1868, to Martha Williams. She was born in Branch county, Michigan, and when fourteen years of age removed with her parents to Mower county, where she was married. Mr. and Mrs. Kenerson have had five children, of whom three are living: Era A., aged thirteen years; Roy and Ray, twins, aged seven years; Jessie died in infancy, and Daniel at the age of two years and five months. Mr. Kenerson's mother died in Troy, New York, at the age of thirty, and his father in Rochester, in this State, in 1878, when seventy-five years old. Mrs Kenerson's parents reside in Dexter, Mower county, and she is the eldest of their ten children. Mr. Kenerson came to Armstrong in the fall of 1881, and is engaged in the grain business, and also owns a grocery store. He was appointed Postmaster in June, 1882.

Frederick Leonhardi is a native of Illinois, born in Palos, Cook county, in 1856. When he was three years old his parents removed to Chicago, and ten years after, a short distance from there, to Lake View, where Frederick attended school six years, then clerked in the Post-office two years, and afterwards in a grocery store. In 1876, the family came to this county and settled in Nunda. The subject of this sketch was joined in marriage on the 16th of July, 1882, to Henrietta Eikhorst. She was born in Wheaton, Du Page county, Illinois, in 1864, and resided in her native place until twelve years of age, then came with her parents to Mansfield where the marriage ceremony took place. She attended school in Illinois and also in Minnesota. Mr. Leonhardi moved to Pickerel Lake and settled on a farm in the spring of 1882. His mother died in Nunda in February, 1877, and his father still lives in the latter place. He and his wife are members of the Lutheran church.

W. C. Norton was born in Chicago in 1834, and when four years of age removed with his family to Burlington, Wisconsin, where he was reared and educated. He was also married there to Bell Bradshaw, a native of Vermont. In the fall of 1858, they removed to Pickerel Lake, and located a farm in section thirteen which is now their home. They returned to Wisconsin after living here four years, and remained six years, since which time this place has claimed them as residents. They have had four children, three of whom are living; Eva C., twenty-three years of age; Cora A., eighteen; Willie A., thirteen; and Mattie C., died at the age of one year and and eight months. Mr. Norton has been Chairman of the board of Supervisors for several terms, Town Assessor, and a member of the school board several terms.

John Ruble is one of the early settlers of the county, and a pioneer of this township, having come in the spring of 1856, and is now one of the most extensive farmers in the county. He is a native of Mifflin county, Pennsylvania, born on the 15th of September, 1827. When he was an infant his parents moved to Ohio where his father died and the sons carried on the farm for many years. Mr. Ruble was married on the 20th of August, 1849, to Miss Harrietta Fleck, and the same year came to Rock county, Wisconsin, where they resided on a farm until coming to Pickerel Lake. He first took one hundred and sixty acres about three miles from Albert Lea, and it has since been his home, but is at this period greatly changed. The homestead now contains six hundred acres with fine buildings and a beautiful yard; our subject also owns a farm and milling interests in Martin county. In an early day Mr. Ruble commenced the sale of agricultural implements, in which business he has been quite successful, having an office and warerooms in Albert Lea. He has a family of ten children.

Charles H. Ruble, a son of John Ruble, was born in Wisconsin on the 13th of July, 1852. He came with his parents to this township when four years old and has since made it his home. He was elected Town Clerk in 1879, and is school Director in District No. 39. He was united in marriage on the 29th of of November, 1881, with

Miss Eliza Heising. Their farm is in section two and is one of the finest in the township.

William Schneider was born in Germany in 1833, received a common school education and learned the cabinet maker's trade in his native country. In 1853 he came to America and worked at his trade for two years at Batavia, New York, then came to Farmington, Iowa, and resided six years. He was married in 1860 to Julia Bruman, who was born in New Orleans, where her father was the first German Methodist preacher. She came to Iowa when young, and there received her education. Her father died when she was three years old, and her mother now lives in this State. In 1861, Mr. Schneider enlisted in Company B, of the Third Iowa Cavalry, and served sixteen months; was then discharged in Memphis, Tennessee, for disability, and returned to his home in Iowa. After a short time he removed to Pickerel Lake, and located in section seven, where he now resides. He owns three hundred and sixty-five acres of land, with two hundred improved, and has a new large brick house and a good barn. He has held every local office except constable, and is now clerk of his school district. He organized the first Sabbath school in this part of the town, himself and wife being members of the German Methodist church. Mr. and Mrs. Schneider have had nine children, seven of whom are living: Emma H., aged twenty years; George A., eighteen; Matilda, twelve; Sarah C., ten; Willie K., eight; Walter S., six; and Edward H., four. Annie J. died at the age of one year, and William F. at the age of one year and four months, and both are buried in the cemetery near their home. Emma, the oldest child became deaf from the effects of scarlet fever, and when ten years old entered the Faribault institute, and in seven years graduated.

John George Widman, is a native of Germany, born in 1844 and reared on a farm. He emigrated to America in 1863, located in Wisconsin and engaged in farming there nine years. He was married in 1869, to Annie Lampert, a native of that State. They came to this township in 1872, and settled in section twenty-three, which is still their home, having a farm of two hundred and ten acres. They have seven children; Margaret, aged twelve years; Katie, ten; George, eight; Annie, six; Lizzie, four; Frank, two; and Lida, an infant. Mr. Widman has been Chairman of the board of Supervisors, and a member of the school board six years. He and his wife are members of the German Methodist church.

August Yost, a native of Germany, was born on 11th of February, 1849. He emigrated to America when seventeen years old, and directly to Minnesota, locating in this township. He was employed on farms, and made his home with Christian Pestorius, until buying his present place in 1876. He was married on the 1st of December, 1869, to Mary, daughter of C. Pestorius, and they have a family of five children. Mr. Yost's farm contains two hundred acres, situated in section nineteen, and has a good frame house and barn. He is Clerk of school district No. 69.

RICELAND.

CHAPTER LXXII.

GENERAL DESCRIPTION—EARLY SETTLEMENT—ITEMS OF INTEREST—POLITICAL—STATISTICAL—EDUCATIONAL FACILITIES—BIOGRAPHICAL.

Riceland is one of the eastern towns of Freeborn county, lying in the second tier from the north, as well as the eastern county line. Its contiguous surroundings are as follows: Geneva township on the north; Moscow on the east; Hayward on the south; and Bancroft on the west. It is a full congressional township of 36 sections or square miles, containing about 23,040 acres.

The western part of the town is what would be called burr and jack oak opening land, which is interspersed with natural prairies and meadow land. The general inclination is to rolling, and here and there are many egg-shaped mounds covered with timber. At one time the lake was bordered with a heavy growth of timber, but these miniature forests have been greatly reduced. The heaviest timber at present is located in sections twelve and sixteen, which is cut up into timber lots and owned by various parties. The northeastern part of the town is marshy and not subject to cultivation. A large marsh extends across the southwest corner, which the Indians claim was originally a lake of great depth and large. It is also said that the water, or the greater portion of it, suddenly ebbed away and disappeared, leaving boats and canoes on dry land, as if by magic. There are several places in this slough where it is claimed no bottom can be found to the water sink holes.

The soil of the town is generally dark loam; but on the knolls there is a marked tendency to clayeyness. A good acreage is under a high state of cultivation; yet it is somewhat below the average of the townships. The low lands are brought into excellent use as hay land and the crops raised are as abundant as valuable.

Rice Lake is one of the larger lakes of Freeborn county, and we are in doubt as to whether the name of this suggested the name for the town or *vice versa*; but it is certain the name originated among the Indians from the abundance of wild rice in this locality. The lake lies in the northeastern part of the town, and several small streams find their way from it through the marshy tract to the east.

EARLY DAYS.

We here with present a sketch of the early events of the town, which about covers the ground we should have filled had it not been for this. It was prepared by D. G. Parker, and read by him to the old settlers at their annual re-union in 1877, as follows:

"Ole C. Olson and Ole Hanson first settled this town in August, 1856. The former put up a log house in the same month, and opened the first farm in the latter part of that season. Samuel Beardsley, a blacksmith, commenced business in the same year, and was the first mechanic. George P. Bracket was the first merchant, and opened business in 1857. In 1859 Amy Baker taught in a private house the first public school. The first schoolhouse was built in 1864. In 1858 the Rev. Mr. Mapes held the first religious services. The Methodists, in 1859, established the first organization. Stephen Beardsley and Sarah Croy were the first parties married, George P. Bracket performing the ceremony. In April, 1858, the first child was born, in the person of Caroline Olson. The first death was that of Mr. Shortledge, who was frozen in April, 1857. Isaac Baker was the first Chairman of Supervisors, and a Mr. Snyder the first Clerk. In regard to the first acquired title to land, there is some question whether it was Amy Beardsley or Victory B. Lossee. The evidence seems to be in favor of the latter, who selected a tract upon section twelve, and proved up

May 7, 1856. The town was organized at the January session of the county board in 1858."

While the above is in the main correct, yet many points will be found corrected in another column. The statement as to the first settler is especially criticised, and many, in fact all, say it is wrong, and that the Beardsleys were the first settlers. Among others who were prominent early settlers the names are remembered of a few who will be briefly mentioned.

Samuel A. Beardsley and John Hull, his son-in-law, together with their families, came by ox team from Illinois, brought considerable stock, and settled on the south side of Rice Lake. Beardsley remained until about 1860, when he removed to Wisconsin, and from there went to Otter Tail county, Minnesota, where he yet is. Hull remained a short time and went to Wisconsin where he has since died, through an accident with a gun.

Ole Halvorsen, Hans Larson, and Ole Christianson were the first Norwegians to settle in the town.

In 1858, we find a number of Americans had settled in the township, among whom were Charles Williams, —— Brackett, Joseph Neil, Nels and James Snyder, Nick and John Reims, and Thomas Walaska, who have all long since gone to more congenial climes.

In 1858, quite a family of pioneers put in an appearance in the persons of Deacon Isaac Baker, his good wife Phœbe and their children, William H., Charles E., Margaret N., Amy J., Rhoda, and Sarah E. Baker. They settled upon section twenty, and in about seven or eight years the father removed to Austin, where he has since passed away. The two boys, William H. and Charles E., still live in Riceland, and are among its most prominent and intelligent citizens.

Soon after this party had got settled, Nathan P. Amy and Charles Bartlett, from the eastern States, arrived, the former bringing the first team of horses. They have both left.

William L. McNish was another early settler, and still lives in the township.

About 1860 the Norwegians began crowding in, as the Americans crowded out, and now there are only three of the latter in the town.

DECEASED.

Deacon Isaac Baker.—On the 24th of November, 1879, this estimable man closed the book of natural life, at the age of 73 years. His first apppearance on this stage of action was at Wood Creek, Washington county, New York, on the 24th of December, 1806. At the age of six his father's family moved to Pennsylvania. When 22 years of age his marriage took place with Mrs. Phœbe Beardsley. In February, the year of his death, the golden wedding was observed. In 1843, he removed to Shirland, Winnebago county, Wisconsin, and from thence to Riceland, where he remained until 1870, when he removed to Austin. Mr. Baker and his wife were two of the six constituent members of the Baptist church at Shell Rock.

ITEMS OF INTEREST.

The first birth in the township took place on the 23d of April, 1858, and Caroline Oleson came into existence. She was a daughter of Mr. and Mrs. Ole C. Oleson, who lived upon a farm in section thirty, and the child yet lives.

The earliest marriage of which there is any record, took place on the 1st of January, 1858, and joined the future destinies of Stephen Beardsley and Sarah Croy.

It is claimed, and is undoubtedly a fact, that the first death that occurred within the limits of Riceland, was that of Martha Hull; aged about 16 months, in October, 1857, of Scarlet Fever.

The next was the demise of Miss Sarah Baker, on the 18th of July, 1859, from a stroke of lightning. It seems that two sisters, Amy and Sarah, were sleeping near a stove, and toward morning a thunder-storm arose, which scattered its bolty messengers with a profusion that was terrific, and a bolt struck the house, ran down the stove pipe and glanced across the room, striking the girls and instantly killed Sarah, severely wounding her sister, Amy. The bolt then passed through the floor and down a studding into the ground.

The first school taught in the district, was held at the residence of Harry Beardsley in section sixteen, in the summer of 1859, Miss Amy Baker being the instructor.

The first religious services held in the township were presided over by the Rev. Mr. Phelps, in the spring of 1857, at the residence of Samuel Beardsley.

The township of Riceland originally bore the name of Beardsley, in honor of an early and prominent pioneer; but it was finally changed by the residents to Riceland, suggested by the name of the lake.

Blacksmith Shops.—The first blacksmith shop in the town was opened in the fall of 1857, in a little log hut in the northern part of section fifteen, by Samuel A. Beardsley.

John Peterson, a Norwegian, in 1880, erected a one story, 18x20 foot, frame building in section eighteen, and opened a shop for shoeing, repairing, and blacksmithing generally, which he still continues.

Saw-Mill.—In 1857, buildings were erected on the south shore of Rice Lake, or rather a shanty, by Samuel A. Beardsley, who moved machinery from Rice county and commenced operating a steam saw-mill. The establishment continued turning out lumber for about one year when it was removed to Itasca, When the machinery was first moved from Faribault, Rice county, it was placed upon a wagon, with shelves or runners placed underneath to prevent the load from dropping out of sight in the deep mud, and in this shape, behind a big yoke of cattle, the trip was made.

Wind-Power Mill.- In 1880, N. P. Bartelson, a native of Denmark, erected a structure, put in two run of stones, and attaching it to a sixteen foot winged wind-mill, commenced grinding feed, etc. The stones are what is here termed hard-heads, and were dug from the ground in the vicinity of the mill, and manufactured into buhrs by Mr. Bartelson. The establishment cost about $300.

Fairfield Village.—A village under this name was platted by Samuel Beardsley, on the south shore of Rice Lake in section fifteen, on a proposed road from Fairfield to Shell Rock. A Post-office was established and a regular mail route; it was on the same section as was the saw-mill, and everything looked lovely for rapid growth; but that looked for railway never came and the village became a thing of the past.

Riceland Lodge of Good Templars.—This society was organized in the spring of 1871, at the house of Frank Ross in section twenty-eight, by members of the Moscow Lodge. The society continued here until December following, when the base of operations was changed to what was then the village of Sumner; but the following year, the interest waning, the charter was surrendered.

Seventh Day Adventists.—The first preaching to the adherents of this faith took place in 1865, at the house of Nels Hanson, with the Rev. John Mateson as minister; and after this, services and Sabbath school have been held regularly in private residences and schoolhouses. In 1880, the church was erected, size, 20x30, at a cost of $500. At the time of organization the society had about thirty-five members. Regular quarterly services have been held since October, 1865. The present elder is Hans Rasmusson, and the Sunday school Superintendent and Class Leader is Hans Johnson. The Sunday school now consists of about forty members. Preaching is held about once each month by itinerants.

There is a burial ground in connection with the church, which was laid out in 1872. The first burial here was of the remains of Andrew Peterson.

POLITICAL.

As stated elsewhere, this township was originally known under the caption of Beardsley. The first town meeting was held at the residence of Samuel A. Beardsley, but as the records for the early years are entirely destroyed, or effectually misplaced, any statement we might make as to their proceedings would be merely "hearsay." It is claimed the first officers were: Supervisors, Isaac Baker, Chairman, Charles Williams, and James Harris; Clerk, James Snyder. The names of the balance of the officers have been forgotten.

The matters pertaining to the town have always been in capable hands and have been attended to with commendable zeal and honesty. The last town meeting was held at the house of N. P. Bartelson, on the 14th of March, 1882, and the following township officials were elected and are now serving: Supervisors, John J. Jerde, Chairman; P. Iverson, and William H. Baker; Town Clerk, Knud Ingebretson; Treasurer, C. Jacobson; Assessor, B. K. Winjum; Justices of the Peace, L. T. Bell and O. O. Bagaason; Constable, C. E. Baker. The gentleman named as Justice of the Peace, L. T. Bell, has just been nominated by the Republican County Convention for the position of representative of his district in the lower house of the Minnesota Legislature.

STATISTICAL.

The Year 1881.—The area included in this report takes in the whole town as follows;

Wheat—4,384 acres; yielding 55,376 bushels.

Oats—686 acres; yielding 24,101 bushels.

Corn—699 acres; yielding 29,867 bushels.

Barley—130 acres; yielding 3,146 bushels.

Potatoes—49 acres; yielding 8,735 bushels.

Sugar Cane—6 acres; yielding 511 gallons.

Total acreage cultivated in 1881—5,626 acres.

Apples—number of trees growing—1086; number bearing—399; yielding 92 bushels.

Grapes—15 vines; yielding 30 pounds.

Sheep—243 sheared; yielding 948 pounds of wool.

Dairy 417 cows; yielding 34,750 pounds of butter.

THE YEAR 1882. -Wheat, 3,557 acres; oats, 732; corn, 230; barley, 144; rye, 6; buckwheat, 2; potatoes, 57; sugar cane, 9; total acreage cultivated in 1882—4,327.

Apple trees—growing, 874; bearing, 419.

Grapes -vines bearing, 30.

Milch cows—337.

Sheep - 214; yielding 836 pounds of wool.

Whole number of farms cultivated in 1882—106.

POPULATION.—The census of 1870 gave Riceland a population of 633. The last census, taken in 1880, reports 783 for this town; showing an increase of 150.

EDUCATIONAL FACILITIES.

DISTRICT No. 25.—The first board of school officers in this district was as follows: Clerk, H. Ing; Treasurer, O. Henry; Director, John Johnson. In 1872, the first schoolhouse was erected at a cost of $700, size, 18x20 feet, which answered the purpose for about ten years, when it was dispensed with, and the present neat frame building was erected, size 26x36 feet, at a cost of $800, the location being in the southeastern part of section seven. The present officers are: O. Henry, J. Jacobson, and John Johnson.

DISTRICT No. 26.—The first school taught in this district was by Miss Williams, with twenty-five pupils present. In the summer of 1861, the citizens of the district were called out, and the first schoolhouse erected in section twenty-nine, by subscription, size, 16x22, of logs. A new frame building is now in process of erection in section twenty-nine, which will be 18x28 feet. The last school was taught by Mr. Arthur Grow, with thirty-nine pupils present.

DISTRICT No. 27.—This is one of the younger districts of the township, and embraces the territory south of Rice Lake. The present schoolhouse was erected in 1878, a frame building, located in the northeastern part of section twenty-seven.

DISTRICT No. 88.—The first schoolhouse was erected in 1867, of logs, in section nine, size, 16x20, and cost $250, the logs being furnished by subscription of the citizens. The last term of school was taught in this district by Robert English, with fifty-two pupils enrolled. A new schoolhouse was completed this year at a cost of $800, size, 20x32 feet, in section nine, although, as yet no school has been held there. The present school officers are as follows: Clerk, Christian Larsen; Director, Jonas Ingvardson; Treasurer, Christian Hanson.

DISTRICT No. 91.—Embraces the territory in the southeastern part of the township, with a schoolhouse located in section thirty-five, which was erected in 1872.

NORWEGIAN SCHOOL.—This educational medium originated in 1869, in the spring, when Knud Ingrebretson called the first school to order, consisting of about forty pupils, and the institution has continued ever since.

BIOGRAPHICAL.

WILLIAM H. BAKER, one of the early settlers of Riceland, is a native of Pennsylvania, born in 1837. When he was about five years old his parents moved to New York, and a year later to Winnebago county, Illinois. In 1857, the family came to Minnesota and settled in this place, William taking land in section twenty where he has since made his home. He was married in 1861, to Miss Mary E. Stark, a native of New York. They have had two children, one of whom is now living; Frank E.

CHRISTAIN ULRIK CHRISTENSON was born in the central portion of Denmark, on the 15th of January, 1852. At the age of eighteen years he enlisted in the Danish army, served one year, and then after a period of six months re-enlisted for another year. In April, 1873, he came to America and directly to this county, settling in Geneva. On the 5th of July, 1879, he was joined in matrimony with Carrie Mary Christenson and they have two children, a boy and a girl. In 1880, they removed to this township and bought a farm in the east half of section ten.

NILS A. NILSON, deceased, one of the pioneers of

this place, was born in Norway and brought up on a farm. When first coming to America he settled in Wisconsin, but after a short time came to this place where he lived until his death, which occurred in 1869. He left a wife and four children; Nils, Bertina, Andrew, and Martin.

BOTLER K. WINJUM was born in Bergen, Norway, on the 5th of March, 1833. When he was twenty-one years old he emigrated to America, and was engaged in agricultural pursuits for four years in Dane county, Wisconsin. In the fall of 1858, he was united in wedlock with Miss Maria Bell, and the same year they came to this township. They have had eleven children, eight of whom are living. Mr. Winjum owns a farm in section thirty-one. He has served as Assessor for several years.

OLE NELSON WIGDAL is a native of Denmark, born in 1853. In 1871, he emigrated to America, landed in Portland, Maine, and came directly to Dane county, Wisconsin. He was married in 1873, to Miss Mary Wigdal, and the result of the union is two children; Susan and Annie Christina. In 1877, they came to Riceland and settled on the farm which they have since made their home.

SHELL ROCK.

CHAPTER LXXIII.

GENERAL DESCRIPTION—EARLY SETTLEMENT—EARLY SETTLERS DECEASED—EVENTS OF INTEREST—STATISTICS—SHELL ROCK VILLAGE GORDONSVILLE VILLAGE—SCHOOLS—BIOGRAPHICAL.

The town bearing this name is one of the southeastern of Freeborn county, lying contiguous to Iowa on the south, London township on the east, Freeman on the west, and Hayward on the north. It is a full congressional township, containing 23,040 acres.

Shell Rock is mostly a prairie town, although in many places is found the oak opening land, so common throughout this region, or in other words, prairie land interspersed with groves of burr, black and scrub oak timber. The surface is generally rolling, but there are no hills or bluffs sufficiently abrupt to be detrimental to agriculture. The soil is a light loam, well adapted to the prevailing mode of agriculture. The farmers throughout the town are in comfortable circumstances, and many fine and costly residences dot the valuable and fertile farming country.

The name of the town was taken from that of the river, Shell Rock, which flows through the eastern part from north to south.

The Minneapolis & St. Louis Railway also traverses the same part of the town, running in the same direction.

EARLY SETTLEMENT.

This township witnessed the first actual settlement ever made in Freeborn county, and contained for about one year the only inhabitant of the same. The settlement first began in the southwestern part of the town, the first man being Ole Gulbrandson, or, as he was often called, Ole Hall, a Norwegian, who, through the influence of a brother in Northwood, was induced to come to this locality in search of a place, arriving in June, 1853, and locating upon a large farm in section thirty-three. He was accompanied by his family, and at once erected a log house, the first dwelling ever erected in this then unbroken county. This house is still standing, and at present is, and has been for years, the residence of P. J. Miller, Esq., one of the well-known old settlers of the county.

He also commenced improvements, and by the

time the government survey was made, in 1854, he had broken seven acres of land, put in a crop, and had it fenced. This plowed and cultivated field being the only one in the county it was entered by the surveyors upon the government survey map. In the fall of 1855, Mr. Gulbrandson and his wife, having had trouble and discouragements, finally separated, and it is said her father gave him, in the words of our informant, a "h— of a lickin" for treating his wife so. The following spring Gulbrandson sold his place and moved to Decorah, since when he has been lost trace of.

Thus the settlement of this locality remained until September, 1855, when an addition was made to it. The first was John Stanley, a native of the New England States, but came direct from California and took a claim on the corner of sections nineteen, twenty, twenty-nine, and thirty. He brought with him quite a herd of cattle; but as he had but little very poor hay, it is claimed that all of the stock died. The farm he settled upon is now the property of T. Porter.

Stanley remained three or four years. He then went east and brought back with him the two Smiths, John and James A., natives of Canada, who both took claims in sections twenty and twenty-one, but have since left the locality.

Then in the spring of 1856, came the next settler in the person of William Beighley, who had been here the year previous, accompanied by his brother Jacob, T. J. Gordon, and E. Maybee, in November, looking for a suitable location, and decided to make this place his future home. So, as stated above, in April, 1856, he again made his appearance upon the scene, and bought the claim which Gulbrandson had settled on. In May his brothers, Jacob and S. P. Beighley, came with teams, bringing William's family, and they at once selected claims, the former in sections thirty-two and thirty-three, and the latter in thirty-three and twenty-eight, where they both still hold forth. William Beighley is still living in the township, and is one of the prominent old settlers of the county.

With this party came J. B. Gordon, who selected his claim in section thirty, west of the river; but when his father, T. J. Gordon, a native of Pennsylvania, arrived in the fall and fall made himself comfortable in section twenty-eight, the son moved over and still makes his home there.

A little later in the season—1856—James Allen came in and settled in section thirty, on the town line, and remained for about one year when he disposed of it to Peter Beighley, and finally went to Tennessee. The latter named gentleman also took a claim in section thirty-two, where he lived until the time of his death in 1872 or '73.

Chris. Oleson, a Norwegian, late from Pennsylvania, made his arrival substantial by planting his stakes on a farm in sections thirty-one and thirty-two, in June, 1856. He was a blacksmith by trade and still holds the fort on his original claim.

In the spring of 1857, Warren Barber, a native of New York, pushed his way within the limits of the township, and taking his slice of the government domain in section twenty-nine, continued his sojourn there until after the war, when that insatiable mystery, Death, secured him, and he was called hence.

But, in the meantime, the northern portion of the township began its evolutions toward civilization, and by the time of the last mentioned arrival it counted a goodly number as a neighborhood. Early in the spring of 1855, William Rice came from Wisconsin and commenced the settlement in the northern part of the township by taking a claim in section eight. In the spring of the following year he went to St. Nicholas, in Albert Lea township, and started a hotel there under the sign of "St. Nicholas Hotel." He was mail carrier for the village, and on one of his trips, on the 3d of December, 1856, he got lost, and after wandering about for three days brought up at Plymouth; but he was so badly frozen that he died in a few days, and his remains were deposited in the Greenwood cemetery. This was the second death in Freeborn county.

Almost immediately following Rice, a little colony from Wisconsin made their appearance and swelled the Shell Rock settlement, arriving in June, 1855. This party consisted of Gardner Cottrell and family, George Gardner and family, Madison Rice with his mother and her family, C. T. Knapp and family, and a couple of others whose names have been forgotten. The first mentioned, Gardner Cottrell, stopped for a time on the Rice place, which he soon after took for himself and remained upon it for about one year when he opened the first store in Shell Rock village. After managing the business for a number of years he retired and has since passed to the great beyond, while his wife and several children still live in the village.

George Gardner located upon section six, where he remained until 1880, when he went to Northwood, where his lamp still holds out to burn.

Madison Rice, with his mother, made himself at home in section eight, and here remained until after the war when he took up his goods and chattels and removed to Wisconsin where he yet lives He married the daughter of C. T. Knapp.

Mr. Knapp was not behind the rest of the party and immediately after his arrival took a farm in section thirty-six, just over the line in Albert Lea township. Here he lived until 1877, when he removed to the village of Shell Rock, and in the year following opened the meat market which he still continues.

The next spring--1856—F. L. Cutler and John Smith came, arriving in May. Butler was an eastern man coming from Iowa to this place, and bought the claim settled by Gardner. He finally, after service in the Minnesota First during the war, sold his place and went to Freeborn, and from there drifted down to Missouri. He was quite a sport and jockey, and took great delight in fast horses.

John Smith took land on both sides of the town lines of Shell Rock and Freeman.

About this time came Joseph Marvin, John Wood, and John Eddy.

In May, (1856), Mr. Anthony C. Trow, a native of New Hampshire, came from Mitchell county, Iowa, and after looking the country over on foot finally located on section seventeen, where he still continues his sojourn. He selected a quarter of the same section for his brother, Elisha, who arrived the same month and settled, remaining a couple of years and then moved away. He now lives in Kansas.

Joseph Marvin and his son-in-law, Daniel R. Young, natives of Massachusetts, arrived on the 10th day of July, 1856, and selected claims. The former, in 1876, was called upon to cross the dark river of death, and the latter still lives in the township.

With these, or at about the same time, came Aszel Young, Uriah Grover, and Robert Budlong, who all secured homes.

On the 11th day of July, 1856, A. H. Bartlett made his appearance, and the village of Shell Rock, through his energy and capable management, sprung into existence. He yet resides in the village, one of the prominent public men of Freeborn county, and a man capable, trustworthy, and efficient in every respect.

E. P. Skinner and Mr. Beattie arrived in early days, and taking a good deal of land commenced speculating and continued for many years. The latter, Mr. Beattie, was for years known to the residents, and, in fact, everyone, as the "One-Legged Speculator."

In 1857, A. M. Burnham drifted upon the scene and erected the first bridge thrown across the Shell Rock River, and with him came a number from Albert Lea. The population grew very rapidly and the country settled with a good class of inhabitants. An idea of the ingress can be formed from the fact that in 1857, 100 votes were cast at the general election.

EARLY SETTLERS DECEASED.

Rev. Walter Scott was an early settler at Shell Rock, coming in the summer of 1856. In 1857, he was licensed to preach by the Methodist Episcopal church. On the 24th of November, 1877, he died, at the age of 53 years, leaving a wife and six children. He had removed to Northwood.

John S. Corning was born in St. Lawrence county, New York, in 1827, where he lived until 1855 when he came to Minnesota, and erected the first frame house in Shell Rock, and for two years did two men's work—run a saw-mill, kept a store, and managed a hotel, and afterwards kept the Webber house in Albert Lea. For twelve years before his death he kept a hotel in Austin. When 52 years of age, on the 10th of October, 1879, the gong sounded for him to retire from this world forever.

Mrs. Nancy M. Brown, wife of Watson Brown. A singularly noble character with an even disposition. She was the oldest of ten children, and was married in 1859. New York was her native State. Her eyes were closed in death on the 10th of February, 1881, at the age of forty-eight years. She fully realized the value of early instruction, and was particularly active in Sunday school work.

Mrs. Lucretia Weeks, grand-mother of Mrs. H. T. Chase, of Shell Rock, finished her earthly sojurn on the 7th of December, 1871, at her home in Pennsylvania, at the age of 93 years. Her descendants at the time of her death were, nine children, fifty-eight grand-children, and one hundred and four great-grand-children, and six of the next generation.

> "Thou hast for many a lengthened year,
> Life's weary pathway trod;
> Seen generations disappear,
> Laid low beneath the sod
> *　*　*　*　*　*
> We bid thee, aged friend, adieu;
> Our friend of many a year.
> We laid thee here beneath the yew,
> And leave thee with a tear."

HOPKINS B. RIGGS was introduced into this world in the state of New York, on the 21st of May, 1820, and transferred to the next on the 9th of June, 1875, after a lapse of 55 years. At 14 years of age he went to Michigan, and lived there twenty-five years. At first he joined the Methodist church, and then the Baptist, and was a true man, considerate of the rights of others. As he was breathing his last he said, "I am in the waters: let me go."

VARIOUS MATTERS OF INTEREST.

EARLY BIRTHS.—Early in the spring of 1854, the first child born in the county came into existence at the log cabin of Ole Gulbrandson, the first actual settler, who lived in the southwestern part of the town, as treated in full elsewhere. The youngster was a girl, christened Bertha, and at last accounts was living healthy and robust.

Another early birth was the minor arrival of Susan, a daughter of Mr. and Mrs. William Beighley, on the 13th of April, 1857. She is now married and living in Dakota.

A girl was born to Mr. and Mrs. James Luff, who lived in the village of Shell Rock, where they kept a tavern. The child's nativity was early in the spring of 1857, and was christened Minnie. She now lives in the West.

In November, 1855, Willie Andrews, son of Oliver and Mary Andrews, who the July previous had located in the township of Hayward, was born, being the second white child, and the first male, to commence its existence in Freeborn county.

EARLY MARRIAGES.—The first marriage in the county took place here, early in 1857, or late in the year previous. Hannibal Bickford, or as he was generally known "Bunk," walked to the State line, where he procured a horse and brought his proposed, Miss Maria Colby, to Shell Rock, where the ceremony making them one was duly performed by William Andrews, Esquire. Mr. Bickford still resides in Manchester, one of the solid men of the county, with two children. Mrs. B. died several years ago.

EARLY DEATHS.—We will let A. H. Bartlett, in the words used by him in his recent speech to the Old Settlers in their late reunion, in Albert Lea, relate the story of the first sad event of this kind.

"Mrs. Fannie Andrews, wife of William Andrews, Esq., a well known and prominent early settler of the county, and the mother of a large family of stalwart pioneers, who accompanied her and her husband and settled in the county in July, 1855, after a brief residence of nearly two months, living in their wagon while their habitation was being erected, was suddenly called for by the inexorable tyrant, death, and her immortal spirit, so lately filled with grand and hopeful expectations, winged its flight to its eternal home above, while the entire community, as weeping mourners, followed her earthly remains to their last resting place, the grave, to be known no more on earth, forever. The sculptured marble (now to be seen in Greenwood cemetery, in the town of Shell Rock) has for years reared up its front, proud to perpetuate her name and virtues, and rehearse to the passing traveller that on the 21st day of December, 1858, the earthly remains of death's first victim from the pioneers of Freeborn county, was here consigned to its last resting place, the tomb." And again Mr. Bartlett adds:

"On the 3d of December, A. D., 1856, William Rice, (the second settler in Freeborn county) while carrying the mail across the broad and bleak prairie, lying between the Cedar and Shell Rock rivers, was caught in a severe snow storm, and lost his way. He wandered around, over the trackless prairie, without shelter or protection from the severity of the storm, until he froze to that extent, that he died of his injuries, some three or four days afterward. This calamity was followed in quick succession, on the 20th day of the same month, by Byron Packard and Charles Walker, (a part of the company who laid out and founded Shell Rock City) being caught in a terrific storm, on the same broad prairie, while hauling a steam boiler to its destination at Shell Rock, and both perished from the severity of the storm and the extreme cold. Their bodies, frozen stiff and cold in death, were found four days afterwards, lying upon the frozen crust of the deep snow. Their bodies were carried to Shell Rock, and there buried upon the town site they had so lately helped to lay out and form. No relatives were there to attend the funeral obsequies, and mourn their sad fate, yet sorrowing friends and brother pioneers, composing the entire community, assisted in performing the last duty to the untimely departed. No preacher of the gospel could be found in the county to speak words of consolation to the sorrowing and bereaved friends and associates, and our friend, Jacob Hostetter, one of Freeborn county's earliest pioneers, feelingly and eloquently addressed the early pioneers there gathered, upon the sadness and suddenness of their bereavement; upon the mysterious and inscrutable ways of an overshadowing providence, in which no one can tell why, in the prime of vigorous and useful manhood, when hope, the ministry of life is most buoyant, and future expectations in the coming life of usefulnes is most prominent, that a mysterious power should step in with its dread mandates, and the brightest and most promising life should be consigned to oblivion and the grave. These sad bereavements, and others which happened in the county about that time, caused by the unparalleled severity of the winter of A. D 1856, cast a sad and sorrowing gloom over the young settlement of Freeborn county. Some few of the settlers became disheartened and discouraged and early the following spring returned to their former eastern homes."

TOWNSHIP OFFICIALS FOR 1882.—Supervisors, G. W. Gleason, Chairman, I. R. Flatt, and M. Mackin; Clerk, S. Messinger; Treasurer, A. C. Grow; Assessor, H. H. Gordon; Justices of the Peace, J. W. Prichard and James Abbott; Constable, Jud. Randall.

SHELL ROCK GRANGE No. 310.—This society was organized on the 9th of July, 1873, with a charter membership of thirty. The following were the first officers of the lodge: Master, O. C. C. How; Secretary, Ira A. Town; Overseer, W. G. Barnes; Stewart, G. T. Knapp; Assistant Steward, E. E. Budlong; Gate Keeper, E. T. Kelly; Ceres, Mrs. E. E. Badlong; Pomona, Miss Matilda Howe; Flora, Mrs. J. Presswell; Lady Assistant Steward, Mrs. George Hyatt. This grange has reached a membership of 135.

RELIGIOUS.

The Methodists have held services in the township almost since the first settlement. About the first gathering was held at the residence of William Beighley in the winter of 1857-58, by the Rev. Mr. Mapes, an itinerant Methodist preacher, with a congregation consisting almost entirely of Beighleys. A class was organized about the same time with William Beighley as leader. Services were continued at various places until the schoolhouse of district No. 50 was erected in the northeastern corner of section thirty-two, since which time services have been held part of the time every Sunday, and again irregularly; as a rule by the pastor from Shell Rock village.

DANE CEMETERY. This burial ground is located in the southeastern corner of section twelve, having been laid out in 1878, and the same year the remains of Mrs. Mary Nelson were deposited here, making the first interment. The grounds contain one acre, well fenced and neatly laid out with groves, occupying a high point of land.

HOYT WILL CEMETERY.—Is situated upon a high rise of land in the northeastern part of section twenty-four, containing something less than one acre, which was laid out in 1872. The first burial here was of Daniel S. Hoyt, in 1867, and it was on his land and by his wish that the cemetery is located here.

STATISTICS.

Below we present an extended list of the acreage and product, together with other items of interest compiled from the Auditor's report to the Commissioner of Statistics of Minnesota, and elsewhere, which will prove of interest:

THE YEAR 1881.—Showing the acreage and yield in the township of Shell Rock for the year named:

Wheat—4,076 acres, yielding 35,362 bushels.

Oats—1,388 acres, yielding 40,589 bushels.

Corn—1,162 acres, yielding 46,860 bushels.

Barley—178 acres, yielding 2,026 bushels.

Rye—82 acres, yielding 444 bushels.

Buckwheat—8 acres, yielding 43 bushels.

Potatoes—62 acres, yielding 7,487 bushels.

Beans—½ acre, yielding 13 bushels.

Sugar cane—30½ acres, yielding 3,852 gallons.

Cultivated hay—245 acres, yielding 307 tons.

Total acreage cultivated in 1881 —7,232.

Timothy seed—37 bushels.

Apples—number of trees growing 2,456; number bearing 532, yielding 251 bushels.

Grape vines bearing—28.

Sheep—75 sheared, yielding 550 pounds of wool.

Dairy—302 cows, yielding 32,792 pounds of butter.

THE YEAR 1882.—Wheat, 3,596 acres; oats, 1,503; corn, 2,337; barley, 436; rye, 39; buckwheat, 21; potatoes, 100¾; sugar cane, 2¾; cultivated hay, 99; flax, 3. Total acreage cultivated in 1882—8,321.

Apple trees—growing 2,259; bearing 772; grape vines bearing, 18; milch cows, 324; sheep, 72. Whole number of farms in 1882—100.

Forest trees planted and growing—118½ acres.

POPULATION.—The census of 1870 gave Shell Rock a population of 512. The last census, taken in 1880, reports 1,013 for this town; showing an increase of 501.

SHELL ROCK VILLAGE.

Or, as it is called by the railroad company Glenville, lies in the northwestern part of the township of Shell Rock, in sections six and seven, on the river bearing the same name and on the Minneapolis & St. Louis railway. The site the village occupies is all that could be desired, the river furnishing a limited water-power, and the surrounding country is rich and productive to those who follow agricultural pursuits.

EARLY DAYS.—The settlement of the locality surrounding the village has been treated at length in another place; so it will be unnecessary to refer to it here. In July, 1856, A. H. Bartlett came through this region in search for a village site and a suitable place for the construction of a mill. He was pleased with the locations of both St. Nicholas and Northwood; but money would not induce the proprietors of these prospective places to quit claim to their interests. In following the river Mr. Bartlett came to the site of Shell Rock, and commenced laying plans for the establishment of the village. John Smith and Frederick Cutler each donated 20 acres to the project, and Mr. Bartlett at once proceeded to survey and record eighty acres in lots and blocks as the village of Shell Rock. He next commenced the erection of a water saw-mill on the banks of the river, with a building 20x80, frame, equipping it with a 56-inch buzz saw. The water power did not succeed as anticipated, so a steam power of 30 horse was placed in it and the mill for two years continued piling up sawdust, when the timber became exhausted and the property was sold to William Morin and moved to Albert Lea, from where it has since continued its journey toward the setting sun.

Just before the saw-mill was completed, and while Mr. Bartlett was in the East procuring machinery, E. P. Skinner laid out a town under the caption of Shell Rock, a short distance north of Mr. B.'s proposed site, in the town of Hayward.

This promised to be quite a formidable rival to the present village, as a Post-office and store were established there; but on Mr. Bartlett's return negotiations were entered into which were finally completed, by which E. P. Skinner got one-fourth interest in Bartlett's site, and the Post-office, store and goods were removed to the latter place. At that time the store was run by R. A. Cornish, who was also made Postmaster. This store was continued for a number of years under the management at different times of Skinner, Hall, Brown, and Smith; but finally, soon after the war, the goods were removed to Albert Lea.

George Whitman next put in a stock of goods and kept a store for about one year, when he went out of business. Hon. A. H. Bartlett then bought the buildimg and got Victor Gilrup to open a store. Mr. G. still continues in the mercantile business, and now owns the entire establishment.

But little was done toward the development of the town until the railroad was built through in 1877, when the progress really took root.

W. H. Peck came with the railroad, and opened a provision store which he continued for three or four years. He is now in Jackson.

H. G. Koontz also came about the same time, and opened the business he still continues under the sign of "Variety Store."

L. B. Woodruff opened a general merchandise store, and is still in the village, although not in business.

P. F. Brown opened the first hardward store, and sold to W. H. Peck, who in turn, in 1881, turned it over to Greengo & Landis, the present proprietors.

John Haugh started a harness shop here which he still manages.

In the spring of 1878, C. T. Knapp opened a meat-market, and still handles the beefsteak.

The first hotel was erected in 1856, by James Luff, and consisted of logs and clay. In this Mr. Luff entertained travelers, and supplied them with bad whiskey. When the railroad was constructed, E. P. Kelly remodeled it, and it is now run by H. T. Chase.

In 1877, Dr. H. H. Wilcox opened a drug store which is yet in operation.

A hotel was erected the same year by William Beatty, which is now run by his wife, as he went to bed soon after its completion, and has never since been up: although the doctors say nothing ails the man.

Hon. A. H. Bartlett is the first and only lawyer of Shell Rock.

SHELL ROCK POST-OFFICE.—This office was established in 1856. It was the intention of A. H H. Bartlett, who laid out the village of Shell Rock, to have a Post-office at once established at his embryo village: but while he was in the East, purchasing machinery with which to equip his mill, E. P. Skinner took time by the fore lock and played "check mate," by having an office established at a point in Hayward township, a short distance north of Shell Rock, where he proposed the commencement of a village. When Mr. Bartlett returned from the East and discovered the state of affairs, he went to Skinner and offered him one-fourth interest in Shell Rock, provided the office should be removed to that point and the proposed opposition town site abolished. The offer was accepted and the office was removed to Shell Rock as soon as the papers from Washington were received, with E. P. Skinner as Postmaster and A. H. Bartlett, deputy. It was held in Bartlett's house, on the river, for one quarter, the business in the meantime amounting to $18 and a few cents, when it was removed to the store of Skinner & Cottrell. The mail was carried by William Rice, from Mitchell through to Albert Lea, and finally, in 1857, a regular mail route was established from St. Ansgar to Mankato, by way of Shell Rock and Albert Lea, carried by A. B. Davis of Albert Lea. Skinner held the office until the spring of 1858, when, through the influence of A. H. Bartlett, R. A. Cornish became Postmaster, with the office at the same place. Next came Esquire William Andrews,—who, by the way, was the first Justice of the Peace in the county and married the first couple, -and he held the office for three or four years, when Edward Town received the appointment, and following him came the present Postmaster, Victor Gillrup.

VILLAGE OF GORDONSVILLE.

This hamlet is located on the Minneapolis and St. Louis railroad, in the southwestern part of Shell Rock township, and about one mile east of Shell Rock River. It was laid out in 1880, by S. P. and Jacob Beighley, containing four or five acres, divided into four blocks: two of them on the east half of the northeast quarter, belonging to Jacob; and two on the west half of the northeast quarter of section thirty-two, belonging to S. P. Beighley. It was named after the Post-office, which was established years before.

In the year 1879, John Fallen started a blacksmith shop which has since been running under various managements.

Soon after the railroad was finished J. W. Abbott put a small stock of groceries in one end of his residence, and in connection with the Post-office, which had in the meantime been removed to this point, opened the first business house in the place.

In the summer of 1882, Heman Frost erected a one story building 24x30 feet, and put in a good stock of general merchandise, also taking the stock of goods mentioned above of Mr. Abbott. The Post-office is also kept in this store.

There are two warehouses; one run by Jacob and S. M. Beighley; the other is owned by S. S. Cargill, of Albert Lea.

There is also a good depot, which is well kept; but agents do not stay here long, as it is a small place, and they are promoted to larger places as they become efficient.

GORDONSVILLE POST-OFFICE. — This Post-office was established a few years after the date of first settlement, with Peter Beighley as Postmaster, and office at his house in section thirty-three. The mail arrived by way of the Northwood and Albert Lea mail route and was carried at first by John P. Beighley. In 1865 T. J. Gordon was appointed P. M., and took the office to his residence in section twenty-eight; after a time his son, W. H. H. Gordon received the appointment and the office was kept at the same place until after the completion of the railroad, when J. B. Abbott was appointed P. M., and the office was removed to the station of Gordonsville, where it is kept in the general merchandise store of Heman Frost, with Mr. Abbott's son, William, as deputy Postmaster.

PUBLIC INSTRUCTION.

DISTRICT NO. 50.—First held school at the house of Peter Beighley on the farm now owned by Joseph Miller, section thirty-two, by one of

Mr. Beighley's daughters, then by Mrs. Catherine Hawk and now Mrs. Charles Grim, of Freeman, with a few scholars present. This commenced in the fall of 1858, with a two months term, and afterward school was held at various places until 1856, when the frame school building now in use was erected in the northeastern corner of section thirty-two, at a cost of about $600. The first school taught in this house was by Jane Buchanan to an attendance of about twenty-five. There is now about seventy scholars in the district and an attendance at school which will average about thirty-five pupils. The schoolhouse is frequently used for the purpose of public meetings, etc., and the school generally goes by the name of the Gordonville district.

District No. 52.—Embraces the territory just southeast of the village of Shell Rock. The first school in the district was held in a granary owned by J. S. Corning on section eight; it was taught by Miss Emily Streeter with an attendance of eight pupils. In 1866 the schoolhouse was erected in the northeast corner of section eight, size 21x30 feet at a cost of $765; in which Miss Bennett taught the first school to an attendance of twelve scholars. The present attendance is thirty-five.

District No. 59.—This district effected an organization in 1856 and embraces the village of Shell Rock and surrounding country as its territory. The first school meeting was held at the house of Lawyer A. H. Bartlett, and the board elected at that time consisted of C. T. Knapp, A M. Young, and A. H. Bartlett. The erection of a schoolhouse was at once commenced under the supervision of Mr. Bartlett, and it was finished on Sunday the 18th day of August, 1857, at a cost of $500 it being a neat and substantial frame building which still stands and is in use as a wood house. The day the house was completed Elder Lowry held the first religious services in the township at the house of A. H. Bartlet, ignorant of the fact that at the same time the boys were hard at work on the schoolhouse, and no one took pains to inform him. One week from the completion of the house the first school was commenced by Miss Emily Streeter, who is now in Oregon. The schoolhouse just mentioned was the first erected in Freeborn county. The school building now in use was erected in 1878, by A. H. Bartlett, size 26x24, and cost $2,200. The last term of school was taught by Daniel Palmer, principal, to a large attendance. The present school board consists of F. F. Carter, George Hyatt, and O. C. C. Howe.

District No. 77.—The first school taught in this district was in 1866, at a granary owned by Mr Bailey, the teacher being Miss Lena Doris with an attendance of eight scholars. The attendance up to the present time has grown but little. The schoolhouse is a neat struture, 16x20 feet, and cost about $400.00.

District No. 100.—Embraces the territory in the northeastern part of the township. The present school edifice was erected in 1876, size 18x20 feet, at a cost of about $500, being furnished with folding desks and the most improved furniture. The first school was taught by Miss Hannah Buchanan to an attendance of eight scholars, which has now grown to fifteen. The schoolhouse is located in the southeastern corner of section two.

District No. 104.—Embraces as its territory the southeastern portion of the township. The schoolhouse was erected in 1878, being a neat frame building, 24x30 feet, and cost about $850, seated with patent seats and equipped with all necessary apparatus. The first school was taught by Miss Elizabeth Beighley to an attendance of about twenty scholars, which is about the same as at the present time. The schoolhouse is located in the southeastern corner of section twenty-seven.

BIOGRAPHICAL.

Alonzo Alford was born in Clinton county, New York, on the 1st of January, 1842. In 1854, he came to Wisconsin where he grew to manhood. He returned to his birth place when twenty years old, and the following year married Miss Helen Richards, a lady of Canadian birth. He returned west with his wife and resided in Hastings until 1876, when he came to Glenville and engaged in the manufacture of boots and shoes, which has since been his business. His wife died in 1878, leaving a family of seven children.

James W. Abbott, a native of Morgan county, Ohio, was born on the 9th of January, 1843. When two years old he moved with his parents to Athens county, where he grew to manhood, and at the age of eighteen years enlisted in the Eighty-seventh Ohio Volunteer Infantry, Company H, went south, was in the Army of the Potomac, and served over three years. After receiving his discharge he returned to the scenes of his childhood where he married Miss Sarah E. Pierce in 1864. Mr Abbott having lost his health during the hardships and exposures of the soldier's life. sought a home in Minnesota soon after his marriage. He located a claim in Oakland and remained until 1872, when he removed to this place and started in the lumber business, afterward opened a grocery store, and three years later sold out and engaged in buying grain and general produce. In 1878, he was appointed Postmaster; has held the principal town offices, and is at present Justice of the Peace. Mr. and Mrs. Abbott have five children.

Edward E. Budlong, a native of Columbia county, New York, was born on the 22d of May, 1829. At the age of five years his parents removed to the western part of the State, where they remained until 1844, then removed west and settled in Dane county, Wisconsin. Edward was united in marriage, in 1854, with Miss Almira Skinner, a native of Essex county, New York. In 1856, they moved to Mitchell county, Iowa, remaining during the summer, and in the fall came to this county, settling in the town of London. In 1864, they came to Shell Rock, and have a fine farm of two hundred and thirty acres. Mr. Budlong takes an interest in all public matters and has held different local offices. He has a family of three children.

Eldad Barber, one of the old and respected citizens of this place, was born in New York on the 21st of December, 1835. His father being a lumberman, he followed the same until the age of eighteen years, when he went to Hartford, Connecticut, and learned the wheel-wright trade. In 1857 he moved to Iowa, and a year later to Minnesota, where his father took the claim Eldad now owns. His parents have both died since coming here. Mr. Barber takes a general interest in the welfare of this place, and has held several offices of trust.

William Beighley, a native of Pennsylvania, was born on the 23d of November, 1824. He was employed at various occupations and grew to manhood at his home. In 1851, he married Miss Emily Gordon and settled on a farm near his father's. He sold out and came west in 1855, locating first in Iowa, but soon after came to this township where he was among the first settlers, taking a claim in April, 1856. In 1865, he purchased his present farm in section twenty and now has it well improved.

Jacob Beighley was born in Pennsylvania on the 5th of March, 1829. In 1856, he came west and became one of the pioneers of this place, staking out a claim in section thirty-three, now owning a farm of two hundred and fifty acres, all improved. He was married the year after coming here to Miss Susanna M. Miller, also a native of Pennsylvania. The union has been blessed with one child, Ruth E. Mr. Beighley owns a warehouse on the B. C. R and N. Railroad, about three minutes walk from his residence, and deals extensively in grain and general produce. His home has always been open to ministers of any denomination and in an early days was used for religious services. As there is no hotel within five miles it is also a convenience for travelers, and none have ever been turned from his door unfed or uncared for.

S. P. Beighley, one of the pioneers of Shell Rock, was born in Butler county, Pennsylvania, on the 12th of July, 1833. At the age of nineteen years he began to learn the trade of tanner and currier, which he followed several years. He was married in 1854, to Miss Louisa M. Miller. Two years later they came to this place and settled in the southern part of the township, where they have since made their home. In 1862, Mr. Beighley enlisted in Company C, of the Fifth Minnesota Volunteer Infantry, served in the Indian Massacre, then went south and remained in service three years. After receiving his discharge he returned to his home and has since devoted his time to tilling the soil. He has a family of ten children, all of whom reside in this township.

A. H. Bartlett, one of the first settlers of this place, was born in New York on the 28th of September, 1829. At the time of his birth his parents were living in a saw-mill, their house not having been completed. His father died in 1833, and when A. H. was eight years old the family moved to a place twenty miles from their former home, where he attended school. At the early age of sixteen years he began teaching, and subsequently entered the Arcade Academy in Wyoming county, remaining two years. In 1852, having for some time been troubled with a lung disease, he was advised by the physician to take an overland trip to California, and after a period of one hundred and seventeen days he reached Placerville, where he remained two and a half years. In 1854, he returned to New York, where he had previously married Miss Anna D. Peet, a native of the same State. In the latter year they came to Iowa, and in 1856, to this county, and Mr. Bartlett platted the town site of Shell Rock. In an early day he read law, and in 1860, was admitted to the bar. He was a delegate to the last Territorial Legislature in 1857, and also the first State Legislature. He has been Judge of Probate several terms and takes an interest in all local affairs. He is the father of four children: Sam, Ida, Jay, and Eva.

T. A. Clow is a native of Canada, born on the 23d of October, 1843. His father is a minister and in 1861 moved with his family from Illinois to Minnesota. After a few years A. F. moved to Winona county, thence, three years later, to Olmsted county and in 1863, took a homestead in Blue Earth county. The same year he enlisted in the Second Minnesota Cavalry, Company H, and after his discharge returned to his farm. He was married in 1856, to Miss Caroline M. Paine and they have a family of four children. Mr. Clow came to this township in 1877, opened a blacksmith shop and now has a good business. He is the father of four children; one son having died in April, 1875, aged seven years and three months.

V. Gilbert, one of the oldest and successful business men of this place, was born near Copenhagen, Denmark, on the 29th of May, 1840. In 1862, he came to America, arriving in New York City and soon after enlisted in the First New York Volunteer Eng., Company G, serving three years. After his discharge he came to Watertown, Wisconsin, and engaged in the mercantile business for two years, then in Albert Lea a short time and from there to Shell Rock, where he was one of the first to open a substantial mercantile business. He was married in 1872, to Miss Lilly I. Carter, a native of Wisconsin. They have had five children, four of whom are living: Hattie, Frank, Harry, and Walter. Burt, aged five years, died in February, 1882.

O. C. C. Howe is a native of Allegany county, New York, born on the 23d of November, 1823. He learned the millwright trade when a young man and in 1852, came west to Iowa. He built a saw-mill which he conducted and also farmed until 1864, then came to this township and bought his present land. He is engaged principally in stock raising. Has held most of the local offices and is a staunch democrat.

Daniel S. Hoyt a native of Ohio, was born on the 3d of March, 1847. At the age of six years he moved with his parents to Iowa and two years later to this State, locating first in Fillmore county and in 1862, came to this township, where they were among the first settlers. His father died in 1878, leaving a large circle of friends to mourn his loss. Daniel came into possession of the homestead at the death of the latter and his mother resides with him.

Charles T. Knapp was born in Medina, Medina county, Ohio, on the 1st of November, 1820. He was married in 1838, to Miss Mary Hamilton. In 1851, they moved to Dane county, Wisconsin, and four years later came to Minnesota, settling in Freeborn county, and Mr. Knapp was the first to use a breaking plow in Albert Lea township. His first wife died in 1870, leaving five children; Betsey E. M., Jane J. A., Chloe, and Margaret E. He afterwards married Miss Jane Wilsey, who died in 1875, leaving three children; J. H., Ada, and Ida. The maiden name of his present wife was Catherine Bates whom he married in 1877. The same year he moved to this township and opened a meat market in Glenville.

Willard F. Marvin, one of the pioneers of this county, was born in Rutland county, Vermont, on the 13th of May, 1825. He resided in his native State until 1846, when he removed to Illinois, and soon after to Wisconsin. In 1859, he was united in marriage with Miss Huldah Wilcox, a native of New York. They came to Shell Rock in 1857, and pre-empted land in section eighteen, which has since been their home. They have a family of five children; Nancy, Curtir, Cynthia, Viola, and Clara.

Morris Marshall, one of the old and respected citizens of this place was born in Monroe county, New York, on the 8th of October, 1830. At the early age of sixteen years, he enlisted in the Mexican War, serving in Company F, of the Eighth United States Infantry for a period of sixteen months. He sailed for the scene of action, and landed at Vera Cruz, on the 5th July, 1847; joined the command of Franklin Pierce and went to Pueblo, participrting in many hard fought battles. After his discharge he came home, and in 1849 came to Wisconsin but soon returned to his native State. He removed to Jackson county,

Michigan, where he was engaged in farming several years. There he was joined in marriage with Miss Joliett Scofield. In 1862, they came to Minnesota, and settled on their present farm, which is well cultivated. They have a family of seven children.

PETER J. MILLER was born in Westmoreland county, Pennsylvania, on the 6th of September, 1807. He grew to manhood in his native county, and learned the art of coverlet weaving. In October, 1829, he married Miss Sarah Cribbs, and for several years was employed in the above occupation. In 1836, he moved with his family to Mercer, Mercer county, in the same State, and engaged in carpet weaving until the Rebellion. In 1866, he came to Minnesota, and purchased "Pilot Grove" farm in Shell Rock township, which has ever since been his home, his house being the first built in the county. Mr. and Mrs. Miller have a family of ten children, five sons and five daughters.

CHRISTOPHER OLSEN, one of the pioneers of this place, is a native of Norway, born near Christiania, on the 20th of June, 1817, and when sixteen years old began to learn the blacksmith trade. He was married in 1840, to Miss Nellie Evenson, who has borne him two children. In 1853, Mr. Olsen came to America, engaged at his trade a short time in Montreal, Canada, then moved to New York City, and later to Virginia, thence to Iowa first living in Dubuque, and afterward in St. Ansgar. In 1856 he came to this place, locating in sections thirty-one and thirty-two, where he built the first blacksmith shop in the township, and has since carried on the same in connection with his farming.

JOSEPH R. PAGE was born in Lycoming county, Pennsylvania, on the 13th of September, 1838. When he was five years old his parents moved to Indiana, and located on a farm in La Porte county, where Joseph grew to manhood. In 1866, he married Miss Matilda Minninm, who was born on the 26th of January, 1841, in Crawford county, Pennsylvania. They have six children: Joseph S., born on the 24th of March, 1867; Ada A., the 11th of December, 1868; John J., the 19th of July, 1870; True R., the 31st of July, 1872; William A., the 29th of January, 1875; and Hugh D., the 21st of October, 1879. Mr. Page is a highly respected citizen, a member of the Baptist church, and always takes an active part in the welfare of the town.

THOMAS PORTER, an early settler of this township, was born in Canada, on the 6th of December, 1829. He was married in 1855 to Miss Almira Smith, and they have a family of ten children; Albert, Bennett, Arvilla, Georgiana, Cynthia Maria, Carrie Viola, George L., Rolan, Alice Minnesota, and Amy. Three are dead; Kilburn, who died on the 14th of June, 1882; William H., the 15th of October, 1862; and Morella, the 13th of April, 1876. Mr. Porter moved from Canada to Minnesota in 1859, and settled on land in section thirty, Shell Rock, which has since been his home, his farm containing two hundred and eighty acres, the greater portion of which is under cultivation.

W. H. RATHMELL, a native of Pennsylvania, was born in Lycoming county, on the 5th of May, 1820. He attended school in the town of Williamsport, and at the age of fourteen began learning the harnessmaker's trade, at which he was engaged several years. He was joined in matrimony with Miss Ann Page, in 1844. Mr. Rathmell was for several years Captain of a steamer on the Pennsylvania Canal. In 1850 he went to California, but two years later returned and settled on a farm near La Porte, Indiana. After a residence of about twenty-five years in the latter place, he came to Iowa, and in 1871 to Shell Rock. He bought a tract of land containing over five hundred acres, and it is now well improved. He erected the first warehouse, as well as some of the finest buildings in the place, having since sold most of his real estate, and for the past nine years has made a business of loaning money. He has raised a family of three children; Mary, Sarah J., and H. C., the latter being located in La Crosse, Wisconsin.

JOHN E. SKINNER was born in Essex county, New York, on the 6th of September, 1838. When fifteen years old he moved with his parents to Dane county, Wisconsin, and in 1855 came to Minnesota, but soon returned to Wisconsin. He made another trip to this State in an early day, remained during one winter, and returned to his home in Wisconsin. In 1862, he enlisted in the Twenty-ninth Wisconsin Volunteer Infantry, Company G, taking part in several important battles, and served three years. In 1865, he came again to Minnesota and settled in this township. He was married the following year to Miss Jane Gardiner, who has borne him four children. Mr.

Skinner has held several offices of trust since his residence in this place.

ANTHONY C. TROW, one of the pioneers of Shell Rock, is a native of New Hampshire, born in New London, Merrimac county, on the 14th of July, 1833. At the age of seventeen years he began working for himself, when not needed at home. In 1855, came west to Iowa, and the following spring to Minnesota. After traveling over a portion of the State in May, he located in Shell Rock, and has since been one of its residents, owning a farm of two hundred and eighty acres, well improved. He came in company with his brother, and they experienced all the hardships of a pioneer's life, using burnt corn for coffee, and grinding corn meal in a coffee-mill.

INDEX.

EXPLORERS AND PIONEERS OF MINNESOTA.

PAGES 1 TO 128.

INDEX.

OUTLINE HISTORY OF THE STATE OF MINNESOTA.

Page 129 to 160.

INDEX.

STATE EDUCATION.

Page 161 to 176.

INDEX.

THE SIOUX MASSACRE OF 1862.

Page 177 to 256.

INDEX.

HISTORY OF FREEBORN COUNTY.

GENERAL HISTORY.

CITY OF ALBERT LEA.

ALBERT LEA TOWNSHIP.

ALDEN.

BANCROFT.

BATH.

CARLSTON.

FREEBORN.

FREEMAN.

GENEVA.

HAYWARD.

HARTLAND.

LONDON.

MANCHESTER.

MANSFIELD.

MOSCOW.

NUNDA.

NEWRY.

OAKLAND.

PICKEREL LAKE.

RICELAND.

SHELL ROCK.

THE

Northern Pacific Country,

FROM THE

GREAT LAKES TO THE PACIFIC,

TRAVERSES

The Great Wheat Belt, Grazing Range, and the Vast Gold and Silver Regions

OF

Minnesota, Dakota, Montana, Idaho, Washington, and Oregon.

The most attractive regions for new settlement are unquestionably the grain and grazing lands along the line of the Northern Pacific railroad in Minnesota, Dakota, Montana, Idaho, Oregon and Washington Territory. No section is settling so rapidly. None offers such advantages to the farmer and stock raiser. The Northern Pacific Railroad company now offers for sale

4,000,000 Acres of the Most Productive Wheat Lands

In the world, adjacent to its completed road in Dakota and Minnesota, which lands are now ready for the plow. No failure of crops to apprehend. **Average yield of twenty-two bushels of wheat to the acre** in Dakota last year. **Twenty-five to thirty** bushels of wheat not an exceptional crop. No agricultural industry is more profitable than wheat farming upon these rich and rolling plains. The country is well watered. Plenty of timber for domestic purposes. Low freight rates on farm products and settlers' household goods.

PRICE OF LANDS. East of the Missouri River, in Dakota and Minnesota, **$4 per acre**, with a rebate of 25 per cent. for acreage cultivated within two years from purchase. West of the Missouri River, along its completed road in Western Dakota and Montana, and in the beautiful valley of the Yellowstone, the company offers a large area of fine farming lands at the government price of $2.50 per acre (with a charge of 10 cents per acre to cover cost of surveying, &c.) admirably adapted for stock raising and general farming purposes. The Northern Pacific is now completed and in operation to a point ninety miles west of Miles City, on the Yellowstone River in Montana, and will soon be opened 200 miles further west. Settlers who go into this new region will have the advantage of a choice of locations and lands, and of the rapid rise in the value of property. The climate of the Pacific country is bracing and healthful.

IN THE MOUNTAIN REGION OF MONTANA

Soon to be traversed by the road there are many lovely and fertile valleys awaiting settlement, and vast wealth in **Gold, Silver, Copper and Iron** offers fine openings in every kind of mining enterprise. Upon the Pacific slope the Northern Pacific railroad is now in operation from Puget Sound to Pen d'Oreille Lake in Northern Idaho. **10,000,000 acres** of magnificent timber and wheat lands of unparalleled fertility in Oregon and Washington Territory are offered for sale by the company in the immediate vicinity of rail and water transportation at the rate of $2.60 per acre.

PACIFIC COAST LANDS.

For information relating to the lands of the company west of the Rocky Mountains, address J. H. Houghton, General Land Agent, New Tacoma, W. T. or Paul Schulze, General Immigration Agent, Portland, Oregon, or A. S. Stokes, General Agent, 52 Clark street, Chicago.

THE NORTHERN PACIFIC COUNTRY.

From Lake Superior to the Pacific Ocean, has unsurpassed attractions to the tourist. It offering an unrivalled field for fishing and hunting. For information and reduced rates for round-trip tourist and excursion tickets, address G. K. Barnes, General Passenger and Ticket Agent, St. Paul, Minn. H. Haupt, General Manager. J. M. Hannaford, General Freight Agent. G. K. Barnes, G. P. & T. A., St. Paul, Minnesota.

MINNESOTA, DAKOTA, AND MONTANA LANDS.

For land seekers' and colonists' rates of fare and freight, and inquiries relating to movements of colonists, and with reference to traveling and land agencies, address P. B. Groat, General Immigration Agent.

For all information referring to location, description, and prices of the millions of acres of cheap lands for sale by this company, and for maps and descriptive publications relating thereto, address R. M. Newport, General Land Agent.

www.ingramcontent.com/pod-product-compliance
Lightning Source LLC
Chambersburg PA
CBHW022029120726
47901CB00003BA/889
* 9 7 8 3 7 4 1 1 2 3 7 3 3 *